VE JUL 2011
AR May 14

MARATHON

Praise for *Marathon*

The book is great fun. Any insider to the sport will relish the race and running descriptions. Any outsider cannot help but be fascinated at the detail and inner workings of a big city marathon.

--Kathrine Switzer, New Palitz, New York

Marathon is a real page turner; when it comes to books, a winner.

--George Hirsch, New York, New York

It's great! When you pick the book up, you don't want to put it down. The characters are rounded, interesting, intriguing.

--Toni Reavis, San Diego, California

With all of the training books on the market, someone finally has written a novel that captures the essence of the marathon.

--Amby Burfoot, Emmaus, Pennsylvania

Even though *Marathon* is fiction, it embodies the building emotion of an actual race. Hal Higdon's entry into fiction writing should demonstrate his ability to draw pictures in the reader's mind.

--Paula Sue Russell, Findlay, Ohio

Quite a fictional universe. It's an engaging book where many different lives cross paths, and it gives us a fascinating glimpse inside the marathon. The novel should appeal to the non-running public as well

--Rosemary G. Feal, New York, New York

Hal Higdon gets into the heart of a marathon. His book will help people who never have run a marathon understand the challenge more.

--Kim Alexis, Wayne, New Jersey

I couldn't put the book down once I started. Very nicely done.

--Gloria Ratti, Boston Athletic Association

A delightful book. Well-developed characters, and I enjoyed turning the pages to see what became of them.

--Donna Deegan, Jacksonville, Florida

MARATHON

A NOVEL BY HAL HIGDON
Contributing Editor *Runner's World* Magazine

Marathon is a work of fiction by *Runner's World's* Hal Higdon. It describes the 72 hours leading up to a major marathon, similar in scope to the best-selling books by Arthur Hailey, *Airport* and *Hotel*.

All of the characters in this book are fictitious, and any resemblance to actual events or persons, living or dead, is purely coincidental.

Library of Congress Cataloging-in-Publication Data

    Higdon, Hal
        Marathon-1st ed.
        ISBN: 978-0-9636346-0-3
        1.   Marathon running – Fiction
        Library of Congress Control Number. 2009908324

Published in the United States by McNaughton & Gunn, Saline, Michigan

Major Characters

In approximate order of appearance and importance

Peter McDonald: Director, Lake City Marathon.
Christine Ferrara: TV3 reporter
Carol McDonald: Peter's late wife
Celebrity X: More famous than Oprah
Redbird: Tracks Celebrity X's movements
Edmund Giesbert: TV3 cameraman
Don Geoffrey: Contributing Editor, *Running Magazine*
Burton Ambrose: Editor, *Running Magazine*
Nelson Ogilvie: Media director for marathon and bank
Noel Michaels: Executive director, marathon
Dennis Lahey: Executive manager, Shelaghi
Patrick (Paddy) Savitch: Shelaghi executive
Miles Wendell: Founder, Lake City Marathon
Yolanda Kline: Christine's roommate
Jonathan Von Runyon: Reporter, *Lake City Ledger*
Matilda (Tilda) Goldberg: Religious reporter, *The New York Times*
Joseph Nduku: Kenyan, defending champion
Kenyatta Kemai: Kenyan, challenger
Moses Abraham: Kenyan, rabbit
Kyle and Wesley Fowler: Rabbits, Northland Racing Team
Steve Holland: Coach, Northland Racing Team
Aba Andersson: World record holder
Bjørn Andersson: Aba's husband
Fiona Flynn: Irish marathoner
Meghan (Meg) Allison: Podiatrist, unknown runner (Husband: Matt)
Tatanya Henry: Russian, defending champion (Husband: Jacob)
Toshi Yamota: Japanese marathoner
Katie Hyang: Marathoner, Northland Racing Team
Mark Mallon: TV3 sports commentator, marathon anchorman
Timothy Rainboldt: Color commentator, marathon telecast
Carolynne (C.V.) Vickers: Color commentator, marathon telecast
Vaughn Johnson: TV3 weatherman
Tom Schorr: Director, marathon telecast
Nicholas Terrence, MD: Medical director, marathon
Leonard Hand: Pacing team leader
Bob Veldman: Air traffic controller, marathoner
Naní: Supermodel, running for AIDS Africa (Husband: Ricco)
Captain Robert Newsom: Directs police protection
Jean Grey: Fire Department lieutenant, helicopter pilot
Damien and Elisa: Interns, marathon office
Mario and Angelo: Bodyguards

Dedicated to the women in my family:
Rose, who has stood by my side all these years;
daughter Laura and daughter-in-law Sharon, proofreaders;
daughter-in-law Camille, computer consultant;
cousins Jean, Irene and Barbara, who corrected early drafts.
One does not undertake a work of this scope
without support from all sides.

PART 1:

THURSDAY

THURSDAY

MARATHON

72:00:00

Late on a Thursday afternoon in early October, the chief executive officer of a large, multi-national organization based in Rome, stepped out of a black sedan at a private airfield southeast of that city and walked purposefully toward the airfield's single building, a stucco structure with a rust-colored tile roof.

The executive checked his watch to determine how much time remained before the arrival of his private jet plane. It was precisely 2:00 P.M., Central European Time, in Rome. That translated to 8:00 A.M., Central Daylight Time, at his destination in the United States: Lake City.

Seventy-two hours remained between that time and the focal moment that served as purpose for the individual's journey. The countdown began.

72:00:00. 71:59:59. 71:59:58.

Where the individual was going and what he planned to do was known to only a trusted few, one of them a close friend who to maintain secrecy had given him the code name "Celebrity X."

The man called X was dressed in black slacks, a black shirt, black socks, black shoes, a black jacket, zipper open almost to the waist. X wore the darkest of dark wraparound sunglasses, so dark you wondered if he could see through them. His cleanly combed hair also was raven black, a hint of his Mediterranean origins, with just a touch of grey at the temples betraying his age, in the early forties. His nose was straight, narrow, slightly hooked, one that would have made Julius Caesar proud. X stood near 6 feet, carried 160 trim pounds and had the straight-up stride of a person who worked out in the weight room as well as ran.

Following Celebrity X closely came two similarly dressed and similarly sized men, Mario and Angelo their names, clones almost, but actually they were bodyguards, who had popped out of each side of the limousine ahead of the man they were assigned to protect, pausing to survey the surroundings before allowing him to emerge. From a distance, you would not know which of the three was the executive and which were the bodyguards, a purposeful deception. Should a bullet be fired from the rifle of a potential assassin, one of them would absorb it. The possibility of getting killed was part of their job description, and they accepted the danger that came with being guardian and companion for one of the most important men in the world.

3

THURSDAY

Celebrity X and his two bodyguards did not enter the stucco structure, but waited nearby. If they knew others might be observing from the edge of the woods, they gave no indication. Within a few seconds, two new automobiles, black sedans, arrived and parked beside the limousine. A half dozen largely anonymous looking individuals climbed out of the cars. They too were dressed in black, like their predecessors.

While all waited, the bodyguard named Mario circled behind the first limousine, opened the trunk and removed a single suitcase. It too was black.

The executive nodded and acknowledged the small courtesy. *"Grazie,"* said Celebrity X. It made him uncomfortable that in his current position, he rarely was allowed to do anything unaided. Even as simple an act as moving a suitcase fell to others. It would be easy to succumb to the privileges of his office and accept the favors it brought, but he could not get used to doing so. X felt crowded, hemmed in, pushed into a closet, molded into a role not willfully chosen but impossible to avoid.

It had been from a desire to negate the pressures of his high profile job and find at least one hour a day of freedom from responsibility that had caused Celebrity X to begin running.

X wondered about the events that would transpire over the next seventy-two hours. Was he foolish to proceed? Was it an act of unnecessary hubris? Of pride? Was what he was about to do dangerous, not only to himself, but to those around him? Ironically, he worried as much about their safety as he did about his own. He knew that his position and his celebrity put him in harm's way—and he was willing to accept that—but he no longer acted or stood alone. He felt the weight of the world upon his shoulders.

X and his entourage continued to stand by the stucco structure at the edge of the airfield. The structure was small, barely more than a single room. Only a slender antenna on the building's roof indicated that it might serve a purpose other than a farm shed. It was the only building at the airfield. No airplane was visible nearby.

Despite their stealthy look, none of those accompanying the executive betrayed any anxiety. None of them smoked. None of them talked to each other. None of them even glanced at a watch to check the time. They knew the time without looking. They simply stood and waited.

Others watched from a distance. Two men concealed at the edge of the woods observed the arrival of the cars and passengers minus motion or emotion, as though they expected this event to happen at precisely the moment it occurred. The two men were armed with assault weapons. Unseen others positioned at intervals around the airfield were similarly armed.

4

MARATHON

Neither of the two held his weapon pointed at those just arrived, particularly not the man central to the group. To do so seemed almost obscene. Trained as specialists in security, they would react rapidly if provoked.

One now raised a pair of binoculars to his eyes and surveyed the scene. He viewed the darkly clad executive and those around him. Yes, it was their employer. He and the other guards had received word of Celebrity X's movement only an hour before, barely enough time to get into position around the airfield. Although he did not want to voice the words, the first man knew that despite all the protection, X was an easy target if someone wanted him eliminated. He hoped that nobody nearby had such intentions.

"*Alloco!*" hissed the first man with the binoculars. *Fool!* "Forgive me for using such a term to describe our leader." The man made the sign of the cross as though to absolve himself. "Does not he know how vulnerable he becomes when he enters the outside world?"

"I don't think he cares," mumbled the second man.

"*Mamma mia,*" said the first. "I care. Where is our leader going?"

"You won't believe me if I tell you."

"Do me the honor. Tell me anyway."

"He may be headed to America to run a marathon."

This comment resulted in a palpable silence. *Santa Maria.* The first man finally commented. You're right. I don't believe you. An assassin's bullet won't be necessary. Don't people die running marathons?"

"Not if they train properly," said the second man.

The first man, the one with the binoculars, said no more, his attention diverted by the whistling hum of a jet airplane approaching the airfield on a landing pattern. Because he had been properly briefed, the man knew that the plane would be a Gulfstream G550, a business jet that could carry a dozen or more passengers, plus two pilots, across the Atlantic Ocean without refueling.

The first man looked away from the men on the runway and began to scan the sky until his eyes caught a glint of white that grew larger in his binoculars as the whistling hum of its engines got louder in his ears. After the plane landed, he knew that the executive would board it and move out from under the umbrella of protection established by those on the ground. Presumably, there would be another umbrella when and wherever the plane landed. Or did the executive hope that secrecy would protect him? That would explain the suddenness with which the trip to the airfield was announced.

Less than seventy-two hours now separated the moment the dark-clad man stepped out of the limousine to the moment when he would become most vulnerable to enemies who meant him harm.

The countdown continued:

71:55:02. 71:55:01. 71:55:00.

5

THURSDAY

Secrecy might not be enough to protect this individual so important to world harmony. The man with the binoculars hoped that he would not hear later on television that someone had attempted to harm the individual he was assigned to protect.

"Marathon?" said the first man. *"Ma che pazzo!* He must be mad!"

71:55:00

A s the man called **Celebrity X waited patiently beside a runway** near Rome, Italy, westward across the Atlantic Ocean the work day had just begun. It was 8:00 A.M. in Lake City, a large metropolis in the central part of the United States. Less than seventy-two hours remained before the start of the Lake City Marathon. Those runners who accessed the race's Web site could see a countdown clock at the top of the home page showing the hours, minutes and seconds slipping away:

71:55:00. 71:54:59. 71:54:58.

That clock and others—including one at the marathon Expo, one in the lobby of the race's headquarters hotel and one each over the start and finish lines—would continue counting until 8:00 on Sunday morning, stopping at *00:00:00*. At that point, runners would begin streaming across the starting line, their movements measured both by the starting line clock and digital watches on each runner's wrist.

The Web site clock reached *71:54:30*, then *71:54:00*, then *71:53:30*. Runners all over Lake City—in fact all over the world, 50,000 entrants from 121 countries—found their lives transcribed by the ticking Web site clock:

71:53:00. 71:52:59. 71:52:58.

And so early on Thursday morning the clock continued, relentless in its countdown.

Peter McDonald, director of the Lake City Marathon, paused briefly on a balcony overlooking a convention hall so huge it could have hangered dozens of airplanes the size of the one now landing near Rome. This was Pritzinger Place, the city's main convention center. The center's North Hall was 452 feet wide by 790 feet long, a total of 369,000 square feet, larger than the playing fields in most stadiums. If you wanted to be a major player in the convention business, you needed exhibit space that large and more. In addition to the North Hall, Pritzinger Place featured three more major halls plus other exhibit space in satellite buildings. Attached to it was a mammoth four-story parking garage that could hold thousands of cars.

Here, the marathon's Health and Fitness Exposition—or "Expo" as most called it—would begin the following day. After set-up on Thursday, the Expo opened on Friday and lasted two days, leading to the Lake City Marathon Sunday morning. Peter, a man in his mid-thirties, a champion runner in high school and college, remembered when he first became director of the Lake City Marathon with barely 5,000 runners, a tenth of the current field. He got the job because of a scandal involving the previous race director that resulted in the loss of the event's main sponsor, a sporting goods company. In terms of respect and finances, the Lake City Marathon had sunk to so low a spot that few within the running community gave it much chance of surviving.

Peter seemed like an unlikely candidate for the top job at even a failing marathon. He had competed with some success on the European track circuit for several years after graduating from Notre Dame University with an engineering degree, but soon realized that matching strides with the fastest in his sport was beyond his ability. Still sorting out his career options, recently married, Peter accepted a temporary job with the marathon and ascended to the position of race director by default—because nobody else wanted the job. Race founder Niles Wendell, who fired his predecessor, told him: "You want the job, kid, you got it. But don't be surprised if your salary checks bounce." None had. Wendell, a wealthy local architect and running fanatic, may or may not have been joking. But the size of those checks remained small Peter's first few years as director. Fortunately his wife Carol had a job working in a bookstore that helped pay the bills.

Peter McDonald was forced, because of lack of finances, to stage the Expo in the basement of one of the downtown hotels, a small space, yet he still had a hard time coaxing more than a few dozen exhibitors to come. It was a measure of how much the marathon had grown that he now used Pritzinger Place's largest hall and filled it with 150 or more exhibitors. Too bad Carol no longer was around to share his success.

Peter could not help but consider the marathon's growth and its position and prominence among city events as he looked down on the booth of the race's current sponsor, the Lake City Bank. The bank's booth had as its centerpiece a JumboTron screen, showing scenes from previous races. Beneath the screen, a clock displayed the time remaining before the start of the marathon:

71:52:57. 71:52:56. 71:52:55.

He liked to think of the Lake City Marathon as *his* marathon, although neither he nor founder Niles Wendell owned the race. (Technically, the Lake City Marathon was the property of a non-profit consortium.) But as director,

Peter was its most visible spokesperson. As the marathon grew, so did his salary, now six figures.

The marathon stood as a key player among Lake City events, particularly when it came to generating revenue: more than $120 million spent in hotels and restaurants and other visitor activities, according to a convention bureau report. Although Lake City had teams in all the pro sport leagues, and although the city hosted hundreds of conventions, large and small, marathon weekend occupied a niche special and apart from all other city activities. Those responsible for making the city hum *loved* the Lake City Marathon. The marathon served as a Welcome-All activity in which most citizens of Lake City could participate—as spectators and volunteers, if not as competitors. It seemed as though almost everyone scattered in workplaces across the city had a friend, or a friend of a friend, who was running the marathon. Monday after the big race, finishers arrived at those workplaces with medals proudly hung around their necks to be welcomed at the water cooler as heroes and heroines. Of course, within a week those same seemingly supportive workers would go back to questioning their sanity, wondering why they felt compelled to run, asking questions like, "How far was this marathon?"

Lake City usually accepted its heroes—politicians, business leaders and gangsters—without insightful analysis. A sprawling and brawling metropolis located on the Great Lakes in the heartland of America, Lake City went from frontier village to major metropolis in the space of a century. Originally a center for manufacturing and transportation, Lake City lately had begun to shed its blue-collar image and attract more and more corporate headquarters and the electronics companies that proliferated around them. The city contained nearly three million inhabitants, triple that number if you counted those within its metropolitan area. Along with Boston, London, Berlin, Chicago and New York, the Lake City Marathon ranked as one of the world's major marathons, each year attracting 50,000 participants to a lightning fast course that almost screamed: "Come set a world record!"

Nevertheless, despite its popularity among the masses, Peter McDonald knew that the Lake City Marathon faced a major financial crisis. This was the final year of the marathon's contract with sponsoring Lake City Bank. A mammoth Irish conglomerate named Shelaghi recently had swallowed that bank and—according to insiders within the world business community—might not continue to finance what bankers from abroad certainly could consider a silly sporting event. The bank contributed several million dollars a year to the race budget, a sum not easy to match, particularly during a down economy. Peter's own contract as race director also ended with this year's event. If the principle sponsor abandoned Lake City, Peter's job and six-figure salary could disappear. Several Shelaghi representatives, including executive manager Dennis Lahey, were in town to observe the marathon and maybe decide whether or not to allow it to continue under the bank's sponsorship.

71:52:54. 71:52:53. 71:52:52.

Another challenge faced by Peter, not to mention every runner in the field, was the weather: hot, hot, hot! He had been in contact with weatherman Vaughn Johnson earlier this morning. Johnson worked for TV3, the same television station that sponsored the marathon telecast. Johnson was a runner who planned to run the marathon himself. He was predicting high 80s and clear skies: Good for the beach, bad for running 26 miles. If temperatures continued to rise, Peter might need to shorten or even cancel the event to protect the health of runners, an unpopular choice he did not want to make.

71:52:51. 71:52:50. 71:52:49.

Also a problem was Peter's main athletic attraction, world record holder Aba Andersson of Sweden. Aba hoped to set another world record; Peter even had hired two rabbits (male pacers) to help her achieve her goals. Late yesterday, he had received a call from Aba's husband Bjørn, informing him that Aba was sick. Neither Bjørn nor Aba knew or would admit why, but she had thrown up and still felt queasy. Food poisoning? The flu? Maybe she would recover in time to run, maybe not. Peter told Bjørn and Aba to skip the noon press conference. "Just get well," he said and added not to worry about the $150,000 already paid her as an appearance fee.

71:52:48. 71:52:47. 71:52:46.

Peter's recommendation to Bjørn that Aba not feel obligated to run just to fulfill a contractual obligation was not entirely altruistic. The Swedish runner's decision to choose Lake City for her world record attempt already had attracted media attention more than money could buy. More reporters had applied for press credentials than any previous year. If Aba failed to run, it offered a problem more for the media seeking story lines than for him as race director. Peter did have one story line he could feed ravenous reporters, another celebrity to attract their attention, although Peter needed to be cautious about revealing too soon the identity of the man he called Celebrity X.

71:52:45. 71:52:44. 71:52:43.

That celebrity was the individual about to board the Gulfstream at the airfield outside Rome. He was a celebrity whose fame was *so* great that his appearance would cause an instant sensation, not only among runners, but among spectators along the course. This was an individual better known by people around the world than Oprah Winfrey, who ran the Marine Corps Marathon one year. More famous than Lance Armstrong, who ran the New York City and Boston Marathons. At the individual's request, McDonald had hidden his identity under a code name: Celebrity X. Nobody on his staff knew

Celebrity X's identity, or even the code name! The celebrity was actually an old acquaintance of Peter's from Lake City's East Side neighborhood where they both grew up. Before X achieved a fame that few could imagine and while both were still young he had coached Peter in high school, and they continued to stay in touch. This most famous of famous men had warned Peter: "If the media finds out, it will make it impossible for me to run."

Celebrity X was the ultimate paparazzi magnet, an individual who needed to be protected from his public, both those who loved him and those who did not. When Peter discussed with Celebrity X the possibility of his running the Lake City Marathon, their major concern was security, how could they get him to the starting line without causing a stampede? People could trample each other seeking to see him up close, touch him, or secure an autograph.

More a problem, Celebrity X could be a target for any number of groups or individuals seeking to protest his appearance, or even do him harm. You cannot easily provide security in a race featuring 50,000 runners and viewed by a million spectators. You cannot surround an individual with several dozen bodyguards. You cannot encase him in bullet-proof glass. The best security, the two finally decided, was total secrecy. If people did not learn about Celebrity X until the moment he stepped onto the starting line, he might be able to run and complete his marathon without disruption. Despite X's fame, maybe because of it, Peter knew the runners would accept his presence instantly and provide their own protective shield. He would have 50,000 bodyguards.

Yet on several occasions, Peter almost picked up the phone to contact Celebrity X and tell him, "No, this is impossible. We'll never pull this off." Preventing Peter from impulsive calls was the wall built around X, the many layers of people protecting both his privacy and his public persona. Though Peter was among the few people in the world who knew X's private phone number, even he did not always get past the protectors.

71:52:42. 71:52:41. 71:52:40.

As the Web site clock continued its countdown in Lake City, Celebrity X's Gulfstream rolled down a runway outside Rome, soon to bridge the distance between two great cities of the world. Peter had asked X to call soon after taking off, but even as the race director stood on the balcony in Pritzinger Place, his mind skipped past the many problems confronting him this year to the task of the moment: an interview with a reporter for TV3, the channel that would televise the race live on Sunday. On the main floor below, McDonald spotted a group of waiting people, one of them a muscular man with a TV camera on his shoulder. He recognized the cameraman: Edmund Giesbert. Edmund, a Vietnam veteran, had been around a long time. The group was waiting in the booth of Metro Foods, one of his sub-sponsors. Next to the cameraman stood a long-legged woman: dark-haired, wearing a red blouse, the uniform of TV3 Sports. She held a microphone in one hand. He did not recognize her. She must be new. Attractive, he thought, but aren't they all?

The woman glanced up toward the balcony and spotted Peter. She smiled and waved to indicate recognition, but maybe also to show just a bit of impatience. *Yes, I'm late*, Peter thought. Nearly eight minutes late, he realized looking at his watch. Peter McDonald politely returned the TV reporter's smile and wave and moved toward a bank of escalators, rehearsing in his mind as he did several bullet points offered him by Nelson Ogilvie, his media director, for this interview and others during the weekend:

- Say as little as possible about the sale of the bank.
- Discuss the weather, but do not panic people with dire predictions.
- Admit Aba Andersson might not run, if and when that fact becomes known, but stress the strength of the field even without her.

Peter would have added exactly one more bullet point: Do *not* say anything about Celebrity X!

Stepping onto the escalator, Peter amused himself with the thought that even Ogilvie did not know about that curve ball, although he might need to warn the media director at least before the start of the race. Ogilvie understandably would be furious at not being on the Need-to-Know list, although for the present that list had only one name on it other than that of Peter McDonald, Celebrity X himself.

71:52:39. 71:52:38. 71:52:37.

The countdown continued and would not stop until the horn blew Sunday morning at 8:00, signaling the start of the Lake City Marathon.

71:52:00

As the escalator lowered Peter McDonald to the main floor of the convention hall, he observed a scene of complete chaos. Boxes big and small, sheets of cardboard, discarded paper and plastic strapping blocked most aisles. Teamsters directing traffic barked instructions adding to a din that echoed upward, reverberating against the steel ceiling high overhead. Fork trucks scurried back and forth, moving shrink-wrapped pallets into booths being hammered together by carpenters. Thursday was the day exhibitors began to prepare their booths for the Health and Fitness Exposition that preceded Sunday's marathon, and for many occupiers of the bigger booths, it was an all-day task. Shoe companies, sporting goods stores, equipment salesmen and people pushing various running-related products all wanted a piece of the nearly 50,000 marathoners who would need to come to the Expo to pick up their race numbers starting the next day.

71:52:00. 71:51:59. 71:51:58.

Stepping onto the main floor, Peter tried to imagine himself as one of the runners who in the next several days would ride that escalator downward into the Expo signaling the start of their big adventure: the running on Sunday morning of a race 26 miles 385 yards long. What had he overlooked? Was there anything he had failed to provide for their comfort? What more must he do to enhance their experiences?

That was McDonald's job description: enhancer of running experiences. Improving the quality of the Lake City Marathon both for elite runners and those in the back of the pack was his duty, as well as obsession. As a former track athlete, Peter knew that you are only as good as your last race. He hoped this year's marathon proved successful, that all the first-timers finished, that the rest set Personal Records or qualified for Boston, making everybody happy, including sponsors, but there were so many variables out of his control, particularly the weather. It would be hot—he knew that—though he tried to push that problem to a back compartment of his mind.

Peter McDonald arrived at the Metro Foods booth offering the trademark grin that many women found irresistible. He was tall, trim, ruggedly handsome with wavy light brown hair. Women took notice when he walked by, but Peter was barely aware of that fact. Since he lost his wife Carol less than a year ago, working late hours had served him as a narcotic to erase memories of a traumatizing event. The few women he dated seemed unsatisfactory compared to his memories of Carol. He rarely asked women out for a second date, much to their disappointment. He lived lately in a shell, which worried many of his close friends. Peter realized that, he needed to move forward with his social life some time soon but, in the meantime, he had a marathon to run.

He nodded to cameraman Edmund Giesbert and extended one hand to the TV reporter, the dark-haired woman first spotted from the balcony above.

"Hi. I'm Peter McDonald. I apologize for being late."

"No problem," said the reporter, looking firmly into his eyes.

No problem, Peter thought. But talk about an icy stare: *Whew!* He could see the woman was irritated by his late arrival. But it was not that the TV3 reporter had been waiting unoccupied. She had someone else in the booth to interview while awaiting him.

The TV3 reporter apparently realized the same. Moment of irritation past, her look softened. She introduced herself: "Christine Ferrara. We're just finishing another interview."

MARATHON

Peter turned to the person being interviewed, a man skinny like all very fast runners, short, bearded, ruddy, his sandy brown hair, sparse and flecked with gray, betraying his age. This was Don Geoffrey, Olympian, past Lake City Marathon champion, Contributing Editor for *Running Magazine,* author of *Mastering the Marathon*, a man nicknamed the "Turtle" despite his speed. During a lengthy and successful career, Geoffrey won most of his races by drifting patiently behind the main pack, waiting for fast-starting runners to self-destruct, smoothly striding past them in the final miles, as in the classic Aesop fable of the turtle and the hare. Geoffrey lived in Lake City and served as training consultant for the marathon.

Responsible for having arranged the interviews was Nelson Ogilvie, who handled media relations for the marathon. "We're just finishing with the Turtle," Ogilvie explained. McDonald stepped back to allow the interview to continue. Edmund the cameraman indicated his readiness to the TV reporter.

"Don, we're standing in a booth at the Expo filled with food," began Christine Ferrara. "What foods should runners eat before the marathon?"

As Don Geoffrey began to discuss the values of carbohydrates, a well-rehearsed response that he seemed to have given many times, Peter McDonald noticed with as much amusement as displeasure that the TV reporter had failed to mention—had *avoided* mentioning—the name of Metro Foods, the sponsor in whose booth they were standing. "A booth." she had said, not "the booth of Metro Fresh." The grocery chain, as part of its sponsorship arrangement, provided yogurt, bananas, chocolate chip cookies and other food items for runners immediately after they crossed the finish line. Not that Peter had expected such a plug. He had been in the marketing business long enough to know that TV stations avoid commercial plugs for which they are not getting paid. Fair enough. The name of the race was the *Lake City* Marathon, almost identical to the name of the *Lake City* Bank, his main sponsor. There was no way you could talk about the race without tying the bank to it. He hoped the new bank owners would comprehend that—if they did not try to change the name of their newly acquired subsidiary, a distinct possibility.

Peter wore a light blue golf shirt, a shirt that matched the color of his eyes, a shirt that displayed the logo of the Lake City Marathon. A logo not large enough to be recognized by anyone watching on television, but an identifying symbol of the marathon organization. The race director also wore sharply creased Dockers trousers, dark blue. Black shoes: Italian, highly polished as they might appear on the feet of a banker. The shoes, ironically, had been a gift from his friend, Celebrity X. Peter McDonald lived in a sartorial world halfway between that of the banker and that of the more casually dressed runner. His only item of jewelry, since he wore no rings, was a silver chain, barely visible beneath the collar of his golf shirt. The chain had been a gift from his wife, Carol. She had brought it back from a charity walk to Africa undertaken with her college roommate. He never removed it. Not to bathe. Not to sleep. If he ever remarried, his second wife would need to live with that chain, or she never would become a second wife. Peter suspected there might be one woman somewhere who could learn to love the memory of Carol as much as he did. Peter had just not met that woman yet. Waiting to be interviewed, he touched the chain lightly as he often did for good luck.

The TV interview with Don Geoffrey continued. The Turtle responded to a second question related to drinking during the marathon after which the TV reporter turned to her cameraman: "Is that a wrap?" Edmund indicated, yes.

Interview over, Geoffrey said to McDonald: "I need to squeeze in a workout between now and the press conference. See you later, Peter."

With the Turtle gone, Peter McDonald and Christine Ferrara turned toward each other. She was a striking woman, he decided, with a very trim figure that her red TV3 blouse helped accent. *Nice legs,* thought Peter. Tall. *I wonder if she runs.* The woman's hair was raven black, tumbling across her shoulders. Straight nose with a tiny wrinkle before the tip. Firm chin. Her skin was unblemished and bore a natural tan, not one that needed the help of a tanning bed. Well, of course, her name was "Ferrara," suggesting Italian roots. Brown eyes that did not glow, did not sparkle, but bored laser-like into his seemingly vulnerable blue eyes. Peter was reminded of Sophia Loren, an actress whose early films he and Carol always enjoyed watching cuddled up on the couch. Carol: Would she forgive him for having allowed his interest in an attractive woman to intrude even briefly on the business at hand? The woman seemed strong-minded, a trait he actually admired. The woman had not hesitated to display her displeasure at his late arrival.

Peter tried to move past that awkward moment. He said quietly: "Where do you want to do the interview, Ms. Ferrara?"

The TV reporter did not answer immediately, considering the question. For a moment, her eyes and his eyes locked. She could sense that he knew she was perturbed. *Well, get over it,* Christine said to herself. Peter, meanwhile, wondered: *What's her problem?* Each shifted their gaze, hers toward another booth in the front center of the hall. She said: "How about moving to the marathon booth?"

"I was going to suggest just that."

While reporter and cameraman gathered their equipment for the move to the nearby Lake City Marathon booth, Peter McDonald turned to Ogilvie, who dutifully had been hovering just out of camera range. "Everything ready for the press conference?" McDonald asked his media director.

MARATHON

"We roll at noon. We'll have a dozen or more top athletes, the usual suspects, sitting in the front rows. The mayor has promised to attend, although he may come late. The chief knows her lines. She'll accept a 'whereas' plaque from the mayor."

McDonald nodded. In the last several years, the Lake City Marathon had achieved a level of respectability within the city that surprised even him. Longtime Mayor Richard T. Danson had not always been a fan of the marathon. The first African-American mayor in Lake City history, the mayor once considered the marathon the sport of wealthy white people, even though runners from Africa usually crossed the finish line first. His department heads for some years had treated the race, its organizers and runners as an intrusion on their business day, a drain on public services. Blocked streets along the 26 mile 385 yard course caused complaints from citizens caught in traffic. Then shortly after Lake City Bank had assumed sponsorship, the Bank's chief executive officer, Robin Carter, sought a meeting with Mayor Danson.

Robin Carter was unique among bankers, not many females having crashed the glass ceilings in corporations, much less elbowed their way to the top of the stodgy banking world. Carter, having started in the bank as a lowly teller with a night school degree in economics, wasted few words. Meeting with the mayor, the bank chief slid a single sheet of paper in front of His Honor's eyes. It was an accounting of how much money runners had spent the previous year on hotels, restaurants, taxicabs and other activities, including shopping. "That's last year," she said. "The dollar figures will increase as the popularity of the marathon continues to increase."

The marathon was not merely a sporting event, it was a convention, the bank chief explained to His Honor. The mayor examined the figures, eyebrows raised, smiled, and passed the sheet back to Carter. "Point made," he said. The following year, services provided by the city improved significantly. The mayor had never attended a pre-marathon press conference before. He began doing so. Banks do have clout, McDonald realized. The bigger the bank, the more clout.

"How's Aba?" Ogilvie asked quietly so the reporter would not hear.

"Still sick," Peter responded in a whisper. "Throwing up. Her husband doesn't know why. I gave them the name of a doctor. We may lose her."

The media director winced when he thought of how much time Peter had spent wooing Aba Andersson and her husband/agent Bjørn, convincing them to select Lake City for her fall marathon. Given all the pre-race publicity, certainly they had gotten value for money offered, but what substitute story could he now offer to the media? He disliked seeing reporters focus on negatives. Not all would understand the reasons offered for why the marathon's main

15

attraction might not run. Baseball and football players play if they catch colds, don't they?

Not coincidentally, when Christine Ferrara began her interview, the first question referred to the world record holder. "The Lake City Marathon has a lightning fast course," she began. "How important is that in attracting elite runners like Aba Andersson to your race?"

"It's important to the elites," McDonald began, but then the media-savvy race director quickly changed direction. "It's equally important to the 50,000 runners finishing behind."

Peter continued: "Everybody wants to run fast. Even someone running a first marathon and hoping to finish in six hours wants their experience to be as pleasant as possible. We have 8,000 volunteers to guarantee that happens."

The race director had done enough interviews for television to know that TV is a medium that thrives on sound bites. Depth is for shows like *Sixty Minutes*. For *The Ten O'clock News*, any response that rambles is liable to either fall to the cutting room floor or be mangled so you do not recognize your message. Reply with more than fifty words, Ogilvie kept reminding him, and you've lost the viewer—if the viewer even gets to hear what you said. More than likely, the reporter will simply not broadcast your comments.

Christine was media savvy enough to know that the race director had dodged her question. *You did that purposely, didn't you?* Christine left that thought unsaid. She did not want to offend her interview subject—yet.

The TV3 reporter offered a series of questions, which allowed McDonald to respond with many of the figures at his command: 50,323 official entries, a few over their 50,000 limit; twenty-nine charities in their charity program, raising $34 million; 1,462,500 paper cups into which would be poured 41,780 gallons of E.R.G. (he mentioned that sport drink's name) along with water from "our beautiful lake."

Christine let the mention of E.R.G. slide past her, somewhat bothered by the commercial implications of the plug, but not wishing a confrontation at this point. She could always slice the E.R.G. plug from the interview as it aired, although she expected that might be difficult to do because he had, almost casually, referenced the sponsor in the middle of a lot of gee-whiz numbers she probably would want to keep.

This guy has been media-packaged, thought Christine. *Probably trained in a room without windows so he could respond to my probing questions. On the other hand, he's drop-dead gorjus!*

"Let's talk about Aba," she asked. "Is it reasonable to expect a world record given the predicted hot weather?"

MARATHON

This girl did her homework, thought Peter. *Most TV sports reporters who followed professional sports would not make the connection between warm weather and slow times.*

"I flunked Meteorology in college," said Peter, sidestepping the question.

She refused to let him do so: "So did most of our TV weathermen."

Peter smiled: "Touché."

"Seriously," Christine continued to bore. "Warm weather; slow times. Yet all of your press releases have promoted the fact that Aba could set a world record on Lake City's fast course."

"Aba's from Sweden. She loves warm weather. Also, seriously, Ms. Ferrara, we have a press conference with Aba scheduled for Saturday noon. I'll let her address your legitimate concerns, which I share. I apologize for ducking your question, something I usually dislike doing."

The reporter nodded, indicating that she accepted his response. But only grudgingly! She suspected that when she returned to the TV studio, she would discover that nothing Peter said related to Aba Andersson and the weather worked as a sound bite.

"One final question," Christine Ferrara offered. She smiled to soften its impact. "The marathon's contract with its main sponsor, the Lake City Bank, ends this year. A foreign conglomerate has just swallowed the bank whole. Has that caused you any sleepless nights, not knowing whether or not they'll be back? Do you feel that the marathon needs something spectacular this year, whether or not a world record, to keep the momentum going?"

Peter McDonald recognized a fact of media life: Reporters always save the tough questions for the end, knowing that if the person they're interviewing gets mad and stalks away, they will at least have answers to the preceding easier questions on tape. He had expected the question, because whether or not the bank, under new ownership, would continue its sponsorship had been the main story in the sports section of the *Lake City Ledger,* the city's main newspaper. The article was the work of Jonathan Von Runyon, a hatchet man, a thorn in Peter's side.

"I'm not looking past Sunday," the race director replied, smiling to show no displeasure. Five words. Not enough for a sound bite. Nothing that could be edited to distort his words or his meaning! Standing behind the reporter, Peter's media director suppressed a grin. *Well done, Peter,* Ogilvie thought. He held up his right hand, thumb elevated, to indicate approval.

Christine Ferrara sighed, making no effort to hide her displeasure. She stood motionless, staring intently at the man she was interviewing. *Does this woman have X-ray vision?* Peter wondered. *If she can read my mind, she may learn about Celebrity X.*

THURSDAY

For a moment, the TV reporter continued to hold the microphone between her and Peter, debating whether to continue to probe or let the subject drop or maybe plunk him over the head with the mike. The investigative reporter inside her clambered for a follow-up question, but in reality she thought the *Ledger* article and its suggestion that the marathon might be in financial trouble if the bank bailed was a stretch, something not worth wasting a lot of air time on before the race. Maybe after. Better to keep comments positive rather than negative going in, especially since TV3 would televise the marathon. *Am I copping out? Maybe.* Christine lowered the microphone and turned to Edmund the cameraman. "That's a wrap."

Turning back to Peter, she looked at him without speaking. Nor did he speak. For one second, two seconds, what seemed like an eternity, neither one spoke to the other.

Christine finally broke the silence with another sigh. "You know, Peter... May I call you Peter?"

Peter nodded, indicating that use of his first name was proper.

Still another sigh, then an admission, "...I'm being terribly rude."

He thought so too, but did not want to say so. "I hadn't noticed."

She knew he was lying, but that was okay. She was in the midst of an apology. "Overslept. Didn't get my second cup of coffee. And..."

Peter finished the sentence for her: "...And I was late."

Christine knew there was another reason related to time-of-the-month, but she was not about to share it with a man she had just met. She offered her hand: "Can we be friends?"

"Let's be," acknowledged Peter, shaking hers, then adding: "I'd offer to buy you that cup of coffee, but I'm on too tight a schedule this morning."

While packing his camera equipment, Edmund had been observing this mating dance with mounting amusement. "I have some coffee in the truck," he suggested.

"Be quiet, Edmund," said Christine. "I'm trying to be humble."

Peter sensed a chance to escape. "Gotta fly," he told the reporter, instinctively touching her lightly on the shoulder. The moment he did so, he worried she might misinterpret that touch.

Apparently she did not. Her response was warm, friendly. "I'll probably see you at the press conference, Mr. McDonald," said the reporter, shifting politely back to his last name.

"I'll be there," Peter replied, "but I need to take a walk through the hall and see how work is coming. Good to meet you, Ms. Ferrara."

Christine Ferrara noticed that he had pointedly failed to address her by the name Christine, despite her obvious invitation to do so. Or maybe he already had forgotten her name. *Men*, she thought.

18

She continued to watch Peter McDonald as he moved away, thinking: *Here I am new in town, without any significant male companionship, no social life because of my career, approaching my 30th birthday, my biological clock ticking, and I act like a clueless teenager with the first good-looking guy I meet.* Christine allowed one final sigh to escape her lips, then began to walk with her cameraman toward the escalator.

71:38:00

As Peter McDonald left Christine Ferrara and stepped into the chaos surrounding preparations for Friday's opening of the Health & Fitness Exposition, the man he called Celebrity X boarded the Gulfstream G550 at the airfield near Rome.

71:38:00. 71:37:59. 71:37:58.

This was a plane pilots referred to as the "G-5," the longest range business jet in the world, capable of cruising 6,750 nautical miles at speeds up to 680 mph at an altitude of 51,000 feet. The décor within the Gulfstream's cabin provided a luxury level equal to that of a penthouse in a five-star hotel.

A man of simple roots, Celebrity X found himself often discomfited by the pomp and circumstances that came with his position, particularly when he considered the plight of so many poor people in the world, particularly the children of Africa, so many suffering from AIDS, but those responsible for his safety expected him to travel in style. They would have been discomforted if he chose to do otherwise.

Moving forward in the cabin, Celebrity X selected one of a dozen swiveling chairs. His bodyguards followed. The two men in black were named Mario Castriota and Angelo Nesci. With everyone seated, the Gulfstream began to move away from the group on the ground. Those left behind watched with practiced impassiveness, as though to exhibit any emotion would betray their profession.

The jet was as anonymous looking as X and those accompanying him. No identifying marks that might make it stand out from any other airplane you might see at airports around the world. It was white, no corporate logos. In fact, the Gulfstream was not owned, but rented. For security reasons, each time Celebrity X needed to travel unnoticed, people in his employ rented a different plane to avoid any identifying patterns.

Money was not a factor. The organization with which Peter McDonald's friend was connected owned trillions, not merely billions, of dollars in assets throughout the world. In comparison, the conglomerate, Shelaghi that had recently acquired Lake City Bank was like a ma & pa Grocery Store. Realistically speaking, the position X occupied with the multibillion-dollar organization was that of chief executive officer; although he did not fit the mold of a typical CEO, and most of the people of the world who knew him by face, name and position might be shocked and maybe even offended if they heard him referred to by that title.

Celebrity X fastened his seat belt as the Gulfstream taxied down the runway to position itself for takeoff. There was no control tower to grant permission, so when the pilots reached the far end of the runway, they simply did a 180-degree turn and pushed the throttles to full power. The Gulfstream's engines screamed sharply as the jet picked up speed, lifting off the ground and soaring out over rolling hills and green trees.

Celebrity X carried a briefcase stuffed with papers, work to consider during a long trans-atlantic plane ride. But rather than open it, he settled back into his seat, staring mindlessly for a few precious minutes as the Gulfstream climbed into a sky clear of clouds.

Instead of concentrating on the many worries of his profession, Celebrity X enjoyed the view of Rome retreating in the distance and thought ahead to the marathon he would run on Sunday. A former track athlete, X had quit running competitively after high school to concentrate on the next stage of his life. He ran recreationally in college and into graduate school, but soon his schedule became so crowded that he had to abandon any attempt to maintain a regular exercise routine.

X did his job well. He was bright and quickly rose to the top. His ascent shocked and even angered many within his own organization, but they soon embraced him. X possessed a natural charisma and a way of charming even those who might have become his enemies, overwhelming any doubts they once might have harbored. He settled easily into his position of prominence. Only then did X start running again to cope with the enormous stresses imposed by his position and fame — and to lose a little weight.

X began by installing a treadmill in a room near his lavishly decorated office in the heart of Rome. His fame tied him to his office and his connected residence. Certainly, it would be impossible for him to run on the twisting streets of the Eternal City; he would stop traffic. So he ran twenty or thirty minutes a day on a treadmill, staring at a TV set to both maintain contact with world events and alleviate boredom.

At various times of the year, X spent time at a castle outside the city, its surrounding grounds at certain times of the day closed to the public. This permitted him to actually run outdoors, usually before sunrise in company with the fittest of his bodyguards, including Mario and Angelo, the two with him on the Gulfstream.

Celebrity X disliked feeling hemmed in and longed for the loneliness of the long distance runner. Sometimes he would sneak out after midnight to run on trails through the hills, lit only by the moon and stars and without bodyguards, but this made the people responsible for his safety very nervous. *Very* nervous. An assassin had attacked one of his predecessors; nobody wanted a similar incident occurring on their watch. He could be killed; he could be kidnapped. Mario would get particularly upset if he learned his "boss" had been out running without him and did not hesitate to complain. "Just call me!" scolded the bodyguard in a tone a teacher might use to correct a disobedient pupil, a tone that might have gotten the bodyguard fired if his employer was without humor or less aware of his own transgressions

Sometimes when he returned home to the East Side, the blue-collar community on the edge of Lake City where he and Peter McDonald grew up, Celebrity X would call his friend and ask that they meet for a run. It was a neighborhood of plain but comfortable homes. X could still walk or run the streets or a grassy park near the high school without causing a commotion. Neighbors did not treat him like a rock star and formed their own wall of protection against those who did.

One morning he suggested to Peter that one of his desires before becoming famous had been to some day run a marathon, not to prove anything, but just to do it. X wondered if he might find freedom surrounded by 50,000 likeminded runners. There seemed something special about completing a journey—some might call it a pilgrimage—of 26 miles 385 yards. It was what attracted so many to the sport of long distance running.

During the length of a run lasting forty-five minutes, he and Peter each had come up with numerous reasons why it would be impossible to run a marathon: impossible to find time to train, impossible to avoid having his plans detected, impossible to participate in such a public event without turning it into a carnival.

Yes, it was impossible, but as the two friends continued their conversation at breakfast in the kitchen of X's widowed mother, a plan developed. That was when he assumed the identity of Celebrity X.

His briefcase beside him, X wistfully stared out the window remembering that moment, simultaneously watching the ground disappear beneath him as the Gulfstream continued to climb to cruising altitude. He was protected, pampered, waited on hand and foot, transported in luxury. People stepped aside and stopped talking when he wandered into the room. It made X uncomfortable, but it was a cross he had to bear.

THURSDAY

Once the jet reached cruising altitude, X could rise from his seat and wander around the comfortable cabin, grab a cup of coffee, a snack from the refrigerator, without having to ring a bell and ask a flight attendant for service. He could talk to Mario and Angelo as equals, ask them about their mothers, their girlfriends, their favorite soccer teams. (The two bodyguards often argued about whose team was best, an argument neither seemed able or willing to win.) Given the distance between their ranks, the bodyguards and X could hardly be friends, but the barriers dropped when no one else could see them or hear their conversations.

X could stroll forward and chat with the pilots, even sit in one of their chairs and fly the plane for a while. The pilots seemed overjoyed to show him how they functioned in their jobs. He could not even begin to describe to them how he functioned in his. Yet in one sense, he was like them: a pilot, but a pilot of men, not airplanes.

Celebrity X looked at his watch, saw that it was 2:30 in the afternoon, and reckoned it to be early morning in Lake City. Fewer than seventy-two hours separated X from what would be his first and probably only marathon.

71:30:00. 71:29:59. 71:29:58.

Peter, who at that moment was wandering through the convention center, had asked that Celebrity X call after he became airborne, but X decided it was still too early in Lake City for him to call. He would delay before doing so and, in the meantime, enjoy the scenery below. The Gulfstream continued to rise toward its cruising altitude, leaving the small airport far behind. The black limousine that had delivered X to the airport already had departed, as had the other limousines, but two men remained at the end of the runway, prior to climbing back on motorcycles to return to Rome.

The first man, the one who had watched Celebrity X's departure through a pair of binoculars, now reached in the pocket of his leather jacket and removed a cell phone. He punched two buttons that automatically connected him to a pre-programmed number. The number he dialed rang twice. The ringing stopped as someone answered.

That person did not speak.

"He's departed," said the first man.

Still there was no response at the other end. A sharp click indicated that the person answering had hung up.

70:30:00

Driving out of the parking garage and past the convention center's main entrance en route to a meeting with bank executives at Hilliard Towers, Peter McDonald spotted someone familiar: the TV reporter who had interviewed him earlier. Following a tour by the race director of Expo preparations that had taken him nearly an hour, it was now 9:30 A.M., less than seventy-one hours before the start of the Lake City Marathon.

70:30:00. 70:29:59. 70:29:58.

Peter was surprised she had not yet left the building. Christine Ferrara stood in the taxi pickup area, looking exasperated. On a morning with no major conventions in town, there were no taxis, because there were few conventioneers to transport.

Peter was driving a minivan with "Lake City Marathon" and pictures of runners wrapped around it. The minivan was gaudy, almost embarrassing to drive, but it came with the job. He slowed and looked toward the TV reporter, who had not yet seen him. She was not exactly the most delightful female he ever had met. The reporter was confrontational with most of her questions, but Peter had become hardened when it came to members of the media with hidden agendas. It was their job. She had apologized at the end—somewhat.

Should he blow the lady off and head to the hotel pretending he had not seen her? He was tempted to do so, but he was not exactly piloting a stealth bomber. She was certain to see him trying to escape. More than that, he could not resist rescuing a damsel in distress.

Peter slid to a stop and punched a button lowering the window on the passenger side: "Can I offer you a ride, Ms. Ferrara?"

The TV reporter allowed a sigh of relief to escape her lips. "Yes," she said. "That would be a help—a *very* big help!"

She added: "I was afraid I might have to run to the hotel or miss the press conference." The TV reporter opened the door and climbed into the van, a move that resulted in her tight skirt sliding higher up her legs than she normally might think proper. Peter could not help looking at those legs: long and well-formed. She was wearing high heels, red to match her TV3 blouse, the shoes hardly suited for walking, much less running the mile-plus separating the convention center from the host hotel.

Peter was about to make that comment, but caught himself, fearful of revealing where his gaze had wandered. He suspected she knew. Women are

23

not dumb; certainly not this one. Peter safely shifted his eyes to his wristwatch: "You haven't been waiting for a cab since our interview, have you?"

Christine smiled. "No, we did some more shots in the hall." Only someone very observant might have noticed her face reddening. She had told a slight fib. After several minutes filming the chaos in the hall, Edmund her cameraman had left for the hotel where the press conference was scheduled to occur in several hours. She sent him ahead, promising to meet him later. Christine's period suddenly had arrived two days ahead of schedule, and she had to rush into the women's rest room, hoping there was a sanitary napkin dispenser on the wall. Fortunately, there was. But this was hardly the sort of intimate information you shared with a man first met only an hour before!

She quickly shifted subject, offering her best smile: "Nice wheels."

Peter resisted the temptation to repeat those exact words. Instead he laughed, responding simply: "Borrowed from the guys in the warehouse. Living in the city, I don't own a real car."

For a moment their eyes locked, the silence saying more than any words. Christine was first to look away, feeling flustered while doing so. She did *not* like this man—or did she? He *was* cute. Christine focused her gaze forward and assumed her best nonchalant pose. Her mother would be proud.

Peter continued to stare at the TV reporter for a few seconds before looking away himself. He said nothing, figuring this was no time for pick-up lines. Not for someone with an obvious chip on her shoulder.

Peter pulled the van into bumper-to-bumper traffic moving tortuously slow along Jefferson Avenue, the wide boulevard leading into the downtown area where it separated Lake City's skyscrapers from park and lake. Drivers were honking. Tempers were rising among people late to work and to meetings. Living in the city presented such challenges, but he loved it. Rush hour should be over. Maybe there was an accident ahead, or some construction project. Probably not the latter, since they were on the marathon course, and it was his business to know about any construction on the course that might impede runners on race day. For the next half dozen blocks heading north toward Hilliard Towers, they would be tracking the marathon in its last mile. Just before the 26-mile mark, the course turned east on Rushmore Road into Dearborn Park. After crossing a bridge over commuter railroad tracks, the course quickly turned north again with the finish line only 385 yards away.

Marathoners who previously had run Lake City called the bridge "Mount Rushmore," even though it caused barely a five- or ten-foot change in elevation. But even that much of a climb might force a struggling marathoner to shift from a run to a walk. McDonald, knowing runners chose his race because of its flat and fast course, wished he could remove even that one bump, but you could not get from downtown into the park without using a bridge over the railroad tracks. Once crossed, however, and with the finish line in view, runners had a slight downhill that caused nearly everybody to pick up their pace and nibble seconds from their times.

For some (the elite runners at the front of the field), even improving their finishing time by a few seconds might mean setting a world record with all the cash that accompanied that achievement. McDonald estimated that when you combined prize money and bonuses, both from the bank and sponsors, a runner setting a world record could earn a half million dollars or more. That was one of the lures he had used in recruiting Abe Andersson to run his marathon. There were also bonuses for men running faster than 2:10 or for women bettering 2:30 to insure that runners ran hard to set fast times.

The media liked to report world records and fast times, and the Lake City Marathon's reputation for having one of the fastest courses in the world attracted runners of all ability levels. If you wanted to qualify for the Olympic Trials, Lake City was the place to do it. If you wanted to qualify for the Boston Marathon (BQ for Boston Qualifier), Lake City was the place to do it. If you wanted to set a Personal Record (PR), Lake City was the place to do it. If this was your first marathon and your only goal was finishing, Lake City also was the place to succeed with the least effort. A fast course and a fast time was part of the reason 50,000 entered the Lake City Marathon, the field closing early in the spring. Would records be set at Lake City this year? Peter McDonald worried that the predicted warm weather might make that difficult. Would slow times for elite runners and those behind impact the success of this year's marathon, specifically its continued ability to attract sponsors? Given the change in bank ownership, how about his own job security? Peter thought his job safe, but a cloud of uncertainty hung over this year's running of the Lake City Marathon.

With all that going through his mind, he forgot for a moment the presence of a pretty passenger in his van. "Penny for your thoughts," she said.

"I'm sorry," he said. "I can't drive even a block on the course without having it grab my attention. I'm not a very good host."

"Is that for background or for attribution?"

"Background only," Peter smiled as they waited for a red light to change. Was she making fun of him? Probably not, but he could not tell. There was a fire in those brown eyes staring back at him. She made him just a bit uncomfortable. But the TV reporter was good looking. Maybe that was part of the problem. He was just a bit frightened of the woman, frightened of all women. Frightened of beginning a relationship, the memory of Carol and how he had lost her still haunting him. Peter knew he needed to move past that painful memory, but it would not be easy.

"What about you?" he shifted the subject. "Why do I not know your name and face? Have I not been paying attention? Sometimes I fall asleep before *The Ten O'clock News*." Having made that comment, Peter decided he probably should not have.

The reporter did not seem offended. "I sometimes can't stay awake that late myself—particularly on days when I have to get up early to interview people at 8:00 in the morning...."

Peter laughed: "...especially people who don't show up on time."

"I didn't say that." Christine smiled, a tight smile, lips closed. "Besides, you were only eight minutes late."

"You timed me?"

"It's my business." Christine allowed the smile to fade from her face. *That was rather pert of me*, she thought. The TV reporter was not sure which way this conversation was going.

"So, I apologize for not recognizing you."

"No need to. I'm the new girl in town. Unless your satellite dish can pick up Peoria channels, there would be no reason to know I existed until several weeks ago, when TV3 gave me a call."

"Peoria?" commented Peter. "Big jump from Peoria to Lake City. Most TV reporters would take years to scratch their way from Peoria to Des Moines to Denver before getting a call from Lake City."

Christine was surprised at her new acquaintance's knowledge of how career advancement worked in the competitive field of TV broadcasting. She replied. "When someone called claiming to be with TV3 in Lake City, I said, 'Yeah, right. April Fool's is past, and I'm the biggest fool at last.' I thought my roommate's boyfriend was making a joke."

She was talking rapidly now, but could not stop herself. "It turned out to be one of the TV3 directors, who luckily did not see how red my face got. He laughed and introduced himself. His name was Tom Schorr."

"He works with us on the marathon telecast."

"Right," said Christine, momentarily uncomfortable because maybe she was talking out of turn to someone just barely met. Nevertheless she could not stop her flow of words: "Turns out Tom had graduated from Bradley University, my alma mater, and was in town for some alumni event. He saw the news at 10:00, and there I was. Tom confessed later that when he returned home, he called the station vice president and said, 'Hire that girl!'"

"Hire that girl?" commented Peter. "Very insensitive. My bosses never would allow me to refer to you as a 'girl.'"

"I was horribly offended too, but only until they told me how much more I would be making. At that point, I suspended what would have been my usual sense of feminist outrage."

26

Peter laughed, something he lately did not often do. Though they had been exchanging mostly small talk, Peter had begun to warm to the reporter. *Maybe she's not that bad after all. At least she has a sense of humor.* "Sports reporter?" He asked.

"General assignment reporter, meaning I do everything. The producer calls a meeting every morning and tells everybody which story to chase—although that can change hour to hour based on breaking news. When hired, I made the tactical error of mentioning that I once had run a marathon. Coincidentally, the station was looking for stories to assign to me until the reporter I'm replacing goes on maternity leave. So here I am."

"Time?"

"Beg pardon?"

"Your time in the marathon? You finished, didn't you? If not, my apologies for asking. I'll send flowers."

Flowers, she thought. *Ummm. Please do!* "You don't want to hear my time. Very slow."

"Actually, you're probably right. I don't want to hear, because this weekend my attention span is about that of a kindergartner. I'd forget your time in three seconds and embarrass myself asking you again the next time we meet."

"Four twenty-one," she said.

"Four twenty-one? You ran that fast in the marathon? You should be running the race instead of covering it. Background or for attribution?"

"I'm sorry?"

"Your time: background or for attribution? Can I mention your time at the press conference?"

"Don't you *dare!* Besides, you've already forgotten my finishing time. Three seconds have passed—unless you weren't telling the truth. People I interview on TV sometimes have been known to do that."

"You're right. I've already forgotten. I never lie, especially to reporters.... Excuse me." McDonald felt a vibration against his hip, his cellular phone indicating a caller. He looked at the name displayed on the phone and told his passenger. "My apologies, but I need to take this call."

The identity of the caller displayed on his cell phone was "X." If Peter had been falling out of an airplane, he would have answered the phone before pulling the ripcord.

"Che paso, amico?" Peter began. What's happening, friend?

"Heading your way," responded Celebrity X. "Where are you at?"

"In a van driving from the convention center to the hotel, a slightly slower vehicle than the one in which you're riding, particularly given Lake City's typically awful traffic."

"I'll trade jobs and vehicles any day. Are you alone? Can you talk?"

THURSDAY

Peter glanced toward Christine: "I'm riding with a TV3 reporter looking for a good story. Got one to offer?"

Christine Ferrara looked sideways at Peter McDonald, wondering why she was being brought into a conversation with someone she did not know. *Men!* They sometimes can be so difficult. She pretended not to have overheard.

"You're not thinking of selling me out, are you, Peter?"

"Avverbio!" What a brilliant idea. Peter directed his attention to the passenger in his van: "Ms. Ferrara, are you interested in a story about some guy running his first marathon?"

Without waiting for her answer, Peter redirected his attention to his phone conversation. "Not interested. She's looking for someone more exciting, a person who knows how to dress. Your outfits—how can I say it—are so déclassé. Besides, you're from out-of-town. She needs someone local."

Celebrity X laughed. How easy it was for the two of them to fall into the old banter of friends from the East Side. "She?" said X. "*She*, Peter? I hope some day there is another 'she' in your life."

Peter's voice shifted in pitch, confronted suddenly with a memory both pleasant and tragic. "It will happen," Peter replied. "When the right...." Peter stopped mid-sentence. He was about to say 'when the right girl comes along,' until he remembered those words might not be understood by the person beside him. Peter offered as substitute: "When it's the right time."

X searched for words and finally said simply: "I miss Carol."

"I do too," said Peter. "Every day of my life."

Unable not to listen to one end of the conversation, Christine wondered what was being said on the other end. She noticed Peter's voice change tone. Was it her imagination, or was there the hint of a tear in his eye?

Then Peter's voice changed again and after several more minutes of what seemed to her guy talk, he ended the conversation. "I need to talk to you about arrangements for Sunday. Can I call you back in a couple of hours? I'll be out of the press conference with more time to talk."

"Let me call you," said X. "I need some nap time."

"I do too. Somehow I don't think I'm going to get it this weekend."

"Ciao, Peter," said Celebrity X.

"Ciao," responded Peter. With a look toward Christine that said excuse me," he began another conversation with a second caller.

The second caller was media director Nelson Ogilvie, who after the TV interviews had left immediately for the hotel to prepare for the bank meeting at 10:30 and noon press conference. "What's up, Nelson?" said Peter, then after a pause, "I'm approaching the hotel. I'll see you at the meeting."

Peter placed the cell phone back on the console, shaking his head. "Cell phones, the curse of our century. After the marathon, I want to find a resort on a Caribbean island, where they have the ability to jam electronic signals. No voice mail. No text messages. Nothing but white sand and blue water and a piña colada in your hand you watch the sunset."

Christine, still irritated at being ignored while Peter had taken two cell phone calls, did not reply. She decided she had said too much already. It was like they had been fencing with each other during the entire length of the ride from the convention center. In a way it had been fun, but theirs was a business relationship: *Right?* She suspected the race director would be happy to get her out of his car.

Peter turned left off Jefferson Avenue at the north end of the hotel, then into the driveway where arriving guests stopped their cars before registering. Several valet parking attendants waited to see if he wanted them to park the van or park it himself in the garage attached to the hotel. He wanted neither, but knew that a ten-dollar bill slipped into the right hand would allow the van to be parked, at least briefly, in the driveway.

"If you don't mind, Ms. Ferrara, I'll let you off here. I need to get something out of the van. I'd offer to buy you a cup of coffee, but I have a meeting with some people from the bank."

"I'll take a rain check on the cup of coffee, and I'll assume that the mention of the meeting with the bankers was for background, not attribution. And this girl from Peoria still answers to the name Christine."

Peter did not answer. He sat motionless, waiting for her to vacate his van so he could get on with his business organizing a race for 50,000 runners.

Christine sensed a slight irritation on his part, but recognized she was being invited to remove herself from his van—as soon as possible! "Thanks for the lift, Peter," she said, offering her hand before opening the door to get out. He accepted it. She smiled and closed the door behind her.

"My pleasure," he said and watched as she started to walk toward the revolving door leading into the hotel. They were parting on a rather sour note. Continuing to watch, he pushed the button to lower the passenger window. As it slid downward, he called after her:

"Christine!"

She turned to look at him, puzzled. "Yes, Peter."

"Four twenty-one," he said.

The TV broadcaster laughed, waved and disappeared through the revolving door, into the hotel lobby. As Christine walked along a deeply carpeted hallway, she noticed a rest room on the left that she should now visit. After she came out, Christine could call the station to see if they had received this morning's interview in time for *The Noon News*. Edmund her cameraman should have emailed the Expo interviews to the station by now.

THURSDAY

Busying herself inside the rest room, Christine Ferrara found herself having difficulty concentrating on her job. Instead, she found herself thinking of Peter McDonald, who had committed her marathon time to memory. *That was so funny*. Christine decided that maybe she liked him after all.

70:00:00

Meghan Allison, D.P.M. arrived at the Metro Fresh store trailing an empty shopping cart, preparing to fill it with proper foods for her final carbo-loads leading to the Lake City Marathon. After finishing her studies as a podiatrist and before going to work in that profession full time, Meg decided to take a year off to train for a marathon. She figured it would be her one and only shot at that race distance.

Matthew Allison, her husband, supported Meg in her marathon goal. In fact, Matt suggested it. Meg had been a talented runner in high school, a state champion, who never quite excelled in college because of suffering one injury after another. Meg admitted she had chosen podiatry as a profession because of her pain-plagued collegiate career. "I've had every running injury imaginable," she claimed. "I should know how to treat them."

Matt, a former competitive swimmer, had a well-paid job as an insurance claims adjuster. Without children, without even a dog, without a car, they did not immediately need her contribution to the family income.

He recognized his wife's unfulfilled athletic potential. One night Matt challenged her: "Why not run a marathon? See how good you can be."

"Are you sure?" worried Meg. "We've got so many loans."

"We'll pay them next year. I'll be married to a rich doctor by then."

"Mmmmm," she said. "Is that why you married me?"

"Truth be told...."

"Quiet!" said Meg, tapping his cheek with her hand to silence him.

Matt and Meg were lying in bed, still wrapped around each other after making love. She later would accuse him of having seduced her into becoming a marathon runner.

That post coital conversation had happened nearly a year ago, and now Meghan Allison had only seventy hours remaining before stepping to the starting line of the Lake City Marathon in a quest to discover just how good a runner she could become.

70:00:00. 69:59:59. 69:59:58.

MARATHON

Her visit to Metro Fresh was part of that quest. Meg had taken courses in nutrition as well as anatomy at podiatry school, figuring running injuries occurred because of a multitude of reasons: bad eating habits being one of them. With three days remaining, Meg knew it was time to focus her eating on three forms of food: carbohydrates, carbohydrates and more carbohydrates. That would pack her muscles with a maximum load of glycogen, assuring peak performance on Sunday. Of course, her success also was tied to a training routine that included double workouts daily averaging 80 to 100 miles a week.

Metro Foods was one of the sponsors for the Lake City Marathon, and she shopped frequently at the chain's Metro Fresh store only two blocks from their apartment on the Near North Side. Smaller than most Metro Foods stores, more tastefully decorated, Schubert playing rather than the Stones, and—many of its customers complained—much higher prices. That was Metro Fresh: Fewer foods, but most of them designed for a specialty market. Better cuts of meat. An expanded delicatessen. Flowers! Few bottles of wine priced under $10. Interesting items like dried cranberries. Where else in town could you find an entire aisle devoted to nuts and dried fruits? No tacky tabloids by the checkout counter. If you wanted to buy toothpaste or toilet paper, better pick another store.

Meg had strategically chosen to shop at Metro Fresh for her next three dinners—Thursday, Friday and Saturday—essential meals, since the first-time marathoner and soon to be podiatrist was in peak carbo-load.

Meg knew you need not eat spaghetti three nights in a row to be able to finish a 26 mile 385 yard race. She understood sports nutrition and, despite her skinny frame, possessed a voracious appetite. Matt once had accused his wife of having the feeding habits of a shark. Meg got a little irritated at him saying it at a party, particularly when he added that she walked through their apartment with her mouth open absorbing all loose calories in sight.

"Matt!" she had said in a half-hearted effort to silence him, but the first line got a laugh so her husband continued: "Meg can empty the contents of a refrigerator simply by opening the door and inhaling."

More laughter. "Ha, ha, Mr. Saturday Night Live," said Meg pretending to be embarrassed, putting her hand over Matt's mouth so he could say no more, but secretly pleased. Because of her lack of boobs or butt or anything that resembled cellulose, Meghan Allison, naturally blonde, had gone through life with many worried that she might suffer from anorexia nervosa. Or bulimia. Far from it, her mom informed Meg's teachers in elementary school. Mom had used the shark analogy that eventually had been stolen by her husband. *That's me*, thought Meg, *the skinny shark*.

It was Meg's metabolism. Shoveling food into her was like shoveling coal into an all-consuming furnace. Meg remembered the time her high school

31

cross-country coach, Edgar McAnally, had taken her to the track between her freshman and sophomore years. Feeling he might have the makings of a state champion, Coach McNally wanted to introduce her to interval training: fast 400-meter repeats punctuated by slow 400s, ten of them at a time. He asked Meg to wear a heart rate monitor: a strap attached to below her tiny chest that broadcast a signal to a wrist monitor that recorded heartbeats-per-minute every five seconds.

Coach McAnally later told other teachers that watching Meg Allison run was like watching a deer bounding through the forest. You could almost hear Beethoven's Pastoral Symphony playing in the background. Yet when he played back the results of the workout as recorded by the heart rate monitor, he was ready either to send the device back to the manufacturer or to quickly call 9-1-1. Meg's heart rate had spiked at a machine-gun-like 260 during the fast repeats, sinking back to half that number during the recovery interval.

Eventually coach and athlete adapted her training to the reality of a high metabolism. Although her maximum heart rate had declined somewhat as she aged, Meg never worried about having to diet to meet her best running weight, which was 108 pounds draped tightly on a 5-foot-8-inches skeleton, not that unusual for elite runners. Instead, she needed to focus on consuming a significantly high number of calories, particularly as she pushed her weekly mileage up near 100 while training for the Lake City Marathon. In order to fuel her body, Meg needed close to 4,000 calories a day, enough to make most women gain weight rapidly.

Meg Allison knew those should not be empty calories. She balanced her diet at 55 percent carbohydrates, 30 percent fats and 15 percent protein. That was the gold standard. No low-fat or low-carb diets if you want success as an endurance athlete. Her motto, borrowed from a runner's cookbook she owned, was, "Eat a wide variety of lightly-processed foods." Meg learned to distrust anything in the grocery store that came wrapped in plastic. That was one reason Meg enjoyed shopping at Metro Fresh.

As the glass door slid open to welcome Meg, she examined her shopping list. Knowing that Matt might leave if forced to endure three consecutive days of spaghetti, she planned to select foods guaranteed to please his palette and provide her with the carb-calories she needed for marathon success.

Thursday night featured lamb chops, and she knew that runners without a thorough knowledge of nutrition might shudder at the choice of red meat so close to the marathon. But lamb chops come small, and you *do* need fats and protein, even during the carbo-load. Accompanying each lamb chop on the plate would be a baked potato, and she sifted through the potato bin to choose large ones. Add to that asparagus. A salad of greens and tomatoes served in best Italian fashion after the main meal came next. Matt loved to make salads and would shove her out of the way if she dared interfere. Particularly for tonight, she would warn him not to overdose on olive oil. For dessert, yogurt topped with peaches.

Oh, and a glass of wine. Surprise: a pinot grigio by King Estates in Eugene, Oregon, the so-called "track capital of the world." She enjoyed hanging out in the more than ample wine department of Metro Fresh, playing the role of connoisseur. Neither she nor Matt drank much, but they did fancy a fine wine with dinner. Add candles: two. Light them and dim the lights. Every evening with Matt offered an excuse for romance.

Friday night she planned to have fish. Her parents raised her as a proper Catholic for whom anything other than fish on a Friday night was an abomination. The church no longer forced that obligation upon its members, but she still clung tenderly to the tradition. Salmon seemed a good choice. A pinot noir accompanying. Many believed that fish demanded to be eaten with white wine, not red. Meg never had heard any fish complain, so selected a noir: Erath Reserve from Salishan Hills on the Oregon coast.

Saturday night before the marathon, what else? Pasta with marinara sauce. Wine? Cabernet Sauvignon: Estancia, from Paso Robles, California Should she have a glass? Would that much alcohol hinder her performance on Sunday? Her brother Aaron Kennedy was coming to dinner with his fiancé, Moira. Aaron planned to run the first half dozen miles with her as pacer, mainly to hold her back so she did not go out too fast. Meg did not want to seem like some running geek who lived a Spartan life. The Spartans drank wine before they went off to battle, didn't they?

Everything else, Meg noted as she rolled her shopping cart out of Metro Fresh, she had pretty well covered. Even the marathon. Nobody expected her to do as well as she planned. Meghan Allison would surprise them.

69:30:00

Hilliard Towers occupied an entire block on Jefferson Avenue overlooking the park and lake, also overlooking the start and finish lines of the Lake City Marathon. With two dozen floors and nearly two thousand nicely appointed rooms, the Hilliard served each year as the race's headquarters hotel. Partly for that reason—but more because of closeness to the epicenter of race activity—the block of rooms reserved at the Hilliard for runners disappeared rapidly each year.

THURSDAY

For good reason: Unlike point-to-point races such as Boston, New York and Grandma's Marathon (a popular race in Duluth, Minnesota), Lake City featured a loop course with start and finish lines conveniently close to each other and close to downtown hotels, including the Hilliard. No long bus rides or sitting around for hours in staging areas. No standing in lines to use portable toilets that took on distinct odors as the starting time grew near. Waiting to use the toilet was a major inconvenience for runners, particularly at the biggest races. New York even featured an open trough for urinating men, a favorite Photo-Op for many women with cell-phone cameras.

No risk of exposure at Lake City, since runners could stay in their rooms until the last minute, make one final stop in a nicely-tiled toilet, head for the elevators and arrive at the starting line within minutes. At the end of the day, those same runners could return to the hotel to take an ice bath while waiting for room service to deliver a post-marathon snack. If you wanted a room at the Hilliard for next year's marathon, you needed to book it within a few weeks of last year's marathon, otherwise look to find lodging elsewhere.

The hotel had been built in 1908 and named after its principle investor, Timothy Hilliard, a well-known Lake City business executive, founder of Hilliard Steel, a mill on the lakefront near the city's East Side neighborhood. Hilliard Steel no longer existed, its ancient blast furnaces uncompetitive with those of other countries, specifically China. The steel company had vanished, its buildings torn down for scrap metal. But Hilliard's name remained on the hotel and probably would indefinitely, the hotel now listed on the National Register of Historical Places. A plaque in the lobby entrance commemorated that fact. Hanging in that entrance also was a digital clock telling guests in the hotel the precise time in hours, minutes and seconds before the start of the Lake City Marathon.

69:30:00. 69:29:59. 69:29:58.

Stepping into an elevator, McDonald pressed the button for the twenty-fourth floor, entirely given over to the Presidential Suite, in which he and several of the other important officers of the bank were lodged. Over the years, many United States presidents beginning with Teddy Roosevelt had stayed in those same rooms, hence its name. The Presidential Suite was where his scheduled meeting with the executives from Shelaghi, the Irish conglomerate that now owned Lake City Bank, would occur, beginning at 10:30. He was a few minutes late. Peter was not entirely certain of the purpose of the meeting other than to greet and press flesh with those executives, but he knew it was important that he attend, even if it meant shortening his preparation for the press conference following at noon.

34

MARATHON

On the twenty-fourth floor, Peter McDonald walked into a high-ceiling living room whose most elegant feature, other than a grand piano tucked into one corner, was a wall of picture windows overlooking Dearborn Park and the lake. The view was exceptional, and few people could walk into that room without being drawn almost magnetically toward those windows and the balconies to which they led. Even with snow on the balconies midwinter, Very Important People staying in the Presidential Suite or using it for receptions would thrust the glassed doors open and step out into the cold air to absorb the view, surely equal to any in Lake City.

The air certainly was not cold today, Lake City being gripped by an unseasonable warm spell. A half dozen executives dressed in business suits, like the people Peter McDonald had seen in the lobby on this day before most marathoners had arrived in town, stood on one of the balconies. One of them turned now and moved toward Peter: Nelson Ogilvie, his media director. "Peter, I'd like you to meet our guests from Ireland." An exchange of names and handshakes followed.

Observing these bank executives whose decisions in the next month, particularly in the area of budget, could affect his ability to maintain the Lake City Marathon in its preeminence among world races as well as affect his own livelihood, Peter noted that few of them possessed the skinny builds of runners. More like Gaelic football players, or at least fans of that Irish game.

Central to the group was a man who Peter recognized as Dennis Lahey, his title executive manager, his role second in command to the conglomerate's chief executive officer back in Ireland. In briefing Peter prior to the meeting, Ogilvie had suggested that while all of the visitors from Shelaghi were important, Lahey was most important of them all. A lurking hulk of a man with curly short hair and a ruddy complexion, Lahey was the one to whom heads would turn when it came to making critical decisions, specifically related to the marathon's future role within the broader corporate picture. Ogilvie quickly introduced the two.

"You have a very beautiful city," Lahey told Peter McDonald while shaking his hand. Lahey lingered over the world "bee-yoo-ti-ful," the lilting flow of his Irish accent converting an ordinary English word into a Gaelic roller-coaster ride. Lahey continued to distribute blarney: "One of the pluses of Shelaghi's acquisition of Lake City Bank, certainly, is that it gives me an excuse to visit, particularly this time of year."

"It's a bit warmer than usual," Peter conceded. "The leaves are late changing, but we won't be seeing snowplows for another several months. October is a perfect month to visit Lake City—and to run a marathon."

"Your Mayor certainly deserves praise," said Lahey, skipping past the marathon reference. Ogilvie had warned Peter that the Irish executives seemed to be showing reluctance about maintaining the bank's connection with the race. If Shelaghi should pull the plug on funding, Peter would face a crisis in finding a new sponsor. That disturbed him less than people might think. As an athlete, Peter had thrived on competition, usually running better in the end-of-season meets that counted vs. those mid-season.

Lahey continued his praise of Lake City: "A lot of people in our part of the world recognize the beauty of Paris and Rome. We are just beginning to acknowledge that cities off the beaten tourist path also can be an attraction."

"The mayor will be at the press conference."

"Ah, yes, the press conference. We'll have a chance to meet the favorites in the race, including the world record holder."

Peter glanced toward Nelson Ogilvie, but the media director was avoiding eye contact.

"Unfortunately, Aba is sick and may not run." Peter's mother always had cautioned him: When in doubt, tell the truth.

"Sick? That *is* unfortunate."

"And even if she does run, a world record attempt seems unlikely."

Lahey stroked his chin, pondering that fact, his banker's mind having just clicked in. "The bank, I'm told, has spent a considerable sum of money attracting the Swede to your race." He let that comment hang in the air, waiting for Peter to react. The Shelaghi executive manager had come to town to judge the marathon and its impact on business, but also its race director.

Peter winced inwardly at the reference to 'your race' and to 'the Swede,' as though Aba had been among Vikings who had pillaged Ireland in the ninth century, but he tried not to react. "We've already reaped the benefit of Aba agreeing to run Lake City. The advance publicity. The large number of reporters you'll see in another hour attests to that. But the big sums of money in her contract are tied to performance: her ability to win the race and to win it in a fast time." Peter prided himself on the fact that, unlike many other road races, he refused to pay excessive appearance fees. If you wanted to earn big money at Lake City, you had to do so between the start and finish lines. The best of world athletes recognized that fact.

"There's a plus side to Aba not running, Dennis." The comment came from an executive standing by his side. The man's name was Patrick Savitch.

"And what would that be, Paddy?"

"That opens the door for our Irish Lass."

"Ah!" Lahey's face brightened. "A good point."

The Shelaghi executive had referred to Fiona Flynn, Ireland's best, fourth behind Aba Andersson at 10,000 meters in the recent European Championships, a solid runner at distances up to the half marathon. Lake City would be Flynn's debut in the full-distance marathon.

36

Lahey turned back to McDonald. "What are Fiona's chances, Peter?"

"If Aba cannot start—and we still hope she will—then that opens the door for a number of runners, Fiona Flynn being one of them. I'd call her a good choice, but I might say the same about several others: Tatanya Henry. Toshi Yamota. Katie Hyang."

"I'll put my money on Fiona," said Savitch, "particularly if it comes to a kick in the last hundred meters."

"Here, here!" echoed several others.

Turning toward Savitch, Peter noted his slight build, the only one among the group that looked like he might belong in a marathon.

"Paddy is our marathoner," Lahey explained. "Quite a good one, if you will. A former county champion."

"Are you running Sunday, Mr. Savitch?" asked Peter, thinking that someone should have informed him of that fact."

"Yes I am."

"Tell him your time, Paddy."

"Two thirty-seven," said Paddy, not without some embarrassment at being that fast. Not Kenyan fast, nevertheless fast by the day's standards.

"But he had the wind at his back," added Lahey, prompting laughter from the group, all familiar with the Irish blessing, *May the road rise to meet you, may the wind be always at your back.*

"That I did, Dennis. That I did."

"Can we get you a starting position in one of the front corrals, Paddy?" Peter asked, switching to the familiar nickname used by the other Shelaghi executives. "Or have you already secured one?"

"I have one, thanks Peter, but that 2:37 was years ago when I was a school boy and more serious about my running. I'll be starting well back and happy with any time under three hours."

"We tried to talk Paddy into pacing Fiona Flynn," said Lahey, "but it appeared his wife Molly objected."

"That she did, Dennis. That she did."

The group was in good humor, Peter noted with pleasure. Lahey added: "Ms. Flynn does cut a fine figure—as a runner, I might add. It appears Ms. Flynn's mother needs to feed her some more corned beef and cabbage."

Lahey shifted the tone of the conversation to business: "We do have some questions about financing."

"I'll be happy to answer them," Peter replied.

"If you could find a gap in your schedule later today...."

Peter removed the digital phone from his pocket, tapping it with his thumbs to access a schedule. Peter knew the schedule by heart, but did not want to appear too available: "After the press conference?"

THURSDAY

The Shelaghi executive manager turned toward Patrick Savitch. No words passed between the two, but Paddy nodded.

They already have something planned, thought Peter.

"One-thirty?" asked Peter. "Back here in the suite?"

"Excellent," said Dennis Lahey. "Paddy will represent us."

"I'll do just that," said Patrick Savitch.

Peter could not help thinking that he had just been handed off to one of the lesser players. The race director wondered if that meant the marathon was not at the top of the Shelaghi priority list. Peter decided that he should not try to think ahead, but be ready instead to react to what they asked of him.

After an appropriate time exchanging small talk, Peter McDonald excused himself and headed downstairs to get ready for the press conference. He hoped it would not be his last.

68:40:00

Jonathon Von Runyon turned off his computer and watched the screen go dark. The veteran sports reporter for the *Lake City Ledger* stood, smoothing his sharply-pressed tan trousers as he did. A short and slender man of an indeterminate middle age, Von Runyon rolled down his shirtsleeves, buttoning them at the cuffs. He reached for the jacket hanging from a hook on the wall of his tiny but primly organized office on the nineteenth floor of the newspaper's skyscraper headquarters. The jacket was emerald green, reminiscent of jackets awarded to winners at the Masters Golf Tournament in Augusta, Georgia each spring.

Von Runyon considered himself, first, a golf writer. Most of the bylined columns and articles by Jonathan Von Runyon were those he wrote covering the major tournaments and the players who appeared in those tournaments, gentlemen all. He loved golf, the manicured courses, the people in and around that sport, the fact that they drank bourbon, not cheap beer, yet you could light a cigar in their presence without being insulted.

You could not do that among runners: the athletes and pseudo-athletes in the sport he would be covering this weekend. He appreciated the athletes: those who combined talent and training to succeed at the highest levels of the marathon world. He had less appreciation for those for whom running was a hobby, not a profession. They could be a scratchy bunch. Place a cigarette in your mouth among a gathering of runners, and the glares would begin. Invariably some oaf would tell you—not always politely—to extinguish it. Some-

38

times, to trigger such a response, Von Runyon maliciously would remove a cigarette from the initialed silver case he carried in his breast pocket, waving it like a saber even though he had no intention of lighting the cigarette. He tolerated runners, tried to treat them and their sport with respect, but he'd much rather be golfing.

Covering the Lake City Marathon this weekend was not necessarily a chore Jonathan Von Runyon dreaded; it was simply less pleasurable than covering a golf tournament. Running remained a secondary beat for him. A professional, he would accept the marathon as his assignment this one weekend. Any time Von Runyon sat down to write, no matter what the subject, he gave that subject his first-class attention. But he approached running with a certain cynicism, knowing that the $100,000 paychecks paid the marathon winners (male and female) and boasted about in press releases was barely a tenth of what a professional golfer would receive for winning a comparable tournament. And that golfer could go on to equally lucrative tournaments the following weekend, or the weekend after that. In contrast, an elite marathoner might only run one or two marathons a year with prizes that high. There were no Tiger Woods in the runner's world. The blacks winning marathons came from Eldoret, Kenya, not Cypress, California, thus were much less interesting to the public. As a professional sport, road running simply did not compare with his first love golf — and it never would, in Jonathan Von Runyon's judgment.

Von Runyon tried not to let his cynicism infect his writing about the Lake City Marathon, although it was not always easy. His article in the *Ledger* this morning about the marathon possibly losing its sponsor was a case in point. He suspected that the article had ruffled feathers not only at the marathon office, but also at Lake City Bank. Comments had drifted back to him already that certain high-positioned executives, who regularly supervised the placement of full-page ads in the *Ledger*, were not happy. Fortunately, the newspaper's publisher did a good job of insulating the editorial department from the advertising department. Sources at the marathon office and bank temporarily might become less available to him for interviews, but the story was legitimate. The marathon *was* in the last year of its contract with the bank. A European conglomerate, whose plans and motives remained unknown, had acquired the bank. The story cried to be told, and he had told it. If this had been a golf tournament, there would be a half dozen corporations lining up for the privilege of attaching their name to the event. Running and golf: A small sport that wished it had the corporate clout of the larger sport.

So be it, thought Von Runyon. Writing the occasional running story was the price he paid for the privilege of spending much more time writing about golf and having the title "Golf Writer" appended to his byline not only in the *Ledger*, but in columns syndicated to newspapers and carried via the Internet around the world. Von Runyon prided himself on the fact that his words were read by the people who count in countries as diverse as South Africa and Japan. Sometimes his reports would appear even in Scotland, the center of the athletic universe as far as he was concerned.

Von Runyon looked at the plaque on the wall above his desk, awarded to him by the American Association of Golf Writers, not for his play (at best, he shot in the 80's), but for his writing about that sport. The plaque contained a clock, one you wound instead of plugged into a socket. Von Runyon wound the clock each day upon arriving at the office. The clock indicated the time to be 11:20, signal for him to head to the marathon press conference scheduled for noon at the Hilliard.

68:40:00. 68:39:59. 68:39:58.

Collecting his laptop computer, Von Runyon slipped out of his office and closed the door behind him. Not that anybody from the editorial staff would *dare* invade his inner sanctum. Even the cleaning ladies would do little more than empty trash from the wastebasket, placed by Von Runyon near the door at the end of each day so they need not intrude further.

Von Runyon walked the length of the newsroom, nodding occasionally to a colleague who glanced up to see him pass. He was not well-loved in a sports department most of whose reporters cared more about mainstream sports such as baseball and basketball and football. They played golf, but rarely read about it or even watched golf on TV. Not while a NASCAR race was on the tube. Von Runyon arrived at a wall to which was attached a plastic bulletin board containing his name and the names of other reporters. He used a felt pen to identify his destination: "Marathon Press Conference."

Von Runyon stopped at an elevator bank, pressed "Down" and waited for a passing elevator to answer his call. When this happened, he got in, checking to see that the ground floor button already had been pressed. It had, but once a detail man, always a detail man. He pressed the button a second time, just in case. The elevator car was itself a work of beauty with an Art Deco frieze, its brass highly polished, but Von Runyon had ridden that elevator up and down too many times to notice. Fine art was lost on him. Green, manicured fairways served as his *objets d' arte*.

The elevator reached the ground floor. Its doors slid open. Von Runyon strode through the lobby and exited the building through a revolving door. He paused briefly on the sidewalk in front of the *Ledger* skyscraper to absorb the beauty of the moment. The sun shone brightly in a cloudless sky, the temperature unseasonably warm for October. Von Runyon was among the few on the street wearing a jacket, particularly a green one. What a beautiful day to be golfing, thought Jonathan Von Runyon. That the 50,000 runners might consider warm and sunny weather unsuitable for their marathon experience did not concern him—at least for the present.

Jonathan Von Runyon hailed a taxicab and climbed into the back seat. "Hilliard Towers," he instructed the cab driver.

68:20:00

Looking at herself in the mirror, Fiona Flynn liked what she saw. On top, she wore the long-sleeved turquoise sweater with zippered front given to elite women competitors in the Lake City Marathon. She had requested a sweater one size smaller than respectable to emphasize her lithe figure. *La Femme Fiona* (a nickname given her by one disreputable British tabloid) also wore black, butt-hugging Capri pants and real shoes with high heels, not the running shoes she knew the other elite athletes would wear at the noon press conference, set to start in twenty minutes.

68:20:00. 68:19:59. 68:19:58.

She understood that she should arrive on time but Flynn wanted to examine herself in the mirror a few minutes more to guarantee that the heads of every man at the press conference would turn when she walked into the room. A daughter of Ireland, educated in a convent school in Cork, Flynn wondered what the nuns would say if they saw her now. Fiona ran one hand through her blazing red hair, short but fluid as the waves of the Irish Sea. Despite time training in the sun, her skin was white, like milk, punctuated by the tiniest of freckles. Blue eyes. Straight nose. Thin lips, but very kissable. Long neck.

Around that neck, she wore an exquisitely crafted silver necklace, one she had picked up in Paris when the World Championships were held in that city. That was about all she got that year at the Worlds in Paris, having dropped out of the 10,000 meters on the track. Well, she had a quickie affair with a Russian shot-putter, but that was no accomplishment in Paris.

For earrings, Flynn wore a pair acquired at an Indian store in Albuquerque, New Mexico, where she trained. Turquoise: a perfect match for the sweater. Lucky she had brought the earrings along, although she did not know until arrival what clothing would be required for the press conference. The elite men had been given red sweaters. Seemingly, that would have served to complement her hair, but maybe she would talk race director Peter McDonald into giving her an extra sweater later. She could use an excuse to talk to him. You never knew what might develop. She had dated him once or twice in Europe when he was still single and traveling on the track circuit. That was before his

41

marriage. Dear Peter did not show much interest, so they never got past a cheek-peck, but he was damaged goods now following the death of his wife Carol. Unfortunate, she felt, but it was time to get over that, Peter.

She ran her fingers up the front of her body from her thighs and over her crotch and stomach to her breasts, small, but accentuated by the tight sweater. She played gently with the breasts and felt her nipples come alive. She wore no bra, and the outline of pointy nipples showed through the sweater. Nice effect, but she was not sure how to maintain it while being interviewed by reporters under hot lights and clicking cameras. She pulled the zipper down to just under the breast line, not low enough to allow anything to show — since, quite honestly, there was not a lot to show — but she had enough to attract attention. Fiona knew she was sexy as hell.

And, God, was she horny. Tapering for a marathon did that to her. During the long weeks and months of training, as she averaged more than one hundred miles a week, Flynn could keep her sexual desires under control — somewhat — but as soon as she cut back mileage tapering for the race, she was ready to explode! Earlier this morning, Fiona had a massage from a male massage therapist, and with his hands stroking her back, legs and buttocks — even though he had done so as a true professional — she was ready to fly off the table. Was there a danger that her testosterone level might rise to beyond the point where she would flunk her post-race drug test? Probably not, but Fiona fantasized for a moment on how that testosterone level might be reduced with the aid of a good man. Unfortunately, this was a road race, not a track meet, so there were no Russian shot putters.

Perhaps she should forget her fantasies and focus instead on winning the race. That would not be easy, since Lake City was her first marathon, and it had world record holder Aba Andersson in the field.

Fiona Flynn had won many races during her career, having come from Ireland to the U.S. as a young girl of nineteen to run cross-country and track at Arkansas State University. ASU won the women's NCAA cross-country title her second year in school, but Fiona did not return the following season, deciding to turn professional. She now spent winters training at altitude in Albuquerque, returning to Europe in late spring for the track season.

She had achieved some success as a track runner, but quite frankly the routine of jetting from Oslo to Rome to Brussels to Helsinki to Paris to Tokyo, sometimes running as many as two or three races a week, had grown old after a few seasons. If this is Tuesday, it must be Bislett. You could race that often if you confined yourself to distances between 800 and 3,000 meters, but unless you were winning and setting records, the money was not all that good: a second place here, a third place there; a Euro here, a yen there. Being a spear-carrier sucks, Fiona decided.

MARATHON

Fiona Flynn knew that if she wanted to stay in the running game, eventually she would need to move up to the marathon. There were too many gamins coming into the sport, girls even skinnier than she and with better base speed. Fiona possessed more endurance than speed, more slow-twitch muscles than fast-twitch muscles. Her forays into the 5,000 and into the 10,000 had taught her that. Her former coach at Arkansas State kept saying whenever he saw her, "Fiona, you're a marathoner. When are you going to figure that out?"

Well, she had figured it out several years before. But she had not acted on that knowledge. She had not entered a marathon, partly because she feared the 26-mile distance. She had talked to enough women who did make their career running marathons and other road races to know that something happened to your body once you got past 20 miles. Even the best trained runners sometimes failed badly. The great Norwegian runner Grete Waitz once had stepped off the course a few miles from the finish of the Boston Marathon while leading the race. Fiona did not want to fail. Yes, she would run a marathon, but only on her terms, when she knew she was ready, when she was positive that not only would she post a time faster than 2:30, but also win the race and collect a sizable prize as well. Marathoners at the elite level usually could achieve success only if they ran 26 miles 385 yards no more than once or twice a year, maybe as few as three or four great races a career, carefully pointing for the few races they ran at that distance. She had considered carefully where to run her first marathon.

And so Fiona Flynn had chosen Lake City. It might not have the prestige of New York or Chicago or the other major marathons, but the prize money was equal to the best: $100,000 to the male and women winners with time bonuses for those capable of breaking 2:30, which she knew she could do. She often ran faster than that pace during long runs in practice without extending herself to the limit. The businesswoman in Fiona Flynn understood that whether or not she could win Lake City, she would place high enough and run fast enough so that she would be able to negotiate more money with her clothing and shoe suppliers next year. First place seemed questionable, because after Fiona agreed to come, race director Peter McDonald invited Aba Andersson. Thanks, Peter!

Fiona worried for a while that she would be going head-on again with the world record holder, a woman she never had defeated. But there was a silver lining. Aba's presence apparently scared away several other top female marathoners, causing them to choose marathons they thought they might more easily win. They overlooked the fact that there was good money to be claimed for placing second or third behind Aba, and today Fiona heard that Andersson was sick and might not run at all. A perfect set-up for the Irish Lass. There were several fast Russians along with Japanese, Kenyan and Ethiopian runners who would push Fiona, but she still felt she could win.

Another factor in choosing Lake City was the question of sponsorship. She was enough of an insider through her friendship with Peter to know that the marathon's contract with Lake City Bank had ended. The Bank recently had been swallowed by Shelaghi. Peter aggressively recruited her on the premise that she was Irish, as was the conglomerate. "No promises," Peter had said, "but it would benefit all to have someone Irish in front of the field."

Right, Peter, then why the hell did you invite that Swedish bitch?

Fiona thought that, but did not say it. She actually liked Aba and her adorable husband Bjørn. Too bad she had not seen him first.

Peter had a point about how it would benefit negotiations with Shelaghi if she won the race, or at least stayed close enough to be captured on the telecast back to Ireland. She had not yet met any of the Irish executives, but she knew that several were in town for the marathon, determining whether or not to renew the sponsorship. She knew that the sight of an Irish Lass with flaming red hair crossing the finish line first would be a strong inducement to renew. She even planned to run the Lake City Marathon wearing her national team sports bra featuring shamrocks rather than polka dots in case anyone from the conglomerate failed to get the point.

Yes, Fiona Flynn was ready. She took one final look in the mirror, ran her fingers through the flaming hair and departed the room, heading for the elevator. The press conference was due to start in a few minutes, and it was time for *La Femme Fiona* to make an appearance.

68:10:00

Just before noon, a little more than sixty-eight hours before the start of the Lake City Marathon, the elite runners and reporters assigned to write about those elite runners began to arrive at the Hilliard Towers. This included Don Geoffrey, who though a former Olympian had achieved greater fame as Contributing Editor for *Running Magazine*.

Listed by that title on the masthead of what arguably was the most influential running publication in the world, Geoffrey did not serve as a full-time editor, nor did he live near the magazine's New York offices. Geoffrey worked as a freelance writer and lived with his wife Emily in Lake City, on the city's south side near the campus of Lake City University, where he taught part time in the English department. In addition to his writing, Geoffrey also served as a consultant for the Lake City Marathon, providing training programs for those running the race. Geoffrey did not train elite runners at the front of the field, but rather those with more average ability, who finished hours behind. In connecting his considerable celebrity to the back of the pack, Geoffrey utilized the self-deprecating nickname: the Turtle.

"There are more slow runners than fast runners," the Turtle often told reporters, who sought quotes for newspapers and TV. "That does not mean those slow runners don't want to run faster, but to do this, they need well-organized programs." Geoffrey knew how to use the media to plug himself, since a fair share of his income came from selling runners training programs. Pay $49.95, and for the next eighteen weeks you will get an email from the Turtle telling you how to train. That morning, Don Geoffrey's clients received an email suggesting they run 2 miles at a very easy pace.

The Turtle's electronic advice continued: "Carbo-loading begins in earnest: Pasta, rice, potatoes, cereals, fruits. Don't make radical changes in your diet, but now is not the time for filet mignon. Cut back slightly on your food intake, since you will be burning fewer calories by running fewer miles this final tapering week."

As a closing tip, he added: "When you pack, don't forget your running gear, including shoes."

Simple and obvious advice, Geoffrey knew, but in helping runners at all levels, he realized they liked being coddled and told precisely what to do each day for eighteen weeks. They did not want to *think*, something they were forced to do constantly in their professional lives. Unlike the elite, running was for pleasure, not for profit. Let somebody else do the thinking.

Geoffrey, now in his late fifties, no longer competed at or near the front of the pack. He ran with the mid-pack for recreation, sometimes pacing four-hour-plus runners. Because of his oft-seen byline in *Running Magazine,* the Turtle remained highly visible among the running community, a guru to the masses. During marathon weekend, not only would Geoffrey appear at the Expo to autograph books and deliver several lectures, he also planned to run the marathon, leading one of the pacing teams. Fast runners achieved fleeting fame, cashing big paychecks, seeing their pictures on the cover of *Running Magazine* this year, fading to obscurity the next. Geoffrey, though not quite as fast as the sport's champions, past and present, had established a niche that allowed him to outlast them all. His close friendship with Peter McDonald permitted him to maintain his visibility in Lake City, but he worried whether that would continue if the marathon lost its major sponsor.

Climbing out of the taxicab that had brought him to the Hilliard, Geoffrey handed the driver a twenty-dollar bill and asked for ten back along with a receipt for tax purposes. The Turtle nodded politely at a doorman who opened the taxicab door, noting that the doorman, like many other employees of the hotel, was wearing a bright blue Lake City Marathon jacket, the same jacket offered to volunteers, provided by one of the marathon's sub-sponsors, Nitro Sports, a shoe and apparel company based in New England.

Glancing back just before entering the hotel, Geoffrey saw that the passenger descending from the taxicab immediately behind was Jonathan Von Runyon, reporter for the *Lake City Ledger*. Geoffrey knew Von Runyon, but saw no need to wait to walk into the hotel with him, or even offer a word of greeting. The Turtle enjoyed friendly relationships with most reporters, but resented Von Runyon for his attitude.

One example of Von Runyon's attitude was this morning's article about the possibility that the marathon might lose its bank sponsor. As one reporter viewing the work of another, Geoffrey could not condemn Von Runyon for accuracy. His facts were correct. It was more a matter of tone, a negative approach that was too typical of the *Ledger* reporter. Or maybe Geoffrey was colored by his distaste for an individual whom he felt had no love, or even respect, for the sport of long distance running.

68:10:00. 68:09:59. 68:09:58.

Geoffrey pushed through a revolving door, passed a digital clock counting down the time to the marathon's start, and ascended an ornate staircase to a balcony above the main lobby where two staff members from the marathon office sat at a table with a checklist of those invited to the press conference. They were interns, hired for the last several months before the marathon. One was named Damien; the other, Elisa.

Before he had a chance to offer his name, Elisa recognized Geoffrey as the Turtle and handed him not one, but three press badges to dangle around his neck. The badges would offer him access to various areas in the park as well as the media center. Geoffrey thanked the pair and entered the next room. Another intern offered him a backpack bearing the marathon logo. Contained within it was a Media Guide crammed with facts and statistics, a notebook and a ballpoint pen, all bearing the Lake City Marathon logo. Everything he needed to cover the race. That plus a free T-shirt. *It doesn't get much better than this,* thought the Turtle.

The media center already had begun to fill with reporters, who saw each other regularly at major marathons. At ease with each other, they chatted about the weekend activities and swapped information on who was fit and who was not. Geoffrey greeted several of them, but did not stop to talk.

He moved through a foyer and into the media center's main room. At one end of the room were a half dozen computer terminals, a handful of reporters seated in front of them checking emails. Also at the room's end, several long tables had been positioned like Conestoga Wagons defending against the Indians. Protected within this area, staff from the marathon office hunkered down waiting to offer support for the large group of reporters now finally drifting into the room.

Geoffrey sidestepped a bank of TV cameras and walked down a center aisle between rows of chairs on each side. In doing so, he encountered TV3 reporter Christine Ferrara and Edmund her cameraman patiently waiting for the press conference to begin.

Christine greeted him, "How was your run?"

The Turtle was impressed that the TV reporter remembered his plans to work out after their interview at the Expo earlier this morning. "Every run is a good run," he said pleasantly, but kept moving.

Only half the chairs had yet been occupied. He saw Burton Ambrose, the editor of *Running Magazine*, busy talking to photographer Steve Victor and TV journalists Carolynne Vickers and Timothy Rainboldt. The pair would provide color commentary for the race telecast on TV3. Geoffrey might have joined them in conversation, but instead continued moving toward the front of the room with its dais featuring a lectern in the middle and a half dozen microphones, three on each side.

Signs before the microphones indicated who soon would sit there. This included defending champions Joseph Nduku and Tatanya Henry. Nduku, like so many road running champions, was from Kenya. Tatanya Henry was Russian, her maiden name Kamarenko. The more simply pronounced Henry came from her marriage to a British track athlete, Jacob Henry, now retired, who served as her agent. Neither athlete had taken their place on the podium, nor was anyone seated behind the third placard on the left side, a seat reserved for Aba Andersson, who did not seem to be present. Geoffrey wondered why.

Placards on the right side of the podium indicated it to be the domain of non-runners: Bank Chairman Robin Carter and Mayor Richard T. Danson. Peter McDonald would occupy the third seat, sharing it with Mark Mallon, TV3 sportscaster and anchor of the marathon telecast, also emcee for the press conference. Athletes of lesser fame than those on the dais had been invited to sit in the front several rows to be introduced, but without fanfare. "Invited" in the sense that their contracts stipulated that they appear for the press conference and make themselves available for interviews. Not to do so would result in a fine of several hundred dollars. To a golfer or baseball player, that might seem a trivial sum. Not to a runner from Kenya or the former Soviet Union. Among those Kenyans seated in the front row was at least one, Kemyatta Kemai, who felt he had a chance to upset Nduku, perhaps with the help of the runner seated next to him, Moses Abraham, one of the rabbits assigned to pace the runners through the early miles.

THURSDAY

But few of the reporters knew Kemai's hopes and ambitions yet.

A large banner on the wall behind the dais exhibited the name of the Lake City Marathon along with the logo of the sponsoring bank. The bank's logo also was attached to the front of the lectern so that unless those manning the TV cameras tightly framed the face of the speaker, that logo would be visible in any telecasts. Other sponsors of the marathon were afforded lesser positions on side walls, position and size of banners governed by the size of their contribution to the race budget.

Standing at the room's far corner was race director Peter McDonald, changed into a dark suit that would not have looked out of place in the Board of Directors room of any bank or corporation. Beside him was his media director, Nelson Ogilvie, who held in one hand an agenda for today's press conference. It listed the order in which people would speak, what they would speak about and how much time they had to speak before yielding the microphone to the next speaker. Any deviation from this schedule, and Ogilvie would alert McDonald, who would move as subtly as possible to push the program forward. It was noon, time for the press conference to begin.

Staying on schedule was important, since this was the kickoff to the weekend's activities. Additional press conferences involving other athletes were scheduled for Friday and Saturday, but this opening conference on Thursday noon set the tone for what followed. Ogilvie knew that Peter McDonald demanded that they stay close to the preplanned timeline. Peter wanted to know immediately about any delays so he could correct them. Not only did the Chairman and Mayor need to get on to other business, but so did members of the media filing reports for *The Four O'clock News* or the next day's newspapers or blogs on the Internet. Delayed reporters are unhappy reporters, and McDonald wanted to keep them happy.

By this time, Geoffrey had made his way to the front of the room. He greeted McDonald, shook his hand, but saw that the race director was busy so only lingered long enough to ask the one question in his mind, which he did quietly. Peter answered by whispering in Geoffrey's ear. The Turtle nodded, then turned to shake the hands of Ogilvie and two athletes standing nearby, the defending champions. Having made his presence known, the Turtle retreated to a seat next to Burton Ambrose in the center of the room.

"Where is Aba?" Ambrose wondered.

"Aba seems to have the flu. She's been throwing up."

Ambrose's eyebrows rose noticeably. "Can she run?"

"She can run," began the Turtle, pausing for effect. "The question at hand is, can she run fast enough for another world record?"

MARATHON

The two defending champions, Joseph Nduku and Tatanya Henry, looked nervous as they waited to take their seats. They would rather be running instead of giving speeches and talking to reporters As part of the press conference, they would be handed the numbers (1 and 101) that each would wear in the race. Joseph Nduku, the Kenyan, had won last year's race in 2:06:20, fastest time of the year. He spoke and understood English well, but like so many of the Kenyans talked softly and with an accent that frustrated reporters trying to collect quotes for their stories. Tatanya Henry, the Russian, despite being married to an Englishman, apparently spoke little English and responded to questions through her husband, which did not make for good TV sound-bites.

Peter McDonald worried about the fact that foreign athletes dominated road running. If only some of these foreign runners, particularly women from the former East Block countries, would realize how much their paychecks would be enhanced if they did speak English, maybe they would enroll in language classes between training runs, rather than sitting around watching game shows on TV. He wished that there were more fast Americans who had majored in Communications at Midwest universities. Unfortunately, they were few in number. No American seemed likely to win Lake City this year, and that included a South African, now an American citizen.

Two young runners, twins, from the Northland Racing Team, showed promise — but only promise. Kyle and Wesley Fowler were not running the full distance. Peter had hired them to serve as rabbits to assist Aba in her world record attempt, but their services now might not be needed. Seated next to them was another young runner from Northland: Katie Hyang. He hoped Katie ran well, but did not expect her to challenge the leaders.

Peter glanced at a young Japanese girl seated in the first row — and girl was the correct name for Toshi Yamota, only seventeen years old and with the tiny body of someone a half dozen years younger. Japanese TV was covering the Lake City Marathon live. Some of the correspondents from Japan hinted that Toshi would be the next great marathon phenom. Maybe so, Peter conceded, but she had run few marathon races and had a PR slower than 2:30. She did speak excellent English, but he did not want to subject the impish Toshi to public scrutiny this early in her career.

Aba Andersson, though Swedish, did speak unaccented English, but was absent. The placard featuring her name remained positioned in front of the chair next to the podium. Peter had not yet replaced it on the chance that she might show despite his suggestion otherwise to her husband Bjørn. The race director planned to postpone any announcement of her not starting until tomorrow, hoping to delay any unfavorable press, particularly from Jonathan

Von Runyon, who he saw walking up the center aisle. Von Runyon undoubtedly would concoct some conspiracy that would be well forgotten after the damage had been done.

Ogilvie nudged McDonald: "About that seat for Aba...."

"She's certainly not coming," replied the race director. "Bjørn would have contacted us by now."

"An empty seat does not look good."

"Agreed. Unless pressed, I don't want to explain why it's empty."

Peter looked out over the audience and saw a familiar face and figure now moving toward the front row where athletes with less celebrity than those on the dais would sit. If anyone could be plucked out of that elite mass and asked to make everyone forget Aba, it was her. Fast. Good looking. Red hair. An incorrigible flirt, good for attracting the attention of male journalists. And another plus, considering his new conglomerate bosses, she was Irish!

"Nelson," Peter told his media director, "ask Fiona Flynn if I can talk to her for a minute."

68:00:00

At the same time the press conference was being held at Hilliard Towers in Lake City, Celebrity X's Gulfstream jet had arrived at a point high above the Atlantic Ocean. As though aware of this fact, X stirred from his nap and glanced out the window to see if he could spot the last landfall for continental Europe: Ireland's craggy West Coast. Too late: he already had passed that point of no return. His course was set.

68:00:00. 67:59:59. 67:59:58.

For a few minutes X allowed himself to be hypnotized by the blue of the Atlantic Ocean, punctuated by the whitecaps of waves that, seen from an altitude of 40,000 feet, looked like speckles on an Impressionist painting. He pondered the fact that as recently as a century ago, this view was not available to man. And five hundred years before that—Copernicus be damned—many still believed Earth to be flat with the Sun revolving around it. How much have our views changed in so few years, and how much new will we learn about the universe in fifty more years? It was a thought for philosophers, not a simple man en route to his first marathon.

No cloud in the sky, little turbulence, perfect for flying. Perfect for sleeping. Soon, Celebrity X fell back to sleep.

MARATHON

The Gulfstream's flight plan had taken it from northern Italy across the Alps and into the air spaces above France and England then across the Irish Sea to a point near Shannon Airport on the western coast of Ireland before leaving land behind. Air traffic controllers below could view the Gulfstream on their radar screens, though they had no idea who might be passengers in that plane. As the Gulfstream flew out over the Atlantic Ocean aimed at North America, however, its flight was being monitored by at least one private individual who took a special interest in all of Celebrity X's movements.

The individual also used a code name to hide his identity: Redbird.

Redbird's residence, actually one of several he used, was not far off the flight plan of the jet carrying Celebrity X. This was more by coincidence than by design, but watching the blip on the computer screen that represented X's plane departing the continent, Redbird had noted with some amusement that if he stepped onto the patio behind his residence with telescope in hand, he might actually have been able to pinpoint X's plane in the sky high above.

Redbird had been tracking the Gulfstream carrying Celebrity X since its takeoff from the private landing strip near Rome several hours before. He had been the silent one called by the two observers who had followed X to the airport on their motorcycles. As much for his amusement as from a need to know X's whereabouts, Redbird wandered from his study every fifteen or twenty minutes into the side room that contained electronic equipment equal to any air traffic control centers in the world.

Equipment capable of tracking peoples' precise movements did not come cheaply, nor was it easy to acquire without embarrassing questions being asked. You needed money as much to insure secrecy as to purchase the equipment. As a highly placed executive in an organization with vast wealth, Redbird did not lack for money. His country residence in County Limerick was proof of that. Furnished with antique furniture and priceless tapestries on the wall, it was a fifteenth-century castle. Redbird did not own the castle, but inhabited it at convenient times, when he wanted to avoid public scrutiny.

This was his country residence, but Redbird also had a residence in Dublin as well as an apartment overlooking the Tiber River in Rome plus several other properties in different parts of the world about whose ownership even he was uncertain, because it made little difference to one who only needed to speak a word or move a finger and something happened.

The country residence, certainly, was Redbird's favorite, because of its beauty, its convenience, and because his roots remained planted deeply in the dark sod of western Ireland. His study overlooked the ocean; he could step out onto a balcony and see waves crashing on the rocks below. In terms of convenience, Redbird needed only to press a button on his desk and within minutes a limousine would usher him to Shannon Airport, only ten minutes away. Within hours, using a private jet, he could be in Dublin, or London, or Rome or any other big city in the world.

At this particular moment late on a Thursday evening, Redbird's thoughts were directed toward Lake City, since that's where he suspected the individual who lately had become the focus of his interest was heading. Although tracking the man Peter McDonald called Celebrity X, Redbird did not know him by that name yet or even know why that identity had been created.

Where, where, my dear friend, are you going? Redbird pondered that question. *More important, why are you going there? And if on a mission involving public contact—highly unlikely considering your covert departure—how much will it increase your level of vulnerability?*

Redbird knew that X grew up near Lake City in a community called the East Side, but why such secrecy?

Although seemingly he would be most vulnerable staying in a private home near an area of the city noted for its high crime rate, Redbird knew that X was relatively safe among friends and relatives. The reason might be called the rule of the jungle, one followed even by the Mafia. You do not attack a man when he is among his family, among innocent women and children. You do not invade his private space. But do today's terrorists play by such rules?

As he considered these facts, Redbird sensed someone standing in the doorway. The individual just stood there as though afraid to interrupt him. This obsequiousness often irritated Redbird, but he accepted it as the price he must pay for his lofty position and the influence he wielded in world circles.

"What is it?" said Redbird, trying to conceal his irritation.

"Our friend made one telephone call after take-off," said the intruder as he handed Redbird a paper with the number on it.

"And?" asked Redbird.

"To an individual living in Lake City named Peter McDonald."

Redbird examined the number on the paper. It certainly suggested that the final destination of the jet plane now well over the Atlantic Ocean was, indeed, Lake City. But the name Peter McDonald meant nothing yet to Redbird, who hated incompetence more than he hated obsequiousness. Why had his staff not provided him with information about this Peter McDonald, and why would the man whose movements they were following so closely be calling him immediately after takeoff?

"Find out more about this Peter McDonald."

The individual who had brought him the message turned to go, but halted briefly before exiting the room to hear Redbird's final instructions.

"...And determine *why* our friend should be calling him."

MARATHON

67:15:00

Toward the end of the press conference, media director Nelson Ogilvie glanced out into the crowd and saw Jonathan Von Runyon, reporter for the *Lake City Ledger*. Ogilvie wondered: *Is water-boarding still legal?* Von Runyon's article on the bank's sponsorship crisis seemed designed to cause trouble, particularly with executives from Shelaghi in town. What would the *Ledger* reporter write next? It probably would relate very little to what had just been offered in the press conference. As it wound down, just over sixty-seven hours remained before the start of the marathon. *67:15:00. 67:14:59. 67:14:58.*

The press conference, Ogilvie decided, had gone smoothly by any standard. The mayor had been introduced, the bank chairman said a few words, and a framed "Whereas" document drafted by the City Council passed from one hand to the other. Where all those "Whereas" plaques landed after the marathon, even Ogilvie did not know. He wondered whether some day far in the future one might appear on Antique Road Show.

Following the exchange, Mark Mallon talked briefly about TV3's plans to cover the race, then introduced Vaughn Johnson, weatherman at the same station. The forecast was grim, Johnson said, not for people who planned to barbecue outdoors on Sunday, but for those running 26 miles 385 yards. Sunny, not a cloud in the sky, winds from the southwest, maybe 10-20 mph, temperatures rising into the 80s by noon with large numbers of runners still on the course. A cold front lurked off to the west, but probably would not arrive in time to do much good. The dangers of heat exhaustion would stretch the medical personnel to their limits. As for the possibility of any world records, Johnson allowed the reporters to draw their own conclusions.

Nelson Ogilvie was grateful that the weather forecaster did stick to the facts and made no attempt to editorialize. The press conference had continued on schedule. Peter McDonald thanked Mallon and Johnson as he took the podium to introduce the defending champions, Joseph Nduku and Tatanya Henry. Nduku's comments were precise and polite, praising the city, the mayor, the Bank Chairman and the race sponsors as he had been programmed by his agent to do. The Kenyan spoke English quietly, but possessed a natural charm that Ogilvie found endearing, even though a lot of reporters complained they had a hard time understanding the East African athletes. Those same reporters (Ogilvie thought but did not say) spent most of their careers covering baseball and football games, whose players often did not speak English as well as the Kenyans. As for Tatanya Henry, she offered a pleasant smile as she spoke in her native Russian, and if her husband did not translate her words exactly, who in the room would notice? Maybe Jonathan Von Runyon; it would be just like the *Ledger* reporter to bring with him a translator and complain about what was said and not said.

Then it was Fiona Flynn's turn, and *La Femme Fiona* lived up her reputation. She began, "I'm only up here because I'm Irish—as are the new owners of the bank." Fiona continued with a short monologue that was both hilarious and semi-obscene, including her plea to have a massage therapist (male preferred) sent to her room. About running her first marathon, she turned to Peter and told him: "I'm not sure I can run more than two hours without peeing, Love. Can you arrange a porta-pottie at 20 with a shamrock on it?"

Then leaving the podium, La Femme Fiona planted a big kiss on Peter's cheek that lasted just a millisecond longer than it should have—punctuated by whistles and cheers from the elite runners up front, who were quite familiar with Fiona's reputation. To everybody's amusement, Peter turned beet red. *Good,* Ogilvie thought, knowing how Peter had struggled to get his life back in order after losing his wife, Carol.

La Femme Fiona got the loudest round of applause from the usually blasé press corps, but Ogilvie suspected there was not a single quote that could be used in a news story or shown on TV. That was all right with him. With Aba possibly sidelined, he speculated on the marketing implications if the Irish Lass actually won the race. It might help in negotiations with Shelaghi.

Peter followed with introductions of the other invited runners and announced that all would be available in the next room for interviews. This included Kenyatta Kemai, who sat in the front row looking forward to his showdown with Joseph Nduku on Sunday. Kemai's training had gone well; he knew he was in peak condition.

Moses Abraham, one the runners assigned as rabbits to pace the leaders, nudged Kemai: "Next year, it will be *you* occupying the seat of honor."

Kemai mumbled his agreement. The exchange, spoken in their native language, was not understood by those seated around them. Abraham and Kemai purposely had chosen seats away from the rest of the Kenyan contingent. What they did, they would do on their own.

In closing, Peter invited everybody to eat at a buffet set-up on the balcony, noting that the elite athletes would be available for interviews.

Leaving the dais, Fiona passed Peter: "How was that, Love? Do you want to hug me, or strangle me?"

Peter laughed: "Let's say, Fiona, you made everybody forget Aba."

"I'll make them forget her on Sunday too," said Fiona, touching Peter lightly on the arm before moving into the crowd of reporters.

Watching the Irish Lass walk away, Peter, like Ogilvie, wondered whether or not her winning the race would influence Shelaghi to continue its sponsorship. Unfortunately, he suspected that decision already may have been made.

As reporters gathered around the better-known athletes for interviews, others returned to their rooms. This included a pair of twins who ran for the Northland Racing Team: Kyle and Wesley Fowler. Their coach, Steve Holland, who had not yet arrived in town, felt that the twin brothers had the potential to succeed at the upper levels of American distance running, although their PRs of 2:10 and 2:11 left them well behind the fastest Kenyans.

Among those still in the room was Christine Ferrara. The new TV3 reporter stood, microphone in hand, next to her cameraman, Edmund Giesbert. Earlier, using the press conference as background, she had provided a live introduction for some of the footage shot at the Expo, the interview with Peter quoting numbers connected with the race: numbers of volunteers, numbers of paper cups, gallons of E.R.G. poured into those paper cups by numbers of volunteers, and he had not been punished for letting the name of that sponsor roll effortlessly off his tongue. It remained part of the package.

Not knowing any of the athletes, a rookie in the world of sports reporting, she wondered which ones to choose for interviews. Or did it matter? It was then she looked up and saw Peter McDonald moving purposely toward her. "Hi, New-Girl-In-Town," he said with a smile.

"You realize, Peter, that I am terribly offended that you apparently have forgotten my name."

"I know that, Christine, but thought you might offer absolution if I suggested you talk to Fiona Flynn."

"Oh, really?" said Christine, showing what might be described as a cynical frown. "Let's see if I can remember which one she was. Oh, yes: The Irish lady with the red hair and the zipper lower than it should be."

"Your audience would like that."

"Our audience would like that too much. I can get Edmund to cut her off at the neck."

"I meant your audience would like her Irish accent."

Christine laughed: "So would your new bosses."

"You're onto me, but Fiona has a good chance to win the race."

"Even with Aba in the field?"

"Inside tip. Fiona is now the favorite, but it didn't come from me."

"I'll talk to her."

"Good idea. Maybe I'll see you at lunch."

THURSDAY

Offering a final smile, Peter slid past Christine and entered the other room where Jonathan Von Runyon abruptly appeared to block his path. Unlike many of the other reporters, Von Runyon used neither tape recorder nor notebook to record responses to his questions. His memory of the questions he asked and what subjects responded was precise and invariably accurate. Truman Capote played similar memory games. Some suspected Capote did it mainly for bragging rights, not because it improved his journalism.

Von Runyon's first question involved Aba Andersson: "Aba skipped the press conference. I've heard she may not run."

"Aba appears to have a cold," said Peter. "I told her to get well."

"When will we see her?"

"Tomorrow's press conference."

"If she's sick, will she run Sunday?"

"I'm hoping she will."

"Obviously you paid a lot of money to get her here."

Peter simply shrugged, feeling that the remark did not need an answer.

"With or without Aba," Von Runyon continued, "who do you see as favorites to win the race?"

Peter slid smoothly into what might have been a rehearsed response. "You can't overlook our defending champions. Both Joseph and Tatanya are in top form. Joseph won the Philadelphia Distance Classic last month. But he has competition on his own team. Tatanya's time of 1:06:12 winning the 20-K in New Bedford shows she hasn't lost a step. Don't bet against her, even with Aba in the race. Long shot: Fiona Flynn."

"In her first marathon?" Von Runyon frowned. "That would be rare."

"Fiona *is* rare, Jonathan."

Glancing over Von Runyon's shoulder, Peter noticed Christine Ferrara talking to Fiona. Christine had followed his advice. Temporarily distracted, he almost failed to hear Von Runyon's next question: "The bank's new owners certainly would enjoy having an Irish champion."

"Say again?"

"The conglomerate that now owns Lake City Bank. Would you like to comment on my story this morning suggesting that Shelaghi might be less than enthusiastic about continuing its sponsorship of the marathon?"

"Jonathan," Peter replied, trying hard not to be testy. "In all honesty, I have been *so* busy this week, I have not had a chance to read the newspapers, yours or others. Regardless, any talk about sponsorship would be premature until after this year's marathon."

Peter's comment about not reading Von Runyon's article was both true and not true, since Ogilvie had read the story to him earlier this morning at the convention center. To prevent a follow-up question, Peter broke eye contact with the *Ledger* reporter and addressed a Japanese woman standing with microphone in hand and TV cameraman by her side. "Did you want to do that interview now?"

Von Runyon knew that Peter had dodged his question, but he expected that to happen and bore him no malice. In fact, although Peter McDonald might be surprised to hear it, Jonathan Von Runyon admired the race director for his success in bringing Lake City to its current level of prominence among world marathons. Von Runyon enjoyed the give and take between reporter and subject, particularly if there was an edge to it. Controversy attracts readers. Plus it kept him from getting bored covering running instead of golf.

Von Runyon surveyed the crowd to see whom he might talk to next and spotted Niles Wendell. Wendell, a prominent architect, had helped found the Lake City Marathon three decades before, providing the seed money to get the race started. A man with a perpetual sun tan, even through winter, Wendell wore only shirts with French cuffs and sports jackets with brass buttons and handkerchiefs in the breast pocket. His shoes shone so splendidly that they could inflict eye damage if you gazed at them too long. Von Runyon liked Wendell because he looked like a golfer, whether he played that game or not.

The reporter moved to talk to him. Wendell noticed him coming and extended his hand: "Jonathan, what a pleasure. I always enjoy your stories, your insights, your style. You are the consummate craftsman."

Von Runyon knew Wendell spoke sarcastically, that the race founder despised what he wrote, but he had not come to argue, only to chase leads and tips, anything that would give him insights that he could share with his readers. Von Runyon returned the race founder's pleasantry, then asked: "Any comment on the possibility that the bank might part company with the marathon as a result of its new owners?"

Wendell responded: "Jonathan, I read your article this morning in the *Ledger*, a superb job of reporting. But in all honesty, I've been out of the loop now for several years. I'm happy now to watch from the sidelines and cheer what continues to be one of the world's best marathons."

The *Ledger* reporter began to frame a follow-up question, but before the words could leave his mouth, he found his hand being shaken a second time as a prelude to Wendell sliding away into the crowd. "Jonathan," Wendell said as he slid, "I hope you received an invitation to our Founder's Party tonight at Wendell House. If not, consider this a personal one." Wendell's eyes already had drifted away from those of Von Runyon as he mentioned the name of the mansion that served as headquarters for his architectural firm. "I'll look forward to seeing you there."

And then Miles Wendell stepped away. The ultimate politician, thought Von Runyon. *Says everything, but says nothing.* He turned and pushed his way through the crowd of athletes, reporters and hangers on, debating as he went whether or not to go for the free lunch in the next room.

As he disappeared, Christine Ferrara asked Fiona Flynn about Sunday. "I plan to win," the Irish lass responded. No guile there, the TV reporter thought.

"I'd like to shoot some footage of you running," Christine suggested. "I don't want to interfere with your training this close to the marathon, but do you plan to work out later this afternoon?"

"All the serious training is done, Love" replied Fiona. "Any running I do in these last few days is play. I have to grab a bite to eat, attend a meeting about drug testing and get a massage. I'll probably head out to run on the lakefront some time around 4:00 or 4:30."

Perfect, thought Christine. She could meet Fiona and do some action shots to blend with the talking-head shots. It might be tight to try to make *The Four O'clock News*, but her station had continuing news broadcasts at 5:00 and 6:00 before yielding to situation comedies and detective shows. Reporter and athlete debated where to meet. Fiona appeared to know the Lake City lakefront better than Christine and suggested a small park several miles from the hotel. Edmund said he knew how to get there. The two women exchanged cell phone numbers, each pulling out their phones to punch in numbers. Christine was surprised how cooperative the woman who Peter pegged as possible winner was in offering her time. I suppose that's part of being in an activity that has to fight for headlines on the sports pages.

Meeting decided, Christine moved to the crowd of reporters talking with defending champion Joseph Nduku. After several minutes, he answered a question she posed, but said little, though he was polite. *There's a response that will land quickly on the cutting room floor,* Christine thought sadly.

The TV reporter continued to eavesdrop and collect background information that might be used on one of TV3's many news broadcasts later that afternoon or evening or in the next several days. TV was a ravenous beast that feasted on news like a vulture feasted on carrion. She was sure she could patch together something that would make her bosses happy. She lowered her mike and said to Edmund, her cameraman, "Let's head back to the office."

But before they could move, Christine felt a hand on her elbow. "Can I buy you lunch, Ms. Ferrara?"

She turned and found herself looking at Peter McDonald. Christine Ferrara realized that suddenly she was very, very hungry.

MARATHON

67:00:00

Peter McDonald felt the cell phone in his right pocket vibrate. Still listening to the lunchtime conversation, or seeming to listen, he pulled the phone from his pocket, trying to attract as little attention as possible. Peter glanced down at the screen identifying the caller. The screen showed a single letter: X.

"Pardon my rudeness," Peter whispered to Christine Ferrara, seated beside him. "I have to take this call." The race director pivoted in his chair, so he was facing away from those at the circular table on the balcony of Hilliard Towers. He would need to be cautious so others at the table, still talking, would not be able to identify the person calling. In his position, Peter was accustomed to being discreet.

Because he knew the identity of the caller and because he also knew the caller too was aware of that fact, Peter did not waste time with greetings. "Where are you?" he asked.

"High above the Atlantic Ocean," Celebrity X responded. "I'll be touching down at the Hampton Airport, crossroads of the world, tonight."

Hampton Airport was a small airport bordered by the lake on the north, an expressway on the south and steel mills on the remaining two sides. Hampton Airport had been built on landfill, slag from the furnaces, partly for the convenience of executives from those steel mills. It was not quite a public airport, but was not quite private either.

"ETA?" asked Peter.

"Pardon?"

"Sorry. Do you know your Estimated Time of Arrival?"

Celebrity X smiled at having failed to recognize the acronym. He decided he had been living in a sheltered world too long. "Not sure," X replied. "The pilot claims we're bucking headwinds and may have to dodge around some thunderstorms."

"Do you need a ride to your mom's house?"

"Taken care of."

"Did you remember your passport?"

"We arranged for that issue before we filed our flight plan."

"More important: Your running shoes?"

"Packed."

"Listen, how's your training?"

59

THURSDAY

"Terrible. I'm going crazy. Nearly three weeks since my 20-miler, and I know I should taper, I know I should rest, but I want to be out running."

Peter laughed, recognizing a symptom common to marathon runners, dubbed "Taper Madness" by Don Geoffrey. In training for a marathon, runners spend four months or more increasing their long-mile dose week after inexorable week: 6 miles, then 7 miles, eventually up to 20. Then after that final peak week, they cut back on their training for three weeks as they gather energy for the race. Like an addict coming off heroin, these deprived runners begin to suffer anxiety and find themselves with more time on their hands than they would like.

Also part of the problem is that on the eve of achieving their goal, they realize that once that goal has been attained, they may need to move on to the rest of their lives. "I don't know what I'm going to do for amusement after the marathon," said X, articulating this feeling. Both he and Peter knew that this would be the only marathon he possibly could do.

"You'll find something," Peter replied.

There was a moment of silence as Celebrity X considered that statement. He asked: "Are the plans all in place? Pardon my pushiness."

"In place. I can't say much now, since I'm at lunch with friends. Get some rest after you land. I miss your mom's spaghetti. Tell her I love her. I'll give you a call tomorrow if I find a gap in my schedule. If I fail, and I've been known to do so, you call me."

The two old friends exchanged quick goodbyes, and Peter punched the red button on his cell phone, ending the call. He replaced the phone in his pocket and returned his attention to the lunchtime conversation, although his mind was skipping ahead, reviewing how he would handle Celebrity X to avoid negatively impacting the experiences of those running around him. It was sixty-seven hours before the start, and he still had much on his mind.

67:00:00. 66:59:59. 66:59:58.

Peter found himself staring into the sparkling brown eyes of Christine Ferrara. The TV reporter returned what was a blank gaze with a smile. "A friend?" she said, not that she actually wanted to know.

"A friend," Peter responded, shutting down further comment. He thought how surprised she and the others at the table would be if he told them the identity of the friend calling. He was not about to do that and hoped that their security remained tight until Celebrity X found his place on the starting line Sunday morning. There, his presence would be disguised somewhat by 50,000 surrounding runners. But not for long. Not for long.

Christine smiled, realizing that the race director was not going to tell her who that call was from. *But why should he?* She turned away, directing her attention toward others at the table.

60

Peter did the same, but for a moment he worried. *Am I getting too friendly with this woman? Is she, like most reporters, trolling for information that she has no business knowing?* Peter finally decided, no. She was merely being friendly to an acquaintance just met.

"Got to go," he announced and stood up, a signal that caused others at the table similarly to do the same. Not pausing to shake hands, Peter began to move away from the table, then stopped and looked back at Christine Ferrara. He touched her lightly on the shoulder: "I'll see you later this week, Christine. On TV, if not elsewhere."

Christine felt the light touch of his hand on her shoulder. It was like being struck by lightning, she later would tell her roommate Yolanda. But at that moment, she could do little more than smile again, because the race director already was moving toward the elevators.

67:35:00

Walking away from his luncheon companions, headed toward the elevators, Peter McDonald realized that he may have executed a too sudden departure from a newly met female who seemed both interesting and interested in him, but these last three days before the marathon were critical to the race's success, especially the meeting he was about to have in a few minutes. Christine Ferrara certainly was bright enough to realize that. She would understand—or so Peter hoped.

Also nagging at him was the memory of his late wife Carol—and the agony of how she had left him. Was he ready to move beyond the memory of her? Pressing one hand against the top of his dress shirt beneath the tie he had donned for the press conference, Peter could feel the silver chain she had given him. *Am I living too much in the past?* He quickly banished that thought from his mind.

An elevator door slid open, and he stepped inside. Peter's meeting, planned for 1:30, was with one of the Shelaghi executives, Patrick Savitch, Paddy as they called him. Not the top man, nor necessarily even close to the top man. A marathoner though, running the race on Sunday. Good enough to break three hours, too. He could be counted on to understand what went into the organization of a major marathon, but the insertion of a layer of authority between him and the Shelaghi executive manager both bothered and worried Peter. *Was this a hint of a decision already made?* Peter liked Dennis Lahey. He suspected most men felt the same on first meeting. He appreciated the ex-

61

ecutive manager's bluntness, his directness, his hale-fellow-well-met charm, and most of all, the lilting Irish accent that certainly had helped propel him to the top of world banking circles. But what lurking thoughts lay beneath the surface charm? That worried Peter most.

Paddy, a fellow runner, most likely would be sympathetic when it came time to resolve the pending sponsorship decision. But in all honesty, did it still make sense for the foreign bankers to continue pouring money into the event? Peter thought so, but would they?

Dennis Lahey apparently would make the final decision, but Peter could not read the Shelaghi executive yet. Nor did he have much time this weekend to attempt to do so. Peter's best strategy, he finally decided, was to focus on the ordinarily prosaic details of good organization. Make the marathon work. Run it as smoothly as possible. Create an enjoyable event for runners, volunteers, spectators and sponsors despite the threat of warm weather and the tumult sure to be created the moment Celebrity X stepped onto the course.

Could X's presence tip the scales in his balance? Peter thought so, but did not know. More important: he did not want to promote X's running the race as some publicity coup or reduce it to a photo-op. It was not Peter's style.

In the elevator Peter punched the button that would take him to the twenty-fourth floor. Stepping out, he encountered an empty corridor. Savitch had not yet arrived. Just over five minutes remained before their scheduled meeting.

Peter pulled a plastic card from his wallet and used it to enter the Presidential Suite. The card had the marathon logo on it, a nice touch thought up by Noel Michaels, his executive director. It made the card a keepsake. Maybe some day he would see the hotel's marathon cards offered on eBay. The thought amused him.

Although several others on his staff also had access to the suite, including two sleeping rooms off a balcony over the main room, the suite now was unoccupied. Peter placed his attaché case containing instructions for the weekend on a coffee table before an unlit fireplace. Despite his busy schedule, Peter could not resist walking to the full-length glass doors and staring out for a few seconds at the lake and park. He focused his gaze on Burnham Fountain, a major attraction for tourists visiting Lake City. Tents on both sides filled the grassy areas near the start and finish. Tomorrow, precisely at 10:00 AM, the police would block Columbia Drive so that his staff, led by Michaels, could take possession of that street to ready it for Sunday. In less than three days, Peter mused, the pavement would feel the feet of nearly 50,000 runners.

67:35:00. 67:34:59. 67:34:58.

Peter returned to the living room. Nearly 1:30. He hoped Savitch arrived on time. He had other tasks scheduled, including a meeting soon with elite athletes to brief them on plans for the weekend, including drug testing.

Even as his mind shifted forward to that meeting, Peter heard a polite tapping on the double door he had left open. "Hello," said someone with a voice that raised images of the green fields of Ireland. Patrick Savitch was a man of medium height with a runner's build and the dark hair of the Black Irish. *He might be a runner, but he dresses like a banker,* Peter noted.

The two exchanged greetings. Peter suggested they move to a cluster of upholstered chairs on both sides of a coffee table and before a fireplace that on this balmy afternoon was more for show than for warmth.

"Can I get you something to drink, Paddy?" asked Peter.

"Rare is an Irishman who says no to so kind an offer, Peter, but I know you're busy. Dennis asked me to discuss the finances of the marathon with you. He thought that both of us being runners, we might be able to communicate more quickly than he could."

In other words, Peter thought, *Lahey would rather assign unpleasant tasks to others on his staff.*

Savitch settled slowly into one of the chairs as Peter claimed another. The Irishman tried to remain nonchalant, although Peter could see Paddy's eyes darting left and right as he absorbed again the suite's opulent furnishings, including its Grand piano. Having access to such a suite would impress some executives, or it could make them believe you were wasting money on unnecessary extravagance. In truth, the hotel offered the suite free to the marathon as a thank you gesture for filling its rooms with runners on what might otherwise be a slow weekend. Peter would not explain in detail the hotel/marathon business arrangements to Savitch. He did not want to burden the Irish banker with unnecessary detail. Let the Shelaghi executives find out later—if they continued their sponsorship.

"Let me move quickly to what I believe to be the reason for our meeting," said Peter reaching into the attaché case on the coffee table between the two men. Savitch nodded to indicate he agreed and watched calmly as Peter extracted a sheet of paper from the case. "Numbers. We can start by discussing some of the costs of producing a race as large as Lake City,"

"Exactly what I want to know," replied Savitch.

"I'm going to paint a broad picture."

"Agreed."

"Feel free to ask questions."

Peter explained what Savitch certainly already knew: that it cost $110 to enter the Lake City Marathon. "We raised the entry fee—not without some serious discussion—from $90 the year before in an attempt to keep pace with the spiraling costs of organizing the event."

"Why $110? Why not a rounder number like $100?"

"We wanted to think ahead, so we don't need to raise fees every year."

"Smart."

"At the same time, we raised the cap to allow 50,000 into the race compared with 40,000 the year before. Believe it or not, that caused more controversy than charging everybody more money."

That puzzled Savitch: "Why was that?"

"Because the experienced runners, the veterans, those who were running this race when we had only 5,000 starters—a tenth of today's numbers—felt they were being crowded off the course by hordes of newcomers who started running three months ago after deciding to raise money for some charity."

Savitch chuckled. "I know exactly how they feel."

"Our sport is in the midst of a boom because of these newcomers, but it's an uneasy truce between them and the veterans who can remember races costing only $5, and you could show up ten minutes before the start and slap your bill down on the table to pick up a number."

"Many of our races in Ireland are still like that."

Peter continued: "The arithmetic is simple, Paddy. Multiply 50,000 times $110 and runners pay $5.5 million for the privilege of running Lake City. Complaints aside, we actually filled the field sooner this year compared to last year despite more spots available. It's a case of demand overwhelming supply. In the last decade, Lake City has positioned itself near the top of world marathons. I want to say *at* the top, but I'm trying to stay modest."

"I would agree to 'at the top,' Peter. I don't intend to be modest when I relay these numbers to Dennis."

Peter resumed his analysis. "But to be honest with you, Paddy, there is an undercurrent of resentment about the increased difficulty runners now face in entering at least the major marathons. Somewhere near 13 percent of our field will not start the race, even though they have paid their entry fees."

"I think I know why," said Savitch, but tell me anyway."

"The fact that races such as ours limit entries forces runners to enter early: in the spring for a fall race; in the fall for a spring race. But by race date, their situation changes and some decide not to run."

Peter listed some of the reasons why this might happen: "Runners become injured. Their plans change. They get halfway through their training and realize completing a 26-mile race is more difficult than imagined. A roommate from college calls and says she is getting married in Hawaii, and would you like to be my bridesmaid? You would not believe the number of reasons—or excuses—runners offer requesting a refund. Unfortunately, we can't return their entry fees."

"Because?"

"Because we've already spent the money."

Paddy nodded to indicate he understood.

"More arithmetic, Paddy: With 50,000 runners and 13 percent who fail to make it to the starting line, that's 6,500 runners who have trusted us with $110, or $715,000 invested in our race by no-show runners. Some of them feel they're being ripped off, and maybe they are. I like to think of it as an investment in the right to run through the streets of Lake City unimpeded by traffic, protected by police and pampered by volunteers for up to six or seven hours. The cost of providing this experience is high, very high."

Peter shifted quickly and expertly into an explanation of the major cost items involved in producing an event as large as the Lake City Marathon. This included the salaries of the nearly two dozen full-time employees that worked in the marathon office as well as money paid a half dozen part-time interns, usually college students, hired the last month or two to handle the increasing number of tasks leading to race day. One line item included rent for office space, nearly a full floor in one of the bank's several buildings. "The bank obviously owns the building and our office, but we still need to include rental as part of our budget," explained Peter.

"Nothing comes free," Savitch agreed. "At least not with line-item costs."

Peter handed a cost spreadsheet to the Irish banker, pointing to large sums connected with T-shirts and other clothing offered volunteers, rent for the convention center, electronic clocks and signage on the course and rental charges for the warehouse in which all the equipment necessary to run a marathon needed to be stored. "The mayor loves us," McDonald said. "We dump $100 million into the economy. But he does not love paying the salaries of all the policemen standing on corners without which we could not run through town without having the Hell's Angels cross the course on their motorcycles."

Savitch smiled at the reference to the motorcycle gang, known even in Ireland, but said nothing, preferring to listen rather than talk.

McDonald continued: "Even the million or so spectators who line the course and make all our sponsors happy would get in the way if we did not find some way to control them. Leave them unwarned for a few minutes and they edge further and further into the streets and into the way of the runners. Controlling them costs money, and the mayor lately has been forced to pass more and more of those costs to us. We don't like it; he doesn't either."

"Do you pay for the police, or does the city?" asked Paddy.

"We pay," Peter replied. "They are off-day officers who volunteer to work marathon day. It's called a 'Hire-Back' program so the city is not exposed by taking police away from their regular duties. We hire about 800 policemen and pay them time-and-a-half at a cost of approximately $300,000."

Savitch nodded. Peter noticed that the Irish banker had yet to write down a number or make a note of a fact that he might later share with Dennis Lahey. Perhaps Paddy had a photographic memory for details—or perhaps he was there mainly as cover prior to a negative decision. Peter could not assume that. He resumed his recital of numbers related to the marathon.

"We pay the Park District more than $100,000 for use of the park, not merely race day but for set-up that begins nearly a week before."

Savitch again nodded, showing that he understood.

Peter hoped so. He continued to move from line item to line item, explaining each and showing how costs had continued to escalate. "We have suffered a deficit budget the last two years," said Peter. "That was one reason we felt obligated to raise entry fees, to pass the cost on to the runners. But you can only do that so much before you begin to reach resistance."

"And the increased number of entries?" wondered Paddy Savitch. "You mentioned that your veteran runners are concerned about crowding."

"They should be," conceded Peter. "We gave a lot of thought this year to reconfiguring the starting grid with additional corrals for fastest and faster runners, those with pre-qualified times. We made a number of operational changes that most runners don't realize despite promoting those changes on our Web site. Even if your previous marathon time is only four hours—and I use the term "only" advisedly—we'll position you on the starting line to almost guarantee you a smooth start.

"We've also narrowed the gates at the starting line funneling runners over the chip mats through a narrower opening than last year. This will delay runners spilling out onto the course. While this seems counterproductive, once across that line, they can begin to spread to the full width of Columbia Drive. The result, less crowding."

Peter paused and looked up to see if Savitch was absorbing the information offered him. Savitch seemed to be, so Peter continued: "Our research suggests that we can handle 10,000 more runners without diminishing the experience for all entrants, no matter their times."

"And if your research is wrong?" asked Savitch, then hastened to add: "I'm not trying to say it is."

"If we're wrong, runners will vote by next year, running Chicago or New York or Marine Corps or Twin Cities, and Shelaghi as sponsor might not like it if our numbers go backwards. But cutting back is a disservice to those who want to run Lake City. And a lot of people do."

The pair had been talking for nearly a half hour. Simultaneously sensing that little more remained to be said, both stood up. Patrick Savitch offered

Peter his hand, thanked him for his time, and headed toward the elevators. Their meeting over, Peter began to think forward to his next meeting, one with elite athletes in another half hour. Before that meeting, he would need to return a number of telephone calls. During their discussion, he had continued to feel the vibration of his cell phone. It indicated that different people—some of them important, some of them not—wanted to talk to him.

Peter McDonald knew he had force-fed Patrick Savitch with more numbers than even the smartest banker could absorb in a single setting. But it was less the numbers, he wanted to impress on the Irish banker, and more the fact that the Lake City Marathon, indeed, was exceptionally well organized and one that the Irish conglomerate could afford to continue to be associated with. He suspected that Patrick Savitch knew that. He only hoped that the message would get through to Dennis Lahey.

66:00:00

He hates me!" sighed **Christine Ferrara. Back at the TV3 studios,** preparing to edit the interview with Fiona Flynn, Christine first decided to call her roommate and confessor Yolanda Kline. The two women had roomed together in college. After moving to Lake City, Christine accepted an invitation to stay with Yolanda, at least until she decided whether or not to get her own apartment.

66:00:00. 65:59:59. 65:59:58.

"Hello," responded Yolanda in a singsong voice that betrayed bemusement. Having graduated from Bradley University with a degree in criminology, Kline now worked for the Lake City Police Department as a computer data analyst. "Who is this mysterious creature calling me without offering some word of introduction? If you want to sign me up for a credit card, whoever you are, I already have sixteen such pieces of plastic."

Another sigh: "Hello, Yolanda."

"Aha! The mysterious creature reveals herself as my sometime roommate. Hello Christine."

"I'm sure he hates me."

"And who is this hateful person, Christine? A stalker? A serial killer? Someone you slandered on *The Four O'clock News*?"

"His name is Peter."

"The stalker has a name?"

"He is absolutely gorgeous. I couldn't keep my eyes off him."

Yolanda let out a shriek that momentarily startled a detective in the next cubicle. She gave him a wave to indicate that this was girlfriend talk, and he better not listen if he valued their friendship. The detective lost interest and returned to the sports section of the *Lake City Ledger*. He was reading about the local N.F.L. team, not Jonathan Von Runyon's story suggesting the marathon might lose its sponsor.

"The stalker not only has a name, but also he is gorgeous?"

Christine began to describe Peter McDonald as though he were some perpetrator, who might at some time be brought to justice: his approximate height, his weight, the color of his hair, what he was wearing, that he seemed to be in his mid-thirties, at least a few years older than her. Most important from a woman's perspective: he did not seem to be married. "At least he wasn't wearing a ring."

"You checked?"

"I checked, and I think he caught me doing so, but that's okay, because later I caught him looking at my legs when I got in his car."

"You got in the stalker's car?"

"He offered me a ride to the hotel."

"Hotel? Roomie, I'm calling your mama."

"The press conference was at the hotel. The marathon is this weekend, Ms. Dirty Mind. He's race director. That's why I was interviewing him."

"And checking his marital status. And letting him see your legs."

"I chose too short a skirt this morning. Most of my clothes are still in Peoria. And I had to climb into one of those vans with a running board."

"At which point you exposed yourself. I hope you were wearing clean underwear, Christine."

"Yolanda!"

"What I don't understand is why, after noticing you checking on his marital status and getting a good look at your legs, this man hates you?"

"He probably doesn't really hate me, but he should. I was rude. He was late for the interview, and I'm afraid I showed it. It's that time of the month, but I know that's no excuse. Later at lunch...."

"Excuse me?"

"Later at lunch...."

"You had lunch with him?"

"Yes."

"This gets better and better. I know I'm going to call your mama. You meet this man. He is gorgeous. You check to see if he is married. He is not. Did you ask if he was divorced? That might be a deal breaker...."

"Yolanda!"

"...You climb into this man's car, flagrantly exposing your legs. You go to a hotel. You have lunch together."

"It was at the press conference. A buffet."

"Buffets still count as an eating encounter with or without wine and candles. And yet you tell me he hates you?"

"Well, probably not. He should! He was talking on his cell phone to someone he said was a friend, and I couldn't help overhearing at least his end of the conversation, because he was seated right next to me, and I think he sensed that and got a bit defensive."

"Friend? Like in girlfriend?"

"I don't know. But I don't think so. It sounded more like guy talk, but I felt guilty listening in."

"So it is revealed: The stalker is being stalked. What else do you want me to not tell your mama?"

"He remembered my marathon time."

"He remembered your marathon time? If that's all it takes to seduce a woman, there would be more babies in the world than there are now."

"Yolanda, I have not been seduced."

"Thankfully. If it happens, I know I will call your mama."

"Bye, Yolanda."

"Bye, Christine. I'll see you after work."

"Okay, except I'm going to a party. Peter might be there."

"Christine!!!"

The detective in the next cubicle looked up from reading the sports section and shook his head. *Women!* He thought.

65:30:00

As the elite athletes gathered in the Marquette Room on the third floor of Hilliard Towers, Peter McDonald could not help thinking how much time and money was wasted on keeping them honest. Not that those running the Lake City Marathon were dishonest. Not that they wanted to cheat each other. But each runner, male and female, was possessed by paranoia, the worry that others less honorable might cheat them out of their rightful honors as endurance athletes. It was less about winning either titles or money and more about self-respect and the knowledge that all their hard training, the miles run in practice, their talent, their dedication to the sport, their sacrifices, could be squandered if forced to compete against cheaters.

THURSDAY

The problem was drugs: not recreational drugs, but performance-enhancing drugs that might allow individuals with less talent or who had trained less intensely to defeat them by chemically enhancing their skills.

To prevent this, the U.S. Anti-Doping Agency (USADA) and the U.S. Track and Field Federation (USATF) spent millions annually monitoring not only American athletes, but foreign athletes competing in the United States. That sum was in addition to even larger sums spent by the International Amateur Athletic Federation (IAAF) and the World Anti-Doping Agency (WADA). Plus this year, Peter was committing more money to test deeper in the field than usual in most major marathons.

Drug testing, however, was only one item on the agenda for the Thursday afternoon briefing of elite athletes. Peter needed to provide them with detailed information on what to expect Sunday and also answer any questions. It was a mandatory meeting for invited athletes, who had received travel expenses or appearance fees. Should any fail to attend, they could be fined as much as $500, the money to be deducted from prize money. Those arriving in town late still could attend a secondary briefing meeting on Saturday, but most invited runners had arrived several days before the marathon for the noon press conference just completed.

Apart from drugs, the agenda involved mostly mundane matters such as what time the hospitality suite opened race day morning (4:00 AM), what food would be available (coffee, rolls and various carbohydrates), how the athletes would get from the hotel to the starting area (buses), where they could warm up (in front of the starting line) and when they needed to position themselves (immediately after the wheelchair competition began). The wheelchair racers started at 7:55 A.M., the runners at 8:00 A.M. Because of their ability to move faster on their specially designed chairs, the first wheelchair athletes would finish long before the first runners.

As Peter continued to talk to the elites, there remained approximately sixty-five-and-a-half hours before the start of the Lake City Marathon.
65:30:00. 65:29:59. 65:29:58.

Once the race started, other details impacted the ability of runners to compete successfully. They needed to be given "splits," their times for each mile, as well as every five kilometers, foreign runners being more used to the metric system. They needed to be provided special liquids, not merely water and E.R.G. in cups on tables, but in plastic bottles that they could grab on the run, because it is a lot harder to drink if you are running 5:00 miles than if you are running (and walking) 10:00 miles. To insure fast times, Peter provided "rabbits" for the top runners. Rabbits were individuals who would lead the pack at a fast pace for 10 or 15 or 20 miles, then move out of the way. This removed the burden of leading from those capable of winning the marathon.

Peter had contracted for a half dozen rabbits to pace the men's field; two more for the women, their specific task to help Aba Andersson set a world record. Aba's rabbits—Kyle and Wesley Fowler—were seated in the back row, Kyle text-messaging his coach back in Minnesota about Aba's illness. The Swedish runner had failed to show for the elite athlete meeting. Her husband Bjørn attended in her place, still saying Aba hoped to run Sunday, but Peter was not sure whether or not to believe him. After all his hopes for a world record, Peter wondered whether it would happen. Given the weather forecast, pacing plans might prove obsolete, not only for elite runners like Aba but for citizen runners behind, many who relied on pacing teams to fulfill their BQ and PR dreams. It did not make much sense to send runners out at a 2:05 pace (men) or 2:15 pace (women) or 4:00 pace (midpack) if temperatures soared into the 80s. In fact, it could be dangerous.

Peter would need to worry about that later, since the next item on the agenda was drug testing, a necessary evil of today's racing scene. Peter despised being forced to test for drugs, not only because testing siphoned money out of the sport, but also because it diverted the public's attention, as well as the attention of potential sponsors, when runners got caught.

And they *would* get caught if they tried it at his race, and Peter needed to warn them of that.

"We're going to do more testing for drugs than at any other marathon before," Peter began. "For openers, we plan to test the first ten across the line, men and women. Not just the first three, the first ten! That's automatic."

Peter allowed that information to be absorbed by the athletes before continuing. He noticed several of them talking to each other in their native languages. Good, he thought. Peter wanted the message to get out. After the buzz began to decrease, he continued:

"There will also be random testing, and it will be less random than in the past. If you are sitting in this room, the chances of your being picked out of the finishing chute and tested 'randomly' is near one hundred percent.

"That includes rabbits," added Peter. He realized that he was using what his mother used to call her "Teacher's Voice." Peter's mom had worked as a schoolteacher. There were times, she claimed, when it was necessary to address the class in a voice where they knew she meant business. Not loud, but firm. Of a pitch that if taken to the next level would shatter glass!

"I don't want to be embarrassed if any of you have been taking drugs and get caught. I don't want our sponsors to be embarrassed. Don't think that you can fool our testers. You cannot, and even if there's a slight chance that you might slip through the cracks, don't even try. If we catch anyone, I guarantee that you will never run another major road race again. Never! Your career will be over. You'll be banned for life. Since I consider all of you my personal friends, I do *not* want that to happen."

The elite athletes responded with silence. They did not talk. They did not move, as though the subject was disrespectful. Peter waited a beat before making his final point: "If you have been taking anything to improve your performance, I do not—repeat, *not*—want you to dirty my race. Even if you come jogging across the line in three hours, we'll spot you and catch you. If anyone does decide not to start, no questions will be asked. *Period!* Do I make myself clear?"

Again, Peter McDonald paused. The buzz had returned, those who could understand English interpreting for those who could not. Finally, one of the athletes, a black athlete from Kenya, raised his hand. It was Joseph Nduku, the defending champion.

"Mr. Peter," Nduku said with a voice that was softly gentle, betraying the accent of one raised in the Rift Valley.

"Yes, Joseph."

"For all the other athletes who love to run, from my country and from the countries of others..." Nduku stopped, weighing the impact of his next words. The Kenyan then said simply, "I would like to thank you."

Spontaneously, the room erupted with applause.

Peter was moved. "Thank you, Joseph." With no more questions, the athletes began to disperse in groups, some to head back their rooms for naps, others to go for an easy workout, a last minute shaking of their legs.

The Kenyans left in a group, all trailing Joseph Nduku, as though they recognized him as their leader. This included Kenyatta Kemai, who anticipated that he, not Joseph, would be the leader when they completed 26 miles 385 yards of running on Sunday.

After most had left, Peter McDonald found Bjørn Andersson standing before him. "We both know there's a chance Aba will be unable to run Sunday."

Peter indicated that he knew.

"I do *not*, Peter, want her not-starting to be interpreted as ducking the drug tests. You know how much Aba despises cheaters."

Peter knew; he responded: "We can arrange that Aba also be drug-tested before she leaves town."

"That would be first rate," said Bjørn.

Peter added: "But I'm still hoping she can run."

MARATHON

65:00:00

Joseph Nduku had been sitting in the front row when Peter McDonald launched into what on the surface seemed a harsh condemnation of the long distance running scene, where wins and world records sometimes seemed to be the property of those able to afford the best and latest ergogenic aids.

Joseph Nduku hated drug users. He absolutely detested them. He hoped that none of his fellow competitors in the marathon scheduled to start in little more than sixty-five hours used them.

65:00:00. 64:59:59. 64:59:58.

The defending champion did not use drugs, and he was not aware of any of his teammates who used them. Not even Kenyatta Kemai, who Joseph suspected would like to upset him. *No, not Kenyatta.* Not any of their brothers who ran under the black, red, green and white flag. Kenyans did not use drugs, Nduku truly believed. Some might think Joseph had his head stuck in the sand of the Rift Valley, but the Kenyan felt: *We don't need them! We're good enough without them!* And those younger Kenyans still a year or two away from making the team that wins the World Cross-Country Championships year after year after year are too poor to afford them!

Athletes from other countries who took drugs, he abhorred their cheating! If a beggar in the slums of Nairobi stole the wallet out of his pocket, Joseph Nduku might feel anger toward the beggar, but at least would rationalize that the poor man now could feed his family. Other runners who needed drugs to win not only stole from him, they stole from his family, his brothers and sisters and cousins and uncles and aunts now living on the land he had begun to purchase in the Rift Valley with his prize money.

Nduku's experience was typical of many Kenyan runners. Growing up near Eldoret, high on a mountain plateau, running became a means of transportation. Nduku attended a missionary school five miles from home. He ran to and from school barefoot, because he owned no running shoes.

After becoming a successful distance runner, winning world championship medals on the track and in cross-country, Nduku had read a column in *Running Magazine* written by Don Geoffrey: "If we want to end Kenyan dominance in distance running, all we need do is ship a thousand yellow school buses to that country. Make the Kenyans ride to school instead of run."

Other of his teammates might have felt insulted by that politically incorrect statement, but it made Nduku chuckle. Later, Joseph told the writer: "I read what you wrote about yellow school buses. True, Mr. Donald. It is true!"

Truth be told, it was more than a lack of yellow school buses that made Kenyans great runners. It was their build. They were small people. Nduku stood 5 feet 5 inches tall and weighed 122 pounds. The wrong build for playing in the National Football League; perfect for winning the Boston Marathon. Nobody played football in Kenya, at least not American football. Succeed as a runner in Kenya, and you climbed to the top of the athletic pedestal. In that third world country, the average annual income was less than $1,000. That financial disparity between the haves and have nots drove the Kenyan runners to success, just as it did black basketball players in the United States. It helped also that most of the best Kenyan runners lived at altitudes near 5,000 feet. They possessed highly developed cardiovascular systems. Athletes from other countries often moved to high altitude locations or slept in oxygen tents that simulated high altitude in the belief that it would train their blood to process oxygen more efficiently. Foolishness, felt Joseph. Pitiful, he believed. A better approach was to be born at altitude and live there growing up.

As a boy, Joseph Nduku never anticipated being a world champion. He was too humble to allow such a thought to enter even his dreams. Nevertheless, Joseph remained quite aware of the great tradition of Kenyan distance runners, beginning with Kip Keino, who won the 1500 meters at the 1968 Olympic Games in Mexico City. Keino became the first Kenyan Olympic champion and the first African winner on the track (although Abebe Bekila of Ethiopia had won the marathon at the two previous Olympics).

Those two Africans from two different and not always friendly countries were harbingers of so many great African distance runners following. Henry Rono at one time held every world record from 3,000 to 10,000 meters. Paul Tergat won five consecutive world cross-country championships and later broke the world record for the marathon, running 2:04:55. The list of great Kenyan distance runners was long, almost endless, and currently Joseph Nduku was on top of the heap because of wins with fast times at Boston, Chicago and last year at Lake City. The world record in the marathon thus far had eluded Joseph, but he hoped to add that to his résumé at some point, if not Sunday when it might be too hot to run fast. He did not fear the heat. Coming from Africa, he knew hot weather was just one more opponent to be defeated, one more excuse for those whom he would defeat.

Joseph Nduku knew he would win the Lake City Marathon on Sunday. The Kenyan did not even consider defeat. And he would accomplish that goal without the aid of performance-enhancing drugs.

Following the elite athlete's meeting, Joseph Nduku returned to his room. After changing into his running clothes, Joseph rode the elevator down to the lobby to meet his teammates. They would go for an easy run of half a dozen miles, and it would be an *easy* run, as slow as the slowest joggers entered in Sunday's marathon. Despite what the running public believed, Kenyans did not run every workout at a pace faster than five minutes a mile.

In the lobby, Joseph encountered Kyle and Wesley Fowler from the Northand Racing Team. The Kenyans often met Northland athletes at other running events, and an easy friendship had developed between runners from the two countries that transcended race and nationality. As Joseph Nduku and his teammates headed out of the hotel for their run along the lakefront, he fell into stride with the two Americans.

"You two may be out of a job if Aba fails to run," said Joseph.

"Then we'll help you, Joseph...." offered Kyle Fowler.

Wesley Fowler continued the comment without missing a beat. "...We'll be waiting at the finish line to hand you your warm-up suit."

"If the weather forecasts are correct, none of us will need warm-up suits," said Joseph ruefully.

64:30:00

As the Gulfstream carrying Celebrity X neared the coast of Greenland, the waters of the Atlantic Ocean slipping effortlessly behind, one of the men accompanying X to Lake City, Mario, moved to the front of the plane and placed a tray containing a plate of pasta on the table beside him. The pasta, fettuccini splashed with a marinara sauce, had been prepared before departure by one of the chefs who worked for the organization X headed. It had been tasted before being put on the plate and sealed with shrink-wrap. This was a precaution made necessary by the fact that there existed evil people in the world who might seek to kill Celebrity X.

For so important an individual, it was a simple meal. In addition to the plate of pasta, the tray contained a smaller plate containing a single piece of French bread, no butter. Beside it sat a salad that was mainly lettuce, touched lightly by an olive oil dressing. No dessert. If X had been eating back in his quarters in Rome—for security reasons, he rarely ate in restaurants—he might have capped his meal with a fine wine from Tuscany, but not before a marathon. Alcohol, he worried, could dehydrate you. He did not want to go into a marathon dehydrated, particularly if what his friend Peter McDonald had told him of the weather reports proved true. His beverage of choice for the Atlantic flight was an orange drink.

X looked up at Mario and offered a simple, *"Grazie tante."* Before removing a fork from the napkin in which the silverware was wrapped, X made a quick sign of the cross and said Grace, silently so none in the plane would hear. Those accompanying X to Lake City, his bodyguards Mario and Angelo, who also were running the marathon, had not yet started to eat. Their meals would be slightly more lavish than his, including that fine Tuscan wine. Only after he finished, would the pair feel comfortable eating.

He ate quickly, aware that their eyes were upon him. No sooner had he taken his last bite than Angelo moved forward to retrieve the tray. It was almost as though the two vied for the honor of serving him, X noted with some amusement. He politely said no to a request for dessert or coffee and picked up again the book he had been reading, a scholarly analysis and history of the Middle East, an area of the world that occupied more and more of his attention lately. He read only two paragraphs before the ponderous subject caused his mind to drift to the marathon he would be running in less than three days. Was he prepared? Had his plans remained secret? Nervous, X wanted to call Peter, but he knew his friend was occupied with organizational duties. *All this power*, X thought, *and I still do not want to seem intrusive.*

X stared placidly out the window and spotted a bank of clouds low on the horizon ahead. As the Gulfstream continued to approach the clouds, he saw land beneath: the coast of Greenland. In a few hours, he would arrive in Lake City. Looking at his watch, he saw that it was 9:30 in Italy. *What is the time difference? Six hours?* X turned and asked one of his traveling companions, who confirmed it to be 3:30 in Lake City.

64:30:00. 64:29:59. 64:29:58.

Given his importance as chief executive of one of the world's most influential organizations, X should have had a Rolex, or some other expensive timepiece, on his wrist. Instead, he wore a plastic watch, black with multiple buttons, so similar to watches worn by other runners. He began punching buttons to change his watch time to destination time.

The time was 8:30 on the west coast of Ireland, that edge of continental Europe that X's Gulfstream had streaked across several hours before. The sun had set. The sky was darkening. Redbird, still in his study even at that late hour, gazed out a window at waves crashing on rocks below. He had a single sheet of paper on the desk before him, but he looked beyond it, not at it, as though his view of the endless ocean would calm his mind and allow him to understand better the words written on the paper.

MARATHON

Immediately after being informed that the passenger in the Gulfstream had phoned a man named Peter McDonald, Redbird swiveled his chair and googled that name, as might anyone with Internet access trying to identify someone. That was a joke, Redbird realized. He found 9,020,000 references to individuals so named, including a well-known Irish actor born in Dublin, whose mother, according to one Web site, was a cookery writer, his father a seller of bailer twine. Another Peter McDonald worked as a camera operator (second unit) on one of the *Batman* films! *Was there no limit to the amount of useless information available on the Internet?*

Redbird had turned away from the computer, aware that his subordinates soon would bring him the information he needed. And in ten minutes they did just that. Several Peter McDonald's lived in Lake City; the one in question had attended the same high school as the man called Celebrity X, although several years later. They also grew up in the same neighborhood. Apparently the two were friends, and it made sense that the individual who interested Redbird would contact him before a visit to his parents.

But one other tidbit of information caught Redbird's attention, and he could not let it go. The sheet of paper reprinted an article identifying Peter McDonald as director of the Lake City Marathon. Not too coincidentally, the passenger in the Gulfstream, the focus of Redbird's attention, once was a track athlete and kept in shape by running, usually a half hour a day. Lately, however, he had increased his time spent exercising, sometimes going for long runs of several hours around the gardens of his estate outside Rome.

Was it possible, wondered Redbird, *that the man he was tracking had in his mind the running of a marathon?* He would be out in the open, exposed, vulnerable, part of a crowd. His bodyguards could hardly protect him.

"Foolish boy," said Redbird continuing to gaze over the Atlantic.

64:00:00

Peter McDonald once told Don Geoffrey that if he did his job properly for 364 days leading up to the marathon, he should be able to head home Saturday night, sleep late Sunday morning, prepare breakfast, read the paper, then turn on TV and watch the winners cross the finish line without doing anything that day other than relax and let the marathon happen.

Geoffrey had been writing an article for *Running Magazine* about the amount of time and effort it took to organize a major marathon. The reporter shook his head. "You're not serious," said Geoffrey.

Peter shrugged: "I'm too anal to let that happen, but theoretically it's true. If some dread disease dumped me into bed with a 104-degree fever, it would have zero effect on the 50,000 marathoners running my race."

"Perhaps."

"Not perhaps," Peter replied. "I have a number of assistants I've worked with for years. Noel Michaels, for example." Peter was referring to the marathon's executive director. "She's best in the business, which is operations: making the marathon work. Noel probably should be earning half a million dollars a year working for some Fortune 500 company."

"I'll tell her that."

"Don't you dare!"

Peter continued: "Look, it's like being conductor of a well-rehearsed symphony orchestra. If the players know their Mahler and Mozart, the conductor can stand back and listen to the music."

"But it helps if the conductor waves his baton, then bows to the audience after the last movement."

"The applause makes the musicians feel good," conceded Peter, "but my job involves more what goes on before the marathon than during."

Geoffrey eventually would use Peter's quote in his article in the September 2009 issue of *Running Magazine*, titled, "How to Be a Race Director." Geoffrey also described Peter as having a spread sheet in his computer titled "Things to Do" listing more than 150 items that needed to be accomplished to assure the marathon's success, everything from obtaining insurance certificates to balloons and bagels. Each time a task was accomplished—usually not by himself, but by a person assigned to that task—Peter red-marked the line item. By the last week before the marathon, the Excel sheet would be all red, otherwise he had not done his job. He then handed off to Michaels, who had her own spreadsheet focused on specific activities during the final seventy-two hours leading up to the start.

During those final hours before 50,000 runners took to the streets of Lake City, Peter would get very little sleep. The perfectionist in him required that he continue to monitor those trusted assistants and be on call in case they encountered any unexpected problems, which always seemed to occur no matter how much you planned in advance.

64:00:00. 63:59:59. 63:59:58.

At 4:00 on Thursday afternoon with sixty-four hours before the start of the marathon, Peter met three key members of his staff in the Presidential Suite on the twenty-fourth floor of Hilliard Towers. The relatively small group included Noel Michaels; Brad Keyes, director of the Health & Fitness Exposition; and Nelson Ogilvie, the media director. Everyone else responsible for Sunday's marathon reported through those three.

Peter opened the meeting by offering the latest weather report. He had spoken to TV3 weatherman Vaughn Johnson only ten minutes ago, just before Johnson stepped onto the set for *The Four O'clock News*. The TV weatherman confirmed reports of rising temperatures, possibly into the 80s by noon on Sunday. At that point (four hours into the race), the elites would have finished their work, but tens of thousands of less biomechanically perfect runners would be out on the course, still struggling toward the finish line, their time goals probably abandoned, yet determined to finish 26 miles 385 yards. Hopefully, they would have heeded warnings to slow down and drink amply, but Peter knew from past experience that risks rose exponentially with the heat. He could not put any numbers on it, but for each degree the temperature rose, another several dozen, maybe several hundred, runners would need to be taken to the Medical Tent.

Some of them might not even make the Medical Tent. They would collapse on course and need to be transported to hospitals. Even in normal years, he could figure on several hundred runners needing medical assistance after finishing. This would not be a normal year. Peter hoped that nobody would die. That happens occasionally for various reasons, and the media invariably reports these deaths, glossing over the fact that while one individual might have shortened his lifespan by running a marathon, 49,999 others will have improved their lives by embracing a lifestyle that includes exercise.

Thus in his talk to his key executives, he stressed preparation one more time, focusing particularly on the threat posed by hot weather. "We need to offer more water at all the aid stations," he said. "And E.R.G." Without a sponsor for water, Peter had planned to tap into fifteen fire hydrants at as many aid stations. But they still needed more cups. He also had put in a call to their supplier for E.R.G. "They've agreed to increase their commitment by 50 percent," said Peter. "On a hot day, even that may not be enough.

"Ambulances," he continued. "We're going to need more. And backup to those ambulances. And backup to the backup, particularly in the last miles."

Fortunately, the marathon course came near several medical centers in those miles. That would allow for quicker transport to emergency rooms, but while the first fallen runner was moved by ambulance, one, two, or more runners might fall in his footsteps. Later that afternoon, Peter had another meeting scheduled to discuss the problems caused by hot weather in more detail with those responsible for the runner's safety, including Nick Terrence, M.D., the marathon's medical director.

Clipboard in hand, spreadsheet on that clipboard, Peter had moved quickly through a discussion of race day logistics both before and after. "Before" in-

cluded collecting clothing bags from the runners to staging them on the starting line and organizing the waves that let them clear the line as rapidly as
possible. "After" included food and drink in the area immediately behind the
finish line to returning those bags. Given the warm weather, runners probably
would bring fewer items of clothing to the start than normal. That probably
meant less clean-up problems for clothing discarded in the first few miles, but
that was small consolation for other problems caused by the warm weather.

Peter set the clipboard down on a table. "Now I'm going to surprise you.
throw you all a curveball. It concerns the appearance of a celebrity, a very
well-known celebrity whose identity I still can't reveal—even to you."

"Peter," was Nelson Ogilvie's shocked response. "That's not a curveball.
That's a spitball."

"Sorry, Nelson. If word leaks that this person plans to run our race...."

Peter paused. He did not mention the code name, Celebrity X. Among the
group in the meeting, nobody yet knew even the code name. Until the meeting, the code name was simply one more line item on his spread sheet.

Peter resumed: "If word leaks that this person plans to run our race, it will
make it impossible for he or she to do so."

"He or she?" laughed Ogilvie. "You're not offering us many clues."

"You do *not* want to know the celebrity's identity, Nelson, because if word
does leak from any other source—and it might—you do not want any fingers
pointed in your direction."

"Correct," said Ogilvie.

"If this celebrity..." Michaels began.

"I refer to this person as Celebrity X," Peter interrupted.

"If this Celebrity X is as famous as you suggest, once he—or she—steps
onto the starting line, the word will spread quickly among the surrounding
runners. But when will we know?"

"I need to inform the police at roll call Friday morning that *a* celebrity will
be in the race. They will not be offered a name, and I suspect they will not
care. The police are used to handling movie stars and presidents, and are not
easily impressed—or pretend not to be. Other than that, you will not learn
Celebrity X's identity until all the other runners do."

Nobody offered an objection. If they questioned the reasons for this secrecy, they respected Peter's need to keep the information private. How much of
an impact could the appearance of any one celebrity have on a field of 50,000
anyway? Oprah had run the Marine Corps Marathon, and it caused a small
buzz for a while, then she simply became one among the pack. Oprah got her
picture on the cover of *Running Magazine,* but so do ordinary runners. Everyone had trained too long and too hard to allow even the most famous celebrity

to interfere with their plans. Running a marathon was too personal an activity for that. The race would go on with or without Celebrity X.

Or would it? A more pressing question—but one that nobody in the room dared ask—was what effect would the acquisition of Lake City Bank by the Irish conglomerate have on the marathon and their own job security? Would they be selling shoes in a running store by this time next year?

Peter stood up indicating that the meeting was over. Pure business, and with only a handful of no-nonsense people attending, it had lasted little over fifteen minutes. Nobody wasted time chatting afterwards. They headed to the elevators. With the last one gone, Peter sat down and responded to a series of telephone calls that had landed on his cell phone. Scrolling through a dozen messages, he was reminded of a call received several hours earlier from the just-discussed Celebrity X. *Where would he now be*, wondered Peter: *Probably high over the Atlantic Ocean.*

Although it was not planned that way, X's running the Lake City Marathon could have an incredible impact on the bank's new owners. The tremendous publicity connected to X's appearance might be the tipping point in any negotiations. Some rolling of the Red Carpet upon his arrival at the finish line seemed almost necessary, but X had killed anything that smacked of exploitation when Peter had raised that point several weeks before.

"I just want to run my 26 miles and jump back on the plane and head back home," said X. Peter smiled when X told him that since that was the goal of so many other runners. Peter would love to spend time with his friend, but knew that to be a totally impractical idea. Peter hoped only that they had a chance to talk even briefly before X returned to work in Rome.

Peter realized that it was time for *The Four O'clock News* on TV3. Past time, but sports coverage usually came halfway through the show. He clicked the television on, lowering the volume so he could continue to make telephone calls while watching out of one corner of his eye. He was engaged in a conversation with his contact at the Police Department, Captain Robert Newsom, planning his appearance the next day at roll call, when he saw that the station's sports coverage had begun. Sports anchor Mark Mallon opened with baseball and golf—major sports, unfortunately, grabbing the attention of the public more than running—then the logo of the Lake City Marathon appeared behind Mallon, signaling a switch to that sport.

"Fifty thousand runners have entered this year's marathon," Mallon began. "Christine Ferrara is standing by on the lakefront at Cushman Park…."

Immediately, the telecast had Peter's full attention. He ended his conversation with Captain Newsom and focused his gaze on the TV screen.

THURSDAY

63:44:00

Christine Ferrara and cameraman Edmund Giesbert waited beside a bench in Cushman Park, named after an airman killed during the Vietnam War. The park on a peninsula jutting out into the lake disguised, to a certain extent, a filtration plant. The plant purified water sucked from the lake and transported to the bathrooms and kitchens of Lake City citizens. Many if not most of the runners passing probably did not know the name of the park, its purpose, or why it was named.

It was 4:16 in the afternoon, *The Four O'clock News* presently being telecast to homes all over Lake City. Christine had just been alerted by the director that they would be cutting live to her in ninety seconds so she could introduce her package on marathon nutrition, shot earlier that morning at the Expo. *63:44:00. 63:43:59. 63:43:58.*

Christine never had visited Cushman Park before. As they waited, Edmund, a Vietnam veteran, pointed to a brass plaque at the entrance to the park. "Too many people were killed in that dirty little war," said Edmund.

"It happened before I was born," conceded Christine. All she knew about the Vietnam War came from history books and a few conversations with her parents, from the same generation as the cameraman. Her father had used various deferments to escape Vietnam, and, despite remaining an anti-war activist, he never seemed proud of that fact. Christine decided she better not mention her father's views. She sensed in Edmund a rough edge not entirely smoothed in the decades since that dirty little war ended.

Christine read the lettering on the plaque several times, pondering the twists of fate that had caused one young man, an airman, to lose his life, while others returned home. Some day she must read more about America's recent history if only to put into perspective the news she offered viewers. So much of what she previously had reported while working in Peoria was local rather than national news: fires and car crashes and family arguments. She suspected the news focus would remain the same now that she had moved to Lake City and its much larger market. TV3 billed itself as *"The* Local Station," emphasis on *"The,"* as though news of international importance could be obtained elsewhere, such as on CNN. Perhaps some day she would work for a station that focused on issues of importance. Are car-bombings in countries halfway around the world more or less important than car crashes in your own hometown? It depended probably on whether someone you knew was involved in, or cared about, that crash. Producers, not reporters, decided what stories their stations featured or even carried. Or maybe it was the advertising department. Until the unlikely time when she moved into a corner office signifying celebrity, Christine would content herself reporting on a marathon in which people would not get killed. Some might consider that a frivolous activity, but life was full of frivolous activities.

Following the press luncheon at Hilliard Towers, Christine returned with Edmund to the TV3 offices to check the editing of her morning's work to be aired on various newscasts later during the day. She already had done her live shot from the press conference used on *The Noon News*, her interview with Peter recorded at the Expo. She was about to do another live shot for *The Four O'clock News* standing on the lakefront, introducing the interview done with Don Geoffrey, also at the Expo. For *The Five O'clock News*, she planned to use the interview of Fiona Flynn from the press conference—and Christine hoped Fiona would show up in a few minutes so they could record her running on the lakefront to add to that package. Then she would head to the TV3 studio a few blocks away, to appear live in studio.

Mark Mallon, the regular sports announcer, had told Christine that during *The Five O'clock News*, they would chat with each other and also weatherman Vaughn Johnson, who planned to run the marathon. Happy Talk, Christine thought. She did not like it, but apparently viewers did, as did TV executives hoping to please those viewers. Happy Talk and the Car Crash or Fire of the Day. *Why are you being so cynical, Christine?* she asked herself. *If you do not want to be a TV reporter, they're hiring at Wal-Mart.*

Before heading home and to the party later that evening, she also needed to select stories for the 6:00 and 10:00 news telecasts, or at least variations using different soundbites from one of the stories already used. TV producers hated to repeat what already had aired under the assumption that someone who had turned their TVs on immediately after getting out of bed at 6:00 AM would still be watching TV3 before going to bed at midnight and would switch to another channel if they saw something already viewed. That made little sense, and it also made more work for everyone involved. She hoped that by the time her 10:00 report—whatever it was—aired, she would be in bed fast asleep.

Christine needed her rest. She expected to be busy the next several days with marathon coverage, although she could just as easily be called away to cover some breaking news story. She wondered why any healthy male would want to date a female TV reporter who might call fifteen minutes before their date for dinner in an elegant French restaurant, reservations required six weeks in advance, to announce that she had to cancel. No wonder she was about to celebrate her 30th birthday without a ring on her finger or a man on her arm. Christine Ferrara was convinced that she would die a spinster, and she knew her mother harbored similar worries. Of course, Peter McDonald had just entered her life—or had he?

Christine had chosen the interview with Don Geoffrey for *The Four O'clock News*, because it focused on the foods runners ate. A food package should work particularly well during that show with an audience predominantly female halting during their day's activities between picking kids up at school and preparing dinners for their families. Food always served as a good subject on *The Four O'clock News*. At least it did in Peoria, and she had no doubt the same would prove true in Lake City.

Waiting to go live with an introduction to that package, Christine allowed Peter McDonald to drift into her mind. Peter showed an obvious interest in her, and that interest seemed to transcend the fact that she was a TV journalist who could treat his race kindly. Or was Peter merely being polite? Was he just another wolf? She hoped the latter was not the case.

Peter had said little when she asked him whether the bank might lose its sponsor. What was his response? "I'm not looking past Sunday." The perfect non-answer and later at the press conference she had posed the same question to bank CEO Robin Carter and had gotten almost the same response, though said more sweetly as befitting a female executive who wants to appear tough, but not too tough. In still another interview with one of the Shelaghi executives—his name was Patrick Savitch—she got several minutes of what might be described as pure blarney. How she loved those Irish accents, plus Savitch had the look of a leprechaun. Sweet man and in parting, he had offered to buy her a pint of Guinness if he saw her at the bank's Friday-night party tomorrow. She did not think he was trying to pick her up, but he might have been.

Her mind adrift, Christine suddenly heard a voice in her earpiece, and it startled her. "Ten seconds, Christine." It was the news director back in the TV3 Studio. She was about to go live, and instead of thinking what she would say, she was thinking about men. *What is it about men that causes them to invade our minds so frequently?* The station had her Don Geoffrey tape ready to roll, so all she needed to do was introduce it with fifteen seconds of patter. Christine flashed five fingers twice to alert Edmund that they would be live in ten seconds. She did not need to. True professional, he had been holding his camera aimed at her for the last several minutes.

The next voice in her earpiece was that of Mark Mallon: "Fifty thousand runners have entered this year's marathon. Christine Ferrara is standing by on the lakefront at Cushman Park to tell us what they plan to eat between now and Sunday's race."

"Carbohydrates, Mark," Christine began. "And more carbohydrates. And still more carbohydrates." She paused for slightly more than a second to allow those words to sink in, feeling at the same time a chill ripple down her spine, aware that scattered around Lake City tens of thousands of viewers were waiting for her next words. More than in Peoria.

Christine continued: "Olympian Don Geoffrey serves as training consultant for the Lake City Marathon. Earlier today I had a chance to talk to him about what foods runners prefer for their last suppers."

As the studio tape rolled, Christine stood almost not blinking, concentrating on Don Geoffrey's words and hers recorded earlier. At the segment's conclusion, she supplied a quick tag: "So if some day you want to run the Lake City Marathon, mind your spaghetti." Studied pause. "This is Christine Ferrara, reporting live from the lakefront for *The Four O'clock News*." She heard Mark Mallon's voice thank her by name and lead into the next segment, an NFL player arrested last night for drunken driving—thank goodness the marathon was more important than that ugly piece of news—and then Mark's voice cut out to be replaced by that of the news director.

"Crisp, Christine. We'll see you back in the studio."

"I have another shot to record for the package scheduled for 5:00."

"Right," replied the director, somewhat brusquely. "Thanks for reminding me." Her earpiece went dead. *I guess he did not need to be reminded,* thought Christine. *Well, welcome to the Big City, Small Town Girl.* She turned her attention southward along the lakefront to see if she could spot Fiona Flynn. The Irish Lass had promised to appear at 4:30. Christine hoped she would not be disappointed. She was not used to dealing with the promises of professional athletes. But at that very moment, she thought she sighted a female runner with red hair approaching in the distance.

63:30:00

At the same time Christine Ferrara noticed the red-haired runner approaching, her cellular phone jangled a Mozartian melody. She reached into her purse and silenced the ringing by pushing a green button, answering with her name, "This is Christine." The individual calling identified herself as Fiona Flynn. "Sorry I'm late, Christine," began Fiona. "I got delayed. You should see me running toward you in just a minute."

"I do see you, Fiona," replied Christine, amazed that one of the favorites in the Lake City Marathon, might actually run carrying a cell phone. Christine was new to running, certainly new to any contact with the sport's fastest athletes. Was staying wired common practice for the running elite?

"See you in a minute, Love," said Fiona.

THURSDAY

Christine returned the phone to her purse. "I do not believe this," Christine said to Edmund, shaking her head. "That was Fiona Flynn."

Edmund merely smiled without comment. The cameraman had worked in the TV industry too long to be surprised by strange behavior.

Christine focused her attention on the red-haired athlete, slender as a deer, approaching at a pace she could not even imagine being able to duplicate. Not for a mile. Not for a hundred meters. Would athletes in other sports bother to notify a reporter they might be late? Not according to her colleagues on the sports desk. Athletes in other sports invariably were late for appointments and, arrogantly, did not seem to care. Runners, on the other hand, participated in a sport ruled by the clock, so perhaps possessed a more precise knowledge of how long it took them to get from Point A to Point B.

As Christine watched Fiona approach, it was now 4:30. *The Four O'clock News* had just ended to be followed the next half hour by *Jeopardy*. Sixty-three and a half hours remained before the start of the Lake City Marathon.

63:30:00. 63:29:59. 63:29:58.

Without being told, Edmund, ever the professional, had his shoulder-held camera focused on the runner. By then, Fiona had approached to within a hundred meters of the waiting TV3 journalists. Christine, equally profession-al, recognized this as a photo-op. Holding the microphone, she positioned her-self between Edmund and the approaching runner. "Frame me," she said. "Cue me when you have both of us in the picture."

Edmund nodded that he understood. After a pause of a few seconds, the cameraman said, "Now!"

Christine began without missing a beat: "With only three days to go before the marathon, the lakefront seems almost quiet. Most local runners have be-gun to taper for their Sunday race. But one individual from Ireland was out training this afternoon. Her name is Fiona Flynn."

And at that precise moment, the Irish runner arrived and slowed to a walk. Christine turned: "Hello, Fiona."

La Femme Fiona responded in kind. Without saying so, Christine mar-veled that despite the speed at which she had been running, Fiona did not seem out of breath, nor was she sweating despite the unseasonably warm weather. *Is this woman human?* Christine explained to Fiona that they would like her to jog past the camera a few times just so they had some images to accompany her words from the press conference. Edmund, meanwhile, was reviewing the just-shot footage of the runner with Christine's voice-over. "Good lead-in, Christine," he said, indicating it would not need to be re-shot.

Christine asked Flynn to back up twenty or thirty meters on the path and run past. When the Irish runner did that, Christine asked her to do it again, then again. "Thank you, Fiona," said Christine finally, offering her hand once again to the runner. "Look for yourself on *The Five O'clock News*."

Fiona seemed almost puzzled by the brevity of the encounter. "That's all?" she said, pleased that she was released to continue her run. "You're fast."

Christine smiled and said, "So are you." Then as Fiona Flynn began moving away down the lakefront path, Christine repositioned herself between cameraman and runner. "Frame me," she said. Edmund shifted his camera and indicated that she had been framed.

Christine began without missing a beat. "For many runners in the Lake City Marathon, particularly first-timers, the goal Sunday will be to finish. But Ireland's Fiona Flynn has a loftier goal." Christine paused for effect. "She wants to win."

Christine continued smiling at the camera for a few seconds more while the red-headed figure of Fiona Flynn grew smaller behind her, then added: "This is Christine Ferrara reporting from the lakefront."

Edmund lowered the camera from his shoulder and offered a smile. "I can see how you got promoted to this job," he said.

"Thank you, Edmund," Christine replied sweetly, "but my ego is large enough without you feeding it more." She turned and began staring down the lakefront path in both directions, looking for a different location where they could capture extra footage of runners training. But there were simply not that many running on a Thursday afternoon. Most of Lake City's runners seemed to be resting for Sunday's race. Or maybe everybody was at work. A few runners did pass, not pausing, but staring at the reporter and cameraman, wondering what story was being shot. "Hey, make me famous!" shouted one.

Christine waved back at the runner without speaking. She had not been in Lake City long enough for him to recognize her as a media celebrity. She was thankful for that fact and dreaded a time some weeks or months from now when she would not be able to walk into a bar or restaurant without someone nudging and pointing. Christine had attained that level of fame in her last job in Peoria, and she *detested* being even a local hero. She sometimes tried to disguise herself by combing her hair in a bun and wearing Granny glasses. It did not always work. That was a bit like Snow White trying to look ugly so the Queen would not feed her a poisoned apple. Christine could not complain. She realized before entering her profession that lack of privacy was one of the penalties she would pay for ascending to the top ranks. If you want to be the next Barbara Walters, don't complain if someone asks for an autograph while you're fixing your face in the women's rest room.

Then there was Fiona Flynn, definitely a piece of work, looking more fashion model than marathon runner. A lilting accent combined with confidence in her ability that bordered almost on arrogance. "I'm planning to win the race," Fiona had told Christine earlier that afternoon, not *hoping* to win the race, *planning* to win the race. Even the presence of Aba Andersson in the field did not seem to bother the Irish Lass. Well, there remained some doubt as to whether the ailing Aba would run. Although he had not said so, even Peter seemed to have those doubts since he had pointed her toward Fiona as a possible winner. *Wouldn't he love that to happen with his new bosses and the runner both being Irish?*

Christine wondered about the relationship between Peter and Fiona. They seemed friendlier than one might expect. *Why had he chosen Fiona to take Aba's place on the dais? Why had he suggested Christine interview Fiona? Did Peter have some secret agenda? I saw that kiss she gave him. Was that more than your usual air kiss? Maybe the correct question should be: What right do I have to be suspicious of a man-once-met?*

Christine turned and looked northward along the lakefront. The path used by runners moved away from Lake Shore Drive and dropped down a ramp and onto a breakwater low to the water that paralleled the Drive. She could see for nearly a half mile and with only a handful of runners occupying that part of the lakefront, Christine thought she would certainly still be able to spot Fiona's red hair. She could not see the Irish lass. Fiona had only left them a few minutes ago and had obviously not dived into the lake to continue as a swimmer. *How could anyone,* Christine wondered, *run that fast?* She could not even begin to imagine the combination of talent and training that would permit someone to do so. And three days before a marathon when most of the 50,000 runners entered in Lake City were resting for their ordeals, Fiona was out running a workout that would incapacitate ordinary human beings.

Christine Ferrara did not dwell long on the thought. She turned to Edmund: "Let's grab a few scenics before we head back to the station."

63:25:00

Fiona Flynn continued her run along the lakefront, oblivious to the fact that the TV3 cameraman was focusing his lens on her retreating backside. Interview completed, *La Femme Fiona* was back in marathon mode and oblivious to everything except the road ahead. Like most elite runners, Fiona was obsessed with her training. She ran twice daily and rarely missed a workout, averaging well over 100 miles a week, the price you pay if seeking success at the upper levels of the distance running sport.

MARATHON

Normally, it would be an inconvenience for Fiona to stop mid-workout. If asked for an interview, she simply would say, no! But with the marathon so close, Christine's request had given her an excuse to take a break, to signify that today, three days out, was a day to run easy, even carry a cell phone, silly for a serious athlete to do, she conceded. Sometimes Fiona needed to remind herself that rest was as important a training ingredient as speed and distance.

Nevertheless, the seconds sped by as she ran.

63:25:00. 63:24:59. 63:24:58.

Stopping to have her picture recorded had delayed Fiona less than she expected, barely five minutes. And it offered a chance for a photo-op, always appreciated by her sponsors. The TV reporter had said the interview would air on *The Five O'clock News*, probably midway through the show. Fiona would be back in her hotel by then. If the feature played well, Fiona would call the reporter—she had Christine's cell phone number—and request that a copy be sent to her agent, useful for thanking sponsors.

The Irish Lass's workout today was 6 miles. One workout today, not two. She would run at a relaxed pace and let the run come to her. Although Fiona wore a GPS watch that allowed her to monitor both pace and distance and her heart rate, she would not look at it until the end of the workout and then only to record those numbers for future reference.

Like many runners, fast and slow, Fiona Flynn liked to keep records both on paper and in a computer log of everything running-connected she did. She was compulsive in this respect, but running *was* her profession, unlike most of those running that afternoon on the lakefront.

Today Fiona allowed her body to dictate the pace at which she ran, even if that pace seemed inhumanly fast to other runners she passed, her short red hair flying behind as though blown by a dryer, her skinny butt barely quivering as it propelled her relentlessly forward, the slightest trace of a smile betraying the pleasure she felt from her movements. There were few pleasures in life as intense as a fast run. Well, one other, but that better be left unsaid.

As she ran, such was Fiona's speed that she swept past runners both coming to her and running the same way. She barely gave them a glance, because as she ran, her entire mind was focused on moving one fast foot in front of the other. Fiona knew that intensely focusing your mind was the secret to running fast, both in practice and in races. Other runners on the lakefront might as well have been animated figures in a video game, computer clutter, passing through her peripheral vision without triggering a reaction. The scenery along the lake, particularly on a clear day, was spectacular: monarchal high-rise buildings on one side, sun-sprinkled lake on the other. Fiona did not see the scenery. She might as well have been running through a tunnel. Fiona did not acknowledge approaching runners, nor did many acknowledge the Irish

THURSDAY

Lass—even if they recognized her, which most did not. Her status as a stranger probably would change after the TV3 interview aired and particularly if she ran well Sunday. She hoped this happened, since it would cause money to fall into her bank account. But in the meantime, Fiona Flynn remained largely unrecognized and happy about that fact.

On a less crowded path, Fiona might have nodded or even offered a word of encouragement while encountering another runner. She did not want to seem aloof or disdainful of those less gifted. Part of being an elite runner capable of earning endorsements is marketing oneself. But rules of common courtesy change on crowded paths, such as on the Lake City lakefront. With so many runners, you could not greet all, so you greeted none. You would not wave or do much more than smile unless it was someone familiar to you, a friend or training companion. So went the rules of the road.

Truth be told, most of the runners sharing the lakefront with Fiona on this Thursday afternoon were not marathoners, or at least probably were not running the Lake City Marathon this weekend. They were recreational runners, many of them running for fitness, motivated merely by a desire to keep their waists slim or to stay in shape for other sports. Running made them feel and look good. Most had little desire to race competitively, although that did not mean that a charitable cause or other incentive might not lure them to a marathon starting line some time in the future.

Yet there was at least one fast runner sharing the lakefront this afternoon with Fiona Flynn. If Fiona was largely unknown to the average citizen of Lake City, this individual was completely invisible, not even a pulse beat on the running celebrity scale. It was Meghan Allison, and as Fiona ran north along the lakefront, Meg ran south, almost on a collision course with the Irish Lass. At the moment when Meg looked up and recognized Fiona because of her flaming red hair, perhaps a hundred meters separated the two female runners. Since Meg was running almost as fast as Fiona Flynn, that ground was bridged in a matter of seconds.

Fiona swept past without a side glance. If she noticed the other runner, Fiona gave no indication. Meg also offered no hint that she might have recognized Fiona. She did, because the two had run against each other several times in college. On those occasions, Meg had finished far back in cross-country races won by Fiona Flynn. After they passed, each woman's speed propelled her away from the other. The space separating the pair grew rapidly like celestial bodies tossed by gravitational forces into different corners of space, not to meet again until gravity once more exerted its pull.

An impartial observer seeing both runners sweep past each other might have had a hard time knowing which was more gifted. They both had slender runners' bodies, long legs and strides that allowed them to brush the pavement rather than strike it. Certainly, Meg Allison had talent—perhaps more than Fiona Flynn. What she lacked was achievement.

At least a few times, Meg Allison had showed her speed, but her entire career had featured one injury after another: pulled hamstrings, sore knees, plantar fascitis, Achilles tendonitis. Despite her smooth stride, Allison was fragile as fine china. She wore orthotics to correct various biomechanical deficiencies. She used an inhaler to control exercise-induced asthma. She had been forced to slow down in many races, particularly early in her career, because she could not breathe. And despite that single state championship and the best hopes of her college coaches, Allison never quite attained the level of success that everyone anticipated of her. Such was her self-esteem that it never seemed to bother her, at least on the surface. But a tiny voice inside Meg Allison echoed the famous words uttered by Marlin Brando in *On The Waterfront*: "I coulda been a contender."

Allison ran regularly during three years of podiatry school and four years interning as a surgeon. On a reduced diet of mileage and without the stress of racing each weekend, her injuries began to disappear. Running became fun again. She even had an easier time breathing, partly because of improved inhalers but also because of a relaxed lifestyle, particularly after she married her college sweetheart, Matthew.

After starting to train seriously, Allison had concentrated on gradually increasing her mileage from 30 to 40 to 50 miles a week, still less than she had been forced to run in college. This mileage build-up occurred through the winter when cold weather combined with ice and snow forced her to bundle up and slow down. As the weather warmed, Meg stabilized the number of weekly miles run between 60 and 70, allowing her to run some of those miles at a faster pace. A test 5-K race early in the spring produced a time nearly equal to those she had run in college. It was a small 5-K race with only a few hundred runners in one of the western suburbs, and her winning time attracted little attention even among the local running community. Meg figured that everyone would think the course was short.

Satisfied by her progress, Meg returned her concentration to training, adding speedwork, though staying away from the track. On days when she did speedwork—repeat 400s or 800s—she did them on a straightaway on the lakefront path, the distance having been measured by her husband who did not trust GPS watches, so he used a steel tape. Weekends, when she did long runs up to two hours, but rarely much longer, he would bicycle beside her offering water and E.R.G. They often talked about his work or their plans for the future, what they would do when she resumed her career as a podiatrist. They began, also, to think of a family.

THURSDAY

Her goal at the start of the marathon training was simply to run and finish the race, possibly getting a Boston Qualifying time of 3 hours 40 minutes, although she doubted whether she could carve out enough time in her busy schedule after this one year off to ever run that race. But as her training continued, she began to visualize a time significantly faster, perhaps under 3 hours, or faster still than that. Was she dreaming? Meg did not know. In May, she participated in an 8-K race that many local runners used as a tune-up for the marathon. With approximately 20,000 runners, she placed third behind two invited runners from Eastern Europe, finishing ahead of several others on the elite circuit.

After the award ceremony, Peter McDonald stopped Meg as she and Matt were heading to their car in the parking lot. They chatted. Peter praised her. Meg thanked him. Matt beamed, delighted at his wife's success, not in the slightest bit threatened by her having outdone him as an athlete.

"I know who you are, Meg Allison," said Peter. "You don't fool me. I remember how well you ran in high school."

"...And how poorly I ran in college," Meg finished the sentence.

"It looks like you've got your high school legs back."

"They're good legs," suggested Matt. Meg gave him an irritated look.

"I appreciate your comment, Mr. McDonald," she said, "but I'm trying to fly under the radar."

"Meg, you're so far under the radar, you're down in the subway." Peter paused, then asked the question he had been leading up to.

One word: "Marathon?"

"I'm not sure," Meg Allison replied.

Peter handed her his business card. "Let me know. We'll give you a free entry and a spot in the Top 100 Start Corral."

Meg Allison promised him she would get in touch, but she did not want the pressure of mingling with the elites, whether deservedly or not. Several weeks after that and just before the Lake City Marathon met its cap of 50,000, she quietly paid her entry fee of $110. Later in the summer, she ran a small half marathon in one of the suburbs. With fewer than a thousand in the field, she finished first female, even though not going full speed. Meg only wanted to run faster than 1:25:59, the time that would qualify her for Start Corral A, the first corral behind the elite runners. She bettered that time by several minutes, feeling she could have run much faster if she had gone full out. Given her history of injuries, that was the last thing Meg Allison wanted to do. "Smart race, honey," Matt said after the race, hugging her after she exited the finishing chute. She smiled and later that week submitted her qualifying time to the marathon office to secure her position in Start Corral A.

MARATHON

Her entry did not escape the notice of Noel Michaels, who dropped it on Peter McDonald's desk. Peter recognized the name and time. "It's our Below-Radar girl," he told Michaels. "She obviously does not want to call attention to herself. We'll treat her like everybody else."

Meg Allison was both like and not like everybody else. She was a more streamlined and faster version of everybody else, just like Fiona Flynn. Running fast, unmindful of her speed, Meg reached the turnaround point for her workout, coincidentally near the park where Christine Ferrara earlier had interviewed Fiona. Christine and her cameraman had just finished packing equipment into their TV3 van preparatory to returning to the studio. Meg slowed, walked, stopped to drink from a water fountain, then started back toward her apartment, first walking, then jogging, then gradually picking up the pace. Meg had learned from experience never to make fast pace changes, never in a workout, only sometimes in a race. Most track athletes have the ability to make one fast move in a race, sometimes surging in the middle, but more often waiting until the last lap when grabbing a lead of a few strides may make the difference between victory and defeat. In terms of her running career, Meg Allison's year off from school and work was that one fast move that might allow her success in the Lake City Marathon.

Christine glanced at the runner, thought she recognized her, but only after Meg Allison had begun to disappear from sight did the TV reporter realize it was the clerk who had sold her a pair of running shoes two weeks earlier.

And as Meg headed northward home, she found herself once more on a collision course with Fiona Flynn returning south toward her hotel. Fiona, moving swiftly, looked up and saw Allison approaching, also running fast. Fiona remembered the runner from a few minutes before, and it was the Irish Lass who offered a brief greeting as the two approached to within a few feet of her. "Looking good, Love," said Fiona, a standard greeting offered by runners to each other whether they looked good or not.

Meg was startled, not expecting the elite athlete to say anything, and *La Femme Fiona* almost had passed before Meg Allison offered a weak reply. "Hey," she said. The two runners, who would not seem to be competitive equals on Sunday, continued to move apart from each other.

They would meet again.

THURSDAY

62:15:00

S tanding in the shower of her friend Yolanda's apartment, Christine
Ferrara allowed the warm water to cascade down her body. She used a
woolen sea sponge to massage herself all over, to firmly cleanse her
every pore, to scrub away the stink and stress of her workday.

Christine had bought the woolen sea sponge on the way home, stopping at
a home furnishings store several blocks from the TV 3 studio before boarding
a bus heading north toward the trendy Near North Side where singles new to
the city first land. Since moving to Lake City two weeks ago, Christine had
been staying with her old Bradley University roommate, Yolanda Kline. Yolanda wanted Christine to move in permanently and share expenses. Christine
enjoyed Yolanda's company, but suspected that eventually she would want to
secure her own and more private housing.

Christine stepped dripping out of the shower and reached for a fluffy towel, lavender colored, another purchase that afternoon from the home furnishings store. Rubbing herself dry, Christine moved to a position in front of a
full-length mirror and let the fluffy towel slide to the floor. She allowed herself a moment to examine her naked self, from still-wet raven-dark hair to the
same-colored patch of hair in a neat V between her legs. No man had yet been
permitted to reach this sacred area of Christine's body. She was a virgin. She
was not a militant virgin, or even a reluctant virgin, or one who like the Catholic schoolgirl she once had been, wore her virginity on her coat sleeve. She
was simply a somewhat virtuous woman who did not want to sell her tail to
just anybody offering dinner and a ticket to the latest rock concert.

Christine wondered if she was missing something, particularly during late
night talk sessions with her friends, married and unmarried, when after a few
glasses of wine, they began to talk first shyly, then more openly, about what it
was like to go to bed with a man. *It sounds like a lot of fun,* thought Christine,
but it also could turn into a lot of trouble. She shuddered at the thought of a
college friend who got pregnant by a guy she had dated only a few times, then
dropped out of school to have an abortion. Hardly ever saw the guy again.
That bothered her greatly—and she was not even pro-life!

Was she the only remaining virgin in Lake City? Or the only virgin about
to turn 30, her biological and matrimonial clock ticking? She doubted that, but
certainly there was pressure to shed your inhibitions when you moved to a big
city and into your own apartment (not yet, but soon) where it was you who

made the decision as to who stayed the night. For the time being, she decided it would be: Nobody! Would it be put-offish if she pinned a poster to her wall saying: "Don't even ask!"

Why am I thinking this? Christine reached down for the towel, rubbed it vigorously on her hair, then began blow-drying the hair with a thin-toothed plastic brush. Because of her hair's full body and length, drying it often became a task that consumed more time than she would like, but her mother would freak out if she ever cut it short. So would she. *I wonder what Peter would think?* Too early in the relationship to ask.

She pulled her hair from the back so that it fell across her shoulder, long enough so that it covered her left breast. Then she pulled it back and over to fall across her other shoulder, covering her right breast. *Okay, Christine. What is it going to be: a left-breast night or a right-breast night?* She could not help herself. She laughed, knowing she was being silly.

Hair finally dried, a few more whisks of the brush caused it finally to fall into place almost as though there existed a computer program titled "Drop-Dead Gorjus." Christine wasted a few more seconds to observe the result of her hair-grooming efforts. Although she would never voice the words so someone else might hear, the TV reporter decided she looked like she belonged in a shampoo ad. But that would be unprofessional.

Christine moved from the bathroom to the bedroom, still naked, and threw the towel onto a chair. Glancing at the red numbers of the digital clock beside her bed, she thought: *I'm going to be late for the party, except the only reason I'm going to the party is to see one man, and he might not even show up. Or if he does, he will be too busy to talk to me. How silly is that?*

The clock on the dresser displayed the time as 5:45.

62:15:00. 62:14:59. 62:14:58.

Christine directed her attention to an open suitcase that occupied a corner in the bedroom. The suitcase still was half stuffed with clothing, mostly the parts of her wardrobe that men supposedly were not permitted to see. *Two weeks in town,* thought Christine, *and I still haven't unpacked!* Rummaging through the suitcase, she extracted a silken pair of black bikini panties and the scanty same-colored bra that accompanied them.

Five minutes later, dressed in a clingy black cocktail dress, she returned to the bathroom to assess in the mirror the results of her dressing. Christine attached dangling earrings. She held a necklace around her neck, rejected the choice and selected another. She applied make-up, not excessively because she did not need to. She stepped back for one last self-examination. Christine looked great, and she knew it.

Be on guard, Peter: I'm coming after you! But what am I thinking? Christine, get a grip! This is a man you met for the first time this morning. Am I that desperate for a male to drape on my arm? Christine gave that question a few seconds thought and finally decided: *Yes!* Particularly someone as attractive as Peter. But what was it about this Peter McDonald? She had known many attractive men in her young life, but few that succeeded in attracting her. Something clicked when they first met each other this morning. And it had not been just *her*, it had been *him* too. She was a good enough judge of human behavior to recognize that fact. Maybe the stars were in alignment—Venus and Mars in a straight line—but would the alignment remain the same after this hectic weekend?

Just as Christine was about to leave, she heard a key sound in the door. Her roommate Yolanda stepped into the apartment carrying two plastic bags full of groceries from the Metro Fresh store. Seeing Christine, Yolanda stopped, her jaw dropping to mouth-wide-open. "Oh my God, look at you. It's the stalker, isn't it?"

"Yolanda! Peter is not a stalker."

"I'm talking about you, girl. *You* are the stalker."

"I am not stalking Peter. He's just a very nice man I met earlier today."

"Very nice man? And you are a very nice woman: the perfect pair."

"Yolanda!"

"So tell me where you are going, and what are your intentions related to this very nice man once you get there?"

"I'm going to a party, and Peter probably won't be there."

"Probably won't be there. I'm sorry, Christine, but do you expect me to believe that? Because *nobody* looks that good unless she has very ulterior motives. You've found him: Mr. Right! Poor guy, he doesn't have a chance. It's like sending Wonder Woman up against a pickpocket."

Though amused by the banter, Christine wanted to go. "I'm late," she offered as an alibi. "Talk to you when I get home."

Yolanda followed her roommate out into the hallway and watched her descending the stairway to the street. "Take notes, Roomie," Yolanda shouted after Christine. "You know how, don't you? You're a reporter."

Christine failed to turn or respond. If Yolanda had seen her roommate's face, she would have seen that Christine was rolling her eyes.

MARATHON

61:30:00

The stately mansion at 1340 Astor Way had been built toward the end of the nineteenth century by Anthony Astor, a distant descendent of John Jacob Astor, at one time reportedly the wealthiest man in America. The original Astor had amassed at least part of his fortune by importing opium from the Far East, though he later shed that illegal business in favor of New York real estate, even more profitable. Enough of John Jacob Astor's wealth filtered down to Anthony so that he could live in comfort without ever holding a traditional job.

Anthony Astor invested wisely in the stock market and moved to Lake City, where he built his 70-room mansion in the neighborhood just north of downtown, a favorite nesting ground for the carriage trade. In deference to Anthony Astor's stature as a businessman and in return for a considerable investment in his political campaign, Lake City's mayor named the street in front of the Astor Mansion after him.

Ownership of the mansion passed through several generations of progressively less wealthy descendents. Unable to maintain their home at 1340 Astor Way at anywhere the level of its previous splendor, the family allowed it gradually to decay. In the mid-1970s, architect Niles Wendell, founder of the Lake City Marathon, acquired the mansion at 1340 Astor Way, renaming the property after himself: Wendell House.

The new owner retained a basement swimming room, but remodeled the rooms on the top floor into offices for his staff. He used the mansion as part home, part office, mostly business deduction. Wendell tried to convince the mayor to rename the street on which he lived. He liked the thought of having an address, 1340 Wendell Way, but the price of political bribery had risen in the years since Anthony Astor. The mayor declined, citing the mansion's listing on the National Register of Historic Places.

Christine Ferrara was unaware of this history as she slid two shapely legs out of the taxicab that had brought her to this destination. A couple emerged from the mansion and hailed the cab and climbed in, presumably off to home or another party. As the taxicab departed, Christine thought: *I'm late. Here I am arriving and people already are leaving.*

Plus she did not know anybody—not a single soul! Well, hardly anybody. The only reason she even bothered to come to the party was because of the possibility of encountering a man met only that morning, a man who probably was too busy to show, or to stay long, because he was responsible for 50,000 runners this weekend. Less than sixty-two hours remained before the start of the Lake City Marathon.

61:30:00. 61:29:59. 61:59:58.

On the top step, she was greeted by a doorman, who smiled and welcomed her to Wendell House. Christine paused to examine a bronze plate on the gleaming mahogany door. "*Carpe Viam*," it said.

Christine had never studied Latin in school, but was familiar enough with the expression *Carpe Diem* to know it meant, "Seize the day." She was not so sure about "viam. She asked the doorman what it meant.

The doorman smiled. "Seize the way," he responded. "Actually, 'seize the roadway.' It's a reference to Mr. Wendell's being a runner."

The doorman further indicated that the party was on the second floor: "Take the staircase to the left or the elevator to the right." Because she prided herself on her fitness, Christine chose the staircase on the left, but paused before ascending it, her eye caught by a black-and-white drawing. She moved close to the drawing to determine whether it was an original or a print. It was a print, numbered 8 out of 25, but she could not even begin to imagine how much a numbered print signed by Pablo Picasso would cost.

Ascending the stairway, Christine thought, *This has got disaster written all over it.* TV3's new girl in town entered the mansion's main ballroom, a room almost cumbersomely large with a fireplace at one end and a piano in the center and more drawings and paintings on the wall that looked like they should belong in some art museum instead of in a private home. Scanning the crowd, she noticed the host, Niles Wendell, talking with guests, but she felt uneasy about approaching him. He seemed engaged in a conversation with someone else anyway, an individual she remembered from the press conference, except she could not put a name to him.

Winding her way around people she did not know, moving slowly and in a serpentine direction to occupy time, smiling at one or another person as she passed, Christine stopped to accept an hors d' oeuvre and napkin from a waiter with a silver tray. She stood eating it for a moment, since to continue walking with the hors d' oeuvre might invite crumbs falling on the polished parquet floor. Having consumed it, she headed toward a bar in the corner, waiting her turn, then instructing the bartender: "I'll have a white wine."

"Chardonnay?"

"Yes, please." Christine thought chardonnay was white, probably so or the bartender would not have offered it. She wondered if she could find a book through Amazon.com on the subject: *How to Act Sophisticated at Parties Populated by Stunning People.*

MARATHON

It was then that Christine felt a hand lightly touch her arm, the arm not holding the Chardonnay.

She turned and it was Peter McDonald. "Hey," said Christine, upbeat, suddenly cheerful. She reached up to smooth her long, dark hair that flowed smoothly across one shoulder to enticingly cover one breast. Before leaving the apartment, she had decided it would be a right-breast night

"Hey," repeated Peter, warmly, inviting.

They stood staring at each other for what to Christine seemed like an eternity, each wondering in which direction to send the conversation. "You've shed the TV3 blouse," Peter finally said, thinking immediately that that was a stupid thing to say.

Christine apparently did not think so. "The studio takes them back at the end of the work day," she said. "My TV3 blouse currently is being worn by the anchor on *The Six O'clock News*."

Peter smiled, but immediately changed the subject: "I saw your report on Fiona. Nice job. You actually talked her into posing on the lakefront?"

"I was surprised too. Are runners always that cooperative."

"Not always, but they're fighting an uphill battle for publicity in a world that prizes more the antics of professional football players and NASCAR drivers. If a marathon runner got arrested for having an AK-47 in the backseat of his car, nobody would even notice."

The professional in Christine surfaced. Eager to get some tip that could lead to a story, she asked: "What do you think about Fiona's chances of winning? She's bubbling over with confidence, but is it realistic?"

Peter shrugged: "We'll find out Sunday."

A real non-answer, Christine thought. *But why am I interviewing him? Act like you're at a party, Christine, not still at work.*

"I don't know anybody here," she smoothly shifted gears.

"I'll introduce you," promised Peter, placing his hand inside the arm not holding the Chardonnay. "You're my date for the evening."

When he said that, Christine thought she might wet her pants.

And for the next ten minutes, Peter worked the room with her at his side, and Christine realized that she did know a few people. There was Don Geoffrey, the writer from *Running Magazine*, and Burton Ambrose, the editor of that publication. She had sat at their table at lunch, and they even remembered her name and offered several minutes of conversation before moving on. Peter introduced her to two others from the press conference she had not yet met: Timothy Rainboldt and Carolynne Vickers. The pair were in town to provide color commentary for the marathon telecast. Christine did not know that, even though she also had been assigned to the telecast. Hopefully someone would tell her what to do at the production meeting scheduled Saturday. She was on a quick learning curve since moving to Lake City,

"We'll look forward to working with you, Ms. Ferrara," said Carolynne Vickers, politely, before she and her companion—or was he her husband—moved on to another group.

After a handful of hellos and goodbyes to people who would not remember her nor would she remember them, Christine and Peter drifted toward Vaughn Johnson, the weatherman from TV3. Johnson greeted his new co-worker warmly and introduced her to his wife Barbara, a slender and attractive woman with brown hair.

Peter started to excuse himself. "I would tell you I have to talk to somebody important, which is partially true, but in actuality I have to visit the men's room."

"Vaughn and Barbara will take care of me," announced Christine.

"I also need briefly to talk to our host," said Peter nodding toward Niles Wendell, who on the other side of the room was engaged in conversation with *Ledger* reporter, Jonathan Von Runyon. "Don't stray too far."

When Peter emerged from the men's room, he noticed that Von Runyon no longer was talking to Wendell. Glancing toward Christine, he signaled his intent to talk to Wendell alone and moved toward the man who three decades before had been one of the founders of the Lake City Marathon. Peter knew that some on his staff considered the race founder a curmudgeon, but Wendell had hired Peter, and the race director always treated him with respect.

Two others at the party temporarily had Wendell's attention, but as they moved away, the founder beckoned Peter to follow him to a side room for a private conversation. Closing the door, Wendell commanded him in a soft voice, "Tell me about the famous celebrity who's running Sunday."

A leak, thought Peter. *We've got a leak*. He wondered how much Niles Wendell knew about the identity of Celebrity X.

Peter worried about the problems it would cause if his friend's identity became public knowledge before X stepped inconspicuously onto the race course Sunday morning. Peter wondered whether Von Runyon had been the source for Wendell, or Wendell the source for Von Runyon. Most likely, they each knew something and wanted to discover more: Wendell, because he loved gossip; Von Runyon, because it would offer him a front-page story—and it would be front page!

Peter certainly had no intention of providing Wendell or anyone else with that information. Fortunately, fearing that someone would learn of the code name, he had prepared a cover story. It was another celebrity—not quite as high on the pop charts as Celebrity X, but one whose name and face appeared with embarrassing frequency in the tabloids. That person had agreed to keep secret for a while her plans to run Lake City allowing any who penetrated Peter's veil of secrecy to believe she was Celebrity X.

"Can't talk, Niles," said Peter, displaying his best poker-player face.

"Not even me?" Niles Wendell probed.

"Not even you, Niles." Peter thought, *especially not you, Niles*.

"I understand," said Niles, hiding his hurt without success.

Peter felt he had to offer the race founder a clue. Fortunately, he had his cover story. "Niles, will I see you at the bank's party tomorrow night?"

"Give me a reason to attend."

"You'll see me with someone. I'm not saying she's the celebrity in question, but you'll recognize her."

"Oprah?"

"Five-letter word for famous runner? No, too many letters."

"But a woman," said Wendell. "You've at least cut the list of famous celebrities in half."

Peter smiled. Wendell had taken the bait. *No, not Oprah*. Peter's faux celebrity was the famous supermodel, Naní, who was probably in the air headed to Lake City at this moment.

Returning to the ballroom, Peter and Niles Wendell parted. Peter made one final grab at a passing hors d' oeuvre tray, thinking woefully that this was his dinner for tonight. Too bad, because there was someone here with whom he would like to spend some alone time in a restaurant with candles on the table and a bottle of wine. That would need to wait until another weekend. He scanned the room until he spotted Christine Ferrara. No longer talking to Vaughn and Barbara, she had fastened herself to another group, including Nelson Ogilvie, his media director. Peter paused before joining them, overcome for a moment by the thought that Christine reminded him of his late wife Carol. He was not sure what it was about her. They really did not look the same. It must be his imagination.

At that moment, Christine turned. Her smile lit the room. Still clinging to the glass of Chardonnay with one hand, its level barely reduced an inch, the TV reporter slowly raised her other hand and offered a soft wave. Peter smiled and moved toward this captivating woman.

Peter joined the group without offering much to advance the conversation and, during a lull, pulled Christine to one side. "You've switched."

"What?" she said, puzzled.

"Your hair. When I left, it was over your right shoulder. Now it's over your left."

I can't believe he noticed, thought Christine. Moving from one group to another, she apparently had shoved her hair to the back, then pulled it to the front, this time to cover the left breast. It was something she often did without thinking, almost like smoothing her skirt. Yolanda used to laugh when she saw Christine toy with her hair, suggesting it was akin to a lion in the jungle, stalking its prey.

All Christine could think to say was, "You amaze me, Peter."

"It's you who is amazing, Christine." Then after a pause that neither of them seemed to want to fill, the race director assumed his business face. "Listen, date-for-the-evening, this is terribly rude, but I need to pick somebody up at the airport. Can you find a ride home?"

Christine indicated she would, disappointed that he was leaving without her, but not wanting to reveal that fact. She would wait five minutes, then have the doorman downstairs call a cab. She had achieved all she had needed by attending the party.

No hug, because they did not yet know each other well. They touched hands. No more. After he left the ballroom, she moved to a window with a view of the street. She wanted to make sure Peter had safely left the arena before she did so herself. She watched and saw him emerge on the steps below and move between two parked cars to onto the street where he hailed not a cab, but a stretch limousine that apparently had been waiting for him. The stretch limousine was white. It moved toward him and Peter got in. Not exactly the gaudy van he had used to transport her from the convention center to the hotel earlier in the day.

Christine thought: *Whomever Peter is meeting at the airport must be very, very important.*

If Christine Ferrara had remained at that window a few seconds later, she might have seen another car move from a nearby parking space as though to follow the limousine. Two men occupied the car. But even if Christine had noticed the car or the men, she probably would not have suspected them to be following Peter McDonald. Christine returned her attention to the party. If anything, it seemed to be only beginning, but tomorrow was a working day. She would thank Niles Wendell for the invitation to attend and head home. Yolanda would be surprised to see her back so soon.

60:30:00

The private jet slid into Bob Veldman's view when it descended beneath 13,000 feet, approximately 50 miles from touchdown in Lake City. Veldman did not actually see the plane. He worked in a building without windows, so the plane carrying an important celebrity into town appeared only as a blip on his radar screen coupled with an identifying number so he knew what kind of plane he would be directing: a large airliner or small private plane. In this case, Veldman recognized it as the latter.

Veldman's job was that of an air traffic controller, assigned to Lake City Terminal Radar Approach Control (TRACON), located not near the main Lake City airport, but monitoring traffic into it and several smaller airports whose planes utilized the same airspace.

Though Veldman had on his screen the descending jet, that one plane was not his only responsibility. The controller also was tracking nine other airplanes flying in the airspace above and around Lake City at the same point in time. Working near him in the windowless building were ten additional air traffic controllers tracking fifty-four planes flying near Lake City. Assuming these controllers did their jobs—and they almost always did—the approximately 11,000 passengers in these planes coming and going would all arrive at their destinations safely to the relief of families and friends.

But Veldman's was a high-pressure job, since if you made a mistake, people died. Most of the air traffic controllers working at TRACON at 7:30 on a Thursday evening would not want to make that blunt a statement, but it was true. Despite an average salary of $90,000 a year, attrition was high among controllers who typically lasted twenty years in the job, then moved on to less stressful positions. Air traffic controllers had a relatively high degree of alcoholism and divorce because of their jobs.

Veldman did not fall victim to such stresses. He relieved the demons in his head by running. The hour or so the controller ran most days of the week provided him with an inner peace. His wife knew that, and if she caught the man she loved skipping his workout for more than a day or two, she would tell him: "Bob, get out of the house. You're driving us crazy!" The Veldmans, married sixteen years, had two children and lived in a farming community twenty minutes down the road from where he worked. Veldman had run sixteen marathons with a best time of 2:30:32, achieved at Lake City the year before. He was running the Lake City Marathon again this weekend with dreams of finally cracking the 2:30 barrier on Sunday.

60:30:00. 60:29:59. 60:29:58.

Except he did not like reports garnered most of the week from associates who monitored weather for the airlines. Warm weather, they warned, was predicted for the weekend. *Very* warm weather. "Can't you guys do any better than that for me?" he pleaded while chatting with them at the coffee bar.

"No," they replied, smiling, going along with his fiction that they as weathermen somehow bore responsibility for slowing his marathon time, defeating him in his bid for success, thwarting the months of training that had gotten him, Veldman thought, into the best shape of his life.

"Let it be on your heads if cooling breezes fail to appear," he warned.

"There's a cold front up over the mountains and headed this way," claimed one of his colleagues.

"Will it arrive by Sunday?"

"Unlikely."

"Then don't tell me about it." Veldman refilled his coffee cup—one bearing the logo of the Lake City Marathon—and headed back to work.

Veldman's thoughts this Thursday evening were far from the marathon as he watched the blips identifying airplanes on his radar screen. He dare not allow his attention to drift. Controlling air traffic was like running a marathon. You achieve the greatest success if you totally focus your mind on the task at hand. He was focused at this moment on the private jet now in its final approach, not to the main Lake City airport on the northwest edge of town, but rather to Lakeport, a much smaller field used by private airplanes, a single runway only 9,000 feet long, occupying a spit of land jutting into the lake near the city's convention center, Pritzinger Place.

Having vectored aircraft for this approach hundreds of times, Veldman turned the jet so the pilot could intercept the final approach course ten miles from the airport. This would allow the pilot to adjust his approach by instruments to Lakeport so that his passengers barely noticed the turn.

As the jet approached the outer marker and began its descent on the final approach course, Veldman had done his job. He transferred the aircraft to the Lakeport control tower, ending with his customary, "Take care." The pilot wished him well and flipped his radio switch to that of the Lakeport tower. The controller shifted his attention to other airplanes in his sector.

Veldman had no way to know it, but one of the passengers in the descending jet he had just cleared to land was an individual also planning to run the marathon, a well-known celebrity whose name was not contained in the official list of 50,000 entries, because race director Peter McDonald did not want the public yet to possess that information. Peter, having just left Niles Wendell's party, was seated in a limousine heading toward Lakeport.

Peter did not realize that others were interested in his movements that evening. The race director had become the target of two individuals following in a bland sedan that would attract no attention. The pair had tracked him from the hotel, wondering why Peter would choose a garish limousine rather than a more anonymous vehicle like theirs. Maybe he had nothing to hide. Maybe their assignment in watching the race director was a waste of time. Whether or not it was did not concern them. They were merely following orders, relayed to them only a few hours ago from the organization in Europe that sometimes employed them.

MARATHON

The pair worked for Redbird. At that moment (12:30 AM Greenwich time), Redbird slept peacefully in a castle on the western coast of Ireland, confident that those in his employ would find out why Peter McDonald had received several telephone calls the last several hours from the individual who interested him most. As the stretch limousine departed Wendell House, the two watchers moved their car into a position a half block behind it. When the limo carrying Peter turned onto Lake Shore Drive and headed south on the expressway paralleling the lake, they followed. They did not follow too closely, because the white limousine clearly stood out among other traffic on the road. They also had been using electronic equipment to monitor Peter's telephone calls during the day, soon after he received the first call from Celebrity X. They would get to the same destination as Peter, but they did not need to get there exactly at the same time.

As the limousine neared the airport, the private jet, a Cessna Citation, was in its final approach, now under the control of the Lakeport tower.

The pilot of the jet now confirmed his plans to land: "Lakeport Tower, Citation 64213 is five miles out from landing."

"Roger, Citation 64213," responded a controller in the tower. "Winds are two-four-zero at five knots. You are cleared to land."

"Citation 64213, cleared to land."

Arriving at the airport, Peter and his companion stepped out of the limousine. Choosing to wait outside the terminal, the two positioned themselves beside a fence. The individual with Peter was an executive with The Field Store, Lake City's largest department store. Not a runner, she was the store's media manager, one of those responsible for a fashion show sponsored by the store the next day.

The two men that had tracked the limousine to the airport did not go near the terminal for fear of revealing their identity. Instead, they waited on an access road nearby, parking their car in a position where they could quietly observe the action using powerful night binoculars.

"Are they doing anything?" one man impatiently asked the other.

"Just waiting," the second replied.

At that moment, the Cessna Citation slid past overhead and touched down near the end of the runway, the screech of its wheels striking the asphalt interrupting the silence of the night. The Cessna was painted light blue with the word *Zest* boldly written in red on both sides of the fuselage. The man with binoculars focused his attention on the plane as it slowed at the end of the runway, eventually turning back toward the terminal. The shrill sound of jet engines dropped in pitch, then stopped. Parked in front of the terminal, the jet's door dropped, providing stairs for its passengers to descend to the parking apron. Two people stood at the top of the stairs, a crewman and a woman.

THURSDAY

Peter and the individual accompanying him moved from behind the chain-link fence and approached the plane. The crewman descended to the ground, then turned to help a female passenger behind him.

The man with the binoculars lowered them. "That's not our man," he said, speaking of the individual as in Italian, *il uomo nostro*.

"Who's the woman?" said the other.

"I have no idea. And what's the meaning of *Zest?*

"It's a magazine. Fashion. Fitness. Scantily clad models, hardly something our man would want to be associated with."

The man with the binoculars pondered what he had seen. "Then why are we following this Peter McDonald?" he wondered.

Far from their hearing, Peter moved toward the woman. She had long legs and wore tight-fitting jeans, a silver belt holding the jeans in place. She wore a lavender blouse, unbuttoned at the neck, tied in a knot at the waist. A purple scarf loosely wrapped around her slender neck completed the woman's outfit. Her black hair was cut tight showing natural curls. Her glowing skin was a combination of milk and chocolate, the heritage of her white American father and her Tanzanian mother. Although the men watching from the end of the runway could not make out her face even with the help of night binoculars, it was a face that readers of *Sports Illustrated*, particularly those partial to its annual swimsuit issue, would have recognized instantly.

Peter grasped the woman lightly with both hands, gave her a quick hug and planted a soft kiss on one cheek. She reciprocated with a smile.

"Thanks for coming, Naní," Peter told the woman, one of the world's most famous supermodels. "It's a pleasure to have you in town."

"It's my pleasure to be here, Peter," responded Naní. "But I had hoped for cooler weather."

"We all did," sighed Peter, then switched subjects. "How's Oprah?"

"The taping went well. We talked about the marathon, but I dodged the question of whether I was running. The show airs tomorrow afternoon."

"I hope I can find time to watch it."

"Ricco's planning to tape the show."

"When will he arrive?"

"Saturday. He said he wanted to see me suffer."

Peter laughed. As the pair talked, the store executive directed the limousine driver to collect the supermodel's luggage. Naní had brought two bags, light blue, the exact color as the airplane. The driver placed the bags in the trunk of the limousine. Quickly, it left with its passengers headed downtown.

"Driver," asked Naní. "Can we drive through the park en route to the hotel. I want to see Burnham Fountain all lit up."

"Yes ma'am."

MARATHON

As the limousine moved out of sight, one of the two men watching looked at his watch. It was 8:00, sixty hours before the start of the marathon.

60:00:00. 59:59:59. 59:59:58.

The two puzzled men at the end of the runway did not follow the limousine. It no longer interested them. One of the men had dialed a cell phone as soon as he saw the passengers.

"Wrong plane," he reported to the person who answered the phone. "Our man seems headed to another airport."

The man with the cell phone stood silent, then punched the red button to hang up without saying another word. He turned to his companion: "They've got it covered. We're through for the night. Let's go get a beer."

As the pair drove away, the Gulfstream carrying Celebrity X approached Hampton Airport, further south and around the bottom of the lake.

After landing, the Gulfstream stopped in front of the terminal, and its passengers descended to the pavement. This included Celebrity X and his bodyguards, Mario and Angelo. X still wore his dark glasses even though the sun long had set. He and his entourage were met by a white-haired man dressed in jeans and an Aloha shirt, a red cap on his head bearing a patch for Hilliard Steel. He held out a hand. Celebrity X, wheeling his own black suitcase, smiled and shook it.

"Welcome home, Tony," said the man.

"Thanks for picking me up, Herb."

"Let me take your bag."

"Wouldn't think of it," said Celebrity X, wrapping one arm around the man's shoulders as they walked toward a pick-up truck parked nearby.

Watching them from a nearby roadway were two men, clad in dark clothes, similar in many respects to the two who had watched Peter McDonald at the first airport. As one lowered a pair of binoculars, the other dialed a cell phone. "We've got contact," he said simply, then hung up.

Heading toward the pick-up truck, Celebrity X passed a pair of employees who worked for the corporation that managed Hampton Airport. "Good evening," he greeted them.

The employees responded to his greeting, at first not knowing or caring who the man wearing the dark glasses might be. It was only after Celebrity X passed that one of them did a double-take.

"Do you realize who that was?"

"I didn't notice," said his friend.

The first man paused, astounded at what he was about to say:

"It was the pope!"

PART 2:

FRIDAY

FRIDAY

MARATHON

50:02:00

The sky over the lake was black turning gray when Peter McDonald rolled over, noted that the red numbers on his alarm clock would within a few minutes reach 6:00:00, six o'clock, and decided it was time to get up. *Friday!* Two days before the Lake City Marathon and the culmination of a year's work for the race director and his staff. He both anticipated eagerly the moment when the horn would sound Sunday morning, sending 50,000 runners off on their individual 26-mile-385-yard odysseys, and dreaded it. The best of times. The worst of times. So many moments to savor. So much to fear with questions about sponsorship, the weather and (most challenging) Celebrity X.

50:02:00. 50:01:59. 50:01:58.

Before going to bed—alone—in his bedroom in the Presidential Suite of Hilliard Towers, Peter had set the alarm to sound at 6:00, but he rarely heard an alarm buzz any more. Invariably, no matter how tired, no matter how late gone to bed, he would roll over before his programmed wake-up call and rise voluntarily rather than submit his sensibilities to a sleep-shattering alarm.

Peter shifted the button on the clock from "Alarm" to "Off" and hoisted himself from the mattress. Feet finally on the ground, he paused a few seconds to clear his head, then staggered sleepily to the bathroom.

The marathon race director could have used an extra hour or two of sleep. Peter had worked with his executive director Noel Michaels past midnight to insure that her crew was ready to move rapidly as soon as the city shut down the area on the southernmost stretch of Columbia Drive, where the marathon would finish. That would happen precisely at 10:00 A.M., forty-six hours before the start, with everything related to set-up flowing from that moment.

Should he worry? Not really, because Michaels knew well her job. He would merely need to stand by and allow Noel to do the heavy lifting. Still, he never found himself able to relax the last few days before the marathon, nor could he relax until the last slow-shuffling runner crossed the finish line late on Sunday afternoon.

As he stood tottering before the toilet bowl, he thought of the day's schedule. The craziness that was marathon weekend had begun. Sleep would be scarce these next three days, yet Peter had no important appointments before 8:00. Peter had time to run, then he would grab a quick breakfast downstairs, bury his head in the newspaper, offer polite hello's to anyone he knew who passed, hoping they did not sit down at his table and interrupt his reading, then head over to the TV3 studio for an appearance on *The Morning News*. From there, he would go to the convention center to arrive just before the first runners appeared to pick up their numbers.

This would allow him some wandering time. He could walk through the hall to make sure all the volunteers were in place, all the booths were up and operating, that everything had begun to happen the way it had been programmed to happen during the many months leading to this weekend. Peter McDonald felt confident that peace and harmony would prevail, that all those connected with the marathon would do their jobs as instructed, but the perfectionist in Peter would not allow him to relax for the next three days. From this point Friday morning until the post-race party Sunday evening, Peter would be on call full-time.

Peter could not unwind. He could not loosen his grip on the controls of the juggernaut he had created. Any sleep Peter could catch would need to come in short snatches. He would arrive at that post-race party Sunday exhilarated but exhausted, happy yet drained of energy, more fatigued than if he had run the marathon himself, but that was one of the penalties he paid as race director for an event that attracted 50,000 runners.

One day a year. That was his focus. And 364 days leading to that one day a year. Peter took pride in making that day as perfect an experience as it could be for all those runners who were both his customers and his superiors.

Yet there was another factor that propelled Peter McDonald from his comfortable king-sized bed in a suite much too luxurious for ordinary mortals.

He could not go back to bed, even to lie awake and contemplate the day ahead, because there was a ghost in that bed with him. Peter was haunted by the ghost of his late wife, Carol. Even though she had been gone now for nearly a year, when he slept in the double bed in the condo they once shared, he slept on "his" side of the bed, not "her" side. This was quirky behavior, Peter realized. A psychoanalyst would have a field day with his phobia, but the few times he tried to cure himself of the habit and move to the middle, the bed felt cold. He felt cold. He shifted immediately back to his narrow part of the half-empty marital bed. This was particularly ridiculous in a luxury suite like the one he occupied at the Hilliard. In its king-sized bed with a half dozen pillows, he slept perilously close to the edge, almost in danger of falling off, the remainder of the bed untouched by his body.

What must the maid think when she stumbles upon his one-third-slept bed? Peter consoled himself with the thought that hotel maids certainly encountered evidence of much more bizarre activity when they cleaned up after departing guests.

MARATHON

It was not that Carol's memory troubled him. Even as he left the bathroom and returned to the bedroom section of the suite, he touched the chain she had brought back from Africa. Every time he touched the chain, it was like a prayer sent her way. He never took it off, not while awake, not while asleep. It was a permanent part of him.

Peter loved to gaze at the photo of him and Carol on the mantle of his apartment, their marriage photo, a picture taken during their honeymoon in Hawaii. Even to touch the checkbook in the desk drawer caused Peter sometimes to shiver, because Carol had handled the checkbook. Her fingerprints remained on it. When he touched the checkbook, he sometimes felt that he was touching her. It was not an entirely unpleasant experience.

Nevertheless, to lie in bed upon awakening and be conscious of the empty space beside him somehow unsettled him. Since Carol's death, no other woman had occupied that space. Peter had opportunities, but he was not ready to accept the fact that some new woman might one day replace her, might warm the space that she had left cold.

Would it be the TV3 reporter he had met yesterday at the Expo? Almost against his will, Peter had found himself hovering over her yesterday, both at the press conference and later at Niles Wendell's party? She seemed attracted to him, although maybe she was merely being polite to someone who could feed her news sources. Christine Ferrarra. He liked the sound of her name, but he quickly banished it from his thoughts, because the ghost of his late wife still haunted the other half of that cold bed. Was she smiling or frowning as she read his mind. *She should be able to do that from Heaven, shouldn't she?*

The best and only way to exorcize his demons was to run. Removing the oversized T-shirt he had slept in, Peter pulled open the bottom drawer of the hotel room dresser in which he had placed his running gear. He pulled on a pair of navy blue shorts and a gray T-shirt bearing the name Nitro, the shoe company that served as one of the race sponsors. Even in the middle of a heat wave, he knew it would be cool before dawn, so Peter layered a long-sleeved shirt over the T-shirt. It announced Lake City Marathon. He had numerous shirts that said Boston or New York or London, since like many of those involved in the running sport, he could hardly go off to a race on business without people thrusting goods and equipment at him, but he tried not to advertise other races in places where people would see him. Even in the dark before dawn, people would see him.

Peter took the plastic room key and thrust it into a zippered back pocket in his shorts and, as his last act before leaving the room and the ghost of his dead wife, grabbed an iPod off the dresser and clipped it to his shorts, fitting the earpieces around his ears as he headed to the elevator. He pushed the down button and an elevator door opened instantly, as though the car had been assigned for his personal use. He rode quickly to the lobby.

Though still half asleep as he pushed through the revolving door that opened onto Jefferson Avenue and the park to the east, the rush of brisk air finished the job of awakening him. "Good morning," offered a doorman wearing a marathon jacket. Peter politely returned the doorman's greeting and headed for the lake.

Rather than turn left toward to the staging area where his staff had begun to direct the movement of goods and equipment the finish line, Peter decided to turn right, knowing that he could bypass this scene of race-related activity. Otherwise, he would feel obligated to stop and chat. No, he needed this run. He needed this one last workout along the lakefront before the serious business of making the marathon happen. Despite having donned the iPod, Peter had not activated the device, but now he pushed the button starting the music.

Billie Holiday. One of his favorite albums. Her biggest hits. The black singer somehow seemed even more popular today than during her lifetime that had ended prematurely in the 1950s. Carol had loved Billie's music. That's one of the things that had first attracted him to her, the fact that she owned a half dozen albums from an oddly-voiced singer who had been dead nearly forty years—so he had adopted Billie Holiday too. Why, if he was trying to escape the memory of his late wife, did he continue to play music that reminded him of her?

In my solitude, you haunt me, With dreadful ease of days gone by.

Peter ran as the music continued. He ran up a set of stairs that led to a bridge crossing the railroad tracks and from there down into a tunnel that ducked under Columbia Drive. He discovered a police car parked at the head of the tunnel, protection for any runners rising early, although the policeman in that car appeared to be sleeping. Peter ran past without interrupting the policeman's slumber and moved up a ramp, then across a grassy knoll into an area of the city known as Museum Campus, because of its cluster of museums: an aquarium, a planetarium and a museum of natural history. He crossed in front of the aquarium, then down a ramp and onto a concrete breakwater below that building. This took him along a peninsula jutting out into the lake beside a boat harbor. The peninsula led to the airport where he had picked up the supermodel Naní in a stretch limousine last night, but Peter was thinking of another woman, prodded by the music flowing from the iPod.

In my solitude you taunt me. With memories that never die.

Peter and Carol had talked about having children. There was never any doubt in either of their minds that they would raise a family. "Two seems the right number," said Carol.

"Me too," Peter agreed. Then they would chatter about whether it was better to have a boy first or a girl first. Boy first appealed to Peter, since he could protect his younger sister. Girl first appealed to Carol, since a more sensitive girl would be able to guide her younger brother. Obviously, they both knew they did not have a lot of choice in the matter.

"As long as she's healthy," said Carol. Peter agreed. They were not sure when to start. They enjoyed their unencumbered lifestyle, plus they had careers, but Carol did not want to wait too long. At some point, they would pull the plug on their birth control and see what happens. "Soon," they each agreed, and their talk about a little Carol, or a little Peter, often continued into the darkest hours of the night, most often after making love.

But there never had been a little Carol, and now there never would be. If they had known Carol's fate in advance, would they have decided to create another human in her image? Would it make it easier if a part of the woman he loved remained on this planet, or would it make it harder to raise a child who never would remember, as he still did, the sweet scent of her mother.

As Peter's run on the lakefront continued, the sky changed from blue to gray to pink, and now the rim of a sun began to show over the waves, creating on those waves sparkles of golden light. As he continued to and around the planetarium and turned back past the airport, the Lake City skyline filled his view, the buildings themselves bathed in the gold glow of the rising sun, the multitudinous windows reflecting its orange rays back at the sun. Peter and other runners were blessed to be able to encounter such views with a regularity that they too often took for granted.

The song Billie sung had long since been replaced by another melody and a melody after that, but that one song had been his and Carol's favorite, so it lingered in his mind as he returned to Hilliard Towers and pushed the button on his iPod turning it off before passing through the revolving doors leading to the lobby. He touched again his chain without realizing he had done so.

As Peter broke from run to walk, the doorman greeted him again: "Have a good run, sir?"

"Yes, thanks," Peter responded with a smile, and it was true. His demons had been exorcised, although Billie's words lingered unsung in the air:

In my solitude, I'm afraid. Dear lord above, send back my love.

FRIDAY

49:30:00

Christine Ferrara sincerely believed that the people on this planet could easily be divided into two groups: those who promptly bounce out of bed when the alarm sounds each morning and those who hit the snooze button, once or twice or more, to steal a few more minutes of sleep. That ignored the fact that many people in the Third World not only do not have digital alarm clocks, but do not have electrical outlets into which they could plug such a device of the Devil. Socioeconomic arguments aside, Christine definitely fitted into that second category of snooze-buttoners, rarely rising from bed before the second or third buzz, sometimes holding out to the ultimate buzz after which her digital alarm clock would surrender, convinced that its mistress was beyond help, soon destined to be unemployed if she did not remove her heavy head from the pillows and leave for work.

49:30:00. 49:29:59. 49:29:58.

This snooze-buttoning used to drive Yolanda Kline crazy. It was more a problem at college when the two seemingly incompatible females shared a single sleeping space in their sorority. After a few ignored buzzes, Yolanda sometimes would scream: "Roommate, you either get out of bed or I'm coming at you with a bucket of water guaranteed to de-curl your pretty locks."

That was an idle threat, and both girls knew it, but it was partly their incompatibilities that kept the pair together. Yolanda knew that by tolerating Christine's ignored buzzes, she could go one-up on her roommate, meaning that Christine would need to tolerate her indiscretions, which usually meant studying with the light on until way past midnight while Ms. Never-Had-To-Cram-for-an-Exam placidly slept.

Sometimes Christine would roll over and see her roommate still studying. "Yolanda, go to bed," Christine would plead. "You're keeping me awake."

"Roommate, you could sleep through an earthquake," Yolanda would counter. "Nothing short of the Apocalypse could keep you awake."

"Roommate," Christine responded. "*You* are the Apocalypse. One of these days, you are going to wake up after your latest Late Night to find all your books scattered on the grass beneath the window."

Their arguments rarely escalated to a serious disagreement, but merely proved the rule that opposites do attract.

Yolanda was a big black girl from the inner city, whose high school had been almost totally devoid of whites, unless you counted Latinos, which for

116

some reason not everybody keeping statistics on urban integration did. Christine, despite hair even blacker than Yolanda's, was unmistakably white, having come from a small town with few minorities, unless you counted Catholics. Somehow the two opposites survived four years and sincerely liked each other to the point where Yolanda, since Christine's arrival in town, had been pleading with her friend to forsake thoughts of a separate apartment.

"Being free and single ain't as much fun as you think," Yolanda argued. The fact that Yolanda occupied a two-bedroom apartment, paying double rent since the departure of a previous roommate, prompted that offer. With two bedrooms, Christine could play snooze button as much as she wanted without disturbing Yolanda.

Christine could have continued to doze this Friday morning, since she did not need to get to the TV station until several hours later. But she wanted to get up and run. She needed to run. The time she had spent among runners Thursday had motivated her. Plus, she had met Peter. Might not they have a running date some time in the future? He seemed such an accomplished runner. She better get in shape, lose a few pounds. *Would he slow to my pace?* She suspected she might find a way to entice him to do so.

Moving the alarm switch to "Off," Christine lifted herself out of bed and shuffled to the bathroom she shared with her roommate, whose bedroom door remained closed. Plopping down on the toilet seat, Christine rested a minute, tinkled, then stood to splash water on her face. Despite her dozing habits, Christine could become instantly awake when it suited her purpose.

Christine was in the middle of her period, uncomfortable, but not enough to slow her down. After changing her tampon, Christine returned to the bedroom, sorted through her recreational gear and found an outfit featuring matching shorts and singlet. Clothing conscious, Christine liked looking good even when nobody was looking to see she was looking good.

From last night's weather reports, she knew that it would be warm even in the early morning hours. Well, maybe slightly chilly until the sun came up. She would only need those shorts and singlet plus socks and her running shoes. The singlet provided a pocket for her iPod, which she popped into place, fitting the device's earpiece into her ear.

Just before departing, Christine clicked into her Facebook page, providing the several hundred Friends connected with her on the Internet with some important information related to her activity of the minute:

"**Christine Ferrara...** is running on the
lakefront on a beautiful, sunny morning."

Heading out the door, Christine began a planned two-block walk to the lakefront, before starting to run. She punched the start button on her iPod and heard the voice of Tony Bennett from one of her favorite albums: *Tony Bennett on Holiday*, songs associated with Billie Holiday.

When a woman loves a man, sang Tony. *Tell her she's a fool. She'll say yes, I know. But I love him so.*

Christine paid little attention to the lyrics, hardly heard them or thought much about their meaning. She actually would have been embarrassed if she realized they might, at least some time soon, apply to her. Music was simply something that went along with running. She could not run without music. It would be absolutely impossible for Christine to plant one foot in front of the other, she thought, without sounds in her ear.

But it was running that brought Christine peace. It allowed her escape. It offered a form of freedom from the responsibilities of the everyday world. It also provided empowerment, important for a female attempting to survive in a business world with rules designed by men. The act of running created a corner from which she could not easily be pried. Christine revered running for its ability to provide one hour a day when she could shove her business commitments aside and just run free. She had friends who used their daily shower as a refuge for escape. Yolanda was one of them. She even enticingly had it on her answering machine: "I can't talk to you now. I'm in the shower."

That girl is going to drown some day, thought Christine. *Do I really need to share Ms. Submariner's water bill?* But taking a shower, even for an aquaphile like Yolanda, only buys you five or ten minutes of peace. Stay under the water longer, and you emerge feeling and looking like a prune. You can also only waste so much time sitting on the toilet with or without the latest issue of *InStyle*. Running, on the other hand, allows you to escape for longer periods of time. Thirty to sixty minutes of peace: maybe longer on weekends, while doing long runs. *I can't talk to you now. I'm training for a marathon. And please do* not *leave a message!*

Arriving at the park, Christine paused and waited for the traffic light to change from red to green. Her small town ethic did not permit Christine to ignore traffic laws. Even when everybody else was rushing across a street empty of traffic, she waited nervously on the curb, certain that a sinkhole would open beneath her feet should she shift even one foot onto the right of way. She owed that attitude in life to her mother, who never would allow her or her brothers or sisters to move from the curb until the light changed.

"Mom, no cars are coming."

"Hush, Christine. Laws are meant to be obeyed."

That was one reason why Christine remained a virgin. She reasoned: Moses must have brought the Ten Commandments down from the mountain for some reason other than to provide a plot line for a best-selling book and assorted films following.

MARATHON

When the light did change, Christine walked across the street, stepped onto the gravel path frequented by runners and began slowly, but purposely, to run. Many others had preceded her to the path during this morning hour, not marathoners because they would be resting for Sunday's race, but others among the large number of runners living in Lake City for whom a day begun without a morning walk or run was unacceptable.

The many runners and walkers around her each ran or walked at different paces, slower or faster, and she could have latched onto one, matching that person's pace as an aid to moving forward, but Christine ran without an awareness of those nearby. They did not exist. She moved as though in a plastic bubble, separated from those around her, the sounds of Tony covering Billie floating in through one ear and out the other.

And that's how it goes, when a woman loves a man.

Christine might have been surprised to learn that almost precisely at the moment she stepped onto the lakefront path on the near north side of Lake City, Peter McDonald was running on the extension of that same path several miles away, south of downtown. Had Peter headed north and had Christine headed south, the pair actually might have met somewhere in the middle. *When Peter Met Christine:* Great title for a movie. But fate did not intend for any blissful encounters that morning, and Christine's run took her further north and away from her someday (she hoped) lover. She followed the path as it twisted between trees just beginning to show their fall colors, passing beneath Lake Shore Drive and a half dozen lanes of traffic filled mostly with commuters heading early to jobs in town.

Emerging from the tunnel, Christine ran past a mammoth boat moored to the concrete shore of a small harbor. The boat served as a yacht club for those using the harbor. The harbor was crammed with sailboats and powerboats not yet moved to winter storage. The yachtsmen owners of those boats, when on them, existed in a dimension apart from passing runners. Their outlook was toward the lake, not activities within the park beside the lake. If they thought much of the marathon this weekend, it would be mainly to worry whether runners jamming the streets and stalling traffic would prevent them from getting promptly to and from their boats.

After coming to the end of the harbor, Christine passed a totem pole and a dozen or more people doing exercises in cadence, being shouted at by an individual dressed in fatigues with a voice like a Marine Corps Drill Instructor, urging them to various degrees of distress, although those doing push-ups certainly paid the instructor a fee for punishing them. That they occupied a grassy space beside the totem pole made it seem they were worshipping the Indian gods depicted on the pole, but such was not the case. Theirs was the God of

Fitness, one to whom human sweat was Holy Water. On reaching the exercisers, Christine decided to turn back for no particular reason other than her body said it seemed time to do so. Despite the instructor's abrasive voice, she barely had been aware of him or his pupils supine on the grass.

Christine returned at a faster pace. She was warmed up now, fully awake. She passed slower runners, although she saw them less as rivals and more as fellow aerobic travelers. The sun was rising over the lake, bathing her with its pleasant glow. *Bennett on Holiday* had run its course. Her iPod had shifted without being told to Yo Yo Mah playing Brazilian melodies. If someone had asked Christine moments after she stopped what she had been listening to while running, she would not have been able to tell them.

Music, just music.

Do you find the scenery beautiful along the lake?

Yes, of course. Very beautiful.

Did you encounter any activity along your running path, Ms. Ferrara, someone shouting like a Drill Instructor, for instance?

Sorry, I was in my plastic bubble.

Christine returned to her apartment and started dressing for work. The shut bedroom door indicated that Yolanda Kline still was sleeping.

49:00:00

As both Peter and Christine completed their separate workouts on the lakefront, the man called Celebrity X slept the sleep of the innocent in a plainly appointed bedroom in his mother's house in a working class neighborhood on the industrial edge of Lake City, a neighborhood referred to as the "East Side." The long flight from Rome to Lake City had tired him, as it always did, but at his mother's house, X could sleep as much as he wanted. Forty-nine hours remained before the marathon, but that important encounter with ordinary life did not trouble the sleeping moments of the man most of the world knew by the unpretentious name, Pope Tony.

49:00:00. 48:59:59. 48:59:58.

No duties demanded Pope Tony's attention. Had he been back at his quarters in Vatican City, he would have risen well before dawn for prayers, sometimes a treadmill run, a light breakfast and more prayers before taking on the worries of the World in his position as Holy Father, bishop of Rome, head of the college of bishops, chief of state of Vatican City, his Holiness, successor to Peter, vicar of Christ, head of the Roman Catholic Church, the pope.

MARATHON

Those were titles X never had aspired to, nor desired, but once the church's top office had been thrust upon him, he humbly donned the vestments and accepted in his hand the scepter, the same staff once clasped at least symbolically by the first individual to have held his job. *"Tu es Petrus,"* the cardinal electors meeting in conclave had proclaimed. "You are Peter!"

How a relatively young American became pope both stunned and puzzled most observers of the church. Pope Tony had turned forty only a few months before. Because of the strict secrecy surrounding the conclave of cardinal electors, X's ascension to pope was a story that probably never would be told—at least within the lifetimes of those involved.

The birth name of the man called Celebrity X was John Anthony Molina. His father's name had been Anthony John Molina. His grandfather's name had been John Anthony Molina, actually Giovanni Antonio Molina, X's *nono*, or grandfather, having been born in Italy, coming to the United States with his parents as a child.

For countless years members of the Molina family, who lived in a tiny mountain village in Calabria, had shifted first and second names back and forth from generation to generation, a practice followed in many Mediterranean countries. This traditional first-male-child name change transpired over so many decades and even centuries that nobody in the Molina family could remember the first Giovanni Antonio, or maybe the first Antonio Giovanni. When it came time to choose the name by which X would be identified as pope, he saw no reason to upset family traditions. There had been twenty-three previous Pope Johns and two recent John Pauls, but no John Anthonys, so he became the first Pope John Anthony. And the first American pope, seemingly a *huge* break with ecclesiastical tradition despite a recent pope who was Polish and another who was German.

That became an immediate topic of discussion soon after the puff of white smoke fluttered out of the Sistine Chapel window, indicating that the college of cardinals, after nearly two weeks of deliberation, finally had made their choice. *Time* magazine, among other publications, devoted a cover story to the young American's ascension to the papacy, trying to guess what motivated the cardinals meeting in conclave to choose him of all people as pope. Reading the *Time* article after its publication, the pope could only smile and acknowledge that the magazine's reporters had not even come close to discovering the actual facts, a tribute to Vatican secrecy.

The Vatican press corps, nevertheless, continued to probe into the reasons why he, a complete unknown, a nonentity, had been chosen to lead the church at this critical point in its history. Most persistent in her questions was Matilda

Goldberg, a reporter for *The New York Times* and a Vatican regular, who insisted that the world deserved more information as to why the church, at this critical point in its history, would choose a young man—and she used that term—as its chief prelate. Pope John Anthony shrugged amiably when Goldberg asked this question during his early meetings with reporters who covered the affairs of the Vatican on a regular basis. Media-savvy, he had agreed to a press conference, that itself a departure from Vatican protocol.

The new pope, prompted by Goldberg, conceded that his having been Italo-American might have softened the surprise and diluted the outrage among certain cardinals and others within the Roman curia, those who formed the *governatorato* or government of the church. X did not say "Italian cardinals," but Goldberg and her colleagues knew who he meant. Forty-seven cardinals lived and worked in Vatican City, almost all of them Italians.

The pope told Goldberg and the other curious reporters that his mother was Latina, her father having crossed the border from Mexico illegally to work in the steel mills near Lake City. "Instead of referring to me as the first American pope, or the first Italo-American pope," said John Anthony, betraying the tiniest smile to suggest he was joking, "perhaps you should identify me as the first Latino pope."

The Vatican observers, used to dealing with more staid individuals in his position, did not know whether to take that comment seriously—or even report it. But popes are, first, teachers, rabbis. The new pope hoped to impress on the reporters—and through them the people of the world—that he had roots in several cultures, and that they should accept him for what he was, and is, and abandon prior stereotypes and any prejudiced perceptions of what the bishop of Rome should be.

"Pope John Anthony seems, first, a man of the people," Matilda Goldberg wrote in *The New York Times* after that first group interview. "What the people think of this charismatic, young American will be determined in coming years." Goldberg noted that, given his age, Pope John Anthony could remain bishop of Rome for a long, long time and certainly would outlive those responsible for his election, some of them nearly twice that age.

What to call the new pope also had become a matter that worried those Vatican observers who attended his first media appearance. Pope John Anthony, of course, but his nickname growing up—they quickly learned—had been Tony, the same as his father. Those among X's circle of high school friends often jokingly referred to each other by the first name of their parents rather than their given names. So his closest friends called him Tony, not John. After ordination, he found himself being referred to most often as Father Tony, a name that didn't displease him. While serving at various churches, including St. Stanislaus Church in his parent's neighborhood on the East Side, parishioners comfortably called him by that name. Now transferred from that humble parish to Vatican City with all its majesty, Father Tony suggested that he might retain that unimposing nickname.

"Would it be proper to refer to you," worried one Vatican reporter, "as Pope Tony?" The reporter, Italian, actually used the name *Papa Tonio*.

"Call me as you wish," responded Pope John Anthony, adding: "I'm merely the messenger, not the message. Respect the office more than the man occupying the office."

And so the man known as Celebrity X became officially Pope John Anthony, more familiarly Pope Tony, that short title handy for newspaper headlines. Many church members, particularly those within the country that had yielded so many popes, at first were shocked, even horrified, that the college of cardinals had chosen a man so young, in his forties, and *mama mia*, an *americano!*

Bloggers worried how much damage an American pope might do to the church's credibility. Was he, despite his Roman collar, some flaming revolutionary? A "Che" in disguise? They feared he might push the church into accommodations with an increasingly indifferent and immoral public, rather than guiding that public to the teachings of Christ.

Nevertheless, so great was Pope Tony's humility and what might be described as a certain boyish charm, it required only a few public appearances before he won over most of his detractors. He also spoke Italian, thanks to his grandfather's origins, with a sub-Neapolitan accent, which branded him as a man of the people. "Jesus Christ was only thirty-three when he founded the church," laughed dark-haired men sipping coffee on the Via Veneto, "and now He has chosen someone in his own image."

Goldberg of the *Times* pointed out that popes are not chosen for their office by the cardinals as they are by the cardinals *inspired by God*. "If you understand that," wrote Goldberg, "you know there must be some reason why this young American has been picked at this particular time to lead the holy Roman Catholic Church."

Pope Tony was not quite sure he understood the reason himself. He had grown up in the same neighborhood as Peter McDonald. (Ironic, that his good friend should have the name Peter.) Tony was nearly a decade older than Peter and, in addition to his parish duties, a part-time teacher at a high school on the south side of Lake City when Peter arrived as a freshman, a talented yet still not quite mature member of the cross-country team. Father Tony coached the team and became Peter's mentor, guiding him toward the right classes and the right classmates. Even as a teenager, the soon to be Pope Tony already had begun to show leadership ability.

The high school Tony taught at and Peter attended was Carmel Catholic, run by Carmelite priests, located near the epicenter of a neighborhood where gangs circled like vultures, ready to land on any carrion in sight. Yet parents from the white suburbs still sent their sons to the all-boy's school, not only because of the education the Carmelites provided, but because of the strict discipline that accompanied it. The fact that Carmel Catholic possessed one of the best football teams in the city, winning frequent state championships, also served as a lure for students who enjoyed the thrill of victory.

That Carmel Catholic also won a state championship in cross-country Peter's senior year failed to attract as much attention among bill-paying alumni as its victories on the gridiron, but runners, more introspective than extroverted, did not need to have their victories witnessed by 10,000 paying spectators. At one point his senior year, Peter considered the priesthood and discussed the subject with his mentor.

"I have a calling," Father Tony told him. "Do you?"

Peter decided not and chose the career route that eventually led him to race director for the Lake City Marathon.

Father Tony's career route led him after several years of teaching to a job as assistant at a different parish, but the bishop already had identified this personable young man, whose homilies parishioners actually listened to, as an individual who might better serve the church at a higher level. The bishop soon recruited him for the diocese office. Father Tony spent a year working as assistant to the bishop. The bishop next sent him to Rome to study canon law. After Tony's return, the bishop had him enroll in law school at Notre Dame University, also assigning him as administrator for two small, rural parishes. Peter was running for Notre Dame at the same time, so their friendship continued. Despite his busy schedule, Father Tony graduated with honors in less than three years.

During his earlier stay in Italy, Father Tony also had attracted the attention of several high executives in the Roman curia, including the cardinal camerlengo, whose job might be likened to Secretary of the Treasury, although he also supervised Vatican security, including the Swiss Guards. The cardinal camerlengo, in an example of increased diversity of the Vatican, was an Irishman: James Connolly, named after a great uncle who had been hung by the British for his part in the Easter Rising in 1916. This latter-day James Connolly was a man of peace, unlike his famous ancestor, one-time commandant of the Dublin Brigade, a man still revered on the Emerald Isle. Nevertheless, some of the rebelliousness of the early-day Connolly remained with the cardinal camerlengo, who felt control of the church must be shared with others beside the Italians.

It was the cardinal camerlengo who administered the properties and revenues of the Holy See and who, upon the death of a pope, would supervise the election of his successor. After Father Tony's first stay in Rome, the camerlengo permitted him to return home, allowing him several years more of parish work, all the time keeping his eye on him. Eventually the camerlengo brought Father Tony back to work in the Roman curia.

After a year's stay, the camerlengo requested that the talented American be allowed to remain another year. This both pleased and displeased the bishop back in Lake City, who had chosen a somewhat different direction for Father Tony, but how could he say no? Tony also wondered about being compelled to labor in the bureaucracy of the church. He considered many of his new companions in the curia (priests as well as laymen) worker ants. Dressed in cassocks or black suits, they mostly processed paper for their superiors. He longed to return to parish life and contact with real people.

Nevertheless, luck, fate, or some might call it the hand of God, had positioned Father Tony in the perfect place for his next career move. It happened after the death of the sitting pope. "When his predecessor died," Matilda Goldberg reported, trying to analyze for readers of the Sunday *Times Magazine* the events that followed, "John Anthony Molina was in Vatican City attached to the camerlengo, arguably the Vatican's most powerful administrator."

Goldberg continued: "It is the duty of the cardinal camerlengo to certify the pope's death. Ceremony required that the camerlengo call the pope by his birth name three times to see if he responds. Actually, the medical staff verifies the death after which the camerlengo seals the pope's apartments and arranges for the ring of the fisherman and papal seal to be broken. He then prepares for the funeral rites and the *novemdieles*, nine days of mourning."

The *Sede Vacante*, the period when the Holy See was vacant, began.

Meanwhile, the Swiss Guards, following custom, had hung a heavy black chain across the entrance to the courtyard of the papal villa. *"Il papa est mort."* The pope is dead. The word spread quickly. The cardinal camerlengo next called cardinals all over the world to convene in Rome to select the pope's successor. The college of cardinal electors consisted of 120 men, the maximum number allowed, none of them over age 80 as prescribed by the rules of election.

While Catholics throughout the world waited and after several weeks of sermons and meditation in their home churches as to what kind of pope the church needed, the college of cardinals met in conclave under strict secrecy in the Sistine Chapel, which had been swept to detect and eliminate any listening devices. This guaranteed that no news of the meeting would leak to the outside during the conclave. All within were pledged to *never* reveal afterwards the discussions that resulted in the choice of a new pope. To break that pledge would result in automatic excommunication.

As a result, little information leaked about how Father Tony became pope. As per custom, after each vote the ballots were burned, the cloud of black smoke emerging from a window in the Sistine Chapel signaling to those waiting outside that no choice yet had been made.

The cardinals voted twice each morning and twice each afternoon and after three days devoted a day to prayer so each could examine his own conscience as to whether his choice would prove best for the church. During most of this period of stalemate, Father Tony remained outside the conclave, continuing to assist the camerlengo within, shuffling requests and messages in and out, as the voting continued. Despite his close connection, he had no clue as to what was transpiring within.

Vatican observers continued to speculate about which cardinal might emerge from the conclave as new pope. In daily reports and eventually in the article she wrote for the *New York Times Magazine*, Goldberg tried to analyze what went on behind closed doors. The bishop of Palermo seemed to be the leading candidate, she thought, particularly among the Italian delegation, who after several non-Italian popes wanted a return to power. Some among the media suggested that the cardinals might look toward the Third World, perhaps picking an African, though more likely someone from Latin America. Although nearly two-thirds of Catholics now lived in the developing world, half the cardinals (and this included the Italians) remained Europeans.

"It seems unlikely that the conclave will select an American," Goldberg originally wrote. "Given the powerful economic and military presence of the United States in the world, the cardinals certainly will avoid that choice." Dismissing any American's chances of becoming pope, she also mentioned recent sexual abuse scandals within the American Catholic Church.

Because the oath of secrecy eliminated any accurate description or analysis of what occurred within the conclave, Goldberg and other observers could only guess later why the seemingly conservative college of cardinals might choose not only an American, but one so young that he conceivably could rule the Church for three to four decades!

Goldberg wrote later that the selection of Pope John Anthony, a man not even a cardinal at the time the previous pope died, could only be explained as a fluke, or at best as a compromise to placate two warring factions within the conclave: the conservatives and the liberals. In that opinion, the *Times* reporter probably was close. As the deliberations carried into their second week, one of the cardinals from Asia celebrated his eightieth birthday, thus reaching the age when cardinals became ineligible to vote. With the conclave already started, he probably could have retained his position, but as a point of honor decided to excuse himself. That dropped the number of electors from 120 to 119, and while a replacement was not necessary, the camerlengo chose to bring Tony into the conclave as elector, even though he was not a cardinal.

Was it a joke that several days later with the vote still stalled between two powerful candidates, the bishop of Palermo and the bishop of Rio de Janeiro, someone offered Father Tony's name in nomination? And was it some perverse act of fate that on the next vote a few midstream cardinals shifted their votes to Father Tony almost in protest to the candidates backed by the conservative and liberal wings. He received a total that put him well behind those candidates, but suddenly heads began to turn Father Tony's way.

Maybe the cardinals opened themselves to the grace of the Holy Spirit. It was during the next vote that a significant number of cardinals, most of whom knew Tony only as a pleasant and intelligent fellow, shrugged and said maybe this was the man who God wants.

"Tu es Petrus!" they informed the American. Tony was stunned, almost speechless, but he had been made an offer that he could not refuse.

Whether or not the vote happened this way, nobody knew, but this was the explanation that Matilda Goldberg offered the readers of the *New York Times Magazine,* and given the oath of secrecy, who would say that she was wrong? Cardinals do not normally write Op/Ed articles for the *Times.*

None of the members of the college of cardinals meeting in conclave, however, suspected that the man they chose as bishop of Rome would some day decide to run a marathon.

47:55:00

L et me suggest your worst nightmare, Peter," Mark Mallon, co-host of *The Morning Show*, teased his guest. "Your front runners are on world record pace. Three miles to go! You're riding the lead vehicle. You round a corner and encounter a sewer project. The street looks like a war zone. There's a bottomless ditch for 50,000 runners to hurdle."

It was just after 8:00. *The Morning Show* was the most-watched program in Lake City at that hour, seen by more people than any of the national news broadcasts. Mallon, normally TV3's sports director, not the regular host, was filling in for a colleague on vacation. That the marathon was less than forty-eight hours away was a happy coincidence.

FRIDAY

47:55:00. 47:54:59. 47:54:58.

Peter McDonald smiled at the question, realizing that the always well-prepared Mallon already knew the answer, but thousands of viewers tuned to *The Morning Show* probably did not. "Mark," Peter began, "if there's a ditch, I'll jump in. You shovel sand on my back so the leaders can cross."

Mallon's co-host, Louise Twill, laughed. "Sewer projects blocking traffic? That's an unfortunate side effect of city life. Can you guarantee no blocked traffic, Peter? A lot of our commuting viewers would like to know how to get such a guarantee."

"Louise, the Bureau of Streets & Sanitation offers the guarantee. We have good coordination with the Bureau through the mayor's office. Earlier this week, I met with the department heads and discussed possible problems."

As always, Peter had numbers committed to memory to prove his point: "Last year, there were 335 active construction projects within a few blocks of the marathon route. We run across bridges, run under overpasses, run across railroad tracks. Working with the Bureau, we make sure all the projects get addressed timely. Sometimes the Bureau needs to push a contractor to bump priority on a project, but race day everything is in place."

"So you don't need to ride the course race day morning with a shovel in the back of your pick-up truck," Mallon commented.

"Sunday morning, if you're on the course at 3:30 A.M., Mark, you just might see me drive past, but that's mostly nervous energy on my part."

"At what time does the City close the streets so you can begin your preparations?" asked Twill, her voice assuming a more serious tone. "I'm talking about the start and finish lines, Peter. You can't wait until Sunday."

"That's correct, Louise." Peter looked purposely at his watch: "In less than two hours, after rush hour, we'll block Columbia Drive. Starting last weekend, we already had begun to erect tents in the park and stack merchandise nearby: cups, medals, Mylar blankets, medical supplies, mostly items that don't spoil. If you wander into the park this morning, you'll see port-a-potties sprouting like weeds. Perishable items from Metro Foods that need refrigeration come later." Without subtlety, Peter had mentioned the name of that sponsor. He knew that some TV journalists become irritated if and when you plug a product live, often warning against it. He knew that the TV3 people would allow the slight plug to slide, because there was a legitimate connection to his response. Peter knew exactly how and when to mention sponsors without seeming so much a pitchman that he endangered his own credibility.

The race director continued: "Once we have Columbia Drive blocked, we move everything into place, positioning tables that race day will be covered by food and drink. We'll erect booths for TV and radio broadcasts: your booth, Mark. We construct the bridge where photographers take pictures of runners finishing for their walls back home."

"Everyone wants a photo of their first marathon finish," Mallon interjected, shifting the subject slightly.

"Not quite everyone, Mark, but close. RunFoto, the outfit that has the contract to take course and finish line pictures of runners tells me the number is 70 percent for first-time marathoners." Another number; another sponsor. Peter knew how and when to push the buttons.

"Incredible," said Twill.

"It's like hanging your M.D. or Ph.D. degree on the wall," added Mallon, who loved having an articulate guest on the show, because it made him look good. "You've accomplished something. You want everybody to know."

"Back to shutting the streets, Peter," Twill moved the interview forward, having received a signal from the director indicating they had two minutes more to talk. "On race day, when do the streets close? A lot of people want to know this so they don't get caught in traffic."

Peter responded with a well-rehearsed answer: "One hour before the start Sunday, police will begin blocking the course. We do this progressively, mile by mile, so as to inconvenience citizens as little as possible."

"The police know their jobs," suggested Mallon.

"We have 800 police officers that work race morning," answered Peter, using still another number from his reservoir of statistics. "It's a huge contribution by the city to the marathon's success. I'm due at a police roll call later this morning so that the officers know where to deploy their men."

"Security? I hate to mention it, but we live in the Post 9/11 era."

"Obviously I can't offer details, Mark, but the police are well equipped to react rapidly to any threat."

"Still, you have 26 miles of streets to secure."

Peter allowed the remark to go unanswered. He hoped that what he said about the police reaction time was true, particularly when it came to the real dangers that Celebrity X, his identity still hidden, might encounter. Peter had not yet informed the police about Celebrity X. He would do so later that morning without mentioning that X was his close friend, Pope Tony. Neither he nor Tony wanted the media focus to shift from the front of the pack to the well-known man in the middle.

Twill steered them to safer ground: "If you had to start tomorrow, and you never had organized a marathon before in this city, if you had to create an event for 50,000 runners, how much of a task would it be?"

Peter's face registered mock shock, as though asked the impossible. "Louise, you must first consider that the marathon in this city started thirty years ago with a few thousand runners. And it grew gradually, allowing the race organization to gradually grow with it. Those responsible for the race—my predecessors and 8,000 volunteers—also gradually acquired the expertise necessary to accommodate everybody in this year's race."

"Hopefully without hitches."

"It's not the big tasks that cause problems. Stack 3,000 pounds of ice in the medical tent? I've got it covered. Stuff 1.62 million items in goodie bags? Tell me something difficult to do. More a worry is someone calling the alderman or the mayor's office, and her daughter's getting married, and she's worried about the reception guests getting stuck in traffic."

"She should have scheduled the wedding another weekend."

"Try telling that to Mom." That prompted laughter from both interviewers. "So I usually inform Mom what time the street in front of her house will close and how soon, after 50,000 runners have passed, it will open. One way or another I'll find a way to resolve the problem."

"You'll send Mom flowers?" asked Twill.

"Not a bad idea, Louise. I'll send TV3 the bill."

"But *you* personally will resolve the problem?" probed Mallon. "Not some intern hired two weeks before?"

"The week before the marathon, I'm the only one in the office without a job. I'll often pick up the phone first. I want to know where we've made mistakes, not learn about it second-hand in a staff meeting after the race. People with problems often are shocked to find they're talking to the race director."

"You're the one in charge of wedding plans?" asked Twill.

"I'm the one who keeps the mother of the bride happy. When the bride sends thank-you notes for all of the gifts, I'll probably get one too."

The director signaled one minute remained.

"But don't you get complaints?" Twill continued the thought. "Shutting down 26 miles of streets for most of the day must inconvenience more than a single mother of one starry-eyed bride."

"When I first took this job, when fewer than 10,000 ran, we used to field a hundred or more complaints after the marathon: 'I couldn't park my car in front of my house! I had a flight to catch and missed it, because the street was blocked by all those stupid runners! There were empty cups everywhere! All those runners spooked my dog!'

"But eventually the spirit of the marathon took over the city. Residents knew the marathon was coming. They planned for it, including lawn parties to watch the runners pass. Within a year, complaints were down from several hundred to only a hundred. Then fifty. Then maybe a dozen angry people. Now, two or three, because you can't please everyone."

The director indicated thirty seconds.

"The people of Lake City love the marathon runners."

MARATHON

"And the runners love the people of Lake City," said Peter. "That's one reason why even with a 50,000 cap, our field closes earlier each year."

The director sliced a finger across his throat: time to cut to commercial.

Mark Mallon turned from his guest and addressed a camera showing a red light, that camera providing the shot being watched by viewers all over Lake City. "We've been talking to Peter McDonald, race director of the Lake City Marathon. Our race coverage begins 7:00 Sunday morning, an hour before the start of the race. Be sure you tune in. Peter, thanks for coming."

"Always my pleasure, Mark."

The red light on the camera disappeared, allowing two minutes for Peter to exit the set while the co-hosts switched to a different desk and another guest appeared to occupy the seat Peter was about to vacate. It was a woman who had written a book about ADHD, Attention Deficit Hyperactivity Disorder. Peter had met her in the Green Room before heading to the set, and she told him that physical exercise—not necessarily running marathons—was not a cure for ADHD, but it helped moderate some of the symptoms. Peter wondered if she would make that point on camera. On his way to his next appointment, too busy to look at a TV screen here or somewhere else, he would not find out. He stood and allowed one of the production assistants to remove the tiny microphone from his coat jacket. He began to move off the set, noticing at the other end of the studio one of the TV3 weathermen, who undoubtedly would begin by talking about the warm weather expected for Sunday. *Does anybody have a magic genie in a bottle they could loan me?* Peter did not need three wishes; one would be enough.

Peter grabbed the paper cup containing coffee he had been drinking, saw it to be empty, crushed it in his hand and, as he walked off the set, began looking for a wastebasket into which he could deposit the cup. It was at that point he noticed Christine Ferrara standing near one of the cameras, blocking the path to the exit, a smile on her face to indicate that he would not get by without stopping to talk.

"Buy you another cup of coffee?" Christine asked Peter.

"You can," said Peter. "Next week. Unfortunately, not now. I need to be at another TV station in fifteen minutes."

"Traitor!"

"Normally, I'm easier to live with. But this week…." He let the comment dangle in the air between them.

"A deferred date is better than no date," said Christine.

"Deferred it is then. In fact, not merely deferred, I expect to accept the cup of coffee with relish."

"Relish is for hot dogs at the ballpark, Peter."

"I have a friend with box seats. Maybe next summer."

"Maybe next summer."

Christine smiled, recognizing the development of a relationship, the two of them obviously mutually attracted and enjoying the moment for what it was. They were fencing with each other, and it was fun. Dare she hope that she and Peter might have a life together after their coffee date? After "next summer?" But her offer of coffee was for business rather than personal reasons. "You mentioned a police roll call."

"Eleven o'clock. Police headquarters."

"I'd like to attend."

"I can't give you permission, but...." Peter removed a cell phone from his pocket and punched several buttons. "Write down this number." He held the phone up so Christine could see the small screen.

Christine pulled a notebook and pen out of her purse. She wrote down the number, as commanded.

Peter identified the owner of that number: "Captain Newsom. Towering black. Brusque voice. If you were doing something wrong, you would *not* want to meet him. Pretends to be ill-tempered, but it's an act. Mention my name. Notice how quickly the voice turns to butter. State what you want. It shouldn't be a problem, but in case you can't get through, do you have my cell phone number?"

"I suspect it is about to be provided."

Peter offered the second number. Christine wrote it in her notebook, an exclamation point beside it. This was one number she did *not* intend to lose.

"You really do want that cup of coffee," Christine told him.

"No sugar. No cream."

"Noted for future reference."

"If I totally ignore you before or after the roll call, it's not because I'm busy, it's my general lack of manners."

"Manners lack noted. Rudeness anticipated. I know where I can find an etiquette coach to help improve those manners, Peter."

Peter smiled, suspecting she was the etiquette coach. He liked fencing with the attractive reporter too, "One important point; in fact, a *very* important point, Christine. I'm going to be discussing some sensitive information, so sensitive the police do not know it yet. I may need to ask you to turn off the camera and suspend your pretty reporter's brain."

"*Pretty* reporter, Peter?"

"I shouldn't have said that."

"Do I look offended?" Christine said coyly.

Peter gazed in her eyes for a moment. No, she was not. He finally spoke: "Look, let's be honest. We're both hitting on each other."

Christine sighed. Am *I that much of a flirt?* "Guilty as charged."

They both paused, each not knowing what to say next. Peter finally filled the void: "Coffee date?"

"Coffee date."

Another pause, then Peter spotted a wastepaper basket and flipped his crumpled coffee cup toward it. *Two points!* Peter raised his hand triumphantly, fist clenched, then unclenched the fist and waved it toward Christine as he headed toward the studio exit. Before walking out the door, he paused. That corner of the studio was dark. Commercials over, the telecast had begun again, the weatherman talking—as Peter expected—about the warm weather.

Peter turned back toward Christine and spotted her still looking at him. He could tell that she was embarrassed at having been caught doing so. Retracing his steps at a slowed pace, he reached out with one hand. She lifted her hand to meet his. They stared at each other without speaking. Gently, he raised the hand to his lips and kissed it.

Still holding the hand, he spoke softly into her ear so as not to interfere with the continuing telecast: "That was very unprofessional of me, but what do you expect of a man with bad manners?"

Then Peter was gone, and Christine stood staring at the door he had just passed through. *Stunned!*

In the corridor, Peter's mind churned with thoughts of his schedule for the remainder of the weekend: Meetings. Appearances. Parties. Worry about the weather. And Celebrity X. Some of those he could control; others, he could not. Exiting the studio, looking for a cab to take him to his next interview, Peter wondered about his world record holder. He hoped Aba was feeling better, but he did not want to call the Swedish star's hotel room and risk waking her up. He would wait and hope her husband Bjørn called him with good news. With the potential loss of his principle sponsor hanging over his head like a sword of Damocles, he could use some of that.

47:30:00

Aba Andersson gazed at the ugly mess in the toilet bowl and grimaced. The Swedish athlete had just thrown up, something she was not used to doing. Never at the end of even the most strenuous races. Rarely even when she was sick from the flu. And since she rarely drank more than a glass of wine during quiet dinners with her husband Bjørn, Aba *never* vomited because of alcohol abuse. Drugs? She abhorred them, hated the people who took them. Growing up in Gothenburg, Aba had witnessed too often young people staggering into alleys to unload what they had just eaten or drunk. Swedes had an unfortunate reputation for excessive drinking. She swore that she never would fall into the trap of such behavior, nor spend much time around people who did.

47:30:00. 47:29:59. 47:29:58.

The women's world record holder owed her first name to her mother's love of the Swedish rock group, ABBA. Her birth certificate listed her name as Abba, with two "b's." Aba got tired of people making funny comments about how she spelled her name, so at age sixteen deleted one "b" to silence them. The rock group got its name from the first names of its musicians: Anni-Frid, Benny, Bjørn and Agnetha. Later, after meeting and marrying Bjørn Andersson, she claimed that the "b" she had deleted was Bjørn, so she would have room for a real person in her life with that initial and name.

Even if Aba had not become a runner for whom drinking could be a detriment to performance, she still would have held to that belief. Fortunately, Aba had found a man who shared her respect for the human body.

The world record holder prided herself on her stomach, not merely strong muscles, what some fitness buffs refer to as tight abs, the "six pack" coveted by those obsessive about how their bodies looked, but the ability of that stomach to take punishment like a prizefighter.

Aba pushed the toilet handle and watched as a swirl of water removed from her sight the repulsive remnants of her last meal. What was the cause of the sickness that had sent her reeling toward the bathroom the last several days since they had landed from Europe?

Aba Andersson moved from toilet to washbowl and turned on the water, not bothering with a glass, scooping water with one hand into her vomit-stained mouth to take at least some of the sour taste out of it. She was too lazy to brush her teeth. Her husband would have to tolerate her smelly breath, but that was okay. She thought now she knew the reason for the upset stomach that had kept her from the press conference the day before. Aba knew her own body well, since it so much was the focus of her daily life.

She looked at her reflection in the mirror, the fat-free body of a world-class female runner. When last measured, Aba had tested only 7.2 percent body fat, almost enough to brand her as anorexic were it not the fact that she was naturally skinny, lifted weights each day, ran 180 kilometers a week (112 miles, American) and functioned like a garbage disposal unit when sitting at table with food in front of her. Looking at her own naked body, Aba stared at her own breasts, barely pancakes, like those of many fast females. She could hardly remember the last time she had a period. Two years ago, when a stress fracture limited her training, and she had gained a few pounds.

MARATHON

Aba turned and headed back into the hotel room and slipped under the covers next to her husband Bjørn, also naked like her. As she did, she squeezed him gently between his legs. Bjørn moaned, but did not move. They had made love last night before falling asleep with a passion, as they always did. But when Aba awakened in the morning, hardly knowing the time because her body was still in Sweden, her churning stomach forced a flight to the bathroom.

Aba squeezed Bjørn one more time between his legs, resulting this time in a response. "I know what you want," he said. "You're like a caged animal when you're tapering for a marathon. Like last night at 3:17."

"How do you know it was 3:17?"

"Because after you rolled off me and passed out—I thought you were dead for a minute—I looked at the clock."

"I thought you were asleep—or at least half asleep."

"I was faking it. I like it sometimes when you do all the work."

Aba gave him a playful slap on the cheek. "Bad boy."

"Want to make love?" Bjørn could feel his passion rising

Aba could feel that same rising against her body, but she burrowed her head against his neck, holding him tightly. "I just want you to hold me, if you don't mind holding Puke Face. I want to feel your naked body against mine."

The two lovers held each other, the only sound their gentle breathing. "Still sick?"

"Still sick. And it's your fault."

"Morning sickness?"

"Morning sickness," Aba confirmed, then said with startled voice, "How did you know?"

"I know your body better than mine."

"Naughty boy." She paused: "I think I'm pregnant."

"Good," answered her husband. "Then substituting placebos for your birth control pills did work."

Aba gave his cheek another playful tap. "You did not! I thought we were going to wait until after the Olympics to start a family."

Bjørn pulled back and stared in her eyes. They were blue, just like his, as certainly would be those of the baby if his wife were correct about her being pregnant. "Some things don't happen on schedule," he told her.

"I'm supposed to run a marathon on Sunday."

"You might not be pregnant."

"No, I am. I know I am, Bjørn. I want to bring your baby into the world, Bjørn. Our baby. I don't care about Sunday's race, or the Olympics."

"I don't either," said her husband, still looking in her eyes. He kissed her gently on her lips. "Whew. You do need to brush your teeth."

She aimed another slap at his cheek, but he ducked. They both started laughing then there was a long period of silence. Aba finally whispered in her husband's ear: "Can you imagine me a nursing mother? I wonder what it will be like to have tits again?"

Bjørn slowly lifted the sheets and stared at the barely perceptible bulges that served as breasts, surely soon to increase in size.

"I can't wait."

47:02:00

For the second time in just over twenty-four hours, Peter McDonald found himself standing on the balcony overlooking Pritzinger Place's North Hall, site of the Health & Fitness Exposition for the Lake City Marathon. The doors would open in two minutes at 9:00, signaling the official start of the marathon weekend, at least as it would be experienced by the 50,000 runners entered in the race. *Then the fun begins*, thought Peter.

47:02:00. 47:01:59. 47:01:58.

Observing the scene below, order had replaced chaos. The litter of cardboard and plastic that had blocked aisles Thursday morning had vanished to areas unseen, awaiting transport to a landfill. Teamsters no longer buzzed back and forth on forklift trucks delivering goods to booths. Certainly, they remained in the building, but had shifted to work their magic on a different convention in another of Pritzinger Places's mammoth halls.

Compared to the clatter heard yesterday, the hall today seemed eerily silent. Listen carefully and you could hear the humming of the heating and air conditioning system, but that existed only as unobtrusive white noise. The humming would cease to be heard within a few minutes, since as soon as the doors opened, the hall would fill with chattering runners, excited about their missions to run 26 miles 385 yards. So many people; so many of them new to the sport. Nearly 40 percent (analysis of race entries revealed) would be running their first marathon. Peter hoped each of them, along with the other veteran marathoners, achieved their goals. He knew it would not be easy given weather reports.

The Expo, Peter mused as he continued to observe the North Hall, could be classified as a work of Pop Art. No need to visit Lake City's Museum of Fine Art this weekend; here was where art was happening. The various booths in nine separate aisles running the length of the quarter-mile long hall contained everything from shoelaces on sale for a dollar to luxury cars costing tens of thousands of dollars.

While the central competition this weekend would be Sunday morning between runners vying for a half million dollars in prize money, an equally active competition existed among the exhibitors, each one competing with their neighbors for the attention of 50,000 runners. At this moment, the first of those registered runners stood outside in the hallway, waiting for the doors blocking their access to the Expo to swing open at precisely 9:00 AM. When the Web site clock and various other countdown clocks clicked over to 47:00:00, the Expo would begin. Runners would rush into the hall and descend one of the escalators near where Peter was standing to begin their marathon experience. It was about to happen: everything for which he and his staff had prepared for nearly a year.

There remained one minute before the doors would open. Using this last minute of unclaimed time, Peter allowed his eyes to wander to the booth of Metro Foods, the grocery chain that was one of the marathon sponsors. It was that booth where he and Christine Ferrara first had met. Given their respective positions—he the race director of a large sporting event, she the reporter for the TV channel that covered that event—it probably was inevitable that the two eventually would have encountered each other, but would some day they be telling children that Dad and Mom had met in a food store booth, amidst bananas and apples and oranges?

Peter could not *believe* he had allowed that thought to enter his mind. Without realizing he was doing it, Peter reached up and placed his hand over his neck chain, Carol's last gift to him. Twenty-four hours ago, when he thought of women it was to look backwards to the loss of his wife. And in that brief span of time, he suddenly found himself looking forward to the woman who might replace her. *Was there such a thing as love at first sight?* Does one, like the Italians claim, get struck by a lightning bolt: *un colpo di fulmine?* He tried to think back to the day that he and Carol had first met, then stopped the thought process. He was tired of looking back. Peter needed to look forward. He could almost hear Carol whispering in his ear: *Get over me, Peter. Get over me!* It was time for that empty space in Peter's bed to be filled with another woman.

And at that moment, the doors opened. Runners swept past Peter toward the escalator, the surge coming from those hoping to be first in line, most of them local runners, who would grab their numbered bibs and T-shirts, then head to jobs downtown, not stopping at any of the booths because they needed to get to work. A few of the businessmen looked at these runners rushing in and out as lost customers, but quite a few would return Saturday, often accompanied by one or more members of their family. Two to three times as many runners appeared on Saturday vs. Friday, although for some runners, the attraction of the Expo lured them both days. For runners accompanied by families, the Expo was like a circus, except with shoe and clothing companies in place of lions and tigers.

As runners moved onto the escalators, most failed to look at Peter or recognize him as race director for the Lake City Marathon. While always eager to promote the race, Peter preferred to keep a low profile. Although he granted reporters frequent interviews and appeared often on television because it was part of his job, Peter was without ego. He knew it was the race that was paramount, not him. Still, he did enjoy the interchange with his public and had agreed to do four lectures explaining the marathon course, two each of the two Expo days. Those who had been participating in the Lake City Marathon did know his face. A few greeted him while rushing past:

"Peter, thanks for putting this together."

"It's my job," he replied with a smile.

"Peter, saw you on TV this morning. You've assembled a great field."

"You're my 'great field,'" responded Peter.

"Peter, we know you have connections. Could you change the weather?"

"Working on it," Peter acknowledged the subject on the minds of all runners. "Tried the Man Upstairs, but all I get is His voice mail."

The runner laughed and turned away as the escalator propelled him downward. As to connections with the Man Upstairs, Peter thought if anyone could claim a direct connection it would be his friend Celebrity X, *Papa Tonio*, Pope Tony. Peter suspected even the pope might have a difficult time moderating the weather. It's probably easier to change water into wine.

So far, security was tight. His friend's visit to town had not yet been revealed. Nobody had spotted him landing at the private airport south of town, or, if they had, they chose not to talk. Neighbors in the neighborhood where Tony grew up did not easily welcome strangers, particularly reporters.

Nevertheless, Peter could not help but wonder what the reaction would be when runners discovered who was running the marathon with them. Certainly, the word would spread as soon as Pope Tony stepped onto the course. Potentially, if too many runners attempted to get near the pope it could cause a gridlock that might stall the rear of the race. Peter hoped and assumed that would not happen. When Oprah had run Marine Corps and Lance Armstrong had run New York City, their fellow runners certainly had become excited by their presence, but each individual in the field was on his or her personal mission. They were not like paparazzi whose income demanded their getting close to marketable celebrities. Peter suspected that more than a few pictures would be taken of Pope Tony both by professional photographers and runners carrying their own cell phones or digital cameras. He wondered if the TV3 people would be mad for his not having given advance warning of this biggest of world celebrities. The marathon's TV contract was up for renewal this year, and renewing it was important for the success of the race.

Regardless, any public relations slight would quickly be forgotten in the excitement of having the pope in the race. Should he tell Christine? *Definitely not!* In fact, if they did later become an item, he would need to be very careful not to favor her over others within the media, who might see their connection as a conflict of interest.

Time to get on with my work, Peter decided. He moved toward the escalator and joined those descending. Peter turned to the runner on the step behind him, a man dressed in casual clothes. The man's name was Bob Veldman, his job an air traffic controller. He had driven in from the suburbs to secure his bib early, then do some sightseeing with his family later in the day before checking into a hotel for the weekend.

"What's your goal Sunday?" asked Peter.

"PR," answered Veldman. "Or it had been until I watched the weather report last night."

"What's your PR?"

"Two-thirty."

"I'm impressed."

"Thanks. I had been hoping to slide into the 2:20's, but...." Veldman allowed the comment to hang in the air.

"I assume you requested entry to Start Corral A."

"Done that. Not sure I plan to use it."

"Do you want my best advice?" asked Peter. The escalator had brought them to the lower level. The two stepped off to one side together.

"I'm listening."

"Run Sunday as a workout. Either the full distance slow or sixteen at race pace, then step off the course."

"Makes sense."

"Given your PR, you certainly can secure a last-minute number for New York. If you have any problem, give me a call—after the race."

Veldman laughed at that last comment. "Peter, I appreciate your concern. Everybody I know values all you have done to make this marathon what it is."

"It's my job," said Pete McDonald, shaking hands with Bob Veldman before heading into the hall.

FRIDAY

46:00:00

Precisely at 10:00 AM and with rush hour past, an officer with the Lake City Police Department, strode purposefully onto the street at the intersection of Columbia Drive and Rushmore Road, near the 26-mile mark of the marathon, and indicated to workers from the Department of Streets & Sanitation that they now could move sawhorses onto the street. *46:00:00. 45:59:59. 45:59:58.*

Waiting on the other side of the intersection, stopped by a red light after exiting the expressway, drivers suddenly found their direct route into downtown blocked, meaning they would need to waste time detouring left across the Rushmore bridge and onto Jefferson Avenue.

Not all seemed pleased. One irritated driver rolled down his car window and shouted, "Hey, what's the deal, Officer?"

"Marathon," the sergeant passively replied.

"Right," said the driver. "I forgot." The driver rolled up his window, apparently mollified.

In the last few years of Peter McDonald's tenure as race director, the marathon had attained status in the city akin to motherhood. For citizens like the driver forced to detour, the marathon had become such a constant part of city life—along with other activities such as Taste of Town and the Air & Water Show—that residents simply made small adjustments in their activities to avoid the marathon if they did not want to watch or participate.

Simultaneous to the police officer's action, other officers at separate access points to the finish area also barked instructions for workers to shove sawhorses into blocking positions. The marathon's finish line was now secured and would remain so from Friday morning until mid-afternoon on Sunday, no wheeled vehicles permitted into the area except trucks carrying equipment or golf carts used for transportation by the marathon staff. Members of that staff now began their tasks of directing the construction of apparatus, including a photo bridge over the starting line. Tomorrow, after the police closed several more blocks of Columbia Drive, the marathon staff would continue its occupation of the park, erecting a mammoth mid-street tent for runners to check their bags. It all happened by plan.

On Seventh Street, the avenue leading into the park near Hilliard Towers, the driver of a semi-truck maneuvered his vehicle into position to enter the now blocked start/finish area. He flashed a permit at the officer in charge. Re-

140

cognizing the TV3 logo on the trailer and without glancing at the permit, the officer motioned for one of the workers to move the sawhorses so the driver could proceed. The semi-truck driver tapped his cap to thank the officer and shifted into low, moving slowly forward. The driver planned to drop the trailer at its planned position near the finish line, then leave to retrieve his next load, a refrigerated car containing bananas.

Noel Michaels, executive director for the Lake City Marathon, Peter McDonald's most trusted assistant, watched as the crew she had assembled began the task of turning a busy city boulevard into a sports arena. She noted with satisfaction that the police had shut the street almost exactly at 10:00, as instructed. Having worked closely with the Police Department planning this weekend, she expected no less from them. She loved it when timeline items clicked into place exactly as they appeared on the clipboard tucked under one arm. *Thank you, Police Department,* Michaels thought, allowing a brief smile to cross her unlipsticked lips.

From her position near the corner of Columbia and Seventh Street, Michaels could look toward the finish line without seeing a wheeled vehicle occupying space except by her permission. She now began to walk south and in so doing passed the TV3 trailer being moved into position just behind the line. Guiding the semi-truck driver was Tom Schorr, producer-director of the telecast. The pair exchanged waves, but not words. Schorr had a timeline just as crowded as that of Michaels, focused exclusively on producing the telecast that would be viewed both locally and as far away as Japan, marathoning being a high-interest sport in that country. For the next two days, neither Michaels nor Schorr would get much sleep other than catnaps taken when they could find time. On Schorr's schedule later that weekend was a production meeting that would be attended by the "talent," those individuals with on-camera roles during the marathon. That included Christine Ferrara.

Noel Michaels possessed almost a fanatical passion for perfection. The executive director of the Lake City Marathon expected everyone from staff to volunteers to city employees to perform their assigned tasks on time, exactly as prescribed. She measured their performance by referring regularly to the clipboard timeline. Clipped onto the clipboard were a half dozen sheets of paper labeled "LCM Timeline" (LCM for Lake City Marathon). This pre-prepared timeline allowed the race's executive director to know exactly to the minute, almost to the second, whether or not marathon arrangements were moving smoothly—and if not, she wanted to know why so she could bring her considerable intellect to bear fixing the problem.

Despite her intense knowledge of operations, since minutia was what motivated Noel Michaels in her life work, the executive director depended on the clipboard timeline to keep her and her staff working in synchronization. In notes next to the Street Closure item, Michaels reminded herself: "Contact Peter." She needed to inform her boss that the start/finish area had been secured as scheduled.

There was also a most important column on the left side of the timeline. It said: "Done." Michaels methodically removed a red marker pen from the backpack she carried instead of a purse and placed a check in the "Done" column opposite the Street Closure line. Nearly all the preceding tasks before the 10:00 AM entry, everything from erecting bleachers alongside the finishing area to raising tents in the charity village, had similar checks indicating their completion—or at least that work on them had begun. And most of those missing checks would have their appropriate boxes filled within the hour or Michaels would be on her hand radio wanting to know what was causing the delay. In dealing with staff members, Michaels did not shout, she did not swear, she normally did not punish with even a stern look. But a pensive glance from the tough-minded executive director in response to an unfulfilled task sent ripples of fear through the marathon staff. Everybody liked Noel Michaels, but nobody wished to displease her.

Michaels removed a digital phone from the backpack and with a few quick thumb motions sent a text message to Peter McDonald: "Streets closed." She knew that Peter was busy at the Expo, probably about to begin one of several course lectures. If already on stage, he would not acknowledge the message immediately, not wishing the audience to spot him multi-tasking. As she was about to return the handheld wireless device to her backpack, it beeped at her. A glance at the screen indicated to Michaels that it was Peter responding with a brief, "OK." He must not have started his lecture yet.

The executive director punched a button to delete the message and permitted herself another brief smile, second one in the last several minutes. Should Task continue to match Time as the weekend progressed, Michaels would continue to smile and those on her staff around the executive director also would sport smiles. She expected to stay on schedule with the large number of tasks identified on her clipboard. Everything listed, she could control. She was less certain about what she could *not* control, the major worry being the predicted hot weather. Was the medical tent both staffed with enough doctors and enough equipment in case larger numbers of runners than usual needed treatment? Do we have enough ambulances on call? And given the forecast, was there even the remotest possibility that they might need to shorten the marathon, cut the distance run to an alternate shortcut course? She and Peter had a contingency plan in case this became necessary. (Contingency Plan A.) And another contingency plan to deal with the threat of lightning. (Contingency Plan B.) A decision to shorten the race could come either before the start or even after should temperatures rise and the medical tent overflow.

Noel Michaels had not trained to direct operations for a marathon, nor had the tall and brown-haired executive director, growing up, even run much except as conditioning for volleyball, the focus of her early life. She attended Villanova University on scholarship, starting all four years, her specialty leaping high above the net and smashing the ball back at opponent's faces. Michaels' aggressive play earned her All-American status her last two years with the Wildcats and an invitation to train at the U.S. Olympic Center in Colorado Springs to see if she was good enough to make the national team. Her coach at college and the coach of the national team said she was.

Not interested, Michaels told them. She was tired of leaping above the net, plus her knees ached. Her father, member of a state championship basketball team in high school, had arthritic knees. She did not want to follow suit, so Michaels collected her Bachelor of Arts degree with a major in education and accepted a position as sixth-grade teacher in a suburb of Lake City. She passed on an invitation to assist the high school volleyball team and started to run to avoid gaining weight.

One door closed behind her; another opened in front, because surprisingly, Michaels found she enjoyed running, despite having despised the activity when forced to do it as part of her volleyball conditioning. What appealed most to her was that it was a sport where your success or failure was not dependent on teammates. Running gave back to you exactly what you gave it. More to Michaels' delight, her knees no longer pained her, particularly if she avoided hard surfaces and ran mostly on the crushed limestone paths that drew so many to Lake City's lakefront.

Michaels, however, resisted the temptation to race, although she easily could have won age-group prizes. She had enough of competition as a volleyball player to last a lifetime, but she did enjoy being around runners, so volunteered to assist at several smaller races sponsored by the Lakeside Runners, the umbrella organization that served the sport locally. Her volunteering duties brought her to the marathon and a series of increasingly important positions around the finish line, which resulted in her getting to know race director Peter McDonald.

One year at the marathon, she received the assignment of escorting the women's winner, a Romanian, to the awards ceremony. Because of the telecast, the ceremony was scheduled to occur only a few minutes after the women's winner crossed the line. This was not enough time to allow the winner to recover, since even before the laurel wreath had been placed on her head, she began upchucking a seemingly continuous stream of yellow liquid, all the

E.R.G. she had consumed during the previous 26 miles. Most of the liquid hit the street: some of it splattered Michael's shoes. Stomach emptied, the Romanian smiled at Michaels and offered in accented English, "I'm okay now,"

"My shoes aren't," said Michaels, meaning it as a joke, although the humor in the situation failed to translate well. The Romanian runner became flustered and offered to buy Michaels a new pair of shoes. Michaels laughed and said that was not necessary, free shoes being a perk offered to volunteers. Besides, the Romanian wore shoes other than Nitro, a marathon sponsor. Michaels handed the women's winner off to Peter, who supervised the presentation of a 6-feet-wide cardboard check with the sum $100,000 written on it.

Following the ceremony, Peter descended from the awards platform and, noticing Michaels awaiting assignment to another task, asked her almost in passing: "Why don't you work for us full-time next year?"

"That's reward for having a woman barf on my shoes?"

"No, I'd been thinking of hiring you anyway. The marathon is getting too big for a small staff or volunteers to handle."

Michaels did not know if she wanted a new job. She enjoyed teaching sixth-graders. It was what she had studied for at Villanova. But Peter already was moving in the wake of the winners, headed to a press conference.

"I'll call you next week," Peter promised, and when he did, Noel Michaels protested that she had a contract for the school year.

Peter refused to accept that as an excuse: "Come work for us in June after school gets out." The race director added: "My uncle taught school. He used to paint houses all summer to help support his family. Organizing marathons is easier than painting houses in August."

After her first summer on the job, Michaels was not convinced that was a true statement, but she loved the work and the interface with a staff focused on making the Lake City Marathon not merely the best event in the U.S., but best in the world. She abandoned her career as teacher and after several years, Peter rewarded her with the title executive director and a salary considerably higher than she would have earned in her previous job.

Organizing a marathon, however, resembled school teaching in some ways. As a teacher, you needed a lesson plan: everything you and your students would do each day. As the marathon's executive director, Michaels' lesson plan was the half dozen sheets attached to her clipboard: the LCM Timeline. With a red mark in the Done column beside the line item Street Closure, Noel Michaels regarded the next tasks needed to be completed. Among those planned for the rest of the day were: Elite Athlete Press Conference, which she would attend at 3:00; Security Venue Signage Distribution, scheduled for 4:00 (although that time was flexible, as noted under the Time Sensitivity column); and the Hospitality Kick-Off Reception at the bank, beginning at 7:00, ending at 10:00.

Peter firmly but politely had informed Michaels that her attendance was essential, particularly because of the bank recently having been acquired by Shelaghi, the Irish conglomerate. There were new bosses to be met and schmoozed. Despite a distaste for schmoozing, Michaels would accede to Peter's request to attend, but probably would not stay long. She had a half dozen more tasks to fulfill before she could get to bed later that evening. *If* she got to bed, since who knew what crisis might develop? And although she would never voice the comment, she knew that if the bank's new owners cancelled their sponsorship with the result that most of the staff, including her, lost their jobs, she could always return to teaching.

Michaels was unmarried. She did not live with anyone. Like most of the staff, she was staying at Hilliard Towers, so it was a walk of only several minutes from her work station to her hotel room and as short a walk back Saturday morning when another page of line items defined her day's work.

If everything went as planned, all of the lines on the half dozen pages on Noel Michaels' clipboard soon would have red marks in the "Done" column signifying they had been successfully completed. Only the weather forecasts continued to haunt Noel Michaels.

45:01:00

Captain Robert Newsom towered over the podium as he waited to begin roll call in the main auditorium of the Central Police Station. A former college basketball player, Newsom stood 6 feet 9 inches tall and weighed 235 pounds, maintaining a trim look through regular weightlifting as an example to his men. The roll call gathered policemen assigned to supervisory duties marathon day. It would begin precisely at 11:00, since Captain Newsom did not like wasting time, his or the time of others.

45:01:00. 45:00:59. 45:00:58.

Newsom grew up on Lake City's South Side with dreams, like so many black kids, of playing in the National Basketball Association. These hoop dreams carried him through high school where his size allowed him to dominate play. He got mostly passing grades, because why study when you score 20 points a game? Four years sitting at the end of the bench at Valparaiso University, however, put paid to his hoop dreams. Newsom relieved his bench-sitting frustration by doing something he had never done before: He studied. Much to the police officer's surprise, he found he enjoyed exercising his mind as much as exercising his body, graduating with the degree in criminology that led to his current job.

Reflecting back on this metamorphosis, happily married and possessed of three well-grounded children who did not spend as much time as had their daddy at the playgrounds, Newsom sometimes confessed, "Thank goodness, I never learned how to hit the outside shot." His wife Amanda could only smile and echo, "Amen," although the dangers of her husband's job served as a constant worry for her.

With Peter McDonald standing nearby, Captain Newsom waited for the second hand of the auditorium clock to pass through one more rotation and signal 11:00 before calling roll call to order. Several dozen policemen, most of them sergeant's rank or above, occupied the seats in the front rows. These officers would supervise the lower-ranked policemen who would control traffic Sunday, a force of more than 800 total. The officers sat down front, because they knew Captain Newsom preferred they do so, and that if they sat in the rear, he would call them forward, not without certain embarrassment and ridicule from their fellow officers. Thus, all the front seats were filled with men dressed in blue.

The noise level in the auditorium remained high as the officers waited for Captain Newsom to begin. They chatted freely among themselves about their jobs, their families, but mostly about sports, a safe subject where you could suffer disagreements and still maintain working relationships. These were men who carried guns as casually as regular citizens carried cell phones.

Few discussed the Lake City Marathon, despite that being the subject of today's roll call. In honesty, running as a competitive sport appealed little to the men in blue. Their main interest in the race was that they got paid overtime for spending a Sunday seeing to the safety of 50,000 runners. It cost the marathon nearly a quarter-million dollars to obtain police protection, but you could not run a footrace through the central part of the city without that safety shield. Policemen controlled traffic at each intersection to assure that no cars interfered with the smooth flow of running traffic. They also controlled spectators, who had a tendency to creep forward into the streets, narrowing the lane for runners. Most important, the men in blue provided the first line of support should a runner collapse.

Starting, Captain Newsom offered a few words related to a second roll call planned for all policemen at 5:00 in the morning on race day. He then yielded the podium to Peter McDonald. The race director thanked the policemen for their presence before flicking a button that caused a map of the marathon course to fill the screen behind him. At this moment, Christine Ferrara entered

146

from the back of the auditorium, accompanied by Edmund Giesbert, her cameraman. In the rush of the morning's activities, Peter had forgotten his invitation to Christine to attend. Obviously, she had spoken to Captain Newsom earlier and encountered no opposition. Peter worried about his own impetuousness. Some of what he planned to tell the policemen probably should not leak to the public. As Peter began his talk, Edmund moved to a position where he could film the action. Christine remained in back.

Peter offered a quick review of the course, suggesting that the policemen consult the map in folders provided them. He described how the marathon course wound through and around the central city, a mini-review of the talk he had given earlier to runners at the Expo. Using a laser pointer, Peter identified fifteen aid stations featuring water and E.R.G. and as many medical aid stations, each of them evenly spaced to provide maximum coverage. "Think of this as a series of protective umbrellas over the heads of runners," Peter offered. Ambulances would be parked at most medical aid stations, or could be summoned quickly from nearby hospitals and fire stations.

It was a rolling support system, since as the mass of runners passed the early stations, supplies could be leapfrogged to stations further along the course, particularly to the critical late miles, where help might be most needed for runners pushing themselves to the limit on a hot day. Because the course looped back and forth, medical personnel and ambulances assigned to a single medical aid station could provide coverage at several points in the race. Noel Michaels, Peter's assistant, had carefully chosen these locations. Given the police protection and medical support, runners probably were safer running a marathon than participating in any other activity at any other place at any other time of the year. One research study matching traffic accidents with running incidents even suggested you were more at risk driving the 26 miles of the marathon course than running it!

Heat, however, caused this risk ratio to rise. "It's going to be hot," Peter said. "Even the elite runners will struggle—but they'll be off the course in a couple of hours. Most at risk are those who take three, four, five and six hours to finish. They'll still be running into the afternoon under adverse conditions.

"These are the people you need to protect," emphasized Peter. "And you need to protect them from themselves."

Peter looked toward Captain Newsom and stepped aside, allowing him to talk. Captain Newsom reminded the policemen what they already knew about how to summon medical help, radioing for a technician or, in the most serious cases, calling for an ambulance. "We do have back-up," said Newsom. "When an ambulance heads to the hospital, another ambulance moves to take its place at the medical aid station."

FRIDAY

One of the lieutenants in the front row asked about contingency plans. Peter responded: "We've always had contingency plans in case of terrorists, a fire in a high-rise, a suspicious package, lightning, even a tornado. And, of course, hot weather." He proceeded to describe those plans, most of them unknown to the public. The police did not want terrorists to know preventative procedures related to their threat.

In case of hot weather, Peter explained, the contingency plan was to divert runners back to the finish line over previously established routes: "Unfortunately, marathoners are highly motivated people. Like geese heading south for the winter, they are programmed to get to the finish line. They have trained months for their marathon. For a large number, it may be a first marathon with extra self-pressure to stay the course. Many raise thousands of dollars for charity; they will not want to admit to their supporters that they failed, even for reasons out of their control."

Peter paused, knowing that he had some additional information to provide the policemen assigned to marathon duty, some very important information related to the safety of one individual in the race: Celebrity X. He could not tell them X's identity, otherwise it would be like throwing a match into a parched grass field. The news would spread like a wildfire.

The race director looked toward Christine Ferrara. "Ms. Ferrara, I apologize, but I need to ask your cameraman to stop taping. This is somewhat sensitive information that the public probably does not need to know." Edmund lowered his camera and retreated to the rear of the auditorium. Christine placed fingers over her ears to indicate they were plugged.

Peter began: "An important celebrity will be running the marathon. For security reasons, I cannot offer the individual's name. All I can tell you now is that you will all receive further instructions on Sunday, so that you can pass that information onto your men." Peter paused again to see if any of the officers had a question. None had. They all knew the meaning of the word "security." They would do as instructed. Peter could not predict with any certainty how the public would react to the presence in the race of the pope. He felt as prepared as anyone could be and hoped there would be no problems.

Peter thanked the officers for their attention and allowed Captain Newsom to complete the briefing, confirming that those in the audience knew their assignments, so they could organize the assignments of the larger number of policemen under their command. As the policemen left the hall, Peter observed Christine Ferrara move down the center aisle with Edmund, her cameraman, for a pre-arranged interview with Captain Newsom. He waited at a distance as Christine pointed her microphone at the Captain, undoubtedly asking him some question related to police protection on marathon day. Twenty minutes to complete roll call, less time than he had allowed on his schedule.

44:40:00. 44:39. 44:39:58.
He just might have time for a cup of coffee before heading back to work.

44:39:00

Because Starburst was one of his sponsors, Peter McDonald knew there was a coffee shop only two blocks from the Central Police Station. He asked. She hesitated. Christine Ferrara glanced at her cameraman packing his equipment into the back of the TV3 truck. Edmund pretended not to notice the continuation of this mating dance featuring reporter and race director.

"I need to get on to my next assignment, but...." Christine said to Peter, drawing out the last few words as she looked at her watch.

44:39:00. 44:38:59. 44:38:58.

"What's your next assignment?" asked Peter.

"Fashion show."

"Lake Theatre."

"Right. How did you know?"

"One of the models is running the marathon."

Christine's journalistic instincts momentarily pushed aside her emotional instincts, the fact that she had just been invited to have coffee with a very interesting man. "Would that individual happen to be a supermodel?" she asked that interesting man.

The interesting man failed to respond. He merely smiled, which teased her more. Christine realized that one of the individuals she was scheduled to interview at the fashion show was, indeed, a famous celebrity, one whose face and figure was featured prominently on the covers of tabloids and magazines. Curiosity aroused, she probed: "It wouldn't be Naní running the marathon, would it Peter? You admitted at roll call that a celebrity was running the marathon, someone very famous whose name you could not provide because of security reasons."

Peter continued to duck the question. "Stop being a reporter, Christine. I told you to plug your ears when I made that statement. Anyway, the subject was coffee. We're cutting into the few minutes I have available before heading back to the Expo."

"I don't have a car."

"I can drop you at the theatre on my way back to the Expo."

FRIDAY

Christine still hesitated, worried as a newcomer to the station about proper protocol on the job, whether becoming involved with a source compromised her journalistic ethics. From the inside the TV3 truck came her cameraman's voice: "Christine, I think you need a coffee break!"

A few minutes later, Christine found herself seated opposite Peter at a Starburst Coffee Shop, using a stick to stir cream into her coffee: regular, large, although it actually was their smallest size. Peter ordered the same: regular, large, but no cream. *He's a purist,* she thought. They were not entirely incompatible. *I can live with it.* At least he didn't order some silly flavored blend, probably because neither of them had time to wait for an exotic beverage.

Christine started to sip her coffee. Peter blew into his, seeking to cool it before taking a first sip. *Why hasn't he spoken?* Christine worried. *Why haven't I spoken? He's going to think I'm boring. He'll never ask me out.*

She used a fork to snip off a piece of scone. Peter bit into an oatmeal and raisin cookie. "This is probably lunch for me," he said.

"Me too," said Christine. *Our first meal together,* she thought, although she never would have dared let him know what she was thinking.

The silence continued. Peter finally broke the silence, and it would seem almost as though he were reading her mind: "I'm going to appear foolish admitting this, but I can't think of anything to say."

"I can handle foolish."

"It's just that my mind is cluttered with marathon plans, and here I am seated opposite a very attractive woman, and I'm thinking of it and not her. Am I going to get in trouble admitting that?"

Very attractive. Christine registered that compliment, but she avoided reacting to it: "Peter, you'll never get in trouble with me telling the truth."

"I didn't think I would."

And for precious seconds, Peter and Christine said nothing. Each covered the silence by sipping from their coffee cups, somewhat of an effort for him since the coffee still remained too hot to drink.

"We could stare at each other," Peter said finally.

"What?" Christine was incredulous at his remark.

"Stare at each other," Peter repeated. "People who have known each other for years would not feel obligated to talk. But we've just barely met."

"Not quite twenty-six hours."

"Is that your marathon time? I thought you ran faster than that."

"You said we barely met. That's how long ago it was."

"You're counting?"

Christine paused before admitting, "I'm counting."

MARATHON

44:00:00

In the elite athlete's suite at Hilliard Towers, High Noon, forty-four hours before the start of the Lake City Marathon, two massage therapists pressed strong fingers into the soft tissue of two women runners favored to place up front in Sunday's race.

44:00:00. 43:59:59. 43:59:58.

"Gently, Love, gently," Fiona Flynn instructed the therapist working with her. "Make me feel good, but not too good. I have a race to run Sunday."

"You'll feel good," said the massage therapist. "After I'm done, you can sleep until Sunday morning."

"Not that," cooed *La Femme Fiona.* "I'l save my sleep for Sunday night—after the party."

On the other table was Tatanya Henry, the defending champion. Other than a guttural "Hal-lo" and nod offered to her fellow competitor on first entering the room, the Russian had said not a word. Fiona suspected that Tatanya knew more English than she wanted people to know. Pleading ignorance allowed Tatanya to avoid talking to reporters except through her husband Jacob. And she could avoid fraternizing with her rivals, focusing inward on the simple act of running. Fiona thought that not too bad an approach. *Would people believe me if I now claimed only to speak Gaelic?* she wondered. No, she was too garrulous for that approach.

Fiona and Tatanya lay naked under the sheets. They were being serviced by two female massage therapists. Fiona would have preferred a male therapist, but in the communal setting of the elite athlete suite it worked best female on female, male on male. Too bad, because she enjoyed having a male stroking her body. Yes, massage was not supposed to provide sexual arousal, but Fiona never allowed that prissy attitude to get in the way of a good feel.

"Anything I need to know?"

"Nothing deep," commanded Fiona Flynn, her voice thick as syrup, little more than a whisper. During some massages, her regular therapist would punish the muscles of her back with fingers that seemed as sharp as daggers. From her time on the table, she knew this was a necessary means for relaxing those same muscles. But deep massage was not what she wanted this close to a marathon. "Smooth and easy," added Fiona.

"Absolutely," said the therapist. She too understood that before a marathon her clients needed soothing massages, more than penetrating ones.

151

FRIDAY

Fiona lapsed into silence, preferring to let the conversation lag. She did not know the massage therapist, but felt that talk interfered with the object of a good sports massage: to both relax and heal the muscles. Some clients, she knew from her own therapist, chattered continuously; others fell asleep on the table. Fiona never did. Doing so defeated the purpose of massage.

She liked to concentrate on the parts of the body being massaged, focusing her mind on the point of contact: her hands, my muscles. She felt it helped the healing process. Even when she seemed on the edge of sleep, about to let go from the cliff with her fingertips and plunge into the depths of slumber, she kept one part of her mind awake so she could participate in the massage. To not do so, she felt, was to waste her money, and massage therapists did not come cheap, even though this one was free, supplied by the marathon office.

Yet knowing that, what did *La Femme Fiona* do while being massaged in the elite athlete's suite at the Hilliard? She fell asleep!

Fiona only became aware of that fact when she heard the massage therapist tell her to roll over and felt the sheet being lifted from her body. *What happened to the last half hour?* Fiona wondered.

The Irish Lass followed the therapist's instructions, rotating, moving from lying on her stomach to lying on her back. Fiona allowed a sigh to escape her lips as he did so. She felt herself—buttocks, then back, then calves—sinking into the table warm from her body, white sheets above and below enveloping her as though within her mother's womb. She felt the therapist's hands move beneath the sheets to grasp her left leg by the ankle, pulling it toward her, then pressing upward from ankle to shin to knee to the muscles of her upper leg, almost to her crotch, stopping delicately short. "Give a bit more attention to the quads," Fiona suggested. "I'm going to need quiet quads if I want to meet my goal on Sunday."

The door opened. Eyes closed, Fiona passively ignored that fact until she heard the singsong voice of Katie Hyang, a runner from the Northland Racing Team: "Excuse me for interrupting you, ladies, b-u-t...." The "b-u-t" was drawn out to last several seconds.

Fiona raised her chin and opened her eyes to see the Northland runner standing in the doorway with a broad grin on her face. A huge grin! Fiona knew that Katie's parents were Hmong, an ethnic group that in the last century had been chased during various wars from China to Vietnam to Laos to Thailand and finally to the United States, many settling in St. Paul, Minnesota. Katie was a work in progress, so typically American despite her roots. But hadn't anybody told this sweet young thing that she did *not* barge into someone else's massage. "This better be good, Katie. You just brought me back from Nirvana."

152

Katie giggled before continuing her comment. *You should be on the Disney Channel, Katie*, thought Fiona, who noticed that Tatanya had not stirred, had ignored the intrusion, so typical of the Russian.

"...Aba is P.G."

This caught Fiona's attention. Tatanya still remained motionless, perhaps not having understood the news brought by the young American.

"Aba is pregnant?"

"She's fluttering up and down the corridor waving a pregnancy-test stick with a plus on it as though she were conducting an orchestra."

"Is she still running Sunday?"

"I didn't ask," said Katie. "We were too busy hugging each other."

"Ker-ching, ker-ching," said Tatanya Henry.

"What?" said Fiona, startled at the Russian breaking her silence.

"Ker-ching, ker-ching."

Fiona knew what Tatanya meant and finally had proof that the Russian *did* understand more English than she wanted to admit. Probably knew Gaelic too. With Aba not running—or at least not running world record pace—all of them moved up one place in the standings. And the size of their paychecks simultaneously would increase. *Ker-ching, ker-ching.* The sound of a cash register.

Katie Hyang departed. Tatanya Henry said no more. Fiona Flynn returned her attention to the massage, trying to retreat into her previously held Nirvana, but without success, because her mind now was spinning. How would it affect her strategy? She had gone into the race figuring that with Aba in The field, she had no chance to win. That allowed her to arrive in town possessed of a certain savoir faire, knowing that she could deal with any situation that arose, even with the predicted hot weather. What did she care if high temperatures slowed her down? It would equally affect her other competitors.

But now? Fiona tried to relax under the strolling fingers of her massage therapist, but could not do so. *"Damnú air!"* The American runner's announcement had completely spoiled her massage. Oh well, there would be other days and other massages. Maybe it was time for the Irish Lass to start taking this race more seriously than she had up to this point.

43:00:00

Christine finally figured it out. She thought she knew the identity of the celebrity whose name Peter had so carefully been hiding. He refused to admit it after she quizzed him following roll call, but he did say a model was running the marathon. But not just any model. It appeared to be Naní, the supermodel. *Ta-Tumm! Elementary, my dear Watson.*

43:00:00. 42:59:59. 42:59:58.

Naní certainly was a celebrity whose fame transcended the runway and the covers of women's magazines—or the tabloids. A paparazzi magnet, her appearance anywhere causing photographers to sprout like crabgrass on a water-parched lawn. Should any eligible, or even non-eligible, male step within three feet of the supermodel, he immediately would be misidentified by the tabloids as a latest boyfriend. A regular on the talk shows, including Oprah, Naní's face and figure were familiar to fans all over the country, all over the world, or at least within those countries where couture was important.

Compared to Naní, all the other models appearing in the fashion show sponsored by The Field Store, a department store just down the block from the Lake Theatre, looked like ragamuffins dressed in dishrags. The supermodel was at least six feet tall, and she carried her height with a nonchalance that could only be described as regal. Naní wore an ankle-length white gown that accentuated her cocoa-colored skin. Her smile made the strobe lights that so often recorded that smile seem dim by comparison. A purple sapphire plucked from the alluvial deposits of the Umba River in Tanzania glowed on the third finger of her right hand holding a microphone. Its glow could not match the supermodel's own glow as she provided closing remarks for the show just seen.

"As some of you already know, I'm involved raising both money and awareness for AIDS Africa." Naní paused, making certain she had the audience's attention. "Today, thanks to all of you, your purchase of tickets, plus your pledges, we have raised more than $300,000 for this most worthy cause."

The applause was almost equal to that offered the runway walks and musical numbers just completed. Naní allowed the applause to build, then raised both hands for silence so she could continue: "That's the monetary part of the equation. Money is important. But equally important is awareness. Awareness among people in this country, but also awareness among the people of Africa who have the power within them to help stop the spread of AIDS, particularly among innocent children."

Naní did not explain. She left that statement hang in the air, knowing that in the wake of the glitz and glamour of the fashion show, and despite her beauty and celebrity, even a supermodel could hold an audience's attention only for so long. It was lunchtime. They were hungry. In addition to the show, their tickets allowed them entry to a luncheon at The Field Store. But she had one more important point to make.

MARATHON

"This is also the weekend of the Lake City Marathon. I know a few of you will be running the race. Can I see a show of hands?" A number of hands did go up, including those from a large group in the balcony.

"Through my AIDS Africa Foundation, I've encouraged several hundred runners to come to Lake City and run the marathon. Many are in the audience today." Naní pointed upwards to those seated in the balcony. "Through their donations and the donations of friends, we've raised at least a quarter million additional dollars for the cause." More applause as those seated down front turned to acknowledge those with hands raised in the balcony.

Yes, thought Christine, standing in a side aisle. *Peter's secret celebrity must be the supermodel. Who else? Did Naní say she herself was running the marathon, or did she merely acknowledge the charity runners who would run the race?* Christine was not sure, but it had to be her. Problem solved, but did she dare use this as a breaking story when Peter had pledged her to silence? It did not make sense to Christine. Why make Naní's participation such a secret when Peter had just told 800 policeman a celebrity would run the marathon, and here was this incredibly famous supermodel standing on stage boasting about how much money she had raised for AIDS Africa.

"Excuse me, Edmund," humphed Christine. "Why all the secrecy about some celebrity, when we're staring at a super celebrity right now?"

Edmund smiled: "Don't ask me, Christine. I just point the camera. I leave the commentary to others."

Christine allowed a loud sigh of exasperation to escape her lips.

Naní's interest in AIDS Africa certainly came from her African roots. Her mother had been Tanzanian: Miss Tanzania, if Christine recalled from her infrequent perusal of the tabloids. Trying to remember what she had read about the supermodel occupied Christine's thoughts as she waited to be led backstage by the media manager for the department store sponsoring the fashion show, Sandra her name. As the curtain closed and even before the audience rose and headed toward the exits, thoughts of hors d' oeuvres if not sugar plums dancing in their heads, Christine wondered whether she would get the requested one-on-one interview with Naní. And how much time? She noticed several other reporters with TV cameras in the auditorium and expected that she would need to fight for a few precious moments with the supermodel. Then the media manager magically appeared in front of the TV reporter.

"Naní would *love* to talk to you." The word "love" trickled off Sandra's tongue as though to indicate that, paparazzi-chased or not, *there was no one other than Christine Ferrara that Naní wanted to talk to!*

FRIDAY

Take that you other reporters waiting in line. Christine had not been in town long enough to realize that TV3 had clout. *The Four O'clock News* dominated its time slot, as did *The Five O'clock News* and *The Evening News* at six o'clock. TV3 was local. Other reporters worked for network-based stations. Those might have been more important to the supermodel in raising awareness for AIDS Africa nationally, but the savvy media manager knew that local people, not people out of town, patronized The Field Store and bought clothes. The others could wait while Christine got first call on Naní.

Sandra led Christine and Edmund up a stairway and to a door, behind which stood a security guard. He nodded as the three passed. Pandemonium ruled as models, their well-paid day's work completed, clambered out of fashionable clothing and into jeans and sweatshirts that would make them indistinguishable from people passing on the street. Sandra threaded her way through the pandemonium apparently knowing exactly where she would find the supermodel. And there stood Naní, still so elegant in her flowing white gown, talking to another reporter, a fashion reporter apparently led backstage by another media person. Seeing Sandra approach with her entourage, the fashion reporter took the hint and left without asking, getting a hug from Naní. The two apparently knew each other. Christine, however, approached as a stranger, someone Naní never had talked to before and might never talk to again. That worried her somewhat, except Christine had an inborn confidence that she could go one-on-one with the best and the brightest, and that description certainly fit Naní.

Christine framed in her mind her first question. She only needed one, and it would probably be something simple like: *Tell our viewers why you are here in Lake City?* One of her mentors at the station just left in Peoria had instructed her: "Less important than the question you ask is the answers they give." He told her to be a listener, not a questioner. Her mentor felt that too many novice reporters came to celebrity interviews awestruck with lists of questions in their mind, or even in notebooks, and they would fail to listen to the answers and stumble through the interview almost without purpose.

Christine would not do that. The TV3 reporter opened: "Tell our viewers why you are here in Lake City, Naní. May I call you Naní?"

"That's my name," the supermodel responded politely, and for the next five minutes, she discussed the fashion show, the fashion industry, her joy at being invited to town by The Field Store, but leading into her quest to raise money and awareness for AIDS Africa. Christine could see how important that cause was to the supermodel, so important that talk flowed out of her without Christine's prompting.

MARATHON

As the interview wound down and with The Field Store's media manager Sandra edging closer ready to step in, Christine probed: "One last question, Nani. You mentioned the marathon. Are you running?"

"I'm not going to say," Nani replied in a stage whisper that somehow made her response sound more intimate than conspiratorial. "But I will be at a press conference tomorrow at the host hotel along with Joseph Nduku, the defending champion. I hope you can attend, Miss…"

"Ferrara. Christine Ferrara. Yes, I will."

"It was a pleasure talking to you, Christine." Nani held out her hand. Christine was not yet in Nani's circle of reporters who earned hugs. Christine shook her hand, but the supermodel paused as though not wanting to be the one to walk away. Sandra edged still closer, ready to intervene if this new reporter in town did not get the hint that the interview was done, *finito!*

Christine lowered her microphone indicating that she had gotten the hint, then asked one more question, prompted more by curiosity than by a need for TV3 viewers to know: "Why Lake City? There are other high-profile fall marathons: Chicago. Marine Corps. New York."

"Peter."

"Peter?"

"Peter McDonald, the race director. He twisted my arm, gently. When he asked, I couldn't say no.'

Christine did not recall the name Peter McDonald appearing on any tabloid list of Nani boyfriends. As though she read Christine's mind, Nani added, softly: "I knew his wife."

Christine was stunned, but before she could press Nani for more answers to questions she had no business asking, Sandra intervened to escort the supermodel to her next appearance, the luncheon at The Field Store. Sandra told the supermodel she had several store executives who wanted to meet her. While agreeing and walking away with the store's media manager, Nani said she had to go potty then change into something more comfortable before the luncheon, but the fading conversation was lost on Christine.

His wife! Christine was certain Peter was not married now. He wore no ring. She had checked out that detail within ten seconds of their first meeting. This handsome hunk of a race director obviously was trying to date her. Certain promises had passed between the two of them. If he had a wife, he did not have her now. He then must be divorced, or at least separated. If so, how did that affect her? Was she comfortable dating a divorced man?

As the minutes and seconds continued to tick away to the marathon, Christine Ferrara realized that whether or not Nani was the celebrity running the marathon was not the most important item of news she had learned today—at least from her point of view. There was so much about this Peter McDonald that she did not understand.

42:30:00

Jonathan Von Runyon looked up from his computer to see one of the other *Ledger* reporters standing in the doorway of his cubicle. "Jonathan," said the reporter as a means of getting Von Runyon's attention. It was a reporter from the newspaper's Metro section, not sports.

Von Runyon did not reply verbally, but removed his glasses and raised his eyebrows to indicate he was receptive to whatever information the Metro reporter might have to offer.

"Jonathan," the reporter continued. "I just got a tip from one of my sources within the Police Department. Peter McDonald announced at roll call this morning that an important celebrity was running the marathon on Sunday. *42:30:00. 42:29:59. 42:29:58.*

Von Runyon removed a cloth from his pocket and began polishing the glasses just removed from his nose. "Celebrity? Do we have a name?"

"No name. McDonald offered none to the police. My source didn't know. I already asked. But he had the impression that it was a very important celebrity, one whose identity needed to be kept secret."

Secret identity? *Really!* That the identity of a celebrity running the marathon needed to be kept secret intrigued Von Runyon. *But why?* Each month, *Running Magazine* did a back-page feature on the latest fab person who had just joined the ranks of marathon runners. The list went on and on. Coincidentally, the *Ledger* reporter was just finishing a column mentioning a celebrity, whose single marathon run earlier had profoundly affected marathon running as an industry, if not as a sporting event. But that was over a decade ago. McDonald's secret celebrity certainly was not her.

"Can I call your source and ask him some questions?"

The Metro reporter standing in the doorway smiled: "One reason he remains my source is that I never reveal his identity."

Von Runyon nodded to indicate he understood and would not compromise the relationship. The reporter returned to his desk. Von Runyon continued to stare at the empty doorway for several seconds. Celebrity runner. So important his name must be kept secret. Or her name. A puzzlement.

Von Runyon wondered if this were a Machiavellian move on the part of Peter McDonald: that he might have recruited some super celebrity to grace his race and convince the bank's new owners to continue their sponsorship. The *Ledger* reporter immediately dismissed that idea. McDonald did not think that way. There was a press conference at the Hilliard in just over an hour. If he got a chance to talk to the race director in a corner, he might be able to tease some information out of him without tipping the story to others. If not, that person's identity could wait until later. Did it really matter?

Jonathan Von Runyon turned back to his computer and the column just completed. He pressed "save" then clicked on an "X," closing the file. Attaching it to an email message, he sent it to the newspaper's managing editor. The column would appear Saturday morning in the *Ledger* under the title, "How Oprah Ruined the Marathon."

42:00:00

Dennis Lahey seemed stunned when he learned how much it cost to stage the Lake City Marathon: $15 million! As a banker, Lahey had grown used to dealing with extremely large sums of money, but that seemed a bunch, particularly for a running race. Gaelic football was more Lahey's pleasure, and he still could not quite understand the fascination with running 26 miles 385 yards through the streets of some city. He just did not get it. Did it not hurt? Much better to sit around the pub with the boyyos and watch people kicking the be-jabbers out of each other on the Telly. They hurt, not you. Besides, was not Sunday morning for going to church? Stripping down to your skivvies seemed sacrilegious.

But $15 million: *Jesus, Mary and Joseph!* Shelaghi's executive manager had in front of him a pile of accounting sheets that summarized those costs, provided by Peter McDonald yesterday to Paddy Savitch. In addition to Lahey, a half dozen other Shelaghi executives had come to Lake City to oversee the transfer of power from regional bank to international conglomerate. All now were part of the group meeting in the Board of Directors room on the thirty-second floor of the Lake City Bank's skyscraper headquarters.

No executives from the Lake City Bank had been invited to attend the meeting, which would help determine the fate of the marathon and perhaps Peter McDonald's job. If any of the Lake City Bank executives had asked to attend the meeting, they politely would have been told that this was Irish business—although not exactly in those words. The bank executives, including director Robin Carter, would have been too savvy to ask. Actually, despite the marathon's dominating presence this weekend, its future was merely one line item on a crowded agenda. And only one of the Shelaghi executives actually was running the marathon, now forty-two hours away.

42:00:00. 41:59:59. 41:59:58.

Patrick Savitch, Paddy to friends, was easily distinguishable from the others. He weighed half as much as most of them and also stood a half head shorter than most. Despite his scrawny frame, Paddy Savitch was not someone you would choose to engage in a barroom brawl. More than anyone in the Board room, Paddy bore the look of the long distance runner. Two decades earlier, Paddy had attended Providence College on an athletic scholarship, that Rhode Island school traditionally serving as a magnet for impoverished but swift Irish runners seeking a hand up in the world.

Most of Savitch's college teammates had remained in the United States, but he saw more promise in returning to the Old Sod. It was not so much from a premonition that the Irish economy would boom, but more from a desire to return to his birthplace in Swords, a town outside Dublin, and reclaim his childhood sweetheart, Molly McFarland. Four years away at Providence had been like Purgatory, but as one who studied his catechism, Paddy knew that often you needed to spend time in Purgatory before arriving in Heaven.

Paddy and Molly were married soon after his return, and he went to work for a small bank in Swords, which was swallowed by a larger bank in Dublin, which became part of the growing conglomerate, Shelaghi. Paddy had been carried along from post to post to post from bank to bank to bank, not because he possessed a banker's mind, but because he stood out of the way of people who had those minds, yet still seemed to have the right response whenever one of them needed the answer to an important question. "Paddy, what do you think?" And he would tell them.

"Yes, that makes sense, Paddy. We'll do it."

Yet among the group he had accompanied to Lake City, Paddy was also much the junior executive, only recently promoted to vice president, added to the party mainly because he was a marathoner and might be able to offer a runner's perspective to any race-related discussions. Savitch had planned to run the Dublin Marathon this fall, but quickly agreed to run Lake City. He kept silent as discussions continued that might affect the future of that event. Normally garrulous in a bar with a pint of Guinness in hand, he knew that in the company of more highly placed executives, silence would be more likely to insure his advancement.

"Paddy, you keep your two lips sewed together," his wife Molly had warned him as she kissed him goodbye at the Dublin Airport.

"Ah Molly, I know that," her husband replied. "You'll be the only lass to get a touch of these lips."

MARATHON

"I'm talking about staying silent in business meetings," she scolded. Molly realized her husband knew when to bite his tongue, but nevertheless felt it her duty as a good Irish wife to offer a reminder.

Paddy had smiled and turned toward the waiting jet. The Shelaghi executives had flown to Lake City in a Gulfstream G550, coincidentally the same type jet that transported Celebrity X. Just before boarding, Paddy turned and gave Molly a wink that even a leprechaun could not match.

And now after having spent several days in town, having spent as much time sightseeing as visiting their newly acquired property, the Shelaghi executives finally met to consider the fate of the marathon along with other line items that seemed to provide a cash flow outward and none inward. Support of the Symphony of Lake City: There was another hemorrhage of several million dollars that seemed questionable for those whose tastes in music veered more toward The Furies than Mozart. Dennis Lahey and his cohorts would consider each and every line item, those with the largest numbers getting the brunt of their attention. At $15 million, and because it was happening this weekend, the Lake City Marathon was high on the agenda.

So, accounting sheets centered on the desk between them, the Shelaghi executives discussed the marathon. Lahey encouraged each to speak his mind, but all knew he would make the final recommendation to his superior back in Shannon. At this point, it appeared that Lahey would draw a red line through the $15 million marathon budget, a third of that sum supplied by the bank. The rest of the budget came from sub-sponsors, but sub-sponsors were not always easy to obtain during hard times. Lahey could hardly endorse lavish support of any athletic event at the same time he was allowing several thousand employees to lose their jobs over the next several years through a combination of attrition and outright firing. He would absorb a lot more heat from that action, and already had from the local media, than if he turned his back on this silly fetish of running through the streets in your shorts.

Dennis Lahey was first a businessman, always a businessman. He knew that if the conglomerate allowed the contract with the marathon to lapse, if Shelaghi permitted some other sponsor to move into the vacuum so created, even if the race expired or became diminished in importance because of inadequate finances, it would result in not one less plastic card being inserted into ATM machines around the city.

"Fifteen million dollars," said Lahey, pressing one stubby finger to the paper, tracing it beneath that bottom-line number. "That's a lot of money."

The bank executive now turned to the only individual who had not yet contributed to the discussion. "So tell us, Paddy, what do you think?"

"Dennis, I can't offer an honest opinion," replied Patrick Savitch. "You know I'm running the marathon, so I'm biased."

FRIDAY

"Ah, Paddy. We all have biases. It's just that we know yours."

41:00:00

C ompared to Thursday, a smaller group of reporters gathered in the media center at Hilliard Towers for Friday's 3:00 press conference. Waiting for Peter McDonald to start, Nelson Ogilvie knew that with Aba Andersson standing in the wings, he certainly did have a juicy news item to feed the press. One that might move the story off the sports pages and into another section of the paper more related to lifestyle. Ogilvie liked that. The bankers would like that.

Ogilvie looked toward Peter and got a sign indicating it was time to start. The media director nodded agreement. Peter tapped the microphone to make sure it was live, then began: "Forty-one hours to the marathon."

41:00:00. 40:59:59. 40:59:58.

Peter glanced to the side where Aba waited with her husband Bjørn. Aba had a smile on her face that would have made the Cheshire Cat envious. Bjørn offered a more contained smile, much more Scandinavian. Looking at him, Peter could not help but think that Bjørn filled a very necessary role in Aba's life: agent, lover, confidante, a man who was always there, but never got in the way, Aba's greatest supporter. All runners should be so fortunate.

"We are excited to have at our marathon this year, Aba Andersson," the race director continued. As though not willing to wait for more introduction, Aba stepped forward and moved to a position beside Peter by the podium. This caused the normally reserved reporters to offer a smattering of applause. As the world record holder, she did deserve a level of respect not offered to more mortal runners.

Jonathon Von Runyon's hands, however, remained folded in his lap. He considered it undignified to applaud for athletes at a press conference. He would never applaud for Tiger Woods, would he? Well, maybe for Arnold Palmer or Jack Nicklaus, but they were true athletes and gentlemen and millionaires to boot. However, a Swedish marathon runner? He would treat her with respect, but not act like some silly teenage rock fan.

Von Runyon's article in the *Ledger* this morning had continued the theme established on Thursday, that the Lake City Marathon might be in trouble both financially and artistically. Financially, because if rumors proved true that Shelaghi planned not to renew its contract, Peter McDonald would need to work fast to find a replacement sponsor. Artistically, because this year's

162

field did not seem as strong as in years past, particularly if compared to Berlin, Chicago and New York. Joseph Nduku was past his prime, Von Runyon thought. If the *Ledger* reporter was a wagering man, he might be tempted to put his money on another Kenyan, Kenyatta Kemai, who seemed hungrier than the defending champion. Von Runyon also sensed that the two Kenyans were not close friends, although this was a story line that would not interest his audience. It barely interested him. Now if Tiger Woods had someone as a sworn enemy, *that* would be something to write about.

And what was this about a celebrity, not yet identified? What celebrity on the national or world scene today possessed such fame that his or her identity needed to be masked from the public, that identity not revealed at roll call earlier this morning, according to the newspaper's source? Was that lead worth chasing? Did Peter have some trick up his magician's sleeve, one conjured so as to increase the possibility of Shelaghi extending its sponsorship. No, that seemed unlikely. The secret celebrity's identity could probably wait until Monday morning's newspaper.

Von Runyon also suspected that Aba Andersson was about to announce that because of some undisclosed illness, she would not start the race. The *Ledger* reporter would soon find out if that were true, as Peter continued his introduction of the world record holder.

"One of the reasons Aba agreed to run the Lake City Marathon—and despite what some cynics might think, it is not always about money—was that we have a flat course, a fast course and generally good weather in October." Peter said this even though good weather would not be present this year.

He continued: "Lake City offered Aba an opportunity to break her own world record. Fast course. Fast lady. If you were heading to Las Vegas, that's about as close to a sure bet that you could get."

Peter paused for effect, then added: "It won't happen, but it's not because of the warm weather." He turned to the runner by his side whose Cheshire Cat smile showed no evidence of fading. "I'll let Aba tell you why."

Before stepping aside, Peter lowered the microphone to compensate for Aba's height. She began to giggle. Tears began to form in her eyes. She glanced toward Bjørn, as though needing his permission to continue. She turned back to the now puzzled press and raised both arms as she might crossing the finish line in that now cancelled world record attempt.

"I'm pregnant!"

As the world record holder continued to talk about her pregnancy, discussing the possibility that she might still run the marathon, but well back in the pack, subject to a doctor's approval, except she did not yet have a doctor in Lake City, but Peter promised to find her one, Jonathan Von Runyon wondered why he had bothered to attend the press conference if this was all the hard news that the marathon had to offer. His bosses would have been better off sending one of the women reporters from the *Lifestyle* section than him, a serious sports journalist.

Really! In reporting on his favorite sport, Von Runyon did not waste much time covering golfers incapable of breaking 100, yet in the sport of long distance running, joggers often received as much attention as world-class runners finishing hours in front of them. An insult to the most talented, he believed.

Von Runyon thought of the tip offered by his colleague, Peter McDonald's so-called secret celebrity. Once Aba finished her discussion of news fit only for women readers, he would press Peter privately on that issue. Not because he really wanted to know. Mainly because Von Runyon wanted to prove to Peter that he was still on top of his game.

40:15:00

C hristine Ferrara did not get it. Earlier this morning, Peter had told the assembled policemen at roll call that an important celebrity would be running the Lake City Marathon. But he would not reveal the name of that celebrity, claiming security considerations. *Sigh!* None of the policemen questioned this reason, or seemed to have much curiosity as to the celebrity's identity. But she did. Was it her reporter's nose for news or simply feminine curiosity? Maybe a bit of both.

Later, when Peter offered to drive her to the fashion show, he admitted that one of the models was running the marathon. He would not identify the model nor admit that she might be the celebrity mentioned to police. Yet only one model in the fashion show came even remotely close to being famous: Naní. It seemed obvious that the woman whose face and figure had launched a thousand tabloids was the celebrity.

Or was she?

When Christine interviewed Naní after the fashion show and asked if she were running the marathon, the supermodel did not duck the question, but she had not exactly answered it either. Naní said she would appear at a press conference tomorrow with Joseph Nduku, the defending champion to say—what? *Strange. Strange. Strange!* Perhaps Ms. Supermodel had taken a vow of silence concerning her marathon intentions until after that press conference. News was news, and organizations like Lake City Bank like to control news. That's why they have public relations staffs. As the marathon approached,

Christine wondered whether Naní's running it would be the major buzz story—or would it be something else?

40:15:00. 40:14:59. 40:14:58.

Worrying Christine further was learning from Naní that Peter had been married before. When was Mr. Right going to admit that fact? Okay, she was being picky and naive. When he first extended his hand yesterday at the convention center, should he have announced: "Hi, I'm divorced." Her roommate Yolanda would have rolled her eyes in both directions like a Fourth of July pinwheel if told Christine expected that information on first skin contact. "Girlfriend, you go get your brain fixed," Yolanda would have said.

Maybe that was Christine's problem, her woman's brain. She had seen a funny video on the Internet by a comedian whose name she already had forgotten, but his routine focused on differences between the brains of men and the brains of women. Men's brains, claimed the comedian, consisted of a series of boxes. Each box was stuffed with information on one specific subject. And one box never touched the other. They never met. Men focused on one problem at a time. With that problem solved, they moved on to another.

Women's brains, on the other hand, were a jumble of wires, all of the wires interconnected, so that their brains constantly were going *bzzzt, bzzzt, bzzzt*, processing all available information. Their problems were intertwined, connected, jumbled together. This was one reason why women could be multi-orgasmic but not men, claimed the comedian straight-faced.

Still clinging cautiously to her virginity, Christine knew nothing about that. She was suspicious, however, wondering if some other reason brought Naní to town, if there was a relationship between Peter and the supermodel. "I knew his wife," Naní had said. *Is that all, Ms. Supermodel?* Christine realized that she was being silly. She only met this man yesterday, and already she was picking out silverware.

More to the point: why the big fuss over Naní running the Lake City Marathon? Why hide the fact, then hold a press conference? Her attraction to the paparazzi aside, was the supermodel that big a celebrity? Would her running Lake City cause people to stop eating their breakfast and rush to the curb to watch her pass? Would she attract as much attention as did Lance Armstrong and P. Diddy running New York, or Katie Holmes and Will Farrell running Boston or when the biggest celebrity of them all—Oprah—ran the Marine Corps Marathon?

And that was the person who Christine Ferrara was staring at now: Oprah, whose daily TV program appeared in Lake City just before *The Four O'clock News*, although on another channel. Christine, having skipped the just completed press conference, was editing the package featuring Naní at the fashion show when director Tom Schorr stuck his head into her cubicle and said to check out Oprah: "Guess who she has as guest?"

"Who?" Christine started to ask, but Schorr already was heading back to his office. *Who? Who? Who? Dammit, Tom, don't leave me hanging.* Christine sighed, a sigh so ferociously loud that it would have fluttered curtains all over the newsroom had there been any curtained windows. Sigh released, the reporter rose from her desk and moved to a wall featuring a dozen small TV screens, each tuned to a different channel. A large screen featured the TV3 telecast, currently a soap opera. Picking a remote off a table beside the wall, Christine punched buttons until the Oprah Winfrey Show replaced the soap opera on the large screen.

Sitting on the set with Oprah was—surprise, surprise—Ms. Supermodel talking about the Lake City Marathon, restating what she had said earlier in the day on the stage of the Lake Theatre, that she would be at the marathon with a group of several hundred runners who had raised more than a quarter-million dollars for her pet charity, AIDS Africa. "It's not about money," Naní told Oprah. "I want to promote awareness of the serious health problem faced by the children on that continent."

Christine was puzzled. She had just finished talking to Naní only two hours before, and there was no way to get from Lake City to Chicago (where Oprah taped her show) in that short a time. Was Oprah in town? Was she the celebrity running Lake City? Then it dawned on Christine—*bzzzt, bzzzt, bzzzt*—that the show had been videotaped earlier in the week. *Duhhh!* More than likely, Oprah's people made Naní pledge to stay silent about the marathon until the show aired. That would explain the supermodel's reluctance to reveal her plans—if she had plans. *Was she really running the marathon, or not? She had not exactly said so.* Christine began to feel more kindly toward Naní—unless there was something between her and Peter!

Oprah and Naní discussed AIDS Africa for several minutes before accepting questions from the audience. Naní insisted that AIDS in Africa was not a problem involving homosexual men, but rather heterosexual men infecting their wives, who then passed the disease to children not yet born. "The men are very proud," explained Naní. "They do not want to be instructed about sexual behavior, but they must if we are to halt the spread of this disease."

Serious business over, Oprah asked Naní if she planned to run the marathon herself? "Are you planning to beat my time?" Oprah's time of 4:29:30 had become a benchmark for many running their first marathon, particularly men. When P. Diddy ran New York, he appeared on Oprah's show and identified that as one of his goals.

MARATHON

Oprah had scolded the rapper: "You have to run your own race. You have to run to the rhythm of your own soul." P. Diddy did just that, running 3:42:46, which surprised many doubters.

Naní, however, refused to reveal her plans, whether she would run 26 miles with her group or stand on the sidelines cheering them on.

Oprah refused to allow Naní to sidestep the issue. "I can offer you immunity, put you under a Witness Protection program. Didn't one of your relatives run the marathon for Tanzania in the Olympics?"

"My uncle. We see each other on those occasions when I return home to my mother's village on AIDS Africa trips. I can tell you that he was more in awe of your performance than his own. He told me to wish you best the next time I appear on your show, which is broadcast in Dar es Salaam. Everybody loves you in Tanzania, Oprah."

"That is so sweet," said the world's most famous celebrity marathoner to date. "Thank you for coming, Naní, and we'll be back after this break." The picture broadened to show the full set, then shifted to the audience applauding, followed by a commercial for a women's hygiene product.

Christine continued to watch during the commercial break in case Oprah had more to say about the marathon, but when the world's most famous marathoner returned to the air, another guest was seated in the chair vacated by the supermodel. The next subject was food: how to prepare a delicious dessert for dinner guests. Interesting transition, thought Christine. At that moment sportscaster Mark Mallon, script in hand, appeared in front of the door leading to the studio. "Christine, you have that fashion package with Naní coming up on the next show?"

"Right, Mark!"

"Fade out by speculating on whether Naní plans to run the marathon. Or even Oprah. That will lead into my segment about Aba being pregnant."

"Aba is pregnant?"

"She just announced that fact at the press conference."

"Is she still running?"

"Wouldn't confirm the fact," said Mallon over his shoulder as he headed toward the set. "Has to talk to her doctor. But probably, yes."

Christine decided that TV3 did not need to broadcast soap operas. One was happening in the middle of the marathon. *Is she, or isn't she? And who is Peter's celebrity?* Christine figured that she would need to approach that subject carefully so as not to break her oath of confidentiality.

Christine tried to busy herself with preparations for the telecast, but her mind was not on what she would say on *The Four O'clock News*. All the electronic connections in her brain were going *bzzzt, bzzzt, bzzzt*. She wondered when her new boyfriend would finally admit he once had a wife.

FRIDAY

40:00:00

Being a male, **Peter McDonald's brain consisted of boxes separated** from each other, not a tangle of electronic connections as with females. Or so went the joke. Peter had not seen the comic monolog comparing male and female brains, but he would have agreed with that assessment if informed by Christine Ferrara.

Peter was too preoccupied with preparations for the marathon to access the box in his brain recently dedicated to Christine. There would come time for that later. Meanwhile, Peter could focus on the non-touching box that, if brain boxes had labels, might have been marked, "Warm Weather."

Forty hours before the start of the marathon, it remained the single most vexing problem that faced him. In contrast, whether or not he would lose the bank as sponsor was a problem to be faced at some later date. Aba's sickness? Done Deal. His media director Nelson Ogilvie conceded that they would probably get more good publicity out of that story line than if she had set another world record. Celebrity X? He was on hold. Peter was more worried about the welfare of the runners, his people, than the welfare of the race, which he knew would survive in some form or fashion regardless of decisions made by Shelaghi executives in town for the weekend.

The countdown clock on the marathon Web site continued to tick away the hours, minutes and seconds remaining before the moment when 50,000 runners would begin moving across the starting line to face one of the most hazardous tests in their lives: a long run on a too hot day.

40:00:00. 39:59:59. 39:59:58.

If Peter wanted to protect the runners entered in his race from heat-related problems, he needed to react quickly. Or be prepared to react. That is why he had convened a meeting at 4:00 in the Presidential Suite on the twenty-fourth floor of Hilliard Towers. A small meeting: three people. Three *key* people! Only Peter and Noel Michaels and Nelson Ogilvie. Race director, executive director and media director respectively. Those three key people plus TV3 weatherman Vaughn Johnson and medical director Nick Terrence, standing by in case Peter needed to reach them quickly on their cell phones.

Peter had just gotten an update from Johnson about weather predicted for Sunday morning. They had talked just before the weatherman headed for the studio to appear on *The Four O'clock News*. Peter had the TV set in the suite tuned to TV3 with the sound off. Johnson told Peter that he would set his phone on vibrate: "If you have an urgent question, call during a commercial."

Peter suspected that no question would be that urgent. The TV weatherman informed Peter that the forecast for mid-day temperatures in the 80s and high humidity held—although there were some systems still hundreds of miles from Lake City that might disrupt predictions. A mass of hot and dry weather off to the southwest might collide with a spiral of cold and moist weather up in Canada to produce high winds and thundershowers.

"If there's lightning striking anywhere near downtown," Johnson commented, "you might beg to have the warm weather back."

That was true, Peter agreed. If you have 50,000 runners scattered over 26 miles of city streets, you cannot protect them from all possibilities. He was not sure that any previous marathon had faced the problem of lightning striking. The race director remembered a cross-country race in high school. He and his teammates had run to get under a tree, before their coach (ironically Pope Tony) yelled to get into the school bus. Watching a golf tournament on TV, he remembered it being delayed because of lightning. Each year in the United States, lightning kills an average of 62 people and injures 250 more.

Golfers and cross-country runners might pause in their activities to wait out a bad storm passing overhead. With highly motivated marathoners, who had trained months for their moments of glory, not all would want to step off the course with the clock still running. Thanks to Noel Michaels' foresight, they had a contingency plan for routing runners into shelters, mostly schools and public buildings along the course. But forcing runners to abandon their dreams and goals to run for shelter, even with lightning striking around them, would not be an easy task.

Also at risk were people not running a marathon. Medical emergencies occur to ordinary citizens all the time. Peter shuddered when thinking of what the city's response—any city's response—might be if faced by a true disaster: a terrorist attack, a nuclear holocaust, or some natural catastrophe such as an earthquake or tornado hitting downtown. We should be more prepared after 9/11 than we are now. *Would it take several more airplanes crashing into skyscrapers to wake this nation up?*

More likely than a terrorist attack was the more routine threat posed by hot weather. The Lake City Marathon Web site displayed the USATF Guidelines related to heat: "There may be times when we feel it is unsafe to proceed with the race. While we recognize the aspirations and commitment of those that have entered the race we will make decisions about the race based on the participation population as a whole."

The statement continued: "Specifically, when weather or other physical conditions present a danger to participants as a whole, we will maintain the right to cancel the race."

Peter wondered how many runners bothered to read that statement. It was like agreeing to accept the terms of new software for your computer: Most people clicked "accept" without reading what they had just accepted. Yet in an emergency, he might need to either stop the race or not even allow it to start! That had happened recently at the Western States Endurance Run, a 100-mile race through the Sierra Nevada mountains near Squaw Valley, California. Because of wildfires burning nearby, organizers cancelled the race, offering everybody entry for the following year. But only four hundred or so runners are allowed entry each year into Western States. It would not be as easy for a marathon that had accepted the entry fees of 50,000 runners to say, "don't start," particularly after their entry fees already had been spent on operations. You can't take down several dozen tents in Jefferson Park and not pay the companies from which you had rented them.

Peter worried that the city, conscious of liability issues, might force this choice on him as late as race day morning. Runners who had paid $110 for entry and hundreds of dollars more for airline tickets and hotel rooms would not take such a decision kindly, even if made for their own safety. It might cause a mini-riot with runners forcing their way onto the course, running without the normal city-provided protection. Peter could not imagine conditions so extreme that he would cancel the race, but it seemed more and more likely he might need to shorten it, at least for runners back in the pack.

The actual act of closing the course had worried Peter when they discussed this contingency several months earlier. He asked Michaels: "How do you stop people who demand to continue?"

"You don't," Michaels replied. "But you make it increasingly difficult for them to do so." Peter's assistant pointed out that back in the pack, gaps inevitably open. "You slide a wooden barrier into the street. A few runners may dodge around the barriers, but during the next gap you slide a few more barriers across until the entire street has been blocked. Next, you drape the barrier with banners—and we have some from the Expo we can use. That will prevent runners from ducking under the barriers. Spectators will start moving onto the street adding to the wall. Most runners will comply."

"A few will not," Peter had suggested to Michaels.

"They'll find themselves running in a vacuum. If they look a quarter mile ahead and a quarter mile behind and see nobody running with them, they'll begin to wish they had made the turn."

So the course closing had become Contingency Plan A. Peter could decide to execute that plan before the start of the marathon, shortening the race even for the elite runners. That would be a very unpopular decision, one he hoped not to make. Most likely, they would allow most runners to go the full 26 miles and only ask the slowest one to stop short.

A second plan, Contingency Plan B, involved a temporary suspension of the race: sending runners to shelter to wait out a severe thunderstorm involving lightning. In his talk to the group, Peter mentioned B only briefly.

Peter shifted to another problem, one involving Celebrity X. "Jonathan Von Runyon somehow has caught onto the fact that a secret celebrity is running the marathon. He confronted me at the end of the press conference, out of the earshot of others apparently because he does not want to tip them."

"Does he know the celebrity's name?" asked Ogilvie.

"No."

The media director laughed: "Then don't come to us for sympathy, Peter, since you haven't even told us that fact!"

Michaels asked: "Do you expect a leak in the marathon office?"

"No, nobody knows even as much as you do. But it's hard to keep secret the fact that a celebrity is running the marathon, when you make that information available to 800 police officers."

"But they don't have a name."

"No."

"So worst case: Our beloved reporter discovers the name and announces it to a breathless public."

"Then Celebrity X doesn't run."

"You call him Celebrity X? You haven't ever shared that information with us until now," said Ogilvie, more amused than angry.

Peter did not answer. He merely shrugged.

"Then it's not a problem. If Von Runyon learns this Celebrity X's identity and reveals it, he kills his own story and looks foolish doing it."

"True," said Peter, rising from his chair to indicate the meeting was over, "but he may not be smart enough to realize that, and I do not intend to be the one to tell him."

39:15:00

N ice transition," offered Mark Mallon. The TV3 sports director stopped while passing Christine Ferrara's cubicle following *The Four O'clock News*. Mallon was referencing Christine's fashion show interview with supermodel Nan. She had ended the package by saying: "Everybody's favorite supermodel came to town not only for a fashion show, but she also is here supporting a group of runners running the Lake City Marathon to raise money for AIDS Africa. But is Naní running the marathon? I asked her, but she just would not say."

Christine stretched those last four words for emphasis: "...just... would... not... say."

Christine and the anchorman discussed that question briefly before the commercial break. After that break, with Christine off the set and Mallon now in her chair, the two men continued the discussion after which the sports director slipped smoothly into the news that world record holder Aba Andersson was pregnant. That led into a clip from Aba's press conference earlier that afternoon. Mallon closed by mentioning that TV3 would cover the marathon live Sunday starting at 7:00 AM., an hour before the start.

39:15:00. 39:14:59. 39:14:58.

The shift from news to anchor to sports had gone as smoothly as the one-two-three of a Strauss waltz. And Christine knew it. She responded to the compliment: "Thanks, Mark."

But there must have been an edge to Christine's response, since he repeated the compliment. "I meant that sincerely."

Christine smiled and repeated her thanks: "I realized that, Mark."

Mallon worried he was not getting through to the new reporter. "I was a bit abrupt before the show. My wife keeps telling me to relax. You would think that after twenty years in this business, I would not get edgy, but I do."

"Only you?" Christine laughed. "Mark, you do *not* want to cross me on one of my bad days."

Mallon laughed, then swept his hand overhead to suggest we're both in a crazy business before heading toward the coffee bar.

Christine returned her attention to her computer to view a clip planned for *The Five O'clock News*, same subject but slightly different footage from that just offered on *The Four O'clock News*. For *The Six O'clock News*, she had an entirely new package, the one shot at roll call earlier this morning, minus any reference to an unknown celebrity running the race—but wasn't that slinky cat already out of the bag? The secret celebrity had to be Naní, but Christine could not say anything without Peter's permission because of the promise she had given to gain access to roll call. *Damn journalistic ethics!* Maybe she could use her need to obtain permission as an excuse to call Peter. *No, no, no, he would see right through that.* Besides, he was too busy. So was she, but with her day's work almost done, she could soon head home and get ready for the bank party. Maybe her roommate Yolanda would accompany Christine. Did she still want to attend?

MARATHON

Actually, despite her comment to Mark, this *was* one of Christine's bad days. For one, she was right in the middle of her period with accompanying cramps, headaches and discomfort. *Damn it, Eve, why did you eat that apple in the Garden of Eden?* For another, there was the disturbing news about Peter: that he once had been married. That troubled the Catholic schoolgirl in her; she knew also it would trouble her mother, bless her heart. His being involved with a supermodel was merely a secondary worry. But should she be so upset? She only met the man a day and a half ago. It was not like they were engaged. Probably they never would be. She had arrived in Lake City only two weeks ago. There must be many men as interesting as Peter.

On the other hand, maybe not.

She had to get her mind off Peter and back to her work otherwise, despite Mark Mallon's good wishes, she would be on the streets looking for another job soon and probably not in TV. She wondered if McDonald's was hiring. Suddenly Christine became aware of Tom Schorr, the director for the marathon telecast standing in the spot just vacated by Mark Mallon.

"What's this about a celebrity running the marathon?"

"Pardon?"

"A celebrity. One of my uncles is a police lieutenant. He called and said Peter announced at roll call that some celebrity was running the marathon on Sunday, but for security reasons Peter could not reveal his name."

"Did your uncle say, 'his?'"

"I'm not sure."

"Because it might be Naní."

"It might and it might not."

"She said she would be at the press conference with Joseph Nduku tomorrow to talk about AIDS Africa. Maybe she's planning to run."

"Exactly, so why the secrecy?" commented the director. "Besides, is Naní that hot a celebrity, compared to others who have run marathons?"

"I don't know, Tom. I honestly don't know."

"You were at roll call?"

"I was, but I only got in the door by making certain promises. One was to not say anything yet about a celebrity running the marathon. Of course, now that your uncle told you, does that relieve me of any obligation?"

"No, we can sit on the story, and you *do* need to protect your sources," Schorr conceded, "but I just don't get it."

"I don't either."

Christine began to think maybe the celebrity was someone else, not Naní. The TV reporter did not share that information with the director. She still felt restrained by her promise to Peter.

"Production meeting tomorrow," said Schorr. "Peter will be there. We'll ask him again. If he doesn't confess, we'll simply waterboard him."

"Tom!"

Schorr began to head to his office, then stopped. "By the way, Christine, we're putting you on a golf cart Sunday."

"What?"

"Don't worry: I've hired one of my nephews to drive the cart. Edmund will be riding shotgun with his camera. All you need do is ride along and pretend you're a princess."

"I am a princess. Didn't you read my resumé? Why a golf cart?"

"I want some middle-of-the-pack shots. Right in the runners' faces. So close, that viewers with high-definition TV can see them sweat. Some up-close interviews too. Can't use a motorcycle. Too much exhaust. And while you're on your cart, maybe it will offer you a chance to get close to Naní—or whoever this celebrity is."

But if not Naní, then who? She suspected Peter would not tell. In fact, she hoped he would not tell. That would provide more pressure than she deserved after only two weeks on the job. Director Tom Schorr disappeared to his office, leaving Christine puzzled. The learning curve on her new job seemed to be getting steeper. *Welcome to the Big Leagues*, thought Christine Ferrara.

39:00:00

After learning about Pope Tony's plans—or what he now surmised to be those plans—Redbird debated his next move. The phone call had come earlier that afternoon just before dinner on the western coast of Ireland. Given the five-hour time difference, that was just after noon in Lake City. Not wishing to interrupt dinner, Redbird had allowed several hours to pass before making any move. He could not delay much longer.

One of Redbird's informers—and he had many scattered in positions of importance within and without the church—tipped him on the fact that Pope Tony had been running more miles than usual in recent weeks. That plus his cell phone calls to Peter McDonald, race director of the Lake City Marathon, suggested that the pope planned to run that race on Sunday—without warning anybody responsible for his security.

Amazing, thought Redbird, that this man who has been anointed head of the world's most prominent religious body, had the audacity—or perhaps naiveté—to believe that, confirmed into that office, he could continue to behave like a normal human being. He might be able to so behave, but each step that he took had a rippling effect felt by the tens of millions who looked to him for guidance. Was the pope divine, a saint in his own right before canonization, or was he merely another human who could move among his public, who could attend movie shows, who could eat out in restaurants, who could walk down the street and wander into stores unnoticed, who could enter and run marathons. This particular pope seemed to think so. But when he did move into the public arena without the protection of bodyguards or outside the bulletproof womb of the popemobile used when he appeared at St. Peter's Square, he became vulnerable. And while there were many in this world who venerated this pope, many did not. This was a violent age, an era where terrorists sought to seek control of the world, to create chaos. Pope Tony's behavior did not make sense in this era of terrorists.

Or did it? Maybe Pope Tony's message to the terrorists was to say to them, "Here I am. I walk among the people. You cannot harm me. And even if I do, my successor would rise up to smite you with my staff." Was this not Jesus Christ's attitude when he walked unguarded into the Garden of Gethsemane to pray on the night of his betrayal by Judas Iscariot. Would the Lake City Marathon be Pope Tony's Garden of Gethsemane? Does this foolish boy have some agenda that transcends our own idea of how the most powerful, yet powerless, leader of the world should act?

One of his recent predecessors, Pope John Paul II, had acted with similar brazenness: often making clandestine trips to the Italian mountains to hike, even to ski at the resort in Ovindoli. On one occasion he departed Castel Gandolfo packed in the back of a tiny car with several other prelates, hiding behind a newspaper so the Swiss Guards would not recognize him. And few on the ski slopes recognized him either, but it was easier to hide bundled in ski clothes than nearly naked running a marathon. Was that dignified?

These thoughts had tumbled through Redbird's mind as he ate dinner not because of hunger, but to postpone the decision he knew he must make. Redbird had eaten little of the fine meal presented to him, pushing the food around his plate more than consuming it. He sipped from a pint of Guinness, but did not finish the brew. Eventually he pushed it and the plate of food away from him, rising from his chair, not waiting for the cup of coffee that usually signaled the end of his meal each evening.

Redbird passed out of the dining room and through a pair of glass doors that led to a lawn so lusciously green that it would have inspired Ludwig von Beethoven to write another Pastoral Symphony had he seen it. Redbird walked through the gardens of his castle and along a path until he came to a stop at a lookout that offered a view of the Atlantic Ocean, waves crashing on the beach far below, the sun settling toward and into the horizon, casting an orange glow on the water.

So Redbird waited and watched the sunset, seemingly wasting precious moments when he could be acting based on information now gathered about Pope Tony's plans on Sunday. But he could not act without knowing how to act, and as the sun dropped below the horizon, still coloring the clouds above, fading gradually from blue to black, Redbird determined what he must do.

Turning, he began the walk back to his office, reaching into a pocket for a cellular phone that would connect him with a member of his staff within the castle. He could have waited to see that individual in the two minutes it would take him to retrace his steps to his castle, but now that he had made his decision, seconds seemed more precious. They no longer could be wasted.

"Get me an airplane," Redbird told his assistant. "I'll be leaving for Lake City immediately."

Now several hours later, Redbird was seated in that airplane, not coincidently a Gulfstream 550 similar to the one that had transported Pope Tony to the same destination only a day before. High over the ocean, Redbird regarded his watch and said to his assistant, who had packed hastily so to accompany his superior on a trip whose purpose he did not know. "What time is it in Lake City?

Five hours difference thought the assistant. Ten O'Clock in Ireland. Five O'Clock in Lake City. The assistant announced that fact to Redbird.

39:00:00. 38:59:59. 38:59:58.

With one hand Redbird adjusted the time on his watch to the time at his destination. It was a watch you would expect a man of substance to wear, one with a gold band, not the plastic watch worn by runners and even Celebrity X. Thirty-nine hours now remained to the start of the marathon. Would Pope Tony join 50,000 runners running through the streets of Lake City on Sunday morning? Or did he have some other secret agenda? As his jet continued its journey across the ocean, Redbird wondered about that fact.

36:00:00

Just before leaving for the Lake City Bank party, Christine Ferrara confessed to her roommate Yolanda Kline that she did *not* want to go to the party, and it was *not* because of the normal fatigue from a busy week at work, and it was *not* because she still had her period. "I just do *not* want to go," she told her roommate.

176

"Did I hear the word 'not'?" asked Yolanda.

"I am so disappointed."

"Offer me the source of your disappointment, dearest roommate. I'm not good at guessing games."

"Peter McDonald."

"Mr. Right?"

"Mr. Wrong!"

"That was a short romance, Christine. I better call The Field Store and cancel that order for a 32-piece silverware set."

"You're making fun of me."

"I've been known to do that, but you're an easy target."

Christine stuck her tongue out at her roommate.

"Does this mean *we* are not attending the party," continued Yolanda, "and if *not*, why have I spent all afternoon at Saks shopping for this dress?"

"You bought that dress at Target, Yolanda, and we are going to the party anyway, but I am *not* planning to have any fun."

"You're already no fun, Christine, but what's the problem with Peter?"

"I learned today—not from him—that he was formerly married."

Yolanda frowned. "I am trying to focus on the word 'formerly.'"

Christine told Yolanda what Naní had let slip at the fashion show: that Peter once had a wife, apparently a woman known to the supermodel. But it hardly seemed appropriate to pump a woman she was interviewing on television for details, so Christine had none to offer her roommate.

"Are Peter and Naní—ummm—involved romantically?" probed Yolanda.

"I don't know. I don't think so."

"You don't think so, but you don't know."

"I don't think so, because why would Peter be hitting on me—which he obviously is—with her coming into town?"

"Let me offer the unapologetically feminist answer that immediately pops into my addled mind: Because he's a man?"

"If you expect me to rise in defense of the male species, that's not going to happen—at least tonight, not before we leave for a party where I have pre-programmed myself to be miserable."

"Miserable, Christine? You look like you just stepped out of the pages of *Vogue*, yet you're miserable?"

"Not only miserable, but rejected, unwanted, betrayed."

"Could I add the word 'silly?'"

Christine slid past Yolanda's comment. "Not only that but foolish, irrational, immature! Oh, Yolanda: Why am I going on like this? Two weeks in town, and the first man I meet is less than perfect Welcome to the real world. Let's go to the party and be miserable together."

FRIDAY

"You be miserable, Christine. I'm going to the party to have fun and aim darts with my eyes at your Mister-Right-Turned-Wrong."

Twenty minutes and one cab ride later, the two roommates found themselves standing outside the Lake City Bank's downtown skyscraper with thirty-six hours remaining before the start of the marathon. They knew that fact because of a display window promoting the marathon with male and female mannequins dressed in running gear. And over the mannequin's heads, one of the many digital clocks in town announcing the countdown to the marathon start in hours, minutes and seconds:

36:00:00. 35:59:59. 35:59:58.

The pair pushed their way through a set of revolving doors that allowed them entrance to the bank lobby, where they found themselves staring down a long corridor with shops on both sides. Two young interns from the marathon office waited behind a table with nametags to greet them. The interns were named Elisa and Damien. Christine had two invitations, acquired from director Tom Schorr at the TV station to insure their entrance to the party. Upon offering her name and that of her roommate, Christine discovered that nametags already awaited them. Peter must have phoned in the names, since she had not. How did he know the name of her roommate? Had she mentioned it to him during their brief stop for coffee this morning? She must have, because there was the evidence. *Amazing*, she thought. *Peter McDonald obviously was a man who realized the importance of small details.* He knew more about her than she knew about him. But how was she going to face him tonight?

"The party is on the forty-third floor," said Alisa, handing Christine her nametag. "Take the center elevator."

"Have a nice night," said Damien, handing Yolanda hers.

Walking past the greeters, the roommates stopped before a bank of elevators featuring golden doors decorated by a bas-relief done in a style that seemed borrowed from the Acropolis. Only a single elevator out of a group of eight was operating, carrying guests from the lobby to the party above. A guard stood before the elevator. They had to wait for it to descend, then had to wait inside for several other just-arrived guests to collect their nametags.

At the forty-third floor, the golden doors slid open.

Christine and Yolanda paused after exiting the elevator, not yet knowing which way to proceed. They found themselves standing in a waiting room that contained a circular desk, probably occupied during the day by a receptionist or security guard, although none were evident now. Beyond the desk a long hallway stretched in two directions to large rooms at each end. Christine and Yolanda decided to explore in one direction. They encountered at one end of the floor a room with tables where people were eating and drinking and talking. The room had two bars and a table with desserts, though not solid food. Retreating, they found food in a side room, but bypassed that room wanting to explore the party before pouncing on the banquet tables.

If the first end room visited had been the sit-and-eat room, and the second side room the fill-your-plate-with-food room, Christine decided that the next room they entered at the other end of the hallway might be defined as the talking-and-drinking room. The music was louder—hard rock vs. soft rock—the talk louder still. There were tall, circular tables, but no chairs. There was a balcony above, though no people on it, nor any apparent route to reach the balcony. Christine and Yolanda accepted two chardonnays from a roaming waitress and began to pass with serpentine movements through the crowd of people clad in clothes that resembled those seen at the fashion show that noon. Had they all rushed to The Field Store immediately after the show demanding to be clad in what they had seen on stage?

Then Christine saw him: Peter McDonald, talking to a couple that had shared the elevator with her and Yolanda earlier. And by Peter's side, the supermodel: Nani. *Was she with him? His date for the night? Hummmph!* Christine needed restraint to prevent her mouth from flopping open, her eyes from widening like those of a child exposed to presents beneath the tree on Christmas morning. *Have I ever seen anyone more beautiful?*

Nani was clad in a gown that was Beyond Category. It was African in its color and design, but few on that impoverished continent could have afforded such a gown or worn it the way Nani did that evening. Peter, beside her, seemed to be beaming. Who wouldn't be in the presence of such a beauty? *How could she, Little Christine from Peoria, hope to compete?* As though to match Nani in elegance, Peter wore a tuxedo. Christine suddenly felt underdressed, her basic black cocktail dress unable to equal the clothes of the glitterati. *Were Peter and Nani touching? His shoulder against hers?* Then as though to confirm her worst fears, the supermodel reached inside the crook of his arm and cradled it. She wanted to cry. She wanted to leave!

Yolanda too had stopped to regard with wide eyes the presence of Nani. "Will you look at her?" said Yolanda conspiratorially.

"I'm looking at *him*," replied Christine.

"That's—"

"Peter!"

And as though he sensed his name having passed across her lips, Peter McDonald turned and spotted Christine Ferrara. He raised his hand and started to beckon her toward him, then apparently decided upon a more polite approach. He said something to Nani. Leaving the side of the supermodel, sliding out of her arm, Peter walked toward Christine. Nani turned as Peter did so, then seeing the reason for her abandonment, smiled gently and re-turned to the conversation with several other people.

Christine, meanwhile, was paralyzed with fear as Peter approached: *What am I going to say? How am I going to act?*

She felt his hand pressing gently against her hand, felt also the touch of his cheek against hers. If anyone had been watching, it would seem the greeting of two friends if not lovers—yet they had met only the day before. Christine closed her eyes as though it might help burn the memory of this moment into her hard drive.

"I was afraid you might not come," she heard him whisper in her ear. She mumbled something in return, and he moved his cheek away turning toward her roommate. Christine forced her eyes to pop open, not wanted to be re-vealed in an instant of carnal desire.

Her senses barely functioning, Christine became aware that Peter had re-tained possession of her hand with one hand while simultaneously offering his other hand to Yolanda. "Ummm, Peter this is my roommate."

"Yolanda," said Yolanda when it appeared Christine was too paralyzed to provide any further information.

"Yolanda Kline," added Christine, quickly recovering.

"My pleasure," said Peter, comfortably.

"Enchanted," said Yolanda, evilly aware of Christine's discomfort.

Peter sensed that too, but pressed on: "There's somebody I want you two to meet." He emphasized the word "two," so as to include Yolanda. Gently, he tugged Christine by the hand, Yolanda following.

Oh, my God, worried Christine. *I'm not up to this. Why did I leave Peoria?*

The two groups merged, Peter presiding over introductions. Christine held out her hand to shake the hand of the supermodel, saying perfunctorily, "We've already met."

"I remember," said Naní offering a smile that was more radiant because of its contrast against the brown of her skin. She turned toward Peter: "Ms. Fer-rara interviewed me this afternoon at the fashion show."

"I missed the interview. We were in a meeting."

"Not that you have anything important on your mind this weekend, Peter," cooed the supermodel, sliding her arm back into his.

Christine noticed and was temporarily outraged, though she tried to give no sign. *Is she reclaiming him?*

Yolanda also noticed that Peter was attached by hand and arm to two at-tractive females, but tried to remain a detached observer. *Do I detect a fight brewing? Can I choose the weapons? Hairspray at five paces?*

Then as easily as she had clasped Peter, she released him. Peter seemed not to notice. Naní spoke to Christine: "I owe you an apology."

"Apology?"

"You asked about the marathon. I dodged that question."

"I saw you on Oprah. You dodged her too."

Naní laughed: "Equal rights."

Peter interrupted: "Before Naní says too much, and at the risk of being accused of suppressing Freedom of the Press, let me remind everybody that she will be at a press conference tomorrow afternoon with Joseph Nduku, our defending champion."

"Important announcement," conceded Naní. "At least very important to me, as you know, Peter."

Is the news the fact that Naní is running the marathon, wondered Christine, and, if so: *Why is that all so important?* But let's talk about something else, like: *Why does this famous model have her eye on Peter?*

Small talk followed, then Christine saw Nelson Ogilvie, the marathon's media director, approach. He whispered something in Peter's ear, then moved away from the group. Peter stated: "Excuse me. Command performance. Some people from Ireland have indicated an interest in our presence." Peter took Naní by the hand to show that she was indicated in the "our," but obviously not Christine.

Sensing that his abandoning her needed additional explanation, he looked at Christine and said, "Don't go too far." Then Peter and the supermodel retreated to another part of the room.

"Fifteen more minutes, girlfriend," said Yolanda, "and you're going to have to feed me."

"Oh hush," said Christine. "Let's have fun."

"I thought you said you were *not* going to have fun "

"I lied, Yolanda, I lied. Even though the man I love is in the arms of another woman, I am going to have fun tonight."

Yolanda Kline let out a shriek so loud that it caused several people standing nearby to turn her way in puzzlement. "You go, girl!" the one roommate said to the other.

35:30:00

Friday was always Date Night for Meghan Allison and her husband Matt, almost a sacred evening for them. It signaled the end of the work week for him and the school week for her, and even if he had to go into the office Saturday morning or she had to spend all weekend with her nose stuck in a book cramming for an exam, they usually went out to eat Friday night, sometimes with friends but more often just the two of them alone, because, well, they liked each other.

During her sabbatical year away from podiatric duties preparing for the marathon, Meg saw Matt most mornings before he left for work and before she went for her run. But because Friday was a rest day, or at least an easy day, she always slept in on Fridays allowing Matt to empty the dishwasher, brew the coffee and fix his own breakfast before leaving for work. Usually he would plant a kiss on her cheek half buried beneath the covers before leaving the apartment. Half the time she did not feel the kiss until she woke up, the half memory of his lips still upon her.

Then when she crawled out of bed and stumbled into the living room, she would spot a sheet of paper on the floor, a parting message from the man she loved: DATE NIGHT!! Matt was so adorable.

For this Friday night, Meg decided she did not want the pressure of eating out, of going to a crowded restaurant and being forced to wait an extra half hour for a table even if they had made a reservation. Normally she enjoyed standing at the bar with Matt and sipping a glass of Chardonnay, but not with the marathon so near.

"We're staying home tonight, right?" she mumbled earlier that morning when Matt brushed her cheek with his lips before leaving for work.

"Whatever."

"I don't feel like fighting the crowds."

"Me either."

That ended the conversation, since Meg fell back to sleep, although she vaguely remembered hearing the door to their apartment close as Matt exited. Meg had not stayed long in bed, because she wanted to go early to the Expo to pick up her number. Stumbling through the living room, she had spotted Matt's note on the floor: IT'S STILL DATE NIGHT!!

I love him so much, she thought. *Will making love tonight make me run faster or slower on Sunday? Too bad either way.*

For the evening meal and, because it was Friday, she chose salmon as her main course. No longer did Catholics have to eat fish on Fridays, but Meg's mom was a traditionalist, and so was she. To insure sufficient carbohydrate to go with the fish heavy with protein and fat, she cooked rice mixed with green peas. Matt provided his usual salad featuring Boston lettuce plus spinach, sprinkled with almonds. She threatened him with bodily harm if he put too much olive oil on the salad, which he usually did. He smiled and placed the olive oil bottle beside the vinegar bottle on the table next to the candles, which he lit before dimming the lights. "Not too dark," she warned.

MARATHON

She had a single glass of the Erath Reserve pinot noir; he had two. Dessert was a bit over the top for someone running Sunday: apple cobbler, but at least she did not cover it with ice cream, which Matt did, the beast!

Afterwards they did the dishes, then went for a short walk holding hands to the lakefront and back mainly to relax and aid digestion. The sun already had set, the skies to the west shifting from pink to blue to black during their walk. All the trees on the street where they lived still had their leaves. Autumn seemed late this year, perhaps because of the warm weather.

It was 8:30 by the time they returned to their apartment, less than thirty-six hours before the start of the marathon, Meghan Allison's big test.

35:30:00. 35:29:59. 35:29:58.

They watched a film rented from Blockbuster, a spy thriller whose name and plot Meg would not remember the next morning because she fell asleep on her husband's shoulder halfway through. Though uncomfortable, Matt tried to remain as still as possible so as not to disturb his wife.

The film ended and Matt pushed the button on the remote to turn off the TV. He looked down at his wife still sleeping. She looked so beautiful, so comfortable, Matt almost was tempted to leave her alone. But she probably would awaken at midnight with a crick in her neck and be mad at him. Finally, he shook Meg to half wakefulness: "Hey, Beautiful Lady, you better not fall asleep in the marathon on Sunday."

It took her a few seconds to reply. "Let's go to bed."

Back at the Hilliard, many other runners entered in the marathon were making the same decision, some early, some late. In offering advice over the Internet, Don Geoffrey always stressed the importance of getting sufficient sleep the night before the night before the marathon. "You're going to be anxious the night before," the Turtle advised his followers. "You'll be nervous, worried. You'll probably get up to go to the bathroom a half dozen times, because you drank too much fluid during the day. Add to that a too-early wake-up call. That makes even more important that you go to bed early the night before the night before and that you get up late."

Kyle and Wesley Fowler were not aware of the Turtle's advice. They did not own any copies of his books, nor did they visit his Web site or the Team Turtle Bulletin Board. Yes, they knew who Geoffrey was because of his record as a runner and his writing in *Running Magazine*, but he never had interviewed him for that magazine, and it was unlikely Sunday that he would.

They were only rabbits.

35:00:00

Nine O'clock proved to be the tipping point for the party on the forty-third floor of the Lake City Bank. At 8:59 everybody seemed to be enjoying the splendor of an elegant event: eating, drinking, talking with old friends, meeting new ones. At 9:00, while few actually looked at a wristwatch, couples did exchange glances: Time to head to the next party. Time to relieve the baby sitter. Time to go to bed, particularly those racing on Sunday. For members of the marathon staff, time to return to work. Time to just *leave*, because we've been here two hours, seen everybody and run out of fresh conversation.

At 9:01, a subtle shift toward the exits began. It would be ten or twenty more minutes before the drop in noise and numbers became noticeable. And another forty or fifty minutes before the last party-goers departed, taking the elevator down to the lobby to accept gifts as their reward for being part of the evening's festivities. This year's gift was a Tiffany glass bowl with Lake City Marathon and the race date etched on the bottom. With the contract soon to expire, this could be the last bank party, the last gift offered to guests.

Peter McDonald was too involved with problems connected with this year's marathon to worry about next year's race, whether funded by the bank or not. After leaving Christine and Yolanda, he had introduced Naní to Dennis Lahey and the Shelaghi executives, then slipped away to another group, leaving the supermodel to charm them if she so desired. He felt somewhat uncomfortable about doing this, as though he were pimping her to secure sponsorship, but she was above that, and he suspected that the Irish bankers also were the same. He moved to still another group of important people, shifted to a different group after that, and while surfing the room for people he knew and people he should know, Peter looked to find Christine, not wanting to abandon her a stranger in a strange land, but each time he caught a glimpse of Christine and her roommate Yolanda, they were on another side of the room and apparently engaged in conversations with other party-goers who they might not have known before this evening. *I need to get back to her*, thought Peter, but it did not happen and at the tipping point of the party, Peter stepped into a side meeting room with several key associates. Nine o'clock, and there remained at that point thirty-five hours before the marathon.

35:00:00. 34:59:59. 34:59:58.

MARATHON

By the time Peter exited the meeting, he could not find Christine. *Where is she?* He told her "don't go too far," then he had abandoned her. She was hardly his date for the evening, and she had come to the party with a roommate, and she had seemed to be busy with a number of new people met, so Christine should not be mad at him, should she? He thought of what Carol would have said following similar treatment. She would not have been too shy to tell him, before rolling over to the other side of the bed, announcing, "I'm tired." *Whoops!* Peter knew what that signaled. But Christine was not Carol. She had only come into his life yesterday, but he sensed it was an important coming-into-his-life, and he suspected she felt that way too.

He would need to call and apologize for being rude.

Was she still in the building, perhaps down in the lobby accepting her Tiffany bowl? Was she in a taxicab heading home? Was she already home? Impulsively, Peter decided that he had nothing to lose by dialing her cell phone. He stepped into a corner to do so. The phone rang four times, then clicked over to voice mail.

"Hi, this is Christine. Please leave a message."

At that precise moment Christine was downstairs in the lobby. She had just accepted a boxed Tiffany bowl, but she put it back down on the table when the phone in her purse began its Mozartian jangle. Removing the phone, she glanced at the display, which told her who was calling.

"It's Peter," she said to Yolanda.

Yolanda watched incredulously as Christine continued to look at the display without punching the button which would allow her to talk.

"Well?"

"He's leaving a message."

"And you are not going to answer?"

"No."

"Girlfriend, why not?"

"Because if I did, I would get back into that elevator and return to the party, and I do not want to get back into the elevator and return to the party."

Yolanda frowned: "I could debate man-catching strategy with you, but I suspect you do not want to discuss man-catching strategy."

"No, I do not."

Christine replaced the cell phone in her purse and indicated a desire to go home. The expression on her face might best be described as a pout. She picked up the box containing the Tiffany bowl and, cradling it with one arm, took Yolanda's arm with another and began moving toward the revolving door that led outside. She hoped that they could quickly hail a taxicab. She was tempted to slam-dunk the bowl into a trash can, but did not see any.

FRIDAY

Outside Yolanda asked her, "You're not going to cry, are you?"

"I am *not* going to cry in the taxicab. I am *not* going to cry when we get home. I *am* going to cry as soon as I can find some place to do so alone without making a total fool of myself."

A taxicab quickly appeared. The two got into it. Yolanda gave the driver their address, then put her arm around her roommate. "Roomie," said Yolanda. "You're better than any supermodel."

PART 3:

SATURDAY

SATURDAY

MARATHON

24:00:00

Most of the rooms below the eighth floor at Hilliard Towers were dedicated to activities other than sleeping. Meeting rooms occupied several of the floors; offices for hotel management, part of another. Over the years as more and more executives brought workout gear with them on business trips, the hotel catered to them by expanding its fitness center on the sixth and seventh floors. Once offering only a treadmill, an exercise bike and a few other machines featuring pulleys and weights in a tiny, windowless room, the Hilliard's fitness center now overlooked the lake through picture windows and boasted dozens of state-of-the-art exercise machines. These were located on a balcony above an Olympic-size swimming pool. A real pool, where you could swim laps, not merely one for lounging around sipping piña coladas. Beside the pool sat a whirlpool and cold-water bath. Locker rooms for men and women contained separate steam rooms and saunas.

Normally on weekday mornings, the fitness center was crammed with guests working out before seeing to their business needs, but this was Saturday. Moreover, few of the marathoners who had filled the Hilliard to capacity wished to engage in any aerobic activity this weekend other than running 26 miles 385 yards on Sunday.

Thus, the fitness center was nearly empty as one hotel guest clad in a Speedo bathing suit that barely covered his butt moved from the locker room to the pool deck. It was Peter McDonald, who bent to test the temperature of the water. It was warm, near 80 degrees. Placing his towel on a nearby chair, Peter sat down on the edge of the pool and slipped into the water. He was not looking for a workout in the traditional sense. He simply wanted to relieve his mind of stress ranging from the sponsor crisis to hot weather to secrecy surrounding Celebrity X.

The clock on the wall indicated the time to be 8:30 A.M. Peter figured he could swim for ten or fifteen minutes before getting on with the rest of his day. Twenty-four hours remained before the start of the Lake City Marathon. *24:00:00. 23:59:59. 23:59:58.*

Peter pulled goggles down over his eyes, fitted clips on his nose and began to stroke the water: gently pulling with his arms, barely kicking with his legs, breathing every third stroke from one side or the other. Despite his running ability—or maybe because of it—Peter was an atrociously slow swimmer. Nobody would mistake him for Michael Phelps; he did not particularly care.

189

SATURDAY

Peter paused at the far end of the pool, took a few seconds to catch his breath and started back the other way. No kick turns for him. During his competitive days, Peter rarely went near a pool and spent little time during the summer hanging out at the beach. That was something done by non-athletes. In high school under the control of a domineering coach, he ran twice daily, averaged 110 miles a week, and had little time in his life for anything other than running. And studies. He always got good grades. But few dates with girls. None serious. It was not until after college that he met the woman who taught him other things in life besides running mattered. Carol: She kept slipping into his thoughts. Even here in the pool. *Especially* in the pool when his mind floated free of his body. Perhaps that was what brought him down to the swimming pool on a Saturday morning.

Coming to the end of another lap, Peter paused longer than usual; long enough to allow him to touch the chain around his neck. It brought him peace. And, he hoped, just a touch of good luck given the challenges this weekend.

Strange, but now that the focus of his life revolved around organizing the running of others, Peter discovered much to his surprise that he enjoyed swimming. Previously, he believed that swimming laps might prove tedious. Unlike running on the lakefront, his wake-up activity yesterday, there was no scenery to enjoy; all you did was stare at a black line on the bottom of the pool. *B-O-R-I-N-G!* But lap-swimming somehow was not boring—or if it was, maybe he needed some minutes of boredom in his otherwise busy life. Enveloped in a womb of water, Peter could forget. And there was much that Peter needed to forget.

As he stroked his way back to the end of the pool, Peter noticed the clock on the wall. It was a clock with hands (not digital numbers), and the hands moved to signify the march of time. The clock did not show the time of day, nor the time remaining to the marathon. It just offered miscellaneous minutes and seconds, so those swimming laps could time their fitness ritual.

Peter McDonald was beholden this weekend to ticking clocks. At this time tomorrow morning, the elite runners, including defending champion Joseph Nduku, would explode across the starting line bound for glory, not to mention the $100,000 awarded to the victors. Peter had spent most of the night working with his assistant Noel Michaels. Should a reporter ask either what they had accomplished working so late, neither would have been able to offer a precise answer. Not without referring to the checklist on their clipboards. Once a task was completed, it became a "done" entry, a red mark on their checklists. No looking back. On to the next task

Returning to his room at 4:30 A.M., Peter had managed to capture a few hours sleep before rising. After his workout, he would grab a bite to eat, visit the start/finish area on Columbia Drive and then head for the Expo. He had a course lecture to give at 10:00. At the bank party last night, several of the Shelaghi executives had discussed whether or not to drive the marathon course in advance. Patrick Savitch, the only one of the visitors from Ireland running the race, had encouraged them to do so. "It'll give you an excuse to see the city," Savitch insisted.

Savitch's plea seemed to fall on deaf ears. Executive manager Dennis Lahey had other business, he claimed. Or maybe it was disinterest. Peter confessed to them he often drove the course around 3:00 or 4:00 race morning, partly because he could not sleep. The thought of rising that early to view the course had prompted laughs from the Irish contingent and no volunteers to accompany him.

Peter could not read the Shelaghi executive manager, who appeared both friendly and distant. Peter feared that Lahey planned to pull the plug on the bank's sponsorship, but did not want to press for an early decision. Monday morning might bring bad news. Still, you do not easily kill a race as well received among runners as the Lake City Marathon. Fifty-thousand runners can't be wrong, rationalized Peter. Lahey might not agree. If so, Peter would face serious problems in the year following as he attempted to match the largesse of his current sponsor during a down economy. It would be a challenge, but as a competitive runner Peter was used to facing challenges.

Peter never tracked how long he swam. He allowed himself to be ruled by instinct. After a dozen or so laps, he stopped, removed his goggles and nose plugs, set them on the side of the pool and began running laps in the chest-deep water. And with the shift in activity, his mind shifted to thoughts of Christine Ferrara. He had become enamored of the TV reporter, a woman he barely knew. *What was it about Christine?* He had met many bright and beautiful women in the period since his wife Carol died. *Why her?* It was totally irrational, but is love ever rational? Why should he be so attracted to a woman whom he had met barely forty-eight hours before?

The warm water swirling around his body relaxed Peter, but so did thoughts about Christine—thoughts about what might be, or what might not be! He had acted badly last night. Yes, he had duties associated with the evening's event, specifically escorting Naní, introducing the supermodel to as many important people as possible, including the Shelaghi executives. In doing so, Peter shoved Christine and her roommate aside without meaning to do so. And after the meeting he had with Michaels and Ogilvie, she was gone. When he tried to call her, she did not answer. He wanted to call again before coming to the fitness center, but you do not call people you barely know at 8:00 on a Saturday morning. He might have text-messaged her but he did not want to seem pushy. Is that how young people measure levels of intimacy? First, the cell phone number. Next the email address. Next, invite them to your Facebook page. And after that....

Peter, still married to a memory, was not sure he was ready to consider the "after that."

Getting out of the pool at the end of his workout, Peter decided that he would shower when he returned to the room, get dressed and call Christine some time after breakfast.

23:59:00

Emerging from the operations trailer in Dearborn Park just after 8:00 on Saturday morning, Noel Michaels congratulated herself for staying on schedule—so far. Less than twenty-four hours before the start of the Lake City Michigan, and Peter's executive director was ready. More than ready. She could handle any task he threw at her. Even the predicted hot weather. They might have to shorten the race, which would make a lot of runners very unhappy, but she was prepared for even that extreme decision, if hot weather forced their hands.

Twenty-four hours. *Less* than twenty-four hours!

23:59:00. 23:58:59. 23:58:58.

Michaels had just eaten breakfast: a cup of coffee and two donuts from Starburst to jump-start her day. Peter's signing a coffee chain to a sponsorship was an act of genius, but would he have equal luck retaining Lake City Bank as main sponsor? That was not her worry; she had other things on her mind.

She had managed a brief nap of several hours during the middle of the night, but few people on the marathon staff would get much sleep during the remaining twenty-four hours before the start of the race. Strangely, she looked forward to going sleepless in Lake City. It was part of the challenge—even the thrill—of her job. Seventy-two hours of intense work, then they could begin planning for next year. In between, she had an invitation to lecture at a race director's meeting connected to the Honolulu Marathon.

Michaels had reservations about accepting such largesse, but when she expressed her doubts to Peter, he looked at her straight-faced and said: "Noel, it is very simple. Unless you go to Hawaii and represent me at the meeting, you're fired." Nice man. She loved working for him and, along with others on the marathon staff, she was delighted—absolutely *delighted*—to notice that a new woman had entered Peter's life. It would be fun watching that romance develop over the coming months. What was her name: Christine Ferrara? The staff was buzzing with the news. Office gossip. Everybody loved office gossip. Whether or not the two eventually connected, at least Christine had gotten Peter moving in the right direction. Michaels made a quick sign-of-the-cross in an attempt to call down blessings from above.

Coffee cup still in hand, Michaels continued to allow herself a few minutes of relaxation, walking through a grove of trees behind the trailer to look over the tops of tents in the charity village toward a sun rising high over the lake. A stunning sight. Like most runners who trained regularly on the lakefront, she loved the sight of light sparkling on water, especially at sunrise. But the sun this morning and tomorrow would be both beauty and beast, its rise upward in the sky accompanied by a rise upward in temperatures. Mother Hen Michaels worried about its effect on the 50,000 runners under her care.

Many runners had come to Lake City anticipating the usually perfect weather in October. They had trained hard. That plus one of the flattest and fastest courses in running usually guaranteed that runners could achieve Boston Qualifying times, set Personal Records or finish their first marathons with minimum discomfort. They had spent months of training that, this year unfortunately, would result in less than satisfactory achievements. She felt bad for everybody entered, but there was little she or others could do about it. They would muddle through and look down the road toward their next goals.

Michaels worried less about those whose goals coming to Lake City were lofty than she did for those runners, who for various reasons had not trained enough, who were not heat-acclimated, who were not experienced enough to know how much to drink and when to slow down if faced with extremes of hot weather. Those were the ones whose failures might overwhelm their medical facilities. Fifty-thousand runners had entrusted their safety to her, and Michaels hoped that she and her staff were up to the task facing them Sunday.

The marathon executive director took another sip of coffee, discovered it was cold and dashed the remnants of the cup toward a nearby bush. She regarded once more the rising sun lighting the water and the tents of the charity village, then returned to the operations trailer. A full day of hard work awaited her, then another night with very little sleep.

23:00:00

The buzz on the bus Saturday morning centered on the hot weather expected the next day. For those riding the shuttle bus between Hilliard Towers and Pritzinger Place, site of the Expo, hot weather was

SATURDAY

Conversational Subject # 1. There existed no Conversational Subject # 2.

Most of the 50,000 runners entered in the Lake City Marathon, even the elites, had been checking weather.com frequently over the last week, looking for some glimmer of hope, some hint that maybe the forecasts were incorrect, that a frigid front centered over Manitoba might shift course and head their way. No luck! When they turned on their television sets and tuned into *The Morning News*, there stood TV3's Vaughn Johnson giving the worst news possible: "Warm weather makes watching marathons more fun, but it's a lot less fun for those running the race."

Yuck!!!

Johnson, many realized, would be running the marathon with them on Sunday. Could not the weatherman do better than that?

Before boarding the bus at the Hilliard, runners had passed the lobby countdown clock. It continued to remind them how many hours, minutes and seconds remained before the start of the Lake City Marathon.

23:00:00. 22:59:59. 22:59:58.

The heat wave meant slower times, significantly slower times. The majority of runners perform efficiently at temperatures between 45 and 65 degrees. Much colder or much warmer, and the body wastes energy retaining or dissipating heat. It is easier to cope with cold than heat, because in cold weather you can add clothes to stay warm. In warm weather, your options for staying cool are more limited: you can only remove so many clothing items without getting arrested.

Many of the 50,000 entered had come to Lake City because of the promise of a fast course and fast times. That promise would not be fulfilled, although not everybody was willing to accept that reality. They had come to Lake City to set PR's and achieve BQ's or (the most admirable of goals) to go the distance. Now this might be taken away from them. More to worry, word had begun to spread about a contingency plan that the race director had to shorten the race from its cherished 26 miles 385 yards.

"What's this about closing the course early?" grumbled one runner to another as they rode the bus to the Expo.

"They can do it," explained his friend.

"No way."

"They can even cancel the race."

"What?"

"You agreed to that when you signed the waiver."

"I didn't read the waiver."

"Not everybody does. More to the point: Given the heat, are you still going for that Boston Qualifier?"

"Don't ask me that question." The first runner fell silent, contemplating the training he did over a period of four months to prepare for peak performance. Was it now to be wasted?

Listening to their conversation, but not adding to it, was Matilda Goldberg of *The New York Times*. As a reporter of world events based in Rome, she was used to looking and listening as much as asking. But she wondered about her own race. Tilda had planned to start with the 4:00 pacing group. *Did that still make sense?* Maybe she would de-seed herself to 4:15. She was not sure yet about that strategy. She would pick up a 4:00 number at the pacing team booth. Maybe she would wait until just before she headed to the start to see just how hot it was going to be before switching to 4:15.

Awaiting Tilda and the approximately 7,500 others who would utilize pacing teams to aid them in reaching their marathon-related goals was Leonard Hand, who served as pacing team coordinator for the Lake City Marathon. That was not his full-time job. Lenny Hand spent most of his work hours designing video games, being well paid for doing so. This allowed him the luxury of serving the marathon as a volunteer, his job each year to recruit approximately a hundred experienced pacing team leaders (or "pacers" as they most often were called). The purpose of these pacers was to pace people through the race, to help them to finish, or to finish fast. Regardless of whether you wanted to run a 3-hour or a 6-hour marathon—or somewhere between in 10- and 15-minute increments—Lenny Hand had a pacing team for you, a total of sixteen teams for that matter.

The most popular team was that for runners hoping to break four hours, since being able to say you ran 3:59:59 or faster conferred instant status on anyone having achieved that goal. Very few of today's recreational runners would approach the next hour goal—2:59:59—so breaking four hours, to many, became a huge achievement. The Holy Grail. Not quite BQ status, but close. For this year's marathon, Lenny expected that 500 or more runners might join the 4:00 pacing team. He had recruited eight leaders to pace them.

As runners filed into the Expo, Lenny enjoyed the calm before the storm. He knew that after acquiring numbers and T-shirts they would begin to cruise the aisles. Many would find their way to the pacing team booth to sign up for one of the popular teams that he helped organize.

As marathon running increased in popularity, pacing teams had become de rigueur in most of the biggest marathons. Runners looking to run fast times often chose marathons based on whether they could join a team whose leader could keep them on pace toward their goals. Despite being a nice addendum to any marathon, not all race directors took the time to add them, or had the personnel to staff them. Peter McDonald was not one of those race directors;

he valued greatly Lenny Hand's role in adding an extra dimension to the Lake City Marathon and never missed an opportunity to tell him so.

Lenny was tough on his pacers. He expected them to cross the finish line 30 seconds plus or minus their planned time, but also to hold a steady pace throughout the race. Fast starts by pacing team leaders particularly irritated him, since he did not want people signed up for the teams to get dropped in the first miles—or to run those miles too fast and pay the price later. Better to start slowly for the first two or three miles. Lenny instructed his leaders to gradually make up lost time during the next ten miles so as to pass the half marathon mark on time, or very close to it. "Then hold that pace," he insisted. This was a requirement to help people being paced meet their goals. Pacing team leaders who failed to achieve Lenny's strict standards would not be invited back the following year.

"I'm a bit of a curmudgeon," Lenny once admitted to Peter McDonald. "I have little tolerance for incompetence."

Peter told Lenny that was his attitude too: "If anybody complains, simply refer them to me."

That never had been necessary. With increasing numbers of runners arriving at the pacing team booth, Lenny Hand's job was both over and just begun. Recruiting the hundred runners who would lead the teams at Lake City had been his first task, accomplished many months before. With the Expo open, Lenny's job was to greet runners signing up for the teams, registering them by name and answering all their questions, helping them also in their choice of teams. Particularly for first-time marathoners, Lenny tried to encourage them to set conservative goals. "Your goal should be only to finish," Lenny said over and over again, "not to finish fast."

Lenny also provided special numbers for runners to pin to the back of their singlets. These pacer bibs serve an important purpose. Runners wore them on the back in addition to the race numbers worn on the front. Each pacer bib identified the runner by the team to which he had assigned himself: 3:00 for someone running with the 3-hour team; 3:10 for someone running with the 3:10 team and so forth. This made it easier for runners to rejoin their team if separated from them at an aid station or after taking a potty break. The pacer bibs also allowed runners who might not have signed up for a team to judge their pace. Lenny realized that not all runners who hoped to benefit from a pacing team wanted to be so identified. If you had a 4:00 number on your back and found runners wearing 4:15 or 4:30 passing you, it could become very embarrassing.

Each of Lenny's pacing team leaders was required to work a three-hour shift in the booth over the two days of the Expo talking to runners about their pacing strategies, answering questions about where and when to meet and how to keep in contact. The day before, he had sent emails to his leaders, warning them of the problems anticipated because of the predicted hot weather. They needed to encourage runners to forget planned finishing times and drop back a team or two. A series of speakers were scheduled each half hour for the main stage talking about everything from training to nutrition to the course, a topic Peter McDonald usually saved for himself. Lenny would give seven of those lectures and in each one he would caution runners to pace themselves properly.

He hoped they would listen.

Back at the Hilliard, two other pacers not members of Leonard Hand's team dressed to go running. Because Aba Andersson no longer planned an attempt on the world record, Kyle and Wesley Fowler were rabbits without a cause. Based on their contract, race director Peter McDonald could assign them to pace one of the other women runners, or even join with the lead men, but the expected hot weather seemed to have cancelled all pacing activities for the elites, men or women. Peter told the twins that he would have a final decision by this afternoon's elite athlete meeting whether or not their services were needed, but that left them dangling.

Complicating the twins' problem was the fact that their coach, Steve Holland, had not yet arrived in town because of Friday teaching commitments. Earlier, Kyle had text-messaged their coach and caught him driving the team van to Lake City. He text-messaged back for them to train this morning as planned. That meant an easy two-mile jog with some strides and stretching in the middle. After they met with McDonald at the elite meeting, they could decide upon their race plans for Sunday.

Gazing at the digital device, Kyle parroted Coach Holland's words to his twin brother, Wesley: "Coach said not to worry. We still get paid."

Wesley shrugged: "Does it look like I'm worried?"

"Yeah, let's go run."

22:20:00

Christine Ferrara could hear her cell phone ringing, but could not find the infernal device. When that happened, as it too often did, it drove her crazy. She stumbled out of bed and finally found the phone, still ringing, in her purse on the dresser, left on all night, not wise because that meant her battery would be low on a day when she would need the phone. She was scheduled to attend a press conference for the marathon that morning and a production meeting later in the afternoon. Still bleary-eyed, TV3's new girl in town looked at the screen showing the identity of the caller before deciding whether or not to push the green button to talk.

Peter!

Why is he calling me this early in the morning? What time is it anyway? 9:40! I can't believe I slept this late.

Christine decided that she never should have stayed up late reading a book, but she had to do something after the disappointment she felt after attending the bank party, seeing Peter spend more time with that supermodel than he did with her. Jane Austen! What am I doing at this stage in my life reading Jane Austen, especially *Pride and Prejudice*. She had read that book one summer in high school, read it again in an English Lit course in college and grasping something off the shelf, anything off the shelf, Jane Austen had fallen into her hands. Did she want to read *P&P* one more time? Would it impress friends, if she could quote from memory whole passages from the Austen classic. She had seen the recent movie twice—once in the theatres and once on DVD—and knew the ending. *Is Peter my Darcy? No, he's too well-mannered, plus I don't think he lives on an English estate with three dozen bathrooms.*

The phone stopped ringing. *He's probably listening to my voice telling him to leave a message,* Christine decided. *Now, he's leaving a message—at least I hope he's leaving a message unless he's mad for my not replying last night. Apologize, Peter, apologize. Tell me you'll never see that supermodel again!*

Christine did not want to press the green button and start talking to him, because she was standing in her sleeping pajamas in the middle of her bedroom. Not that he could see her, but somehow conversing half-naked to a man you just met two days ago seemed indecent. Her mom would not approve. Besides, she was still perturbed about his actions last night.

Christine jumped back into the bed, still holding the cell phone in one hand, and curled up under the comforter, allowing her to feel somewhat more decent about a phone conversation not held. Waiting long enough to assure he had hung up, she punched the appropriate buttons and heard Peter's voice.

"Hi, Christine. Sorry I couldn't spend more time with you last night, but we had an important meeting. Story of my life—at least this weekend. I am truly, truly sorry. See you at the press conference? If not, I assume you'll be at the production meeting?"

22:20:00. 22:19:59. 22:19:58.

Well, half an apology was better than none. "Truly sorry." In fact, two truly's. Not bad for a man supposedly without manners. *Okay, he's forgiven.* Replaying the message once more and analyzing its content, Christine noted that her almost-acquired-new-boyfriend failed to leave a phone number suggesting he did not expect her to call him back. *Good!* On this day before the marathon, she did not want to bother him anyway. And yes, she would see him at the press conference, if not talk to him. But the press conference posed hazards, particularly since a prominent person at that press conference would be Naní. And up at the front of the room as though expecting everybody to genuflect. Should members of the press wear sunglasses to avoid eye damage? *Why have you jumped off the front pages of the tabloids and into my life to haunt me, Naní?* Later this afternoon, the production meeting. Fewer people, so easier to avoid having awkward conversations heard. *Why do I want to avoid Peter?* Christine wondered. *Didn't I tell Yolanda he was Mr. Right? Maybe he still is.*

Naní. Naní. I want to strangle that woman. Still, she did seem friendly. Do I not have all the facts in front of me?

Christine remained under the comforter for at least five more minutes, her mind churning with thoughts about her and Peter and his supermodel friend. Finally, she could no longer stand talking to herself and decided to take a shower. She threw on a robe, because Christine did not even like her female roommate seeing her in her jammies. Besides, she still had her period, which always made her feel somewhat uncomfortable, as though cursed.

She stayed under the shower too long to the point that she wondered why Yolanda, normally a world-class shower-taker, had not offered to throw her a life preserver. After stepping out of the shower, Christine realized Yolanda's bedroom door was open, meaning her roommate was off doing some errand.

Christine threw on her crummiest pair of jeans and most tattered T-shirt, a maroon one, fading, extra large, with Bradley Braves splashed over the front. Sitting down in front of her laptop computer, Christine turned it on. *Who is this man Peter McDonald? Is googling him indecent?*

She decided to do so anyway.

Within a few minutes, she began to cry!

21:55:00

During the several days before a marathon where they serve as color commentators, Timothy Rainboldt and Carolynne Vickers haunt the elite athlete suite, particularly during the morning hours when runners might drop by the suite for breakfast. In this, they were somewhat unique among their colleagues covering the running sport. Most reporters, the broadcast pair noted with just a touch of pride, don't go (or run) the extra mile. "They're content with what the media person hands them at the press conference," so claimed Vickers in one interview.

Carolynne Vickers—or C.V. as her closest friends often called her— made that point to a reporter from *TV Guide*. The reporter interviewed C.V. in New York before she and ex-husband Timothy were scheduled to do the telecast of that city's marathon. Timothy sat in on the interview, adding comments when appropriate and also when not appropriate. The subject of the article was women who had penetrated the once male-only domain of sports reporting.

C.V. never anticipated that sports reporting would become her life work. As a girl growing up in Owensboro, Kentucky, Carolynne Vickers always assumed she would become an elementary school teacher, like her mother and her grandmother. But Carolynne could run. Without particularly trying, she outran most of the boys in her grade school class. This was during the 1970's when few sports were offered girls in school, but C.V. had a boyfriend, who talked her into joining him in a summer road race. She won a trophy; he did not, and their relationship soured soon afterwards.

Beginning in the late 1970s, women's road running had begun to blossom in the United States, though not yet in the rest of the world. Recruited to train with a team sponsored by a shoe company, Carolynne moved to Boulder, Colorado, becoming a much-needed role model for female runners, partly due to her ability, partly due to her good looks and trim figure. *Running Magazine* featured her on its cover.

This taste of celebrity plus the decision of the I.O.C. finally to add the marathon to the 1984 Games in Los Angeles inspired Carolynne to train much harder. Obsessed, averaging more than a hundred miles a week in twice-daily workouts, she reached the best shape of her life and proved it by almost beating Norwegian Grete Waitz at the New York City Marathon. Unfortunately, a sore Achilles tendon aggravated by her overtraining forced Carolynne out of the Olympic Trials won by Joan Benoit, who then won the gold medal at the Olympics. It would be years before C.V. could overcome the feeling that Benoit had stolen a medal that should have been hers.

Carolynne's running career waned. She bailed out of a bad marriage with a 5,000 meter runner and returned to college, hoping finally to make Mom happy. C.V. briefly did become a school teacher in the Denver school system, keeping her house on the edge of Boulder so she could continue to run recreationally in the trails winding up into the Front Range. It was while running the trails early one morning that she met her next husband, Timothy Rainboldt.

A South African and former winner of the Comrades Marathon (a 52-mile race between Durban and Pietermaritzburg), Timothy Rainboldt had moved to Boulder to train with the many foreign athletes located in that distance-running Mecca. Away from the running trails, Timothy's specialty was statistics, teaching classes in that subject at the University of Colorado. The pair eventually married.

Because of her previous fame as a marathoner, but more because of her talking ability coupled with good looks, C.V. soon found herself asked to serve as a color commentator on marathon telecasts as the sport achieved increased popularity through the 1990s. She worked the World Championships, the Olympic Games. She talked several TV stations into hiring Timothy to supply running facts and statistics. "I was a cheap hire," Timothy claimed. "They already had paid for her hotel room."

One year at the Pittsburgh Marathon, another commentator came down with a hacking cough and begged off the job. The producer asked Timothy to substitute and found that his knowledge of the sport combined with a crisp South African accent made him the perfect commentator. Soon, Carolynne and Timothy found themselves in demand as a telecast team.

Unfortunately, their marriage had begun to unravel. They split, reconciled, then split again, all the time prospering broadcasters in demand at most of the major marathons, including Lake City.

So they had come to town. On Sunday, the not-always-happy couple would sit for four hours on either side of anchorman Mark Mellon, describing alternately the men's race and the women's race.

During the interview with the reporter from *TV Guide*, the discussion shifted to the extra attention the pair brought to their jobs. It was because of their backgrounds as elite runners. Few of the other reporters covering marathons would think of stalking runners in the elite athlete suite. Timothy and C.V. did this all the time, sometimes running with them on workouts.

C.V. added: "Most mainstream reporters see the athletes at a press conference, watch them on TV during the race and interview them afterwards, but never get into their souls or learn what motivates them to excellence."

Her fellow commentator and sometime husband Timothy offered an anecdote to the *TV Guide* reporter: "Take Joseph Nduku. To most reporters, Joseph is just another black face, someone who not only speaks accented English, but speaks it softly."

Carolynne continued Timothy's thought as though working from a script: "See Joseph running at the front of the pack in Boston with a dozen other Africans, all black, all short, all skinny, all wearing the same uniform, and he's indistinguishable."

"...But sit down with Joseph and ask about his life outside running, and you learn that he has a wife and two small children...."

"...Some day, Joseph will retire to Kenya, and his prize money will allow him to live a life above those of his poorer countrymen."

SATURDAY

Timothy could see that the *TV Guide* reporter had stopped writing, her glazed-over eyes indicating that all this carefully presented information by the articulate pair was incidental to the main thrust of her magazine assignment: women in sports reporting.

The *TV Guide* reporter asked: "All this detail about life back in Kenya might be interesting for The Discovery Channel, but how would you use it during a sports broadcast?"

Carolynne Vickers paused a moment, somewhat irritated by the question, though she was too media-savvy to show that irritation. "I *might not* use it," C.V. responded. "In a four-hour telecast, we *might* have a half dozen thirty-second segments when Timothy or I *might* have a chance to say something other than who is leading and who *might* catch whom. But it's important to me to learn as much as I can. You never know when you will need to fill with details about someone who has just won the race, except you can't get to him, because he's throwing up, or someone from BBC snuck ahead of you, and the volunteer guarding the winner does not know who the hell you are..."

"...because the volunteer follows the NBA instead of marathons."

Oh shut up, Timothy, thought Carolynne, her irritation at the reporter spilling into irritation with him and his perennial habit of stepping on her lines, something he did all the time during telecasts, which always pissed her off. After broadcasts, Carolynne would tell Timothy that, but it never seemed to enter the man's statistic-crammed brain.

Timothy finally did shut up, because he noticed that the *TV Guide* reporter's pen was moving rapidly across her notebook. He wondered whether she was writing down what he just said or what C.V. just said. Timothy hoped the latter, because he knew she hated getting misquoted.

The reporter had one more question: "But why spend time interviewing a male, Carolynne, when your job is to cover the female marathoners?"

"We share," said C.V. tersely.

"We share," echoed Timothy impishly, waiting to see how his television partner would respond next.

"But I don't just cover 'the women's part of the marathon.' I cover the marathon, period, both men and women. Although the anchorman might defer to me while the women are on screen, and he might defer to Timothy with men on screen, if I have something to say about the men, I say it. If Timothy has something to say about the women, he says it."

"We step on each others lines," said Timothy, smiling.

"We've been known to scream at each other during commercial breaks for doing just that," said Carolynne in a moment of self-revelation.

"Sometimes C.V. can be such a...." Timothy paused

"Don't say it...."

"I hadn't planned to, dear."

Carolynne and Timothy continued to smile sweetly at each other.

The *TV Guide* reporter closed her notebook though somewhat puzzled. Wasn't this couple married, or once married, but divorced? She decided not to ask, because it was an embarrassing question, its answer unimportant to her story, which featured *her*, not him.

When the article eventually did appear in *TV Guide*, it focused mostly on female commentators who covered the so-called popular, male-dominated sports from football to basketball to ice hockey to baseball. One paragraph featuring Carolynne Vickers did appear:

Women reporters often bring a different dimension to the world of sports reporting. Carolynne Vickers, a color commentator for marathons, takes time to know each of the runners, talking to them about their homes and families, not merely their fast times. "You never know when you might need to fill with details," claims Vickers.

When Carolynne read the article, it did not anger her as much as exasperate her. C.V. immediately called Timothy, who was not living with her at the time. "Did you read what that bitch wrote?" she said without bothering to introduce herself.

"Don't use that word, C.V." Timothy chided his ex-wife good-naturedly. "It's not a word nice girls use."

"I'm not a nice girl."

"Nice women then."

"Don't patronize me, Timothy."

"I would never do that."

"How long did we talk to that reporter? Achh! She had a tape recorder going. She scribbled constantly in her notebook And look at the tiny paragraph and tiny quote. Wait, let me count. A dozen ousy words."

"Eleven. I already counted."

"Damn it, Timothy. You know me better than my mother. You realized I would call as soon as I read that article"

"I also know you're going to be in New York next week for that planning meeting before the marathon. How about dinner afterwards?"

"You know I'm going to say yes. Who pays?"

"No matter. Whoever does will put it on an expense account."

Carolynne sighed before responding. "We're supposed to be divorced, Timothy. You're not supposed to ask your ex-wife out on dates. You'll probably ask me to sleep with you."

"That thought entered my mind."

"And I'll probably say yes."

"It depends on how many glasses of wine you've had."

SATURDAY

"My limit is two glasses after which I'm out of control."

"That's why I'm planning to order the most expensive wine on the menu, a Chardonnay from Stellenbosch. Cost doesn't matter…"

"…because it's going onto an expense account," they said simultaneously,. C.V. hung up the phone without bothering to say goodbye. God, she couldn't wait to get in bed with him again.

That conversation was typical of ones between Carolynne Vickers and Timothy Rainboldt, who, several months after the *TV Guide* article, arrived in Lake City to serve as color commentators for the marathon. And though staying in separate rooms on different floors of the Hilliard Towers, and without previous thought or planning, they both headed for the elite athletes' suite on the twenty-first floor of the Hilliard Towers at precisely the same time.

C.V. stepped onto the elevator and encountered Timothy's smiling face. "Oh, God. This is scary."

"Good morning, C.V." said Timothy. "Did you sleep well?"

"I always sleep well—alone!"

The suite was empty except for one or two members of the marathon staff, but Carolynne and Timothy had learned patience in their dual jobs as commentators. They would sip coffee (C.V.) and tea (Timothy) and nibble on danish (Timothy) and bagels (C.V.) and talk to anyone who wandered into the suite, whether athlete or agent—and sometimes they got the best stories from the agents—or even a massage therapist, who might let slip the fact that someone had a stiff hamstring or calf muscle, or how excited certain top women were on learning that Aba was pregnant, because it meant they would move up a place in the standings and earn more prize money.

Visiting the food table first, the sometimes couple moved to a room with a view of the lake, sitting down in separate couches, close to each other, but not too close. At that moment, a runner arrived, so black that his skin glowed. He came to the suite at 10:05 still dressed in his running gear, certainly not sweating. It was Joseph Nduku, the defending champion.

21:55:00. 21:54:59. 21:54:58.

Nduku's smile was so broad, his teeth so white, that he could have been the perfect pitchman for a TV commercial for toothpaste—that is, if advertising agencies used Kenyans for TV commercials. "Miss Carolynne," said Nduku. "Why am I not surprised to see you here?"

"Because you know the coffee is free."

"Hopefully it is Kenyan coffee."

One of the marathon staffers, who had been placing press releases on a table adjoining the food table, felt obliged to interrupt: "Actually, it *is* a brand of Kenyan coffee. Peter McDonald insisted that we offer it."

"Mr. Timothy," said the Kenyan runner, offering the broadcaster his hand. "So good to see the two of you together again."

"Don't you dare say another word, Joseph," warned Carolynne.

The Kenyan shrugged, "It's just that sometimes you are together and sometimes you are not together. And even if you are together, I don't know whether you are not together." Nduku sat down in a chair near the two broadcasters and put his coffee and bagel on the table, indicating he would spend some time talking to old friends.

"He knows us too well," Timothy admitted to Carolynne.

"We're not together this morning," said Carolynne, "but we're also together." Saying that and seeing Joseph's smile, she could not help thinking that a lot of reporters covering the marathon would be surprised to know that even the fastest of the fast Kenyans might have good senses of humor.

"As long as you are here," began Joseph, "I might as well tell you about an announcement I plan to make at the press conference in another hour. It's about what I plan to do with my prize money from Sunday's race."

"Tell us, Joseph," asked Carolynne. When he did, friend to friend, she was amazed at the humanity of this Kenyan runner, so little known by most Americans, who only saw him on TV or read about him in the sports pages.

21:45:00

Peter McDonald's 10:00 lecture at the Expo had gone smoothly. Several hundred people filled the seats in front of the main stage. He spoke for about fifteen minutes, offering a quick tour of the marathon course, complete with images flashed on the screen behind him. Peter had given two course lectures yesterday and had one more to do later in the afternoon. Various other experts and celebrities would lecture throughout the two days of the Expo.

"I need to rush back to the hotel for an 11:00 press conference," Peter admitted to his audience at the conclusion of his talk, "but I'll be happy to answer a few questions."

His time today was precious, but Peter did not want to seem eager to flee the stage. He had a van awaiting outside a nearby exit. Traffic should be light on a Saturday morning. Ten minutes for questions, and he would be out the door to his next task.

21:45:00. 21:44:59. 21:44:58.

SATURDAY

While waiting for hands to go up, Peter twisted open a bottle of water he had purchased at a concession stand before mounting the stage. The air in the hall was dry, and he had much talking to do this weekend. Unless he hydrated as carefully as the runners, his voice would be little more than a rasp whisper by Sunday evening.

Peter drank from the water bottle, replaced the cap and waited for someone to ask a question. Nobody wanted to be first.

Runners might wonder *why*, on such a busy weekend, Peter McDonald would take time to stand in front of a crowd, particularly when a JumboTron screen over The Lake City Bank booth displayed continuously a video tour of the course, cameras rushing over it in fast forward mode, visually covering 26 miles 385 yards in two minutes and 30 seconds. But it was more than vanity on Peter's part. He was (in marketing parlance) "an entitlement."

Entitlements sometimes consisted of signs along the course, ads in the program and links on the race Web site. In selling sponsorships, the marathon office found that attaching a sponsor's name to a lecture featuring Peter or one of the other clinic speakers sometimes provided just that extra perquisite that cinched the deal. In return for its fee, the sponsor became *entitled* to attach its name to that of Peter McDonald, who as director of the Lake City Marathon was its most visible and most valuable spokesperson.

There was another more important reason why Peter found time for the lectures: He *enjoyed* doing them. He liked the interface that talking to a crowd provided. It gave him a direct connection to the running public, his true bosses. He learned from questions asked by the audience. It was feedback that otherwise might not so easily be obtained. Peter knew it was too easy to get locked into procedures because you always did it that way. But that ignores the fact that there might be a better procedure, if you took time to identify it.

A runner in the front row raised his hand: "How do you measure the course, so we know it is accurate? I assume it is."

"Very accurate," Peter responded. "As close to 26 miles 385 yards as we can get. The course needs to be at *least* that long otherwise any records set on it—world records or your Personal Records—would not count. But you don't want the course long either, since that adds seconds to the time needed to qualify for Boston."

Peter quickly described the technique necessary to measure a course accurately and get it certified for world record purposes. "We ride the course with a bicycle, several bicycles actually. By counting the number of revolutions and calibrating that to a previously tape-measured mile, we can guarantee everybody gets to run the right distance."

"Do you need to re-measure the course each year?"

"Only if we change the course, and sometimes the mayor's office asks us to make small changes. Lake City is a dynamic city with projects continually happening. The course has remained the same for three years, and we have not re-measured during that time. We would after a world record to make sure the distance was correct."

Peter left unstated the fact that predicted hot weather made records unlikely, but after several additional questions related to aid stations and spectator viewing points, someone touched on that subject:

"Several years ago during a hot weather marathon, officials actually stopped runners early, bussing them to the finish line. Would you do that?"

"We have contingency plans. We hope not to be forced to use them."

Peter did not elaborate on those contingency plans, and no one seemed to want to press the issue, perhaps not wanting to consider the thought that their marathon Sunday would end before 26 miles 335 yards for reasons out of their control. A new speaker was waiting to offer the next lecture. Peter thanked his audience again for their attention and descended from the main stage, shaking hands with several runners he encountered at the bottom of the stairs, staying in motion, knowing that if he stopped a crowd might gather and prevent his getting to the press conference due to start in a half hour.

Walking down the center aisle, he passed the *Running Magazine* booth. A line had formed in front of Don Geoffrey autographing race numbers and copies of his book. Spotting the race director, the Turtle shouted: "Peter, did you see the column by Jonathan Von Runyon in this morning's *Ledger*?"

"I'm not sure I want to hear about it," said Peter, not breaking stride.

The Turtle called after Peter, quoting the headline over Von Runyon's column: "How Oprah Ruined the Marathon."

Peter could only shake his head as he continued to move toward the exit. "I was right," he told the Turtle. "I did *not* want to hear about it."

21:05:00

S eated toward the back of the Marquette Room, waiting for Saturday morning's press conference to begin, Timothy Rainboldt read the *Lake City Ledger*. He just had been handed the newspaper without comment, by Carolynne Vickers seated next to him. Timothy's attention, as C.V. knew it would, had been drawn immediately to a column bannered on the front page. The time was five minutes before the hour Peter McDonald had just arrived from the Expo and was talking to several people at the front of the room, including defending champion Joseph Nduku.

21:05:00. 21:04:59. 21:04:58.

Carolynne noted with amusement that the column bothered Timothy. As he continued to read, C.V. heard him mumble angrily several times:

"Ridiculous!"

And: "What an idiot!"

Finally: "I simply cannot believe that a responsible newspaper would print such garbage!"

Carolynne knew exactly what disturbed Timothy, having just finished reading the column herself before passing him the newspaper. The column, irresponsible though it might be, amused more than angered her. She played dumb, suppressing a smile: "Responsible newspapers do not exist anymore, Timothy. What's your problem?"

"All this does is pander to a public that thrives on negativism."

C.V. peered over Timothy's shoulder as though to determine the cause of his anger. "Consider the source, Timothy."

The column with its provocative headline read:

How Oprah ruined the marathon

By Jonathan Von Runyon
LEDGER REPORTER

Watch on TV or from sidewalks at various locations around town this weekend, and you will see in the Lake City Marathon la crème de la crème. Race director Peter McDonald has done his usual superb job recruiting an elite field.

See how they run. The fastest of fast runners from Kenya, including defending champion Joseph Nduku. The swiftest of the swift females, even though world record holder Aba Andersson, pregnant, plans not to compete.

They streak through the streets with the grace of deer in motion.

But get to the course early, because soon after the deer pass come the snails and the turtles and the elephants, runners possessed of little grace, hideous to observe in motion.

If you want to appreciate a marathon run in style, you need to arrive on time—and leave on time as well.

For even as the champions step before the cameras to accept the spoils of victory, the Lake City Marathon will start to get ugly, like all major marathons these days. Not all these arriving at the finish line afterwards possess the élan of the superbly trained leaders.

Some cross the line arms raised as though in victory, but what victory is it when you finish an hour or more behind the leaders?

Others stumble across that line, spent, exhausted, faces contorted in agony. They puke their Gatorade on the shoes of finish chute volunteers, who somehow have been coerced into being part of this disgraceful spectacle.

And many—too many in my mind—do not even reach the line. Woefully undertrained, coerced into running too long a distance by charities greedy for donations, attracted to the sport of long distance running because of its being chic and because "anybody can do it" (even if you're overweight and only gave up smoking last week), these unwashed masses have brought disgrace to a noble sport.

Blame Oprah.

Oprah is the one who ruined the marathon!

The marathon once was a sport of aficionados in the best meaning of that word. Forget for a moment that the first marathoner in ancient Athens, Pheidippides, supposedly died at the end of his run. His was a Greek historian's fantasy, but at least those who followed in Pheidippides' legendary footsteps respected his ethic. If not always of Olympic caliber, marathoners through the first half of the last century trained hard and raced with pride.

In the era before Frank Shorter won an Olympic gold medal, the Boston Marathon had no standards—and needed none for the few hundred who ran it each year. All could finish within an hour of the winner, and the officials could pocket their stopwatches and head to the taverns early.

No more! With his victory, Shorter changed the marathon ethic, but he and Bill Rodgers, another American hero of his time, did not ruin it. The pair inspired Baby Boomers to get off their couches and train relentlessly to lose weight and lower their times, and if that improved their health, so be it.

These nouveaux marathoners were almost entirely male. In the same year as Shorter's victory (1972), only 1,220 men ran the Boston Marathon. And five females, women having just been permitted entry to Boston that same year.

Then came Oprah!

In 1995, the woman who is arguably the world's best known talk show host appeared unexpectedly at the starting line of the Marine

Corps Marathon. And made it to the finish line too, completing the race in 4:29:20.

Give Oprah credit. She trained hard for the race under the direction of a personal trainer, Bob Greene. Never possessed of fashion-model slimness, she lost weight, pounds and pounds of it rolling off as she upped her mileage. She modified her diet, serving as a positive role model for so many females.

Unfortunately, in Oprah's wake came many less prepared, lured to the marathon by the siren song: *If Oprah can do it, so can I.*

But while many of those entered in the Lake City Marathon tomorrow can do it, few can do it well.

Consider the effect that Oprah has had on the time standards of most major marathons. In the era of Frank Shorter, the median time for runners doing marathons (according to Running USA) was 3:32; now that time has sunk to a barely respectable 4:20. Hordes of joggers in their quest for mediocrity have slowed the marathon, once a competitive race, now an exercise in self-improvement.

Two streakers, so called because they have run and completed each Lake City Marathon since its founding in 1979, comment upon the degradation of the marathon sport.

"The bar is set so low," says one, "everyone becomes a winner."

"If Oprah could run a marathon," so says another, "shame on anyone who cannot."

I hide their identities to protect them from the verbal abuse they might get from those who think finishing in four, five, six and even more hours is perfectly acceptable behavior. It is, if you have no respect for the skill and dedication it takes to finish in half that time.

The effect on the front of the field has been as negative as on the back. Frank Shorter and Joan Benoit Samuelson won Olympic gold medals. Bill Rodgers won Boston and New York four times each. Alberto Salazar won each of those races in record times. In the quarter century following those champions, American runners have fared poorly against the best of the world.

In Sunday's marathon, once the elite runners pass, observe those trailing. Despite rules that supposedly ban the use of iPods, too many runners will be wearing these devices, listening to canned music to divert their minds from the subject at hand. Could you imagine Tiger Woods wearing an iPod at the Masters Championships? Roger Federer at Wimbledon? Or any other respectable golfer or tennis player for that matter?

What about racers in the Indianapolis 500: Expect to see any of them come hurtling toward the turns at 230 mph to the music of Bon Jovi? Yet runners wear iPods saying it distracts them from the pain of their sport.

Perhaps the marathon would be less painful if they properly trained for it.

Timothy Rainboldt stopped reading, closed the paper, and began shaking it at Carolynne Vickers as though he were scolding a puppy that had just soiled the carpet. "Can you imagine the effrontery of this oaf?"

"Now Timothy," said C.V., simultaneously nodding to an individual who with the press conference about to begin had just arrived, claiming a seat in the front row. "Comes the dragon."

Timothy glared at Jonathan Von Runyon. "What think you, Carolynne? Shall I take this paper and ram it down the evil man's throat?"

She looked at him and laughed. "No time for that, Timothy." Peter McDonald had moved toward the front of the room to begin the press conference. With him came defending champion Joseph Nduku and, to the surprise of many, one of the most glamorous women in the world.

Timothy Rainboldt immediately lost interest in throttling Von Runyon. "What is Naní doing here?" he asked Carolynne Vickers.

"If you pay attention, Timothy dear, perhaps we'll find out."

21:00:00

Jonathan Von Runyon arrived at the press conference in the Hilliard's Marquette Room almost precisely at 11:00, choosing a seat in the front row, as if to announce by his presence, *Now that I am here, it is all right to begin.*

Many among the media disliked Von Runyon, even despised him, for the attitude that he, a respected golf reporter, was doing the sport of running a favor by covering it. His column on how Oprah had ruined the marathon might not have angered reporters who thrived on sensationalism, but it was hardly designed to make any friends among those who covered road racing regularly like Don Geoffrey or Timothy Rainboldt and Carolynne Vickers. Nor was it likely to improve his esteem among those running the race on Sunday, now twenty-one hours away.

21:00:00. 20:59:59. 20:59:58.

SATURDAY

Despite Von Runyon's perfectly timed entrance, he was barely noticed as he moved to his front-row seat, a shadow figure when compared to the woman standing with Joseph Nduku and Peter McDonald in the front of the room: Naní! All eyes had shifted to focus on the face that launched a thousand tabloid headlines.

Even the women were stunned by Naní's majesty. The fashionable fashion model was dressed in a mostly black dashiki kaftan, the buttonless dress and floor-length garment favored by West African women. The garment both hid the supermodel's slender figure and tantalizingly offering hints of what lay below the cloth, her simmering sexuality presented almost with innocence rather than with any attempt to seduce. The male reporters, who had seen Naní posed frequently in skimpy bathing suits in the *Sports Illustrated* annual swimsuit issue, certainly had no difficulty picturing what the kaftan failed to reveal. A black, green, yellow and blue scarf thrust almost carelessly around her neck highlighted the outfit. Gold Tanzanite earrings punctuated it.

Only a few of the sports reporters knew that black, green, yellow and blue were the colors of the Tanzanian flag, Naní's mother having come from that country. Timothy Rainboldt, being South African, knew, but so did Jonathan Von Runyon, because Von Runyon knew everything.

Christine Ferrara did not know. She had not given the subject of African flags much thought. Christine stood apart from her trusted cameraman Edmund Giesbert in the back of the room, because she did not want to get too close to Peter, not after what she learned about his wife after googling his name earlier this morning. A single word described her: *embarrassed*. Embarrassed for doubting him.

At age thirty-two, though not yet ready for AARP, Naní might have seemed past her prime matched against the barely-old-enough-to-drink models who haughtily heel-stomped down the runway at the Lake Theatre the day before, but nobody could convince any of the men in the room of that fact. The Hilliard's air conditioning system had been successfully coping with the heat wave in Lake City to this point, but seemed to have failed in the Marquette Room as the press conference began.

At the front of the room, there was no podium. Several hotel workers had begun to wheel a podium into place, but media director Nelson Ogilvie told them to remove it, figuring he did not want a piece of furniture, even with the bank's name plastered on it, standing between the eyes and cameras of those attending and their female celebrity. The room was small. No mike was needed, not even for someone as soft spoken as Joseph Nduku.

Peter McDonald wasted little time in offering introductions, nodding toward Nduku as he did: "Most of you previously have met, and interviewed,

212

our defending champion, his winning time a course record 2:05:37 last year."
Nduku smiled, his white teeth against ebony skin sparkling like a flashbulb.

Peter began to turn, his movements away from the Kenyan athlete as slow
and precise as a revolving rooftop restaurant. When he stopped, his eyes now
focused on the tall woman by his side. "We also have with us today...."

The race director paused, almost as though hers was a name that could not
be said aloud without proper inflection.

"...Naní!"

To Christine's surprise, almost to her dismay the mostly male reporters
spontaneously began to applaud. Even the women! Even Jonathan Von Runyon politely padded his hands together.

Is this not a press conference? wondered Christine. *We are journalists. We
are not supposed to applaud people we cover.* Christine thought she learned
this in Journalism 101, a course she had aced while a student at Bradley. *Yes,
Ms. Supermodel is fabulous, guys, but are you not being just a bit sexist?*

As Peter's attention shifted back to Joseph Nduku, Christine found herself
almost against her will staring at Naní. Had she noticed a look pass between
the supermodel and Peter? Was she being jealous? Had she any right to be?

Still focused on Naní, the words spoken by Joseph Nduku at first failed to
interrupt her thoughts. But the subject was not running. Speaking softly with
an accent as rippling as the effect of the wind touching the grasses of the Se-
rengeti, the Kenyan talked not about running, but about the problem of AIDS
and the children of Africa. He discussed the fact that this devastating disease
had claimed millions of lives and would continue to claim more unless the
world paid more attention. And unless the men of Africa, the tribes of his
country and tribes throughout that continent, educated themselves as to why
AIDS spreads from heterosexual males to cohabitating females and eventually, and tragically, to the offspring of their unions, the children. "The innocent
children of Africa," said Joseph Nduku. He spoke with such sorrow and such
emotion that even though his voice was like a whisper, its words were immediately understood even by the male reporters who finally had shifted their
attention away from Naní.

But Joseph's next words were so astounding that even the supermodel's
beauty would not distract from what he said. "To help the children of Africa,"
said Joseph, "I am donating my prize money to AIDS Africa."

The magnanimity of his offer struck like a laser beam. There was a pause.
Could silence be visible? This one was.

"Your prize money?" one reporter finally asked, as though he had heard
the words, but did not understand them.

"Yes."

"One hundred thousand dollars, if you win?" asked another reporter. It was Jonathan Von Runyon. Even he seemed stunned.

"Yes."

And for the next several minutes, the reporters peppered Nduku with questions, obviously impressed that a man whose country was among the most impoverished in the world would donate such an immense sum. The head of a local investment firm only a few days before had donated $25 million to Lake City University, but that now seemed almost like a trivial sum compared to the commitment of this humble African.

For the second time, the journalists applauded.

One not applauding was another Kenyan runner who attended the Saturday afternoon press conference not as a matter of obligation, but more from a sense of curiosity as to what his rival might say. Kenyatta Kemai, seated next to his cousin Moses Abraham, would not offer his thoughts to the reporters present—if they even cared—but Joseph's seemingly generous offering offended him. *Just one more instance of Joseph grandstanding,* he thought. Joseph would not donate the money out of his sizable (for a Kenyan) fortune; he would get one of his sponsors to do so.

Kemai knew one way he could cause Joseph's contribution to be less than promised. He would beat him! Simple as that. He and Abraham already had plans to insure that Joseph Nduku would not cross the finish line first.

Even Christine Ferrara, journalistic principles notwithstanding, had joined her colleagues applauding Nduku's last announcement. Now, as she edged her way up the side wall to be closer to the action, she saw the reporters shifting their attention back to Naní. Christine now found herself forgetting about the plight of the children of Africa. Her own personal plight somehow seemed more important: *How can I compete with someone so famous and glamorous?* And, *Is Peter interested in her?*

More to the point: *Is she interested in him?*

As Naní began also to talk about AIDS Africa, Christine—she would feel guilty about this later—continued to focus on her own personal crisis, or what she perceived to be a crisis. She knew that she should not worry. She should simply do her job, and if Peter or some other Mister Right came along, that would be fine. It was not that Christine was incapable of attracting men. Her worry, given the celebrity of her job, was more attracting too many men. Or the wrong kind of men.

Naní expanded on what Joseph Nduku had said during this flight of Christine Ferrara's imagination: "But we are also here to talk about running. Yesterday on her TV show, Oprah Winfrey asked me about my running. Oprah knew I was headed to Lake City to join a wonderful group of runners, several hundred of them planning to run the Lake City Marathon, each of them raising money for AIDS Africa. She asked, was I running the marathon myself? And I would not respond, although Oprah knew the answer because I had told her my plans backstage, pledging her to secrecy."

Speaking those words, Naní directed her attention to the side of the room until Christine thought the supermodel almost was staring at her. In fact, Naní *was* staring at Christine!

"And I have to apologize to Christine, because yesterday at the fashion show she asked the same question, which I refused to answer."

Christine froze as eyes in the room shifted from Naní to her. She felt her face begin to turn red, as red as her TV3 blouse. Not quite, but close, as Edmund would tell her later. *Naní remembers my name?* That surprised Christine at first. *Well, duah, we talked yesterday at the fashion show and later at the bank party, but Naní must meet and be introduced to hundreds of different people over the course of a year, thousands! Ms. Supermodel either possesses an excellent memory, or Peter told her about me. But why? Our relationship has barely reached the flirtation stage, and in the meantime he seems to have a more famous "her" fluttering around him. Is Peter worth my fluttering?* Christine decided she would suspend judgment at least until after this weekend, by which time her rival presumably would have fled town.

The questions and answers between the press and the supermodel continued for several more minutes. After that, still photographers and reporters with TV cameramen attached moved into place, each seeking a minute of Naní's time. One of them was Christine, who in her flustered state of mind would not remember immediately afterwards what was said between the two of them. She would review the interview when she got back to the studio.

As the press conference ended, Christine saw Naní move to one corner to talk with Peter and Joseph Nduku. She conferred briefly with Edmund her cameraman. He planned to head back to the studio. There was no *Noon News* on Saturday, so she said she would stay: "I want to hang around the hotel to absorb some of the color." Christine did not feel hungry, figuring she could snatch a bagel and a Diet Coke at the media center later. Except Naní had disengaged herself from Peter and was walking toward—*me!*

"Christine," said Naní, so sweetly that Christine wanted to melt. "Have you got a few minutes?"

Have I got a few minutes? The woman whose image and words everyone wants to capture is asking me, do I have a few minutes?

"Yes," said Christine, rather weakly.

"Good," said the supermodel, "because *you* and *I* need to have a girl-to-girl talk..."

Cradling Christine's arm as to ensure that the TV reporter could not escape, Naní added: "...about a mutual acquaintance."

Christine looked back over her shoulder to where she had last seen Peter, as though needing his approval, but he already had departed the room.

20:30:00

Naní tugged Christine out of the room, avoiding as politely as she could several reporters who sought interviews. "Hungry?" Naní whispered conspiratorially in the hallway. Christine responded that she was "famished." She was not, but who could refuse an invitation to lunch with the supermodel?

20:30:00. 20:29:59. 20:29:58

"I have to carbo-load for my race tomorrow," Naní explained. "Have you run a marathon, Christine?"

"Once. Not very fast."

"Perfect. I need to talk to a fellow not-very-fast runner."

But will we talk about running? Christine thought not.

Still hanging onto Christine's arm, the supermodel marched her toward a bank of elevators and pushed the "down" button. Waiting for an elevator to arrive, the two women said nothing to each other. An elevator door slid open. It was crowded, mostly with runners who muscled each other out of the way to allow two very beautiful women join them.

One of the runners said to Naní: "I hear you're running the marathon, Naní. Good luck."

Naní turned toward him astounded. Her voice rose an octave: "You heard that? We just announced that barely five minutes ago!"

The runner held up his digital phone as though to indicate that the news had travelled around the world via the Internet in that brief span of time. "How are we to keep any secrets?" Naní shook her head in astonishment. "The people living in my mother's village back in Tanzania probably know already. Once, we communicated by drums."

The elevator arrived at the ground floor. Exiting, the two women debated their options, including an outdoor café on Jefferson Avenue, pleasant eating given the warm weather. But that seemed too public, given pedestrians passing back and forth. Finally, they chose to eat at the lobby restaurant opposite the main desk, figuring they could disappear among the sea of runners, all measuring their carbohydrates against proteins and fats.

What is she about to say? worried Christine, as they walked toward the restaurant. She noticed heads turning, people recognizing the supermodel. *She has no privacy, thought Christine. And probably only a handful of individuals, whom she can call close friends. Peter apparently is one of them.*

The hallway overflowed with runners, wandering back and forth, standing in small groups talking, waiting in line to check in. A friendly maitre d' spotted Naní and allowed the supermodel and her somewhat less famous companion to bypass a line waiting for tables, waving them to the front. Though this temporarily embarrassed Christine, Naní seemed used to celebrity treatment and handled it well, apologizing to those being bypassed, who did not seem offended. Naní requested a table, "in the corner," so they could talk quietly without being pestered by autograph-seekers and picture-takers.

Christine ordered a Reuben sandwich and an iced tea. Naní ordered a bowl of minestrone and a Caesar salad "with dressing on the side," and "bring lots of rolls," and "iced tea for me too."

As the waiter departed with their orders, Christine folded her arms, placing her elbows on the edge of the table and leaned forward, waiting for their planned girl-to-girl talk to begin. But it did not come. Naní merely looked pleasantly toward her, sipping from a plastic water bottle she had fished out of her purse, hydrating for tomorrow's race. They exchanged several pleasantries, forgotten within seconds after the words left their mouths. They talked about the press conference. They talked about the weather, everybody's main topic of conversation that weekend.

The waiter returned with a plate of rolls and two glasses of water, the promise of iced teas to come later. Naní placed her water bottle back in her purse. Apparently having gathered courage and realizing that if she took one more sip of water, she would be up all night peeing, Naní leaned forward so their conversation would not be overheard by people eating nearby.

"I know you're interested in Peter, and Peter is interested in you."

"We've just met," Christine protested.

Naní offered her sternest look. "Don't deny it, Ms. Ferrara. My grandmother was a witch doctor, and I possess her psychic powers. I saw what happened when you walked into the room last night at the bank party. You looked at him, and he looked at you. The lightning discharge was measurable. You could see the lights dim."

"You could not," argued Christine. But she was disarmed as Naní's stern look melted into a gentle smile. "Was it really that obvious?" asked Christine, her voice a whisper as though worried someone at the next table might overhear them.

"Mmmm-*hmmm*," said Naní.

"Did Peter notice?

"Are you kidding?" huffed Naní. "Men are clueless."

Why is she telling me this? wondered Christine. *She doesn't seem angry. Is Peter her lover, or is he not?*

The waiter brought the iced tea. Naní took a sip, continuing, "Then did I not notice the arrival at the party of—*ta-tummm*—the Green-Eyed Monster?"

"The Green-Eyed Monster?"

"Jealousy!"

Christine sighed. It was a very loud sigh. It said more than words. *Naní is about to say something, but what?* She hoped it was not bad news.

"Because you worried that Peter and I were—may I pause for emphasis?—an *item?*"

"Yes." It was a very weak yes.

"Because you worried that Peter loved me, and I loved Peter."

"Yes." Weaker still.

"And we do..." Naní paused before continuing her thought.

During this briefest of brief pauses, a chill began to run down Christine's spine for fear that the news would, indeed, be very, very bad.

Then Naní completed her thought: "...like a brother loves his sister. And like a sister loves her brother in return."

"Oh." Barely audible.

"Peter and I are very close friends. But merely friends!"

"Oh." A volume increase.

"Tell the Green-Eyed Monster, he has no business interfering with our friendship: I with Peter; hopefully now, I with you."

Christine did not know what to say, but so far the girl-to-girl talk was not going badly. She began to reach for a roll, but decided that was a stalling tactic in the conversation between two women whose relationship might not be what she feared.

"Besides, I'm married," Naní said. "Happily married, I should add."

"Married?"

"To the publisher of *Zest*."

"Ricco?" This shocked Christine. She knew the name of the man who was as well known in his circles as Naní in hers. "I didn't know that."

"Not everybody does. You would need to read the tabloids very closely to realize that fact."

"I hate reading the tabloids."

Naní laughed. "I think we're going to be friends. I *know* we're going to be friends, Christine." The supermodel paused again. The smile on her face disappeared to be replaced by a sad expression. "I could use another friend. I lost one recently."

Christine felt her head spinning. The waiter reappeared with a bowl of mine-strone for the carbo-loading supermodel, a Reuben sandwich for the less diet-fastidious TV reporter. Simultaneously, they thanked him, both eager that he leave them to continue their conversation.

"Can I get you anything else?" asked the waiter.

"No," they responded together, not even looking at him. *Who was this friend that Naní lost?* wondered Christine. *Tell me! Tell me!* The supermodel did just that:

"Peter's wife."

"Oh, Naní!" Christine's eyes suddenly filled with tears.

Naní's eyes too clouded. She reached out and put one hand over Chris-tine's on the table. "You know about Carol?"

"Yes."

"Did Peter tell you?"

"No."

"But you found out somehow."

Christine reached for her napkin, using it to temporarily stem the flow of tears. "I'm embarrassed to tell you how I found out."

"Try me."

"I googled him."

Naní's shook her head in amazement more than amusement. "That is *so* precious. Wait until I tell Peter."

"Don't you dare!"

"Maybe I won't, but..." Naní paused again, her voice more serious. "If you googled Peter, maybe you learned how Carol died."

"I did and probably cried for five minutes afterwards."

"That doesn't come close to the number of tears I shed, Christine. Carol was my roommate in college. She was like the sister I never had."

"I didn't know that."

So the supermodel began to talk about the woman who chance had chosen as her roommate when both attended Hamilton College in New York more than a dozen years before. Some administrative assistant pairing females had de-termined that the two would be brought together, and the two young women had become instant friends, lifetime friends as it would happen. One lifetime shortened; another, continuing. The words poured out of Naní, as though she had been waiting since her roommate's death for someone to absorb her grief.

Peter came along later after the roommates had graduated, Naní explained. She had pursued a career as a model, despite her degree in political science;

SATURDAY

Carol, having majored in English literature, became salesperson then assistant manager of a book store in Lake City. Carol had grown up in a northern suburb, Christine learned. The store where she worked was downtown, and one day this man walked into the store seeking a book, which the store did not have in stock. Carol, dutiful salesperson that she was, said she could order it for him, and Peter later admitted that he might have sought to purchase the book at another store down the block, except ordering it gave him an excuse to return and see again this attractive woman who waited on him. She was not in the store several days later when he returned for the book, so he paid for it with a credit card, but kept returning until she was.

"It was love at first sight, for both of them," said Naní, the supermodel's forehead now only inches away from that of the TV reporter. Their eyes locked. Naní had reached forward to cover one of Christine's hands with her own. Food on the table temporarily was forgotten. "That's what Carol told me later, as though she knew that this man who walked into the store soon would be hers, and he knew she would be his."

Naní learned about Carol's new boyfriend first in emails and later in long telephone conversations and later in person when her exploding career as supermodel brought her through Lake City—and she kept finding excuses to flit through town. She liked Peter instantly. She found him to be polite, considerate, humble, yet ambitious, qualities not always found in young males, the prototypical Mr. Right. The romance blossomed, thoroughly documented by emails back and forth that Naní wished she somehow had saved. "I miss her, Christine. I truly and honestly do. I know Peter misses her more, but she left a vacuum in my heart."

When Carol walked down the aisle to appropriate music by Mendelssohn, Naní was there to fuss with her train as the two friends she loved most pledged to spend the rest of their lives together, but neither realized how short that life would be for one of them.

Ironic, but Naní might not be raising money for AIDS Africa had it not been for Carol. The supermodel was in Aruba for a photo shoot that would result in her appearing again in a swimsuit on the cover of *Sports Illustrated,* when her former roommate text-messaged her, "I'm going to Tanzania."

Tanzania! Naní's mother had been born in Tanzania, had met her archeologist father there, had earned a modicum of fame as Miss Tanzania. But fame was not always a blessing in Africa, where people who had little wanted your "more," and sometimes took it at knife or gunpoint, and sometimes you did not survive the taking. Her parents moved to Paris, where, growing up, she learned to converse fluently in French, an asset in the fashion business. Naní came to the U.S. to attend college. It was after graduation that Naní was discovered by a photographer and encouraged toward a modeling career.

As her career blossomed as a supermodel, Naní never found time to visit the country of her mother's birth. They did not hold too many fashion shows in Dar es Salaam. Her mother did not want to return to that country, having closed that chapter in her life, and Naní gave traveling to Africa little thought until she received the text-message from Carol McDonald.

Naní quickly responded: "Why are you going to Tanzania? When are you going to Tanzania?"

"AIDS walk," Carol text-messaged back. "Next February. Join me."

And after more text-messages and emails and telephone calls, Carol explaining that she was participating in a five-day walk around Mount Kilimanjaro to raise money to combat the growing problem of AIDS in Africa, Naní carved enough time out of her busy schedule to join her college roommate. It had been a mind-changing experience.

Naní worried that two wealthy Americans would not be welcomed in the country of her mother's birth. On the East Coast of Africa, south of Kenya on the Indian Ocean, Tanzania is home to 38 million people, most of them living off the land, 90 percent of the workforce farmers. They belong to 120 different tribes, but share a common language, Swahili. Carol had raised $12,000 in contributions from friends of hers and Peter's so that she could make the trip. Naní raised considerably more, because it was not difficult to get people in the fashion industry to contribute to a charity for AIDS. All the money collected went straight to an AIDS foundation, participants covering their own travel expenses. Carol expected to travel in the back of the plane. Naní insisted that she had enough frequent flyer points to move to the front where she would be less likely to be badgered for pictures and autographs. "I'll handle the first-class tickets. You don't need to reimburse me." Actually, Naní had paid for the upgrades, but did not want Carol to know that fact.

Wealthy Americans or not, they and the group of several dozen AIDS Africa walkers found themselves instantly welcomed by people so much poorer. "*Jambo,*" the children of Africa greeted them, that being the word for hello. It brought tears to Naní's eyes as the children would gather around them, not wanting candy or money, merely hoping to touch them, to brush the dust and dirt from their clothing, gathered during their walk around Mount Kilimanjaro. "They led us on adventures down steep ravines to see the colobus monkeys," Carol later would write in her journal. "They taught us their dances and showed us their schoolbooks and let us take photos so they could marvel at their own faces on our camera screens. We visited schools and community centers, orphanages and hospitals. We were truly *karibu*, or welcome."

Naní visited her mother's village and met uncles and aunts and nephews and nieces and cousins many times removed, and she was welcomed as a lost child, as certainly she was. The supermodel had offered all the details of the trip on her Facebook page. She and Carol had laughed a lot, but they also had cried a lot at the plight of the children of Africa, not for anything they had done, but because of the sins of their parents, particularly the men in that male-dominated culture who would not use protection. And now Carol was gone, but it pleased Naní that she was able to utilize her celebrity as supermodel to commemorate their friendship and to preserve the sights and smells and sounds of that trip while raising money for AIDS Africa.

She would run the Lake City Marathon, and how fitting that was, it being directed by her departed roommate's husband. *And here am I, less than twenty-four hours before that race, seated at lunch with the woman who might be destined to be Carol's replacement—not merely for Peter, but maybe for me as well.* As the two new friends hugged in parting, Naní thought: *We sat together in this restaurant, and I did nothing but talk and talk and talk.*

And Christine thought: *We sat together in this restaurant, and I did nothing but listen and listen and listen.*

Naní and Christine left each other, promising to continue their conversations later after the marathon, both realizing that they had found a new friend. "I'm adding you as a friend on my Facebook page," said Naní in parting. "But I hope our friendship goes far beyond that."

Christine walked toward the lobby leading to Jefferson Avenue, planning to catch a cab to the TV3 station. She needed to put together a package from the press conference about AIDS Africa to be used on *The Four O'clock News*. How much could she use from her lunchtime conversation with the supermodel? Christine knew she would need to be cautious to not let her personal life invade her professional life, and vice versa. Christine also wanted to review her notes before the production meeting later that afternoon to plan for the marathon telecast. Might Peter be there? She hoped so, but she was not about to text-message him to find out for sure. After her just completed girl-to-girl talk, and all she learned about his late wife, she did not know what she would say to him. Maybe she would just smile and enjoy listening to the thunder caused by the lightning striking around them.

Naní headed to the bank of elevators off the lobby, but stopped before boarding an elevator up to her room. She planned to spend the afternoon relaxing for tomorrow's marathon, but before doing so, she pulled a digital phone out of her purse. The supermodel rapidly punched the keys with her thumbs. She was not hesitant to text-message Peter, teasing him with news about her lunch companion.

Lunched w Christine, Naní thumb-punched. *Guess who we talked about??*

An elevator door swung open. Naní entered, putting the digital phone back in her purse as she did She pushed the button on the console for her floor. While waiting for the door to slide shut, she stared at the miniature TV set above the console, showing a broadcast from CNN. Incredibly, she saw herself and Joseph Nduku talking about AIDS Africa. As quickly as they appeared onscreen, they disappeared to be replaced by racing machines roaring around a NASCAR track. The door began to close just as someone dressed in standard runner's attire approached. She could have allowed the door to close and rode the elevator to her floor alone. Instead, she pushed the "open" button and held it, permitting the runner to enter the car. The door closed, and the elevator started up.

The runner did not react immediately to the celebrity beside him, then he slowly turned and confirmed the sighting. "Aren't you?" he began.

"Yes, I am," responded the supermodel with a smile.

"Good luck in the race tomorrow," said Bob Veldman.

Naní thanked him pleasantly, but could not help thinking, *My life is an open book.*

20:15:00

Aba Andersson wanted to run the Lake City Marathon. She had trained hard for the race and felt she deserved to earn payback from that training, not financially as much as psychologically. In this respect, the world record holder's motives were similar to those of the slowest runner in the race, whose main goal was to finish. Granted, the world record attempt was unfeasible. But running to Aba, apart from any financial consideration, was fun. So why not run?

Well, she was pregnant The morning sickness suffered by the Swedish runner the last several days had been the first sign. Initially, her husband Bjørn thought it the flu, or maybe a touch of food poisoning. Not Aba. She knew her own body too well. She recognized almost instantly the cause of her vomiting. She was pregnant. The pregnancy test confirmed it.

Aba decided against consulting a local obstetrician, who may or may not have understood running. That could wait, she and Bjørn decided, until after their return to Gothenburg. But now with less than twenty-one hours to go before the start of the marathon, the couple sat in the office of Nicholas Terrence, M.D., the marathon's medical director. Though a cardiologist, Dr. Terrence well understood the peculiar demands pregnancy made on a woman's body and whether or not it was safe to run the next day.

20:15:00. 20:14:59. 20:14:58.

The swift Swede easily could have walked away from Sunday's race without refunding the considerable appearance fee she already had pocketed. Race director Peter McDonald told her that after the press conference where she announced her pregnancy. "Have your baby, Aba," said Peter. "You're welcome back any time — on your terms."

That was so sweet of Peter, and so typical. She had difficulty holding back the tears, but she was Scandinavian and not supposed to display her emotions. Aba knew she would return to Lake City and not even ask for an appearance fee. She and Bjørn already decided that. You treat decently the people who treat you decently.

"Maybe I'll run in the back of the pack," Aba had suggested. That's when Peter recommended that she and Bjørn visit Dr. Nicholas to make certain there were no dangers, especially given the predicted warm weather.

"No dangers," said Dr. Nicholas when the couple met him at his office. "Yes, if your body temperature were to rise over 101 degrees. How fast do you plan to run?"

Aba did not know. "Three hours? Four hours?"

"For a trained athlete like yourself," Dr. Nicholas, conceded, "that's like a stroll in the park. You probably run that far and that fast in practice."

"She did last weekend," said Bjørn. "An easy 30-kilometer workout through the woods near home."

"Pretty fast too. I was feeling good. And I was pregnant then, but didn't yet know it."

Counting back, Aba and Bjørn figured that she was six weeks pregnant. Morning sickness usually commences about that time, agreed Dr. Nicholas. That time frame coincided with a vacation trip to Monaco where Aba foolishly had forgotten to throw her birth control pills into her travelling case. They both hated his having to wear condoms, so Bjørn said, "Let's chance it." They had, for an incredible weekend of skin-on-skin sex. And although most of the couple's previous discussions about starting a family had concluded in a decision to wait another few years after this Olympics or that World Championships, there was always another Olympics or another World Championships. Subconsciously, maybe each of them wished to start their family now. Even though not going for the world record could cost her a half million dollars or more in bonuses and endorsements, was not a child worth much more? So Aba was exultant when she passed, not failed, the pregnancy test, and it was obvious that her husband felt the same. She still could run, though obviously not as fast.

"Maybe four hours," Aba suggested how fast she might run.

"Maybe you shouldn't think time," Bjørn argued. "Maybe you should simply get out and run and let the time come to you rather than setting some artificial schedule."

"That would be smart," Dr. Nicholas agreed.

One of Aba's predecessors as marathon world record holder had been Ingrid Christiansen of Norway. One year, Christiansen had appeared at the World Cross-Country Championships the favorite, but finished far back from the winners, what she considered a rather lackluster performance. After returning home, Christiansen realized she had run the race while several months pregnant. "Elite women with low body fat percentages often don't have periods," Dr. Nicholas explained. "So they miss the early signs that would alert them of their pregnancy.'

It was quite normal—and healthy—the medical director explained for women to run while pregnant. Exercise allowed them to strengthen their bodies and avoid excessive weight gain, allowing for what might be considered a more normal delivery. "In the third trimester," said the doctor, "many women switch from running to walking, mainly because they feel off-balance or uncomfortable, but you're a long time from making that decision."

"So Aba is cleared to run?" asked Bjørn.

"Cleared to run," said Dr. Nicholas.

Bjørn offered: "I'll find a sign to pin on your back: *Bäbis ombord*."

"I think I know what that means," said Dr. Nicholas, "and I don't speak Swedish."

The couple had left Dr. Nicholas's offices with his good wishes, laughing and holding hands and delighted that some months further, they would be parents, and what shall we name her, Bjørn wondered. *Him* said Aba. "I don't think we have much choice," said Bjørn. She had never been more relaxed the day before a marathon. She never had been happier.

Truth be told, Aba Andersson welcomed the opportunity to abandon her record-setting plan and run a pressure-free race. So many times before, she had gone to the starting line of marathons paralyzed with fear. In the race where she had set her world record, Aba remembered being so scared of not fulfilling her potential, worried about not reaping the rewards from long months of training, that she could not even warm up! She had tried to warm up, had jogged a few hundred meters, then turned back, so emotionally distraught that, fleeing into a porta-potty, her fourth visit, she actually had begun to cry, an emotion she tried to hide from her fellow competitors, not wanting to buoy their confidence, not wanting to allow them to think that they stood even the slightest chance of defeating her.

And they had not. Because despite Aba's fears and worries, once the horn sounded, she exploded off the line! Even without warm-up, she hit full stride in a matter of seconds. And although the faster men moved out ahead of her, she stayed well ahead of her female competitors that day. They never even got a sniff of the perfume she applied before heading to the line, an unnecessary feminine flourish since she would sweat it off almost immediately.

Fear was part of her running life. It was unpleasant to endure in those last hours and minutes and seconds before the start of a marathon, but fear also inevitably was what drove her to perfection. And as the countdown continued to the start of the Lake City Marathon, Aba felt relieved that she could go to the starting line minus fears normally felt.

The runners who normally finished behind her—not her elite competitors but those *far* behind—Aba envied them. Did they experience fears as they stood deep in the pack on the starting grid? They probably did, to a point. They had their goals: to finish the marathon, to finish it in fast times, even if "fast" for them was four and five hours. But their fears certainly had to be less than hers. If they had a bad day and found themselves in the closing miles of the race—as happened to her once in the World Championships—seated on the curb crying because cramps had made it impossible to continue, the news of their defeat would not be broadcast around the world on TV and on the Internet. They would not have to worry about bloggers, who never had run as far or fast as she, second-guessing their performances. She was beyond that for this one marathon. She could lower her personal bar to three or four hours and run in the back with people with lesser fears, if not lesser goals.

"Woo-hoo!" shouted Aba the minute she and Bjørn reached the street leaving Dr. Nicholas's office. She shouted it in Swedish, of course.

20:00:00

S o this is the East Side," said Redbird. He knew a great deal about this blue-collar neighborhood near the bottom of the lake on the southeastern border of Lake City, because it was the boyhood home of Pope Tony, but Redbird never before had a chance to visit until drawn here by the pope's decision to run a marathon, now only twenty hours away.

20:00:00. 19:59:59. 19:59:58.

226

"Signore?" asked Luigi, Redbird's driver, not knowing whether the comment about the East Side had been directed his way.

"Non presti attenzione," Redbird responded to the driver. "I'm talking to myself."

"Capito."

The two in the car, driver and passenger, had driven to the East Side by tracing southward the curving edge of the lake from downtown. Redbird was casually attired in tan slacks and an emerald green golf shirt, looking as though he had just stepped off the links at Killorglin. Given the warm weather, he wore no jacket.

Sleeping late, Redbird had breakfasted with Bishop Nolan before calling Pope Tony, apologizing at once for his effrontery in trailing him to Lake City. Pope Tony, more amused than offended, had shrugged off the apology and invited Redbird for lunch. "It's your job to worry about me," conceded the pope. "I was wondering how quickly you might discover my plans. My mother will want to meet you."

How quickly he put me at ease, Redbird thought after the conversation. *Maybe that was one of the reasons we chose him.*

Redbird had been present when the college of cardinals met after the death of the previous pope to choose his successor. In fact Redbird, whose actual name was James Connolly, served as the most eminent of eminent members of the college, the cardinal camerlengo. It was he who had supervised the voting in the Sistine Chapel that after several weeks finally resulted in a complete unknown, John Anthony Molina, ascending to head of the Roman Catholic Church. Redbird was Connolly's nickname, acquired from the computer-savvy cardinal's username on the Internet. It touched Cardinal Connolly how quickly after his rise, the new pope had switched from calling him "Your Eminence" to the much friendlier "Redbird." And Tony resisted Redbird's calling him "Your Holiness," except on public occasions. "You know my given name, my dear Redbird. Continue to use it at your pleasure."

Among the cardinal camerlengo's varied duties was security: supervising the Swiss Guards who protected the pope. That duty had brought him to Lake City, where he now found himself being driven by one of those guards over a high steel bridge on the toll road leading to and through the East Side. Staring out the car's windows, Redbird could not help but be fascinated by the sights ahead and below.

From his moving vantage point more than a hundred feet above an industrial river that pierced the neighborhood, Redbird could see a steel mill, a power plant, a golf course as well as the lake ahead to the left; a casino in the distance in front of him; and the roofs of simple bungalows below and to the right. The mills and the occupants of those bungalows, mostly with Eastern

SATURDAY

European roots, had been linked to each other for more than a century. Immigrants had spilled into Lake City in the early 1900's seeking work, hoping to escape poverty back home. They provided fodder for the foundries, although as production shifted to China and other countries, the lives of their sons, daughters, grandsons and granddaughters changed.

The cardinal camerlengo already knew much about this neighborhood from discussions with its best known on-time resident, Pope Tony. And as the sedan began to descend the far slope of the bridge, Redbird continued to gaze out the window, enthralled by this view of the city, hardly scenic compared to the Cliffs of Moher, but the home of working class people so important to the propagation of the faith. Though he had not visited the East Side before, Redbird had supervised security measures for those occasions when Pope Tony might return home to see his widowed mother and their family, including his sisters. These would be family visits, unannounced visits, the pope insisted: "I don't want to be trailed by journalists or advisors as with most visits of state."

That made sense, figured Redbird, and normally he was forewarned of these private visits so he could arrange security, but why not this time? The running of a marathon, and Pope Tony had not told anybody.

Redbird only uncovered the pope's plans after tracking him to the airport in Rome and in the air. He felt embarrassed about having to spy on his friend and master, but it was his duty. After discovering that Pope Tony planned to run a marathon, Redbird had been drawn to the East Side partly from a sense of duty, a desire to protect the pope from his worst instincts, but also because of a curiosity about the neighborhood from which he sprung.

How did this man become pope? wondered the cardinal camerlengo. *I had a hand in it, certainly, but was God guiding my hand?*

Supervising security was no easy task when the man he was committed to shield sought to sidestep his protection. It was incredible, thought Redbird, that despite the small but effective intelligence operation possessed by the Vatican, Pope Tony's plans to run a marathon had gone undetected. Totally undetected! *Perhaps that is a good sign,* rationalized the cardinal camerlengo. *His enemies must be in the dark too.* And Pope Tony had enemies, not because of his views but because of what some people expected the views of a relatively young priest elevated to the highest of high positions in the Church might be. All considerations aside, maybe he should keep an open mind and, in terms of security for this marathon, trust the man now considered by many to be infallible.

After arriving late last night, Redbird had stayed in town at the residence of the archbishop of Lake City, an elegantly furnished nineteenth century mansion near downtown. Flying toward Lake City, Redbird had called his friend,

Archbishop Sean Nolan, requesting a humble palette on which to sleep. The archbishop had claimed to possess no palettes, only beds. Redbird accepted, and fortunately his host was asleep by the time he arrived, so he did not need to explain the purpose for his visit. At breakfast the next morning, the cardinal camerlengo easily dodged a single question directed toward that matter. Knowing further inquiry would be fruitless, his host smoothly switched to less sensitive subjects. The word "marathon" did not enter the conversation as the two prelates shared coffee and rolls and talk about the church, its difficult role in today's society.

Following breakfast, the cardinal camerlengo had telephoned the home of Pope Tony's mother, incredibly a public number, one that anybody could look up in the directory and call. *Unbelievable*, thought Redbird. *In Italy, this man is surrounded by walls and guards, his every move attracting thousands of the faithful. Here in America he moves like an ordinary human being. Maybe he is an ordinary human being—Jesus was for a time—so perhaps we emphasize too much the trappings of the office.*

Liliana Molina, the mother of John Anthony Molina answered the phone. Call the pope and you reach first his mother, a remarkable woman in her own right. Mrs. Molina's husband, Tony's father, had been killed in a mill accident. In addition to one son, she had four daughters, three of them married with children. With their husbands, they lived near her on the East Side.

When Pope Tony finally came to the phone, he seemed neither surprised nor displeased that the cardinal camerlengo had tracked him to Lake City. Perhaps it had been a test. Whether or not true, the pope issued an immediate invitation to lunch, but cautioned Redbird to come alone so as not to attract attention. "I already brought two bodyguards," warned Pope Tony, "and don't need any more." Redbird doubted that, but acceded to the pope's request, bringing with him only a driver, Luigi Fabbricatore, a member of the Swiss Guard. Redbird chose for his transportation a two-door sedan, an anonymous grey, borrowed from the archbishop. Not wishing to appear pretentious or to attract attention, Redbird had rejected Sean Nolan's offer of a black limousine in favor of the smaller car.

After leaving the toll road, the cardinal camerlengo and his driver found themselves traveling south on a residential street of three-flats, cars parked on both sides narrowing the one-way street to little more than a single lane. The driver slowed as they approached a bungalow surrounded by a brick and iron fence. That precise moment, their arrival apparently having been observed by unseen eyes within the bungalow, the gate of the iron fence slid open. Simultaneously, the double door of a garage attached to the home rolled up. There was an empty space within the garage. Fabbricatore did not need to be told. He drove the car into the garage. Even before he could turn off its engine, the garage door slid shut behind them. It was a heavy door, steel, meant to not be breached easily.

The cardinal camerlengo noted that fact with satisfaction, then stepped out of the rental car at the same time a door into the kitchen of the house opened. "Your Eminence," said the woman standing in the doorway. It was Liliana Molina, the pope's mother. "Jimmy, you are like an old friend, even though we never have met."

Redbird smiled at the woman's being unperturbed by his arrival on short notice. "Mrs. Molina," he said, easily shifting into family mode. "It is a pleasure to visit your home." He held out his hands, clasped hers, and presented his cheeks, one on each side for air kisses in the Italian tradition.

Standing behind was her famous son, the man Peter McDonald had dubbed Celebrity X. Pope Tony greeted Cardinal James Connolly with a smile, the same as might a little boy who had done something naughty, only to be caught. "My dear Redbird," said Pope Tony. "What a pleasant surprise."

Redbird spread his hands as though giving a blessing and raised his eyes toward the ceiling as though there was only one higher power who could offer the reason why he was in this place at this point in time.

"You have much to explain, my friend. You have much to explain."

19:30:00

After the press conference in the Hilliard's Marquette Room, Peter McDonald abandoned the scene hastily, not taking time to engage either Naní or Christine in conversation. Not taking time to say good-bye, or even to offer a see-you-later. Not taking time, because the race director had little time to spare.

His rapid retreat seemed ungracious, but each of the women currently in his life knew how tight his schedule was. Was Christine mad at him, because he had given her so little attention last night? Because he spent more time attached to Naní? But surely she realized that was at least partly business? Maybe that was a poor assumption on his part. Christine had not returned his calls, but then he purposely had not left a number, indicating no obligation on her part. He did not understand women—or at least not this woman yet.

Interestingly, Naní and Christine seemed to have found each other without his having intervened. Peter noticed them talking in one corner of the room. And it hardly looked like a standard interview of a celebrity by a TV reporter. Peter wondered what they were saying to each other and wished he could eavesdrop. *Oh, to be a fly on the wall*. But he had to make a hello-only stop at a luncheon for other race directors who had come to Lake City to view his operations. After that, he would return several phone calls while en route to the park for a scheduled meeting with Noel Michaels at the operations trailer. This of all weekends was no time to allow his personal life to interfere with his business life. It was nearly 12:30 when he passed through the lobby beneath the digital clock that continued to tick down the time to the marathon.

19:30:00. 19:29:59. 19:29:58.

Leaving the Hilliard by its main entrance, Peter walked the half block from the hotel to Seventh Street, the closest street leading into Dearborn Park. That street now was blocked to traffic. Four sawhorses effectively closed access. A security guard stood beside the sawhorses, closely scrutinizing trucks and trailers attempting to invade this private space as Michaels' crew continued their work erecting tents, positioning trailers and organizing the mass of materiel necessary to manage 50,000 marathoners before their starts and after their finishes on Sunday. From the park entry point, Peter had a few more blocks to walk to the operations trailer. Normally, he would have covered this distance on foot, but he radioed for someone to meet him in a golf cart, mainly to save a few minutes.

Impolitely, Peter did not offer more than a few words to the person driving him, an intern, a young woman named Elisa. As they rode past crates and tables and boxes, he reviewed in his mind some of the issues he needed to discuss with Michaels, the most important their continued plans to cope with the expected warm weather. But mainly it was a chance for him to confer with his key assistant, so the two could assure each other that their schedule was being met. And if not, who could they assign to fix any problems? He still had not offered his assistant any details about Celebrity X. He wondered what Tony was doing today, but did not have time to phone him and find out.

"Thanks for the ride, Elisa," said Peter hopping off the cart at the operations trailer, not looking back as the intern drove away to her next task. He took the three steps leading into the trailer as though racing up a mountain. Michaels was sitting in front of a computer displaying the spread sheet of her tasks to be completed in the coming hours. She clicked on a box that colored red a line that said she had a "meeting with Peter" at 12:30. He was several minutes late, which was almost uncharacteristic of him, but she did not lack for tasks to accomplish while waiting. Michaels now marked the meeting as "done," even though it had not begun. She spun in her chair to greet him, but began their discussion without the need to say hello.

As they talked for nearly a half hour, Peter grabbed a ham and cheese sandwich and a can of Diet Pepsi from the snack table for staff using the operations trailer. It was cheaper to provide food and drinks than to allow staff members to wander off to one of the cafes on Jefferson Avenue. "Most important," Michaels had said, explaining the line item in a planning meeting two months before, "we don't lose an hour of their time while they eat."

This was Peter's quick-grab lunch for the day, but as he and his assistant reviewed the check list on her spreadsheet, he felt the cell phone in his pocket vibrate, indicating a message just received. Peter set down the Diet Pepsi and fished the phone from his pocket without interrupting his conversation with Michaels. Miss Manners would have disapproved at such an imperious action, but Michaels, a world-class multi-tasker herself, took no offense. Peter's sideglance allowed him to identify the caller as Naní. She probably wanted to tell him of her talk with Christine. Dying to know what the two had discussed, her message was in the category of gossip. He should not allow it to engage his attention in the middle of a business discussion.

Several minutes later, his talk with Noel Michaels complete, Peter exited the operations trailer and walked north past a line of tables in the center of the street that extended nearly two city blocks. This was where runners Sunday would check their bags before the marathon. Set-up seemed complete. Signage looked good. Drop the bag containing your warm-up clothes at the position marked 12,000 - 12,999 and pick it up three to four to five to six hours or more later. Simple enough, but requiring much organization to make it run smoothly. Nobody manning the tent yet, but several hundred volunteers would be there Sunday morning. One of the line items on Michaels' spread sheet was feeding those volunteers between bag acceptance and retrieval. That was not on Peter's spread sheet, so he continued his walk, remembering that he had received a message while talking to his executive director.

The name NANÍ in capital letters remained in the display window. Text-message, not voice mail. Without breaking stride, Peter punched a button on the phone to see what the supermodel had to say.

Lunched w Christine. Guess who we talked about??

Peter could not help laughing. He had no trouble guessing about the girls' topic of conversation. If anyone else but Naní had sent him such a message on the next-to-most-important day of the year, Peter probably would have deleted it less from anger than from being in talk-to-me-next week mode. Walking from Point A to Point B, however, it was easy for him to punch three letters into the phone followed by a question mark.

Moi?

Naní was back in her hotel room stripped down to her underwear, silky black, supplied by one of the fashion companies that used her images in ads, lying in bed, under the covers, watching a golf tournament, sound turned down low, watching not because she liked golf, but because it filled the screen while she rested for her marathon. The supermodel figured that fifteen minutes of golf would be enough to put her to sleep. Jonathan Von Runyon would have been outraged to hear this, but the supermodel and *Ledger* columnist did not know each other, and Naní would instantly have disliked him if she did.

A ding indicated an incoming message on her cell phone. The display indicated PETER. She one-punched the phone to retrieve his three-letter-one-question-mark message and laughed when she did.

Naní rolled over on her stomach and propped herself up on her elbows for ease in replying to Peter's message and in doing so positioned one of the shapeliest behinds in America between cell phone and televised golf game.

Naní typed rapidly with her thumbs: *I love your new girlfriend*. If Peter planned to respond, he would need to do so soon, because she was one 5-iron shot away from falling asleep. She punched "Send."

By then, Peter had arrived at the TV3 trailer and was talking to Tom Schorr, director of the marathon telecast. They had a production meeting scheduled for later that afternoon, and he wanted to make sure he understood what the director needed before departing for the Expo where he had one more course lecture to give.

A vibration in his pocket indicated another message. It was the third incoming call since he last had text-messaged Naní. Two of those messages were important, but needed no response, so quickly were deleted. When Naní's message arrived, Peter ignored the vibration until he completed his talk with Schorr. Multi-tasking certainly was an accepted vice in their professions, but Peter wanted to take no chance of riling the TV director, whom he had not yet told about Celebrity X.

The meeting with the TV director completed, Peter stepped out of the trailer, which was located near Burnham Fountain. He could not help but pause for a few seconds to regard the fountain that was one of Lake City's most photographed landmarks. Many of those running the marathon told loved ones to meet them at the fountain, then had difficulty connecting because so many others had picked the same meeting place.

Peter stepped into a van marked with the Lake City Marathon logo, the same van he had driven while giving Christine a ride from the Expo to the hotel only two days before, their first serious conversation. While walking past the line of baggage tents earlier, he had radioed to have the van waiting after his meeting with Schorr so it could take him to the Expo. He did not have time to take a cab.

The van was driven by a different intern, Damien. Peter slipped into the passenger seat, offered a perfunctory hello to Damien, then as the intern drove them toward the convention center and not without some guilt on Peter's part, he pulled out his digital phone to see what Naní had to say.

I love your new girlfriend.

Peter swore that this would be the last text-message from the supermodel that he would access. She was only responding to him, because he was responding to her. One of them needed to have the courage to end the dialog. He thumb-tapped a response and pushed "Send." As he did, Damien pulled the van out onto Lake Shore Drive, the traffic heavy on a Saturday afternoon. Five minutes more and he would be at Pritzinger Place, a different milieu. Peter replaced the digital phone in his pocket and stared out at the lake to the left, sunlight glimmering on the waves. It would be warm Sunday, and he hoped that they were ready.

Back at the Hilliard, Naní failed to see the 5-iron shot roll into the hole, because her eyes were closed. Not yet asleep, she heard the tinkle of her cell phone. *If I'm going to get any sleep, I need to turn the sound off,* Naní thought, but she glanced at the display and saw it was Peter. Doesn't that man have anything to do today?

Peter's message was simple: *I love her too.*

That is so sweet, she thought, but decided no response was necessary. And she dare not forward that message to her newfound friend, Christine. Time to step out of the way and allow the two lovers to connect without her playing matchmaker any more. Naní punched the red button on the phone causing it to provide one final melodious tune as it said goodbye.

Naní closed her eyes again, pulled the covers on the bed tight around her and prepared to fall off the cliff into Dreamland. Then the phone rang. *Damn,* thought Naní. *Why didn't I tell the hotel to hold all calls? Who knows I'm in this room anyway?* Then she remembered: her husband, due to arrive from the West Coast about this time, arriving at the same airport and using the same private jet that brought her to Lake City two days before.

She groped for the phone, clumsily allowing it to fall to the floor, then had to lean half out of bed to retrieve it. Pulling the receiver to her ear, Naní groggily tried to gather herself to speak.

The person on the other end of the line spoke first: "Aren't you at least going to say hello?"

It was him. Her husband. She was so relieved he finally had arrived in town. "Hello," she said sleepily. "Where are you, Ricco?"

"At the airport. I'm in the limousine headed your way."

"Mmmmm."

"What are you doing?"

"I'm in bed."

"Good, that's exactly where I want you to be."

"Don't you dare, Ricco. I have a marathon to run tomorrow."

"Like I didn't just fly 2,000 miles to kiss you after you finished."

"How about kissing me before I start? I've just reconsidered my previous comment."

"Don't fall asleep."

"If I do, you know how to wake me up."

18:30:00

Surprise! Now that he had come to the East Side and discussed the dangers that running a marathon with 50,000 runners and a million spectators posed to the pope, Redbird conceded the point: Surprise offered the best protection against people who might cause him harm. "Until just after 8:00 tomorrow morning, nobody will know my plans," explained Pope Tony. "That's the time when I'll step onto the starting line. Once that happens, I'll have 50,000 bodyguards, not just the two I've brought with me."

18:30:00. 18:29:59. 18:29:58.

The cardinal camerlengo grunted. *It is an outrageous plan,* he thought. *Outrageous! Outrageous that Pope Tony had not confided in me, but maybe I'm merely disappointed at not being included on the need-to-know list. Yet, apparently that list contained only two people: Pope Tony and this Peter McDonald. From what I've learned of him in the last few minutes, the marathon race director knows what he's doing. An old friend. Coached by Tony in high school. They grew up in the same neighborhood. The two hatched this plan together, and so far their planning has proved flawless. Even with all my connections, I only learned at the last minute.*

Yet it was Redbird's job to be suspicious. "My dear friend, what if surprise is not enough?"

The man whose identity was hidden under the cover Celebrity X smiled: "I almost hesitate to use this word, but we abort."

"Abort?" The word was equally repugnant to the cardinal camerlengo, but he conceded its use in the current context.

"I'll walk away. *Finito!* Any leak to the press, any suggestion that others may know our plans, and I'll join you watching the race on television."

"That would disappoint you."

"Enormously. It would be a *huge* disappointment.'

"But you would humble yourself," jabbed Redbird, the twinkle in his eyes suggesting that he had begun to accept what at first to him had seemed a preposterous plan.

Pope Tony alertly sensed the shift in his mentor's mood. The hint of a smile lit his face: "Absolutely! He that humbles himself shall be exalted."

"Touché." Cardinal Connolly admitted, but frowned: "I do *not* quite understand the compulsion that causes otherwise sensible men and women to run 26 miles. I can't imagine how difficult it must be to train for such a feat. I understand that among Olympic athletes. Didn't an Italian recently win the marathon gold medal?"

"Stefano Baldini. Athens, 2004: 2:10:55."

"You quote times to me. I am amazed. You truly do care about this sport of running."

"When one runs on a treadmill for an hour or more, not all one's thoughts concern the worries of the world, I unhappily confess."

"I understand the lure of an Olympic gold medal. But what causes people of—can I say—lesser talents to flagellate their bodies?"

"The training program I used lasted eighteen weeks. Not that difficult. Truth be told, training with a single goal in mind is much more enjoyable than those who have not run marathons might think. Compare the time spent training to forty days fasting in the dessert."

Redbird laughed at the analogy. "I hope you are not trying to link running and religion."

Pope Tony shrugged: "It is possible to dip into the Bible and justify almost any good deed and, unfortunately, some bad deeds as well. St. Paul once said, 'Do you not know that those who run in a race, all indeed run, but only one receives a prize...'"

"...So run as to obtain it," the Cardinal Camerlengo completed the quotation. "Corinthians 9:24."

"I suspect if it comes to a theological debate, my respected friend and mentor, you will win. But let me force you to hear my confession: I worry I am a victim of my own pride for what I intend to do Sunday."

"Pride?"

"Yes, pride."

Redbird pondered this admission on the part of the Holy Father. "I'm afraid we all are guilty of that most vicious of the seven deadly sins. I admit to feeling irritated at you, my dear boy, for not including me in your planning for this…. Will I insult you if I call it an impetuous decision to run a marathon?"

"No, you will not."

"But if I am irritated, maybe it is because I allowed *my* pride to interfere with rational thought."

"You are about to quote Thomas Aquinas," Pope Tony impishly offered.

"Obviously, your papal powers include an ability to read men's minds."

"No, my cardinal camerlengo, only *your* mind!"

The two men chuckled, amused that their discussion had drifted from the sport of running into theology. Pope Tony enjoyed religious discussions with his mentor, and he knew Cardinal Connolly did the same. Both men had in their minds what the theologian Thomas Aquinas had said about pride.

Redbird confirmed that fact: "Aquinas defined inordinate self-love, or pride, as being the cause of every sin."

"The root of pride is found to consist in man not being, in some way, subject to God and his rule," countered Pope Tony.

"I can't see how your running the marathon would get you in trouble with Thomas Aquinas."

"My pride could get me in trouble with Peter '

This caused Cardinal Connolly to blink. "Are you talking about Saint Peter, your predecessor?"

"Peter McDonald."

The Irish prelate wondered about mention of a man about whom he had become aware only hours ago: "Explain!"

"I don't want to turn his race into a carnival."

"There is some risk," Redbird agreed. "Sometimes it is necessary to assume risk to save our own souls, if not those of others." The cardinal camerlengo did not say it, but he thought the greatest risk was that Pope Tony, stepping forward into public, increased his vulnerability, not just for physical harm, but harm in the public mind. Should someone in such an exalted position lower himself to a level where sports and the worship of the human body—fitness—rules? What does this do for the image of the papacy, of the entire Holy Roman Catholic Church? On the other hand, Tony was the first pope to have a page on Facebook. Redbird wondered if he had posted to it today. Probably not, since he was disguising his intentions this weekend.

Cardinal Connolly knew Tony not to be universally loved within the church, particularly by those within the hierarchy who considered this American an interloper. Several highly placed people within the College of Cardinals considered Tony's elevation to the papacy an abomination. At a critical time in church history, when Holy Church was under attack because of priestly pedophiles, this youthful-thinking American had arrived with who knew what radical changes in mind. *Would he allow priests to marry? Would he ordain women priests? Would he embrace homosexuals? And consider the enormously divisive quarrel over abortion. What damage could Pope Tony do to the church's traditions, particularly since, being young, he might occupy his position for three or four decades?* It seemed an irreverent thought, but at least some members of the hierarchy would like to see this *Papa Tonio* disappear. This was, indeed, a frightening thought for Cardinal Connolly and those closest to the man whose plans this weekend still remained hidden under the identity of Celebrity X.

Those thoughts flashed quickly through the mind of the cardinal camerlengo, but they went unspoken. Tony broke the brief silence between them:

"Pride goeth before the fall."

"Pride goeth before destruction," Redbird corrected him. "and an haughty spirit before a fall."

"I stand corrected."

"Better it is to be of an humble spirit with the lowly, than to divide the spoil with the proud. Proverbs: 16-19."

"True, but I do not run like a man running aimlessly," said Tony, countering with another quote from the Bible.

It was not unknown to his friend. "That's from St. Paul again," said Redbird, identifying the saying from First Corinthians, verse 9:25. "St. Paul must have been quite an athlete in his day."

"Or, he appreciated athletics at its purest level: the urge to perfection. In runners, the urge to maximize our talents, to succeed, each of us, at our own level, even though not able to match in ability a Stefano Baldini."

Redbird nodded, now in agreement. The cardinal camerlengo loved these discussions with a man younger, yet in many respects very wise. He continued to quote from Corinthians: "Everyone who competes goes into strict training. They do it to get a crown that will not last; but we do it to get a crown that will last forever."

"You obviously aced your courses in Theology at seminary, my dear Redbird," said Pope Tony. "You should have my job."

"I'm happy with the jobs I have, one of which is protecting you—although you do not always make it easy." Redbird raised his arms over his head and shook his hands vigorously, as though trying to frighten a flock of overhead sparrows. Pope Tony merely smiled. For a moment, they both fell silent, their bag of Biblical quotations related to running, temporarily depleted.

During their talk, the pair had been seated near a picture window offering a view of the street, unremarkable scenery compared to that from the pope's apartment in Vatican City or from the windows of Castel Gandolfo southeast of Rome with its overlook of Lake Albano. Bungalows. Well-manicured lawns. Each home with a tree in front, its leaves soon to turn with the approach of winter, although you would not know that winter was near given the temperatures this weekend. *A nice neighborhood,* thought Cardinal Connolly, temporarily distracted because of something just seen.

The cardinal camerlengo had noticed a car pass, almost out of the corner of one eye. There was nothing remarkable about the car. Mid-sized. Light blue, Could be a rental car. The car with a woman driving had not stopped, but had slowed. And in moving slowly past, the woman driving the car had stared impulsively at the home. She could not see them because the picture window constructed of bullet resistant-glass nearly three inches thick was reflective. The car passed slowly, then sped away.

Curious, thought Redbird. *It could simply be an ordinary sightseer, who knows Pope Tony's mother lives here. She may or may not know the pope is in town. Or are his plans now known to others beside me?* Redbird knew he was beginning to display a certain paranoia, but that was part of the cardinal camerlengo's job description.

"Excuse me," said Redbird. He stood and moved across the room to the picture window. Seated nearby, also watching out, was one of the two bodyguards who had accompanied Celebrity X to Lake City, Mario Castriota.

"A problem?" asked Pope Tony.

"Problems only become problems if you don't consider them problems," said Redbird. Moving to Mario's side, he whispered a few words. Mario nodded, stood up to move closer to the window and reached for a radio, speaking several words in it that caused the other bodyguard, Angelo Nesci, to enter the room. Both men stood on alert.

Pope Tony watched with some amusement. He felt secure during his visits to the East Side. The people in this neighborhood did not treat him as a celebrity. They had watched him grow up. To them, he was simply an old friend and neighbor, someone who showed up to say mass at Saint Stanislaus Church without warning. Truth be told, Pope Tony had more than two bodyguards in this neighborhood. Although his neighbors did not possess bullet-resistant windows, their eyes peered out for signs of any suspicious behavior. Slowing down in a car while passing might be that, might not.

Except within a few minutes, the light blue car reappeared and this time stopped across the street. The woman in the driver's seat had a notebook in hand and seemed to be writing in it, Redbird noticed. That certainly was more than suspicious. Was she a reporter who had become aware of Pope Tony's arrival in town? Did she know he was running a marathon? If so, that would prevent him from doing so tomorrow morning, which would not make the cardinal camerlengo unhappy.

Redbird nodded toward Mario, indicating that he exit the home, cross the street and ask the woman why she had stopped, and if she sped off, catch her license plate. Mario, radio in hand, moved toward the front door, but even in that instant someone else was doing the same.

"I told you I possessed extra bodyguards," laughed Pope Tony.

His neighbor from across the street, knowing that the pope was visiting his mother, also had noticed the car stop. It was a man with silver hair and a stomach suggesting an appetite for beer while watching TV. It was the same individual who Thursday had picked up the pope at the airport.

"That's Herb," said Pope Tony. "A Vietnam veteran. You probably should put him on the payroll."

"We might just do that," mumbled Redbird, who watched as Herb stepped in front of the parked woman's car, preventing any move on her part to depart hastily. He made a rotating movement with one hand, indicating he would like her to roll down the window. She obeyed, and the two began to talk. Mario by now was out the door moving toward them without haste, not wanting to appear threatening. He stood behind Herb, apparently not willing to interfere unless provoked. *Well trained,* thought Redbird.

Mario raised the radio in his hand and spoke into it, communicating with Angelo still in the house. Angelo's radio crackled, the words unclear to Redbird and the pope. Angelo relayed the message. "Apparently just a sightseer. She seems embarrassed and is very apologetic."

"Nevertheless, get her name," said Redbird. Angelo relayed the order to Mario standing in the street. Angelo asked the woman. It was Matilda Goldberg, a name offered willfully by a woman who seemed frightened for having been caught doing something wrong.

"Aha," said Pope Tony.

"You know the woman?"

"I have yet to meet her personally."

"Refresh my mind."

"She's a reporter for *The New York Times*."

"I remember. Our media people have talked to her. Doesn't the woman want to write a biography on you?"

"Correct."

"It would be unauthorized."

"True," said Pope Tony. "She attends press conferences along with other reporters. You've probably seen her before."

"I know her now. The woman wanted to interview me after your selection. Naturally, I informed her I could not. She apparently expected that answer, but felt compelled to ask, probably because of requests from New York."

"If you remember the article in the *Times* about why the college of cardinals chose me, it was remarkably accurate."

"I don't remember reading the article," admitted Redbird, "but her requests for personal interviews, at least to this point, have politely been declined. We did not want to favor one outlet over the other."

"Makes sense, but at some point we may need to modify that policy."

"Shall I chase her away?"

Pope Tony smiled. "My dear Cardinal Connolly: Where is your Irish sense of hospitality? If my mother discovers you have no manners, it will be *you* she will usher out of the house."

The cardinal camerlengo shrugged as though not knowing what to do or say next. Pope Tony told him:

"Why don't we invite Ms. Goldberg in for a cup of coffee?"

18:00:00

Are you awake?" Ricco whispered, brushing Naní's bare back with his fingertips. He did not want to awaken his wife if she was not, but her stirring ever so slightly had prompted the inquiry. "Mmmm," replied Naní, signaling some level of wakefulness, but indicating no desire to move from her prone position, cuddled comfortably between the sheets, head buried beneath not one, but two pillows in an attempt to shut out the daylight.

Ricco had slid into bed beside Naní almost immediately after arriving from the airport. The clothes he had worn on his flight from the West Coast were scattered all over the floor between door and bed. Because they had not seen each other in several days, their lovemaking had been intense. Then they both had fallen asleep.

He had awakened before her. Good, he thought, because the woman he loved needed to rest for the marathon tomorrow. *How much time remained before her race?* He did not know, but it did not matter. She would tell him. *18:00:00. 17:59:59. 17:59:58.*

This weekend was all about her. He would play the role of dutiful husband, obeying her every command. He knew how much preparation she had put into this marathon, how important it was because of her commitment to AIDS Africa, her desire to run in support of those runners who had contributed to the charity. In planning for his attendance at the marathon, Ricco several weeks ago had told Naní, "I'll be your slave."

"*Hen*-ry," she said, offering several admonishing tongue clucks. (She only used his given name Henry when displaying displeasure.) "That is politically incorrect. Slavery is outlawed in this country."

SATURDAY

He had been born Henry Jones, switched to Ricco, since that sounded more appropriate for someone who photographed beautiful models in swimsuits for *Sports Illustrated*. After founding his own magazine, *Zest*, that combined fitness and fashion, he often reverted to his born name to assure his privacy and that of the supermodel he married. When Naní had checked into the Hilliard, she did so offering the last name of Jones. She loved thinking of herself as Mrs. Jones, not Ms. Supermodel with a single name, not two. As Christine proved earlier, only the most demented tabloid followers knew she was married, much less married to Ricco, and she hoped to keep it that way.

"I'm awake," she finally admitted, "but don't tell anybody." His one hand remained touching her back between the two shoulder blades. He lightly rubbed his fingernails over her taut skin, knowing she loved to have her back scratched. She indicated a thankful awareness by releasing a barely audible sigh. Not sure whether this was a signal for more lovemaking, he allowed his hand to drift sensuously downward along her spine to past her waistline, pausing finally on the upward swelling of her body two of his fingers within the top of her crack. "Don't get any more funny ideas," she warned. "I'm running a marathon."

He laughed, but did not move his hand, allowing the warmth of her sexuality to flow into him and his into her.

"Wait until I tell you about Peter."

"Peter?"

"He's got a girlfriend."

"Hmmm. About time."

But his wife did not seem willing to expand on that information. Within a few minutes Naní had fallen asleep again. Only then did he remove his hand. Ricco lay there, eyes closed, not moving, no desire to rise from the bed and hang his clothes thrown hastily on the floor in the closet. *I am the luckiest man in the world,* he thought.

17:30:00

Matilda Goldberg was so mortified. Ashamed! Embarrassed! Humiliated! The religion reporter for *The New York Times* had been caught stalking the pope! Stalking his mother's house! Invading their privacy! What would the guardians of journalism ethics sitting in their Ivory Towers say? What would her editors back in Manhattan say? Not a punishable-with-dismissal offense; more a roll-of-the-eyes offense: "Tilda, next time check with us when you get any more bright ideas."

And what was the purpose, the gurus of journalism might ask? The *Times* reporter suspected Pope John Anthony was back at the Vatican and nowhere near his boyhood home on the East Side. Goldberg felt no particular need to see that home, except she was in town to run the Lake City Marathon, so why not take a look on a Saturday afternoon when she had nothing better to do?

17:30:00. 17:29:59. 17:29:58.

So Tilda had driven her rental car across the high expressway bridge to the East Side home, had circled the block once, then parked in front, taking notes in case she needed to describe that house some time either in an article for the *Times* or in the book she hoped soon to write: a biography of the American pope. Goldberg did not yet have a contract with a publisher, but her agent Jeremy Kaplan claimed interest on the part of several editors. They might even do an auction.

"Will the pope let you interview him?" Kaplan had inquired.

"I asked. The Vatican claims the pope does not do interviews," Goldberg had been forced to admit. "At least that's present policy."

"Too bad," said the agent. "We might still swing a deal for an unauthorized biography, but if you could get him to sit down and talk, I could probably get you seven figures."

Seven figures? Like a million-dollar book deal? *Gulp!* Everyone in Tilda's class at Medill School of Journalism dreamed of being the recipient of such contracts, but realistically: Does it happen to real writers, notoriously an underpaid lot? Do you need to encounter a burning bush to have your agent swing such a deal?

"It helps that you're Jewish," her agent had added.

"*What?* Jeremy, that's outrageous!"

"Nevertheless, it would be a plus in marketing the book. Consider the sell line: A nice Jewish girl's look at the Catholic Church's hunk pope? Guaranteed talk-show time, sweetheart."

Goldberg swallowed her sense of outrage long enough to concede that her agent possibly was right—but what does that say about the taste of the American public? Now, with the thought of seven figures swimming in her head (but almost more important. the chance to do *the* definitive book explaining how this previously unknown American had ascended at such a relatively young age to such a lofty position), the nice Jewish girl had been caught notebook in hand, *esposta*, parked in front of Pope John Anthony's home. No cameras. No hidden recorders. Just ballpoint pen and a notebook she bought at Office Max, evidence enough. Hardly a Mortal Sin More a Venial Sin?

SATURDAY

Matilda Goldberg was a slender wisp of a woman, barely five feet tall, weighing less than a hundred pounds, small breasts but well rounded hips, shapely legs, feet so tiny she had a hard time finding shoes to fit, a nice build if you liked elves. Or liked female runners, except Tilda's marathon time was an hour or more slower than the best of the skinny crop at the front of the field. What Tilda lacked in bulk from the neck down, she compensated from the neck up. Curls! Enough raven black curls for a dozen jealous women sitting in beauty shops pleading with their hairdressers for more body. A face that was sweet, if not gorgeously beautiful. Tilda never had any trouble attracting male companionship during or after college.

After graduation from Medill, Tilda had headed to New York bent on a career in journalism, but got sidetracked after marrying an Equity actor, who found it easier getting cast into road shows than those running on Broadway. His birth name was Morty Goldberg, not Morton Goldberg, but "Morty," although he used as a stage name Gilbert Morton, as though it was necessary to disguise his Jewishness to get a job in the New York theatre. *Really!*

Dutifully, Mrs. Matilda Goldberg abandoned her low-profile job as little more than a secretary with *Newsday* and followed Morty from theatre to theatre. It was fun if your husband was booked into Chicago for a year playing Pharaoh opposite Donny Osmond in *Joseph and the Amazing Technicolor Dreamcoat*; less fun, if he was an understudy and part of the chorus with the touring company of *Le Miz*: in Jacksonville one night, Orlando the next, Miami after that. A week on the beach working on her suntan was not enough to compensate for riding the bus between gigs, not all cast members supportive of accompanying spouses.

After becoming pregnant, Tilda returned to New York, gave birth and settled into a life that combined part-time editing jobs with a part-time husband. She was most happy when her husband was out of work or in artsy roles Off Broadway, thus around the house—she loved to cook for him—but a dozen years into the marriage Morty told her that he had decided on a career change that would take him to Hollywood. Tilda confessed a lack of excitement to moving west to which his response was, "You're not invited."

Other than that, the Goldbergs parted amicably.

Morty achieved success not in front of the camera, but behind it, doing mostly voice-overs for animated features. If you watched the credits roll at the end of *The Lion King*, you could spot the name Gilbert Morton. "He was one of the hyenas," Tilda spitefully told her girlfriends.

So much for Matilda Goldberg's marriage. At least the union between Tilda and Morty had left her with a lovely child, Ephraim, a junior at Brandeis University, thankfully studying accounting, not theatre. Her next long-term relationship with a male might best be classified as an *affair d'coeur,* because (both once divorced), they did not choose to sanctify their union by marrying. His name was Albert Finn, a career diplomat attached to the United Nations. Tilda followed her boyfriend-not-husband to Washington, then to Rome, but when he moved to Lebanon as assistant ambassador (definitely a career boost), she chose to stay in Italy. It was not the danger of that war-torn country that made Tilda pause, but more because part-time work as a correspondent in Rome for *The New York Times* evolved into a full-time job as that paper's bureau chief, her major assignment the Vatican. When assignments brought Tilda to the Middle East, as it frequently did, she and her boyfriend would find time to see each other. Despite Albert's pleas for her to join him, even get married, Tilda preferred her work in Rome. She loved having an *affair d'coeur*, but loved even more receiving frequent text-messages from Ephraim at Brandeis. Ephraim had text-messaged Tilda this morning to wish her good luck in the marathon.

Tilda had begun running soon after her divorce from Morty, mainly to retain her sanity. She abandoned the activity briefly after taking up with her diplomat lover, resuming it after he left for Lebanon, running before the start of each day through the Villa Borghese near her Spanish Steps apartment. Matilda Goldberg figured that if offered the choice between sex and running, she probably would choose number two. She now lived a mostly chaste life, suitable given her current role covering the Vatican. She had no immediate plans to become a nun.

But how long could she hang on at the *Times* now that she had been caught stalking the pope? *Oy vey!*

Everyone had been so polite. Seemingly, there was little or no security at the pope's boyhood home. No Swiss Guards with halberds and sabers blocking the front door. She noticed the seeming lack of security on her first drive-by and thought it curious. *A simple house by any standard, but larger than those surrounding,* Tilda wrote in her notebook. Most East Side bungalows, she noticed, were crammed together on 33-foot lots. One look at the pope's family home might have been enough, but Goldberg decided to circle the block and return for a second look. Interesting, the speed bumps on surrounding streets. Could they be detonated to prevent assassins from escaping? *I've seen too many Hollywood thrillers lately,* decided Goldberg.

But as she parked, writing in her notebook, Tilda Goldberg suddenly discovered that security was tighter than she imagined. First, it was a man who came out of the house across the street. Smile on his face. He did not look like a Swiss Guard, but he had popped out his front door like a jack-in-the-box. Apparently a neighbor. Tall. Muscular. White-haired, matched by the colorlessness of his underwear top. Straps, not sleeves; very ethnic. An *AARP Magazine* subscriber, certainly. Maybe National Rifle Association too. Spoke with an indeterminate accent that probably was Eastern European. Rather than write these impressions in her notebook, Matilda Goldberg made mental notes in case she ever needed to write about this encounter, which could become decidedly unpleasant.

Or maybe not. The neighbor's smile had not faded. One front tooth seemed to be steel, not gold. After pausing in front of her hood to insure she did not speed away, he moved to the passenger window of her rental car. Less threatening than if he had confronted her by the driver's window. Made motions with one hand indicating he wanted her to open the window. She fumbled for a button that would allow her to lower the window, but the mid-size car had no automatic button to ease that happening. Goldberg needed to lean over and roll down the passenger window by hand. She thought she noticed him looking down the front of her blouse as she did so. *Maybe I should stay in this position to distract him*, she thought. Except she did not have much there with which to distract. Then his eyes lifted to hers.

"No intent to alarm you," began the man. "You're certainly within your rights to park here. It's simply that we tend to be overprotective when it comes to our neighbor."

And with good reason, Goldberg thought. But as she fumbled to offer an apology, she saw another man approaching from the driver's side of her car, and he *did* look like a Swiss Guard, albeit dressed all in black instead of in the colorful colors of that unit. He also carried in one hand a radio, as though he could call down a missile strike on the roof of her rental car.

She rolled down the window on the driver's side, and as she did the neighbor vanished from the passenger's side, apparently to return to his front window viewpoint. The man in black acted with an air debonair that seemed *so* Italian! She would learn later that his name was Mario. He maintained a pleasant politeness as he both talked to her in accented English and in Italian to an unseen someone in the pope's boyhood home. She was both stunned and fearful when finally he smiled and said, "Would you like a cup of coffee?"

"Coffee?"

Mario gave a so-Italian shrug of his shoulders. "Cappuccino? Your beverage of choice. Don't be alarmed. It's just a friendly invitation." He smiled. "We simply would like the opportunity to talk to you."

Talk to me? We? *Does the Vatican condone waterboarding? Well, not since the Spanish Inquisition, and I have no secrets other than I'm a curious female.* But what could Tilda say, other than yes to an individual who despite his dark clothing seemed so charming. *God, Italian men are so good looking!* Too bad the invitation for coffee had not been made on the Via Veneto.

Goldberg rolled the window back up and got out of the car, notebook still in hand. Mario smiled again and pointed at the notebook. "You won't need that." That comment landed with a clink! It seemed less a threat and more a request, so Matilda Goldberg set her notebook on the seat, swallowed her pride and followed Mario walking toward the home of Pope John Anthony. She did not bother to lock the car. There seemed no need.

Before they reached the door, it opened. Another man dressed in black, smiling, seemingly offering no threat. Escorted into the living room, she stopped as two men she recognized stood to greet her. One was Cardinal James Connolly, the cardinal camerlengo. And next to him to her complete surprise, Pope Tony. He was walking toward her, holding out his hand. She did not know whether to curtsey or to kiss his ring. Instead, she simply shook it. A very American thing to do. But then they each were Americans.

"Ms. Goldberg," began Pope Tony. "I recognize you from Vatican press conferences."

He knows my name? He recognizes me? Matilda Goldberg was more than shocked. *And look how I'm dressed. I would never walk into the Vatican looking like a slut. Shorts with my ass half hanging out. A blouse, open too low because it's hot. Do I care button it to display less skin? No, that would be too obvious. Thank god I'm wearing a bra.*

Pope Tony continued, nodding toward the cardinal camerlengo: "Have you met Cardinal Connolly?"

She had on several occasions, including one recent meeting when she had requested an interview with His Holiness, her request refused, albeit with Irish good grace. Should she address the cardinal as His Eminence, the pope as His Holiness? Back at the Vatican, she would have done so, but was there a special protocol to follow when you have been identified and captured as a stalker? Neither man seemed to show any anger at her presence, and the man in black had quietly moved to a position near the picture window, presumably to guard against other threats. She decided to relax. Waterboarding apparently was not on their agenda.

Hospitality was. "Would you like a cup of coffee?" asked the pope. "Some tea? I can ask my mother to put on a pot?"

"No," Goldberg responded. Weakly. "Maybe a glass of ice water."

Then, fumbling for words, even though she hardly needed to justify choice of beverages, Goldberg added: "I'm running a marathon tomorrow."

"A marathon?" said the pope, looking toward the cardinal camerlengo as though this piece of information was new to him.

The cardinal camerlengo had an impish smile on his face. The *Times* reporter did not notice, nor had she noticed, would she have known why. "The Lake City Marathon, Holiness."

"Yes, I remember," said the man whose identity Celebrity X was known only to a few. "Tomorrow, isn't it?"

The *Times* reporter acknowledged that to be true. It hardly offered her much of an excuse to be prowling around the East Side. And neither of the two prelates seemed interested in probing the reasons for her doing that. Instead, the cardinal camerlengo waved for her to sit down. He took his seat and Pope Tony took his as Mario exited toward the kitchen to obtain the promised glass of water.

"Running a marathon?" said Pope Tony, turning toward Redbird. "Imagine the amount of training it must take to accomplish such a feat."

"Like forty days fasting in the desert," Redbird replied.

The irony of those words went well over Matilda Goldberg's head, although reflecting on what was said and this very special moment later, she would laugh at her own naivety.

17:02:00

Sitting in the front row of the Marquette Room on the third floor of Hilliard Towers with the technical meeting about to begin, the twins— Kyle and Wesley Fowler—wondered what effect Aba Andersson's pregnancy would have on their own plans Sunday. The Swedish runner understandably had abandoned her world record attempt. The warm weather would have made that difficult, if not impossible, to achieve anyway. But what did that mean for them as rabbits?

They expected to find out soon. Race director Peter McDonald was conferring in the corner with his assistant Noel Michaels. She had just checked her watch. Instinctively, each twin looked at his. If there had been an Olympic event for Synchronized Time Checking, the twins would have scored a 10.0. The meeting for elite athletes was due to begin in two minutes, each noted. Just over seventeen hours remained before the Lake City Marathon.

17:02:00. 17:01:59. 17:01:58.

The pair from the Northland Racing Team had been hired by Peter McDonald to pace Aba to a world record. Kyle and Wesley had looked forward to doing just that. The twins considered it an honor to have been asked. They never had met the world record holder prior to this weekend, but had discussed strategy with her husband Bjørn by email. The perfect assignment: to run 20 miles attached to a running icon and get paid for doing so. The Fowler twins each had been promised a fee of $5,000 plus bonuses if Aba succeeded. Not promised: it was in their contracts!

Would McDonald now ask them to pace one of the other women? They were ready. Would they even be required to run? Apparently they still would get paid, but there remained some question about for what? The two young runners were on tight budgets. They needed the money. Neither had yet scored a big pay day. Like many developing American runners, the twins scraped by working as part-time accountants, hoping to improve to a point to where they could match the paychecks of the runners they paced as rabbits.

The term "rabbit" was used to describe those runners hired to run ahead of the lead runners at a set pace, serving as windbreaks in case of headwinds. The purpose of a rabbit—and this was understood by all the elite runners— was to force them to run fast times, to keep them honest, to assist them in achieving those fast times. The term came from the artificial rabbits used at greyhound races to lure greyhounds around racetracks. Rabbits were most common on the European track & field circuit at meets like *Bislett* in Oslo and *Weltklasse* in Zurich, where the paying fans demanded fast times along with close competition. Rabbits were running's equivalent of the *domestiques* used in the Tour de France. For several years after graduating from college, touring the European race circuit, Peter McDonald sometimes rabbitted races to help with expenses.

Peter preferred that his rabbits not go the full distance. For the men, he often used four or five rabbits, assigning different individuals to lead at 10 miles, 13.1 miles (half marathon), 16 miles or 20 miles. If the final rabbit could remain in front, still holding pace, to 21 miles or 22 miles or even 23, Peter would provide a bonus.

Most rabbits knew their jobs and performed them well, sometimes rabbitting in one race as a workout to get ready for a later marathon in which someone else would be assigned as their rabbits. Many of the rabbits Peter had hired for the Lake City Marathon were Kenyans but for several years he also had been using the services of runners connected with Steve Holland's Northland Racing Team.

Because of a smaller pool of women capable of running up front, Peter and other directors often used males as pacers. A female capable of staying near Aba to even halfway probably could go to a lesser race and win more money, and certainly more glory, than she could serving as a *domestique*.

The Fowler twins were perfectly matched for Aba, being a half dozen minutes (about a mile of running) faster. Wesley was a 2:10 marathoner who had placed in the top ten at Boston two years before and also had competed in the World Championships. His twin brother Kyle had a slightly slower time, but had finished in front of Wesley at Boston. At the World Championships, the twins had run together, finishing within a few seconds of each other, Wesley ahead of Kyle. By prior agreement, the Fowler twins determined that there would be no ties between them in races, that each brother would do his best with no hard feelings afterwards.

They had planned to use this 20-miler with Aba as a fast training run to get ready for the New York City Marathon, a month later. But with Aba's not running, now what? Unfortunately, their coach Steve Holland had not yet arrived in town. Depending on what Peter McDonald decided, they would need to confer with their coach to discuss Sunday's strategy.

Peter McDonald addressed their questions immediately after starting the technical meeting, precisely at 3:00.

"First," said Peter, "you need to know that I'm releasing the rabbits." And he quickly said why. "It's too warm for world records. It's too warm for following any pace other than that dictated by your own body." Left unstated was the fact that a pregnant Aba Andersson would not be chasing a fast time at Lake City, although he had just heard from Bjorn that she still planned to run, but well back in the pack. Private discussions with those women (including Tatanya Henry and Fiona Flynn), who in Aba's absence might now contend for the $100,000 first prize indicated that none wanted the pressure of matching even a heat-adjusted pace. They would race each other instead of the clock. As for Joseph Nduku and the Kenyans, Peter knew they marched to their own drumbeat. He did not know what plans Kenyatta Kemai and rabbit Moses Abraham had for the race, because they had not told him, nor had they told their fellow countrymen. Kemai and Abraham certainly had not said anything to Joseph Nduku.

Seated in the first row of seats, Kyle and Wesley Fowler glanced at each other. Kyle shrugged his shoulders as if to ask, what next? Wesley shook his head to indicate, he did not know.

Noticing the reaction of two of his rabbits, Peter added: "You'll still get paid as per contract, whether you run or not." The race director indicated his need to know everybody's intentions either after the meeting or some time later this afternoon.

"Moving ahead," Peter continued, "I'd like to walk you through the schedule for Sunday morning: getting you to the starting line, facilities in the waiting area, and where you'll be able to warm up. I also hope that everybody brought their bottles so we can have them ready at the aid stations. We're collecting them at the back of the room."

As Peter continued to talk, Kyle leaned toward his brother Wesley and whispered: "What do you think, Bro?"

"I think we should run, and at a decent pace," Wesley told Kyle, "but let's see what Coach says."

16:30:00

J **onathan Von Runyon stroked the ball smoothly and saw it roll in a** curving line toward the cup. The *Ledger* reporter applied his best body English—a hip swing to the right—to try to nudge the ball sideways, but his putt rimmed the cup and stopped inches away from earning him a par four on the ninth hole of the East Side Community Center's golf course. A gimmee. He'd take it. Von Runyon shook hands with the others in his foursome, strangers who had shared a few hours with him on a Saturday afternoon, and penciled the final score on his scorecard.

Thirty-nine.

He could have played better on the easy nine-hole course, but Von Runyon was happy. What was there not to be happy about playing a round of golf on a warm and sunny day?

16:30:00. 16:29:59. 16:29:58.

The *Lake City Ledger* reporter had come to the East Side to sneak in a few holes of his favorite sport, golf, after the press conference. It was mid-afternoon, the marathon sixteen-and-a-half hours away, but that event was far from his mind. In fact, Von Runyon had chosen golf as the best way to get away from the marathon. Not all his peers, he surmised, appreciated the "Oprah" column, but that was their problem. Oprah's name in headlines certainly attracted more readers to the story than would have the names of Joseph Nduku or Aba Andersson or even Naní.

And that raised an interesting question: Who was race director Peter McDonald's secret celebrity? McDonald had alerted the police at roll call that a famous person would be running the marathon. On the surface, Peter's celebrity would seem to be the supermodel, Naní, but realistically: Was she celebrated enough to stop traffic away from events where the paparazzi lurked? He thought not.

Von Runyon should not care, although the fact that McDonald apparently was hiding something intrigued him. It intrigued the *Ledger* reporter less by being important news and more from being a puzzle to solve. Like solving *The New York Times* crossword on Saturday, which he always did. Crossword completed earlier today, he now could enjoy his golf—even nine holes of it on a mediocre course.

The East Side course certainly was far from fancy compared to better-manicured courses in the suburbs, courses the *Ledger* reporter did play with

251

some frequency. As a golf writer, he was welcomed as guest on courses not merely in Lake City but around the world, even St. Andrew's in Scotland.

Still, golf was golf. What was the classic comment? Describe the worst day you ever had as a golfer: *Fabulous!* The course at the East Side Community Center possessed considerably less character than St. Andrew's. For one thing, it was only nine holes, crammed onto a patch of land reclaimed from the lake by dumping slag from the steel mills on the shallow lake bottom and covering it with dirt and grass. The one-time exclusive (no blacks, no Jews) East Side Country Club had been built for the convenience of executives who worked in the mills rimming the bottom of the lake, the smokestacks of Hilliard Steel clearly visible from most tees.

But after most of the steel companies closed, or moved their mills elsewhere, the more prosperous East Siders migrated toward the suburbs. Before departing, they donated their bankrupt country club with its golf course, tennis courts, beach and ball rooms to the city, which converted the private club into a public community center for people whose ethnic mix never would have allowed them to become members a generation or two before. Maintenance of the golf course, alas, had deteriorated under Department of Parks management. That missed final putt might have found its way into the hole had the green been less bumpy, but Von Runyon cared little. He played the East Side course mainly from nostalgia. Growing up in the neighborhood, he had caddied at the club to earn money during high school. The course being only nine holes also suited his purpose on a Saturday afternoon, given the limited time he had following the press conference.

Von Runyon wheeled his clubs to a car parked in a lot overlooking the lake, its surface speckled with sailboats, their owners taking advantage of what might be one of the last warm weekends of the season. He placed his clubs in the trunk. Opening the passenger-side door, he sat down to change out of his golf shoes, allowing his mind to briefly wander back to the marathon he would be covering tomorrow. He thought less about the runners up front and dwelled again on the tip that a celebrity might be running and, more specifically, why Peter McDonald would think that person's identity important enough to keep secret. Political figure? The president plays basketball. Rock star? Movie star? TV star? So many so-called celebrities exist today, it is possible that there are *no* celebrities—at least none important enough to care about. No, not Naní. No secret about the supermodel. She clearly had announced her attentions to run the marathon. If someone else more famous, or infamous, who? The *Ledger* reporter decided not to care.

A glance at his watch told Von Runyon that if he did not dally too long at the golf course—no nineteenth-hole scotch and soda—he could catch 4:00 mass at St. Stanislaus Church before a planned dinner engagement back in town. Nostalgia again ruled his decision to go to Mass. Growing up on the East Side, he had served as an altar boy at the church. After Mass, he would call his mother living down in Florida and let her know he had taken communion at St. Stan's. It would make her happy.

16:00:00

St. Stanislaus Church occupied an entire city block in the East Side neighborhood where Pope Tony had grown up, a convenient two-block walk from his mother's home. After Matilda Goldberg left to return downtown and prepare for her marathon (no wiser of the pope's Sunday plans than before), the man called Celebrity X suggested to the cardinal camerlengo that they participate in 4:00 mass at St. Stan's. A simple call to the pastor, Monsignor Alphonse Kostka, secured them spots at the altar. Usually when Tony served at his home church, he preferred to do so without warning and in a secondary role, which surprised Cardinal Connolly when appraised that fact.

"You walk into the rectory and don a deacon's vestment?" asked Redbird.

"I try not to upstage Monsignor Kostka," explained Pope Tony. "He was pastor of St. Stan's when I attended school here. I still look up to him."

Redbird smiled, realizing that here in his old neighborhood was the single church in the civilized world where Pope John Anthony could walk in the door a few minutes before mass and have nobody make a fuss over him.

16:00:00. 15:59:59. 15:59:58.

And that is exactly what happened. A quarter hour before the scheduled start for Mass, the two prelates left Pope Tony's mother's home and walked to church, she accompanying them. Liliana Molina and her boy, Tony. *Some things never change; Some things never should change*, thought the cardinal camerlengo. Pope Tony's two bodyguards hovered safely behind so as not to advertise their presence. Those among Tony's neighbors who spotted him while driving past or getting out of their cars in the church parking lot simply waved. A few shouted, "Hey, Tony." It was "Tony," not "Pope Tony."

Liliana offered return waves to some, hugs to a few. Tony did the same. It was obvious from the look on his face how much pleasure he received from the interchange with friends and neighbors, his delight watching his mother showing off her son, as though to say, *Look how well my son turned out.* Nothing wrong with that.

Marvelous, thought the cardinal camerlengo, *simply mar-vel-ous.*

SATURDAY

St. Stanislaus Church hardly compared in splendor with the many churches and cathedrals in Rome, even in Cardinal Connolly's own country, Ireland. St. Stan's had not been constructed centuries ago, nor had it been built over a period of decades to serve as focal point for a metropolis like Rome or Dublin. It was just a neighborhood church. It dated back to the early 1900s. Soon after arriving in Lake City and claiming the East Side as their own, the mostly Polish and mostly Catholic residents of that neighborhood realized they needed a church as a gathering point for themselves, their children, their grandchildren, now their great grandchildren. The first St. Stanislaus Church had been wooden, erected over a single weekend by men employed at nearby mills, men who had brought simple skills with them from the Old Country. Muscles and an ability to withstand the heat emanating from the blast furnaces; that's all it took.

They recruited a priest from back home. He said masses in their native language. St. Stanislaus provided a link to the land the new people of the East Side had left as they and their families struggled for acceptance as Americans by people who had preceded them to the New World by only a generation or two. Scots, English, Germans, Irish. They had come before. Italians, Mexicans, blacks, Asians; those newer immigrants would come later.

Within a few years after its construction the church burned, a fire begun when a careless altar boy lit a candle too close to some flammable drapery. The embers were hardly cold before the parishioners of St. Stanislaus, whose lives had begun to achieve a level of blue-collar contentment, decided to construct a more permanent and fireproof church, one in the architectural style of the great cathedrals they remembered from Wroclaw and Gdańsk and Poznań. They built their next church from bricks carried to the New World as ballast in ships bound for the steel mills at the bottom of the lake, most specifically Hilliard Steel, one of whose chief executives was Karol Kostka, grandfather of the current monsignor. It was Karol Kostka's donations during the dozen years of construction that helped convert St. Stanislaus from an ordinary block of brick into a structure suitable for welcoming The Lord each Sunday—or this weekend, a visiting pope.

Cynics, the old men who still gathered for coffee at the shopping center, claimed Kostka's donations were less to insure his pathway into heaven and more as penance for the clouds of dark smoke belching from the mills, blackening any laundry hung outdoors to dry for more than a day, blackening also the lungs of those who hung the laundry. The air on the East Side was cleaner now, because, alas, Hilliard Steel no longer existed, its smokestacks surviving only as symbols of a simpler industrial age, its antiquated foundries unable to compete with more modern ones in Asia.

MARATHON

Karlos Kostka, nevertheless, had left his artistic imprint on St. Stanislaus Church. A hand-carved crucifix high in the apse that could have been in a museum, the apse itself gilded with gold. Bas-relief stations of the cross along the interior walls. A baptistery carved from Carrara marble. Solid oak pews in the nave. No padding on the wooden kneelers as though those using them needed no pampering. Finally, stained-glass windows which, when the sun shone from certain angles, showered the altar with all colors of the rainbow. The altar was thusly lit now as Pope Tony exited the sacristy behind Monsignor Kostka with Cardinal Connolly by his side. They wore simple white, cotton vestments, unlike the magnificent garments they might have worn saying mass at St. Peter's in Rome. Pope Tony preferred simplicity over elegance. Ceremony certainly was one of the major attractions of the Roman Catholic Church. Tony knew that, but understood that his predecessor, St. Peter, wore no fancy garments. In the first century, of course, the church was under attack, but in many respects the church was also under attack in the twenty-first century, often because of its own flaws. When Pope Tony thought of the church's future, he often wondered: Is there some way to maintain the traditions centered in its great cathedrals while returning to the simplicity of those years when Jesus Christ had walked the Earth?

The organ was playing now, the choir singing a song that Tony loved, *On Eagle's Wings*, particularly appropriate considering his plans for Sunday.

You who dwell in the shelter of the Lord,
Who abide in his shadow for life,
Say to the Lord,
"My refuge, my rock in whom I trust!"

After their entry from the sacristy, the three priests walked in procession behind three altar boys dressed in red cassocks, covered by crisp white surplices. They walked toward the front of the church. One altar boy in front carried a cross. The other two marched solemnly behind, hands clasped before them in positions of prayer. Thinking of the direction the church must turn in years to come to maintain its credibility with the world's changing populace, Pope Tony wondered what he must do and what he must not do. Many new Christians were simple people in third-world countries, whose struggles to fight the devastation heaped upon their shoulders during wars and famines challenged the church. How could he reach out to them? How must he relate to others living in prosperous nations, bombarded daily by visual temptations so intense he worried for them and their children and their children's children.

And he will raise you up on eagle's wings,
Bear you on the breath of dawn,
Make you to shine like the sun,
And hold you in the palm of his hand.

SATURDAY

Reaching the front of the church, the procession turned, then turned again, moving up the center aisle, the altar boys still leading the way. And they were altar *boys*, not altar girls, Monsignor Kostka believing firmly that only males could be acolytes, not females. What would the good monsignor say if told that Pope Tony had begun to grapple with the question of whether women some day must be accepted as members of the Holy Priesthood? And a more contentious question: Whether priests could marry? He had not voiced these thoughts even to his closest advisors, not to his mentor, Cardinal Connolly. Would he be the pope who would cause this transformation?

The snare of the fowler will never capture you.
And famine will bring you no fear;
Under his wings your refuge,
His faithfulness, your shield.

Was this too radical a break with tradition? Could he accomplish this and other reformations during his lifetime? Given his age, he might continue to guide the church even into the second half of the century. But how long would that lifetime be? He had enemies within the church that considered his ascent at best an accident. One does not impeach a pope like one might impeach an American president for his misdeeds, but there are other ways to remove from office individuals whose policies you dislike. The cardinal camerlengo had followed him to Lake City out of fear for his safety. Was his decision to run 26 miles 385 yards foolishness? Many might think so.

You need not fear the terror of the night,
Nor the arrow that flies by day;
Though thousands fall about you,
Near you it shall now come.

As the procession reached the altar, the three priests circling around behind it to begin Mass, altar boys moving to their positions, the lead acolyte placing the crucifix into a stand, Pope Tony found his mind assailed by doubts. Would even his mother's friends and neighbors accept his moving the church in a radical direction? Often it was the women who sustained the church, who lit votive candles, whose prayers were most sincere, while the men stood outside on the front stairs. That was true in Italy literally, true in America figuratively. Yet it was the men, not women, who rose to positions of authority. Partly for this reason, nuns, the brides of Christ, hardly existed any more, at least in the American church. If women achieved acceptance as priests, would one some day be among his successors?

For to his angels he's given a command
To guard you in all of your ways;
Upon their hands they will bear you up,
Lest you dash your foot against a stone.

As the hymn neared its end, the sound of the organ and the voices of the parishioners of St. Stanislaus echoing off rafters overhead, Pope Tony decided not to worry. God would guide him. *God guided the college of cardinals when they placed me in this role.* Or at least he liked to think so.
And he will raise you up on eagle's wings,
Bear you on the breath of dawn,
Make you to shine like the sun,
And hold you in the palm of his hand.

Sitting toward the rear of the church was an individual, just arrived after playing golf. A former parishioner, he was not surprised to discover who was serving Mass. He knew Pope John Anthony Molina had grown up nearby. He also knew Pope Tony had run in high school and later coached Peter McDonald, who reportedly was trying to keep secret the fact that a very important celebrity planned to run his race. *Hmmm.*

Jonathan Von Runyon finally realized who that celebrity might be.

15:45:00

Lightning lit the monitor, so startlingly **bright that for a millisecond** the screen went blank. Pure blinding light that bathed everything in sight like the flash of a strobe. It made weatherman Vaughn Johnson blink. And instantaneously, the crash of thunder:

CRUMMPP!!

Then another flash. Then more. Thunder and lightning. Each flash and roar blending into the one following:

BOOM! BOOM! BOOM!

A summer storm was brewing off to the West. With luck, if the storm moved east toward Lake City, it could bring relief from the threatening heat wave. *A cold front certainly would be welcome,* Johnson thought.

The weatherman watched mesmerized, realizing he was observing a display of nature rarely caught as effectively on camera. Between the flashes and crashes, the scream of a siren could be heard. Two men stood silhouetted in the light, seen only during the flashes. He knew one of them: Arthur Hailey, Ph.D., a meteorologist at Northern Nebraska University. Dr. Hailey and a graduate assistant stood on a roof staring at a menacing cloud that darkened the screen. *Arthur, get off that roof!* Johnson wanted to scream, even though he knew what he saw had happened several hours before.

The TV3 weatherman was watching a storm captured on video earlier that day, now viewable online, thanks to Hailey. The storm had struck a city west of Lake City. Less than sixteen hours to the marathon. Would the weather system that produced the storm reach Lake City, and if so when? The answer to those questions remained unclear. You could never be sure about thunderstorms as severe as this one. Vaughn Johnson would need to continue to monitor the storm's eastward progress.

15:45:00. 15:44.59. 15:44:58.

During one of the flashes, he detected black bulges along the bottom of the approaching cloud, as though some supernatural entity within was trying to escape. *Flash:* A bulge. *Flash again:* No bulge. *Flash a third time:* The bulge reappeared, and in the several seconds of light supplied by one, two, three strikes, Vaughn could see the bulge metastasize into a twisting funnel.

It was a tornado!

The two men on the roof recognized the twisting cloud for what it was. Despite the rising roar that accompanied the approaching tornado, Johnson could hear Dr. Hailey shout to his assistant: "We better get off the roof, Mitch!" *Very wise idea, Arthur*, thought Johnson. The next time lightning lit the screen, the two men were gone. Johnson watched spellbound as the funnel, lit now by almost continuous lightning flashes, rose above the horizon, descended, rose, then descended, doing untold damage as it ripped a path along the ground, all the time growing in size during its approach toward the rooftop camera capturing its image. The screen flashed white, then black, then white, the continuous light shifts like those at a disco dance, the sound now rising to a decibel level that even the most demented guitar player would find difficult to match. And in one of the flashes, the screen went blank.

Johnson punched stop. Fortunately, Hailey and his assistant had fled before that point otherwise they both might have been killed. That they were not, Johnson knew because the pair had returned to the roof. In passing overhead, the tornado had destroyed the camera, but Hailey and his graduate assistant had retrieved from the camera an undamaged flash drive with its images preserved. Dr. Hailey, whose main specialty area was violent storms, had uploaded the video to his Web site, which is how weatherman Vaughn Johnson was able to view it. The cold front that spawned the tornado was headed in the general direction of Lake City.

Johnson knew that when a cold front hits, temperatures can drop ten or twenty degrees in as many minutes. What a relief if the front arrived before the 8:00

marathon start. Unfortunately, Johnson suspected that would not happen. Or perhaps fortunately, if the front spawned a tornado. His projections suggested that the cold front would not reach Lake City until late Sunday evening. It seemed to be both weakening and slowing. At least the runners would not be threatened by lightning or the accompanying tornado that caused several million dollars damage and killed four people in the city where it hit.

The storm that Johnson had watched in the safety of the TV3 studios had created nearly 90,000 thunderbolts, according to the National Lightning Detection Network. At peak, during the moments captured on camera, the storm fired as many as 800 bolts a minute, and that counted only those hitting the ground! Johnson found that amazing. There was almost no precedent for such a storm, suggested Dr. Hailey, the professor who had captured it on camera. The adventurous part of Vaughn Johnson yearned to have been standing on the roof beside the professor and his graduate assistant; his more cowardly part would have caused him to run for shelter earlier than had they.

The current storm, whether headed his way or not, was the result of a build-up of heat and humidity, not dissimilar to current weather conditions in Lake City. Clouds capable of creating a tornado contain positively-charged ice crystals at the top and negatively-charged water droplets below. This volatile mix results in electrical tension, a powder keg. When warm and moist air floats upward into the high clouds, it is like touching a spark to the powder keg. Result: frequent lightning strikes, accompanied often by high winds.

Johnson replayed the storm video again. An amazing storm, perhaps a once-in-a-lifetime occurrence, but although the cold front seemed headed in the general direction of Lake City, Vaughn Johnson figured that the marathon runners would neither benefit nor suffer from that front.

Vaughn Johnson looked at his watch. Forty-five minutes remained before he was due at the production meeting for the marathon telecast. He needed to be at the TV3 trailer beside the course by 5:00. Only a mile separated the station's studios from the trailer. Normally Johnson would have enjoyed walking that distance, but not the day before he was scheduled to run a marathon and not when the weather was so warm. He would catch a cab. He could put it on his expense account.

Leaving the newsroom later, he noticed Christine Ferrara standing beside her desk. "Going to the production meeting, Christine?"

"As soon as I can get my act together."

"Care to share a cab?"

"Love to."

SATURDAY

15:30:00

Fiona Flynn pushed open a door leading to the interior of Our Lady of the Lake, a modern church, little more than a chapel, constructed for the convenience of people who worked downtown or who were staying like her in a downtown hotel. The church was dark, brightened only by light filtering down from windows above the front entrance, plain windows because there existed no congregation to pay for stained glass. The homeless people who wandered in to rest or to warm themselves on cold days did not carry wide wallets.

15:30:00, 15:29:59. 15:29:58.

A single mass was scheduled for later in the afternoon, but *La Femme Fiona* had come to Our Lady of the Lake not to attend church and fulfill some perceived obligation, but merely to seek a few moments of solitude. In that respect, she was akin to the homeless.

Despite having been recipient of a religious education while growing up in Cork, Ireland, Fiona did not consider herself a spiritual being. She did not attend church regularly. She could not remember the last time she had gone to confession. She did not know how to pray. She could recite the words, but that was not praying, was it? While kneeling in a pew, she knew it was proper to say a few Hail Mary's and Our Father's to signal God, "Hey, I'm here," but she could not do it. She could not recite rote prayers. Most often while visiting church to attend mass or, like today, to settle her mind, she allowed that mind to go blank. If there is a God, does he respond to silence? If so, the Irish Lass just might be in touch with Him.

Moving down the center aisle toward the altar, Fiona paused in front of the steps and bowed her head. She moved next to a side altar in the right transept, one that had behind it an image of the Blessed Virgin Mary, the mother of God, the Lady of the Lake after which the church had been named. Fiona had come not to pray, but only to light a votive candle, which she did after stuffing a dollar bill in the slot for offerings.

She did not kneel, but stood in front of the rows of burning candles, each in red holders bathing the altar with an ethereal light. She stood silent, hands clasped before her, not prayerful, more in tranquility. Was this prayer? Fiona did not think so. To pray for victory, she felt, was obscene. She winced when she saw athletes being interviewed on TV after winning races, who credited Jesus for their victories. What about those finishing behind? Did they lose because they did not have as direct a line to Jesus? If she won the Lake City

260

Marathon tomorrow and earned $100,000 as her human reward, it would be because of her actions not because she had bribed the Man Above. He (or "She," Fiona thought impishly) had provided her with certain talents. She had chosen to make use of those talents. She would succeed or fail tomorrow because of her ability to maximize the talents she had been given at birth. Maybe *He* should thank *her* after the marathon.

Okay, Jesus, I think I get it now. We're in this together. If I run the race so as to obtain the prize, as St. Paul suggests, will you offer me a sip of wine when I show up for mass next Sunday? Fiona decided she better not ask that; it was tantamount to offering Jesus a bribe.

Fiona forced herself not to think such dark thoughts. She tried to abandon metaphysical delusions. She focused on emptying her mind of all opinions, judgments, beliefs, feelings, bad vibes. And after satisfying herself that she had allowed her mind to go blank for at least a few purifying seconds, Fiona bowed her head once more and exited the church to return to her hotel.

Tomorrow, with the grace of God, Fiona would do the best she could, and if that "best" resulted in a prize worthy of St. Paul, she would be fulfilled.

15:00:00

The "studio" for TV3's marathon telecast was located in a tent on a wide walkway between Columbia Drive and the lake, conveniently halfway between the start several hundred yards to the north and the finish line several hundred yards to the south. To the west loomed the skyline of Lake City, buildings so tall, several of them over one hundred stories, that they could be seen at least on clear days across open water from the other side of the lake, nearly forty miles away. Not far from the TV3 tent to the east was Burnham Fountain, water spurting skyward. Stepping out of the taxicab that had brought her and Vaughn Johnson to the scheduled production meeting for the marathon telecast, Christine's eyes were drawn almost magnetically to the fountain as she waited for the weatherman to settle their fare.

They had a few minutes before the start of the production meeting at 5:00. The start of the marathon now was only fifteen hours away.

15:00:00. 14:59:59. 14:59:58.

Such a beautiful city, thought Christine. *I must get to know it better.* Despite having attended college little more than a hundred expressway miles away, she only had visited Lake City a handful of times. Given her current position with TV3, Christine had begun to realize that certainly she would

261

spend the next several years in Lake City, maybe longer than that. In her profession as TV reporter, there were only a few markets—New York, Chicago, Los Angeles, maybe Atlanta—that offered a step upward. Would she some time in the future take that step, or was there a good reason to remain in Lake City, some compelling incentive to stay in town.

Turning back from the fountain, she saw the taxicab driving away, Johnson standing beside the curb placing the change from a twenty-dollar bill back into his wallet, and beyond him a golf cart driven by an intern from the marathon office, Alisa, her only passenger the man who might offer that compelling incentive not to take her TV career too seriously.

Peter.

She could see that he looked tired from the continued stress of preparing for an event destined to be run under less than perfect conditions. During the ride over from the TV3 studios, weatherman Vaughn had updated her on the changing weather conditions, the cold front headed their way that unfortunately, he said, probably would not arrive in time to offer any relief. Peter looked sleep-deprived, Christine observed with some amusement. He obviously was in nap mode, his eyes were closed, his head bobbing. He had not seen her yet. Christine wondered with some amusement how long the cart ride could have been? A minute from somewhere else in the set-up area. Sixty seconds of sleep? I suppose that when you are fully occupied organizing an event over a period of seventy-two hours, you catch snatches of rest whenever you can grab them.

"Good morning, Mr. McDonald," said Christine teasingly, as Peter's cart stopped near the TV3 tent studio.

At the sound of her voice, Peter's chin lifted, his eyes popped open, the sight of her brought a smile to his face. "Good *afternoon*, Ms. Ferrara."

Stepping out of the cart, Peter thanked Alisa for the ride and turned toward Vaughn, offering a hand and a greeting familiar to the weatherman. "How's the weather, Vaughn?"

"Continued warm, I'm afraid," Johnson responded. "One update, which I'll address during the meeting."

Peter could have asked for a quick preview of that update, but chose not to do so. "Tell Tom we'll be inside in a minute," said Peter, referring to director, Tom Schorr.

We? thought Christine. *Hmmm. How am I going to handle this?*

Johnson caught the hint, sensing that Peter had something private to say to Christine Ferrara. The buzz in the newsroom was that the pair had been spied exchanging a kiss after his appearance on *The Morning Show* yesterday. It had been in a dark corner behind a couple of cameras, an air kiss only, but eyes had been on them, nothing escaping the notice of the nosy workers at TV3, friends of Peter, who, remembering the traumatic death of the race director's wife a year ago, had been hoping beyond hope that someone would arrive and help him move past that painful period. The talk at the coffee bar had been so intent yesterday, that Johnson suspected the ears of both lovers—dare he think of them as such—had been burning with an intense flame. The weatherman offered a hand wave and entered the tent studio.

Neither Peter nor Christine saw him go. Their eyes were only on each other. "You had lunch with Naní?" Peter began.

"You talked to her?" asked Christine.

"Text-message," he said, patting the phone attached to his belt.

Christine could not conceal a wicked smile. "I am now the subject of your text-messages, Peter?"

He laughed. "Let me say that Naní is a *very* special friend of mine, Christine. I believe you understand better the relationship now." Then to make sure she did, he added: "Her husband just arrived in town. Hopefully you'll get a chance to meet Ricco after the race tomorrow."

Tomorrow. He had made an assumption about her availability tomorrow. Christine smiled again, temporarily amused as to how rapidly their relationship was developing during this most important weekend of both their lives. But the smile on her face froze. Talk about text-messaging reminded her of what she had discovered while seated in front of her computer earlier that morning. Her eyes grew moist.

Peter noticed. "Something wrong?"

"I...." Christine let the word dangle.

Peter sensed what the TV reporter was about to say. Inadvertently, he reached up to touch the silver chain his late wife Carol had given him.

Christine's tears were now real. A single tear began to escape one eye. It had reached halfway down her cheek when the words tumbled from her mouth: "I'm so sorry. I'm so *very* sorry."

Christine could not bear to utter his late wife's name. Neither could Peter. "Naní told you?"

"No, I...."

A second of silence. Two seconds as Christine groped for words. Peter removed the hand touching the necklace and placed it on the tear halfway down Christine's cheek, allowing the drop of fluid to move from her face to his hand. Her head spun so fast she worried that it must fly off her neck and shoulders. The contact of his hand on her still moist cheek provided a feeling more passionate than anything she had experienced in her life this far. *Is this love? Is the feeling as intense with him as it is with me? Will the feeling grow?* She knew it would. She *hoped* it would.

Then Peter broke the silence: "You?..."

SATURDAY

It was a request that she finish the sentence just begun. She did, not without some embarrassment:

"I googled you."

"You googled me?"

"I googled you."

Peter looked deeply into her eyes, momentarily amused, but neither he nor Christine wanted to admit what she had learned from her search. Neither had spoken his late wife's name, and neither wanted to devote time to discuss the facts of Carol's death—at least not at this point in time. There would come time for that later, thought Peter. Christine thought the same.

After brushing the tear from her eye with his hand, Peter had allowed the hand to drop to lightly clasp hers. Now he gave that hand a tug. "Christine, I love that you did that, and there is so much I want to tell you, but we're late to the production meeting."

Peter obviously did not want to talk—at least now. Christine was relieved, but said nothing. Still holding hands, the pair began walking toward the tent studio, speaking no more, each one caught in their own thoughts. Peter's mind had skipped forward, reviewing plans for the telecast, his role during the four-hour show and how he would balance the greedy demands of the media with the normal organizational tasks of insuring for nearly 50,000 runners that their marathon experiences were as good as they reasonably could expect, given the threat of warm weather. Worries about sponsorship? That did not concern him now; it was a problem to be dealt with some time after the last runner crossed the finish line. Celebrity X? At some point, probably soon after 8:00 tomorrow morning, the TV people would learn the identity of this all important individual. Not yet.

Christine had not yet begun to think of the telecast. Her thoughts were centered on this man who walked beside her toward the studio tent. He allowed her hand to slip from his as they arrived at the production meeting, just before the eyes of those involved in the telecast turned toward them.

Christine Ferrara realized that her life had taken a sudden and unanticipated turn in the three days since she met Peter. She thought: *He cares for me as much as I care for him. I've never wanted anything more intently than I've wanted this man.* Lucky that each of them had so much else going on in their lives, Christine thought, or she could really get herself in trouble!

MARATHON

14:30:00

S o how fast do we want to run—or do we even want to run at all?"
That was the question posed by Kyle and Wesley Fowler to Coach
Steve Holland. The question had been weighing on the twins' minds
since the technical meeting. With the start of the marathon less than fifteen
hours away, the two runners wondered what their coach wanted them to do.

14:30:00. 14:29:59. 14:29:58.

Affecting their decision was the fact that the twins were running the New
York City Marathon in another four weeks with a goal of breaking 2:10.
Coach Holland had figured that their rabbiting in Lake City would provide a
stepping-stone for peak performance and a good paycheck in New York.

"Tell me again what Peter said," asked Holland. The coach had arrived late
in town, because he had Friday classes to teach at Northland College. The
Northland coach left the Twin Cities driving the team van early morning with
a group of other runners he coached, thus missed the technical meeting. Those
runners had less lofty goals than that of the twins, or their fast female teammate, Katie Hyang, but Holland enjoyed working with runners of all abilities.
He found that the fast and slow runners on his racing team meshed well, each
encouraging the others. The older runners also helped with fund-raising, necessary in preparing promising runners to achieve Olympic-level objectives.
The Fowler twins had come to his room before heading out to dinner. They
would be carbo-loading tonight with several who planned to finish somewhere between three and six hours. This huge gap in aspirations seemed to
make little difference when the Northland Racing Team sat down to eat, or to
down a beer or two after a race.

"Mr. McDonald offered us the day off," said Kyle.

"We can run or not run," added Wesley.

"But he still plans to pay you?" Businessman and agent as well as coach,
Holland knew that the twins were to each receive $5,000 for bringing Aba to
20 miles on pace, after which she would continue to the finish line unaided. If
the Swedish runner broke the world record, the twins would receive a $2,500
bonus. Fail to maintain the steady 5:10-per-mile as planned, and they would
be penalized, their paycheck tied to the number of miles they stuck with her.

Kyle informed Coach Holland that they still would receive their paycheck
although no bonus. "Mr. McDonald released the rabbits in the men's race
too," added Wesley.

265

SATURDAY

"Too hot," said Kyle.

"Joseph Nduku told Mr. McDonald that with temps spiking above 80, he had no desire to follow a pace determined three months ago. The rest of the Kenyans seemed to agree."

"Makes sense," said Holland.

"It's going to be a free-for-all," said Kyle.

"We're not getting in *their* way," said Wesley.

"They'd chew us up and spit us out like *ugali*," said Kyle, mentioning an African porridge made out of corn.

"It probably will be a better race without rabbits."

"Slower time, better race."

As his twin athletes nervously chattered, Coach Holland pondered the problem posed by their no longer being needed as Aba's rabbits. All their training plans had been predicated on a fast run at sub-marathon distance this weekend. He asked his runners about the other top women.

"Tatanya would never use us," Kyle began, mentioning the Russian.

"She would elbow us if we even came close," echoed his twin.

"Toshi is too much the free spirit," Kyle said of the Japanese runner.

"She considers it a disgrace for a woman to rely on a man."

"Katie?" asked Holland, mentioning their teammate.

"We discussed it. Katie felt it put her in the embarrassing position of being paced by teammates."

"Like we'd be running interference."

"It might not sit well with the other women runners."

"And it wouldn't look good on TV—assuming Katie gets on TV."

Coach Holland said he agreed, then asked about Fiona Flynn.

"She said she wanted us..."

"...But not as pace-setters."

Their coach laughed at that remark. *La Femme Fiona's* fondness for male companionship was well known on the track, and now road-running, circuit. But that left his runners without a pace to set, neither for others, nor for themselves. Resting did not make sense to Holland, not with New York coming up. They needed a hard run at 20 miles this weekend, although warm weather compounded the problem of deciding exactly how hard. Maybe a 5:10 pace for 20 miles was too fast given the expected warm weather.

"How about 5:20 pace?"

"That makes sense, Coach," Kyle agreed.

"Carry that pace through the half marathon, maybe to 15 miles. If the heat doesn't bother you—and it shouldn't at that pace—pick it up to near 5:10 pace for the final five miles. Then stop short, as planned."

"That makes sense, Coach," Wesley echoed his brother.

The trio continued to discuss plans for the weekend—and beyond the weekend—training that they would do leading into New York. They had rested today, Saturday, jogging no more than a couple of miles in the morning. Run Sunday, but at a controlled pace, as just discussed. "I'll be out on the course to keep you honest," said Coach Holland, "but I'm going to give Katie more attention."

"No complaint from us," said Kyle.

"She's racing for money," added Wesley.

The Northland coach had brought a bicycle with him on the team van and had plans to intersect the course at various locations. He could do this by taking shortcuts and using parallel roads. Monday would be a day totally away from running. They would need this not so much after what should be for them an easy 20-miler, but more from the stress of travel. Runners needed rest, felt Holland. Sometimes they fail to realize this, trapped by their diaries and desires to make each week a hundred-mile week or more. It's not the number of miles you run, believed the Northland Racing Team coach, it is the *quality* of those miles that counts.

He considered this sound advice even for the slower runners he coached, those planning to finish in four hours or more. Holland worried about them the most. They would be out on the course and under the hot sun twice as long as the elite runners. Long after Joseph Nduku and his countrymates had returned to the hotel, many of the other runners would still be struggling.

Elite or sub-elite, this was no time to stick with pacing goals set three or four months ago. His runners would need to recognize the fact that when temperatures climb into the 70s and 80s, you simply cannot run as fast as with temperatures in the 50s and 60s. The elite runners in the club understood this better than the so-called citizen runners. Elite runners usually focus on place, not on time. They are more likely to run against their fellow competitors than the clock. Citizen runners more often run against the clock than their competitors. This could lead them to fatal mistakes.

Wesley Fowler interrupted Coach Holland's thoughts by announcing, "C'mon Coach, let's go eat."

14:15:00

Trying not to be caught doing so, Peter McDonald slipped the cell phone from his pocket. The phone's vibrations had alerted him to the arrival of a text-message, one of probably a dozen that had clicked into the phone in the forty-five minutes since the start of the TV3 production meeting. The meeting was dragging w-a-a-a-y too long, as meetings often did. Peter needed to get back to the hotel in time for the pasta party scheduled for 6:00. No need to dress fancy. None of the runners expected to see him in a tuxedo. Aba was speaking. He could arrive late, trusting his staff to get the party moving, but he hated being late even when he had good reasons.

14:15:00. 14:14:59. 14:14:58.

No identifying name. He apparently did not have the caller in his directory. The phone number displayed had a Minnesota area code: 612. Peter suspected he knew who was calling. He pushed the green button and saw a short text-message from Steve Holland, the Nitro/Northland coach.

Twins plan to run 20, fast workout only. See you tomorrow.   --Steve

Peter considered the message for a few moments. There was no need for him to acknowledge, but he did so anyway, thumb-tapping: *OK.*

That makes sense, thought Peter. He knew Kyle and Wesley Fowler planned to peak at New York in four more weeks. They lost the chance of a bonus check when Aba cancelled her world record attempt, but the twins were being well rewarded just for showing up. Maybe if Kyle and Wesley continue their improvement, next year he can hire a rabbit to pace them to a fast time.

Peter started to replace the digital phone in his pocket, then had a better idea. Standing, showing the phone, he said simply, "Gotta go."

"We're almost wrapped," said director Tom Schorr, then just as Peter was about to exit, asked: "Nothing more to announce?"

"Nope," said Peter, knowing Schorr was trolling for info on Celebrity X.

"No secrets to confess?" Schorr probed maliciously, smiling to indicate he expected no confession.

"I forgot to floss my teeth this morning," said Peter, straight-faced, producing a laugh from the group.

Christine blushed slightly at learning this intimate detail about her soon-to-be (she hoped) boyfriend's bathroom habits. *Flosses teeth,* she thought. *I'll note that in my Peter File.* Christine had perfect teeth, never a cavity, and rarely flossed, much to the consternation of her dentist—and Yolanda.

Peter left, briefly making eye contact with Christine before doing so. No smile from either to indicate a developing relationship, although that relationship had become more than obvious to those in the room.

During the meeting Peter had offered no information about whether or not a yet unidentified celebrity was running the race. Seemingly, this most important celebrity was Naní, except the supermodel had announced her plans at the press conference earlier this morning. So if not Naní, then who? Despite his question, Schorr had decided that to probe further was a waste of time. He quickly moved through the last few items on his checklist, then asked, "Anybody have any more questions?" Nobody did, so he indicated that he would see everybody tomorrow morning.

Christine had been seated next to Carolynne Vickers and Timothy Rainboldt. They rose simultaneously. "Going to the Pasta Party?" asked C.V., meaning it as a conversational gambit more than from any desire to know.

"Not really," Christine responded, the response leaving the subject of her dinner plans open. She probably would head home. She had no Saturday-night date, nor did she want one. Christine definitely did *not* want to attend the Pasta Party, since that was where Peter was heading. She did not want to appear to be chasing him. Time enough for that next week.

"Neither are we attending," C.V. smiled and turned toward her telecast partner. "In fact, Timothy just agreed to take me to dinner."

"I did?"

"You did, darling, to a fashionable and expensive restaurant not likely to be frequented by runners, because it does not serve Italian food."

"Fashionable and expensive?" said her sometime husband. "That must mean, I'm paying."

"You are, and it was very thoughtful of you to suggest that we ask Ms. Ferrara to join us. You will, won't you, Christine?"

The offer sounded promising, certainly more promising than whatever leftovers awaited her at home. But wearing Capri pants and a pastel blouse that was neither fashionable nor expensive, Christine hardly seemed dressed for a night on the town. "Look at me," said Christine to suggest that fact.

"I have been," smiled Timothy.

"Shut up, Timothy,' C.V. rebuked him, though without anger. "Okay, fashionable and expensive is out. Look at us: We're not dressed any better."

"Fashionable is out," said Timothy.

"Out," said C.V. "I refuse to go to a restaurant where a maître d' might rebuke me for my taste in clothes."

"Expensive is still in."

"Hard to avoid in Lake City," acknowledged C.V, turning back to Christine. "You are accompanying us to dinner, are you not?"

Christine smiled, amused by the banter. "Do I have a choice?"

"You do *not* have a choice. We need to discuss tomorrow's telecast."

"Somehow," mused Timothy, "I sense tonight's dinner will find its way onto an expense account,"

"Very perceptive. Have you ever met an expense account, you did not like, my dear ex-husband?

"Still-husband," Timothy corrected C.V. "You never signed the final divorce papers."

SATURDAY

"They're on my desk back home, wherever back-home is these days. Text-message me Tuesday morning, and I promise to put them in the mail." Carolynne folded her arm inside that of Christine. "Come, my fair lady. You and I are going to find someplace to freshen up while this terrible man worries about securing a taxi."

Christine Ferrara allowed herself to be tugged she did not yet know which way. Certainly this was going to prove a more enjoyable evening than one at home with Yolanda's leftovers.

14:00:00

They began lining up before the doors to the International Room at Hilliard Towers ten or twenty minutes before the Pasta Party's scheduled start. By 6:00, the line waiting to get into the ballroom was backed down a stairway to the first-floor corridor, snaking around a corner past an Irish bar, a gift shop and a restaurant almost to the main entrance of the hotel. There, the lobby digital clock continued to display the hours, minutes and seconds left before the start of the Lake City Marathon.

14:00:02. 14:00:01. 14:00:00.

Precisely at 6:00, the three marathon office staff members guarding the three entrance doors to the International Room opened them and began accepting tickets. Runners flowed rapidly into the mammoth ballroom, its gilded ceiling dominated by glittering chandeliers high above a parquet floor. Mirrors on sidewalls made the room seem even larger than it was. Within a few minutes almost all the tables, except for several up front near the podium marked "reserved," had been claimed by groups of runners, only a few scattered seats remaining for those arriving late.

Those entered in the marathon were hungry, eager to eat, ready for their ritual feeding, the final carbo-load before being released to run Sunday morning. But the dinner offered at Lake City was more than the ordinary carbo-load offered at lesser marathons. They would not stand in a line to have spaghetti dumped on plastic plates to be eaten with plastic forks. No paper napkins. *This was a feast!* No buffet line. Fine china. Silverware that was silver. Cloth napkins. Along the edges of the ballroom, tuxedo-clad waiters hovered ready to serve three types of pasta—fettuccini, linguini, rigatoni—plus a minestrone soup, a green salad and a sherbet dessert. Bottles of E.R.G. in center baskets. Coffee to come. Tea if you asked for it. A cash bar, should your choice be an alcoholic beverage. Add to that: Aba Andersson as after-

270

dinner speaker. Finally, a raffle with the grand prize two expense-paid trips to the Honolulu Marathon. *Woo-hoo!* Nobody would be leaving early.

Everything about the event radiated elegance. Peter McDonald took pride in hosting what he considered the running world's best Pasta Party. The International Room seated 900; tickets to the Pasta Party had been sold out for months, available now only on eBay at inflated prices.

Heading to a reserved table in front of the podium, Peter worked the room, taking a serpentine course, going from table to table, saying hello both to those he knew and those who knew him, the consummate politician, not stopping, limiting conversations to a few brief sentences, moving inexorably forward. Several Shelaghi executives had accepted invitations to the dinner. That included Paddy Savitch though not the key man, Dennis Lahey. That seemed worrisome, though Peter was too busy with other race-oriented tasks to give the matter much thought. He could see Paddy in conversation with Aba. She seemed to be charming him and the other Shelaghi executives. He needed to join his dinner guests.

13:45:00

On another floor at the Hilliard, in a smaller ballroom, several hundred marathoners running for AIDS Africa gathered for their final carbohydrate feast, a meal identical to that offered at the official Pasta Party hosted by Peter McDonald. In making arrangements Naní, knowing Peter's menu, simply told those planning her party to duplicate it. "I'll have what he's having."

Just as Peter had strode through the International Room shaking hands with a flair worthy of a practiced politician, Naní also moved from table to table, making sure each of the runners, who as a group had raised more than a quarter million dollars for her charity, would have reason to say later to their friends that they had met *her*, the supermodel. These were people who *cared*, and Naní appreciated their support. As the race drew nearer, she found herself eager to join them on the starting line, to get to know at least a few of them during the 26 miles they would spend on the course together.

13:45:00. 13:44:59. 13:44:58.

Naní remembered tearfully the week when she and Peter's late wife, Carol, her college roommate, had walked around Mount Kilimanjaro meeting the children of Africa. Strange, but Naní had learned more about Carol in that one week than she had in four years rooming with her. They parted at the Dar es

Salaam airport, taking separate planes, Carol back to Peter, she to Europe for a fashion show. That was the last time Naní had seen Carol. Naní attempted to visualize Carol with a stupid hat on her head worn around the mountain waving goodbye, offering that silly giggle of hers that sometimes had driven Naní wild in college, handing her ticket to an attendant, then vanishing into the gantry connecting terminal to the plane. Naní tried to call back that image in her mind, but it was fuzzy, getting fuzzier. She wondered what images Peter still held in his mind. She hoped he had high-definition recall.

In the several months after the AIDS walk, she and Carol had talked on the phone. They had text-messaged each other. But that moment in the Dar es Salaam air terminal was the last time they had touched, the last time they had looked in each other's eyes, the last time they offered good-girl hugs, promising friendship forever. If Naní missed Carol that much, she could imagine how the loss had devastated Peter. She truly hoped that Christine Ferrarra could help him erase a bad memory. Christine did seem perfect for Peter, but even if not, it was a step for him in the right direction.

"Are you planning to win the race tomorrow?" teased one of the runners at a table where she had stopped.

"Goodness, no," Naní responded with a laugh. "I'm not that fast."

"Didn't you have an uncle who ran for Tanzania in the Olympics?"

"A cousin. A distant cousin."

"A long distance cousin," another runner corrected her, delighted at this contact with the supermodel, so much the celebrity yet such a warm person when met away from the lenses of the paparazzi.

"I probably have two hundred cousins," confessed Naní. "You're talking about John Stephen Akhwari. Cousin John finished more than an hour behind the rest of the field."

"But that's not the entire story," prodded the first runner, who obviously wanted her to tell it.

"No, it's not, and it's a story I love to tell—and will probably retell when I address the group after we eat."

At the 1968 Olympic Games in Mexico City, Akhwari fell, cutting his knee and dislocating his joint. Still, the Tanzanian marathoner continued, limping to the finish line. He finished last out of seventy-four runners, his time: 3:25:17. Asked afterwards by filmmaker Bud Greenspan, why he had continued to run, Akhwari replied: "My country did not send me 7,000 miles to start the race. They sent me 7,000 miles to finish it."

The questioning runner said: "With that slow a time—relatively speaking—you surely could beat it?"

Naní smiled: "There would be no honor in doing so. He is revered in my mother's country. On another occasion, Cousin John ran 2:15."

"Whew!"

"I will be happy to run near four hours."

"That's still fast."

"You are too kind," said Naní, "but I need to get back to my table. I'll see you on the starting line tomorrow."

She had noticed the tuxedoed waiters beginning to move forward with plates of food. Most of the waiters were from the same group that had waited tables at Peter's larger Pasta Party at the International Ballroom, their movements from one banquet to another cleverly scheduled by a manager in the kitchen. Peter had promised Naní that he would stop by and say hello to the AIDS Africa charity runners, but it needed to be a Kiss-And-Fly, he warned. He had made a similar promise to another charity group in another ballroom running to raise money for the American Cancer Society.

Naní sat down at a front table beside her husband Ricco. For a moment, they gazed at each other without speaking. He covered her left hand, the one that for tonight contained their wedding band. He always wore his; she wore hers only when with him. It was an arrangement suggested by her agent. She loved being possessed by a man, loved having the band signifying that fact on her third left finger, wondered why it was so necessary for her image to disguise the facts of her marriage. Her not wearing the band did not seem to bother Ricco, who never betrayed any jealousy that her fame exceeded his. Her husband was worth millions because of his magazine, *Zest*, but he seemed to relish being the man in the background when she took the stage.

"Excited?" he asked.

"Yes."

"Nervous?"

"No."

Ricco squeezed her hand. "If you're excited about the marathon, why aren't you also nervous?"

"I'm not excited about the marathon, I'm excited about meeting Peter's new girlfriend this afternoon."

"Naní!" Ricco removed his hand from hers and raised an index finger to shake it, scolding her. "You are not a matchmaker."

"If I were, guess who I might match?"

He cradled her shoulder, kissing her on the cheek as he did. It was a lingering kiss, one not quickly removed. He whispered in her ear: "You are so much the woman, yet still the little girl."

"Don't you like the little girl?"

"Sometimes. I like the woman even more. You don't suppose anybody would notice if we suddenly ducked under the table."

Naní covered his mouth with her hand, scolding: "I'm not going to listen to you. Eat your spaghetti, Ricco! It's getting cold."

13:30:00

aturday evening, as runners throughout Lake City looked to their carbo-loading options, members of Team Turtle trickled into the Iroquois Room at Hilliard Towers for a reception sponsored by Don Geoffrey. Some had eaten before; some would do so afterwards. The reception started at 6:00; Geoffrey arrived a half hour later.

13:30:00. 13:29:59. 13:29:58.

No stated dress coast existed. Some came straight from the Expo dressed in traditional runner's garb: jeans, T-shirt and running shoes. Others had visited their rooms to shower and change into slacks and collared shirts or nice blouses. A few wore coats and ties, dresses with jewelry, suggesting that their appearance at the Team Turtle reception was merely the first stop en route to a more elegant affair elsewhere. They paused in the entrance to the Iroquois Room, allowing themselves to be properly greeted by the greeters, next signed a sheet on a clipboard: real names and usernames. They accepted paper badges: *Hello, my name is....* Then began the game of wandering from person to person, trying to connect names and usernames on badges with avatars (or pictures) they had become familiar with online.

A bartender stood in one corner. He had been warned in advance by the banquet manager to stock only beer, wine and soft drinks, that runners normally did not consume hard liquor.

And so they came to the Team Turtle party. Arriving soon after the doors opened at 6:00 was Natasha, a music teacher from Covington, Kentucky. And Gloria from Bethesda, Maryland: her husband worked for the C.I.A. (although they did not want anybody to know it). Behind her came Sophie from Carmel, Indiana, who discovered Team Turtle several years ago while searching the Internet for a cure for shin splints before her first marathon. Sophie ran the race anyway and learned later she had a stress fracture. The advice she received on the Team Turtle Bulletin Board allowed her to avoid injuries while training for later marathons. Suzanne arrived from Punta Gorda, Florida. She had smoked for a dozen years before starting to walk to help kick the habit. Walking led to running and then to the challenge of the marathon. Both Suzanne and husband Carter had qualified to run Boston, though at gatherings of runners they usually liked to be asked rather than boast of that fact.

Barry from Seattle, Washington had played football all through college, then had spent nearly fifteen years becoming increasingly sedentary and obese before deciding to train for a marathon. His greatest achievement, he liked to say, was not his fast times, but that he had lost forty pounds and kept them off. Barry had set four successive PRs coming into this race, lowering his best time to 3:42, not good enough to qualify for Boston, but he hoped to meet that goal before turning forty in three more years. Ian, though born in Manchester, England, lived in Los Angeles, California. Lured to the U.S. by the prospects of a film career, Ian found more success working in the pharmaceutical industry. He started to run after getting a golden retriever. "It was easier to run with the dog rather than get my arm pulled off."

Daniel from Pensacola, Florida, a former smoker, had ballooned to 215 pounds before turning forty. Forced to renew his insurance policy, he started running to avoid flunking the medical exam. He arrived with Frederick, also from Pensacola. Several married couples who had met them at previous Team Turtle gatherings wondered if the pair were "partners" (to use one euphemism for gay couples). Nobody wanted to be the first to ask, fortunate, since they were merely good friends who enjoyed running together.

Terry from South Milwaukee, Wisconsin was a computer scientist whose previous exercise had consisted of moving between office cubicle and coffee bar. His wife Carla signed up for a 5-K and talked him into joining her. Enjoying the experience, impressed with the energy of those around him, Terry ratcheted his way up to the marathon, although Carla continued to compete only in 5-K races. Austin was a Team Turtle member who lived, ironically, in Austin, Texas. He used "Austin Austin" as his username. He had just graduated from the University of Texas and was running Lake City as his first race, claiming he also liked rock climbing and jumping out of airplanes. His older brother Kelly was terrified by heights, but had run a dozen marathons; he planned to pace Austin Austin to a "fabulous time," not finishing time, but the enjoyment of spending several hours surrounded by 50,000 friends.

Bob Veldman, an air traffic controller, who lived in a northwest suburb of Lake City, suggested to people who had flown into town that he might have provided instructions for the pilots landing their airplanes. Clarence, a stock broker from Chicago, spent time chatting with Georgia, a stay-at-home mom from Omaha, whose husband dutifully was up in their room with a snoozing child, hoping that he could join her later at the party. Tilda from Rome arrived wearing a floor-length gown that clung tightly and quite sexually to her broomlike body. She was *dying* to tell everybody about the famous person she had met and talked to earlier that afternoon, but a reporter's discretion for not spilling news before it became news caused Tilda to hold her tongue. "So you're not Italian," commented Bobby from Des Moines, Iowa, who had assumed that to be the case from her avatar.

Also attending the party was a man whose paper badge said: "Hello, my name is Jimmy." He came from St. Paul, Minnesota, but nobody recognized the name, because he was a lurker, never posting to the bulletin boards, only reading the posts of everyone else. In a conversation with one group, he admitted to having attended the same college as the Turtle, Northland, "but a decade later." He was hoping to qualify for Boston with a time under 3:20, weather permitting. Pleading a previous commitment, he left just as Norris, a sociology professor at Lake City University, arrived. "Pleased to meet you, old sport," said Jimmy barely breaking stride en route to the elevator.

Brad from Mishawaka, Indiana once had run a 4:17 mile in college, but claimed he only ran marathons for "fun." A few others had competed as runners earlier in life. Daisy ran cross-country and track while attending high school in Louisville, Kentucky, but disliked the pressure of competition and jogged mainly to maintain her Size 6 figure. Lake City would be her second marathon. Her husband Tom, a former football player from Yale, had come to cheer her. Howard lived in Kansas City, Kansas and did not start running until his mid-thirties, prompted to do so because of the poor health of his father. He did not want to die of a heart attack at age fifty-seven as had Dad. So far this year, Howard had run six marathons, losing twenty-five pounds. From Colorado Springs, Colorado came Warren, whose father was a runner. He had started running at age seven, but he still had not matched his dad's best times.

Sara Ann lived in Cleveland, Ohio. A graduate of Wellesley University, she had been inspired to run the Boston Marathon after her first year in college, seeing runners in that race pass Wellesley, the halfway point. Sara Ann's remaining three years, she had run Boston as a bandit starting without a number. At least she was respectful enough to wait for the entered runners to clear the starting grid. Because she had talent, she finished in front of many of them. After graduation and marriage and two children, she properly qualified for Boston and ran it a half dozen times, almost breaking three hours once. She still was embarrassed about previously having run as a bandit. Cornelia played the horn in her high school band growing up in Whittier, California, Richard Nixon's birthplace, but recognized the life of a concert artist was neither easy nor financially rewarding. She recently returned home after spending a year with the touring company for *Evita*, managing the company, not playing in its orchestra. Needing a break, Cornelia decided to spend the next year reading books and training for a marathon.

Sharon, a high school librarian from Portland, Oregon, considered herself first a triathlete, but ran marathons to prepare for that sport. She hoped some day to qualify for Ironman. Frank from Columbia, South Carolina had as his goal running fifty marathons in fifty states, and this was number forty-three. He was saving Hawaii for the last and had extracted from his wife a promise that she go too. Normally she disliked the marathon scene and had not accompanied him to Lake City. In return for her allowing him his hobby, he offered no objection to her going on bird watching expeditions with her similarly obsessed friends.

All these people came to the Team Turtle party Friday night before the Lake Shore Marathon. When the Turtle arrived, he leafed through the guest book rapidly, smiling at comments accompanying names, until he realized people who had signed the book were standing nearby with smiles on their faces, waiting to meet him.

The Turtle arrived late and stayed for only a half hour, the time it took him to grasp every hand thrust his way, to give hugs to those he had met at previous Team Turtle parties, to pose for pictures on demand. Eventually, he apologized it was time to go eat. He was meeting Burton Ambrose, the *Running Magazine* editor for dinner. They planned to avoid the various carbo-loading parties and the hotel restaurants, opting for a Greek restaurant guaranteed to have no spaghetti-obsessed runners among its diners.

The Turtle's departure provided the tipping point. People began to leave in twos and threes. One large group had reservations at a restaurant nearby, *Giocci*. By 7:00, the Iroquois was empty except for a few people chatting in a corner, but none had drinks in hand. The bartender began to place on his cart the beer and wine unconsumed. Not a group of drinkers, mused the bartender. His tip jar was light. Wheeling the cart to the kitchen, the bartender knew that he would have better evenings. The hotel would be host to more garrulous and more generous conventioneers after the runners departed on Monday.

13:15:00

A sudden flash of flame. *"Oopa!"* shouted Christine in cadence with Timothy and Carolynne, her dinner companions at the Acropolis Restaurant in Greektown, on the western edge of downtown Lake City. They had shouted in response to the waiter igniting a dish of saganaki just brought to their table. The TV commentators had suggested that they eat Greek rather than Italian as one means of avoiding the long lines at restaurants whose specialty was pasta. "No respectable runner would want to be seen in a Greek restaurant the night before a marathon," opined C.V.

"Are you suggesting, *Cara*, that we are not respectable?" asked Timothy.

"That's a given, my beloved."

Christine could do little more than laugh at the broadcast couple's banter, but the couple proved correct. Timothy, Carolynne and Christine had walked into the Acropolis without a reservation and had been escorted to a table almost immediately. Timothy suggested they first order a bottle of wine. Coming from Stellenbosch (wine country in South Africa), he knew exactly which wine to order: a Boutari Santorini, a dry white. That and the flaming saganaki. "For show," admitted Timothy, smiling coyly. It was now fifteen minutes before seven o'clock, an hour since leaving the production meeting. The trio had filled their time together discussing the race and telecast. "Tax purposes," admitted C.V. The trio still had not ordered their main course.

13:15:00. 13:14:59. 13:14:58.

Christine, dateless on a Saturday evening, was happy to have accepted an invitation to eat Greek. Timothy and Carolynne were so very knowledgeable about their profession, her profession; she was learning a lot that she could put to use during tomorrow's telecast. Christine had phoned Yolanda to announce her plans, but got only her roommate's answering machine. Christine suspected Yolanda had a date with one or more of her boyfriends, but was not sure. Of the two females, Yolanda seemed more attuned to Christine's current romance than any of her own. That was okay. Christine's head was spinning after arriving in town only a couple of weeks before. New job. New boyfriend (she hoped). Maybe after a few weeks in town, her life would settle into a steady pattern. Or would it? Chaos was not necessarily bad.

The waiter appeared again, ready to accept their orders. Christine had barely glanced at the menu, but Timothy seemed willing to offer guidance. He chose an egg-lemon soup. Christine did the same. C.V., as though to exercise her independence, decided on lentil. A side order of kotopitakia, which the menu identified as boneless chicken and vegetables wrapped in phyllo. What *on earth is phyllo*, wondered Christine. She better not ask. A second order of braised octopus, cooked with tomatoes, herbs and wine. *Ooooo. They do not serve that in Peoria, but I don't want to act like a small-town girl and pass.* The main meal was easier. You can't go wrong with lamb. To be somewhat different, Christine chose roast loin of lamb, which came with rice pilaf, after Timothy had selected lamb with artichokes. C.V., claiming that she was on a diet, asked for dolmades: vine leaves stuffed with rice, meats and herbs, flavored by an egg-lemon sauce. *Diet? I better start one after tonight.* Timothy said that they would reserve judgment on dessert, but certainly would want to finish with coffee. *Dessert. I can't imagine dessert after all that food.*

MARATHON

Reaching into the ice bucket beside their table, the waiter topped off their glasses, emptying the bottle, turning it upside down in the bucket. Timothy reacted by suggesting he bring another bottle. Christine decided that she was glad the couple would be taking a taxicab back to their hotel, although she might want to stop by the TV3 trailer to retrieve and review her notes, which she somehow had forgotten. *Am I an airhead? Only on special occasions. I better not tell Peter* A cell phone call to Tom Schorr in the cab coming over determined that he had the notes in hand. He would be in the trailer all night, and give him a nudge if he was asleep on the floor.

After they finished ordering, the conversation switched subtly from TV and the marathon to a subject not entirely to Christine's pleasing: *Herself.* Not only that: *Herself and Peter!*

Timothy and C.V. obviously had known Peter McDonald for some time. She gathered they were close friends. After Timothy returned the menus to the waiter, offering a toast to a successful telecast, Carolynne set down her wine glass and initiated a conversation by directing her eyes at Christine and asking: "Tell us about Peter."

Oops!

Christine stumblingly protested that she only had met Peter two days earlier, *blah, blah, blah*, so being single she certainly was attracted to him—his good looks, his personality, his manners—nothing much had transpired between them, not even a First Date.

"Uh huh," said C.V., immediately admonished by her telecast partner.

"Carolynne, we've only met this nice young lady and you have no right to inquire into her...." He paused politely. "Can I say 'love life?'"

"Hush Timothy. I am not inquiring into her love life, I am inquiring into the love life of a man we admire. Christine, am I being obnoxious?"

"Carolynne has been known to...."

Christine was not sure she liked the direction the conversation was going, except this couple—were they married or divorced or does it matter?—seemed so charming and interested in her career and also so much fun to be with. She did like C.V., and Timothy reminded her of someone she had seen on *Masterpiece Theatre.* One of Jane Austen's kinder characters, certainly. Besides, now into her second glass of wine and without much in her stomach except the saganaki and after an inadequate lunch, and being normally a nondrinker, Christine already had begun to feel a bit woozy. *I had better be careful. I do not want to wake up tomorrow with a hangover, not with an early-morning telecast to do.*

"Well, I do like Peter," confessed Christine, "but we only met each other two days ago."

"Christine, you are so lovable, I want to hug you myself," countered C.V. "And Peter is like a favorite uncle, I love him so much. But the two of you: *tsk! tsk! tsk!* Kissing in the studio during the morning news."

"Carolynne," protested Timothy, but C.V. ignored him. She could see that her comment had caused Christine to blush, but their dining companion did not seem particularly offended.

"We..." said Christine, but could not think of words to describe her emotions that ratcheted rapidly between stunned, worried, mortified and, yes, pleased. She had a very pleasant memory of that moment in the studio. *Why deny it?* Arms crossed as though for protection, shoulders hunched, leaning forward, breasts pushing against the table, Christine looked upwards over her eyebrows at her accusers, allowing a smile to creep across her face Her brown eyes twinkled. No, she did not look mad at being caught *flagrante delicto*.

"It was only an air kiss," Christine offered as her alibi, a quick giggle revealing that it was a memorable air kiss.

This encouraged Timothy. His smile might best be described as wicked: "I am embarrassed to reveal that some snoop spotted you two."

"The gossip mill at the studio is all over the story," said Carolynne.

"Crime. Politics. The economy. World affairs. Paris Hilton." Timothy shrugged. "How could ordinary news compete with juicy office gossip."

"Out of control."

"Like a wildfire in the California hills."

"I'm so embarrassed," said Christine, her voice barely a whisper. Though secretly, she remained delighted.

"Do not be," said Carolynne. "Christine, you cannot even *begin* to imagine how many people are cheering in your corner."

Christine sighed. "I think I know why."

The pair spoke almost in unison: "We weren't sure you knew, but...."

"His late wife. Carol."

"Everybody loved her..."

"...and understood what she meant to Peter."

"I only found out about Carol today," admitted Christine. Almost without realizing what she was doing—and why—she reached for the now refilled wine glass, but paused before taking another sip.

At a table on the other side of the restaurant, a waiter ignited a plate of saganaki. *"Oopa!"* cried Timothy, lifting his wine glass high. *"Oopa!"* C.V. and Christine echoed his toast.

"I thought you promised we would encounter no runners in a Greek restaurant. Look who's sitting over there: The Turtle and Burton Ambrose!"

`"We will ignore them and hope that they do the same for us."

The toast broke the spell. Turning back from the flames, the three stared at each other, not sure whether or not to allow the conversation to continue in the direction it had been heading.

As she often did, Carolynne took the lead: "Did you see that woman at the table with the saganaki? How can anyone fit into a dress that small?"

13:00:00

Meghan Allison's older brother, Aaron Kennedy, had flown in from Boca Raton earlier in the day, along with his fiancé Moira. The couple joined Meg and Matt for a 7:00 dinner, her final carbo-load, a spaghetti feast, the third of three meals on three consecutive days designed to stuff her muscles with enough glycogen to carry her through the 26 miles and 385 yards of the marathon, its start only thirteen hours away.

13:00:00. 12:59:59. 12:59:58.

Aaron, an editorial cartoonist with the *South Florida Sun-Sentinel*, had come to Lake City not merely to bear witness to his sister's pre-race feast; he planned to run the race, at least part of it. Aaron hoped to stay with Meghan for the first half dozen miles, then drop out.

A soccer player in high school, Aaron figured six miles was probably just about as far as he could stay with his faster sister. Meg wanted to run 6:00 per mile, which would bring her through 10-K in about 37:00. Aaron's PR for that distance was only a few seconds faster, which meant he needed to be as well prepared as she.

In the months before the marathon, Meg and Aaron frequently text-messaged each other with reports of their training. Matt joked that Aaron served as her pseudo-coach. Aaron was hardly that, but he knew she reported her workouts to him to motivate herself, to know that someone other than Matt and her computer training log was paying attention. Aaron was astounded by the reports of her training, much tougher than anything he could ever do, but Little Sis (as he often called Meg) was a natural talent. And she *did* need his help, or so he convinced himself. That was why he was in town. Earlier in the summer, Meg had defined Aaron's role in a text-message: "Your mission, should you decide to accept it, Mr. Kennedy, is not to help me run *fast*, but to run *slow!*" Inexperienced at road racing, Meg feared going out too fast and dying. "If you catch me running faster than 6:00 pace, grab the back of my shorts and slow me down."

281

SATURDAY

Meg had ended that text-message: "Your digital phone will self-destruct within five seconds."

Meghan Allison felt she could comfortably run the first six miles at 6:00 pace, then determine whether to speed up or slow down. Unfortunately, the predicted warm weather offered an added variable confounding her pacing plans. Also unfortunately, Aaron had not run as fast in the past year as his sister, fast times determining positions on the starting grid. Using a half marathon time run in Orlando, Aaron had qualified for Start Corral B; Meg would start ahead in Corral A. Meg probably could have gotten Aaron bumped up a group had she chosen to contact race director Peter McDonald. Earlier in the spring, McDonald had offered to seed her into the elite athlete's corral. But Meg did not want to call attention to herself. She had a fear of failing based on her lackluster college career.

Nevertheless, with only 1,500 in Corral A, the brother and sister team hoped he could quickly bridge the gap between B and A. Once joined, the plan was for Aaron to run beside Meghan and, using his GPS watch, remind her to keep it in cruise control. Once he dropped out, she was on her own. By then, Meg expected to have established a rhythm, a comfortable pace, which she could maintain to the end. That is, if any pace in a marathon could be comfortable. She did not know, not having run that far before, not even in practice. But she had done the math: A 6:00 pace carried to the end would get her a time in the high 2:30s. A more realistic goal, assuming some fade toward the end, was to break 2:40, not fast enough for prize money, but finances did not figure in her reasons for running the Lake City Marathon.

Strategy dominated the discussion as the two couples sat in the living room of Meg and Matt's apartment before dinner, three of them sharing a bottle of Cabernet Sauvignon by Estancia that Meg had purchased at Metro Fresh on Thursday. Meg stuck with ice water, breaking from the group finally to say, "If we don't stop talking, I'll never finish dinner."

Aaron followed her into the kitchen. "Can I help?"

"Get out of my kitchen, Aaron," she said, giving her brother a friendly push toward the door. "You're our guest, not the cook."

He turned to leave, then stopped in the doorway. "I'm so proud of you, Little Sis."

"Out! Out! Out! You won't be proud of me when I'm throwing up on your shoes after finishing."

Aaron laughed and returned to the living room. Meg turned to her final preparations. She had been puttering in the kitchen most of the last few hours. Cooking relaxed her, allowing Meg to push the marathon from her mind. Sauce for spaghetti was simmering on the stove.

MARATHON

Eventually judging the sauce ready, Meg turned off the flame and allowed the sauce to cool slightly. She planned to cook a pound of spaghetti. She broke the thin spaghetti shards in half, throwing them into a pot. Eight minutes and the spaghetti would emerge properly *al dente*, "to the tooth."

Matt had wandered into the kitchen to prepare the salad, so she removed a string of spaghetti and commanded him to taste it. "Perfect," he said. Knowing he would say "perfect" no matter how chewy the piece, she tasted it herself. He was right.

Aaron and Moira followed Matt to the kitchen, standing around, continuing their conversation. She used them to test the sauce. It too was perfect. Matt's salad featured lettuce, celery, green onions, tomatoes, olives with an oil and vinegar dressing, sprinkled with seasoned salt. "Don't use too much olive oil," she warned him.

"Meg always says that," Matt commented. "I'm going to buy her a talking bass with that message to hang on the wall."

Meg drained the spaghetti in a colander, transferred it to a bowl, covered it with the sauce just prepared, placed more sauce in a dish in case her guests wanted more. Another dish contained Romano cheese, which she preferred to parmigiano, because it was stronger. And so her dinner was done. Later, they would have sherbet with chocolate sauce.

The four positioned themselves around the table: Meg and Matt at the ends, Aaron and Moira on the sides. "Can I tempt you with a glass of wine, honey?" Matt asked.

His wife held up two fingers. "No more."

After the wine had been poured, Matt led the group raising their glasses. *"Carpe viam!"* he said.

"Carpe viam!" the three responded.

They drank. Putting down her glass, Moira looked puzzled. "What does that mean?"

"Sieze the road," said Matt, looking proudly at his marathoner wife.

Meghan Allisson looked lovingly back at her husband, Matt. *I will*, she told herself. *I will*.

12:45:00

While many of the runners staying at the Hilliard attended one of several pasta parties for their final carbo-load, or went out to eat at one of the many Italian restaurants in and around downtown, the

SATURDAY

Kenyan runners, male and female, gathered for their meal at the elite athlete's hospitality suite. They could have used the meal coupons provided by Peter McDonald to eat in the downstairs restaurant, but Joseph Nduku, the defending champion and leader of the Kenyan delegation, had decreed otherwise.

"At best downstairs, we'll get the same spaghetti that everyone else staying here in the hotel can get by ordering off the menu," explained Joseph. "But we are special. We are a team, not a group of individuals. We are here representing Kenya, and we should eat a Kenyan meal."

The Kenyan delegation gathered at 7:00 and took their places around a dining table in the elite athlete suite. There remained now less than thirteen hours before the start of the Lake City Marathon.

12:45:00. 12:44:59. 12:44:58.

Joseph Nduku also took it upon himself to supervise the preparation of the meal, which centered on *ugali*, a traditional food, also called *ngima* by members of the Kikuyu tribe in Kenya. Italians knew the same basic food staple as *polenta*, similarly made from corn or maize. Maize was an easy crop to cultivate in even the driest sections of Africa. Without ugali, many could not survive. Rolled into a ball and placed in the center of the table so all gathered around could access the food, ugali could be wrapped around chicken or various vegetables or dipped into a stew. Whether you ate it with your hands or with spoon, knife or fork depended upon the traditions of your tribe. Joseph Nduku enjoyed this meal the most while also sipping *chai*, a habit his family had acquired from the British who once ruled Kenya. Although many in Africa resented their departed colonial masters, Joseph tried to remember the Brits for the positive benefits they had left, particularly the rule of law that allowed Kenya to become the most successful and peaceful of all the African countries south of the Sahara. Unfortunately, that rule of law had been tested and found wanting after recent presidential elections resulted in a rift between various tribal groups, Kikuyu vs. Kalenjin. Kenya's best runners were Nandi, a branch of the Kalenjin people. People from both tribes had died during the turmoil, several of Joseph's friends, including one Olympian, having been murdered by mobs of angry people. *Nothing is perfect in this troubled world*, thought Joseph Nduku. Many of the Kenyan runners needed to leave the country to continue their training. It had bothered Joseph to do so, since it had left his family vulnerable at home. Fortunately, all had avoided trouble.

But while to the world Kenyan distance runners presented a monolithic front, there remained rifts even among them, small slights that had been magnified by the violence that had engulfed this once peaceful country. Thus, not all members of the Kenyan delegation approved of Joseph's leadership. This included two runners who with several others in Lake City formed a separate clique. The two were Kenyatta Kemai and Moses Abraham. Ironically, though cousins, one was Muslim, the other Christian, as suggested by his Biblical name. Their family and tribal connections overruled any religious differences that might have separated the two. Those handicapping the race figured that among the Africans present, Kemai had the greatest chance to upset Joseph and win the first-place prize of $100,000. Abraham was one of the rabbits, not expected to battle for first place or even start, since he had been relieved of that obligation by Peter McDonald.

Neither runner wanted to challenge Joseph, but they continued to resent his assuming the mantle of team leader. Apart from the fact that he had run the fastest times and won the most prestigious races (Boston, Lake City and one world title), who appointed him, who chose him? Yet neither cousin could deny how the younger Kenyans looked up to Joseph, so they could hardly defy his authority. Still, he could be beat—they hoped.

Part of the conflict between the pair and Joseph was the fact that he was proudly nationalistic, a leader in the training camps that prepared emerging runners for their annual and usually successful assault on the World Cross-Country Championships. While athletes and fans in other countries might give more attention to the Olympic Games, or the World Track & Field Championships, or Grand Prix races in Oslo and Berlin and Zurich, or marathons from London to New York to Chicago, cross-country titles offered the most appeal to the nationalistic Kenyan distance runners and their supporters. And the Kenyan runners rarely disappointed their followers, their only serious challengers being the Ethiopians.

It was Joseph Nduku who dictated the pace of most of the punishing workouts on the roads around the village of Eldoret in the Rift Valley. Joseph did not necessarily *lead* each workout, or attempt to *win* each workout; it was more that he *controlled* each workout by his presence. As they ran along the dirt roads and paths around Eldoret, most of the runners looked nervously over their shoulders at Joseph before attempting to push the pace or break loose, as though it was only by his permission that they were able to seek success. Even when Joseph shifted his racing away from the world cross-country trails or the European tracks to the more lucrative world of road racing, a visit by him to the training camp caused everyone to stand aside and pay him homage, as though he blessed them by his presence. Joseph Nduku definitely was the Alpha male of the Kenyan distance runners.

Kemai and Abraham still seethed over an incident in the 10,000 meters run one year at the World Track & Field Championships. The pair had come to the biennial meet not representing Kenya, but Qatar. It was a matter of money that caused them to shift countries. They got paid to represent the Arab country in important international meets. They did not move to Qatar, but accepted passports and ran wearing the maroon singlets of Qatar instead of the red, black, green and white singlets of Kenya. With five laps to go in the 10,000, Kemai moved into the second lane to pass Joseph and another Kenyan running second and third behind the Ethiopian, Kenenisa Bekele. And in that instant Joseph held out a single finger to warn Kemai not to pass, to get back in his place, to not interfere with his countrymen. Joseph had not blocked Kenyatta Kemai. He had not pushed him. He had not elbowed him. But that finger moved into Kemai's lane was like a wall that the runner representing Qatar could not hurdle. Intimidated, Kemai fell back, eventually finishing sixth and out of the medals. Joseph captured the silver, Bekele securing the gold for Ethiopia. *I could have beaten Bekele*, Kemai raged after the incident. *I could have won the gold. Even though for Qatar, it still would be a Kenyan victory.* Or so Kemai thought. Joseph would have disagreed.

That incident had occurred nearly a half dozen years before, but Kemai refused to forget—or forgive! And so as the Kenyan runners entered in the Lake City Marathon finished their meal of ugali, he thought of how he might seek revenge. He could achieve revenge by winning the race. He felt that. He knew that. And his cousin Moses would help him.

12:30:00

After the pasta party speech by Aba Andersson, Peter McDonald rose from his seat at the front table, intending to skip the raffle that would award a trip for two to the Honolulu Marathon. Standing beside a circular drum that had just been rotated by an intern, Aba waited to be handed a number to determine the winner of one of the preliminary prizes, a race jacket. Peter waved at the world record holder to signal his departure.

Aba glanced at him and smiled, simultaneously announcing, "For a race jacket, number six-oh-one."

Toward the back of the room, a woman rose from her seat and held a ticket overhead, one that matched the winning number.

"We have our first winner," said Aba.

As the woman came forward to claim her prize, Peter said to Paddy Savitch, seated next to him. "Have a great race tomorrow, Paddy."

"And the same to you, Peter," responded the Shelaghi executive.

"If you or Dennis need anything, you know how to reach me."

"We know you're busy this weekend. Dennis was *truly* sorry he could not attend this dinner." The word "truly" rolled across Paddy's tongue like rain caressing a peat bog.

Peter hoped Dennis Lahey's sorrow was sincere. It still worried him that the Shelaghi executive manager had chosen to skip the pasta party. Was that a hint of bad news to come? Too much was scheduled Sunday for him to worry about what might or might not happen Monday and beyond.

"Number four-seven three," Aba announced a second winner.

The second winner, a man seated near the center of the room, stood and said plaintively, "Damn!" Friends at his table laughed. The man had won a jacket, but if he wanted to run Honolulu, he would need to pay his own way.

Trying not to draw too much attention to himself, Peter moved from one sponsor table to the next. shaking hands, apologizing for being forced to leave early, explaining that he had two other dinners to attend. He had a good alibi, but it still embarrassed him not being able to be three places at the same time. Maybe he could be cloned in time for next year's marathon—if there was a next-year's marathon.

"Number eleven-thirty-three," announced Aba as Peter exited the ballroom. It took him only a few minutes to reach the dinner sponsored by the American Cancer Society in another room of the hotel. He stayed long enough to talk briefly to that charity's organizers and offer words of encouragement for those running the marathon. Then on to still another dining room and the AIDS Africa party, hosted by Naní. It was nearly 7:30 when he entered the room. A quick hug for her, a handshake for Ricco, more encouraging words for the charity-raising group, another apology that he needed to return to the park to check on preparations. He had no doubt that Noel Michaels was lock-step with the spreadsheet on her clipboard, but he was too hands-on to relax and let plans proceed without him.

Before leaving, Peter wished Naní well in the marathon, figuring he might not see her before the start. "What's your goal?" he asked, more for conversation than from any need to know.

"I'm joining the four-hour pacing team," she told him.

"That's going to be a very popular team," stated Peter, thinking not only of her, but also of the other individual who also planned to run with the four-hour runners: Celebrity X, his boyhood friend, Pope Tony. Peter had not talked to Tony since yesterday, but the pope was a big boy and could take care of himself. Celebrity X would be brought to the starting line minutes before the horn sent nearly 50,000 runners on their way. After that, nobody could predict what might happen. At least thus far, there had been no leaks. Could he keep the lid on for a dozen more hours?

SATURDAY

Peter departed the party and took a side stairway down to the lobby rather than wait for an elevator. Full of nervous energy, he decided to walk to the marathon's operations trailer rather than have a golf cart meet him at the park entrance. He needed the walk to both stretch his legs and clear his mind. *What have I forgotten? Nothing, and even if I have, Noel has my back. Thank God for her spreadsheet.*

Exiting the hotel, Peter passed the clock in the lobby, still counting down the time remaining until the start of the marathon tomorrow morning.

12:30:00. 12:29:59. 12:29:58.

Peter did not give the clock a glance, being busy scrolling through the messages left on his digital phone. Most he could either ignore or return after he got to the operations trailer. One he could not. It was a text-message from Nelson Ogilvie, his media director. Peter paused under the canopy in front of the hotel near the taxi queue to read the message.

"Taxi, sir?" asked the doorman.

Peter shook his head. The message read: *Call Dennis Lahey in his room ASAP. Room 2210.*

Peter wondered: *What could that be about?* Rather than call from his digital phone, Peter decided to double back into the hotel to use one of the house phones in the lobby. It would allow him a few minutes to think, but Peter still had no idea what to expect as he used the lobby phone to dial 2-2-1-0. The Shelaghi executive manager answered after the second ring.

Lahey did not waste time explaining the purpose for his call. "Peter, in talking with Nelson, I have become convinced that the best platform from which to view the marathon is the press truck in front of the lead runners."

"Best place and worst place," explained Peter. "You'll see the lead male runners, but not much more. Certainly not the lead woman, and I understand your interest in Fiona Flynn. Most of the so-called 'press' now watch on TV in the media center."

"Nelson explained that, but I'm as interested in everything that goes on around the race, the spectators."

"Your customers."

"Absolutely!"

"Then let me issue an invitation to ride the press truck. Can I help with credentials?"

"Nelson took care of me."

"Then I'll see you tomorrow morning on the back of the truck."

"I'll be there," said Laehy and hung up the phone.

Peter replaced the hotel phone in its cradle, but made no effort yet to move. *Is this a sign that Shelaghi actually might continue its contract?*

Leaving the hotel, Peter McDonald allowed any worries related to sponsorship to slip from his mind. It was a beautiful evening, the moon near full in a clear sky. Warm. Delightfully warm. Too warm. Even though the sun had set, the heat of the day continued to radiate from the buildings bordering the park. It would have been a beautiful evening to stroll through the park with someone on his arm, someone he loved. It used to be Carol. They delighted their walks in the city at all hours and in all sorts of weather conditions, even wind and snow in the middle of winter. Still clinging to the past, he imagined Carol on his arm as he continued toward the operations trailer, greeting briefly a security guard that stood near the barricades preventing automotive traffic from entering the park.

"Beautiful evening," said the guard.

"Yes, it is," Peter McDonald agreed.

His digital phone indicated another incoming call, actually a text message. Peter glanced at the display on the phone.

"Shit!" he said. Only rarely did Petr McDonald use swear words, but the brief message on his phone was very disturbing.

The message was from Jonathan Von Runyon: "It's the pope."

11:30:00

At the same time the approximately **50,000 runners entered in** the Lake City Marathon were finishing their final carbo-loads and heading back to hotel rooms or homes within town, Tom Schorr dropped a just-delivered copy of Sunday's *Lake City Ledger* on the desk in the operations trailer where Christine sat before a computer monitor reviewing past marathon programs.

"Your boyfriend is not going to like this," said Schorr.

"Ex-*cuse* me, Tom," Christine responded, irritated by the TV director's assertion. Obviously her pending romance was news on the street even before it was news. "Peter is not yet my boyfriend."

"Sorry," Schorr responded. "Our common friend and admirer—at least admirer of one of us—is not going to like this."

Christine sighed: "What is our common friend and admirer not going to like, Tom?"

He pointed at the headline: "LAST LAKE CITY MARATHON?"

SATURDAY

"That news is so—yesterday. Peter ducked my question about the possible loss of bank sponsorship when I asked it Thursday. Whether bogus or not, I felt it got in the way of what was happening this weekend."

"I agree," said Schorr. "The bank sponsorship may or may not come up during the telecast. Since you'll be out on the course, you probably won't need to address the issue. I just wanted you to be aware of it."

"Thank you, Tom," said Christine, as the TV director returned to his work. She only had come to the operations trailer because of having forgotten her notes after the production meeting earlier in the evening. She could have headed back to her apartment immediately after reclaiming them, but decided to use a computer in the trailer to look at past marathon news reports, more to get her in the mood for tomorrow's telecast than from the need to know anything. But it was late, she was tired, and just maybe she had one glass of wine too many at dinner. Christine looked at her watch: 8:30.

11:30:00. 11:29:59. 11:29:58.

Time to head home. Early to bed for this boring reporter. Prospective boyfriend, but no date for Saturday night.

Preparing to leave, Christine slipped the notes from the production meeting into her purse. She did not want to forget them again. Standing, she started to sign off, when a link caught her eye. It was under a series of video-links labeled "Related." One of the links had an identifying headline that seemed puzzling: "CM Traffic Camera." *CM? Chicago Marathon? No, hardly that. Couldn't be. And what was the meaning of "Traffic Camera?"* Almost without willing it, Christine pointed her mouse on the link and double-clicked.

What she saw would sicken and horrify her.

It was a common scene: a city street. Parked cars. Relatively little traffic. Black and white, rather than color. A nighttime scene lit only by streetlights. Early in the morning, since there seemed to be little traffic. A few cars passing from either direction. Hardly the precise focus you would expect from a TV camera. Then she got it: Traffic Camera, one of so many cameras that provided surveillance of streets in Lake City. Almost an invasion of privacy when you think of it, city government spying on its citizens, but the promoters of surveillance cameras claimed they prevented crime, or at least recorded crime, supposedly making identification and capture of criminals more likely.

There was a pick-up truck parked near the intersection. Its door opened. A leg appeared, the driver about to get out. Then suddenly onto the screen flashed a fast-moving cyclist, traveling in a lane reserved for bicycles. The cyclist hit the open door. The bicycle flipped, rear wheel rising over front wheel, the cyclist thrown from the bicycle as though propelled from a trampoline. And in a moment that passed so swiftly it seemed almost impossible to

290

measure, the cyclist—she seemed to be a woman—flew over the pick-up's open door, feet now high over her helmeted head, twisting, descending, landing on her head. There was no sound on the video, but Christine could almost hear the blow delivered to the exposed neck.

"Oh my god," she said in horrified realization what "CM" meant: Carol McDonald. She was watching the death of Peter's wife, captured somehow on this video, preserved for who knew what reason.

Then it got worse.

After the woman's head hit the ground, the body above crumpled, still descending, sliding sideways, bouncing once, twice, into the lane of oncoming traffic. Then suddenly a car appeared in that lane and—Christine could not believe what she was seeing—struck the now prone body, crushing the body, Carol, beneath its wheels.

Christine screamed!

Wishing to stop the horrible video, fumbling for the mouse, unable to find it and also unable to move her eyes from the screen, Christine saw the car skid, too late, its brake lights finally flashing, too late, coming to a halt, too late, door opening, a woman climbing out of the car now. The man from the pick-up also now stood in the street, not moving, the body in the street not moving, the woman from the car that had run over Carol's body approaching slowly, apparently now only realizing the enormity of what she had done. The woman had one hand covering her mouth, as though she might vomit any minute. In the other hand, she held a cell phone. She began punching it with one finger, apparently dialing 9/1-1. The video suddenly stopped, going to freeze frame.

Thank God, thought Carol, still staring at the screen, still fumbling for the mouse to erase from her sight the frozen screen. But before she could do so, what she had witnessed began to repeat itself—this time in slow motion.

"Oh, no!"

At that moment she felt a hand placed reassuringly on one shoulder. It startled her, but it allowed her to remove her eyes from the screen, where she saw Tom Schorr.

"I'm sorry you saw that," said Schorr.

"I didn't...."

"I know you didn't." Schorr kneeled beside her. With his one hand he reached for the mouse that had eluded her touch. He maneuvered the mouse's pointer onto an X in the screen's upper right corner. *Click!* The video image disappeared. "We should have deleted these images long ago." Removing his other hand from Christine's shoulder, he began typing rapidly on the keyboard. *Click!* Christine was barely aware that the link disappeared. Schorr continued typing, accessing a file that had moved to a recycle bin. *Click!* The file disappeared, presumably still stored in the main computer back at the TV3 studios, but now it would take someone versed in the mysteries of computers to retrieve it.

Christine turned to look at the TV director. He had tears in his eyes, as she did in hers. "Evidence," he said.

"Evidence?" she wondered.

"Pre-trial evidence."

"There was a trial?"

"No, just a hearing."

Schorr rose from his position kneeling on the floor. He spotted a box of tissues on a nearby table, offered it to Christine and, after she took several tissues, he took several himself. And while doing so, he explained the existence of what was, yes, a surveillance camera capturing the death of Peter McDonald's wife and why the video images remained in the TV3 archives, accessed accidentally by Christine Ferrara.

There had not been a trial, just a hearing to determine whether there should be a trial, either of the man who opened the pick-up truck door that Carol had struck or the woman who had run over her body. The pick-up driver had not been alert, should have looked back before opening it. But it was in the dark before dawn, late autumn, a month after last year's marathon. Carol commuting to work on her bicycle. Maybe Carol should have been more alert herself, although you hate to blame the victim.

The woman seemed most guilty. She had been talking to a friend on her cell phone almost for thirteen minutes, filling an otherwise boring commute to work with conversation. The phone records proved that. She needed to end her conversation to dial 9-1-1.

"The woman was never charged?" asked Christine.

"Analysis of the video suggested that Carol broke her neck the moment her head hit the pavement, before the woman hit her. Maybe she did; maybe she didn't. The prosecutor's office reviewed the video. We manipulated the images close-up and in slow motion. That's why we had a copy. It was at Peter's request, although he declined to view the video."

"I can understand why."

"The prosecutor's office said it would be near impossible to get a conviction—even if the woman were guilty. Peter did not want to pursue her, feeling the woman would need to live with what happened the rest of her life."

"I almost feel sorry for her."

"So we all moved on, but a lot of us who knew Carol closely continue to retain warm memories of her. Supposedly, Carol's death was quick and painless, but is any death quick and painless to the person who dies? We never know, do we?"

"No, we don't."

"The video never aired, Christine. Those of us who labor in the media sometimes are accused of sensationalizing even the most personal of events. Sometimes we are guilty, and sometimes we are not."

"Thank you, Tom."

Christine picked her purse off her desk. Touching Schorr under his chin, she kissed him lightly on the cheek. It was a kiss without passion, a thank you kiss for his having heard her scream and come to her rescue. The image was gone from the computer, but could she erase it from her memory?

"Can I call you a taxi, Christine?"

"No, you go back to work. I need some fresh air. I need to walk. I'll walk over to near the Hilliard and catch a taxicab there."

"See you in the morning."

"See you in the morning."

She paused: "Please don't tell Peter I saw this."

"I won't." promised the TV director.

Christine exited the trailer, head still spinning, stomach churning. Descending three steps to the ground, she halted. She did not feel well. What she had seen sickened her. She could not erase from her mind what she had viewed. The death of a woman! The death of a woman loved by the man she now loved! Would she be able to replace her in his mind? Did she want to?

Beside the trailer stood a grove of trees, a dark area. Christine walked, almost staggered over to the grove. She placed one hand on the first tree to steady herself. And the instant her hand touched the tree, everything she had eaten in what had been such a pleasant evening erupted from her mouth and onto the grass. And erupted again. And erupted again.

Inside the trailer, Tom Schorr could hear Christine vomiting. And knew why she was vomiting, and it almost tempted him to do the same. He debated whether to go outside and offer consoling words, but decided, no. She would not want anyone to see, to hear, to know. The vomiting continued. And after a while, it stopped. Then there was silence, so Schorr suspected she had started home. He would see Christine tomorrow morning, and neither would mention what had occurred.

It was warm outside. Looking past Burnham Fountain toward the lake, Christine could see the moon, nearly full, rising from the blackness of the lake into the blueness of the evening sky. The gold of the moon reflected on the wine dark surface of the lake. Such a beautiful sight. Christine stood for a moment trying to absorb the moon's energy. It helped a little. Not much.

SATURDAY

Using a tissue to wipe speckles of vomit from her chin, Christine passed a waste container and dropped the tissue in. If she could only wipe the sight from her mind that easily. She turned and began to walk toward Jefferson Avenue, moving through an area that she knew tomorrow morning would be crammed with 50,000 runners. She noticed only a few people, workers responsible for the staging of the marathon. Certainly, others were scattered in tents and in trailers over the nearly mile-long stretch of Columbia Drive that had been closed to accommodate the start and finish lines. Somewhere among them was Peter McDonald. He had work to do, work that would occupy his mind. She had work to do and hoped it would occupy her mind before she saw him next.

Christine felt tears in her eyes, but she would not let them flow. *I'm not going to cry. I'm not going to cry,* she told herself. And the tears did not come. There would be time for crying later, Christine knew. And time for laughter too.

PART 4:

SUNDAY

SUNDAY

MARATHON

08:00:00

Twas the night before the marathon, when all through the house, not a creature was stirring, not even a louse. The singlets were hung on the chair backs with care, in hopes that the weather soon would be fair. The runners were nestled all snug in their beds, while visions of PR's danced in their heads. And Mama in her negligee and Dad in his cap had just settled down for a short evening's nap.

At midnight, as Saturday became Sunday, those sleeping at the Hilliard Towers and elsewhere in and around Lake City had only eight hours to go before the start of the marathon.

08:00:00. 07:59:59 07:59:58.

The lobby of the Hilliard was deathly quiet, almost *unnaturally* quiet, for midnight on a Saturday evening. A security guard strolled past the desk where guests check in, no attendant visible. The bar was open, but with only a single bartender and two clients to serve. The TV set over the bar showed the replay of an auto race that nobody was watching. The restaurant in the lobby was devoid of customers, just having closed. It would open again at 4:00 A.M. to service those runners planning to top their tanks with a final shot of carbohydrate. Don Geoffrey, the Turtle, usually recommended that runners eat a light snack approximately three hours before a marathon. The *Running Magazine* writer, himself asleep in tailored pajamas on an upper floor, generally favored orange juice and/or coffee plus a bagel, or some form of easily digestible carbohydrate. Most members of his Team Turtle and runners who trained using Geoffrey's programs would follow their guru's lead.

Peter McDonald, arriving from the operations trailer near Burnham Fountain, passed through the lobby and under the countdown clock around midnight, and headed straight to the elevator bank, showing his plastic room key with the Lake City Marathon logo on it to a security guard to gain entry.

"Have a good night," said the guard.

"I will," Peter politely responded, although as he stepped into the elevator his mind whirled with thoughts of the day to come. His day would start with a drive of the course. Peter still needed to cope with the threat of warm weather, but there remained little more he could do. Peter's biggest worry was Celebrity X. Peter had not talked to his friend all day. Was Tony crazy to run a marathon? Would people consider the pope's doing so a stunt? Worries about sponsorship, specifically whether Shelaghi would cancel its relationship with the race, were something to address in the weeks and months to come.

There was also the problem posed by Jonathan Von Runyon, who apparently and puzzlingly had figured out the identity of Celebrity X! Peter studiously had avoided responding to the almost snickering text-message from Von Runyon earlier in the evening. Trolling for information, the *Ledger* reporter simultaneously had contacted media director Nelson Ogilvie. When Peter and Nelson talked a few minutes later, they agreed that the best way to handle the situation was with silence, no denials that Von Runyon could manipulate to his own ends. The reporter's message actually seemed more statement than question to which he expected an answer. *Gotcha!* The pair suspected—or hoped—that Von Runyon would not run with a story that was little more than an educated guess. Nobody could have leaked the news, because nobody but Peter knew. His media director remained as shocked as anybody at Von Runyon's revelation: "You're not even going to confirm it with me?"

"Nope," Peter responded. "You need to preserve your deniability."

Ogilvie conceded his point.

And apparently their gamble had succeeded. Nothing related to Celebrity X's true identity yet had surfaced on the Internet. Nothing on the *Ledger's* Web site, or Ogilvie would have contacted Peter. The deadline for getting breaking news into the final editions of Sunday's paper—9:00 according to Ogilvie—had passed. "For something truly newsworthy," the media director explained, "the *Ledger* might extend its deadline, but marathons usually don't qualify for someone shouting, 'Stop the presses!'"

If Von Runyon's scoop was not online yet, it would not be in newspapers delivered to subscribers beginning at 4:00 A.M. But the battle was only half won. Ogilvie promised to keep monitoring the situation. Peter hoped Pope Tony did not need to cancel his plans. Ironically, if he did, that would make moot any scoop Von Runyon thought he had, since Tony would not run. Peter could hardly have told Von Runyon that, since the *Ledger* reporter probably would have considered it a threat, causing more problems.

Arriving at his suite on the 24th floor, Peter Mc Donald stripped to his underwear and collapsed into bed. He would shower and dress after he woke up—in a few hours. Those were almost too few free hours to justify a return to the hotel, except Peter knew that if he failed to get away from where work continued, he would be drawn into that work. Three hours of sound sleep with his alarm set for 3:00. A wake-up call posted for that same time for insurance. Given his obsession for punctuality, Peter probably would need neither.

Rather than occupy his usual spot on the far side of the bed, Peter dove into the middle. Was this a betrayal of his late wife Carol or a belated recognition that it was time to retrieve the social side of his life? Before drifting off,

Peter tried to imagine Christine in bed beside him, but even that pleasant prospect failed to keep him from sleep for more than several seconds. His breathing became measured, heavy. He slept.

Christine Ferrara, demurely wearing spaghetti-strap shirt and PJ pants, had gone to bed several hours before Peter McDonald, but her sleep was more fitful, troubled, colored by the ghastly video she had viewed by accident at the TV3 trailer. *Why did I click on that link?* Christine did not dream of Peter. She did not dream of Carol. The anxiety dream that caused her to toss and turn in the early hours of Sunday morning featured herself!

She was on a bicycle, hurtling down a busy city street in the dark before dawn. Her bike had no lights. No reflectors. It was pouring rain. Thunder sounded in the distance. Lightning flashed. She wore no helmet. Her long, dark hair cascaded behind. She was soaked. The bike was propelling her forward against her will, a reluctant participant in a devilishly-designed video game. Rain clouding her vision, she wove past cars and vans and trucks, moving faster and faster as though on a steep downhill, no control, and suddenly the door of a parked pickup truck opened. She could not avoid it.

SMAAAKKK!!!

The video game was over! She had lost.

Christine jumped like a jack-in-the-box. Straight up in bed. Horrified. More than a simple anxiety dream. More than night terrors. This was real; it had to be real. She covered her face with her hands for protection as, still half dreaming, she tumbled through space, turning, turning, turning, hard pavement below. If she struck the pavement, she would die—just like the woman she had seen in the video.

"Help!"

Christine screamed, then collapsed back in bed, sobbing, unable to stem the flow of tears.

Barely seconds passed, before her roommate, Yolanda Kline, rushed into the room and sat on the edge of the bed, tender arms pressed lightly on Christine's shaking shoulders. "Christine! Christine!" Yolanda had arrived back at the apartment only minutes before after a night out with friends, but had decided to page through a fashion magazine before retiring.

"Roommate," whispered Yolanda. "Sweetheart! What's the matter?"

Christine gasped: "It was horrible."

"It must have been horrible. In four years together, I never heard you scream like that before."

"I saw something."

SUNDAY

Yolanda wondered for a moment if that "something" was connected with Peter, but decided she did not want to go there. "Do we need to talk?"

"I'm okay. It was a bad dream. A *terrible* dream, but it's gone."

"Are you sure?"

"I'm sure. We'll talk tomorrow."

Yolanda continued to hold her college roommate and felt Christine's breathing still, her sobbing stop. As abruptly as Christine had screamed and awakened, she fell back to sleep. Relieved, Yolanda covered Christine with the bedcovers and rose to return to the living room. She picked up the fashion magazine from the floor, where she had thrown it, and started to read again, but the words and pictures made no sense any more. She thrust the magazine into a bag for recycling. She returned to Christine's room, but her roommate seemed to be sleeping, bad dream past. Yolanda went to her own bedroom, undressed and crawled into bed. A half hour later, she remained awake, the echoes of Christine's scream still ringing in her ears.

Throughout Lake City, many of those running the marathon suffered anxiety dreams, a common theme being difficulty finding the starting line. Bob Veldman, the air traffic controller, was among them. Veldman hoped to crack 2:30—or at least that had been his goal before he heard the weather reports. In his dream, Veldman found the starting line—then got lost running the race. After visiting a portable toilet, Veldman exited to find himself alone on the course. The air traffic controller dreamed he was running through a canyon of skyscrapers, not a person on the streets. No runners; no spectators. A single policeman, who pointed ahead as if to say, "They went thatta way!"

Veldman came to an aid station that stretched two city blocks. An indescribably long table with what seemed like 50,000 cups on it, but no one to drink from those cups. He grabbed a cup, and it was empty. He grabbed a second cup: empty too. Angered, he struck the cups with one hand, and all the cups on the table tumbled like dominos.

Another policeman appeared before him. "You have to leave the course," instructed the policeman.

"What did I do wrong?" pleaded Volkman.

The policeman ignored the question: "You have to seek shelter."

"Is the race over?" worried Volkman. "Is it the weather?"

Then the skyscrapers vanished, and Veldman was running on a flat plateau, no variation in elevation, not a millimeter's worth of climb or descent on a 360-degree horizon, the flattest of flat courses, and the air traffic controller realized that he was on a runway at Lake City International Airport with airplanes landing on all sides, their landing patterns dangerously intersecting, as though all the controllers were taking a coffee break and had left the pilots to fend for themselves.

Veldman, still dreaming, looked to one side and found himself no longer running alone. Matching stride with him was a slender black man, his sweat-soaked skin so ebony dark, it shined. Veldman recognized the black man as a Kenyan. The man spoke in a tightly-clipped British accent. "Are we going the right way, Bob?" asked Joseph Nduku. Veldman could not find words to answer, but looked over his shoulder and saw 50,000 runners behind mouthing the same words:

"Are we going the right way, Bob?"

Airplanes circled, landed, took off, still with no apparent guidance, and as the air traffic controller desperately searched for a way to lead 50,000 runners and Joseph Nduku off the runway, a corporate jet slid past overhead, wheels narrowly missing his head, and screeched to a stop. It was a G-5. White. No identifying markings. Veldman stopped. Joseph Nduku stopped. All 50,000 runners stopped, mesmerized by the scene before them. Climbing from the G-5 were three men, each dressed in black, carrying identical briefcases, looking like they might be part of some secret organization. Veldman thought he recognized the first of the black clad men. His face looked familiar. He could not attach a name to that face.

On the East Side, a man who, were dreams real, might have been that black-clad man, slept peacefully, dreamlessly. Celebrity X (a.k.a. Pope Tony) knew he had trained hard, so why worry? Sleeping in a room near him were his two bodyguards and training partners, Mario and Angelo, wearing shorts and T-shirts, the shirts bearing the logos of their favorite soccer teams, their sleeping outfits sufficiently modest so they could jump from bed and into defensive postures without embarrassing anybody. The pair might have had difficulty sleeping given the measure of their responsibility, except Redbird (Cardinal Joseph Connolly, the cardinal camerlengo) had insisted during his visit Saturday afternoon on supplying additional bodyguards, at least overnight and at the start when the pope was most vulnerable. Pope Tony had agreed, partly because he knew it would allow Mario and Angelo to sleep more soundly. Two new bodyguards assigned by Redbird sat inside the house looking out. On the street outside, two additional bodyguards sat in a blandly anonymous rental car looking in. Herb had told the bodyguards that if they wanted coffee, he would leave a pot brewing. At two-hour intervals, the bodyguards switched positions with each other and with two additional sleeping bodyguards to allay the boredom that came with their job.

Redbird wanted to provide more security during the marathon, but Pope Tony insisted it was overkill. "There will be 800 policemen on the course, my dear Redbird," said the pope, adding: "Peter tells me they have security cameras at every intersection. The marathon's security net will cover me every step of the way. They even have a helicopter to cover gaps." Despite being perturbed at not being trusted with information surrounding Celebrity X's plans, Redbird conceded that total secrecy had worked smoothly—so far.

Jonathan Von Runyon slept on a sofa in his living room. The *Ledger* reporter had no intention of spending the night before the marathon on the sofa, but he had fallen asleep watching the telecast of a TiVoed women's golf tournament from Maui. The TV set shined ghostly grey, but he slept on.

It irritated Von Runyon that neither Peter McDonald nor Nelson Ogilvie had responded to his text-message earlier that evening trying to coax from them a confirmation that Pope Tony was Peter's secret celebrity. Von Runyon suspected that fact to be true, but had no way to confirm it. He might have constructed a story out of their silence, but Von Runyon did not want to play that game. He liked news, not rumors of news. So he had allowed the 9:00 deadline when the story might have made the Sunday-morning edition to pass. Nevertheless, he did take time to patch together a story with background on John Anthony Molina as a runner and friend of Peter. He had not posted it to the *Ledger's* Web site, as he easily could have done with a few key strokes. Instead, it sat in his computer as background detail, waiting for a more appropriate time. Being first to break the story offered little appeal to Jonathan Von Runyon. Bloggers and twitterers more often were first to report stories these days, but they rarely won Pulitzer Prizes. More important to Von Runyon than getting the story *first* was getting the story *right*. That both McDonald and Ogilvie would know he got the story and sat on it, awaiting confirmation, was probably most important of all. For once, covering a marathon seemed almost as much fun as covering a golf tournament.

Von Runyon stirred and realized that the golf tournament from Maui had vanished from his TV screen. He pushed the button on his clicker to turn off the TV and rumbled toward his bedroom. He anticipated a busy day covering the marathon.

Back at the Hilliard, the woman who briefly had visited Pope Tony's mother's house on the East Side lay awake, clad in a lacy black nightgown. Before going to bed, the meticulous Matilda Goldberg had positioned her running uniform on a chair near the bed: singlet with bib attached on the back of the chair, shorts on the seat of the chair, running shoes and socks below the chair. Tilda was ready to run! If an alarm sounded in the hotel, she could jump instantly from bed and slide out of the nightgown and into her running gear.

302

MARATHON

What kept the reporter from *The New York Times* awake was not an anxiety dream, but anxiety itself, her inability to decide which pacing group to join. Tilda had discussed that question at the Expo with pacing team coordinator Leonard Hand. At the Team Turtle party, she and other runners had agonized over their race plans. All decided that she should de-seed herself: that she should forget about time given the hot weather and just run to finish, not finish fast. Tilda knew that to be sound advice, but she was having difficulty swallowing it. Pinned to the back of her singlet draped on the bedside chair was a secondary number: 4:00. It identified her as running with that pacing group. In previous marathons, Tilda had broken four hours without problem. She considered being a "three-hour runner" a badge of honor, so that when asked her marathon time, she could coyly begin with the number, "Three...."

Instant respect!

But did that make sense given the weather predictions?

At the party, Tilda had asked Don Geoffrey what to do: Should she still try to break four? Geoffrey had tugged at his beard with one hand, as though offering permission for a smile to show. The Turtle said: "It's like buying a yacht. If you need to ask the price, you can't afford one."

The group around them had laughed. She was not sure whether she wanted to hit the Turtle or hug him. A funny response, but *soooooh* true. Rolling over in bed for the seventy-eighth time, Tilda glanced at the digital clock on the table beside the race-uniform-draped chair and saw red numbers. In that very instant, they clicked from 12:14 to 12:15. *Fifteen!* Tilda was being sent a message, one that included the number 15. Perhaps the Turtle himself had rigged the clock. Or maybe it was Yahweh text-messaging her. She decided that en route to the starting line, she would stop by the pacing team tent and request a 4:15 number to replace the 4:00 number pinned to her singlet.

Elsewhere in the Hilliard, runners expecting to run significantly faster than Matilda Goldberg lay in their beds, some of them asleep, some of them not, some of them dreaming, some of them not. One fast asleep was Fiona Flynn, naughtily naked. On going to bed nearly two hours earlier, *La Femme Fiona* bemoaned the fact that she had no male in bed beside her for assistance in falling asleep. Fiona decided on the next best thing. It worked. She dozed off, allowing the vibrator to slip from her hand. But now she rolled over in bed and struck her hip on the phallic device still beside her.

"*Damnú air!*" said Fiona, cussing in Gaelic, testily shoving the vibrator aside and off the bed, hearing a clatter as it struck the floor below. Fiona worried she might have broken the device, but no matter. If she won the marathon, she could afford to buy a better model, maybe one with tunes like on her iPod. Or maybe she would forget about battery-powered devices and attach herself to the real thing. *Is Peter seeing anybody? All the good men are taken. Will the convent back in Cork accept me back if I can't catch a male?*

Among Fiona's rivals, one woman did not need to rely on battery-powered substitutes. Tatanya Henry said to her husband: "Rub my back." The Russian runner spoke English, which she used when desiring something special.

"Do you want to make love?" whispered her husband.

"Nyet."

Jacob Henry positioned himself behind Tatanya, so their naked bodies touched. He began gently to stroke her back. He knew that she loved to have her back scratched, particularly at the bra line. "I'll rub your back, but only if you promise to win the race."

"I'll give you all my prize money if you rub my back."

"Am I your male prostitute?"

"No, my massage therapist. Be quiet and rub my back."

"I love you, Tatanya," he said, kissing her on the neck.

She sighed in response. Soon they both fell asleep.

Meghan Allison, wearing a shortie nightgown with a flower pattern, had no trouble sleeping. Meg felt no pressure to please anyone other than herself. Husband Matt, however, would awaken several times during the night to find the woman beside him in bed motionless. He marveled at his wife's ability to totally tune out an event to which she had devoted an entire year of training time. Matt hoped Meg did well, but even if not, he would continue to love her. Eventually they planned to have children, but he was thinking of giving her a dog for her next birthday, one that they both could run with. He was thinking of a golden retriever.

Other elite athletes slept or lay awake, depending on their anxiety levels. Joseph Nduku, confident of his ability, lay motionless in bed, mouth open, breathing shallowly, barely burning enough calories to stay alive until morning. Joseph, clad in an ankle-length garment similar to a dashiki, dreamed the sweetest of dreams. The defending champion lay like a crocodile beside the bank of an African river, submerged, only the eyes and nostrils visible above the surface, masquerading as a log, seemingly harmless, but ready to pounce on any game that drifted to the river to drink. A stray impala would do. Since no impala approached, Joseph the Crocodile continued to sleep undisturbed.

In another room, rabbit Moses Abraham, clad only in khaki boxer shorts, slept dreamlessly, because his task to pace his friend and running companion in the next bed offered little pressure. But Kenyatta Kemai, also wearing boxer shorts, lay on his back, eyes open, staring at the ceiling. Did he really have the audacity to think he could defeat the great Joseph? *Yes, I can!* Kemai kept saying to himself. But did he believe it?

In one more room on the same floor, the twins. Kyle and Wesley Fowler, lay peacefully asleep. Kyle wore Spider-Man pajamas; Wesley, the Incredible Hulk. Christmas presents from their little sister Holly, but wearing those gag pajamas had become a pre-race ritual. They had no reason for anxiety. The twins would simply cruise the first twenty miles of the marathon at a steady pace and step off the course as directed by their coach, Steve Holland. That evening, they had attended the premiere of a movie, *The Spirit of the Marathon*, directed by Jon Dunham, then returned to their room to play video games for an hour, hurtling in motorcycles through the streets, dodging cars and vans and trucks.

Director Tom Schorr would have loved to run Lake City, but his duties obviously prevented that from happening. Instead, he intended to run New York a month later. At the TV3 trailer, he lay fully clad in a corner on the floor, not sleeping, just resting. Schorr remained blissfully unaware of how much the presence of Celebrity X would complicate his day.

Weatherman Vaughn Johnson, wearing silk pajamas, slept in his apartment north of downtown. Before going to bed, Johnson had accessed his computer for a final weather check on the Internet. The low-pressure system that might produce cooler temperatures lingered far to the west, immobile as though caught in a whirlpool. He suspected it would arrive in Lake City too late to offer much help for late-finishers.

Color commentators Timothy Rainboldt and Carolynne Vickers occupied separate rooms on separate floors in the Hilliard. Fidgety, C.V. considered calling Timothy for "you-know-what," but decided, no, she did not like him tonight. She wanted to dislike him just a bit in the morning too, knowing that the edge between them made both better broadcasters.

Wearing a nightgown with a picture of two pandas on the front, C.V. rose from her bed and moved to the window overlooking the lake and also the area of Columbia Drive encompassing the start and finish lines. To aid in preparations, the area was brilliantly lit by spotlights. Trees blocked her view of workers who continued to prepare for the arrival soon of 50,000. C.V. stood staring toward the park and lake for several minutes Eventually, she turned and returned to bed. She soon fell asleep.

In a few hours, the sun would rise over the lake. Runners would fill the streets of Lake City. The dawn of a very hot day approached. None of the dreamers, however, had any idea what that day would bring.

SUNDAY

05:00:00

Peter McDonald slept well during the several hours he managed to steal from his busy schedule. He had set his alarm clock for 3:00, since he wanted to drive the course before the race, a ritual designed to both calm his nerves and assure himself that no problems existed on the course. No potholes. Nothing that would block the flow of 50,000 runners. As per custom, Peter awakened a few minutes before the alarm would have startled him to action. Five hours to go before the start of the marathon.

05:00:00. 04:59:59 to 04:59:58.

Peter showered, shaved and quickly dressed. Exiting his room, the race director encountered a runner in the corridor dressed in shorts carrying a bucket of ice, designed for a purpose other than chilling champagne. "Good luck today," Peter told him.

"And to you," said Bob Veldman.

Arriving in the main lobby, Peter greeted the same security guard he had seen three hours earlier. "Have a good day," said the guard.

"I will," Peter politely responded.

Peter walked toward the hotel's side entrance, leading to the parking garage. A van wrapped with the Lake Shore Marathon logo awaited him. After showering, Peter had called to have the van ready. Climbing into the vehicle, Peter recalled dropping Christine Ferrara at this entrance after offering her a ride from the Expo. Thursday morning. Three days ago. Not even seventy-two hours. Had they known each other that short a time? Yet he already had begun to hope she would become his girlfriend, that as soon as the marathon was past, their relationship would blossom. He suspected Christine felt the same.

But that was for tomorrow. He had a marathon to run today. Peter guided the van onto Jefferson Avenue. Very few cars occupied the usually busy street. Traffic would be light. Peter figured that it would take him somewhere around ninety minutes to cover the 26 miles 385 yards of the marathon course. It amused him that this was only marginally faster than the best runners in the field would run later in the day.

Access to the park was blocked, so Peter continued on Jefferson parallel to the starting grid where in a few hours runners would begin gathering. Eventually, he turned onto a side street that allowed access ahead of the starting line.

MARATHON

Peter looked backwards toward the line overhung by a sidewalk-to-sidewalk banner emblazoned with the name, *Lake City Marathon*, containing also the logo of Lake City Bank. Fences that would separate spectators from the runners also were blanketed with the bank name and logos. There were, in fact, signs and banners with the bank's name on it all over the course. Peter wondered whether he would need to replace the signs and banners next year.

Now on the course, Peter entered a tunnel that would take the 50,000-runner field beneath several blocks of skyscrapers, before crossing the Des Plaines River, a waterway runners would encounter a half dozen times during their 26-mile odyssey. The bridge floor was steel grating, not easy on the feet of light-shoed runners. A red carpet, wide enough for two or three runners, had been laid on the bridge to soften some of the impact for those runners able to fit onto it. Mainly, the rug was for the elite field. Elites were more likely to compete in racing shoes weighing as little as 5 ounces. Most runners were content to use training shoes, two or three times that weight. Heavier shoes slowed the runners somewhat, but also protected them from the pounding their bodies would absorb during 26 miles of running. It was a trade-off that each runner needed to make each time he or she walked into a running store.

In the early miles, the course wound through downtown and past the offices of Lake City Bank before heading north. As he continued, Peter passed the locations of aid stations, none of the volunteers yet having arrived, none of the tables with cups yet having been set in place. Mile markers had not yet been erected. Position them too early and they would disappear.

He drove through a neighborhood of condos, restaurants and small shops and moved into Wilson Park just past the 5-mile mark. The road here was narrow and winding, compressing the field, often forcing runners to slow their pace. Like weight of shoes, the park posed another trade-off. Peter could have designed the course to bypass the park, but he chose not to do so, favoring the more scenic option. An opposite problem was that later in the race, the course passed through several industrial neighborhoods featuring wider streets, but with no shade, definitely unfriendly under a sun rising on a hot day.

He exited the park, passing a tall condominium building with balconies, only a few lights showing life inside, most of the occupants asleep. Reaching the northernmost point of the course, Peter turned left, then two blocks later left again, returning south toward downtown. The mammoth Target Tower, brightly lit, could be seen far away, looming above the roofs of stores and apartments. The Tower would be in the sights of runners for nearly five more miles before they reached the half marathon mark. That was the point, depending on the temperature rise, at which Peter might need to not allow runners to continue. Those failing to reach halfway by a set time would be turned toward the finish line, failing to reach their goal of covering a fully certified 26 miles 385 yards. For many, this would be a traumatic experience. But, another trade-off: Do you allow the marathon to continue as planned, if large numbers of people land in the hospital? The Angel of Death is an infrequent visitor to marathons, but deaths and serious health-related problems do occur.

Warm weather was less a problem for the elites, who would be off the course in just over two hours. Others would take a significantly longer time to finish, and they were most at risk. Peter could not help but muse over the fact that organizing a marathon the size of Lake City required a subtle balance. He needed to cater to the elite athletes—the Joseph Nduku's and the Aba Andersson's of the world—because they generate headlines and attract sponsors. But if he overlooked those filling the streets behind the elites, the *lumpenproletariat* of the sport, or ignored the spectators cheering from the sidewalks, he did so at his own risk. They would write angry letters, displeasing to sponsors. They would choose other cities for their fall marathons in future years, something he hoped would not happen.

It was nearly 5:00 A.M. when Peter arrived back at the hotel, having cut the course at several corners. That was a timesaving luxury he allowed himself, but any runners who tried cutting the course would almost certainly be caught and disqualified. His assistant Noel Michaels would catch them, even though it might take her several weeks to identify those who failed to cross all the timing mats on the course. Identifying fifty or sixty cheaters absorbed staff time and cost money, but Peter considered this a necessary expenditure to maintain the integrity of the sport. He knew almost every other director of a race big or small felt the same.

Returning to the Hilliard, Peter knew he had exorcized his demons, having convinced himself that all was ready for the moment, now only three hours away, when nearly 50,000 runners would challenge themselves to meet their personal goals. As Peter stepped out of the van up to the curb, a parking garage attendant wearing a Lake City Marathon jacket greeted him.

"Have a good day," said the attendant.

"I will," Peter responded, still wondering what the day would bring.

MARATHON

01:00:00

At 7:00 AM, with only an hour to go before the start of the Lake City Marathon, Matilda Goldberg stopped by the pacing team tent. It was located near the gate where runners entered the starting grid. This was the domain of team coordinator Leonard Hand, where he met with team leaders and runners before sending them to the line. If you had failed to sign up for a team at the Expo, you still could do so by visiting the tent. Tilda already had pinned to her back a number indicating commitment to the 4:00 team, but she had second thoughts.

"Can I sign up for a different team?" she asked a woman standing behind a desk covered with numbers representing times from three to six hours. The woman indicated she could and asked to which team Tilda wished to switch.

"4:15."

The woman offered a 4:15 number. It was colored light blue vs. light green for the other number, further differentiating the different pacing teams. The entire purpose of the numbers worn on the back was so that pacing team members could find each other, particularly if they became separated while going through aid stations. Similarly, all the pacing team leaders wore lime green caps and singlets to easily be spotted by members of their teams. Some even ran carrying the large, circular overhead signs (called lollypops) used so runners could find them on the starting grid.

Leonard Hand was standing near the table gathering signs to be given his pacers. Lenny planned to lead the 4:00 team, but he did not regret losing Tilda to the next slower team. He complimented her: "Good choice."

"Thank you."

"I wish everybody today had the common sense, given the weather, to join a slower team." He offered the comment in a loud voice, hoping that other runners lined up for numbers reconsidered their own strategies.

Tilda said no more. She merely smiled. Her stomach was churning, and she knew she would have to visit the toilets once again before going to the line. At least she could remove her singlet and switch numbers in the privacy of one of the portable toilets. She walked out of the tent and toward a grassy area containing row after row of porta-potties, bright blue in color, dozens of them. *Hundreds* of them, if you counted all the porta-potties in the immediate area of the start and finish. But *thousands* were lined up to use them. Appraising the lines, Tilda estimated she would need to waste ten or fifteen minutes standing in line. Then there was the smell once you got inside. *Ewww!* Should she suck it up? Yes, because she did not want to be forced into a pit stop during the race, so she needed to stop. Tilda seriously considered returning to her hotel room, but a glance at her watch caused her to reject that option.

01:00:00. 00:59:59. 00:59:58.

Matilda Goldberg, however, possessed talents beyond those of the 50,000 or so other entrants in the Lake City Marathon. She was a reporter for *The New York Times*, a journalism school graduate, most important: an investigative reporter! *Hold your applause, please.* Surely, some of the porta-potties had lines shorter than others. If she spent two or three minutes wandering between the lines of blue-painted outhouses—that was what they were, let's be honest, outhouses—she certainly could find the one with the shortest line. Tilda decided to amuse herself by doing just that.

As Matilda Goldberg left the pacing team tent on a quest for a short line, Don Geoffrey entered that tent from another direction. The Turtle prided himself on never having to use a porta-potty, not immediately before the start of a marathon, certainly not during one. Having run dozens of marathons and hundreds of road races at other distances, the Turtle understood—almost to the *gram*—the kind and amount of food and drink to imbibe that would allow complete digestion and elimination before leaving his hotel room. No poop. No pee. Forget fast times, that was his goal in entering any marathon: never to enter the sordid, blue chambers.

The Turtle knew that the fear of failure that came before any important race often caused digestive upset. But he had long since conquered that fear. Also, because he planned to run with the 4:00 pacing team, a pace well within his capabilities, the Lake City Marathon for him would serve mostly as a stroll in the park. Warm weather was for the Turtle less a problem than it would be other less anal athletes in today's marathon.

Without the need to eliminate, and not wishing to mingle with the masses, many who would want to say hello or ask to have their pictures taken with him, the Turtle searched for a spot to be alone with his own thoughts. Spotting a chair in one corner of the tent, behind the tables and away from the activity, Don Geoffrey went to sit down.

The Turtle was amazed by today's generation of runners. The Olympian knew that many trained just as hard as he had during his elite years. Maybe not as fast or as far, but with the same dedication. For eighteen weeks leading up to their marathon, whether first or fiftieth, they focused their attention on the programs he designed for them. Training for the marathon became their obsession. They became fixated on setting a PR or snatching a BQ or (for first-timers) merely finishing with honor. Yet they also ran with digital cameras and cell phones and iPods that had nothing to do with fast times. They ran with slogans on their backs and names on the front of their shirts, so those lining the course could cheer them by name. "Go, David!" "You can do it, Danny!" "Looking good, Angela!" *Doesn't that get old by the tenth mile or so?* Yet they were wonderful. They were his people. He loved every one, and hoped none came to any harm today. Not on my watch! Not under my care!

Geoffrey looked up and saw Lenny standing nearby. The pacing team leader waved, then completed his conversation with a runner asking advice about which team to choose, "A slow team," Lenny advised. He then directed his attention to the Turtle.

"There'll be a celebrity running with the 4:00 team," began Lenny.

"Thank you, Lenny," the Turtle responded dead-pan. "You don't need to feed my already considerable ego."

"No," said the pacing team leader. "A real celebrity."

The Turtle looked hurt. "Lenny!"

"Aba Andersson stopped by the booth yesterday. She's pregnant."

"I know. I decline responsibility."

Lenny pressed on like a boulder rolling down a mountain. "She still wants to run though and wondered if it would be okay if she ran with one of our pacing groups. I didn't know whether to hug her or ask for an autograph."

"I would have preferred the hug."

"But she might not be the only celebrity."

"Lenny, no hug from me."

"Naní might be running with us too."

"Really," said the Turtle. "Okay, I'll reconsider my stand on hugs."

But neither Lenny nor the Turtle yet knew that a third celebrity might be accompanying them through the streets of Lake City.

A quarter block away, race director Peter McDonald strode into the operations trailer and approached the tiny room occupied by Noel Michaels, its door open. His executive director was alone. Peter tapped politely on the edge of the door. Michaels, talking into a headset, turned to look at Peter and waved him toward a chair. Peter closed the door, which surprised Michaels.

"What's up?" she asked.

"Let me tell you about Celebrity X."

00:45:00

The charity village for the Lake City Marathon occupied several dozen acres of land in Wilson Park east of the finish line. Trees surrounded the plot on its outward edges, but mostly it was grass, flat, well-manicured, containing baseball diamonds, eight of them, a popular gathering spot for recreational softball players throughout the summer.

For the marathon, however, tents filled the grassy area, each one hosting a different charity. Twenty-nine charities used the marathon to raise money, some of the tents large, some small. Among the 50,000 entered in the Lake City Marathon, approximately 7,000 were charity runners, who would raise $34 million for organizations around the world. They did this by asking friends and relatives to donate money in their names to a charity-of-choice, in effect sponsoring their participation in the race. One of the perks offered charity runners was a tent, where they could gather before and after the marathon. They could talk to each other. They could check their bags. They could utilize porta-potties with lines shorter than elsewhere in the park. Some of the larger charities even provided massage therapists and post-race refreshments.

Among the medium-size tents in the village was that for AIDS Africa. Readying herself for the race forty-five minutes before its start was Naní. On the runway of a fashion show, at a film festival premiere, or on the cover of *InStyle*, Naní served as the ultimate paparazzi magnet. In the marathon environment, however, the supermodel was just another skinny babe. Yes, the AIDS Africa runners knew of her fame. They reveled in her celebrity, the fact that they were running the marathon with this incredibly glamorous female, but they allowed Naní her space. They knew how nervous they felt before running a marathon on a warm day, so they were not about to bother her with questions or requests for autographs and photos. That could wait until after the race. When it came to using the porta-potties, Naní waited in line just like everybody else. She preferred it that way.

00:45:00. 00:44:59. 00:44:58.

Her husband Ricco, who had accompanied her to the tent, watched his wife double-knot her shoes and fuss with her shorts and singlet to make sure they fit right. Ricco smiled and said, "I know what you're thinking."

"Yes, isn't it great *not* to be famous."

"Enjoy it while you can."

She put her arms around him. "I've always been amazed at your ability to stay out of the spotlight." They hugged. Overcome with emotion, Naní had tears in her eyes.

"Time for you to go the line," Ricco whispered in her ear. "See you after you finish."

"*If* I finish."

"Hey, no negative thoughts."

Another hug. A kiss on the cheek.

They parted.

Many of the AIDS Africa runners already had begun to file out of the tent. Naní attached herself to a group of several dozen, all similarly clad in yellow uniforms with the charity's logo emblazoned on their singlets. Brightly attired, they would be easy to spot by friends. They walked slowly, some chatting in whispers, others jabbering loudly to cover their nervousness. One or two broke into a jog to loosen their legs, but soon returned to the group.

A half mile separated the charity village from the gate where they would enter the starting grid. Once inside, each participant would seek runners near equal in ability. Signs beside the course in the general starting area attempted to define areas for those running 8:00 (per mile) pace, 9:00 pace, 10:00 pace and so forth, but not everyone paid attention to the signs. Ahead of the general starting area were four more strictly monitored corrals for faster runners, who had qualified for those corrals by having posted fast times at various distances. Naní had learned at the Expo on Saturday that leaders for the various pacing teams would signify their team assembly points by holding large, circular signs overhead. Fortunately she arrived at the same time Leonard Hand and his team leaders marched into the starting area, numbered signs raised high like flags at the opening ceremony for the Olympic Games.

Naní spotted Lenny carrying a 4:00 sign. *One worry out of the way,* she thought. Yesterday, he had told her it would take roughly ten minutes after the race began for the 4:00 team to reach and cross the starting line. Talking with Lenny, she had the feeling that he was just *dying* to ask for an autograph, but felt it unprofessional to do so. If her race went well, she would find some way to reward him. Maybe a kiss on the cheek in the finish chute. Maybe an autographed photo in the mail. Maybe both. She hoped she did not have problems staying with the team. First marathon or not, she really wanted that 3:59:59.

She noticed Paddy Savitch standing nearby, one of the Shelaghi executives who might determine whether or not the Irish conglomerate would continue its sponsorship. *Would Peter want me to offer a final schmooze?* Naní decided, probably not. Then Paddy glanced her way and waved. She returned the wave with a five-finger wiggle and her shyest of shy smiles. *Okay, that schmooz taken care of.*

Naní wore a floppy hat partly for disguise, so she would not have to talk to anyone other than those with AIDS Africa. She was too nervous to make polite conversation, but she suspected a lot of the others felt the same. Naní planned to discard the floppy hat after the start in favor of a simple yellow sweat band across her forehead. Ricco had promised to intersect the course at several points along the race to cheer for her. He claimed to have a map that showed him how to do so. Naní hoped Ricco did not have trouble spotting her. She needed his support.

Peter had told Naní at the press conference—in confidence, he said—that there might be another celebrity joining her group. He had not offered a name; she did not ask for one. Later, she learned world record holder Aba Andersson also might join the 4:00 group. *Was she the celebrity? If so, why the secrecy?*

At about the same time Naní left the charity village and began walking toward the starting grid with members of her AIDS Africa group, Aba and husband Bjørn left the Hilliard, headed in the same direction. Had Aba been bent on a world record attempt, she would have ridden a bus with other elite athletes to a special compound near the starting line, separated from those with less impressive Personal Records. She would have been allowed the privilege of warming up in the open area in front of the line, forbidden ground to other runners doing Lake City. She still could have accepted those privileges of rank, but had chosen not to.

00:44:00. 00:43:59. 00:43:58.

Bjørn Andersson walked a half step behind his wife. A former world-class cross-country skier, Aba's husband often trained with his more famous wife, doing long runs, but Bjørn almost never raced, enjoying more the role of supporter/spectator. He never had run a marathon! But when Aba decided to run though pregnant, aiming at a time somewhere in the four-hour range, Bjørn decided this was too good an opportunity to resist. He talked Peter into giving him a number. He wore on his chest the totally anonymous 51,138.

Peter told him. "You have the highest number of anyone entered."

"I'll try not to finish in that place," Bjørn promised.

Though secretly delighted that Bjørn planned to accompany her, Aba (who had been issued number 101) chided him for his decision to compete. "Are you running with me, or running with our baby?" she had asked.

"Both," Bjørn responded.

And although the Swedish world record holder hoped to run in the back of the pack with some anonymity, as she and Bjørn headed toward the starting corral, she found many runners smiling at her and offering comments.

"Aba, congratulations on your pregnancy."

"Thank you." (Said shyly.)

"Boy or girl, Aba?"

"We haven't decided yet." (Said with a smile.)

"We're so proud of you, Aba."

"I'm proud of *you!*" (Said sincerely.)

"Aba, are you really running back of the pack with us?

"No, we're all running back in the pack together!" (Mutual laughter.)

"I ran all through my pregnancy, Aba."

"Really?" (Said with amazement.)

"Not entirely. The last month or so, I mostly walked."

"Then *you* and *I* have a lot to talk about."

The Swedish runner linked arms with the other woman, Natasha from Covington, Kentucky. A member of Team Turtle, Natasha had signed up for the 4:00 pacing team, mainly because she heard that her mentor Don Geoffrey would be running with that group.

Bjørn, walking now two steps behind his wife and her newfound friend, watched with amusement and amazement as the two women chatted animatedly. His wife, so typically Scandinavian, usually was very shy among people she did not know well. She was fanatic about protecting her privacy. Bjørn never had seen Aba this happy at a race before. This marathon was going to offer a very special moment for the two of them.

After leaving the operations trailer, Peter McDonald began to walk north toward the starting line. With less than forty-five minutes to go, he knew that movement soon would become difficult, not merely because of 50,000 runners, but because of near equal numbers of spectators and family members crowding the sidewalks.

00:43:00. 00:42:59. 00:42:58.

It only had taken a few minutes for Peter to brief Noel Michaels on plans for Celebrity X, who should be arriving by car—unmarked, unpretentious—at the cross street near the starting line within the next fifteen minutes. Captain Robert Newsom would be there to supervise X's arrival. Nobody connected with the Police Department, not even Newsom, yet knew the identity of Celebrity X, nor had he shared that information with Michaels.

"You're still not going to tell me the identity of this Celebrity X?" she had probed during their meeting.

"When you find out his identity, you'll understand why."

"*His* identity. That immediately narrows the field to half the people in the world. So it's not Naní."

"No."

315

SUNDAY

"When will I learn?"

"At the same time everybody else learns."

"Everybody else in the world?"

"Exactly."

Peter departed his assistant's room in the operations trailer, fearful that he already may have said too much. He knew he could trust Michaels, but the walls were thin. He had kept plans for Pope Tony running the marathon secret this long; no sense offering too many hints this close to the moment when his boyhood friend would step onto the course.

Peter continued toward the starting line. In a few minutes, Celebrity X would arrive at the corner where Haydon Street intersected Lake Shore Drive. Haydon was the side street, now occupied by the lead vehicles, including the press truck on which he planned to ride. The press truck was scheduled to remain in position until 7:30, the time at which anybody planning to ride the truck was scheduled to be on board. One person who had told Peter he might ride the press truck was Dennis Lahey. Peter wondered whether the Shelaghi executive actually would show.

At 7:30, the press truck and other lead vehicles would move off Haydon to a position on Columbia Drive ahead of the runners. With the departure of the lead vehicles, the side street would be nearly empty. All eyes would be on the starting line nearby. Celebrity X could warm up, if he wanted with little chance of being seen. There was even a portable toilet, locked and closed to the public, a police officer assigned to guard it.

Once the horn sounded, the elite runners would move quickly off the line, 50,000 following. It would be a magic moment. Everybody's attention would be on the passing parade. At the appropriate time, Pope Tony and his two bodyguards would jog to the starting line. There was a gate in the fence, guarded by two trusted interns from the marathon office, Elisa and Damien. Peter personally had recruited the pair for this special assignment, not offering any hints as to the importance of their task. They would open the gate when Celebrity X appeared. If all went well, this would occur as the 4:00 pacing team approached the line.

He walked past the TV3 tent near Burnham Fountain, where the telecast team was primed to go live. The tent was festooned with signs and banners plugging the station. Within the tent and on a raised platform was a table, behind it chairs where anchorman Mark Mallon and his two color commentators, Carolynne Vickers and Timothy Rainboldt, would sit. In front were cameras, their usage dictated by Tom Schorr, who would direct the telecast from a control trailer nearby. The control trailer, with its nearly two dozen monitors, was a miniaturized version of control rooms at the TV3 studios downtown.

316

MARATHON

As Peter passed, he looked through an open side of the TV3 tent at the three key telecast members, the "talent." They stood talking to each other and Schorr, discussing last-minute instructions or maybe, knowing Mallon, which teams were likely to win in the NFL today. Peter could not help wondering how they might react when they learned about Celebrity X. *Have I kept Tony's identity secret for my own pleasure in being the only one to know?* That thought crossed Peter's mind, but he dismissed it instantly.

He failed to see Christine Ferrara and wondered for a moment where she might be. He had not seen her since last night, but he could not take time to search for this new woman in his life. Peter had to keep moving. The sidewalks surrounding the starting area were becoming more crowded. He needed to reach the side street where the press truck was parked, where Celebrity X may already have arrived.

Christine Ferrara had left the TV3 studio less than a minute before Peter appeared. She was only a hundred yards ahead, also walking toward the starting line. Christine needed to reach the golf cart she would ride during the race along with cameraman Edmund Giesbert. It was parked with its driver on the side street nearest the starting line, across the road from Peter's destination.

00:42:00. 00:41:59. 00:41:58.

She carried earphones with microphone attached, but had not yet donned them, partly because they were cumbersome and partly because she did not want to call attention to herself. Christine wore a red golf shirt with a TV3 logo as did the rest of those who would be seen on camera, but that was almost too much identification for her comfort. She also wore hung from her neck a plastic credential that would provide access to all areas, but Tom Schorr told her to tuck it into the front of the shirt so the credential would not be seen on camera. She tried that, but the scratchy piece of plastic dangled between her breasts in a most uncomfortable position. Christine sighed: *Well, if that's all I need to worry about today, I should do fine.* Nervousness aside, she did feel confident about her ability to do the job.

The plan was for her to stay near the starting line for at least a few minutes after the start. There was a wooden platform, access restricted, on which she could stand with her cameraman. Mallon might throw to her for a comment or might not, Tom Schorr had said. But immediately after her report, she needed to jump into the golf cart and hustle to another location near the aid station across from the Field Store, then to still another location further on the course as runners doubled back and forth through downtown. Eventually, as the pack began to string out, Christine would need to move the golf cart out onto the course. That would be a delicate maneuver.

"Please try not to run over any runners," Tom had warned her. "If some-one sues, we'll need to take the settlement out of your salary."

"Tom!" Christine had protested. She knew Schorr probably was kidding. He usually was. The director had come up with the innovative idea of imbed-ding a reporter (her) and cameraman (Edmund) unobtrusively among mid-pack runners, ordinary mortals, not the elite up front. When Tom approached Peter about using a camera vehicle within the race, the race director vetoed the idea of a motorcycle with sidecar, which would have forced the tightly packed runners to inhale its exhaust. The director came up with the idea of a golf cart, which Peter approved.

Arriving opposite the starting line, Christine approached a gate guarded by two young members of the marathon staff, interns. Christine never had met Elisa and Damien. She reached for her credential to display it for entry, but Damien smiled and said, "Good morning, Ms. Ferrara."

"Good morning." *He knows me? I've only been in town two weeks.*

"We'll look forward to your reports from the course. I've set the TiVo back at my apartment."

"I hope I have something interesting to report on."

"I'm sure you will."

"Break a leg," said Elisa, offering the traditional good-luck expression used in the theatre.

Christine laughed. "Better me than any of the runners." Passing through the gate, she moved across the no-man's-land in front of the starting line to cross to where she would meet her cameraman and the individual assigned to drive the cart. She could see Edmund standing with his camera atop the plat-form waiting for her. The golf cart was not immediately in sight; she assumed it to be parked behind the crowd to facilitate a quick escape.

As Christine left the interns, Elisa said to Damien: "So that's her."

"Yep. She's the one causing the buzz the last few days."

"I am so-o-o-o-h very happy for him."

"So is everybody. Apparently, Mr. McDonald has not been a lot of fun to be around this last year."

"Small wonder."

"Yep."

"I love office gossip."

"Me too."

318

MARATHON

00:30:00

Precisely at 7:30 A.M., a half hour before the start of the Lake City Marathon, the lead vehicles began to move into place on Columbia Drive in a long line in front of the runners. This procession included (in order) a half dozen police motorcycles, a convertible containing timing officials, the press truck on which Peter McDonald planned to ride, a TV camera truck and a TV camera motorcycle (which would move from front to side to behind the runners to catch them from different angles). Another motorcycle had as passenger a photographer from *Running Magazine*, who also would shift back and forth capturing still photos for that publication. The TV camera truck (the vehicle closest to the runners) had a countdown clock mounted on its roof showing at this moment how much time remained before the start. Once the race started, the clock would shift to counting forward, displaying the running time.

00:30:00. 00:29:59. 00:29:58.

Arriving at the starting line, Peter McDonald stopped at the gate that Celebrity X would use to access the course. It was not only for Pope Tony's benefit. Officials and elite athletes would use it too, but Peter wanted to make sure that when Celebrity X arrived, nobody tried to block him. It seemed inconceivable that anyone would fail to recognize the pope, but Peter wanted to avoid any snafus. Seeing the two interns from the marathon office, Elisa and Damien, perched on each side of the gate, like the pillars of Hercules, he stopped to give them final instructions:

"There will be three runners. Expect them to arrive five or ten minutes after the start. They will have credentials hung around their necks for identification—although you'll probably recognize one of them."

"You can't tell us who it is?" wondered Elisa.

"Nope."

Elisa looked at Damien and shrugged.

"Once they're through the gate, nobody else gets in. *Nobody!* I don't care who they claim to be."

"Okay," Damien agreed.

"The three plan to join the 4:00 pacing team as it passes. That should not be a problem. If it becomes one, you take charge."

SUNDAY

Peter certainly expected no problems, but he could not predict how the nearly 50,000 runners and a million spectators would react once they realized Pope Tony was running the marathon.

He moved to go, then stopped, turning back toward the interns. "One final item: They won't want to run wearing their credentials, so will probably hand them to you." Peter smiled. "You might want them as souvenirs."

As Peter departed, Damien turned towards Elisa, a puzzled look on his face. "Do you have any idea what this is all about?"

"I'm clueless."

"Rock star? Hollywood idol? The President?"

"Dunno."

"I'm thinking about those credentials. Something to sell on eBay?"

The two interns laughed.

Walking out into the no-man's-land before the starting line, Peter glanced back and forth as though looking for some overlooked detail that he could fix. Nothing remained for him to say or do. Noel Michaels had done her job. A half dozen officials responsible for the start stood nearby, including Ted Morgan, a retired coach from Lake City University. He greeted Ted and the others, but did not stop to talk. Several wheelchair athletes waited near the starting line. There was a wheelchair race within the marathon. They would start five minutes before the runners at 7:55. Several dozen wheelchair athletes were entered, and the top three finishers in men's and women's divisions would receive prize money. They raced in three-wheeled vehicles, crafted with the precision of spaceships. The best wheelchair athletes would finish as much as a half hour in front of the runners. Peter organized a separate race-within-a-race for these handicapped athletes and wished he could offer them more in terms of publicity and prize money, but the Lake City Marathon remained a runners' event.

The elite athletes had not yet arrived, or at least had not made their presence known. Bussed from the Hilliard, most should be waiting in a holding compound on the left side of the starting line. Some would have run from the Hilliard, using that as their warm-up. Within the next five or ten minutes, they would begin to jog out onto the course, a privilege accorded only them, because allowing 50,000 runners to access that area for their warm-ups would result in chaos. Lack of warm-up was a penalty most runners paid when they entered major races. When Peter raced track, he usually spent an hour or more jogging several miles, stretching, doing short strides at race pace, to make sure he was ready to run. He tried to offer the opportunity to do just that for the fastest runners; the others simply had to adapt, and they usually did.

MARATHON

Peter looked to the left and saw Christine Ferrara standing on a platform next to her cameraman. Christine did not see him. Peter considered walking over to say hello or text-messaging her to "turn around." He was being foolish. He had a race to supervise. He was not being paid by the bank to plan romantic liaisons. He turned away from the TV reporter and headed to the right side of the street. The last of the lead vehicles, including the press truck, had moved onto Columbia Drive ahead of the starting line.

Haydon Street was now empty, but only for a moment. Peter saw three new vehicles—bland looking sedans—pull to the point on Lake Shore Drive where entry to the side street was blocked by sawhorses. A policeman approached the vehicles to check for proper credentials. That confirmed, he waved for the three cars to enter the side street just vacated.

Good, thought Peter, *everything is working smoothly—so far!*

The three cars moved to a point in the middle of the street and stopped. Doors opened from the first and third cars, not the second whose doors remained closed. The men who exited the first and third cars all wore identical nylon jackets, a luminous orange color so they easily could spot each other in a crowd. If you looked closely—and you would have had to look *very* closely—you would have seen that each of the men had earpieces and throat microphones. Once out of the cars, the men moved in different directions, positioning themselves between the outside of the area and the second car, whose doors still remained closed.

Peter could not help thinking: *This is how the Secret Service protects the president*. He knew that additional bodyguards had been added to the protective umbrella surrounding the pope, at the insistence of Cardinal Connolly. Peter thought that the extra bodyguards might prove superfluous. The most effective bodyguards would be the stream of 50,000 runners surrounding Tony. Or so Peter hoped. He did concede that the extra bodyguards might prove handy at this critical time before Tony stepped onto the course. And maybe also after he finished.

Turning, Peter suddenly found himself staring at the man he had been trying to avoid since receiving his text-message late yesterday afternoon. "Jonathan," said Peter, less surprised than he might have been.

"Peter." The *Ledger* reporter had a cackling smile on his face, as though he had cracked the riddle that would lead him to the Holy Grail. Von Runyon indicated with a wave of his hand the three vehicles parked in the center of the street and the men dressed in black surrounding them. "So this is your secret celebrity. Was my guess correct?"

Peter sidestepped the question, answering only. "Whether correct or not, you apparently chose not to break the news."

SUNDAY

The smile remained on Jonathan Von Runyon's face. "I'm not into breaking news, Peter. I'm into journalism."

Peter sidestepped that comment too. "When did you figure it out?"

"Mass at St. Stan's. You know, Peter, I grew up on the East Side too."

Peter laughed. A slight break in security, but he hardly could have told Pope Tony not to attend Mass. "You realize, Jonathan, that if the news had leaked, Celebrity X would have chosen not to run today."

"I considered that, one reason why I sat on the story." Von Runyon paused. "You call him Celebrity X?"

Peter nodded to concede that true.

"Celebrity X? Delicious. Quite frankly, Peter, the story of how you kept secret the identity of your Celebrity X interests me most about his presence here today."

Peter stood silent, not yet sure whether he could trust the *Ledger* reporter. Of all the journalists who covered the Lake City Marathon, Jonathan Von Runyon irritated him the most.

Jonathan broke the silence, "I'd like to talk to your Celebrity X, if only for a few minutes."

Peter frowned: "I can't offer you an exclusive interview."

"You owe me, Peter."

"Is that a threat?"

"No, just a polite request."

"He has a marathon to run, Jonathan."

"That fact occurred to me, Peter."

Peter did not immediately respond. He could feel the grip of Jonathan Von Runyon's slimy hand on his most precious body parts. Would the *Ledger* reporter squeeze? *If the identity of Celebrity X were made public, would it really matter at this late point?*

Peter began, "I try to treat all members of the media equally."

"Like dirt—except when you need us."

Peter McDonald laughed. "Jonathan, you just hit on the very essence of public relations." Still, Peter knew that Von Runyon had done him a favor—a huge favor—by keeping his mouth shut. Would it hurt to throw the dog a bone? The race director turned toward the car containing Pope Tony. "He's probably nervous," said Peter, as much talking to himself as to the *Ledger* reporter. "Sitting in there waiting for the race to begin. Why don't I introduce you to him, Jonathan. He'd probably love the opportunity to talk—briefly—to someone from the old neighborhood."

MARATHON

00:15:00

Meghan Allison had been surprised by how few runners she saw
on the elevated train earlier that morning. She, Matt, Aaron and
Moira had been late leaving home. Her fault. They were out the
door, when Meg decided she needed one last trip to the toilet.

Matt had freaked out: "Honey, you're going to be late!"

"*Hon-eee*, do you want me to pee in my pants?"

At least they all had gotten seats on the train. Maybe everybody else entered in the Lake City Marathon worried more about arriving at the starting
line on time than she. Matt certainly did—and he was not even running! But
Meg had a bib number that permitted her entry into Start Corral A, the first
corral behind the elite runners. She had qualified for the corral based on having run a fast half marathon time earlier in the summer. Her brother Aaron
would be behind her in Start Corral B, based on his somewhat slower qualifying time in another half in Florida. There might be a thousand or more runners
vying for upfront positions in each corral, but so what? Like everybody else,
she wore a chip on one shoe. It would catch her correct time from start to
finish. Why rush to the start, when all it means is standing around much too
long in a crowded corral?

Or at least that's what she kept telling Matt. He appeared much more nervous than her, more nervous than her somewhat nervous brother, Aaron. Way
more nervous than her future sister-in-law Moira, who never had watched a
marathon before, so did not know what to expect. Matt had provided Moira
with a "Go Meg Go!" sign, promising that he would cue her when to raise it
overhead and scream like a banshee. Matt anticipated seeing his wife at least a
half dozen times along the course.

The two couples left for the El station near their apartment around 7:00, or
soon after. Meg did not even look at the clock, but she noticed Matt's panic
level rising to Red Alert, so finally had yielded to his request that they depart.
Then her toilet break. After that, they had spent another fifteen minutes or so
walking to the station and waiting for a train. It took somewhat less than that
time to reach downtown. Matt had scouted out what he called a secret toilet in
the underground pedestrian walkway that connected train station to the park.
"Better than standing in line outdoors," he insisted, and it had been, except
she only dribbled a bit. By the time they reached the starting line, only fifteen
minutes remained before the start of the race.

SUNDAY

00:15:00. 00:14:59. 00:14:58.

Walking past the front corral reserved for the elite athletes, Meg noticed only a few runners, none she knew. She did not spot Fiona Flynn, encountered running on the lake three days before. Presumably, most of the elites were waiting in some private area with their own toilets. She did not care. Meg did not regret turning down race director Peter McDonald's offer of a low number and access to the elite area. At the time, she did not consider herself worthy. More to the point, she did not want the added pressure that a low number and the perks accompanying it might present. She was free to fail. Passing the gate that allowed entry to the elite corral, she now wondered whether she should have said yes to McDonald. She quickly put that thought out of her mind and approached the gate allowing access to Start Corral A. Before entering she gave her brother Aaron one final hug. He promised to quickly catch her, so they could run together until he dropped out at 6 miles. She said she would go out slow allowing them to connect.

"Run on the left, so I'll have an easier time spotting you."

Meg promised she would.

"Good luck, Sis," Aaron said before continuing to Start Corral B.

Meg wore a singlet displaying, appropriately, the name "Fast Feet." It was the name and uniform of the running store for which she worked. Red. Easy for her support team to spot. On it was pinned her number, 1459, yellow, guaranteeing access to Start Corral A. Showing her number to the volunteer guarding the corral, Meg entered, but did not immediately go to stake out a position among the other runners. She sat down on a curb to conserve energy.

That lasted two minutes, then she popped up, feeling maybe she needed some warm-up. Since most of those in Start Corral A were at the front of the corral trying to edge as close to the elites as possible, that left an open area between them and Start Corral B. A wooden gate separated the two corrals, so runners could not move forward from one to the other, at least until the proper time. Like all the other fencing, it was draped with a Lake City Bank banner. Meg supposed the fence would be lifted or opened before the start of the race, but she was not sure how or when or if Aaron, could sneak forward to join her before the start. Maybe if she had read the instructions that came with her bib, she would know.

Meg started jogging, but went only three or four steps before coming to a halt. She was exhausted. She could not move, not even walk. She wondered what would happen if the race started and she was left standing like a pillar of salt with 50,000 runners forced to dodge around her while she slowly melted in humiliation. During her podiatric studies, Meg had run so few races—and specifically so few important races—that she honestly did not know.

324

MARATHON

Then she remembered how she had felt standing on the starting line her senior year in high school at the state cross-country championships, the race she had won, arguably the last good race she had run. Like today, she had been paralyzed by fear, certain that the gun would sound and she would be unable to lift her lead leg off the ground. But the gun had sounded, and the leg had lifted, then the second leg, and, all fears forgotten, she had run like a deer! Meg tried channeling memories of that single most important victory in her career. She thought of Mr. McAnally, her late coach from high school: *Mr. M, are you up there watching me? I don't care if I win. I don't care if I run a fast time. I just want to finish and not embarrass myself.*

She decided that she would dedicate today's race—win or lose, fast or slow—to the coach who had given Meg her start in running.

Meg started to jog again. Eight steps before she could go no further. *Good,* she thought, *I'm improving. I might make it across the line before those 50,000 runners trample me.* She wondered how much time remained to the start. They had just announced that fact over the loudspeaker but, spaced out, she had not heard. She could not look at her watch, because Meg had chosen not to wear a watch, not wanting to follow a set pace, especially not on a warm day. The announcer had just announced the start of the wheelchair race, with resulting cheers from the crowd. That must mean five minutes remain. Once more, Meg started to jog. Eleven steps, then near collapse.

00:05:00. 00:04:59. 00:04:58.

She moved again to the rear of Start Corral A, hoping that she might spot Aaron in the corral behind, still separated from her by the un-lifted gate. She could not see her brother. She could move backwards through the field, but that would be like trying to swim up Niagara Falls. The entire front row of Start Corral B seemed to be occupied by muscular men, taller than her, heavier than her, probably faster than her, frothing at the mouth, ready to shove and elbow her if she got in their way.

Instructions continued to alternate on the loudspeaker with music. Meghan failed to hear either. Playing now was *Summon the Heroes,* an anthem composed by John Williams for the 1996 Olympics in Atlanta. Meg failed to recognize it, or its significance. She had other things on her mind.

What if Aaron and I fail to connect? What if I start too slowly, and he passes without seeing me? What if I start too fast, and he fails to catch me?

She turned and almost bumped into another runner, also was jogging back and forth in the open area between Start Corrals A and B to warm up.

"Meghan?"

She was startled. *Do I know him?* The face looked familiar. Her mind churned trying to attach a name to the face. Someone she had fitted for shoes while working at Fast Feet?

SUNDAY

Sensing her puzzlement, the runner offered his name: "Bob Veldman."

Still no recognition. Neither the name nor the face.

"The 8-K," he offered.

"Oh."

"We ran together for most of the race."

"Oh!" She finally did remember.

At a local 8-K race in the spring, Meg and another runner—him apparently—had hooked up in the second mile, running together for the rest of the race, no words exchanged between them, she totally focused, him the same, mostly a half step behind, hanging onto her pace, but that was okay, because she used his presence to push herself to a fast time. They had shared water going through one aid station, but she had pulled away in the last half mile, surprising herself by finishing in third place.

She had waited at the end of the chute for her unintended pacing partner to emerge. They had hugged and thanked each other for the support. He seemed more excited by her success than she. Meg had introduced him to Matt, and he had left to find his wife. Veldman said he worked as an air traffic controller. Matt thought that interesting and wished later they had time to get to know each other, to share a beer or two at the post-race party. Their paths had not crossed since spring. Apparently he did not buy his running shoes at Fast Feet. Maybe he lived in the suburbs. And now, this chance meeting?

"I'm surprised you're not up with the elites."

"I'm not that fast."

"You could have fooled me last spring."

"I just want to finish."

He laughed: "I've heard that before."

Meg held up her wrist: "No, seriously. I'm not wearing a watch."

"And you've been injured all summer, and you've had to stay late at work, and you have a cold—no, the flu—I've heard all the excuses."

"How fast are you running?" Meg at least was curious about that.

Bob Veldman shrugged. "I trained to break 2:30. Eighty miles a week. A half dozen 20-milers. But there's *no* way I'm running that fast in this heat. So maybe I'll drop out and run New York in another three or four weeks."

Smart man, Meg thought, but before she could voice that thought, the runners began to move forward. With only a few minutes to go until the start, the gates were being lifted one at a time, allowing the runners to fill the empty spaces separating corrals. Maybe now was the time to look for Aaron.

"C'mon," said her new friend, placing a hand on Meg's back to gently push her forward. "We're going to get swallowed by Corral B if we don't move quickly." The fence separating them from that corral had not yet been lifted, but it would in a few seconds.

She hesitated. "But...."

"C'mon, Meghan," Veldman urged. "You're too fast to stand this far in the back of the corral."

He pushed her forward, still gently. Meg decided not to resist. "Fast lady!" he shouted, embarrassing her. "Fast lady!"

Incredibly, as though Moses had pounded his staff on the ground commanding the Red Sea to part, runners who had been waiting for a half hour or more, moved aside.

"How fast?" one grumbled.

"Sub-three," Veldman announced.

"Wow!"

"Maybe faster than that: 2:50? 2:40? 2:30? Faster than Aba!"

"No, really...." protested Meg.

"Third at the 8-K last spring, Let this woman through."

Meg thought she would melt into the pavement, but she allowed herself to be pressed forward.

"I remember her," said one of the runners moving to let Meg pass. "Hey, what's your name?"

"Meg Allison."

"Didn't I buy a pair of shoes from you?"

Oh my God, thought Meg Allison.

"I'll look for you in the results. Hey, let this woman through!"

The countdown clock continued to tick off the few remaining seconds before the start of the race.

00:00:02. 00:00:01. 00:00:00.

The horn sounded. The clock reversed itself, displaying now the time since the start of the race:

00:00:00. 00:00:01. 00:00:02.

The Lake City Marathon had begun.

00:00:00

The Lake City Marathon has begun," announced Mark Mallon, anchorman for the TV3 telecast. After that opening comment, Mallon fell silent, knowing that often pictures are better than words. As a sports broadcaster, Mallon felt that sometimes the worst sin you can commit was talking too much. There are times when it is best to sit back and watch what the viewers are watching, at least until you have some important titbit to offer: a fact or comment that will enhance their viewing pleasure.

The various clocks associated with the race instantly shifted from counting the time remaining *to* the race to counting the time *in* the race.

0:00:00. 0:00:01. 0:00:02.

The color commentators sitting on each side of Mallon—Carolynne Vickers and Timothy Rainboldt, professionals both of them—saw no reason to fill the void. They would talk when Mallon wanted them to talk. Unless one or the other had something profound or important to add to the commentary, the pair would allow Mallon to dictate the pace of the telecast. All three, however, would take their cues from Tom Schorr in the control trailer nearby. As the marathon began, Schorr stood, arms folded, in a room that resembled the cockpit of the Starship Enterprise. The trailer was crammed with electronic equipment and operatives who sat with hands on switches and levers. They stared at more than two dozen wall monitors, each with a different image from which Schorr could choose for his live feed.

"Hold on Camera 1," said Schorr, speaking to an operative seated in front of him. "Widen."

The live feed being shown two seconds into the race to viewers all over Lake City and to selected markets throughout the United States plus to several countries around the world, including Japan, showed the elite runners sprinting away from the line. Many of those in the front row, including Joseph Nduku, were Africans, a few Europeans and Asians, several from Mexico and other countries in Latin America, a trio of Brazilians, one runner from Australia. No American males were expected to finish anywhere in the top ten, except for one naturalized citizen, born in South Africa.

"Sound up," Schorr addressed another operative. "I want to hear the roar of the crowd."

Two seconds into the race, no women appeared on the Camera 1 view of those leading. Not Fiona Flynn. Not Tatanya Henry. Not Toshi Yamota. Each of the three female favorites had started the race lined up beside each other in the front row, several dozen other fast women, including Katie Hyang of the Northland Racing Team, clustered nearby, but once the horn sounded the top women instantly disappeared from sight, lost among a sea of swifter men. Approximately two seconds into the race, Meghan Allison crossed the starting mat, which instantly registered the moment her shoe, chip attached, touched the mat, recording that touch within a hundredth of a second, but no recognizable image of Meg appeared on any of the several dozen screens in the TV3 control room. For the time being, her presence would remain a mystery.

0:00:03. 0:00:04. 0:00:05.

"Sound down," said Schorr. "Mark, set the scene."

MARATHON

"Fifty-thousand runners. Twenty-six miles and 385 yards. The fastest runners in the world, off and running through the streets of Lake City."

"Camera 2," said Schorr. The live feed shifted to a shot of the lead runners, but this time from a side angle as seen from a camera held by a cameraman on the back of a motorcycle.

On the set, Mallon turned toward Timothy Raintoldt, offering him permission to talk. "The fastest runners in the world, Mark," Timothy began, "and the Kenyan runners already have moved to the front. Kenyatta Kemai. The rabbit, Moses Abraham. I don't yet see Joseph Nduku, but he may not feel any need for a fast start—particularly on a warm day.'

"Camera 4," said Schorr, skipping past Camera 3, which was on another motorcycle also with the lead runners. Once the pack spread, it would drop back to cover the lead women. Camera 4 was mounted on a bridge above the course and showed a wide-angle view from ahead of the entire 50,000-runner field, slowly beginning to move across the line.

Carolynne Vickers spoke: "That *is* a good strategy, Timothy, and as we look at the rest of the runners crossing the line—those we might impolitely call the 'non-elite'—let's hope they adopt a similar strategy."

Mallon smoothly continued the commentary: "Because it is hot. Too hot! I can't tell you *how* hot, because our TV3 weatherman Vaughn Johnson is somewhere out there in that sea of humanity."

Timothy interrupted him: "Seventy-nine degrees, Mark, and sure to rise in the next several hours."

The anchorman smiled, showing no irritation at the interruption. He had worked with the two commentators before and enjoyed the back-and-forth between them, each bringing a different dimension to the telecast. "Always quick with a statistic, Timothy, and we'll be talking to Vaughn by cell phone later in the race, but in the meantime, look at all those runners. It's amazing!"

Mallon fell silent, again allowing the picture to speak for itself. The screen was filled with runners, all dressed differently, many dressed in bright colors, hoping it would help friends and relatives along the course spot them. The appearance was that of a pointillist painting, 50,000 points of light. But with background music supplied by Bruce Springsteen, *Born to Run*. Some of the runners shed garments worn to the starting line, throwing them joyously overhead or sideways toward the gutters.

The highway's jammed with broken heroes
On a last chance power drive
Everybody's out on the run tonight,
But there's no place left to hide.

"Sound up," said Schorr. The cheers had ceased as each of the runners crossing the line directed his or her attention to the task at hand, shifting from standing to walking to running, cautiously at first because of the dangers caused by being packed closely together. As they crossed the line they rocked to Springsteen's music.

Some day, girl, I don't know when,
We're gonna get to that place
Where we really want to go,

"Cue Christine, Mark," said Schorr.

Mallon obeyed. "Christine Ferrara is standing by the starting line. What's the view like down there, Christine?"

"As soon as the horn sounded, the lead runners exploded off the line, and if you're a Bruce Springsteen fan like me, you *know* they were 'born to run.' You mentioned Joseph Nduku, and despite his being defending champion, Nduku positioned himself in the second row and seemed to be in no hurry to rush to the front, Mark."

"Smart move, Christine."

"Among the women, Tatanya Henry, Toshi Yamota and Fiona Flynn were standing right in front of me on the left side of the line. They all got off to a good start, but a good start on a day like today may have been the more conservative one by Nduku...."

"...Whoops, somebody just fell!"

"Two minutes to commercial," said Schorr.

"Watch out for yourself, Christine," said Mallon, "and whatever you do, don't get in the way of the runners. From what you tell us, it's a madhouse down there."

"Camera 1," said Schorr.

Mallon continued: "It will take nearly a half hour for all 50,000 runners to cross the line and perhaps that long or longer before we begin to get a picture of who the likely winners might be."

And we'll walk in the sun,
But till then, tramps like us, baby, we were born to run!

00:00:30

Tripped, Aaron Kennedy felt himself pitch forward and lifted his arms to break the fall. He hit the pavement—hard! *"Uhhhhh,"* Aaron grunted as forearms, hip, thigh, knee, ankle, scraped across the unyielding concrete. *Ouch*, that hurt, and there would be blood and bruises, but it could have been worse. Instinctively, Aaron had rolled while falling, a protective movement to soften the fall he had learned as a high school wrestler.

Well, at least something I learned in high school stuck.

Meghan Allison's older brother was not immediately certain why he had tripped. Only later would Aaron realize that in the excitement of the start, someone—wait, make that some *idiot*—had discarded a T-shirt by throwing it joyously into the air, but what goes up, comes down, and the T-shirt lurked like a booby trap on the pavement when he reached that point on the course. Aaron Kennedy stepped on it *seconds* after he crossed the timing mats on the starting line. *Seconds!* Only seconds after the chip on his shoe precisely had recorded his start to the one-hundredth of a second. A half minute maybe after the horn sounded! Starting in Corral B, it had taken him somewhat less than that to reach and cross the line. Then, *Whoomp!*

00:00:30. 00:00:31. 00:00:32.

Aaron had not seen the treacherous T-shirt, because he was running heads-up up trying to spot Sister Meg. He had Sis in sight just before the start, then lost her. Because of the crowds, he had failed to push to the front of Starting Corral B, but, looking over the heads of other runners, he had spotted Meg warming up at the rear of Starting Corral A. Aaron had shouted her name, but with the loudspeaker blaring, Meg had not heard. After the gate between the two corrals lifted, allowing the runners in B to merge with those in A, he tried to move forward as fast as possible.

No luck. Everybody else had the same idea, crowding as close to the line as possible, as though that somehow might allow them to run a faster time.

When the horn sounded and everybody started to move, Aaron thought he saw Meg's blonde ponytail bobbing in the sea of heads before him. Whether her or not, Aaron figured that if he just relaxed and stayed on the left, he should be able to make contact with Little Sis. A half minute behind? He could make that up in the first mile. His assignment for the half dozen miles he planned to run was to hold Meg to a pace of 6:00-per-mile, or slower. Meg did not want to go out too fast, she had warned. *Six minutes per mile?* To him, that seemed like warp speed. Was his little sister really in that good shape? When they rode the elevated train earlier, she had told him that if she was running too fast, grab hold of her pony tail and tug her backwards.

Then he tripped. For an instant lying on the ground, Aaron did not move, too stunned to do so. Then he felt someone's hand reach under his left armpit and start tugging. "Get up! Get up!" shouted his rescuer. A second runner snuck a hand under his other armpit, and like a fish being pulled from the depths of the ocean, Aaron found himself being scooped off the pavement and placed on his feet in a running position.

SUNDAY

"Are you okay?"

"Yeah"

"I hate those stupid fools who throw their shirts in the air."

"Tell me about it."

"Sorry to be rough," said the first runner, "but if you hadn't moved, there would have been 100,000 footprints on the back of your singlet."

"Yeah," said the second, "with you lying in the morgue."

"Thanks," Aaron mumbled, then turned to offer thanks to the first runner, except he was gone, moving rapidly away. The first runner wore the number 3:00 on the back of his shirt, indicating a desire to achieve that finishing time. But that was slower than Meg's projected pace, much slower! Aaron tried to keep pace with his rescuers and the other runners passing, but he could not. His knee was bloody. So was his elbow. And he could no longer see his sister's blonde ponytail bobbing before him.

With her starting-line segment done, Christine climbed into the golf cart and told the driver: "Let's roll."

"Hang on," said the driver, whose name was Jake, one of director Tom Schorr's nephews, a high school senior, chosen, Tom claimed, because of his heavy left foot. "Jake's already leading the family in speeding tickets."

"Thanks, Tom. You're trusting my life to a maniac."

"He's family, Christine. This is Lake City. Nepotism prevails."

Once clear of the crowd, Jake quickly had the golf cart at full speed, which was only 15 mph going up the bridge over the railroad tracks, considerably faster going down. At Jefferson Avenue, Jake slalomed past a pair of sawhorses blocking traffic. *Whoah! Where's the seat belt on this vehicle?* The light was green, although Christine suspected it would have made little difference to Jake. No traffic fortunately. They tore down the middle of the street.

Calculating earlier, Christine figured it would take the front runners somewhere around eight or nine minutes to reach the aid station. *Three minutes gone now in the race,* she noted, looking at the watch she had started when the horn sounded. Only two blocks now separated them from that point on the course. It would be tight, but Jake seemed to be doing his job.

00:03:00. 00:03:01. 00:03:02.

A cyclist pulled up beside them. "Going my way?" the cyclist asked.

Christine looked at him. The cyclist seemed familiar. *Where have I seen him before? Have we met?* The cyclist wore black cycling pants and a yellow shirt with black and red vertical stripes. Emblazoned in front of the shirt in red was "Northland," beneath it in smaller letters, "Racing Team."

"You're Steve Holland."

"Guilty."

332

MARATHON

The Northland coach had not attended any of the press conferences, but she recognized him from an article by Don Geoffrey several months earlier in *Running Magazine*. Christine had done her homework. Three runners from the Northland Racing Team were running the race. Two guys and a gal. Except the guys were—what did they call them?—rabbits. Twins, and they were planning to pace Aba to a world record, except she was pregnant. So what do rabbits do when they have nobody chasing their fuzzy tails? She would need to ask, except the cyclist had started to pull away. Christine shouted after Holland: "If you're going to the aid station, I'd like to talk to you on camera!"

Holland slowed briefly, turned and shouted to Christine, "See you there."

Foolish! Foolish! Foolish! As he passed the 1-mile mark at the back of the lead pack, "foolish" best described how Joseph Nduku felt. He had run the first mile in 4:47, and he was probably a second or two behind the leaders, his countrymen, Moses Abraham and Kenyatta Kemai.

00:04:47. 00 04:48. 00:04:49.

Abraham had come to Lake City as a rabbit, but they had the day off. Joseph believed that Moses Abraham should have been sitting back in the hotel sipping an iced tea and watching the Cartoon Network. And regardless of what prompted Moses to bolt into the lead, what was Kenyatta Kemai thinking by accompanying him, the two Kenyans shoulder to shoulder at the front of the pack? And everybody else had played along. Without counting, there must be fifteen to twenty foolish souls, running like it was 50 degrees, and we had a tailwind at our back on a downhill course.

Of course, I am one of those foolish souls, so I can't complain.

Joseph decided that he would play along with this strategy for one more mile, no more, then let Abraham and Kemai go—planning to catch them later. *Hoping* to catch them later.

The leaders came to the first turn on the course, left off Columbia Drive and west onto a cross street, Garfield Avenue. Running two strides behind the pack, Joseph had no one pressing him from either side. He focused intently on cutting the turn as tightly as possible, wasting not a step, not a half step, not an inch. Who knew at the end of the race whether or not he would need that inch saved in the early miles?

The move brought him closer to the other runners in the pack, some of them forced to slow slightly to avoid bumping shoulders. Joseph Nduku shifted his pace almost imperceptibly to preserve the gap between him and the front pack, allowing himself within the next block of running to slide backwards off that pack a stride, then another stride. They approached an underpass beneath Jefferson Avenue. It would be dark beneath the underpass, difficult seeing as their eyes adjusted from bright sunlight to dark shadows. He did not want to twist an ankle stepping in a pothole that he failed to see.

Joseph shifted several body widths to the right, just enough so he had a clear line of sight looking a block ahead. Clear of the underpass, he raised his eyes and aimed toward the next left turn to be executed in two more blocks onto Lake Street. Another saved stride, or saved half stride, or saved inch. Joseph Nduku believed that to succeed in the marathon, he needed to concentrate his mind on every step taken.

That was the route to success.

00:07:00

Hang on, Dennis," Peter warned the Shelaghi executive manager as the press truck on which they were riding approached another left turn, one that would bring them back through downtown, several blocks west of the park where the Lake Shore Marathon had begun seven minutes before. A digital clock on the roof of the TV3 truck between the press truck and the lead pack indicated the running time:

00:07:00. 00: 07:01. 00:07:02.

"Grab the railing," Peter shouted, but Dennis Lahey already had figured that out on the first turn, where he briefly had lost his balance. Peter needed to grab Lahey's shoulder to steady him, otherwise he might have gone down. Dennis was not mad; he came up laughing:

"Peter, when I signed up, I didn't realize you were asking me to ride a roller coaster."

As they swung through the second left-hand turn, the Shelaghi executive handled it better. The secret, he decided, was to stand legs wide, knees slightly bent, and hold onto something solid. Fortunately, the press truck— open air with three separate levels like grandstands—had railings built into each of those levels so riders could cling to them. The ride was turning out to be a buzz. The Shelaghi executive was glad he had accepted Peter's offer, issued yesterday, to ride the press truck rather than hang around the V.I.P. Tent. Nothing to do there but eat omelets, drink Mimosas and watch the race on television. This was more like Irish sports back home.

Peter too was pleased that the Shelaghi executive had accepted his invitation, even though it had been delivered with a caveat. The race director told Lahey that he probably would see more of the race if he watched on TV. Although it rode ahead of the runners, the so-called press truck was separated from those runners, the stars of the show, by a truck carrying the main TV camera that sometimes blocked viewing. Various other vehicles — cars, trucks, motorcycles — sometimes filled the space between press truck and runners. Occasionally the press truck drifted back to within 20 or 30 yards of the runners, but then pulled ahead to a position further in front. Only a handful of photographers sat on the tailgate snapping pictures of the lead pack. And only a few reporters rode the truck. Jonathan Von Runyon of the *Lake City Ledger* was not one of them, feeling he could see more of the race from the media center in the Hilliard, which offered twin feeds of the men's and women's races. That plus splits and statistics that made it easier to meet deadlines.

Peter, however, felt viewing the race from the press truck provided the opportunity to capture the "feel" of the marathon: to see spectators lining the course as well as runners. In many respects the spectators *were* potential customers for Shelaghi. He hoped Dennis Lahey understood that.

Compared to the impressive numbers of people at the start, fewer spectators lined the course at least in the first few miles. Lahey could see that most of the viewing positions along the curb were occupied, but not three and four deep as he had expected based on claims that a million people watched the marathon. Peter had explained why. Relatively few people lived in and around downtown compared to the neighborhoods they would soon pass through. And not all spectators had yet claimed the prime viewing positions. They were less interested in seeing the front runners than in seeing those trailing far behind, many of them their friends, relatives and neighbors.

"Is the one million estimate accurate?" Lahey asked.

The race director offered an honest answer: "Reporters ask for a figure. The police offer us one. We tell the reporters. They print what we say. But it's not a rock concert. We don't sell tickets, so can't count who comes."

"Best free show in town, I would say."

"We think so, Dennis. But another factor complicating crowd estimates is that the person you see cheering by the course near 2 miles might appear again at 4 miles and at 10 miles and at 20."

"They can intersect the marathon that easily?

"It's not easy. The most active spectators need to do some running as the course cuts back and forth through downtown. Or they can jump on an elevated train and shift between the northern or southern ends in five or ten minutes. We even give them maps telling them how to do that."

"Maps with, I hope, the Lake City Bank logo on it?"

"You're onto me, Dennis."

The Shelaghi executive manager's eyes sparkled. The press truck rumbled once more across a bridge crossing the Des Plaines River, its tires humming on the steel grill. The lead runners shifted to where a red carpet had been laid to protect their lightly shod feet from the grill's rough edges.

Coming into downtown, the lead pack consisted of nearly two dozen tightly packed runners with other packs forming behind. The pace was fast: insanely fast, Peter thought. Much too early to determine who might emerge as winner in 24 more miles. Most of those on the press truck had not noticed defending champion Joseph Nduku sliding off the back of the pack. Peter had. After the last corner, Peter watched runners coming around the turn through a pair of binoculars and discovered that Nduku was two strides back. He could see daylight between the pack and Nduku. Peter did not waste time speculating on what that meant. Instead, he turned and looked ahead on the course.

"Look forward, Dennis. We're coming into an aid station."

Dennis Lahey had not seen an aid station before. There was row after row of tables and row after row of cups on those tables and more than a hundred volunteers awaiting the horde of runners yet to arrive. Two full blocks of tables and cups on both sides of the street. As the press truck passed, the volunteers started to cheer, aware that their moment of glory was about to begin. Lahey never had been cheered before. And it almost brought tears to his eyes.

They passed a woman holding a *Go, Meg, Go!* sign.

"That's a good Irish name," remarked the bank executive.

As the press truck slid past the tables of E.R.G. and water, Peter spotted aid station manager Harry Chandler, who saluted him as though he were a general passing in review. Peter saluted back at the Fast Feet store owner. At the end of the tables, there stood Christine Ferrara. Peter waved at Christine, but if she saw, she offered no response. Microphone in hand, the TV3 reporter seemed to be getting ready to interview somebody. The press truck, elite runners trailing, had passed through the aid station before Peter realized the interviewee was Steve Holland, coach of the Northland Racing Team.

How did Christine ever connect with him? Peter wondered. The Northland coach was not even at any of the press conferences this week. *Remarkable woman,* he decided.

"Cut to Christine," said Tom Schorr from the control room.

Mark Mallon cued her: "Christine Ferrara is standing by on the course. Where are you, Christine?"

"I'm at the first aid station, Mark."

"First aid, as in Red Cross, Christine?"

"First aid as in water and E.R.G. The first station on the course where marathoners can stop to drink—and they need it today, Mark!"

"How did you get there so fast? We just saw you at the starting line." Mallon knew how Christine had gotten from Point A to Point B, nearly two miles into the course, but he wanted the viewers to know.

"I have a golf cart, but no clubs if you're worried about my plans this morning. I'm standing here at the first aid station—*initial* aid station, if you please—and the lead runners have just arrived, Mark."

Christine paused. Her cameraman Edmund had positioned his camera to capture Christine in the foreground, the passing runners in the background. Moses Abraham and Kenyatta Kemai remained in front, Joseph Nduku in back, the defending champion having allowed the gap to widen further between him and the leaders. Christine made no effort to identify the runners. The talent back in the studio could do that, as Schorr had pointed out to her at the production meeting. She allowed them to pass, then turned instead to a man with a bike standing beside her. Edmund adjusted his shot to include interviewer and interviewee.

"I'm here with Steve Holland, coach of the Northland Racing Team, who is chasing his runners by bike. But what's the deal, Steve? It's hot, and I didn't see any of the lead runners take any water.'

"Some did," Holland claimed. The TV3 reporter had grabbed the Northland coach almost the moment she arrived at the aid station. Holland was torn between cheering his runners and promoting his team, but he figured he could waste a few minutes on public relations before leapfrogging to the next vantage point. He told Christine, she could have sixty seconds of his time, no more. She agreed, since that was all she wanted anyway.

Holland continued: "The aid station is two blocks long, so they could have taken water earlier. Joseph Nduku did grab a couple of cups, emptying them over his head."

"To cool himself off?"

"Correct," said Holland, then interrupted himself. "Wait, here come two of my runners." The Northland coach turned to cheer Kyle and Wesley Fowler as they passed. They waved, broad smiles on their faces as though out for a Sunday stroll. Holland returned his attention to the interview, asking, "Sorry about that. Where were we?"

"Fluids," prompted Christine.

Watching from the control trailer, Schorr could not help but be amused by the juxtaposition between talk and action. *Nice touch,* he thought.

Holland continued: "The answer to your question is that the elite runners have separate tables for their fluids. They're in the middle of the street with plastic bottles placed on the table for them."

"Hey that's not fair, Steve. I paid my $110 entry fee, and I want some special attention. Why can't I get someone to hand me a plastic bottle?"

SUNDAY

The TV reporter was playing Devil's Advocate, which Holland recognized. "Actually, nobody can hand an elite runner a bottle. It's against the rules to accept assistance from people standing on the sidelines."

"I didn't know that." Actually, Christine Ferrara did know that to be the rule, but she preferred having Holland offer an explanation, which he did including the fact that although he was riding the course by bicycle, if he wanted to cheer any of the runners he coached—including the two just passed and another fast woman following—he would need to get off the bicycle to do so, and, "I definitely cannot ride beside my runners offering advice." As they talked, the top women passed, Tatanya Henry in the lead, shadowed by Toshi Yamota and a half dozen others, although several already seemed to be struggling to stay close to the Russian.

"There go the top women," commented Christine, pausing briefly to allow them to be seen over her shoulder. Christine noticed that Fiona Flynn was not among the top females, but it was not her job to comment on that fact.

"Thank you, Steve. Go chase your runners, so they don't get lost."

The Northland coach moved several steps away. Another Northland runner appeared, easily identifiable by her bright, yellow shirt. "Go, Katie!" Holland cheered, offering several more words of encouragement before climbing back on his bike. He departed, pedaling hard. Having scouted the course, he knew he could intersect the trio at another point as the course turned back north: a mile of running for them, three blocks of riding for him.

Christine Ferrara ended the interview by saying to Mallon that she was going to hop in her golf cart and see if she could follow Holland around the course as the Lake City Marathon continued.

"Grab a cup of water before you go, Christine, and we'll talk to you later," announced Mallon. "The Lake City Marathon continues with more than a dozen runners in the lead. We'll be back right after this message." A commercial for a soon-to-appear-in-theatres film filled the screen, at least as seen by viewers at home. The feed seen by those watching from the control room and in the media room at the Hilliard remained that of runners at the front of the race. Joseph Nduku seemed to have dropped further behind.

"Good segment, Christine," said Schorr from the control trailer. "Where did you find that coach?" But the director did not expect an answer, nor did Christine respond, because Schorr began signaling a switch in the main feed: "Camera 3. Mark. We'll come out of the commercial break with the lead women. C.V., get ready to I.D. those in front. We'll help you with an insert of the top five as soon they pass the 2-mile mark."

Meghan Allison was not among that top five. Nor in the top ten. In fact, the podiatrist-turned-road-runner did not know what place she occupied, and did

338

not care. She purposely had not looked at the digital clock at the 1-mile mark, passed several minutes before. She wondered how come Brother Aaron had not caught her, but only for a second, because she had picked up another pacer. Bob Veldman, the runner who pushed her to the front of Start Corral A, was running a half step behind, hanging onto her pace, drafting, considered unfriendly by some runners, except it was okay with Meg, because he had asked permission, which she had granted as long as he promised not to talk to her or offer any splits. "I do *not* want to know how fast or slow we're running," she said, tapping him on the shoulder to emphasize that point. The air traffic controller agreed to those terms.

Approaching the aid station, she spotted Moira standing with her *Go, Meg, Go!* sign, pumping it up and down, shouting, repeating the words on the sign. Standing beside Moira was Matt, also shouting, jumping up and down like a cheerleader at a Northern Indiana football game. Meg waved but did not slow down. She was in what Matt liked to describe as her "Deer Mode," running as effortlessly as a deer bounding through the forest.

"Oh-my-gosh," said Matt after his wife passed.

"What's wrong?" Moira wanted to know.

"I can't believe she's running this fast."

"How fast is she running?"

"I honestly do not know." Not near a mile marker, Matt had no way of judging his wife's exact pace, but he told Moira, "She is moving *very* fast."

"Where's Aaron?"

"I don't see him."

Meg swept past the E.R.G. tables without stopping. Her stomach often became upset if she took too much sports drink, so she would sip some at later aid stations, but not now. Reaching the water tables, she grabbed a cup, took little more than a sip, then poured the rest down the back of her singlet. Cold, it chilled her for a few seconds, no more.

At the end of the tables, Meg spotted Harry Chandler. "Hey, boss!" she shouted in passing.

Chandler, assisting volunteers, had not seen his employee approach. Her appearance startled him, but he reacted quickly: "Go Meghan!" Chandler immediately thought: *Meg's started way too fast. She's going to crash!*

"There he is!" shouted Moira.

"Where?"

"Coming right now."

"Oh-my-gosh. He's all bloody." Matt stepped off the sidewalk and onto the street so his brother-in-law could see him. "Aaron, what happened?"

Meghan's brother slowed slightly and moved toward the sidewalk. "I fell. Where's Meg?"

"She just passed a minute or so ago."

"I'll catch her," said Aaron, grabbing a cup of E.R.G. before moving back into the center of the street.

Watching as Aaron limped away and remembering how fast Meg had been running, Matt thought: *There is no way that is going to happen.* "Grab your sign," he told Moira. "Let's try to intersect them at the next side street."

As more and more runners appeared, the press truck continued in front of the lead runners, turning right several blocks past the aid station, turning right again several blocks further to head north away from downtown.

00:10:57. 00:10:58. 00:10:59.

Peter McDonald's cell phone rang. He glanced at the caller-ID, saw it was Tom Schorr, and knew immediately why the TV director had called. Peter smiled at Dennis Lahey and said, "This will be fun."

Fun? wondered Lahey.

Peter pushed the green button on his cell phone. "I was expecting your call," he said without waiting for the caller to introduce himself. Peter spoke no more, content to just listen to what the caller had to say.

Watching Peter listen silently, Lahey could not avoid wondering what the hell was being said. The caller apparently was angry, talking loudly so the Shelaghi manager almost could hear the one-way conversation, though not quite. Yet Peter continued to smile, a cat-that-ate-the-canary smile. The angry shouts ceased. Lahey imagined a phone being slammed down at the other end, although you do not slam down cell phones as you might phones with ordinary receivers. *What's that all about?* The race director did not seem perturbed as he replaced the cell phone in its belt holder.

Peter continued to smile, finally saying: "He's on the course!"

This puzzled Dennis Lahey even more: "Who's on the course?"

00:11:00

Leonard Hand was stunned as he reached the starting line and discovered who was about to join his pacing team. Peter McDonald had warned Lenny yesterday to expect someone well known, but he had not offered that individual's name, nor his code name, Celebrity X.

"Naní?" Lenny had probed. "You must mean Naní."

MARATHON

"No, not Naní."

"Then Aba?" continued Lenny, suggesting another female celebrity best known by her short, first name.

"Not Aba. Not Naní. Not even close," teased Peter. "This is not a crossword puzzle, Lenny."

And it was true that Naní and Aba had chosen to run with the 4:00 team, as had a third celebrity, Don Geoffrey, the Turtle. But that trio had arrived without fanfare, each to be greeted with delight by team members though they were apparently not *the* celebrity about whom Peter had warned.

So the pacing team leader stopped guessing, accepting Peter's recommendation to wait until this most famous celebrity emerged from the crowd at the starting line and joined his team as it shifted from walking to running mode. Now that the moment of truth had arrived, Lenny was stunned at the identity of the man called Celebrity X.

He gasped: "Oh, my God!"

"No, just one of His servants," laughed John Anthony Molina, offering a hand in greeting as he stepped onto the course. Unless you looked closely, you might not have realized he was someone famous. Pope Tony was dressed blandly in brown shorts and white singlet with "Carmel" (also in brown) written across the front, the uniform he had worn as a member of that school's cross-country team. Carefully preserved in a box in the attic by his mother, it smelled of mothballs, but Tony would not criticize his mother's squirrel-like habits. He told her he could think of no more significant uniform to wear.

"Your father loved how you looked in your uniform."

"I know, Ma."

Tony wore on his singlet number 91, it too having a special significance.

As the 4:00 pacing team moved across the timing mats, the overhead clock indicated that nearly eleven minutes had elapsed since the start of the marathon. The lead men were well beyond 2 miles; the lead women just reaching that point on the course. It would be another twenty minutes or more before the entire field of 50,000 runners cleared the starting area.

00:11:00. 00:11:01. 00:11:02.

Pope Tony fell in step with the pace team leader, who continued to run with the 4:00 sign held overhead to make it easier for team members to spot and stay near him. Lenny expected to lose 30 to 60 seconds per mile off perfect pace for the first few miles because of the crowd. That was acceptable, and planned. By starting slow, runners under his command would preserve glycogen, permitting a reservoir of this most efficient fuel for the final miles. Once the crowds thinned, he would ever so gradually increase the pace to recover lost time. Lenny expected to reach the half marathon mark in two hours and would be disappointed if he missed that goal by more than a few seconds.

341

SUNDAY

Pope Tony's two bodyguards, Angelo and Mario, moved into positions one step behind the man they were assigned to protect, one on each side. They were dressed anonymously, singlets bearing the crests of Italian soccer teams. Tony introduced Angelo and Mario without disclosing their role as bodyguards. Lenny instinctively understood the purpose of the pair and wondered whether other bodyguards were operating nearby. He decided not to ask. He understood now why Peter had been wary about offering information about this most-famous celebrity.

Was he in danger running next to Pope Tony? In these troubled times, he suspected the Roman Catholic Church's number one prelate was not universally loved. He could be a target for any number of terrorist groups. Maybe, but Lenny pushed negative thoughts out of his mind.

But Leonard Hand was a man of precision, and one thing worried him most about the man who would accompany his pacing team for the next 26 miles 385 yards: *What should I call him?*

Lenny voiced that thought.

The question amused Pope Tony. People did worry about etiquette. He responded with a smile: "If you were visiting me in the Vatican, protocol certainly would require your addressing me as, 'Your Holiness.' That's a bit stiff. Here on the marathon course, 'Tony' works quite well."

Near the gate where Pope Tony accessed the starting area stood Jonathan Von Runyon, a smile of satisfaction upon his face. Two of Peter McDonald's interns were guarding the gate. They had just informed several surprised reporters that they would *not* be permitted entry until after the 4-hour pacing group, including Pope Tony, had cleared the line. Observing, Von Runyon chuckled, quietly, so none around could hear. He had what he needed. He had scored a scoop, a big scoop, a very big scoop. The moment Pope Tony crossed the starting line, the reporter punched "submit" on his handheld device, sending his previously written story about the pope running the marathon to the *Lake City Ledger's* Web site. Von Runyon knew that within seconds after his story appeared on *lakecityledger.com*, it would also post as a link on Google News and other Internet content news providers. Von Runyon's story about Celebrity X was being read at this instant by people all over the world.

Von Runyon considered himself a print journalist. Usually he scorned the instant reporting and gossip journalism that passes for news these days. But he conceded there sometimes were advantages to being instant on the Internet. Jonathan Von Runyon returned the handheld device to his shoulder bag and headed toward the Hilliard.

The lead runners, both men and women, had passed the 2-mile mark by now. He would catch up with that story after he reached the media center.

And update his news-breaking story, adding some quotes from Pope Tony, offered during the several minutes they had chatted in the back of his car. The pope had been more than gracious, particularly when he learned the reporter came from the East Side and had spotted him at 4:00 Mass. "Perhaps I should have worn a mask," joked Pope Tony, then explained that if Von Runyon had broken the story, it would have made it impossible for him to run.

"Impossible?" asked Von Runyon.

"Neither Peter nor I wanted to turn my running the marathon into some public relations stunt."

The *Ledger* reporter nodded. If Tiger Woods ever decided to run a marathon, he certainly would do the same.

Continuing to walk toward the Hilliard, the *Ledger* reporter congratulated himself for making the right choice when it came to holding the story. He also decided that covering the marathon today might be more fun than expected. His next round of golf could wait.

The word spread. Not as might a wildfire. Gradually. From runner to runner, within the field of the Lake City Marathon.

"Hey, the pope's running!"

"The who?"

"The pope!"

"You mean..."

"Yeah, Pope Tony."

"Are you serious?"

"Check it out. He's running right in front of us."

"Holy cow!"

"Holy pope."

"He grew up in Lake City, didn't he?"

"Right."

"I didn't even know he was a runner."

"He is now."

Runner told runner. And those carrying cell phones began calling and text-messaging friends to spread the news. A few spectators in the first few hundred yards noticed Pope Tony passing and recognized him quickly, but then Tony moved toward the middle of the road and became less easy to find in the crowd of runners surrounding him. At first, Mario and Angelo remained nervous. In other areas of the world, they had witnessed how not only members of the Roman Catholic Church, but people of all religious faiths had been drawn to their spiritual leader. He *was* the world's most famous celebrity, all those Hollywood movie stars not withstanding. The common people wanted to see him, to touch him, to hear his word. This could prove dangerous, the bodyguards knew, not because of people wanting to *harm* Pope Tony, but of people wanting to *love* him. He could fall victim to their love. The greatest danger was to those drawn to him, the admiring masses. People sometimes got trampled in crowds. It happened at soccer matches. For that reason, the pope's appearances in public had to carefully be controlled for the safety of those around him as much as for the safety of Pope Tony himself.

But it was *straordinario*, the two bodyguards eventually commented to each other. The runners around Tony allowed him his space. Whether instinctively or not, they realized that in starting this marathon, he had accepted the same challenge as they: not merely running 26 miles 385 yards, but training to cover that distance with some level of comfort. They smiled at him. They shouted encouragement at him. But over the next several miles as those in the 4:00 pacing team and those around the 4:00 pacing team reacted to the pope's presence, they did not reach out to touch him, unless he reached back to touch them. In any normal appearance by Pope John Anthony Molina, he would greet the tens of thousands his presence attracted on an altar or on a platform or on a balcony so everybody could see him, his words magnified by loudspeakers so all could hear, but separated from the masses by guards and often bulletproof glass for his protection. In the Lake City Marathon, he was not above the masses, he was part of that mass, floating as might *una barca*, a boat cast adrift in a river, a wide river, floating peacefully toward the sea. He was one with the 50,000 runners in the field of the Lake City Marathon, and each of those runners was one with him.

Tom Schorr learned of Pope Tony's presence almost the moment he stepped onto the course. One of his cameramen shooting from in front of the starting line noticed a commotion the moment the 4:00 pacing team reached the line. Nothing startling, just a ripple of sound and movement in the river of runners, as participants recognized Tony and swiveled their heads to look at him, almost drawing away as they did, allowing him for a moment to exist in an open space. The cameraman zoomed in with his lens and recognized instantly the reason for the commotion.

"Tom! Put me live: Now!"

Schorr's attention had been on the main feed. For an instant, he hesitated: "We're live on the leaders."

"Look at the picture, Tom. Recognize anybody?"

"Holy shit," said Schorr, hesitating no longer. "Camera 5!"

The live feed featuring front runners vanished, replaced by a shot of the masses moving across the starting line: Pope Tony framed in the center of several dozen runners.

Schorr spoke into the intercom that connected him to Mark Mallon on the main set: "Mark, check the picture. It's Peter's celebrity."

Mallon paused in a discussion with Timothy Rainboldt about the front runners. "We just spotted someone who everyone should recognize...." Then he paused again, because by now Pope Tony was moving away from the starting line. All Mallon could see was the back of Tony's head.

Timothy, amused, filled the vacuum: "...except we can't identify him, because all we see is the back of his head."

Carolynne Vickers, however, had immediately recognized the identity of the man called Celebrity X: "It's Pope John Anthony." Her words calm, controlled, almost hushed.

"Confirmed, Mark," said Schorr on the intercom. "Go with it!"

That said, Schorr switched radio channels to talk to the cameraman on the bridge ahead of the runners. Camera 6 had been focused wide angle, presenting the marathon as an epic struggle by 50,000 runners. But it was also 50,000 individual struggles, and one of those struggles, Schorr understood immediately, was that of Peter's Celebrity X. Suddenly, the marathon had become more than a sports story.

Schorr told the bridge cameraman to zoom in on the 4:00 pacing team sign. The cameraman followed instructions, but struggled to find Pope Tony among the bobbing heads. The live feed remained the earlier shot of Pope Tony's retreating head.

"It *is* Pope John Anthony Molina," Mark Mallon said smoothly, nodding toward C.V. to thank her for the quick identification. "And I am amazed—as I know is everybody." Ever the master of the silent moment, Mallon allowed his comment to hang in the air. In the moment of silence, the bridge cameraman finally found Pope Tony. Head and shoulders, no strain yet on his face, chin bouncing, its rhythm synchronized to the movement of legs below, eyes straight ahead, focused on some Xanadu, movements precisely the same as any one of 50,000 runners ahead or behind him crossing the line.

Mallon continued to allow silence to tell the story, as though covering the launch of a rocket into space. Too bright a light for words. Or was it that like many viewers watching the show, the TV anchorman was stunned, lost for words or trying to find words equal to the spectacle? The silence continued to speak for itself. Finally the TV anchorman spoke, his tone not excited, more reverential: "We had heard, C.V., that a celebrity might be running the Lake City Marathon..." A dramatic pause. Mallon had found himself. "...but until this moment, this *exact* moment, we had not heard *who* that celebrity might be." Mallon looked toward Carolynne, not certain yet which way to go, hoping she might find for them a direction.

And she did, smoothly, professionally, and with such a grace that people employed with the station viewing the tape of the show later remarked that it almost seemed as though she was reading from a teleprompter.

"That's correct, Mark. Rumors had been flying all weekend that someone well known—*very* well known—might be running the Lake City Marathon. We thought at first it might have been Naní, the supermodel, who is running to raise money for AIDS/Africa."

"A good cause," filled Mallon, "and we'll be talking about that later."

"Or maybe world record-holder, Aba Andersson. First, she was running, then not running because we learned she was pregnant, then running again, but back in the pack."

"We'll be talking about Aba too," said Mallon, the main feed remaining the shot from the bridge in front of the runners. For a moment Mark Mallon reverted to becoming a witness to history, not a chronicler of it. All thoughts of the race up front were for the moment forgotten.

C.V. continued: "But there was a third celebrity, Mark, and race director Peter McDonald—much to his credit, I might add—was playing his cards close to his vest..."

"Under his shirt," laughed Mallon.

"...and not until this minute, not until this *very* minute, did any of us *guess* that Pope John Anthony Molina would be running the Lake City Marathon..." As she talked, Carolynne Vickers had been observing her sometime husband Timothy Rainboldt tapping his laptop furiously. She knew Timothy was like a human vacuum cleaner when it came to sucking up data. And now both Mark and Carolynne directed their attention to Timothy, whose raised hand and beaming face told them he had just struck bedrock gold.

That gold included the story posted only seconds ago by Jonathan Von Runyon on the *Lake City Ledger* Web site. Von Runyon told in a few short paragraphs how race director, Peter McDonald had hidden the identity of his boyhood friend under the nom de plume Celebrity X. Rainboldt was astounded: *How did that toad Von Runyon get the news first?* There was even a quote from Pope Tony describing how he sometimes trained on the roads near Castel Gandolfo after midnight. *Incredible! Well, we'll just steal that quote and make it our own.*

Timothy Rainboldt began: "...but hindsight, C.V., tells us that we *should* have known better," Timothy said triumphantly. "The pope grew up in Lake City. He attended the same high school as race director Peter McDonald. The pope later actually *taught* at that school, Carmel Catholic, and coached Peter. Patently, if there was any other world celebrity that Peter McDonald knew better than anyone else, it was his Holiness, Pope John Anthony Molina."

"Patently."

"But, let's be honest, C.V., none of us knew that Pope Tony was even working out."

"The Vatican failed to send us a press release," joked Mark Mallon.

"Or more important, Mark," said C.V., "that he had plans to run the Lake City Marathon."

"So credit to Peter," said Timothy. "You've given us a pleasant surprise."

"A *most* pleasant surprise," Mark echoed. "So let us now watch the Bishop of Rome as he begins a journey that will end 26 miles 385 yards later."

The camera on the bridge continued to focus on Pope Tony as he came closer, then disappeared passing under the bridge, heading into darkness where the course moved beneath several blocks of skyscrapers, eventually to emerge in daylight as runners crossed the river. "We'll be right back," announced anchorman Mark Mallon as TV3 broke for another commercial.

That was when director Tom Schorr had called Peter, riding the press truck.

It was a one-way conversation, an angry conversation, a shouted conversation: "Why didn't you tell me? I can't believe you didn't give us at least a few minutes warning! This is unforgivable, Peter! When I figure out how the hell we're going to cover your secret celebrity and still follow the race up front, I'll call you back. In the meantime, Peter, I'm pissed off as hell!"

It was with that comment that Schorr punched the red button ending the conversation, the same moment when Peter had pocketed his cell phone and turned to Dennis Lahey, saying, "He's on the course." Lahey had been puzzled by this comment, but not long, the news of Pope Tony running a marathon already beginning to spread.

Back in the control trailer with one minute of the two-minute commercial break remaining, Tom Schorr's mind was skipping ahead to how TV3 would cover the marathon given the bombshell dropped in his lap. Schorr had told Peter that he was pissed off as hell, but that moment had passed, and the director realized now he had been handed a golden opportunity to cover a marathon that had become more than a race. It had become a Happening. For newspapers all over the world, their front-page headlines tomorrow would read: POPE RUNS MARATHON. But in the meantime, the pope had disappeared into a tunnel and even when he emerged, Schorr did not have a single camera on the course in front of him for the next several miles. *Maybe I still am pissed off at Peter. He could have warned me!*

But the director calmed. There was one solution. The girl in the golf cart. He spoke into his radio, this time calmly and sweetly:

"Christine? Where are you, honey?"

00:14:59

Approaching the 5-kilometer mark, Joseph Nduku allowed his gaze to shift toward a digital timing clock by the sidewalk in time to see it click from 14:59 to 15:00 to 15:01, that last number displayed at the instant his foot (with chip attached) crossed the electronic mat on the street. Positioned several strides behind the lead pack, seemingly running without stress, Joseph was quickly past the electronic timing device, which continued displaying the elapsed time since the start of the marathon:

00:15:02. 00:15:03. 00:15:04.

Joseph's having reached 5-K in 15:01 also was now displayed on the computer screens of anyone tracking the progress of the elite runners on the Internet, accessible around the world. This included Timothy Rainboldt seated on the TV3 set. The Internet also revealed the defending champion, Joseph Nduku, to be in 16th place, though but a few seconds behind the leader, at this moment Kenyatta Kemai.

The fact that Nduku was that many places and that many seconds behind Kemai was meaningless at this early point in the race. For all practical purposes, the two Kenyans and fourteen others of various nationalities still running together in the lead pack were tied. In his commentary, Timothy Rainboldt made that point: "They're tied, Mark," he said. After the commercial break, the telecast returned its focus on the leaders, leaving the story about the pope running the marathon to be resolved later.

Mallon responded to Rainboldt's point, adding: "It's a horse race."

"A very fast horse race, Mark."

"Foolishly fast on a day this warm," Carolynne Vickers added.

Timothy agreed: "We'll soon see runners falling off the pace, maybe as early as another mile, or two, or three."

"But look at Joseph Nduku, Timothy. Joseph is two strides behind..."

"...And has been two strides behind almost from the start..."

"...Which means he's either struggling to hang on..."

"...Or he's smarter than the others."

"It may take two more hours before we learn which," added Mallon. "Meanwhile, we also have some fast women, headed by Tatanya Henry."

"Camera 3," barked Tom Schorr in the control trailer.

MARATHON

Whether the main feed featured him, the lead women, or midpack runners mattered little to Joseph Nduku. He had come to run. Time was irrelevant. Having glanced briefly at the time display at 5-K, the defending champion would not check another timing clock until 10-K—and maybe not even then.

Joseph usually paid little attention to pace. He ran instinctively, not from some preconceived plan. The defending champion had passed three previous timing clocks thus far in the marathon (one each at 1, 2 and 3 miles) and had not looked at any of them. Nor did the running time as displayed on the camera truck in front of the leaders concern him. *Too much information is bad,* Joseph believed. *It interferes with your natural talents. Running is simple. Why corrupt it with mathematical formulas that say, I can do this, but I cannot do that?* The display clocks—black with flickering red numbers, rectangular, positioned eye height—appeared as images in his peripheral vision, but the numbers failed to penetrate to Joseph's inner brain, the brain that dictated his pace and strategy, his every footfall for the length of the marathon.

Joseph knew that pre-set strategies often failed to take into account course difficulty, weather variations (heat and wind) and particularly other runners with other strategies, athletes from Kenya and different countries, who might have the audacity to believe they might defeat him.

They might finish in front of me on some occasions, Joseph Nduku believed, *because we all have talent and train hard and possess a will to win, but they will never defeat me. I can only defeat myself if I fail to achieve my potential on any given day.*

If I fail to do that, the great Kenyan runner believed, *the slowest runner in a field of 50,000, the one last across the line whose only goal is to finish on his or her hands and knees, can defeat me. We all select our goals, or have our goals selected based on the gifts God gave us. Achievement can only be measured by that standard.*

At the same time, Joseph Nduku wanted to win the marathon today, particularly since he had dedicated his prize money to AIDS Africa—but how fast must he need run to fulfill that desire? While considering that question, he shifted his attention to a half dozen tables in the middle of the road featuring plastic bottles containing fluids for elite athletes. Kemai and the runners in front of him had begun to split in two groups, based on where they anticipated finding their personal bottles, ones they had delivered to the elite athlete's meeting yesterday.

Position on the table was dictated by bib numbers: odd numbers left; even numbers right. As defending champion, Joseph wore number 1 on the front of his singlet. His rival Kenyatta Kemai wore number 3, based on ranking by fast time. Because Joseph wore that lowest of low numbers, he could expect to locate his bottle at the near end of the table. There it was! Standing almost alone. Most of the other low-numbered runners ahead of him already had grabbed their bottles. The bottles were set three or four feet apart to avoid one runner inadvertently knocking over the bottle of another.

Joseph snatched his solitary bottle and, without breaking stride, raised it to his mouth. His first bottle contained not sports drink, but water. As planned, he would take sports drink at the next table in another five kilometers and at every other elite table for the rest of the race. But he liked for his first drink to be water. Not bottled water, but water from the tap in his hotel room. From the lake. Perhaps he was superstitious, but Joseph always selected tap water when filling his bottles. Best not to make the local gods angry. He felt that way even though he was baptized a Christian.

The Kenyan drank deeply, ran for a dozen or more strides to allow the water to settle into his stomach, then drank deeply again. Then a third time, because it was hot—way too hot! Temporarily satisfied, he pulled the cap off the bottle, raised it overhead and emptied the remaining contents onto the billed cap he wore to keep the sun off his face. The water cascaded down over his shoulders. *Aaaaaaah,* sighed Joseph, allowing himself a moment of pleasure, though maintaining the same incessant stride. He hurled the bottle toward the curb, not wanting someone following in his wake to trip over it.

The bottle took a funny bounce, striking the leg of a spectator standing beside the course. Embarrassed, Joseph turned his head and shouted, "Sorry!"

The spectator waved to indicate no offense, then as Joseph disappeared from sight, bent to pick the plastic bottle out of the gutter. He handed it to a small boy standing by his side. "It looks like we've got a souvenir."

The boy cradled the bottle, almost reverently. "I hope he wins the race."

"That seems unlikely. He's pretty far back."

As Joseph Nduku continued, still separated from the front pack by several strides, he allowed his mind to dwell on the time he had seen passing the 5-kilometer mark: 15:01. Quickly, he did the arithmetic. Joseph had scored all A's at the missionary school he had attended in Eldoret. Rudimentary math. Fifteen minutes times eight, and that's two hours for 40 kilometers. (Joseph always thought in meters, not yards.) Add six or so more minutes for the rest of the race distance (42.2 kilometers), and it gives you a time of 2:06:00. Or thereabouts. That for the leaders. Somewhat more than that for himself. He was on, say, 2:06:45 pace. That time for the marathon was well within his capabilities and also within the capabilities of several within the field, especially Kenyatta Kemai, still in front pressing the pace, Moses Abraham at his side. He doubted Abraham could run that fast, but, yes, Kemai. Although not on a day like today with the temperature expected to peak in the high 80's, maybe even into the 90's by the time everybody finished.

MARATHON

Joseph Nduku never wore a heart monitor, either in training or races. Joking with his teammates, he sometimes referred to them as "devices of the devil." On several occasions, he had agreed to be tested in exercise physiology laboratories: running on a treadmill with various wires attached to his chest. Most recently, he had been tested by Wilbur Melvin, Ph.D., director of the human performance laboratory at Old Dominion University in Norfolk, Virginia. Don Geoffrey was doing an article for *Running Magazine* on the physiological differences between elite and mid-pack runners. Joseph agreed to be a guinea pig partly as a favor to the Turtle, but more because his cover picture would result in a $5,000 bonus from Nitro, his shoe sponsor.

Dr. Melvin determined that Nduku had a resting pulse of 29 and a maximum pulse of 160. Geoffrey explained in his article that well-conditioned mid-pack runners might be ten or twenty beats higher at each end. Their cardiovascular systems could not match those of elite athletes. And even among elite athletes, some had better cardiovascular systems than others. That was one reason they defeated other runners—but only one reason.

Had Dr. Melvin been able to measure Joseph Nduku's heart rate as he passed 5-K in the Lake City Marathon, the scientist would have discovered that his heart hovered near 140, about 85 percent of maximum. Not much of a strain for an elite runner. In workouts back in Elderot, Joseph could run for several hours at that steady state. But not on a hot day!

Joseph did not know the numbers, but he knew his body. He knew that he could not continue at his current pace for nearly two more hours without suffering dire consequences. And he suspected neither could his rivals. He knew that; apparently they did not.

After passing the aid table, because he wanted to relax and drink, Joseph Nduku had allowed those in the main pack to get two, three, four, even five strides in front of him. Easy enough for him to rejoin the pack, but now Joseph made the tactical decision to let Kemai, Abraham and the other leaders go. Masoi, Kipkuruit, Rutich, Cherrito, the other Kenyans. He trained with them all the time. He knew their capabilities; they knew his. They were running 4:50 miles, he a pace only slightly slower. And while anything was possible, he did not believe they or any others in the race could maintain a pace that much faster than 5:00-mile pace for the full distance. They would crash. They would crumple, allowing a smarter runner paying attention to his body, not captive of some electronic training device, to catch and pass them. Brains would triumph over brawn on days as hot as this.

Joseph decided to let them go.

Joseph slowed ever so slightly, allowing the distance between him and the impetuous runners to grow to 50, then 75, then 100 meters as the electronic

351

timing device continued ticking, now well behind him. As long as he did not allow the lead of Kemai to grow too greatly, he still might win.

He *would* win!

As Joseph slowed to 5:00 miles, letting his rivals go, his heart rate stabilized, then began to slide downwards slightly to 136. But all this was lost to the defending champion who ran by instinct. He would not let numbers dictate his comfort level.

Still maintaining concentration, still fixated on every footfall, Joseph allowed the backs of those ahead to blur. Out of sight, out of mind—at least until they drifted back to him. Also sliding out of his vision was the clock atop the TV truck. He did not want to know the time. Today's race would be won by the competitor capable of running the most intelligent pace given race conditions. He believed that competitor to be himself.

Joseph withdrew inside his body, visualizing himself now as a crocodile immobile and invisible beneath the waters of a flowing river.

I am crocodile. I am crocodile, Joseph Nduku chanted to himself, recalling his dream from last night. *I am crocodile, and I will wait beside this brown and flowing river until some animal, an impala, a herd of impalas, comes close to drink. Then I will pounce. And if all the impalas ahead of me err in their pace, I will win. I am crocodile. I, Joseph, am crocodile!*

Running beside Aba Andersson, Natasha felt like she had been dunked in a whirlpool. It was hot, so hot. And she was hot, so hot, hotter than she could remember being in any previous race, especially in a marathon. And how long had they been running? Barely 5 minutes. She was ready to quit, although that was not in her nature.

Natasha looked toward Aba, now conversing with another woman. The world record holder had not yet begun to perspire! Her body was dry on a day when simply standing stationary caused you to sweat. Natasha decided that was one of the reasons Aba held the world record in the marathon.

"Christine, where are you, honey?" She heard Tom Schorr's voice echo sweetly in her earpiece.

"Approaching 5-K. The lead men just passed. Sorry I'm late."

"Not important. Have you heard yet?"

"Heard what?"

"Never mind. Are the lead women in sight?"

"Not yet."

"Good. Tell Edmund to focus on the gals approaching. Don't worry who's leading, but it's Tatanya Henry with a half dozen others right behind. As soon as we have them on camera, Mark will cue you. C.V. will have I-D'ed the leaders, so you don't need to."

"Got it."

"Think of something to say."

"Thanks, Tom. I'm glad you reminded me."

Jake stopped the golf cart past the aid tables. Christine moved into position between the camera and the tables. Someone, not Schorr, told her to shift two steps to the left, then another step. "Perfect," said the operator.

The next voice was that of Tom Schorr. "Cue Christine, Mark."

Mallon spoke: "The lead women have just passed through 3 miles and are approaching the next aid station. Christine Ferrara is on the scene."

"Camera 4!"

"On the scene and thirsty, but I dare not grab any water bottles off the tables you see behind me, because those belong to the elite women, Mark."

Christine stopped talking, allowing the picture to tell the story, as the lead women swept past, each of them grabbing a bottle. All the bottles had numbers on them; many had ribbons or other identifying marks to allow an approaching runner to spot which bottle was his or hers. Tatanya grabbed her bottle. Toshi Yamota, hers. As instructed, Christine did not mention them by name, although she recognized them from the press conference. She did not recognize several of the other women running in the same pack, runners more anonymous but capable of achieving fame if they paced themselves correctly today. Rogers from New Zealand. Hyang from the U.S. Gurmu from Ethiopia. Barely five feet tall, she looked smoothest of the group, but it was not Christine's job to offer that analysis.

The lead women had a group of several men attached to them like barnacles on the hulls of ocean liners; either drafting their pace, or hoping to be shown on TV, perhaps both. These drafting men had peeled off to one side. None of the bottles on the tables were theirs. They lacked status. Though able to match pace with the lead women—at least to this point—they were well behind the leading elite men and would not figure into the top places or earn any prize money. Christine succinctly explained the elite aid station set-up as other runners passed in the background, several more women and more men. Fiona Flynn passed at this time, but Christine failed to see the Irish Lass, because she was looking at the camera while talking.

"Watching these women refresh themselves and, as hot as it is, I'm going to get a drink myself. There's a Starburst on the corner, Mark."

"Given the *extremely* hot weather, Christine, you better order iced tea. That was Christine...."

The live feed in her ear stopped. As it did, Christine thought: *I can't believe I just did that. I mentioned a sponsor. Tom is going to be pissed.*

SUNDAY

The next voice was that of Tom Schorr. And he was pissed—though not at her. "You won't believe the trick your boyfriend pulled on us."

"Tom, Peter is *not* my boyfriend. We just met."

"And he probably never will be your boyfriend when you learn what Mr. Pompous Race Director did."

A couple standing nearby suddenly started screaming.

"Repeat that, Tom. It's getting noisy here."

Christine put one hand over an ear to limit the noise. Tom Schorr began to update Christine Ferrara about Pope Tony, providing plans for covering him as the couple beside her continued to scream:

"Go, Meg, go!"

00:20:00

What?" shrieked Matilda Goldberg. "I don't believe it!" Tilda had just learned the news from a runner nearby, a man named Terry, she had met at the Team Turtle party. He wore headphones and a radio, apparently listening to the broadcast of the Lake City Marathon. They had just emerged from the tunnel near the start where surrounding concrete temporarily blocked radio reception. Crossing the bridge over the Des Plaines River, she was treading carefully so as not to trip on the steel grating, when she heard the runner next to her say simply, "Wow!"

Ever the news-gatherer, Tilda inquired: "Why 'wow?'"

"The pope is running the marathon," Terry explained.

"The pope?"

"Yeah, the pope. What's his name: John Anthony?"

"Are you serious?"

"Yes."

That's when Tilda shrieked in disbelief, which caused Terry to react defensively, explaining he just heard it on the radio: "It's true."

Which caused an apology from Tilda, who explained to Terry she did not doubt what he said, but merely was registering surprise over the fact that Pope Tony might be running the marathon. Tilda was about to add that she had talked to the pope yesterday about her marathon plans, and, *yada-yada-yada*, he had said nothing about his, then decided, *No, I do not want to go there.* She would be forced to spend the next mile explaining to some stranger why she, a distinguished reporter for *The New York Times*, had been snooping around the pope's boyhood home on the East Side.

"Where is the pope now?" she asked instead. "Can we see him?"

Terry held up one finger to tell her to wait, as though that information was being broadcast to people all over Lake City at this precise moment. Others nearby, who had heard what Terry had said about the pope running the marathon began to show the same sense of astonishment as had Matilda Goldberg.

"The pope?"

"No way."

"I heard he works out."

"Yeah, but a marathon?"

"He grew up in Lake City."

"That is *so* awesome!"

Finally, Terry accumulated sufficient information to share with runners crowding together. "He should be right ahead of us."

"Should be?" Tilda stirred with anticipation, "Can you see him?"

"He's running with the 4:00 pacing team, so we're not far behind."

Tilda groaned. If she had not decided to switch teams, she could be running with Pope Tony right now. *Million-dollar book contract: bye, bye.*

Then she thought of the conversation yesterday with Pope Tony and the cardinal camerlengo at his mother's house. She had told the pope that the reason she was in town was to run a marathon. And what was his comment?

"Imagine the training it must take to accomplish such a feat."

And the cardinal had added: "Like forty days fasting in the desert."

Oy vey!

Craning her neck, Tilda could see the sign for the 4:15 pacing team bobbing up and down a hundred yards ahead. Delayed while making one last porta-potty stop, she had not quite made it through the crowd to where the 4:15 team was gathering. She did not consider that important at the time, figuring she could catch up within a few miles if necessary. But now, given her instincts that this would become a front-page story not only in the *Times*, but in newspapers around the world, it was not merely necessary, it was essential that she catch up.

Could she do it? Especially on a day that was, oh so hot? It had taken Tilda a dozen minutes to reach the starting line. A glance at her watch (activated crossing the line) indicated her to have been running nearly eight minutes. She had not yet reached the 1-mile mark. Twenty minutes total. The elite men had passed 4 miles; the elite women soon would reach that marker.

00:20:00. 00:20:01. 00:20:02.

But more important: How far behind the 4:00 pacing team was she? And would she be able to bridge the distance lost through her foolishness? She could see the 4:15 sign; but being woefully short, she could not see the 4:00

sign further ahead. Terry was tall. Maybe he could catch a glimpse of the pack with the pope and provide an estimate. "Can you see them?"

"No, not quite. Wait: There's the 4:00 sign, about to turn the corner."

"Tell me when."

"Now!"

Tilda noted the time on her watch. When she made the turn on that same corner, it would allow her to estimate the time separating her from the 4:00 team, the pope, and a possible front page story. *Sixty. Seventy. Eighty. Nearly ninety seconds!*

How would she ever catch up? Why had she changed pacing teams at the last minute? Why had she decided on one last toilet trip? *Can I cut the course and catch him?* Tilda tried to recall the map of the marathon course that had come in her goodie bag. The course wound back and forth through the downtown area and elsewhere through the city. Yes, she could take shortcuts and jump to a point in front of the pope, but was that ethical behavior befitting a religious reporter with the *Times?*

No, she might get away with it if she worked for the *Lake City Ledger*, but not the *Times*. So she would be patient. She would pick up her pace—slightly. She would not dodge around slower runners, because that would waste energy. She would look for openings and press ahead. She was faster than a 4-hour marathoner. She would narrow the gap over a period of time. Suppose it took her five or ten miles to catch the pope. This is a marathon, not a 5-K, and in a marathon the patient runner wins the race.

Patience, Tilda, patience!

Christine Ferrara stood leaning against the golf cart near the 5-K point on the course waiting for further instructions. Director Tom Schorr had just told her Peter's dirty little secret, that Pope Tony was running the marathon. She was stunned, but Schorr said not to move until he figured out what to do next. Tom said he would call back in two minutes after he had a chance to talk to Peter McDonald again. But that two minutes had passed, and she was still waiting. And getting more frustrated as each second ticked away!

00:22:00. 00:22:01. 00:22:02.

Peter's failure to warn them about his surprise celebrity definitely put them in a bind. The pope: she could not believe it! Peter has some explaining to do.

Her plans to float along on her golf cart in the middle of the pack cherry-picking mid-pack runners needed modification. Should she be angry at Peter? Probably not. *We all knew some celebrity was planning to run Lake City. We just were not prepared for how important that celebrity would be.*

Maybe that was the point. She could not imagine the extent of the security preparations needed any time the pope stepped beyond Vatican walls. Except, apparently from what Tom said, Pope Tony was running without security.

Why doesn't Tom call back? Arrrgh! Time's a wasting!

She looked at Edmund, her cameraman. He was perched on the seat of the golf cart, waiting for instructions. He seemed much less perturbed than her, probably because he was getting paid for a day's work no matter how many celebrities appeared in shorts and singlets. Edmund nodded with his head toward a Starburst shop nearby. "Have we time to go for coffee?"

Christine knew Edmund was joking, but replied: "No, Edmund. We will stand patiently here beside the course, fuming, until some genius back at Mission Control next tells us what to do."

Christine turned her attention to the couple standing nearby, the pair who had been screaming so loudly before. They had lowered their "Go, Meg, Go" sign and were waiting to cheer another runner. Busy with her phone call, she had not paid much attention to the "Meg" they had been cheering, except the woman who flashed by so quickly seemed vaguely familiar.

"Who were you cheering?" asked Christine.

"My wife, Meg," responded Matt.

Whoever this Meg was, Christine thought, *she was running pretty fast, probably not much more than a minute or two behind the lead women. Did I see her at one of the press conferences?*

She asked that question, but Matt responded, no. "She's a podiatrist."

That meant nothing to Christine. New in town, not running much, she had no reason to visit a podiatrist. *So why does she look familiar?*

"She works part-time at Fast Feet," added Moira.

Christine suddenly realized the identity of the woman and pointed down to her feet, "She sold me this pair of shoes."

"That's my wife, the shoe salesman."

But more than that, realized Christine, dipping deeper into her hard-drive collection of unrelated events. *She was also the woman I saw running on the lakefront when I interviewed Fiona Flynn. That was less than 72 hours ago, and how much my life has changed since then.*

The couple suddenly lost interest in talking to the TV reporter, apparently having spotted another runner to cheer. A man. Limping. Blood streaking one leg, apparently from a cut on the knee. Christine had seen someone fall at the start. *Could it have been him?*

Her phone rang. She looked at the display. Not Tom: *Peter!* She frowned, sighed so loudly that it startled Edmund, who had been watching runners stream by during her conversation with the couple. The runner with the bloody leg stopped to talk to them.

SUNDAY

The phone continued to ring. She ignored its ring, but offering another sigh, finally pushed the green button.

"Get in the cart and head up the course," commanded Peter.

"Like, *hello*, Peter! Shouldn't it have been, 'Hello, Christine?'"

"Hello, Christine."

"Tom is really pissed at you, Peter."

"No, he's not. I just talked to him again. He was pissed for maybe 30 seconds, until he realized I had handed him the biggest story of his life."

"Speaking of 30 seconds, you couldn't give us 30 seconds warning?"

"No, and you'll understand why when I explain it to you."

"...Over dinner next weekend?"

"Over dinner?"

"Over dinner!"

"You are asking me out on a date, Christine."

"No, I am demanding retribution."

"Retribution?"

"Retribution! Dinner. With a fine wine."

"Only if I get to choose the restaurant."

"They don't serve wine at Burger King, Peter."

"Why are we fencing with each other?"

"Because we like each other, and you need to tell me where to go."

Silence on the other end. Then laughter.

"Okay," said Christine, offering a third sigh. "Let me rephrase: At what point on the course do you wish me to position myself and for what reason?"

Peter, shifting to business mode, instructed Christine to motor several blocks further north to where the road divides, planters separating opposing lanes. "Police will direct the runners into the right lanes. The left lanes will be open: No traffic. Spectators behind barriers on the left sidewalk."

Christine also had shifted into business mode. "I understand."

"You'll be able to ride parallel to the runners for more than a mile."

"Ummm-hummm." Christine was trying to visualize the course from the map she had studied yesterday. She was not yet that familiar with the city, but her driver, Jake, the teenage Indy 500 clone, should be able to position them even with Pope Tony to capture him on camera. Perhaps she could coax him into an interview. She asked Peter if that were possible.

"I can't promise that."

"I understand."

"I don't have direct contact with Tony. Only with his bodyguards, and I don't want to distract them."

Tony?

Peter continued: "Once the course turns into the park, you won't be able to stay with the runners. Too many turns. Take the street that parallels the park. You can pick up Tony exiting the park around 6 miles."

"You call the pope 'Tony,' Peter?"

"We went to high school together."

"I didn't know that."

"There's a lot about me that you don't know, Christine."

Peter thought of his late wife Carol as he said those words. Without realizing he was doing so, he reached up and felt for the chain, her last gift to him. "Gotta go," he said finally. "Tom will be in touch."

He hung up. No goodbye. *Well, what do I expect? Shape up, Christine. You're supposed to be working, not acting like a love-struck schoolgirl.*

Christine punched the red button on her cell phone and looked to find her driver. She finally spotted Jake off to one side watching the race. "Hey, Darrell Waltrip!" she shouted at Jake and waved for him to return to the golf cart. She figured they needed to get moving before the large bulk of runners arrived and made it more difficult for them to maneuver on the course. The couple she had been talking to a few minutes ago also had departed, probably to intersect the runners several miles further into the race. Too bad, she would have liked to interview them. A podiatrist running the marathon—especially a fast one—would have made a good story.

But the story at hand was better. Climbing back into the golf cart, Christine thought ahead to Pope Tony. *Tony, indeed!* Would she be able to get near him? Would he be willing to talk while running? Or would so many runners want to run with this world-famous celebrity that the entire race might grind to a halt. She hoped not. Hopefully before the moment that Pope Tony appeared within range of her camera, Schorr would call with more instructions.

00:24:00

Meghan Allison slowed her pace slightly as she came to the next aid station, moving to the first table on the right. She had only a handful of runners around her, sub-elite men, so she had nobody in her way when she reached for one of the cups filled with E.R.G., the replacement drink. Because of male runners blocking her vision, she could not see any of the faster women ahead, but did not expect to, given her plans to run a conservative pace. A hundred or so yards up course, it looked like another woman—or was it merely a man with long hair tied in a ponytail? It was sometimes hard to tell the women from the men in road races, the fastest women having skinnier butts than most of the men. But she did not care, should not care. *Isn't it my plan to run within myself and not worry about racing other runners?*

When she had seen Matt and Moira near the 5-K mark a few blocks earlier, her husband had not told Meg what place she might be in—if he knew. Matt did say that her brother Aaron had tripped at the start, one reason why Big Bro had not caught her. But a bigger reason was that once the horn sounded, she momentarily forgot about Aaron. *Totally!* She found herself caught up in the excitement of the moment, swept along like driftwood in a roaring river. Meg actually was scared, frightened, worried that if she slowed her pace relative to those around her, she would be trampled by those behind.

This might not have occurred if she had positioned herself near the back of Start Corral A, but the one runner had pushed her forward. He was merely being helpful, she knew. And she had not resisted, but when the gate between her corral and the elite corral lifted and everyone moved forward, she found herself standing not that far behind the fastest runners on the planet, which definitely was *not* something she planned to have happen.

And the heat, the heat! She knew the weather forecasts. She knew the temperature already was up in the 70's, and would go much higher, but she did not feel warm—yet. Would she? And how soon? Should she respect the weather forecasts and slow down even though she still felt comfortable, even a bit chilled because of her low body fat? Meg did not know. The marathon remained uncharted ground for Meghan Allison, each step forward leading Meg toward an uncertain result.

All this kept playing and replaying through Meg's mind during the first few miles until finally, she had to tell herself: *Get out of the past, Meg. You can't change what happened. Think of what's in front of you, not what's behind! Concentrate!*

But even that mindset presented perils. Would she pay for her pacing error later in the race? Would she hit that "wall" at 20 miles that everyone talks about? She did not know. She had no clue. She had never run a marathon before, so how was she expected to pace herself? *Aaaiiieee!* Meg finally decided that she needed to stop thinking and start running.

A cup of E.R.G. in hand, she downed half its contents, the rest spilling all over her front. *Yuck!* Since the aid tables were long, she had time to grab a second cup off a later table. This time, she squeezed the top of the cup so less spilled. *I'm learning,* thought Meg. Then she was at the tables with water. She grabbed a cup and downed most of it, using it as a chaser for the E.R.G. Then grabbed another cup and used its contents to splash in her face and wash off the sticky stuff. *Wheeew!* That feels better.

Then she was past the aid station, except the runner who had been running with her since the start—Bob Veldman, he had identified himself—was offering her another cup. He held two in his hands.

"Don't you want it?" worried Meg.

"I'm probably going to drop out and run New York."

She remembered him saying that, so accepted one cup and threw its contents down the back of her singlet. "*Oooooh:* That's cold!"

Veldman laughed and did the same with his remaining cup of water. Those would be the last words they spoke to each other for several more miles. *Time to run and not to talk,* thought Meg. Her running companion obviously felt the same. They remained close to each other through the 4-mile mark, not from any preconceived plan, but because the pace felt comfortable to both. Also comfortable for several other men running near them. Passing the electronic timing device at 4 miles, Meg did not look to see the time.

00:24:00. 00:24:01. 00:24:02.

Yes, she was getting her act together, subtly shifting from deer mode to racing mode. Meg directed her attention to the runner with the long hair in the group in front of her. She decided it was a woman and not a man. A skinny-butted woman. Judging from the distance now separating them, Meg was about to catch her. Not in the next stride, but maybe in the next mile if both continued their present pace. *But why do I care? I do* not *want to tie my pace to some runner I do not know, and certainly not this early in the race.*

Memories of her successes as a high school cross-country runner began to guide her footsteps, although only at a subliminal level. Meg barely was aware of what she was thinking, but during her successful, younger years it was always *her* running, not others. Meg achieved success as a singularity. A selfish singularity. It mattered little what others around her did, not even her teammates. To be successful, Meg knew she needed to run for herself and not for Matt or Aaron or Moira or even that nice man who had handed her a cup of water a few blocks back. *Thank you, but I can do this alone now.*

Meg stopped looking at the woman in the group ahead and narrowed her focus to an angle of one degree. All that interested her was the pavement ahead, not any of the runners who had crossed it before or who would cross it afterwards. *One step at a time,* she reminded herself. *One step at a time!*

Seated in the residence of the archbishop, the cardinal camerlengo, James Connolly, a.k.a. Redbird, watched the Lake City Marathon as shown on TV with satisfaction. He enjoyed the look on Archbishop Sean Nolan's face when the commentators discovered the presence of Pope John Anthony Molina in the marathon and announced that fact to their viewers. There had been a close-up shot from the starting line with Pope Tony running amid a group of runners, then a second head-on shot where you could almost see him, not quite, and then the horde of mid-pack runners had vanished into an underground section of the course. Pope Tony had not appeared on screen again as the commentators continued with descriptions of the race up front—both men and women—but that was how it ought to be. From discussions yesterday, Cardinal Connolly knew that his friend and superior did not want what he was doing perceived as some sort of stunt.

Archbishop Nolan was incredulous: "Did you know his plans?"

"I only learned two days ago."

"You didn't try to stop him?"

Redbird laughed: "Do you think I would have succeeded? One does not treat the Bishop of Rome as some child who follows orders."

"Even when he acts like a child?"

"Even when he acts like a child."

"But the danger. The security risk. My dear Cardinal Connolly, you are in charge of security. How about his bodyguards?"

"Two running with him. You know them: Mario and Angelo."

"Good men."

"But look." Redbird gestured toward the TV set. It was a gesture one might have made while lecturing to the congregation at Christ Church Dublin. "He has 50,000 bodyguards."

The archbishop did not seem convinced. The only runners he saw on screen were a dozen or so very fast runners, most of them black. Then the picture shifted to one showing a larger group of runners, most of them white. The archbishop, who had given little attention to the sport of running until this point, did not understand what they were doing. And Redbird offered little help. Eventually, the two prelates realized these mid-pack runners were grabbing cups off a table and drinking. It seemed like some pagan ritual. Or, let's be charitable: The Last Supper? Regardless: *Was this something in which the leader of the Holy Roman Catholic Church should take part?*

"How far is this marathon?" asked the archbishop.

"I think it's around 40 kilometers?

"How far is that in miles?"

"Twenty-six."

"I can't even begin to imagine running that far."

The cardinal camerlengo chuckled: "Have faith, Bishop Nolan."

Then the cameras caught him: Pope Tony. And he was grabbing water just like the others, a shepherd among his flock. And there: He dumped a cup of water over his head. Hardly the dignity any of his predecessors displayed dressed in regal white in St. Peter Square. *But we elected this crazy American pope, didn't we? Obviously, we got more than we bargained for.* The archbishop let his head roll back until he was staring above him as though to seek the help of some higher being in understanding what was happening. His loud laugher echoed off the ceiling overhead.

Redbird merely smiled. Without admitting it to Archbishop Nolan, he remained somewhat concerned about security arrangements. Pope Tony had suggested yesterday that once the race began, Redbird should visit the area between the start and finish lines to observe standard race security. (A quick phone call to Peter McDonald secured proper credentials to something called the unified command tent.) Unstated was the recommendation that he not interfere. Tony even had suggested: "You can wander over to the finish line and watch me finish."

Wander? Redbird had grimaced. *He wants me to "wander" and ignore potential threats to his safety?* The cardinal camerlengo finally had decided to do what Americans often suggested in times of stress. He would "chill out!"

Now on Sunday morning, properly chilled, Redbird checked his watch. "We're only three blocks from the marathon course, aren't we?"

"I didn't know that."

"From my study of the map, and what our young American friend told me about how fast he planned to run, we just might stroll over the course and offer our esteemed leader a cheer."

"And how shall we cheer him?"

"How about, 'Go, Pope, Go!'"

00:30:00

TV3 remained firmly focused on the lead Kenyan runners, Kemai and Abraham. "Through 10 kilometers with a time just under 30 minutes," announced Mark Mallon. "What do you think, Timothy: Are they running too fast?"

29:59:58. 29:59:59. 30:00:00.

"Normally, I might have thought so," Timothy Rainboldt responded, "but that was before Kenya's Samuel Wanjiru won the 2008 Olympic marathon in a time of 2:06:32 in conditions not much better than today. Kemai is on pace for a time equally as fast."

"True, Timothy," interrupted Carolynne Vickers, "but Kemai does not have Wanjiri's marathoning chops."

"Third at the World Championships in the 5,000 meters."

"Five-thousand meters is *not* 42.2 kilometers, Timothy."

SUNDAY

"But...."

"No buts, Timothy. You know I'm right. What about Moses Abraham? Talk about no chops. He came here as a rabbit, but Peter gave the rabbits the day off because of the heat. What's that all about?"

"Maybe, C.V., the pair are working together. Kemai and Abraham have ignored the rest of the field for the first half dozen miles. I've long since given up trying to put 'limits' on Kenyans, even those minus so-called chops."

"You might not believe in 'limits,' Timothy, but we may witness a large explosion—almost a sonic boom—when the lead pair reach 20 miles."

Mark Mallon was content to listen to the pair argue. He loved it when they disagreed, but felt it was time to steer the conversation in a safer direction: "What about our defending champion, Timothy?"

"Camera 2," said Tom Schorr in the control trailer. A shot of Joseph Nduku now filled the screen; he was running alone. The motorcycle with the second cameraman had dropped back to cover Nduku. The defending champion had just reached the elite aid tables. Collecting a plastic bottle, he raised the bottle to his lips, continuing to run as he drank.

"Break for commercial, 30 seconds," warned Schorr, his words heard through earpieces worn by the trio on the set.

"Joseph is gambling," Timothy opined. "But it's a risky gamble. If he lets Kenyatta Kemai get too far out in front, he'll never catch him."

"It's a gamble worth taking on a day like today."

"We'll see," said Timothy, seemingly irritated at being challenged, although he should have known C.V. would do just that. His once-dearly-beloved would have favored Kemai if he had taken the opposite view. Seeking the last word, he played his trump card:

"Remember Constantina Tomescu-Diţă, also at the 2008 Olympics. She made a move in the middle of the race, also a gamble, and nobody covered the move. She's the one with the gold medal."

Before C.V. could challenge that statement, Mallon interrupted. "In the women's race, similar to the men, Tatanya Henry is leading with Toshi Yamota on her shoulder. We'll see that battle after these messages."

"Camera 3," announced Schorr. The main feed switched to that of the lead women, Henry and Yamota in front, a half dozen other women behind, a dozen or so men part of the pack. The picture faded, replaced with a screen showing the marathon logo, then a commercial for erectile dysfunction.

As the commercials rolled, C.V. snapped at Timothy: "No way Kemai wins this marathon."

"His gamble could work," her fellow commentator defended himself.

"Could work? *Could* work? No! Smart money's on Joseph."

"Smart money's on Kemai."

"Sorry, your man's going down!"

"Put your money where your lovely lipsticked mouth is, my dear."

"What are we betting?"

"If Kemai wins, you treat me to dinner."

"If? That's a huge 'if,' my dear, opinionated, never-been-wrong Timothy. When *Joseph* wins, you treat *me* to dinner!"

Mark Mallon leaned back in his chair and roared with laughter.

"Hey you three clowns," interrupted Tom Schorr. "Thirty seconds."

Carolynne Vickers became suddenly serious. "But where is Fiona Flynn? We haven't seen her on camera lately."

Timothy began pecking at his laptop showing the lead runners as they crossed the electronic map at 10-K. "*La Femme Fiona* is in the same position in the women's race as Joseph in the men's."

"Which of us is going to pick her as winner?" asked C.V.

"Let's flip a coin."

"Five-four-three-two-one," signaled Schorr.

TV3 went live with a picture of the lead women, Tatanya and Toshi. Mallon opened, but quickly deferred to C.V. Timothy stared at his laptop as it registered times and places of the leading women. Six runners showed on the screen, then two more, another, finally after a long period the tenth. The tenth possessed a high number and a name he did not immediately recognize.

Number 1459: Meghan Allison. Not an invited athlete, judging from her number. Good enough for Start Corral A, not the elite corral. A computer glitch? Someone running over her head? Even someone who cut the course? Timothy decided he would make no note of Ms. 1459 until certain she was legitimate, not some impostor looking to get her name mentioned on TV.

00:40:00

Naní had met John Anthony Molina once before, when he was an ordinary priest assigned to the Vatican, before Tony's elevation to the highest post in the Roman Catholic Church. They had collided, so to speak, both having arrived in Lake City at the same time: she on a modeling assignment, he on vacation from Rome. Naturally, once Peter and Carol McDonald learned Naní planned to be in town, it had resulted in an instant invitation for dinner.

Then Father Tony called, also coincidentally in town, also invited for dinner with the young couple at their near north side apartment. Tony arrived accompanied by an Italian priest, who spoke no English, but smiled a lot. Later, Naní was more shocked than anybody to learn that this neighborhood friend of her college roommate's husband had been appointed pope! Talk about 6 degrees of separation.

And she was almost as shocked when, crossing the starting line, someone pointed to the man who had just joined the 4:00 pacing team.

Peter never told me!

Of course, Peter had told *nobody* about Celebrity X. The supermodel did know some secret celebrity was scheduled to run the marathon. Naní also knew Peter had used her surprise presence as part of his cover for Celebrity X.

But the pope?

As they moved onto the course, Naní wondered if Pope Tony would remember her from that dinner, but only a few minutes off the line, he had glanced her way, showed instant recognition, waved and mouthed the words, "We'll talk later." At the time, he was still responding to hello's and thanks-for-coming's from those as surprised and mystified by the appearance of the pope in a marathon as she was.

That was three miles and a half hour ago, and they had not yet talked, because runners had been helloing and thanking her as well as him, doing the same also to Aba Andersson and Don Geoffrey, also part of their pacing team. Normally, Naní hated paparazzi, but she hoped someone captures a picture of the four of us running together.

00:40:00. 00:40:01. 00:40:02.

They passed through the 3-mile checkmark at 40 minutes into the race. Eleven minutes to reach the starting line, twenty-nine minutes for the distance just covered. That was slower than the 27:28 (9:09.2 per mile) it should have taken if on even pace. Thus, they were a minute and a half slow, but pace team leader Lenny Hand said that the slow start was part of the plan. He expected them to make up the lost time over the next ten miles.

"We'll be right on pace by 13.1," Lenny promised everybody.

Only after the winding course headed north out of downtown, crossed the river a third time and reached a point where the road divided, planter separating opposite lanes, did Pope Tony drift her way, two Italian-looking runners drifting with him. Bodyguards, she supposed, but she would not ask. Tony held out a hand, "Good to see you again, Naní."

"With all the people you must meet, I'm surprised you remembered me," confessed the supermodel.

He laughed: "I might have said the same about you."

I get my picture on the cover of Sports Illustrated, thought Naní, but *he gets his picture on the cover of* Time *as Man of the Year*. Naní did not voice that thought as Tony introduced Mario and Angelo.

"The last time we met, you didn't need bodyguards."

"They come with the office. All the attention bothers me. I like to think of Mario and Angelo as friends, training partners."

"When I realized you were Peter's secret celebrity, I was so mad at him for not telling me."

"It was necessary."

"I understand that now."

Pope Tony changed the subject. "I admire your work with AIDS Africa."

"Unfortunately, it's just a drop in the bucket."

Tony shrugged, indicating he knew. "At least it's a drop. One of the items on my agenda is to direct more attention to Africa. Not to send missionaries. That doesn't always work. But to provide help."

Naní momentarily was breathless, not from the running, but from a vision of what this man could do. "We should talk," she said, realizing the moment the words left her mouth how audacious a statement that had been.

Apparently, Pope Tony did not think so. "We *will* talk," he said.

This time it was Naní's turn to change the subject. She did not want their encounter on the marathon course to turn into a business discussion. "Have you met Peter's new girlfriend?"

"I didn't know he had a girlfriend. When I called him the other day, there was a woman riding in the car with him."

Naní pointed across the divide to the half of the street not filled with runners. "Coincidentally, that's her." She indicated a woman riding in the back of a golf cart wearing earphones and microphone. "Her name's Christine, and she is very sweet."

"I'd cross over to say hello, but I suspect it would make Mario and Angelo very nervous."

Naní understood, realizing more than before how necessary had been Peter's secrecy. "They met only seventy-two hours ago, so it may not last. But he seems to have come out of the shell he's been in since Carol's death."

"I'm still in shock myself," said Pope Tony.

"Excuse me," said Naní. Her eyes had begun to fill with tears. "Every time I think of Carol, I start to cry, and I can't afford to lose any fluids on a day like today."

No! She could not do it. Matilda Goldberg would not cheat. Running several blocks behind Pope Tony, she would not cut the course to catch up with him. How could she, Tilda, respected religious reporter for *The New York Times* commit such a crime? It would be a moral outrage. A sin. It offended her sense of decency, made a travesty of everything that was right in this world. Had not Moses come down from the mountain with tablets in his hands containing ten tenets to live by, one of which was "Thou shall not bear false witness against thy neighbor?" Now if Tilda were Catholic, she could cut the course, catch the pope and have him hear her confession before they finished. Instant redemption. But she was Jewish, thus more obsessed by guilt related to transgressions against the Law of Moses. Tilda laughed out loud at the audacity of that thought.

This caused the runner next to her, the one listening to the race as reported on his radio, to turn down the sound and ask, "Something funny?"

"I was just thinking that if I cut the course, I could catch the pope."

"Don't do it."

"I won't. But he can't be more than a minute or two ahead?"

"If that."

"If I speeded up, maybe 5 or 10 seconds per mile, I could catch him."

"Good luck," said the runner. "Maybe I'll see you at the finish line."

Christine had been traveling in the golf cart in the open half of the divided street for nearly a half mile, Edmund's camera relaying pictures back to the control trailer. Her half of the street was empty, neither runners nor spectators. Police controlled the spectators, who cheered as they saw the pope approach. Between her and the runners were planters filled with flowers, part of a beautification program by the mayor. When she arrived in Lake City two weeks before, Christine had been amazed at the beauty of the city by the lake that she had visited only a few times. Yes, it will be fun to live and work here.

Peter had told her that the divided avenue would run approximately a mile before the runners turned off and entered the park. Could she, during that time, move into the lanes filled with runners? Probably not, because of the dangers of collision. She had told Jake to drive as close to the planters as possible, but Tom Schorr soon countered that order. "We get a better image when we see both planters and runners," he said.

Christine had just finished doing a short report on the pope running the marathon, what she knew about Peter's plans—which wasn't much. Later, she would get Peter on the phone and see if he could offer more information. *Can he talk to me? All he's doing is riding on a press truck in front of the lead runners. What else does he have to occupy his mind?*

While those thoughts were rattling through her head, Christine suddenly noticed Nani disengage herself from a conversation she apparently had been having with Pope Tony. Coming to a side street, the supermodel crossed from the runner's side of the road to Christine's side.

Moving to a position beside the golf cart, Nani offered a hand to Christine. "The pope says, 'Hi.'"

"Hi? Just like that? *Hi?* To me?"

368

"Tony and Peter are old high school friends. Tony apologizes, but his bodyguards would become nervous if he moved to your side of the street."

"Understood."

"Maybe later in the race."

"But you, I've got *you!* I'm not going to let you go back to running your marathon until you give me the best interview of your life. Let's talk AIDS Africa, the reason you're out here."

Naní laughed. "You're not shy, are you Christine?"

But Christine already was talking to Tom Schorr back in the control trailer, informing him she was riding beside Naní. Finishing the conversation, Christine returned her attention to the supermodel: "We're on a commercial break. As soon as we're finished selling a few luxury automobiles, it will be you and I, old friends of twenty-four hours, up close and personal."

"Stop!" pleaded Naní. "I can't run laughing like this."

00:45:00

S mooth, Christine. Smooth!" said Tom Schorr after the Naní interview. Christine started to thank him for the compliment, but realized the TV director already had left the line. The live feed now showed the lead men approaching 15-K, now 45 minutes into the race.

00:45:00. 00:45:01. 00:45:02.

Eight men remained in the lead pack, Kenyatta Kemai and Moses Abraham continuing to control the pace as though it was only the two of them on the course and not 50,000 runners, some fast, most not. Timothy Rainboldt checked his laptop for the identities of the top ten as they passed 15-K: a Croatian, a Moroccan, a Brazilian, a South African (now a U.S. citizen), and three Kenyans. That was eight with two others split from the pack, but not that far behind. The next Kenyan appeared on Timothy's screen as he read the list of leaders for the TV audience. Finally, an Ethiopian filled the top ten.

Yet, incredibly, not yet Joseph Nduku. As a trickle of additional elite runners reached 15-K, Timothy expressed his surprise that the defending champion had allowed the lead pack to escape him this early.

"Do you think Joseph is hurting," asked Mark Mallon, "or does he feel the pack will come back to him?

"I honestly don't know Mark. If Joseph were carrying a cell phone, we could dial him up and ask."

"I don't think he's carrying a cell phone, Timothy," said C.V.

369

"Certainly not, but without an ability to peer into the inner realm of his brain, we can only guess."

The live feed being shown to viewers had switched from the lead runners to the three commentators seated in the studio tent near Burnham Fountain. Wise to the ways of television, Timothy spotted the red light on the camera pointed at him and looked into the camera. He shrugged, indicating to the television audience that he did not know.

C.V. offered her opinion: "My guess, Timothy, is that Joseph is biding his time. He's the pro. He's the experienced runner. He knows that in this heat, Kenyatta and Moses cannot maintain this fast pace much longer—and they may come back to him."

"They may, but wait. Here's Joseph coming through 15-K." Timothy had heard Tom Schorr call for a switch to Camera 7, mounted at that point on the course. The main feed switched to a shot of Joseph Nduku as he arrived at the elite aid table. The defending champion grabbed a plastic bottle from the table, drank from it, carried the bottle for a few more strides, drank from it again, a long drink, then he twisted the top off the bottle and emptied the remaining contents over his head.

"I hope that's water," said C.V. swiftly. "I don't think he would dump E.R.G. over his head."

Mark Mallon laughed. He loved working with this pair. The anchorman returned quickly to the business at hand. "But how far behind is Joseph Nduku, Timothy? Can he make up the ground he's lost?"

As Mallon anticipated, Timothy Rainboldt had the answer. "Kenyatta Kemai and Moses Abraham passed in about 45 minutes, Nduku just under 46. Since he was running with them at 5-K, he's lost a minute in the last six miles. That's a lot to lose. If the lead pair continue at that same pace, they'll finish in 2:06, Joseph in about 2:09."

"That's a big 'if,' Timothy," argued C.V.

Mallon interrupted the pair before they could continue the debate. He enjoyed it, and he suspected so did the viewers, but he had just heard Tom Schorr announce in his earpiece that they had thirty seconds to the next commercial break.

"In the interests of transparency," said the anchorman, "let it be revealed that during one of the commercial breaks this jolly pair beside me bet on the outcome of today's Lake City Marathon, possibly an ethical violation. I don't want to reveal too many of our secrets here in the booth, but what were the stakes, C.V.?"

"Loser pays for dinner tonight," she responded

MARATHON

"At the risk of compromising my journalistic integrity, I want a piece of that action. You get Joseph Nduku, C.V. You get Kenyatta Kemai, Timothy. I get the rest of the field."

"Five seconds to commercial break," said Schorr.

For a moment, Mallon was tempted to admit that no matter who wins and who pays, the cost of dinner would find its way onto an expense account. But there was no reason to reveal that dark secret. "We'll be back after this message."

00:52:00

Meghan Allison had moved into tenth place by the time she reached 10-K, as noticed by Timothy Rainboldt when he checked places on his laptop computer, but she was unaware of that fact and did not remain in the top ten long. Five kilometers and approximately seventeen minutes later, she had slipped back to fourteenth place without having lost much ground to the leaders, who remained too far in front to see.

00:52:00. 00:52:01. 00:52:02.

That was true because, by 10-K, Meghan had moved into a pack with five other women. Several miles before that mark, she had caught the pony-tailed woman just ahead of her. The two of them caught three others. Without any signal being passed from one to another, they became a trail pack, absorbing energy from each other. Several men ran with the women, including Bob Veldman, thus it became a unisex pack. Eventually there would be a sorting out, but for a time, the group ran together as one entity.

Meg had moved into tenth only because just before 10-K, the other women slowed to grab bottles off the elite table. Being a woman without privilege, Meg had no bottle. Thus, she temporarily popped ahead just before the timing mat. It was then that Timothy Rainboldt noticed her in the top ten.

Almost immediately, the pack formed around her again: a pleasant womb of similar-minded runners, each willing to help the others—for the time being. Meg's position in the women's race dropped to fourteenth. Continuing, she was twelfth, then thirteenth, then eleventh, and fourteenth again, except there was no way of recording these slight shifts in position, because no additional mats had been laid between 10 and 15 kilometers.

There was little talk among those in this pack: not the women among women, not the men among men, not the women among men. This did not surprise Meg, because she never had talked with her competitors in track or

371

cross-country races. You were not enemies, but talk was something left for afterwards. She thought everybody knew that, so was surprised earlier in the summer when she and Matt ran a 5-K together at his pace. It amused Meg how much runners near them chattered, particularly given the subjects they discussed as though nobody could hear. *Whew: That one better find a new boyfriend!* She and Matt had been talking too, enjoying each other's company. Dissimilarities certainly existed between average and elite runners. Talking while racing seemed to be one of them. She also could not imagine why anybody would want to wear an iPod. But she knew there were times when average runners shut up and just ran. And times when elite runners talked.

Shortly after she joined the pack, she found herself running beside a woman with oriental features. The other runner wore a bright yellow uniform with red and black stripes down the side. Those were the racing colors of the Northland Racing Team, the club coached by Steve Holland. Meg remembered an article about Northland written by Don Geoffrey in *Running Magazine*. She vaguely recalled that in a photo of the otherwise white club from, Minnesota, one of the runners was Asian, but she could not recall the woman's name, which was Katie Hyang.

Hyang broke the silence. "Are you for real?" No accent there. Hyang might look Asian, but she definitely talked American. Her parents were Hmong refugees, who fled Laos after the Vietnam War and settled in St. Paul, Minnesota. Hyang attended Northland College on an academic scholarship. Only after she went out for cross-country as a sophomore ("because my roommate ran and it seemed cool," the Turtle quoted her) did Hyang discover in herself a natural talent.

The other runner's comment startled Meg. "Huh?"

"Are you for real?" repeated Hyang, pointing toward Meg Allison's bib.

"Oh," said Meg, realizing that the Northland runner was reacting to her high number: 1459. All the other women in their group wore triple-digit numbers in the 100's. "I entered late."

"Oh-*kaaaay*," said Hyang, drawing the comment out so that it covered twenty or thirty yards of running. Hyang ended the conversation by saying, "Good luck, 1459." She offering an open palm to be slapped.

"And to you," said Meg, slapping the palm.

The exchange occurred as the group was still heading north. Soon after, she spotted Matt and Moira—and there was Aaron!

Meg was past them before that fact sank in. He never had caught her, but she was too busy dealing with the race to give that fact much attention until now. The course turned west, but only for a few blocks before turning south to return downtown.

She soon encountered again her cheering section with Moira pumping the "Go, Meg, Go!" sign overhead. Matt's strategy she knew, had been to take the elevated train to near the northernmost point of the out-and-back course. With only a few blocks between the out-and-back legs, they could see her twice before jumping back on the El to return downtown. It was a strategy employed by many spectators following their favorite runners.

Having only waved the first time, Meg impulsively decided to detour to the curb and reward her husband with a hug.

"Hey stop that," said Matt. "Get running!"

Meg did, but then looked back over her shoulder toward Aaron. "What happened to you?"

"I fell."

"Aaron, you are such a klutz!"

In greeting her family, Meg allowed herself to fall several strides behind the group with which she had been running. Moving back to the middle of the road, Meg decided there was no hurry to catch up. They were approaching another aid station at 15-K. There might be jostling as each of the other women went for their bottles. She did not want to get in their way.

Am I for real? Meg asked herself. She did not know. She realized she was wearing a four-digit number among women with three-digit numbers. *Do I belong with this group?* Meg knew she was running smoothly. She felt little fatigue so far. And the heat did not bother her, also so far. She believed that if she picked up the pace even slightly, she could leave the four women behind. *Dust them!* She remembered how good she felt after her final 20-miler, but: *Am I kidding myself?*

Suddenly Meg burst into tears. She did not know why she burst into tears, it just happened. Perhaps it was more fear of success than fear of failure. Fortunately this temporary emotional breakdown happened at a point when she was running alone, otherwise the pack might have interpreted her outburst as a sign of weakness. She refused to exhibit weakness. She would be strong. It still did not matter whether she finished ahead of them or they finished ahead of her in whatever place, but she would run to the best of her ability in this race of 26 miles 385 yards, then get on with the rest of her life.

Meg accelerated slightly and within the space of a quarter mile recovered the distance she had foolishly squandered hugging her husband.

It was while catching back up that she crossed the next mat recording time and place. Meg passed a digital clock at 15-K, but did not look at it. And even if she had, she would not have understood the numbers. Despite getting A's in math all though school, Meghan Allison never had been able to comprehend differences between miles and kilometers.

SUNDAY

One individual who understood the difference was seated on the TV3 set near Burnham Fountain. There was little about statistics that Timothy Rainboldt did not comprehend. And as Matt Mallon and Carolynne Vickers discussed the women's race up front, he checked on the women's race further back. Tatanya Henry and Toshi Yamota still looked strong in front of a lead pack of a half dozen, but where was Fiona Flynn? Fiona hardly had been a factor today. Then, *La Femme Fiona* appeared on his computer screen in seventh place, a minute behind, still in contention.

He raised a hand to signal C.V. and caught her attention still talking about Tatanya and Toshi. He pointed at his computer screen, the line with Fiona's place and time. C.V. nodded to both indicate she understood and to thank him for the heads-up.

"We still haven't seen Fiona Flynn today, Mark."

"Yet she was one of the favorites."

"Only after Aba learned she was pregnant and decided to run today's marathon for fun rather than money."

"But a first-time marathoner, Carolynne? Fiona's among the world-best at 5,000 and 10,000 meters on the track, but 26 miles on the road presents a different challenge."

"I couldn't agree more, Mark, but somehow I think we'll be seeing *La Femme Fiona* in the final sprint for the finish."

"Meanwhile, speaking of the world record holder," Mallon shifted the subject, "Christine Ferrara is on the course tracking Aba Andersson. We'll talk to the expectant mother after this message."

Timothy continued to stare at his laptop as its screen filled with the identities of the remaining top-ten women runners. A Kenyan. An Italian. An Ethiopian in tenth place. As expected. All solid runners, but probably not capable of winning today. The name of the runner with the four-digit number did not appear. By pecking at the keyboard and shifting screens, he could continue to explore the identities of runners further behind, but saw no reason to do so. The appearance of a four-digit runner in the top ten certainly must have been a computer glitch. With so much to report, especially with supermodels and popes on the course, there seemed no reason to mention her name. How long had they been running? Fifty-two minutes. Much more than the usual fifteen minutes of fame allotted to all the rest of us.

MARATHON

01:04:30

Joseph Nduku had been surprised by the welcome received passing the cheerleaders between the 10- and 11-mile marks, heading back toward downtown. He did not know the name of the street, nor did he know the name of the neighborhood. Gaytown, it was called, due to large number of homosexuals and lesbians living there. The Kenyan did recognize that the half dozen large-breasted cheerleaders standing on a platform dressed in glittering outfits cheering him were men not women. That neither offended nor amused him. The presence of large numbers of gays in what was an upscale neighborhood was part of living in a big city. He was surprised, however, by the enthusiasm of their cheers.

Then one of those cheering ran for several strides beside him, shouting: "Hey, Nduku: We're proud of what you're doing for AIDS!"

Of course. Joseph smiled. After the Saturday press conference, it probably was in that morning's newspaper about his promise to contribute any prize money he won to AIDS Africa. When Naní and others running for that charity came along in another hour or so, the crowd would cheer with as much enthusiasm. Probably a lot more!

Joseph, indeed, was generous, but ironically when he passed the cheerleaders he was running somewhere around twelfth place, not destined to win much money, certainly not the $100,000 he had earned winning last year. And there would be little bonus money either, Joseph suspected. Two miles later, Gaytown behind, passing west of downtown, Joseph reached the half-marathon (13.1 miles) point. He had moved up a few places during those miles, but although he did not look at the digital clock in passing, the numbers displayed showed his time would not be fast enough to increase his paycheck.

01:04:59. 01:05:00. 01:05:01.

Runners breaking 2:10 earned an extra $1,000 with additional bonuses for those breaking 2:09, 2:08, 2:07, or still faster with an ultimate bonus of $25,000 for a world record. The women received equivalent bonuses for times under 2:30. Given the weather, few bonuses would be paid today.

But Joseph saw no reason to worry. He would maintain his steady pace, whatever it was, and if he guessed correctly, in another half dozen miles, many of the runners currently in front of him would soon be put behind him. And if he caught and passed enough runners, he would win. If he did not pass enough runners, he might not finish in first place, but he still would win, because he would have run to the limits of his ability on a very warm day. *I am crocodile,* Joseph continued to remind himself. *I am crocodile.*

Just before the 14-mile mark, he came to another aid station, one for ordinary runners, not the elites. Joseph did not care. He snatched a cup off the tables for water and took several sips, throwing the rest down his back for whatever cooling it might provide. He grabbed another cup off the last table and repeated his actions.

I am crocodile, but even crocodiles must drink to survive.

Less than a half minute after Joseph Nduku passed that mark, two runners from the Northland Racing Team followed his actions, grabbing and drinking water wherever they could find it. Kyle and Wesley Fowler knew they were trailing Joseph. They could see him on what might be considered the edge of their viewing horizon. They recognized him partly because of the color of his outfit—he was wearing a yellow AIDS Africa singlet—but more from the effortlessness of his movement. Nobody ran as smoothly as Joseph: It was as though he were on a rail, moving effortlessly along a glass-smooth plain.

They were aware he had dropped off the back of the front pack soon after 5-K. They wondered if he was in trouble, as he gradually drifted back toward the pair. But then the defending champion's pace had stabilized, matching theirs, except he retained his lead over them of thirty or so seconds. They had no idea how much further ahead were the leaders. Planning to stop at 20 miles, the front pack was not on their radar screen. This was only a workout, they kept reminding themselves. In most races, their coach Steve Holland provided tactical information, but they had only seen him a couple of times and only in the early miles. Coach Holland apparently felt his time was best occupied supporting their teammate Katie Hyang in the women's race, where she had a good chance to finish high in the top ten.

They would see Joseph, then not see him. He would turn a corner and move out of sight. When they turned that same corner, they would see him again. Then he would turn another corner and disappear. After they reached that corner, there Joseph would be again. Always the same distance ahead.

Except after turning one corner, Kyle sensed they might be catching Joseph. He said to his brother: "Is he slowing down?"

"I think we're speeding up," Wesley replied.

"Should we do that?"

For several seconds, Wesley failed to respond, then said, "I don't know."

The twins continued running without saying more. Just before 15-miles, the course turned left and headed south. Joseph disappeared from view. Wesley looked at his watch. When the pair hit the corner, he looked at the watch again. "Twenty-one seconds," he announced.

Two blocks later, Joseph turned left again, heading back towards downtown. Wesley looked at his watch. When the pair hit the corner, he looked at the watch again. "Nineteen seconds."

"We're catching him."

"Should we slow down?"

"I don't think so."

"If Coach were here, he could tell us."

"He's probably busy with Katie."

"True."

"We're smart enough to figure this out on our own."

"Yes."

Silence for a block. Then another block. They passed 25-K and the elite aid station in the middle of the street. Kyle's bottle was on the left; Wesley's bottle on the right. Even though they had no plans to go the full 26, Coach Holland still made them prepare special bottles, good practice for New York in another month.

They carried the bottles for several blocks, then flung them toward the gutters. Silence for another block.

"Comfortable with the pace?" It was Kyle asking the question.

"Yes."

"So am I."

"Despite the heat?"

"It's not that hot."

"Bravely spoken for a Minnesotan."

"You *betcha!*"

Silence for a half block. Kyle again: "Why not turn this into a 3/1 run?"

"Hmmm," said Wesley.

Continued silence while they both considered the idea. A 3/1 run was a long distance workout done every second or third week during peak training. In a run of 20 miles, you do the first three-quarters of the distance (15 miles) at a relaxed pace, then during the final quarter (5 miles) pick up the pace slightly to finish faster than you had begun. It was a good workout strategy, but also a good race strategy whether elite or not.

"Let's catch Joseph and offer some support."

"I'd like that."

The twins were well past 15 miles and had less than 5 more miles to run in their workout. More silence for several more blocks as the two Northland runners considered the 3/1 option. It was not like they could read each other's minds, but they thought alike. Without breaking stride, Wesley simply turned over his left hand to expose a palm and presented it to his brother. Kyle raised his right palm and whacked his brother's palm sharply.

"Ouch, that hurt!"

"If you think that hurt, wait until you feel the next 5 miles!"

"Yeah," Wesley chortled. "Let's get ugly."

01:06:00

As word quickly began to spread that Pope Tony was running the marathon, residents of Lake City, the devout and the curious, began to trickle toward the course, hoping to get a glimpse of him passing. The crowds would continue to grow. If a million watched the marathon under normal conditions, two million might watch today, particularly given the warm and sunny weather: bad for running, perfect for spectating.

01:06:00. 01:06:01. 01:06:02.

As the course turned into Wilson Park, Christine Ferrara told Jake to move off the course and try to jump ahead of the pope using side streets. She then returned her attention to her conversation with Tom Schorr: "You *what?*"

Schorr repeated a comment just made: "I sold you to CNN"

"Tom!"

"CNN discovered the pope is running the marathon. It's all over the Internet. They saw your package and bought it. We're 'Breaking News.' I have CNN up on one of my screens. Your name is on the bottom: *Christine Ferrara reports on pope marathoner*. You're being watched right now by people in Tokyo, Khartoum, Buenos Aires."

"Really?"

"Yeah, really. They think you're the new Erica Hill."

"I'd rather be the old Christine Ferrara."

"Maybe you can be both."

"I don't want to move to New York!"

"Then Erica's job is secure."

"Do I get paid?"

"*We* get paid, and you get a share. It's in your contract. Page 7, subparagraph 12a. Enough money to take your boyfriend out to dinner."

"Tom: Peter is *not* my boyfriend!"

"Did I offer the name, *Peter?*"

"Oops."

"Regardless, get your pretty little—uhhh, golf cart—out on the course in front of Pope Tony. Stick your microphone in the Holy Father's face. CNN wants to know why he's running the marathon, and so do we."

"Tom, the crowds are enormous — and it's getting worse. I'm not sure how much longer I can stay close to the pope. Jake claims we can jump ahead before he exits the park, but I don't know how long that will be possible."

"We're onto it," said Schorr.

"Onto it?"

"I'm negotiating to get you a helicopter."

"Say what?"

"Helicopter, Christine. Flying object with rotating blades overhead."

"I know what a helicopter is, Tom. I've just never ridden in one before, and I'm not sure I want to."

"Page 11, sub-paragraph 14c."

"Tom, you're making these numbers up. Aren't helicopters dangerous? They don't have wings, do they?"

"Life is dangerous, Christine. Stop talking and listen. Give Peter a call on the press truck. He promised to background you on why Pope Tony is running the marathon. It'll help you ask intelligent questions."

"I always ask intelligent questions."

"I know that, sweetheart. That's why you're working in Lake City and not Peoria. Do you have Peter's cell phone number?"

"He's in my speed-dial."

Schorr paused for a second, saying finally: "I am not going there."

"Oops again."

"One final item: Pope Tony is wearing number 91. Why? There's probably a reason. Find out what it is."

"Does CNN want to know?"

"No, your favorite director wants to know."

Christine was about to counter that comment, but realized Schorr had hung up. Within a few minutes, they reached the point where the runners exited the park and spilled out into city streets. Blocked, Jake halted the cart between several rows of spectators. Christine said to Jake: "See if you can slide us out onto the course without running over anybody."

"Coming through!" shouted Jake. Several spectators at first looked at Jake without compassion even though he was driving a cart carrying a reporter and TV cameraman and waving his credentials hoping it would elicit some respect. Seeing his plight, a policeman shouted for people to get out of the way and moved a sawhorse to ease the cart's passage.

"Thank you, Officer," said Christine in passing.

"I watch you every night on *The Ten O'clock News*," said the policeman, who had a cheery red face.

I'm not on the Ten O'clock News, thought Christine, then realized he was referring to the program, not her as an individual.

SUNDAY

Jake soon had the golf cart moving at an even pace within the flow of runners, who did not seem overly disturbed about sharing the road with someone with a camera. "Hey, make me famous," several shouted. Christine offered her best smile, but made no promises. She instructed Jake to slow slightly. She figured the pope was running a minute or two behind them, thus if she timed it right, he soon would catch up. Before that happened, she needed to call Peter. She wondered what she would say to him.

01:14:54

Timothy Rainboldt considered the information shown on his laptop, the list of female elites, first through tenth places, the last two names having just posted within the last several seconds as the women positioned in ninth and tenth crossed the mat at the half-marathon mark in 1:14:54. Ninth was Katie Hyang, a member of Steve Holland's Northland Racing Team, someone whose name he recognized.

The other runner in tenth was the one with the four-digit number and a name still unfamiliar to him. Impostor or not? He did not know. Tenth at 10-K. Out of the top ten at 15-K and 20-K, so he figured she had drifted back into obscurity, or maybe even dropped out. But here was the Mystery Girl again, back in tenth at the half-marathon and with a split that predicted a sub-2:30 finish. *Who is that masked runner?*

01:14:54. 01:14:55. 01:14:56.

Mark Mallon and Carolynne Vickers were discussing the lead women, Tatanya Henry and Toshi Yamota, still up front, although the half dozen or so runners who had stayed with them during the first half of the marathon were losing contact. *Yes, the serious racing has begun.*

"Tatanya and Toshi look like they may be breaking this race open."

"And surprisingly, Mark, one of the pre-race favorites, Fiona Flynn, has yet to make a move."

"This is her first marathon?"

"So maybe she's being a bit timid."

"Or smart?"

"Or smart."

Timothy knew his fellow commentators had no immediate use for his input. C.V. could talk for five minutes without taking a breath, so he was free to research the credentials of this number 1459, Meghan Allison, before introducing her to the viewing public.

MARATHON

Accessing Ms. 1459's splits and places as she crossed the timing mats to this point, Timothy quickly confirmed that her splits were even, remarkably so, within a few seconds of each other. Her position in the race had jumped back and forth, but this was because she was running within a pack, which included five other runners. He realized now it was chance whether she crossed a mat in ninth or fourteenth place.

A few more taps on Timothy's keyboard revealed not much of a racing record for the Mystery Girl. She had won the women's division in a local half-marathon this summer, though in a time slower than she had just covered that same distance! But here: third in an 8-K that Lake City Bank sponsored in the spring. Finished close to a couple of Russians. So she has speed if not endurance. With a performance like that, it seemed strange that Peter McDonald would not offer this Meghan Allison a number lower than 1459, one that would offer access to the elite corral? *Was the Mystery Girl not planning to run the full distance?*

Timothy would need to seek the answers to those questions later, because the main feed had just switched from the leading women to the leading men, and Mallon had just directed a question his way:

"Kenyatta Kemai and Moses Abraham are still forcing the pace, Timothy, but Joseph Nduku is nowhere in sight. What do you think?"

"What?" Meghan Allison asked the runner next to her the one in the bright yellow singlet with Northland Racing Team on the front. Meg still did not know that runner's name.

The Northland runner, Katie Hyang, seemed startled, particularly since this runner with the high-numbered bib had run beside her for most of the previous four miles without saying a word, not a single word. The two communicated with side looks, each judging her pace off the other. It was comfortable to run that way, and there was no need to communicate verbally.

Hyang assumed the other runner was asking about the man who had hopped off his bicycle to shout words of encouragement as they passed the half-marathon mark. "That's my coach," she replied.

"I know, but what did he say?"

"He said I was in ninth place and told me to maintain a steady pace."

"Uhhhh, yeah. That's what I thought he said."

"So that means you're in ninth or tenth place too."

Meg fell silent for several strides more. "Are you serious?"

"Ye-e-e-s-s-s!" Hyang allowed her answer to slide slowly off her lips.

"They give prize money for the top ten, don't they?'

"Ye-e-e-s-s-s!"

The pair continued to run side by side for several more strides, Hyang finally breaking the silence. "Are you from Outer Space?"

"My husband sometimes thinks so."

Katie Hyang reached out with one hand: "Tell your husband, he's got it right. My name is Katie."

"And mine is Meg."

Introductions complete, Meg Allison shifted her attention back to the act of running. Her short discussion with the Northland runner had occupied less than a minute, but she knew that for her to stay in the top ten—if her new friend was correct—she needed to concentrate intently on each step. That was true when she ran cross-country for Coach McAnally in high school; it certainly still must be true while running a marathon.

Meg looked ahead and saw another female runner a hundred meters up the course. The runner had been positioned that far ahead for most of the last few miles. If the two of them were in ninth and tenth place, that other runner was in eighth place. She was running the same pace as her and Katie, but never quite in contact with them, as though she lived in a parallel universe.

That eighth-place runner was wearing a green singlet and had fiery red hair, and Meg suddenly realized that it was the same runner she had passed coming and going on the lakefront three days before: Fiona Flynn! One of the race favorites, even interviewed on TV. *What was she doing back in eighth place, but more to the point: What am I doing this close to her in tenth place?* Then suddenly, ninth place, because after their brief discussion, Katie Hyang had moved to a position behind her. One stride behind, then two, then three. *Did I unconsciously speed up? That was unfriendly. Maybe I should slow down. Or maybe I should see if I can catch Fiona.*

Contemplating whether she should commit to a faster pace, Meg Allison decided that with nearly half the race to run, that might be too risky. *Where is Matt? He could tell me what to do—if we had time to talk.*

Meg Allison finally looked back over her shoulder toward the Northland runner. She modified her pace slightly, just slightly, in a conscious decision to let the other runner catch up. "Come on, Katie. We're in this together!"

01:20:00

Standing on the press truck, rushing along the Lake City Marathon course ahead of the elite runners (Kemai and Abraham still in the lead), Peter McDonald savored the sights ahead and behind in his race. *I know* *it's arrogant of me,* Peter thought, *but I made this race what it is today. With a little help from my friends.*

Despite forebodings, everything was going as well as could be expected. His main challenge—that of getting Celebrity X into the field without discovery—could not have been better met. Aba Andersson's running while pregnant seemed a more enticing story than if she had set one more world record. It did not appear to be as warm as predicted—he was not even sweating—but Peter was a poor judge, riding on the back of a truck that created its own breeze. The issue of whether to shorten the race would need to be addressed later, after the elites finished. Weatherman Vaughn Johnson was somewhere back in the middle of the pack, running with a cell phone. Peter would need to call Vaughn soon and ask how he felt. Dennis Lahey seemed like an engaging man, but even if Shelaghi bailed, there were other sponsors. Peter would never say so, but an Irish conglomerate might find it difficult to walk away from a marathon blessed by the pope. He only wished Fiona Flynn was doing better. On last report, *La Femme Fiona* was far behind the leaders, "but that could change," he warned Lahey.

Truth be told, the reason for Peter feeling so upbeat was the sudden presence in his life of someone who might shift the direction of that life. Someone who, following his just-completed conversation with TV director Tom Schorr, should call any minute.

01:20:00. 01:20:01. 01:20:02.

His cell phone rang, and there was her name in the caller-ID window: Christine. He knew why she was calling, so he did not waste words: "I need to background you on Pope Tony, Christine."

The person who had just called did not immediately react. "Hello, Christine," she said, mockingly.

"Hello, Christine," he repeated, realizing he should not have started talking in the middle of a conversation.

"Hello, Peter," she said, this time more sweetly.

"I need to background you on Pope Tony," Peter said again.

"Yes, that's why I called."

"Christine, you're incorrigible," said Peter, saying it without malice.

Wait until you know me a little longer, she thought. but this was no time to play cute. So she listened as Peter told about having been coached by Tony in high school, Tony's sudden elevation to the papacy, his having started running again to relieve stress, his decision to run the marathon, and there never was any question which one he would choose. Without taking notes, Christine imprinted the information in her memory.

"One other question, Peter. Tom wants to know the reason for the number he's wearing. Why 91?"

"You need to ask him that."

"Peter, are you still keeping secrets from me?"

The moment those words left her mouth, Christine remembered the video she had seen last night of Peter's wife getting killed. She realized how rude those words must seem to him. Peter had failed to respond immediately. She filled the silence:

"I'm sorry," she said softly.

Peter realized the reason for Christine's apology, but decided he did not want to react—at least not this early in their developing relationship.

He skipped past her apology: "Just ask him. There's an interesting reason for the number. In fact, two reasons. Better that you don't know them until after you ask Tony the question."

"You sound like my instructor for Journalism 101."

"You took Journalism 101? No wonder you're such a good reporter."

Good, we're back to fencing again. "I'm hanging up, Peter."

"Before you do, did you get an invitation to my suite after the race?"

"Peter, we just met."

Good, thought Peter, *we're back to fencing again.* "There'll probably be a hundred people. You know what I mean, Christine."

"I do."

"If you need directions, call me on my cell phone after the telecast."

"You're on my speed-dial."

A sudden buzz on the line told him that this time Christine had hung up, without saying goodbye. She did that purposely. *Women!* It's good to be starting a relationship with one again.

Peter redirected his attention to the race as seen off the back of the press truck. Kenyatta Kemai and Moses Abraham continued to hold their lead. The collection of other runners who had stayed with them in the early miles, one by one, had dropped away. In fact, the lead of the two Kenyans had grown to the point where he could barely see the third or fourth runners. He knew neither was his defending champion, Joseph Nduku. Too bad, because of all the Kenyan runners, he liked Joseph the most. He had the best sense of humor. He talked to the press with grace and style. But having promised his prize winnings to AIDS Africa, it would be embarrassing if Joseph had little or no money to donate.

Several of those riding the press truck had radios, probably listening to the marathon broadcast. They would know how Joseph was doing, but Peter felt disinclined to ask them. He liked being disengaged from the race-in-progress at least for the few hours he rode the press truck. Once they reached the finish line, he would need to return to his persona of race director, but in the mean-

384

time he could ride along and enjoy the warm weather; enjoy it, he knew, much more than would the runners.

His cell phone rang. Looking at the display he saw it was Noel Michaels. The subject was weather. "Good news and bad news," she told him.

"Start with the good news."

"That cold front lurking out west suddenly has accelerated. Best estimates are that it might arrive as early as noon, dropping the temperature as much as 10 or 20 degrees when it hits."

It did not take Peter long to do the calculation. The front would arrive too late to provide much relief for those finishing under four hours. But most of these finishers, he rationalized, were better trained than those further behind. Knowing relief was on the way probably meant that they could avoid shortening the marathon, meaning everybody would have a chance to finish, if not finish in a fast time.

But his executive assistant had begun by saying there also was bad news. After she told him, Peter decided that the good news might not be good enough to balance the bad.

01:32:00

"Approaching 19 miles," said Mark Mallon, "Kenyatta Kemai and Moses Abraham continue to turn this into a two-man race." The anchorman was coming out of a commercial break. "The two Kenyans had company until a few miles ago, but one by one the other contenders have drifted backwards."

"Toward oblivion," suggested Timothy Rainbold.

01:32:00. 01:32:01. 01:32:02.

The live feed featured Kemai and Abraham shoulder to shoulder, little strain showing on their faces, betraying no emotion, eyes focused forward rather than on each other, arms moving in smooth synchronization with their legs, the pair seeming to float above the road rather than touching it as they drew inexorably closer to the finish line of the Lake City Marathon.

"We thought the heat might be a factor," continued Mallon, "and although temperatures have climbed into the low 80's—predicted to go higher—it has not slowed these two brave Kenyans down."

"But it seems to have taken a toll on defending champion Joseph Nduku," responded Timothy. "He simply has *not* been a factor today."

SUNDAY

"Camera 2," came the voice of director Tom Schorr, unheard by the viewing audience. *"Split screen."*

The two leaders continued to be shown on the left half of the screen, Joseph on the right. For a few moments, Mallon allowed the picture to tell the story, then turned to Timothy, "How does Joseph look?"

"As smooth as the leaders. Looking at his stride, his cadence, he looks to be matching Kemai and Abraham step for step, but...."

Timothy paused and melodramatically allowed the phrase to dangle, then continued, "And it is a big 'but...'"

Another pause before the commentator continued: "...Joseph may soon be running out of course. Over the first half of the race, beginning around 5-K when Nduku allowed the lead pack to distance itself from him, he lost two minutes to the leaders. That's nearly a half mile and a lot to make up in the miles remaining."

"But...." Carolynne Vickers interrupted. "And it's another big but, Timothy. We're still a mile shy of 20 miles, that mythical mark where runners often explode if they have gone out too fast."

"True," her partner conceded.

Mark Mallon leaned back in his chair, a smile on his face although it was unseen by viewers, the split screen showing the three Kenyans still in place. He would allow the two color commentators to argue for a while.

C.V. continued with her point. "I've been watching the splits, Timothy, as I know have you. And it's easy to see that Joseph made a conscious decision around 5-K to let the leaders go. They were on a 2:06 pace and, since we can't look inside his head, we can only assume that he felt there was no way Kemai—and particularly Abraham—could run that fast on a day this warm, with temperatures climbing."

"Agreed."

"So Joseph slowed to a more rational 2:09 or 2:10 pace."

"Gambling," Mallon joined the discussion, "that he could win with that slow a time."

"'Slow' being a relative term, considering that there will be runners finishing at six or seven hours today."

"Or *not* finishing," said C.V. "Given the warm weather, race director Peter McDonald might choose to cut the race short for those too far back. It is one of his contingency plans. But back to the leaders. Beginning at 5-K and through the half marathon, up to around 25-K, Kemai and Abraham continued to build their lead. Then that lead of about two minutes stabilized..."

"...not because Joseph was running faster—you're right, C.V—but because the leaders were running slower..."

"...slightly slower..."

"…but faster than the other dozen or so runners in the lead pack…"

"…who have begun to struggle…

"…so again comparing their pace to that of Joseph…"

"…within a mile, or two, or three…"

"…our defending champion, currently in eighth place…"

"…could soon be in third…"

"…or maybe second, since we don't know how long Abraham, who came here as a rabbit, can match the pace of his countryman, Kemai."

During this exchange, Mallon felt that he was like an umpire seated in a high chair above the net, watching a long volley at Wimbledon. He had just learned from director Tom Schorr that the motorcycle with Camera 2 was about to pull slightly forward from its position beside Joseph Nduku to a point where it could look back at him head on. From that position, Schorr informed him, viewers could look past the defending champion at two other runners closing on him. And surprisingly—although nobody would dare to make such a politically incorrect comment either on camera or off—they were white!

"And here's an interesting development," offered Mallon, "because we can see two other runners not that far behind Joseph Nduku."

"We can't tell how far behind because of the camera angle," said C.V.

"But they seem to be catching Joseph," Timothy pointed out.

"Which means," said Mallon, "they're running faster than Joseph, faster than the leaders."

"An interesting development."

"Very interesting, but remember: Joseph is still in eighth place, well behind the leaders…"

"…but maybe catching up…"

"…or being caught…"

"…or both…"

Mark Mallon interjected: "It is said that the first half of the marathon lasts 20 miles. The second half is six miles. This may prove true today."

Timothy had been pecking at the keyboard of his computer. "I'm trying to identify the pair."

Unseen by him, C.V. rolled her eyes. She had been looking at the TV screen rather than at a computer. "Those are the yellow shirts of the Northland Racing Team, Timothy…"

"…Kyle and Wesley Fowler…"

"…Rabbits!"

"Clarifying that term," said Mallon, "a rabbit is a runner hired to pace other runners, at least for an agreed-upon mileage—then stop."

"Thirty seconds to commercial break," warned Tom Schorr.

SUNDAY

C.V. explained further: "The Fowler twins—Kyle and Wesley—came to Lake City to help pace Aba Andersson to a world record. With Aba pregnant, race director Peter McDonald released them from their duties. We spoke to their coach, Steve Holland, yesterday, and he said the twins still planned to run 20 miles, then drop out. They expect to run New York City next month."

As she spoke, Nduku was shown on screen moving toward a table in the center of the road, grabbing a plastic bottle from the table. He began drinking from it, then turned to observe the two runners trailing as they also grabbed bottles from the table. Joseph appeared to slow down, as though waiting for the twins to catch him. When they did, the three runners began moving in tandem. Joseph held out a hand to a twin on one side, a second hand to the twin on the other. The trio could be seen talking to each other.

"What's that all about?" wondered Mark Mallon.

"Too bad we don't have them miked, so we could listen to their conversation," said Timothy.

"Kenyatta Kemai and Moses Abraham might want to listen to that conversation too," added C.V.

"Ten seconds to commercial break," warned Tom Schorr.

Mark Mallon began a tease: "Meanwhile, there are some interesting developments on the women's side. "Tatanya and Toshi are still leading, but the trail pack is far from out of it. And a mystery runner has moved into the top ten. Local girl, interestingly enough. And more: Weatherman Vaughn Johnson is running the race with a cell phone. He tells us, 'It's hot out.' We'll be back with those stories after these messages."

As viewers of the telecast were forced to endure a series of commercials for fast food stores and car companies, Joseph Nduku began a brief conversation with the two Northland runners who had just joined him.

"What took you so long?"

"We forgot our map," said one twin.

"We took a wrong turn coming out of the park," said the other.

Joseph smiled, white teeth shining against glistening black skin. "Then you two truly must be fast to have caught me." He gestured forward. "Run ahead and tell Kenyatta to explain why he is running so much faster in this heat."

One twin: "We're only running 20 miles, Joseph."

"Ahhh."

The other: "If we keep going, our coach threatened to tackle us."

"Ahhh."

The three ran together silently for another ten seconds, Joseph thinking.

"Then I will let you run with me to 20 miles," he said finally. "No more."

"Thank you, Joseph."

"Maybe"

"No tricks, Joseph."

The three continued to run together, the brief conversation having ended, their movements no longer seen by the television audience watching commercials at that moment for an insurance company.

During the commercial break, the two color commentators seated on each side of Mark Mallon debated the legitimacy of a so-called "Mystery Girl," now in tenth place. C.V. worried that this woman with the four-digit number might be another Rosie Ruiz, the impostor who had "won" the 1980 Boston Marathon, stealing the race from Canadian Jacqueline Gareau, until officials discovered Rosie had run only the last mile leading into the finish line.

"She's legit," argued Timothy. "Her split times track perfectly. I just got off the phone with Noel Michaels. There is no way, Noel says, that she could have cut the course."

"Then who is she?"

"Save that question for when we come back live," Mallon interrupted.

"Ten seconds," warned Tom Schorr, through their earphones.

Mallon told his fellow commentators: "Tom also has been talking to Christine, who knows this Mystery Girl. A foot doctor: would you believe that?"

"What?"

"We'll be cutting to Christine as you two try to figure out the mystery. And Vaughn Johnson is somewhere out there with a cell phone waiting to explain why it is hot without the help of a green screen."

Timothy and Carolynne looked at each other and shrugged.

"So many story lines," said Timothy.

"And that's not even including the pope," added C.V.

Mallon chuckled as he heard the voice of Tom Schorr in his earphone: *"Five, four, three, two, one...."*

01:43:00

As he drew near, now only a block behind her, Christine Ferrara first worried about how she should address the pope. *Your Holiness*, if she remembered correctly from parochial school. But that seemed *so* formal, particularly for someone who was a close friend of Peter. And running without white vestments or that funny, pointed hat.

SUNDAY

The pope and those surrounding him were ten miles into the marathon. At the point where he had emerged from the park, the runners were too thick around Pope Tony for her to blend into the pack, so she had cut the course to intersect it doubling back toward the city. The course was on a wider street. More room to maneuver, but still too many people for comfort.

01:43:00. 01:43:01. 01:43:02.

Christine continued to consider the protocol of papal interviews. *Dare I call him Tony? Probably not—or not yet, assuming Peter and I have a future.* In newspapers and on TV, reporters and commentators usually refer to him as "Pope Tony." But would you say that to his face?

Darn you, Peter. If you only had given me a few hours warning, I could have googled an online gossip columnist. Oh, that man!

But as the distance between her golf cart and the pope diminished to a half block, then to a quarter block, finally to less than that, Christine realized there was no possible way she could conduct an intelligent interview within what she later would describe to viewers as a "maelstrom of love."

It was the noise!

An intense, noise. Loud. Unbelievably loud. A piercing noise. Off the decibel scale. Like an elevated train passing overhead. Like the most obnoxious rock concert ever attended. Like an airport runway. Like inside a tornado.

The noise came from the cheers of people lining the course, people living within a few blocks of the marathon route, or even miles away, who after learning on radio or TV that the pope was running decided to rush to the course to see him. And as he ran past, they cheered. The noise had been less a factor an hour earlier when she had ridden parallel to the pope on the divided street, but now the crowds of spectators had doubled, maybe tripled, the noise level also doubling and tripling.

Now with the pope so close, Christine placed a cautionary hand on the shoulder of her driver, Jake. "Don't get anyone killed!" she warned him.

Jake looked back over his shoulder: *"What?"*

Christine could only shake her head and raise her palms in despair. If she could barely communicate with her driver, how could she ask questions to the man who was the center of the maelstrom.

Then he was almost close enough to touch. The wall of noise moved with him. With the runners immediately around the pope, she could see that it had become increasingly difficult for her driver to avoid interfering with them.

The pope began to pass. He was in the middle of the road. She riding in the golf cart, on the side of the road, Edmund's camera recording his every moment. If her driver angled the cart slightly to the right, she could talk to him. Even that close, they would barely be able to hear each other, nor would the TV audience be able to hear any conversation they had.

Then the pope looked in her direction and smiled. And waved.

Edmund caught it on camera.

Christine smiled. And waved back. For a moment, the pace of her cart equaled the pace of the pope, although she could see that spectators stepping off the curb to get a better view might make it difficult to keep pace. The danger was that the entire race at this point might bog down, and the pope and would find it impossible to continue. Policemen at each intersection were trying to control the crowd, successfully coping so far, but what if more and more Lake Citians come out to participate in this love fest?

After his wave, Christine saw the pope speak to a runner by his side. There seemed to be two runners, both looking very Italian, keeping pace with him. Probably bodyguards, she decided. The runner nodded toward the pope, then began angling toward her. Other runners nearby yielded.

Mario, moved to a position beside the golf cart and said something. Christine could not hear, because she was wearing earphones. She removed the earphones and realized that the earphones had been protecting her from some of the noise. It was even more intense. Now she was inside the screaming jet engine, but at least she could hear what the bodyguard said:

"Christine?"

He knows my name? "Yes?"

"He can't talk."

"I know."

The bodyguard shrugged. It was a full-body shrug, arms sweeping high above shoulders. It reminded Christine of her Uncle Massimo, now gone. Italians know how to shrug better than any other people in the world. The bodyguard started to move away, back to his position beside and behind the celebrity he was assigned to guard.

"Wait!"

Mario returned to running beside the cart. Christine hoped she was not taking him away from his duty, that she was not putting the pope in danger by diverting his bodyguard's attention. But she had to know:

"The number?"

The bodyguard looked puzzled by the question, so Christine patted herself several times in the area of her body where she would be wearing a number if in the race. "*Numero? Numero?* Why number 91? *Novantauno?*" Saying that, she realized it was silly to try to communicate with the bodyguard in the few words of Italian she had learned from her mother. Initially, he had addressed her in English.

The bodyguard finally realized what she was asking. He smiled. It was a wide-toothed Italian smile. Even though Mario was a Swiss Guard, he came from the Italian-speaking corner of Switzerland.

"High school," he said.

High school? Christine wondered, then she understood. The pope was running in a uniform of the high school he and Peter had attended. It was probably Pope Tony's year of graduation. But there had been a second reason for his choosing the number 91.

During the exchange, Christine had kept one hand on Mario's shoulder so he could not return to the pope's side. She asked about a second reason.

"Psalm 91," he said.

Psalm 91? But she could not ask Mario to explain, because he had slid away from under her hand and was returning to his main duty the side of the pope. *Psalm 91?* Should she know the words of that psalm?

Then it came to her. It was a hymn based on that psalm she had sung frequently in church, one of her favorites. She could even remember the words, so ha, ha, Peter McDonald! But could she quote those words exactly?

And he will raise you up on eagle's wings,
Bear you on the breath of dawn,
Make you to shine like the sun,
And hold you in the palm of his hand.

Yes, like eagle's wings. She even had seen those words on the back of T-shirts, very appropriate for running in a marathon, particularly if you are head of a church with nearly a billion members.

Jake had slowed the cart because of the large number of runners trailing the pope, who had begun to slide away from her, carried on the tip of a glacier. Fortunately, the noise was moving with him. At the next intersection she would ask Jake to leave the course and find some quiet corner away from runners and spectators. She would do a report, ending it with the meaning of the number. Christine hoped Tom Schorr had someone in the studio who could confirm if her memory of the hymn's words was correct.

Her cell phone rang. Looking at the display, she saw it was her director. "Tom, this is impossible," she began talking without saying hello. "The crowds. The noise. I'll never get near him again."

"Don't worry, Christine, we've got your back. I'm switching you and Edmund to a helicopter."

"What???"

MARATHON

01:46:30

Somewhere around 18 miles, Meg Allison realized that Katie Hyang, the Northland runner who had run with her for most of the last ten miles, suddenly was gone. They were hardly close friends. Not even friends. They had not spoken a word to each other until somewhere around the half-marathon mark, where they had acknowledged each other's presence. They had exchanged few words after that. But it was like we knew each other.

And now Katie was gone.

And Bob Veldman, the runner who had pushed her to the front of Start Corral A, was gone. *Did he drop out as planned?* She could not remember when she last saw him. Not that she was paying much attention, but Meg was on her own. Running without company, and it made her uncomfortable. *Am I going too fast? Am I going too slow? I never ran a marathon before. Help!*

Meg looked quickly over her shoulder and realized that Katie had fallen thirty, maybe forty, yards behind her, and seemed about to lose more ground. It did not make sense for Meg to slow that much. This was supposed to be a race, not High Tea. Katie still was close enough so Meg could see from the expression on her rival's face that she was hurting. Maybe she had a stomach cramp. Still moving at a good pace, but hurting. Meg sometimes got cramps in training, like a knife stuck in your stomach one minute, then with some massage or some deep breathing, it went away. She hoped Katie could stay close, maybe even catch back up.

If this had been a high school cross-country race and she had surged and broken a rival, Meg might have been tempted to gloat. At least to herself: *Yeah, I beat her!* But this was a marathon, and although she had not run one before, the rules of engagement seemed different. She noticed that runners around her—men and women—communicated with each other. Not much, and not about frivolous matters, but they talked, like she had with Katie.

In cross-country or track, runners communicated more often with their elbows. Cut someone off going around a turn and you might get shoved into the next pole. Of course, once each of you crossed the finish line, you immediately turned and apologized to each other in the chute. That's why she and so many other runners loved high school cross-county. But this is not high school cross-country, Toto. It's road racing, where competitors seemed to be racing against the distance as much as against each other. Nobody had shoved an elbow into her side yet, and she suspected nobody would.

393

SUNDAY

How dumb am I? Meghan did not even know how much prize money she would win if she held her position. She thought she was maybe seventh now. Or was it sixth? Katie's coach had shouted out the placing to them the last time they saw him on his bicycle, but now that Katie had vanished from her athletic universe, Meg no longer would be recipient of such information. She hadn't seen Matt and Aaron and Moira for the last half hour, so who knows where they were. Matt had said something about the pope running. *Was he kidding?* Maybe they're off chasing the pope. She would be too if she was not out here running.

Meg was having a hard time concentrating. Her mind had begun to drift, now that she was running alone. She had begun to lose focus, and she did not want to do that. She forced herself to look forward not backward and realized she was about to catch another runner. The runner was black: Kenyan, or maybe Ethiopian. Meg did not know her new rival's name, because she was clueless, just running on instinct and talent. The black runner was fading off an early pace that had been too fast for her. Sensing her weakness, Meg increased her own pace slightly to catch the black runner. High school cross-country instincts cutting in again.

Meg pulled even with the black runner just as they passed the mats at 30-K. Meg looked up at the numbers on the digital clock when they passed, but the numbers meant nothing to her.

01:46:30. 01:46:31. 01:46:32.

The two runners ran side by side but only for a short time. As they came to a table in the center of the road, the black runner swerved toward it and picked a plastic bottle off the table. She began drinking. Meg had no plastic bottle on the elite athlete's table, because she was not an elite athlete—at least in name. She kept running causing her to gain several strides on her rival. Looking at the front of her rival's singlet, she now saw that she was Ethiopian. Her name was Gurmu, because in addition to numbers on their bibs, the elites also were identified by last name. In contrast, Meghan Allison remained an anonymous 1459, though she sensed that if she maintained this pace, she would not maintain that anonymity longer. *What is this going to do to my podiatry career?* That was a silly thought, so she immediately dismissed it. *Concentrate, Meghan! Concentrate!*

Past the elite aid table, the Ethiopian increased her pace slightly and caught Meg, so as not to yield another position. Or maybe Meg subconsciously slowed down slightly to allow her to be caught, permitting some company for the next few miles. Gurmu had carried her plastic bottle past the aid station and continued to sip from it. She carried the bottle in her right hand. Meg looked at the Ethiopian runner, who was incredibly tiny, her head barely up to the American's shoulders.

Meg smiled at Gurmu, who smiled back and said something in a language that Meg could not understand, except her new rival reached over with her left hand and tapped Meg's number, 1459, then smiled. Meg suspected it was the Ethiopian equivalent of the question posed by Katie Hyang when Meg pulled even with her: "Are you for real?"

"Yes, it's me the stealth bomber," Meg responded, knowing there was no way Gurmu would understand that comment.

And that's when Tsutsu Gurmu offered her plastic bottle to the American whose name she did not know. It surprised Meg. *This is not cross-country.* The Ethiopian understood that if the runner beside her did not have elite status, as shown by her relatively high number, she also must not have bottles on the elite tables. It was a pure, but not that unusual, act of friendship from one runner to another.

Meg accepted the bottle, and drank from it. *Ugh! What is this liquid. It is awful!* She gulped and handed the bottle back to Gurmu with thanks. She hoped the Ethiopian did not notice her reaction to the taste of whatever homemade concoction was contained in that bottle. *Please don't offer me that bottle again!* Meg thought she might upchuck and wondered how soon they would come to an aid station, so she could wash the taste out of her mouth.

It was from a desire not to share fluids with the Ethiopian that caused Meg to pick up the pace ever so slightly. She did not want to surge, because that was wasteful of energy, and they still had a long way to go. Just a slight pace increase—and it worked! Gurmu fell behind a stride, then another stride, then she was gone, the same as had happened to Katie Hyang a mile before.

Victims!

Meg found herself now running in another vacuum, not even any men nearby. No-woman's-land. Everybody seemed to be slowing down at this point in the race except her. Yet it's much easier to run with someone else, she had learned. You can work together. *The last half dozen miles are liable to be very lonely,* thought Meg Allison.

Except....

Meg looked ahead and saw another solitary runner, a woman. She had red hair and an emerald green singlet. A mile later, just before 20 miles, when a slight pace increase allowed Meg Allison to catch and pull even with the runner with red hair, that runner seemed startled, as though she had not expected to be caught. She looked at Meg, then down at her number.

"Who are you?" asked Fiona Flynn.

01:58:00

Niles Wendell loved Marathon Sunday. He had founded the Lake
City Marathon, had presided at its birth, had breathed life into it on
several occasions when it appeared the marathon would not survive
for lack of sufficient funds from sponsors. Niles had served as savior, throwing some tax-deductible cash at the race at appropriate moments, assigning
one of his assistants to help with organization, eventually hiring Peter McDonald as race director. No big deal for a businessman of his stature, who knew
everybody connected with the mayor's Office. The marathon prospered even
after he stepped away from micromanaging the event. Why interfere, when
Peter was best in the business? As a result, he could show up at the V.I.P.
Tent on Marathon Sunday and enjoy the fun without having to do any work. It
doesn't get much better than that. He now was standing at the coffee table,
having refilled his cup. Moving, cup in hand, back to where he had left his
guests, Niles looked up at one of the TV sets showing the race. A couple of
Africans leading; no surprise there. The ticking clock at the bottom of the
screen indicated the time as approaching two hours.

01:58:00. 01:58:01. 01:58:02.

That would put the leaders at close to 24 miles. Only ten minutes away. He
needed to remind his guests that they could go out to the grandstand beside
the finish line and watch the winners come across. A few more sips of coffee,
and Wendell would head that way too. He had been invited, as founder, to
hold one end of the banner that the winner would break crossing the line.
Bank CEO Robin Carter would hold the other end, her last race-related duty
before pulling the ripcord on her golden parachute and landing on the Cayman
Islands. She was somewhere else in the tent, schmoozing customers important
enough to be offered VIP access.

Next year with Shelaghi, things might be different. *Will I stay on the A
party list?* Wendell had searched the tent earlier for Dennis Lahey, but learned
he had chosen to ride the press truck with Peter McDonald. At least they had
warm weather. One year he had ridden the press truck on a day when it
snowed. He would have frozen if Peter had not loaned him a pair of gloves.
That should not be a problem today.

Lahey's future plans for the marathon had not yet been revealed to him,
just as Peter had not revealed the pope was running. Clever boy. Wendell understood now the need for security. Would the pope's presence in the race be

one factor in determining Lahey's decision? Would it help if Fiona Flynn won the women's race? It might, except the Irish Lass had been back in fifth place the last time he looked. Some Russian was leading; no surprise there.

Don't Americans know how to run? It's always foreigners coming to our races and taking home $100,000 paychecks. How long had it been since an American had won the Lake City Marathon? Niles could not even remember. Someone who probably is now a member of AARP.

That did not stop Americans from staging the best parties. He had been to the London Marathon. He had been to Berlin. Their V.I.P. Tents did not come close to matching the one in which he was standing in now.

The spread was equal to any you might encounter in the best country clubs. Sliced ham. Roast beef. Two chefs cooking multi-ingredient omelets. The finest in pastries. Niles liked best the almond croissants. Everything from soft drinks to martinis (shaken not stirred) at two bars, one on each side of the tent. This year in deference to the Shelaghi visitors, Wendell had suggested to Peter that they add Guinness to the beer menu. The cup of coffee he had in his hand was as fine as in the city's most elegant coffee bars. A coffee from the high plateaus of Mount Kenya. Peter claimed he had to serve Kenyan coffee otherwise the runners from that country would refuse to come to Lake City. A bad joke, of course, but good coffee.

Placing his half empty cup on a tray, Niles walked past the TV set again, this time pausing to see who was leading. The elite runners had their names as well as numbers on their bibs, so it was easy to tell. "Kemai," was the name on the bib of the lead runner. *Boring race*, thought Niles. He's been leading since the start with the other Kenyan, Moses Abraham, a rabbit, who was no longer running at Kemai's side.

Or was that Abraham? The distortion of the telephoto lens made it difficult to determine distance. If that was Abraham, who were those two other runners? They did not appear to be Kenyan, and that *would* be a surprise.

Niles Wendell moved closer to the TV set so he could listen to the announcers. With everyone talking, it was hard to hear. Bad luck: Break for a commercial. Wendell knew he needed to get out to the finish line if he wanted to hold the tape for Kenyatta Kemai or some other Kenyan.

"Ten seconds," warned director Tom Schorr. "Five, four, three, two, one...."

Mark Mallon picked up the cue: "We're back live and will stay live until we have a winner." Mallon directed his attention to Timothy Rainboldt sitting beside him. "And, Timothy, up until a few minutes ago—in fact, until we broke for commercials—I would have assured our viewers that the winner would be Kenyatta Kemai."

"Camera 1!"

SUNDAY

Timothy responded: "It looked like a lock, Mark. Kemai and his partner Moses Abraham have led from the start. Several miles back Moses stepped off the course, his rabbiting work apparently over."

"Moses no longer was leading Kenyatta to the Promised Land."

Timothy winced visibly, but continued, "Since that moment, Kenyatta's pace has dropped from 5:08 to 5:17 to 5:31 for the last three miles. Those times might sound pretty fast if you're a Sunday jogger..."

"...Or a pope," interrupted Carolynne Vickers.

Timothy ignored her comment, continuing his flow of statistics, "...but up until the moment Abraham abandoned ship, they had been running 4:50 miles, nothing above 5:00."

"Kemai hit the wall," said Mallon.

"At least he brushed it. A lot of runners in this race can identify with how that feels. But more to the point, that opens the door for.... I yield to my superior, who may yet win our office bet."

"...Joseph Nduku," offered C.V. triumphantly.

"Camera 2!"

The live feed shifted to Joseph Nduku running purposely, looking no more fatigued than he had two hours ago. But he was not alone. Running with him were two other runners, both wearing yellow shirts with red and black stripes.

C.V. continued, excited by the scene she saw on the TV monitor: "Joseph Nduku closing fast on Kenyatta Kemai is not the surprise. Kenyatta went out at what has been revealed now as a too-fast pace on a too-hot day. Joseph went with him for maybe 5-K, then backed off to what also has been revealed as a sensible pace. So that's not the surprise, Mark and Timothy. The surprise is the two runners running even with Joseph Nduku!"

02:05:00

Steve Holland was amazed when he reached the 20-mile mark, climbed off his bike and saw the Northland Racing Team's van parked exactly where he had left it last night, in a parking lot used by tourists visiting Chinatown. The plan was for the twins to run the first 20 miles of the marathon and stop. The van would be sitting there, and they could use it to drive back to the hotel.

Other than seeing them a couple of times in the opening miles, he had not paid Kyle and Wesley Fowler much attention as he biked around the course. They twins were only running a workout. Others in the club were actually running the marathon and deserved more of his time. Katie Hyang, was flying. Katie was in fifth place when she passed him at 20, headed for a PR even in this hot weather—and a good payday if she could hold on. And it looked like she could. The sixth-place runner, an Ethiopian was now more than two minutes behind and struggling. Holland remained by the side of the road to check on her competition, planning to cut the course to catch Katie one more time before heading to the finish.

He looked at the time on his watch. The elite men probably were within a mile of the finish line, but he did not have a horse in that race.

02:05:00. 02:05:01. 02:05:02.

Holland had leaned his bicycle against a lamppost. Before departing, he decided to check the inside of the van. The warm-up gear belonging to the twins was still in the back seat. The Northland coach pulled out his cell phone and speed-dialed Kyle's number. He heard the phone ringing in the glove compartment. They had not been here, but if so: where were they? Maybe they were nearby, cooling down. Maybe they had decided to spare themselves a hard run on a hot day and drop out before 20. No, that was not like them.

The coach decided that he could not waste more time worrying about the twins, who could take care of themselves. He needed to move if he wanted to intersect Katie at 23 miles to update her about her competition. He climbed out of the van and received another surprise:

"Son of a bitch! Somebody stole my bicycle."

Joseph Nduku would not let them stop. Just before they had reached 20 miles, the point where the twins planned to drop out, the defending champion challenged the pair: "Don't stop. Run one more mile with me."

The twins had run hard over the last 5 miles to catch Joseph and were not sure they could go even that much further. Still, Kyle told Wesley he still felt strong and Wesley told Kyle he could probably go one more mile—but not much more, particularly since they would need to jog back a mile to get to the van they planned to take to the finish line.

"C'mon, guys," Joseph challenged them. "Rabbit me another mile."

"Okay," said Wesley, "one more mile."

Then they reached 21 miles and Joseph grabbed Kyle by his singlet. "One more mile. I'm not letting go."

"Joseph, we can't," pleaded Wesley. "We're supposed to run New York next month. Our coach will kill us."

"Hey, rabbit," argued Joseph. "Earn your money. Look!" He pointed toward Moses Abraham, walking by the side of the road, his race apparently over. But when Moses saw the three go by, he started jogging again.

"One more mile," said Joseph. "Come on, brothers. Let's catch Kemai."

SUNDAY

He repeated that plea at Mile 22. It caused Kyle to remember the story about Alberto Salazar's classic duel with Dick Beardsley at the 1983 Boston Marathon. After running with Salazar all the way from Hopkinton to the last of the Newton hills, Beardsley appeared beaten with only five miles to go, but he would not quit and kept telling himself "one more mile" at each marker. Beardsley did not win that day, but he finished only two seconds behind.

So it became almost a joke when Joseph said again at 23 miles, "One more mile." The twins echoed his comment, "One more mile!" Weakly. The heat had taken its toll. They were hurting, but so was Joseph, and so was Kemai, although that had not yet become apparent, since he still had a large lead.

At 24, the three chanted "one more mile" simultaneously. And laughed doing so. They were running in rhythm. Or staggering in rhythm. It was not pretty. Each of the three still ran at a pace that he would not have been able to hold, if forced to run solo at this point in the marathon.

By 25, they did not need to remind each other to run one more mile. Joseph could point ahead to the single runner in front of them: Kenyatta Kemai, who had slowed his pace noticeably since Moses Abraham had fallen behind. Plans aside, the twins would finish the marathon today. Forget New York! Coach Holland would forgive them when he saw their paychecks.

Just before the 26-mile mark, the course turned right off Jefferson Avenue and onto Rushmore Road and the bridge over the Metra railroad tracks. It was the slight incline that runners had labeled "Mount Rushmore." His pace still deteriorating, Kenyatta Kemai struggled up the slope. Joseph, eye on his prey like a crocodile who had just spotted an impala drinking from his river, flew up the slope, the twins behind him, each drafting the defending champion.

The 26-mile mark was right at the corner, where the course turned left onto Columbia Drive. As they turned the corner, the trail trio had caught Kemai!

02:08:24

The press truck had sped away from the leaders at 24 miles, led by a motorcycle policeman, sirens screaming, a necessary move to get members of the press and others on the truck to grandstands opposite the finish line in time to watch the winner cross that line.

"Hold on, Dennis," Peter McDonald had warned as the press truck suddenly accelerated.

The Shelaghi managing director had to grab the railing to avoid pitching backward. He placed one hand atop his head to prevent losing his cap, a green cap bearing the conglomerate logo.

"It looks like we have a winner," suggested Dennis Lahey, referring to the runner who had led the Lake City Marathon from the first step: Kenyatta Kemai. It was as much question as statement.

"Maybe."

Lahey nodded to indicate he understood. "Wasn't it one of your philosophers who said, 'It's never over until it's over?'"

"That was a baseball coach, Dennis."

"Same thing."

But indeed, the identity of the winner remained in doubt. As the press truck had sped away from him, Kenyatta Kemai did seem to have the victory in his pocket, although Peter had noticed the Kenyan beginning to struggle. Looking down a long straightaway to far behind the leader, he could see what appeared to be two or three runners starting to close the gap. But it was a large gap, several blocks, too far for him to even identify this chase pack. Peter could have asked one of several riders listening to radios to identify them, but he did not. He liked being surprised. The instant when the leader or leaders rounded the corner at Mile 26, finish line finally in sight, was a magic moment not only for runners, but for those cheering them.

After crossing the bridge on Rushmore Road, the press truck pulled off the course. A worker rolled a ladder into place behind the truck so riders could descend to the ground. Most riders melted into the crowd headed for seats in the grandstand. Peter indicated for Lahey to walk with him on the course, the last 385 yards on Columbia Drive.

"It's faster. You'll never make it to the line if you stay on the sidewalks."

Fences on the sidewalks prevented spectators from spilling onto the course. And there were more spectators than Peter could remember seeing at any previous Lake City Marathon. Was it the pope or the weather? Temperatures in the 80s made it difficult for runners, but more pleasant for those cheering them. Grandstands behind the fences were jammed. Others stood in open areas between grandstands. In these last few minutes before the lead runner — or runners — appeared, there was a notable buzz of anticipation. Music alternated with announcements over the loudspeaker system.

Walking with the Shelaghi executive on the course between the grandstands, Peter saw the finish line as the runners would see it when they turned the corner. It was like a scene out of a Renaissance painting, an exercise in perspective, all lines intersecting at a point under a photo bridge to which was attached a digital clock: the ultimate digital clock, the one that would record the times of all those crossing the line. Race director and bank executive were not yet close enough to read the numbers shifting on that clock, but looking at his own watch, Peter judged that Kenyatta Kemai would have passed 25 miles by now, meaning he should finish in the next five minutes.

The climax of a year's work, thought Peter, yet there were multiple climaxes. The wheelchair athletes already had finished. The women would finish soon after the men, another climax. The pope was still out on the course, another climax. Each of the 50,000 runners crossing the line created their own climaxes. Then it would be time to prepare for another year, assuming there was another year.

They were close enough to the finish line now for Peter to see the Jumbo-Tron clock beside that line. Kemai remained in the lead. Then the scene shifted to several runners behind—and apparently they were not that far behind. *That's a shocker!* Peter easily recognized Joseph Nduku, his defending champion, but *what?* Who are those running with him? The twins! *Why are they still in the race?*

The scene on the JumboTron shifted again to a shot taken by a cameraman positioned high on a crane looking down on the so-called Mount Rushmore. *Incredible!* All four runners in the same picture. Peter began to jog toward the line. Lahey tried to match the race director's pace, but gave up after a few strides. *If I decide to get serious about this marathon thing*, thought the Shelaghi executive, *I'm going to need to get in shape.*

Reaching the finish line, still stealing glances toward the JumboTron, Peter saw Niles Wendell Robin Carter standing on that line with the finish banner. The banner was perhaps a dozen feet across, wide enough certainly for a single runner, or two, but three or four?

Standing just behind the pair holding the banner was Edward H. Morgan, the retired track coach from Lake City University. "Ted," as everyone called him was head referee. It was a necessary position in case any disputes arose concerning interpretations of USATF. rules, but Ted rarely had to exercise his authority. He also served as finish line judge, except little was required in that job either, close finishes being rare in marathons. Ted had been part of the race organization since Year 1. Originally, he and a single assistant recorded finishing numbers on a clipboard. They handed out tongue depressors with numbers hand-written on them to be able to tell who finished in what place. Chip technology made that practice obsolete. Never one to leave anything to chance, Peter had as backup a video camera as well as a photo finish camera, the same as those used in track meets.

And now looking up at the JumboTron, Peter decided he might need all of them to determine the winner.

But then Peter no longer needed the JumboTron. He could look down the straightaway and see four runners rounding the corner. Shoulder to shoulder, like sprinters in a 100 meter dash. And a fifth behind them.

02:08:24. 02:08:25. 02:08:26.

Niles Wendell called out: "Peter, next year I think we need to order a longer banner!"

02:09:24

"T his is in-*cred*-i-ble!" said a stunned Mark Mallon. The live TV3 feed showed four runners rounding the corner onto the final straightaway, a fifth runner not that far behind. Mallon continued: "I don't normally deal in superlatives, but…"

"…We're entitled to some superlatives, Mark." It was Timothy Rainboldt.

"Four runners—now *five—and* any one can win the Lake City Marathon, the finish line only 385 yards away."

"Beyond incredible," offered Timothy. During his career as color commentator, Timothy *never* had seen a tighter marathon finish. He suspected nobody else had either, but left that thought unsaid.

And for seconds more, Mallon did the same; then he began to summarize in an almost hushed voice what had led up to this climactic point: "For nearly twenty-two miles, Kenyatta Kemai and Moses Abraham dominated this race, not allowing anyone else to head them—not for a step! Then Abraham apparently dropped out. And Kemai faded…"

"…Dramatically!"

"…To be caught by Joseph Nduku. And the biggest surprise, Timothy: two rabbits, the twins, Kyle and Wesley…"

"…Expected to run only 20. We don't know that story yet, Mark…"

"…And apparently they pulled Abraham along, because, my goodness, he's back in the hunt. Twenty yards behind, but…"

C.V.'s turn: "…Don't count Moses out yet!…"

"…We thought we were watching a long distance race, but this looks like 400 meters at the Olympics. Let's see what happens."

Joseph Nduku focused on the narrow corridor ahead of him, the last insulting 385 yards of the marathon. The entourage of motorcycles and cars and trucks had moved aside. He had a clear view of the finish line clock, though he was not yet close enough to read its numbers through sweat-drenched eyes.

SUNDAY

The crocodile, tail thrashing for propulsion, had made his move, a classic move, a come-from-behind move, a startlingly swift move for such a somnolent beast. *Impalas beware!* His prey would pay for their audacity thinking they could defeat him. On the final straightaway, Joseph increased his leg turnover rate an almost imperceptible amount, but enough to allow him to edge ahead of the Northland racers, one on each side. Kemai tried valiantly, heroically, to stay close, but began to see victory sliding away. As the leader for 26 miles faded, Abraham closed the gap in fifth.

With less than 300 yards remaining, Joseph achieved full sprint. He could go no faster, but neither could the twins, camped on his shoulder like water skiers riding the crest of his waves. Had exercise scientists measured his pulse, or the pulse of his rivals, that scientist would have noted they had achieved maximum heart rate and VO_2 Max, the point where the heart can no longer push blood through the cardiovascular system any faster.

Each of the five leaders had reached VO_2 Max at varying points coming across the bridge before turning onto the final straightaway. Joseph's heart rate had peaked at 160; he and the others were flat-lined. Running at max, their cardiovascular systems began to fail, no longer able to remove the poisons piling up in their bloodstreams. The waste products of energy combustion included lactic acid, which leaked hydrogen ions, clogging the system. The ions had begun to collect in the muscle cells, causing fatigue by interfering with enzymes involved in energy production. The muscles of the leading runners no longer could produce energy as rapidly as needed to sustain optimum pace. In unscientific terms, their muscles had begun to seize. They were crashing. They hurt. Badly! Soon, they would be unable to go a step farther.

"This is the moment," said an emotional Timothy Rainboldt, "when talent doesn't count, when training doesn't count, when what you ate for dinner doesn't count, when all that counts is: Which runner wants it the most?"

And for a moment with 200 yards to go, that runner appeared to be Joseph Nduku. His lead on the twins grew—imperceptibly. Kemai seemed beaten, though he hung on gamely. Abraham appeared too far behind to recover in time to claim victory.

Kyle Fowler felt victory slipping away. His brother felt the same. But they had not come to Lake City expecting to contest for first place. What they and everyone watching the finish were experiencing at this point was an anomaly: something that should not have happened!

Each twin was running as hard as he could, also flat-lining. Their once smooth form had been left behind on the course. Every system that normally allowed them to cover huge stretches of ground with minimum effort had begun to deteriorate. Intellectually, each twin knew that smooth running was fast running—their coach, Steve Holland, kept reminding them of that fact—but they could not run smooth. They could only run ugly.

Running ugly hurt. It truly hurt. It did. Runners often defensively claim that their sport is not painful. Normally, it is not. But it was now. It was like being a running back and being tackled by someone 100 pounds heavier than you. It was like being a batter and getting hit on the helmet by a baseball thrown at 95 mph. It was like being a point guard and going up for a rebound and having someone else's elbow meet your teeth. It was like 385 yards of childbirth. Without anesthesia!

Their shoulders ached. Their hands tingled. *Is somebody sitting on my chest, or is this a heart attack?* The legs of the twins felt like someone had poured molten iron into their bloodstreams. Their quads hurt. Their calves hurt. Someone was stabbing needles into the soles of their feet. They had begun to suffocate, as though underwater, unable to suck oxygen into their lungs. And as they got closer to the moment when they would be allowed to stop running, their mouths opened wider and wider, as though this might help them breathe better It did not. Their vision began to fail. Surely, they would soon go blind. *Is my brain about to explode?* No way could either twin run faster. Joseph's rush to the front widened the gap between them, still measured in inches, soon to be measured in feet, maybe measured in yards by the time they reached the finish line only 100 yards away.

It was the second twin, Wesley, who found a reservoir of energy, a molecule or two of glycogen not yet consumed that allowed him to pull even again on Joseph's shoulder. They could not see each other; they could only sense each other. Each runner's peripheral vision had been narrowed to maybe two or three feet of finish line 50 yards away, 40 yards away, 30 yards away, Kyle sensed his twin's move. He moved with his twin brother. The crocodile had company, and those were not easily digestible impalas by his side.

Locked together, the three rushed painfully toward their destiny, the two who had led for so long behind, forgotten, out of contention. Twenty yards. Ten yards. A few footsteps from victory or defeat.

"Let the banner go!" Peter shouted at Niles Wendell and Robin Carter, the two honorary holders, fearful they would be run over if they did not back up. The pair retreated. For a moment the banner with "Lake City Bank" printed on it floated in midair.

02:09:22. 02:09:23. 02:09:24.

The banner wrapped around Joseph Nduku's chest as he reached the line, his foot with chip attached planted firmly on the electronic mat, his body balanced above that foot. Kyle Fowler reached the line in the same instant and lunged forward, diving, falling, sliding beneath the banner. He hit the ground hard, the few breaths within him allowing a scream to rise from his lungs. A primeval scream.

"Aaaaaaah!"

Tumbling, he accidentally collided with Joseph Nduku, who also fell, in turn tripping Wesley Fowler. All three lay on the ground when an exhausted Kenyatta Kemai crossed the line to similarly crumple, as though not having a single step of running left in his body. As Kemai hit the pavement, Moses Abraham dodged around him, the only runner to remain upright. Moses slowed and began a staggered walk into the chute, leading into the area beyond the finish line. Then, deciding that to be an ungracious act, the Kenyan turned to assist finish line workers get the fallen runners off the ground. Except they did not want to get up. They lay on the ground gasping for air.

Abraham bent and lay one palm on the chest of his friend lying on the ground as though to say, *Well done, brother, but I believe we failed.*

"Oh, my!" said Mark Mallon, unable to say more.

Timothy Rainboldt never was at a loss for words: "This is not the Lake City Marathon, Mark. This is NASCAR!"

C.V. remained speechless, thinking: *The women are still three miles away. How can they possibly match this?*

Medical personnel, finish line workers and photographers hovered over the downed runners, who still resisted efforts to help them up. It would be some time before large numbers of runners would appear on the final straightaway, so they were allowed to lie. Kyle Fowler probed for broken bones, found none, but his lower left arm was covered with blood where he scraped it hitting the ground. He lay on his back, mouth open, gasping for breath, trying not to cry, not with cameras focused on him.

A medic asked, "Are you okay?"

Kyle nodded to indicate he was.

Joseph Nduku rolled over toward Kyle, but was too exhausted to speak.

"Did you win, Joseph?" asked Kyle.

Joseph opened his mouth, but no words came out of it. He wrapped his arm around Kyle's chest and allowed his head to rest against Kyle's shoulder, as though seeking a pillow. It was the respectful gesture of one dying gladiator to another. Each man lying on the ground had given his all. There was no more "all" to give.

Wesley had bounced the other way and lay on his back wondering whether he had won, or had finished second, or had finished third. No worse than that, certainly. Looking up at a clear sky overhead, he mumbled, "I love this sport."

MARATHON

Peter McDonald turned from the runners still on the ground toward the man who would be called upon to sort all this out. Referee Edward H. Morgan chuckled and said "I'm going to earn my money today."

A quarter mile away, Steve Holland showed a permit to a policeman blocking access to the park. The policeman examined the permit and moved a sawhorse aside so Holland could park his van in an empty space. The Northland coach still wondered why the twins had not taken the van as planned, but did not dwell on the question. Holland needed to rush to the finish line to see Katie Hyang come across. He hoped Katie could hold onto fifth place. That would be a big boost for the team.

Holland stepped out of the van, pushing a button on his keypad to lock the doors. The vehicle had a combination lock. If the twins got back to it, they could retrieve their clothes and the phone from the glove compartment.

The Northland coach began walking into the park. Happy. Anticipating Katie's success. Maybe she might even get fourth. Third seemed a stretch. Second? First? Unlikely, but a lot can happen in the last few miles of a marathon, even in the last 385 yards.

There were so many people crowding the finish area. So many. More then he remembered from any other marathon: New York. Chicago. Boston. There existed no easy route to the finish line, where his credentials would allow him access to the grandstand. Holland had to patiently weave around people blocking his way. He passed an electronic signboard that should have showed the names of the top male finishers. No names had been posted yet, which Holland thought strange. Surely, the men had finished by now. In this electronic age, their names and times should have been posted instantly. It would be a while before the women appeared. He hoped he had time to stop in the VIP Tent to grab a cup of coffee.

Holland showed his credentials to two staff members guarding the tent entrance and headed straight to the coffee table. Niles Wendell stood beside that table, cradling a steaming cup of coffee in one hand, waiting for it to cool. Wendell had a broad grin on his well-tanned face. He would be heading to his condo in Ponte Vedra Beach later in the week.

"Great race, huh?" commented the race founder.

Steve Holland removed a cup from the tray and positioned it under the spigot of the coffee urn.

"Yeah," wondered the Northland coach. "Who won?"

02:20:00

S o, explain again who won?" Jonathan Von Runyon asked media director Nelson Ogilvie. The results of what had been the closest marathon in history (five runners crossing the line within two seconds) had been posted to the results board at the end of the room. Ogilvie was standing in front of the results board answering questions from puzzled reporters. The results *were* confusing, based on times posted beside each name. The fastest time was that of the third-place finisher. Second fastest was the runner in second. Third fastest was that of the winner! *Huh?*

Von Runyon wondered why: "Excuse me, Nelson, if I confess to some confusion based on what I see on the board. The numbers don't jibe."

Ogilvie smiled. It was indeed striking for the *Ledger* reporter to admit even the slightest bit of confusion, but it was an extraordinary day. Always the diplomat, the media director admitted: "We're all confused, Jonathan."

The *Ledger* reporter continued: "You have Kyle Fowler posted as winner, Joseph Nduku second, Wesley Fowler in third, yet..."

"I know what your 'yet' is going to be, Jonathan."

"...Yet Wesley has the fastest chip time, Joseph next fastest, Kyle the third. I believe I understand why, but humble me with an erudite explanation."

Ogilvie did his best to explain: "As you all know—or should know, excuse me for talking down to you—position in a road race is determined not by chip time, but by who reaches the finish line first. Wesley apparently started in the second row behind his twin brother, so crossed the starting line a half second later than Kyle or Joseph. Thus technically, he has the fastest chip time, but it won't get him the first place prize of $100,000."

The media director added, "Of course, it stays in the family."

"I'm still confused," said another reporter. It was Burton Ambrose. "Joseph also had a chip time faster than that of your winner."

"We're still sorting that out," Ogilvie admitted. "But again, as you all know..." (Good natured booing from the reporters.) "...chip time is determined by the moment your shoe bearing that chip crosses the mats on the finish line. Stay with me here, because I'm trying to repeat what Peter just told me by radio: It is *not* when your lead foot hits the line that determines whether you win or lose, but when your torso crosses the line, as in a 100 meter dash. Think Olympic Games. Kyle dove at the line, thus his torso hit that invisible, chest-high line before the torso of Joseph.

"Kyle's official winning time is 2:09:23.97. The time of Joseph in second, 2:09:23.95. Wesley in third, 2:09:23.52. All times as per rules rounded up to 2:09:24, so it will not confuse your readers."

Ogilvie added, "Those times and places are unofficial, but almost certainly will stand under review by the referee, Ted Morgan. As backup, we have a videotape as well as a photo-finish shot."

"Which will be made available to us?"

"Which will be made available to you, probably within the next five or ten minutes. Meanwhile, the women are out on the course, and we'll be watching them for the next ten minutes or so…"

02:20:00. 02:20:01. 02:20:02.

Ogilvie pointed toward one of two screens at the front of the room. For most of the last two hours it had shown the men on one screen, the women on the other. Now both screens showed the women. "…And as you can see on the screen, we suddenly have a new leader, Fiona Flynn."

The Irish Lass was easily recognizable by her emerald green singlet with the shamrock on the front. Less recognizable was the woman running beside her. "I have no idea what that other runner with the high number is doing running beside her."

Ambrose knew. He had checked her number, 1459, in the program. Her name was Meghan Allison. Listed as living in Lake City. No biography in the Media Guide. *A complete unknown. Like a rolling stone,* Ambrose turned to Von Runyon standing beside him: "It doesn't get much better than this."

Maybe not in a marathon, thought Jonathan, charitably not offering a rebuttal. *But you never saw Tiger Woods sink a long putt on the 17th hole at The Player's Championships.*

"I've got you and Edmund another ride, Christine," director Tom Schorr informed her by cell phone.

"You're not…"

"…Comfortable seats. Air conditioned. Bubble windows…"

"…going to expect me to climb into a helicopter?"

Schorr ignored her response and began to give directions to a hospital near the 15-mile mark where, he said, a Fire Department helicopter with two empty seats would pick her up. "Bright red. We chose that color, because it matches your shirt."

"You're really not doing this to me…. Are you?"

"Best view of the marathon."

"Tom, did I tell you I suffer from motion sickness?"

"There's a barf bag in the back seat," he told her and hung up. Schorr did not want to waste time discussing what already had been decided: his having arranged with Peter McDonald to have the helicopter containing Police Captain Robert Newsom pick up his reporter and cameramen. It was a Bell 206, a JetRanger. It was a five-passenger helicopter with the back seats vacant. Still, Schorr had to plead with the captain to divert briefly and pick up Christine and her cameraman. TV3 would be promoting the Fraternal Order of Police Christmas Party with vigor this holiday season. Meanwhile, the women were into the last two miles of their race, suggesting a finish equally as dramatic as that of the men, and he had to turn his attention to covering them. Most exciting, a total unknown—local, no less—was running in the lead with race-favorite, Fiona Flynn.

Meghan Allison, was starting to hurt. Big time! They had just passed 24 miles, she and *La Femme Fiona*, side by side, stride by stride. Meg never had run that far before, not in a race, not in practice. Twenty miles had been her workout limit, following the advice of Don Geoffrey as posted on the Internet. The Turtle claimed, "One dare not run further than 20 miles unless you have a number pinned to the front of your singlet." Well, she did have a number pinned to the front of hers, but it was a lowly four-digit number: 1459, one guaranteed to garner her little respect. Fiona was among several runners who wondered about her identity. "Who are you, the Mystery Girl?" The question was said in jest earlier, just after Meg had caught Fiona. Meg had not taken offense, offering a brief explanation that triggered another comment by Fiona:

"Didn't I see you running on the lakefront a couple of days ago?"

Meg acknowledged that to be true. She was surprised Fiona noticed.

"Yeah, you looked fast," admitted the Irish Lass. "I wondered if you might be running the marathon, and now it seems you are."

Meg acknowledged that to be true.

Fiona paused allowing several hundred yards to pass before continuing the conversation. "Have we ever raced before?"

"NCAA Regionals. Terre Haute. A half dozen years ago. I was running for Northern Indiana."

I won that race, thought Fiona, but decided it would be impolite to offer that information. "How did you do?"

"Fourteenth place—behind you."

"How did you do in the NCAA?" Fiona had won that race too. She hoped her new companion did not think she was engaged in one-upmanship.

"I didn't run."

"Didn't run?"

"Injured," admitted Meg. "Story of my life."

"Hmmm," said Fiona, looking sideways. "Well, you don't look injured today, Love, so let's get it on." *La Femme Fiona* offered a fist to slap.

410

Meg fist-slapped her back. *Toto, I have a feeling we're not running cross-country any more.*

Meg had pulled even with Fiona at 30-K, and those were the last words the two exchanged until 35-K where Fiona grabbed a plastic bottle off the elite athlete table in the center of the road. Meg had been forced earlier to go to the aid station used by ordinary runners to get her liquids. Fiona noticed this and after she had sucked enough fluid from her bottle offered it to Meg, not saying a word. Meg drank, offered it back, saying simply, "Thanks, Fiona."

It was a mile later before Fiona spoke again, just after they had passed a fading Toshi Yamota without even a nod, as though to acknowledge the Japanese runner's presence on the course was to admit weakness. And Toshi failed to acknowledge their passage either. Soon she drifted behind them, but in doing so yielded the second-place position that she had held up until 24 miles.

Only one runner remained in front of them: Tatanya Henry. Fiona said in a reserved tone of voice, "I'm going to burn that bitch!"

That shocked Meg, but Fiona must have sensed that. She added: "I'm normally not that nasty, only in the last few hundred yards of races."

Meg Allison nodded to indicate she understood. She saved her words. So did Fiona. Only in the last few steps of the marathon would the pair find it necessary to communicate again.

02:29:33

Later, with Meghan Allison sitting on the stage in the media center back at Hilliard Towers, an ice pack wrapped around her foot to still the pain, one of the reporters asked her and Fiona Flynn to recreate the last mile of their race: what went through their minds, how their bodies felt, as each battled the other for victory in the Lake City Marathon. Matt later said it was the reporter from the *Lake City Ledger*, Jonathan Something-or-Other.

Matt had to argue his way into the press conference, because as the husband of a woman whose race number was 1459, he had little status. Eventually, Peter McDonald sent one of his media assistants out to intervene when after fielding several questions, Meg asked in all innocence, "Has my husband shown up yet?" Matt got in, but not Aaron and Moira, who had to wait nearly another hour because Meg had to be drug-tested after the press conference.

"Do they really want us to pee in a bottle?" she had asked her new friend, Fiona, who smiled tolerantly and responded:

"You'll get used to it."

Meg suspected she never would, but that was after she and Fiona had answered the "Last Mile" question. Fiona went first and Meg probably should have listened to what the Irish runner was saying, but that was when she spotted Matt in the back of the room, each of them waving at each other and acting foolish, but she had earned the right to act more than a bit foolish.

She woke up when the same reporter turned to her. Fiona must have been finished with her reply: "How about you, Ms. Allison?"

"Excuse me?"

"The last mile? What were you thinking when you saw the sign saying you had only one mile to go?"

"I don't remember seeing it."

"It was when you passed the convention center."

"I don't recall passing the convention center. Did we?" She looked at Fiona, who smiled and shrugged.

"The two of you were running in first: You knew that, didn't you?

"Actually, I didn't. We were passing runners, but I wasn't counting."

Meg wrinkled her forehead and opened her eyes wide, what Matt sometimes referred to as her "clueless look." *Last mile? Convention center? Running in first place? I just want to go pee.*

Only days later when the enormity of her achievement, being able to stay close to one of the world's most accomplished female runners until that pivotal last mile, did Meghan Allison remember some of the small details of what went through her mind. Only then did the questions asked her by Jonathan Von Runyon and other reporters at the post-race press conference seem to make sense. At the time, she just wanted to laugh; she just wanted to cry.

Coming out of a commercial break after having wrapped up the story of the men's race, including the presentation of a $100,000 check and a quick interview with surprise winner Kyle Fowler, Mark Mallon set the scene for the women's race. The main feed showed Mallon with Timothy Rainboldt and Carolynne Vickers on each side of him:

"One mile to go, C.V., and a few minutes ago the three of us agreed that it would be difficult to match the drama of the last men's race, but we may need to take back those words."

"True, Mark, because while we do not have five battling for the lead, we do have three. Any one of them could claim victory, although judging from how rapidly Fiona Flynn and the woman we might call the Mystery Girl have closed the gap in the last several miles, the number of contenders may soon be down to two."

"Camera 3," instructed Tom Schorr. The main feed switched to a shot of Tatanya Henry running in front, Fiona Flynn and Meghan Allison twenty or more yards behind.

"Let me recap the race for the benefit of those who just joined us in the last half hour, because you heard the race was heating up..."

"...Or heard the pope was running," said Timothy impishly.

"That too," conceded Mallon, "And we'll be getting back to Pope Tony later, but let's talk about the women. Carolynne?"

On the shot shown viewers, Meg and Fiona had cut the gap between them and the leader to ten yards. "Tatanya Henry has run in front almost from the start, Mark. Not always first, but close to that position. Not setting the pace, but controlling it. For the first half of the marathon, Tatanya had nearly a dozen other women nearby, but it always seemed like they were deferring to her, trusting the Russian's judgment to maintain what seemed like...."

C.V. paused briefly, "I almost hate to use the term."

"Use it," coaxed Timothy, as she knew he would.

"...A pedestrian pace..."

"...That pace understandable given the warm weather..."

"...But it meant Tatanya failed to put away her rivals..."

"...They drifted away, bruised but not beaten..."

"Camera 1," said Schorr. *"Keep 3 in the corner."*

The live feed returned to the three commentators seated in the studio tent, the shot of the runners reduced to the right corner of the screen.

"...And that's where we are with less than a mile now to go. By not pushing the pace earlier—and I'm not criticizing her for doing so, it *is* hot out there—Tatanya Henry let the door swing open for Fiona Flynn and..."

"...The Mystery Girl..."

"...Number 1459..."

"...And I have no idea who she is or her history as a runner."

Mallon interrupted the two color commentators. "Fortunately, Timothy does. During the last commercial break, our esteemed colleague has been frantically working the phones and rattling his computer keyboard."

"He's good at that," said C.V. sweetly.

Timothy ignored what was intended as an elbow in his ribs and reached for a clipboard containing notes he had made: "Meghan Allison. State champion in cross-country. Attended Northern Indiana University, but accomplished little, mainly because of injuries. Graduated Pre-Med. Attended Podiatry School. Residency in Surgery. And after getting her degree went to work part-time for a running store, selling shoes."

"What?"

"In fact, Christine Ferrara bought a pair of shoes from her last week at Fast Feet. I just got finished talking by cell phone to the owner of that store, who organizes one of the aid stations, and he told us our Mystery Girl reportedly had been injured so much of her career, she wondered if she could achieve something if she took off a year and did nothing else but train."

"And now she's running third in the Lake City Marathon," said a flummoxed Mark Mallon.

"Not just third any more, Mark. Our Mystery Girl—and I guess we should start calling her by her right name, Meg Allison—has just moved into first ahead of Fiona Flynn and an apparently well-beaten Tatanya Henry."

That surge had happened as the three cruised down Jefferson Avenue with three-quarters of a mile left in the race. It happened partly by accident, because when Fiona caught Tatanya, the Irish runner had actually slowed down and called over her shoulder: "Come on, Tatanya. Run with us."

Meg did not quite understand at first, because only a mile before the woman they call *La Femme Fiona* had called the Russian woman a "bitch"—and now she was encouraging her?

Fiona's doing so had caused Meg to move temporarily into the lead, but not for long because Fiona quickly was back at her side, saying: "Now it's my turn to detest you!"

Okay, I get it. It's all about competition, isn't it? It's not about her or me, and it's not even about money, it's about using every element available to motivate yourself to do the best you can. It's the ultimate expression of love/hate. Obviously, Fiona loves to race. She loves to compete. It's what she lives for. A feminine form of man-a-mano. And despite what Meg had thought earlier, marathon running was not that different from cross-country. She had read once in *Running Magazine* (an article by Don Geoffrey) that cross-country runners often make the best marathoners. She now understood why.

"Did you see that, Timothy," commented C.V. "When Fiona caught and passed Tatanya, she suddenly turned and shouted at her."

"Too bad we didn't have a mike on her," commented Mallon.

"That caused her to lose a stride on our Mystery Girl, then when she caught back up, she had something to say to her too."

"I think we can assume they were not discussing the latest Paris fashions."

"Camera 3 and hold it," said Schorr. *"Guys, you're making too many not-that-funny jokes. Let's get serious for the last mile."*

414

MARATHON

Meghan Allison did not know that she had been nicknamed the Mystery Girl, nor would she have cared. All she knew, as she and Fiona ran together between crowds of cheering people in the last mile was that she hurt.

Hurt badly. Worse than she ever had hurt in her life. Well, she had not yet experienced pregnancy, so she could not say much about that, but she could not imagine that giving birth could be too much more painful. Is it?

First, it had been her hips. Her hip flexors to be more precise, important muscles for moving the legs forward. Her hip flexors began to ache back around 20 miles when she was closing on Fiona Flynn, perhaps because unconsciously she had picked up the pace to catch Fiona. The left hip more than the right hip. Once at Fiona's side, the pain went away, perhaps because she had slowed, or maybe they both had sped up. She could not remember, but suddenly the pain in the left hip disappeared only to reappear again this time in her right knee—and that made absolutely no sense at all, except that she had heard similar complaints from runners who appeared at clinics while she was in podiatry school.

"Where do you hurt, Dr. Allison?"

"My body."

"Your body?"

"Right, my entire body."

"Well, of course, Dr. Allison. You're in the twenty-second mile of a major marathon, racing skinny butt against skinny butt with a woman who once placed third in the World Championships."

"Oh, I forgot."

Her adductors. She knew all the names of these body parts, because she had taken Anatomy, scored an "A" in the course, because she always earned A's. The muscles at the front of her body that allowed her to raise her legs off the ground with each stride, stride after stride, thousands of strides—how many, she did not know—in an event like the marathon. The pain in her adductors eventually went away, overridden by other pains multiplying almost faster than she could catalog them. She was falling apart.

Her quads. She knew the quadriceps muscles threatened to melt during the closing miles of a marathon, but she never had been in the closing miles of a marathon before, so had no concept of how much they would hurt. Like somebody had just poured boiling oil over the front of her legs. *I've never had Third-Degree burns on my legs before. Is that what it feels like?*

Her right ankle. She once had twisted it in a cross-country race over muddy ground. New Prairie Invitational, which she won, of course, because she won almost everything in cross-country. Lost half a season because of it, and now like the Ghost of Christmas Past, it had returned to haunt her.

SUNDAY

Stomach cramps. Nausea. *I think I'm going to puke in another minute, and it won't be because of some home remedy handed me by an Ethiopian.*

Her groin. Or rather the inside of her legs below that delicate part of her body. Chafed. Badly chafed. Happened during several of her long runs. Caused her to scream it hurt so bad when she lowered herself into a post-run ice-bath. Skin ointments do not work. *I'll have to write the manufacturers and complain. Or maybe they do work, but not for me and not for 24 miles.*

Sunburn. *The sun has been beating on my back for all this distance. I'm naturally blonde. I tan badly. I'm going to look like a beet after I finish—if I finish. Less than two miles to go. I could collapse.*

Fiona could not be feeling pain like this. *I know she doesn't. She was nice to me for a few miles while I was helping her catch that Russian, whatever her name is, but now I'm her enemy. She's in hate mode. She even told me. I'm afraid to look at her. She'll think it a sign of weakness. Maybe she'll sign my race poster after we finish. Matt can frame the poster and hang it in our living room as a symbol of what might have been.*

"They've made the turn on Rushmore with a quarter mile to go," said Mark Mallon, following Schorr's suggestion that they provide viewers with minimal information. "Two great runners. Shoulder to shoulder. The great Irish champion, Fiona Flynn, and our own Mystery Girl."

"Meghan Allison," added Carolynne Vickers as if a more precise identification at this late point in the race were necessary.

"Whoever wants it the most," said Timothy Rainboldt, almost in a whisper as though he did not want to distract with his words the attention of viewers from the battle on the screen.

All three fell silent at the moment Meg and Fiona turned the final corner onto Columbia Drive: 26 miles down; 385 yards to go. Spectators in grandstands on both sides of this final 385-yard insult could look away from the JumboTron and stare up Columbia Drive and see the two women runners live. Several struggling male runners saw the speedier women coming and moved right or left, yielding to them the middle of the road.

One moment the pair was running even, and the next moment one had surged into the lead. A surge so fast that if you blinked, you missed it. A surge so fast that it seemed like your TiVo skipped forward. A surge so fast that it belonged in a 5,000-meter race on the track or in a cross-country race coming out of the woods, the New Prairie Invitational, instead of in the closing stages of a 26-mile-385-yard marathon.

Meghan Allison, mystery no more, had the lead.

416

Fiona Flynn began losing ground. Tom Schorr switched cameras from the side shot to head-on to keep the Irish Lass in the pictures. Except head-on failed to reveal how much Fiona was falling behind. It was 5 yards, then 10 yards, then 15, then 20.

La Femme Fiona was being blown away. She was being destroyed. Chewed up and spit out on the last straightaway of the Lake City Marathon.

"Oh my God!" shouted Carolynne Vickers. She forgot for a moment that she was talking into a microphone, her shout almost blowing the earphones off the heads of her fellow commentators.

"Calm down, C.V." said Tom Schorr, almost a reflex reaction since he too was mesmerized by what he saw on the control room screens.

Meg could not *hear* the screams of spectators. She could not *see* their wide open and trembling mouths. She could not *view* the JumboTron looming overhead that showed her as its only sight. She could not *think* of what was happening to her or to Fiona behind, how far behind she did not know, and she did not want to look. *Is she on my heels, waiting to slingshot around me in the closing yards, or have I beaten her? Have I won?*

She swept past Matt, Aaron and Moira standing by the fence screaming, Moira with the "Go, Meg, Go" over her head jumping up and down as though on a trampoline. She did not hear them. She did not see them. She could not see the finish line, though she knew it was up there somewhere. She increased her arm pump, hoping her legs would follow. She had weight-lifted for the last year for this moment, for these last 385 yards.

The pain intensified. Meg could not breathe, although oxygen must still be coursing through her lungs and through her blood and into her muscles, otherwise she would not be able to keep moving. Her heart beat had soared past 200 beats a minute, flat-lined, the highest it could go without exploding inside her body. Her entire focus was on a photo bridge on which was hung a sign saying "finish" and below, a ticking digital clock, its shifting, red numbers a blur. Then they came into focus. Unwillingly, because she *did-not-want-to-know!* Numbers would interfere with her ability to sprint as fast as her body would allow. Nevertheless, the thought passed through her brain for only the tiniest fraction of a second: *I am about to break 2.30. I am about to win the Lake City Marathon.*

But she had not won yet.

02:29:30. 02:29:31. 02:29:32.

It was at that precise moment that Meghan Allison screamed: *"Aaaahhh!"*

The pain was intense, as though somebody had not merely stepped on her left foot, but had driven a nail through it. Her right foot came down, and there was no pain. Her left foot came down, and Meg screamed again. She could not help it.

SUNDAY

"Aaaahhh!"

She slowed. She limped. She stopped. She looked up at the people standing on the finish line not much more than 10 yards away and all were screaming at her to finish, to keep going. Open mouths. No sound coming out of them. At least none she could hear, because she was close to unconscious. Meg's eyes would have been filling with tears, except she had no moisture left within her body to create tears.

"Aaaahhh!"

And with the finish banner with Lake City Bank written on it so close she almost could reach out and touch it, Meg began to pitch forward. She caught herself, stumbled, then began to pitch forward again. The pain was unbelievable. It was at this point that a near delirious Meg Allison heard another woman scream behind her:

"No! No!"

She suddenly felt Fiona Flynn's arms wrap around her body.

"Finish! You've got to finish!!!" Meg would say later that she could not remember Fiona Flynn saying those words, which had been heard clearly by those standing nearby, the two banner holders, Dennis Lahey and Mayor Richard T. Danson, words also captured on TV by those capable of reading lips. Nor could Meg remember exactly what happened next, except she had this feeling that the Irish runner had thrown her across the line and into the banner with Lake City Bank written on it. Actually, the two clinging women crossed the line together taking the finish banner with them as they fell to the ground. Even as medical personnel waiting at the line surged forward to assist fallen runners for the second time, a revived Tatanya Henry rushed past the prone pair into the finishing chute — in third place.

02:29:33. 02:29:34. 02:29:35.

Peter McDonald moved back to allow the medical technicians to do their jobs. The two runners gasping for breath seemed more stunned than hurt, although something seemed to have snapped in Meg Allision's left foot that caused her collapse.

He looked toward Dennis Lahey who had been holding one end of the finish banner, and he could see from the Shelaghi executive's look that he was wondering who had won, whether the Irish Lass or not. Would it matter when it came to the conglomerate's continuing its sponsorship? That would need to be decided later, and it hardly seemed important now. Mayor Danson had stepped back, a look of shock on his face as he recognized the sacrifice one runner had made for another. "She gave away first!" he would say later to others in the VIP Tent. "She gave away first!"

Or had she?

MARATHON

Peter McDonald turned toward Ted Morgan, his referee, who once more would be needed to sort out the placings of the top runners, with or without the benefit of chip times, video cameras or photo-finish devices. Morgan seemed unperturbed, as though it happened all the time in track and cross-country meets where he had officiated.

"Looks like a tie to me."

Television coverage continued as both women were led away from the finish line. After Tatanya Henry in third, the next runner was Northland's Katie Hyang, who passed a fading Toshi Yamota on the final straightaway. Tom Schorr ordered a replay of the finish featuring Fiona and the Mystery Girl, and another, and another after that, as they waited to see if they could get an interview with the winners. Neither Fiona nor Meg were immediately available, the former so spent she could barely talk, the latter apparently having suffered a stress fracture in her left foot. Not serious, treatable, and apparently she had given medical personnel a precise diagnosis of the injury.

"I'm stunned," said C.V.

"I'm breathless," Mark Mallon agreed. "What next?"

"We still have the pope," Timothy Rainboldt reminded him.

"And Christine Ferrara up in a helicopter," came Tom Schorr's voice in their earphones.

"And we have Christine Ferrara up in a helicopter," repeated Mark Mallon. "We'll be talking to Christine when we return after these commercials."

02:45:00

The cardinal camerlengo, after watching the pope pass, had taken an elevated train with Archbishop Sean Nolan to the finishing area. He wanted to observe security arrangements. The archbishop had suggested they not bother with anything as pretentious as a limousine. "Jesus didn't travel by limo," insisted Nolan. "Besides, in this traffic, the El is quicker—at least quicker than a donkey."

He had been proven correct.

Now the two prelates stood in what Noel Michaels referred to on her spreadsheet as the unified command tent, side flaps down, darkened to make it easier to view the half dozen TV monitors, 42-inch, flat screen, mounted on inside walls. Michaels had shifted her work station from the operations trailer to the tent immediately after the start.

419

SUNDAY

Each monitor offered multiple images of the race in progress. The monitors covered street intersections along the course, showing runners and crowds viewing runners. The images changed continuously, flickering from one street-corner camera to another. Michaels explained to the two visitors how she could manipulate the cameras, rotating them, pointing them in different directions, zooming into scenes that caught her eye. Should a runner collapse and need medical attention, she could expedite a response. Several other staff members and city traffic employees assisted her in this operation.

At two hours and forty-five minutes into the marathon, most of the elite runners had crossed the finish line. They were safe, but the bulk of runners remained on course with temperatures still rising.

02:45:00. 02:45:01. 02:45:02.

"The cameras enable us to focus on and zoom into intersections and see how police are handing traffic," Michaels told her two visitors. "We can track ambulances moving to and from Med Tents. We can monitor all 911 calls taking place in the city. Toward the end of the race, we can spot stragglers."

Redbird was stunned: "The city has a camera on every street corner?"

"Most corners," conceded Michaels.

"Most?"

"Where gaps exist, we cover them with a Fire Department helicopter. Currently, that helicopter is tracking the pope."

Redbird could not help but wonder: *Is there a single corner in this world where we cannot be observed? Big Brother has found us.*

But it also gave Redbird confidence that Pope Tony was right. The massive security preparations that might have been necessary to protect him on visits to London or Paris or Berlin or some troubled Third-World country were not necessary during this marathon. He was surrounded by 50,000 runners who provided their own protective shield. And 800 policemen protecting those runners. Could he do anything more to improve security?

"So the pope is never out of your sight?"

"Not merely the pope," Michaels explained. "Every runner falls under our security umbrella. TV3 tracks the front runners. We track the rest."

"I'm comforted by your vigilance," Redbird conceded, "but playing devil's advocate: Isn't all this camera coverage overkill?"

"Somewhat," Michaels conceded, "but I'm going to take the position that each of the 50,000 runners is as important to us as the pope."

"I have no argument with that."

"Given the warm weather, surveillance today is extra vital. No matter how hard they trained, a certain number of runners will suffer heat exhaustion. Fifty runners who collapse represent one-tenth of one percent of all runners in the field, but we don't want to lose one of them."

Redbird looked toward the archbishop and nodded to indicate he was impressed. The cardinal camerlengo decided that once this marathon was over and they had Pope Tony tucked safely on a plane headed home, he would invite this executive director to Rome to consult with him about Vatican security arrangements.

Noel Michaels turned her attention back to the monitors displaying intersections throughout the second half of the course, the ones that still had runners moving through. And one specific screen that currently displayed the shot from the helicopter, now tracking the pope. Michaels was concerned because Captain Robert Newsom was in that helicopter along with Christine Ferrara and her cameraman. With a thunderstorm approaching from the west, that might not be the safest ride in town.

03:00:00

Peter McDonald walked into the medical tent past the finish line and looked for his medical director, Dr. Nick Terrance. The tent stretched for over a hundred yards and contained more than fifty cots. Only a few overheated runners were lying on the cots. Most of those finished at this point had broken three hours, a significant accomplishment on so warm a day. They were the most talented, the best trained runners, but anyone can get in trouble on a hot day. Not everybody heeded the advice to forget personal goals and run conservatively. And the weather predictions proved accurate. The temperature was rising steadily: 84, 85, 86. If it reached 90, it might be a wise idea to shorten the race, diverting the slowest of the slow runners to take a shortcut back to the finish line? Peter feared making such a decision.

03:00:00. 03:00:01. 03:00:02.

He saw Dr. Terrance standing beside a cot next to a runner, who looked embarrassed to having been forced to seek medical care.

"How's he doing?" Peter asked.

The medical director laughed, "Blisters."

"Yeah, I know," grumbled Bob Veldman, who had decided to run the full 26 miles, not drop out at 16 as planned.

"He'll be out of here before the real casualties hit," said Dr. Terrance.

"How's the Mystery Girl?" Peter asked his Medical Director.

"Stress fracture. Not serious. And it turns out, believe it or not, she's a podiatrist. She told me exactly which bone cracked. She said she's going to volunteer for the medical tent next year. I put a bubble cast on her foot and sent her off in a cart to the media center."

Peter switched subjects to the real reason he had come to see Dr. Terrance. "What numbers can you give me?" He was inquiring about numbers of runners treated along the course. He knew his medical director stayed on top of those statistics.

"Not as bad as you would think given the weather, Peter. Numbers are actually slightly less than last year with cooler temperatures. Most runners seem to have accepted the advice to slow down and drink."

Peter thanked his medical director and left for the command tent to see Noel Michaels. *Three hours into the race,* he thought. *Those passing the half-marathon mark would finish in six hours—or slower.* He still could use his contingency plan to divert them and others scattered all over the course on a shortcut back to the finish line, in effect, stopping the race. But now it appeared he might not need to execute that plan, particularly after what Michaels told him about the approaching cold front.

As Peter left, he heard the runner with blisters ask Dr. Terrence, "Who's the Mystery Girl?"

Christine Ferrara gripped her seat in the Bell 206 JetRanger tightly as though doing so might offer an extra degree of protection if the Fire Department helicopter in which she was riding suddenly plummeted to the ground. The 206 was a sleek machine, like a ski resort gondola with a slender tail behind and two mammoth blades above that chattered as they followed the marathon course. She was sitting behind the pilot, Jean Grey, a lieutenant with the Fire Department. Her cameraman Edmund sat behind Captain Newsom, who was monitoring traffic control, particularly as it involved the pope, talking by radio to policemen on the ground. She wondered about the level of clout Tom Schorr must possess to get them a last-moment ride.

Fear aside, she had to admit that Tom was right: the view was stunning. As they hovered several hundred feet above the marathon course, moving barely as fast as the runners below, she was able to view Lake City from an angle available to few other than the birds. Even those flying into town failed to see the streets, houses, apartments, back yards, trees as close as this. Not even from the city's highest skyscrapers. People below, even some of the runners, waved as they passed overhead. Off to the east, the lake shimmered in sunlight. Off to the west, rooftops stretched all the way to the suburbs.

Yet despite the view she was frightened. "Have you ever been up in a helicopter, Edmund?"

"Too many times."

"Too many?"

"I served as a medic in Vietnam."

"Wasn't that dangerous?" She asked innocently.

Edmund smiled: "Only when they shot at us."

"Oh!"

Christine could think of nothing more to say. She pulled her seat belt tighter, hoping this would offer her an extra degree of protection. But as she continued to look toward the west, she saw something that frightened her even more than the seeming instability of the helicopter. The sky along the horizon was dark blue, almost black. Something nasty was headed their way. Weatherman Vaughn Johnson had predicted thunderstorms later in the afternoon. *Were they here already?* Christine Ferrara hoped that she was not still up in the helicopter when the storms hit.

Sitting on the stage at the media center, Fiona Flynn sipped a soft drink so she could produce some urine for drug-testers and get the hell out of here. Seated beside the Irish Lass was Meghan Allison, bubble cast attached to one foot. Although she usually enjoyed the give-and-take between reporters, Fiona did not want to be forced to field too many more questions right now. She just wanted to go somewhere and lie down.

She hurt. She hurt real bad. Never before had *La Femme Fiona* run a race that had drained her so much. The heat! The heat! Certainly, the heat had been factor, but this being her first marathon, Fiona had no explanation for how badly she felt: Like a truck had hit her. Fiona figured it would take a week of massages before she could even contemplate running again. *Why didn't somebody warn me?*

"What were you thinking when you stopped to help the runner you were racing?" asked Jonathan Von Runyon of the *Lake City Ledger*.

"I wasn't thinking," admitted Fiona.

"You regret helping her."

"No, I wasn't thinking; I was reacting."

"You gave away first place."

Fiona Flynn nodded over her shoulder at the results board: "Says up there I'm first. We're both first. End of story."

"But it could have been *you* exclusively," Von Runyon continued to probe. The *Ledger* reporter considered what happened incomprehensible. Golf players never tie in tournaments. They come back to play on Monday.

Fiona said she did not consider it a big deal. She shrugged and looked sideways at her fellow first-place finisher: The Mystery Girl, they called her. Meghan Allison had this huge grin on her face. Not huge, *mammoth!* Same grin she displayed while officials were rolling her through the chute in a wheelchair. Grinning, despite a broken foot. Fiona could not begin to imagine how much *that* must have hurt, but Meg seemed not to care. Well, why not? Each of them was just about to cash a $100,000 check. Peter said they both deserved the top prize. You can buy a lot of Tylenol with that kind of money.

Fiona gave her new friend a gentle shove. "Get on with you, Love. Stop smiling." Meg did, then started giggling.

Fiona rolled her eyes, looked away from Meg and redirected her attention at the *Ledger* reporter. "Look, consider that if it weren't for your so-called Mystery Girl, I might not have finished. At 20 miles I was roadkill. I wanted to sit down on the curb and cry. She came along and rescued me."

"Rescued you?"

"Yeah, I finally had someone to run with, and it picked me up. I thought, 'Whew: At last!' This was my first marathon and, quite honestly it was even tougher mentally than it was physically. The leaders got away from me in the first mile. Okay, I let them go. Good strategy, but I fell into a no-man's-land with nobody around me."

"No-woman's-land," prompted Meg.

"Thank you, Mystery Girl."

The two winners high-fived each other.

"My point, Love, is that as soon as Meg caught up, we could work together and catch the leaders. Otherwise, I wouldn't be talking to you now. I'd be up in my room crying."

A different reporter had his hand up: Burton Ambrose from *Running Magazine*. Fiona pointed at him.

"Have you two first-timers thought about your next marathon?"

The pair said simultaneously: "You mean we have to run another?"

"Yikes! That's my roommate!" screamed Yolanda Kline. "I can't believe it!" Yolanda was sitting with a tableful of friends in a Starburst coffee shop near her apartment on the north side of town discussing their last-night bad dates, how difficult it was finding a good man these days.

Nobody was paying much attention to the overhead TV toward the back of the coffee shop. Yolanda, sipping on a Latte Supremo, was about to launch into a monolog about new roommate Christine cruising into town only two weeks ago and already latching onto the rightest of Mr. Rights, when she glanced up at the screen and there was Roomie. On CNN! And Christine didn't even work for that network!

"BREAKING NEWS," it said on the screen.

The picture showed a headshot of Christine, who at that moment—believe it or not—was up in a helicopter over Lake City, tracking Pope Tony. She had a microphone in front of her face and was talking loudly into it in an attempt to make herself heard over the chatter of the helicopter blades. With the sound turned off in the coffee shop, Yolanda could not understand what Christine was saying or why she was saying it.

"That's Christine!" repeated Yolanda. "Aaaiieee! Ms. Dreamgirl is going to have some explaining to explain when she gets home tonight." Immediately, all Yolanda's girlfriends at the table forgot about bad dates and started shrieking. Others in the coffee shop began staring at the crazy women.

Matilda Goldberg veered off course and into a different Starburst coffee shop just past the 20-mile marker. Considering her split, she figured she finally was on target. Tilda had begun to see and pass more and more runners with 4:00 on the backs of their singlets. Many simply had failed to match the pace of that pacing team, but it was a sign that she was about to catch the pope.

But she could not hold it any longer. Tilda felt that she would burst. Unfortunately, all the porta-potties passed in the last several miles had long lines. Even in this hot weather, people were drinking too much, and that included her. Then a burst of inspiration: She would stop at the Starburst's Coffee Shop she saw ahead, duck into a toilet used by normal people and be back on the course in less than a minute. *Ta-tumm!* Her *Times* investigative reporter skills had triumphed again.

No: Someone in the women's room. And two runners standing in front of the men's room, otherwise Tilda would have claimed unisex rights to that. She waited. And waited. She looked at her watch: 30 seconds gone. The pope was pulling away while some woman in there was powdering her nose.

"Hey!" A man seated in front of a laptop computer called to her.

"Me?"

"You!" said the man. "You're on a sub-four pace."

"What?"

"I just plugged your race number into the computer and pulled all your splits," the man explained. "You're on pace to run 3:59."

"Not if I continue standing here," she said heading out the door to continue her chase of the pope.

03:15:00

Walking toward the command center, Peter McDonald could not help but notice how evil the sky looked. Its colors ranged from a cloudless light blue overhead to a blue so dark to the west that it might have been midnight, a sign of bad weather brewing. But how soon would bad weather strike? Until the last hour, Peter's weather worries had centered on warm temperatures, always a danger to marathoners, but to that still-present worry was now added the threat of stormy weather.

It was the bad news mentioned by Noel Michaels earlier as accompanying the good news that a cold front might cause temperatures to plummet. Hooray for that, but Vaughn Johnson now suggested that the cold front might bring with it thunderstorms, maybe even a tornado. Earlier, Peter had called Johnson running the race on his cell phone and talked him into leaving the course to help them decide how to handle the approaching weather. "I'll send a golf cart to pick you up," Peter promised. Johnson, overheated, quickly agreed.

Now, Peter found the TV3 weatherman sitting in front of a computer in the command center, Michaels looking over the weatherman's shoulder.

03:15:00. 03:15:01. 03:15:02.

Peter did not waste time: "Give me an update on the weather."

"Nasty," Johnson replied. "Very nasty. Exceptionally nasty! When the front hits , you may wish the problem was only warm weather."

"Cooler temperatures?"

"A drop of 10 or 20 degrees. Good, but your medical people will need to switch to treating hypothermia, rather than hyperthermia."

"Cold body temperature rather than hot," explained Michaels, as though Peter did not know.

Johnson pointed to the computer screen showing a map of rural areas to the west and southwest of Lake City. Overlaying the map were bands of color, red over the far suburbs indicating precipitation. It was the same kind of map viewers tuning into *The 10:00 News* might see. "Add to the rain, high winds."

"You mentioned tornados yesterday out west?"

"That threat seems to have diminished. None seen today as the front has moved westward toward us. But tornados resist the best efforts of us weathermen to predict them."

"If there's any hint of a tornado, we need to start clearing the course." Peter thought of Pope Tony, last reported passing Mile 21. They had a contingency plan where police could rapidly shelter runners in schools and warehouses. They could hide the entire remaining field in the parking garage at Pritzinger Place near 25 miles. The problem was getting highly motivated runners to obey police commands. Sounding sirens would set them moving in the right direction, but also might unnecessarily cause a panic.

Johnson continued: "I can't predict what will happen when the cold air rushing at us collides with the warm and moist air over the lake."

"Lightning?"

Peter thought for several seconds, although it seemed like minutes to Johnson and Michaels, who both waited for him to make a decision.

"Tell me when the cold front will hit," he told Vaughn Johnson. It was less a question and more a command.

"You're asking me to guess."

"I'm asking you to guess."

"Noon."

Peter turned toward his executive director: "How much time to clear the course and get everyone into shelters?"

"Fifteen minutes."

Peter, who seldom let even the minutest detail of race planning to slide by unrecorded, knew that. He had asked that question mainly to allow himself a few more seconds to think. He began to talk—slowly as a means of holding center stage—but it was his decision to make, and his decision only. Peter wanted to be sure he made the right decision.

"Noon.... Four hours into the race.... More than half the field still out .... Twenty-five thousand runners.... More than that.... A lot of people to move.... Fifteen minutes to clear the course.... Eleven-forty-five?..."

"That makes me nervous," said Michaels, reading his mind.

"Eleven-thirty. Barring some sudden shift in the weather...

"...which I don't expect," said Johnson.

"...we'll tell police to execute Contingency Plan B."

Peter looked at his watch and saw that he was due to be interviewed on TV at that exact moment, and was late. He did not like being late. "I'll be back in fifteen minutes. If you don't hear from me, because I'm talking on TV or the radio, push the panic button. Start clearing the course."

"The runners won't like it."

"They'll like even less getting hit by lightning. Besides..."

"Besides?"

"After four hours running in this heat, they might like to spend some time in the shade."

"Good point."

The race director placed his hand on the door, displaying an eagerness to head to the TV tent. "Anything else?"

"Go!" said Michaels.

Peter pushed open the door and started to leave, but Vaughn Johnson called after him: "If you have a hot line to Pope Tony, you might ask him to pray for us."

Out on the course, like so many other runners around him, Pope Tony had lapsed into survival mode. One foot in front of the other. That's all it takes. Keep placing one foot in front of the other. Tony knew he had trained hard for this marathon and should have floated the distance faster than this, but the necessity to interact with others had drained him. And *the noise, the noise*. He had not trained to endure the noise, the cheers of those supporting him. It was almost frightening. Just when things seemed darkest, Mario or Angelo would give him a pat on the shoulder or offer a word of encouragement, spoken in Italian. They kept him going. He wondered if they realized how important they were to his success today. One can't survive in this world without the support of others. That sounded like the theme for a bad homily.

Forty days in the desert? That sounds like a vacation!

One foot in front of the other. That's all it takes. Tony knew he could pray, but isn't that too self-serving: to pray for your own success, when so many other people and causes need his prayers? To keep going the last two miles, Tony returned again to the mantra he chanted to himself when maintaining pace became difficult: *Wings of Eagles. Wings of Eagles. Wings of Eagles*. One foot in front of the other.

Running within sight of Pope Tony, Don Geoffrey visualized the sell line on the cover of *Running Magazine*: "Pope Tony Did It, So Can You!" The Turtle loved it when one of his articles made the cover. It fed his ego, but he got a $1,000 cover bonus above his usual exorbitant writing fee.

For the entire marathon, Geoffrey had hovered in the wake of the pope, rarely more than a hundred yards behind, more often almost close enough to touch him. At one point, he apparently had gotten too close for the comfort of the bodyguards running on each side of the pope. One of the bodyguards had looked at him as though to say, *Who are you?* Geoffrey offered his given name and explained he wrote for *Running Magazine*.

The bodyguard smiled and said, *"Tartaruga!"*

Geoffrey began to explain that he did not speak Italian, so Angelo translated for him, "Tur-tell!"

That caught the attention of the pope, who reached over and offered a sweaty palm: "I read your articles every month, Don."

Okay, thought the Turtle, nominally Protestant. *I'll convert.*

They said no more to each other. Geoffrey did not want to sully his journalistic credentials by buddying up to the subject of an article he knew he would write. He imagined the blurb that would lure people into reading it: *Hoping to get a scoop on The Most Famous Person Ever To Run A Marathon, the author discovers that Pope Tony is just a regular runner.*

The Turtle moved back to a respectable distance and became an observer, not a participant in the story. He hoped he could remember the words of encouragement deluging the pope not only from cheering spectators but also from those running with him, a movable feast of admirers.

"Tony, we love you in Kansas City."

MARATHON

"Tony, you're an inspiration."

"Tony, I'm running my first marathon too. C'mon, we can make it."

The Turtle often wrote as he ran, composing paragraphs that after he returned home would move from mind to computer, eventually into print. He imagined how he would describe Pope Tony's reaction to this adulation:

> You can tell that Pope Tony would rather be concentrating on the marathon than responding to everyone, but he tries to be civil. Over and over again, he gives a little wave with his right hand. But mostly he keeps his eyes down and keeps chugging.

As the pope and the entourage surrounding him drew closer to the finish line, Geoffrey heard one spectator shout: "One mile to go!"

The Turtle laughed within himself. They had just crossed the 24-mile mark a few minutes before, so he knew that there was more than a single mile to go. He hoped the pope realized that too. They did not have that much further to go in a marathon that would be heralded on TV broadcasts today and in newspapers tomorrow all over the world. He hoped at least a few people were patient enough to wait to read his report in *Running Magazine*.

In these closing minutes, Geoffrey found himself running next to a runner wearing a bright green singlet, displaying a shamrock. From his dress and looks, certainly Irish. The runner spoke: "This is an incredible experience." Yes, from his accent certainly Irish.

The Turtle did not like wasting words in marathons. He offered a single word response: "Absolutely." He did not want to offend with his aloofness someone who read his books or used his training programs.

The Irish runner had no intent to continue the conversation. Paddy Savitch was thinking: *Somehow I need to convince Dennis to continue our sponsorship of this race.*

Preoccupied with survival strategies, neither runner thought to look sideways at the darkening skies, now finally being lit by flashes of lightning. If they had, Geoffrey and Savitch might have begun to worry whether they would finish before the storm struck.

One block behind, Matilda Goldberg felt frustrated. She had been pushing the pace harder than she wanted for more miles than she wished and still had come no closer to catching the pope. One problem now past was having to pee. It was hot. Too much to drink. Long lines at porta-potties. *Help!* Finally, modesty aside, she ducked off the course and dropped her drawers between two parked cars. *Oh, did that feel good! I hope nobody caught me on their cell phone camera.* Got piss all over her, but she was able to mini-shower at the next aid station by throwing a cup of water down the front of her shorts.

SUNDAY

At one point less than an hour ago, Tilda saw the pope far ahead being interviewed by some female reporter riding in a golf cart. Pope Tony must have slowed while doing the interview, because Tilda found herself getting closer. Then with the interview over, he surged ahead to again disappear among runners who wanted the thrill of running near the most celebrated individual ever do a marathon.

Tilda thought: Only a few more miles to go and still not close. *Why didn't I start with the 4:00 pacing team? Will he give interviews afterwards?* Like Don Geoffrey and Paddy Savitch, Matilda Goldberg was so focused on catching the pope that she too had not looked over her shoulder. She remained innocently unaware of the storm that threatened to engulf those remaining on the course past four hours.

03:30:00

At precisely 11:30, three-and-a-half hours into the marathon, Noel Michaels, having talked to Peter McDonald minutes before, called the Police Department's Captain Robert Newsom flying in the Fire Department helicopter above Lake City with Christine Ferrara and told him to execute Contingency Plan B. "And get that chopper back to the ground before the storm hits! It is going to get nasty: *Nas-tee!*"

03:30:00. 03:30:01. 03:30:02.

Captain Newsom told Michaels that he had his eye on the approaching storm and would take no unnecessary risks. But he needed to remain overhead as long as possible to supervise the course closing. Once he put Contingency Plan B into motion, it meant that the 800 officers under his direction would need to convince close to 30,000 runners (those still out on the course) to stop running and seek shelter. No easy task, but all anybody needed to do was look west. The black clouds heralding the thunderstorm's approach now dominated the western sky.

Less than a hundred yards away at the TV3 control trailer, Peter McDonald was watching those same clouds, worrying whether or not he had delayed too long pulling the plug. The approaching storm was both friend (since it promised cooler temperatures) and foe (since it threatened the safety of anybody in the open). More to the point, it threatened the safety of an individual who in the last several days had become very dear to him.

430

MARATHON

"Christine's in that chopper, Peter," said Tom Schorr. Peter had placed the call to Noel Michaels from the TV3 control trailer during a commercial break.

"I know," Peter responded calmly, trying to hide his concern.

Schorr turned his attention to the commentators in the booth: "Thirty seconds, coming out of break." Peter left the control trailer to join the trio on the set. He would explain to the television audience reasons for the course closure, then do the same on radio. That message would not get through to those still running. He hoped all obeyed police orders. He hoped also that the helicopter containing Christine got back on the ground, and quickly.

The helicopter hovered above the Barack Obama Expressway near the point where the course crossed the expressway and doubled back on itself. The back seat of the 206 was wide enough to seat three, but Christine still worried that each time they went live, all viewers would see was her eyes, nose and the microphone in front of her mouth. When she expressed this worry to Edmund, he claimed that his wide-angle lens would capture "The Whole Christine"—but she was not sure.

A few minutes earlier, Captain Newsom had contacted his dispatcher, who activated a pre-recorded message transmitted instantly to the radios of every policeman below assigned to traffic control, repeating continuously the message: "Contingency Plan B. Clear marathon course. Direct runners to nearest shelters. Repeat: Clear marathon course!"

"How long will the response take?" wondered Christine.

"Just watch," said the police officer confidently.

The 206 offered four doors, each with wide windows. Christine looked below and what she saw amazed her.

At that precise moment, she heard Tom Schorr's voice in her earphones: "Five, four, three.... Throw to Christine!" With the chatter of the helicopter blades, it was hard for her to hear, but she knew filters would silence most of the noise, and viewers would hear her voice clearly.

She barely heard that of Mark Mallon: "The Lake City Marathon continues with more than half the runners still out on the course. For the last several hours, Timothy and C.V., the threat to runners was hot weather. Suddenly, we have a new threat: stormy weather. Christine is not merely *out* on the course, she is *above* the course in the TV3 helicopter. Where are you, Christine?"

"I'm hovering above the expressway near the point where the marathon course turns back toward downtown and with a good view of two or three miles of runners, literally thousands of them, all hoping to finish, but that might not be possible today, Mark."

SUNDAY

"Christine, Peter McDonald just informed us he executed what he called 'Contingency Plan B.' If not exactly cancelled, the Lake City Marathon has been put on rain delay, like might happen at a baseball game."

"Looking below, I can see the stadium for our last-place team, and it is about to fill with runners instead of baseball fans, Mark."

"Presumably they did not enter in search of beer and hot dogs."

Christine ignored Mallon's attempt at humor. With a better view of the dark clouds on the horizon than he had from the anchor set, she was, quite frankly, scared to death. The TV reporter had never flown in a helicopter before. If the engine on your airplane dies, you might coast to a safe landing on the expressway, or even in the lake. With a helicopter, there are no wings. You drop straight down. But engine reliability was much less a problem than the high winds headed their way. The dark clouds to the west did not to Christine look friendly. Christine tried not to let the fear she felt within show in her voice as she described what she was witnessing.

"I am seated behind Captain Robert Newsom of the Lake City Police Department. 'Lake City's Finest,' I might add. Barely two minutes ago, I heard him tell his dispatcher to execute Contingency Plan B. Naïve that I am, I had not even heard such a plan existed, Mark."

"You're not the only one, Christine."

"So I asked Captain Newsom, how long will it take to clear the course? His response was, 'just watch.' So I'm watching, and I am amazed."

Christine explained how, almost within seconds of the command, policemen began to shove sawhorses onto the course to block approaching runners. "Some ducked around the sawhorses, but most stopped and seemed willing to follow directions toward already identified shelters."

"I did not know runners were that obedient," commented Mallon.

"All they needed to do was look over their shoulders at the storm aimed at those same shoulders. Quite honestly, the clouds are ink black, lit by flashes of lightning. Scary, very scary. But if you need one other reason to understand why runners might be willing to bail on their dreams to finish a marathon, consider that the weather has been hot as…. My mother won't let me use the word to describe what it has been hot as, but it is, Mark."

C.V. jumped in to ask: "Where are they going, Christine?"

"Many of the shelters are schools, public buildings. Obviously, somebody has the keys. The baseball stadium I already described, with or without hot dogs and beer. The football stadium, closer to you. Plenty of room for the runners to wait safely under the grandstands until the storm clears. The parking garage attached to Pritzinger Place, the convention center. Many of the spectators who live nearby apparently are returning to their homes. Or to their cars. Or they're being directed to follow the runners, C.V."

"Christine," said Mallon, "we just talked to Peter McDonald, who told us that with the storm expected to hit shortly after noon, runners hoping to finish faster than four hours on the clock above the finish line are being allowed to continue running toward that goal." Although the anchorman failed to explain it, that included runners who might have taken ten minutes or more to cross the starting line, meaning most of the last runners expected to finish before the storm hit actually had chip times of 3:50 or faster.

"Where is the pope?" he asked.

"He's still running, I'm being told, with the 4:00 pacing team, those on pace to finish in that time. They're headed toward the convention center parking garage—and that's where we'll be going in a few minutes, landing on the open roof, Mark."

"Twenty seconds to commercial, Mark," spoke Tom Schorr.

"Don't stay up in the air too long, Christine," said Mallon, who shifted his attention to viewers. "We have been talking to Christine Ferrara in the TV3 helicopter above the marathon course. The Lake City Marathon is on hold with Pope John Anthony Molina and tens of thousands of others still on course. If anybody wonders why, just look to the west. Although, maybe you should consider instead seeking shelter in your basement."

"Five, four, three...."

"We'll be right back after these messages."

Mark Mallon turned to C.V. on the left and Timothy on the right and raised his arms into an almost prayerful position. "But where do we go? We're sitting in a tent in the middle of a park with trees and lampposts all around. We don't have a basement."

"Prayer might be appropriate," said Timothy Rainboldt.

Sirens began to sound.

04:00:00

For several minutes, policemen and volunteers at intersections passed by the pack with which Matilda Goldberg was running had been warning about dangers posed by the approaching storm—high winds and a threat of lightning—and that within a few blocks everybody would be diverted to shelter for their own safety. "But only for ten or fifteen minutes," promised policemen and volunteers. As soon as the storm passes (they assured everybody), runners would be welcome back on the course and allowed to finish, and finally, "We are sorry for the inconvenience."

"Sorry?" commented Barry, a runner from Seattle, who had been running by Tilda's side for the last few blocks. Both had been at the Team Turtle party, but did not recognize each other. "Nobody needs apologize to me," said Barry. "Get me out of the sun and into the shade!"

"Not your first marathon?" Tilda asked.

"Lost count," laughed Barry. "When I get home, I'll count T-shirts and text you the exact number."

The New York Times reporter offered some solace: "Once the front passes, it should get colder."

"Thank God for that!"

Thank God. Speaking of which, Tilda ruminated, *one of his appointed messengers is running just in front of me. Will I ever catch Pope Tony?* She had been close to doing just that before the sirens began to sound, but what happens once we are diverted?

04:00:00. 04:00:01. 04:00:02.

At that moment, four hours into the marathon, Tilda looked ahead and saw two policemen begin to move a sawhorse into the street, effectively blocking the path of several dozen runners ahead of her and several hundred or more runners behind. Apparently her group was about to be directed to a nearby shelter until the storm passed. Fair enough, but those who had gotten past the sawhorse before it was moved into the street were being allowed to continue on course, probably to another shelter, which made sense, except Pope Tony was in one pack, she in another. *Unacceptable.* That just would not do!

Of course, try telling that to the cops.

Most around her had shifted from running to walking mode, apparently feeling no need to keep running if forced to wait out the storm in some shelter. Tilda too slowed her pace, while considering her options. Volunteers had shoved a second sawhorse into place. Runners ahead of her obediently began to turn off course as directed, calmly following orders even as the sky to the west grew darker still.

Approaching a policemen standing arms folded, guarding the gap between sawhorses, Tilda wondered how she might dodge around him. Making the turn, then cutting back onto the road was one possibility, but that act of lawlessness offended her moral code. Did the officer have a Taser to deal with perpetrators who misbehaved? She could identify herself as a reporter with *The New York Times* (too bad she did not have her press pass), but, no; she doubted if anyone in Lake City read the paper that employed her.

Distasteful as it was to her feminist nature, Matilda Goldberg finally decided to rely on women's wiles. "Officer," she pleaded. "My husband's in the group ahead. We got separated at the last aid station. I need to catch him."

No further discussion was necessary. The police officer moved aside, allowing Tilda past. "Okay, but don't get caught in the open." He pointed at the radio in his belt. "We just got word of a tornado sighting."

Sirens continued to wail.

Tilda slipped through the gap as the officer turned to discourage several others from following. "Her husband's up there," he said. She began running again, because she definitely did *not* want to get caught in the open with lightning flashing all around. The pope was somewhere in the pack ahead, that pack now being diverted into a giant parking garage. Did she actually believe that even if she caught him, the pontiff would have anything to say that could be classified as "All the News That's Fit to Print?"

Tilda looked over her shoulder at a sky undeniably dark. Dark on dark. So dark that if a tornado were part of the menacing clouds, it was beyond her ability to detect it. And now, the frightening sound of something loud approaching. *Pup-pup-pup-pup-pup!* It was a helicopter, red, "Fire Department" on its side in large letters. Tilda watched mesmerized as the chopper passed hardly more than a hundred feet over her head. Given the threat of a tornado, Tilda was glad not to be riding in that helicopter.

"Get that chopper on the ground!" snapped Peter McDonald. "Quick!" He had gone from being worried to being angry. "Right now!"

"Relax, Peter," said Noel Michaels, trying to remain calm.

The fact that Christine Ferrara was passenger on that helicopter certainly added to his anxiety. "What the hell is Captain Newsom thinking?"

Michaels recognized the reason for her boss's anxiety. And she was anxious too, because weatherman Vaughn Johnson had just revealed that a tornado apparently had been sighted not more than five minutes ago, fewer than a half dozen miles to the southwest. It had not touched down, but might any minute. Most of the personnel connected with the marathon had only tents over their heads for protection and while Peter had ordered as much of the staff as possible to seek shelter in the underground garage, she and key people within the marathon organization remained at their posts.

The executive director offered the news just received from Captain Newsom that the helicopter was headed toward the convention center, planning to land on the top deck of the parking garage.

"Tell them to run for cover as soon as they land," instructed Peter.

I think they know that, thought Michaels, but she dutifully repeated what Peter had said into her radio.

Satisfied, Peter left the command tent and headed to the finish line. He began to jog through the area that at this point in the marathon normally would be crowded with runners having Mylar blankets wrapped around their shoulders and medals hung around their necks. It was eerily quiet: the calm before the storm. Only a few runners trickled across the line. Volunteers told them to keep running and seek shelter.

Peter moved through the chute and across the mats on the finish line. He stood for a moment contemplating what to do. He noticed a golf cart parked by the fence, abandoned at least temporarily by its driver, hopefully now in shelter. Peter could commandeer it and drive to the parking garage, but that act bordered on the insane. He looked south at the swirling clouds that menaced that garage. He thought for a moment he saw an extra bump of blackness at the bottom of those clouds. The first phase of a tornado, or was it his imagination? He stood motionless, knowing all he could do was wait until the storm passed.

Back in the command tent, weatherman Vaughn Johnson tracked the same clouds as radar-generated images on his laptop. The screen showed a mix of colors, the most ominous of which was red identifying the heaviest winds, the most rain. "It looks like the point of the storm will pass a mile to the south," he told Noel Michaels.

"Good news for us," she replied.

"But bad news for those a mile south."

"The convention center."

"And its parking garage."

"I sure hope that helicopter is on the ground."

The weatherman decided not to comment on what would happen if the helicopter containing Christine Ferrara was engulfed by the storm.

The Fire Department helicopter slowly began to descend toward the concrete surface that served as top deck for the parking garage. Free of parked cars, it offered a wide and flat landing area. "Aim for a spot near that stairwell," Captain Newsom instructed the pilot, Lieutenant Jean Grey. She moved her controls gently, hoping for a soft landing.

"Hang on," said Grey.

Pup-pup-pup-pup-pup! Christine Ferrara might be more frightened than any time in her life, but her voice betrayed no emotion as she reported on the evacuation of the marathon course.

"Five minutes ago, Mark, I could look out the side window of this helicopter and see thousands of runners in the last few miles of their marathons. And, tens of thousands of spectators standing on sidewalks cheering those runners. And, all the volunteers without which an event the size of the Lake City Marathon could not successfully be run.

"And now..." Christine paused, allowing her words to hang in the air.

"...Nobody! Nearly nobody! The streets are empty, vacant, abandoned, everybody having run for cover. I do not even *know* where they all disappeared to, but the Police Department obviously knew what it was doing. It gives you confidence that if ever again we are faced with a more serious disaster drill, the people of this town will be well served, Mark." Christine did not offer the words "terrorist attack;" she did not need to.

"Where are you, Christine?" asked a worried Mark Mallon.

"About to land on the..."

Suddenly the helicopter shook, as though struck by a missile. Edmund would say later that it reminded him of Vietnam.

"Uhhhh!" Christine reacted.

"Christine?" called a very worried Mark Mallon.

The helicopter went up, then down, as Lieutenant Grey fought to regain control. High winds! Rain! Hailstones! They were under attack!

Christine was frightened. Very frightened. *Why did I let Tom talk me into getting into this thing?*

The noise of the storm was intense, like the breath of a dragon.

Then another sudden drop.

BOOMP!

"...I guess we've landed on the roof of the parking garage."

"Get out! Get out!" shouted Newsom. "Run for the stairwell!"

Christine, momentarily stunned, fumbled for the handle that would open her door. It would not move. She tried again. What am I doing wrong? Then the door slid open, pulled by the pilot.

Christine did not as much climb out the door as she fell out the door, slipping to the ground, her fall broken by forearm and elbow. *Ouch! That hurt!* She was instantly soaked, pummeled by the rain and hailstones. The fluttering sound of the helicopter blades had been replaced by a roar that would have shattered any decibel meters attempting to measure it.

She felt hands grabbing under both armpits, the hands of the pilot. She did not so much help Christine up as she yanked her up. "Run! Run!" the pilot shouted, pushing Christine toward the door of a stairwell, Captain Newsom standing beside it, holding the door open. Edmund, lugging his camera as though he might be charged if he returned it damaged, preceded her through the door almost tripping over a ledge as he did so.

As she ran toward what she hoped was safety, the dream Christine had last night of tumbling through the air after striking a car door on her bicycle flashed through her mind. This was worse than the worse anxiety dream, but Christine did not want to take time to scream.

SUNDAY

———

Mallon's hands were shaking. He tried to calm himself by gripping the desk with one hand and the microphone in with the other. The anchor attempted to maintain control of his voice as he instructed: "Christine. Do *not* waste any more time talking to us. Get *out* of that chopper as quickly as possible!"

Silence.

"Christine?"

Silence.

"Let's hope she heard you," offered Timothy. "Look."

He pointed southward in the direction of the convention center. The black clouds that had darkened the sky to the west now had enveloped downtown. Out the open end of their tent, the three announcers had a clear view south. A bump suddenly appeared along the bottom of the black clouds sweeping across the city to the south of them. The bump suddenly exploded into a tail aimed at the ground, twisting, finally striking the ground. Even as far away from the tornado as they were, the three announcers could hear its roar as it cut right across the marathon course.

"Shit!" muttered Mark Mallon. Fortunately that four-letter word, which might have earned him a reprimand from the station boss despite the circumstances in which it had been uttered, was not heard by those still viewing the marathon telecast. The grid of several square miles that included the park suddenly lost power. They were temporarily off the air. It would take several minutes before backup generators provided power again.

The digital clock over the finish line had gone blank. No runners crossing the line or spectators who normally might have been watching them remained to look at the clock, its last numbers:

04:01:33. 00:00:00. 00:00:00.

04:01:33

Matilda Goldberg had both the best and the worst view of the tornado, because she was still sprinting for shelter seconds before it hit. A policeman probably saved her life. After foolishly dodging around a sawhorse earlier, Tilda had hoped to beat the storm and catch the pope, only to fall short. A block short. Looking ahead, she could see that Jefferson Avenue for the entire length of the block ahead of her was empty. For the first time since she started this ill-chosen marathon four hours ago, no runners. No spectators. No helpful volunteers. All smarter than her, because they had run for cover. She had not.

04:01:33. 04:01:34. 04:01:35

From a distance, she had watched the last runners in the pack trailing Pope Tony duck into the parking garage at Pritzinger Place, but she was still out on the course struggling, legs dead, incapable of moving any faster. And it had begun to rain: hard!

And hail!

Tiny particles of ice. Bouncing off the streets. Bouncing off *her*. And it hurt! *Oy vey iz mir!*

She ran down the center line, stranded, abandoned, unprotected in a void between safe havens with the sounds of the storm locomotive loud in her ears, and as her curly crop of hair began to tingle with electricity, it seemed like she was experiencing every runner's worst anxiety dream. Except this was no anxiety dream: For Tilda, the dream was real. She might not wake up from it.

Are we there yet?

Fatigued, brain not functioning any better than her legs, muscles locking like a relay runner at the end of his 400-meter leg, Tilda found herself unable to shift to a higher gear. There was no higher gear, and the lower gears were not working too well either.

If my body lands somewhere over the rainbow, can they still sit shiva?

It was then she heard the policeman: "Lady, get off the course!"

Except where? How? What do I do?

Tilda's brain cells, still in slumber mode after nearly twenty-five miles of mindless running, could not be summoned to shift into intelligent thought. At this moment with the storm about to suck her up its throat like a whale swallowing krill, she could do little more than place one foot in front of the other and the other foot in front of that.

That's when the police officer grabbed Tilda by the arm and yanked. It was an unfriendly yank, one the cop might have used to immobilize a perpetrator. As he tugged her from the street toward the sidewalk, Tilda in her marathon-fogged mind wondered if he would ask her to put two hands on a squad car roof while he informed her she had the right to remain silent. Then the policeman threw Tilda into a doorway and covered her with his body so hard that the breath went out of her body.

He was a huge man and her head, hair still tingling, stuck out from beneath one armpit, allowing her to watch wide-eyed as the tornado's black funnel brushed the top deck of the parking garage while it moved oh so slowly across her armpit-limited field of vision.

Only a *meshuggeneh* would have thought she could outrun a tornado.

SUNDAY

That's when she saw the helicopter rise up off the deck and it caused Tilda to wonder why its fool pilot would want to take off into the vortex of a storm so fierce. Then she realized the helicopter was not involved in a man-directed takeoff, but rather it was being vacuumed into the vortex, tumbling over and over as it disappeared in the blackness above. She hoped that whoever had landed the helicopter atop the garage was out of the machine and under cover.

The tornado roar began to diminish as the front of the storm pushed past the doorway where she remained pinned unable to move. Now came the near equally loud roar of hailstones—huge hailstones—bouncing off the pavement. Forget the tornado: If a hailstone hit your head, you still might die! Hailstorms and rain so thick, she might as easily be standing in the cave beneath Niagara Falls. Matilda Goldberg would describe the experience as such in her first-person feature for *The New York Times* about what it was like to nearly fall victim to a tornado.

As the police officer relaxed his claim on her, allowing Tilda to breathe more freely and observe the aftermath, she discovered the street covered with debris as though the storm earlier had passed over a construction site in its passage across Lake City and sucked up everything not tied down to deposit miscellaneously along its path. She wondered where the helicopter would come back down to earth.

"Thank you, thank you," Tilda kept repeating to the policeman as she moved back into the street, not running but stepping cautiously over the boards and roofing and even bricks. She failed to get his name. Or badge number! How could she call herself a reporter and fail to do so?

Thank you, Mr. Policeman, and I hope your wife did not mind how much you pressed me into the corner of that driveway. If you got a free feel, you deserved it.

It felt to Naní like her head might explode any second. The pain was intense. More than intense! As though someone had clamped a vise over her head and started to press against her ears. Twisting the screw to inflict maximum pain. Isn't this what they did in the Middle Ages to force confessions out of sinners? *But I am guilty of no sin! Look who I'm running with.*

Naní swallowed, then swallowed again, because that's what she did instinctively while landing in an airplane when a change in air pressure caused a similar reaction to her ears. Later, after comparing how she felt with others sheltered in the parking garage, all agreed it had been the sudden change of air pressure from high to low. Someone standing next to a water fountain said the water had literally *exploded* out of the fountain, bubbling onto the concrete deck of the garage.

440

People around the supermodel were crying not from fear but from relief because the storm had passed, the noise of the tornado now replaced by the noise of heavy rainfall. *At least nobody here got hurt,* thought Naní looking at those around her, many struck to silence, others beginning to babble as though the low pressure system had affected not only the water pressure, but also their tongues.

"Anybody hurt?" runners began to ask each other. But it appeared nobody among the 4:00 pacing group suffered any injuries.

Lenny Hand looked at his watch and noted that they had been on the course for just over four hours. "Looks like I can't award myself a bonus for bringing you across the line on pace," He said.

04:10:00

S he got out of the helicopter in time," Noel Michaels advised Peter McDonald. The executive director had just received a report by radio from Captain Newsom, standing on the top deck of the parking garage now that the tornado had passed. Michaels quickly called McDonald on his cell phone to relay the good news.

"Say what?" said Peter.

"Christine," repeated Michaels. "She's safe. Everyone else too."

"What happened to the helicopter?"

"Captain Newsom claims we owe the Fire Department a new one."

"Are you serious?"

Peter's assistant laughed at how absurd had been what the police captain had just told her. "The helicopter: It's gone!"

"Gone?"

"*Just gone!* Everybody from the helicopter—Newsom, his pilot, Christine, her cameraman—ducked into an enclosed stairwell. *Barely!* After the tornado passed, they went back onto the deck, and the helicopter had disappeared."

"Disappeared?"

"The chopper must have gotten sucked up into the tornado. Who knows where it is now—maybe at the bottom of the lake."

"And Christine is safe?"

"Yes, except she fell getting out."

"Oh my god!"

"And she left her purse on the back seat of the helicopter, Newsom told me. He laughed while telling me about it, so everybody may still be scared,

441

but at least they're in a good mood. Newsom said Christine's wallet was in her purse. She has no money, so you're going to have to lend her cab fare."

Peter placed one hand atop his forehead and closed his eyes, unable not to think about how he had lost one woman to a terrible accident, and now had come close to losing another.

"Where is she now?" he asked his assistant.

"Apparently, Christine ran down into the parking garage. She wants to get an interview with the pope."

Peter thanked his assistant and punched the red button on his cell phone, hanging up. He quickly speed-dialed Christine. The phone rang four times and clicked into her voice mail. If still in the garage, thought Peter, Christine must be surrounded by foot-thick concrete. *She can't get a signal.* He closed the cell phone and put it into his holder.

The rain that had been so intense a few minutes ago was down to a trickle. Luckily, he had grabbed an umbrella leaving the command tent, otherwise he would be soaked—and cold. As the storm front passed, the temperature had not dropped, it had plummeted! Like on a summer day, stepping from under a blazing sun and into an air-conditioned building. Those still out on the course would enjoy the last few miles a lot more. They probably were moving from shelters and headed his way, but although a few workers and volunteers had begun to reappear, the entire 385 yards on Columbia Drive leading to the finish line remained devoid of runners. Not a single one! Looking above at the finish line clock, Peter noticed it had resumed counting the running time. The power must be back on. He hoped the time was correct.

04:10:00. 04:10:01. 04:10:02.

Storm past, the marathon would return to normal. Runners soon would complete their day's work. The closest of them, including Pope Tony, Peter knew, had stopped at the parking garage at Pritzinger Place, only a mile away. Ten minutes of running. Perhaps he would go out and greet his boyhood friend. He saw again the golf cart next to the fence, wisely abandoned by someone on his staff fleeing the storm. The key was still in it. Climbing into the cart, Peter turned the key and began to drive backwards on the empty course toward the convention center.

Christine Ferrara knew they had barely—just barely—made it out of the helicopter in time. She shuddered while returning to the parking garage's top deck from the stairwell, and it was not from the refreshingly sudden cold.

She wanted to retrieve her purse, but the helicopter in which she had been riding was gone.

Gone!

MARATHON

In the last minute before the storm hit, it seemed almost as though it had accelerated in an attempt to grab them. Captain Newcomb apologized: "Sorry. I cut that too close. I'm used to taking risks, but I should not have submitted you to that experience."

Christine told him not to worry. As a journalist, she claimed also to be used to taking risks. That was reassuring and a nice thing to say, but it was hardly true. As reporter with a TV station located in Peoria, her most dangerous previous experience was dumping a full cup of coffee on her lap during a commercial break for *The Ten O'clock News*.

This was earlier, before Peter tried to contact her by cell phone. The TV3 reporter was soaking wet. Running across the roof with the pilot tugging her to safety, Christine had looked up and actually saw the metamorphosis of what merely had been dark clouds turn into a killing funnel. Fortunately they made it into the stairwell and slammed the door behind them just in time. Covered on all sides by concrete, they could not have been safer, even the roar of the passing tornado seemed muted. Had the concrete garage actually shaken, or was it her shaking?

But that was past. She had a job to do. She nudged her cameraman, beside her in the stairwell: "C'mon, Edmund. Let's go downstairs and locate some articulate runner looking for fifteen minutes of fame."

04:30:00

The last mile became a triumphal march by marathoners, many who had come to Lake City with time goals, lured by its flat course and normally perfect weather. Well, the weather had proved far from "perfect," but nobody seemed to care any more about shattered time goals or the discomfort suffered in the heat of the first 25 miles. They would have tales to tell to their friends, who had not been "lucky" enough to choose Lake City this year for their fall marathon. The bragging had already begun among those who had run with cell phones, who could call and text-message friends and family to assure them that, yeah, I'm okay, but what an amazing experience. Their comments to friends and family:

"You'll never believe what happened!"

"The tornado passed right overhead."

"Lucky we were in a parking garage."

"I was standing right near the pope when it hit."

"Figured with Tony nearby, we had God on our side."

443

"Talked with the supermodel. Can you believe, she's like normal?"

"Ran with the world record holder. She's pregnant."

"No, I haven't finished yet. But I will."

And so the pack of runners, who had found shelter in the parking garage returned to the course. A mile of asphalt remained to be run, but nobody yet seemed eager to run it. They stood in groups in the middle of Jefferson Avenue talking, comparing stories, as though waiting for a signal from someone to begin their journey. Christine Ferrara did find several individuals willing to describe what happened for the viewing audience. After finishing one interview, she turned and found Peter sitting in a cart, wide smile on his face.

"Would you like a ride, Christine?"

"Peter!"

"Or bus fare? I can give you exact change."

She began to cry, realization only beginning to set in.

"Or maybe just a hug." He climbed out of the cart and moved toward her.

"I'm all wet."

He put his arms around her. "Let's be wet together."

And for what seemed like the longest time, Peter and Christine just stood holding each other. Edmund decided to look the other way.

"Tony, where's Tony?"

It had become "Tony" for all those who had run with him today.

"He's coming."

Without anybody having spoken the words, those who had sought shelter in the parking garage decided to wait for the pope, so he could continue to serve as their shepherd. They would not start running until he started running in front of the group.

Pope Tony emerged from a crowd of runners. They began to cheer, to applaud, to whistle. He laughed and raised his hands in thanks. Had he been Italian, like most previous popes, he probably would have fluttered his hands toward himself, in a gesture that might seem to many Americans that he was calling for more applause. Instead, Tony's palms were positioned outward as though to reflect the applause backwards on those who had joined him on such a memorable morning.

04:30:00. 04:30:01. 04:30:02.

Time and place meant nothing any more, even to those who had arrived at Lake City with time-based goals. They would finish. Everybody would finish. Only a mile to go. One foot in front of the other. The cold front had passed. Perfect running weather.

Pope Tony moved forward. But before beginning, he motioned for Naní, standing nearby to join him at the front of the pack.

And Aba. "Where's Aba?" asked Tony, and she moved to his side. Several members of Team Turtle shoved Don Geoffrey up to the front.

"Any famous people we forgot?"

"Someone find Lenny." And they did. Leonard Hand, still clasping the lollypop sign with the identifying 4:00 on it, moved to the position he had assumed for the previous twenty-five miles, the front of the pack.

Matilda Goldberg chose not to run with the leaders, even after spending most of the race trying to catch Pope Tony. She decided that her role was that of detached observer, a simple reporter, one who writes about all the news that is fit to print, not one who creates it.

Slowly, the pope and his followers began to walk, then to jog, then to run. Purposely, it was at a near pedestrian pace so as to leave no runner behind. Moving in front of them but off to one side was Peter driving the cart he had commandeered at the finish line, Christine in the seat beside him, Edmund riding on the back of the cart, camera pointed at what were now the leaders of the race, all of them born to run.

"Coming out of the commercial, Mark, cut to Christine," said Tom Schorr. "Five, four three...."

"This has been a remarkable marathon," began Mark Mallon. "And we have a remarkable woman covering it. Christine Ferrara decided it might be safer to switch from helicopter back to golf cart. Christine?"

"...And I have seated beside me in that golf cart, Mark, the race director of the Lake City Marathon, Peter McDonald, who certainly in his wildest dreams could not have anticipated the events of this weekend...."

Not in my wildest dreams, thought Peter as Christine continued with her introduction. *Not in my wildest dreams, Christine. And the wildest dream of this weekend happens to be you!*

"...so talk to us, Peter, about the man you called Celebrity X."

And so did Pope John Anthony Molina complete the journey that had begun in secrecy and ended with more people watching the last mile of a marathon —the TV3 coverage now being beamed around the world by CNN and other carriers—than any other race before, not even at the Olympic Games.

Spectators, who had abandoned sidewalks and grandstands because of the storm, returned to their posts to cheer Pope Tony's coming. So did many marathoners who had finished before, now returned from shelter to the finishing area. Tony turned off Jefferson and crossed the bridge and made the final turn toward the finish line 385 yards away as the chant not only of people on both sides but of the runners following began: *"To-nee! To-nee! To-nee!"*

445

Then the man once known as Celebrity X was across the line and into the chute. Peter parked the golf cart near where it had been before. Christine climbed out of the cart to offer her final impressions, then back to Mark Mallon so he could wrap the show. Despite the spectacle of a pope running a marathon, that story was now ancient history. A National Football League game was about to begin, and TV3 dared not miss the opening kickoff.

Christine handed her microphone to Edmund and turned back to Peter, who sat leaning against the cart, smiling. "Still need that bus fare, Christine? Or would you prefer taking the elevated train."

"I'm not sure I want to get that high off the ground for a while."

"Coming to the party?"

"You've only asked me a dozen times, Peter."

"Maybe I'm insecure."

"For no good reason." She smiled. An enticing smile.

Christine brushed both hands through her hair, wet as though she had just stepped out of a shower. Her soaked TV3 shirt clung revealingly tight on her body. *When I signed up for this job, I didn't anticipate it would include a wet T-shirt contest.* She wondered if Peter noticed; she hoped he did.

"I'm a mess."

"A very attractive mess."

"Flattery will get you everywhere."

"Messy or not , are you still coming to the party?"

"Peter, if you ask me that one more time, I'll..." She paused.

"You'll what?..."

Christine turned to leave. Soaked and getting cold, she figured she could grab a Mylar blanket on the way back to the TV3 set and maybe Tom or someone could loan her a dry shirt. She remembered his having a box of extra TV3 shirts in the trailer.

"I'll..." A pause. A sigh.

"...I'll see you at the party."

08:00:00

One or two or three or four or even five or six hours after the diving finish in the men's race, after the embracing finish in the women's race, after Pope Tony survived the tornado and led his flock across the finish line in an event already being discussed and debated on the Internet, those involved with the Lake City Marathon wandered up to the 24th floor of Hilliard Towers. They went there to celebrate.

It was Peter's party.

08:00:00. 08:00:01. 08:00:02.

The directors of the London and Berlin Marathons were off in a side room playing pool, sometimes joined by others, mostly playing each other. A bartender stood behind an ornately carved bar in the corner of the same room watching the pool players out of boredom, because there seemed to be little demand even for the free drinks. This was a party of marathoners, not convention-goers; the bartender knew his tip jar would go light tonight.

In the main room, a brightly polished grand piano, no one playing. A fireplace, no logs burning. A spread of hors d'oeuvres and sweet treats, few people eating. They had come to be among each other more than for food and drink. It was a meeting of the clan after the clan's biggest and most spectacular event of the year.

A crowd of mostly young people gathered around a TV set showing a replay of the marathon coverage. Peter McDonald had obtained a DVD of the telecast from Tom Schorr before heading back to the hotel. At various and appropriate moments, the crowd in front of the TV cheered the action on the screen as though they did not know who would win. When Joseph Nduku walked out of the elevator and into the room, everyone stood and cheered, much to Joseph's embarrassment. He blushed deeply, although with his dark skin it was difficult to tell. He also walked with less dexterity than one might have expected from a well-trained Kenyan. Joseph had arrived with supermodel Nani and her husband, Ricco. She was walking more smoothly than he. Ricco arrived with a smile on his face that never dimmed.

Others among the winners received equal ovations as they entered the room, including the Mystery Girl, her foot still in a bubble cast. "What did you say your name was?" someone shouted, causing everybody to laugh. Meghan Allison explained that she planned to have surgery on her foot tomorrow, but it was a minor procedure, one she probably could perform on herself if her husband Matt would allow. "It would make him sick," Meg said.

Aba Andersson sat at the end of a long table, tall candles on the table, its polish matching that of the grand piano. Occupying the table were seven or eight women, mostly wives of executives with the bank or the marathon office. The conversation centered on childbirth, not on world records. All of the women had children and opinions on subjects related, which Aba absorbed with maternal fascination. Her husband Bjørn was off in another corner of the world talking with Jacob Henry, husband of Tatanya. Both served as agents for their wives and harbored strong opinions related to world sport. When it came to soccer, the Swede, ironically, was a fan of Manchester United, but was being chastised by Jacob, who considered that team and its fans a band of thugs, robbers, criminals. "How could you, Bjørn?"

One not at the party was Pope Tony, already flying back to Rome in a Gulfstream G-5 that had brought him to Lake City barely seventy-two hours before. Not the same G-5, a new one, the switch being made for security purposes at the request of Redbird. Bodyguards Angelo and Mario were asleep in the back of the plane, the stress of the day's events finally having caught up with them. Tony had offered Redbird a ride home, but the cardinal camerlengo demurred, saying he planned to hang around town and do some sightseeing. Besides, Cardinal Connolly had his own G-5. Before saying goodbye, the two prelates embraced, Redbird telling Tony to expect a strong rebuke from the college of cardinals for not revealing his plans. The pope promised "never again," although he meant keeping secret counsel, not running another marathon. Already playing in his mind was the thought of running seven marathons on seven continents, including Antarctica, which might allow him to deliver a message to the world related to global warming. Given so many problems in the world, climate control was not a church issue, yet he thought just maybe it should be.

Also not at the party was Matilda Goldberg, busy at her computer in another room at the Hilliard, writing an article about the day's events. Her editor back in New York warned her against doing, *I Ran with the Pope.* "Leave that to *Running Magazine*," he said.

Christine Ferrara had not needed money for the El, a bus or the subway. Tom Schorr assigned one of his assistants to drive her, still soaking wet, back to Yolanda's apartment in a TV3 van. "You were incredible," he told her, still feeling guilty for having put her in that helicopter. Yolanda wanted to know everything, so the two roommates sat and talked for an hour while Christine told her everything. Christine was exhausted and probably needed a nap before getting ready for Peter's party—there was no way she was going to miss that—but she was totally wired by the day's activities and suspected she would not be able to sleep. After the talk with her roommate, she headed to the shower, but stayed in it too long, soaking up the warmth of the water too long, then fussed over what to wear too long, then had been forced to wait for a taxicab too long, because all the cabs were busy ferrying finished runners home. She probably could have gotten to the Hilliard faster by elevated train, but she still wanted to keep her feet planted firmly on earth. Even having switched to high heels took her almost up higher than she wanted to go. Eventually a taxicab heading back downtown stopped and accepted her as a passenger. Within fifteen minutes, she was stepping out of the elevator on the

24th floor of Hilliard Towers and walking into Peter's party, which seemed to have been going on a long time without her.

A quick survey of the room identified where she could obtain a glass of chardonnay. No Peter yet, though she swiveled her head so much people must have thought her a U-Boat commander looking for a target to sink. Christine drifted over to the group watching a replay of TV3's race telecast, herself now on camera explaining the meaning of the pope's wearing the number 91. Silly reason: his high school graduation year, but also a reference to Psalm 91 and "wings of eagles." But she pulled it off well, and none in the crowd realized it was her both in front of and behind them.

She turned around before they discovered that fact and found herself staring at Tom Schorr. "You were brilliant," he told her.

"Thank you, Tom," she replied sweetly, wondering if it was a comment delivered frequently to feed a talent's ego.

Schorr must have read her mind, because he countered, "No, I mean it, Christine. I was on the phone with the station chief. He said the same. He wanted to make sure we had signed you to a long-term contract."

"He's not worried I might leave for CNN, is he?"

"No, he's worried that he might need to pay you what you're worth."

"Tom, I am *so* not going to listen to you any more!"

Before they could continue the conversation, everybody began not merely applauding, but cheering—loudly! A stairway led down into the suite's main room from what Christine surmised were sleeping rooms upstairs. Peter was descending the stairway, embarrassed at the stir his appearance caused, smiling, waving like a political candidate, absorbing the crowd's well wishes for another marathon well-run. It was a descent into a room that might have been made by a crown prince.

They locked eyes instantly. He smiled. She smiled back. She could not hear his voice, but she could read his lips: *I was worried you would not make it to the party.*

And he could read hers, reproaching him: *Peter!*

It took him a while to reach her side, although she could see he was trying. Too many other people wanted a piece of him. She wondered if she should move toward him, but decided, no, Yolanda would disapprove. So would her mother. Soon enough he was standing in front of her.

"Hey," he said.

"Hey," she said.

Not quite a full hug, but his cheek against hers. Mutual smacking of lips to simulate a kiss. No kiss yet.

"I'm sorry I'm late," he said.

"I just got here," she said.

"Tom told me you were brilliant."

"He's lying."

"He's not, but we can discuss that later."

The word "later" hung in the air between them. She noticed that he had not let go of her hand, nor had she let go of his.

"But in the meantime, Dennis Lahey wants to talk to me."

"I'm not going anywhere," she assured him. *Not without you..*

She released his hand, and he moved away. She drifted in another direction, slowly snaking through the room, smiling at people she knew and did not know, not pausing, eventually coming to the long table occupied mostly by the women talking with Aba Andersson. *This looks like a safe haven,* Christine decided, then realized the women were not talking running, but rather childbirth. *This is a subject I do* not *want to consider for a few more years,* thought Christine.

She walked toward one of the windows overlooking the park. More than eight hours after the start, and runners still were finishing. Christine had not stood by the window for more than a minute when she felt fingers on the small of her back. She did not need to turn to know it was Peter. Still without turning, she asked, "How did your talk with Shelaghi go?"

"Is that for background or for attribution?"

She smiled, a smile unseen by Peter, because he was still behind her, fingers still on her back, but applying no pressure. She remembered their conversation the first day they met, barely seventy-two hours ago, when he offered her a ride from the convention center to the press conference. How much had happened in her life since then.

She finally turned and their eyes met. "Background only," she said.

"There's good news and good news."

"Tell me the good news."

"Which good news? The first good news or the second?"

"We're fencing with each other again."

"I like fencing with you, Christine."

She did not reply immediately. She smiled. She put one hand on his chest. Lightly. She looked at the chain he was wearing. In the few days observing Peter, she noticed he sometimes reached up to touch that chain, although she did not yet know why. Bravely, she allowed her fingers to slide upward until they touched the chain around his neck.

He let her.

"Tell me the first good news, Peter."

"Shelaghi is going to end its sponsorship of the marathon."

She raised her eyes from the chain to his eyes, worried: "How can that be good news?"

"Because of the second good news: Dennis told me they want to *buy* the marathon. He said he made up his mind while riding the press truck and seeing the enthusiasm of the spectators. Customers, he called them."

"Why does Shelaghi want to buy the marathon?"

"Stop being a reporter, Christine. It's an accountant's thing. Tax purposes. Tell your business editor to call me tomorrow. No, make that Tuesday. I plan to spend all day tomorrow in bed, sleeping."

Christine could have made a comment about that too, but chose not to. Yolanda would be proud of her. So would her mother.

"Let's go out on the balcony," suggested Peter, so they did. And stood. And said little. They looked out at Dearborn Park toward where workers had begun to dismantle the finish line, even though few competitors in the marathon remained on course. Peter knew that Noel Michaels would see that every person finishing had his or her time recorded, even if she had to stand by the line and use her own wristwatch. He appreciated the applause offered when he descended the stairway, but he knew the marathon was more than him.

It was cooler now, easier for the few left on the course to finish. The photo bridge already was gone. So was the storm that had passed off to the northeast, off across the lake.

Christine and Peter looked toward Burnham Fountain, the water flowing upward out of it, sparkling in the light of the late afternoon sun. The fountain was near the TV3 compound. One of the TV technicians claimed that when the storm arrived, the fountain stream had exploded upward, reaching a height twice as high as usual. Vaughn Johnson explained it was because of the low pressure. Less air pressure pushing down against the water allowed it to spurt upward, he said. Never having taken meteorology, Christine was not sure she understood what he meant, but there was a lot about today that she did not understand. She would have time to learn, and she suspected she could find a good tutor.

Peter had one arm around her waist, pressing her gently back toward him. She had placed one hand over that arm, the other hand still clinging to the glass of chardonnay, even though she had taken not more than a few sips. His right cheek was against her left cheek although, she noted, he had made no effort to advance them romantically even though they were alone on the balcony. She did not know how many eyes were upon them; she did not care.

Peter finally broke the silence. "I need to warn you, Christine, that I never kiss on the first date."

"I never do either, Peter. My mother would disown me. She says that nice girls do not behave that way."

"My mother would agree with your mother."

"Still...."

SUNDAY

"Still?..."

"This is not exactly a first date."

"Are you suggesting the possibility of a loophole?"

Christine saw no need to respond. They were fencing again. Was it time for one of them to shout, "Touché?"

She turned her head, ever so slowly, and lifting her chin, closed her eyes. She felt the press of his lips on hers.

Tom Schorr interrupted them: "Hey, you two lovebirds. Come help us cut the cake. It's the Turtle's birthday!"

There he goes again. Christine turned to correct him: "Tom, we are not...." Then she stopped. *Why deny the obvious?*

"I hope the cake is angel food," said Christine Ferrara.

"My favorite too," said Peter McDonald.

EPILOGUE

Eight months after they first met, Peter McDonald and Christine Ferrara were married in the Sistine Chapel, their wedding ceremony presided over by Pope John Anthony Molina. Yolanda Kline served as Christine's Maid of Honor; Naní served as Peter's best man. It did not strike anybody that having a female best man might be in any way unusual.

Peter remained race director of the Lake City Marathon for only one more year. After the International Olympic Committee picked Lake City as an Olympic host, Peter assumed the chairmanship of the Games. Noel Michaels was given his job as race director.

Christine continued her career for several more years, resisting an offer from CBS to move to New York to join the cast of *Sixty Minutes*, her having decided it was time to start a family. She and Peter named their first child, a girl, Carol.

Naní and Ricco flew to Lake City for the baptism, serving as godparents. By then, Naní had abandoned her career as supermodel in hopes of living a somewhat normal life. Her husband Ricco sold his interest in the magazine *Zest* so the two of could start a foundation to focus on AIDS as a disease, not only for children in Africa but for men and women around the world. Many years later after a cure was discovered, they were honored at a special banquet hosted by the United Nations.

Matilda Goldberg took a sabbatical from her job as religious reporter for *The New York Times* and moved back to Brooklyn to finish her biography of Pope Tony for which she had received a six-figure advance. Titled *The American Pope*, it stayed on the *Times'* Best-Seller List for ninety-one weeks.

Tom Schorr received an Emmy for his work as director of the marathon telecast. Mark Mallon got a better-paying job with ESPN. Timothy Rainboldt and Carolynne Vickers continued fighting and living together—sometimes!

Dennis Lahey became enamored with the marathon and decided to sponsor a race on the west coast of Ireland on a course featuring the Cliffs of Moher. The Shelaghi Marathon attracted 7,000 runners in its first year.

Fiona Flynn never ran another marathon. "I'm quitting while on top," *La Femme Fiona* told friends and reporters. She met a nice boy from Galway Bay, settled down and had six children, all of them with red hair.

Meghan Allison never ran another marathon, although she continued to run with a golden retriever, which she and Matt named Fiona.

Aba Andersson never ran another marathon. She found motherhood much more fulfilling, although she still continued as a spokesperson for the sport she loved.

Joseph Nduku never ran another marathon. He had planned to run Boston the following spring, but a knee injured in his finish line fall at Lake City made it difficult to train. He returned to Kenya and founded a training camp for young Kenyan runners, hiring Moses Abraham as his assistant.

In Joseph's absence, Kenyatta Kemai won the next Boston Marathon.

Tatanya Henry won the gold medal in the next Olympic marathon.

Steve Holland continued to teach music at Northland College and coach runners through his racing team and play the clarinet at jazz clubs in St. Paul.

The twins, Kyle and Wesley Fowler, never let their coach forget that he had missed their diving finish at Lake City. The following year, they won the Honolulu Marathon, deciding at the last minute to tie by holding hands crossing the line.

Katie Hyang wrote a memoir about her Hmong family's journey from China through Vietnam, Laos and Thailand to the United States. Hauntingly written, it failed to attract a major publisher because, unfortunately, nobody cared about the Hmong.

The issue of *Running Magazine* featuring Don Geoffrey's article about running the marathon with Pope Tony sold more copies than any previous issue, even the one featuring Oprah on the cover.

Jonathon Von Runyon went back to covering golf tournaments. One evening at a reception, he found himself chatting with Tiger Woods and asked, "Did you ever consider running a marathon?"

John Anthony Molina served as pope for two decades, then in an unprecedented move resigned, because he wanted to teach and return to parish work. During his time as pope, the Roman Catholic Church revised its rules to allow women to become priests and priests to marry, although he never did.

All the other characters in this book lived happily ever after.

About the Author

Hal Higdon, Contributing Editor for *Runner's World*, has written for that magazine longer than any other writer, an article by him having appeared in that publication's second issue in 1966. Author of 35 books, including the best-selling *Marathon: The Ultimate Training Guide*, Hal also has written books on many subjects and for different age groups. His children's book, *The Horse That Played Center Field*, was made into an animated feature by ABC-TV. He ran eight times in the Olympic Trials and won four world masters championships. One of the founders of the Road Runners Club of America (RRCA), Higdon also was a finalist in NASA's Journalist-in-Space program to ride the space shuttle. He serves as a training consultant for numerous races and answers questions online for TrainingPeaks, also providing interactive training programs. At the American Society of Journalist and Author's annual meeting in 2003, the Society gave Higdon its Career Achievement Award, the highest honor given to writer members. An art major at Carleton College, he also exhibits his work, painted in a Pop Art style. Hal's wife, Rose, hikes, bikes, skis and supports him in his running and writing. They have three children and nine grandchildren.

Training

Hal Higdon offers training programs for races from 5-K through the marathon, free on his Web site: *halhigdon.com*. Interactive versions of those same programs are available through TrainingPeaks. Higdon also answers training questions on his Virtual Training Bulletin Boards, accessible either through his Web site or through the Web site of *trainingpeaks.com*.

TWILIGHT
of the
HABSBURGS

To Jim.
Love always,
Ma

TWILIGHT
of the
HABSBURGS

The Life and Times of

EMPEROR FRANCIS JOSEPH

───────────

Alan Palmer

Grove Press
New York

To Anna, László and Judit,
György and Eszter,
in gratitude and affection

First published in Great Britain in 1994 by Weidenfeld & Nicolson
First Grove Press edition, March 1995

Printed in the United States of America

FIRST PAPERBACK EDITION

Library of Congress Cataloging-in-Publication Data

Palmer, Alan Warwick.
Twilight of the Habsburgs: the life and times of Emperor Francis
Joseph/Alan Palmer.
Includes bibliographical references and index.
ISBN 0-8021-665-1 (pbk.)
1. Franz Joseph I, Emperor of Austria, 1830-1916.   2. Austria—Kings
and rulers—Biography.   3. Austria—History—Francis
Joseph, 1830-1918.   I. Title.
DB87.P25 1995   943.6'04'092—dc20   94-40982

Grove Press
841 Broadway
New York, NY 10003

10 9 8 7 6 5 4 3 2 1

CONTENTS

Map of Austria Hungary 1878–1918   vi
Illustrations   vii
Family tree of the Habsburgs   viii
Preface   x
1   Schönbrunn 1830   1
2   A Biedermeier Boyhood   12
3   Year of Revolution   28
4   Apotheosis of the Army   49
5   Marriage   64
6   'It Is My Pleasure . . '   80
7   Italy Without Radetzky   98
8   'Power Remains In My Hands'   114
9   In Bismarck's Shadow   130
10   The Holy Crown of St Stephen   148
11   Facing Both Ways   165
12   A Glimmer of Light   180
13   The Herzegovina and Bosnia   195
14   Father and Son   214
15   Golden Epoch   228
16   Mayerling and After   246
17   Spared Nothing   267
18   The Belvedere   286
19   Two Journeys to Sarajevo   300
20   War   325
21   Schönbrunn 1916   340
22   Into History   345
Notes and Sources   350
Alternative Place Names   374
Index   375

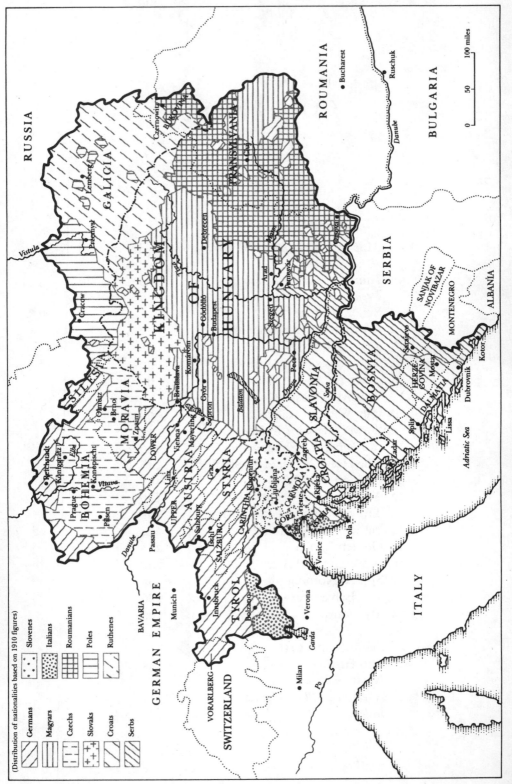

(Distribution of nationalities based on 1910 figures)

Germans	Slovenes
Magyars	Italians
Czechs	Roumanians
Slovaks	Poles
Croats	Ruthenes
Serbs	

Austria Hungary 1878–1918

ILLUSTRATIONS

Elizabeth and Francis Joseph on horseback[1]
Francis Joseph with nephew, Charles I, 1894
Francis Joseph at wedding of Charles and Princess Zita[1]
Francis Joseph in his study at Schönbrunn[2]
Emperor in old age[1]
Funeral procession of Francis Joseph[1]
Francis Joseph as huntsman[2]
Francis Joseph and companions during hunting trip[2]
Elizabeth and dog[2]
Francis Joseph and two of his children[2]
Schönbrunn[1]
Archduchess Sophie[3]
Radetzky[3]
View of Schönbrunn through avenue of trees[1]
Villa Schratt at Bad Ischl[1]
Katharina Schratt[1]
Francis Joseph as Hussar officer[1]
Emperor's visit to the pyramids[2]
Court ball[2]
Archduke Francis Ferdinand and family[1]
Francis Ferdinand[1]
Acclamation of Hungarian parliament[2]
Mayerling[1]
Stephansplatz, Vienna[1]
Kaiservilla at Bad Ischl
Emperor and Empress, 1855[2]

[1] Weidenfeld & Nicolson archive
[2] Mansell Collection
[3] Austrian National Library

Unacknowledged photographs are taken from private collections. The publishers have attempted to trace copyright owners. Where inadvertent infringement has been made they apologise and will be happy to make due acknowledgement in future editions.

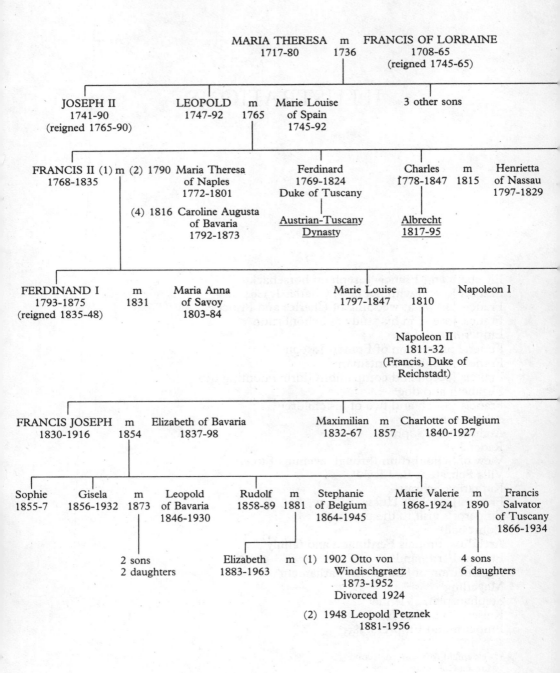

MARIA THERESA   m   FRANCIS OF LORRAINE
1717-80   1736   1708-65
(reigned 1745-65)

JOSEPH II   LEOPOLD   m   Marie Louise   3 other sons
1741-90   1747-92   1765   of Spain
(reigned 1765-90)   1745-92

FRANCIS II (1) m (2) 1790 Maria Theresa   Ferdinard   Charles   m   Henrietta
1768-1835   of Naples   1769-1824   1778-1847   1815   of Nassau
             1772-1801   Duke of Tuscany   1797-1829

      (4) 1816 Caroline Augusta   Austrian-Tuscany   Albrecht
           of Bavaria   Dynasty   1817-95
           1792-1873

FERDINAND I   m   Maria Anna   Marie Louise   m   Napoleon I
1793-1875   1831   of Savoy   1797-1847   1810
(reigned 1835-48)   1803-84

                                   Napoleon II
                                   1811-32
                                (Francis, Duke of
                                Reichstadt)

FRANCIS JOSEPH   m   Elizabeth of Bavaria   Maximilian   m   Charlotte of Belgium
1830-1916   1854   1837-98   1832-67   1857   1840-1927

Sophie   Gisela   m   Leopold   Rudolf   m   Stephanie   Marie Valerie   m   Francis
1855-7   1856-1932   1873   of Bavaria   1858-89   1881   of Belgium   1868-1924   1890   Salvator
                      1846-1930   1864-1945   of Tuscany
                                                            1866-1934

               2 sons   Elizabeth   m   (1)   1902 Otto von   4 sons
               2 daughters   1883-1963   Windischgraetz   6 daughters
                                        1873-1952
                                        Divorced 1924

                               (2)   1948 Leopold Petznek
                                     1881-1956

Rulers in Vienna capitalised. Note: Francis II was
the second Holy Roman Emperor of that name but
the first emperor of the new style Austrian empire.

Simplified genealogical table of the Habsburg dynasty

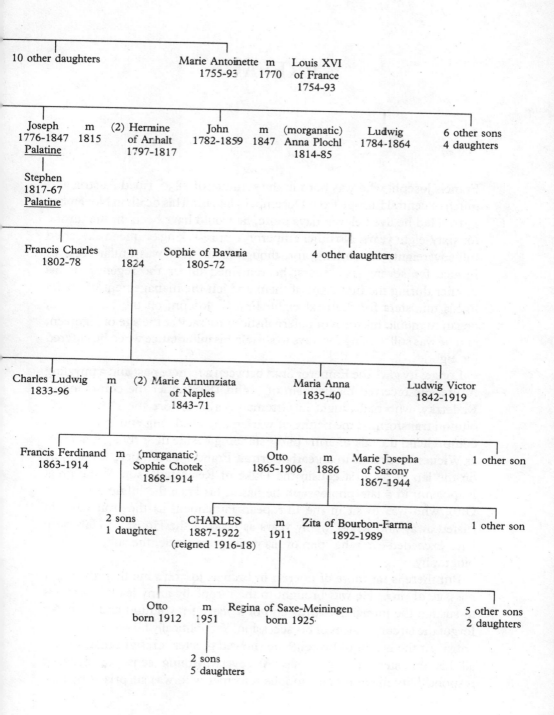

10 other daughters

Marie Antoinette m Louis XVI
1755-93 1770 of France
1754-93

Joseph m (2) Hermine John m (morganatic) Ludwig 6 other sons
1776-1847 1815 of Anhalt 1782-1859 1847 Anna Plochl 1784-1864 4 daughters
Palatine 1797-1817 1814-85

Stephen
1817-67
Palatine

Francis Charles m Sophie of Bavaria 4 other daughters
1802-78 1824 1805-72

Charles Ludwig m (2) Marie Annunziata Maria Anna Ludwig Victor
1833-96 of Naples 1835-40 1842-1919
1843-71

Francis Ferdinand m (morganatic) Otto m Marie Josepha 1 other son
1863-1914 Sophie Chotek 1865-1906 1886 of Saxony
1868-1914 1867-1944

2 sons CHARLES m Zita of Bourbon-Farma 1 other son
1 daughter 1887-1922 1911 1892-1989
(reigned 1916-18)

Otto m Regina of Saxe-Meiningen 5 other sons
born 1912 1951 born 1925 2 daughters

2 sons
5 daughters

PREFACE

Francis Joseph, who was born in the summer of 1830, ruled Austria and much of central Europe from December 1848 until his death in November 1916. Had he lived eleven days more, he would have been on the throne for sixty-eight years. No other emperor, empress, king or queen exercised full sovereignty for so long; for, though Louis XIV was titular King of France for seventy-two years, he remained under the regency of his mother during the first eight of them and left the management of affairs to his ministers for the next eight. Francis Joseph, on the other hand, began to mould his form of paternalistic autocracy at the age of eighteen, and he was still looking for ways to sustain his inheritance when he entered his eighties.

Longevity gave the Emperor links between a remote past and a puzzling future. He received his baptism of fire in 1848 under the command of Radetzky, who had fought in Ottoman Serbia before the French Revolution transformed the nature of warfare: he lived long enough to try to comprehend the talk of army pilots standing beside their flying machines at Wiener Neustadt. In an early portrait Francis Joseph perches happily on the lap of his first cousin the Duke of Reichstadt, son of the great Napoleon: in a late photograph he has at his knee the infant Archduke Otto, who was to sit in the European Parliament as the Iron Curtain rusted away and whose many years as head of the House of Habsburg have exceeded even the span of his great-great-uncle, the subject of this biography.

But there is far more of interest in Francis Joseph's life than the sheer passage of time. He was brought to the throne by army leaders anxious to sustain the monarchy at the end of a year of revolution and he never forgot the circumstances of his accession. Yet politically he was no obscurantist. At the height of his reign he showed greater foresight than almost all his ministers and generals. An overwhelming sense of dynastic responsibility made him a cautious reformer who was surprised by new ideas, but he was willing to think them over and use them if he did not see them as a threat to the well-being of the multinational community over which he presided. He was not the remote, cardboard cut-out figure of historical legend, a humourless bureaucrat able to endure personal tragedies because he lacked the human warmth to feel their impact deeply. Nor was his intelligence so limited as some writers insist; for, while he rejected pretentious intellectualism with brusque common-sense honesty, he took pains to master several languages and to perfect an astonishingly detailed memory.

Shyness and inhibition made him publicly aloof, and only gradually – long after his death – has the publication of letters and diaries confirmed the agreeable simplicity of his inner character. Like Queen Victoria, he was a compulsive writer of letters but, in contrast to her (and her grandson in Berlin) he never became a natural correspondent, with a spontaneous style in which the ink brims over with underlining. Rather he was a chronicler, choosing to narrate what he saw and did each day in long accounts to the three women who were closest to him: his mother, Archduchess Sophie, who died in 1872; his wife and first cousin, the Empress Elizabeth, who was assassinated in 1898; and the actresss, Katharina Schratt, whose intimate companionship for over thirty years he valued too dearly to cheapen by a physical relationship. It has been a pleasure, in writing this biography, to read the printed editions of these letters, and I feel a deep sense of gratitude to their editors: Franz Schnürer, Georg Nostitz-Reineck, Jean de Bourgoing and Brigitte Hamann. Count Egon Caesar Corti made the first detailed studies of the Emperor-King and his family, using sources which in some cases were lost during the Second World War, and no one can attempt an assessment of Francis Joseph's qualities without quarrying into Count Corti's pioneer works. While writing this biography I was deeply conscious, too, of how much my interest was stimulated many years ago by the late Dr C. A. Macartney, with whom I once had the privilege of collaborating on a preliminary study of independent Eastern Europe.

Long ago I realized that in histories of central Europe the rendering of proper names poses problems for English readers and leaves an author liable to accusations of bias favouring one or other nationality of the region. In this book I have, in general, followed the principle of using the familiar, modern form of a place name, readily identifiable in today's atlases, even though it may be anachronistic to write of 'Bratislava' or 'Ljubljana' etc. during the earlier part of Francis Joseph's reign. Readers will find alternative place names given in an appendix. Dynastic names are anglicized, thus 'Francis' for 'Franz' and 'Charles' for 'Karl', but I have retained the name 'Ludwig', as I do not think the English equivalent

'Lewis' would be readily recognizable when applied, for example, to the eccentric rulers of Bavaria. Somewhat illogically, I refer to Francis Joseph's soldier cousin as 'Archduke Albrecht', partly to distinguish him from other princely Alberts – but also, I suspect, from force of habit, after passing the Archduke Albrecht Monument on the Augustinerbastei so many times.

I wish to acknowledge the gracious permission of Dr Otto von Habsburg to make use of material from his family archives in Vienna, and especially for allowing me access to the journals of Archduchess Sophie. I would like also to express my gratitude to the General Director of the Haus-, Hof- und Staatsarchiv and his staff – notably Dr Elisabeth Springer – for their patient advice during my visits to the Minoritenplatz. There are others, too, in Austria to whom I am indebted for kind assistance, though unfortunately I do not know their names. I remember, with particular thanks, the lay sister at Mayerling who drew my attention to the fresco above the high altar.

In England, I feel a particular debt to Lord Weidenfeld for suggesting, in an inspirational flash, that I should write a life of the Emperor Francis Joseph, a task which has given me much pleasure. Good fortune brought me the editorial aid of Christopher Falkus, a friend with long experience of historical biography. I am grateful to him, to Catherine Lightfoot, editorial co-ordinator at Orion House, and to John Mclaughlin and Charlotte Bruton for their wise counsel. The staffs of the Bodleian Library and the London Library have once again offered me ready help, much appreciated. Since my wife, Veronica, accompanied me on more than a dozen trips to the former Habsburg lands, she has been able to give me advice, chapter by chapter. She also undertook the formidable task of indexing the book at a time of considerable difficulty for her. Even so, these instances of practical help constitute only a small part of the support she has given to me during this absorbing enterprise. My greatest debt remains, as ever, to her.

For more than twenty years we have enjoyed the friendship and frequent hospitality of a Hungarian family, in four generations. Their companionship, in person or by letter, has warmly enriched our experience and broadened our understanding of central Europe, past and present. Sadly, the head of that family, László Szőke Snr., a doctor who served devotedly the young people of the Hatvan district, died prematurely four years ago. In dedicating this book to his widow Anna, and to his sons, László and György, and their wives, I wish also to honour his memory.

Alan Palmer
Woodstock, July 1994

Chapter 1

SCHÖNBRUNN, 1830

The summer residence of the Habsburgs lies barely three miles from the centre of Vienna. Like Versailles, Schönbrunn was originally a hunting lodge; it was converted into a palace by the Empress Maria Theresa, to whose achievements it offers a finer memorial than any sculptured statue in a city square. Yet unlike Versailles, which the greatest of revolutions had left forlorn and neglected, Schönbrunn remained the home of a reigning dynasty. It was, of course, more modern than Louis XIV's prototype; and, in an odd way, it was more elegantly easy-going and self-assured, despite over fourteen hundred rooms and a long facade stretching for an eighth of a mile towards the slopes of the Wienerwald. No steep angled chapel roof buttresses Schönbrunn into oppressive grandeur, as at Versailles, for Maria Theresa's feeling for natural spaciousness ensured that the palace would always look subordinate to the landscaped parkland behind it. In August 1830, fifty years after Maria Theresa's death, the ochre stonework was still new enough to glow with pristine splendour in the sunshine. At sixty-two the reigning emperor, Francis I, could remember how on sunny days in her last years his grandmother would sit beneath the open arcade of the palace, facing the clipped hedge-shaded walks which led to the newly completed colonnade of the Gloriette. A box holding state papers was strapped to her chest so as to form a portable desk, and to them she would turn conscientiously, oblivious of the bustle around her. It was rarely quiet at the palace which the most businesslike of empresses had created.

All that, however, was by now more than half a century ago. Recent history associated Schönbrunn in name with a foreign conqueror rather than with Maria Theresa. For on three occasions – before and after Austerlitz, and following his hard-won victory at Wagram – Napoleon I made the palace his headquarters. Ironically, it was in one of Maria Theresa's exquisite salons that an Austrian plenipotentiary was forced to sign the peace treaty of 1809, which cost her grandson more thalers than his treasury could afford, lost him three and a half million subjects, and forced what remained of the Habsburg Empire into dependence upon France. That humiliating episode passed swiftly, and within six months Emperor Francis's daughter, Marie Louise, became Napoleon's second wife; but the defeat at French hands left scars which the reversal of Habsburg fortunes in the campaigns of 1813–14 never healed. For two generations men and women who remembered the shock of occupation dominated Viennese society, with the poet and dramatist Franz Grillparzer outstanding among them. The public figures of the war years survived the return of peace. In 1830 Emperor Francis was still on the throne; and Metternich, the Rhinelander whom Francis appointed foreign minister while the French were in Schönbrunn, was still Chancellor of his empire.

There were other reminders of the occupation, too. Gilded French eagles, mounted on Napoleon's orders above the pyramidical columns of Maria Theresa's time, continued to overlook the palace courtyard (as they do today). Since both empires made proud use of eagle symbolism, it was tempting to leave them in place even if, in heraldic ornithology, the *Aquila Bonaparta* has a single head while the Habsburg species boasts two. More romantically evocative than gilt symbols was the Eaglet himself. For *l'Aiglon* – 'the Son of the Man' and Marie Louise – had his home at Schönbrunn, although for much of that summer he was at Baden. The boy, who upon his birth in 1811 was proclaimed King of Rome, had been parted from his father before his third birthday and educated as a Habsburg 'Serene Highness'. His baptismal name was dropped in favour of 'Franzl', the German diminutive of his second name, and at the age of seven he was created Duke of Reichstadt. Though Emperor Francis petted this first-born grandson, enjoying long walks and talks through the parkland of Schönbrunn, Franzl's status was anomalous. Occasionally, he seemed placed on a pedestal; when in 1826 the Viennese artist Leopold Fertbauer was commissioned to paint 'Emperor Francis and his Family', the fifteen year old Reichstadt was placed at the centre of the group, between his grandfather and Marie Louise, so that the eye at once focuses on him. In Court precedence, he ranked immediately after the Habsburg archdukes. But Reichstadt's origins continued to worry Chancellor Metternich, who made certain that his secret police kept the intelligent young man insulated from Bonapartism and its agents. Not surprisingly, Reichstadt was eager to shake off Court restraint. If he could not return to France as Napoleon II, he hoped to serve in his grandfather's army. Although Franzl was delicate, he was promised a colonelcy in the foot guards at the age of twenty.

Yet, however generous the Emperor's sympathy with a half-Bonaparte might be, he was preoccupied with the immediate prospects of his own dynasty. For although fifty-two Habsburg archdukes and archduchesses had been born in the past hundred years, the future succession remained in doubt. Francis had married four times and fathered thirteen children, but only two sons and five daughters survived infancy; all were the offspring of his second wife, Maria Theresa of Bourbon-Naples, who was doubly a first cousin. Such inbreeding had disastrous genetic consequences. Francis's heir, Crown Prince Ferdinand, was a good and amiable simpleton and an epileptic, with no inclination to marry. The Emperor's other surviving son, Archduke Francis Charles, was a kindly nonentity, slightly brighter in intellect than his brother but dominated by his wife, Archduchess Sophie, who was a daughter of King Maximilian I, head of the Wittelsbach dynasty and the first sovereign King of Bavaria. If anyone could give the dynasty a new lease of life, it was Archduchess Sophie, as all Vienna recognized. She, too, is prominent in Fertbauer's group canvas, almost edging out her sister-in-law, poor Marie Louise; and in these sultry August days of 1830 Sophie's well-being was Emperor Francis's chief concern.

Over the centuries Habsburg and Wittelsbach had frequently intermarried. Indeed, the reigning Empress-consort – Francis's fourth wife, Caroline Augusta – was Sophie's half-sister. Officially the Church frowned on such a relationship, but between Francis Charles and Sophie there was no close consanguinity, and their wedding in Vienna in November 1824 was welcomed as yet another affirmation of the links between the two principal German Catholic dynasties. Disappointment followed; for in her first five years of married life the Archduchess suffered a succession of miscarriages: would she prove barren, like her half-sister? But when, early in 1830, pregnancy was confirmed, the Archduchess – who was still only twenty-five in that January – began writing back to her mother in Munich with calm confidence. Before the end of the month she was even prepared to give Monday, 16 August, as her child's probable birthday.

Sophie was reluctant to abandon her social life. But fate was against her. There was little gaiety in Vienna that winter: a bitter February, with the Danube frozen, gave way to a thaw on the last night of the month and unprecedented flooding, with loss of life in the low-lying suburbs, on the eve of *Fasching*, the pre-Lenten carnival. Briefly, after Easter, Sophie was able to go to the theatre and opera, but at the end of April the Emperor's doctors clamped down on her movements. Despite particularly pleasant weather, for the next fourteen weeks she was expected to remain at Schönbrunn, walking gently in the gardens, with no exciting distractions permitted. To climb the sloping path up to the Gloriette colonnade, 150 feet above the parterre, was inadvisable. The Archduchess may, too, have avoided the western side of the park, near the zoological gardens; for a tale, which Sophie's letters show troubled her over several years, maintained that her husband's youngest sister Archduchess Marianna – only seven months older than Sophie – owed the hideous disfigurement of her face and her virtual imbecility to a pre-natal incident when her mother was startled by an escaped orang-utang while walking in the gardens. In 1830 Archduchess Marianna was still living at Schönbrunn, a rarely seen presence secluded in the labyrinth of smaller rooms.

The Emperor's concern for his daughter-in-law's health is understandable. His fear of madness, deformity or epilepsy increased as her time of confinement drew nearer. Most of her days were spent in the pleasantest wing of the palace, her bedroom on the first floor of the east terrace looking directly out across the main courtyard. Yet if Sophie hoped for privacy she was disappointed. Even the relatively human task of getting born could not pass without ritual observance; and by mid-August the pregnant Archduchess was the light around whom the planetary Habsburg Court revolved. On the Monday afternoon – 16 August, as Sophie predicted – her child's birth seemed imminent. The principal midwife told Archduke Francis Charles he would be a father that evening; the Archduke duly informed the Emperor in Vienna; and Francis at once left for Schönbrunn. The palace became a hive of activity, with bustle and confusion everywhere. Prayers for the mother's safe delivery were offered up in the chapel; but still the Archduchess was not in labour. Members of the family hurried to the bedroom; Court officials and well-wishers from high society waited in crowded antechambers, an initial noisy excitement giving way to a no less noisy impatience. Many were still there twenty-four hours later, by which time the midwives had wisely decided against giving any more forecasts. In the chapel, votive candles were lit once again.

By Tuesday the Emperor was so nervously restless that he refused to go to bed, spending a fitful night on a sofa. As ever, dutiful functionaries sought to emulate their sovereign's example and slept wherever they could. Apparently in all this suspended animation no chronicler bothered to notice the expectant father – that was Archduke Francis Charles's fate throughout his life. By eight on Wednesday morning, when cries from within the bedroom let her audience know that the Archduchess was at last in labour, the palace corridors were full of weary men and women. At a quarter to eleven the shrieks ceased. A few moments later Empress Caroline Augusta brought them her half-sister's good news: 'It's a son – and a healthy, well-formed child, too,' she announced. Francis Joseph – throughout his reign the most punctilious of timekeepers – had arrived on Wednesday, 18 August, some forty hours behind schedule. Not that the long wait mattered now; his tired grandfather was delighted. Although technically third in line of succession, from that moment onwards the newcomer was treated as an Archduke destined soon to rule.

He was born into the most historic dynasty on the continent. The House of Habsburg had provided Germany with twenty emperors and gave rulers to Spain, the Netherlands and much of the Italian peninsula. From 1438 until its abolition in 1806, the 'Holy Roman Empire of the German Nation' was virtually a Habsburg hereditary possession, and in 1792 Emperor Francis had been duly crowned in Frankfurt as 54th successor to Charlemagne. But Francis was under no illusions; he needed more precisely defined authority than this curious relic of feudal obligations could provide. Within ten weeks of his coronation, a republic was proclaimed in France. The revolutionary upheaval and Napoleon's subsequent imperial aspirations, made him seek a new title which would assert his sovereignty over all the Habsburg lands, and in April 1804 he was proclaimed 'Francis I, Emperor of Austria'.

In many respects Francis's new realm was a hasty improvisation; and the changing fortunes of war delayed a final settlement of its frontiers until 1815 when the map of Europe was redrawn at the Congress of Vienna, under the chairmanship of his foreign minister, Prince Metternich. The Empire of Austria became the largest country in Europe apart from Russia, spanning the centre of the continent. It linked in common allegiance to the dynasty towns as far distant as Milan in Italy and Czernowitz (now Chernovtsy) in the Ukraine. All of present-day Austria, Hungary, the Czech Republic, Slovakia, Slovenia and Croatia fell within its frontiers at the time of Francis Joseph's birth. So too did such cities as Lublin in Poland, Cluj and Timişoara in Roumania, and Venice, Verona, Mantua and Trieste in Italy. In the provinces of Lower Austria (around Vienna) and Upper Austria (around Linz) the population was almost exclusively German, while in Lombardy and Venetia it was overwhelmingly Italian. Everywhere else the nationalities were mixed; even in Vienna there was a considerable Czech minority in the outer districts. Germans could be found in every province; they constituted about a fifth of the total population of the empire – in 1830 some 6.5 million out of a total 34 million. Sometimes the Germans were a majority in a province, as in Tyrol (with an Italian minority) or in Styria and Carinthia (Slovene minorities); but often they were so concentrated as to form Teuton islands in a Slavonic, Magyar or Roumanian sea. The empire could therefore never be described as a Germanic institution, even though German was the first language of sovereign and Court. Throughout Francis Joseph's reign his empire was always to have more Slavs – Czechs, Slovaks, Croats, Serbs, Slovenes, Ruthenes, Ukrainians, Poles – than Germans or Magyars or Latins (Italians and Roumanians).

But on 18 August 1830 it was German Catholic churches around Schönbrunn that first celebrated the good news from the palace. Bells rang in jubilation in neighbouring Hietzing. Soon they were pealing in Vienna, too. Guns thundered a first royal salute; crowds streamed into the outer palace courtyard at Schönbrunn, cheering with satisfaction and waving flags. Archduchess Sophie was far from popular in the capital, where her peremptory manner and Bavarian Sunday piety aroused a certain mistrust. But, for the moment, that hostility was forgotten. The birth of the young Archduke provided an excuse for more celebrations in Vienna's Auergarten and Prater, the open land which the 'reformer emperor' Joseph II (Maria Theresa's son and Francis's uncle) presented to the city. In this vast area south of the Danube there were already some forty restaurants or taverns, certain to attract good custom on a warm summer evening.

Prince Metternich heard of the Archduke's birth while working in his study at the state chancellery in the Ballhausplatz. The gun salutes must have pleased him – 'I have a great weakness for the sound of cannon', he once confessed – but there is no evidence he showed any great interest in the news from Schönbrunn. He was, of course, glad that Archduchess Sophie could bring new hope to the dynasty he served, for he recognized that hereditary kingship was the best constituted source of authority for the rule of law in a post-Jacobin age. But, while Emperor Francis had been impatient for the birth of a Habsburg grandson, his Chancellor was looking farther afield, anxiously waiting on events hundreds of miles from Vienna. More than once Metternich lamented living in such an 'abominable epoch'. Reports from France and from several of the Italian states left him in little doubt that the 'tranquillity and repose' which he believed essential were about to be disturbed yet again by violent assertions of popular sovereignty. To combat the moral anarchy of Revolution he urged collaboration between the three eastern autocracies – Austria, Prussia and Russia.

Metternich never expected to be in Vienna when Francis Joseph was born. Arrangements had been made for him to conduct government business that August from Königswart, his country estate in Bohemia. But while he was there, late in the evening of 4 August, he received news through the courier service established by the Rothschild brothers to serve their banking interests: on 27 July the people of Paris had risen in revolt against the reactionary policies of their Bourbon king, Charles X. Metternich was shocked by the news, briefly collapsing in despair. But he soon rallied: 'When Paris sneezes, Europe catches cold', he was heard to remark. There could be no summer holiday in the quiet of Königswart that year. He set off back to Vienna at the end of the first week in August and was at his desk in the Ballhausplatz long before Archduchess Sophie went into labour.

His forebodings were justified: Europe did, indeed, catch cold. On the day Francis Joseph was born, the last legitimate Bourbon King of France, newly landed in England, was on his way to exile in Edinburgh; and the Archduke's first months of infancy coincided with a period of protracted tumult across the continent. In Paris a Constitutional Charter provided for Louis Philippe, head of the Orleanist branch of the Bourbons, to accede as 'King of the French by the Grace of God and the Will of the People'. When Francis Joseph was nine days old, rioting in Brussels and Liège marked the outbreak of a national revolution against Dutch rule in the Belgian provinces which, as Emperor Francis and his Chancellor could well remember, had been the 'Austrian Netherlands' less than forty years earlier. Before the end of September, rulers were dethroned in Brunswick, Hesse-Cassel and Saxony, where German liberals followed the example of the French and Belgians in demanding constitutions; and it became clear that, before the winter was over, there would be grave unrest in Italy, where Metternich had sought to stamp out the embers of a national patriotism fired by Napoleon. But the most dramatic challenge to Metternich's European system came in the last days of November, when an army revolt in Warsaw sparked off a national insurrection in Poland. The uprising was aimed principally at the Russian puppet 'Congress Kingdom', created at the end of the Napoleonic Wars. But as Russia, Prussia and Austria had jointly partitioned historic Poland in the eighteenth century, and some two million Poles lived within the Habsburg Empire, what happened in Warsaw mattered deeply in Vienna. The revolt placed the Polish Question firmly back on the agenda of Europe. It was to remain unresolved throughout Francis Joseph's lifetime: indeed, the search for a solution became the last diplomatic problem to trouble him in his dying days.

No echo of these events disturbed life in the young Archduke's nursery, where Sophie remained proudly protective of her infant son's interests. There was little trouble in the heart of the Habsburg Empire: Metternich's chief of police, Count Sedlnitzky, reported all was quiet in the Austrian lands, apart from habitual grumbling at heavy taxation; even in Galicia the Poles made no open moves to aid their compatriots in Warsaw. But before the end of the year Archduchess Sophie was disturbed by one unexpected aspect of Metternich's policy. At first it seemed harmless enough: the Chancellor began to encourage the Emperor to affirm the status of his eldest son, Ferdinand, by presenting him for coronation as King of Hungary at a meeting of the bicameral Hungarian Diet in the autumn. There were plenty of occasions in Hungary's past when the sovereign's designated successor had been crowned while his predecessor was alive. But Metternich had another purpose in advocating the coronation: if Francis showed a special regard for his Magyar subjects, he hoped that their spokesmen would respond by authorizing the recruitment of additional soldiery from the Hungarian counties.

All went as well as Metternich had hoped, perhaps even better. Less than six weeks after Francis Joseph's birth, his simple-minded uncle was crowned King of Hungary at Pressburg, the fortress city some 40 miles down the Danube from Vienna, known as Pozsony to the Hungarians and Bratislava to the Slovaks (whose capital it is today). Ferdinand fulfilled his duties adequately and with a certain pathetic dignity, thanks to the careful guidance of his father's sixth brother, Archduke Joseph, Palatine of Hungary for the past third of a century. The Diet agreed to authorize the enlistment of 28,000 recruits in return for procedural concessions, notably the use of the Magyar language rather than Latin in official communications. Here too, as in Poland, was a pointer to future problems; the 'language question' was to be raised time and time again during Francis Joseph's reign.

Barely a month after Ferdinand's return from Hungary, it was made known at Court that the imperial physician, Dr Stifft, had become convinced there were no medical reasons why the Crown Prince should not marry. The news, totally unexpected, startled Archduchess Sophie; if Ferdinand married and had a son it was unlikely that either her husband or her child would become Emperor. More disturbing still was the announcement in December of the Crown Prince's betrothal to Maria Anna of Savoy. Only after Dr Stifft had assured Sophie that it was unlikely the Crown Prince would ever 'make any attempt to assert his marital rights' was the Archduchess mollified. When Ferdinand and Maria Anna were married in Vienna at the end of February 1831, she felt a genuine sympathy for the bride, coupled with indignation over Metternich's cynical manoeuvres. No one in the imperial family really believed that poor Ferdinand's disabilities would allow him to accept the strains of married life. These doubts seemed confirmed when the Crown Prince took to his bed on the day after the wedding. His bride – kind at heart, dutiful and singularly plain – was left with the doubtful consolation of accompanying Sophie on an evening visit to the Schönbrunn nursery, where she could admire the wonder child in his cot. Metternich, it was thought, wished to safeguard Ferdinand's succession, confident that a figurehead sovereign would leave the business of government in his experienced hands.

Despite her worry over Metternich's intentions, the Archduchess was more immediately concerned with the health of her child. To her great relief, throughout his first winter, Francis Joseph remained astonishingly robust and lively, by Habsburg standards. He had golden curls and a rosy complexion: 'a strawberry ice with a topping of whipped cream', was Reichstadt's happy description of his infant cousin. But before the boy's first birthday Sophie was seized by a fear common that year to families in every social class throughout central Europe. For during 1830 the first great cholera epidemic had been advancing remorselessly across Russia, causing near panic in Moscow in October and sweeping into Russian Poland, where it killed the Tsar's brother and his wife, and the Russian commander-in-chief. By the early spring of 1831 cholera had reached Galicia, soon crossing into the northern counties of Hungary, where it was especially virulent. So gravely did the disease strike Hungary as a whole that, during the year, it was to claim the lives of 1 in 25 of the population.

Early in July 1831 cholera was confirmed in central Vienna. Archduchess Sophie was thoroughly alarmed: 'God's scourge of the cholera threatens us', she had already warned her mother. The imperial family gathered in Schönbrunn, cordoned off from the evil-smelling River Wien – virtually an open sewer in the 1830s – and from all contact with the city. In Vienna the authorities responded to the epidemic much as if it were the plague: isolation was imposed with such rigour that cholera made less impact on the city than in London a year later. Nevertheless both Sophie and her husband were eager to get away from the capital. The Archduchess had a firm belief in the therapeutic qualities of the Salzkammergut's saline springs and at the end of July, husband, wife and child set out for Gmünden and the clear mountain air of Ischl, farther up the valley of the Traun.

The village of Ischl had prospered in the previous century, when wealthy salt refiners built elegant houses along the north bank of the River Traun and raised a fine parish church, at much the same time as Maria Theresa was watching the scaffolding come down from the Gloriette at Schönbrunn. In 1821 a fashionable Viennese medical practitioner, Dr Wirer, began to praise the saline waters of the Traun valley. Sophie was impressed by Wirer's 'discovery'. She visited Ischl after the last of her miscarriages and fully agreed with Wirer. Ischl delighted her, reminding her of home; and small wonder, for the Bavarian mountains she had known in her girlhood are an extension of the same alpine range. On this first visit with her child, she told her mother (in English) of Francis Joseph's high spirits, describing to her how he would sit astride a huge, good-tempered dog belonging to the director of the salt works, riding the hound like a pony. In later years Francis Joseph made Ischl his summer holiday home for as much of July and August as official duties would permit. Seventy years after this nursery visit 'dear Ischl, so beautiful and so green' could lift his tired spirits, much as did the magic of Osborne for the widowed Queen Victoria.

Before the autumn rains came, Archduke Francis Charles took his wife and child northwards to Bohemia. Prague was officially free of cholera, and the family stayed for some weeks in the Hradčany, where a royal palace of some 700 rooms was stamped with the unmistakable embellishments of Maria Theresa's reign. From the Hradčany, the family moved southwards to Laxenburg, on the Danubian plain barely ten miles from Vienna. Laxenburg was a natural hunting-ground, where the child grew accustomed to the sound of his father shooting wild duck around the lakes in the well-timbered parkland. But before Christmas they were back in the capital. As spring approached in 1832, they prepared to return to Schönbrunn.

By then, Sophie was again pregnant, her baby due early in July. During these months of waiting, she became less self-centred. More and more she wrote and spoke about Franzl Reichstadt. So much was he in her thoughts that gossip then and in later years suggested the young and romantic Duke was father of the child she was expecting. Such an easy assumption of an improbable sexual relationship fails to understand the nature of the attachment binding the Archduchess to the twenty-one-year-old Eaglet. At heart both Sophie, as a young woman, and poor Franzl remained interlopers at the Habsburg Court. Her character was shaped by a typical Wittelsbach mixture of family ambition, dreamy melancholia and realistic common sense to which, in an intellectually lack-lustre Court, she added a cautiously restrained mental curiosity. Misfortune had made Reichstadt devious, shyly hesitant, and suspicious of those around him, but he was highly imaginative and eager to discover if he had inherited the creative genius which lifted his father so far above the mediocre talents of the other men in the Bonaparte clan. In the winter before Francis Joseph was born, the Archduchess was frequently escorted to the opera and theatre not by her philistine husband but by her nephew; the two outsiders came to trust each other, sharing enthusiasms and exchanging ideas freely. Their confidences were those of a brother and an elder sister rather than of lovers.

Tragically, Sophie's second pregnancy coincided with the relentless advance of Reichstadt's tuberculosis; and it was the knowledge that she was creating life, while disease was eating away his health which accounts for the devotion she showed to her young companion at this time. Some rooms in her own apartments at Schönbrunn were given over to him, so that he could catch the lingering sunshine in the late afternoon that spring. So long as she could do so, Sophie would visit the sickroom on Reichstadt's bad days and read to him, even though at times she was overcome by the heat of the room. 'How tragic it is to see someone so young and beautiful slowly wasting away', she wrote to her mother in Munich, 'At times he looks as if he were an old man'.

He had helped amuse Francis Joseph in that first year in the nursery, and Sophie believed there was a deep bond of affection between the two cousins. In June she took the 'little one' with her on a brief visit to the Schönbrunn sickroom because, as she told her mother, Franzl Reichstadt 'so desperately wanted to see him, as he is so much alone'. The young man's condition grew worse but he rallied, as if he was determined to cling to life until Sophie had her baby. On 4 July – a humid Wednesday morning – the Archduchess paid her customary visit to the sickroom, but the heat was too much for her, and she did not stay long. Later in the day the midwives were once more on duty, and on the Friday Sophie's second son was born; he was called Ferdinand Maximilian (although the first name was rarely used). A few doors away, in what had once been Napoleon's study, Reichstadt heard the news of Max's arrival, and smiled with evident satisfaction. He never saw the boy – a cousin destined to become disastrously ensnared by a Bonapartist misadventure in Mexico while still only in his thirties.

Reichstadt never saw Maximilian's mother again, either. For, though Archduchess Sophie's confinement had been much easier this time, she collapsed physically and mentally when the ordeal was over. Her doctors would not allow her to leave her bedroom for three weeks. Early on 29 July, the third Sunday after Maximilian's birth, Archduke Francis Charles broke to his wife the news she had dreaded: only a few minutes before, he had been with his sister Marie Louise at Reichstadt's bedside, as the Eaglet's lungs gave up the fight for life. Now there was only one 'Franzl' in the palace. Rather strangely, within an hour of her son's death, Marie Louise was with his young cousin in the nursery above the Schönbrunn guardhouse. To the one-time Empress of the French there was comfort in the chatter of a little boy who could not probe memories half-forgotten of loyalties half-fulfilled.

Chapter 2

A BIEDERMEIER BOYHOOD

Regimentation and orderliness shaped the daily life of the young Arch-dukes from their first weeks in the nursery. Their father had little influence on his boys' upbringing, though he was later to impart to his eldest son the skills from which he acquired so many hunting trophies. Inevitably it was Archduchess Sophie who set the form and pace of Francis Joseph's education, a responsibility she fulfilled with methodical care, knowing that, in contrast to her own girlhood in Munich, he would gain little intellectual stimulus from the Court life around him. Sophie was proud to play the Emperor-maker, conscious – perhaps too conscious – that her hands possessed the strength to mould the Monarchy.

The Archduchess held no theories of her own on education. For, though the most cultured woman to brighten the Court for many decades, she was in no sense a child of the Enlightenment. Music and the arts could count on her patronage, and with Reichstadt she read and discussed novels and poems upon which the Imperial Censorship frowned. But she was a conventionally devout Catholic, sentimentally pious and always respecting her spiritual confessor, Abbot Joseph von Rauscher. Sophie knew that her son's active imagination should be cultivated, but she took care to see that any sign of enthusiasm was held in check: for it was essential he should learn to show iron self-respect in the face of adversity. From Sophie's letters to her sister in later years it is clear that she gave top place in any ideal curriculum to linguistic skills.

Even in infancy, the Archdukes had their own household. Both were entrusted to the care of the same governess ('Aja'), Baroness Luise von Sturmfeder, a spinster with a firm and equable temperament, sixteen years older than Sophie, and herself the sixth child in a family of eleven, from the lesser Prussian nobility. Her young charges remained personally devoted to the Baroness, whom they affectionately called 'Amie'. As she also won and retained the trust of the boys' mother, she must have been a woman of good sense and tact. Subordinate to the Aja were a nurse, an assistant nurse, a cook, a chamberwoman, a general purpose maid, a scullery maid and two footmen. Much detail of these early years can be reconstructed from an edited selection of Luise von Sturmfeder's dotingly reverential jottings, published some forty years after her death, but while Francis Joseph was still on the throne. Her diary vividly recalls exaggerated fears over minor happenings, such as the near panic at Schönbrunn one afternoon in early November when 'Franzi' arrived back from a walk in the park with his hands blue as no one had given him gloves. We learn from Baroness von Sturmfeder and from the Archduchess's correspondence of Franzi's happy disposition, of his delight in looking down from a gallery on his first masked ball and of seeing his father riding back from a hunt, and of the pleasure he gained from the tambourines and toy drummer-girl left as presents beneath a Christmas tree when he was still too young to talk. As the young Archdukes passed from infancy into boyhood, their mother's letters show the difference in temperament between the brothers. For, while Max became fascinated by the animals, birds and flowers at Schönbrunn and Laxenburg, his elder brother absorbed the soldierly ceremonial around him. With sentries pacing beneath the nursery window each day and the sound of bugle calls from neighbouring barracks thrown back by the palace walls, it is hardly surprising if, from birth, Francis Joseph seemed a natural parade ground officer. In Austria, unlike Prussia or Russia, there was no tradition of educating the heir to the throne first and foremost as a soldier.

A well-known portrait by Ferdinand Waldmüller shows the future emperor at the age of two, wearing a frock but holding a toy musket in his right hand, with a child's helmet above his blonde curls, and his left hand firmly grasping by its wooden head a carefully carved officer doll in trim white uniform. By the age of four he was often dressed up in uniform himself, while toy soldiers became his principal playthings: his Christmas presents in 1834 included a large model of the palace guard from his grandparents, and a hand-painted set of officers and other ranks in finest parade ground order. Boyhood letters to Max, when the brothers were separated by illness or the demands of family itineraries, mention bombardments of forts in the nursery, but the toy soldiers were not mere playthings. Gradually Francis Joseph built up a collection in which every regiment of the army was represented; soon he came to know the detail of every uniform. Not one of these toy soldiers was broken.

'No peace at all around the little ones', Archduchess Sophie complained often enough, especially after the birth in July 1833 of Charles Ludwig, her third son in three years. A daughter, baptized Maria Anna, followed Charles Ludwig in October 1835, but she was extremely delicate. To her mother's grief she soon showed signs of epilepsy and she was to die shortly after her fourth birthday. But, apart from this tragedy to a much-loved little sister, Sophie's sons had a happy childhood. At Ischl they wore *lederhosen* and followed a simple life in contrast to the traditionally strict Court etiquette of Vienna. In practice, however, the 'Spanish' ceremonial stiffness had eased under Emperor Francis and there was a certain cosy domesticity during the winter months.

In the third week of December 1834 Francis Joseph was allowed to join his grandparents at dinner in the Hofburg. His mother was well satisfied with her son's natural confidence in what to a four year old might well have proved a disastrous ordeal. Franzi was, of course, used to the presence of his imperial grandfather. The old Emperor had never stood aloof from childish pleasures and often visited the nursery, chatting happily with the boy who would eventually succeed to his crowns. But by that December everyone at the Hofburg sensed he was unlikely to live much longer; a note of valedictory gloom runs through the pages of more than one diary chronicling events at Court that winter. Stories began to circulate in Vienna which emphasized the middle-class bonhomie the Emperor readily affected and which always pleased his subjects. It was said that he had complained openly of the 'silliness' of the government's censorship. There was a slightly mocking undertone to the phrase '*Der gute Kaiser Franz*', which was so often heard in Vienna in the early 1830s; but there was a loyal affection in it, too.

'Good Emperor Franz' survived the Christmas of 1834 and the bitterly cold January which followed. On 12 February, with his grandson standing briefly beside him, he looked down benevolently at the Court Ball which celebrated his sixty-seventh birthday. Eleven nights later the Emperor and Empress went to the Burgtheater. On that Monday a sharp north wind was blowing into the city from the frozen plains beyond the Danube; less than forty-eight hours after leaving the Burgtheater the Emperor was confined to bed with pneumonia. Archduchess Sophie was touched by her son's concern; for when, on Thursday, Franzi heard his Grandpapa was so ill that he could drink only tea, he decided, in a nice gesture of family solidarity, that it was his duty also to drink nothing but tea. Over the weekend the Emperor's strength rallied, but by Monday afternoon it was clear he was sinking fast, and his grandson was taken on one last visit to the sick room; he died that night, in the small hours of 2 March, plunging Vienna into mourning on the last day of the Fasching carnival.

The imperial titles passed to the unfortunate Crown Prince Ferdinand. But on his deathbed Francis had signed two documents, addressed to his successor: one enjoined Ferdinand to defend and uphold the free activity of the Roman Catholic Church; the other was a political testament, insisting that Ferdinand should 'not displace the basic structure of the

State', and should take 'no decision on public affairs . . . without consulting . . . my most faithful servant and friend Prince Metternich'. More surprising than this recommendation was the dying Emperor's counsel over dynastic questions. Francis I was survived by six brothers, three of whom were far abler than himself: Archduke Charles, respected throughout Europe as a military commander; Archduke Joseph who showed rare skills of diplomatic tact as 'Palatine' (governor) of Hungary; and Archduke John, who was a good soldier and a discriminating patron of the arts in Graz (where he delighted the Styrians, and shocked his family, by morganatically marrying the daughter of the village postmaster of Bad Aussee). But Francis's political testament passed over all three gifted Archdukes and recommended as Ferdinand's guide the youngest of the brothers, Archduke Ludwig, dull and unmarried. To Sophie's dismay, the testament gave no status to Francis Charles, the heir apparent. Not that she had any illusions over her husband's abilities: she merely wished him at the centre of affairs as trustee for their eldest son's interests.

Francis I's death made an impression on a small boy of five. His uncle Ferdinand, the new Emperor, was kind and gentle but a pathetic sight on those rare occasions when he took the salute or wore the robes of sovereignty. By contrast, the young Francis Joseph conjured up in his mind an image of his grandfather as an ideal ruler, though in reality he had been a very ordinary monarch – and knew it. 'My son has still no attachment so strong as that which he bears to the memory of his grandfather', the Archduchess told Frances Trollope two years later. But the first months of the new reign coincided with the emergence of Francis Joseph from the nursery to the schoolroom. Count Heinrich Bombelles, who became his principal tutor was a soldier-courtier, trained as a diplomat. Metternich warmly approved of Bombelles: 'one of the few men who thought as I thought, saw as I saw, and wished as I wished', he recalled a few years later. Bombelles was assisted by Count Johann Coronini-Cronberg, who as personal Chamberlain was primarily responsible for the young Archduke's military training. The Coronini family estates were in Gorizia, a province part-Italian and part-Slovene. Coronini was a good horseman, stiffly unimaginative and, like so many senior officers, totally non-national; he was a servant of the dynasty rather than in any sense an 'Austrian' by sentiment or conviction. Since Francis Joseph's main interest as a boy was in soldiering, Coronini had a greater influence in shaping his character than did Bombelles.

It was, however, Bombelles who presented the Archduchess with the first of several elaborate programmes of study. Her eldest son would be expected to progress from 18 hours a week spent over his books at the age of six to 36 or 37 hours at the age of eight, 46 hours at eleven, and between 53 and 55 hours a week at the age of fifteen. As an educational programme, the scheme had grave defects, even by the standards of the time: there was too much rote-learning, too little emphasis on how to think, and – apart from his brothers – virtually no contact with other youngsters in a classroom. Despite half a century of social upheaval there was little difference between what Francis Joseph was learning in the late 1830s and what his grandfather had been learning sixty years before, except for increased attention to minor languages within the Empire. Training in spiritual matters was entrusted in the first instance to a Court chaplain, Joseph Colombi, but the Archduchess sought advice from the ultramontane Abbot von Rauscher, who personally supervised the young Archduke's instruction in moral philosophy from the age of fourteen onwards. By then, too, the Bombelles scheme had been revised by Colonel Franz von Hauslaub, but not in any liberal spirit; Hauslaub's programme was specifically designed to include 'instruction in military science.'

This programme of education remained far narrower than the syllabus followed by Albert of Saxe-Coburg some twelve years earlier and was in marked contrast to the precepts laid down by Baron Stockmar in 1842 for the Prince of Wales. Even in Berlin the future Emperor Frederick – fifteen months younger than Franzi – was, thanks to his mother's insistence, receiving a more liberal and scientific education to offset his Potsdam military training. Fortunately, while every lesson in history, philosophy and Christian apologetics emphasized to Francis Joseph the divine omnipotence of kingship, he was also taught that imperial sovereignty carried obligations and that it was his duty to protect his subjects from injustice as well as to uphold monarchical rule. Neither character nor training inclined him to despotism.

Francis Joseph showed greater academic promise in boyhood than the familiar word portraits of the mature Emperor would lead one to expect. He was a good linguist. Even before his eighth birthday he was writing letters in French to his mother which seem to have been his own work, for he asks the recipient to let him know if his grammar or choice of words are at fault. Occasionally, too, he lapsed into a German phrase, as if he could not think how to express himself in French. In 1841 he was sufficiently confident in the language to tell his mother what he regarded as an amusing incident: the noise made by the boys at their early morning gymnastics in Schönbrunn aroused his widowed grandmother's septuagenarian chamberlain whose anger, while draped in a dressing-gown, 'made us laugh'. By that spring Francis Joseph was already learning Magyar and Czech as well as French; before the end of the year he had begun Italian, too. A thin veneer of classical studies soon followed, with a little Latin acquired at twelve and less Greek at thirteen.

He possessed a natural aptitude for drawing. Some sketches made in northern Italy soon after his fifteenth birthday, and later printed, may well have been touched up by the lithographers who reproduced them: a priest astride a donkey outside an inn looks almost too carefully well-fed and the fetlocks of a horse in a second drawing seem professionally tidy. But, though the draughtsmanship may not be entirely original, the composition of the sketches is good, and it is interesting that earlier scribbles in the margin of letters to Max show a similar sense of fun and attention to detail. Francis Joseph had a sharp eye and a ready perception of the ridiculous. He enjoyed, too, a finely appreciative sense of landscape, simply and naturally expressed in his boyhood letters to his mother. When in the early autumn of 1844 he travelled to the Vorarlberg and the Tyrol, it is hardly surprising to find him as excited by a steamboat trip on the Bodensee as any other fourteen year old would have been, but his greatest enthusiasm was reserved for the magnificent alpine scenery around Merano, Bolzano and Innsbruck. In particular, he admired the Stubaital, 'the loveliest valley I have seen'.

Yet, though both Archdukes responded warmly to the beauties of nature, their mother feared they would become as antipathetic to the finer aspects of cultural life as their father. They liked the theatre (as had Francis I); it is true that early letters show more interest in the mechanics of scene changing than anything on the stage, but this is hardly surprising among boys of their age. Their mother, however, sought to counter incipient Habsburg philistinism by welcoming selected writers and performers into the family circle. Thus the three Archdukes listened to Hans Christian Andersen telling them his stories in the Hofburg itself, and much later – when Francis Joseph was fifteen – Jenny Lind was treated as a personal friend by the Archduchess, who vainly hoped that the soprano's presence at Schönbrunn would break through Max's wall of tone deafness and arouse in her elder son a taste for harmonies more rhapsodic than the steady beat of a military march. Nothing could make Francis Joseph appreciate good music. He did, however, enjoy dancing, even as a boy: 'Tomorrow Papa is giving a Ball in the Gallery, where 20 couples will be able to dance to the enlivening strains of Herr Lanner's music', runs an excited letter to Maxi in May 1841; and other correspondence and diary entries show that he took the floor himself at an early age. He liked going to the ballet, too, when he passed into adolescence. During Fanny Elssler's short season at the Kärntnertortheater in the spring of 1846 he saw her dance in *La Esmeralda*, *La Jolie Fille de Gand* and in a showy divertissement of Jules Perrot, *La Paysanne Grand Dame*. Like his cousin Reichstadt before him, he became an Elssler fan, continuing to acclaim the ballerina on her return to her native city until she retired, three years after his accession.

In admiring the dancer-actress from Gumpendorf the young Francis Joseph was following the fashionable taste of the Viennese public. So it was, too, with much else that he liked and disliked. This was a period of theatrical achievement but not of great innovative drama, as in the previous decade. Joseph Schreyvogel, the modernizer of the Hofburg Theatre, died when Francis Joseph was still a baby, and Grillparzer gave up writing plays when his comedy *Weh dem, der lugt!* flopped in March 1838. During the early years of Emperor Ferdinand's reign, the theatre-going public enjoyed the Volkstücke dialect plays at the Theater an der Wien and the Theater an der Leopoldstadt, the earlier refinements of traditional comedy lapsing into farce, liberally intermingled with song. The almost insatiable demand for these Volkstücke plays was matched by the mounting popularity of the rhythmic, gliding music of Joseph Lanner and the elder Strauss: it was a happy culture, if not a subtle one, and Francis Joseph shared it to the full. Long after he reached maturity he would use Viennese dialect phrases in conversational moments of relaxation; but this particular habit is more likely to have come from the affectations of an officers' mess in his adolescence than from early days in the nursery. Luise von Sturmfeder was too conventional a Prussian to tolerate vernacular usage.

In the late 1850s a more earnest generation began to ridicule the style of life which had prevailed at the end of Francis I's reign and throughout the early years of his successor. *Fliegende Blätter*, a humorous journal published in Munich, invented a naive character called Gottfried Biedermeier, the 'worthy Meier' (which, sometimes as Maier or Meyer, is one of the commoner surnames). He was first portrayed as a poetaster, perpetrating sentimental verse, some of it the genuine surplus doggerel of a well-meaning village schoolmaster in Bohemia. Sustained satirical attacks were then mounted on all that Biedermeier was held to represent: the virtues of thrift, diligence and cleanliness; the limited vision of an unambitious middle class content to seek a quiet life in comfortable domesticity. From Bavaria these lampoons crossed into Austria, where the emerging tastes of a thriving middle class had set new fashions in provincial cities, as well as in Vienna. Nowadays the graceful paintings, furniture and porcelain of the Biedermeier era, with its decorative clocks, lyrical landscapes and smug portraiture are accepted as a cheerful expression of bourgeois faith in stability and progress. But at the height of Francis Joseph's reign 'Biedermeier' was a term of amused contempt, the elevation of mediocrity into a generalized style of expression. The myth became rapidly extended until the dismissive adjective 'Biedermeier' began to be applied retrospectively to all the decorative arts and archi-tecture, painting and music which emerged from the new social order after the Napoleonic Wars. An Age of Stifled Revolt could not forgive the Biedermeier era for being an Age of Acquiescence. From so preposterous a misreading of recent cultural history it was easy enough for the youthful intellectuals of the early 1870s to scoff at their sovereign's limited attain-ments: Francis Joseph became a Biedermeier figurine in uniform, exalted in his polished saddle astride a horse groomed to perfection.

The caricature was, of course, unfair. It ignored the Emperor's sense of duty and discipline, the inner conviction that accession to the throne required an immolation of personality for fear that any display of feeling, or any impulsive action, might impeach the dignity of monarchy; his character was more clearly defined than he would reveal on public occasions. But the Biedermeier image was not entirely false. From his letters it is clear that the interests which Francis Joseph retained in later life were shaped by the fashions of his boyhood. This is not surprising: temperament and taste always respond more readily to the contemporary mood than to the formal teaching of precepts in an improvised code, however well intentioned. Twelve years of Francis Joseph's early life were spent in absorbing the facts presented to him by his tutors but, apart from a desire to widen his vocabulary in the four foreign languages he studied, there was no stirring of intellectual curiosity. By the age of eighteen a fine memory was excellently trained. The mind, however, was not disposed to analyse ideas or to question acknowledged truths.

These limitations remained with Francis Joseph throughout his life. They explain why his inclination was towards chatter rather than serious conversation, why he respected musical virtuosity and not originality in composition, and preferred tableaux vivants to histrionic declamation on the stage. But his education made him a perfectionist in matters of detail, and he expected high standards; a slipshod performance of Schiller at the Burgtheater would incur an imperial rebuke, especially if an actor forgot his lines. Despite his boyhood skill at drawing, he never pretended to be a connoisseur of the visual arts. Painters, he instinctively felt, should be decorators, their pictures celebrating military victories or faithfully reproducing the colour and contours of familiar landscape, notably in the Salzkammergut. His mother had admired the works of Ferdinand Waldmüller and Peter Fendi, who depicted the Archdukes in their infancy with cosy sentimentality. Waldmüller, in many respects the archetypal Biedermeier artist, received imperial patronage for the first quarter of Francis Joseph's reign; and, though Fendi died six years before his accession, the Emperor approved of the work of his pupils, notably Friedrich Treml. There was, however, another side to the Fendi school of painting, not without influence on Francis Joseph; for Fendi could record domestic incidents among the poor in Vienna's outer suburbs without resorting to contrived or condescending pathos. This aspect of the Biedermeier tradition Francis Joseph, too, absorbed. It helped sustain embers of compassion which a less reserved monarch would have kindled into human warmth of feeling.

That human warmth, so rarely shown by Francis Joseph after his accession, was still present when the fourteen-year old Archduke took part in his first military review. On the eve of his thirteenth birthday he became colonel-in-chief of the Third Dragoon Regiment, and in late September 1844 he was considered sufficiently proficient as a horseman to ride at the head of his regiment when it was participating in exercises in Moravia, close to the historic battlefield of Austerlitz. The Dragoon officers were impressed by their honorary colonel. Archduke Albrecht – himself only twenty-eight – wrote to Francis Joseph's father praising his cousin's 'natural friendliness' and tact, his ability to speak easily when in company with the regiment while maintaining 'a certain bearing and dignity such as I have never seen at his age'. When, a year later, the three young Archdukes – Franzi, Maxi and Charles Ludwig – were sent on an official tour of Lombardy-Venetia, Francis Joseph again scored a personal success. Their host was the most respected veteran commander in the Habsburg army, Field Marshal Radetzky, who had fought against the Turks nearly sixty years before and, as Austrian chief-of-staff in 1813, drew up the strategic plans for the campaign which culminated in Napoleon's defeat at Leipzig. Now, with equal application, he staged military reviews, firework displays and exhibitions of horsemanship for his young imperial visitors; there were conducted tours of the defensive bastions of the Quadrilateral, the fortresses Radetzky was modernizing at Peschiera, Mantua, Legnano and in Verona itself. From the Roman arena in Verona the Archdukes watched a military reconnaissance balloon ascending into the sky. Radetzky was convinced of the importance of aeronautics. Four years later he authorized the first use of airborne missiles, with explosive balloons released from the mainland to harass Italian patriot insurgents besieged in Venice.

The presence of the Archdukes in Verona, and later in Venice, posed a security risk, even though Radetzky himself thought it unlikely that Italian hostility to Austrian rule would endanger their lives. He was right. Girls threw flowers from balconies of the houses in central Verona and thousands of Venetians cheered the three brothers as they were escorted down the Grand Canal by a small fleet of gondolas, late on a warm September evening. The combination of torchlit palaces, bells ringing out from a hundred churches, moonlight over the lagoon, and – for the first ever time – gas lamps in the Piazza San Marco excited Francis Joseph, and (as he also wrote to his mother) he was gratified at finding the four bronze horses, filched from Byzantium by a thirteenth century Doge and carried off to Paris by General Bonaparte, 'back in their rightful place' above the central doors of the basilica. There were no patriotic liberal protests in Venice, whose citizens were criticized in the more ardently nationalistic towns of central Italy for their lukewarm response to the national cause.

If their journey was intended to introduce the Archdukes to the complexities of the Italian problem, it failed. The Kingdom of Lombardy-Venetia was the most highly industrialized region of the Monarchy at that time, a development which, over the following three years, heightened the struggles between the north Italian peoples and their sovereign's representatives. But, not surprisingly, the young Archdukes kept away from Milan, where anti-Austrian feeling was already intense, and they saw nothing of industrialized Lombardy. Apart from the military instruction accorded to Francis Joseph by Radetzky's staff, the boys were essentially tourists on an educational holiday, an experience which made the most sensitive of the three brothers, the thirteen-year old Maximilian, an Italophile. Francis Joseph – older, more suspicious by temperament, and ready to accept unquestioningly all he was told by the veteran Marshal and his staff – did not share his brother's enthusiasm for everything south of the Alps. Francis Joseph recognized that there was a natural antipathy between German-Austrians and Italians. Yet he failed to understand how deeply the people of Lombardy and Venetia resented the presence of the Austrian 'whitecoats' among them. One in three of the infantry battalions under Radetzky's command at the time of the imperial visit were Italian, and the Marshal assumed that their military honour would ensure their lasting loyalty. In 1848 Francis Joseph was both surprised and disillusioned by what he regarded as a rebellion in his imperial uncle's Italian-speaking kingdom. Almost half of Radetzky's Italian infantrymen fought against the dynasty, a transfer of allegiance which hardened the mood of the old Marshal in the last years of his long life and intensified the young Emperor's hostility to the Italian cause.

From the daily journal she began to keep in 1841, it is clear that Archduchess Sophie was amused rather than perturbed by the totally different response of her sons to their brief visit to Lombardy. In that autumn of 1845 Italy was not yet a pressing problem for the government in Vienna; the agitation against the Habsburg yoke only became dangerous in the peninsula as a whole after the election of the allegedly liberal pope, Pius IX, in the following June. The Archduchess was determined that Francis Joseph should be well-versed in current problems, for ten years of Ferdinand's nominal reign had convinced her – and most of the Court –

that the accession of a young and assertive emperor could not long be delayed. Sophie remained in close touch with political affairs, her influence strengthened by the firm backing she received from the long-suffering Empress Maria Anna, who was painfully aware of her husband's inability to understand state documents or political argument.

Sophie's ambitions never again sustained so sharp a blow as the rebuff of 1835, when Emperor Francis's will excluded her husband from the central council of government. There followed some eighteen months of political in-fighting, in which Archduke John methodically and unobtrusively undermined the primacy of Metternich. By Christmas 1836 the Archduchess was satisfied by the creation of a 'Staatskonferenz' – a virtual Council of Regency – consisting of Archdukes Ludwig and Francis Charles, Chancellor Metternich and minister of state Count Kolowrat-Liebsteinsky, a great Bohemian landowner, whose skilful financial retrenchment over the previous six years made him a potential challenger to Metternich's long ascendancy. So intense was the antagonism between the two statesmen that the Staatskonferenz was threatened with permanent paralysis. If the Archduchess may be believed, effective government was possible only through the enterprise and initiative of Francis Charles: 'Whenever a decision has to be taken, Uncle Ludwig needs my husband's support to counter his modesty and timidity', she claimed. There is no other evidence that Francis Charles played so active a role in government. He may, however, have been encouraged by his wife and the more far-sighted 'absentee' Archdukes – his uncles Joseph, Charles and John – to stiffen Ludwig's resistance to Kolowrat; for only a stubbornly obtuse chairman, deaf to plausible argument, could have checked a Minister of State who showed such super-efficient mastery of detail at the council table.

So weak was the centre of government that, in practice, the day-to-day running of the Monarchy depended on the rulings of a larger council of seventeen specialists, co-opted from the principal departments of state, rather than on the Staatskonferenz itself. But, ultimately, executive authority remained vested in the Staatskonferenz; and in this political confusion the role of the Archduchess Sophie, speaking ventriloquially at the conference table through her husband, became all important for Metternich, despite his earlier misgivings at the prospect of a Bavarian-born princess meddling in government. From the closing weeks of 1836 until the opening months of 1848 there was, accordingly, a tacit pact of political convenience between Archduchess and Chancellor; the way would be smoothed for the early accession of Sophie's eldest son, under the veteran statesman's tutelage.

As parents, Metternich and Sophie encouraged a certain companionship between their children. For, although the Chancellor was sixty-seven in 1840 and a grandfather, he was also the father of four youngsters: his second wife had died within a fortnight of giving birth to their only child, Richard (eighteen months older than Francis Joseph), but in 1831 he married for the third time. Princess Melanie Metternich, a Zichy-Ferraris by birth, was the same age as the Archduchess, and in six years she became the mother of a daughter (named after her) and three more boys, one of whom died in infancy. Melanie was imperious and supremely tactless, a natural sparring partner for the Archduchess Sophie. But she saw the social advantages of close association with the dynasty. Her journal entry for 8 May 1838 records Franzi's first train journey (on the earliest completed section of the Vienna-Brno line) and her determination that the young Metternichs would not miss such an occasion: 'Went with the children and mother to look at the locomotive. Clement had been on a trip by train along with the Dowager Empress, Archduchess Sophie, the Archdukes – among whom we found even the little Archduke Francis Joseph – and Count Kolowrat. The excursion by this new device was eminently successful and everyone was well pleased with it.' At Christmas 'the little Archduke' and his two brothers were invited to the children's ball at the Chancellery, a regular event in their lives over the next few years. Richard Metternich and his half-sister would always be among the selected group of boys and girls invited to the archducal birthday parties at Schönbrunn.

The youngsters never became close friends, as children or as adolescents. Francis Joseph fettered his leisure hours, exhorting himself to work harder, even on days when most boys were content to enjoy themselves. His journal for 18 August 1845 reads: 'My birthday, and more important still my fifteenth. Fifteen years old – only a little more time to go to get educated! I must really pull my socks up (*muss ich mich sehr anstrengen*), really mend my ways'. These resolutions, it should be added, did not keep him away from a birthday stag-hunt with his father. He cannot have been such a really impossible prig for, though he may have felt inadequate beside the precocious Metternichs, he could make friends of his own choosing. Closest among them, from the age of sixteen onwards, was his cousin, Prince Albert of Saxony, but at twelve or thirteen he liked to play with 'Charly' and 'Franzl C.', the sons of his instructors, Bombelles and Coronini; they remained his personal companions until the upheaval of 1848. Dénes Széchényi, a young offshoot of the large and culturally distinguished Hungarian family, joined his circle of intimates when Francis Joseph was sixteen. So, too, did 'Eddy' Taaffe, a mischievous lad with a keen sense of fun, three years his junior. Eventually Taaffe won a slightly puzzled respect in Europe as Count Eduard Taaffe, the part-

Irish nobleman who 'muddled through' as Austrian prime minister for fourteen years. But in the 1840s he was the young Archduke's riding companion, his skill sharpening Francis Joseph's desire to raise the standard of his horsemanship even higher. By contrast, Richard von Metternich was staid and studious, the dutiful son of his father, just as Francis Joseph was a dutiful son of his mother. In this relationship there could be mutual respect, but never easy understanding. For a few months, immediately following the Archduke's seventeenth birthday, they were jointly initiated into statecraft by Richard's father at weekly sessions in the state chancellery. But, by then, Prince Metternich's hold on European affairs was weakening. It is doubtful if either young man profited greatly from such high-powered instruction. In all, there cannot have been more than twenty hours of these tutorial sessions.

In Hungary, the Habsburg lands whose peoples most resented the Chancellor's centralist theories of government, Metternich made use of Francis Joseph even before he became his occasional pupil. Hungary was constitutionally unique, a kingdom within the Empire which possessed an elective system of county government as well as its bicameral Diet; and members of the Diet jealously safeguarded its ancient right to accord its sovereign the Hungarian soldiery and revenue his ministers required only in return for royal approval of its laws. The emergence of a Hungarian reform movement, moderate in the 1820s but intensely nationalistic twenty years later, convinced Metternich of the need to 'so manipulate the constitution that it becomes possible to govern Hungary in the regular manner' (as, in 1841, he told a session of the Ministerial Council, the seventeen specialists who advised the Staatskonferenz). Thereafter Metternich sought to create a neo-conservative political group of Hungarian magnates, who would emphasize loyalty to the Habsburg dynasty. He intended this creed to serve as an alternative to the Magyar patriotism so warmly invoked by the popular idol, Lajos Kossuth, and accepted by many Hungarian noble families as well as by the middle classes in town and country. When in the second week of January 1847 Archduke Joseph died, after half a century in Hungary, Francis Joseph was sent to Ofen (Buda) for the Palatine's obsequies, with Bombelles to advise him. The young Archduke's evident progress in learning Magyar and his tact and apparent interest in all that he saw in this first brief journey into the Hungarian lands made a favourable impression, which Metternich was determined to exploit.

Yet there could be little doubt of the real feelings of the Hungarians; a fortnight after Francis Joseph's visit to Buda, students across the river in Pest set fire to the German theatre, burning it to the ground. To send the Archduke back to Buda in the autumn as Ferdinand's representative at the installation of the new Palatine – Joseph's son, Stephen – showed great confidence in his bearing and personal nerve. On this occasion he delivered a speech in Magyar which was well received, even by Kossuth personally. A few weeks later Francis Joseph was among the Hungarians once more, on this occasion at Bratislava for the opening of the momentous Diet, which was to be dominated by Kossuth and his radical reformers. Even in the Diet's honeymoon days, when defiant rebellion was still a long way off, Francis Joseph could sense the mounting excitement, the 'terrific agitation' as he wrote at the time. When revolution shook the Monarchy a year later, he was not so much taken by surprise as puzzled by its persistence. He had seen for himself more of the troubled regions of the empire he was to inherit than historians generally acknowledge. But mere acquaintance does not in itself bestow insight.

By now he was spending less hours in the study. Often in the spring and summer of 1847, and increasingly during the winter, he was in uniform. All too frequently he would have a black armband around the sleeve of his white tunic, for there was a high Habsburg mortality rate in the eleven months after the Palatine's death. In early May Francis Joseph was at the head of his regiment for the funeral of the great army commander, Archduke Charles; six months later he attended the funeral of his host on the moonlit gondola procession in Venice. Archduke Charles's third son, Frederick, the nominal commander-in-chief of the Imperial navy; and Francis Joseph went into mourning yet again shortly before Christmas, when his aunt Marie Louise was buried in the family vault of the Kapuzinerkirche. But he was also experiencing – and enjoying – military life away from the parade ground. That autumn he joined his regiment for field exercises in Bohemia, staying on the Taaffe family estate and meeting, for the first time, Prince Alfred Windischgraetz, the commanding general in Prague. At seventeen he was making high claims on his reserves of confidence, assuming a dignity of bearing in the regiment which concealed the diffidence he felt among contemporaries whose upbringing had been less carefully regulated than his own.

Archduchess Sophie's diaries record a mother's pride in her eldest son, slim and handsome in his Hussar uniform. But she was never dotingly foolish; there were blemishes on that proto-imperial image, and she knew it. In his mother's company – and even more under the disparaging gaze of Melanie Metternich – Francis Joseph became woodenly self-conscious. He was too stiff and lifelessly impassive during receptions at Court, the Archduchess complained. With the best of intentions she set about overcoming his inhibitions. Early in December 1847 she hit upon a fitting solution. Amateur theatricals had been a popular feature of German Court life for over a century: why should not Francis Joseph immerse himself in some light-hearted comedy? A romping role, full of wit and humour, played privately in the Hofburg before the imperial family, the Metternichs and other luminaries of Court would teach him how to present himself happily and easily. The Bertrams of Mansfield Park, in Jane Austen's novel, chose Augustus Kotzebue's *Lovers' Vows* for their amusement, and it was to Kotzebue that the Archduchess, too, turned; he had, after all, been director of the Hofburg Theatre long before that unfortunate day in 1819 when he was assassinated as a police spy by a German theological student in Mannheim. But Sophie settled, not for *Das Kind der Liebe (Lover's Vows)*, but for the, sightly older, five act farce *Wirrwarr (Confusion)*. Her eldest son could play Fritz Hurlebusch, a country squire's roguish heir and ward.

Francis Joseph disliked the idea intensely. From a reading of the play, one sympathizes with him: Hurlebusch is a habitual joker, amiably polite in the family circle, while throwing aside sardonic comments to the audience; in the final scene he must hide under a table, where he hears his cousin Babet, who had spurned his advances, avow her secret love for him; the curtain falls as they are about to marry and live happily ever after. Francis Joseph told his mother that Maximilian was ideal for the role and coveted it, but she was adamant: Richard Metternich could be in the cast; Dénes Széchényi and Charly Bombelles, too; Marie Széchényi was to play Babet; and, at fourteen, Charles Ludwig might be the night-watchman; but Franzi was to play Hurlebusch. Not even the death of Marie Louise could save her nephew from the stage debut he dreaded; the performance was not cancelled. It was postponed until the end of court mourning.

Wirrwarr was duly presented in the Alexander wing of the Hofburg at 10 pm on 9 February 1848. 'A wonderful production', the Archduchess noted in her diary. She said nothing of Francis Joseph's acting. Nor did Melanie Metternich in her journal, though she questioned the choice of title: why 'confusion' at such a time in the Monarchy's history? From the awed admiration with which Francis Joseph later commented on good theatrical presentation, he probably hated every minute on the stage, though he dutifully learned his lines. None of Hurlebusch's waggishness was grafted on to his character, perhaps fortunately. Yet the evening of theatricals proved a turning-point in his life. Never again did he need to accept his mother's ruling on how to present himself. Events overtook his adolescence. Five weeks after watching the play, the Metternichs were fugitives from revolution, hurrying westwards to find sanctuary in England; and within 300 days of his curtain-call, the reluctant actor was to receive the homage of his father and mother, his brothers and all the paladins of the army as their sovereign emperor. Effectively *Wirrwarr* marked the end of Francis Joseph's childhood.

Chapter 3

YEAR OF REVOLUTION

A persistent legend maintains that throughout the winter of 1847–8 Francis Joseph's mother sought the downfall of Metternich and a transition to constitutional government. 'Events enabled a court faction, led by Archduchess Sophie, to pressure Emperor Ferdinand into jettisoning Metternich', a distinguished modern American historian has written. So, certainly, Princess Metternich believed when she looked back on the recent past from the bitterness of exile; she convinced herself that the Archduchess let Kolowrat know he could count on support from a 'dynastic Opposition' if he tried to defeat the Chancellor's proposals at meetings of the Staatskonferenz. She may well have held dark suspicions of a dynastic intrigue as early as the second week in February, when the two women sat watching the private theatricals in the Hofburg; for by then *The Sybilline Books out of Austria*, an anonymous pamphlet blaming Metternich for the sterility of Austrian politics, was the talk of the salons. Rumour correctly identified the author as Captain Moehring, tutor to the five sons of the Viceroy of Lombardy-Venetia, Archduke Rainer. More sensationally the pamphlet carried a dedication to Archduchess Sophie. Could Moehring have put her name forward in such a way without foreknowledge of her convictions? It seemed unlikely.

Yet the dedication, like so much that happened during the spring, took the Archduchess by surprise. There is no evidence she was ever prepared to make any active move against Metternich, nor did she show sympathy for Kolowrat, the ambitious spokesman of a particularly narrow circle of German-Bohemian landowners. Throughout the 1840s she had kept abreast of Europe's affairs. Family letters afforded her an insight into Germany's problems: a half-brother was King of Bavaria; her twin sister was Queen of Saxony; and their elder sister was married to Frederick William IV of Prussia. As well as these private sources, she read the main German newspapers and several French periodicals, defying the Austrian government's clumsy censorship. She was aware of the mounting discontent: the impatience of the younger generation of politicians with Metternich's negative conservatism; the widespread resentment at the arbitrary imposition of taxes; the confusion caused by the election of a so-called 'liberal Pope'. Within the Monarchy she could see for herself the spread of a linguistic, cultural nationalism and the growing frustration of the commercial class in many towns at the bureaucratic barriers hampering the spread of trade. By Christmas 1847 the Archduchess was deeply pessimistic: 'God knows what the future holds for our poor country', she wrote in her journal. But gloomy jottings in a diary are a sign of passive fatalism rather than active conspiracy. Sophie, and the Court with her, waited anxiously upon events.

So, for that matter, did Metternich. On 2 January 1848 he drew up his 'political horoscope' for the year: radical forces would emerge and throw society into confusion, he predicted; the danger-spot was Italy, he insisted, and more precisely Rome. He dismissed the significance of events in Germany or France and the familiar problems of Hungary. At first it seemed as though he was right. Reports reached Vienna of insurrection in Sicily, the grant of a constitution in Naples, and the spread of a liberal agitation through Tuscany and the Papal States. But when, on the last Sunday in February, it was confirmed that Radetzky had proclaimed martial law in Lombardy-Venetia there were also rumours in Vienna of a revolution in France. Next morning – Monday, 28 February – there was a rush of panic selling as soon as the stock exchange opened. By Wednesday the Chancellor, still as imperturbable as ever, felt he should reassure his luncheon guests. Were he to be dismissed from office, he explained, Revolution would have come to Vienna; and that, of course, as he assumed every visitor to the Ballhausplatz must realize, was unthinkable.

Meanwhile the Hungarian Diet, whose opening ceremonies Francis Joseph had attended in the city now known as Bratislava early in November, remained in session. It was on Friday, 3 March, that, with news of the fall of the monarchy in Paris confirmed, Lajos Kossuth made the most historic of all his speeches to the Lower House of the Diet. He urged the establishment of a virtually autonomous Hungary, with a responsible government elected on a broad franchise. It was not a fiery call to arms. He spoke respectfully of the dynasty as a unifying force, welcoming in particular the first steps taken by Archduke Francis Joseph to win the love of the nation; but Kossuth was not the man to compromise. To safeguard Hungary's historic rights for all time, it was essential to change the character of government in the Monarchy; and he called for 'general constitutional institutions which recognized the different nationalities'.

Reports of Kossuth's proposals soon reached Vienna. They produced a triple response: a plea for civil rights and some form of parliamentary government from the Diet of 'Lower Austria' (*Nieder Oesterreich*), the province including the capital and its suburbs; petitions to Emperor Ferdinand from several professional bodies, seeking the removal of police surveillance; and demonstrations by university students for the abolition of censorship, more freedom in education, and liberty of public worship. For the first time there were signs of dynastic Opposition to the Chancellor, but it was not inspired by Archduchess Sophie. She was increasingly alarmed by the unrest: as early as 9 March she recorded in her journal the fear that Vienna would soon suffer the horrors experienced by Paris in 1793 (though one would have thought 1792 a more alarming parallel). It was the popular and pragmatic Archduke John rather than Sophie who began to rally the dynasty; 'Uncle Johann' was induced by a member of the Lower Austrian Diet to come up to Vienna from Graz in the hope that he would give sensible advice to the Staatskonferenz. John found, as he wrote, that Metternich 'was the only person to whom you could talk and he remained convinced he could handle the situation by writing memoranda and delivering long speeches. Everyone else was impossible'.

The events of 1848 were to mould Francis Joseph's character and determine the pattern of his life. But at first, during these heady days of March, there was little change in his customary Hofburg routine. On Sunday afternoon (12 March), while the students awaited news of a petition presented to Ferdinand by two liberal professors, Francis Joseph escorted his mother through the gardens, strolling down to the bastion of the old palace, where they were seen and cheered by some of the demonstrators. There was no positive response from the Court and overnight the mood of the students turned uglier. By nine on Monday morning thousands were gathering outside the Landhaus in the Herrengasse, where the Lower Austria Diet was to meet. A Tyrolean with powerful lungs read Kossuth's speech in a German translation, amid repeated cheers and angry calls for Metternich's resignation. A second deputation went to the Hofburg and the Emperor summoned his Chancellor to the palace soon after midday. But Metternich did not intend to surrender office: he was prepared to talk to the leaders of 'the rabble'; but he urged his fellow councillors to stand firm. It was decided that the thirty-year old Archduke Albrecht, as military commandant of Lower Austria, should close the city gates, for there were rumours of a general attack on property by unemployed labourers squatting outside the walls. When Albrecht's men sought to clear the Herrengasse, some shots rang out: a student and two artisans lay mortally wounded on the cobbles; a journeyman weaver died from a broken skull; and an elderly woman from an almshouse was crushed to death when the demonstrators fled in panic down the narrow street.

The sound of shooting could be heard in the Hofburg, where there was already great confusion. Archduchess Sophie – who had to allow 13, 14 and 15 March to pass before finding time to write up her journal – gathered her sons around her protectively in one room, suddenly emphasizing the immaturity of Francis Joseph, of whose manliness in uniform she had been so proud over the past year. Empress Maria Anna, a close friend ever since she came to Vienna as Ferdinand's bride, was by now convinced of the need for her husband's abdication and assumed that Francis Charles would renounce the succession in favour of his eldest son. But Sophie insisted that the time had not yet come for such a dramatic palace revolution. During Monday afternoon she met Prince Windischgraetz, the commanding general in Bohemia who – though on a purely private visit to Vienna – was summoned to the palace when it was feared Albrecht's inexperience might put the fate of the dynasty at risk. To Windischgraetz Sophie carefully explained that Francis Joseph had not yet attained his majority, 'being more or less still a child'. 'We must set things in order first, before letting him take the reins', she added.

For most of this historic Monday 'the child' was therefore necessarily an onlooker. But not entirely so. During the early evening Archduke Ludwig, the customary chairman of the Staatskonferenz, at last turned against Metternich and asked for his resignation. The Chancellor refused to go unless his sovereign and the Archdukes in line of succession should personally absolve him from the oath he had taken before Emperor Francis's death that he would give loyal support to Ferdinand. Such a gesture of absolution required the presence of both Francis Charles and his eldest son around the Staatskonferenz table; and in this curious way Francis Joseph was ushered into the inner counsels of government. From that moment until his death in 1916 he remained close to the heart of affairs.

Metternich's resignation was announced at nine o'clock on the Monday evening, even though it was Tuesday afternoon before he was able to slip quietly away from the capital with his family. Archduke John returned to Graz, confident he could check the spread of unrest through Styria. Nominally Windischgraetz was given full powers to keep order in the capital, but he never exercised them; unexpectedly Francis Charles emerged as chief spokesman for the government, effectively succeeding Ludwig as chairman of the Staatskonferenz. It was Francis Charles who summoned a special conference, at eleven on Tuesday night, at which he spoke in favour of a constitution; once the Emperor had made such a great concession, Francis Charles argued, all later political demands could be refused on the grounds that these matters must wait until agreement had been reached on the basic instrument of government. The Archdukes Francis Joseph and Albrecht, as well as Windischgraetz and Kolowrat, were present at this conference. Significantly Archduchess Sophie, though not herself present, made it clear that she was unhappy over her husband's proposal; she did not wish to find that, when their son came to the throne, his freedom of action would be constrained by any earlier concessions. Nothing, however, was done that night; far better wait until the celebrations of the Chancellor's fall were over and the popular agitation died down.

Accordingly, on Wednesday afternoon, Francis Joseph joined his father and Emperor Ferdinand for a carriage drive through the inner city which was to test the public mood. That morning the Palatine had arrived in the capital with a large deputation from the Hungarian Diet, intensifying the widespread excitement. There were cheers once more, especially for the good-natured 'Kaiser Ferdl', but outside the Hofburg itself the crowd seemed sullenly suspicious. The drive settled doubts left unresolved at Tuesday night's conference. Some two hours after the carriage's return, a mounted herald rode out to the Michaelerplatz and proclaimed the Emperor's resolve to convene a constituent assembly 'as speedily as possible'. Cabinet government came to Austria on the following Monday, with the appointment of Kolowrat as head of a 'responsible ministry'.

Metternich's fall meant different things to different groups of people, but most hailed it as the end of a supranational repressive system. The pace of revolution quickened, notably at Bratislava where, in the last week of March, the Hungarian Diet carried through a series of sweeping constitutional changes which required their sovereign's assent to the establishment of responsible government in the historic Lands of the Hungarian Crown, too: there would be a Hungarian minister of war, a Hungarian minister of finance and a Hungarian minister 'resident around the King's person'. When the Palatine brought details of these proposed reforms to Vienna the Court complained that, if they became law, the Magyars would share nothing with the other peoples of the Monarchy except the person of the sovereign.

These demands were bad enough for the Court in Vienna. Yet however vexatious they might be, Hungary's striving for independence was at least a recognizable cause, steeped in past history. Other nationalities posed unfamiliar problems or raised old questions in a new form: thus Cracow, a 'free city' until absorbed into the Empire in 1846, remained a seedbed of Polish patriotism; and there was uncertainty over the loyalty of the Roumanian and Serbian minorities. In Zagreb representatives of the

'Triune Kingdom of Croatia, Slavonia and Dalmatia' asserted claims for acceptance of their national identity in a continued voluntary union under the Hungarian crown and reigning dynasty, but they unanimously entrusted executive authority and military command to their chosen governor (*Ban*), Baron Josip Jellaçić; while in Prague the Czechs put forward demands which threatened the power of the great landowners, the German magnates of Bohemia and Moravia. Nor could Vienna entirely escape the Pan-German enthusiasm, which surfaced so dramatically in Berlin and Frankfurt.

In one form or another, each of these issues continued to confound politics throughout Francis Joseph's life and reign. But the most immediate problems were raised by the Italian Question, as the exiled Chancellor had foreseen. The eruption of radical rebellions in Milan and Venice made the Risorgimento a sustained threat to Habsburg primacy in the peninsula. Less than a fortnight after Metternich's fall, King Charles Albert of Sardinia-Piedmont felt in honour bound to answer the call of Italian patriots for a crusade which would sweep the whitecoats back across the Alps. It was this challenge which thrust Austria into war for the first time in a third of a century.

The Austrian army, accustomed to quelling isolated rebellions in the cities of the peninsula, was surprised by the extent of the anti-Habsburg rising. By the third week in March Radetzky, who had already evacuated Milan and fallen back on the fortresses of the Quadrilateral, was appealing to Vienna for military aid; he could count on only 50,000 loyal troops to hold Verona, Peschiera, Mantua and Legnano and protect his communications from Venetian raiders at the head of the Adriatic and guerrilla attacks in the South Tyrol. But before the army could receive reinforcements the Piedmontese claimed a victory, at Goito on 8 April. In Vienna the Kolowrat government seriously considered granting Lombardy independence and Venetia autonomy, in the hopes that the troops deployed in the peninsula could be used to maintain order elsewhere in the Monarchy. But, from a sense of pride and prestige, the army would not willingly pull out of so familiar an arena of battle. Archduke Albrecht, whose father had fought against Bonaparte with distinction in northern Italy half a century before, left Vienna to command a division of Radetzky's army. Understandably Francis Joseph, who was intensely proud of his Hussar commission, wished to accompany his cousin to the Italian Front.

Not yet, however. To his mother's evident relief, the government needed Francis Joseph in Vienna, where the removal of press censorship was stimulating the growth of radical journalism. An uneasy calm prevailed with sudden displays of dynastic loyalty which may – or may not – have been sincere in intention. Thus when Archduchess Sophie and her son took an afternoon drive down the Praterallee they would hear the coffee-house orchestras suddenly switch from a popular tune to the Habsburg anthem, *Gott erhalte Franz den Kaiser*, as the carriage approached and there would be cheers from the townsfolk out walking. But many stolidly respectable Viennese families were ready to affirm their Pan-Germanic sentiments and copied the university students by wearing the black, red and gold cockades of the Frankfurt liberals. Politically, these were confusing days.

By early April Kolowrat seemed about to quit office in despair, although he did not resign until the middle of the month, largely because it was by no means clear who – or what – would succeed him. Meanwhile, to appease the radical trouble-makers, he encouraged Baron von Pillersdorf, his minister of the interior, to go ahead with the preparation of a constitution for early publication and discussion. Both Francis Charles and Francis Joseph were asked to examine Pillersdorf's first drafts and amplify his proposals, if they wished, but neither father nor son made any written comment on what was to them an alien document, difficult to comprehend. Yet, though it was clear Francis Joseph remained ill-prepared for such matters, the Kolowrat government persevered with the attempt to draw him gradually into political life; and on Thursday, 6 April, he received his first official post, Governor of Bohemia.

Kolowrat assumed that the appointment would enable the young Archduke to complement Windischgraetz's military authority, perhaps even to contain it, for the civilian landed magnates of the northern provinces felt a certain mistrust of their colleague's ambitions. But Francis Joseph had no chance to familiarize himself with the tasks ahead of him. He was at once plunged into the complex problems of Czech government. A group of 'German Bohemians resident in Vienna' was quick to seek the new *Staathalter*'s protection for the German language in Bohemia's schools. He received a deputation, but the meeting with Francis Joseph was unproductive, one delegate sadly admitting that the great hope of the dynasty 'did not appear to know what it was all about'. Kolowrat seems to have had second thoughts; for on Saturday morning the ministers went back on Thursday's arrangements. 'In the circumstances ... it would be better' for the Archduke 'not to hurry to take up his appointment', they declared.

Hungary's affairs were more pressing; and on Tuesday Francis Joseph was on his way down the Danube by steamer, accompanying Emperor Ferdinand and his own father to Bratislava for the closing of the Reform Diet. In later years the champions of the dynasty regarded Ferdinand's speech at the ceremonies on the following day as a humiliating surrender to the demands of the revolutionaries, for he gave formal consent to all the thirty-one measures enacted by the Diet over the past six months. Yet at Court there was some hope that these April Laws would give the Monarchy an effective balance of government: there is no evidence that Francis Joseph disapproved of the attempts by his cousin, the Palatine Archduke Stephen, to strike a working compromise with Kossuth and the parliamentarians. The liberals in Vienna were optimistic, too; once again warm cheers greeted the imperial carriages as they sped back to Schönbrunn from the Prater landing-stage after the steamer's return from Bratislava on 13 April. But the Palatine had his critics. Archduchess Sophie consoled herself with the curious constitutional doctrine that, although her son might have witnessed Ferdinand's acceptance of the April Laws, he had not given the reforms his assent and was not therefore bound to uphold them. She noted with approval the subsequent decision of Archduke Stephen's Chamberlain to resign office because he thought the Palatine too sympathetic towards Magyar nationalism. Soon she found room for the ex-Chamberlain, Count Karl Grünne, in her personal service. He was a forty year old devout Catholic, more stolidly conservative in politics than Bombelles, and in character and training a parade-ground officer certain to win her eldest son's warm regard.

On 19 April – Wednesday in Holy Week, and also Emperor Ferdinand's birthday – the Archduchess received a visit from Windischgraetz, who was about to return to Bohemia. The sixty-one year old Prince, who in his boyhood had witnessed the flight of French emigrés from the Revolution, expressed doubts over the wisdom of having the imperial family grouped together in the capital during Easter week: it was a time of traditional open air gatherings in the Prater and this year, on the Tuesday, the text of the Pillersdorf constitution would be published. He therefore warmly backed Francis Joseph's plea to be allowed to join Radetzky's army in Italy, and the Archduchess relented. She had never met the old Field Marshal, but she wrote a letter to him on Easter Eve, expressing confidence in the troops under his command and commending her eldest son to his safe-keeping: 'He is a good and honest boy', she wrote, 'and ever since his childhood has set his heart on a soldier's career'.

Francis Joseph travelled slowly down to the Italian Front, stopping overnight at Salzburg, Innsbruck and Bolzano on the way. He reached field headquarters in Verona before dawn on Saturday, 29 April. Next morning he rode out beside Radetzky to reconnoitre the Piedmontese positions south-west of Verona. 'My most precious possession, my life-blood, I entrust to your faithful keeping', Sophie had written in her letter to the Field Marshal.

One's sympathies go out to the veteran commander, with such new and unwanted responsibility thrust into his hands. On that same Sunday his troops, dangerously depleted in strength, suffered a rebuff at Pastrengo; and he was painfully aware that they were facing a well-equipped Piedmontese army supplemented by 5,000 enthusiastic volunteers from Tuscany, and awaiting the coming of several thousand men from the Papal States and a large contingent of Neapolitans who were on their way northwards. It is true that, though heavily pressed at Peschiera, the Austrians still held the Quadrilateral fortresses. Moreover, at the turn of the month, Radetzky was encouraged by news of the appointment in Vienna of a vigorous war minister, General Count Latour-Baillet, who made the sending of reinforcements to Italy a matter of urgency. But, for the moment, the Field Marshal could grumble at having his headquarters littered with sword-rattling princelings; for the five young Archdukes already there were now joined by the great hope of the dynasty, full of fire and fervour, eager – as he told his mother – to see 'the Piedmontese swept from our two provinces' and 'the double-headed eagle flying over Turin'. He was attached as an ordnance officer to Baron d'Aspre's corps, covering the approaches to Verona from Mantua.

Francis Joseph received his baptism of fire on 5–6 May, when the Piedmontese army launched three stubborn assaults on the Austrian positions in the suburban village of Santa Lucia. The Archduke was well to the north of the centre of the fray but several cannon-balls fell close to him; he remained cool and totally unperturbed, though urged to seek cover. The victory came as a great morale booster for Radetzky's troops and for dynastic loyalists throughout the Monarchy. Santa Lucia was no Austerlitz or Leipzig; no one reckons it among history's bloodier battles and there were less than 350 Austrian casualties, dead, wounded and missing. But the Santa Lucia positions were strategically important: had the defences been breached, the key fortress of Verona would have been in danger.

To a seventeen year old Hussar, barely two months out of the schoolroom, this experience of battle was a great occasion. 'For the first time I have heard cannon-balls whistling around me and I am perfectly happy', he wrote to his mother. But thereafter discreet postings kept him away from the firing line. He had, however, an opportunity to meet Radetzky's protégés, his 'military children'. Among them were an intrepid brigade commander, Prince Felix Schwarzenberg, and a gifted regimental officer who despised military theorizing, Colonel Ludwig von Benedek. Yet the Archduke's chief service was as a correspondent, someone to emphasize to the Court that, given reinforcements, victory would come swiftly and decisively. Radetzky suspected the government of seeking a compromise settlement, ceding Lombardy to Piedmont. This suspicion seemed confirmed when, as the month ended, he was forced to pull out of Peschiera.

By then, Vienna was again in revolt. Pillersdorf's constitution seemed inadequate, for it did not even specify who would have the vote. On 10 May radical student leaders set up a Central Political Committee and five days later columns of students and labourers marched through the inner city carrying a 'storm petition', demanding a constituent assembly elected by universal male suffrage. The government, short of reliable troops and alarmed by the rapid growth of a National Guard loyal to the Central Committee, capitulated; and on Tuesday, 16 May, the people of Vienna were informed that the Emperor had accepted the student demands, even promising that, from Thursday onwards, the National Guard should share sentry duty at the palace with the regular garrison.

These concessions alarmed both the Empress Maria Anna and Arch-duchess Sophie. Parallels with the great French Revolution were in everyone's mind: there were rumours of a student mob planning to force an entry into the Hofburg, set it ablaze, and murder the imperial family. 'Here we are held like a mouse in a trap', the Archduchess declared; they would wriggle free before the first National Guard sentries went on duty. On Wednesday the Emperor and Empress set out for an afternoon drive; and so, soon afterwards, did Francis Charles, Sophie and their younger children. But this time the carriages did not make for the Prater; they turned westwards out of the city and through the suburbs. In France, fifty-seven years before, Emperor Ferdinand's great-aunt and her royal husband had been ignominiously intercepted at Varennes and returned as virtual captives to Paris. Now, in this year of revolution, the Habsburg refugees were taking no chances. Their carriages sped throughout that night and all Thursday until, in the failing light of their second evening, they reached Innsbruck. There, behind the familiar yellow ochre stone-work of a far smaller Hofburg, the Court was to remain in residence for the next three months.

Francis Joseph warmly approved of the move to Innsbruck; it left the family free from any threat of intimidation by radical students in the capital. Indirectly, however, it also ended his participation in the Italian campaign. Now that he had won wide respect as a courageous young officer under fire, there was a good case for bringing him back to Court and grooming him for the tasks which would confront him after his accession. He might, it was felt, take up his post as Governor of Bohemia; and he certainly needed to be abreast of affairs in Hungary, where Count Lajos Batthyány was striving to keep in office the loyal constitutional government envisaged by the April Laws. By the second week in June Francis Joseph was in Innsbruck.

Sophie was relieved to have her 'most precious possession' restored to her unharmed. She was pleased, too, a week later, when her sister Ludovika, Duchess in Bavaria, arrived in Innsbruck with her daughters Helen, fourteen, and Elizabeth, ten. It was the first time Francis Joseph had met his Bavarian cousins; they seem to have made no impression upon him whatsoever. Elizabeth ('Sisi') fascinated his younger brother, Charles Ludwig, but the Santa Lucia veteran had no time to spare for a little round-faced girl, who was still so much a child that she brought with her in the coach a pet dog and a cageful of canaries. Day after day the Archduke seemed content to remain closeted with General Grünne, whom Sophie induced her son to appoint as his personal chamberlain. Grünne confirmed the High Tory prejudices which Francis Joseph absorbed at Radetzky's headquarters: to both men 'constitutions' were the invention of the devil. When a deputation from Vienna persuaded Ferdinand to appoint Archduke John as his personal representative in the capital, Francis Joseph echoed his mother's disapproval of such contact between dynasty and rabble.

While the Bavarian Princesses were staying at Innsbruck the Court received the first news of effective military backing for a counter-revolution. Not surprisingly it was Windischgraetz, the military commander in Bohemia, who seized the initiative. For several weeks in the late spring he had sought full powers from the government to stamp out the embers of revolt in the capital and the more restless cities of the Empire, but his pleas had always been rejected. In June, however, unrest in Prague gave him the opportunity to strike a blow for the old order at a time when elections for a constituent Reichstag were taking place throughout the Austrian lands.

During the Metternich era Prague was never reckoned one of the more explosive cities of the Empire. Local magnates from German princely families backed a Czech cultural and antiquarian movement which was, at times, sentimentally Slavophile but never aggressively Panslav in sentiment. The growth of factory industries had thrown many home craftsmen out of work and by late May 1848 there was high unemployment in the mills because the delivery of American cotton, normally landed at Trieste, was disrupted by the fighting in the north of Italy. Yet politically Prague remained true to the dynasty, mistrusting 'the rebellious people of Vienna'. When on 1 June a Slav Congress was opened in the city, its leaders wished to emphasize to Ferdinand the loyal support of Slavonic peoples of his Empire, and their conviction of the need for an 'Austria' freed from dependence on Germans and Magyars. Other nationalities proved less cool-headed than the Czechs: Poles, Slovaks, Ruthenes, Serbs, Slovenes and Croats all had different objectives, while radical delegates from outside the Monarchy urged support of Panslav ambitions which presupposed a need to dissolve the Empire entirely. The Congress got out of hand, and Windischgraetz put his troops on the alert, a provocative move with fatal consequences. Clashes between the army and demonstrators became serious on 6 June, and over the following days there were some four hundred casualties in a series of confused skirmishes at hastily improvised barricades. Among the dead was Windischgraetz's wife (who was also a sister of Felix Schwarzenberg); she was hit by a stray bullet as she stood at her window, trying to observe what was happening in the narrow streets below. This misfortune settled Windischgraetz's line of conduct. He refused to receive two missions of would-be mediators sent from Vienna and began shelling central Prague. The city surrendered unconditionally to Windischgraetz on 16 June: martial law was imposed; and military tribunals meted out harsh punishment. The 'conqueror of Prague' received, not a reprimand for insubordination, but a warm letter of gratitude signed by Emperor Ferdinand. From St Petersburg came further congratulations and a high military decoration; Tsar Nicholas I saw himself as the custodian of the old order now that Metternich was gone, and he recognized in the army commander of Bohemia a natural ally against Revolution.

Archduchess Sophie welcomed the news from Prague: had she not emphasized to Windischgraetz in March the 'need to set things in order' before her son came of age? Sophie remained in close touch with Windischgraetz. She was heartened, too, by the attachment to the Emperor's suite of Felix Schwarzenberg, as spokesman for 'Papa' Radetzky and the army in Lombardy-Venetia. That, after all, was the decisive battle-front: 'All Austria is in thy camp' ran a line in Grillparzer's famous ode to Radetzky, published in the *Donauzeitung* of 8 June; and Schwarzenberg emphasized the truth behind the poetic apostrophisation. Certainly after 25 July, when Radetzky defeated the Piedmontese army at Custozza, there was no more talk, either among the ministers in Vienna or at Innsbruck, of seeking a compromise peace with King Charles Albert. Within a fortnight the whole of Lombardy had been cleared of the invaders and Charles Albert was glad to accept an armistice. This was a decisive moment in the counter-revolution. Latour, the war minister, no longer had to find troops to send down to Verona; there was some prospect that, in the near future, units could be withdrawn from Italy to restore order elsewhere in the Monarchy.

Meanwhile, three days before Radetzky's victory, a newly elected assembly (*Reichstag*) met in Vienna's imperial Riding School. Delegates came from every part of the Empire, except Lombardy-Venetia and Hungary (which had its own Diet, opened by the Palatine Archduke Stephen in Buda early in July). Although there was friction between some national groups in the Reichstag and scuffles broke out in the narrow streets around the Riding School, there seemed no threat of further violence in the capital. The most lasting achievement of the Reichstag – the emancipation of the peasantry from feudal dues and obligations – was carried through peacefully in the second week in August. Archduke John, the ministers and the deputies, all urged the Court to return to the capital, and Ferdinand and the Empress duly left Innsbruck as soon as the report of the armistice with Piedmont was confirmed. Francis Joseph accompanied them as far as Ischl where, with Grünne now acting as his chief adviser, he called on Archduke Ludwig, who chose to remain in the Salzkammergut and leave affairs of state to more active members of the family. Not entirely, however. News of a plan for Francis Joseph to visit England, where Metternich had settled in exile, stirred him into strong opposition: it would be far better for Franzi to wait upon events in Austria, he told Sophie.

It was therefore at Schönbrunn that Francis Joseph passed his eighteenth birthday and reached the age of majority. Outwardly there was nothing unusual about the day itself or the festivities which continued for much of the week. From his parents he received a gift of two beautifully decorated meerschaums, for he was already a habitual pipe-smoker; he attended a Te Deum and a military parade to celebrate the victory in Italy. Yet affairs were far from normal. Tension remained high: the troops drawn up for inspection came, not only from historic regiments in the garrison, but from units of the National Guard, the citizen militia established in March; and a relaxed day with his younger brothers at a village festival was cut short by a plea from Grünne to return to the palace, as there were clashes between unemployed and soldiery in the poorer districts of Vienna. Worse rioting followed in mid-September, when the University was put into a state of indefinite vacation in the hope of dispersing the students and keeping them away from allegedly left-wing academics. The Reichstag, too, came under suspicion when by a narrow majority it threw out a proposed vote of thanks to Radetzky, for his victories in Italy. The rebuff angered the veteran Field Marshal. Unlike his colleague in Bohemia, Radetzky liked to stay so far as possible above politics, but he resented this gesture by the Reichstag; he told war minister Latour – himself a General of the old school – that he would never tolerate attacks on the honour of the officer corps, and he expressed alarm at the prospect of decisions over the future of the army passing into 'the hands of mere boys and contemptible agitators'.

There was no precedent for a military coup in the whole history of Imperial Austria. Over-ambitious generals had been effectively discouraged for the past two centuries, deterred perhaps by the fate of

Wallenstein in the Thirty Years War. Yet by September it seemed clear to outside observers – including the British ambassador – that the future of the Monarchy depended on its military commanders and, allegedly, on a camarilla of generals and courtiers with influence over the young Archduke. Here the key figure was thought to be Windischgraetz: he insisted on holding autumn manoeuvres in Moravia, thus massing a large army within a few days march of Vienna; and he strengthened his links with the Court through the appointment in late August of a trusted staff officer, Prince Joseph Lobkowitz, to serve as adjutant-general to the Emperor. Recent historical scholarship has played down the role of the camarilla, emphasizing the discord between the rival commanders, but Windischgraetz personally had little doubt of his objective. He would lead a counter-revolution, designed to perpetuate aristocratic rule in central Europe through the agency of the Habsburgs. He presented Lobkowitz with a contingency plan in case the imperial family had to flee the capital a second time: no more slipping away to the alpine provinces, as in May; 'the Emperor and all the imperial family' must head northwards 'by way of Krems to Olmütz, not in flight, but under the protection of the army'. 'Then', Windischgraetz added in confidence, 'I shall conquer Vienna, the Emperor will abdicate in favour of his nephew, and I shall proceed to occupy Ofen (Buda)'.

Hungary determined the pace of events that autumn. Throughout the summer the Hungarians behaved with exemplary loyalty, within the constitutional structure of the April Laws: Archduke Stephen remained Palatine; Count Lajos Batthyány served as prime minister of a coalition which included the cultural 'father of his people' István Szechényi and the cautious lawyer Ferencz Deák as well as the more radical Kossuth. In early June Batthyány travelled to Innsbruck, where he promised to raise funds for 40,000 recruits to swell Radetzky's army in Italy. Yet, though their prime minister might be treated with respect, the Court looked on all Hungarians with suspicion. If the Batthyány ministry made the April Laws really work, then the centre of the Habsburg Monarchy would effectively shift from Vienna to Buda, with the Magyar magnates succeeding to the privileged position held by the Germanised Bohemian nobility. It was therefore in the Court's interest to encourage the discontented non-Magyar peoples of historic Hungary, both 'backward' nationalities like the Slovaks and historically more assertive communities, such as the Roumanians of Transylvania and the militant Serbs of the Voivodina, where the Serbs could count on covert backing from Belgrade. Fighting spread across southern Hungary in the second week of June and continued intermittently throughout the summer.

The key figure in these troubled south-eastern lands of the Monarchy was Colonel Josip Jellaçić, the Ban of Croatia. At midsummer the Court at Innsbruck disavowed the Ban as a disobedient and independently minded troublemaker, but he received some encouragement and funds from Latour, officially for the well-being of the 'frontier folk', military families settled along the historic Croatian-Bosnian borderland. The worsening situation in southern Hungary bolstered the Ban's status, making him indispensable to the so-called camarilla in Vienna. He was promoted General and on 11 September led a Croatian army across the River Drava and marched swiftly northwards to Lake Balaton, having achieved a working alliance with some 10,000 Serbian irregulars in the east. This South Slav ('Yugoslav') invasion rallied the Hungarian parliamentarians who, on Kossuth's prompting, voted funds for an army of Home Defence, numbering 200,000 men. The Palatine's well-intentioned appointment of Count Lemberg to negotiate with Jellaçić went tragically wrong; on 28 September a nationalistic mob in Pest seized and lynched Lemberg. Archduke Stephen, who was in Vienna, had already determined to step down as Palatine because of the hostility he encountered at Court; and Batthyány also resigned soon afterwards. The fate of Hungary was in the hands of Kossuth, as head of a Committee of National Defence.

Francis Joseph, with Grünne at his elbow, was well briefed on events in Hungary, receiving Jellaçić's proclamations as soon as they reached Vienna and passing them on to his mother (who, in her journal, already called the Ban of Croatia 'that admirable Jellaçić'). Emperor Ferdinand, at Latour's prompting, issued a manifesto on 3 October giving Jellaçić command of all troops in Hungary and proclaiming him as representative of the sovereign in the absence of a Palatine. This appointment soon proved an embarrassment. Hungarian resistance stiffened north of Balaton, thanks largely to the enterprising young General, Arthur Görgei. After three days of heavy fighting, the Croat army was in urgent need of reinforcement. Latour ordered a regiment to be sent by rail from Vienna into Hungary on the morning of Friday, 6 October. The troops mutinied. There was shooting at the railway station. By midday rioting had spread to the centre of the city.

As in March and in May, the imperial family was gathered in the Hofburg. Alarming reports reached Lobkowitz, who was entrusted with their safety. Angry groups of workers and students were hunting for the two most unpopular men in Vienna: Alexander Bach, a liberal reformer who had accepted office as minister of justice; and Latour, the war minister. Bach escaped the mob: he changed into women's clothes but, refusing to shave off his moustache, was induced to accept the role of gentleman's gentleman instead. Latour was tricked into emerging from the war ministry and was seized by the mob who repeatedly stabbed him, stripped him naked and strung him up on a lamp post in the square known as Am Hof. News of this bestial murder, less than a quarter of a mile from the Hofburg, convinced Lobkowitz of the need to get his charges out of Vienna. They left under heavy escort at half past six on the Saturday morning.

Once clear of the city, the imperial 'caravan' (as Archduchess Sophie called it) moved slowly, conscious that Windischgraetz's troops were heading southwards to give the family greater protection and restore order in the capital. Sunday was spent at Sieghartskirchen, barely twenty miles west of Vienna, and it was not until the following Saturday morning that the caravan reached its destination, the garrison town of Olmütz (now Olomouc), a natural centre for the fertile farms and small industries of northern Moravia. The imperial family occupied the palace of the Prince Bishops, a spacious Baroque residence built some 180 years previously. Both the German townsfolk and the Czech peasantry in Moravia were as effusively loyal to their 'honoured guests' as the people of Innsbruck had been a few months before. In later years Francis Joseph remained suspicious of Vienna's artisans and students and continued to look on Hungarians and Italians as natural rebels – but not the good folk of Moravia, the Salzkammergut or the Tyrol.

The sudden departure from Vienna and the week-long journey through an army massing to avenge the murder of Latour and the alleged affronts to the dynasty left a deep impression on the Archduke's mind. Once again he was, in his own eyes, a professional soldier; he chafed at the restraints which prevented him from marching 'to conquer Vienna' beside Windischgraetz (whom Emperor Ferdinand created a Field Marshal two days after the Court reached Olmütz). By the last week in October the new Field Marshal concentrated 59 battalions of infantry, 67 squadrons of cavalry and 200 guns on the outskirts of the capital. There he joined forces with Jellaçić, who was glad to have sound strategic reasons for leading his Croats westwards out of Hungary as Magyar resistance stiffened. The Honved, an essentially National Defence force, was reluctant to cross the frontiers of historic Hungary in pursuit of Jellaçić, but its commanders raised the hopes of the beleaguered Viennese by tentatively probing forward as far as Schwechat – where Vienna's airport now stands – before falling back at the approach of the main Austrian army.

By 31 October Vienna was in Windischgraetz's hands. The Field Marshal set up his headquarters in imperial Schönbrunn, while Jellaçić's ill-disciplined troops were left to break down the last improvised barricades in suburban Leopoldstadt. Almost a quarter of Vienna's inhabitants had fled the city before Windischgraetz tightened the noose, many heading northwards to Moravia; but some two thousand Viennese perished in the fighting, and twenty-five alleged ringleaders were subsequently shot. Throughout the winter the city remained under strict military control.

Windischgraetz was dictator of the Monarchy in all but name. For him it was enough to be invested by Emperor Ferdinand 'with the necessary plenipotentiary powers to restore peace in My realm'. Outwardly the months of November and December 1848 marked the apogee of Habsburg militarism; and in several provinces there was a brief popular cult of WJR, a symbolic trinity of soldierly saviours and of the dynasty, formed by the initials of Windischgraetz, Jellaçić and Radetzky. But, in reality, the three generals had little in common: Jellaçić, a far inferior soldier, was mistrusted politically by both colleagues; Radetzky complained that Windischgraetz's politics were impossibly reactionary; and Windischgraetz, for his part, undervalued the victor of Custozza's generalship. The WJR combination never sought to establish a purely military oligarchy for the Empire as a whole. Ministerial government had not been swept away: the septuagenarian diplomat Baron Wessenberg, appointed prime minister in July when Pillersdorf retired from the political stage, followed the Court to Olmütz, and he was joined there by most of the cabinet. Nor were the delegates to the constituent assembly sent about their business: the Reichstag sitting in the Vienna Riding School was prorogued on 19 October, with its members given a month to make their way to Moravia, where the assembly would reopen at Kremsier. This was a town some 25 miles south of Olmütz in which the Prince-Bishop had a summer palace, with large halls and galleries to accommodate the deputies. Yet in one respect, Windischgraetz left a decisive imprint on active politics in Moravia: once Vienna was in his hands, he secured the nomination of Felix Schwarzenberg as prime minister in succession to Wessenberg. For Windischgraetz's political future this was a mistake. If Schwarzenberg felt any obligation at all towards the mythical WJR trinity, it was to the old Field Marshal he had served in Italy rather than to his brother-in-law.

Francis Joseph, though steeling himself to show no strong feelings over any question, liked and respected the forty-eight year old brigade commander whom he had first met in the forts outside Verona. Schwarzenberg was a Byronic cavalry officer beginning to look slightly seedy from the ravages of typhus. He had been a career diplomat and still possessed ideas of his own as well as the skill to express them convincingly. To come from the most illustrious family still in attendance at Court was also an advantage for him. 'A man of authority, but in no sense an absolutist', Metternich's protégé Baron Hubner wrote contentedly in his journal after hearing Schwarzenberg expound his views for the first time.

He was strongly opposed to Windischgraetz's extreme Toryism and, since he was more sympathetic towards constitutionalism than Grünne, he slightly broadened Francis Joseph's political horizon during those weeks at Olmütz when Windischgraetz's star seemed in the ascendant. Above all, Schwarzenberg acknowledged that his experience of domestic politics was limited: and in Olmütz he looked for advice to Count Francis Stadion, a genuine believer in parliamentary government, and the lawyer Alexander Bach who, though regarded as a renegade by Vienna's radicals, was one of the ablest administrators who ever operated Austria's cumbersome bureaucratic machine. When Schwarzenberg announced his cabinet on 21 November, he found in it posts for Stadion (Interior) and Bach (Justice) as well as for Baron Bruck (Commerce), the entrepreneur who had already created for Austria a new port at Trieste. Unlike the Empress and Archduchess Sophie, who still believed Windischgraetz was the soldier-statesman of the coming reign, Schwarzenberg saw no reason to look to the WJR combination for guidance. And, under his tutelage, neither did Francis Joseph.

Windischgraetz, in Vienna, remained unaware of the day to day shifts in power and influence at Olmütz. He did not realize how rapidly Schwarzenberg established an ascendancy at Court. Long ago both men had agreed that Ferdinand should abdicate in favour of his nephew; and Schwarzenberg accepted office only on the understanding that a change of emperor was imminent. Empress Maria Anna and Archduchess Sophie also recognized that the time had come for Francis Joseph's accession. But the long-suffering Empress retained a certain pride. She did not wish to see her husband nudged off the throne for a new monarchy based upon popular sovereignty. An act of abdication must condemn the revolutionary leaders who had induced Ferdinand to whittle away his powers, she insisted; and she wished it to emphasize that, in renouncing the throne, Ferdinand was ensuring that his nephew could begin his reign unfettered by concessions exacted from his predecessor. Windischgraetz fully agreed with the Empress. He assured her of his conviction that the Schwarzenberg government would respect her views: 'You need have no scruples over advising the Emperor to abdicate', he wrote.

Schwarzenberg did not see political life in such simplistic terms. Neither the Empress nor Windischgraetz seem to have known of the speech he delivered to the Reichstag at Kremsier five days after becoming prime minister, when he told the deputies that the government wished 'to place itself at the head of' the movement in favour of representative institutions. 'We want constitutional monarchy sincerely and unreservedly', Schwarzenberg declared. Perhaps he even meant it, for there was no reason why a 'constitutional monarchy' need necessarily concede popular sovereignty. But the speech made no attempt to condemn the Revolution; the prime minister's sentiments had little in common with the straightforward Toryism shared by Maria Anna and her sympathetic correspondent in Vienna.

On the evening of Friday, 1 December, Windischgraetz and Jellaçić arrived in Olmütz from the capital, knowing that the change of monarch was imminent; the third paladin, Radetzky, could not leave the Italian war zone. In the evening Windischgraetz discussed the Abdication Act and the accession ceremonies with Schwarzenberg. He seemed satisfied by all he was told, for Metternich's close assistant, Kübeck, had drafted a stern preamble to the Act, denouncing the sins of Revolution.

The presence of the Court in Olmütz had drawn the diplomatic corps to northern Moravia, and the town was already packed. It was clear some ceremony was to take place next day, for the garrison was ordered to turn out in full-dress uniform at half past nine. Few people were in the secret, certainly not Archduchess Sophie's younger sons: Maximilian, not unreasonably, assumed that his brother was to be invested as Governor of Bohemia-Moravia. There was an element of improvisation right up to the last moment. Only on Friday morning was it agreed in talks between the prime minister and the Emperor-to-be that he would retain his two baptismal names as sovereign, reigning as 'Francis Joseph I' rather than as 'Francis II' (as styled in the first draft of the proclamation): both men liked to associate 'good Kaiser Franz' with the reformer emperor, Joseph, who was also an active soldier.

The date chosen for the ceremony was hardly auspicious: 2 December was the anniversary, not only of an upstart Emperor's coronation in Paris, but of the humiliating defeat he inflicted a year later on the Austrian and Russian armies at Austerlitz, scarcely thirty miles away from Olmütz. But, for different reasons, both Windischgraetz and Schwarzenberg were in too much of a hurry to worry about anniversaries: the Field Marshal wished to march on Buda before winter made the roads impassable; and his brother-in-law believed he could curb the giddier flights of constitutional fantasy at Kremsier by emphasizing that there was, once again, a central authority prepared to exercise real powers.

Only a small gathering of people witnessed the ceremonies in the salon of the Prince-Bishop's palace on that Saturday morning: the imperial family, the government ministers and the two soldier paladins. With a weary voice, halting between words and placing emphasis at times on the wrong syllables, Emperor Ferdinand read out the Abdication Act which Schwarzenberg handed to him. Windischgraetz, who was not listening carefully, thought the reading took less time than he had anticipated, and when he received the official copy of the gazette he was able to see why;

for Kübeck's preamble condemning the revolution had dropped out of the speech. 'Important reasons have led Us to the irrevocable decision to lay down Our Crown in favour of Our beloved nephew, Archduke Francis Joseph ...', Ferdinand declared, surrendering his Austrian imperial titles and the crowns of Hungary, Bohemia, and Lombardy, although retaining the personal style and dignity of Emperor. Schwarzenberg read Archduke Francis Charles's formal renunciation of his claims, with its assertion that, at this grave moment in the dynasty's history, a younger person was needed on the throne; and family, generals and ministers gave homage to their new sovereign lord. 'It is thanks to you that all this is possible', Francis Joseph said, simply enough, to Windischgraetz. Afterwards Ferdinand recorded all that he remembered in his journal: 'The function ended with the new Emperor kneeling to his Emperor and master – that is to say myself – and asking for a blessing, which I gave by laying my hands upon his head and making a sign of the Cross'. Sophie heard Ferdinand say, 'God bless you, Franzi. Be good. God will protect you. I'm happy about it all'. Then, as Ferdinand wrote in his journal, 'We went away to our room ... and heard Holy Mass in the chapel of the Bishop's Palace ... After that I and my dear wife packed our things'.

At two in the afternoon Emperor Ferdinand and Empress Maria Anna left for Prague and took up residence in the Hradschin Castle. Meanwhile in Olmütz Francis Joseph's accession was proclaimed to his subjects with a flourish of trumpets outside the Rathaus and again on the steps of the cathedral. Schwarzenberg later read a proclamation of accession to the Kremsier Assembly: 'Long Live the constitutional Emperor, Francis Joseph' responded Franz Smolka, the Speaker of the Reichstag, with conviction. Only from Hungary came the firm voice of dissent: the change of throne was 'an affair of the Habsburg family', Kossuth insisted. Hungary would acknowledge no other King until a successor swore to uphold the constitution as defined in the April Laws and received on his head the Holy Crown of St Stephen.

Legend depicts Francis Joseph as returning from the ceremony with the sad comment, 'Farewell my youth', and bursting into tears. Perhaps so; though, for the past nine months, moments of light-hearted frivolity were already rare; and thus life continued for him. He remained at the heart of the family circle in the Prince-Bishop's apartments, along with his mother and father and three brothers. But, long before dawn each morning, the Emperor was working at his official papers. For a fortnight he buried himself in documents of state, trying to make sense of reports from his commanders in the field and sending off holograph letters to the sovereigns of Europe. On 16 December came the grave news that Windischgraetz had led an army of 52,000 men eastwards into Hungary, confirming that the Monarchy was racked by civil war. That evening the self-control which was second nature to the young ruler momentarily broke, exacting a curious price. A ball thrown to one of his brothers by the six-year old Archduke Ludwig Victor cracked a mirrored door in the episcopal palace. The boys, fearing a scolding or worse, appealed to Francis Joseph for sympathy and support. Unexpectedly the Emperor felt an urge to join in their romp. Turning to his mother, he asked for her permission to smash the door down; and, with astonishing indulgence, the Archduchess allowed her children to do as they pleased. A frenzy of glass-breaking followed, until the door was shattered. '*Sa Majesté se donna à coeur joie*' ('His Majesty went at it to his heart's content'), Sophie wrote in her diary that night. What the Prince-Bishop said is not on record.

Chapter 4

APOTHEOSIS OF THE ARMY

Army officers had brought Francis Joseph to the throne, and for the first months of his reign the future form of the Monarchy remained in their hands. Windischgraetz's invasion of Hungary from the west held promise of a speedy victory, especially as Jellačić seized the opportunity to launch a second offensive on the southern front. By 5 January 1849 the Austrians controlled Buda and Pest, forcing Kossuth to move his revolutionary government 120 miles eastwards to Debrecen. 'Whoever today holds the capital in his hands is master of the land', Windischgraetz proclaimed. Offers by a Hungarian delegation to discuss a compromise settlement were contemptuously brushed aside: there would be no negotiations with 'rebels', Windischgraetz insisted. At the end of the third week in January the emperor approved an official bulletin for publication in Monday's *Wiener Zeitung* which proclaimed the glorious conclusion of the campaign in Hungary. Thus, within fifty days of his accession, the paladins handed Francis Joseph the swift and tidy victory he had sought, achieved with little cost in men or material. Or so it seemed.

Meanwhile, Vienna and Prague remained under martial law, the Court was still at Olmütz, and in neighbouring Kremsier deputies continued to dabble with constitutional drafts. 'Our Reichstag at Kremsier has become very docile', Schwarzenberg smugly told Windischgraetz on the day his troops entered Pest: 'Every victory, every step forward in Hungary, broadens its political horizons and adds more maturity to its capacity for law-making'. But a week later the prime minister's tone changed. For the deputies were not marionettes, responding to his pull of the strings; in Kremsier, as earlier in Vienna, they were concerned with fundamental principles of government; the Emperor enjoyed sovereignty through the will of the people rather than 'by grace of God', they declared. Such doctrines smacked of political heresy. 'In the last few days the Reichstag has shown itself so naturally malevolent that any hope of reaching the planned objective, the working out by it and with it of a constitution, is fast disappearing', Schwarzenberg wrote to his brother-in-law; and grimly Windischgraetz responded, 'If they will not hear of the grace of God, they must learn of the grace of cannon'.

But neither Francis Joseph nor his ministers would let Windischgraetz's guns loose on Kremsier. They preferred a political solution, and by the end of January the government had an alternative constitution ready, in case the deputies remained tiresome. Stadion, as minister of the interior, collaborated with Alexander Bach, the minister of justice, to produce a draft constitution which would be centralist and pan-monarchical in character, while providing both for a bicameral elective parliament and a Reichsrat, a council of advisers to the Emperor nominated by himself. For the moment, however, the Kremsier deputies were allowed to continue with their debates: Schwarzenberg had assured his brother-in-law that no constitution would be presented for the Emperor's signature without field headquarters' approval, and Windischgraetz remained opposed to all talk of parliamentary government. Moreover, despite January's confident bulletin in the *Wiener Zeitung*, there was still no prospect of imposing a unitary constitution on the whole of the Monarchy: General Görgei was massing the Honved volunteers along the line of the Tisza; General Damjanics held in check the Austrian-Serbian-Croatian force in southern Hungary; and Jozef Bem, the exiled Polish General who had offered his services to Kossuth, was virtually master of Transylvania and even led a foray into the Bukovina. With such uncertainty around the eastern frontiers, it was felt at Olmütz better to wait upon Windischgraetz, even though there was some disquiet over the slowness with which he responded to Görgei's continued challenge. No doubt, in time, the saviour of Prague and Vienna would give his blessing to a modified draft of Stadion's constitution, and present his Emperor with a positively final victory in Hungary.

In the last days of February the Austrians inflicted a tactical defeat on the Honved at Kapolna, forcing Görgei back across the River Tisza and silencing Windischgraetz's critics. Three days later the Kremsier deputies completed work on a draft constitution which promised the establishment of a democratic multi-national empire (though not in Hungary, where it was assumed the April Laws still prevailed): 'All political rights emanate from the people', the Kremsier blueprint declared, defiantly. The deputies hoped the constitution would be approved by the Emperor and published on 15 March, the first anniversary of Metternich's overthrow. But Francis Joseph would have none of it. Rather than allow 'the people' to assert their sovereignty, he backed Stadion's proposals and on Sunday, 4 March, formally approved the centralist constitution drafted a few weeks earlier. On Tuesday Stadion himself travelled to Kremsier to let the deputies know that the Emperor had graciously endowed his subjects with a constitution which rendered their continued labours superfluous. The Reichstag was dissolved, he announced; they could all return to their families. By Wednesday morning a battalion of grenadiers was patrolling the streets of the little town, while sentries paced the silent galleries of the Prince-Bishop's palace.

Within three weeks Francis Joseph was celebrating a genuine military victory; but not against Kossuth. On 14 March Charles Albert of Sardinia-Piedmont unexpectedly denounced the Armistice. Six days later he attacked the Austrian positions in Lombardy. It was a brief campaign, decided as early as 23 March by Radetzky's crushing response to the would-be invaders on the battlefield of Novara, some ten miles inside Piedmont, a disaster which led Charles Albert to abdicate that same evening. The octogenarian Radetzky became once more the hero of the hour at Court: why, it was asked, had not Windischgraetz, who was twenty-one years his junior, shown a similar initiative in Hungary? Grünne, the Emperor's military adjutant, was no great champion of Radetzky, but he was by now even more critical of Windischgraetz for failing to mop up the Magyar rebels he so despised; and Schwarzenberg, long impatient of his brother-in-law's political obscurantism, was irritated by Windischgraetz's constant pleas to seek help from Tsar Nicholas in stamping out the Hungarian insurrection. Emperor and government were 'absolutely opposed to foreign aid in restoring order within the monarchy, even when the source was so intimate and friendly an ally', Windischgraetz was told, before the battle of Kapolna. His influence at Court, paramount five months before, was fast slipping away as Damjanics's southern army launched a successful flank attack on Austrian positions around Szolnok, forcing Windischgraetz to pull his forward troops back across the open steppe-land of the Alföld towards Pest and the Danube.

Far worse followed a month later. Görgei, moving swiftly across the featureless countryside in a scimitar manoeuvre, came down from the north on Komarom, threatened the main artery between Vienna and Hungary, and compelled Windischgraetz to abandon Pest. The Hungarian successes prompted Kossuth to make the decisive break with the Habsburgs. On 14 April the independence of Hungary was at last proclaimed in the Calvinist church at Debrecen, with Kossuth recognized as Regent President of the Kingdom.

Military defeat sealed Windischgraetz's fate. In the third week of April he was replaced by Baron von Welden: 'I . . . rely on your patriotism and self-sacrificing devotion to my house and to Austria to accept this step, which causes me endless pain', Francis Joseph wrote in the letter informing Windischgraetz of his recall. The proudest High Tory in central

Europe dutifully accepted his dismissal, but he did not hesitate to let the Emperor know he thought he deserved better treatment 'for the sacrifices I have made for the Imperial House'. In the remaining thirteen years of his life he continued to blame his brother-in-law for his humiliation.

Windischgraetz's bitterness was intensified by Welden's total failure to check the Hungarian advance. By late April the Austrians were back to the lines they held five months earlier, before the march into Hungary. Welden remained in command of the army for only five weeks. Before the end of May he was himself superseded by Baron Julius von Haynau. The new commander was one of Radetzky's most competent generals but, as the 'beast of Brescia', he was already notorious abroad for cruelty to men, women and children across northern Italy.

Like many of his contemporaries, Windischgraetz had assumed that his Emperor remained a cipher, responding to ideas put before him by Prince Schwarzenberg or Count Grünne, or even by his mother. But Francis Joseph had acquired remarkable self-confidence in the past twelve months; he was hungry for authority and eager to accept responsibility. The Emperor presided over meetings of his ministers in person, until Schwarzenberg himself was heard grumbling privately, more than once, that he had not intention of being a mere 'hack' for the throne: 'No one knows better than I how many ministerial proposals he sends back on the ground of faultiness', he complained to Metternich in the following summer. There were moments when Francis Joseph affected a family sentimentality which pleased his mother: thus, when she went with his brothers to Prague soon after Easter in 1849, she received a letter from him emphasizing how much he missed her company, especially at the breakfast table, where he was accustomed to joining her after several hours of early morning tedium at his desk. But already the young Emperor was acquiring an iron reserve of character, a conscious awareness of sovereignty. The sentimental note to his mother was written soon after he had penned that hardest of all letters, in which he sacked the saviour of the monarchy from his military command.

For Francis Joseph there was no distinction between the prestige of the army and of the crown. Like his first prime minister – and in sharp contrast to his two predecessors on the throne – he was rarely seen in public out of uniform. The ideal of the Russian and Prussian autocracies, in which the sovereign was accepted as a Supreme War Lord, appealed to him. On the last day of April the war minister in Vienna was notified that the Emperor, who was still at Olmütz, had taken over the supreme direction of the army and was setting up a personal military chancellery. But no Supreme War Lord could conduct military affairs from the heart of Moravia. On the following Saturday Francis Joseph arrived back in

Vienna by the train from Brno and went into residence at Schönbrunn. It was thirty weeks to the day since Lobkowitz's hussars had escorted the imperial 'caravan' out of the troubled city.

In those seven months much had changed in the capital. The Viennese themselves, though vexed by the retention of martial law, were politically quiet and complaisant now that Windischgraetz had been rusticated to his estates and 'that admirable Jellaçić' was back in Zagreb, working for the creation of an 'Illyrian Kingdom' under Habsburg suzerainty. But, as General Welden could still warn Schwarzenberg, 'the fate of the capital city, and with it that of the Monarchy, hangs in the balance'. For the Hungarians, who had threatened outlying Schwechat in the autumn, were once more a mere forty miles away from the outer villages; and there is ample evidence from contemporary journals and diaries of a near-panic in government circles during the first week of May. Until the Hungarian insurrection was suppressed there could be no return to normal life; and so long as Hungary asserted its independence of Habsburg rule, the institutions promised to the Empire as a whole in Stadion's centralist constitution could exist only on paper. A peaceful settlement was even more pressing now than at the Emperor's accession.

Barely a week after returning to Vienna, Francis Joseph left Schönbrunn to spend three days with his troops along the border with Hungary. His presence put heart into his sadly depleted army at a time when he was especially anxious to emphasize the bonds linking Emperor and soldiery. For, shortly before leaving Olmütz, he at last took a step which Windischgraetz had long recommended, but which he and Schwarzenberg consistently rejected: on 24 April the Emperor agreed to seek Russian help. A few days later, in a personal letter to Tsar Nicholas I. he urged the immediate despatch of a Russian expeditionary force which would destroy that 'rendezvous of the lost children of all ill causes ... and, above all, the eternal Polish conspirators enrolled under the banner of Kossuth'; only thus, Nicholas was told, could the 'glorious fraternity' in arms of the Habsburg and Romanov empires 'save modern society from certain ruin, ... uphold with firm resolution the holy struggle of the social order against anarchy' and 'prevent the Hungarian rebellion from becoming a European calamity'. The plea was eloquently phrased, but at great cost to the young Emperor's dignity. Schwarzenberg had always insisted that for governments to seek foreign assistance in order 'to restore order in their own house' was to risk losing 'all credit, both domestic and foreign'. Much of Francis Joseph's behaviour through the second half of the year sprang from the pique of a young ruler at having to reveal to the doyen of autocrats how defective was the army in which he took such exaggerated pride.

Soon after his visit to the Front, he set off for Warsaw and a conference with the Tsar and Marshal Paskevich, his Viceroy in Poland. It was not the first time the two rulers had met. When Tsar Nicholas paid a surprise visit to Vienna soon after Emperor Francis's death he had taken tea with Archduchess Sophie and affectionately bounced her eldest son on his knees. Ten years later they met again, with the Tsar on this occasion admiring the young archduke's bearing as a Lieutenant of Dragoons. The Tsar did not anticipate much satisfaction from the Warsaw meeting or from the proposed intervention in Hungary: 'I see only envy, malice and ingratitude ahead', he told Paskevich, ' and I would certainly not interfere ... if I did not see in Bem and the other rascals in Hungary not only enemies of Austria but also ... villains, scoundrels and destroyers whom we must root out for the sake of our own tranquillity'. But when Francis Joseph reached Warsaw, at the start of the fourth week in May, he scored a striking personal success. The visit coincided with bad news from Hungary, where the garrison, which had held out on Buda's Castle Hill after Windischgraetz ordered the general retreat, was forced to surrender to Görgei's troops on 21 May. Nicholas was impressed by his guest's calm dignity: 'The more I see of him and listen to him, the more I am astonished by his good sense and by the soundness and rectitude of his views', the Tsar told his wife. Francis Joseph emphasized the importance of upholding monarchical solidarity so as to safeguard 'order and justice' across Europe. But however much these sentiments might please the Tsar, nothing could speed up Russian mobilization. Six weeks elapsed between the Tsar's approval of intervention and the southward movement of Paskevich's cumbersome army, which was ravaged by cholera.

The delay at least allowed Haynau to take the initiative and push Görgei's vanguard back from the Austrian border. Against the advice of both Schwarzenberg and his own mother, Francis Joseph again visited the Front in June, accompanied on this occasion by his brother Maximilian. Schwarzenberg, who from his days at Verona well knew the Emperor's imperviousness to danger, accompanied the imperial party, 'fussing around him like an old hen with a prize chick', as Archduke Max wrote back to their mother: 'The Emperor was splendid, always to the forefront of the battle; you can imagine the soldiers' enthusiasm at seeing him sharing their danger and fatigue'. On 29 June he led his troops into the town they knew as Raab (now Györ) across a bridge already licked by flame; 'the burning bridge of Raab' became a set-piece of Habsburg legend, as prone to artistic licence as the famous assault by Napoleon on the bridge of Lodi in his first Italian campaign. By 9 July when, to Schwarzenberg's relief, Francis Joseph and his brother were safely back at Schönbrunn, the Hungarians were in full retreat.

Most of the fighting in that summer was between Haynau's army and the Honved units, for the Hungarians skilfully avoided pitched battles with Paskevich's Russians. But when, in the second week of August, independent Hungary could hold out no longer and Kossuth escaped to Turkey, it was to the Russians that General Görgei capitulated at Vilagos, not the Austrians. Paskevich's subsequent message to Tsar Nicholas, 'Hungary lies at the feet of Your Majesty', was doubly unfortunate: it used courtiers' licence, for some citadels held out for several weeks; and it infuriated Francis Joseph, his government and his generals, all of whom regarded the Russian presence as supplementary to their own efforts.

There followed a bleak two months in the history of Hungary and of Francis Joseph's style of government. At first the Emperor left Haynau to punish his rebellious subjects but, knowing the General's notorious reputation for brutality, he gave orders that no death sentences were to be executed without authority from Vienna. Haynau was aghast at such restraints; he protested that to be an effective deterrent 'Justice' needed swift implementation on the spot; and in this instance Haynau was supported by the prime minister. Legend maintains that, when urged to show mercy in Hungary, Schwarzenberg replied, 'Yes, it is a good idea, but we'll have a little hanging first'. Although the remark is apocryphal, it conveys the sad essentials of a policy of repression to which Francis Joseph weakly assented. The requirement that death sentences needed endorsement from Vienna was revoked; and it was not until the last days of October that the Emperor curbed Haynau's powers, insisting (despite the general's further protests) that there should be no more executions. By then 114 Hungarians had been shot or hanged. Among them were thirteen generals, executed at Arad on 6 October: those who surrendered to the Russians were hanged, while those who gave up their swords to the Austrians had the privilege of being shot. General Görgei, under the personal protection of Tsar Nicholas, escaped with banishment to Carinthia; he was still alive when Francis Joseph began his last year on the throne. The Emperor hardened himself against appeals for clemency not only from the former Palatine, Archduke Stephen, but even from his brother Maximilian. The execution of Count Lajos Batthyány, prime minister of Hungary under the April Laws, was particularly resented. More fortunate were 75 Hungarian magnates who had safely fled the country and were symbolically hanged in effigy. Among them was Count Gyula Andrássy.

Görgei capitulated at Vilagos on 13 August. Fifteen days later the Republic of St Mark surrendered to Radetzky, and the Austrians re-entered Venice, which had been tightly blockaded for almost a year, enduring a steady – though erratic – bombardment since early May.

Radetzky, who had twice concluded armistices with Piedmont and on both occasions showed a wise moderation, did not exact vengeance on the city or its defenders, for he had more foresight than either Haynau or Schwarzenberg. Alone among the military paladins the veteran Field Marshal's reputation was untarnished. In Venice his qualities were not appreciated; only a single Italian – a priest – was in the Piazza San Marco when he made his formal entry into the city. But in Vienna, where war with the Italians stirred deeper feelings than the civil war with Hungary, Radetzky remained a popular idol. On the last day of August in 1848 a 'Grand Impressive Victory Festival ... in Honour of our Courageous Army in Italy and to benefit the Wounded Soldiers' had been held, and for the occasion Johann Strauss 'the Elder' composed a march dedicated to the man of the hour. When, thirteen months later, the capital honoured the twice victorious Field Marshal with a banquet in the Hofburg, it was expected that Strauss would provide a 'Radetzky Banquet March' to complement this earlier work. That second march was never completed; for Strauss fell gravely ill with scarlet fever and died three days later. But the most famous and liveliest of his marches was played at the celebratory banquet; and in the years ahead it was played again and again. No tune became more popular with the Emperor than the *Radetzky March*.

There was a serious purpose behind Radetzky's visit to the capital; for the imperial army needed re-structuring now that it was under the Emperor's personal command and serving soldiers deplored the influence on Francis Joseph of Count Grünne, a staff officer who had seen no active service. To their relief, Radetzky's prestige enabled him to persuade the Emperor to appoint Baron Hess as Quartermaster-General and his personal chief-of-staff, a post the Field Marshal assumed would check the ascendancy of the military chancellery and prevent the rapid promotion of Grünne's nominees to high command. 'Hess is clever, industrious and absolutely convinced that control of the army should be in my hands', Francis Joseph reported to his mother, in a note which shows how well Radetzky had emphasized the qualities most likely to appeal to his sovereign. But, although the Emperor, his QMG and the head of his military chancellery all worked in harmony for some months, Hess was never able to dislodge Grünne entirely, for the Count remained a favourite of Archduchess Sophie. She approved of Grünne's innate conservatism, shared his anti-Hungarian prejudices, and was glad if his devout Catholicism strengthened Francis Joseph's personal religiosity. The Archduchess's whims had little impact on day-to-day politics – Schwarzenberg made certain of that. But at Court it was different. Grünne and his circle would refer to Sophie privately as 'our Empress', and she basked in her status as First Lady of the Monarchy.

In one respect her tastes left a lasting mark on inner Vienna at this time. The private apartments of the Hofburg, though perfectly adequate for the Emperors Francis and Ferdinand, had long seemed drab to her eyes. Once peace and order returned to the Monarchy, Francis Joseph willingly agreed to her suggestion that she should supervise their redecoration. By the following spring the inner rooms of the Hofburg were as impeccably baroque as she could induce mid-century craftsmen to design them. For the Archduchess, dignity could never be compromised for the sake of modernity.

When, in November 1849, Baron von Kübeck was invited to dine with the Emperor and his parents, the Hofburg apartments were not ready and the family was at Schönbrunn. Kübeck, the painstaking civil servant who became Metternich's financial counsellor, was not impressed by the table-talk that evening: 'the apotheosis of the army', he wrote gloomily in his journal. Yet can he really have been surprised? Schwarzenberg was himself a soldier as well as a diplomat. He believed that, even if other institutions failed the Habsburgs, the Emperor should always be able to depend upon his army to maintain order at home and give purpose and meaning to the demands of Austria's diplomatic envoys abroad. Francis Joseph, for his part, had made it clear within a few weeks of his accession that, as he regarded the army as the most important manifestation of state power, he would keep it under his personal control.

From exile in England and Belgium, Metternich's letters criticized Schwarzenberg's inclination to rattle the sword: why had he failed to give the Emperor an alternative to the military regimes which still controlled the great centres of the Monarchy? In the winter of 1849–50 martial law prevailed in Prague and Cracow as well as in Vienna; Radetzky had been re-appointed military and civilian Governor of Lombardy-Venetia on 17 October; Haynau was confirmed as military Governor of Hungary on the same day, with the country divided into six military districts, each under the control of a general. A similar administration functioned in Transylvania, while from Zagreb Jellaçić continued to control Croatia and its frontier marchlands, although mistrusted by Vienna for his 'Illyrianism'. The Stadion Constitution was neither scrapped nor implemented. It was ignored.

For Schwarzenberg such matters were overshadowed by an unresolved problem threatening war along yet another border: how should the Emperor respond to the German Question and, in particular, to the mounting rivalry between Prussia and Austria? Germany's national revolution, symbolized by the attempts of the Frankfurt Parliament to draw up a constitution for a united Germany, lost all impetus when in April 1849 King Frederick William IV of Prussia turned down the offer of the crown of a liberal 'small' Germany, which would have excluded the Germanic lands of the Habsburg Monarchy. Throughout the summer Tsar Nicholas I, an anxious observer of all that was happening in central Europe, assumed that General von Radowitz (Prussia's prime minister) and Schwarzenberg would both wish to restore the old German Confederation which had functioned in the Metternich era. In this he was mistaken. Schwarzenberg at first hoped for a Greater Austrian Confederation, one which would recognize the pre-eminence of the Habsburgs over all central Europe, Germanic and non-Germanic. Radowitz, on the other hand, favoured the establishment of an enlarged German Confederation, organized in two loosely integrated units: there would be a small 'Germany', dominated by Prussia, and the Habsburg Monarchy, serving as an ally and economic partner. To advance this policy Radowitz set up an embryonic confederation, the Erfurt Union, in March 1850. Radowitz's initiative was unpopular with the rulers of Bavaria, Saxony, Hanover, and Württemberg as well as with the government in Vienna, and yet for several months it seemed possible that Prussia would risk a war to impose the Erfurt Union on Germany, assuming that Francis Joseph could not spare troops from Hungary and Italy to meet the threat.

At heart Schwarzenberg was more concerned over the shaky state of Austria's finances than over the possibility of defeat by Prussia. Already military expenditure was twice as high as in the last years of the Metternich era. A long war would bring state bankruptcy and was out of the question, but in the autumn of 1850 he seemed willing to take a gamble on a brief campaign: there was even some skirmishing between Prussian and Austrian units in a dispute over the right to give 'protection' to the Elector of Hesse against his more rebellious subjects. Ultimately, however, both Frederick William IV and Francis Joseph shrank from such a 'war of brothers': Radowitz was dismissed, and Schwarzenberg held in check by the young Emperor's firm resolve to keep the peace. On paper the Austrians gained a diplomatic victory; for a compromise settlement was reached at Olmütz, in late November: the Erfurt Union was dissolved and a new Prussian prime minister, General von Manteuffel, agreed to Schwarzenberg's sponsorship of a series of conferences in Dresden to discuss the future of Germany.

But at Dresden Schwarzenberg was convincingly defeated. The other German states, though wary of Prussia, equally mistrusted an army-run Austria: they rejected proposals from Vienna for a strong executive authority to be set up by the German Confederation and they refused to allow the Austrian Empire, as a single entity, to join the Zollverein, the German Customs Union. The best Schwarzenberg could achieve was a

Prusso-Austrian mutual defence pact, signed on 16 May 1851, valid for three years and renewable thereafter.

When the Dresden Conference opened in late December 1850 Schwarzenberg had urged his Emperor to propose the establishment of an all-German parliament. But Francis Joseph was aghast at the suggestion and brought his prime minister sharply to heel, and during these long months of confrontation with Prussia he became increasingly uneasy over Schwarzenberg's general policies. He would always defend the good name of the army, dismissing complaints of harsh conduct as malicious gossip, and Schwarzenberg found that, over military matters, he invariably met a stubborn hostility to change. In particular the Emperor long chose to give Haynau the benefit of the doubt when the prime minister denounced the Governor-General's ruthless policies in Hungary. Reluctantly Schwarzenberg had to turn to Grünne for support on this issue, knowing that the Count's duties as military adjutant ensured he was in constant attendance on the Emperor and that casual conversation would influence him more than matters raised in any formal audience. Haynau had been Radetzky's nominee rather than Grünne's, and the Count held no brief for him. The joint campaign succeeded. In June 1850 Haynau was abruptly recalled from Hungary.

Yet, though Grünne and Schwarzenberg might ally against an independently-minded general, their political views were poles apart. Despite the disdain with which Schwarzenberg had sent the Kremsier Reichstag about its non-business, he looked upon representative institutions with limited powers as safety-valves for an over-centralized monarchical system. But he knew he was inexperienced in domestic affairs and, with Stadion out of his mind and in an asylum, he became dependent for technical advice on one-time liberal reformers like Alexander Bach and Baron von Schmerling, men whose presence was barely tolerated at Court, even though they were by now firm upholders of the established order. No one was more hostile to the ministers than the egregious Grünne. For, while Schwarzenberg still paid lip-service to constitutionalism, Grünne was at heart an absolutist. It was natural for Grünne to encourage Francis Joseph to indulge his current inclination and create a Russian-style autocracy in Vienna.

The Emperor never intended to put the Stadion constitution into full operation. But he was prepared to establish a Reichsrat, the nominated council of advisers which Stadion had envisaged (and which strongly resembled the Tsar's Council of State). In late October 1850 he entrusted Kübeck with drafting statutes to define the form and purpose of the Reichsrat; and on 19 November he was more specific. Kübeck was told that the Emperor wished the Reichsrat 'to supersede, and in some ways replace, the Constitution'; the advisory council would thus afford the Monarchy a firm basis of government, which would encourage foreign bankers to give Austria the credit essential for the reconstruction of the Empire after years of upheaval. This made good sense to Kübeck, and he dutifully did all that was expected of him. Understandably, his ideas provoked strong opposition from the prime minister and his colleagues in the government. The draft statutes were, in effect, a constitutional counter-revolution and discussions continued for several months. It was clear that the nominated Reichsrat would abolish ministerial responsibility which, so Kübeck argued, was a pernicious concept rooted in popular sovereignty. Once again ministers would become mere servants of the Emperor, reduced to the status of departmental chiefs, as at the height of the Metternich era. So drastic were these proposals that, in the last week of June 1851, Kübeck noted in his diary that Francis Joseph was 'apprehensive of the possible resignation of Prince Schwarzenberg'. But if he went, who would take his place? Kübeck, the provincial tailor's son, was already the Emperor's choice as chairman of the Reichsrat. There was, however, as court and politicians well knew, a more illustrious elder statesman hovering in the wings. News had just reached Vienna that Prince Metternich, though not yet on Austrian soil, was back on his estate in the Rhineland.

Francis Joseph was spared the need to look for a new chief minister. For, though other members of the government left office, both Schwarzenberg and Bach were prepared to stay on, accepting most of the proposed changes. Four decrees, printed in the official gazette on 26 August 1851, revoked basic reforms conceded at Olmütz: out went ministerial responsibility and innovations in municipal administration and the legal system; while a Reichsrat committee would re-assess the remaining promises of the Stadion constitution. Francis Joseph's own views may be gathered from a letter sent on that Tuesday to his mother: 'When you read the *Wiener Zeitung* you will see that we have taken a big step forward', he wrote, 'We have thrown all that constitutional stuff overboard, and Austria has only one Master. Now one must work even harder. After three years we have almost reached the point we wanted to, thank God'. For a young ruler, just twenty-one and only now trimming a thin moustache for the first time, the tone of the letter rang with astonishing self-confidence.

Some of Francis Joseph's optimism derived from the reports with which Schwarzenberg regularly fed him. More than once Kübeck's journal grumbles at the prime minister's glowing accounts of progress in the previously disaffected regions of the Monarchy. But the Emperor did not entirely rely on his diligent desk reading. He was by now travelling increasingly across his empire: northwards to Prague and the Bohemian cities, to all the German-Austrian provinces, and, more than once, southwards to Trieste, Lombardy and Venetia. 'The farther I went from Vienna, the better I found the attitude', he wrote to his mother from Trieste, 'In Graz quite good and calm. In Laibach [Ljubljana] excellent, just as though there had been no revolution, and here all is enthusiastically Austrian.' Only in the capital was he uneasy: 'Here the mood grows worse every day, but the people are sufficiently cunning to avoid an armed clash', he told his mother in September 1850, 'On Sunday a great church parade on the glacis, just to let the dear Viennese see that troops and cannon still exist.' And yet, even when living among these 'cunning people', he found moments of relaxation: no one could recall a more light-hearted carnival than in February 1851, with the Emperor continuing to gain real pleasure from dancing at the numerous balls. At times he liked to escape from it all to Laxenburg, while Ischl remained a favourite retreat. He found solace from the problems of government by stalking chamois or stag in the mountains and using his sharp eye and steady hand to bring down the black alpine wood grouse he would often hunt at sunrise.

By now his brother and one-time companion Maximilian had decided to serve as a naval officer; he made a villa above Trieste his home. The Habsburgs had long neglected their fleet and Maximilian sought to interest the Emperor in the service, either by letter or by word of mouth when he was on leave. In May 1850 Francis Joseph spent a 'delightful night' at sea off Venice and he was with the Adriatic squadron again in the following March as well as visiting Venice in September 1851, during a protracted tour of the Italian provinces. But an unfortunate experience in March 1852 confirmed his prejudices against the navy. While sailing in the northern Adriatic aboard a steam-powered warship, the Emperor and his brother were caught in a violent storm which raged for twenty-six hours and wrecked one of the smaller vessels in the squadron. The naval authorities were blamed for putting to sea at such a time of unruly winds and waves and thus endangering the lives of both their sovereign and his brother, the heir-apparent. To Maximilian's intense chagrin, the navy was thereafter treated as an auxiliary of the army, despised by the veteran generals at the war ministry and at Court. Only in the autumn of 1854, when the twenty-two year old Archduke was himself promoted to Rear-Admiral and appointed commander-in-chief, were serious attempts made to modernize the fleet.

While the Emperor was in northern Italy in September 1851, the Metternichs returned to Vienna after three years of exile. Francis Joseph paid an unheralded private visit to the ex-Chancellor at his villa on Sunday, 3 October, and Melanie arrived home from Mass to find him 'asking Clement's advice on a great many topics'. But the Emperor was readier at asking advice than at heeding it. Shortly before Christmas he sent Metternich Kübeck's latest draft proposals for the Reichsrat. An accompanying note, from 'your faithful pupil and friend', invited comments; and, in his leisurely way, Metternich began to prepare a 2,000 word memorandum, urging the setting up of provincial consultative diets, from which spokesmen would be chosen to serve in the Reichsrat.

He was still working on the memorandum when it was overtaken by events. For Francis Joseph was in too much of a hurry to await the considered verdict of the doyen of elder statesmen. On New Year's Eve – Sylvesterabend in German-Austria – the so-called 'Sylvester Patent' was made public. It comprised three pronouncements, in the form of a message from the Emperor to his chief minister: the Constitution of March 1849 was abolished, without ever having been put into practice; 'fundamental rights', conceded by the Emperor under threat of revolution, were annulled (though freedom of worship was guaranteed and no attempt was made to re-impose feudal obligations on the peasantry); and centralization of the administrative system was completed by the abolition of all locally elected councils and the application of Austrian codes of law to every part of the Monarchy, including Hungary. Now at last Francis Joseph had achieved his first ambition. He ruled as a benevolent soldier autocrat, Austria's Tsar in his own right, not the nominee of a military camarilla. In St Petersburg the Russian Tsar warmly approved. On the desk of his St Petersburg study, Nicholas I kept a statuette of the young man whom he liked to regard as not so much Metternich's pupil as his own.

Schwarzenberg adapted himself to this newest shift of constitutional emphasis with no great heart-searching. He remained prime minister, as of right. Everyone knew he was more interested in statecraft than in forms of government. At fifty-one he was still looking to the future. With railways and the electric telegraph linking Vienna more closely to other capitals, he dreamt of seeing the city accepted as the natural centre of Great Power diplomacy. But the strain of government was taking more out of him than he recognized. The Metternichs, the Radetzkys and, indeed, the Habsburgs themselves enjoyed longevity; the Schwarzenberg family did not. On 5 April 1852 he was felled by an apoplectic stroke as he buckled himself into a tight-fitting hussar uniform for a court ball.

Francis Joseph genuinely mourned the soldier-statesman. Over half a century later, he recalled Schwarzenberg as 'my greatest minister'. A well-known lithograph shows him kneeling beside the deathbed, with Archduke Charles Ludwig, Count Grünne and Alexander Bach sharing the grief of their sovereign, who is said to have been in tears. 'I must make an effort not to lose my composure', he wrote next morning to his mother, who was in Graz; 'I must uphold the principle of order, which cannot be allowed to sink into the grave with this great man.' These were fine sentiments, no doubt; more practical ones followed. 'Now I shall have to do more things myself, for I cannot rely on anybody as I used to rely on Schwarzenberg', the Archduchess was told. And in a revealing afterthought her son added, 'Perhaps that is all to the good'. For the next seven years Francis Joseph was to rule without a prime minister.

Chapter 5

MARRIAGE

For Archduchess Sophie the death of Felix Schwarzenberg intensified a personal dilemma of which she had been uneasily conscious over many months. She knew she fulfilled the role of First Lady in the Empire excellently, adding a lustre to Court life unknown for thirty years. The heads of distinguished families served as Grand Master of the Household, Grand Chamberlain, Master of the Horse, and so on; but it was the Archduchess who made certain that the Court machine purred smoothly. The Emperor's daily timetable was submitted to her for approval: she said where and when meals were to be served and, in the last resort, she decided such tricky matters as the guest list at the imperial table or the floral decorations for State and Court Balls during carnival time. She ensured that a new and young Emperor rode in smartly refurbished carriages, with coachmen and postilions once more elegant in the yellow imperial livery, for she believed in parading the triumph of counter-revolution for all Vienna to observe, and to accept as right and natural. These tasks would increase if her son's insistence on being both head of the army and head of the government reduced still more the time he gave to the outer trappings of royalty.

Yet the Archduchess was only an Acting First Lady. Her son would soon have to marry, as she sadly recognized. If the future of the Monarchy looked assured in 1851–2, what of the future of the dynasty? Had well-placed guns killed both her elder sons at Raab in the summer of 1848, or had they perished at sea in that storm in the northern Adriatic, the task of moulding an Emperor would have begun all over again, with the succession passing to the Archduke Charles Ludwig. This was a challenge no bereaved mother could contemplate. She remained deeply concerned over Francis Joseph's safety. His courage was admirable: unflinchingly he set out on long visits to inner Hungary, Transylvania and Croatia soon after Schwarzenberg's death. But was this headstrong bravery foolhardy? He seemed at times to be courting assassination. Sophie, despite her superficial silliness of sentiment, was a realist at heart. There was no doubt in her mind that Francis Joseph needed a bride and children to safeguard the succession. The intrusion on his daily life of family responsibilities might mellow that stern sense of duty to the state which made the Emperor so much more like an institution than the father of his peoples.

In adolescence Francis Joseph had absorbed Catholic doctrines on the sanctity of family life, with moral precepts given him by Rauscher or Colombi and endorsed by his mother. Like most children of his day, whether noble or commoner, he received no sex instruction whatsoever, and he may well have been surprised by some aspects of barrack life when he was first attached to the Hussars. But he was a normal and healthy full-blooded young man and in the following winter it was left to Count Grünne to rectify lapses in the Emperor's education, with the apparent approval of the Archduchess. Gossip later elaborated a *Giselle*-esque sequence of secret assignations in deepest Bohemia during army manoeuvres. Perhaps there was some basis for these tales but, if so, the girl whom Grünne vetted for his sovereign would have been a 'hygienically pure' countess rather than a simple, starry-eyed peasant Whatever the truth about these well-regulated escapades, it is at least clear that Francis Joseph was not without some sexual experience before he set out in earnest to look for a wife.

Inwardly he had already convinced himself that he would choose a companion whose charm and qualities appealed to him alone. He would, he thought, ignore the promptings of his mother or her trusted agents at Court; and, almost inevitably, his first attachment startled both the Archduchess and Grünne. For, at the time of Schwarzenberg's death, he was captivated by a beautiful young widow, Princess Elizabeth of Modena, a first cousin five months his junior in age but already the mother of a two year old daughter. What alarmed Sophie was not the Princess's tragically brief experience of married life but her childhood background, for she was a daughter of Archduke Joseph, the long-serving Palatine of Hungary; she was therefore a half-sister of that Palatine-Archduke Stephen, whose fair-mindedness towards the Hungarians had caused Grünne to resign from his service. Briefly Francis Joseph's infatuation for his cousin seemed likely to soften his attitude towards his Hungarian subjects. In the spring of 1852 he appeared at a state ball in Hungarian Hussar's uniform and allowed the Csardas to be danced at Court in Vienna for the first time in five years. But the romantic attachment did not last out the summer. It is probable that the entrenched anti-Hungarian prejudices of Sophie and the Court were too formidable a challenge for the young widow to face; two years later she married another first cousin,

Archduke Charles's second son, and settled down happily enough in Moravia.

In the autumn Francis Joseph visited Berlin. At Charlottenburg he met the King of Prussia's niece, Anna. Politically a Prussian marriage appealed to the Austrian foreign minister, Count von Buol-Schauenstein, and his mentor, Metternich; dynastic links would ease Austro-Prussian relations after the tension of the Schwarzenberg years. But by Christmas it was clear the Prussian marriage project was a non-starter. There were three grave obstacles to any such union: Anna's staunch Lutheranism; her prior betrothal to the widower Margrave of Hesse; and the fierce opposition to an Austrian connection of the old guard of Prussian conservatives. With Berlin off the list, Archduchess Sophie encouraged her son to go to Dresden and court Princess Sidonia, one of the six sisters of his close friend and cousin, Albert of Saxony. But Sidonia's health was poor and, in contrast to Elizabeth of Modena and Anna of Prussia, she seemed awkward and low-spirited: there was no Empress in the making to be found at Dresden.

After these setbacks it was natural for Sophie to return to the fond hopes of earlier years and dream of arranging yet another Habsburg-Wittelsbach marriage. Letters to her sister Ludovika, in Bavaria, gave due attention to what Sophie believed were Francis Joseph's likes and dislikes in a woman: graceful movement, a ready smile, lightness of laughter and, above all, confident horsemanship: 'There is nothing the Emperor admires more in a woman than an elegant seat on a horse', reported Sophie. At once Ludovika insisted that her elder daughter, Helen, should take more riding lessons. But 'Néné' would never match the skills of her sister 'Sisi' in the saddle.

Francis Joseph had shown no interest in his Bavarian cousins since their brief visit to Innsbruck, and he does not seem to have suspected his mother of rekindling the Wittelsbach flame that winter. During the first months of 1853 he was again up to his eyes in desk-work: there were long despatches for him to consider from London, Paris, St Petersburg and Constantinople over the evident weakness of Ottoman rule in the Balkans, and in particular the harsh treatment of Christian communities in Bosnia; and there was a renewal of Italian nationalistic feeling in Milan. He remained in residence at the Hofburg after the Carnival season was over, taking regular walks around the old fortifications for exercise in the afternoons. It was while he was strolling beside one of the outer bastions on the second Sunday in February, that Janos Libenyi, a twenty-one year old tailor's apprentice, attacked him from behind, thrusting a long knife into his collar. Fortunately the heavy golden covering embroidered on the stiff collar of the Emperor's uniform deflected the blow, saving him from death but leaving him bleeding from a deep cut. A civilian passer-by, Dr Joseph Ettenreich, came to his assistance while his military aide, Count Maximilian O'Donnell, seized Libenyi and held him until police guards took him into custody: 'Long live Kossuth', Libenyi shouted (in Magyar), as he was led away. Francis Joseph insisted that the police should not maltreat him on the spot, but when the young Hungarian was condemned to death, there was no reprieve and he was hanged on Simmering Heath. Characteristically the Emperor granted a small pension to his would-be assassin's mother.

The attempt on Francis Joseph's life aroused widespread sympathy for him in Vienna. The churches were crowded that evening as rumours spread through the city and suburbs. Archduke Maximilian, serving with the naval squadron at Trieste, was so alarmed by the news that he hurried to the capital; he found his brother in bed with a high fever, but so angry at the sudden arrival of the heir-presumptive in his bedroom that he gave him a good dressing-down for leaving the fleet without permission. Despite this rebuff, the Archduke was deeply affected by the attempt on his brother's life and launched an appeal for subscriptions to build a thanksgiving church, close to the site of Libenyi's attack. Maximilian did not live to see the church completed, but the tapering twin spires of the neo-Gothic Votivkirche remain a familiar feature of Vienna's skyline, a graceful monument to the uncertainties of those first years of the reign.

The Emperor's narrow escape from death stirred sentiments of loyalty in the capital as well as in more distant provincial cities, where his popularity had never been in doubt. Despite his courage and fortitude on the day of the attack, he suffered from delayed shock and was weak from the loss of blood. It was almost a month before he was able to leave the Hofburg. When, on 12 March, he drove in a Victoria carriage to St Stephen's Cathedral for a service of thanksgiving at his recovery, crowds along the street gave him an enthusiastic reception. It is said that, on this occasion, he resolved to relax the military regime which still ordered affairs in both Vienna and Prague, but the restrictions of martial law were not finally lifted until early September.

Francis Joseph was soon himself again. In the second week of May he was host to King Leopold I of the Belgians, who had known Vienna before and during the Congress. The Emperor's bearing and personality made a deep impression on the King, a shrewd judge of character. 'There is much sense and courage in his warm blue eye, and it is not without a very amiable merriment when there is occasion for it', Leopold wrote to his niece Queen Victoria on returning to Brussels, 'He is slight and very graceful, but even in the mêlée of dancers and Archdukes, and all in uniform, he may always be distinguished as the *Chef*' [dominant man].

'This struck me more than anything, as now at Vienna the dancing is also that general mêlée which renders waltzing most difficult. The manners are excellent and free from pompousness or awkwardness of any kind, simple, and when he is graciously disposed, as he was to me, *sehr herzlich und naturlich*' (very cordial and unaffected) ... 'I think he may be severe *si l'occasion se présente*' (if called upon to be so); 'he has something very *muthig*' (mettlesome; self-assured). 'We were several times surrounded by people of all classes, and he was certainly quite at their mercy, but I never saw his little *muthig* expression changed either by being pleased or alarmed.'

Franz Grillparzer, with a poet's instinct for deeply felt sentiments, celebrated the Emperor's escape by addressing a short ode of thanks-giving, not to the wounded convalescent, but to his mother. Libenyi's knife thrust on 18 February shocked the Archduchess; in the last years of her life she never let the anniversary pass by without giving thanks in her diary for her son's preservation that Sunday. The attack intensified her determination to see her son married soon; family life, she believed, would domesticate the imperial institution, thereby making it more acceptable and secure. In June an invitation was sent to Duchess Ludovika in her summer residence at Possenhofen. Sophie suggested that her sister might leave the delights of the Starnbergersee for a few days in August and bring her two elder daughters through the mountains to the Salzkammergut to help celebrate their cousin's twenty-third birthday. The roads were not difficult in summer; and, as it happened, Ischl was actually nearer to Possenhofen than to Vienna.

Despite his insistence that he would not be pushed into marriage, on this occasion Francis Joseph welcomed his mother's initiative. As he regarded himself as the paramount German prince, he had never seriously considered looking outside the German dynastic system for a bride, for his passing infatuation with his widowed Habsburg cousin seems basically to have sprung from a rush of carnival blood to the head. At nineteen his Bavarian cousin Helen was the right age for him; close consanguinity never troubled him or his mother – doubts over such matters could be set aside by papal dispensation. At Innsbruck she had meant nothing to him, a sharp-featured and slightly morose youngster, with little enough to say for herself. Yet by now there seemed nothing but praise for Néné's qualities, even from the Austrian envoys in Munich. So eager was Francis Joseph for the meeting that he insisted on having the speediest horses from the Schönbrunn stables saddled for the journey to the Salz-kammergut. With Grünne as his travelling companion he reached Ischl in nineteen hours rather than the usual day and a half.

By contrast, Duchess Ludovika and the Princesses Helen and Elizabeth arrived an hour and a half late, for it had been a wet August in the mountains, and rain and mud slowed down their coachmen. Even so, they outpaced the carriage containing their luggage boxes and Ludovika was travel weary and ill-at-ease when, on the afternoon of 16 August, she brought her daughters to join the Archduchess and her sons for tea, with Ludovika's elder sister, Queen Elise of Prussia (Elizabeth's godmother) also there. Socially it was not the easiest of family gatherings. Néné, fully aware of the plans made for her, succumbed to an embarrassed shyness and could only exchange conventional pleasantries with Francis Joseph. Sisi, on the other hand, had no such high expectations to inhibit her. She behaved naturally, her oval face alive with changing expression as she speedily took up the childhood friendship with Charles Ludwig which so amused the family at Innsbruck five years before. The tense awkwardness of a contrived reunion thawed. Yet even before dinner was served that evening both the devoted Charles Ludwig and Sisi herself realized that the Emperor had grown tired of small talk with Néné. Instead, he was fascinated by her sister's untarnished elfin qualities, by the long auburn hair and the challenge of those dancing eyes, quizzically unfathomable beneath straight, black eyebrows. Throughout the meal he seemed to be looking intensely at Sisi, who had always hated to be drawn into the limelight and lapsed into a silence. That evening Charles Ludwig, with a sad pang of jealousy, reproached his mother: 'Mama, Franzi likes Sisi very much, far more than he does Néné. You'll see; he will choose her rather than the elder one.' This, the Archduchess thought, was sheer nonsense: 'What an idea!', she replied, 'As if he would look twice at that little imp!'

But Charles Ludwig was right. When next day Francis Joseph saw his mother before breakfast he could talk of nothing except Sisi's natural charm. The Archduchess's diary – with these pages more faded than any others, as if they had been read and re-read time and time again – still conveys her son's excitement that morning. She urged him to be in no hurry, not to rush matters, for there was no need for an immediate betrothal. It was no use; her son had fallen irretrievably in love with his cousin. Even in the sober light of a rainy morning, the passion was still there; and in seeking to refute his mother's arguments, he sought to express himself in a poetic lyricism remote from every earlier experience in his life. The words are trite and the imagery ludicrous, but there is no questioning the sincerity of his emotions. He could not accept his mother's contention that she was too young for him. 'No, see how sweet Sisi is!', he insisted, 'She is as fresh as a newly peeled almond, and what a splendid crown of hair frames such a vision! How can anyone help loving such tender eyes and lips like strawberries!'. The Archduchess was reluctant to give up the fight. 'Don't you find Helen intelligent, and with a beautiful slim figure, too?' she claims to have asked her son. 'Yes', came the reply, 'but, although she is pretty and agreeable enough, she is serious and tongue-tied. Now, Sisi- Sisi – there is something really attractive; that modest girlishness; and yet such high spirits!' The Emperor was not infatuated. He was bewitched.

Not that Elizabeth consciously strove to enchant him. She was puzzled and surprised by his attention. At the first ball in Ischl, which both Archduchess Sophie and Duchess Ludovika had expected to be a triumph for Helen, it was with Sisi that the Emperor insisted on dancing the cotillion; and he presented her with every bouquet. Her governess asked her if she was surprised by this gesture: 'No', she replied, 'only embarrassed.'

By the morning of Francis Joseph's birthday, the Archduchess acknowledged defeat. Carefully planned dynastic marriages had a habit of going slightly awry: fourteen years previously Queen Victoria chose 'dear Albert' rather than his elder brother, Ernest (whom her half-sister had thought more suited for her); and now Francis Joseph was attracted to Elizabeth with a not dissimilar stubborn intensity of passion. Yet there was an all important difference between the two royal romances: Albert of Saxe-Coburg was twenty at the time of his betrothal, mature beyond his years and trained to assume responsibilities greater than any son of a minor German princeling might be expected to encounter; Elizabeth of Bavaria, who would not be sixteen until Christmas Eve, still romped like a child, and was, as yet, totally uncoached in the role of Empress. Francis Joseph brushed aside these objections and others, too. By the time he had spent most of his birthday in her company and sat beside her as he was serenaded by Tyrolean singers in the early evening, he was convinced he had met his bride. All he would concede in conversation with his mother was that 'My position is such a difficult one that God knows it can be no pleasure to share it with me.' He insisted that no one should put pressure on the young Elizabeth to accept him as a husband. She must weigh up such matters herself, he said, with what he assumed to be a kindly understanding of his cousin's dilemma.

Yet he had not even begun to understand her temperament. When Francis Joseph was fifteen he could pen a diary entry regretting the speedy passage of time, which left him with only a few years in which to mend his ways and complete his education. Happily, at that same age, Elizabeth was untroubled by so priggish a conscience, though she remained dutifully devout in her strictly religious observance. But Elizabeth was a puzzling girl, with a character much more high-powered than her aunt appreciated. She was a romantic, already given to writing verses which were restlessly pining rather than sentimental in form. When happy she was young enough to radiate a spontaneous joy in living, a natural antidote to Francis Joseph's cool, disciplined professionalism. But she was a creature of impulse. Often her response to events or to meeting people was either a passionate enthusiasm or a long and childish hatred. At Ischl, in these perplexing days she needed good advice. 'Yes, I am already fond of the Emperor', she told her governess, 'But if only he were not an Emperor!' she sighed.

Her mother and her aunt, though disappointed that Helen had been brushed aside, were too committed to the idea of a Bavarian marriage not to encourage Elizabeth; and Sophie, ignoring the truculent set of her niece's stubborn chin, thought Sisi still young enough to be moulded into character. The Archduchess carefully noted her response to all that was happening: her resentment of the hovering presence of the sardonic Count Grünne beside the Emperor on their expeditions, and the moments when she seemed awkward, diffident and shy; and Sophie's journal also records Elizabeth's significant reply to the good wishes of Countess Esterhazy, the Court Mistress of the Robes: 'I shall need a great deal of indulgence at first'. Everyone at Ischl spoke of the Princess's marvellous good fortune. Had her father, an eccentric and wildly independent hedonist, accompanied his daughters to the Salzkammergut he might have given wise counsel to his favourite child. But would he have advised her to turn her back on the greatest marriage in Catholic Europe? As it was, he was consulted by telegram. Willingly, he gave his approval.

Officially the betrothal was made public at the end of Mass in Ischl's parish church. Francis Joseph led Elizabeth by the hand to the altar steps, presented her to the priest as 'my future wife', and asked for his blessing. The *Wiener Zeitung* carried the news next day, prompting a rash of speculative artistry by painters who had never seen the Bavarian princess but cashed in on local knowledge of the Salzkammergut to give their work scenic verisimilitude. For the rest of August the Emperor lingered happily at Ischl, on fine days showing Sisi the countryside he particularly liked. 'It is lovely to see such youthful radiance shining in such a wonderful landscape', Queen Elise remarked after the whole party dined beside the Wolfgangsee.

'It was hard and depressing to make the leap from the earthly paradise of Ischl to a desk-bound existence and masses of state papers. with all the cares and troubles they bring me', sighed Francis Joseph in a letter to his mother as soon as he was back in Vienna. The romantic idyl had come in the midst of a grave international crisis, with Russian troops threatening to invade the Ottoman Empire and controlling the lower waters of the Danube. Throughout the eight months of his engagement to Elizabeth, it was the Emperor's misfortune to be plagued by elaborate memoranda, some expressed at great length by the indomitable elder statesman, Metternich. To what extent should Austria assert independence of Russia? Was it possible to benefit from dynastic goodwill without lessening the Empire's protective influence over Catholic communities in the western Balkans?

The Tsar gave him little peace. Nicholas was even willing to travel down from Warsaw for several days of top-level talks. Accordingly, less than a month after saying farewell to Elizabeth at Ischl, Francis Joseph was back in northern Moravia, riding beside the Tsar as the two sovereigns inspected troops encamped outside Olmütz, and their foreign ministers sought compromise solutions of the long-term disputes between Russia and her Ottoman neighbour. There followed a brief, and unconvincing, show of solidarity by the three eastern autocrats in Warsaw, where the Emperor found the King of Prussia as reluctant as himself to join the Tsar in a formal military alliance. Then, as soon as he could decently escape from Poland, Francis Joseph was on his way to Bavaria to see the Princess at Schloss Possenhofen, her much-loved home on the Starnbergersee. With her family he would go into residence in Munich, where he could pay his respects to yet another cousin, Maximilian II, King of Bavaria.

Possenhofen – 'Possi' as the place was affectionately called – remained tucked away from the outside world; and this seclusion enabled Francis Joseph and Elizabeth to find even more satisfaction in each other's company than at Ischl. It was while riding beside the Starnbergersee that the Emperor discovered for the first time how fine a horsewoman he was marrying, as skilled a rider sidesaddle as anyone in Europe. The brief visit to Munich was more trying: Elizabeth could not disguise her boredom at having to receive the whole diplomatic corps, assembled to offer felicitations on her forthcoming marriage; and when the Emperor and Princess entered their box at the opera house, the reception was so rapturous that Sisi was overcome with shyness and sought to sink back into the shadows rather than face the appraising eyes of Munich high society. However, at the Court Ball on the following night she carried herself with a natural dignity and poise. Francis Joseph remained enchanted by her, although he was surprised at the casual indiscipline of life at his fiancée's beloved Possi. The tone of his letters to Archduchess Sophie was ecstatic: 'I love Sisi more every day and feel more certain than ever that there is no other woman who would suit me as well as she', he wrote with refreshing simplicity.

He returned to Vienna in the last week of October to find the international crisis intensifying day by day. Already the Russian and Ottoman armies were in conflict along the lower reaches of the Danube, and on the last day of November a squadron from Sebastopol destroyed the Sultan's fleet at Sinope. No one doubted that France and Britain would soon become involved in a war to deny Russia naval mastery over the Black Sea and the Straits. The Austrians were subjected to intense diplomatic pressure from both sides, and the Emperor presided over a succession of cabinet meetings to discuss ways of safeguarding commercial and strategic interests along the Danube, while stopping short of a war which would have brought the Monarchy close to bankruptcy. Yet, despite these worries, Francis Joseph was able to reach Munich in the small hours of 21 December, in good time to celebrate Elizabeth's sixteenth birthday.

On this occasion the couple exchanged portraits, each having been painted on horseback. And for Christmas itself there were flowers brought by express courier from the hothouse conservatories at Schönbrunn, together with a green parrot – a present which especially delighted Elizabeth, and which she was to insist on being brought back to her in Vienna before her wedding. Archduchess Sophie sent a fine garland of roses which, with a tactful gesture, Elizabeth held with her left arm while posing for a birthday portrait by Franz Hafstaengel. A slight note of Elizabeth's wilfulness crept into Francis Joseph's reports to his mother, though he assured her that Sisi's teeth were now admirably white; back at Ischl in the summer, Sophie had mentioned to Ludovika that she thought them too yellow. Detailed arrangements over the wedding were settled, for the most part, by the two mother-sisters; and in March, barely a month before the marriage, Francis Joseph came once more to Munich, bringing the diamond and opal necklace the Archduchess had worn at her own wedding and now wished to pass on to the future Empress.

This third visit to Bavaria in six months emphasizes Francis Joseph's extraordinary ability to keep a public and a private life detached in his mind. He was still effective head of the government and head of the army, and in Vienna he recognized that, as in the first months after his accession, the Austrian Empire stood at a crossroads in its affairs. Count Buol, faithfully echoing the views of Metternich, sought to follow the policy of 1813; he would stay clear of war until Austrian intervention could be decisive. But there was, too, a powerful military party in the capital, pro-Russian in sentiment and recommending an alliance with St Petersburg on the assumption that Austria would receive a free hand in the western Balkans and the certainty of continued partnership against revolutionary liberalism. As so often when his generals spoke out, Francis Joseph found in their arguments much to attract him. In the end, however, he backed Buol. Nevertheless he accepted the need for partial mobilization, and throughout the celebrations of the following weeks, his troops stood on the alert in Galicia and along the Empire's eastern borders.

Would the marriage have been postponed had Austria gone to war? Did the thought of Possenhofen and his marriage compact tilt the balance of judgment towards peace and arbitration? It is hard to say. At all events, he was able to put such grave issues out of his mind once he travelled to Bavaria. To his mother he wrote back from Munich, much as he had done ten years before, when first excited by the mountains of the Tyrol: 'It was a wonderful sunny day', he reported, describing how he joined his aunt Ludovika, Sisi, Néné and four other cousins, 'all bundled into one carriage so as to drive off to Possenhofen. The snow-covered mountains reflected in the deep blue lake looked near enough for us to be on their slopes, and clouds of wild geese were flying over the water'; and he added, 'It was all very jolly, especially after dinner when the youngsters had more champagne than they were accustomed to drinking.'

On Thursday, 20 April 1854, an offensive and defensive alliance between Austria and Prussia was concluded in Berlin, a key treaty which was to help localize the Crimean War. Yet, however important this pledge of 'intimate understanding' between the two sovereigns may have become, it aroused little interest at the time in the German lands and even less in Austria. For on that same Thursday Princess Elizabeth left Munich for her marriage on the following Monday, and during the rest of the month there was a constant round of festivity in Vienna and many other cities of the Empire, too. It was hoped finally to heal the bitterness left by the revolutionary years. Church charities in the worst ravaged lands received a gift of 200,000 florins. The Magyar nobility were invited to send delegations to the marriage ceremony and receptions, wearing what Archduchess Sophie sourly called their 'fancy dress costumes', while the Emperor-bridegroom granted an amnesty for 380 political offenders and promised that, from 1 May, martial law would be lifted in Lombardy-Venetia.

In Vienna itself, every effort was made to encourage Prater gaiety and to restore the neo-classical image of an imperial capital city. Streets and squares were to be decorated with flags and flowers and illuminated on the eve of the wedding as well as on the day itself. 'Several nobles have gone to an enormous expense in the external decoration of their palaces', reported Thomas O'Brien, the (frequently sardonic) correspondent of *The Times*, adding that 'the Papal Nuncio has taken advantage of the festive occasion and had his palace whitewashed, of which kind attention it has been in very great need for many long years'. In planning the ceremonies old traditions were maintained: the bride would, as was customary, go into residence at the Theresianum in Wieden as soon as she arrived in the capital and, like other imperial brides, she would be officially

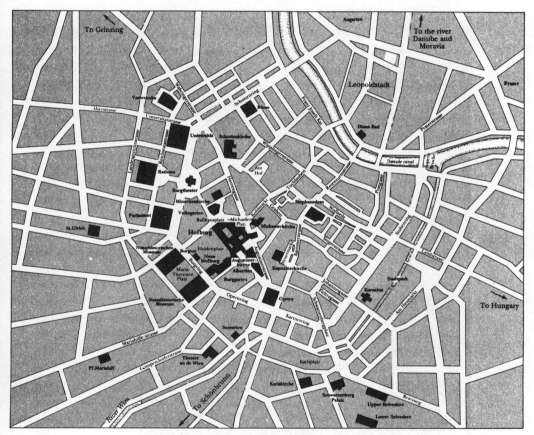

Francis Joseph's Vienna (c. 1900)

received by the city authorities on the day before the wedding. But there were novelties, too. Elizabeth was to come down the Danube aboard a paddle-steamer, named after the Emperor. And, having welcomed her to Austrian soil at Linz on the Friday evening, he would then travel back to Vienna in time to greet her on Saturday afternoon at an ornate landing stage constructed on the quayside at Nussdorf.

Even before Elizabeth left Munich, an ominous incident in Vienna was noted down by the Archduchess in her journal. Sophie's half-sister, the widowed Dowager Empress Caroline Augusta, had come up to the capital from Salzburg where she had lived for most of the nineteen years since her husband's death. Leaning forward to inspect a beautifully shaped diamond tiara which was to be Francis Joseph's wedding present to his bride, the poor woman's mantilla was caught on one of the diamond stars and, as she stepped back, the tiara went crashing to the ground. Fortunately the court jeweller succeeded in repairing the damage before Elizabeth arrived in Vienna and there is no evidence that she ever discovered what had happened. Thereafter, however, all went well with the arrangements, except that it took the paddle-boat half an hour to moor at Nussdorf because of the strong current in the Danube.

The Times correspondent was at the quayside to comment on all that happened. As soon as the landing bridge touched the vessel, Francis Joseph 'rushed on board and, in the presence of a vast crowd of onlookers, tenderly embraced and kissed his bride. The youthful Monarch yielded entirely to the dictates of his feelings, taking no pains whatever to conceal the delight he felt at the safe arrival of the Princess, whose hand he never quitted until he placed her in the carriage in which she drove with the Archduchess Sophie to Schönbrunn ... The Princess Elizabeth smiled and bowed to her future subjects as if every face on which her eye rested belonged to an old and valued friend. Some straightlaced critics would have preferred a more dignified and reserved deportment, but what has a young girl of 16, whose heart is overflowing with love and kindly feeling, to do with dignity and reserve?'. And, with some satisfaction, Thomas O'Brien observed that 'the military colouring which for so many years has been given to everything here was entirely wanting'. But the army was there in strength on the following afternoon, when the Princess made her grand entry into Vienna, taking two hours to cover the densely packed mile and three-quarter route from the Theresianum to St Stephen's Cathedral. The procession, so O'Brien reported, 'was headed by 2 or 3 squadrons of lancers'; and, remembering that *The Times*'s readers would have the war with Russia in their minds, he added, 'Would that the Allies had a dozen such regiments in Bulgaria!'.

The wedding was solemnized at four o'clock in the afternoon on

Monday, 24 April, in the Augustinerkirche, the fourteenth century court church in the shadow of the Hofburg. The imperial couple were married by the Archduchess's spiritual adviser, Joseph Othmar von Rauscher, who had been consecrated Archbishop of Vienna in the previous year. More than 50 mitred bishops formed a huge semicircle around Rauscher as the rings were exchanged and saluting cannon on the Augustinerbastion fired the first salvoes to join the pealing church bells in letting Vienna know that Austria had a new Empress. Rauscher, an ambitious prelate with a cardinal's red hat in his sights, made the most of the occasion by delivering a thirty minute address on the virtues of family life – a sermon 'evidently too long for at least one of the parties present', *The Times* archly reported.

There followed a fifty yard procession down the carpeted street to the Hofburg, where for two hours the Emperor and Empress were expected to receive the loyal homage of their guests: princes and princesses, dukes and duchesses, the old aristocracy and the new and the surviving military paladins, Radetzky, Windischgraetz and Jellaçić. At last, between ten o'clock and eleven, dinner was served, purely for the family. The bride, however, had little appetite. She had seen Habsburg court life only on holiday in Ischl; the reality in Vienna stifled her. Nor were the wedding festivities yet complete. One traditional ceremony remained, duly noted by the Archduchess with the slightly prurient sentimentality so typical of her journal entries: Ludovika 'and I escorted the young bride to her room. I left her with her mother and waited in the anteroom, next to the great chamber in which was the marriage bed. I then fetched my son and led him to his young wife, as I now accepted her to be, so as to wish them a good night. She hid her natural loveliness, for only a wealth of beautiful free-flowing hair buried in her bolster caught my eye, like a frightened bird lying low in its nest'.

Such intrusiveness came naturally to the Archduchess, and she thought nothing of Elizabeth's shy discomfiture. Nor, indeed, did Francis Joseph himself. Some twenty years later, when the Empress could rely on her own hand-picked ladies in waiting, she told them of the embarrassments she experienced in these first weeks of married life: there was no honeymoon; and she was horrified to find she could never rely on having a private breakfast with her husband in the mornings. Perhaps she exaggerated the extent to which Francis Joseph was, in domestic matters, still under his mother's thumb. But there can be no doubt of the lack of privacy at such an intimate time. Once more, the evidence is there, in Sophie's journal: 'Tuesday, 25 April . . . We [the two mother-sisters] found the young pair at breakfast in the lovely writing-room, my son radiant and full of himself, a picture of happiness (God be thanked). Sisi was deeply affected as her mother embraced her. At first we wished to leave them alone, but the Emperor stopped us with a heart-warming summons back again'. There was one question to which both mothers anxiously sought an answer. Elizabeth had no intention of satisfying their curiosity. But in such matters Francis Joseph understood the older generation better than the younger. On Thursday, 27 April, the Archduchess's journal records that Elizabeth had excused herself from the communal breakfast; and later the Emperor came to his mother privately, and let her know that 'Sisi had fulfilled his love'.

Francis Joseph did his best to make his sixteen-year old wife happy. The international crisis ruled out any honeymoon distant from Vienna, he insisted. But, just as he had sought to amuse her with a new parrot before their marriage, so on the Saturday after the wedding he escorted her to the Prater for a command performance by the Circus Renz, the finest display of trick horsemanship in the world: sixty horses; a firework display; more than forty balloons released into the night sky; twelve greys and twelve blacks dancing a horse quadrille; and Ernst Renz himself giving a superlative exhibition of *haute école* on his Arab mare. 'It really was too lovely for words', Sisi was heard to remark to her husband as she left; and she added, 'I really must get to know that man Renz'. Such a suggestion shocked her mother-in-law.

Next morning Elizabeth's mother, father and sister left Vienna to return home. The Emperor, though still puzzled by the child bride's reactions to what seemed to him the natural way of life in the capital, recognized that she was close to physical and nervous collapse. On that Sunday afternoon he acted decisively: his spell of formal residence in the capital was over; he would take his bride fifteen miles out into the country at Laxenburg, and travel every morning into the Hofburg, returning to his wife each evening. Sisi, so he told his mother, was overtired; and no doubt she was, at least within the Hofburg. But she was fit enough to go out riding that same evening. Laxenburg, with its grotto and Gothic bridge and the small wooded lake dotted with artificial islands, lacked 'dear Possi's' spaciousness; but to get into the saddle again after eight crowded days in Vienna brought an almost electric vitality back into her being. She became once more the firebird, as entrancing as at Ischl.

This was, of course, the conduct of a spoilt child, as Francis Joseph knew at heart. But, though rigidly bound by disciplined codes of behaviour himself, he was ready to show a generous complaisance towards his wife's moods. And thus, almost casually, he set standards to which he was to adhere in later years, too. For however much her self-indulgent whims might try his patience, throughout their married life the Emperor loved Elizabeth's individuality so intensely that he never tried in earnest to curb the firebird's flight.

Chapter 6

'IT IS MY PLEASURE . . .'

Francis Joseph was trained to fulfil dutifully whatever tasks circumstances dictated to him, and he possessed an iron constitution anyone might envy. Throughout his life he remained astonishingly fit, rarely needing medical care once he shook off spells of faintness which occasionally afflicted him in early manhood. Yet, despite these advantages, there can be little doubt that he found the first years of married life supremely taxing. Increasingly stern portraits follow each other through the late 1850s: the mouth becomes harder set and side-whiskers, first cultivated in 1855, offset a hairline which photographs show fast receding by the end of the decade. The strain is not surprising. Other people might pursue professional careers and find relaxation in private domesticity: an Emperor of Austria could not expect to have his days so tidily divided, not even if newly married and still in his early twenties. The nature of imperial kingship obliged the young ruler to function at an extraordinary number of levels within a short span of time: as supreme autocrat, he was responsible for deciding issues of peace and war which could enhance or destroy the dynastic heritage handed down to him; as the living embodiment of a divinely instituted sovereignty, he was the ceremonial light around whom the planetary pageant of Court revolved; and as self-appointed president of the council of ministers he was, for much of the day, a desk-bound notary-extraordinary, with reports and memoranda to be read, and decrees and commissions awaiting his signature of authority. To this burden of work there was added each evening the task of placating an adolescent bride, who was bored with Laxenburg, angered by ladies-in-waiting she had not herself chosen, and quite incapable of understanding why her husband should remain so long at the Hofburg, immersed in the humdrum business of government.

Since the Emperor remained passionately in love with his wife, he dealt patiently and sympathetically with her grievances. They would ride together at the weekends and one day he took her with him to the Hofburg, but the experiment was not a success; Elizabeth became ill-at-ease once she was left in what still remained so visibly the home the Emperor's mother had created. Some twenty years later Elizabeth would list the Archduchess's enormities for her chosen companions to hear and record: the rebukes for troubling Francis Joseph with petty matters in these months of crisis; the astonishment that she should wish 'to chase after her husband, driving here, there and everywhere as if she were a young subaltern'; and, conversely, the insistence that an Empress could not expect privacy, that she must not remain hidden away from her husband's subjects in the inner gardens of Laxenburg. The Archduchess, in her 'malice' (*bosheit*), exaggerated trifles, so Elizabeth complained.

Many of these tales find echoes in Sophie's correspondence. It is clear that at times she could be tiresomely silly, especially in the late summer and autumn of 1854 once Elizabeth was known to be pregnant. Old worries surfaced again, including the pre-natal misfortune which had allegedly disfigured Sophie's sister-in-law, Marianna: 'I feel that Sisi should not spend too much time with her parrots', the Archduchess wrote to Francis Joseph, 'If a woman is always looking at animals in the first months, the children are inclined to resemble them. Far better that she should look at herself in the mirror, or at you. *That* would have my entire approval'. Yet there is no malice and little envy in the Archduchess's writings. Her diary preserves the proud – and sometimes exasperated – affection she felt towards Elizabeth. She rejoiced over the success of a state visit to Bohemia and Moravia made by the Emperor and Empress soon after their marriage, and her journal entry for 15 June 1854 is full of praise for Elizabeth's bearing in the solemn Corpus Christi Day procession through the heart of Vienna: 'The young couple looked perfect, inspiring, uplifting. The Empress's demeanour was enchanting; devout, quite wrapt in humble meditation.'

Not all of the Emperor's preoccupations were so solemn. Thus, in a note to his mother a fortnight later, he apologized for not having written to her earlier in the day by explaining that on his journey back from the capital, he had gone to Mödling, a small town three miles from Laxenburg, and 'for the first time swam' in the 'swimming-school' there. Occasionally he went shooting and in late July, to Elizabeth's great relief, they were able to get away to Ischl. Yet in that summer of 1854 there could be little holiday.

Increasingly, week by week, it seemed as if Austria must be swept into 'the war in the East'. For over nine months the army had been mobilized in Slavonia and Transylvania and, shortly before his wedding ceremonies, the Emperor agreed that the Third Army in Hungary should be placed on a war footing. By the middle of May the Fourth Army, too, was fully mobilized in Galicia – and the whole military budget set aside for the year 1854 was already used up. Responsibility for all military dispositions lay with the Emperor, who had kept the post of minister of war vacant since the previous spring as he had no intention of allowing his authority as supreme master of the armed forces to be questioned. Grünne, head of the military chancellery, would speak for the army and navy at ministerial conferences, though General Hess was also normally present as Master of the Ordnance.

Francis Joseph did not appreciate the full significance of the policies he advocated that summer. He sought independence, allowing Austria to work with the British and the French, or to put forward a specifically Austrian solution to Balkan problems – and perhaps to German affairs – if Tsar Nicholas could be induced to abandon his role as 'gendarme of Europe'. At heart he believed he was fulfilling the testament of Schwarzenberg in freeing Austria from a dangerous dependence upon Russia and recovering the Empire's key position as arbiter of the balance of power on the continent. But he was wrong, as eventually he came to recognize. Since he could never collaborate with governments who gave sanctuary to radical exiles from Hungary and Lombardy-Venetia, the Empire would not so much gain independence as drift into dangerous isolation. In effect, Francis Joseph gave an impetus to the diplomatic revolution which was soon to bury the last relics of the Holy Alliance, abandoning the ideal of peace through collective responsibility which had been pursued by Europe's statesmen, however imperfectly, for the past forty years.

Yet, at the time, the policy made good sense. The Emperor accepted the political strategy first recommended to him by his foreign minister, Count Buol, earlier in the spring: Austria would avoid entanglement in any war in the East, but put pressure on St Petersburg to force the Russians out of Moldavia and Wallachia, the Sultan's semi-autonomous 'Danubian Principalities', occupied in the previous summer; Austrian troops might then, it was hoped, police the Principalities, standing guard along the lower Danube. Their presence would create a buffer between the Russians and their Ottoman enemy; it would also ensure that, in any postwar treaty, Austria could insist on international guarantees of free navigation along the great river.

On 29 May 1854 Francis Joseph, who would shortly be leaving Vienna for the state visit to Bohemia, convened a ministerial conference. At the head of the agenda was the need to settle details of an ultimatum which would require Russian evacuation of Moldavia and Wallachia on the grounds that the peaceful development of the Principalities was essential to Austria's vital interests. The conference minutes show that General

Hess was firmly opposed to sending any form of ultimatum whatsoever: Austria, he argued, was as yet unprepared for war on a battlefront stretching from Cracow, around the foothills of the Carpathians and across to the Danube delta. The Emperor, however, was convinced the Russians would not fight, for they too could not face a general war in the heart of the continent. Accordingly Francis Joseph overruled Hess's objections, but he also insisted that his ambassador in Constantinople should be instructed to seek an agreement with the Sultan authorizing Austrian troops to enter Moldavia and Wallachia as a guarantee that the Russians would not return there. The ultimatum was duly despatched to St Petersburg five days later. It required the Russians immediately to end military operations in Bulgaria, south of the Danube, and agree on talks to decide an early date for evacuation of the Principalities.

Tsar Nicholas, who for a year had conducted an increasingly acerbic correspondence with Francis Joseph, was infuriated by the ultimatum. With a characteristically dramatic gesture, he turned a portrait of the young Emperor to the wall and wrote across the back, *Du Undankbarer* ('You Ungrateful Wretch'); and he seriously considered rejecting the ultimatum. But not for long. Francis Joseph was right. Nicholas's generals could wage a localized war around the Black Sea, but they dared not risk opening up a new front in Europe. In August the Russians evacuated the Principalities. By the Convention of Boyadji-keuy, negotiated and ratified before the end of June, the Austrians were thereupon able to occupy Moldavia and police Wallachia jointly with the Turks, although no Austrian units were stationed in Bucharest itself.

Briefly, Francis Joseph believed Austria might gain even more from the war, possibly the permanent incorporation of the Principalities in his Empire. Early in October he explained to his mother that 'despite the political confusion, I am full of hope for, as I see it, if we act strongly and energetically, only good can come to us from this whole eastern affair. For our futures lies in the East, and we are going to push back Russia's power and influence behind the frontiers from which, solely through the weakness and disunity of earlier times, she was able to advance so as to work slowly but surely for ruin, perhaps unconsciously on the part of Tsar Nicholas'. Already Buol had moved as closely as possible to France and Great Britain; a formal alliance was under discussion; and, in consultation with the French, Buol formulated a peace programme – 'the Four Points' – which included a European guarantee of the Principalities and free navigation on the Danube, as well as assurances over the future of the Bosphorus and Dardanelles and of the status of the Sultan's Christian subjects which were of more immediate concern to the western allies. Francis Joseph personally would not have shrunk from waging war in the East. In the late summer of 1854 he ordered General Hess to prepare contingency plans for an attack on Russia next spring, with the main thrust coming between the rivers Bug and Vistula, and on 22 October the Emperor authorized total mobilization, even though Hess still thought he was setting the Monarchy on a dangerous course. There followed conferences in the Hofburg on 26 October and 15 and 17 November at which it was made clear to Francis Joseph that, although Archduke Albrecht shared his bellicosity, his ministers were inclined to agree with General Hess. Could troops be spared from Lombardy-Venetia, for Radetzky had already written personally to the Emperor in August asking for the return of a brigade which was on its way to Galicia? Could the Monarchy sustain the cost of war without plunging into state bankruptcy? And – the most telling of arguments – now that the arena of battle had shifted away from Bulgaria to the Crimea, was there a change of emphasis in the whole purpose of the war? A Lower Danubian War was a matter of deep concern to Austria: a Crimean War, fought primarily over the question of naval power in the Black Sea, was not. At the end of November 1854 Francis Joseph acknowledged the good sense of these arguments; there was to be no more contingency planning for a spring campaign in Poland.

Nevertheless Buol, always ready to assert Austria's importance as a Great Power, still occasionally pirouetted on the brink of war. On the sixth anniversary of Francis Joseph's accession a new Treaty of Vienna bound the Empire in alliance with Britain and France 'in case hostilities should break out between Austria and Russia', but it did not commit Francis Joseph to entering the conflict. Intermittent peace talks continued in Vienna, with Lord John Russell and the French Foreign Minister, Drouyn de Lhuys, attending an abortive conference which met under Buol's presidency in March and April. Russell, writing home to the British foreign secretary, reported that he found Francis Joseph's 'manner singularly agreeable, his countenance open and prepossessing' and added, somewhat patronizingly, that he showed 'an intelligence and a firmness of purpose which may enable him to rule with ability and success'; and Drouyn, too, was impressed by the Emperor's sincerity. But nobody had a good word to say for Buol. Although Austrian mobilization tied down in Poland a considerable Russian army which would otherwise have been deployed in the Crimea, the general feeling in Paris and London was that the Empire sought the fruits of victory without having to fight for it. This conviction was increased when financial necessity induced Francis Joseph to stand down his reservists at midsummer in 1855, a time when the British and French were mounting their most costly assaults on Sebastopol. At the start of the following year, it was under threat from Austria of an immediate declaration of war that the Russians finally agreed to end the fighting. But the ultimatum came too late to boost Austria's prestige; for, though the peace preliminaries were signed in Vienna, the Peace Congress was to be held in Napoleon III's Paris.

Once his minister's had persuaded him not to risk full-scale participation in the war, Francis Joseph seems to have lost interest in the 'eastern affair', despite his recent assurance to his mother that it was where 'our future' lay. He was, after all, first and foremost a German prince, constantly concerned over Prussia's reactions to the turn of events. Moreover his freedom of initiative remained limited by the circumstances of his accession. The autocratic system improvised by Schwarzenberg was still on trial. Much of the resistance to any forward policy in the east sprang from ministerial doubts whether the centralist forces upon which the regime depended for success were strong enough to check simultaneously national and social opposition, wherever it might occur. In many regions of Hungary, for example, the gentry and townsfolk remained passively uncollaborative, ridiculing the efforts – and decorative uniforms – of administrative officials drawn from other parts of the Monarchy who were unable to speak or understand their language. The Croats, who had expected much from Baron Jellaçić's loyalty to the dynasty, found themselves little better off than their Magyar neighbours. It is true that, so long as the industrial boom of the early 1850s provided jobs in the mills and factories, the urban areas of Austria and Bohemia-Moravia were quiet and contented, while the peasants were satisfied with the great land reform of 1848 which freed them from feudal obligations (though not until 1853 was their legal status as freeholders finally determined). So long as there was a surface prosperity, and a reasonably efficient administrative bureaucracy, Francis Joseph had no need to fear any challenge to the system; but throughout this 'decade of absolutism' he had to move with extreme caution: the Monarchy could not hope to survive another 1848. Fortunately the Emperor's confidence in his ability to fulfil his mission as a ruler remained undented.

He made no change in his circle of close advisers. Over most issues he still respected Grünne's opinions, though the Count was under a cloud in the autumn of 1854 because of allegedly pro-Russian inclinations. And only rarely did the Emperor question the stern rule of Radetzky in northern Italy, for he shared the respectful awe in which the army was encouraged to hold its legendary hero. As Governor-General of Lombardy-Venetia Radetzky lived in vice-regal splendour at Monza, the royal palace eight miles north of Milan which had been built for Francis Joseph's great-uncle in the heyday of benevolent despotism, and the Field Marshal had also been assigned 'perpetual' personal apartments in the Vienna

Hofburg. His administration was unimaginative and illiberal rather than harsh, but he was far too old to modify well-tried policies to meet the changing needs of the two provinces. Yet not until Radetzky entered his ninetieth year did the Emperor begin to heed the advice of those who favoured a more conciliatory attitude towards his Italian subjects.

The most outspoken advocate of a new approach was the heir to the throne, Archduke Maximilian. It was in September 1854, when Grünne was out of favour, that Francis Joseph had made his eldest brother a Rear Admiral and commander-in-chief of the navy, an appointment which pleased their mother and caused dismay among the old guard of military paladins. The Archduke, with his headquarters at Trieste and all the resources of the old Venetian naval yards to draw upon, at once began to seek money and imperial backing for the modernization of the fleet as a matter of urgency; and he received it. At Maximilian's insistence a new naval base was created in the fine natural harbour of Pola, while in the Trieste dockyards a 91-gun warship, her wooden hull protected by iron plates and her design incorporating the lessons learnt from the fighting in the Black Sea, was built and ready for launching in little more than a year. The navy remained a subordinate department of the Ministry of War and, almost inevitably, the warship was named *Radetzky*.

However much the old Marshal might merit this honour, the liberal-minded Archduke continued to chafe at the inadequacies of his government in Lombardy-Venetia. Maximilian had been an Italophile since boyhood and, as a naval officer, he came to like and respect the Triestini. On the outskirts of the city he built his dream villa, the castellated palace of Miramare, at far greater cost than he could afford but in confident expectation that this beautiful stretch of Adriatic littoral would remain as much a Habsburg possession as Laxenburg or Schönbrunn; this was a reasonable assumption, for Trieste had been in Habsburg hands since 1382, apart from the interlude of Napoleonic upheaval. In visits back to Vienna during 1854 and 1855, Maximilian stressed the importance of Trieste and the loyalty of the Slovene and Italian population throughout Istria. But Francis Joseph remained sceptical over his brother's assumption that the establishment of a benevolent regime in Milan and Venice, where the population was overwhelmingly Italian, would bring as good results for the Monarchy as in Trieste, where Slovenes pushed the Italians into a minority. For the moment there would be no change in the responsibilities of either Radetzky or Maximilian.

The Emperor already appreciated the significance of Trieste both as a port, set to challenge Marseilles and Genoa for the commerce of southern Europe, and as a Habsburg outpost beyond the Alps and the mountains of Venezia Giulia. The whole region formed, together with Görizia and

Carniola, a separate administrative 'crownland', totally independent of Lombardy-Venetia. In his first years on the throne it would, indeed, have been difficult for Francis Joseph not to give some attention to the likely future of the region for Baron von Bruck, the far-sighted Rhinelander whose financial wizardry had converted what was little more than a fishing harbour into a major port, served until the spring of 1851 as minister of commerce in the Schwarzenberg government. Under Bruck's auspices, the Emperor visited Trieste in May 1850 to lay the foundation stone of the railway station, although it was not until June 1857 that the vitally important strategic link with Vienna was completed. The Semmering Pass section, a pioneer engineering achievement, was ready by the autumn of 1854. By then, however, the *Sudbahn* was in financial difficulties and work was further delayed by the difficulty of cutting through the mountains between Ljubljana and the coast. That the line was finished at all was largely thanks to Bruck's persistence, for the Baron returned to the administration in May 1855 as minister of finance and masterminded the implementation of a Railway Concession Law, approved by the Emperor in the previous year and authorizing the sale to private companies of an extensive network of state lines.

Francis Joseph remained impressed by Bruck's understanding of monetary matters and, on his return to office, allowed him virtually a free hand to reform the fiscal system and ensure the solvency of the Empire. Bruck did nothing to curb the money supply but imposed heavier taxation and improved the exchange rate by putting on sale state property and bonds. Within two years Bruck had come nearer to his ideal of a central European free trade area based upon Vienna, for in 1857 a currency treaty provided for monetary union between the Empire and the Prussian-dominated *Zollverein*. But Bruck's most lasting achievement in these years was the establishment of a Vienna-based credit institution. In the summer of 1855 he convinced Francis Joseph that the surest way to stimulate private industry and safeguard the imperial state finances was by establishing a bank, backed by the Rothschilds and with its investments confined within the borders of the Monarchy. Once the Emperor was won over to his arguments, Bruck sought the help of Anselm Rothschild, and the two financial experts moved quickly, not least through fear of French competition: the *Oesterreichischen Creditanstalt für Handel und Gewerbe* (Commerce and Trade) received a charter on the last day of October 1855; shares were made available for public subscription on 12 December; and by the end of the month, when the board of directors of the Creditanstalt met for the first time, the share value had more than trebled, heralding almost two years of golden harvest for speculators. The bank's founders steered investment towards large-scale development of private enterprise, especially for railways and public works.

This apparent improvement in the availability of credit may finally have induced Francis Joseph to approve a project long under consideration. The possibility of razing the remaining ramparts of Vienna, and thus encouraging the outward spread of the city so as to include the cluster of suburbs immediately behind its walls, was first mooted by bankers and industrialists when he was a boy of nine, though the Volksgarten had been laid out, on the site of a fort destroyed by Napoleon I, a few years before he was born. Military diehards in the bureaucracy strongly opposed any such change: how could the centre of imperial power and the residences 'of the most prosperous and contented subjects of the State' be safe-guarded against looting and attack by 'the brutal, licentious general trade and factory people' except by strong fortifications? Even Francis Joseph, who at first agreed with such a view, was forced to admit that the experience of 1848 did not support the argument at all; the military experts now contended that, so far from providing the Court with a safe refuge, the old bastions had enabled the radical revolutionaries to hold out even longer against Windischgraetz, Jellaçić and the regular army.

On the eve of his marriage, when so many post-revolutionary restraints were being relaxed, the Emperor began to waver. He conceded the prin-ciple that the inner fortifications need no longer be preserved, provided demolition was, in each instance, related to the completion of earthworks for an outer girdle of defences. This cumbersome relationship held good for three years. But practical necessity was already forcing changes around the glacis: on 24 April 1856, for example, the Emperor and his brothers attended the laying of the foundation stone for the Votivkirche, built at the point along the ramparts where Libenyi had sought to assassinate Francis Joseph.

There was, too, as so often in Austrian history, an architectural chal-lenge from France for the Viennese to emulate. These were the years when Napoleon III and Baron Haussmann opened up Paris, thrusting broad boulevards with straight vistas through the old quarters of the inner city. Archduke Maximilian, sent to Napoleon's Court in May 1856 with his brother's congratulations on the birth of the Prince Imperial, was deeply impressed by what was going on around him: a historic city, little changed in six centuries, would soon be basking in the spacious dignity of an artificially created planned capital, like St Petersburg. If long, open avenues were the hallmark of imperial grandeur then, potentially, Vienna possessed an advantage over Paris; for in the Habsburg capital there was no need to sweep away picturesque winding-streets or demolish homes in districts where there was already a shortage of housing for a rapidly growing population. In Vienna, it would be enough to raze the bastions, fill in moats and ditches, and level the glacis. Then the architects and planners, bankers and contractors could compete for the privilege of constructing on this readily prepared surface a wide, circumambient boulevard, more a horseshoe than a ring, which would provide the imperial city with a parade prospect of public buildings.

Five days before Christmas in 1857 the Emperor made his great decision, taking both Alexander Bach (his minister of the interior) and the department of engineers by surprise. A letter-patent, using the characteristic phrasing of benevolent autocracy, informed Bach: 'It is My Pleasure that, as soon as possible, preparatory work should begin on the extension of the inner city of Vienna so as to establish an appropriate link with the suburbs, and that, at the same time, consideration should be given to the regulation and embellishment of My Residence and My Capital'. And he added, 'I give My Permission to abolish the walls and fortification of the inner city, as well as their surrounding ditches.'

Unfortunately the momentous decree coincided with a tightening of credit, following several crises of nerves on Wall Street, in the banking houses of London, Paris and Frankfurt as well as Vienna. But seven weeks after the decree was signed, a government commission invited architects to draw up plans for expanding and 'embellishing' the city; and within two months the first ramparts came down and a fine avenue was laid beside the Danube Canal. Work continued throughout the most critical years of the Emperor's reign. It was easy enough to extend the Volksgarten and create a Stadtpark, which was opened to the townsfolk in 1863 and covered waste ground between one of the eastern bastions of the wall and the River Wien. Even the Ringstrasse itself was completed by the spring of 1865 when Francis Joseph and Elizabeth drove along the boulevard in a flower-bedecked coach on May Day. But the great buildings came later in the reign: the Opera House, begun in 1861, was not opened until 1869; the two museums (Kunsthistorisches and Natural History) went up between 1872 and 1881; Parliament and the Rathaus were not finished until 1883; and work on the Burgtheater dragged on from 1872 until 1888. The process begun at Francis Joseph's 'pleasure' in those closing days of 1857 transformed the Austrian capital into a city as spacious and beautiful as any in Europe. No other missive sent from Emperor to minister had such enduring consequences as that letter-patent to Bach.

Foreign observers, reporting to their governments in the mid-fifties, attached greater importance to a far different initiative by the Emperor, the conclusion of a Concordat with Rome. Some diplomats thought that the privileged position which he gave to the hierarchy was the tired gesture of a harassed young man anxious to please his mother. But this view (which has influenced several historians) is misleading. Francis Joseph had always been dutifully devout, accepting from Colombi and Rauscher in his boyhood the current assumptions of a reactionary Church: lay control of moral teaching led to atheism and the break up of society; the only hope of crushing the demon of revolution was to acknowledge the sovereignty of Holy Church over all temporal rulers. The circumstances of Francis Joseph's accession made him even more inclined to respect the Church's code of government.

The famous Napoleonic Concordat of 1801 had taken several months of preparation: the Austrian Concordat took six years. Within six weeks of coming to the throne Francis Joseph received a petition from Cardinal Schwarzenberg (brother of the then head of government) seeking imperial authority to convene a conference of bishops who would recommend to their sovereign the conclusion of a Concordat with the Pope. The bishops' conference opened in Vienna on 30 April 1849, the day the Emperor assumed supreme command of the army, and it was still in session when he returned to Schönbrunn from Olmütz a week later. Cardinal Schwarzenberg and Rauscher between them were convinced that they possessed sufficient influence over government and Court to sweep aside all concessions made to modern thought by the Emperor Joseph II seventy years before; they sought to bind the Empire in a spiritual tutelage unknown since the Counter-Reformation. A working agreement was reached with the government as early as April 1850, and in July 1851 the Jesuits were allowed back into the Empire after a lapse of nearly eighty years. The death of Felix von Schwarzenberg did not impede the discussions over a formal treaty with the Holy See, for the bishops could still count on support from several government ministers, notably Bach and the equally devout minister of education and religious affairs, Count Leo Thun-Hohenstein.

Even so, the proposals put forward by Rome were so overbearing that Francis Joseph jibbed at accepting them; the terms of the treaty had not been settled when Rauscher preached his thirty minute sermon at the Emperor's marriage. But the Holy See was adamant: the Austrians gave way over eleven points on Church-State relations and seven on doctrine, some of which even Rauscher queried. The state surrendered all control over the Church and its relations with Rome, left to the Church the right to punish priests guilty of civil offences, and agreed to allow marriage laws to be interpreted by ecclesiastical courts. The hierarchy was given the right to ban books on moral or religious grounds, while the clergy exercised supervisory rights over education at all levels. The state recognized Church property as sacrosanct and inviolable, and undertook not to alter confessional laws without the Church's consent, while the Emperor promised not to tolerate derogatory remarks against the faith or Church institutions.

When, on 18 August 1855, Francis Joseph sent a telegram of thanks to his mother at Ischl for her birthday greetings, he added the information, 'Today the Concordat was signed'; and there is no doubt that, even if the Archduchess was not the prime mover in seeking an understanding with Rome, she found the news gratifying. Over purely political affairs she had long ceased to have any real influence, but she remained the matriarch of the dynasty, the most formidable figure in the family. It was not in Sophie's nature to question the fundamental values upon which her life was modelled. For her the indisputable truths of the Church emphasized the role of the family, and her diary jottings reveal a genuine gratitude for the God-given understanding of mind and spirit vouchsafed to her at the Habsburg Court. Read in retrospect, the simple sincerity of her sense of mission softens this tone of self-righteousness, which is present in her letters as well as in her journal; but it is easy to see how, in life, the practice of her precepts must frequently have made the Archduchess intolerable. Familiarity with the ways and wiles of her niece and daughter-in-law strengthened her inner satisfaction at having been a wiser mother than Ludovika. It also convinced Sophie of the need to regulate the nursery routine of her grandchildren and supervise the matchmaking of her remaining sons.

Sophie had suffered several miscarriages in her earliest years of marriage. But all seemed to go well for Elizabeth. On 5 March 1855 she had her first child, a girl rather than the Crown Prince needed to guarantee the succession to another generation; and almost inevitably the baby was named Sophie. Within five months the Empress was again pregnant: a second daughter, the Archduchess Gisela, was born on 12 July 1856, at Laxenburg. Should Elizabeth continue to give birth to girls, the succession would pass to Francis Joseph's brothers and any male descendants they might have; for, despite the reverence shown to the memory of Maria Theresa, legalistic pedantry ruled out the accession of a sovereign's daughter. The Archduchess Sophie intensified her matchmaking and, soon after Gisela's birth, pulled off a second family triumph: Archduke Charles Ludwig, disappointed in his childhood attachment to Sisi, was betrothed to yet another first cousin, Princess Margaretha, the fifth daughter of Sophie's sister, Queen Amalia of Saxony; and in November 1856 they married in Dresden.

The youngest son, Ludwig Victor ('Bubi'), was only fourteen in 1856, but he was already his mother's spoilt pet, with no interest in girls, then or in later years. A more immediate family problem was the Archduke Maximilian, ten years older than Bubi. The independently minded Maximilian was at first disinclined to be pushed into marriage. On his sea voyages he fell in love with Princess Maria Amalia of Brazil, who, though a granddaughter of Archduchess Sophie's eldest sister, was also a great-granddaughter of the Empress Josephine. Sadly, the Princess died from consumption in Madeira before their betrothal was announced. Maximilian then followed his mother's advice and visited Brussels in late May 1856 to meet Princess Charlotte, the only daughter of King Leopold I of the Belgians. A link between the Habsburgs and the newest Catholic kingdom in Europe had been established in 1853, when Leopold's eldest surviving son, the Duke of Brabant, married the Palatine Archduke Joseph's youngest daughter; and Sophie was impressed by what she heard of the Court at Brussels and of the intelligent, pretty and deeply religious Princess Charlotte in particular. But Maximilian remained in no hurry to marry. Charlotte may have found the sailor Archduke a romantic figure but, though he treated her graciously, he was not excited by her presence, as he had been in his brief courtship of poor Maria Amalia. He resumed his naval duties at Trieste and Pola, concentrated on the building of Miramare and in October sailed off with the fleet down the Adriatic. Their engagement was not made public until December, after Charles Ludwig had returned with his bride from Saxony.

The Emperor and Empress were away from Vienna in that month; they spent much of the autumn and winter of 1856–7 undertaking state visits to the southern provinces of the Monarchy. A week in Styria and Carinthia early in September was followed by a nine day visit to Ljubljana and Trieste in October and by four and a half months of formal residence in Lombardy-Venetia. The Carinthian expedition was in part a holiday, allowing both Francis Joseph and Elizabeth to relax and find a natural exhilaration in the mountain scenery of the Grossglockner. Relations with the matriarch in the Hofburg had become strained over the previous year, and Elizabeth insisted on having the children's nursery removed from the immediate proximity of their grandmother's apartments to the imperial wing of the palace. On returning from Carinthia, Francis Joseph wrote more firmly to his mother than on any earlier occasion: he deplored her habit of virtually confining the two little girls to her own rooms and bringing them out as show pieces, for he had a horror of having them turned into vain little madams. Specifically he asked her 'to treat Sisi indulgently when she is perhaps too jealous a mother – she is of course so devoted a wife and mother'. He backed Elizabeth in her determination to take little Sophie with them on the journey to Italy, arguing that the child, who was delicate, would benefit from the warmer winter climate south of the Alps: Grandmamma demurred.

When riding in the Prater, or at ceremonial occasions in Vienna, the

Empress often seemed ill-at-ease, reluctant to have prying eyes staring at her. But in Styria, Carinthia and Carniola she was free of such inhibitions. Her gracious charm and beauty readily aroused popular enthusiasm. It was therefore hoped that in northern Italy her personal magnetism would offset the hostility which it was assumed would be aroused by the presence of her husband. This, however, was asking a lot from Elizabeth. Resentment at individual acts of harsh repression over the past eight years continued to smoulder in Venetia and even more in Lombardy. When, on 25 November, the Venetian State Galley bore the Emperor, Empress and infant Archduchess to the landing stage in front of Doge's Palace there were no cheers. As Francis Joseph inspected the Guard drawn up in the Piazza San Marco, only the orchestrated hurrahs of the troops broke the cold silence. A gala at the Fenice Theatre was half empty, and three out of every four Venetian patricians declined the imperial invitation to the first Court reception. There was a mood, not so much of rebellion, as of proud indifference among the people of the old republic.

The Emperor had not realized the extent to which the army retained administrative control over the two provinces. He was glad he went to the Italian provinces, as he later told his mother, 'for it was high time to clean up the mess in Verona', still the centre of military command for the region. Within ten days of arriving in Venice he gave approval to a widespread amnesty and to measures providing for the restoration of sequestered property and encouraging the return of political exiles. Rumour rightly credited the Emperor with planning a general administrative change of system; and by Christmas the atmosphere in Venice had become less tense; Emperor and Empress were applauded when they entered the Fenice, now full to capacity. To win and retain the confidence of the Venetians was a hard task; but for Francis Joseph the burden was eased by Elizabeth's attention to small details, and in particular, her tact in persuading him to accept petitions from men and women in the crowd, ignored by his military suite. But when, in early January, the imperial couple moved into Lombardy the good work had to begin all over again. In Bergamo the police hurriedly erased graffiti proclaiming, 'The Emperor arrives at 1500. We will get him at 1600'. Elizabeth's most winning charms could not thaw the hostility in Brescia, while in Milan some patrician families sent surrogate servants to a gala at the Scala, providing them with gloves of purple or black, the shade of mourning. Only an administration genuinely sympathetic to Italian culture and the needs of the local community could even hope to coax the Lombards back from the seductive nationalism of Cavour in neighbouring Piedmont.

It was clear that Radetzky would have to go. As soon as he landed in Venice, Francis Joseph saw that the Governor-General was in his dotage –

'horribly changed and in his second childhood', he wrote back to his mother nine days later. But who would take his place? It took nearly three months for Francis Joseph to reach a solution which had already occurred to such disparate foreign observers as Lord John Russell and King Leopold. On 1 March 1857 it was the Emperor's 'pleasure' to announce publicly in Milan that the Archduke Maximilian would succeed Radetzky as Governor-General of Lombardy and Venetia. Characteristically, however, he did not wish to offend senior officers by giving the military command to a reforming 'Sailor Archduke', and Maximilian was therefore given far less power than Russell or King Leopold had envisaged. The Archduke was a purely civilian viceroy: the army would be commanded by Field Marshal Count Gyulai von Maros-Nemeth, a nominee of Grünne whose inadequacies Radetzky had been too old to perceive. At heart Francis Joseph was uneasy over the arrangement: 'I feel a little happier, but not fully reassured. Everything remains very uncertain . . .', he told his mother next day, 'Let us hope Maxi's tact will do some good.'

The Emperor and Empress arrived back in Vienna on 12 March, convinced that their long residence in the troubled provinces had proved a successful experiment. 'On the whole Sisi and I have enjoyed our stay', Francis Joseph insisted. At once they planned a further expedition. Elizabeth wished to know about Hungary: she admired Magyar horsemanship; she found several of the Hungarians at court to be lively and interesting companions; and, even before leaving Bavaria, she had begun to learn their language. Now she persuaded her husband to encourage further reconciliation with his Hungarian subjects by planning a month's visit to the kingdom. And this time, ignoring renewed protests and well-intentioned advice from Archduchess Sophie, both little girls were with their parents when, on 5 May, the Danube steamer brought them to Pest.

A state entry into Buda followed, across Adam Clark's suspension bridge and up the steep, cobbled streets to the royal palace above the river. That night the bridge was festooned with lights while an enterprising Levantine financier paid for an ambitious firework display to welcome Hungary's King and Queen. Once again there was an amnesty and the restoration of confiscated property; and once again Elizabeth set about pleasing all whom she was allowed to meet. But Francis Joseph himself was less inclined to forgive and forget than in Italy. He scarcely bothered to flatter national susceptibilities. Similarly, many of the greater families remained irreconcilable – for it was, after all, only seven and a half years since the royal prime minister and the president of the upper house of parliament were shot and Hungary's generals publicly hanged at Arad.

Sentimental writers claim that Elizabeth fell in love with Hungary at first sight and the Magyar people at once took 'Erzsebet' to their hearts.

In reality, after the first two days, she was distracted by mounting worries over the health of her children, although she resolutely sought to give the Emperor the support he needed. Gisela went down with measles but was soon well on the way to recovery. Her two-year-old sister Sophie, who was more delicate, caught the measles and seemed so weak that the parents postponed their departure for inner Hungary. On Saturday, 23 May, with Sophie said to be out of danger, Francis Joseph and Elizabeth set out for the pustza plains of the north-east, leaving the children in the palace at Buda. By Thursday the royal progress had reached Debrecen, the Calvinist city in north-eastern Hungary where in 1849 Kossuth had proclaimed the deposition of the dynasty. There they received a telegram summoning them back to Buda, 140 miles away, which they reached soon after ten next morning. Nothing could be done to save the poor child's life. 'Our little one is an angel in heaven', Francis Joseph was forced to telegraph to her grandparents late that night, 'We are crushed'.

The Hungarian royal progress was cancelled. Back at Laxenburg, Elizabeth shut herself up, full or remorse for having taken the child with them to Buda in the first place, and then for having set out for Debrecen. The tragedy confirmed Archduchess Sophie's worst fears: children should be kept in the nursery, not carried on long journeys to strange cities. Francis Joseph went back to Hungary later in the summer to complete the tour of the kingdom: but it was ten years before Elizabeth could face the prospect of returning to Buda.

This first personal disaster of the reign cast a shadow over the summer of 1857, for the Empress remained secluded and in deep mourning. She would ride and walk alone, her mind dazed, her nerves numb, her eyes lustreless. Francis Joseph was infinitely patient, but so concerned was he for her health that he pressed Ludovika to come from Bavaria and draw her back to the serenity of daily life in the peace of Laxenburg. These days of anguished introspection could not be prolonged; in early August the Court had to come out of mourning and greet Maximilian and Charlotte, as they passed through Vienna after their marriage in Brussels. The Empress dutifully stood beside her husband at the magnificent reception at Schönbrunn, ethereally lovely in white and as silent as an apparition. Her sombre mood did not help the Belgian Princess transmute into an Austrian Archduchess; and it is possible Elizabeth saw no reason to assist her make the change.

Archduchess Sophie, with whom Elizabeth had little contact during these months, travelled up to Linz to welcome her new daughter-in-law to the Empire. She was pleased to find her both good-looking and sharply intelligent. 'Charlotte is charming, beautiful, attractive, and full of love and affection for me', she wrote in her diary on 4 August, 'I thank God from the bottom of my heart for the delightful wife Max has found and for the wider family they will give us.' The Archduchess already assumed Sisi would have no son and the succession pass to Maximilian and the children whom she was sure that the robust and sensible Charlotte would bear. By contrast, so fitfully did Elizabeth's light flicker, that it was doubtful if she could ever again glow with the ecstasy of happiness fulfilled.

The Emperor and Empress remained deeply conscious of their loss. Six months after Sophie's death Francis Joseph could write to his mother telling her that when, 'yesterday', they saw Gisela sit for the first time in her sister's 'little chair in my study, we wept together'. But this shared sense of bereavement enabled him to show a sympathetic understanding of Sisi's grief: the love that had blossomed at Ischl proved resilient and enduring. By Christmas the Empress knew she was for the third time pregnant: might the baby come on her husband's twenty-eighth birthday? Not quite. The child was born at Laxenburg on 21 August. 'Not exactly beautiful, though well-built and sturdy', Francis Joseph told his parents. Beauty was of little importance this time; what mattered was the child's gender; and Elizabeth had given birth to a son who, on the following Sunday, Cardinal Rauscher baptized Rudolf Francis Charles Joseph. If, as at the imperial wedding, he preached too long on the spiritual rewards of a virtuous family life, on this occasion neither father nor mother grudged the cardinal his pious platitudes.

Towns and villages from Galicia to Lombardy duly celebrated the Crown Prince's birth with festoons of patriotic bunting. There was a further amnesty, and gifts by the child's father to charitable bodies in widely separated regions of his Empire. In Vienna itself Francis Joseph endowed the Rudolfspital, a general infirmary for a thousand patients 'irrespective of family origin and religion'. Some of the rejoicing was officially sponsored, some spontaneous and some commercially opportunist. Josef Strauss soon had a *Laxenburger Polka* on sale and, as the Emperor lost no time in giving his son honorary rank in the 19th Infantry Regiment, the Strauss family made certain that regimental bands would be playing '*The Austrian Crown Prince's March*' long before His Imperial Highness learnt to walk. Yet there was, too, in these August days of 1858 a slightly portentous sense of occasion, perhaps because it was three centuries since an imperial baptism had honoured the founder of the dynasty. Much was expected of the Crown Prince, as the imperial director of theatres speedily acknowledged. On the stage of the Burgtheater a tableau vivant was mounted: with a golden pen the Muse of History inscribed on a huge marble slab the date of Ruldolf's birth; then she declaimed: 'Here stand engraved Year and Day. The rest of this tablet shall be left empty, for space I must leave to record there the famous deeds which, I foresee, he shall accomplish.'

Chapter 7

ITALY WITHOUT RADETZKY

On 18 January 1858 the most impressive military funeral procession ever seen in Vienna made its way across a silent city to the Nordbahnhof. Field Marshal Radetzky, who had died in Italy, was to be interred in the Heldenberg mausoleum in Moravia; and the Emperor wished his subjects to honour their hero in a solemn pageant to match Great Britain's tribute to the Duke of Wellington five winters before. On that November morning in London the weight of the funeral chariot proved too great for the rain-sodden roadway down the Mall, and sixty men and twelve dray-horses had to strain at cables and traces before the cortège could resume its progress towards St Paul's. Francis Joseph would not risk a similar embarrassment on the icy glacis: the Marshal's body was borne in a hearse, not a funeral chariot; but 40,000 men – as many as he commanded on the Italian battlefields – were put on parade, with the Emperor himself riding at their head.

A British diplomat, who some forty years later came back to Vienna as ambassador, watched from a window in Leopoldstadt as the cortège went by, with 'light flakes of snow whirled about by the bitter gusts of wind'. In his memoirs Horace Rumbold was to recall:

No sound but the rumble of the artillery wagons, the tread of the battalions, the clatter of horses' hoofs, the clanking of spur and scabbard, the roll of muffled drums, and – most striking to me of all – the music of the bands playing a solemn strain which seemed strangely familiar and yet had a new and unaccustomed rhythm. Some clever Capelmeister had had the simple, but ingenious, thought of adapting old Strauss's brilliant Radetzky march to a minor key and a dirge-like measure, and, as regiment after regiment filed by, there came up through the frosty air a fresh wail of this famous melody, with just enough of its old original fierceness and wildness left in it to carry the mind back to the days when they had hoisted the octogenarian into his saddle at Custozza or Novara, the troops, as they passed him cheering like mad for 'Vater Radetzky'.

Although old Metternich was still alive, penning memoranda for the

Emperor in his villa off the Rennweg, everyone recognized that the Marshal's death marked the true passing of an era. The Italian Question was once again posed acutely. Cavour's statesmanship and economic policies, together with the increased influence of Sardinia-Piedmont after the kingdom's participation in the Crimean War, made it essential for the Habsburgs to offer a solution of their own, as Francis Joseph had himself recognized when he made Maximilian Governor-General in the previous spring. But the Archduke felt increasingly frustrated. Until the last months of his viceregal term, Radetzky's prestige enabled him to show a certain independence, modifying general policies laid down in Vienna so as to suit the needs of the two Italian provinces (though not always wisely). As Maximilian reminded his mother in a letter, 'For loyalty's sake, Radetzky was disobedient'. Such independence was denied a young and inexperienced Archduke.

Yet Maximilian was astute and perceptive. He spoke Italian fluently and his first speeches emphasized the attachment his great-grandfather, Leopold II, felt for his Tuscan lands at a time when in Turin the House of Savoy-Piedmont showed little feeling for the cultural traditions of Italy. He accomplished much in a short span of time: he secured the establishment of a discount bank to help the silk industry, caught in a severe depression; he saw to it that Milan, like Paris and Vienna, was given a public works programme, with a new square in front of the Teatro alla Scala, and plans for setting off to greater advantage the facade of the cathedral by more than doubling the size of the Piazza del Duomo (a project begun eighteen years later); and he encouraged agrarian enterprises, such as draining the Piano di Spagna marshland at the head of Lake Como. When heavy rain led the Po and Ticino to burst their banks in October 1857, Maximilian supervised some of the relief work, towards the cost of which he contributed money from his personal funds. In Venetia he achieved less, partly through bad harvests, but also because the Venice Arsenal suffered from the loss of naval work he had already assigned to Trieste and Pola. Nevertheless, the record of his first nine months as Governor-General was impressive, not least because of his skill in persuading his brother to sign pardons for over a hundred political prisoners outside the provisions of earlier amnesties. Politically he would have liked to go further: he urged Francis Joseph to seize the initiative and summon a congress of Italian princes at Monza where they might consider the development of specifically Italian railway and telegraph networks and a customs union to match the German Zollverein. But, in Vienna, Buol joined the Emperor's closest advisers in opposing so radical a programme. At such a congress what, they wondered, could be expected from the House of Savoy? And who would speak for the Papal States? Nothing more was heard of the proposed congress.

Yet the Italian Question remained in urgent need of solution. In the week of Radetzky's death and funeral all the European governments were assessing the significance of the Orsini plot in Paris. On 14 January three bombs were thrown at Napoleon III and the Empress Eugenie as their carriage arrived at the Opera House in Paris. Eight people were killed and over a hundred badly injured by this terrorist outrage. The French police had little difficulty in placing responsibility on four Italian exiles led by Count Felice Orsini, a former Mazzinian governor of Ancona who had escaped from the Austrian prison fortress of Mantua five years before. At first it was widely assumed the outrage would put an end to the overt patronage given by Napoleon III to the Italian national cause since the Crimean War. Cavour, who was alarmed by Maximilian's growing popularity and hoping to retain the sympathy already shown by western liberals for the Risorgimento, sent a message to his agents in Lombardy: 'It is urgent that you bring about the reimposition of a state of siege in Milan.' The subsequent publication in the official French gazette of Orsini's letter to Napoleon, appealing to him to follow his uncle's example and liberate Italy from Austrian rule, did not save the Count from execution but it made him a patriot martyr throughout the peninsula, thereby forcing Maximilian's administration on the defensive. But the Archduke refused to retreat into a purely repressive policy. He came to Vienna in July 1858, with proposals for giving Lombardy-Venetia an autonomy unknown anywhere else in the Monarchy. Once again, Francis Joseph was not unsympathetic to his brother's recommendations: he authorized minor reforms in taxation and the system of enforcing military service; but both Grünne and his ministers convinced the Emperor that any major political concession would prompt similar demands from Magyars, Croats, Poles, Czechs and every other nationality, making it hard to prevent the Empire's disintegration.

While Maximilian was travelling back to Monza in the third week of July 1858, Cavour was in France where he met Napoleon III secretly at Plombières, the small spa in the foothills of the Vosges; a verbal agreement, defined more precisely on paper later in the year, promised French support to Sardinia-Piedmont in a campaign to end Habsburg rule in the peninsula, provided Austria could be provoked into launching the war. Cavour's visit soon became known, and over the following three weeks newspapers in Turin, Vienna and London speculated about the talks. Few commentators doubted the two high-level conspirators regarded Austria as their natural enemy. Maximilian, however, wished to press ahead with his limited programme of reforms, particularly in education, and there is some evidence from both Russian and British diplomatic sources that – as Cavour had feared – the Archduke's lenient policies were winning back support for Austrian rule, at least in Lombardy. In Vienna, on the other hand, Maximilian's opponents insisted that reform would weaken the Austrian hold on the provinces. Count Thun-Hohenstein, as minister responsible for education and religious affairs, even encouraged Francis Joseph to wonder if his brother was seeking the crown of Lombardy for himself. Reports of injudicious remarks by both Maximilian and Charlotte criticizing official policy reached Vienna.

On 15 September 1858 Archduchess Margaretha, the eighteen year old wife of Charles Ludwig, suddenly died from a mysterious fever while on a visit to Monza. This latest domestic tragedy intensified the gloom within the imperial family. Charlotte, who like Margaretha remained childless, was especially depressed. The Emperor, pained by the mischievous tales of his brother's open dissent, encouraged Maximilian to go on leave with his wife; and they sailed down the Dalmatian coast to Corfu, discovering yet another idyllic retreat, a ruined monastery on Lacroma, the island off Dubrovnik. When, in late November, the Archduke returned to Milan, he found the Lombard people frigidly unco-operative in his ventures, and he was alarmed at the 'complete chaos' around him. Any confidence he had felt in Count Gyulai as military commander was gone, and he asked the Emperor for more powers in case of war or rebellion. But Francis Joseph refused. In a long and ominous letter on 26 December he explained that he could not risk exposing the Archduke's reputation to the uncertainties of the battlefield; for the moment he was to remain in Milan, carrying out imperial decisions whether or not he agreed with them. Should war come, he might again take command of the fleet in the Adriatic. 'This is the most difficult time I have experienced', the Emperor wrote, 'I am counting, with the firmest confidence, on your loyal support.'

Six days later Napoleon III startled Europe's chancelleries by his famous greeting to the Austrian ambassador, Joseph von Hübner, at the New Year's reception in the Tuileries: 'I am sorry that our relations with your government are not as good as in the past, but please write to Vienna and assure the Emperor that my personal sentiments towards him have not changed.' At first Hübner saw nothing menacing in this urbane and largely meaningless observation, but long before he could send any formal message back to Vienna, the Paris Bourse was full of alarming rumours that the tone of Napoleon's remarks confirmed the imminence of war in northern Italy. Share prices tumbled, first in Paris, later in London and Vienna. At the Hofburg, Grünne urged the despatch of reinforcements to Lombardy. When, two and a half weeks later, King Victor Emmanuel assured his parliament in Turin that he could not 'close his ears' to 'the cry of anguish' reaching him from the oppressed peoples of Italy, Francis Joseph was convinced that war must follow south of the Alps as soon as the winter snows receded and the passes were once more clear.

A wiser, more experienced ruler would have checked the drift into a conflict from which little was to be gained; the Monarchy could not stand the cost of mobilization, let alone the losses in men and material from a long campaign. The ingenuity of Bruck, and the backing given to Austria's currency by the great banking institutions, had allowed the Empire to stave off state bankruptcy after spending so recklessly in 1854–55 for the war in the east which never came. Even so, the military budget for 1857 had been more than halved. But Francis Joseph ignored the lesson of the 1854–55 crisis; he had – at least in these years of unfettered autocracy – a simplistic, old-world belief in treating military threats from abroad like a challenge to a duel, with the honour of the dynasty at stake.

As war loomed in March 1859 Napoleon III seemed to draw back from the brink, and his foreign minister supported Russo-British proposals for a congress to solve the Italian Question without recourse to war. Yet even though Britain, and probably Prussia, would have supported Austria at such a congress, this diplomatic initiative did not appeal to Francis Joseph, who feared international pressure might force him to concede territory – a humiliating prospect. Ten thousand volunteers from all over Italy were in Turin, shouting for war against Austria, and Francis Joseph insisted on regarding them as a serious threat. He warned Maximilian in Monza that he intended to force Piedmont to disarm and told him to 'be ready to send your wife from Italy at a moment's notice'. Charlotte left Milan on 19 April, officially to observe a penitential Holy Week in Venice.

It was at a ministerial council in the Hofburg on Tuesday, 19 April, that Francis Joseph finally decided to risk a war. Next day the Archduke learnt by telegraph he had been relieved of his gubernatorial responsibilities, all powers passing to Gyulai as commander-in-chief. Less than 48 hours later – by then it was Good Friday morning – the Austrian envoy in Turin presented Cavour with an ultimatum: war would follow in five days time unless the Piedmontese army was withdrawn from the frontier in Lombardy and reverted to a peacetime footing. Cavour rejected the ultimatum. By Wednesday, 27 April, Austria and Sardinia-Piedmont were at war; and, after some days of characteristic indecision, on 3 May Napoleon III issued a proclamation calling on the French people to march with him beside Piedmont against the tyranny of Austria. By letting the ultimatum go off to Turin, Francis Joseph thus sprang the trap set for him at Plombières.

Not all the fault lay with the Emperor. His foreign minister had served at the Austrian Legation in Turin and believed that he understood both Cavour and his policy. Throughout the critical weeks Count Buol argued that the Piedmontese were bluffing and that Austria could rely on threats from Prussia to prevent Napoleon III from denuding his eastern frontier so as to wage a campaign south of the Alps. Archduke Albrecht was sent to Berlin to co-ordinate Austrian and Prussian military moves, and as late as 6 April Buol assured the Emperor that he was certain of Prussian support, thereby neutralizing French military backing for Piedmont: Buol argued that, without the prospect of aid from Napoleon, the Piedmontese would meekly accept Austria's demands. Incredibly, Francis Joseph took Buol at his word. To save money, he allowed the ultimatum to be presented in Turin without first ordering the full-scale mobilization which both Grünne and Hess thought essential. If Buol's prediction was correct and Cavour climbed down, the Emperor would gain a prestigious victory on the cheap. If Buol was wrong, he was courting a swift defeat and financial disaster.

In Berlin Archduke Albrecht found the Prussians unresponsive. As Metternich had reminded Buol in memoranda which the foreign minister chose to ignore, neither Prussia nor any other member of the German Confederation was under any treaty obligation to assist Francis Joseph unless he became engaged in a purely defensive war. But Prince Regent William gave Albrecht some slight grounds for hope: Prussia was, after all, an independent Great Power and might be tempted to threaten France, provided the Austrians allowed Prussia a freer hand in purely German affairs. Francis Joseph, by now as angry with Prussia as Nicholas I had been with the Austrian 'ingrate' five years before, offered no tempting concessions; and when the first French army corps headed for the Alpine passes, there was no corresponding movement of Prussian troops across the Rhine and the Moselle.

In January 1858 Rumbold had admired the 'absolute perfection of military trim and equipment' with which Francis Joseph's 'renowned regiments' escorted Radetzky's hearse across Vienna. Fifteen months later Feldzugmeister Gyulai's staff looked no less impressive as they watched five corps, drawn from all the nationalities of the Monarchy, and a crack German-Austrian cavalry division cross the River Ticino to invade Piedmont. But, as Gyulai well knew, these troops belonged to what was essentially a parade-ground army. Numerically they should have had little difficulty in preventing the Piedmontese from emerging from their alpine passes into the plains. But their commander-in-chief was in no hurry. Between Cavour's rejection of the ultimatum and Gyulai's review of the troops beside the Ticino four days elapsed, with no action whatsoever. Gyulai was without a war plan and scarcely on speaking terms with his chief-of-staff. He was also short of rations, support wagons, bridging equipment and trained gun teams for his artillery. An inconclusive month went by, with Gyulai's vanguard at one time advancing to within fifty miles of Turin and encountering little opposition. But the Feldzugmeister was worried by reports that day by day the French were bringing guns, wagons and horses over the Little St Bernard and Mont Cenis passes down to the Po at Chivasso. Fearing that his left flank was over-extended and exposed, on 2 June he ordered the army to pull back out of Piedmont. He would await the enemy east of the Ticino, on Austrian soil.

This aimless marching and counter-marching confirmed Francis Joseph's early suspicions that things were going desperately wrong. At council meetings during the first months of the year Grünne and Hess had urged caution, suspecting that the army was not ready to face a war that spring. They thought (rightly) that, as yet, the single track railway from Vienna to Trieste could not cope with urgent military traffic. Moreover, as Maximilian's reports consistently emphasized, there was still no line linking Trieste to Venice, seventy miles away. Yet both the Emperor and his military advisers were shocked by Gyulai's inability to retain control of an army when faced by unexpected hazards. The late spring of 1859 was exceptionally wet: in early May the Po was already fifteen feet above its normal level; roads were deep in mud, and many of the open fields treacherously swampy. Conditions had been as bad in 1800, during the weeks before Marengo. On that occasion the rivers remained in flood until mid-June, forcing both Bonaparte and the Austrian commander, the septuagenarian General Melas, to adjust the disposition of their troops so as to concentrate on the retention of key bridgeheads. But Gyulai, who had never previously commanded an army in the field, learnt no lessons from the Marengo campaign. The incessant rain and mud demoralized him. By the third week in May Gyulai's desperate telegrams to Vienna convinced Francis Joseph he would have to travel down to the battle-front himself.

He had wanted to leave the capital as soon as it was known that Napoleon III would take command of the Franco-Piedmontese army in person. But Francis Joseph was hampered by the nature of the autocratic structure he had himself created. When he had gone to the front in Hungary ten years before, Schwarzenberg was still chief minister, shaping policies while his sovereign was with the troops. Now, however, he had no chief minister. He had lost all confidence in Buol as soon as it became clear that Prussia would not be entering the war, and Buol was ready to quit office by the end of the first week in May. But who should take his place? So desperate was Francis Joseph that, on several days, he sounded out the Empire's eldest statesman, on one occasion staying for three hours at the villa on the Rennweg. It was largely on Metternich's advice that Francis Joseph appointed Count Rechberg to succeed Buol on 15 May, the old Chancellor's eighty-sixth birthday. Rechberg, a fifty-three year old diplomat of Bavarian origin, was an expert in German affairs and the last of Metternich's protégés. So highly did the Emperor rate the new foreign minister's qualities that he immediately authorized him to act as interim president of the council of ministers as well. A few days later Francis Joseph asked Metternich to draw up secret contingency plans for a council of regency for Crown Prince Rudolf and a memorandum on how the Monarchy might be preserved without an active sovereign on the throne. But these tasks were beyond the ex-Chancellor: his health gave way, and he died on 11 June without drafting this last political testament.

Archduchess Sophie reluctantly accepted the need for the Emperor to go down to Verona once more. Elizabeth did not: his wife and children needed him in Vienna, she insisted. When she found her husband adamant, she begged to be allowed to accompany him to headquarters, again without success; and when at last, on 29 May, he left Vienna, she wept quite openly, like any other young wife seeing her husband off to the wars. The Archduchess disapproved: 'Poor Sisi's scenes and tears only serve to make life even harder for my unfortunate son', she noted in her journal. No sooner had the Empress returned to Schönbrunn from the station than she wrote to her husband, again seeking permission to join him. Long letters followed, almost every day of the campaign. In reply, her harassed husband found time to send Elizabeth seventeen letters in the forty days he was in Italy, most running to a thousand words, several to far more. By contrast his aunt, Marie Louise, had received only scribbled notes of some one hundred words from the great Napoleon as he marched on Moscow.

Francis Joseph, accompanied by both Grünne and Hess, reached Verona late on 30 May, having spoken briefly to Maximilian at Mestre on the way. 'My dearest angel Sisi', the Emperor wrote next morning, 'I am using the first moments after getting up to tell you once again how much I love you and long for you and the dear children . . .'; and after describing to her the journey, telling her that he was now 'in the selfsame room we shared together', and complaining that 'it rains here every day', he praised what he had seen of the army and referred optimistically to Gyulai's success in beating off attacks on his outposts. By then Gyulai had more than 110,000 front-line troops available to check an enemy attempt to penetrate Lombardy, four times as many men as the defenders of Marengo at the start of the century.

A note of disquiet crept into the Emperor's second letter to Elizabeth,

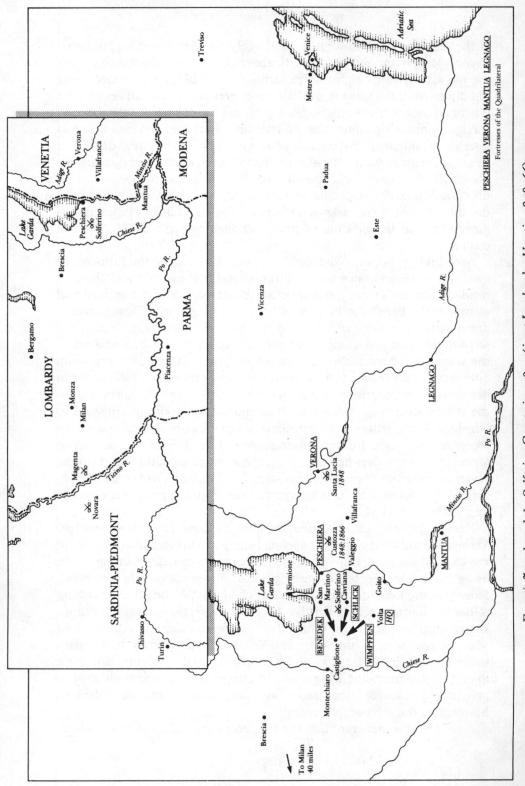

Francis Joseph and the Solferino Campaign 1859 (inset Lombardy–Venetia 1848–66)

PESCHIERA VERONA MANTUA LEGNAGO
Fortresses of the Quadrilateral

Adriatic Sea

Venice
Mestre

Treviso

Padua

Este

LEGNAGO

Adige R.

Po R.

VERONA
Santa Lucia 1848

Villafranca

Mincio R.

MANTUA

PESCHIERA
Custozza 1848: 1866
Valeggio
Goito

Lake Garda
Sirmione

San Martino
Solferino
Cavriana

BENEDEK
SCHLICK
Volta
HQ
WIMPFFEN

Castiglione
Montechiaro

Chiese R.

Brescia

To Milan
40 miles

Inset map:

SARDINIA-PIEDMONT

LOMBARDY

VENETIA

MODENA

PARMA

Lake Garda

Verona
Adige R.

Villafranca

Peschiera
Solferino
Mantua
Mincio R.

Chiese R.

Brescia

Bergamo

Monza
Milan

Magenta
Novara
Ticino R.

Po R.

Piacenza

Chivasso

Turin

dated 2 June. Her latest plea to be allowed to join him was firmly set aside: 'In headquarters which are on the move there is no place for women. I cannot set my army a bad example; and I don't myself know how long I shall be here . . .'; and he hinted that he would soon need to take over the operational command of the army himself. In reality, matters were far more serious than he appreciated. The first clashes had shown French gunnery to be superior to Austrian. Now it became clear that Gyulai's inexperienced sappers underestimated the strength of viaducts and bridges to resist the charges they had laid in them.

On 4 June what began as a sharp engagement between patrols west of the small town of Magenta for bridges over the river Ticino and a neighbouring canal soon developed into the biggest battle fought in Europe for forty-five years. Territorially the fighting was inconclusive on that Saturday for, though the Austrians eventually pulled back from Magenta railway station after twelve hours of bloodshed, Gyulai still commanded the main route towards Milan, twelve miles to the east. His army had, however, suffered over 10,000 casualties, more than twice as many killed and wounded as the French. By now the rains of the previous month had been succeeded by the customary scorching heat of a Lombard summer, and his men were weary, hungry and demoralized; he feared that in a second day's fighting they would be scattered like chaff across the plain. Overnight he decided to abandon Milan and retreat to the River Mincio, around Mantua, where his new positions would be covered by the good, solid fortresses of the Quadrilateral. Francis Joseph was amazed at Gyulai's decision. He sent Hess to field headquarters in the hope that the retreat could be halted. But Hess reported that any attempt to check the retreat of the weary troops short of the Mincio might prove disastrous. On 8 June Francis Joseph, still in Verona, was appalled to learn that Napoleon III and Victor Emmanuel II of Sardinia-Piedmont had entered Milan in triumph. One of the Emperor's aides, sent out to discover Gyulai's intentions, found the commander-in-chief apparently unruffled; he was comfortably housed, with good cooking and a chance to play cards after dinner. Yet Francis Joseph hesitated to get rid of him. Hess, who had served Radetzky brilliantly as a chief-of-staff and was now the Emperor's right-hand man, feared that it would be dangerous for the dynasty if Francis Joseph took command in the field and suffered military defeat. Not until further reinforcements reached the Quadrilateral, giving the Austrians a good prospect of victory under wise leadership, was Gyulai dismissed. On 16 June, at half past one in the afternoon, as Francis Joseph meticulously noted, 'I was driven to Villafranca, where I had summoned Gyulai, and gave him the formal order of dismissal. He was very grateful for it . . .'

News of Magenta and the fall of Milan had caused consternation in Vienna. A sustained press campaign was mounted against the whole absolutist system. Indirectly the Emperor himself came under criticism – particularly as patron of the despised Grünne – and as early as 9 June the council of ministers decided it was their 'sacred duty' to warn Francis Joseph of the mood in Vienna. It was agreed that, if the agitation continued, Rechberg should go down to the war zone and warn the Emperor of the disaffection in the capital; but not yet.

Francis Joseph had, however, sensed the danger already. A letter to the Empress sent soon after Magenta shows a rare impatience with her reports of bickering with the Archduchess and with her failure to do anything useful: 'My dearest one and only angel,' he wrote, 'I beg you, for the love you still have towards me, to pull yourself together. Show yourself in the city now and again, visit hospitals and institutions. You've no idea what a great help that would be to me. It would lift the spirits of people in Vienna and keep up morale, which I so urgently need now.' Throughout these critical weeks her whims continued to worry her husband: how she would eat scarcely any food, and sit up late at night reading or writing letters; and how, during these midsummer days, she would take long rides on her favourite horse, once covering some twenty miles without a stop. Sometimes she was accompanied by her head groom Harry Holmes, a forty-nine year old skilled horseman from the English Dukeries, but these excursions brought a stern reproof from Verona: 'I cannot allow you to go out riding alone with Holmes, that just won't do at all', Francis Joseph insisted. With great relief he heard that Elizabeth did, indeed, visit the capital occasionally. He was pleased to learn that she had converted part of Laxenburg into a hospital for wounded officers, in whose welfare she took a personal interest.

Hess, now chief-of-staff to the Emperor, recommended that the army should move forward from Gyulai's line along the River Mincio to the Chiese, a parallel river some eighteen miles to the west; and for the first two days after superseding Gyulai, Francis Joseph travelled widely so as to get to know the villages, farms and vineyards of this undulating countryside south of Lake Garda. He returned to Verona on the evening of 19 June for what he described as a 'long' meeting with Rechberg, who updated him with news from Vienna and assessments of unrest elsewhere in the Monarchy, notably in Hungary. Francis Joseph believed a battle was imminent, and his letters show a quiet confidence. On Thursday evening, 23 June, he set up headquarters at Valeggio, on the River Mincio some five miles south of Peschiera. His advance troops had still not reached the Chiese, but Valeggio was a good vantage-point: headquarters looked out towards the steep hills around the villages of Cavriana and

Solferino which commanded the plain sloping gently down to Castiglione and eventually to the crossing of the Chieso at Montechiaro. Although Francis Joseph did not know it, Napoleon III had moved French headquarters forward from Brescia to Montechiaro that night.

Francis Joseph was to remember Friday, 24 June, 1859, as 'a harsh, bitter day'. It was the only time he led his army in a major battle against foreign enemies; and he was defeated, with more than 22,000 of his troops left dead, missing or seriously wounded. Yet the day had begun for him as undramatically as its immediate predecessors during the campaign. He was, as usual, up early to attend to his correspondence but when, soon after eight o'clock, he took his breakfast, he could hear a desultory exchange of gunfire, which grew steadily in intensity the opposing armies had stumbled across each other as they advanced over the plain, and there was firing along an unusually broad front. At nine o clock, with breakfast over, the Emperor decided to set out for Cavriana and see what was happening. Remarkably it took another two hours before headquarters appreciated that the full force of the two armies were engaged in battle.

By then Francis Joseph had assumed overall command of the 129,000 troops massed to the west of the Mincio. They were deployed in what might be regarded as a classical defensive position, ready to meet the advance of a slightly larger enemy force, and throw it back towards Milan. General Wimpffen, commanding the three corps of the First Army, was to attempt a turning movement from the left, aiming to reach Castiglione: the four corps of General Schlick's Second Army were to check and repulse the French centre by using the natural escarpment of Solferino; and General Benedek, commanding the largely independent 8 Corps, would engage the Piedmontese on the extreme right of the plateau before the village of San Martino. Francis Joseph established his field headquarters at Volta, on the left of the battlefield, almost fifteen miles from Benedek.

Only once before, at Leipzig in 1813, was a European battle fought over so great an area and with such large numbers of men to control. On that occasion the opposing commanders were soldiers of great experience, yet even they had found the task virtually beyond them, making Leipzig a victory of attrition rather than a striking triumph of arms. Both Francis Joseph and Napoleon III had received a baptism of fire before Solferino, but they remained textbook generalissimos skilled in parade-ground soldiery; they were accustomed to assessing army manoeuvres but not to improvising and executing a co-ordinated strategy dependent on reports from sectors spread across a wide battlefront. The French dutifully stuck to their task; they threw in column after column of infantry to support the guns bombarding Solferino itself; and on the Austrian side Wimpffen mounted two conventional attacks against the French right.

Under the midday heat the fighting was intense but indecisive, with over a quarter of a million men and some 40,000 horses in action. By two o'clock in the afternoon, however, the hilltop defences of Solferino had suffered an intense battering, while Wimpffen's cavalry were exhausted, and the corps commanders were painfully conscious of their lack of reserves. An hour later the French tricolour was flying over the ruined village of Solferino, while from his headquarters at Volta Francis Joseph could see that in the plain Wimpffen's exhausted men had been forced to give ground. Fifteen miles away, almost out of touch with headquarters, Benedek's 8 Corps had spent the morning beating off successive Piedmontese attacks. Had Benedek been able to count on receiving cavalry reinforcements, he was in a position to thrust forward and threaten the main French army with encirclement. But, at half-past three, to his dismay he received from headquarters not the promise of additional cavalry, but an order for all troops to pull back to the protection of the Quadrilateral.

Shells had begun to fall close to the Emperor's headquarters, confirming the enemy's steady and relentless advance across the plain. 'So I had to give the order to retreat' Francis Joseph wrote to Elizabeth on the following Sunday from Verona, thirty miles east of the battlefield:

I rode into Volta, where I stopped briefly, and then through a fearful thunderstorm to Valeggio, from where I drove to Villafranca. There I spent a horrible evening, amid a confusion of wounded, of refugees, of wagons and horses, in which it took a great effort to establish any semblance of order. I was asleep for four hours and at dawn travelled here by railway ... That is the sad history of a terrible day on which much was achieved, but fortune did not smile on us. I have learnt much from what I have experienced, and I know what it feels like to be a beaten general. The grave consequences of our misfortune are still to come, but I put my trust in God and do not feel myself to blame for having made any faulty disposition of troops.

This claim was justified. It might, however, be argued that he had broken off the action prematurely and, in particular, that his judgment of the battle wavered under the shattering news that the 19th and 34th Hungarian Infantry Regiments had deserted, almost to a man, during the day. Kossuth, it was reported, had come to Genoa and was raising a Hungarian Legion to recover the kingdom's lost liberties. The multinational structure of the Monarchy left Francis Joseph unsure of the loyalty of certain units. The German-Austrian and Czech regiments had fought valiantly, and they fell back on the fortresses of the Quadrilateral still in good order. From the Venetian troops there was no real threat of mutiny either, though many Lombards had gone over to the Italian national cause. Although less than six per cent of the rank and file deserted during the campaign, contingents coming from the eastern half of the Monarchy were less reliable than those from the west and north and, after the terrible losses of Solferino, there was little fighting spirit left in any of the South Slav regiments, whether they were raised in Croatia or along the (predominantly Serb) frontier zone to the east. But Hungary remained the greatest uncertainty of all. Francis Joseph knew that Kossuth had been received by Napoleon III in the first week of May; and a German-Austrian and Czech army corps, whose presence in Lombardy would have tilted the numerical balance of forces in Austria's favour, remained in Hungary throughout the war. A French squadron sailed up the Adriatic, ready to support followers of Kossuth in Dalmatia and thus fire the fuse of a Magyar rebellion. But, perhaps fortunately for the Hungarian peoples, no spark of revolt was ignited that summer.

Francis Joseph was deeply shaken by the carnage at Solferino. Archduke Maximilian, who had been at his brother's side ever since the dismissal of Gyulai, wrote to Charlotte on the day after the battle: 'I had never much hope of the outcome, but I did not imagine it would follow so swiftly or be quite so overwhelming. The retreat during the evening formed a scene of desolation I shall never forget. The sight of all the wounded was terrible'. Nevertheless the Emperor was at first prepared to continue the war: the Quadrilateral remained the strongest defensive system in the world; and he was certain Napoleon III would not risk throwing weary troops against the defences of Verona. He had still not entirely given up hope that 'the despicable scum' in Prussia would 'stand by us in the end'; and Prince-Regent William did, indeed, order the massing of six army divisions along the Rhine frontier on the day that the battle of Solferino was fought. If the Austrians had been prepared to allow the Prince-Regent to command all the northern troops of the German Confederation, the Prussians would have marched on Paris. But, though Maximilian liked to pose as an Austro-Italian prince, Francis Joseph still saw himself as the residual legatee of the old Empire of the German Nation: better accept, at least temporarily, the loss of Lombardy than help Lutheran Prussia achieve primacy in Germany.

He was right in assuming that Napoleon III would hesitate before committing his army to a long campaign of probing at the Quadrilateral. Like Francis Joseph and Maximilian, Napoleon was appalled by the horrors of the battlefield, much as his uncle had been after the terrible losses at Eylau. He was worried, too, by the attitude of the Prussians and in particular by threats from Berlin that if a national insurrection flared up in Hungary, Prussia would force France to make peace with Austria so that the German Powers could work together against the spread of revolution. Napoleon, aware that he was becoming involved in problems beyond his control, decided to end the war as speedily as possible. 'I can't hang on in this position', his cousin heard him say, 'I must get out of here'.

In one of her letters the Empress Elizabeth had raised with Francis Joseph the possibility that he might hold talks with the Prince-Regent of Prussia, as a means of putting pressure on France. 'A meeting with the Prince of Prussia, such as you mention, is not on the cards', he replied on 8 July, 'but it could be that another meeting is in store for me which I dread, namely one with that arch-scoundrel Napoleon ... At present Napoleon seems to possess a deep desire for an armistice and for peace ... The evening before last I had already gone to bed when the arrival of General Fleury, aide-de-camp of the French Emperor, was announced ... I leapt out of bed, had myself got into uniform and welcomed the General, who brought me a handwritten letter from his Emperor in which he proposed to me a ceasefire' on land and sea. Next morning Francis Joseph had answered Napoleon: he welcomed a ceasefire pending negotiations and was willing to meet Napoleon to discuss an interim settlement of the Italian question. On 8 July the armistice became effective.

Three days later Francis Joseph set out from Verona soon after dawn, with a group of senior officers, escorted by a squadron of the Imperial Uhlans. A mile to the east of Villafranca he was received by Napoleon III, at whose side he rode into the town, dismounting outside the house which had so recently been his headquarters. In 1807 two opposing emperors – Napoleon I and Tsar Alexander I – surprised the world by meeting on a raft at Tilsit to end a long war and reverse the alliance system, making Russia France's ally rather than her enemy. The Villafranca meeting was intended by Napoleon III to suggest parallels with Tilsit: once more two emperors would startle Europe by coming together privately and deciding the fate of the continent – although, as usual, Napoleon was in far too much of a hurry to spare such matters more than a few hours of conversation. He wished to shun possible mediation by Prussia, Russia or Great Britain and confound the calculations of the European chancelleries with the possibility of a Franco-Austrian detente. Unlike Tilsit – or Plombières – the meeting with Francis Joseph was given great publicity. Journalists were encouraged to clamber round the rubble and craters of Villafranca in search of good copy.

Within a couple of days, Europe's newspaper public could read how Napoleon III and Francis Joseph had gone alone, without advisers or interpreters, into a ground floor room where they talked for about an hour, apparently taking no notice of reporters peering through the windows. They sat at a table smoking cigarettes, and talking fluently in either French or German. No maps were unrolled. Occasionally they would jot down notes on sheets of paper. One journalist claimed to have seen Napoleon III nervously fraying some flowers, and he was certainly less at ease than Francis Joseph; a few days later he admitted to the British ambassador in Paris that, while talking to Francis Joseph, he had no idea 'who ruled what in the various Italian duchies'. By eleven o'clock the meeting was over. The journalists learnt that the emperors had agreed on a preliminary peace. They favoured the creation of an Italian Confederation under the Pope; the cession to France (for transfer to Sardinia-Piedmont) of all of Lombardy, except the fortresses of Mantua and Peschiera; the inclusion of Venetia, which would remain an Austrian possession, in the Italian Confederation; the return of the rulers of Tuscany and Modena to their duchies; 'indispenable reforms' in the Papal States; and a general amnesty 'to persons compromised by recent events'. Refinement of these terms would be made in a definitive treaty later in the year.

Francis Joseph was well satisfied with his morning's work. After signing the 'preliminary peace' he rode beside the 'arch-scoundrel' a short distance down the familiar road towards Valeggio. The two emperors parted courteously, still scrutinized by journalists for whom such occasions remained a novelty. Francis Joseph then returned swiftly to Verona. Three days later he was back in his capital. He had fared better at Villafranca than he dared to hope after conceding defeat on the battlefield. All Radetzky's fortresses in the Quadrilateral remained in Austrian hands, providing him with bases from which he might launch a war to avenge Solferino. He was resigned, for the present, to accept a loss of territory; 'We shall get that back in a couple of years', he was heard to remark a few days later. But in Vienna he found Rechberg still uneasy over the falling prestige of the dynasty. The lost campaign in Italy pierced the mystique of military autocracy cultivated so carefully for the first ten years of his reign. In Prague his uncle Ferdinand, the kindest of ex-emperors, read of the cession of Lombardy and observed, 'Even I could have managed that!'. To win back and hold his subjects' regard Francis Joseph needed to follow retreat in Italy by a phased withdrawal from absolutism in the Monarchy as a whole.

Chapter 8

'POWER REMAINS IN MY HANDS'

Despite the warnings given to him at Verona by Rechberg, the Emperor was shaken by the coolness with which he was received in Vienna on his return from the war. There were no spontaneous cheers in the street and several instances of men failing to raise their hats in respectful salute as his carriage sped by them. The newspapers were, of course still censored, although less strictly than at the peak of the Metternich era, and readers could catch ominous growls emerging from their loosely muzzled columns. The liberal *Neues Wiener Tagblatt*, knowing it could not attack Francis Joseph in person, was outspoken in criticizing his closest advisers, especially Grünne, whom it described as 'a behind-the-scenes head of government' with 'the authority of a Vice-Emperor'. More serious than the press attacks were police reports of assassination threats: some may merely have originated in hotheaded talk after too much drink, but an alleged plot by a footman at the Hofburg who wished to murder both the Emperor and the Archduchess Sophie caused greater concern at Court.

Characteristically, Francis Joseph shrugged off any risk to his person. He stayed away from Vienna, however, for he did not want foreign observers reporting to other governments on what were, in effect, silent demonstrations of disapproval when Emperor or Empress appeared in the capital. Yet, at a time when (as he said) 'our land is suffering from deep wounds', his diligent conscience would not permit him to relax. He therefore changed the normal pattern of Court life: no birthday vacation at Ischl this year, and no lengthy residence at Schönbrunn, for the palace was too public. Instead, he shut himself up at Laxenburg through the last scorching weeks of a sultry summer. The parkland was good for shoots and short rides, but for the most part he chose to immerse himself in the study of memoranda and reports of the 'unfortunate but glorious campaign'. After that shattering experience, he found it hard to feign once more the ebullient self-confidence which had carried him through the first years of his married life. At Laxenburg a morose husband joined a wife who, though still devoted to him, was accumulating more and more grievances over the role she was called upon to play at Court

As early as 15 July Francis Joseph presided over a ministerial Council, the first inquest into what had gone wrong. Later that day he published the so-called Laxenburg Manifesto in which, after informing his subjects of the preliminary peace terms, he held out a promise of reform. He would, so the Manifesto ran, use the 'leisure' hours granted to him by the ending of the war to bolster the Monarchy's welfare 'by a suitable development of its rich spiritual and material resources, and by modernizing and improving the legislature and administration'. But he was in no hurry to complete the changes. During the next five weeks the Council never met once. Two unpopular figures disappeared from the public eye: Bach resigned as minister of the interior at the end of July; while Grünne attended no more meetings of the Council and, in October, accepted the largely honorific Court post of Master of the Horse. A new team of ministers was announced on 21 August: Rechberg remained in charge of foreign affairs as well as being effective prime minister; the indispensable Baron Karl von Bruck looked after finance, trade and communications; and Count Goluchowski, Governor of Galicia for the past ten years, became minister of the interior. Never before had a Polish aristocrat received so high an appointment in Vienna.

Briefly the Emperor seemed to be flirting with liberalism. This was an illusion. He was impressed by a memorandum presented to him by Baron Bruck: it recommended the introduction of constitutional government, with both communal assemblies and an enlarged Imperial Council, and religious concessions to curb the powers enjoyed by the Catholic hierarchy under the Concordat and increase the civic rights of the Protestant and Orthodox churches, so influential among the nationalities around the fringe of the Monarchy. But though Francis Joseph summoned Bruck to Laxenburg to discuss these proposals, over one point he remained adamant: he would never grant a constitution; there must be no more Kremsier play-acting. It was thus impossible for him to accept a genuinely liberal programme of reform. He mistrusted any proposal which might have limited his sovereign powers over the army or foreign affairs. On the other hand, he respected Bruck's judgment of affairs and he agreed with him that local assemblies in the provinces might have a valuable administrative function. He therefore sounded out two highly trusted members of the dynasty, his cousins the Archdukes Albrecht and Rainer; both emphasized the need for something to be done to calm the mounting political excitement in Hungary. Significantly, Francis Joseph took little notice of Maximilian. There had been a brief meeting with him and Charlotte, under Archduchess Sophie's auspices, but Max's ideas remained too drastically reformist, and a popular cult in Buda and Vienna of the 'liberal Archduke' – together with a certain jealousy between Sisi and Charlotte – heightened Francis Joseph's doubts.

Bruck had given the Emperor the views of a bourgeois Protestant: Goluchowski was an astute, Jesuit-educated Catholic, whose religiosity ensured that his political opinions were treated with some indulgence by Archduchess Sophie. For Goluchowski 'Germanization' was the curse of the Monarchy. If he favoured any system of government at all, it was a multi-national benevolent aristocracy. By contrast Rechberg, though a Metternichian conservative in general policy, had the faults and virtues of a slightly pedantic bureaucrat. He acknowledged a need for the Emperor's government to consult the peoples of the Monarchy over regional and local problems, but his main concern was with Austria's status as a European Great Power. In particular, he wished to define anew the traditional Habsburg role in Germany. None of these three ministers – Bruck, Goluchowski, Rechberg – would support a second round of war in Italy.

Nor, indeed, after November, when the Peace Preliminaries were defined more precisely by the Treaty of Zurich, did Francis Joseph want another campaign. He could see that the intensity of Italian nationalist feeling had already ruled out many proposals conjured up so easily in the tobacco smoke of Villafranca; and he did not want to become involved more deeply in the affairs of the peninsula so long as they were in such a state of flux. The army needed to be re-equipped, notably with better rifles and field guns. Before facing new battles, he wished to be certain of the loyalty of all his nationalities.

The first of the reforms promised in the Laxenburg Manifesto were announced on 23 August and followed Bruck's recommendations closely. Local assemblies (*Landtage*) were to receive increased administrative powers; and the Protestant and Orthodox Churches were promised greater freedom. In November Francis Joseph approved proposals to abolish many of the remaining restrictions on the Jewish communities of the Empire (a topic Bruck had not raised in his memorandum). Before the end of the year the Emperor established a State Debt Committee, to examine the financial structure of the Monarchy, for he agreed with Bruck on the need to re-assure foreign investors. Finally, on 5 March 1860, it was announced that an enlarged Reichsrat (to comprise 20 notables appointed by the Emperor and 38 elected representatives from the *Landtage*) would meet in Vienna at the end of May, with the immediate task of settling a national budget. Apart from a group of Magyar magnates, the Hungarians were slow to respond to Francis Joseph's modest reform programme; and the Viennese liberals were suspicious of Goluchowski as an aristocrat, a clericalist, and a Pole. But there were hopes of Bruck and Rechberg together introducing some form of central representative government.

Bruck, however, was dead before the 'Reinforced Reichsrat' met. The enquiry into the lost war had revealed peculation and corruption in high places, with the Quartermaster-General of the army the chief culprit, although he committed suicide before the inquiries were complete. Among financial figures arrested were several directors of Trieste companies with whom Bruck was once linked; and in mid-April 1860 Bruck was summoned to give evidence at the trial of an eminent banker accused of embezzling government funds (and eventually found innocent). The sustained smear campaign by Bruck's enemies made him offer his resignation to the Emperor, on the grounds that a finance minister should not in any way be associated with a trial of this nature. In a private audience, the Emperor assured Bruck that he enjoyed his complete confidence, and he persuaded him to stay in office. But Francis Joseph always remained brutally unimaginative in handling personal relationships. Others at Court – almost certainly Grünne among them – suggested that Bruck was right: he should give up such a sensitive office while the inquiries were continuing. On the evening of 22 April, Bruck returned with his family from a theatre visit to find awaiting him a brief note from the Emperor: 'As you requested, I have decided to put you on the retired list for the time being'; and he was told that one of his senior officials, Ignaz von Plener, would succeed him as minister of finance. So shaken was Bruck by this curt message that he seized his razor and cut his throat. Subsequently, a detailed investigation of the Baron's papers and documents exonerated him from all scandal.

Bruck's suicide deepened Austria's chronic financial crisis, for his prestige among Europe's bankers had been high, and the exchange rate of the thaler fell sharply at the news of his death. Never again would Francis Joseph find such a far-sighted economist to manage the Monarchy's finance and commerce. Politically, too, his death was ill-timed. When the Reinforced Reichsrat began, very cautiously, to discuss a more representative system of government, the balance was tilted in favour of the aristocratic federalism favoured by Goluchowski and a group of Hungarian 'Old Conservatives'.

Francis Joseph was angry that the topic had been raised at all: 'I cannot allow any curtailment of monarchical power through a constitution', he told his ministers in June, 'I would face any storm rather than that. The possibility may not even come up for discussion.' At Reichsrat sessions two Archdukes and Cardinal Rauscher tried to ensure that the Emperor's wishes were observed, but without success. In the last week of September the Reichsrat presented two recommendations to the Emperor: a majority report favoured federalism; a minority report recommended centralized government under an even larger Reichsrat. The Emperor accepted both documents but, for over a fortnight, remained silent about them. He had, however, agreed to meet the rulers of Russia and Prussia in Warsaw on 21 October to discuss a common autocratic Front against the Italian Risorgimento and other manifestations of national liberalism. There was – so he was told by Count Szécsen, spokesman for the Magyar Old Conservatives – a danger of unrest in Hungary if he did not give the Reichsrat a clear answer. On the other hand, Szécsen assured the Emperor that if his compatriots knew their historic Diet was to be restored, they would co-operate with the other nationalities and treat the Monarchy as a unitary state. Francis Joseph did not want his standing at the Warsaw meeting weakened by reports of trouble in Hungary, for that would recall too sharply the first months of his reign. Accordingly, he appointed Szécsen a government minister with the task of drafting, within a few days, 'a new settlement for the Empire as a whole' based upon the recommendations sent to him by the majority in the Reichsrat.

It was a tough assignment. Yet, after consulting Rechberg and Goluchowski, Szécsen completed his task some thirty hours ahead of Francis Joseph's departure for Warsaw. The 'October Diploma' was a fundamental law which strengthened the provincial Diets, giving them legislative authority over matters previously determined by ministers of the interior. It provided for them to send delegates to the Reichsrat, which would be recognized as the principal legislature of the Empire. Supplementary to the basic Diploma were more than twenty 'Sovereign Rescripts' which established electoral bodies to prepare for the Diets in the various provinces – thereby tacitly sanctioning open discussion in towns where, for twelve years, a discreet instinct of well-being had precluded political debate. On paper, at least, the Emperor had abandoned absolutism, while still avoiding use of that accursed word 'constitution'.

'We are certainly going to have a little parliamentary life, but the power remains in my hands', Francis Joseph wrote to his mother, a few hours before leaving for Warsaw. His confidence re-assured the Archduchess, who had read the details of the October Diploma earlier that day. The past twelve months had been hard for her. She had seen earlier protégés, like Grünne and his nominees, discredited and the political clericalism which brought about the Concordat called in question. It was a blow to her that she could not smooth down the mounting mistrust between her eldest sons for, though she thought Franzi right and Max wayward, her second-born child was her favourite. Saddest of all to the Archduchess was the rift with her niece and daughter-in-law, which broadened every week.

The worst disputes concerned the upbringing of the Crown Prince. Archduchess Sophie remained convinced that Elizabeth was too immature to supervise the education of the heir to the throne. As soon as Rudolf left the cradle, his grandmother planned for him precisely the same early training as she had laid down for Francis Joseph and Maximilian. Over such matters the Emperor did not question his mother's wisdom. At heart he, too, still looked upon 'my heavenly Sisi' as a child-wife, his 'one and only, most beautiful angel'; he seems indeed always to have loved an immaturity of spirit she never completely shed. But the Empress was too strong-willed to remain a pet. She resented 'interference' in the nursery routine and, in her indignation, convinced herself that her mother-in-law would stop at nothing to humiliate her. This was unfair: there are many instances in Sophie's journal of sympathy and affection for the niece whose moods she could never understand. Yet the Archduchess must have been a trying companion with whom to share a palace, for her approbation tended to spice Bavarian sentimentality with an astringency all her own: thus, on 24 December 1859, she could describe 'Sisi at a Christmas party for her 22nd birthday, looking as delicious as a sugar bonbon, in a strawberry pink dress of watered silk (*moiré*)'. Was this praise, or criticism of the young Empress's dress sense?

At all events, by the following autumn, when her husband was trying to make up his mind over 'the new settlement for the Empire', Elizabeth had lost much of that bewitching vitality on which her strained nerves had drawn in the first years of marriage. Her reluctance to eat more than a few mouthfuls of the meals set before her – a trait which first caused concern while Francis Joseph was in Verona – had grown into a positive loathing for all food. Each day she would take vigorous exercise on gymnastic apparatus; she feared that she would soon look like her sister Néné, whom she considered overweight but who was, in reality, a comfortably proportioned mother, happily married to the Prince of Thurn and Taxis.

In a modern adolescent a similar instance of eating very little and constantly fighting an imaginary weight problem might well be diagnosed as a form of anorexia nervosa. But in 1860 the science of human behaviour was still in its infancy. That the Empress was ill, there was little doubt. When she took a holiday at Possenhofen in mid-summer her mother and brothers were deeply worried; she was 'a bean-pole', Ludovika told her. As for the cough which she could not shake off, that seems to have been as much a nervous gesture as a symptom of trouble in the throat or lungs.

Elizabeth certainly had grave matters on her mind. Everyone at Possenhofen was concerned over the future of her eighteen year old sister, the Queen of Naples, who bravely decided to stiffen her weak-kneed husband's resistance to the menace of Garibaldi and his thousand redshirts. Elizabeth found it galling that, because of Austria's losses in the Solferino campaign, the Emperor would not sanction intervention in southern Italy. Francis Joseph joined her at Possenhofen in late July; he enjoyed playing billiards with his Bavarian kinsfolk and he was glad to relax in the family circle; he expressed admiration for the Queen of Naples's fighting spirit, but nothing could induce him to send ships or men or material to uphold the independence of the Two Sicilies. And, at this very moment of disillusionment with her soldier husband idol, Elizabeth's enemies at Court seem to have made certain that she picked up rumours of his passing attachment to a Polish countess, resident in Vienna during the previous winter and spring. Whether there was any truth in these tales remains unclear: from Marie Walewska onwards, seductive Polish countesses flit across historical romance at the drop of a fan. But, given the circulation of these rumours, it was unfortunate to have chosen Warsaw for a summit conference that autumn.

The Warsaw meeting, which formally opened on 22 October, was unproductive. Prince-Regent William of Prussia and Francis Joseph treated each other with a cool, mutual suspicion, while Alexander II was too concerned with Russia's internal affairs to trouble himself over a revival of 'the revolution' and the alleged need for the Holy Alliance powers to crusade against liberalism in Italy. Alexander was not sorry to disoblige Francis Joseph, for bitterness over Austria's 'ingratitude' during the Crimean War lingered on. The sudden death of Alexander II's mother gave the Tsar an excuse to cut the meeting short and return to St Petersburg. By 28 October Francis Joseph, too, was back in his capital. He found Sisi in a state of nervous collapse.

A modern biographer of the Empress has claimed that, while her husband was in Warsaw, Elizabeth decided to seek the opinion of an outside physician on the state of her health. 'Heavily veiled and under an assumed name, the doctor may not have guessed at her identity and therefore told the truth, namely, that she was suffering from an unpleasant and contagious disease. To learn that Francis Joseph had not only been unfaithful but had contaminated her as well would have filled her with such horror and disgust, as to explain, not only her behaviour at the time, but her whole attitude in the future.' No authority is given for this tale, the details of which sound highly unlikely. More probably, with winter approaching after months of worry and frustration, the Empress experienced on a greater scale than in earlier years the claustrophobic escapism that had in the past impelled her to ride long distances non-stop in a single day. It would seem that Elizabeth was suffering from a mental illness rather than from any disease, and that the physical symptoms she showed were attributable to emotional causes. 'I must go far, far away, right out of the country', she told Francis Joseph. Villas in Istria or the southern Tyrol were too accessible. She wanted a remote island where no one could reach her. Madeira was her choice. Reluctantly, but with the tolerant kindness he reserved for Sisi, Francis Joseph concurred.

An official medical bulletin informed the public that Her Imperial Majesty was suffering from a grave infection of the lungs which required her to winter in a warm climate. Archduchess Sophie seems to have known nothing of the illness, nor did she hear in advance of the plans for rest and recuperation. 'I was shattered by the news' she wrote in her journal on the last day of October; she could not understand why Sisi wished to leave her husband and children 'for five long months'. As no Austrian ship was said to be ready or available for the voyage to Madeira, Queen Victoria put her royal yacht at the disposal of the Empress. Francis Joseph accompanied Elizabeth through Bavaria and as far as Bamburg. She then travelled on to Antwerp with her personally selected ladies-in-waiting and equerries and with the foreign minister's brother to act as a personal secretary. The Emperor paid a brief courtesy visit to the King of Württemberg in Stuttgart and by the end of the week was back at Laxenburg.

The mystery of the Empress's illness remained unresolved. A fringe observer with a long experience of royal maladies attended her at Antwerp. 'Yesterday before daybreak I . . . paid the Empress a visit, and then I took her to your beautiful ship', King Leopold wrote to Queen Victoria, on 22 November, 'She was much struck with it . . . I saw the Empress already dressed for her departure, but I think there is something very peculiar about her, which is very pleasing (sic). Poor soul, to see her go away under, I fear, not very safe circumstances, as she coughs a great deal, quite grieves one'. The wintry voyage down the Channel and across the Bay of Biscay was exceptionally rough. While most of the imperial suite were seasick, Elizabeth developed a hearty appetite for meals cooked and served by the Royal Navy, her own chef being far too ill to attend to her delicate needs. For several weeks after landing at Madeira, she revelled in the delights of the island like a child on a seaside holiday. And then, as Christmas and her birthday approached, she became bored and depressed once more. 'She often shuts herself up in her room and cries all day . . . She eats alarmingly little . . . the whole meal, consisting of four courses, four sweets, coffee etc. does not last more than twenty-five minutes', her secretary wrote back to Vienna in a private letter. Not all these details were made known to Francis Joseph but, as the year ended, it became increasingly clear to him that, so far from finding reassuring relief in Madeira, Sisi still believed herself wracked by an illness that tormented her spirits.

This protracted crisis in his private affairs coincided with the most perplexing political problems Francis Joseph had as yet encountered. Szécsen had assured him that the October Diploma would be well received in Hungary. He was wrong. The group of Magyar Old Conservatives at the Vienna Court had no following in Hungary. As soon as self-government was re-introduced into the Hungarian counties, there was a rush of patriotism to the head throughout the kingdom and a firm refusal in the towns and the countryside to pay any taxes unless the validity of the constitutional concessions granted in April 1848 was acknowledged. Some districts in Hungary, mocking the whole system, nominated absentees as their 'elected' representatives; the names put forward included, not only Kossuth, but even Napoleon III and Cavour. Nor were the Hungarians the only nationality to find the October Diploma inadequate: the Germans thought it too feudal, too clericalist, and too sympathetic to the Czechs (who, for their part, complained that the Diploma failed to acknowledge Bohemia's historic State Rights); and the Poles felt aggrieved because Goluchowski did not secure for Galicia the privileged status which they maintained Szécsen had won for Hungary. With every nationality disgruntled, Francis Joseph's 'little parliamentary life' proved stillborn.

On 14 December 1860, eight weeks after the Diploma was announced, Goluchowski arrived at his ministerial office to find a letter of resignation awaiting him on the desk, ready for his signature. Szécsen, too, was unceremoniously dropped; immediately after Christmas Francis Joseph held conversations in Vienna with two much respected Hungarian reformers, the lawyer Ferenc Deák and the novelist Baron Josef Eötvös. Both men had been moderate liberals in 1848–49 and both had important roles to play in the course of the coming decade, but for the moment their chief value was in giving their sovereign some insight into genuine Hungarian hopes and fears, rather than the rarefied feudalism of the Old Conservatives.

Francis Joseph was not prepared to tear up the October Diploma – why publicly admit political bankruptcy? He chose instead to have the Diploma's proposals 'elucidated' by a supplementary series of enactments announced on 27 February 1861, and therefore known as the 'February Patent'. These modifications were primarily the work of Baron Anton von Schmerling, a liberal who had once chaired the Frankfurt Parliament, and who took the place of the ousted Goluchowski (although in the first week of February Archduke Rainer officially took over as head of the government). They preserved the institutions proposed by the October Diploma but changed their composition and responsibilities, so as to make the new system more centralized. A bicameral Reichsrat was created, with the lower house comprising members sent to Vienna from the provincial diets under an indirect electoral college system of representation. To the disquiet of many professional army officers, this nominated chamber of deputies was intended to have control over the military budget. But the Emperor was not surrendering his prerogatives. Once again he rigidly insisted that real power remained in his hands: under no circumstances, he told his ministers when the February Patent was under discussion, must they allow the lower chamber to trespass into matters left properly to the foreign ministry and the army High Command. As the legislative programme of the following four years shows clearly enough, Francis Joseph retained a right of veto over contentious legislation and used it freely. He neither liked nor trusted parliaments, but he was prepared to let public opinion have a safety-valve if it minimized the risk of a democratic explosion. The Reichsrat was opened on 1 May with a speech from the throne in the ceremonial Redoutenhalle of the Hofburg. Thereafter parliamentary business was transacted in a specially constructed wooden building, popularly dubbed 'Schmerling's theatre': there seemed no point in commissioning a permanent chamber.

On that May Day of 1861 the Empress was in Seville. She had left Madeira three days before, having decided of her own volition to end the self-imposed exile. Her homeward voyage took her briefly to Malta and then to Corfu, where the beauty of the island entranced her. At last she reached Trieste and, on 18 May, joined Francis Joseph, Maximilian and Charlotte at Miramare, the Archduke's villa outside the city. She seemed fully recovered in health when she completed the journey by train to Vienna. But old grievances returned swiftly. Why was she at once absorbed into the routine of Court life, resuming the formal receptions which she found so tedious in the past? Why were Gisela and Rudolf expected to adhere to so rigid a daily programme that their mother seemed like a visiting guest to her own children? Nursery routine centred upon Grandmama and her two nominees, Countess Sophie Esterházy (the Empress's Mistress of the Robes ever since her wedding) and Baronness Caroline Welden, Rudolf's Aja. At almost three years old, the Crown Prince was devoted to 'Wowo', as he called the Baroness all his life.

The well-ordered life at the Hofburg became intolerable for Elizabeth within a matter of days. Less than a week after landing at Trieste, her health gave way again. Court receptions and state dinners were cancelled. Hurriedly she was moved out to Laxenburg, with her doctors in attendance. Had her recovery been more apparent that real? Or, as the more cynical Viennese began to speculate, was her illness less real than apparent? Soon she was refusing most of the food cooked for her, and her personal physician said she was feverish. In tears, she begged Francis Joseph to allow her to go away once more: not to Madeira, but down the Adriatic, back to the sunshine and peace of Corfu. Though wretchedly depressed himself, Francis Joseph as usual let her have her way. On 23 June he travelled to Trieste with her, leaving Maximilian to take her to Corfu, aboard an Austrian vessel. The fever had gone down and her appetite was picking up again even before she reached Corfu. When she disembarked, it was six weeks to the day since her first visit to the island.

Francis Joseph realized that this second flight of the Empress cast doubts on the future of Court life in Vienna, and indeed on the survival of his marriage. He therefore insisted on regular medical reports from Corfu and sent special couriers down the Adriatic to see what was happening on the island; some emissaries, notably Grünne, were poor choices. Far more welcome to Elizabeth was a visit from her sister, Helen of Thurn and Taxis, in August. When she passed through Vienna a month later Princess Helen urged Francis Joseph to travel to Corfu himself. He was at once attracted by the suggestion. Even though he had amused himself shooting and stalking deer with Helen's husband while she was staying with Elizabeth, he had spent a laborious summer trying to hold in check the mounting German liberalism in 'Schmerling's theatre' while encouraging his ministers to find new ways of asserting Austrian primacy within the German Confederation. Moreover Hungary remained a problem. Despite Deák's calming influence, the Hungarians still refused to take part in the Reichsrat's deliberations, while in Zagreb a new Croatian patriot, Ante Starčević, began to campaign for 'Croatia's historic rights'. Even had Elizabeth not been in Corfu, an escape to the peace of the Ionian Islands would have been welcome.

'I should like to spend early October paying a rapid visit of a few days to my dear Sisi in Corfu', the Emperor felt obliged to explain to his mother on 30 September, 'I feel the greatest longing to be there after such a long separation'. He arrived a fortnight later; soon he was writing back to the Archduchess in rhapsodies over the beauty of 'this earthly paradise'. The short sojourn in Corfu was the only occasion Francis Joseph visited territories which acknowledged Queen Victoria's sovereignty, for the Ionian Islands had been a British protectorate since the Congress of Vienna; and it is inevitable that, though he paid tribute to Corfu's scenic delights, he was more interested in the way the British had modernized the Venetian fortifications and developed the shipping facilities than in the laurel-woods, cypresses and craggy blue coves which so uplifted Elizabeth's spirits. The visit enabled husband and wife to talk long and calmly, with Francis Joseph showing great patience. He tempted her to return home with messages from the children as well as personal pleas, emphasizing his own need for her company. Elizabeth remained concerned for the well-being of the Empire, recognizing the validity of her husband's argument that her absence lowered his prestige as head of a historic dynasty. She kept up her regular lessons in the Magyar language as well as improving her Italian, and now sought to learn modern Greek, too. But she firmly refused to go back to Vienna, believing that to go into residence at the Hofburg again would lead to social disaster. The most she would concede was an agreement to winter in Venice, where she could hope to see Gisela and Rudolf occasionally, free from the brooding presence of their grandmother.

To have the Empress resident in Venice promised some political advantages, as Francis Joseph was quick to perceive. If his ministers were to concentrate on German affairs and on seeking an accommodation with the Hungarians, then it would be as well to preserve peace along the Monarchy's southern borders. Francis Joseph consistently deluded himself over Italian affairs. When the Kingdom of Italy was proclaimed in March 1861 he refused to acknowledge the new state, even arguing that the sentiment of nationalism in the peninsula was a fleeting enthusiasm which would soon give way to indignation over conflicting local interests. He believed Venetia was not quite lost to the Empire; the merchant class, with their traditional shipping interests in the Levant, might have more to gain from the improved railway network of central Europe than they could expect from competition with neighbouring commercial communities in the new Italy. Five years previously, Sisi's tact and charm melted the glacial patrician attitude of the old republic's ruling class towards the first imperial visit. Was there still a dormant strain of spontaneous wizardry crushed within her temperament? Moreover, if she became the First Lady of Venice, spending a Christmas season in the city for the second time in her life, she might well recover the social confidence which had always deserted her at the Hofburg and Schönbrunn.

In fact it was too late for any Habsburg to win acceptance. Elizabeth arrived in Venice at the end of October 1861 and remained in the city for six months. Never was she able to arouse any show of loyal support from her husband's Italian subjects. To them she was an outsider, a visitor wintering on the lagoon. Elizabeth's children were brought to her, and Francis Joseph paid several visits: 'They appear to be as much in love as in the first days of their marriage', Baron Hübner observed when he passed through Venice shortly before Christmas. Yet Elizabeth continued to worry the Emperor: the Crown Prince's trusted 'Wowo' earned her grudging approval, but she found Countess Sophie Esterházy as insuffer-able as ever, constantly insisting that the regime laid down by the Arch-duchess for the children's upbringing must be observed, even when they were away from Vienna.

In January the Emperor at last agreed to Elizabeth's request for the removal of the Countess from her household, after nine years in office. Henceforth the Empress would have around her only women she had chosen herself. But the dismissal of the Countess temporarily widened the rift with the Archduchess, for Sophie Esterházy was her closest friend and confidante. The Emperor could see that Sisi was not yet able to return to Vienna; and her behaviour seemed increasingly odd. She had started collecting a picture album of the (allegedly) most beautiful women in Europe, even asking her husband to use the services of the Austrian ambassador in Constantinople to obtain likenesses of the women of Sultan Abdulaziz's harem. These portraits she would study in admiration or envy. They brought little pleasure. According to her ladies-in-waiting, she again spent long hours alone in her room in tears. As spring approached, the reports sent back to Vienna and Possenhofen made Elizabeth seem so unwell that Duchess Ludovika took the most sensible decision ever recorded of her; she travelled down by train to Venice and, after lengthy consultation with Francis Joseph, whisked her daughter back to Bavaria for medical advice from Dr Fischer, who had cared for her in childhood.

The Emperor spent much of the late spring and summer of 1862 considering reforms in the judiciary and in banking and taxation, put before his ministers by the Reichsrat. He was faced, too, by an unexpected problem over which there were long family discussions. Since the previous December Napoleon III had been pursuing a forward policy in Mexico, where the radical government of Benito Juarez had suspended payments due on foreign debts. Although Mexico's financial viability was of great concern to France, and to a lesser extent to Spain and Britain, it did not touch any vital Austrian interests. But Napoleon believed that a monarchical Mexico, ruled by a European prince with the support of France, would open up a Latin American market to European commerce and political influence at a time when the United States was weakened by the Civil War. At Napoleon's prompting the property-owning clericalist party in Mexico was prepared to invite Francis Joseph's eldest brother to become sovereign of a new empire.

At first Maximilian, a restless romantic at heart, was inclined to accept the offer from Mexico, but he hesitated over leaving the exquisite home he had created at Miramare and he was conscious of the strong opposition of most of his family and his oldest advisers. Francis Joseph himself wavered: he acknowledged that opponents of the Mexican venture had a good case, but he knew that Maximilian and Charlotte had received some encouragement from Brussels, London and Paris to press for the creation of a dynastic satrapy within the Monarchy; better their hopes of a royal title should be realized outside Europe than in an autonomous kingdom of Greater Venetia or a virtually independent kingdom of Hungary. Moreover, though Francis Joseph looked on Napoleon as a 'rogue', he accepted that collaboration with France would help Austria emerge from politically dangerous diplomatic isolation. Yet he could not make up his mind. He was still uncertain over the course he should pursue in Mexico – or the merits of the Reichsrat's reform programme – when, in mid-July, he travelled to Possenhofen to judge for himself the true state of Elizabeth's health.

Here at least he received clear, and reassuring, advice. Dr Fischer was less gloomy than the Austrian physicians. No Bavarian Court doctor, accustomed to Wittelsbach eccentricities, tended to take alarm at relatively mild manifestations of nervous tension in any member of the family; and the doctor could find nothing wrong with the Empress's lungs or with her constitution in general. He was mainly concerned over her anaemia, a condition for which he recommended annual courses of hydropathic treatment at Kissingen. She had recently returned from a visit to the spa when Francis Joseph arrived at Possenhofen, and he was delighted by her progress. But, when it was suggested that the Empress might go back with her husband to Ischl, her ankles puffed up and she seemed once more a sick woman. Yet he was not despondent – merely, as he said at the time, 'hungry and thirsty for mountain hunting and mountain air'. For this deprivation he speedily found a simple remedy. As ever, it was the wildlife of the alpine crags and woodland which gratified the imperial craving for good sport.

Francis Joseph was soon back in Vienna; and, fortunately, too. For Elizabeth was unpredictable. Suddenly, without any warning to her ladies-in-waiting, she arrived by train in the capital on Thursday, 14 August, accompanied by her favourite brother, Karl Theodore. The Archduchess Sophie was in the Salzkammergut, where she had the tact to remain for several more weeks. Elizabeth was thus settled at Schönbrunn for the celebrations of her husband's thirty-second birthday and her son's fourth birthday three days later. The people of Vienna, by no means sympathetic to the Empress over the previous two years, welcomed her with as warm a reception as on the eve of her wedding. Their enthusiasm may have been genuine, but it was perhaps influenced by some liberal newspapers which gave the (over-simplified) impression she was at heart a progressive in conflict with a clericalist, reactionary mother-in-law. On the Sunday after her return – the eve of Francis Joseph's birthday – the imperial couple were serenaded by a choir of three hundred singers, and when dusk fell there was a torchlight procession in which between 14,000 and 20,000 people took part.

Elizabeth was extremely nervous, as her ladies soon discovered. For the next four or five months she wanted some member of her Bavarian family with her, either her brother or one of her sisters. But, as each week passed and Elizabeth remained still in residence, Francis Joseph became more optimistic. With his wife beside him and his mother discreetly absent, he found a new delight in playing the role of family father. Soon after Sisi's return, he took the four-year old Crown Prince with him for the annual inspection of the Wiener Neustadt military academy. He made certain that Rudolf was in uniform, just as he would himself have been at that age. When the cadets raised their caps to give three cheers for their Emperor, and Rudolf followed their example, Francis Joseph found the occasion so moving that tears came into his eyes. For several minutes he could not speak.

In many ways the Emperor remained a simple regimental officer who doted on wife and son and was, at heart, as sentimental as his mother. Yet an inbred conservative acceptance of the demands of duty and a pride in dynastic honour made him acutely conscious of the momentous responsibilities he bore. When he assured the Archduchess that 'power remains in my hands' he was satisfying not only his mother but his own conscience. Gradually, however, some principles she had instilled into him were modified, perhaps to a greater extent than he realized. As yet he would make no concession to the growing popular awareness of nationalism throughout his Empire, rightly perceiving that so powerful a force for change represented the negation of the Habsburg ideal. But, under the influence of Schmerling and the German-Austrian bourgeois liberals, his resistance to parliamentary politics at least began to show a certain elasticity of prejudice. When the Reichsrat ended its first session, a week before Christmas in 1862, he had accepted reforms of the commercial code as well as laws improving personal civil rights, freedom of the press, reform of local administration and the competence of the law courts. But perhaps the most interesting comment on the barely perceptible modifications to the form of the Monarchy came on the eve of the new session of 'Schmerling's theatre'. For on 26 February 1863 a gala performance took place at the opera house in Karntnertor to celebrate the second anniversary of the February Patent. The Emperor, who had at first been so alarmed at the intrusion of the Patent on his sovereign authority, was in the opera house that evening. Beside him, 'radiant and smiling' as foreign envoys noted, was his Empress, returning at last after three years to grace Court Balls and public receptions with her charm. What no ambassador could have predicted that February was how, in little over three more years, Elizabeth would possess the vision and skill to coax Francis Joseph into accepting the greatest of all changes in the structure of his Empire.

Chapter 9

IN BISMARCK'S SHADOW

In September 1862, while the Austrian Court was waiting anxiously to see if the Empress would settle once more in Vienna, the monarchy in Prussia faced a major political crisis. King William I – as the Prince Regent became on acceding in 1861 – shared Francis Joseph's belief that matters relating to the army remained within the sovereign's prerogative and were not subject to parliamentary debate. This contention had kept the King in conflict with liberals in the Berlin *Landtag* since his accession, for William sought army reforms, based upon three years of conscript service, while his parliament refused to authorize funds for changes which they feared would intensify the autocratic character of Prussian government. So disheartened was William by the protracted dispute that he was contemplating abdication when, on 22 September, General von Roon persuaded him to receive in audience the Junker diplomat, Otto von Bismarck, who convinced the King he could form a government which would raise the funds for the reforms without sanction of parliament. Bismarck thereupon became both head of the government in Berlin and foreign minister, responsibilities he held for twenty-eight years.

Francis Joseph had met Bismarck as early as June 1852 when he was sent to Vienna for a brief spell as acting ambassador. The Emperor was in Hungary that month and, after paying his respects to Archduchess Sophie and Metternich, the thirty-seven year old Prussian took the paddle-steamer down the Danube for an audience at the royal palace on Buda hill. The Emperor, Bismarck told his wife, 'had the fire of a young man of twenty, together with sober-minded self-possession'; in other letters Bismarck commented on his self-confidence and on his 'engagingly open expression, especially when he laughs'. At the time, Bismarck made little impression on Francis Joseph: he was, after all, only a stop-gap envoy, seconded from diplomatic duties in Frankfurt. But in 1854, and again in 1859, it was realized in Vienna that Bismarck had greater influence on the shaping of Prussian diplomacy than his duties as an executant of government policies warranted. Bismarck and his circle of Junker conservatives were blamed for Prussia's lack of response to Austrian initiatives both in the Crimean War and in the Magenta-Solferino campaign. It was accordingly with a certain apprehension that Francis Joseph and his ministers greeted the formation of a Bismarck government. On the other hand, there was a widespread feeling that, in defying the Prussian *Landtag* with such contemptuous insolence, the newcomer was courting disaster.

When he received his appointment Bismarck was serving as ambassador in Paris and, in October, he returned briefly to France to present letters of recall to Napoleon III. While in Paris he sought out Richard Metternich, Francis Joseph's envoy to the French Court: Prussia intended to secure political, economic and military primacy in northern Germany, Bismarck insisted in conversation; he preferred to attain this position through an understanding with Austria, he added, but if the government in Vienna opposed his policies he would resort to 'any means without scruple' to ensure Prussian leadership. There was, of course, nothing new in proclaiming such an objective, merely in Bismarck's hectoring tone. A few weeks later, on 5 December, Bismarck had the audacity to propose to Count Alois Károlyi – the Magyar magnate who was Francis Joseph's envoy in Berlin – that the time had come 'for Austria to shift her centre of gravity from Germany to Hungary'; once that was achieved Francis Joseph could count on full Prussian support in Italy and south-eastern Europe, but he warned Károlyi that if Austria rejected his overture Prussia would side with France in any future European crisis.

Neither conversation impressed Francis Joseph or his ministers. Prussia's tone and tactics varied from day to day, sometimes wooing, sometimes cajoling and sometimes threatening Austria: 'It is truly astonishing how swiftly Herr von Bismarck moves from one extreme position to another diametrically opposed to it', Károlyi observed in January. But when Bismarck began to bully the smaller German states into accepting a commercial treaty with France which was hostile to Austria's interests, Rechberg and Schmerling took him more seriously. They had already advised the Emperor to support a reform programme, aimed at reasserting Habsburg leadership of a 'modernized' German Confederation by bringing together delegates from the German and Austrian *Landtage* in a federal parliament. Francis Joseph was hesitant: he did not want to advance the cause of parliamentarianism; and, though always thinking of himself as a German prince, he had the good sense to appreciate the dangers of identifying himself too closely with any particular nationality in his Empire. But in the summer of 1863 he was tempted by a project raised, in the first instance, by Elizabeth's brother-in-law, Prince Maximilian of Thurn and Taxis: the reigning monarchs of the German states would be invited to Frankfurt for a *Fürstentag*, a 'Conclave of Princes', where the future of the Confederation could be discussed by the rulers themselves rather than by their ministers. At such a gathering the princes might well offer the crown of a revived German Empire to the head of the senior dynasty. In late July Francis Joseph made up his mind. On 3 August he paid a courtesy call on William of Prussia, who was taking the waters at Bad Gastein, and invited him to a congress of princes to meet in less than a fortnight at Frankfurt.

The German Princes accepted the invitation, but William temporized. He disliked hustle; he did not fancy the pomp and pageantry of a princely conclave at any time, least of all in August. At sixty-six he was old enough to remember the humiliations inflicted on his father by Napoleon I at the Dresden Congress of rulers. William's doubts were fed by Bismarck, who opposed any initiative taken by the Habsburgs: no acceptance and no final refusal was sent. Francis Joseph, however, was optimistic. He was sure of his fellow German Princes. 'It is the last chance for Germany's rulers, faced by revolution, to save themselves', he told his mother on the eve of departure. His letter rang with cheerful confidence: he felt invigorated by carefree days with Sisi, Gisela and Rudolf in the woods near Schönbrunn, 'the children bathing delightedly in the marvellous water'. When he reached Frankfurt there was still no sign of William, but the Princes warmly welcomed the Emperor and agreed to send their own invitation to the King, who was at Baden-Baden, less than three hours distant by train. King John of Saxony travelled there with a unanimous request that William should join his brother sovereigns.

William was impressed: 'Thirty reigning Princes and a King as a messenger! How can I refuse?', he pointed out to his prime minister. But Bismarck was adamant: to attend the congress would acknowledge Habsburg leadership in Germany; to stay away would wreck Vienna's plans and affirm Prussia's status as a Great Power in Germany and Europe. After a melodramatic dispute which dragged on until midnight, Bismarck had his way. In a letter to the King of Saxony, William politely but firmly rejected the invitation of the 'thirty Princes'.

Without Prussian co-operation there could be little prospect of federal reform or of an imperial coronation. Yet Francis Joseph's visit to Frankfurt was not wasted. The congress forged a loose bond between the Princes, with the Emperor himself accepted as the vital link. Despite William's absence, German affairs were discussed at some length. So long as Bismarck continued treating the Berlin *Landtag* with contempt, Austria appeared less reactionary than Prussia and there was, too, a certain feeling that a multinational institution like the Habsburg Monarchy was better suited to promote unity among the German states than was a narrowly Junker-led Prussia. Francis Joseph and Rechberg were even prepared to champion causes of prime concern to the German states but of little interest to Austria – notably the rights of the German-speaking population in the Danish duchies of Schleswig-Holstein, a topic raised intermittently at Frankfurt over the past fifteen years. Then, too, there was the Polish question. The congress met during the national-liberal insurrection in Russian Poland, which began in January 1863 and reached its peak in March. Most German states were anti-Russian over Polish affairs, but not Prussia. Yet while Bismarck still used the political jargon of the Metternich age, Francis Joseph joined the other states in showing some sympathy towards the Poles, despite his Galician possessions. Not surprisingly, the Princes followed Austria's lead in promoting federal reform. Francis Joseph's warm reception at Frankfurt and in southern Germany, emphasized Bismarckian Prussia's isolation.

So, indeed, Queen Victoria believed. On his way home to Vienna Francis Joseph broke his journey at Coburg, where the widowed Queen was on a protracted visit. It was a curious first meeting. Three days previously the Queen had given luncheon to William of Prussia; she loathed Bismarck and his policies, but she sympathized with the King and convinced herself that he had been kept away from the Frankfurt *Fürstentag* because the Austrians were set on deliberately snubbing Prussia. Francis Joseph was puzzled; he told his mother that, though the Queen was 'very gracious', she became 'quite grumpy ... inclined to have some bees in her bonnet'. The truth was that Victoria thought her son-in-law, Crown Prince Frederick, might soon succeed his ageing father, and she did not want to see his reign open with Prussia confronting a bloc of Austrian-led states.

She need not have worried: not only did William have almost a quarter of a century ahead of him on the throne but, as natural conservatives, both Francis Joseph and Rechberg were determined to shift their policy so as to work with Prussia in matters of joint interest. When, in the closing months of the year, the simmering Schleswig-Holstein question boiled over, German nationalist sentiment in the Confederation as a whole favoured military intervention against Denmark. So, too, did Bismarck's Prussia – though with narrower objectives. Francis Joseph thereupon assumed the role Queen Victoria had pressed upon him at their Coburg meeting; he made certain that, if the German Confederation had to oppose Denmark, the smaller states could at least rely on the backing of both Prussia and Austria. Saxon and Hanoverian troops entered Holstein in the last days of the old year; the Prussians followed a few weeks later, and on 1 February 1864 the Prussians and Austrians jointly marched into

Schleswig. Gradually the larger German Powers took matters into their own hands. In late February it was primarily the Prussians who invaded the Jutland peninsula, while an Austrian naval squadron effectively neutralized the Danish fleet. Little more was heard of Saxon or Hanoverian or Bavarian policies. The future of Schleswig-Holstein was left to British mediation at the conference table and to the diplomatic ingenuity of Bismarck and Rechberg. This was not the happiest of solutions, but there was satisfaction in Vienna that, at all events, Austria and Prussia were working in partnership, despite the rift of the previous summer.

With hindsight, it is clear that relations with Prussia should have been Francis Joseph's constant concern, once Bismarck had begun to press Austria to shift her 'centre of gravity'. But, like Alexander II and Napoleon III, the Emperor underestimated Bismarck: the brash Junker was boasting or bluffing or both, he assumed. A ruler in Vienna could not give more than a cursory glance northwards to the Baltic; Hungary was a more pressing topic than Schleswig-Holstein; and the Emperor continued to question much of the work put before him by Schmerling and the moderate Austrian reformers. There was, too, another problem which could no longer be shirked. The successful naval challenge in northern waters was a tribute to the spirit of enterprise fostered by Archduke Maximilian during his years as commander-in-chief of Austria's small fleet. Yet ironically this achievement came at a time when Maximilian had little opportunity to follow the fortunes of Admiral Tegetthoff's squadron. For in these early months of 1864 the Archduke had to make the supreme decision of his life. A Mexican crown was his for the taking. Should he accept an unstable throne in a distant continent or remain second in line of succession in Vienna?

In the previous August, a week before the German Princes began their deliberations in Frankfurt, Maximilian received a telegram at Miramare from Napoleon III informing him that in Mexico City a 'national assembly' had proclaimed him as Emperor. There was nothing to prevent the Archduke from rejecting the Mexican crown: his father-in-law, King Leopold, though supporting this particular project, had once declined to become the first sovereign of an independent Greece; and several of the Princes at Frankfurt took the opportunity to express doubts over the wisdom of allowing one of their number to become so closely associated with what was, in origin, a neo-Napoleonic project; Archduchess Sophie, Empress Elizabeth, and even Emperor Ferdinand in Prague urged Maximilian to have nothing more to do with Mexico. Reports reaching Europe indicated widespread support in the country for Juarez's republicanism and confirmed that President Lincoln (whose armies were gaining the upper hand in the war against the Confederates) remained hostile to the creation of a new empire in the Americas. Moreover, it became clear that the 'national assembly' which chose the Archduke as sovereign represented, at best, the will of the capital and its surrounding villages. In these circumstances why did Maximilian remain in contact with the Mexican monarchists? Was his obstinacy fed by the ambition of his wife, as his mischief-making youngest brother insisted in a letter to their mother? Perhaps so. Maximilian was not a political schemer; he liked flowers, and seascape gardening. He is said to have remarked to a friend at Miramare, 'If I heard that the whole Mexican project had come to nothing, I should jump for joy – but what about Charlotte?'.

What about Francis Joseph, for that matter? There is no doubt that over Mexico the Emperor behaved equivocally. In letters to Archduchess Sophie, written as early as August 1863, the 'Mexican business' appears as a tiresome distraction from more urgent questions: at heart he disliked the project and mistrusted its patron, 'that man in Paris who, in the last analysis, is the chief enemy of us all'. Yet at no point did he urge Maximilian to give up on the idea entirely, as both Rechberg and Richard Metternich assumed he would do. This failure to intervene decisively has been seen as proof that he welcomed the opportunity to ship a popular brother off to another continent. Consciously or sub-consciously, such motives may have helped shape the Emperor's policy. But these theories over-simplify a complex relationship in which both brothers were troubled by uncertainty. Maximilian, for example, had a higher regard for Napoleon III than did the Emperor; and yet, despite his hostility to Bonapartism, Francis Joseph was alive to the merits of an Austro-French entente in European affairs; he was disinclined to offend the 'man in Paris'. After their earliest talks on the project, Francis Joseph did all he could to please the Archduke. He allowed recruiting in Austria of volunteers who would serve Maximilian in a Mexican imperial army and he put funds at his brother's disposal. Occasionally both Francis Joseph and Maximilian looked upon Mexico as a lost Habsburg inheritance: the first European sovereign of the Aztec lands had been their ancestor, the great Charles V. It has been easy for people, puzzling over the brothers' behaviour, to lose the sight of that particular thread in the web Napoleon III wove around Mexico.

There is another explanation of Francis Joseph's conduct. Knowing Maximilian's character so well, he may have believed that outright opposition would intensify the Archduke's determination to accept the crown; he therefore resorted to less direct methods of persuading him to give up the idea, heavy-handed though they proved to be. Thus in January 1864 Maximilian received a memorandum, drawn up by Rechberg at the Emperor's request, in which it was made clear to the Archduke that, should he go to Mexico, he would lose his rights and titles in Austria, a deprivation which would extend to his heirs, if Charlotte had children. Maximilian protested vigorously at these proposals, which seem to have taken him by surprise. Supposing a disaster struck the dynasty, with both Francis Joseph and Rudolf dying; surely he would then reign as Emperor of both Mexico and Austria? The constitutional experts gave him no encouragement. He was even more outspoken in March, when the original conditions – together with a stipulation that he could no longer receive his annual allowance as a Habsburg prince – were presented in a 'family treaty', which he flatly declined to sign.

At this point Francis Joseph offered him a dignified line of retreat: 'If you cannot consent to this renunciation and prefer to refuse the crown of Mexico', he said, 'I will myself notify foreign countries of your refusal, and in particular the imperial sovereign in France'. But the Archduke believed his honour was involved; there were angry scenes between the two brothers, before Maximilian and Charlotte left Vienna for Miramare with the Act of Renunciation unsigned. A Mexican deputation was on its way from Paris. Already Austrian and French warships were moored off Trieste, ready to escort the newly created Emperor and Empress to Veracruz. But would they sail? For a few days it seemed likely that, even at this late hour, the Mexican project might become one of those rare opportunities which history had the good sense to miss.

Charlotte, however, would not give up the prospect of a crown. She became her husband's emissary, taking the train back to Vienna for prolonged talks with her imperial brother-in-law. She gained some success, securing an amendment to the family pact by which her husband kept his annual income as a Habsburg prince: much of the money was to go towards the upkeep of Miramare, which would be the Mexican sovereign's private retreat in Europe. Her return to Trieste was soon followed by the arrival there of Francis Joseph himself, accompanied by no less than seven Archdukes and his principal ministers. For two hours the brothers remained in the library of Miramare, locked in private conversation. Once, at least, distant observers believed they saw the Archduke on the terrace, looking out to sea, deep in thought. Might he still decide to remain in Europe?

On Saturday, 9 April, he took his irrevocable decision. The Act of Renunciation was signed. There were tearful farewells on the station platform. By Monday he was so deeply affected by the strain that his doctor declared he was suffering from a 'feverish chill' and the departure for Mexico was postponed. Not until the following Thursday did the joint Austro-French flotilla sail out into the Adriatic and set course for Civitavecchia, with a papal blessing awaiting their Mexican Majesties in

Rome. At last, on 28 May 1864, the flotilla reached Veracruz, the port Cortes had dedicated to the 'True Cross' in the year that Charles V was crowned emperor. Back in Austria people soon lost interest in Mexico. Except in the navy, it proved astonishingly easy to forget the most handsome of the archdukes.

Maximilian's departure enabled Francis Joseph to give his attention once again to Schleswig-Holstein, and to German affairs in general. By mid-April the fate of the Duchies was really settled, although an armistice was not signed until 12 May; and the failure of a conference in London led to a second campaign in June and July. No one doubted that the days of Danish sovereignty over a unitary Schleswig-Holstein were over. But the character of the dispute kept changing rapidly. The smaller German states had long maintained that the rightful ruler of Schleswig-Holstein was Frederick, Duke of Augustenburg, who was strongly (if belatedly) supported by the Austrians in the third week of May at the London conference. But by early summer, first Rechberg and later Francis Joseph realized that Austria and Prussia were no longer equal partners, acting as allies in the name of the German Confederation: Bismarck had broken loose on his own, and he was treating Augustenburg's claims with contempt. The geographical position of the Duchies ensured that, over this diplomatic problem, Prussia held the initiative. There was an open cynicism in Bismarck's way of doing business which alarmed Rechberg and puzzled the Emperor: Bismarck might suggest to Austria that 'it was time to begin a policy of mutual compensation', but where? And at whose expense?

Yet, while Francis Joseph deplored Bismarck's methods, he was convinced that 'alliance with Prussia is the only sensible policy' (as he told his mother), and his foreign minister agreed with him. Rather strangely, though a signed convention regulated military dispositions during the campaigns, no formal alliance existed at that moment; and when, in late July, Bismarck travelled to Vienna for talks with Rechberg, the Austrians sought to revive the treaty relationship which had bound the two Powers during the Crimean War and in earlier years, too. But Bismarck was wary of alliance fetters. He preferred to strike specific bargains. Not for the first time, he hinted that Prussia would help Austria recover her primacy in Italy – but only provided he received a free hand in Germany.

Closer acquaintance with Bismarck did not reassure Francis Joseph: why did he persist in 'speaking recklessly and exaggeratedly, trying to frighten people with words'? But the Emperor welcomed King William's decision to visit Ischl in mid-August, and he invited him to celebrate the success of Austrian and Prussian arms in the Duchies by a state visit to Vienna. Although his chief minister would be in attendance, it was hoped that sovereign-to-sovereign talks might draw direct answers to questions of policy rather than the evasive replies with which Bismarck delighted to mystify diplomats who sought enlightenment.

Francis Joseph was at Penzing station to greet the King and Bismarck when – on Saturday, 20 August – they arrived in Vienna, and he escorted them to neighbouring Schönbrunn. On Wednesday there was an excursion to Laxenburg, with boat trips to visit the pseudo-Gothic follies built on the lake islands (for, architecturally, they resembled William's familiar waterfront on the Heilige See, outside Potsdam). But much of the four-day state visit was spent in political discussion at Schönbrunn. Bismarck was prepared to let his hosts do the talking. If Austria allowed Prussia to acquire the duchies what compensation would she receive, asked Rechberg? Help in winning back Lombardy? Retrocession of part of Silesia annexed by Frederick the Great, suggested Francis Joseph? But the recovery of Lombardy would necessitate a major war against France, a challenge neither the Austrian nor the Prussian general staff was prepared to face at this stage; and King William had no intention of handing over land acquired by the most illustrious of Hohenzollerns.

On the final day of talks Francis Joseph at last asked William directly about the future of the northern duchies: did he wish to annex Schleswig-Holstein, or merely secure commercial and strategic concessions for Prussia within them? Reluctantly, and without consulting Bismarck, the King gave his reply: 'I am not exactly thinking of absorbing Schleswig-Holstein. I have no right to the duchies and cannot therefore lay claim to them', he said. This was a startling admission, a conscientious statement of principle which effectively deprived both Bismarck and Rechberg of any opportunity to strike bargains over the duchies; for how could William's chief minister barter territory over which his King denied possessing any rights? Little more could be said around the conference table at that moment. Hurriedly it was agreed that Austria and Prussia should maintain military administration in their respective zones within the duchies until a more definite solution could be found. Rechberg's hopes of securing a lasting treaty relationship, with the Habsburg lands joining the Zollverein common market on an equal footing with Prussia, began to seem totally unrealistic.

The Schönbrunn talks confirmed Francis Joseph's belief that direct contact with Prussia's sovereign could effectively counter Bismarck's schemes. Rechberg's days as foreign minister were numbered. It was not simply that the Emperor lost confidence in his minister's ability to draw Prussia into partnership by conciliatory gestures. More precisely, he felt no need for a minister who possessed ideas of his own. Rechberg had wished to resign in the previous year but had remained in office because his imperial master made it clear he could see no distinction between a minister who, of his own volition, sought to leave office and an officer who deserted his post. By the autumn of 1864, however, Francis Joseph was so confident of his authority within Germany that he was prepared to shape policy himself on a monarch-to-monarch basis, accepting advice from specialist experts in the Ballhausplatz if he chose, but ignoring their views should he believe he might reach an accommodation with King William personally. Accordingly, on 27 October Rechberg was induced to resign, largely through the machinations of two counsellors he had long mistrusted: Ludwig Biegeleben, a conservative Catholic from Darmstadt who was strongly hostile to Prussia; and the fitfully eccentric Count Moritz Esterházy, whom Francis Joseph made minister without portfolio. Briefly the Emperor even considered naming Esterházy as Rechberg's successor. More wisely, he appointed Count Alexander Mensdorff-Pouilly, a soldier-diplomat of fifty who had survived twenty-two battles and two difficult years as ambassador in St Petersburg with equal credit.

The newcomer was respected by the German Princes both for his personal qualities and for his lineage – Mensdorff's mother had been Princess Sophie of Saxe-Coburg and Gotha, thus making him a nephew of the King of the Belgians and a first cousin to Queen Victoria. Like the paladins of 1848–49, he was by conviction *schwarzgelb*, a 'black and yellow man' (the name, derived from the colours of the dynasty, given to devotees of the Habsburg cause). He was not a forceful personality; if a lowly official brought a document or file to his study in the Ballhausplatz, the minister 'would accompany him back to the door and open it himself', a colleague recalled long afterwards. So courteous a gentleman could hardly oppose policies commended by an Emperor whom he was to serve almost too loyally over the following years. At heart Mensdorff understood the nature of the Monarchy better than most of his successors. Austria 'was an empire of nationalities', he told the British ambassador; if concessions were given to any one nationality the whole structure would be in danger; in Transylvania there was 'a considerable Roumanian population' he pointed out; and 'the Prince of Serbia might also claim the Serbs in Austria'.

Yet, as Francis Joseph by now recognized, one 'nationality' within the empire was unique. Alone among his subjects the Magyars of historic Hungary had no 'mother country' beyond the frontier to which they might turn for cultural backing or political assimilation. But the exiled Kossuth was still a danger, as likely to respond to Bismarck's blandishments as he did to those of Napoleon III. It was natural for Francis Joseph to give fresh thoughts to a settlement with Hungary. He had made some progress towards winning the support of Deák and the Hungarian moderates in 1860–61. Now, on Moritz Esterházy's prompting and with the encouragement of Archduke Albrecht, he secretly sent an emissary to Deák shortly before Christmas in 1864 to see yet again if there could be a reconciliation with Hungary. Talks continued slowly well into the new year. They were sufficiently promising for the Emperor to believe that time was on his side, if only the critical confrontation with Prussia could be delayed. Accordingly, while making every effort to win support from the other German states during the summer of 1865, Francis Joseph sanctioned a policy of appeasement towards Prussia. No one in Vienna was prepared to face the prospect of a fratricidal war in Germany so long as there was still the risk of an uprising in Hungary's Danubian heartlands: better to play for time and accept an interim settlement of the dispute over the Duchies. The Convention of Gastein (14 August 1865) provisionally assigned Schleswig to Prussia and Holstein to Austria, while allowing Prussia to fortify Kiel as a naval base, construct a canal across Holstein to link the Baltic and the North Sea and maintain two military roads through Austrian-administered territory. Only Francis Joseph's desire to postpone the conflict until the Monarchy was ready for war justified the signing of such a disadvantageous convention.

He did not fear another military disaster. On the eve of the Danish war he had written to the commanding Austrian General urging him to lift morale by reviving 'the old Radetzky spirit'; and the Austrians acquitted themselves well, whereas the Prussians at first made little impact on the Danish fortified positions. In 1865 he returned from the autumn manoeuvres more than ever convinced that his army could defeat the Prussians. He was especially pleased with improvements in gunnery, notably the replacement of smoothbore cannon by rifled forward-loading light field guns, and he welcomed a change in the side weapons of crack hussar, dragoon and uhlan regiments which marked the end of long outdated pistols. Over military equipment Francis Joseph was less conservative than many senior officers. The new infantry drill manual incorporated lessons learnt from the 1859 campaign, notably the importance of massed bayonet charges. In April 1865 the Emperor watched trials of the needle gun, a breech-loading rifle fired from a lying position, and he appreciated its potential value for the infantry. But where could money be found to equip the army with this new weaponry? Defence expenditure had been cut by almost a third in the four years leading up to the Danish War, largely in response to complaints of military extravagance by a finance committee of the Reichsrat.

To the Emperor this committee seemed to represent all that was unacceptable in parliamentary institutions. With the German liberals still cavilling over funds for rearmament, he made up his mind to get rid of

Schmerling and dissolve his 'theatre', too. In late July 1865 a Bohemian aristocrat, Count Belcredi, was appointed to form a new government; only Mensdorff and Esterházy survived from Schmerling's administration. Six weeks later the Reichsrat deputies were sent about their business: an imperial manifesto declared the February Patent indefinitely 'superseded'. Not that Francis Joseph wished to revert to autocracy. The manifesto anticipated a new political structure for the Monarchy; talks would begin with a Hungarian Diet and spokesmen for other lands and provinces would be consulted about constitutional change in due course. Elections for the Hungarian Diet took place in November. On 14 December Francis Joseph himself opened the first session, with a speech in Magyar.

War did not seem imminent when, on 20 January 1866, the Emperor met the British ambassador. He was in an optimistic mood: 'There were no serious complications on the European horizon for the time being', he told the ambassador, and 'he was confident that the year would unfold quietly and peacefully and that Austria would therefore be able to devote itself almost entirely to its internal affairs'. Nine days later Francis Joseph and Elizabeth went into residence at Buda, remaining in Hungary until 5 March. But military affairs were rarely far from his mind: on the day he spoke so reassuringly to the British ambassador he also gave orders for the infantry to be equipped with the breech-loader needle guns he had seen tested in April. The Austrian ordnance system was, however, a cumbersome machine. Five weeks elapsed before the minister of war drew the Emperor's attention to the regrettable fact that a cheese-paring budget provided funds for only 1,840 new rifles – not enough for a single regiment to begin training with the needle guns. By contrast, each 'regular' Prussian infantry regiment and many militia units were already armed with breech-loading rifles.

Relations between the occupation armies in Schleswig-Holstein remained strained throughout the winter, the tension responding to political manoeuvres at Frankfurt, where Francis Joseph continued to be accepted as rightful leader of the German Princes. Yet it was not until late March that Bismarck's activities caused alarm at the Hofburg. He was known to have links with Hungarian émigré dissidents, and on 21 March Károlyi reported that a high-level Italian military mission was in Berlin. Soon afterwards General von Moltke went to Florence – Italy's interim capital – where, on 8 April, a secret military convention threatened Austria with war on two fronts.

The precise nature of the Prusso-Italian relationship remained unknown in Vienna, but by mid-April Italian troops began massing in Lombardy, half the pincer grip with which Bismarck intended to loosen the Monarchy. Briefly Francis Joseph tried to keep the grasping claws apart by proposing that both Austria and Prussia should reduce the strength of their armies within the German Confederation, a move which he thought King William would welcome. But on 20 April the Austrian general staff presented the Emperor with a memorandum pointing out the need for mobilization in the south, so as to discourage the Italians from entering Venetia. Mobilization in the Habsburg lands was always a slow process. Against Mensdorff's advice, Francis Joseph gave way to his generals; on 21 April he ordered the mobilization of the Army of the South, with Archduke Albrecht in command. Since Bismarck insisted on holding his King to the new commitments to Italy, the call to mobilization along Austria's southern border made certain that all attempts to defuse the tension in Germany itself were doomed.

If there was to be a war, the Emperor was determined to avoid one great mistake he had made seven years before. On this occasion, rather than risk juggling with fortune as a commander in the field, he would remain in the capital, co-ordinating grand strategy. The most respected officer in his empire, General Ludwig von Benedek, 'the new Radetzky', was given command of the Army of the North. An inspired appointment, it was felt; as good as having another 40,000 men in the front-line, declared Bavaria's chief minister. Only Benedek himself demurred. He knew, he said, 'every tree on the road to Milan' but he was unfamiliar with the mountain barriers and plains of central Europe, where Frederick the Great and Napoleon had won and lost reputations. Yet as a stern Calvinist from western Hungary, Benedek dutifully bowed himself to accept the destiny which God and his Emperor imposed upon him. To compensate for his unfamiliarity with Bohemia and Moravia Benedek appointed as his chief-of-staff General Gideon Krismanić, a former head of the army's topographical bureau. Krismanić was recommended to Benedek by Archduke Albrecht, who had found his map-reading skills useful on manoeuvres. Neither the Emperor nor his senior military advisers realized how cautiously defensive were the slow workings of Krismanić's mind.

In mid-May Francis Joseph became impatient. By now he was convinced the Austro-Prussian struggle in Germany would have to be resolved that summer. 'Better a war than prolongation of the present situation', he wrote to his mother on 11 May, 'In any case we must have a result, after spending so much money and making so many sacrifices.' At ministerial conferences he realistically assessed his options. Over one important calculation there was general agreement: Austria might defeat Prussia and Italy together, especially if the campaign in the south could be swiftly decided; but Austria could never hope to defeat the combined forces of Prussia, Italy and France. Something therefore had to be done to buy off that rogue in Paris. In early June Napoleon III hinted to Richard Metternich that Bismarck was prepared to offer an adjustment of the frontier in the Rhineland in return for a Prusso-French alliance, but Metternich saw that French neutrality could be bought for the right offer, a token acknowledgement of Napoleon's decisive role in the Italian peninsula. When the French attitude was reported back to Vienna Francis Joseph reluctantly accepted that the Monarchy might well have to give that acknowledgement and let Venetia go. He was, however, stubborn: no direct negotiations with Italy, for he refused to recognize the unified kingdom; and no surrender of Venetia without a fight, for he believed that if the Austrians could gain a victory in the field against Victor Emmanuel's army, the defeat would prevent the Italians from persisting with future demands for other Italian-speaking regions, such as Trieste and its hinterland or the southern Tyrol. The Emperor therefore authorized Metternich to take up the Venetian question with Napoleon III if Austria defeated Prussia, Francis Joseph would surrender Venetia to Napoleon III (for handing over to Italy), provided he kept France neutral, would guarantee Austria's remaining Italian-speaking lands, and would accept a new settlement in central Europe (probably including the return of Silesia as compensation for the loss of Venetia). On 12 June a treaty embodying these conditions was signed in Paris.

War followed swiftly, with Bismarck repudiating the authority of the German Confederation on 14 June and Prussian troops crossing the borders of the smaller German states two days later. Though Napoleon III envisaged a long war which France would finally settle by armed mediation, military experts in Paris and London as well as Vienna expected an Austrian victory before the autumn. William Howard Russell, the doyen of war reporters, was impressed by Benedek's cavalry, 'the finest by many degrees I ever saw'. No one doubted Archduke Albrecht's skills, and rightly. Within little over a week he telegraphed the Emperor to inform him that the southern army had defeated the Italians at Custozza, the village between Verona and Mantua where Radetzky had gained a decisive victory eighteen years previously. That was the news Francis Joseph wanted to hear, and all Vienna with him. More ominous was the paucity of information from Benedek and the Army of the North.

Benedek and Krismanić established their headquarters at Olmütz on 26 May. Francis Joseph and Crenneville (head of his military chancellery) anticipated that Benedek would move north-westwards from Moravia, carrying the war into the German lands while the Prussians were still engaged with the armies of the smaller German states. When, a fortnight later, there was no sign of any move towards the frontier, the Emperor sent one of his ablest adjutants, Colonel Beck, to Olmütz to stir the northern army into action. But Beck could not make any impression on Benedek and his staff on this occasion, or indeed on a second short visit a few days later. Krismanić insisted that it would be dangerous to take up positions along the frontier until the whole army was massed around Olmütz, a slow task since the military concentration was dependent upon the efficient working of a single railway. Eventually, with nearly 200,000 men and 770 guns at his command, Benedek crossed from Moravia into Bohemia, two days after the Prussians invaded Hanover, Bavaria and Saxony. The first skirmish – on 27 June, near the border of Silesia – ended in a minor Austrian victory; but along the main sector of the front it seemed impossible to halt the Prussian advance, for the rapid and accurate fire power of the needle gun wrought havoc among the massed Austrian formations. On 30 June Colonel Beck arrived again at Benedek's head-quarters on a mission from the Emperor to discover why his huge Army of the North did not engage the enemy in strength.

Beck found Benedek in the fortress of Königgrätz, now the Czech town of Hradeć Kralove. On the previous day the army had suffered a triple setback, with heavy casualties from Prussian artillery at Königinhof and Schweinschädel and a more serious defeat at Gitschin, where a crack Austrian regiment had only been saved from disaster by the intervention of their Saxon allies. Benedek summoned a war council at which he explained to Beck that, since his army was so badly mauled, he had no hope of victory. At Beck's insistence, a telegram was sent directly to the Emperor: 'I beg Your Majesty to seek peace at any price urgently. Catastrophe for the army is unavoidable.' Colonel Beck set out at once for Vienna.

The telegram caused consternation at the Hofburg. It was followed by a second one, from Beck to Crenneville: 'Armistice or peace imperative because withdrawal is hardly possible. My heart is broken, but I must report the truth'. Heads were cooler in Vienna than in Königgrätz: there was no evidence of a 'catastrophe'; the army was not encircled; reinforcements would soon be heading northwards from among Albrecht's victorious troops. Francis Joseph's reply was swift and terse: 'Impossible to make peace. I authorize a retreat in good order, if it is unavoidable', he wired, adding at Crenneville's suggestion, 'Has there been a battle?'. But, though standing firm in central Europe, Francis Joseph finally accepted that he did not have the resources to retain his hold on the Italian peninsula. On 2 July Napoleon III was invited to arrange a ceasefire with King Victor Emmanuel, on the understanding that Venetia would be surrendered whatever happened in Bohemia. The Emperor had decided he needed Albrecht, as well as his troops, in the northern theatre of war if Bismarck's machinations in Germany were to be frustrated.

Benedek spent much of the first two days of July in the saddle, taking stock of his resources. Morale was not so bad as he had feared. He decided to lead his army out from the fortress of Königgrätz, cross the Elbe, and take up positions in the hilly ground east of the river Bistritz, between the villages of Sadowa and Chlum. Early on 3 July the telegraph in Vienna reported that a great battle had begun: never before in European history had such vast numbers contested a single battlefield. Throughout the day the Emperor anxiously awaited wires from Benedek's headquarters. At noon the outcome was still in doubt; the Prussian advance was checked by Austrian artillery fire. But at seven in the evening the dreaded news reached the Hofburg: during the afternoon the Prussian Second Army, commanded by Crown Prince Frederick, had reached the battlefield from the east, forcing the Austrians to abandon their defensive positions in order to avoid encirclement. The battle was lost. 'Fragments of regiments' were seeking safety behind the Elbe, W. H. Russell was to tell his *Times*'s readers a few days later: they were no longer crack troops but merely 'the debris of the army'.

Francis Joseph resolved to continue the fight. He had hopes that Napoleon could be tempted to threaten Prussia along the Rhine and he knew that he would soon have sufficient troops, brought by railway from the south, in order to defend the capital. As a precaution, Elizabeth and the children were sent to Buda and, for the first time in his reign, he was protected by a cavalry escort each day as his carriage carried him from Schönbrunn to the Hofburg for a succession of critical conferences. There were some ominous shouts of 'Long Live Emperor Maximilian' – a sentiment for which, of course, no sceptical Viennese could be accused of showing disrespect towards the dynasty. Not least among the ironies of that summer was the news wired to the Emperor by Admiral Tegetthof on 20 July from Spalato: his ironclads had that morning scattered a larger Italian squadron attempting to seize the island of Lissa; and, in the most memorable episode of modern Austria's naval history, the *Re d'Italia* was rammed and sunk at the height of the battle by Tegetthof's flagship, which bore Maximilian's name. The victory of Lissa made no difference to the outcome of the war; but it gave the Austrians a new hero, an admiral to place on a pedestal rather than a soldier. And it asserted a naval supremacy in the Adriatic which was to be upheld throughout Francis Joseph's reign, and beyond.

Six days later Archduke Albrecht at last took command of Benedek's beaten army, which had fallen back south of the Danube at Bratislava. But the fighting was by then over. Bismarck, who was intent on avoiding a harsh peace likely to perpetuate hostility between Austria and Prussia, succeeded in inducing a reluctant King William to abandon his hopes of entering Vienna in triumph at a time when the most advanced Prussian outposts were on the edge of the old Napoleonic battlefield of Wagram, some 14 miles from the Hofburg itself. A five-day ceasefire along the Danube was agreed on 22 July, while peace terms were discussed. They were more moderate than Francis Joseph had feared, as he told Elizabeth in a letter written hurriedly at six o'clock next morning: 'Whether it is asked of us or not, we shall withdraw completely from Germany – and after what we have seen of our dear companions in the German Confederation, that's a piece of luck for Austria', he wrote ruefully. A preliminary peace was agreed at Nikolsburg on 26 July: apart from Holstein and the cession of Venetia, Francis Joseph lost no territory. He accepted an obligation to pay a war indemnity, the dissolution of the German Confederation and its replacement by a North German Confederation, established under Prussian auspices, and by a Southern German Union from which Austria was excluded. Prussian troops would withdraw from Austria as soon as a final treaty was concluded. The definitive peace was embodied in the Treaty of Prague, signed on 23 August. By the beginning of September the troop trains were heading back across the frontier.

For the second time in seven years Francis Joseph had begun and lost a war. Once again, his subjects held him in low esteem, as he well knew. Yet if he thought he was in any way to blame for the disaster he did not admit it. Poor Benedek was made a scapegoat for the lost battle. As an honourable man, he accepted his misfortune because – as he once told his wife – to justify his conduct would 'be of service neither to the Emperor nor to the army'. While the war was in progress it became fashionable to attribute Prussia's military success to the wonder weapon, the needle gun, while later commentators stressed the genius of Moltke as a staff officer capable of transporting and deploying the huge number of conscript troops in a modern army. The Emperor's greatest folly was his assumption that Austria was in any better position to win a war on two fronts than in the days when his grandfather had faced the challenge of the first Bonaparte.

In an odd way, Francis Joseph sensed the omnipresence of the past. For him the Seven Weeks War came not so much as an isolated conflict as an episode in some long historical serial. He had no doubt of the real villains. They were Austria's neighbours, whose rulers and governments wished to manipulate the popular belief in nationalism. 'We have fallen a victim to refined double-dealing', he wrote to his mother from Schön-brunn the day before the peace treaty was signed. 'Everything was fixed between Paris, Berlin and Florence. As for us, we were very honest, but very stupid.' 'This is a life and death struggle which is not yet over', he added, rallying to that awe-inspiring sense of vocation which was his strength and his misfortune. 'When the whole world is against you and you have no friends, there is little chance of success, but you must go on doing what you can, fulfilling your duty and, in the end, going down with honour.'

Chapter 10

THE HOLY CROWN OF
ST STEPHEN

At Easter in 1865 Archduchess Sophie gave 'praise to God a thousand times over' in her journal for good news which Francis Joseph told her on the eve of his eleventh wedding anniversary; his relations with Sisi had 'at last' reached a peak of reconciliation, or so he 'virtually assured' her. Despite ever returning doubts over Elizabeth's fitness to share her son's great inheritance, the Archduchess was genuinely pleased: happy domesticity around the throne made for contentment in the Monarchy as a whole, she believed.

Everyone could see that Elizabeth had gained poise and authority. Those anxious weeks before Christmas in 1862, when she still needed a brother or sister beside her to face life at Court, seemed far away now. Annual cures at Bad Kissingen, supplemented each morning by carefully regulated gymnastic exercises, strengthened her physically, and her daily life had acquired a purpose and structure. New acquaintances won her trust; notable among them were the principal coiffeuse of the Burgtheater, Fanny Angerer (who became Fanny Feifalik on her marriage a few years later) and young Ida Ferenczy, from a Hungarian lower gentry family at Kecskemét, who in November 1864 was appointed 'Reader in Hungarian to Her Majesty' and was soon accepted as a close confidante. New interests held Elizabeth's attention, enabling her to rein in her impulse to escape on horseback for long, lonely rides in the open countryside. She worked hard at perfecting her Magyar, as Francis Joseph proudly reported to his mother in the autumn of 1863; and she read good literature seriously, enabling her to improve the quality of her own poetry. In the spring of 1863 Fanny Angerer evolved a style of plaiting the Empress's auburn hair which restored a pride in her personal appearance. Such vanity was no doubt deplorable, as she may well have reflected; but, if the Empress lacked confidence in her own appearance, how could she assert her personality either within the family or at Court? In October 1864, when Elizabeth thought her beauty in full blossom, she sat for Franz Winterhalter. A famous portrait shows the Empress in a white ball dress studded with embroidered petals and crowned by the elaborately plaited hairstyle, decked on this occasion with diamond stars. Winterhalter succeeded in making her look both magnificently imperial and shyly imperious. But at the same time Winterhalter painted two more portraits of Elizabeth, each with her hair hanging down over shoulders loosely draped by a simple flowing white gown. These portraits Francis Joseph kept on the wall of his study for the next half-century of his life.

Returning self-confidence bred self-assertiveness. Elizabeth showed her strong will in the first instance over the upbringing of the Crown Prince, although she was slow to respond to a mounting personal crisis. The nursery routine originally instituted, at Francis Joseph's request, by Archduchess Sophie had been modified when Elizabeth secured the dismissal of Sophie Esterházy as head of her household and Rudolf was happy under the daily supervision of his Aja, 'Wowo' von Welden. He was an intelligent child but delicate: an alarming bout of typhoid fever in December 1863 left him frail and in the following summer he suffered concussion after falling from a tree. In his seventh year he was removed from his Aja's keeping and assigned his first tutor, Major-General Ludwig von Gondrecourt, a bachelor of whose high moral principles the Archduchess warmly approved.

As a field commander in the Danish campaign Gondrecourt won a reputation for using shock tactics. These he now applied to his young charge, whom he convinced himself needed toughening up. On one wintry morning Rudolf was forced to drill in the snow long before dawn; and when Gondrecourt thought the boy unduly timid, blank cartridges were fired without warning in his room to test his reactions, an experiment which may have had disastrous psychological effects on the Crown Prince in later life. In the spring Rudolf was again seriously ill, probably with diphtheria; Caroline von Welden personally begged the Emperor to curb the sadistic streak in his son's tutor, which she believed was weakening the boy's constitution. But the Emperor, who could remember his own Aja's affectionate interest in her boys once they left the nursery, played down her concern. Then, at last, Elizabeth intervened. She discovered that Gondrecourt had taken Rudolf to the Lainzer Tiergarten, an imperial game reserve a few miles from Schönbrunn. There Gondrecourt left the boy alone, behind a locked gate, and shouted at him 'Look out, a wild boar is coming!' – at which warning the boy's nerves gave way entirely. So angry was his mother when she heard of this experiment that she told the Emperor outright, 'Either Gondrecourt goes or I go'. The family were at Ischl at that moment, where they had recently celebrated the two birthdays, the Emperor's thirty-fifth and Rudolf's seventh. Yet still Francis Joseph hesitated.

Elizabeth, however, held the whip hand. It was just four months since Francis Joseph had told his mother of the new intimacy of their family life and he was still enchanted by Winterhalter's recent portraits. Now she went to her room at Ischl and sent her husband a virtual ultimatum, in which she did not mention Gondrecourt by name:

'I wish full and unlimited powers shall be accorded me in all matters concerning the children, the choice of their household, of their place of residence, and complete control over their upbringing; in short I alone must decide everything about them until they attain their majority. Furthermore I wish that all matters concerning my personal affairs, such for example as the choice of my household, my place of residence, all changes in domestic arrangements etc., etc., shall be left for me alone to decide'.

Francis Joseph capitulated. The firm, but sympathetic, General Joseph Latour von Thurnburg, was appointed tutor to the Crown Prince, while Gondrecourt received command of an army corps in Bohemia (where unimaginative generalship cost his men heavy casualties outside Königgrätz). Although the Emperor did not formally countersign the 'ultimatum', he was ready to observe the spirit of the agreement, except when he considered his wife's choice of residence dangerous to herself personally or an embarrassment to affairs of state. Elizabeth, for her part, loyally supported him for thirty years of mixed fortunes, even if her restlessness of spirit too often took her from his company.

Until now she had shown no interest in politics, apart from ineffectually seeking support for her sister in Naples. But over Hungary Elizabeth felt strongly, despite the tragic death of little Sophie in Buda. When Francis Joseph opened the Hungarian Diet in December 1865 he agreed that a Hungarian deputation might travel to Vienna and invite their Queen to make a second visit. She received the deputation at the Hofburg on 8 January 1866, wearing Hungarian national costume and addressing the magnates in clear and fluent Magyar. Towering over his companions, and magnificent in their fur-trimmed robes, was Count Gyula Andrássy whom Elizabeth now met for the first time. At forty-two he was a romantic hero who expected to be lionized, but he was, too, supremely accomplished in the art of pleasing women. Elizabeth was captivated. The dark, slender aristocrat, exuding a refined charm which lightly dispelled her shyness, personified the idealized Hungary of her imagination. She respected Deák, but she liked to believe that in Andrássy she had found a genius to reconcile the husband she loved to the people with whom she so passion-ately identified herself. Andrássy, sensing the political value of Elizabeth's capacity for admiration, remained level-headed: was it, perhaps, with gentle irony that he hailed his queen as 'our lovely Providence'? At all events she accompanied Francis Joseph to Hungary before the end of January. For five weeks she endured (as she wrote to Rudolf) 'a most unrestful time', going to the riding school every morning and attending balls, dinners and receptions she would have avoided in Vienna. 'With her courtesy, tact and discretion as well as her excellent Hungarian, Sisi is a great help to me', Francis Joseph wrote to his mother halfway through his visit.

She was a great help to him again during the dark summer days of war, endlessly visiting hospitals around Vienna and making a point of speaking to wounded Hungarians in their own language. A few days after König-grätz Elizabeth travelled to Pest, ostensibly to see the hospitals within Hungary, too. She was met at the railway station by Deák and Andrássy who explained to her the dangers of allowing Bismarck to exploit the Kossuthite radicals and emphasized to her the need for Francis Joseph to give a gesture of re-assurance to the moderate Hungarians at this time. She then went back to Vienna, reported their remarks to her husband, urged him to send for Andrássy and collected Gisela and Rudolf before settling with them at the Villa Kochmeister, in the hills behind Buda. Her letters begged Francis Joseph to 'do something', consoling herself (as she told him) with the thought that even if nothing happened she would 'be able to say to Rudolf one day, "I did everything in my power. Your misfortunes are not on my conscience".'

This appeal, backed by news that Andrássy was taking the night train to Vienna and would await a summons from the palace, was irresistible. Francis Joseph assured her by coded telegram that he was sending for Deák – who was in a remote region of Hungary – and asked her to be discreet in her contacts with the Count. But eventually, at five in the morning of 17 July, he sent his 'beloved angel' the message she confidently awaited: 'Today I am expecting G. A. I shall listen to what he has to say quietly, letting him do the talking and then sounding him out to see if I can trust him ... The old man [Deák, aged 63] can be here tomorrow or the day after.' After ninety minutes of discussion with Andrássy, the Emperor thought him 'good, honourable and highly gifted' but 'wanting too much and offering too little'. Deák, whom he received on 20 July (the day of the battle of Lissa), showed greater consideration than Andrássy for the political needs of other regions of the Monarchy. Yet, though the Emperor believed Deák to be 'honest and devoted to the dynasty', he told Elizabeth that he felt he should talk again to Andrássy, with whom he hoped to take up 'the threads of the negotiations' once 'this luckless war' ended. Francis Joseph seems to have wished to draw up a settlement with

Andrássy – politically more flexible than the legalistic Deák – which would, however, be based upon the 'old man's' principle that Hungary should ask for no more after the war than before it. Yet he understood, as Elizabeth did not, that he would have to move slowly. The Emperor's personal sympathies were with his chief minister, Belcredi, who favoured careful consultation, stage by stage, with the Landtage and the institution of an 'extraordinary Reichsrat', which would need to approve any new status given to Hungary. Such a process was far too pedestrian to satisfy the Empress.

With the return of peace Elizabeth overplayed her hand. She continued to urge her husband to appoint Andrássy as his foreign minister, and she declined to leave the Villa Kochmeister and return to Vienna where the air was unhealthy, she said. Why should not the dynasty have a Laxenburg type residence near to the capital in Hungary, she asked? She had visited a temporary hospital established in a chateau at Gödöllö, some twenty miles north of Pest. It lay in parkland between a ridge of low hills and the wild Puszta steppes, the traditional picturesque Hungary of colourful costumes and fine horses. Elizabeth wondered if Francis Joseph might like to purchase Gödöllö. Andrássy, with whom she sometimes went riding, welcomed the idea.

The Emperor did not. A passing acerbity sharpens his replies to all her suggestions. How could he risk offending his German-Austrian and Slav subjects under Prussian occupation by handing over the conduct of foreign affairs to a Magyar magnate? 'It would be in conflict with my duty to adopt your exclusively Hungarian viewpoint', she was told. He urged her 'not to look over [Gödöllö] as if we were going to buy it, for at present I have no money and we shall have to cut back drastically in these hard times'. Yet he was genuinely worried to learn that Elizabeth was again setting out on long cross-country rides, as in 1859; and a rare note of melancholic loneliness saddens his letters. To reassure him – perhaps to ease her own conscience – Elizabeth returned to Vienna for his birthday on 18 August. But she would not stay. To her mother-in-law's consternation Elizabeth hurried back to the Villa Kochmeister to join her Hungarian friends for the national festival on St Stephen's Day (20 August), which was followed by Rudolf's birthday. Belcredi was aghast at such partisan support of Hungary by the First Lady of the Monarchy.

Francis Joseph could not find it in his heart to be annoyed with Sisi for long. He desperately needed her support, as his letters continue to show. For in late August another, totally unexpected, problem surfaced to vex him in this 'loathsome summer'. Prussia's military ascendancy indirectly called in question the future of Maximilian's empire in Mexico, for Napoleon III had decided he needed back in France the expeditionary force which formed the core of the monarchist army. Common sense inclined Maximilian to abdicate, but his Empress persuaded him to hold on to his throne while she returned to Europe in order to rally support for the monarchist cause. Thwarted in Paris – and as yet showing no public sign that her mind was deteriorating – Charlotte made her way to Miramare, sailing into Trieste where Tegetthoff's victorious squadron lay at anchor, expecting an imperial visit, which was now cancelled. 'At present I cannot go to Trieste', Francis Joseph complained to Elizabeth on 26 August, 'Her Mexican Majesty ... is due to appear there at any moment, so I prefer to remain here, rather than make the journey. Come back soon, my angel.' He had not yet seen his brother's wife; he sought Elizabeth's moral backing before facing a family meeting which he dreaded, for Austria could spare no aid for the unfortunate Maximilian. A week later Elizabeth was home in Vienna with the children. Had she closed up the Villa Kochmeister from fear of the cholera across the river in Pest? Or did she respond to her husband's plea for help in handling Her Mexican Majesty? As with so many of Elizabeth's sudden decisions, no one knows. At all events there was no meeting with Charlotte.

Politically Francis Joseph immersed himself in the Hungarian Question. He would not contemplate appointing Andrássy to the foreign ministry, but with sovereign-to-sovereign diplomacy shown as ineffectual, he wanted a more forceful man at the Ballhausplatz than Mensdorff. Even before Elizabeth returned from Buda, he was in touch with Baron Ferdinand Beust, foreign minister of Saxony on the eve of the Seven Weeks War but dismissed from office at the insistence of Bismarck as a condition of peace. Beust, a hard-headed realist rather than a doctrinaire upholder of outmoded concepts, supported Francis Joseph's German policy before the war, partly because he believed in reforming the German Confederation but largely because of his hostility to Prussia. Although Beust was a liberal and a Protestant, the Emperor respected his loyalty and his talents as a diplomat, which were also commended by Crown Prince Albert of Saxony, Francis Joseph's cousin and close friend. As a possible minister in Habsburg service, Beust had the inestimable advantage of no commitments or group affiliations within the Monarchy, though he soon showed a certain contempt for the Slav peoples, whether western or southern. Francis Joseph explained his immediate objectives to Beust as early as 1 September 1866: he wanted internal peace among the nationalities of the Empire in order to raise the Monarchy once more to the status of a European Great Power; he wanted to improve Austrian contacts with the southern German states to keep them clear of Prussia's orbit; and he intended to give up all ideas of waging war 'for a long time ahead'. After nine weeks of thought and preparation Beust took over the foreign ministry from Mensdorff at the end of October, working in uneasy partnership with the autocratic federalist Belcredi, who remained titular head of the government.

A few days later the Hungarian Diet began a new session. Francis Joseph gave an assurance that he would soon authorize the establishment of a responsible Hungarian administration and appoint a prime minister for the first time since his accession. Deák, whose followers formed the majority party in the Diet, was willing to take part in constitutional discussions but thought himself too old for active politics and recommended Andrássy as head of government. But there was still powerful opposition in Vienna both from Belcredi's circle, who continued to seek the postponement of final decisions until the meeting of an 'extraordinary Reichsrat', and from the army chiefs. Shortly before Christmas, Francis Joseph took the unusual step of sending Beust to Buda-Pest, confident that his foreign minister would reach an agreement with Deák and Andrássy which Belcredi could never even have contemplated committing to paper. The Emperor sought the best of both worlds: 'The government can never satisfy every national group', he told the ministerial council on 1 February 1867, 'That is why we have to rely on those who are strongest . . . and they are the Germans and Hungarians'. He retained Belcredi as prime minister in Vienna because he hoped that he would soothe the ruffled feelings of the Bohemian and German-Austrian aristocracy. But for Beust the situation was becoming impossible; he mistrusted the tactics of Belcredi and Archduke Albrecht. After seven weeks as imperial go-between he demanded a free hand; and on 7 February, 'with tears in his eyes', Francis Joseph therefore asked Belcredi to hand over his responsibilities to the Saxon newcomer. As his deputy Beust secured the appointment of Count Taaffe, the Emperor's boyhood friend, (who remained at the heart of Austrian government for twenty-six years). Andrássy became Hungary's prime minister eleven days later.

The final settlement of 1867 (*Ausgleich*, 'Compromise': or in Hungary, *Kiegyezes*) was speedily worked out by Beust and Andrássy, in consultation with Deák. It was discussed by the Hungarian Diet over the following three months and enacted as 'Law XII' in the last week of May. As an outsider, Beust accepted a fact of political life which the Emperor's Austrian subjects were reluctant to acknowledge: Royal Hungary was a historical entity with an ancient constitution only recently suspended, while other Habsburg lands were provinces of an improvised Empire searching for a cohesive constitutional pattern. Beust could therefore strike a bargain with national leaders who knew precisely what they wanted, even if most Hungarians were to complain that the Compromise merely satisfied their minimum political needs and Deák was disowned by the staunch Kossuthites.

Some Habsburg provinces – notably Bohemia, Moravia and (rump) Silesia, the 'Lands of St Wenceslas's Crown' – could claim historic rights older than those of Hungary though far longer in abeyance, and when Francis Joseph told Beust that he sought internal concord between the nationalities he was conscious of being titular King of Bohemia as well as Apostolic King of Hungary. But Czech nationalism only blossomed in Prague under the next generation, fifteen or twenty years after the Compromise. Czech political leaders were narrowly pan-Slav in sentiment in 1867, and Bohemia was still dominated by the German land-owning minority; there was no single-minded spokesman in Prague with whom Beust could have negotiated a settlement even if the Emperor had wished it. More vociferous were the Croats, another historic nationality with a certain claim on Habsburg gratitude. But Beust felt no obligation towards Jellaçić's compatriots and saw no reason to listen to their complaints. They had experienced a form of 'dualism' in partnership with Hungary from 1102 to 1526, and the terms of the *Ausgleich* left them to strike their own bargain with Buda-Pest.

Territorially Beust's greatest difficulty in Vienna was to overcome the hostility of the army leaders to the inclusion in Hungary of the former 'Military Frontier', for these lands had been virtually colonized by the army since the ejection of the Ottomans. But the Andrássy government received authority over the old frontier regions and Transylvania, too. Francis Joseph made his consent to Law XII conditional on the willingness of the Hungarian parliament to settle a subsidiary 'Compromise' with Croatia and to pass a Nationalities Law, recognizing the principle of national equality. But once parliament began work on the implementation of these details there was no reason to delay royal assent, which was given at the end of July, five months before the basic constitutional laws for the remaining 'kingdoms and provinces' of the Habsburg Monarchy were even promulgated in Vienna.

The *Ausgleich* left defence and foreign affairs as the joint concern of Hungary and 'Austria' (i.e. the rest of the Monarchy, or as it was often called 'Cisleithania', the regions beyond the River Leitha). These matters were placed under a common Austro-Hungarian minister. There was also a 'common' finance minister, although he became a spokesman rather than a decision-maker, since the raising and collection of taxes was the responsibility of the separate finance ministers in the two halves of the Monarchy. The economic provisions of the settlement – a quota system to meet common expenditure, trade, the monetary system, and trunk railway construction – were to be regulated once every ten years, a provision which in practice established a pattern of decennial political crises, recurring when the 'economic compromise' came up for revision or renewal. It was also agreed that the problems arising from the common matters – defence, foreign affairs, and joint finance – would be considered by 'delegations', to be nominated by the parliaments in Vienna and Buda-Pest. The delegations would meet in separate assemblies, summoned alternately to the two capital cities of the Monarchy. Hungarian politicians complained that ministers had to present government proposals to Francis Joseph before making them known to parliament, thus giving the sovereign a veto on what was to be discussed as well as on the final form of legislation. But in 1867 these restraints on Hungary's autonomy seemed slight, especially to the other nationalities within the Monarchy. As Andrássy admitted, 'We are paying 30 per cent of joint expenditure and enjoy similar rights to those who pay 70 per cent'; and on a map the bargain looked even more striking than in any commercial balance sheet. The Compromise ensured that the lands of 'the Holy Crown of St Stephen' formed a unitary kingdom considerably greater in extent than Royal Hungary as recognized in 1848 by the April Laws.

That Holy Crown, surmounted by a primitive Cross, was about to become the centrepiece of a ceremony essential to the new relationship between the people and their king, the first modern coronation held in Buda-Pest. Patriotic legend had long ascribed a unique status to the royal regalia. In the year 1000 the fifth chieftain of the Arpád dynasty, Stephen, applied to Pope Sylvester II for recognition as a Christian King, receiving back from Rome a crown and a cross, which were venerated as testimony of royal sovereignty over the Danubian plains in which the Magyar hordes had made their homes. By the fourteenth century the Apostolic Cross and Holy Crown – given additional dignity by a lower circlet of Byzantine origin – were accepted as mystical symbols of national unity. A doctrine formulated by Stephen Werboczi in the sixteenth century maintained that the actual political entity of Hungary was latent in the Holy Crown, becoming corporate through the mystic relationship between the sovereign who wore the Crown and the nobility who paid homage to the king. An elaborate ritual of coronation was observed at Bratislava for 'King' Maria Theresa in 1741, for her grandson Francis in 1792, and for his son Ferdinand six weeks after Francis Joseph's birth.

With Kossuth's proclamation that the Habsburgs had forfeited the throne, possession of the Holy Crown assumed additional significance. Faced with defeat in August 1849, Kossuth buried it beneath a mulberry tree two miles north of Orsova, near the defile of the Iron Gates on the Danube. From this remote location it was recovered three years later by the Austrian authorities, acting on a tip-off from an indigent émigré.

Thereafter, to the disgust of his Hungarian subjects, Francis Joseph retained the Crown in Vienna. Now that a new contract defined the King's prerogatives and obligations, Andrássy was determined to give fresh emphasis to Werboczi's curious doctrine by treating the Holy Crown with particular reverence, as if to atone for its recent indignities. A chapel was built on the site of the mulberry tree near Orsova and elaborate preparations made for the crowning. Early in March 1867, long before the Diet gave final approval to the *Ausgleich*, it was agreed that Saturday, 8 June, would be Coronation Day.

Traditionally, consorts were crowned in later ceremonies. But on arriving at Buda-Pest in March Francis Joseph found that the revised ritual provided for Elizabeth's coronation immediately after his own. At the same time Andrássy told him that, to mark their joy at the reconciliation with the sovereigns, the Hungarian people had bought a summer residence for presentation to them: Gödöllö could be their home, as soon as renovation of the 120-year-old mansion was completed. 'I can hardly wait . . . for the moment when we are ready to live there', Elizabeth wrote excitedly to her husband on hearing the news. By now she worked at improving her Magyar for hours on end each day. Her enthusiasm for everything Hungarian was taken up by young Rudolf, who idolized Andrássy. Among the Crown Prince's private papers are some, heavily corrected, letters written by him in Magyar that year and a remarkably good sketch of a dashing horseman with wild curly hair and straggly beard, beside which was written the inscription 'Count Andrássy, Ischl, 1867'. When, in the second week of May, Hungary's Queen formally went into residence at Buda-Pest for the coronation season the Crown Prince wrote to ask if there had been 'a right good cheer' as she arrived in the city. His mother's response left no doubt of the Hungarian people's goodwill towards her.

Elizabeth remained in Hungary throughout the month. There was a succession of entertainments to attend – horse races, the theatre, court receptions. But Francis Joseph had to journey back more than once to Vienna. His enjoyment of the summer was darkened by the climax of the Mexican misadventure. Charlotte's mind, brooding over the past and in anguish for the present, lost all power of reason and she remained remote from outward life at Miramare. Meanwhile, in Vienna there was total uncertainty over what was happening in Mexico itself. American reports suggested that Maximilian had been captured by the victorious Juarez and was to be put on trial for treason against the Mexican Republic. President Andrew Johnson, King William of Prussia and Garibaldi were among those who sent pleas to Mexico's republican master; and in the hopes of encouraging Juarez to put his prisoner aboard a ship for Europe,

Francis Joseph re-instated 'the ex-Emperor of Mexico' as an Austrian Archduke before he left for the coronation in Hungary. Perhaps he even believed there might come a time when Max would settle again at Miramare to write his memoirs, but there was an ominous lack of reliable news from across the Atlantic. 'Should the King of Hungary hear of his brother's death, the coronation will not be postponed, but the fêtes and rejoicings will be abandoned', *The Times* correspondent reported authoritatively.

Mexico was not the only shadow to fall over the festivities. Late on Thursday, 6 June, Francis Joseph learnt of another family tragedy. A few days previously Archduke Albrecht's eighteen year old daughter Mathilde, seeing her father approaching and knowing he did not approve of women who smoked, hid a cigarette behind her back. She set fire to her dress, dying from her burns on that Thursday morning. The Court went into mourning for the pathetic young Archduchess and some festivities involving members of the dynasty were cancelled but, with the ceremonies due to begin in less than forty-eight hours, nothing could check the cycle of celebration on either bank of the Danube. The twin cities of Buda and Pest were packed. Among the visitors were foreign newspapermen, for the first time given an opportunity to report all the spiritual self-indulgence of a Hungarian coronation.

In England *The Times* offered readers a four column account on the following Wednesday, some 5000 words of colourful prose written immediately the coronation was over, while 'the centre of the world is just for the time this capital of Hungary on the lordly Danube'. The morning's events had begun with a royal procession from Buda palace along the crest of the hill to Trinity Square and the coronation church of St Matthias, with Andrássy as acting palatine going slowly ahead of the King and carrying St Stephen's Holy Crown reverently on a velvet cushion. Imaginative readers could picture the Hungarian magnates 'mounted, with ostrich and golden pheasant and argus plumes', tunics frogged with 'chevrons of solid silver', and with saddles so splendid that 'whole fields of cloth of gold must have been cut up for shabracks'.

Other newspapers – in Paris particularly – carried full accounts of the crowning itself and of the Coronation Mass, for which Franz Liszt had composed a new setting. *The Times*'s readers could read the prayers in the original Latin (small print only), and a list of dignitaries, before their correspondent was once more entranced by 'white horses and black uniforms' and 'white uniforms and black horses' as a 'dazzling procession' wound its way down the steep hill to the 'yellow Danube'. Francis Joseph, wearing the crown and with the 800-year old faded mantle of St Stephen on his shoulders, rode through the narrow streets and led the cavalcade across the cobbles of the Chain Bridge in to Pest and half a mile along the quay downstream, where an artificial mound made from clods of earth from every county in Hungary stood outside Pest's old parish church. Francis Joseph set his horse up the mound, steadied it on a levelled platform and, brandishing a sword towards the four points of the compass, vowed to protect the Hungarian people and their constitution. The ceremony was 'gone like a beautiful dream', reported *The Times*, 'The crowned King of Hungary ... has passed out of sight just like the hero of some gorgeous fairy spectacle who vanished behind the wings as the audience are dispersing in great contentment.'

Soon afterwards an observant eight-year-old was induced by his tutor to commit to paper a less ethereal impression of the day's events. Rudolf's 400 word account is with the Crown Prince's papers; it is unlikely to have been touched up by Latour since it preserves at least four spelling mistakes in it. At seven in the morning, so Rudolf wrote, 'we went downstairs ... and we were a long time looking for our coach as the square was full of Lifeguards, Archdukes and horses, and among them the King's white coronation steed'. In the church he saw 'many magnates, officers, the Primate and several Catholic and Greek bishops and many other priests ... Mama sat on a kind of throne and Papa went to the altar where a great deal of Latin was said ... Then the mantle was wrapped around him and the Primate gave him the sword and made three strokes ... Afterwards the drums rolled out and Andrássy and the Primate placed the crown on Papa. Then Papa received in his hands the orb and sceptre. Papa and Mama at this point went up to the throne and Andrássy walked out into the middle of the church and three times shouted "*Eljen a kiraly*" [Long Live the King] ... 'A lot more Latin was said' as 'Mama went to the altar' for the Crown to be held over her head. 'We' then joined her 'in a glass coach' and went by steamer down river to see 'Papa spur his horse very nicely at the gallop up the Coronation Mound'. In the evening there was a banquet.

There were banquets on other evenings, too; for the coronation festivities continued for five days and nights. A Coronation Offering of a silver casket containing five thousand gold ducats was accepted by Francis Joseph from Andrássy and then, on the Count's advice, handed back by Their Majesties to the Hungarian people for the support of the widows and orphans of Honved fighters killed in the 1848–9 battles with the Austrians. 'Were it in our power to do so, we two would be the first to recall Lajos Batthyány and the martyrs of Arad to life', Elizabeth told one of Hungary's former rebel bishops. Reconciliation was in the air everywhere, it seemed – although, to this day, the walls of the room at the Hofburg where Francis Joseph presided over meetings of ministers display paintings of his army's victories over the Hungarians at Komárom and Temesvár.

After the Coronation, Francis Joseph and Elizabeth went straight to Ischl to enjoy a holiday with Gisela and Rudolf. They were at Ischl when, on 19 June, Maximilian was executed by firing squad at Queretaro, allegedly for sanctioning the killing of Mexican republicans soon after his arrival in the country. Archduchess Sophie had a premonition of her son's fate on the day that he died but, in Ischl, a strange optimism lingered; the last information, from the American Secretary of State, held out some hopes of a release. News from Mexico took well over a week to reach Europe and Francis Joseph still knew nothing of what had happened at Queretaro when, on 27 June, he heard of the sudden death of his sister-in-law Helen's husband, the Prince of Thurn and Taxis. With Elizabeth, he travelled to Regensburg to console Helen and accompanied her to the family home. It was therefore in Bavaria, three days later, that he received the first telegram giving the dreaded news of Maximilian's execution. He hurried back to Vienna to join his two brothers in seeking to comfort their parents. Although she had suspected the worst, confirmation of her fears numbed Sophie's response to everyday life. She lost her appetite for politics, only seeking to hear from Austrian officers who had been with her second son in these last terrible months. Gradually she gained new fortitude from what she heard: the last entry in her journal that year mourned the loss of 'my beautiful son', but she also gave proud 'thanks to God for the calm valour' with which he met his death.

Francis Joseph ordered Admiral Tegetthoff to sail for Veracruz and receive Maximilian's remains and transport his coffin to Trieste. To humiliate Austria still further, Juarez refused to release the body until the end of November and it was not until February 1868 that the whole imperial court attended the state funeral in the capital. Meanwhile the Emperor had continued policies essential to Austria's well-being, but which his mother thought deplorable. More and more, Austrian businessmen were looking to the Balkans, fearing a loss of outlets in newly unified Italy and Prussian-dominated Germany. As early as 27 July, despite the deep mourning of the Court, the Emperor entertained at Schönbrunn Sultan Abdulaziz and two Ottoman Princes, the future Sultans Murad V and Abdulhamid II. They were travelling back to Constantinople from the great Paris Exhibition, where they were among Napoleon III's guests when the news of Maximilian's execution broke in France. Even more embarrassing to Francis Joseph was a request from Napoleon III himself to be allowed to come to Vienna and offer his condolences. Only the persistent pleas of Beust that Austria needed France to serve as a buttress in western Europe if the Monarchy were to look to the East persuaded the Emperor to be host to 'that rogue'. Not, of course, that he would see him in Vienna nor in Ischl, where his mother and father were nursing their grief. Reluctantly the Emperor settled for a meeting in Salzburg during the third week of August.

Francis Joseph had difficulty in persuading Elizabeth to leave Ischl for Salzburg. She was feeling unwell, she told him; 'Perhaps I am with child.' But, for once, he was unsympathetic: Richard Metternich's letters from Paris had made it clear that Eugenie would accompany Napoleon and was especially eager to meet Elizabeth. Reluctantly she agreed to make the, relatively short, journey and on 18 August the two sovereigns and their consorts greeted each other, amiably rather than cordially, amid the trappings of a grand state occasion. Salzburg was illuminated, with beacons on the surrounding mountains; a banquet was held in a neighbouring castle; the Burgtheater company travelled down from Vienna to present the dramatic poem *Wildfeur*. Political speculation centred on the negotiation of an anti-Prussian alliance while society amused itself by wondering who was the more elegant, Eugenie or Elizabeth? Nothing was resolved, either in diplomacy or the imperial beauty contest. Francis Joseph had no intention of risking a third war in Europe, least of all with the devious Napoleon III as an ally; but he was willing for Beust and Metternich to linger in Salzburg for further talks with French diplomats. The Austrian Court, seeing the Empresses together, felt that Elizabeth carried herself more naturally. On the other hand, Eugenie won praise from Beust for her tact and from Archduchess Sophie for the unaffected sincerity of her condolences; and she even wished to travel privately to Ischl to see the grief-stricken Archduchess. 'The Empress was most gracious', Sophie noted in her journal, her minuscule writing still shaky from emotion.

Beust, who liked fine distinctions, claimed that Austria and France were 'linked together but not bound together'. This union he sought to nurture. With Metternich's support, he persuaded Francis Joseph to accept an invitation for a return State Visit in October. This time, however, Elizabeth would not accompany him; the pregnancy, which in August had seemed a mere excuse, was now confirmed. 'Heaven is once again blessing my marriage, and the gentle hope which is thus offered me imposes the greatest prudence', Elizabeth explained to Eugenie. However, for a journey to Paris in these last weeks of the Great Exhibition, Francis Joseph found willing companions; all were male. Archduke Charles Ludwig, who had married for a second time in 1862, was prepared to leave his wife with their young Archdukes, Francis Ferdinand and Otto; and his youngest brother, Ludwig Victor, also raised no objection to a dutiful fortnight in Paris. And Count Beust – now officially ranked as

Chancellor – felt bound to serve as attendant minister.

The Austrians reached Paris on 23 October. 'I expected much, but I am really thunderstruck by the conquering beauty of it all', Francis Joseph wrote to Elizabeth next morning. Letters, sent almost every day, show his delight in the visit. Although on All Souls Day he remembered at Mass 'both the Maxs' (his dead brother and Maximilian of Thurn and Taxis), he writes for most of the time in holiday mood, intrigued by all he saw, amused by gossip which would not have reached him at home. Eugenie, he wrote on 28 October, 'is mainly concerned in holding King Ludwig [of Bavaria] at arm's length; he has been here three days now and keeps on trying to steal a kiss from her. Apart from that, he is as merry as a cricket'. The next letter reported that Eugenie had 'made a date with Ludwig. Today she is going up with him in the balloon which makes daily ascents from the Exhibition Gardens. There is little risk, as the balloon is a captive one; but the Emperor is to know nothing about it, all the same. *You* would not do that kind of thing behind *my* back.'

A fatherly pride asserted itself: 'The little Napoleon is a bright fellow but a very puny lad. We've got something to show better than that.' Occasionally, too, Francis Joseph laughed at himself. 'At half-past eight I was at the Théatre Français where a long play was performed very well, but I slept a lot and came home at half past eleven', he told her on 26 October, not mentioning the title or the dramatist's name. Next day he was pleased; he had stayed awake through *Mignon* at the Opéra Comique. But two nights later 'the new opera *Romeo and Juliet* at the Théatre Lyrique' proved too much for him: 'I slept very well again', he admitted, though this time he did let Elizabeth know the composer's name – 'Gounaud' (*sic*). It is fair to remember that Francis Joseph was following an exhausting programme of sightseeing, often accompanying Eugenie, as when they went to the Trianon and the Conciergerie, honouring the memory of Marie Antoinette, his grandfather's aunt. And even on holiday Francis Joseph rose early. Most letters were written before six in the morning.

Politically little was achieved by the visit, though Beust's activities kept Bismarck guessing. Francis Joseph was happy to be reunited with his family at 'dear Possi' before returning to work in the Hofburg in the second week of November. Austrian domestic problems awaited him. After six months of intermittent debate a parliament representing the provinces of Cisleithania had produced a series of five constitutional laws which, together with the Hungarian 'Compromise', determined the basic political structure of the Monarchy throughout Francis Joseph's life, and beyond. These measures were approved by the Emperor four days before Christmas and became known as the 'December Constitution'. They introduced the principle of ministerial responsibility, though they safe-guarded the sovereign's prerogative in matters of defence and foreign affairs. The Reichsrat would have two chambers: an Upper House (*Herrenhaus*) of archdukes, ancient nobility, archbishops and certain princely bishops together with members nominated for life by the Emperor: and a Lower House (*Abgeordnetenhaus*), of some 200 deputies chosen by the provincial diets – a system already being challenged before the end of the year and soon modified. Francis Joseph was not displeased by these December Laws: he still had the power to appoint or dismiss ministers (whose responsibility to parliament involved no more than a threat of impeachment for illegal actions); his assent was needed before a bill became law; and he could reject a measure even if it had been passed by both houses. Moreover, Article XIV re-affirmed the concept of 'emergency government' by the Emperor or his nominees. This principle had been recognized in earlier constitutional drafts, but it was now slightly curbed by an insistence that any emergency measure lapsed if not approved by the next parliament within four weeks of its opening. Yet despite his general satisfaction it was a troubled Christmas for the Emperor that year. Already the Lower House was preparing an attack upon clericalism and, in particular, upon the Concordat of 1855. The domestic peace he believed so essential to recovery would need to be bought with liberal concessions which he was far from certain his conscience would permit.

The Empress did not share her husband's fears. She remained passionately Magyarophile in political sentiment and cultural taste. By now she spent as little time as possible in the Hofburg. Nor was she happy at Schönbrunn where, as in her earlier pregnancies, she complained of prying eyes critically staring at her as she took the walks her physicians demanded. Over Christmas she finally decided that her child would be born in Hungary; if she had a boy, he would be named Stephen, after Hungary's first saintly king. The announcement that her confinement would take place in Buda was not made until 5 February, since it was feared (rightly) that it would be extremely unpopular in Vienna. But, with Andrássy's backing, the Empress again had her way. Except, that is, in one respect. For when the child was born in the royal palace of Buda on 22 April, she was a girl, Marie Valerie.

Elizabeth was not disappointed. She claimed that, for the past two months of pregnancy, she was convinced she would give birth to a girl. The Crown Prince was healthy, and so there seemed no urgent need for a second son. Valerie would become, she thought, the family's Hungarian pet, learning Magyar as her first language. Francis Joseph, too, was pleased to be a father again. Rudolf and Gisela, left behind in Vienna, were told in a letter from Papa that they now had a 'beautiful' sister, with 'great, dark blue eyes', so sturdy that 'she hits out vigorously with her hands and feet'. Not surprisingly, the two elder children drew closer together, resenting the fuss being made of the pampered intruder.

Chapter 11

FACING BOTH WAYS

By the summer of 1868 Francis Joseph had lost that 'open and pre-possessing countenance' Lord John Russell commended thirteen years before. His chin remained beardless but, as if to compensate for the loss of hair on the crown of the head, he grew a thick moustache, longer than in later portraits, while the light brown side-whiskers cultivated early in the reign were by now so luxuriant that they obscured much of the collar, straggling down almost to the lapels of his tunic. Though he was not yet forty and still slim and upright in uniform, the face caught by four photographers that year shows streaks of middle-age, with lines of care discernible below the eyes, and with mouth and chin set in a slanting glance, coldly pensive in repose. He kept himself fit: he had cut down his smoking considerably, and he took plenty of exercise, not simply in the saddle, but by stalking in the mountains when he had the opportunity and by swimming; 'the swimming school' at Mödling, 'which I visit every day, is a great blessing', he was to write to his mother two years later, when pressure of work kept him deskbound well into August. Yet it is not surprising if there was a careworn maturity in his general disposition. For, incredible though it seems, Francis Joseph was already the doyen of continental secular sovereigns (although two minor German Princes had ruled their Grand-Duchies for a slightly longer span). Of Europe's crowned heads in 1868, only Queen Victoria was on the throne at his accession; even Napoleon III did not become Prince-President of France until eighteen days after the hurried ceremony at Olmütz.

This prematurely long experience of public affairs had united with an unimaginative conservatism of spirit to mould a temperament which varied little throughout the second half of Francis Joseph's life. He was slow to come to terms with reality and abandon the chimeric illusions of Metternich's day, with their sense of Habsburg mission in Germany and in Italy; and it could be argued that he never completely freed himself from their influence. His mind remained unreceptive to new ideas, many of which he did not even begin to comprehend. This stunting of intellectual capacity hardened innate prejudices: he never lost an interest in art, but he liked painters to show a neo-baroque approach to their subjects, and he wasted little time on innovations in style or technique. In politics he hankered for the absolutism of the Schwarzenberg era. He continued to mistrust parliamentarians, whether from the chambers in Vienna or in Pest; and on several occasions his choice of prime minister in Cisleithania ignored the prevailing inclination of the Austrian politicians.

On the other hand, the bigoted clericalism of his earlier years mellowed. When, in September 1867, an episcopal conclave submitted an address urging the Emperor to uphold the Concordat and condemn liberal demands to free the Church from state control, the bishops were sharply rebuked for making the government's task difficult; they should not excite public opinion; far better that they should tackle questions of conscience 'in a conciliatory spirit of understanding'. With Archduchess Sophie withdrawing from active political life, the septuagenarian Cardinal Rauscher's influence over her eldest son declined. When in May 1868 the Austrian liberals introduced legislation permitting civil marriage, withdrawing the Church's monopoly of jurisdiction in matrimonial affairs, and freeing education from clerical control, the Emperor did nothing to curb these concessions or a further educational law twelve months later.

The Empress, on a private visit to Rome in December 1869, was present at the opening of the Vatican Council. From her raised and enclosed box she felt swamped by the 'ocean of mitres' beneath her and stayed for only one of the seven hours given to the ceremonies. Next day she sent her husband a gently irreverent account of her audience with Pius IX: all 'that down-on-the-knees-shuffling-around' was 'quite comical', she wrote. Not that either Francis Joseph or Elizabeth became any less devout in their religious practices: on Maundy Thursday each year, the Emperor and Empress penitentially washed the feet of more than a dozen elderly pensioners brought to the Hofburg from Vienna's almshouses; and the imperial family continued to observe the public acts of reverence at Easter and Corpus Christi. The Emperor certainly did not intend to accept the growth of a conflict between the Church and secular authority. When, in July 1869, Bishop Rüdiger of Linz was sent to prison for instigating a breach of the peace by an intemperate attack on the new liberalism, Francis Joseph intervened: the Bishop was swiftly pardoned and released. The Austrian episcopate recognized the sincerity of their Emperor's delicate search for a middle way, and at the sessions of the Vatican Council Cardinals Rauscher and Schwarzenberg, together with the Croatian bishop Strossmayer, were outspoken critics of papal claims of supremacy. Francis Joseph and his closest spiritual advisers considered that the proclamation of papal infallibility on 18 July 1870 provided the pontiff with an unprecedented excuse for interfering in the Monarchy's affairs; and within a fortnight Francis Joseph agreed that the Concordat of 1855 should be considered null and void. 'The annulment of the Concordat was hard for me', he assured his mother, but he put all the blame on the wrong headedness of Rome: 'One might despair of the Church's future, if one could not hold firmly to the belief and hope that God will safeguard His Church from further mischief.'

Naturally Francis Joseph recognized that the *Ausgleich* modified the character of the Monarchy. He was fully prepared to spend more time in Hungary and, though he never liked the palace on Buda's Castle Hill, he came to enjoy the weeks of royal residence at Gödöllö almost as much as did Elizabeth. Yet it is clear that the Hungarian Compromise was, for him, a beginning rather than an end. He officially notified Chancellor Beust in November 1868 that his titles were now 'Emperor of Austria, King of Bohemia, etc. and Apostolic King of Hungary'. His grandfather had been crowned in Prague as early as August 1792, barely eight weeks after his Hungarian coronation, and there is no doubt that Francis Joseph intended to follow this precedent as closely as possible – always provided he could reach a political agreement with Bohemia's Germans and Czechs.

When Francis Joseph visited Prague in June 1868 to open a new bridge, he conferred with the veteran Czech historian, Palácky, as well as with his son-in-law, the far less accomplished nationalist spokesman, Franz Rieger. But neither Czech leader possessed the authority of Deák in Hungary nor the political dexterity of Andrássy. Rieger had been in Moscow in 1867 for the first Pan-Slav Congress and he was not prepared to make the concessions which Francis Joseph sought for Bohemia's Germans. Czech nationalism, quiescent for several years, had received a fillip earlier in the spring when the foundation stone was laid in Prague for a National Theatre, and feeling in the Czech provinces became so intense that in the autumn a state of siege was once more proclaimed in Prague. The building of the magnificent neo-Renaissance theatre on the banks of the river Vltava was not completed until 1881, and its construction served as a symbolic inspiration for the next generation of Czech patriots. To emphasize their distinctive 'West Slav' nationality Rieger made certain that all Czech deputies absented themselves from the Reichsrat in Vienna for the first twelve years of its existence. The almost forgotten Emperor Ferdinand and his devoted Maria Anna – 'their Prague Majesties' – could be certain of a polite reception on their walks in the gardens of the Hradčany castle, but Francis Joseph saw that he could not count on the Czechs responding as festively as the Hungarians to another Habsburg coronation.

Nevertheless he persevered in his attempts to secure an agreement with the Czechs. In September 1868 he tried the gambit which had succeeded at Buda-Pest and sent Beust for private talks with the Czech leaders. This was a tactical error: most Slavs, and particularly Czechs, were antipathetic to the Chancellor; and the immediate consequence of Beust's secret mission was the resignation of the Austrian prime minister, who complained that he had not been consulted. Taaffe took over as head of the Austrian government, while the Emperor continued to look for some respected figure who would coax the Czechs into co-operation. Having tried a Galician landowner, Count Alfred Potocki, whose federalist ideas proved unpopular, he eventually turned to one of the Austrian provincial governors, Count Charles von Hohenwart, who at first seemed to make some progress in discussions with Bohemia's politicians. The Czechs themselves at last drew up a series of 'Fundamental Articles', providing for the autonomy of Bohemia, followed the Hungarian model, and in the third week of September 1871 Francis Joseph sent a message to the Bohemian Diet in which he declared 'We gladly recognize the rights of this Kingdom and are prepared to renew that recognition in a coronation oath.' But this gesture provoked a violent reaction. The largely German-Austrian students of the University of Vienna protested so vigorously that there was a threat of riots in the capital; the Silesians complained that, though loyal German subjects of the Monarchy, they were being sacrificed to the Slavs of Prague; the Poles of Galicia saw no reason why the Czechs should receive special treatment; and Andrássy, invited to give his views at a specially convened Crown Conference, declared that the granting of concessions to the Czechs made civil war likely. 'Are you willing to carry through the recognition of Bohemian state rights with cannon?' he is said to have asked Hohenwart, 'If not, do not begin this policy.' Possibly Andrássy spoke less dramatically than this dire warning would suggest. But, at all events, the policy of satisfying the Czechs was abandoned. Hohenwart resigned. Francis Joseph found yet another princely Austrian to head the government of Cisleithania. There was no more talk of a coronation in Prague.

In Francis Joseph's boyhood the Monarchy had been concerned primarily with the German lands in the north and the Italian peninsula in the south. Metternich used to maintain that 'Asia begins at the Landstrasse', the highway eastwards from Vienna – and Asia held no interest for him whatsoever. But this blinkered approach was out of date even before Metternich fell from power. As early as 1837 a pioneer Austrian steamship service linked Trieste and Constantinople; and, after the unrest of 1848–49, improved navigation on the Danube, soon followed by the lifting of most restrictions on foreign banking in the Ottoman Empire, resulted in the growth in Vienna of a lively commercial interest in Near Eastern affairs. Defeat by Prussia in 1866 and the cession of Venetia intensified the need for the Monarchy to face both ways. Francis Joseph's ministers began to show a new sensitivity over what was likely to happen in south-eastern Europe. In 1869 the 'Krisvosije Rising', a series of armed disturbances over conscription in the mountain villages around Kotor, was treated as a major insurrection by the military chiefs in Vienna, not least because the long-neglected Gulf of Kotor seemed potentially the finest harbour for a fleet in the southern Adriatic. At the same time Beust, as Imperial Chancellor, showed an accommodating liberality towards the Balkan peoples: he offered financial assistance to Montenegro, encouraged the Turks to remove their last garrisons from three Serbian fortresses, acted as a mediator in a constitutional dispute between the Serbs and their nominal Ottoman suzerain in Constantinople, and gradually broke down the hostility of government ministers in Vienna and (less successfully) in Buda-Pest to the attempts of the Roumanians to assert their full independence. Very slowly, and with much argument, Beust convinced his colleagues of the value of giving support to a Franco-Belgian consortium which wished to construct a railway from Vienna through the Balkans to Salonika. Completion of this line would, he hoped, ensure that Austria kept a profitable hand on Ottoman trade with Europe.

It was Beust, too, who in 1869 persuaded Francis Joseph to attend the opening ceremonies of the Suez Canal. The invitation was given by Khedive Ismail of Egypt when the Emperor entertained him at Laxenburg in the first week of June. Until he went to the Paris Exhibition Francis Joseph had crossed the Monarchy's frontiers only to visit other German Princes or meet successive Tsars. Now Beust urged him to emphasize Austria's interest in the Near East, not merely by going to Egypt, but by paying a courtesy call on the Sultan in Constantinople, a gesture no Christian monarch had ever made while on the throne. Gradually the itinerary of the 'Imperial Tour in the East' grew longer, until it included other first occasions for a Habsburg sovereign, too: a river trip through the Iron Gates to the lower Danube; a visit to Athens; and a journey to Jerusalem. Originally it was assumed that the Empress Elizabeth would accompany her husband, but she shrank from accepting such a burden of official festivities; the need to appear in public ceremonially so often was more than she dared to face. Young Valerie needed her mother, she maintained; and there were Gisela and Rudolf to be considered, too, she remembered. Unkind gossip insisted that Elizabeth decided against the trip on learning that Eugenie would formally open the Suez Canal, for she could not face a second round in the so-called beauty contest with her alleged rival. At the last moment, when Elizabeth was preparing to say goodbye to Francis Joseph at Gödöllö, she seems to have regretted her decision, but there was no way in which the elaborate arrangements for a six week tour could be adjusted to accommodate her whims.

Not since his accession had Francis Joseph benefited from such an enjoyable and enlightening experience as these travels 'in the East', and yet their significance has been ignored by many later commentators on his reign. He sent Elizabeth twelve letters, with entries written up day by day; for the most part, they read like a travel diary, some 20,000 words long. They enable us, for once, to penetrate the formal mask which, as an essentially shy individual, Francis Joseph created to protect the private face of Empire from public gaze. Their style is a curious mixture; the astonished enthusiasm of an innocent abroad mingles with military assessments from a veteran inspector-general. Sometimes the sheer beauty of the scene overwhelms him; then, a few lines later, he notes the number of gun salutes or the bearing of the jäger battalions, cavalry and field artillery of the Sultan's army on parade.

Francis Joseph reached Turkish soil on 27 October, landing at Ruschuk, the river port of Ottoman Bulgaria. The welcoming ceremonies passed with routine familiarity, but, as he drove into the town, his interest quickened. 'It was a beautiful oriental picture, and I was in the midst of Turkish life, in the World of the East. For me the suddenness of the adventure and the swift change of scene was like a dream.' But when he wrote those words he was already on the Bosphorus: 'I am in Stamboul!', he exclaimed, 'To describe what I am seeing and feeling is beyond me. Only one thought is in my mind, the wish that you were here; my one hope is that you may be able to see it all: this setting for a city; these waters; these palaces; the glorious sunsets; the cypresses; the fleets of boats; the hurly-burly of people in every colour of costume; the women, unhappily veiled but with such eyes that you can only regret they should so be; and as for this air!' His room in the 'imperial palace of Besiktas' amazed him: 'The bed would hold at least three people, and one cannot help constantly thinking of all that must already have happened in it.' He knew his wife's interests, however, for next day he said, 'Soon after I had written to you, I began my sightseeing with the Sultan's stables. I feel certain that's what you would have done'; and he told her about the Sultan's thirty-year-old favourite grey and his 800 mounts, and how even his 'little prince' had 150 horses. Sultan Abdulaziz, so he assured Elizabeth, was 'the most charming host imaginable.'

After four more days off the Golden Horn the imperial yacht *Greif*, followed by two other Austrian ships carrying Francis Joseph's suite and accompanying ministers (including Beust and Andrássy), steamed out into the Sea of Marmora, for the Dardanelles and ultimately Piraeus. 'Here Leander swam to Hero, here Xerxes built the bridge over which he marched against the Greeks, here Lord Byron swam across', wrote the Emperor, stirred by the romantic associations of the Hellespont. As the *Greif* sailed along the coast of Attica he was delighted to see, 'to the right an ancient Greek temple to Diana on a promontory' (the Temple of Poseidon at Sounion, perhaps?). His letters left no temple undescribed, no glory from the monumental past unilluminated. But they carried, too, a modern touch: 'From Piraeus we went by railway in ten minutes to Athens across quite well cultivated plains, with olive-trees, vines and figs'. Francis Joseph was as meticulous an observer as any note-taker employed by Karl Baedeker.

'Four days at sea to reach Jaffa!', he warned Elizabeth in advance. When he landed in the Holy Land he was once again entranced by his surroundings. His party was guarded by several hundred Ottoman soldiers, moving slowly forward in a caravan of camels, while Bedouin horsemen on their lively greys served as outriders. On seeing Jerusalem for the first time, he sank to his knees in prayer. Then, over another four days, he visited the holy shrines in the city and at Bethlehem, went out to Jericho and the Dead Sea, stopped at the River Jordan, and, loaded with relics and holy water bottles, set off back to the coast, bivouacking in tents with their canvas embroidered with gold and silk designs. A lively swell made embarkation difficult: 'I made the trip out to the *Greif* from Jaffa in a small boat manned by local people, and the hoisting aboard in a sling, as horses are, is something I shall never forget for the rest of my days, and I would not do that kind of thing again for a million.' But, at last, on 15 November the three Austrian vessels moored off Port Said, where the official opening ceremonies of the canal were to begin next day.

The principal guest had already been in Egypt for a month, having left Paris nearly four weeks before Francis Joseph set out from Gödöllö. 'So now you are happily united with your beloved Empress Eugenie', Elizabeth wrote to her husband in a lightly mocking tone, 'It makes me very jealous to think of you playing the charmer for her benefit while I sit here all alone and am not even able to take my revenge'. Francis Joseph's response was tactful, though hardly gallant; Eugenie, he informed Elizabeth, 'had grown quite stout and was losing much of her beauty'. The opening ceremonies were, however, Eugenie's great personal triumph. The construction of the Suez Canal had been masterminded by her cousin, Ferdinand de Lesseps, and the whole enterprise was sponsored by the French imperial establishment. It was right for her to be accorded the honours of the occasion, since, as Napoleon III was suffering from stone in the bladder, there could be no question of his coming to Egypt. The French yacht *L'Aigle* headed the procession of ships down the canal, with Francis Joseph following aboard *Greif*; then came a line of nearly forty other vessels, which set out at fifteen minute intervals. Overnight the flotilla anchored in the Bitter Lakes before completing the second stage of what by now Francis Joseph had decided was a 'monotonous' journey down to Suez. At Ismailia there was a Grand Ball – '*Schrecklich*!!' (Frightful), he wrote. There were several thousand people there, so he reported; some were 'quite ordinary guests', including 'Riciotti Garibaldi, the son of the famous Garibaldi'. Eugenie, in a bright red dress and with a crown on her head, entered the ballroom on Francis Joseph's arm. He was, others noted, very attentive to her needs. It was impossible to dance or to make much progress. 'In all our minds there was only one thought: *Aussi mocht ich*' ('Let's get out of here' in Viennese dialect); 'The Empress and I did all in our power to get supper started, which we were bound to wait for, as the most magnificent preparations had been made, and the menu included more than 30 dishes. The meal seemed endless ... I came back aboard *Greif* at 2 in the morning and slept like a log.'

Cairo was more to his liking: 410 mosques, he noted down carefully. Less pleasing was gala night at the new 'Italian Theatre' opera house beside the Nile: 'everyone in white ties' for an occasion which 'cost the Khedive the devil of a sum': 'Act 4 (*sic*) of *Rigoletto*', followed by 'the ballet of *Giselle*, to which I gave my support for only the first act, as I then fell asleep'. Best of all Francis Joseph enjoyed the opportunity to climb the pyramid of Cheops, the highest at Ghiza; this feat he achieved in seventeen minutes, having found that 'my rock-climbing experience stood me in good stead'. 'One Bedouin took me by the hand, another followed so as to push me from behind when the blocks of stone were too high to scramble up, though this was needed only five or six times', he explained to Elizabeth; and he added, 'The Bedouins are very agile, strong and self-assured. As they mostly only wear a shirt, when they are climbing they leave a lot exposed, and that must be the reason why English women so happily and frequently like to scale the pyramids.'

From Cairo it was back to the *Greif* at Alexandria and so, by way of Crete and Corfu, home to Trieste. There Francis Joseph was to see Elizabeth again. Not, however, at the happiest choice of rendezvous: for, with Charlotte in a private asylum in her native Belgium, Miramare had become an Austrian imperial villa, and it was in the rooms Maximilian had designed, looking out on the gardens to which he had given such thought, that his brother and sister-in-law were re-united. Even then, their meeting could be little more than a passing encounter, for during the later stages of her husband's tour, Elizabeth decided she was needed by her sister, the exiled Queen of Naples, who was expecting her first child in Rome; and, accordingly, the Empress had merely stopped briefly at Miramare while travelling to the papal city (and to that opening ceremony of the Vatican Council). Francis Joseph, who landed at Trieste pleasantly elated by all he had seen and done, soon found himself once more 'in harness', to use Elizabeth's phrase. She, on the other hand, avoided public life well into the New Year; from Rome she went directly back to Hungary, and then with her two daughters to Merano; it is hardly surprising if when, in March, the Empress at last returned to the capital, an ironical newspaper article referred to her as 'the resident guest in the Vienna Hofburg'. By then, of course, Francis Joseph had recounted his traveller's tales many times over. Like the gifts he brought with him, their father's adventures excited Rudolf and Gisela at Christmas, and he found he could still share his knowledge of a wider world with his mother, though it was clear her powers of assimilation were beginning to fail.

This new awareness of Eastern affairs soon became of great importance in his shaping of policy. But, for much of 1870, he was compelled to look to the West and the North. There remained a powerful pressure group in the war ministry who hankered for a war of revenge against Prussia. To them the great virtue of Francis Joseph's travels in the East had been the visible signs of friendship and support he extended to Eugenie at Port Said and Ismailia. Unofficial conversations between French staff officers and Austrian representatives were held from time to time during the closing months of 1869, and in February 1870 Baron Franz Kuhn, the first Austro-Hungarian war minister, informed the French military attaché in Vienna that, should France and the Monarchy find themselves at war with Prussia, he could guarantee an army of 600,000 men would be fully mobilized within six weeks. A month later Archduke Albrecht, as titular Inspector-General of the Imperial and Royal army, paid a much publicized visit to Paris, where he unfolded a grand strategic plan to the French minister of war. Provided France kept the Prussians engaged for six weeks and mounted an offensive in the general direction of Nuremberg, the Austrians (and he hoped an Italian expeditionary force) would cross into Saxony, raise the south German states and join the French in a march on Berlin which would destroy Bismarck's Prussia. The French, however, were doubtful of Albrecht's master-plan, not least because of the six week delay it imposed; and when, early in June, a French general returned Albrecht's visit, he received a clear impression that Francis Joseph had no desire whatsoever to risk another war.

This assessment of the Emperor's attitude was perfectly correct. Twice already he had allowed his ministers and generals to hustle him into disastrous wars. Experience made him cautious. Moreover, he could see that there was a conflict around the conference table between Albrecht and Kuhn. Their advice was inconsistent. If the Archduke rattled his sabre, Kuhn insisted that the work of years in preparing the army to face its great challenge was not yet finished. When Kuhn changed his position and began to urge that Austria-Hungary could not stand aside from a coming 'struggle involving all Europe', Albrecht circulated a critical pamphlet, technically anonymous: the army, so the pamphlet asserted, was short of modern weapons, and the parsimony of the war ministry meant that it was ill-equipped for any mobile campaign in the field. Understandably, at this point, the Emperor decided to order an inquiry into the readiness of his troops for war; this task he entrusted to Beck, who had served Francis Joseph so well in the Seven Weeks War, that he was appointed chief of the military chancellery.

Ultimately Beck agreed with Albrecht rather than Kuhn; but before these quarrels could be resolved, the Emperor and all his ministers were shaken by the sudden deterioration in Franco-Prussian relations over the so-called Hohenzollern Candidature for the Spanish throne. On 15 July Richard Metternich was surprised to be informed in Paris that war was certain; 'If Austria realizes what is best for her, she will march beside us', he was told. But Francis Joseph was not going to have questions of peace or war decided for him in Paris. Hurriedly he summoned a council of ministers for 18 July, the day before formal hostilities began between France and Prussia.

Francis Joseph presided over the council himself, and spoke at some length. Beust confirmed that Austria-Hungary retained a free hand and that the French had taken no notice of Austrian pleas not to allow the Hohenzollern Candidature to become transformed into a German national issue. Andrássy thought Russia posed a greater threat to the Monarchy than Prussia, for he maintained that Pan-Slav hotheads were in the ascendant at St Petersburg. If Austria-Hungary was committed to a campaign in southern Germany, the Russians would seize the opportunity to stir up the southern Slavs and press forward with plans to dominate the Balkans and the lower Danube. Kuhn, who had circulated a memorandum in advance of the conference favouring immediate intervention, made a fiery speech which stressed the need for Austria to prevent the permanent siting of Prussian garrisons along the River Inn. Archduke Albrecht wanted immediate mobilization but when, later in the day, he took the chair at a second ministerial conference, there was a strong feeling in favour of neutrality. As a gesture of reassurance towards Andrássy, Francis Joseph ordered defensive measures to be taken along the Monarchy's 500-mile frontier with the Russian Empire.

Before the war began, Beust hoped his influence in Saxony would keep the southern German states from giving military support to the North German Confederation. Here, however, he was wrong. The appeal of German national sentiment was too strong. On 27 July Archduchess Sophie's journal echoed the feeling of the Court: deep sorrow at the 'sad enthusiasm' with which the German states were falling in beside Prussia to fight against the old enemy beyond the Rhine. When, nine days later, press reports indicated that Bavarian units in the Prussian Crown Prince's Third Army were marching on Strasbourg, the Archduchess despaired of her homeland: 'This is the ruin of Saxony and Bavaria', she wrote, 'May God help them.'

Francis Joseph remained at Schönbrunn, presiding over five ministerial conferences in twelve days once the German invasion of France began in earnest. Church-State relations were also discussed at these meetings, for the outbreak of war had coincided with the declaration of papal infallibility. By the end of the first week in August he had little doubt that an Austro-Hungarian entry into the war would be disastrous. After a long conference on 9 August, he stopped all preparations for an imminent campaign. Kuhn thought Austria-Hungary should take advantage of Prussia's pre-occupation with the West by marching into Silesia and recovering lands lost to Frederick the Great. But Francis Joseph was more sympathetic to Beust's argument that the Monarchy stood to gain influence and prestige by staying out of the war and coming forward as a mediator. A ministerial conference on 22 August duly endorsed the policy of armed neutrality – but with a wary eye kept on the Russians, for Tsar Alexander II had complained of hostile troop movements in Galicia. Francis Joseph took note of a warning from Andrássy which confirmed the impression he had formed during his journey to Ruschuk and the Bosphorus: 'Austria's mission remains, as before, to be a bulwark against Russia', the Hungarian prime minister declared, 'Only so long as she fulfils this mission does her existence remain a necessity for Europe.' The army corps in Galicia was kept on the alert.

Yet Francis Joseph could hardly turn his back on what was happening in the West. 'The catastrophes in France are frightful and offer no comfort for our future', he wrote to his mother on 25 August. Worse soon followed: the French defeat at Sedan on 1 September; Napoleon III's capture; the proclamation of a republic in Paris. 'How Eugenie must regret the timidity and vacillation of her husband!' Archduchess Sophie observed. Another long ministerial council on 11 September reviewed the situation gloomily. Beust was sent to Munich in the hopes that, at this late hour, he could persuade the south Germans to stay outside a Prussianized nation state. But even Beust, with all his understanding of German affairs, could achieve nothing. 'I see a very dark future, even more dismal than the present', Francis Joseph admitted to his mother at the end of October. Twelve weeks later a German Empire, from which the Austrian lands were excluded, was proclaimed in the Hall of Mirrors at Versailles. The Habsburgs seemed finally to have lost their voice in German affairs. Not everyone in Vienna was willing to accept the change. Archduchess Sophie, though recognizing the newly elevated status of the ruler in Berlin, denied him his full title: the last volumes of her journal refer to William I simply as the 'Prussian Emperor'.

A second humiliation buffeted Habsburg pride within a few weeks of the ceremony at Versailles. Francis Joseph and his ministers were convinced that Alexander II would take advantage of the European crisis to assert Russia's Great Power status. Rather curiously they seem to have believed he would order his troops into Moldavia and Wallachia, brushing aside the tenuous existence of a semi-independent Roumania. Accordingly when, in November 1870, Russia abrogated the clauses of the Treaty of Paris providing for the demilitarization of the Black Sea, Beust and Andrássy were in a sense relieved, for the Tsar's army would not now be on the move. At a conference on 14 November Francis Joseph agreed with Beust's contention that there could be no question of war with Russia, but it was subsequently agreed that, should there be an international conference over Black Sea problems, Austria-Hungary would seek special status so as to counter-balance Russia. But when, in February and March 1871, these matters were aired at a conference in London, Beust's proposals were totally ignored; even the Sultan's representatives preferred to rely on Germany and Great Britain. Diplomatically the Habsburg Monarchy had been left isolated by the Crimean War and the Treaty of Paris: now, after the Franco-Prussian War and the denunciation of the Treaty of Paris, the Habsburg Monarchy was isolated again.

Beust, however, was a resilient statesman. The definitive peace treaty between the German Empire and France was signed at Frankfurt on 10 May 1871. Eight days later Francis Joseph received a memorandum from Beust setting out a strategy to enable Austria-Hungary to become Europe's pivotal Great Power once more: the Emperor should seek reconciliation with the new German Empire. Side by side the governments of Berlin, Vienna and Buda-Pest could form a central bloc across Europe, ready if necessary to put out feelers to St Petersburg and revive the old understanding between the three northern courts or to unite against revolutionary republicanism should it triumph in France (for Beust was writing while the Communards still held Paris). There must be no more talk of revenge for 1866: on the contrary, the Emperor should realize that Bismarck had created a national empire which might appeal to the

German population of the Monarchy, and thereby threaten its very existence.

Although before the end of the year Francis Joseph was to turn against Beust, for the moment he was willing to accept the principles of the memorandum. Chancellor Beust and Chancellor Bismarck met three months later; and on 11 August Emperor Francis Joseph was on the railway platform at Wels to greet Emperor William I as he made his way to Gastein. It was not the first contact between the two sovereigns since Königgrätz: they had briefly exchanged cold courtesies at Oos in October 1867, when Francis Joseph's train crossed Prussian territory on the way to Paris. But at Wels there was some amiable conversation, and the two Emperors travelled together across the mountains to Ischl, before William went on to Gastein. The reconciliation was carried further when they met again on 6 September in Salzburg. So far, so good; but Francis Joseph had his doubts. Was Beust the best man to carry out the policies he had recommended? Could he subdue his old hatred of Bismarck, for example? Conversely was he still too southern German in his approach to the problems of the Monarchy and, in particular, to the position of the Czechs in Bohemia? In the late autumn Francis Joseph resolved to make one of the sudden and ruthless changes of minister for which he was by now becoming notorious. On 1 November the Emperor asked Beust for his resignation as Imperial Chancellor, the title disappearing with the departure of its holder to serve as ambassador in London. At last Francis Joseph implemented the 'preposterous' suggestion which Elizabeth had put forward five years before: on 9 November Gyula Andrássy moved into Metternich's old room looking down on the Ballhausplatz. For the first time, the Monarchy was to have a Hungarian magnate as foreign minister.

Elizabeth was pleased at the appointment. Yet she was less elated than before her coronation. Her liking for Hungary, its people, language and culture, was undiminished; she now included among her close companions both Ida Ferenczy and the highly intelligent and perceptive Countess Marie Festetics, a confidante of Andrássy. She continued, too, to enjoy hunting at Gödöllö, where Andrássy was a frequent guest. But, after the birth of Marie Valerie, Elizabeth lost her interest in politics, never very great. Once again she earned frowns of disapproval at Court. At the height of the Franco-Prussian War her strong will made her decide that, for reasons of health, she must spend most of the winter at Merano, with little Valerie and at first with Gisela, too. 'My poor son', Archduchess Sophie commented in her journal, on hearing that Elizabeth was heading for the southern Tyrol at such a time. Three weeks later the Archduchess transcribed an unctuous letter she had received from Rudolf, which she seems to have commended: 'So in these difficult days poor Papa must be separated again from darling Mama', wrote the twelve-year-old Crown Prince, 'I am only too happy to accept the noble duty of being the sole support of my dear Papa.' Sophie was fond of her grandson; and there is no doubt that he warmly returned her affection. But in his unhappiness can the boy really have been such an insufferable prig? Did she attribute to him her own sentiments, or was he astute enough to play on her feelings?

In that winter of 1870–71, and in the next, the Archduchess seemed to recover much of her old vigour, making a final bid to preside over high society in the capital. She was, after all, only in her mid-sixties. Every Friday evening she held a dinner-party at the Hofburg, but she did not like new fashions or new ideas. Least of all, could she accept the need for the Monarchy to face both ways, for she deplored the intrusiveness of all those Hungarians at Court. When she entered up her diary on New Year's Eve in 1871 – eight weeks after Andrássy became foreign minister – she followed her usual practice and looked back on the past twelve months. This time she wrote with unaccustomed bitterness: 'liberalism', she complained, was triumphant; and she regretted the omnipresence of its 'worthless shining lights'. 'May God have pity on us!' she added.

It was nearly half a century since Sophie had left Munich for Vienna. Early in 1872, to her great surprise, she learned of the prospect of yet another dynastic link between the Wittelsbach and Habsburg families. At fifteen the Archduchess Gisela was betrothed to Prince Leopold of Bavaria, her second cousin twice over. 'As there are so few Catholic princes, we had to try to secure the only one to whom we might give Gisela with any confidence', Francis Joseph told his mother on 7 April. Sophie was fond of Gisela, who had been an attentive grand-daughter; she also liked Prince Leopold; but she wrote firmly in her journal, 'This marriage is no match'. Elizabeth, too, had doubts, insisting that Gisela was too young – though she was almost exactly the same age as Elizabeth had been when she became Francis Joseph's fiancée. It was accepted that the marriage would not take place for another year, the Empress's critics insisting that, in her craving for eternal youthfulness, Elizabeth wished to put off the reality of becoming a grandmother as long as possible.

Archduchess Sophie did not live to see Gisela married. On Monday, 6 May, she was up at half-past five to set out on a day-long expedition. It was a sharp spring morning and she caught a chill which, at the end of the week, became dangerously bronchial. On Saturday 11 May she began to write up her journal; the effort was too much for her; and, after a few lines, the entry breaks off abruptly. Not that the curtain was to fall suddenly on her. For more than a fortnight she lingered in a sick-room, while her family converged on Vienna, finally gathering in the Hofburg around her.

As Sophie grew weaker, Elizabeth kept a constant vigil, while Francis Joseph put Maria Theresa's rosary in his mother's hands. When at last the Archduchess died – on the afternoon of 28 May 1872 – the Empress had been at her bedside for eighteen hours, contrite for the worry which her wilful ways once caused the dying matriarch. Francis Joseph, deeply shaken by the loss of a mother who was his greatest confidante, admired his wife's dutiful dignity in mourning. Elizabeth's temperament possessed a bewildering facility for swift changes of mood, and he appreciated the sorrowful sympathy which there is no doubt she genuinely felt for all the family around the deathbed. Yet, once the funeral was over, and Sophie's body lay in the vault of the Capuchin church beside the tombs of Maximilian and the Duke of Reichstadt, old convictions sprang readily back into place. Over the following months the Empress liked to gossip about the recent past with her Hungarian ladies-in-waiting, recounting at considerable length the enormities of misunderstanding committed by a bullying mother-in-law in the first years of her married life. Marie Festetics made a careful note of the Empress's spate of reminiscence. Fortunately Francis Joseph was never to read them; the 'dearest, darling angel Sisi' stayed secure on her pedestal in his fondest beliefs.

Chapter 12

A GLIMMER OF LIGHT

The mood of Vienna in Archduchess Sophie's last five years of life changed dramatically, season by season. At first, in 1867, the city was stunned by the lost war against Prussia, slow to accept dethronement from its European eminence. The carnival festivities were muted that winter; it seemed fitting to hold concerts rather than encourage an irresponsible gaiety by the customary series of sparkling balls. Out at the Dianabad-Sall in Leopoldstadt on the middle Friday of *Fasching* – 15 February 1867 – the Vienna Men's Choral Society offered a new choral work, commissioned from Johann Strauss 'the Younger' and frequently changed by him in form and character. It was still without a title when the programme was announced, although words had been found for 'Opus 314' by Joseph Weyl, a member of the Society with a gift for turning out verses for any occasion. This time they were good ones. 'Why are you Viennese sad?', Weyl asked, in effect, 'Why shrug your shoulders in despair? Don't you see a glimmer of light? Carnival time is here; let's be merry and gay'. To this challenge Strauss's music duly responded, a few bars of wistful prelude swiftly giving way to what a leading music critic at once hailed as 'a truly splendid waltz'. Not that Strauss was in the Dianabad-Sall that evening to conduct it. He was with his orchestra at the Hofburg, fulfilling obligations accepted four years previously when he first became *Hofballmusik-Direktor* at Francis Joseph's Court. In the composer's absence the Society's chorus-master, Rudolf Weinwurm, took the baton; and the most famous of Viennese waltzes, hurriedly entitled *An der schönen blauen Donau*, was played for the first time not by Strauss's fiddlers but by the orchestra of the König von Hannover Infantry Regiment, then at barracks in the city.

Three weeks later Johann Strauss conducted the definitive version of *The Blue Danube* in the Volksgarten. Thereafter the waltz was treated as a composition either for piano or for full orchestra; its origins as a choral work were largely ignored until eventually in 1890 Franz von Gernerth,

Elizabeth's life-long riding skills entranced her husband, and she was acknowledged as one of the most accomplished horsewomen in Europe.

Francis Joseph with his great-nephew, who in 1916 succeeded him as Charles I, last of the great Habsburg rulers. A photograph taken by Charles's mother, outside Cannes, 9 March 1894.

October 1911: the old Emperor at the wedding reception on the balcony at Schwarzau, the castle in Lower Austria, where his great-nephew Charles married Princess Zita of Bourbon-Parma.

In his study at Schönbrunn, shortly before his death. He always wore uniforms, except when taking a holiday abroad or in the mountains, but for everyday work he would choose the simple service tunic and trousers of a junior officer.

'The old gentleman'. The octogenarian Emperor passes the 16th-century Schweizertor, as he walks to his apartments in Vienna's inner Hofburg.

The end of an era. The funeral procession of Francis Joseph, 30 November, 1916. It is headed by Emperor Charles and Empress Zita (heavily veiled), with Crown Prince Otto between them; the rulers of Bavaria, Saxony and Bulgaria follow.

Kaiser Franz Josef

Only rarely did the Emperor escape the cares of state. He was a hunting enthusiast, however, and this picture was taken during one of his escapes from the business of government.

Francis Joseph and his companions picnic during a hunting expedition at Gödöllo, in the Habsburg Kingdom of Hungary.

Alongside her passion for horses, Empress Elizabeth was a dog lover too. This photograph shows Elizabeth, in her thirtieth year, with her favourite hound 'Shadow'.

The Emperor with two of his children, Archduchess Gisela and Crown Prince Rudolf, in 1860. The photograph was sent by Francis Joseph to Elizabeth while she was convalescing in Madeira.

Schönbrunn, the enormous 'summer palace' built by Maria Theresa in the 18th century, birthplace of Francis Joseph and chief residence of the Habsburg rulers of a great multi-ethnic empire. In the foreground are the gilded eagles.

Archduchess Sophie of Bavaria, the power behind the throne at the time of her son Francis Joseph's accession and whose ambitions for him were a constant theme of Habsburg politics.

Field marshal Radetzky, one of the greatest of Francis Joseph's commanders, whose control of Italy held back the forces of nationalism at a critical time and inspired the world-famous Radetzky March by Johann Strauss. Radetzky retired in virtual senility at the age of ninety-one.

A view of Schönbrunn, taken from the point at which the Emperor first encountered Anna Nahowski.

The Villa Felicitas, Katharina Schratt's home at Bad Ischl, where Francis Joseph was a frequent, and often inconveniently early, caller on his friend.

Katharina Schratt, the actress who became 'friend but not lover' to the far older Emperor and whose close association with Francis Joseph was actively encouraged by Empress Elizabeth, possibly because she was aware that Katharina gave Francis Joseph a domestic peace which she was incapable of providing.

Young Francis Joseph in his uniform as a Hussar officer prior to his accession. He was trained to love soldiering, uniforms and the military dignity of the dynasty, and this picture reminds us of the dashing figure which contrasted so strongly with the many later images of Francis Joseph as 'elder statesman'.

On his visit to mark the opening of the Suez Canal, the Emperor climbed the pyramid of Cheops, a not inconsiderable achievement despite helping hands.

Francis Joseph receives guests at a Court ball. The glitter and ceremonial of Habsburg Imperial life was one of its chief characteristics, yet did much to alienate the Empress who never disguised her dislike of the formality with which she was surrounded at Court.

Archduke Francis Ferdinand with his wife Sophie and their three children, Maximilian, Ernest, and Sophie.

Francis Ferdinand, heir to the Habsburg throne after the suicide of Crown Prince Rudolf at Mayerling. He himself never entered into his inheritance, assassinated at Sarajevo in a sequence of events that led directly to World War One.

On 8 June 1867, the Austrian Empire became the Dual Monarchy of Austria Hungary. Here, Francis Joseph stands beside the new Queen of Hungary to receive the acclamation of the Hungarian Parliament.

The ill-fated hunting lodge at Mayerling where the scandal and tragedy which took the lives of the Emperor's son Rudolf and his young mistress Mary Vetsera remain largely inexplicable to this day.

Vienna's Stephansplatz, circa 1900. Habsburg power remained intact, but in fact the dynasty which had ruled so much of Europe since the thirteenth century now had less than twenty years before its extinction.

The Kaiservilla at Bad Ischl, a favourite retreat for both the Emperor and Empress.

The Emperor with his young bride Elizabeth, 1855, a year after their marriage. He remained captivated by her throughout their long years of marriage, though her own wayward temperament, not helped by the interfering bossiness of Archduchess Sophie, placed many strains upon them.

another member of the Men's Choral Society, wrote the anodyne travel commercial which has endured for more than a century. But Joseph Weyl's original satirical verses proved extremely apt. He had told the people of Vienna to forget their misfortunes; and this they had good reason to do in the months which followed that première in the Dianabad-Sall. So, too, did the townsfolk of many other commercial centres in the Dual Monarchy. For during the first six years of its existence Austria-Hungary was unexpectedly blessed with an economic miracle. State finance, held for so long in the shadow of imminent bankruptcy, emerged to such astonishing prosperity that between 1869 and 1872 each annual budget closed with a surplus of public funds.

There are many reasons why the 'glimmer of light' so soon became open sky. The abandonment of forward policies in Germany and Italy, together with apparent constitutional stability in the two halves of the Monarchy, helped spread a business confidence which the politicians' skill in remaining at peace in 1870 seemed to justify. Investment came from Britain, the United States and northern Germany, helped by freer trade conditions and the prospect of better banking facilities. More than four hundred banks were founded in the Monarchy as a whole during the six years following the *Ausgleich*, and government approval was given for twenty-nine new railway companies. Nor was this economic progress limited to industry. While there was a rapid spread of factories – with a jump in production figures for coal and pig-iron – agriculture, too, flourished. Yet in this instance the success was, perhaps, a shade fortuitous. A succession of fine summers in central Europe produced bumper harvests in the rich Danubian basin at a time when the yield in western Europe remained low. Surplus cereals were exported at a good price, particularly wheat from Hungary and, to a lesser extent, rye from Cisleithania. There was an astonishing leap in the cultivation of sugar-beet in Bohemia and Moravia, with a consequent rise in the export of refined sugar, particularly to Germany. Moreover in these pre-phylloxera years – and especially in 1868 – the vineyards around Vienna, in Dalmatia and in central Hungary benefited from the weeks of summer sunshine. It is fitting that when, in February 1869, Johann Strauss completed a second waltz for the Vienna Men's Choral Society he should have chosen to honour 'Wine, Woman and Song'.

Like their Emperor, the joint-stock companies looked eastwards; and they were impressed by the prospects for the future. Danubian shipping improved year by year. No one doubted that there were good opportunities for investment in Rumelia ('European Turkey'), Anatolia and the Levant, especially after the collapse of the Second Empire and Napoleon III's speculative ventures; in 1871 two rival institutions – a Banque Austro-

Ottomane and a Banque Austro-Turque – were opened at Constantinople within a few months of each other. But the boom left its most permanent mark on the great cities of the Monarchy, where rash speculation led to equally rash building projects. The demolition of the mediaeval walls of Prague in 1867 enabled a 'new town' to grow rapidly, facing the royal city across the river Vltava; but there were several instances of sharp practice in municipal administration, with the alleged venality of one or other group of developers exaggerated by their political opponents. In Vienna the Imperial Opera House was at last completed in the spring of 1869, ready for opening by the Emperor on 25 April in a gala occasion of pomp and ceremony – even if Francis Joseph did slip away after Act I of *Don Giovanni*. The Opera House had always been intended to serve as a showpiece for a city dedicated to music; but it was anticipated that there would be around the Opera a long line of public buildings, embodying in stone the dignity of a great empire. As yet, however, the Opera stood in haughty isolation; for it was the grandiose palaces of the newly wealthy barons of finance which were spreading rapidly along the Ringstrasse, not the pedimented majesty of imperial institutions.

On the surface, these boom years were happily relaxed. The confidence in stability which encouraged investors also reassured many ordinary wage-earners, in town and country. Once again, all classes of people could be found enjoying themselves in the open spaces of the capital, perhaps sampling the fairground pleasures of the Würstelprater, or quieter moments in the relatively new Stadtpark, where in winter a frozen lake beside the River Wien was a delight for skaters; and it is no accident that this period saw the beginning of the golden years of Viennese operetta, an entertainment by no means reserved solely for the fashionable élite. Yet urban life did not glow so warmly in every level of society. There was an ugly sprawl of wretched homes around most towns, more evident in centres like Brno and Pilsen than in Vienna. And from the capital itself came warning signs; a workers' demonstration through the snow and slush of a bleak Monday morning in December 1869 threw a momentary shadow across preparations for the most affluent Christmas in three decades.

There were warning voices, as well; and to at least one of these the Emperor gave careful attention. Albert Schäffle, a Protestant Württemberger from the University of Tübingen, had recently received a professorial chair at the University of Vienna, where his lectures on the capitalist order of society aroused widespread interest. Professor Schäffle was a democratic conservative, a critic of free-trade liberalism who believed, ideally, in universal male suffrage as a means of holding in check what he called 'the rule of money dressed up in intellectual garb'. He believed, too, in the virtues of an aristocratic federalism which would promote racial equality between the nationalities of the Monarchy; and it was no doubt for this reason that in October 1870 the Emperor invited Schäffle to the Hofburg to explain his theories in a private audience. He came twice, virtually giving Francis Joseph two hours of tuition in ideas totally new to him. The Emperor was impressed. On 6 February 1871 Professor Schäffle was appointed minister of commerce and agriculture. Here, it seemed, was a specialist who could ensure that the economic miracle was not fraudulent.

Schäffle found Francis Joseph 'invariably objective and sympathetic', he wrote in his memoirs some thirty years later. The Emperor would examine 'everything put before him ... conscientiously and in detail ... without prejudging the matter'. Probably Francis Joseph learnt a great deal from the professor, notably his conviction that universal male suffrage was a force for stability rather than change; but the experiment of an academic economist in politics was not a success. Though Schäffle understood trade and investment better than any minister since the unfortunate Bruck, he lacked the Baron's dexterity or his practical experience in handling big business. By the autumn of 1871 the joint opposition of German-liberal newspapers, the 'kings of the Stock Exchange', and the more restrained criticism of his federal ideas from Andrássy left Schäffle isolated. On 13 October the professor offered his resignation, thankfully retreating to the relative calm of academic life. His immediate successors gave no indication that they realized the boom years might soon give way to recession. The Emperor, somewhat bewildered by the seven month experiment, placed all his trust in Andrássy who, on being appointed to succeed Beust at the foreign ministry, also became the co-ordinating Austro-Hungarian minister of finance.

Andrássy looked forward, with habitual confidence, to an era of continued peace and prosperity. Peasants were told they might sow their seeds without fear of finding their holdings ravaged by war; the townsfolk were assured they could continue to build houses, for nothing was going to destroy their homes. He warmly backed plans, already put forward, to hold a World Exhibition in Vienna in 1873, convinced that a great fair of this nature would allow other countries to see the material progress made by the Dual Monarchy in six years.

Francis Joseph agreed with him. He welcomed the chance to be host to his fellow rulers, letting them judge for themselves the vitality of the Habsburg lands. Sovereign and minister knew that such an enterprise would steal a march on Bismarck's Germany, putting Vienna ahead of Berlin; for among Europe's capitals as yet only London (1851, 1862) and

Paris (1855, 1867) had promoted these international shop-windows of industry and commerce. Each exhibition had been larger than its predecessors, with Napoleon III's 'greatest show on earth' in the Champ-de-Mars twice the size of the original Crystal Palace in Hyde Park. Vienna, it was agreed, must present an even greater world fair; 280 acres of the Prater would be set aside for its pavilions, an area five times as big as anything that had gone before. Hotels, pensions, restaurants, cafés and taverns sprang up in and around the capital with astonishing rapidity. More than 6 million people had come to London's Great Exhibition in 1851 and 9 million to Paris in 1867. It would have seemed unpatriotic for any citizen of Vienna to expect less than 20 million visitors by the end of the year, when the Silver Jubilee of Francis Joseph's accession was due to be celebrated.

The naturally sceptical Viennese made fun of the massive rotunda, 312 feet in diameter, going up in their Prater. It was crowned by a cupola which reminded them of a whirl of cream added to an iced cake, for images of confectionery sprang readily to mind. But when to this rotunda were added 28 temporary pavilions and a long central arcade, and when thousands of applications for exhibition stands began to reach the city, the whole enterprise was viewed with new respect. The final catalogue listed 15,000 Austrian exhibitors, nearly 7,000 German, 700 from the United States, and some 27,000 applications for stands from 37 other countries, including Japan. Such a concourse would make the Congress of Vienna seem in retrospect like a village market. A Jewish schoolboy, about to celebrate his seventeenth birthday and go to university, feared the Exhibition might distract him from the qualifying examination he was due to take in June. 'When ... the *Matura* is over, I intend to go there every day', he wrote to a friend, but he could not resist looking in twice before his 'day of martyrdom'. Not that it mattered: he passed 'with flying colours'; indeed, for his translation of 33 verses of *Oedipus Rex*, the examiners gave Sigmund Freud their highest commendation.

Before the opening of the World Exhibition there was an imperial curtain-raiser, which budding radical intellectuals like Sigmund Freud scorned. On 20 April Archduchess Gisela – who was ten weeks younger than Freud – married Prince Leopold of Bavaria in the Augustinerkirche, the parish church of the Hofburg, with Cardinal Rauscher once again officiating. Almost inevitably the bride was upstaged by her mother, who in her obsessive cult of beauty was determined to look even younger than her thirty-five years. In a dress embroidered with silver and with a diamond crown surmounting her thick carpet of hair, Elizabeth moved with great dignity down the aisle, for she now knew how to convey a presence which she had never possessed at her own marriage. Nobody seems to have noticed what her shy and pleasant daughter wore. As usual the festivities began well ahead of the wedding-day. At the Burgtheater there was a gala performance of *A Midsummer Night's Dream* – 'Am *I*, then, the ass?', Prince Leopold asked his Elizabeth; and on 17 April the Emperor, Empress and Crown Prince accompanied the bridal couple to a grand ball given by the city of Vienna at the concert-hall of the Musikverein. The celebrations started with Johann Strauss conducting the Vienna Philharmonic in a waltz composed for the occasion and entitled, rather oddly, *Wiener Blut* (Vienna Blood).

Not everyone was happy on the wedding day. Next morning's *Neue Wiener Tagblatt*, a sympathetic newspaper, commented on the Crown Prince's wretchedness at the railway station as the imperial family said farewell to Gisela and Leopold. Would many boys, approaching their fifteenth birthday, have wept so openly at their sister's departure for a home barely nine hours distant by train? Rudolf, who seems only to have been told the 'facts of life' a few months before, may have been academically precocious but he remained emotionally immature, slow to acquire that public mask of self-control which his father habitually donned. Yet, at parting from Gisela, even Francis Joseph is reported to have had tears in his eyes, as if he felt she had reached womanhood before he really came to know her.

Eleven days later – on Thursday, 1 May, like London's great festival in 1851 – the Emperor opened the World Exhibition in the Prater. At least three witnesses of that earlier May Day ceremony – the Prince of Wales and the Crown Prince and Princess of Prussia – were also present in Vienna twenty-two years on. Unlike Queen Victoria, however, Francis Joseph had the weather against him. 'The 1st of May was a day of well-nigh Siberian cold with a most democratic rain drenching roads and meads', wrote Sigmund Freud, who was there to see the carriage procession drive by, 'No one, with the exception of a few street urchins who sat in the trees, broke into shouts of joy at the sight of the Apostolic Highnesses, while His Majesty's humble and obedient subjects took cover under their umbrellas and hardly raised their hats'. Rain could not spoil the pageantry inside the rotunda where Archduke Charles Ludwig, as Imperial Patron of the Exhibition, delivered a formal speech of welcome before his brother, the Emperor, declared it open to the public. Beside Francis Joseph, Elizabeth and Rudolf on a huge dais, banked with flowers, were the heirs to the thrones of Britain, Prussia, Denmark, and Belgium, together with their consorts, and an array of what Freud irreverently called 'foreign princes ... made up exclusively of mustachios and medals'. Crowned heads of state were booked to come in an exhausting but, for the most part, well-regulated sequence of visits spread over the following five months: King Leopold II of Belgium in May, Tsar Alexander II in June, Shah Nasr-ed-Din of Persia in early August, swiftly followed by the King of the Hellenes, King Victor Emmanuel II of Italy in late September, and the German Emperor William I four weeks later. And there were the ruling princes of Roumania, Serbia and Montenegro to be entertained, and a special emissary from the Sultan, too. Not all were welcome guests: it says much for Andrássy's powers of persuasion that, in the interests of diplomacy, Francis Joseph should have been so well-disposed towards his old adversary from Turin. Nor, as yet, was he entirely reconciled to the Hohenzollerns; a German state visit required a courtesy donning of the helmet, tunic and trousers of the Prussian Guard Grenadier Regiment, of which Francis Joseph remained honorary colonel-in-chief – 'I felt like an enemy to myself', he would grumble when about to go on parade in German uniform. He was happier with his guests from Württemberg and Saxony.

The World Exhibition was dogged with misfortune, starting with an opportunist strike of fiacre drivers and, more grievously, an early cholera scare in the city which turned into a serious epidemic claiming over 2,500 victims. But, for an enterprise planned to promote industry and commerce, the worst setback of all was *Der Krach*, the sudden collapse of the Vienna stock exchange a week after the opening of the Exhibition. Professor Schäffle's grimmest fears were realized: credit resources were hopelessly over-stretched. On 8 May it was admitted that a hundred traders on the Bourse were insolvent. There was a rush to dispose of stock and shares as bubble companies failed hour by hour on that day and the next, 'Black Friday'.

Almost every company caught in the crash was of recent growth: 62 Viennese credit banks founded in the past five years were forced to close and 45 in the provinces; but of 11 older, well-established banks in Austria, only one went into liquidation. There was, as always in such scandals, a wave of suicides among ruined speculators (including one high-ranking general). Subsequent inquiries revealed corruption in high places: the German liberal, Karl Giskra, once an opposition deputy fiercely critical of military budgets and in 1868–70 the minister for home affairs, was totally discredited; and so was a leading member of the Emperor's military chancellery. No one suggested corruption within the imperial family but Francis Joseph's profligate brother, Archduke Ludwig Victor, had speculated wildly – in part with a legacy from his over-indulgent mother – and he lost the equivalent of two years income (in the values of the early 1990s roughly £200,000 or $280,000). Work stopped on many buildings in the Ringstrasse. When on 14 June the Emperor laid the foundation stone of the new Rathaus, people doubted if public funds would allow the completion of Friedrich Schmidt's neo-Gothic monument to his city's self-confident grandeur; and it was, indeed, another nine years before the council's halls and chambers came fully into service.

Ultimately the worst sufferers from the *Krach* were some of Francis Joseph's loyalist subjects, good church-going lower middle-class families tempted into investment by the bright prospects of the boom years. Also pathetically hit were the workers in new factories and casual labourers forced into unemployment by an abrupt halt to building projects and the sudden abandonment of railway lines along tracks no longer needed. The long-term consequences of Black Friday ran deeper than Court or Government appreciated at the time. A relentless search for scapegoats encouraged the spread of both socialism and anti-semitism over the following ten to fifteen years.

A poor summer gave way to a worse autumn: rain ruined the harvest of cereals in both Cisleithania and Hungary; the phylloxera disease began to attack the vines; and valuable timber from the great forests was lost through a species of beetle which bored deeply into good bark. Far fewer visitors came to Vienna than had been anticipated; and the takings at the World Exhibition fell disappointingly low. This run of misfortune troubled Francis Joseph greatly, not least because he always had to minimize its gravity to his eminent guests. The need for frequent ministerial councils, together with the state visits, meant that he was able to escape for only a short holiday, joining Elizabeth at Ischl in August. The strain was also beginning to tell on the Empress. Public appearances remained irksome to her but, realizing the importance of the World Exhibition to her husband in person and to the Monarchy as a whole, she was resolved to give Francis Joseph the support he needed. From Ischl she returned to Schönbrunn at the end of the second week of September, ready to greet King Victor Emmanuel; but on the eve of his arrival she collapsed with gastric fever and spent the following ten days in bed. The illness caused a ripple of friction in her relationship with Andrássy who, knowing Elizabeth's resentment at the ousting of her sister from Naples, believed her indisposition had sprung from pique. But any doubt that she was genuinely unwell was removed when she failed to attend the grand horse show in the Prater. At last in October the imperial family escaped to Gödöllö. Even in these much-loved surroundings her recuperation was slow. Francis Joseph became alarmed: her medical attendants were puzzled by the symptoms, as they had been thirteen years before. She did not look ill but he was afraid that, if Hungary failed to stir Elizabeth, her wander-lust might soon beckon her once more. As yet, however, her physical frailty ruled out foreign travel.

She was well enough to accompany Francis Joseph back to Vienna in time to celebrate the Silver Jubilee of his accession. Exactly a month earlier, on 2 November, the World Exhibition in the Prater had closed its gates, after attracting seven million visitors rather than the twenty million anticipated by the optimists. Already it was clear that the final balance sheet would show a deficit of some fifteen million gulden (about three million dollars at that year's exchange rate). With this newest loss added to the financial embarrassment of Black Friday, it is hardly surprising if the mood of the Silver Jubilee celebrations was austerely chastened.

Nevertheless Vienna did at least acknowledge Francis Joseph's twenty-five years of political improvisation. The streets of the capital were decorated with bunting and discreetly illuminated. On the evening of 1 December the Emperor and his son drove around the Ringstrasse in an open victoria, with the Empress following in a closed carriage. A spotlight from a balcony in the Schwarzenberg Platz picked out the victoria as it crossed the square; the crowd could clearly see the Emperor and the Crown Prince acknowledging their cheers; but the Empress was hardly visible, no more than a graceful silhouette behind the frosty glass of a fiacre's window. Next day, the actual anniversary of the ceremony at Olmütz, the generals and their commander-in-chief exchanged compliments in the Hofburg, with Rudolf standing in uniform beside his father while Archduke Albrecht offered the congratulations of his brother officers. Momentarily, as in the first years of the reign, imperial majesty seemed once more an apotheosis of the army. In the evening, with Elizabeth beside him, Francis Joseph attended a gala performance of *The Taming of the Shrew* at the Stadttheater, where a company directed by Heinrich Laube had enjoyed great success that season. Critics and audience welcomed Laube's new production, but what impression this lively presentation of Shakespeare made on Francis Joseph remains unclear. Though he summoned Laube to the imperial box, he seems only to have managed a conventional 'It was very lovely; it has given me much pleasure'; ever since the architect of the Opera killed himself on hearing disparaging remarks about a building the Emperor thought too dumpy, Francis Joseph's public comments had remained cautiously muted. He did not send for the principal performers, nor even commend the star of the evening, but her time was to come. For the role of Kate was played by a fair-haired grocer's daughter from Baden whom Francis Joseph had never seen before. Her name was Katharina Schratt, and in later years she became the Emperor's warmest friend. In 1873, however, that was unthinkable; a blonde stage-idol of twenty, whose photograph brightened several shop windows along the Kartnerstrasse that December, had no place amid the solemn decor of the Hofburg.

The Empress herself still found the Hofburg oppressive, at least so long as she had to fulfil official engagements there, while her husband was in residence. Immediately after the jubilee celebrations she returned to Gödöllö; and it is hardly surprising if, as in the spring of 1870, the liberal Press wrote, with gentle reproof, of her strange desire to prefer the wintry charms of a Hungarian hunting lodge to the delights of the Austrian capital. The tone of the newspapers annoyed the Emperor (though they were far milder than the attacks on 'England's future king', on sale at London bookstalls in that same month). When journalists from an eminently respectable professional association in Vienna presented Francis Joseph with their jubilee congratulations, the Emperor pointedly emphasized that he considered the private lives of the imperial family a topic on which newspapers should neither comment nor speculate.

Had he in mind the immediate past or the immediate future? Early in the New Year – on 8 January 1874 – Francis Joseph became a grandfather. Princess Gisela's daughter was named Elizabeth after her grandmother, who at once left for Munich, remaining in Bavaria for a fortnight. The Empress was far from pleased at becoming a grandmother fifteen days after her thirty-sixth birthday; her failure, in the months before Christmas, to shake off the effects of gastric fever may well have come from a subconscious sense of dented vanity. 'Gisela's child is unusually ugly, but very lively – not a thing to choose between her and Gisela', Elizabeth wrote back to Rudolf, in Magyar, with a marked lack of maternal solicitude. Francis Joseph was more philosophical; 'Only 44 and already a grandfather!', he sighed, needlessly adding seven months to his age. But at the Court Ball on 5 February – at which the Empress looked 'radiant with youth and beauty' – he showed an active heartiness Vienna had not seen for many years.

Francis Joseph needed every moment of happy relaxation he could find in that winter. Domestic politics were especially perplexing. In Hungary there was a grumbling conflict with the subject nationalities, which was exacerbated by demands from the younger parliamentary deputies that Magyar should be the exclusive language in service on the kingdom's rapidly growing railway system. Francis Joseph instinctively sensed danger in these policies. Moreover, now that Deák had retired and Andrássy was serving in Vienna, he found it difficult to work in partnership with the political spokesmen in Buda-Pest.

He felt more personally involved in narrowly Austrian affairs. A general election in Cisleithania in the autumn of 1873 showed a slight swing to the so-called 'Progressives' and 'Viennese Radicals', but it was not enough to displace the predominantly Austro-German Liberal government, headed by Prince Auersperg. The Liberals followed the scrapping of the Concordat by a series of mildly anti-clerical reforms: a Religious Fund was levied on ecclesiastical property; the State asserted a right to intervene in the education and appointment of priests; and legal guarantees were given to churches and religious groups other than Roman Catholics. But Francis Joseph was unhappy at the draft 'Confessional Laws' promulgated on 21 January 1874. He had already told the council of ministers that he could only approve of absolutely essential changes in the relations of Church and State; care must be taken, he urged, to resist the temptation to placate extremist groups in parliament or among the journalists. He refused to approve a Bill which would have put monasteries and other religious houses under strict state control, and he encouraged the upper chamber to throw out proposals to facilitate 'mixed marriages' between Catholics and non-Catholics. When, in March 1874, Pius IX even warned the Emperor that, in permitting anti-clerical legislation, he was risking excommunication, Francis Joseph could rightly claim that he was promoting calm and dispassionate discussion of the new relationship between Church and State while also protecting traditional Catholicism against modern secular heresies. The German *Kulturkampf*, then being waged so vigorously in Berlin and the Rhineland, would find no echoes inside the Dual Monarchy.

Andrássy, as foreign minister, wished Francis Joseph to remain on good terms with Pius IX, for the papacy was an international institution. But he also sought collaboration with the Italians, who had occupied Rome in September 1870, making the Pope a virtual prisoner within the Vatican. This desire to placate both Romes was politically embarrassing. Courtesy required the acceptance and fulfilment of invitations given to the Emperor by foreign sovereigns during their visits to the World Exhibition; and among these invitations was one from Victor Emmanuel II. But Francis Joseph would not go to the Italian capital, for fear of offending Pius IX. Careful diplomacy delayed the Austrian return state visit until April 1875 and, by then, an alternative rendezvous to Rome had been found. It says much for Francis Joseph's spirit of magnanimity, that he agreed to become the King of Italy's guest in Venice, a city where he had twice been received as sovereign – though never so warmly as on this occasion.

More pressing than the need to please the ruler of Italy was an urgent gesture of reassurance to the Tsar, who mistrusted Austria-Hungary's Balkan policies. Accordingly for a fortnight in February 1874 Francis Joseph endured 'the shivering climate' of Russia. As well as political discussions with the Tsar's veteran Chancellor, Gorchakov, he was expected to attend a succession of lavish entertainments and banquets in St Petersburg, where Alexander II was, at the same time, host to his Danish and English relatives by marriage. Among the visiting guests was the much-maligned Prince of Wales, whose skill in stalking a bear and shooting it in the head the Emperor greatly envied. Four days later, on 18 February, Francis Joseph, with Andrássy beside him, emulated the achievement of 'Wales', a clear note of triumph running through the letter in which he let Elizabeth know of his success. The Prince of Wales's reports home showed great delight in a bear-hunt in which no less than eighty beasts were killed. But it is characteristic of Francis Joseph that he should have preferred the concept of single combat involved in a bear hunt to the mass slaughters to which the Prince and so many owners of Europe's great estates were accustomed.

While Francis Joseph was in Russia the Empress stayed at the Hofburg, partly to counter a mood of resentment that the imperial family had deserted the capital during *Fasching*. It was then that she participated in a well-authenticated episode which reads like a hack's libretto for a sadly unoriginal operetta. On the last day of carnival – as it happened, the night before her husband's bear hunt – Elizabeth went in disguise to the masked ball at the Musikverein, accompanied by Ida Ferenczy who, by the simple expedient of tapping a good-looking man on the shoulder, found for her an agreeable companion. Fritz Pascher was an aspiring civil servant, ten years junior to the Empress. So sure of herself was Elizabeth that, claiming to be a visitor to Vienna, she quizzed the man on the feelings of the people towards Court life in general and their Emperor and Empress in particular, receiving from him the most diplomatic responses. With incredible naiveté, Elizabeth convinced herself that Fritz Pascher did not know her identity and would continue to think of her romantically as his lost yellow domino from the masked ball. She even sent letters to him, signed 'Gabrielle' and allegedly written in London. These letters she entrusted to her sister Marie, the exiled Queen of Naples, who had leased a house in England. Queen Marie, entering into the spirit of the game, arranged for replies sent by Herr Pascher to the General Post Office in London to be collected on her behalf and duly posted them back to 'Gabrielle' in Vienna.

Her secret was well kept. Newspaper proprietors would not have wished their reporters to pry behind the masks at a Vienna ball and Pascher was a perfectly honourable man who made no attempt to exploit 'Gabrielle's' folly. He kept the letters, not making them public until shortly before his death, some sixty years later. For the Empress the evening was an innocent diversion which she did not forget. Her creative mind returned to the masked ball when she was writing sentimental verses some twelve years later, and she told her younger daughter about her brief encounter. Francis Joseph, however, knew nothing of it.

The escapade was a symptom of Elizabeth's mounting restlessness.

Soon after Francis Joseph's return from Russia she left for Bavaria and completed arrangements to follow her sister Marie to England. Archduchess Marie Valerie, by now aged six, was a frail child, suffering from a bronchial weakness, and Elizabeth told Francis Joseph that she needed a holiday by the sea, somewhere with the sun shining but the heat not too intense for the child's comfort. As usual, he allowed Elizabeth to follow her own wishes. She therefore asked Beust, who was serving as ambassador in London, to find a suitable home for a six week summer visit; and on 2 August 1874 the 'Countess von Hohenembs' and her daughter reached Steephill Castle, Ventnor.

The mock-Gothic castle, high above Ventnor's terraced seafront, was in many ways ideal for a summer holiday. For an Empress seeking seclusion, Ventnor had one great disadvantage, however: within hours of her arrival, she was visited by Queen Victoria who was in residence at Osborne, ten miles away. To the amazement of the Queen's Household, Elizabeth subsequently twice declined a royal invitation to dine at Osborne: her health was too poor, it seemed. This unaccustomed rebuff did not incline Victoria to look with particular sympathy on Andrássy's attempts to strengthen Austro-Hungarian contacts with Great Britain. Nor was the Queen mollified by news that the Empress's health was so much better that she felt able to spend the fourth week of August at White Lodge, Richmond, seeing London as a guest of the Duke and Duchess of Teck. By the time Elizabeth returned to Steephill, Queen Victoria had gone to Balmoral. But the Empress was sure that she knew a way of improving Anglo-Austrian relations: 'What a pity you cannot come!', she wrote to her husband, 'After these manoeuvres – of which I thank you for the list of details – you could actually take a fortnight off, see London, make a hurried excursion up to Scotland to visit the Queen, and then hunt a little in the neighbourhood of London. There are good horses for us here and everything to go with them, so it would be a pity not to make use of them'.

It is easy to scoff at the Empress's suggestion. Like most royalty, her husband's itinerary was worked out months in advance: why should he throw over a carefully prepared programme to canter beside Elizabeth in Rotten Row or follow her to Rutland and chivvy foxes from their coverts in the wolds? Yet the idea was not so preposterous as it seems. As a young sovereign, betrothed to a bewitching cousin, he had at times broken loose, hurrying from Warsaw to see her in Bavaria. She knew that the army manoeuvres were to be held around Brandeis in Bohemia during the second week of September and he had no pressing commitments for the remainder of the month. Moreover he had, from time to time, shown some interest in making a visit to England, a project first broached before his accession, during the Year of Revolutions. Elizabeth closed her letter with gentle irony: 'Do think it over for a day or two before, with your usual tendency to play safe, you say "No"'.

Francis Joseph never came to England. No persuasive prompting from Sisi helped him shake off the harness of state. After visiting the Bohemian capital and attending the army manoeuvres he had sporting trips of his own arranged at home, he explained. Elizabeth did not arrive back in Austria until the autumn leaves had fallen, having lingered in Bavaria on the way home. She enjoyed this first contact with English life and particularly with the horsemen of the Midland shires; and she was determined to return. There was no diminution of affection between husband and wife; no intentional separation; only the gradual drifting apart of a wanderer and a self-fettered slave.

While the Empress was riding with the hounds at Belvoir, her husband had been welcomed to Prague, more warmly than in many years. 'God Bring Him Luck' ran the inscription in Czech across a triumphal arch erected outside the railway station and decorated with garlands of flowers and rich green foliage; and there were elaborate decorations, too, down the long length of the former horse-market, which would soon become socially upgraded as Wenceslas Square. He was, of course, not the only Emperor in the city. Germans and Czechs still held Emperor Ferdinand in high regard and, after a quarter of a century, were accustomed to his presence in the Hradčany. In the following April they put out the flags once more for Ferdinand's 82nd birthday. But it was for the last time. Ferdinand died ten weeks later – on 29 June 1875 – and his body was brought back to Vienna for burial in the vault beneath the Kapuzinerkirche. Empress Maria Anna lived on in Prague, surviving her husband by nine years.

In one respect Emperor Ferdinand's death changed the lives of both Francis Joseph and Elizabeth. When he abdicated in 1848 Ferdinand had retained his personal funds, making him the wealthiest member of the dynasty. After legacies providing for the widowed Maria Anna, the residue of Ferdinand's great fortune was left to Francis Joseph who suddenly found himself as rich as any ruler in Europe. Ferdinand's financial advisers had been too shrewd to play the stock market during the boom years and his money was left untouched by the *Krach* and the subsequent depression. The size of his inheritance took Francis Joseph by surprise: 'From now I am a rich man', he remarked to his military adjutant: no personal financial worries need trouble him any more, whatever the mood of parliament might be.

Yet the habits of forty years of cautious spending died slowly. Unlike his brothers Maximilian and Ludwig Victor, he was by nature parsimonious. In the whole of his life there is not a single occasion when Francis Joseph might be accused of personal extravagance. He kept a good cellar and enjoyed good (mild) cigars; he gave his patronage to artists of whom he approved; and he made certain that the best horses were bought for his stables and the best equipment for days when he would go stalking in the mountains. But, apart from the formal banquets, his meals were frugal, he spent his working days wearing the service uniform of an infantry lieutenant, and his palaces remained sparsely furnished. In the Hofburg he slept on an iron bedstead with a camelskin cover, and he used pitchers and bowls for the cold water douche with which he began each morning. In Schönbrunn there was an imperial bedroom with solid jacaranda-wood twin beds and with wall coverings and curtains of blue Lyonnaise silk, first hung in the year of his marriage and not replaced. Although the palace was said to include 1441 rooms and 139 kitchens, Francis Joseph never had a bathroom installed in the imperial apartments at Schönbrunn; he frowned on these luxurious modern inventions.

He was not, however, personally mean. Within days of inheriting this great wealth, he tripled the annual allowance of 100,000 florins assigned to the Empress since their marriage. At the same time he gave her a capital sum of two million florins, which some of the best bankers in central Europe invested wisely for her, mainly in the more profitable railway projects and Danube Steamship Company. He showed, too, a great indulgence towards her passion for building villas of her own and for purchasing the finest thoroughbreds for her to ride to hounds. She never doubted his personal devotion to her. Whether such open-handed generosity made for contented domesticity is open to question. During the ten years after he inherited Ferdinand's fortune Francis Joseph found his leisure hours increasingly spent in solitude and quiet seclusion. The glow of family life chilled rapidly. In the Austrian provinces his subjects began to speak respectfully of 'the old Emperor' while he was still in his fifties.

Chapter 13

THE HERZEGOVINA AND BOSNIA

During the first twenty-five years of his reign Francis Joseph came to know almost every province of his Empire. He possessed palaces or official residences in Lower Austria, Hungary, the Tyrol, Salzburg and Bohemia as well as villas at Ischl and outside Trieste. On several occasions he visited Istria, Carinthia, Carniola, Croatia and Moravia; and he travelled to Galicia, Silesia and Transylvania, too. But there remained one province which he had seen only from the sea, a distant blur on a hazy horizon. The Dalmatian coastal strip from north of Zadar down to Kotor, a region long dependent upon the Venetian Republic, had been assigned to the Austrian Empire by the peace settlement after the Napoleonic Wars but was never visited by a reigning Emperor. Early in March 1875 General Rodić, the Governor of Dalmatia, formally invited Francis Joseph to make an extensive tour of the province. It was decided that, after his April meeting with Victor Emmanuel II in Venice, he would spend a month visiting every important town on the coast and several offshore islands. '*Dann brennt!*' ('Then there'll be a blaze!'), commented General Anton Mollinary, the army commander in Zagreb, when Rodić told him of the Emperor's plans. Rodić smiled knowingly, and said nothing.

Neither general anticipated trouble in Dalmatia itself. There was a strong movement in the province for union with Croatia rather than for continued government directly from Vienna, but it was unlikely to provoke unrest. Uppermost in Mollinary's mind was the political confusion across the Dalmatian frontier, in the Ottoman provinces of Herzegovina and Bosnia. They were separated from the coastal strip by the Dinaric Alps, a limestone karst curtain which virtually isolated the interior from the Adriatic. Yet, though both provinces acknowledged the Sultan's distant sovereignty and were predominantly Islamic in culture, the people were racially southern Slav, kinsfolk of the Orthodox Serbs and Catholic Croats. Indeed, it was said the purest form of Serbo-Croat language was spoken around Mostar, the 'thoroughly Turkish' capital of Herzegovina.

The twin provinces shared a legacy of history as bleak as the mountain ranges which dominated this north-western extremity of the Balkans. They were steeped in legends of heroism and treachery from a bloody past. Before the Sultan's armies overran Bosnia in the summer of 1463 the region had known two centuries of feudal independence; it was the homeland of a schismatic church which, though technically Catholic, owed little allegiance to Rome. Attempts by the Catholic soldiery of mediaeval Hungary to march southwards and stamp out such eccentric beliefs provoked strong resistance and began a conflict which ultimately weakened Bosnia's opposition to the coming of Islam. In many instances the landowners helped the Ottomans, finding that if they accepted Islam they were able to hold on to their estates and feudal privileges. The peasantry were severely taxed and, until 1676, they had to surrender a fixed tribute of boy slaves to serve as infantrymen in the Janissary corps, but they were allowed to retain Christian beliefs, with their religious practices determined by the Serbian Orthodox Church.

To the south-west of Bosnia, an even more barren region, originally known as Hum, served in the fifteenth century as an outpost of Catholic Christendom in the struggle against the invaders. In 1448 the Holy Roman Emperor Frederick III, wishing to stiffen Christian resistance to the Muslim invaders, bestowed a new title on the feudal master of Hum, creating the tough warlord Stephen Vukčić 'Duke of St Sava'. It became natural to refer to these lands as 'the Duchy' – in German, *Das Herzogtum* – a term corrupted into 'the Herzegovina'. It was a German-Slavonic hybrid word, with the definite article soon falling out of common usage. The name has survived even though Vukčić's successors wielded weaker swords than the proto-duke and within forty years Herzegovina was, like Bosnia, overrun by the Sultan's armies. In Herzegovina, too, the Orthodox Church flourished among the peasantry, but there was also considerable Catholic influence, kept alive by the Franciscans who, soon after the fall of Constantinople, had received a charter from Mehmed II giving them a privileged status in the western Balkans.

For four centuries, the twin provinces of Bosnia-Herzegovina formed the north-western frontier of the Ottoman Empire, isolated from the Mediterranean world and yet far enough from Constantinople to show a contemptuous indifference to the reforms of successive Sultans. Real power in the provinces was long exercised by a *kapetane* of forty-eight native Bosnian beys; they still wielded a capricious authority during the first year of Francis Joseph's reign. Not until March 1850 were they finally defeated by an Ottoman army, after a three day battle on the shores of Lake Jezero. Even then conditions in the provinces remained anarchic. Until 1852 the Sultan's governors had sought to rule Bosnia from their fortress at Travnik, while the beys were in control of a town some 60 miles to the south, originally called 'Bosna Sarayi' (Bosnian Palace), a name swiftly modified in general usage to Sarajevo. Access northwards down the river Bosna to the Pannonian plains and southwards along the valley of the river Neretva to Mostar and the Adriatic made Sarajevo a more important city, politically and commercially, than Travnik or any other town in the western Balkans.

At Francis Joseph's accession neither Herzegovina nor Bosnia were provinces a neighbour might covet. Their economic potential was limited. Even in the spacious valleys of northern Bosnia, opening out on to the plains, farming methods remained backward and unrewarding. In several mountainous districts there were rich mineral deposits, with mines partially developed by the Turks. Only heavy investment and skilled engineering could enable these resources to be exploited; and it was questionable whether the yield would justify the expenditure. Yet as early as 1854 the war ministry in Vienna prepared detailed plans for the seizure of Bosnia-Herzegovina; two years later Radetzky urged Francis Joseph to put these plans into operation. It was not that the Austrian generals wished to see the provinces annexed for their own sake; their concern was to protect Dalmatia by securing a land route to safeguard garrisons holding Zadar, Sibenik, Split, Dubrovnik and Kotor in case of a blockade by sea.

A renewed plea for action was made a few years later, when Admiral Tegetthoff urged the Emperor to absorb the hinterland of Dalmatia. His reasoning differed from that of the generals. After his victory at Lissa Tegetthoff discounted the likelihood of an enemy blockade; he saw the Dalmatian anchorages as outlying naval stations for an Austrian fleet sailing into the Mediterranean, and he wanted improved overland communication between the heart of the Monarchy and the fine harbours on the eastern side of the Adriatic. In 1869 General Beck, as head of the Emperor's military chancellery, returned to the familiar theme in a memorandum which stressed yet another reason for annexing the provinces: the need to prevent their falling into the hands of the two Southern Slav principalities, Serbia and Montenegro, should the Ottoman Empire collapse. He was afraid the principalities might become Russian puppets, easily manipulated in Great Power politics to serve the interests of the Tsars. Beck would not be content with Bosnia-Herzegovina: he wanted the annexation to extend eastwards so as to include the Sanjak of Novibazar, a corridor of land separating Serbia from Montenegro. The Sanjak would, he believed, provide a natural route for the construction of a railway down to Salonika, the great Macedonian port on the Aegean Sea.

With these frequent pleas for action reaching him from military leaders whose views he respected, it is surprising that Francis Joseph held back for so long. At the root of his hesitancy lay deep uncertainty over the Southern Slav problem. In 1848–49 Jellaçić, and many of his compatriots in Habsburg service, had believed in an 'Illyrian' kingdom within the Monarchy, which would include Croatia, Dalmatia and the Serb areas of southern Hungary. Ideas had changed during the past thirty years. There were still 'Illyrians', and some intemperate 'Greater Croatia' fanatics followed Ante Starcević; but in 1861 a member of the *Sabor* – the Croatian Diet – had used a new corporate term to describe his kinsfolk; he had spoken of the 'Yugoslavs' (South Slavs), and by the end of the decade the Yugoslav ideal was in the ascendant.

Throughout the third quarter of the century the Southern Slav cause was vigorously championed by an outstanding churchman. Joseph Strossmayer was Bishop of Djakovo from 1849 until his death fifty-six years later and, in western Europe, won the respect of liberals like Gladstone and Lord Acton for his opposition to papal pretensions at the Vatican Council. But in south-eastern Europe Strossmayer's reputation rested on his devotion to the Southern Slav ideal; he founded a Yugoslav Academy at Zagreb in 1867 and a university in the same city seven years later. The Bishop's concept of Yugoslav union embraced, not only the south-eastern provinces of the Habsburg Monarchy and the principalities of Serbia and Montenegro, but the whole of Ottoman Bulgaria as well. He ignored the divisions separating Catholic Croats and Slovenes from Orthodox Serbs, Montenegrins and Bulgars – a distinction, not simply of religious traditions, but even of alphabet and orthography. Although Francis Joseph respected Strossmayer's learning, he remained puzzled by the affiliations of a movement which stressed what was common to Slavs both inside and outside the Monarchy. 'But is he a patriot for me?', Emperor Francis once asked, on hearing a certain Austrian praised as a 'good patriot'. Similar nagging thoughts seem to have troubled Francis's grandson as he observed Strossmayer's cultural activities.

Nor was Francis Joseph alone in these doubts. Strossmayer commanded a great following in Croatia itself, among the Franciscans of Herzegovina, and throughout much of Dalmatia, though not within the influential Italian trading communities represented in the Dalmatian Landtag. On the other hand, his Catholicism made Strossmayer's Yugoslav ideal suspect to successive princes in Serbia and Montenegro and to Bulgarian national leaders who looked for inspiration to a Moscow Slavonic Benevolent Committee established under the Tsar's patronage. The greatest hostility towards Strossmayer's Yugoslav ambitions came from Buda-Pest. After inducing the *Sabor* to approve the *Nagodba* (the Hungaro-Croatian political Compromise of 1868), no Magyar spokesmen would accept any policies which might increase the number of Slavs owing direct allegiance to Francis Joseph as sovereign, for if there were more Slavs brought into the Monarchy the delicate balance between the two master peoples – German-Austrians and Hungarians – would suffer. Andrássy agreed with this sentiment; but it did not prevent his authorizing expenditure of funds to promote Strossmayer's propaganda activities within Bosnia-Herzegovina – the building of Catholic churches and schools would counter the influence of Holy Moscow and the Orthodox priesthood. Grudgingly Andrássy recognized that, if forced to choose between political campaigners, he preferred Yugoslavs to Panslavs.

These nice distinctions were difficult for Francis Joseph to comprehend. When General Rodić had joined Beck in urging the Emperor to make a tour of inspection, Andrássy as usual objected. He did not, however, press the point. 'The Dalmatian trip is a Cisleithanian affair with which I have nothing to do', he remarked to the German ambassador, a shade too ingenuously. Although Andrássy might have been uneasy, he recognized that conditions for such a visit were more favourable than in earlier years. For, by 1875, there could be no doubt that his careful diplomacy had improved Austria-Hungary's standing with the Great Powers and her immediate neighbours. On 6 June 1873 a treaty signed by Francis Joseph and Tsar Alexander II – generally known as the 'Convention of Schönbrunn' – pledged the two Emperors to prior consultation over 'any question on which their interests disagreed'; and four months later the German Emperor, William I, also signed this Convention, thus creating a loosely knit 'League of the Three Emperors'. There was, moreover, closer contact than during the Beust era with both Great Britain and Italy. Finally, in 1868 Andrássy had planted in Belgrade a trusted Magyar agent – Count Benjamin Kállay – who, during the following seven years, secured such influence over Prince Milan Obrenović that by 1875 his political opponents in Serbia were convinced the young prince was in Habsburg pay. If Mollinary was right in suspecting that Francis Joseph's tour of Dalmatia would start 'a blaze', then Andrássy might legitimately feel he had taken every precaution to dampen the tinder and prevent the flames from firing the Balkans as a whole.

Kállay also kept Andrássy informed over the general state of affairs in Bosnia: the province 'is in a state of latent rebellion', he reported as late as the third week in February 1875. There were grievances over agrarian conditions and the harsh incidence of taxation; the discontent was fed by secret societies, backed by the Serbian 'liberal' politicians or by Russian agitators or, especially in Herzegovina, by the Montenegrins. Armed defiance of Ottoman officialdom was traditional in the mountains: 'Blessed is the rifle fired for national freedom' ran a ballad created in

Herzegovina in that year of revolt. It would have been as well to keep the Emperor away from a region where even the most harmless gestures were accorded a special significance. But, like Andrássy, Kállay realized that once Governor-General Rodić had formally invited his sovereign to Dalmatia, nothing could persuade Francis Joseph not to see for himself the southern outposts of the Empire.

The Dalmatian visit marked a historic turning-point in Habsburg policy, with more lasting effects than Kállay, Rodić or Mollinary anticipated. For the first twenty years of his reign Francis Joseph had looked, first and foremost, to Germany and Italy, like Metternich before him. There then followed a brief period, starting with his journey to the East, when the Emperor remained unsure of Austria's true mission. Finally, for the last forty years of his reign he looked determinedly to the East, partly across the Carpathians and towards the mouth of the Danube, but even more to the Balkans and, beyond the mountain ranges, to the two largest Ottoman cities in Europe, Salonika and Constantinople. That last phase dates from 10 April 1875, when Francis Joseph landed from the warship *Miramare* at Zadar and was received by the civil and military dignitaries of his Dalmatian lands.

From the outset the visit attracted the attention of the press, both in Vienna and abroad. The Emperor's letters home gave detailed accounts of welcoming parties, with children 'of Valerie's age' presenting bouquets of flowers beneath triumphal arches in Sibenik or Split and in far smaller towns and villages. As usual Francis Joseph enjoyed his days at sea and what was, in effect, a round of imperial sightseeing, notably at Diocletian's palace. There is no suggestion, in the account of his movements which he sent regularly to Elizabeth, that he was aware of the visit's political implications. His letters describe how he went inland from Split to Imotski, close to the Ottoman frontier; there he received in audience a mixed group of 'Turks' and Franciscans in 'blue pantaloons'; 'A very odd sight', he observed. Two days later he followed the river Neretva from its mouth up to Metković and to 'the border on the road to Mostar'. Here, too, he received a warm welcome. Did he realize how sensitive were conditions in this frontier zone?

By 28 April, when he reached Dubrovnik, he must have sensed the political tension. For there were Franciscans in Dubrovnik in close contact with their brethren in Herzegovina: they did not disguise their hopes that, if Austria-Hungary absorbed the twin provinces, the Emperor would protect the Christian religion and end an allegedly corrupt system of government. 'The local demonstration . . . appeared to me . . . thoroughly Slavish', reported the British consul, 'the imperial visit having been, so to speak, utilized to express the popular native feeling of Pan-Slavism supreme in these parts'. Reports reaching Constantinople of Francis Joseph's triumphal progress so alarmed the Sultan that he ordered his *vali* (governor) in Bosnia, Dervis Pasha, to travel down to the coast and greet the Emperor. Dervis was accorded an audience but had little to say for himself; it was a cold, formal occasion.

Far livelier were the Emperor's two visits – by land and by sea – to the Boka Kotorska (Gulf of Cattaro). He received, so he told Elizabeth, 'a great many deputations'; and on 3 May the thirty-three year old Prince Nicholas of Montenegro, a ruler 'of purest Serbian blood' who enjoyed the confidence of the Herzegovinian clans, came down the mountain paths from his capital at Cetinje to talk to Francis Joseph about the plight of his kinsfolk across the Ottoman frontier. The two men had already met in Vienna, when the Prince was a guest at the World Exhibition. But this time he brought with him 'a large following of military chieftains, senators and adjutants'. What aroused particular interest abroad on this occasion was the presence beside Prince Nicholas of his father-in-law, the colourful Petar Vuković, a formidable warlord hand-in-glove with the most rebellious Herzegovinian clansmen. Francis Joseph told Elizabeth he was glad to find Prince Nicholas 'an excellent man ... very well disposed' towards Austria. Of Petar Vuković the Emperor said nothing; but he showed his goodwill towards the Montenegrins by riding up the slopes of Mount Lovcen and crossing the frontier into Prince Nicholas's eyrie.

After thirty-three days in Dalmatia Francis Joseph arrived back in Vienna in mid-May. His tour of inspection clarified his mind. He was impressed by what he had seen of the Venetian legacy along the Adriatic coast and he understood the advantages of securing the mountainous hinterland. Moreover he was by no means averse to acquiring new provinces for the Empire, compensation for his lost Italian possessions. Mollinary was told to hold himself in readiness to command an army of occupation should Bosnia-Herzegovina appear to be slipping from the Sultan's shaky grasp.

A month after the Emperor's return one of the Franciscans who had crossed the frontier to acclaim him at Metković was murdered, allegedly with Dervis Pasha's compliance. The clan leaders at Nevesinje, barely 20 miles from the frontier districts so recently visited by the Emperor, rose in revolt; they knew they could count on supplies from Prince Nicholas, brought in by sea at Utorina on the Boka Kotorska, an anchorage serviced by the Montenegrins which the Austrians made no attempt to close. By the third week in July the Herzegovinian clansmen were raiding Muslim villages and attacking Muslim caravans wending their way along the Neretva valley to Mostar. The 'blaze' was well alight. Rodić confidently recommended rapid intervention so as to secure Bosnia and Herzegovina for the Monarchy, while in Zagreb Mollinary put the final touches to his plans. But from Vienna there came no order to occupy the provinces.

Francis Joseph habitually listened to the views of those around him, though he might frequently ignore them. So long as he was in Dalmatia he had been in the company of officers who were eager for decisive action in the Balkans. Mollinary, a Croat by origin, and Rodić, a Dalmatian Slav, were soldiers who tended to rattle their sabres precipitately at wild rumours from across the Ottoman frontier. By contrast, in Vienna, Francis Joseph could rely on sound advice from a foreign minister who saw the Herzegovinian revolt in a wider context. He began to have second – or, more accurately, third – thoughts. Emperor and minister were agreed on the need to avoid a general war. Andrássy studied reports of what had happened in the Neretva valley, assessed the impact of the revolt on the Monarchy's relations with Russia and Germany, and sensed danger. Even so, he did not foresee a diplomatic crisis which would pre-occupy Europe's chancelleries for more than four years.

At times during that long period of tension Andrássy's patience was severely taxed. The first proposal he received from the Russian Chancellor dismayed him, for Gorchakov wished to establish an autonomous Bosnia-Herzegovina. To Andrássy this solution seemed an invitation to per-petuate anarchy, with Muslim, Catholic and Orthodox sects ravaging provinces which no central government could hope to control. By the end of the year, however, he had regained the diplomatic initiative: Gorchakov backed the 'Andrássy Note', a series of proposed reforms in the admin-istration of Bosnia-Herzegovina which was circulated to the Great Powers on 30 December 1875 and nominally accepted by the Ottoman authorities six weeks later. But, with the coming of spring, the crisis worsened. On 2 May 1876 a new revolt broke out in several Bulgarian villages deep in the Rhodope Mountains. The insurgents committed atrocities which were equalled or surpassed by Ottoman militia (*başçi bozuka*) anxious to suppress Panslavism in a region far nearer to Constantinople than the troubled valleys of Bosnia. Newspaper denouncement of the activities of the *başçi bozuka* was to shock British (and American) opinion during the fourth week of June, but before the ghastly reports appeared in print there had been a palace revolution in Constantinople, with Sultan Abdulaziz deposed and Turkish liberals demanding the grant of a constitution. Serbia and Montenegro, seeking to exploit the embarrassment of the new Sultan's government, declared war on the Ottoman Empire in the first days of July 1876. At this point it seemed essential for the League of the Three Emperors to co-ordinate policy if the war was to remain localised. Francis Joseph sent Archduke Albrecht to Berlin for talks with William I and Bismarck, while the Tsar and his Chancellor also travelled to the German capital, and Gorchakov asked urgently for a meeting with the other member of the League. Accordingly Francis Joseph invited the Tsar to meet him in Bohemia during his circuitous journey home from Berlin.

On the morning of 8 July Francis Joseph greeted Alexander II and the Tsarevich on the railway platform at Bohmisch-Leipa, some 80 miles north of Prague. It was a hurried conference, Andrássy plying Gorchakov with questions during the five mile coach drive to the imperial chateau of Reichstadt. To the relief of both Francis Joseph and his minister, it was clear that neither the Tsar nor his Chancellor sought a Russo-Turkish war. The so-called 'Reichstadt Agreement', concluded later that day, guaranteed that if the Ottoman armies defeated the Serbs and Montenegrins, Austria-Hungary and Russia would ensure that there would be no changes made in the existing boundaries. Should Serbia and Montenegro force the Sultan to sue for peace, the Ottomans would be virtually expelled from Europe. There were some discrepancies between the Austro-Hungarian and Russian versions of the Reichstadt Agreement, particularly over the precise line to be followed by new Balkan frontiers if Turkey were defeated, but the general pattern was clear enough: Russia would recover southern Bessarabia (modern Moldova) and Austria-Hungary would annex Bosnia; Greece would gain Thessaly and Crete; Serbia and Montenegro would expand so as to meet along a common frontier in the Sanjak of Novibazar; Bulgaria and Albania would receive autonomy. According to Andrássy's notes, Austria-Hungary would also acquire Herzegovina. To his great satisfaction, he thought he had successfully ruled out the possibility of a large Slavonic state in the Balkans – as, indeed, Gorchakov warned the Serbian minister in St Petersburg a fortnight later. Francis Joseph, too, was pleased with the Reichstadt Agreement, believing it would help him acquire the twin provinces without risking war with Russia. An amicable meeting with William I at Salzburg in August ensured that League diplomacy remained in concert.

No one at Reichstadt or Salzburg anticipated that the Serbs and Montenegrins would crumble so soon. Once the Ottoman commanders gave up playing at politics and began a series of counter-attacks, the would-be invaders fell back rapidly. By the end of October the Russians were seriously considering intervention in the Balkans in order to save their Orthodox brethren from Ottoman retribution, and St Petersburg peremptorily ordered the Turks to agree to an armistice with Serbia. So far, Alexander II had carefully kept Francis Joseph informed of each step he was contemplating. But over the winter of 1876–77 the safeguards of the Reichstadt Agreement were increasingly called in question. More and more the Tsar was listening to influential Panslavs, notably General

Nikolai Ignatiev, his ambassador in Constantinople. 'I much desire that we shall reach a general agreement', Alexander II publicly announced in Moscow as a Great Power conference on Ottoman reform was about to open at Constantinople: but he added, 'If this is not possible ... then I firmly intend to act independently ... and may God help us to fulfil our sacred mission'. By Christmas a Russo-Turkish war seemed imminent, although Francis Joseph and Andrássy believed, perfectly correctly, that the Tsar preferred a peaceful settlement of the Eastern Question.

In Hungary there was strong support for the Turks. A judiciously timed restoration of trophies looted from the famous royal library of Matthew Corvinus when the Ottoman armies first advanced across the Danubian plains strengthened the Turcophile inclination of the people during the Eastern Crisis; and there was, too, a fiercely anti-Russian mood seeking 'a war to revenge Vilagos' (as Beck warned Francis Joseph). By contrast, military circles in Vienna favoured close co-operation with St Petersburg: for them the Reichstadt Agreement – a bilateral understanding to which Germany was never invited to subscribe – promised a reversion to a more traditional form of conservative diplomacy. General Beck argued in favour of close co-operation with Russia. For him step-by-step bargaining over complementary expansion in the western and eastern Balkans would secure for Austria-Hungary control over the land-route to Salonika.

A joint memorandum, drawn up by Archduke Albrecht and General Beck, was presented to Francis Joseph in November 1876. It was a strong plea to avoid conflict with Russia: Napoleon's 1812 campaign had shown that there could be no swift decision in the East because of the size of the Tsar's Empire and its reserves of manpower. 'A well-developed industrial state, dependent on universal military conscription, cannot accept the strain of long wars ... There Russia enjoys an advantage over every other Power. Least of all, therefore, should Russia's nearest neighbour, half-encircled Austria-Hungary be among the first to take the field for she cannot, like the Western Powers, withdraw from a war when she thinks fit. Rather she should preserve her full strength to the end, and then the decision will lie in her hands'. This advice – reminiscent of Austrian policy in 1813 and again in 1855 – carried considerable weight with the Emperor and, in essentials, was close to Andrássy's reasoning even though, as a Magyar, the foreign minister was distrusted by both Albrecht and Beck. In January and March 1877 further secret agreements – the Budapest Conventions – provided for Austro-Hungarian benevolent neutrality should Russia be forced into war with the Ottoman Empire; the Tsar agreed that Francis Joseph would have a free hand in dealing with Bosnia-Herzegovina and that, in any re-drawing of Balkan frontiers, 'the establishment of a great compact State, Slav or otherwise, is out of the question'.

Francis Joseph was accustomed to evaluating differing opinions on foreign affairs presented to him in memoranda from his ministers or around the council table. He knew, too, that policy would invariably be criticized in the more radical newspapers. But during the Eastern Crisis he was disturbed by a new development. The German liberals in the lower house of the Reichsrat wished to ensure that parliament was consulted over the shaping of policies which might determine issues of peace or war. In October 1876 no less than 112 deputies signed a demand for a debate on foreign affairs. The Emperor was outraged. The Austrian government had no constitutional right to be consulted over such matters, let alone the deputies in parliament. Foreign policy was the Emperor's prerogative. When, at the height of the crisis, an Austrian minister tactfully explained to his sovereign that the German liberals were uneasy over aspects of Andrássy's policy, he received a sharp rebuff: 'You are constantly talking of Andrássy's policy. It is *my* policy; do not forget it'. There was no debate on the Eastern Crisis in either chamber of the Reichsrat.

Sultan Abdulhamid II, who succeeded his brother Murad at the end of August 1876, refused to bow to foreign pressure and accept a programme of reforms imposed by the European Great Powers. With the coming of spring in 1877 Tsar Alexander II was resigned to the inevitability of a conflict which Ignatiev and the Panslavs had sought to thrust upon him for so long. On 24 April 1877 Russia declared war on the Ottoman Empire and the Tsar ordered his armies to march southwards 'for Orthodoxy and Slavdom'. Towards neither of these causes could his brother sovereign in Vienna feel the slightest sympathy. For the remainder of the year, however, Francis Joseph received reassuring messages from St Petersburg. In the last week of July, when Russia's armies were checked by the stubborn Ottoman defence of Plevna, the Tsar specifically emphasized his intention to observe the Reichstadt Agreement. There would be no permanent military occupation of Bulgaria, Alexander declared, and no encouragement in the Balkan lands of any dangerous 'democratic' movements.

Once the fortunes of war changed, a different note came into the exchanges between St Petersburg and Vienna. In the second week of December, when the last resistance of Plevna was finally broken, the Tsar's messages began to sound ominous. The Serbs, who re-entered the war in that week, would need some territorial reward in northern Bosnia, he claimed; and a Russian army would have to police Bulgaria for at least two years. A month later Francis Joseph, while acknowledging that the

Ottoman Empire had not completely disintegrated and that he could not therefore expect implementation of the precise terms discussed at Reichstadt, hoped that the basic principles behind the agreement and the Budapest Conventions would be accepted. Austria-Hungary was, he said plainly, opposed to any occupation of Bulgaria; and if Russia retained newly liberated southern Bessarabia, the Monarchy would expect to absorb Bosnia.

On 15 January 1878, even before Alexander could reply to this message, Francis Joseph presided over a gloomy conference of ministers in Vienna. The news from the theatre of war was disturbing. The Russians were already in Sofia and advancing on Adrianople; it seemed likely they would be at the gates of Constantinople by the end of the month. Andrássy thought some token military demonstration should be made in order to assert the prestige of the Dual Monarchy, but he found Archduke Albrecht hostile to any anti-Russian move. A further ministerial conference, on 24 February, considered the Tsar's lack of positive response to the Emperor's message. War, it was decided, was out of the question: to risk a protracted campaign was to invite state bankruptcy; even brief operations in the Balkans would require additional funds; nobody could predict the consequences of challenging an Empire with such a lengthy shared frontier as Russia. Only peaceful diplomacy could benefit Austria-Hungary.

As early as 28 January Andrássy wrote to Károlyi, the ambassador in Berlin, setting out the stark alternative in Austro-Russian relations of 'conflict or conference'. Gorchakov, as well as Bismarck, also favoured a settlement of the Eastern Question agreeable to Europe as a whole, and throughout February there was talk among the diplomats of a possible conference, with Baden-Baden as a likely venue. Briefly it seemed possible that Francis Joseph would host a second Congress of Vienna, but in early March it was finally settled that the Powers would meet in Berlin, although the mediatory prestige of summoning the Congress was accorded by Bismarck to Andrássy. Even so, when the invitations went out from Vienna on 6 March, it was questionable whether the other Powers would accept them and it seemed highly improbable that any Congress could stitch together a lasting treaty. Too many governments had objectives of their own in the Ottoman lands to make the attainment of diplomatic compromise easy.

Fortunately for Andrássy the terms of the Russo-Turkish peace treaty signed at San Stefano on 3 March became common knowledge to the European chancelleries by the middle of the month and proved generally unacceptable. Russian field headquarters had not even referred back to the foreign ministry the details of the conditions foisted upon the Sultan's representatives. On paper San Stefano was a triumph for General Ignatiev, the apotheosis of Panslavism; but it ran completely counter to the Reich-stadt Agreement and all the subsequent exchanges between Alexander II and Francis Joseph. A big, satellite Bulgaria encroached on the western Balkans and the probable railway route to Salonika; no territorial com-pensation was offered to Austria-Hungary. In St Petersburg more mod-erate counsellors than Ignatiev realized the folly of San Stefano and were prepared to use the terms of the treaty as bargaining counters for a wiser settlement. Andrássy took heart. With great difficulty in the third week of March he persuaded the Austro-Hungarian Delegations to approve a vote of credit of 60 million florins without indicating in advance whether he intended to use it for a war against Russia or for the occupation of Bosnia-Herzegovina. By the end of the month he was certain he could satisfy the Monarchy's immediate needs in the western Balkans and preserve his sovereign's independence and authority within the League of the Three Emperors.

Francis Joseph, too, still anticipated that he would gain Bosnia-Her-zegovina. Although in mourning for his father – who died on 8 March – the Emperor gave a courteous welcome to Ignatiev, whom the Tsar sent to Vienna on 27 March in the hope that the general could reconcile the Austrians to a Russian military presence in Bulgaria and assure them that St Petersburg would raise no objections to any action taken by the Government in Vienna to secure the twin provinces. Detailed discussions between Ignatiev and Andrássy encouraged the Austrians, but the Rus-sian's brief visit – he was only in Vienna for four days of talks – was neither a social nor a political success. Even after returning to St Pet-ersburg, Ignatiev continued to intrigue, unsuccessfully, against Andrássy, hoping to install a more compliant foreign minister in the Ballhausplatz, perhaps General Mollinary. His activities were so maladroit that he streng-thened rather than weakened Andrássy's position. Francis Joseph was not going to have his foreign minister pushed aside by that 'notorious father of lies', as he told his friend, Albert of Saxony, that the Turks called the Russian envoy.

The Congress of Berlin – a thirty day gathering of Europe's leading statesmen in late June and early July 1878 – was an outstanding personal success for Andrássy, greater indeed than Francis Joseph appreciated at the time. He worked in amicable partnership with the British foreign secretary, Lord Salisbury, and he was accepted by Bismarck as a trusted personal friend. The revised map of eastern Europe satisfied his objectives more closely than he had dared to hope. By the Treaty of Berlin the new principality of Bulgaria was cut to one-third of the size outlined at San Stefano while, on a proposal put forward by Salisbury, the Congress gave Austria-Hungary a mandate to occupy and administer Bosnia-Her-

Francis Joseph's Europe (Frontiers 1878–1912)

zegovina in order to end the endemic state of civil war between the Muslim and Christian peoples of the twin provinces. With some difficulty Andrássy secured treaty recognition of Austria-Hungary's right to station troops in the Sanjak of Novibazar and safeguard communications along the strategic corridor which separated Serbia from Montenegro and gave Bosnia access to the East. At the same time he courted the backing of Serbia and Roumania, both by successfully championing their claims to total independence and by securing territorial concessions for them: the Serbs gained Niš, the Roumanians acquired more of the Dobrudja than under the treaty of San Stefano. Austria-Hungary also secured the sole right to keep clear the lower waters of the Danube, thus ensuring the ready movement of barges and river boats down the great waterway. Serbia and Bulgaria accepted obligations to complete their railway systems in such a way as to ensure links with the Austro-Hungarian network.

Andrássy's sole failure at the Congress was with the Turks. Under pressure from Sultan Abdulhamid and from the *seyhulislam* (head of the Muslim hierarchy in his Empire) the Ottoman delegates refused to permit Francis Joseph's troops to enter either Bosnia or Herzegovina, let alone garrison the Sanjak. Only when Andrássy gave a secret pledge that the Sultan's sovereign rights would not be impaired and that an occupation should be regarded as a temporary necessity, did they consent to sign the treaty; details would eventually be settled in a bilateral Austro-Turkish convention.

'The joining of the two provinces to the Monarchy has overjoyed Papa, as we all knew it would', Crown Prince Rudolf told his old tutor, 'I believe that in Bosnia and Herzegovina he is aiming at compensation for Lombardy and Venetia'. Yet Andrássy did not come back from Berlin with two provinces ready to serve on a plate for Francis Joseph's consumption. He wanted the Ottoman Empire, as well as the newly independent Balkan states, to look to Austria-Hungary both commercially and as a safeguard against further Russian encroachment. He was accordingly just as eager to hold the military aristocrats in check as he had been three years before. There was, he told them, no need for a menacing deployment of troops: far better wait for Ottoman acquiescence before crossing the frontiers; and then simply send in 'two companies of soldiers headed by a military band'.

Francis Joseph held his men back for a fortnight after the signing of the Berlin Treaty. This was a grave mistake: the Turks were still smarting from the humiliating treatment their delegates had received as supplicants at the Berlin Congress (especially from Bismarck); they had no intention of concluding a supplementary agreement with Austria-Hungary at such a time. If the Austrians had moved forward in 1875, after the excitement of the Emperor's Dalmatian visit, the occupation might have been carried through without arousing much immediate opposition. But by the summer of 1878 the Bosnian Muslims had formed their own Home Defence Militia, strengthened by well-armed Turkish troops in mutiny against the Sultan's authority. When the Austro-Hungarian army crossed the frontiers on 29 July it met strong resistance in a terrain ideally suited for defensive operations based upon the Turkish forts built to command the valleys.

Beck and Mollinary had settled for rather more than 'two companies and a band': a force of some 85,000 men entered the two provinces. Within ten days the army was in considerable difficulty; Archduke Johann Salvator (of the exiled Tuscan branch of the imperial dynasty) and the brother of the King of Württemberg, who were serving in a crack regiment, were fortunate to survive an ambush near Jajce on 7 August; and, although plans had been made to present Francis Joseph with a symbolic gift from Sarajevo on his birthday, the Emperor was forced to summon an emergency ministerial council to decide on the course of action in the western Balkans. It took twelve weeks of campaigning before the last Muslim garrison in Bosnia surrendered. By then the army of occupation came to nearly 160,000 men and the Government in Vienna reluctantly had to seek another 25 million florins from a Reichsrat still complaining that it had no voice in the shaping of foreign policy. By the end of the third week in October, when an uneasy peace descended on the provinces, the Imperial and Royal Army had officially sustained over 5,198 casualties, although the actual figure seems to have been almost twice as large; 3,300 killed, 6,700 wounded and an extremely high level of sickness in all units. To Andrássy's dismay Francis Joseph now began to demand the outright annexation of Bosnia-Herzegovina claiming that, after such sacrifices, they belonged to the Monarchy by right of conquest.

'The Emperor does not understand the Eastern Question and he will never understand it', an exasperated Andrássy complained to the Empress Elizabeth. The Muslims in Bosnia were always revolting against the Sultans and they would remain rebels until given orderly government: offensive action against them was readily understood in Constantinople. But to annex the provinces would offend the Sultan and cost Austria-Hungary influence throughout the Near East. Moreover once the provinces were incorporated in the Monarchy the balance of historic nationalities established in 1867 would be lost for all time and Strossmayer's Yugoslavs would become the chief beneficiaries from annexation. Five days after the army first occupied Sarajevo, Andrássy begged the ministerial council in Vienna strictly to observe the letter of the Treaty of

Berlin; and he returned to this theme at other conferences during the winter months.

The strain of continuous office was getting too much for him. When, in 1871, as Hungary's prime minister, he took over the foreign ministry Andrássy was in the habit of doing handstands on Metternich's old desk, so his official biographer claims; but it seems unlikely he was still fit and agile after twelve years at the centre of affairs. For the moment, however, he would not contemplate retirement. He was determined to see the parliaments in Vienna and Budapest give formal support to the Treaty of Berlin (which the Emperor himself speedily ratified). It was not that he felt any responsibility towards parliamentary deputies. As ever, he was concerned with more general questions: obstruction in the Reichsrat delayed any final settlement of the Bosnian question. For so long as the German liberals in Vienna continued to snipe at the autocratic control of foreign affairs, the Ottoman government declined to discuss outstanding questions over the fate of the provinces. At last, in March 1879, the Hungarian and Austrian parliaments approved the Treaty. On 21 April a formal agreement concerning the occupation and administration of Bosnia-Herzegovina was concluded between the Austro-Hungarian and Ottoman governments. The map of the western Balkans now followed the line Andrássy had been seeking for the past four years. He was tired; his estates in Hungary had long been neglected. Within a month of the Austro-Turkish convention he offered Francis Joseph his resignation.

It was refused. The Emperor, angered by the attempts of the German liberals in the Reichsrat to raise issues which encroached on his prerogatives, was contemplating a major switch in Austrian domestic policy, with a reversion to a more conservative and aristocratic administration. He did not want Andrássy to go at such a time, for his departure might be interpreted as a gesture of appeasement towards his political enemies in the Reichsrat. Andrássy therefore agreed to stay in office until later in the year. It was a difficult summer. The League of the Three Emperors seemed to fall apart, with the Tsar showing increasing hostility towards the German Chancellor and the Russians exploiting their privileged position in the eastern Balkans to the discomfiture of Austrian commercial interests. When, at the beginning of August, Francis Joseph completed his change in Vienna by asking Count Taaffe to form a government, Andrássy again asked to resign. He suspected that Taaffe would seek support from the Czechs, and he was not prepared to fight yet another political battle to curb Slav influence in Vienna. On 6 August Francis Joseph agreed that Andrássy could retire in two months time, long enough for him to prepare Baron Heinrich Haymerle, his right-hand man at the Berlin Congress, as a successor.

Unexpectedly, in these last weeks of office, Andrássy achieved a diplomatic victory which, only twelve months earlier, would have seemed improbable. The news of Andrássy's impending departure filled Bismarck with alarm. He, too, suspected that a Taaffe administration might be sympathetic to the Slavs; and he had no wish to see the Reichstadt partnership revived and perpetuated, with Francis Joseph and Alexander II maintaining a basically anti-German entente. Hurriedly therefore he arranged to meet Andrássy at Gastein on 28 August to clarify the situation. Relations between Berlin and St Petersburg remained tense that month: Alexander II complained of a succession of minor affronts by the German Chancellor, and the General Staff in Berlin were disturbed by Russian military movements in Poland. To Andrássy's surprise, when he met Bismarck at Gastein the Chancellor proposed the conclusion of a defensive alliance between Germany and Austria-Hungary, aimed at protecting both empires from a Russian attack. As Andrássy emphasized to Francis Joseph, provided that Bismarck did not subsequently add impossible conditions, this was too good an opportunity to miss.

Francis Joseph welcomed the project. It had a familiar look, a modernized version of the Prusso-Austrian partnership of earlier years. To his satisfaction, Bismarck personally was prepared to come to Vienna in September to complete the negotiations with Andrássy; and it was rumoured (rightly) that when William I demurred from authorizing the conclusion of a secret anti-Russian alliance, Bismarck bluntly informed his sovereign that he could choose between accepting Austria-Hungary as an ally or finding a new Chancellor. The treaty, valid in the first instance for five years, was duly signed in Vienna on 7 October 1879 by the Austro-Hungarian foreign minister and the German ambassador. Next day Andrássy retired into private life.

None of Francis Joseph's other foreign ministers shaped policy so decisively and personally as Andrássy: none left such an enduring mark on the Monarchy's history. The Austro-German alliance survived until the collapse of the Habsburg and Hohenzollern Empires at the end of the First World War, a conflict of which the immediate cause lay in unrest among the Yugoslavs of Bosnia-Herzegovina. Yet it would be a mistake to blame Andrássy for later catastrophes. The terms of the treaty signed by him were strictly defined and, like all previous alignments, limited in time. In 1879 Bismarck's Germany was the suitor, not Austria-Hungary, but this relationship did not last. Whenever ministers and diplomats were faced with renewal of the treaty they accepted it as natural that Germany should be the senior partner in the alliance. Francis Joseph never gained the decisive voice in Europe's affairs which Andrássy's final achievement seemed momentarily to promise him, for Bismarck soon realized that his immediate fears were groundless; he did not need the protection of an ally against an aggressive Russia.

Even less was Andrássy responsible for later events in Bosnia-Herzegovina. His policy for the western Balkans assumed the continuing Austro-Hungarian patronage of a client Serbia, while he was so intent on maintaining good relations with the Ottoman Empire that he even drafted a memorandum for his successor suggesting the conditions under which the provinces might eventually be evacuated and allowed back to the Sultan in full sovereignty. Meanwhile, occupied Bosnia-Herzegovina fell administratively under the authority of the joint Austro-Hungarian minister of finance, who from 1882 until his death in 1903 was Kállay, Andrássy's former representative in Belgrade and the author of a history of Serbia. He became the outstanding proconsul of the two provinces, much as Lord Cromer was the supreme proconsul of British-occupied Egypt, and Kállay consistently followed Andrássy's principles: no region in the Balkan lands made such rapid material progress as Bosnia-Herzegovina, but careful attention was always given to Serb susceptibilities and respect was consistently shown for Islam and its teachings. Only after Kállay's death did Francis Joseph resort to policies which had seemed obvious to him from 1875 onwards. Bosnia-Herzegovina was annexed to the Monarchy in October 1908 and relations with neighbouring Serbia allowed rapidly to deteriorate. Andrássy's careful balance, delicately maintained for so long by Kállay, was irretrievably lost by Francis Joseph's later advisers. As Andrássy had predicted, the Emperor never came to understand the Eastern Question.

Chapter 14

FATHER AND SON

On 2 August 1878, four days after the Imperial and Royal Army entered Bosnia, Crown Prince Rudolf began his active military career, serving in the Prague garrison as a colonel attached to the 36th (Bohemian) Infantry Regiment. Technically his links with the army went back twenty years, for his father appointed him honorary colonel-in-chief of the 19th Infantry Regiment when he was two days old. But Francis Joseph wished his son to have proper military training and service experience: he was therefore not expected to serve in his 'own' 19th regiment, nor was he posted to a fashionable unit of Dragoons or Hussars, for most cavalry officers came from the great aristocratic families and the Emperor thought it undesirable for him to be associated with a socially exclusive set. Rudolf agreed with him. He was content to learn soldiering in a workaday regiment of the line, where there would not be too many noble titles in the mess.

General Latour von Thurmburg, the Crown Prince's principal tutor for twelve years, had done his work well. By 1878 Rudolf was an intellectually curious young man, with keen scientific interests, particularly in ornithology. Barely four months before taking up his post in Prague, the Crown Prince shocked the spiritual authorities at Court by attending a lecture in Vienna given by Dr Ernst Hackel, a Darwinian whose views were unacceptable to all the Church leaders. Later that year Rudolf invited the eminent zoologist Alfred Brehm to accompany him on a short expedition to observe animal and bird life in the Danubian river forests of southern Hungary. With Brehm as his consultant, Rudolf published an account of the expedition *Funfzehn Tage Auf Der Donau* (Fifteen Days on the Danube) that sold better than the title deserved; the author's anonymity was only lightly veiled.

This book, in itself over 300 pages long, was not the Crown Prince's first printed work that year. Shortly before Christmas in 1877 he had accompanied Elizabeth to England. He was a social hit both with the Queen Victoria and with the Prince of Wales: each thought Rudolf 'very pleasing', though Queen Victoria was worried that he 'looks a little over grown and not very robust'. Then, while the Empress enjoyed herself as 'Queen of the Chase' in Northamptonshire, her son set off on an instructive tour, accompanied by a much respected liberal economist, Carl Menger. The Crown Prince met Disraeli, now Lord Beaconsfield, visited the industrialized Midlands and North, southern Scotland, and crossed to Dublin, too; and he made careful notes of the 'English' way of life, whether in the Houses of Parliament, or Billingsgate fish market, the Lancashire mills or newly municipalized Birmingham, or staying with the premier peer of Scotland in east Lothian. After six weeks of travel he sent Latour a long account of his impressions, on notepaper with a 'Queen Railway Hotel, Chester' letterhead: 'I am ... really enthusiastic about England, though I do not fail to recognize grave and very obvious drawbacks in the country', he wrote, 'Life here is magnificent, and I am trying to acquire as much knowledge as possible'. He was fascinated by the role of the aristocracy, the concept of a Tory and a Whig nobility, both socially acceptable, both with patronage in the Commons, both aware of their tenants' needs. Within a few weeks a 50-page pamphlet, *The Austrian Nobility and its Constitutional Mission* 'by an Austrian', appeared in Munich. Subject matter and sub-title – 'A Call to Young Aristocrats' – again left little doubt of the author's identity.

At first Francis Joseph treated his son's intellectual pursuits with paternal indulgence, perhaps even with pride. Latour, who was ten years older than the Emperor, retained his confidence. Francis Joseph supported him against sniping criticism at Court of the unorthodox interests which his old tutor had encouraged the heir to the throne to pursue. Most ruffled of all these conservatives was Archduke Albrecht, Inspector-General of the army since 1867, a hard disciplinarian with no son of his own, who looked out unsmilingly on the younger generation of Archdukes from behind the thick steel rimmed glasses of a graceless pedagogue. Already, in 1876, 'Uncle Albrecht' had sought Rudolf's views on their ancestor, the Emperor Joseph II, and he mistrusted signs of incipient liberalism in his great-nephew's judgments on the past. General Beck shared the Archduke's fears: 'The young, over-excited mind of the Crown Prince, the immaturity of his way of thinking, the extravagance of his undoubtedly high intelligence, make me worry that he will assimilate ideas and tendencies which would not be compatible with the conservative character of a future monarch', Beck wrote in his journal. The military chancellery as a whole was convinced that army service would enable Rudolf to shake off his 'extravagant' ideas. General Beck, meeting the heir to the throne for the first time after he had taken up his post at Prague was satisfied with his progress: 'I have been studying the Crown Prince at Gödöllö', Beck wrote to his wife, 'His mind bubbles over and he wears his heart on his sleeve and has not yet digested many of the liberal teachings of some of his tutors; but otherwise love will soon be his chief preoccupation'.

Beck was not far off the mark. There is a persistent tale that, soon after arriving in Prague, Rudolf was entranced by the beauty of a Jewish girl, who died young and whom he long mourned. But he certainly took his military duties seriously. Within five weeks of joining the regiment he was on manoeuvres under the vigilant eye of Uncle Albrecht. He was attracted, too, by a new intellectual challenge: he had written about ornithology and politics; now he would also become a military historian. 'I shall not be in Vienna for the Hofball', he wrote to Count 'Charly' Bombelles, his father's boyhood friend, who had succeeded Latour as head of the Crown Prince's official household. Instead of leading the traditional defile of Archdukes and Archduchesses into the Rittersaal ballroom, Rudolf chose to immerse himself in study; and with some success. On two consecutive Sunday evenings in March 1879 he lectured the officers of the Prague garrison on the Prussian victory of Spicheren, nine years before. The finest modern book on the Franco-Prussian War devotes 14 pages to the battle: Crown Prince Rudolf's analysis ran to 88 double-sided sheets.

'I am glad I have the lecture behind me', he told Latour on 4 April. He had felt uneasy about it, for he was aware of pinpricks of envy among the more senior of his brother officers. But he was not going to behave like the other Archdukes, he explained: 'Thank God I do not feel within me the call to follow the so-called accustomed paths, the foolish everyday life of my relatives with their blinkers'. He wished to throw himself 'heart and soul into the army, and not just the gaiter legging aspects, but so as to use my head ... These days one must work to deserve to hold a high position; merely to sit in Vienna and keep up a dignified attitude and not know the people, how they are and what they feel, that does not fit into our century'.

These good intentions may have been influenced by a lingering picture of an idealized 'England'. Yet they were hard to uphold. Temperament inclined Rudolf to evenings of amorous amusement, a flaw of character to which the worldly-wise Charly Bombelles, unlike Latour, gave free rein. Already, before going to Prague, Rudolf had acquired a certain notoriety among the courtesans of the capital. He was reluctant to abandon his friends for too long – 'all the beautiful women of Vienna whom I have so much loved', as he called them in a draft will signed eleven days after penning those fine sentiments in his letter to Latour. As heir to the throne he had, of course, duties to perform; and it was these dynastic obligations which brought him back to the Hofburg that spring. On Thursday, 24 April, 1879 Francis Joseph and Elizabeth were to celebrate their Silver Wedding; and at the start of the week the family gathered in the capital for four days of festivity.

The Silver Wedding has a firm place in Viennese popular folklore. It is associated, however, less with the Emperor and Empress than with Hans Makart, the supreme decorative artist of Ringstrasse Vienna, whose allegorical friezes and historical canvases brought a Romantic exuberance to the walls of the new mansions transforming the central city. Makart was entrusted by the Lord Mayor, Julius von Newald, with supervising the costumes, floats and procession of a great historical pageant, which would look back through three and a half centuries to the opulent Flanders of Emperor Charles V. Representatives of every trade and craft, some 10,000 people in all (according to the newspapers) passed in salute before an Imperial Pavilion set up at the side of the Ringstrasse, close to the Hofburg. At the head of the procession, immediately behind the heralds, rode Hans Mackart with a brocaded costume and plumed hat modelled on Rubens originals. The procession, announced for Saturday, 26 April, was postponed because of heavy rain; and it is the Sunday which is still remembered as *Makart-Festzug Tag* (Makart Procession Day), more than a century later.

The imperial family's personal celebrations took place earlier in the week. On the wedding anniversary itself there was a service of thanksgiving in the Votivkirche; and on the previous evening Archduke Charles Ludwig – twice widowed during those twenty-five years, and by now married to Maria Theresa of Portugal – was host at a reception in which he arranged for the staging before his brother and sister-in-law of a series of historical tableaux. Each figure from the past was played by an Archduke or Archduchess. Many of the decorations and costumes were brought for the occasion from the great museums, even from the *Schatzkammer* (Imperial Treasury). In the first scene the Crown Prince, robed to represent his thirteenth century ancestor Rudolf I, wore the real crown of the Holy Roman Empire. He was soon back again, first as Charles V and then as the victor over the Turks, Charles of Lorraine.

'A lasting family celebration for all the peoples of my empire' was Francis Joseph's verdict on his Silver Wedding week. Elizabeth was less pleased: according to one of her nieces the Empress found the protracted festivities exhausting and regarded Makart's procession as an impertinent public intrusion into private affairs. She was more concerned with the future of the dynasty and the search for an acceptable daughter-in-law. Not that Rudolf was in any hurry to settle down. He visited Lisbon and Madrid, gave serious thought to a Spanish Infanta (too plain), and travelled to Dresden, where he momentarily considered a Princess of Saxony (too fat). By the end of July he was back with the 36th Infantry

Regiment at Mnichović, outside Prague; and in his father's birthday promotions' list he was confirmed as commanding officer of the regiment. On 28 August he led his men on parade before their Emperor: 'My most ardent wish has been fulfilled', he told Bombelles; 'I belong to the army heart and soul'. So might his father have written at twenty-one.

Prague was an attractive city, one of the most desirable postings for a young officer. It was also politically a sensitive city during the four years in which the Crown Prince served there. Comments in his correspondence with Latour leave little doubt that he gained greater insight into the problems of the Monarchy than had he remained in Vienna: a twelve-sheet letter in October 1878 shrewdly assesses the effects of the military moves in Bosnia on the Slav peoples, especially on Croat-Magyar relations; while three months later Rudolf filled fourteen pages with an analysis of the current political situation, particularly the growing challenge of social democracy. But it was the Czech problem which most interested him; and Francis Joseph, who was hoping for several years of calm under a government headed by his friend Eddy Taaffe, was pleased that his son should be stationed at such a time in Prague.

At first Rudolf approved of Taaffe's policy. The Count, who was to remain Austria's prime minister from 1879 until 1893, began his term of office with gestures of goodwill towards the peoples of Bohemia and Moravia: language decrees raised the official status of spoken and written Czech in the two provinces; reforms increased Czech representation in the provincial Landtage; and the 500-year old University of Prague was divided into parallel foundations, one German and the other Czech. The promise of these concessions attracted the Bohemian parliamentary parties back to the Reichsrat in Vienna in September 1879, for the first time in sixteen years, strengthening Taaffe's support against the German liberals. But thereafter the Count temporised. No single nationality within the Monarchy was favoured, for that, he thought, accorded with Francis Joseph's wishes and he always saw himself as an executant of his sovereign's will rather than the originator of new policies. Taaffe preferred, as he once said, 'to keep all the nationalities of the Monarchy in a balanced condition of well modulated discontent'. Eduard Herbst, a German-Bohemian parliamentarian bitterly critical of Taaffe's 'weakness' over the Czech Question, complained that the prime minister was constantly 'muddling through' and the phrase stuck, until people believed Taaffe had used it himself. Yet, however pedestrian his style of government, the early 1880s were not entirely barren years: Taaffe introduced improvements in education and social reforms to protect industrial workers; and he persuaded Francis Joseph to accept an extension of the franchise, which gave the vote to the wealthier peasants in the countryside and to small property owners in the towns. Both groups were natural supporters of Taaffe's 'Iron Ring' coalition of conservative Germans and moderate Slavs. In the general election of 1885 their votes strengthened Taaffe's hold on parliament.

Long before then the Crown Prince had lost patience with Taaffe, deploring in particular his sympathy for the more obscurantist Church leaders. At fifteen and sixteen Rudolf had written for his tutor essays which, when published long after his death, read like proclamations of romantic liberalism. But it would be a mistake to deduce from these adolescent airings of the mind that he was constantly in revolt against his father and the whole structure of the Monarchy; and it is too easy to antedate family friction. There was no rift between father and son during Rudolf's first eighteen months with the regiment. At that time Francis Joseph was amused by the attempts of social climbers to ingratiate themselves with the heir to the throne. He did not blame Rudolf, and for the most part he condoned their activities, but one woman went too far, he thought. At Gödöllö, shortly before Christmas 1879, he observed to the Empress's lady-in-waiting, Marie Festetics, that he found the behaviour of Baroness Helene Vetsera 'unbelievable'; 'She is always in close pursuit of' the Crown Prince, 'Today she has actually sent him a present', he exclaimed. The Baroness was a daughter of the Levantine banker Themistocles Baltazzi, who had grown rich from the concession to collect tolls on the bridge linking Stamboul and Galata, in the heart of Constantinople; Helene had made a good marriage to a diplomat at the Austrian embassy in the Ottoman capital. She was eleven years older than the Crown Prince, with two sons and two daughters, Hanna and Mary. Countess Festetics, who jotted down the Emperor's remarks, disliked Helene Vetsera intensely and distrusted her, as he well knew. So, too, did many other ladies at Court.

It would have been inappropriate for his mother or father to reproach Rudolf too severely for his wayward behaviour. The Empress courted admiration, flirting decorously with skilled horsemen at home and abroad, provided they were good-looking. Like her royal Tudor namesake, Elizabeth resented any inclination of her courtiers (male or female) to marry and lead an independent life. Yet, though she would exercise her tantalizing wiles beguilingly in England and Ireland or among her hunting friends at Gödöllö, there was always an element of caprice and pretence in her conduct, and tales of her infidelities which titillated the scandalmongers were probably fictitious.

Francis Joseph, on the other hand, was in these years deeply entangled in the seamiest personal relationship of his life. One morning in June 1875, soon after returning from Dalmatia, he was taking his customary early exercise in the Schönbrunn parkland when he met a young and attractive blonde, who was standing beside the artificial 'Roman ruin' statuary about a quarter of a mile from the palace. It is probable that Anna Nahowski, the newly married sixteen year old wife of a railway official, had every hope of accosting the Emperor: for why otherwise did she, too, decide to take a walk on her own at 6 A.M. in the vicinity of Schönbrunn, where Francis Joseph was known to be in residence? Her tactics were successful. Throughout the months when Elizabeth was in Bavaria or Greece, France or England or Ireland, the Emperor looked for consolation to the plump, blonde Anna and found it. A compliant husband welcomed the steady flow of generous gifts to his wife which enabled the Nahowskis to set up house in Hetzendorf's Schönbrunner Allee just three summers after that first meeting. By 1884 the family could afford to acquire and renovate a large villa in fashionable Hietzing, along what is now Maxingstrasse, overlooking Schönbrunn Park. To this considerable status symbol they eventually added a summer residence at Trahutten, high in the Styrian Alps. It is hard to believe that the businesslike Anna, meticulously noting down in her journal thirteen years of visits, kindled flames of passion; at best she offered the comforting warmth of passing sensuality to a middle-aged man isolated from human contacts. Before the end of the decade, she became an embarrassment for him. But there was no public speculation about the affair; discretion, and ready money, kept the secret for a hundred years or more.

By contrast, there was such widespread gossip about the Crown Prince that it seemed essential for him to find a wife soon, in the hopes of encouraging him to accept the disciplined conventions of married life. Early in 1880 Count Bohuslav Chotek, the Austrian Minister in Brussels, accordingly approached King Leopold II to arrange for Rudolf to meet his younger daughter, Princess Stephanie. The last Belgian marriage had ended disastrously with Maximilian dead in Mexico and Charlotte – Stephanie's aunt – incurably insane. If Rudolf married Stephanie there would be a bond of consanguinity, missing on the earlier occasion: Stephanie's mother, Queen Marie Henrietta, was a Habsburg princess by birth, the youngest daughter of the Palatine of Hungary, Archduke Joseph; she had been among the family guests in Vienna at the Silver Jubilee celebrations. With no great enthusiasm, Rudolf travelled to Brussels in the first week of March 1880. Princess Stephanie, having been told by her father that it was her parents' wish that she should become Empress of Austria and Queen of Hungary, was summoned into his presence, and did not think of challenging her father's decision. She was a gangling 15-year-old, with flaxen hair, plump cheeks and small eyes set close together. Two days after this meeting, on 7 March, Rudolf sent out the telegrams announcing his betrothal. Latour got the news in Vienna soon after eight in the morning, and was pleased. Countess Festetics records that when the Empress received her telegram – at Claridge's Hotel in London – she turned white before letting her know of the betrothal. 'Thank God, it is not a calamity', the Countess said, with relief. 'Please God it does not become one', Elizabeth grimly replied.

'Comely, sensible, good and very distinguished looking', was Rudolf's first verdict on his fiancée in a letter to Latour of less than 70 words. But after his mother had broken her journey home at Brussels and spent four hours with her son and future daughter-in-law, Rudolf became more sure that he had taken the right step: 'I feel intoxicated with happiness and contentment', he told Latour on 11 March, lapsing into informal hand-writing for the first time in a letter to his old tutor rather than using the traditional *Schrift*. Once back with his regiment he was delighted with his reception in Prague: 'The town is decorated with flags. Everything is very correct; no Slav flags, no German; one Belgian; otherwise gold, red and white everywhere.' 'The patriotism here is colossal', he let Latour know in the first week of April, 'Bohemia and Prague have received me as a man betrothed in marriage most graciously and heartily, from top nobility down to the poorest of workers. Never before have I felt such gratitude and love for the townsfolk as in these days ... Whatever the situation, I shall remain a true friend and supporter of this good and beautiful country'. There was no direct criticism of his parents over the following months, only genuine pleasure when he joined his mother in Hungary and found her taking a more active role in social life than in Vienna: 'Tomorrow is the Red Cross meeting', he wrote to Latour from Budapest on 8 June, 'The Empress will herself preside'. It was fitting for Elizabeth to be patron of a society which owed its origin to revulsion at the appalling carnage of Magenta and Solferino.

Rudolf's wedding, originally planned for the summer of 1880, was postponed until the following spring when it was found that Stephanie had not yet begun to menstruate. The Crown Prince remained for the most part in Prague, while his mother again travelled to England for much of the hunting season, staying in Cheshire until March, when she went to Aintree to see the Grand National steeplechase. Rudolf became rapidly disenchanted with the Taaffe government, blaming his father for allowing 'the blacks' (obscurantist spokesmen for the Church) to increase their influence in education. At the same time he privately criticized his mother, now 'an idle, though thoroughly clever, woman'. In a letter to Latour of the second week in February 1881 he showed particular antipathy towards the septuagenarian Cardinal Archbishop of Prague, Prince Frederick von Schwarzenberg, who sought to restrict the Sunday recreational pursuits of the garrison officers and was known to have complained that the heir to the throne frequently kept company with free thinkers and Freemasons. Taaffe, Rudolf argued, had become as illiberal as the Cardinal, while deluding the Czech parliamentarians into believing they enjoyed his support: 'Both feudal gentlemen owe allegiance to no nation', Rudolf told Latour; they 'are dragging the Czech people down into the mud with them', exploiting the Czechs 'for the sake of reactionary and obscurantist aims'. 'The great Slav race, for whom I have much sympathy', he maintained, '. . . are liberal, and the day must come when they will totally disown these gentlemen'. As for himself, Rudolf declared, 'I don't hide the fact that I have no sympathy at all for the Church's pretensions to influence the state . . . I would far rather send my children to a school with a Jewish headmaster than to a school whose headmaster is a priest, an out-and-out supporter of black tendencies'. No heir to the throne since Joseph II had been so suspicious of the conventional Church dogmas which Francis Joseph so confidently accepted. Rudolf was by nature too much a talker to confine these opinions to his private letters. Elizabeth, abroad until a month before the wedding, knew nothing of her son's mounting anger. If Francis Joseph saw any danger signals, he ignored them.

Princess Stephanie spent her first night on Austrian soil at Salzburg and arrived in Vienna on 6 May 1881, four days before the wedding. The popular festivities followed as familiar a pattern as the marriage ceremony in the Augustinerkirche, though the guest list was even more striking: it included both the future King Edward VII and his Prussian nephew, the future Kaiser William II. Rudolf's personal enemy, Cardinal Prince Schwarzenberg, officiated at the wedding, with more than twenty other prelates to assist him. Johann Strauss dedicated his *Myrthenblüthenwalzer* to Stephanie, while Eduard Strauss composed another waltz, *Schleier und Krone* (Veil and Crown). Like his parents, the Crown Prince and his bride spent their first days of married life at Laxenburg. The Empress did not seek to interfere, probably from the kindest of motives, for Elizabeth had vivid recollections of old embarrassments caused by her mother-in-law. But if the Empress did not fuss around them, nobody else did, either. According to Stephanie's memoirs, unseasonal snow was falling when they reached Laxenburg: it was dispiriting to step out of the carriage and be met 'by a breath of air as cold as ice in a cellar', while the predominant smell was 'of mould': 'No plants, no flowers to celebrate my arrival . . . no carpets . . . no dressing-table, no bathroom, nothing but a wash handstand on a three-legged framework'. She and her husband had 'little to say to each other; we were virtual strangers'. The Crown Prince, recklessly loquacious in familiar company, could think of nothing to interest a gauche princess six years his junior. Did he know that his mother had already dubbed her daughter-in-law 'the plain bumpkin' (*das hässliche Trampeltier*)?

All too often, tales of marital discord spring from incidents inflated in reminiscence and recollected in adversity. So it is with the traditional legends of Rudolf and Stephanie's early life together. The evidence of his letters suggests a far happier association. After a week in Laxenburg, they travelled to Budapest, where the Crown Princess was fêted as a granddaughter of the most popular of Palatines. Then back to garrison duties in Prague, where he found Stephanie ready to share his interests. She accompanied him on official visits and occasionally on hunting expeditions and shoots, too. Her vitality of spirit quickened once she gained a solid foothold in Rudolf's topsy-turvy life, as army officer and heir apparent.

In the first year of marriage, he seems to have discussed politics with her. Six months after the wedding he completed the draft of a long memorandum 'On the Present Political Situation In Austria', which he sent to his old tutor, for comment: the Crown Prince was dismayed by the spectacle of parliament and, in particular, by the way in which Taaffe had to strike bargains with political parties which drew their support from the nationalities rather than from the peoples of the Monarchy as a whole; only through the creation of unified Liberal and Conservative parties, with leaders and rank-and-file drawn from all the nationalities in Cisleithania, would it be possible for 'Austria' to secure an orderly administration as coherent as in Hungary. After Latour had replied to Rudolf, praising his political good sense, the Crown Prince wrote back, again at great length, emphasizing how much he had gained from Stephanie's companionship. 'I have never been as happy as I was last summer when, surrounded by domestic bliss, I could settle down quietly to the preliminary studies'. Ought the memorandum to be presented to the Emperor, he asked Latour? 'Might I from then onwards be treated distantly, coldly and sternly; and might this attitude be extended to my wife! She is bright, very observant and sensitive; full of ambition; she is a granddaughter of Louis Philippe (*sic*) and a Coburg! Need I say more. I am very much in love with her, and she is the only person who could lead me much astray!' This is a strangely different Stephanie from the bumpkin lampooned by the Empress and her ladies-in-waiting. The real Crown Princess, her character in many ways still unformed, must be hidden somewhere between these extremes of impression.

Rudolf's letter – which was written on the 33rd anniversary of the Emperor's accession – also contained the sharpest assessment of his father's personality put down on paper since Francis Joseph's boyhood:

'Our Emperor has no friend, his whole character and natural tendency do not permit it. He stands lonely on his peak; he talks to those who serve him of their duties, but he carefully avoids any real conversation. Accordingly he knows little of what people think and feel, their views and opinions. Only those people now in power have access to him, and they naturally interpret matters in the way that is most satisfying for them. He believes we live in one of the happiest periods of Austrian history, he is habitually told so. In the newspaper he only reads the passages marked for him in red and so he is cut off from every human contact, from all impartial and genuinely loyal advice ... There was a time when the Empress ... talked to the Emperor about serious matters, prompted by views diametrically opposed to those he held. These times are past. The great lady no longer cares for anything but sport; and so this source of outside opinions, which were on the whole tinged with liberalism, is now also closed ... Three or four years ago the Emperor was, to some degree, already liberal and reconciled to the nineteenth century. Now he is once again as he was in poor Grandmama's time: bigoted, gruff and suspicious'.

This pen-portrait of his father was unduly harsh. Francis Joseph was indeed eminently isolated, a lonely figure at the head of a spreading dynasty. But it would be wrong to suggest that his political outlook had changed with the contraction of his circle of advisers and confidantes. The Emperor never moved either towards or away from liberalism. Like George Canning earlier in the century, he believed in 'men' rather than in 'measures'; he might appoint a liberal prime minister, provided he was not too doctrinaire; or he might choose a great landowner, if his concepts of political obligation were not too narrow. His ideal remained someone who was not so much a party leader as 'an Emperor's minister'; hence his long support for Taaffe.

There is no evidence that Francis Joseph ever received the Crown Prince's memorandum on the political situation in Austria. This is hardly surprising since, quite apart from Rudolf's fear of his father's cold reaction to such an initiative, the original draft was already out of date when he first sent it to Latour for comment, and he seems to have decided to shelve the matters it raised. For, during the period when Rudolf was preparing the memorandum, the constitutional structure agreed in 1867 was temporarily out of balance. Beust and Andrássy had made certain that the principal government official for the Monarchy should be the common minister for foreign affairs, who was also titular minister of the Imperial and Royal Household and, in the Emperor's absence, presided over the common ministerial council, the Monarchy's 'cabinet'. But from 1879 until 1881 Andrássy's nominee as foreign minister, Heinrich Haymerle, did not have the force of character to maintain this primacy in government. Haymerle was a skilled and patient diplomat. After fifteen months of negotiation he achieved a considerable success. By the secret

League of the Three Emperors' alliance treaty of June 1881 he won from Germany and Russia virtual recognition of Austro-Hungarian supremacy over the western Balkans, including the eventual annexation of Bosnia-Herzegovina. In return Francis Joseph pledged the Monarchy's benevolent neutrality should either of his partners be at war with a fourth Power (other than Turkey). The Crown Prince, like his father, believed during these years that foreign policy remained the prerogative of the Emperor and his chosen minister, and he saw little reason to complain of Haymerle's activities. Disquiet over future trends of policy accordingly led Rudolf to concentrate his criticisms on Taaffe or his Hungarian counterpart Kálmán Tisza, for unlike the foreign minister they were personalities in their own right. Both prime ministers remained in office until after Rudolf's death, but before the end of the year 1881 the balance of the constitutional machine had been corrected; and the Crown Prince increasingly found a new source of dissatisfaction, this time in the Ballhausplatz.

When Haymerle died suddenly, on 10 October 1881, Francis Joseph chose as his successor Count Gustav Kálnoky, the ambassador in St Petersburg, a gifted and hard-working diplomat. Despite his Magyar-sounding name, Kálnoky was a German Moravian landowner, an aristocrat of strong convictions. He was determined to formulate policies himself, after having fed his sovereign with such expert advice from the leading ambassadors that the Emperor was unlikely to question his decisions. This show of expertise so impressed Francis Joseph that Kálnoky remained at the Ballhausplatz for fourteen years, far longer than any other incumbent during the reign. But the Crown Prince did not share his father's admiration for the foreign minister. Kálnoky's ascendancy coincided with a widening of Rudolf's range of interests. A week after Haymerle's death Carl Menger, the economist who had accompanied the Crown Prince on his English tour, introduced to Rudolf an outstanding journalist, Moriz Szeps, editor-in-chief of the *Neues Wiener Tagblatt*, selling some 40,000 copies each day, a good circulation at that time in Austria. By the following spring Rudolf was in regular correspondence with Szeps, who had influential contacts abroad, especially in Paris; his daughter, Sophie, was shortly to marry Paul Clemenceau, brother of Georges Clemenceau, the radical 'Tiger' (with whom, in May 1880, Szeps had had the first of several long interviews). Soon Szeps was to replace Latour as the chief recipient of the Crown Prince's political observations; and in early 1883 the *Neues Wiener Tagblatt* became an unofficial forum in which Rudolf could air his ideas, occasionally through anonymous articles written by himself.

He went to elaborate lengths to keep these contacts secret, for he knew that, on the pretext of protecting him from assassination, the police authorities kept him under virtual surveillance. Letters were carried to Szeps's elder daughter, Bertha, by Karl Nehammer, Rudolf's trusted personal servant who, having shaken off police shadowers by swift changes from tram to tram, would arrive at Bertha Szeps's home posing as her masseur. Conversations with Szeps took place late at night when Rudolf was in Vienna; his guest would be led to the Crown Prince's apartments in the Hofburg through servants' quarters, which were entered through an inconspicuous door on the ramp leading up to the Albertina Collection. When Clemenceau came to Vienna for his brother's wedding, it was by this route that Szeps escorted him to meet the Crown Prince. Yet despite his precautions, the police kept themselves in touch with Rudolf's activities. Taaffe saw no reason to worry the Emperor with the reports they passed on to him.

Thanks to Archduke Albrecht and to Beck (who became Chief of the General Staff in 1881) Francis Joseph had some idea of Rudolf's political contacts; and he strongly disapproved of them. If he had known how deeply the Crown Prince was also interesting himself in journalism, then Rudolf would certainly have been received 'distantly, coldly and sternly'. As it was, the Emperor treated him with indulgence so long as his marriage with Stephanie was not in question. Francis Joseph recognized that he shared Elizabeth's temperament to a greater extent than did their daughters. He possessed Sisi's romanticism and caprice, sometimes enchanting, but often indifferent to the sensitivity of others. But whereas his mother was a cultural dilettante, enraptured by Heine and the dream-world of Greek mythology, the Crown Prince liked to dabble in politics. 'Like his mother', Rudolf's sister-in-law recalled forty years later, 'he had a way of talking that held everybody, and a facility for setting all about him agog to solve the riddle of his personality'.

Occasionally, Francis Joseph was uneasy over the Wittelsbach strain in Rudolf's character. But though the Crown Prince for some five years before his marriage had cultivated a rarefied friendship with his kinsman, the Wagner-omane Ludwig II, the Bavarian king's ill-formed ideas had little influence upon him. To Francis Joseph's great satisfaction, so long as he was stationed in Prague, Rudolf outwardly showed every sign of becoming a good regimental officer, with no alarming eccentricities.

Despite the bitterness which runs through so many pages in the Crown Princess's published memoirs, surviving letters suggest that after two years of marriage Rudolf and Stephanie had achieved a mutual understanding which seemed improbable, given their differences of temperament and background. Szeps noted that Stephanie would be present at some of his early conversations on political topics with her husband; she did not always remain silent. The Crown Princess might enjoy ceremonial occasions more than Rudolf did, and far more than Elizabeth. But that was no fault in the wife of an heir to the throne; indeed, Stephanie's willingness to be present at Court functions won her Francis Joseph's warm approval. Rudolf remained happy in their home in Prague's Hradčany palace. When, after two and a half years of marriage, it was confirmed that Stephanie was pregnant, he hurried to Vienna to tell his father the good news in person.

This journey, too, won Francis Joseph's approval. He saw it as proof of his son's growing sense of dynasty. Just as Elizabeth once planned to give the name of Hungary's patron saint to the second son she never had, so Rudolf in his letters to Stephanie would refer to her coming child as 'Vaclav' (Wenceslas), the patron saint of Bohemia. Was this a private joke between husband and wife, or was it evidence of the Crown Prince's genuine admiration for the Czechs and their historic traditions? There is no indication that the Emperor knew of these exchanges; however, he suddenly approved of new military duties for the Crown Prince, making it certain that Rudolf would be in Lower Austria and not in Bohemia when the child was born.

There was to be no Archduke Wenceslas. On 2 September 1883 Crown Princess Stephanie gave birth at Laxenburg to a strong and healthy daughter. 'Never mind, a girl is much sweeter', Rudolf is reported to have told his wife, who was disappointed not to give the dynasty a male heir. Almost inevitably the Archduchess was named Elizabeth; and she became a favourite of her grandfather. Within the family she was known by the affectionate Magyar diminutive, 'Erzsi'. For, by Francis Joseph's reckoning, there could be no second 'Sisi'.

Chapter 15

GOLDEN EPOCH

For Austria-Hungary the 1880s were a time of promise left unfulfilled. In these years the Monarchy flowered in rich blossom soon blighted by the cold realities of social discontent. There was, at first, an increased prosperity and general stability; the astonishingly rapid growth of railways brought a semblance of economic unity to the Empire as a whole. By the winter of 1885–6, the budget was balanced in both parts of the Monarchy. At the same time, there was a far greater migration of the peasantry to the towns than in the troubled years immediately before Francis Joseph's accession. In central Vienna alone the population increased by 15.5 per cent during the 1880s, with an even larger growth in the inner suburbs. Ultimately urbanization proved a more significant development than the market integration of the economy. In the second half of the decade new mass movements, whose demagogic leaders pandered to popular prejudice and resentment, began to threaten the balance of parliamentary politics so carefully contrived by Taaffe as 'Emperor's minister'. But, before social discontent became a serious threat to stability, the solidly secure wealth of the middle classes provided money to spend on public and private buildings, on the visual arts and on theatre and music. There was a brief golden epoch of decorative pleasure and entertainment in the principal cities, and especially in Vienna, Budapest (a single municipality since 1872), and Prague.

Vienna remained the music capital of central Europe throughout the 1880s. Music could be heard, not only in the concert halls and opera houses, but in parks, wine gardens and beer cellars. Bruckner and Brahms were in their prime; Hugo Wolf, a prolific composer of Lieder, became an influential music critic for a Viennese weekly periodical in 1884; Gustav Mahler completed his first symphony before the end of the decade; while in Prague Dvořák was succeeding Smetana as the musical voice of the Czech people. Popular taste remained lightweight. Operetta flourished, particularly at the Theater an der Wien, where the triumph of

Franz von Suppé's *Bocaccio* in the winter of 1879–80 was followed by Karl Millöcker's *Der Bettelstudent* (Beggar Student), a great success at Christmas four years later. Hungarian audiences, too, enjoyed their light music; and Johann Strauss's *Gypsy Baron*, which delighted the Viennese in October 1885, received an even warmer reception at its Budapest première in the spring.

The artistic taste of the public continued to favour the exaggerated decorative style popularised by Hans Makart, even after his death in 1884, although floral designs and bouquets replaced the neo-Rubens inspiration of the Silver Wedding procession. The most enduring achievements of the decade were architectural. These were the years of the second phase of Ringstrasse building, heavy facades embellished by sculptured figures and offset, where open spaces permitted, by solemnly formal statuary. The Rathaus was finished in 1883 and the massive new home for the University some fourteen months later, fittingly at a time when its faculties of medicine and economics had won great respect throughout most of Europe and north America. Opposite the Rathaus work was in progress for most of the decade on a neo-Renaissance Burgtheater, which in 1888 replaced the smaller, much-loved baroque court theatre in the Michaelerplatz. The pretentions of Viennese architecture were matched by similar ambitious projects in Budapest: thus Austria's neo-classical *Parlaments-Gebaude* was completed in 1883, the year in which work started on its Hungarian counterpart, the grandiose parliament house on the Pest bank of the Danube. Prague, too, was given a neo-Renaissance palace: in 1885 work began on the Bohemian Museum, which was to dominate the newly landscaped Wenceslas Square; it was completed within five years. Trieste had a facelift to celebrate the city's quincentenary in 1882, while in Zagreb the cathedral and many public buildings were given the stamp of neo-Gothic modernity after an earthquake in November 1880 had rocked the Croatian capital and wrecked much of the old town.

Throughout this brief golden epoch, Francis Joseph remained a passive observer of the changes around him. He enjoyed the spectacle of Court balls and welcomed the succession of Strauss waltzes; he was glad to visit the theatre, provided a play did not tax his mind too severely; but he was hesitant over criticizing musical or artistic trends which he knew he had little hope of understanding. Yet he left a mark on the imperial capital, and indirectly on provincial centres which looked to Vienna for inspiration. For there is no doubt that Francis Joseph liked the neo-baroque style of architecture. When consulted over the siting of official buildings around the Ring, he favoured a disciplined orderliness which would preserve distant vistas. The elegant spaciousness of inner Vienna owes more to Francis Joseph's instinctive feeling for landscape than historians who deride his 'heavy and lifeless' lack of taste are prepared to concede.

In 1857 Francis Joseph took the initiative in transforming Vienna into a metropolis with his order for the walls and bastions of the city to be razed to the ground. Thirty years later he was still encouraging the growth of the capital. When, on 30 September 1888, he opened the Turkenschanzpark in Döbling, the Emperor welcomed the completion of this first municipal-sponsored parkland in the suburbs as a step towards the creation of a Greater Vienna, with the last internal barriers swept away; and, as a plaque in Turkenschanzpark still records, two years after his speech the integration of capital and suburbs was, indeed, finally achieved. But after a third of a century on the throne, Francis Joseph asserted his sovereignty less openly than in the early years of the reign. Letters Patent no longer appeared in print with the ringing autocratic decisiveness of the Bach era. Although there was no diminution in the reality of imperial power, during the 1880s the initiative in government lay with Taaffe, Kálmán Tisza or Kálnoky who were, at least in theory, dependent upon the support of the lower house of parliament, both in Cisleithania and Hungary. All matters concerning the army remained within the Emperor's prerogative, and he continued to take the final decision over foreign affairs. By now, however, Francis Joseph was acting circumspectly. In middle age he came to learn more about the practice of politics from that pliable improviser, Eddy Taaffe, than he had gathered in his youth from Metternich's occasional tuition.

Francis Joseph's compulsive sense of duty ensured that he fulfilled every task expected of him. He was at the festivities to mark the completion of the new University buildings in Vienna and he joined Burgermeister Eduard Uhl for the opening of the new Rathaus. He showed respect for musical genius by visiting the workroom of the sculptor, Heinrich Natter, from whom a monument to Joseph Haydn had been commissioned, soon after Natter first began shaping the marble. It was not that Francis Joseph was prepared to express an opinion on the design; he merely wished to inspect progress on a work of art under imperial patronage. Two years later, he duly unveiled the statue outside Haydn's parish church of Mariahilf. A similar sense of obligation ensured that he never missed the international art exhibitions at Vienna's Kunstlerhaus in the Karlsplatz. At a time when Elizabeth was abroad, he dutifully accompanied Rudolf and Stephanie to Budapest for the Hungarian Landesexhibition; a less diligent monarch might well have been content to leave the show of royal support for the exhibition to the Crown Prince and Princess. The truth was that, though he might attend fewer ministerial conferences than in the 1850s and 1860s, he was still setting himself an impossibly high standard of duties to fulfil. Not least among them was the punctilio with which he observed royal courtesies. When Queen Victoria, travelling incognito by railway from Florence to Potsdam, passed through the Tyrol she was surprised to find Francis Joseph on the station platform at Innsbruck to greet her. She was even more astounded to learn that the Emperor had made an overnight train journey of 350 miles solely in order to exchange these brief pleasantries with her.

So long as his ministers enjoyed their sovereign's confidence Francis Joseph actively supported them with personal diplomacy. Often this required a conference with his fellow autocrats, as in the early years of his reign; and he was prepared to make a winter journey into Russian Poland to meet his old adversary, William I, and the new ruler of Russia, Alexander III, at the hunting-lodge of Skierniewice in order to uphold Kálnoky's faith in Bismarck's League of the Three Emperors. Sometimes he had to curb old prejudices so as to facilitate tactical shifts of policy. Although sensitive over matters of sovereignty, he agreed to recognize Milan Obrenović as a King in Belgrade rather than a Prince so as to strengthen Austria's hold on a client Serbia; and when Kálnoky persuaded Francis Joseph of the need to expand the Dual Alliance of 1879 with Germany into a Triple Alliance with Italy, the Emperor swallowed his misgivings over the House of Savoy's appropriation of papal Rome and entertained King Umberto and Queen Margherita on a four day state visit to Vienna. Yet, despite the conclusion of the Triple Alliance in May 1882, Francis Joseph had few illusions over the real feeling of Italian patriots towards the Habsburgs and he was not surprised when, five months later, the police discovered a plot to assassinate him during a tour of the southern provinces. Since Taaffe had already emphasized the need for imperial participation in the quincentenary celebrations at Trieste so as to counter the pro-Italian sentiment in the Monarchy's third largest city, Francis Joseph went ahead with the planned journey despite police fears of further dangerous conspiracies.

The visit did nothing to improve Austro-Italian relations, as both Taaffe and Kálnoky had hoped: the subsequent execution of the principal conspirator, Guglielmo Oberdank, gave the irredentists a martyr-hero whom they idolised for the rest of the decade, despite the formal alliance partnership of Vienna, Berlin and Rome. In retrospect, the most significant aspect of the Trieste quincentenary was the presence in the city of the Empress as well as of the Emperor. For Elizabeth, like Francis Joseph, observed a code of duty, though one of her own making. In 1881 she had gladly handed over some of her drearier responsibilities as First Lady to Crown Princess Stephanie: now she surprised Taaffe with her insistence on joining Francis Joseph at Miramare. It was characteristic of

Elizabeth's concept of dynastic obligation that, while willingly shirking the round of social trivialities in the capital, she had no hesitation in sharing with her husband the dangers of a visit to his remaining Italian provinces. A similar sense of duty once made her cut short a hunting season in England so as to help Francis Joseph comfort the victims of the floods at Szeged; and she had been beside him in the harrowing aftermath of the fire at Vienna's Ringtheater in December 1881, a disaster in which several hundred members of the audience perished. Among the victims was Ladislaus Vetsera, the eldest brother of ten-year old Mary.

The Ringtheater tragedy came barely a week after the Crown Prince wrote the long, critical letter to Latour in which he complained that his mother no longer cared for anything except hunting. This was unfair, as Rudolf must have realized when the family came together at Christmas for Elizabeth's 44th birthday. His mother still spent several hours each day ensuring that she looked young, but she was far less agile than in the first years she went riding in England. Soon she would be forced to curb her constant craving to leap into the saddle; she might even, so her husband hoped, give up those long weeks of foreign travel. No one expected the Empress would be content with fulfilling public duties in the Hofburg or Schönbrunn, and she was always restless at Laxenburg (which, some months later, was badly damaged by fire while the Crown Prince was in residence). But Francis Joseph believed Elizabeth might enjoy the happiness of semi-retirement in a new home on the edge of the Vienna woods. Ever since their first years of marriage, they had gained particular pleasure from rides in the parkland at Lainz; and in the autumn of 1881, Francis Joseph agreed to have a small villa built in a secluded part of the Lainzer Tiergarten. It was intended as a family lodge, free from court ceremonial, tucked away from the public gaze, with life at least as intimate as at Gödöllö, Elizabeth's favourite royal residence. Francis Joseph would pay for the villa from his personal funds and present it as a gift to his beloved Sisi.

The prospect of privacy in a home only a short carriage drive from the parade-ground pomposity of Schönbrunn delighted the Empress. To relieve the boredom of public life she enjoyed creating a poetic fantasy world in which she would identify herself with Shakespeare's queen of the fairies, and she duly called her husband's gift 'Titania's enchanted castle' – a villa in a wood near Vienna made a fine substitute for a flowery bed in a wood near Athens. But there was no Oberon to conjure up a dream palace at the wave of a wand. Prosaically, her generous husband commissioned Karl von Hasenauer, architect of the Burgtheater and many of the museums around the Ring, to design a two-storeyed 'hunting lodge in the imperial and royal Tiergarten'. His first plans were ready for scrutiny in mid-December 1881, when it was accepted that the house would not be ready for occupation for four or five years. Work began in the spring, with the original design of symmetrical stables and guardhouses modified, to lessen the formal appearance of the villa.

Francis Joseph suffered an early disappointment. For the prospect of becoming chatelaine of an enchanted castle seems to have revived Elizabeth's desire 'to wander everywhere swifter than the moon's sphere'. Even before the workmen began clearing the site of the villa, she was off to England for one last month of following the hounds, with a stag hunt at Chantilly on her way home. By now, however, she was riding far less, for she suffered from the first twinges of sciatica. Yet the threat of physical weakness served to intensify her eccentricities. Francis Joseph thought he was giving a splendid horsewoman a hunting lodge of her own; the original plans provided for a small riding school as well as extensive stables. But he still did not understand his wife's temperament. Between 1882 and 1885 Elizabeth's interests changed more dramatically than her way of life. Abandonment of the saddle did not domesticate her. What had begun as a hunting lodge in the Tiergarten became a villa named after Hermes, the winged messenger of the Gods and patron of travellers.

The transformation was gradual. At first Elizabeth persisted with gymnastic exercises every morning. This was to be expected; Francis Joseph had seen to it that the draft plans included a personal gymnasium, next to the Empress's washroom. By the autumn, however, she was supplementing her morning exercises with daily fencing lessons. Soon she began to undertake long excursions on foot, especially when she was visiting her native Bavaria or the Salzkammergut. In the second week of June 1883 she insisted on covering the 22 miles from central Munich to Feldafing on the Starnbergersee on foot along a military road with little shade and under a blazing sun; she protected herself with a parasol, and completed the self-imposed route march in seven hours. To the Empress's exhausted attendants her pace seemed more of a trot than a walk. At Ischl a month later she set herself a target of seven and three-quarter hours walking each day, ordering wagons to follow her, with chairs for the ladies-in-waiting. A 23-mile round trip up the wooded Langbathtal kept Elizabeth walking for almost nine hours. Crown Princess Stephanie's memoirs recall how 'the Empress would never stop for a midday meal, and at the most would drink a glass of milk or some orange juice'. All this activity did not benefit her health. To Francis Joseph's consternation, Elizabeth became pale and thin.

Her mother and father (both by now in their mid-seventies) and her sisters were also alarmed. They were puzzled over changes in her attitude to people. To their surprise she formed a close attachment to her cousin,

King Ludwig II of Bavaria. She had been fond of him in his boyhood but observed his erratic behaviour after his accession with mounting indignation. Now she sympathised with him, as he mourned the death of his idol, Richard Wagner. Long talks with Ludwig in 1883 convinced Elizabeth that he was, like her, a poetic soul sustained by the beauty of a dream world of the imagination. Ludwig told her that he saw himself as an eagle, with his throne the high crag of a mountain; she came to see herself as a seagull, at liberty to glide unrestrained over the oceans. Small wonder if her family was worried.

Other changes were less disturbing. Elizabeth began to read more deeply than for many years. Her passion for the poetry of Heinrich Heine reached a new intensity. With the encouragement of her younger daughter, she once more scribbled verses down on paper. Often she consciously echoed Heine, but sometimes she achieved a certain orig- inality, allowing her pen to sublimate the flow of romantic fancy in which she exulted. With renewed energy, she expanded her education. She was, of course, still Titania, but the fairy queen had a wider vision now; for, with the rediscovery of poetry, came a revived enthusiasm for classical Greece. Soon she was learning Homer by heart and, inspired by Sch- liemann's excavations at Troy, Mycenae and Tiryns, she planned a fourth cruise down to Corfu and beyond. Achilles became her particular hero. When she ordered a copy of Herterich's statue of the dying warrior for the Miramare gardens, it was clear her interests had gone beyond the dogs and horses and huntsmen that filled her idle hours when she first sought a homely villa in the Lainzer Tiergarten.

To respond fittingly to Elizabeth's quicksilver enthusiasms would have been a hard task for any husband. Francis Joseph did his best to please her. Fortunately they retained their shared love of horses, even if he was often alarmed by the risks she took in the saddle. He was prepared to accept her cult of Titania, though after accompanying her to see *A Midsummer Night's Dream* for the first time he had confided to his mother that it was 'rather boring and very stupid'. He was irritated by her admiration for Heine, a dangerous radical by the reckoning of Met- ternich's censors in the Emperor's youth; but he allowed her a statue of the poet in the grounds of their home at Ischl. Her delight in romantic classicism left him unappreciative; 'I find it hard to imagine what you can find to do with yourself in Ithaca for so many days', he wrote when Elizabeth was at last hot on the trail of Odysseus in his native island. Yet, despite this cold douche, 'the main thing is that you are well and happy' he added.

It was in this mood that Francis Joseph continued to indulge her whims over the interior decoration of the Hermes Villa. She might have her

Titania frescoes and her Pompeian murals in the washroom. Above the pediment of the gymnasium door two centaurs achieved curvets worthy of the finest Lippizaners in the Spanish Riding School; and when the Empress awoke in the morning, there above her she could see Zeus's chariot emerging from billowing clouds painted on the bedroom ceiling. It was all rather overdone, as Francis Joseph knew. But he felt bound to consult his artistic advisers, and Hans Makart's taste prevailed. Some of the old egoist's protégés – notably the brothers Gustav and Ernst Klimt – showed an enlightened initiative, adding a touch of grace to elegance robbed of delicacy. But under Makart's influence a home planned as a simple lodge became a compact and cluttered chateau, rich in colours, marble reliefs, thick carpets and heavy drapery. Even today, when the villa is in effect an art museum, the ornate ceiling of 'the Emperor's workroom' stands out in striking contrast to the simple white stucco of his study at Schönbrunn.

On 24 May 1886 Francis Joseph, Elizabeth and the Archduchess Marie Valerie visited the completed Hermes Villa, though another year elapsed before they went into residence. The Emperor admired its finery but was heard to remark 'I shall always be afraid of spoiling things'. The Empress was delighted by the garden. For the rest of her life, she was glad to seek the seclusion of the Tiergarten. But her horizon had broadened by now. Barely two years after this first visit she let her husband know that she wished to have a small palace dedicated to Achilles built for her on Corfu. 'That will do me no good with the Viennese', Francis Joseph confessed privately; but it was a long time since he had denied his wife any request. Elizabeth was duly promised her Achilleion.

When the Empress had resumed her travels in 1882 Francis Joseph sank back into accustomed habits. At Ischl he donned leather shorts, green jacket, thick woollen socks, mountaineer's boots and Tyrolean hat; out came hunting rifles and cartridge belts and he would stalk the mountain slopes for as many weeks as official duties permitted. In the autumn he hunted at Gödöllö or at Mürzsteg, a lodge in Styria about halfway between Semmering and Graz. It was in Vienna that he suffered most from social isolation; he might shoot at Lainz, or ride in the Prater, or take solitary walks around the Laxenburg parkland. But for long weeks he was denied all family life.

At Schönbrunn he could at least still seek the company of Anna Nahowski. His visits became especially frequent in 1884 when – still aged only 25 – she moved to her spacious new house at Hietzing, opposite to the side gate of Schönbrunn's 'Tyrolean Garden'. In the welfare of one of Anna's children, Helene (who was to marry the composer, Alban Berg) he took some interest, giving the mother the very considerable sum of

100,000 Gulden when, in 1883, the girl was born. But though Anna might satisfy Francis Joseph's physical desires, she seems to have been a young woman of limited interests: did they ever have a real conversation? There is no doubt that he tired of her and it is probable that, as he grew older, he found the twenty-nine year gap in their ages increasingly exacting, although he did not finally break with Anna until the end of the decade. However, about the time of Helene Nahowski's birth, he met for the first time the actress he had seen play Kate in *The Taming of the Shrew* ten years before; and soon his friendship with Katharina Schratt was to give him greater solace and a wiser human understanding than any other relationship he experienced.

Fortune had buffeted Katharina Schratt since her early success at the Stadtheater. In September 1879 she married Nicholas Kiss von Itebbe, a handsome Hungarian, who lived well beyond his means in a fourteen room apartment in Vienna's Gumpendorferstrasse. Katharina retired from the stage and a son, Toni, was born in the following summer. But in 1882 Nicholas Kiss, heavily in debt, fled from his creditors, leaving Katharina to face the bailiffs. The Viennese theatres refused to re-engage her. For a year she played in New York, leaving Toni with her parents at Baden; but she was back in the Monarchy by the following spring; an aristocratic admirer found her playing in a company at Czernowitz, a garrison town in the Bukovina, almost on the Russian frontier. Monetary help and graceful hospitality from wealthy friends enabled her to settle again in the capital: Eduard Palmer, presiding director of a mining company, became her financial adviser and helped her to gain admittance to the Burgtheater within six months of being Czernowitz's leading lady. New entrants to the imperial theatre were received in audience by the Emperor. The natural freshness and vivacity of Katharina at this meeting made an impression he never forgot. He began making frequent visits to the Burgtheater. It was noticed he always chose nights when Frau Schratt was listed to appear.

They do not seem to have met again until February 1885, when the Emperor was observed in long conversation with the actress at the annual Industriellenball in the Hofburg's Redoutensaal. Katharina was by no means blind to her opportunities for advancement, for in the following summer she accepted a seasonal engagement at Ischl, where Francis Joseph was accustomed to celebrate his birthday. And on 17 August 1885 the Crown Prince and Crown Princess, Prince Leopold of Bavaria and Archduchess Marie Valerie accompanied him to the Ischl Kurhaustheater for a birthday eve entertainment: Katharina Schratt as Rosel in Ferdinand Raimund's *Der Verschwender* (The Spendthrift), a musical tale of virtue triumphing over a husband's fecklessness. The theme ran close to the actress's heart. Nine days later she appeared before her Emperor and the Tsar in a one-act comedy presented by the Burgtheater company as a command performance in Kremsier during the Austro-Russian summit conference in the Moravian archbishop's summer palace. That evening, at Alexander III's insistence, all three leading actresses joined the Emperors and Empresses for supper.

Elizabeth noticed Francis Joseph's partiality for Katharina Schratt's company, and there is no doubt that she encouraged the attachment. At times she felt remorse for constantly seeking to escape from sharing the Emperor's monotonous round of duty; he deserved lively companionship. She may, perhaps, have known of the Nahowski ménage in Hietzing and have sought a social arrangement less dangerously compromising for her husband. But she will also have been influenced by her current idolization of Heine: in the last year of his life the poet had been cheered and inspired by the platonic friendship of Elise Krinitz, a young social gadfly whom he nicknamed 'La Mouche'; and eighteen months before the Kremsier meeting Krinitz had published, under the pseudonym Camille Selden, her reminiscences of the months when she so successfully lightened Heine's deep depression. Elizabeth read everything she could obtain written by Heine or about Heine. What could seem more natural to her than to look for an Austrian 'mouche' who would brighten her husband's lonelier days? She commissioned a portrait of the actress from Heinrich von Angeli, an artist to whom the Emperor frequently gave his patronage; she would present the painting as a gift to her husband, just as he had presented her with a home in the Lainzer Tiergarten. On 21 May 1886 – three days before Elizabeth became chatelaine of the Hermes Villa – Katharina Schratt was at Angeli's studio when, to her genuine surprise, the Empress brought her husband to inspect progress on the portrait. Sovereign and actress chatted together informally while Elizabeth took a gracious interest in Angeli's other canvases. Two days later Francis Joseph, signing himself 'Your devoted admirer', sent Katharina the first of more than 500 letters. Over the following thirty years, they were to serve as a safety-valve for the suppressed tensions of his inner self.

For the Emperor and Empress the completion of the Hermes Villa and the commissioning of the Angeli portrait were welcome diversions from a protracted international crisis which threatened to plunge Europe into war. At Kremsier Francis Joseph and Kálnoky emphasized their hopes for continued good relations with Russia while Tsar Alexander III re-affirmed his confidence in the League of the Three Emperors, Bismarck's method of maintaining collaboration between the eastern autocrats through a system of common self-denial. But Crown Prince Rudolf – and, rather unexpectedly, his mother – mistrusted the sincerity of the

Tsar's protestations of friendship. A month before the Kremsier meeting Rudolf had written to Latour strongly criticising Kálnoky's appeasement of Russia in the Balkans. He failed to appreciate the delicate nature of Kálnoky's balancing act in the East. In particular, he underestimated the importance of his achievement in drawing Roumania into a secret defensive alliance against Russia in October 1884, with Germany underwriting the treaty.

The Eastern Question was posed again sooner than either Rudolf or his father anticipated. Shortly before the Kremsier meeting Francis Joseph received at Ischl Prince Alexander of Battenberg who, with the backing of the Great Powers, had become sovereign prince of the small Bulgaria created at the Berlin Congress. In September 1885 Alexander showed his independence by proclaiming the 'union of the two Bulgarias', thus linking the predominantly Bulgarian Ottoman province of Eastern Rumelia with his principality. Thereupon neighbouring Serbia, alarmed by the shift of power in the Balkans invaded Bulgaria, only to be defeated by Prince Alexander at Slivnitza (17 November 1885). In this sudden crisis Francis Joseph and Kálnoky strove to keep the peace; they held Austria-Hungary to a common policy of mediation agreed by her partners, Germany and Russia. But their judicious statesmanship was far from popular in the twin capitals of the Monarchy. Andrássy, who was contemplating a return to public life, sent Francis Joseph a long memorandum recommending the imposition of a settlement of Balkan frontiers which would be agreeable to political and commercial interests in Vienna and Budapest.

Neither the Emperor nor Beck, his Chief of the General Staff, were prepared to risk a war in which they could not count on unqualified German support. Not least among their considerations was the mounting threat of two popular mass movements within the Monarchy: the demagogic Pan-German followers of George von Schönerer opposed the dynasty and its chief pillars, the army and the Catholic Church, and would have exploited any rebuff, military or diplomatic; and there had already been two large-scale socialist demonstrations in Vienna. By using diplomatic pressure to halt the Bulgarians after Slivnitza, Kálnoky patiently defused the crisis. A series of ambassadorial conferences in Constantinople patched up the Balkan frontiers by the following spring; and, despite the lobbying of the Russophobes in Vienna, the League of the Three Emperors remained in being, offering Austria-Hungary a certain security in the north and the east.

It was therefore with some confidence of a peaceful summer that, in June 1886, Francis Joseph and Katharina Schratt compared their planned itineraries. She told him of her intention to take the waters at Karlsbad and spend most of July in the Salzkammergut, having leased a villa at

Frauenstein, above St Wolfgang. The Emperor informed her that he would be at Ischl in early July and would visit her holiday home, since St Wolfgang was only an hour's carriage drive along the shore of the lake. This excursion Francis Joseph duly undertook, inviting himself to breakfast at half-past eight in the morning almost as soon as Katharina had completed the long journey south from Bohemia. From surviving letters of that summer and nostalgic references in later correspondence it is clear that over the following weeks he profited from her infectious gaiety, discovering how to chatter over trivialities in an easy, intimate manner he had not experienced since boyhood. He would invite himself to breakfast once or twice a week. On these occasions, despite the time of day, Katharina would slip into a light comedy role, vivacious, sharp-witted and enlivened by mimicry. The best performances of Katharina Schratt's career may well have been at her breakfast table on these mornings in July and August 1886. There was no amatory intimacy: he enjoyed 'sitting together chatting in the comfortable room at Frauenstein' too much to risk cheapening the honour of his newly found friend. Moreover he had not finally broken with Anna Nahowski – whom he was to visit at Hietzing on 23 August, only a few days after his return to Schönbrunn.

The Empress, having kindled the romantic glow of friendship, was not at Ischl in July to watch it burn with a steady flame. That summer brought her little joy. From May onwards, she awaited the unfolding of the year with trepidation, for she had come across an adage predicting that a late Easter brings sorrows before Christmas; and Easter Day fell on 25 April in 1886, the latest possible date in the Christian calendar. At the end of the first week in June she travelled to Bavaria, accompanied by her younger daughter, Valerie. She was therefore at Feldafing on the west shore of the Starnbergersee when the life of her cousin King Ludwig ended in tragedy. On the late evening of 13 June, two days after he had been put under physical restraint for his mental aberrations, the bodies of Ludwig and his attendant doctor were found on the eastern side of the Starnbergersee, almost opposite to Feldafing.

The news was broken to Elizabeth by her elder daughter, Gisela, at breakfast next morning. It was assumed that the King had thrown himself into the lake and that the doctor had died trying to save him. But in the course of the day Elizabeth became deeply agitated: had Ludwig been trying to swim across the lake to her, as the one person who could sympathise with the fantasies of his mind? That night Valerie was shocked to find her mother distraught, lying on the floor of her room. For several days Elizabeth would burst suddenly into tears and accuse the Bavarian authorities of complicity in Ludwig's murder. Often her talk seems to have lacked coherence: Titania was transformed into an ageing Ophelia.

Francis Joseph sent the Crown Prince to represent the Monarchy at Ludwig's funeral. Rudolf was alarmed by his mother's protracted grief and agitation: it was clear to poor Valerie that her brother, though comforting and charming in his manner, was wondering if Mama, too, suffered from the mental instability of the Wittelsbachs; and to what extent were these disorders hereditary? Once she recovered her general composure similar doubts began to trouble Elizabeth. Much of the poetry she wrote in the remaining months of the year showed an obsession with death. At the same time she became fascinated by the problems of the mentally disturbed. A fortnight before Christmas, without consulting Francis Joseph, Elizabeth made a surprise visit to Brundlfeld, the principal asylum serving Vienna; this was the occasion of the well-known encounter with an inmate who insisted that she was the true Empress Elizabeth and that the visitor who received all the honours was an impostor.

During these closing weeks of the year Francis Joseph was preoccupied with renewed tension in the Balkans. The Russians, having decided that Alexander of Battenberg was by nature too independent to serve their interests, kidnapped the Prince in mid-August. At first it seemed as if there would, for once, be no acute crisis. To the Emperor's satisfaction Kálnoky treated this latest coup in Sofia in a firm and conciliatory manner: the Russians were induced to release the Prince and allow him to cross into Austria; but it was agreed in Vienna and in St Petersburg that, for the sake of European peace, 'the Battenberg' should abdicate and allow the Bulgarian parliament to elect another Prince. But, to Francis Joseph's dismay, Alexander III almost immediately sent his aide-de-camp General Kaulbars to Sofia as a personal envoy; and Kaulbars was expected to browbeat and bully the Bulgarian politicians into electing a ruler nominated by the Tsar. 'Unthinkable for Austria-Hungary', Kálnoky declared, fearing that a Russian puppet in Bulgaria would ensure Panslav control over all the Balkans, including non-Slav Roumania, Austria-Hungary's secret ally. Francis Joseph agreed with his minister; in Budapest both Tisza and Kálnoky made threatening speeches; and for two months it seemed probable that the Crown Prince's preventive war pressure group in Vienna would persuade the Emperor to throw caution to the winds. But he was an older, sadder and wiser commander-in-chief than in the days of Buol and Gyulai. Bismarck would do nothing to help his ally; though Kálnoky received some diplomatic support from the British, it was clear that in a general war, the Imperial-Royal Army would have to fight the Russians alone. Thankfully, late in November the Tsar summoned Kaulbars back to the capital. But the Russian foreign ministry had no contact with Francis Joseph's ambassador in St Petersburg; it was as if the two Empires had severed diplomatic relations, an embassy official complained in late December.

Christmas at the Hofburg was gloomy. Francis Joseph had for company a sad Empress, suffering from sciatica and aware she was entering her fiftieth year, and a Crown Prince who showed his impatience at what he still regarded as the indecisive political leadership of his father's ministers. Valerie, her mother's constant solace, was with her parents; but the Archduchess too was unhappy, complaining in her journal of Rudolf's sarcastic manner when conversation turned to finding a suitor for her. Gifts and greetings from Katharina Schratt brought Francis Joseph a childlike pleasure on Christmas Eve; a note of thanks next day emphasized his eagerness to see her star in a worthwhile role: 'I am always pleased when I see your name on the posters or learn from the advance circular that you are to play' in a particular production. A week later, however, he too was depressed. Lack of news from St Petersburg and close proximity to Rudolf's sustained sabre-rattling may well account for the tone of his New Year's Day letter: 'God grant that the year now beginning will be peaceful', Katharina was told, 'Unfortunately at the moment the prospect is poor. I could then hope that last summer's lovely time would be renewed in this year, too, and I would realize the longed-for joy of being able to be near you again, to talk to you again. In these days of deep trouble and heavy work, the recollection of the wonderful times past and the hope of their return come as rays of light for me'.

Elizabeth's 'New Year's Night' poem also anticipated a general war; and at a Crown Council on 7 January Francis Joseph told his ministers that, though he wished to maintain peace, 'all necessary measures are to be taken' in case there should be 'a sudden deterioration of the political situation in the near future'. But Russia did not want a war. Cool, calm deliberation triumphed. By midsummer the danger was over. Although the League of the Three Emperors might be dead, Kálnoky could offer his master three gains from the protracted crisis: a close understanding with Great Britain concerning Mediterranean problems; a renewal of the alliance with Roumania (though there was constant friction between Budapest and Bucharest over commercial tariffs); and a renewal of the Triple Alliance (Germany, Austria-Hungary, Italy) even if the Italians insisted on a supplementary agreement promising 'reciprocal compensation' for territorial gains in the Balkans.

Francis Joseph was not entirely sure if the final settlement of Bulgaria's dynastic problem was to the Monarchy's advantage. For in early July 1887, Sofia's parliamentary deputies unanimously elected an Austrian cavalry officer, Prince Ferdinand of Saxe-Coburg, as their new ruler. 'Illegal', the Russians complained, 'a worthless comedy staged by the most wretched rabble'. Francis Joseph was not displeased at Russia's discomfiture but he, too, was uneasy over the election: Ferdinand had hardly distinguished himself in the 11th Hussars, and the Emperor thought him effeminate, lacking that strength of character he so respected in King Carol I of Roumania. These considered judgments on the Prince may have owed something to the discovery that he had recently sought Frau Schratt's companionship at Karlsbad. But Francis Joseph acknowledged that Ferdinand was unlikely to become a Russian catspaw. As Kálnoky pointed out, the new Prince was a Roman Catholic and he came from a branch of the Coburgs who had augmented their funds by marrying into the extremely wealthy Hungarian princely family of Kohary. Moreover, as a relative of Queen Victoria, Ferdinand might afford the British new reasons for interesting themselves in the maintenance of Balkan stability. Yet, though Francis Joseph learnt to respect 'Foxy Ferdinand's' political dexterity, he never liked him. A certain restraint may have sprung in part from jealousy over Katharina Schratt's lifelong friendship with her 'brotherly friend' in Sofia. Ferdinand was, after all, more than thirty years his junior – and nearly eight years younger than Katharina herself.

Early in July 1887 Francis Joseph's 'longed-for joy' was, as he had hoped, fulfilled; once more he could relax at Ischl while Katharina was at Frauenstein. In that year he had as yet seen little of the Empress, for soon after Carnival time she was on her travels again: down to southern Hungary and into Roumania; then, after a brief family reunion at the Villa Hermes, up to Hamburg in order to visit Heine's sister and across the North Sea for a month on the Norfolk coast. There was a strange contrast in their lives that July. While Francis Joseph was enjoying the coffee and rich pastries Frau Schratt's cooks had ready for him each morning, Elizabeth would come down to Cromer beach from the small bow-windowed hotel annexe she had rented on the cliffs. At Frauenstein the Emperor (as his later letters show) would explain 'how a military manoeuvre is performed' to an actress who, in her turn, amazed him with the tittle-tattle of stage rivalries. On Cromer sands, the Empress would settle in solitary simplicity under her lace parasol, glance out across the same sea that had inspired Heine, and scribble verse after verse on her notepads. She completed 28 poems at Cromer, a literary output which astounded Valerie when a few weeks later her mother read her the verses. Elizabeth was attracted by the quiet little Norfolk town with its church tower landmark; she enjoyed her sea trips and was fascinated by tales of lost villages which had fallen under the waves as the coast was eroded. She wrote sympathetically of a nun whom she saw sitting each day on the shore, and she wrote angrily of a man who persisted in turning his binoculars on her from the clifftop – the verse even threatens she will lift up her skirts and reveal more than the peeping Tom ever expected. But, all in all, her Cromer poems – good, bad, or indifferent – reflect a welcome contentment. She was in a happy mood for the first time since the tragedy of Ludwig. To Francis Joseph's relief she agreed to travel to the Isle of Wight for a courtesy call on Queen Victoria; she would be at Ischl for his birthday. 'My infinitely beloved angel, your dear letter made me very happy', he replied. But from Ischl, a few weeks later, one last poem – *Ruckblick* (Backward Glance) – recalled the 'fine days' she spent at Cromer.

Once back in Austria the Empress amused her ladies (and mildly embarrassed Valerie) by snide remarks over Katharina's robust figure. The Emperor's devotion to his friend ran deeper than Elizabeth had thought possible during their visit to Angeli's studio; and her feelings towards Katharina may have been a shade less generous than is suggested by those open avowals of friendship which her husband found so gratifying. Some verses have survived which mock Francis Joseph's delight in what Elizabeth implies was a feigned simplicity of manner on the part of the actress. But she, too, needed Frau Schratt – for by mid-October the Empress was off again, sailing down to Corfu. It was good to know her husband would not fret in her absence. Almost every letter from him during this period of separation refers to walks or talks with the 'War Minister' (their code-name for Katharina) or includes news from the Viennese theatre world. When Elizabeth rejoined him at Gödöllö in time for St Catherine's Day (25 November) it was she who ordered champagne to drink the absent friend's health on her saint's day. 'I was really surprised to see champagne glasses set on the table', the Emperor wrote to Katharina, 'We do not usually permit ourselves the luxury of this wine'.

There runs through Francis Joseph's letters in this second winter of close friendship an apologetic strain of self-depreciation, mingled with happiness at his good fortune: 'To see you again would make me happy, but of course only if it pleases you, if you feel well and if you can spare the time', he wrote; and 'With what delight I saw you look up several times to my window', after he had watched her cross an inner courtyard of the Hofburg on her way to early Mass. A fortnight later he proclaimed 'Were I not so old and had no cough, I could shout with joy at the idea of meeting you again tomorrow – I hope'. These manifestations of persistent calf-love nearly 40 years since he had said 'Farewell my youth' induced Katharina Schratt to send Francis Joseph, who was in the castle at Budapest, a carefully phrased 'letter of meditation' (*Gedankenbrief*) for St Valentine's Day in 1888 in which she offered to become his mistress. He was flattered ('especially when I look into the mirror and my old wrinkled face stares back at me') and he told her openly, what 'you must at least guess ... that I adore you'. But he insisted that their relationship 'must remain for the future as it has been until now', for 'I love my wife and do not wish to abuse her confidence and her friendship with you'. He added, 'I am too old to be a brotherly friend, but treat me as a fatherly friend'. The letter determined the form of their friendship and therefore made it happier and easier in the future. As he admitted a few days later, 'Frankness is best ... and now it will save me from that stupid jealousy which so often plagues me'. Then he looked out of his window above the Danube in Budapest, saw snow falling and added wistfully, 'If we were walking in Schönbrunn and the slope above the Tyrolean Garden was again slippery, perhaps I might be permitted to take your arm'.

These exchanges with Katharina lifted the Emperor's spirits as the golden epoch approached what he regarded as its climax. For in that spring Vienna's Ringstrasse would be completed and on the anniversary of Maria Theresa's birth he would unveil a huge monument to his great-great-grandmother in a square between museums newly built to house the Empire's finest collections of natural history and art. He intended the ceremony on 13 May to serve as a salute from the dynasty to the woman whose courage had saved the Habsburg crown.

Unexpectedly Francis Joseph, too, needed courage that spring. For while he was still in Budapest, the submerged tensions in a cosmopolitan city came to the surface in Vienna and plunged the capital into a series of street demonstrations which bordered on riot. The *Neues Wiener Tag-blatt* – of which the Crown Prince's friend, Szeps, was the editor – believed it had a journalistic scoop on 8 March: the morning edition announced the death of William I and printed an obituary when the octogenarian German Emperor still had another twenty-four hours of half-existence to endure. The paper's action was interpreted by the Pan-Germans in Vienna as an insult to the first sovereign of a unified Germany; and, with Schönerer at their head, a group of Pan-Germans burst into the newspaper's editorial offices and threatened the staff with violence. Schönerer was a member of the lower chamber of parliament but so disgusted were his colleagues at this behaviour that the House immediately withdrew his immunity from arrest; he was charged with unlawful entry into the *Tagblatt*'s office and sentenced to five months solitary confinement and five years loss of civic rights. The Pan-Germans were indignant. On the evening before the monument was unveiled, thousands of Schönerer's supporters marched along the Ring, passing the draped statue and shouting, 'Down with the Habsburgs! Down with Austria! Down with the Jewish Press! Long live Germany!'. There were fears the Emperor might be insulted in a further demonstration next day. A celebration of the past seemed threatened by an ominous portent – just half a century before the Anschluss.

Never before and never again was there so great a dynastic parade in Vienna. No less than 66 Archdukes and Archduchesses joined the Emperor and Empress for the ceremony. As well as the élite regiments with their bands and the pick of Viennese choirs to sing a *Te Deum*, all the pupils from the Theresian Academy were mustered on parade to honour their founder: 'How handsome they looked!', the Emperor commented soon afterwards. He scorned all thought of insult. Despite the deprecatory comments on his appearance in his private letters, he was still an impressive figure: straight-backed, in a tight-fitting white tunic above scarlet trousers, he looked taller and far younger than he appeared to the townsfolk of Ischl who saw him on the days when he liked to set out for the mountains. Elizabeth, despite hating public occasions, was so moved by the unveiling ceremony that she sought to capture the emotions of the day in a long poem. She was not worried for her husband's well-being: the crowd's ovation emphasized the widespread rejection of Schönerer's mob violence. But Elizabeth was suddenly alarmed by her son's appearance: Rudolf was pale, his eyes were dull and restless, and there were deep shadows beneath them. 'Are you ill?', she asked. 'No, only tired and exhausted', Rudolf replied. She seems to have assumed he was worried over the threats to his liberal and Jewish friends; for she said no more to her son.

Francis Joseph was pleased with the ceremony. The weather was splendid; no member of the family excused himself or herself from the parade; and Kaspar von Zumbusch, who designed and created the monument, had a fine achievement to his credit, with Maria Theresa's counsellors and generals grouped respectfully on the plinth below her. It was right that the crowds should applaud and cheer when their Emperor shook hands with Kaspar. Only one disappointment slightly marred Francis Joseph's day: 'Though you had kindly pointed out to me the privileged stand for spectators, because of the distance and the great mass of people, it was impossible for me to identify you there', he wrote to Katharina Schratt before breakfast a couple of days later. 'Although I especially looked that way, as you perhaps noticed, I had to content myself with a feeling you were there and knowing you were quite close'. But, as he reminded his friend, there would be the banks of the Wolfgangsee in the hot summer months ahead.

Chapter 16

MAYERLING AND AFTER

'On Monday, I will settle at Mayerling', Crown Prince Rudolf told Bombelles on the last Wednesday in July 1887; 'It will suit me very well'. In retrospect the comment seems heavy with portent, for within eighteen months his death at Mayerling was to give the place a tragic notoriety which still provokes occasional headlines in Vienna's tabloid press. But there was nothing sinister in Rudolf's message. The forested hills around Baden and Mödling, less than 20 miles from the capital, had long attracted him. He appreciated the leafy silence of the woods; he once wrote perceptively of their beauty, of changing shades of green in beeches and oaks, 'on a beautiful June evening, when the last rays of the sun throw a golden light on the rounded crest of the hills'. Like other visitors to the region, he was intrigued by relics of its tumultuous past: an isolated watchtower against Turkish invaders standing above the valleys, as if it were a landscaped Gothic ruin; or a monastery set among the lower meadows, enabling (as Rudolf wrote) 'the Angelus to ring out in resonant tones from the lofty spires' and mingle 'with the melancholy sound of the shepherd's horn'. In this enchanting woodland he sought a secluded and compact home. He found it at Mayerling, where a fifteenth century chapel and pilgrim's hospice, twice ravaged by the Turks, had been restored for a third time by Abbot Grunbeck of Heiligenkreuz, the great Cistercian abbey a few miles to the east. Early in 1887 Rudolf purchased the buildings from the white monks for conversion into a hunting lodge. By Christmas his personal stationery carried the letterhead 'Schloss Mayerling' beneath the embossed antlers of a deer. Outside the lodge walls a Holy Sepulchre chapel kept faith with the pilgrim past.

His son's acquisition of Mayerling was of little concern to Francis Joseph, who never visited the Schloss until after Rudolf's death. Yet this indifference to Rudolf's activities did not spring from any conflict of generations, and it would be a mistake to assume that relations between father and son were constantly strained. The Emperor continued to be impressed by Rudolf's wide range of interests. When Count Samuel Teleki wished to give Rudolf's name to the huge lake he had discovered in East Africa, the Emperor gave his approval, seeing the Count's request as a tribute to his son's backing of scientific discovery. And Francis Joseph was well aware that he could not have opened Vienna's prestigious 'Electrical Exhibition' in August 1883 with a speech of such confident authenticity as his son. 'May an ocean of light radiate from this city, may new progress arise from it', were sentiments which encouraged Rudolf's generation; from his socially conservative father they would have seemed derisively insincere. The Crown Prince enjoyed a felicitous gift for public speaking denied to the Emperor and, indeed, to most Archdukes as well.

Francis Joseph welcomed Rudolf's initiative in encouraging the publication of *Die Osterreichisch-ungarische Monarchie in Wort und Bild*, a twenty-four volume encyclopaedic survey of the Habsburg realm 'in word and picture'. The Crown Prince made substantial contributions himself (including the rhapsodic passages on Lower Austria quoted earlier in this chapter). In December 1885 he presented the Emperor with the first printed volume of a project which, though always called 'the Crown Prince's work' was not finished until thirteen years after the Mayerling tragedy. Francis Joseph was also pleased by the publication in Austrian weekly periodicals of several travel articles in which his son showed a detailed knowledge of bird and animal life in the Holy Land (which he had visited shortly before his marriage) and in Corfu and Albania. But the extent of Rudolf's political journalism remained unsuspected by his father.

Despite these strangely varied intellectual pursuits, Rudolf still regarded himself as a professional soldier. Like his father he recognized that the army was the cement binding the provinces of the common Monarchy in an uncommon unity. But there was a marked difference in the attitude of the two men towards the function of the armed forces. The Emperor placed increasing emphasis on the traditional role of his officers as dynastic surrogates bringing a gold-braided splendour to distant towns scattered across a rambling Empire. By contrast, Rudolf sought to promote new ideas in the old regiments, striving for an alert wartime efficiency and encouraging such curious experiments as the creation in 1886 of a 'penny-farthing' bicycle corps. His father, distrusting all such novelties and irritated by his son's advocacy of a preventive war during the Bulgarian crises, thought Rudolf too immature to be entrusted with high military responsibility.

So, on other grounds, did the influential Inspector General of the common army. 'Uncle Albrecht' never ceased to regard the heir to the throne as a rebellious liberal. Rudolf's links with radical journalists both in Vienna and Budapest alarmed the Archduke and prime minister Taaffe, too, although neither man realized the full extent of his contacts. They seem to have thought, with good reason, that Rudolf's volatile temperament inclined him to careless conversation with his intimates, thus making him (in later parlance) a 'security risk'. Rudolf, however, always remained surprised by the hostility of 'the gentlemen who hold the reins of government'. In the spring of 1888 he expected to receive the command of the Second Army Corps, with headquarters in Vienna itself. Instead, he was made Inspector-General of Infantry, a specially created post with ill-defined duties which were carefully monitored by the supreme inspector, Uncle Albrecht. Already, on several occasions, Rudolf had complained privately of persecution by the Emperor's inner circle of military advisers: as he once wrote to Bombelles, 'they fear I may grow out of the common, comfortable pattern and thereby differ from most of my relations'. Now 'they' had shown their power. From March 1888 onwards the Crown Prince's outlook on political life was soured by a deep and bitter sense of frustration.

Much of his resentment was turned against his father. He always exaggerated Francis Joseph's detailed knowledge of the day-to-day life of his officers: there is an odd letter from him to Archduke Francis Ferdinand as early as November 1884, in which he warns his cousin to avoid military escapades, for 'the Emperor knows everything' about such matters. In this assumption Rudolf was totally wrong: Francis Joseph may have had the command structure at his finger-tips; he may regularly have examined requests from commissioned officers for permission to marry; but the meticulous study of reports laid before him gave the Emperor no real insight into garrison life. On the other hand the police chief in Vienna, Baron Alfred von Krauss, knew a great deal about the seamier activities of the younger Archdukes: Mizzi Caspar, the sultry cocotte dancer who for many years offered her favours to Rudolf and his fellow officers (including, on at least one occasion, Francis Ferdinand), found it useful to have among her protectors a skilful lawyer, Florian Meissner; and Meissner was a diligent police informer. Some of the intelligence reaching Krauss from Meissner and other spies was made known to Taaffe but, since the prime minister believed in seeking as quiet a life as politics permitted him to enjoy, he saw no reason to disturb his sovereign master with disagreeable scandal. Francis Joseph knew his son's conduct was far from chaste, but he cannot have realized what dangerous enemies the Crown Prince was making by compounding dissolute behaviour with the ruthless lash of a sarcastic tongue.

Rudolf could still exercise great charm, however. It showed itself in London, where in May 1887 he was his father's representative at Queen

Victoria's Golden Jubilee celebrations, and it frequently permeates his private letters, when he wishes to appear as the family man. He continued to treat Stephanie with indulgent affection, even if their marriage bonds had by now worn thin. The Crown Princess was unlikely to conceive another child despite frequent visits to Franzensbad, a spa in western Bohemia whose waters reputedly countered sterility. Yet she fulfilled all her official duties, often accompanying her husband to the provincial capitals. Stephanie was a woman of courage and determination; she insisted on being with Rudolf when, in June 1888, he defied death threats to visit Sarajevo and Mostar. But on one such journey – to Galicia at midsummer in 1887 – she fell in love with a Polish Count. For the next eighteen months she made as little effort to hide her feelings from her husband as he to conceal his lapses from her. Gossip maintained that late in 1888 Rudolf was seeking divorce, or a papal annulment of his marriage. He is said to have quarrelled with his father over the matter; but there is no written evidence, and it is all unlikely. A tolerance of infidelities, and love for 'little Erzsi', kept the marriage together.

Stephanie remained concerned over Rudolf's health. As winter drew to a close in 1886 persistent bronchitis, together with rheumatic pains, had left him so weak that the Emperor insisted he should spend a month on the island of Lacroma, off Dubrovnik, to build up his strength. But he never made a full recovery. A few months later he told Stephanie, 'I am keeping the cough under control with morphine, although it is a dangerous drug'. Ever since his boyhood fall from a tree, he experienced occasional blinding headaches; their incidence now increased. Soon he seemed dependent on morphia, and began drinking far too much. His handwriting, which in contrast to that of his father and grandmother was always bold and well-formed, deteriorated rapidly. By the time of his visit to Bosnia he looked seriously ill. It is probable that he had contracted gonorrhoea.

There is, however, no convincing evidence for much of the gossip embellished in reminiscences after the Mayerling tragedy. Legend has, for example, perpetuated rumours of serious rifts within the imperial family. Rudolf certainly did not conceal his disapproval of his sister Valerie's determination to marry her childhood friend, Archduke Francis Salvator, from the Tuscan branch of the Habsburgs; although it is by no means clear why Rudolf was so hostile to their distant cousin. But over this question Francis Joseph agreed with his son: the Emperor would have preferred Valerie to seek marriage with the heir apparent of either Portugal or Saxony rather than with a penniless kinsman. Francis Joseph sought to understand all three of his children, but it was hard for a father who was shy of carefree human contacts to attain any intimacy with a son of such unpredictable temperament. Yet, although their personal interests were for the most part so different, Francis Joseph and Rudolf often went stalking together. On one such expedition, made shortly before he acquired Mayerling, the Crown Prince allegedly disobeyed the safety rules; he fired a shot at distant stags which wounded his father's gun-bearer in the arm and narrowly missed the Emperor's head. For such irresponsible behaviour Rudolf is said to have been banned from sub-sequent imperial shooting parties. This tale, however, was not made public until forty years later; even if true in substance, it seems much exaggerated. Only four weeks before his death Rudolf was hunting beside his father in Styria – 'and in the most cheerful spirits', as Francis Joseph sadly recalled in the following autumn.

The Crown Prince's interest in high politics intensified rather than diminished during the years when his health seemed to be deteriorating. He was by now more critical of the Czech political leaders than in his years of residence at Prague and he included among his boon companions several prominent Hungarians. But it would be a mistake to assume he was in any way sympathetic to Magyar claims for independence or for changing the structure of the imperial–royal army. Moreover he was critical of Hungary's treatment of her minorities; he particularly sym-pathized with the Croats, whose past services to the Habsburg dynasty he stressed during a visit to Zagreb in 1888 at which he received a warm welcome. The Crown Prince was more interested in the European balance of power than in the internal affairs of the Monarchy. In April 1888 'Julius Felix' – Rudolf's final pen-name – published in Paris a 15,000 word German language 'Open Letter to His Majesty Emperor Francis Joseph I' on 'Austria-Hungary and its Alliances'. The pamphlet argued that the Dual Monarchy was in danger of destruction in a war caused by Prussian militarism and that the most effective way of keeping peace in Europe was by cultivating the friendship of France and Great Britain. The pam-phlet ended with a patriotic clarion call: 'Away with Prussia! May Austria and the Habsburgs flourish!'

The authorship of the 'Open Letter' was a well-kept secret and there is no indication that Francis Joseph ever read it. Had he done so, he would hardly have agreed with his son's reasoning: 'I believe that, over all political and military questions, the lynchpin of our policies must be the broadest of agreements and the greatest solidarity with Germany', he wrote in a private letter to his old friend, King Albert of Saxony. But Rudolf thought differently: as William II recalled in exile nearly forty years later, 'his soul revolted from the Prussian idea'. On 11 March 1888, four days before Rudolf arrived in Berlin for William I's funeral, Szeps's *Neues Wiener Tagblatt* printed an anonymous obituary, which the Crown Prince had drafted a few years before: it paid grudging tribute to 'a Prussian through and through' who was 'convinced that all his actions, no matter how unjust they might be, were in obedience to God's will ... He saw himself as the protector of all sound conservative ideas, but even so he stole land from his neighbours. Neither his son nor his grandson have any resemblance to him', Rudolf's article concluded, 'With Emperor William died the last of his kind'.

Within a hundred days, there was a second royal funeral in Berlin. Emperor Frederick, gravely ill with cancer at his accession, died on 15 June. His successor, William II – the 'Kaiser Bill' of First World War propaganda – was only six months younger than Rudolf, and the two princes had known each other well since 1873 when 'Willy' accompanied his father and mother on their visit to the World Exhibition in the Prater. On that occasion the German Crown Princess thought her son seemed an uncouth 'bear or a schoolboy beside Rudolf'; but both sets of parents assumed the two fourteen-year olds would become firm friends. They did not; in temperament and outlook on politics they remained poles apart. William deplored Rudolf's 'faults of character', his failure to 'take religion at all seriously': conversely the Crown Prince thought him an unctuous humbug. Rudolf took pleasure in re-telling how, not long before his accession, Germany's new master came on a courtesy call to Austria and borrowed 3,000 florins from him 'for an indefinite time' in order to pay for dubious pleasures in Vienna – a tale which much amused Francis Joseph when he heard of it. More seriously, both father and son regarded the young William II with some suspicion. Francis Joseph could not fail to notice the enthusiasm with which Austria's Pan-Germans welcomed the change of sovereign in Berlin, but he hoped to maintain the close dynastic links forged in William I's final years. Rudolf was less sanguine: he was convinced of William's hostility towards Austria in general and the Habsburgs in particular. 'William II will do well; probably he will soon stir up deep trouble in old Europe', he wrote to Szeps on 24 August with perceptive irony, 'Quite likely in the course of a few years he will cut Hohenzollern Germany down to the size it deserves'.

Yet was Rudolf more depressed than this tone of cynical resignation suggests? On one occasion in that summer he had a strange conversation with Mizzi Caspar, who was then living in the Feldgasse at Mödling, a few miles from Mayerling. The Crown Prince proposed she should accompany him to the 'Hussar Temple', a neo-classical memorial to the bravery of officers who died at Aspern in 1809 which stands on a promontory in the wooded hills south of Mödling. Would she, Rudolf asked, be prepared to die with him? They would, he explained, make a fine gesture, shooting themselves in front of the monument dedicated 'To

Emperor and Fatherland'. Mizzi laughed, dismissing the suggestion as preposterous: for a Crown Prince to dash off Viennese dialect lyrics for tavern songs which lauded a girl's 'dark charms' was flattering, but an invitation to strengthen his wavering courage by sharing the last shots of his revolver was a terminal honour she could not believe he offered in earnest. She was a vivacious extrovert, too excited by life to end it prematurely (though, sadly, her health was to give way and she died at 42). Mizzi maintained that she put the conversation at the back of her mind until she was alarmed by his odd behaviour four months later. Yet did she never mention his strange proposal to any of her close acquaintances that summer? Not all were Rudolf's drinking companions: a ruthless enemy, hearing of his frailty of resolve, might seek and find a young romantic so infatuated with the Crown Prince that she would allow her flame of passion to sear the senses and accept the suicide pact Mizzi had scorned.

Rudolf's soul-searching was totally alien to his father's mode of thought and action. Far lesser problems perplexed Francis Joseph that autumn. How was he to entertain three foreign visitors, the Prince of Wales, the German Emperor and the King of Serbia, as well as his personal friend, Albert of Saxony? The Prince, an attentive host to the Crown Prince in England, reached Vienna on 10 September and spent much of his time with Rudolf, who in a letter to Stephanie admired 'the indefatigability . . . of the old boy'. The imminent arrival of William II cast a shadow before it. 'I am glad to have Wales as a guest', Rudolf wrote to Stephanie, 'but I would invite William only in order to arrange a discreet hunting mishap'. Together Rudolf and the Prince went to the races at Freudenau; they hunted evasive bears in Transylvania; and they shot thirty chamois in seven hours on the crags of Styria. More commendably, with fine contempt for the mounting anti-semitism of the capital, they lunched at the most famous of Vienna's restaurants with the Jewish philanthropist and financier, Baron Moritz Hirsch. They also accompanied the Emperor on a shoot at Gödöllö and joined him for the army manoeuvres in Croatia. Francis Joseph was less appreciative of his guest's company than his son: 'By trotting and galloping I went to some pains to shake off the Prince of Wales but I could not do it', he wrote to Katharina Schratt after the manoeuvres were over, 'The fat man was always with me and held out quite unbelievably, only he got very stiff and tore his red Hussar trousers and, as he was wearing nothing underneath, that must have been very uncomfortable for him'. When 'the fat man' discovered that William II would arrive in Vienna on 3 October, he wished to be there to greet his nephew: they had, after all, been in the city together at the time of Rudolf's wedding. Now, however, their relative ranks were different: the Prince

had spoken privately but unwisely of his contempt for William's pretensions; and the German embassy in Vienna made it clear that their
sovereign was not prepared to meet his uncle during the state visit. The
Prince of Wales, somewhat affronted, withdrew temporarily to Roumania.

For Francis Joseph it was tediously embarrassing. And there was, too,
the problem of Schönerer's noisy followers. The Emperor agreed with
Taaffe that strict precautions should be taken to prevent the Pan-Germans
exploiting the visit of their 'hope for the future, the beacon light of
the German people'. On 29 September Rudolf informed Kálnoky, with
evident satisfaction, that 'the Emperor ordered me today' to make certain
'. . . the German Emperor should not walk about alone in Vienna' for fear
of the excitement his presence might arouse, but 'the matter should be
handled with extreme care so that the real intention cannot be discerned'.
At the same time Francis Joseph summoned Archduke Francis Ferdinand
to the capital in order to support the Crown Prince as he trod the
Hohenzollern trail.

William II's visit was not a success: after attending an Austrian military
review he had the effrontery to criticize in conversation with Francis
Joseph and Elizabeth the turn-out of the infantry and the effectiveness of
its chief inspector, Crown Prince Rudolf. William was only in Vienna for
three days, followed by five wet days at Mürzsteg, but Francis Joseph
found 'the festivities' hard to 'survive', especially once the Empress
escaped to the peace and sunshine of Corfu. His guest's aggressive
ebullience left him ill at ease. With candid relief he let Katharina Schratt
know on 5 October that 'My toast at yesterday's dinner, of which I was
extremely nervous, I managed to deliver without getting stuck and without
a prompter'. After William's departure for Rome, he awaited the return
of the 'fat man' and the coming of the King of Serbia with equanimity.

On 14 October the Emperor and his royal guests went to the gala
opening of the new Burgtheater on the Ringstrasse. In the audience the
Prince of Wales noticed a seventeen-year old girl whom (as he later told
Queen Victoria) he had 'met frequently at Homburg and Vienna' and
whose mother, aunts and uncles he had known 'for the last 16 years'; by
the Prince of Wales's reckoning Baroness Mary Vetsera was 'a charming
young lady and certainly one of the prettiest and most admired in Vienna'.
Others would have agreed with him in London, where Mary had been
with her mother earlier that year. Most enthusiastic race-goers in England
knew of the family, especially Mary's uncles, Hector and Aristide Baltazzi,
one of whom had owned the Derby winner of 1876, 'Kisber'. Although
Francis Joseph had recently warned Katharina Schratt to be wary of
Hector, since he did 'not have an entirely correct reputation in racing and
money matters', the Prince of Wales knew nothing to their social det-

riment. At the Burgtheater he duly 'pointed out' Mary Vetsera to his neighbour, the Crown Prince, 'and said how handsome she was'. To the Prince's surprise Rudolf 'spoke I thought disparagingly of her'. Yet, though the Crown Prince knew her by sight and had been hotly pursued by her mother in his bachelor days, he seems never to have met Mary socially, and his comments were either prompted by hearsay or from the distant assessment of a cynically roving eye. Within three weeks of the Burgtheater gala they had become intimate acquaintances, and it is possible the Prince of Wales first aroused Rudolf's interest in Mary; but it is unlikely that he introduced them to each other, as one of Rudolf's journalist friends maintained. For that fateful connection the Crown Prince's first cousin, Marie Larisch, was responsible.

Countess Marie Larisch was the daughter of Empress Elizabeth's eldest brother, who in 1857 renounced his rights in order to marry, morgantically, the actress Henriette Mendel (created Baroness von Wallersee two years later). The Empress, who treated Henriette with more kindness than other members of the family, grew fond of her niece at an early age; she particularly admired Marie's horsemanship, which was far superior to that of Elizabeth's own children, and in 1875 she invited Marie to become an attendant Lady of the Imperial and Royal Household at Gödöllö, where her musicality and vivacity soon made her welcome. But ambition tempted Marie to overstep the mark. With boundless confidence she threw herself at her cousin, Rudolf, with whom by 1877 she was flirting outrageously. Even more rashly she turned her siren charm on her Aunt Sisi's favourite riding companions. In that autumn the Empress encouraged – or ruthlessly arranged – Marie's marriage to the wealthy Lieutenant Count Georg Larisch von Moennich, the best-natured nitwit in Francis Joseph's army. Thereafter, though the Countess outwardly remained a dutiful niece, she lost all sympathy or gratitude towards her aunt: from scattering spiteful gossip around the outer fringe of high society she graduated in later years to the writing of inventive memoirs in which her malicious venom spared neither Elizabeth nor Francis Joseph.

Yet in a fitful way Marie Larisch was clever. More readily than his closer relatives she perceived the swift changes of Rudolf's temperament. She was also sensitive to the gnawing hopes of others eager for social advancement: indeed, to satisfy them became the mainspring of her oddly warped vocation. In this role she befriended the recently widowed Baroness Helene Vetsera and became the confidante of her daughter Mary, who made no secret of her infatuation for the Crown Prince. In the late autumn of 1888 Marie Larisch arranged a casual meeting between Mary and the Crown Prince in the Prater. Soon afterwards – on Monday, 5 November – the Countess took Mary 'shopping' with her in Vienna, visiting a photographer. In the evening she brought Mary to Rudolf's rooms in the Hofburg, using the back stair entrance to gain admission from the ramp leading up to the Albertina.

Mary Vetsera left a record of that Monday in a private letter which her mother subsequently transcribed and published. It mentions the visit to the photographer and their arrival at the Crown Prince's apartments. The letter continues, 'Marie introduced me, and he said, "Excuse me, but I would like to talk to the Countess privately for a few minutes '. Then they withdrew to another room. I looked around me. On his desk was a revolver and a skull. I picked up the skull, raised it between my hands and looked at it from all sides. Suddenly Rudolf returned and took it from me with deep concern. When I said I wasn't afraid, he smiled'. Other clandestine meetings followed over the next few weeks. Yet, however deep Mary's passion, for two months she can have meant little more to Rudolf than earlier women whom the trusted Nehammer led up the back stairs of the Hofburg. Not until 13 January did Mary know the fearful delight of love fulfilled, as more than one of her pathetic letters testifies. By then their lives had only a fortnight to run.

The Emperor was in Hungary on the Monday, Marie Larisch took Mary Vetsera to the Hofburg, and the Empress was still in Corfu. After what he considered a light day's work – 'a mere 50 audiences' in the old royal palace at Buda – Francis Joseph went back to Gödöllö that evening. Snow showers ruled out all prospect of hunting and, as he wrote to Katharina Schratt, 'I found time to get much pleasure' from reading the 'extremely handsome and fascinatingly written' book she had sent him – *Vom Nachtswachter zum türkishchen Kaiser* (From Night Watchman to Turkish Emperor), reminiscences of theatrical life in Vienna by Karl Sonntag. A few years previously he would never have opened such a book. Now, in the absence of the Empress, he was entranced by the backstage world of the theatre, its feuds, rivalries and superstitions. While Elizabeth sought refuge in the classical past, throughout much of the last quarter of the year her husband also escaped from present realities by 'reviving in my memory so much that I had long forgotten . . . particularly about the Burgtheater', and by discovering in 'what lively and peculiar ways things were done in the theatre' where 'almost everything seems possible'. It was not simply Sonntag's book which sustained Francis Joseph's interest. He continued to seek information on stage affairs, as intrigued by what was likely to happen as a modern devotee of some television soap-opera. 'You make me especially happy when you write to me about the theatre', he told Katharina; characteristically he then felt bound to add, 'That is not very high-minded of me; but it is true, just the same'.

As yet, there were no pressing political problems calling for attention that winter. For the past two years there had, however, been a groundswell of discontent in Hungary after a series of insensitive actions by senior non-Magyar officers of the Budapest garrison (who were publicly defended by Archduke Albrecht). It was therefore clear that when Tisza's proposed Army Bill was ready for presentation to parliament early in 1889, any clauses which favoured Germanic traditions and practices were likely to receive rough treatment from Hungarian nationalists – including Count Pista Károlyi, who was a friend of both Rudolf and the Prince of Wales. But during his long stay at Gödöllö the Emperor was not embarrassed by political demonstrations and received a loyal and royal reception from all the great landowners, including Károlyi. The danger of serious unrest in Budapest seemed less acute than in Vienna, where police agents kept a close eye on the street politicians: Schönerer's Pan-Germans were a noisy threat, but there was also strong following in the capital for the anti-semitic Christian Union, founded by Karl Lueger in November 1887; and the socialists were active, with plans to unify the social democrat factions at a congress to be held at Hainfeld, in Lower Austria, on New Year's Day. More immediately Francis Joseph was worried by family matters and especially by his wife's peace of mind; for he suspected that Valerie would soon wish to marry, and he knew that the prospect of losing Valerie's companionship would sadden Elizabeth. He had to telegraph bad news to the Empress from Munich. Her father, who suffered a stroke in the summer, died on 15 November. It was impossible for her to return to Bavaria for the funeral, but the Court was plunged into mourning. The Emperor and Empress were reunited on 1 December at Miramare where, next day, they quietly celebrated the fortieth anniversary of his accession.

Amid all this relative calm, a political storm gathered around the Crown Prince, for which he was largely responsible. On the last day of October, when Francis Joseph was already in Hungary, a new weekly, *Schwarzgeld*, went on sale in Austria. The name showed impeccable Habsburg loyalty; but the journal was strongly hostile to the Pan-Germans and their Hohenzollern idol; and the tone of the articles echoed the Crown Prince in his more unguarded moments. Foreign observers rightly assumed that *Schwarzgeld* had Rudolf's backing, and there was an inevitable response from beyond the frontier. A scandalous book by the extreme anti-semite Charles Drumont had been published in Paris in October, with a preface which denounced Rudolf's alleged links with Jewish high finance. Early in November, immediately after the first issue of *Schwarzgeld*, Drumont's attack was taken up in two German newspapers with a relatively small readership; they claimed to have knowledge of the Crown Prince's long concealed love affair with 'a Jewess'. On 28 November, when the fourth issue of *Schwarzgeld* appeared, two influential Prussian dailies associated with Bismarck went into action, emphasizing not simply the Crown Prince's involvement with Jewish big business, but the 'envious hatred' which he showed toward Germany's new ruler. Meanwhile the Italian paper *L'Epoca* also joined the fray, with a prurient titbit on 15 November informing readers that the heir to the Habsburg throne 'led a most dissolute life'.

Francis Joseph must have been aware of the general course of this international press war, for semi-official newspapers in Vienna and Budapest responded by printing articles extolling the Crown Prince's virtues. He also knew Rudolf's prejudices too well to believe he was the innocent victim of journalistic spite. But he does not seem to have realized that his son was behind the launching of *Schwarzgeld*; nor can he possibly have imagined the depth of Rudolf's willingness to smear William II's reputation. For, three days after his first meeting with Mary Vetsera in the Hofburg, Rudolf sent Szeps what he called 'an unsavoury article on William II'. This racily written contribution gave details of William's private behaviour during his visit to Austria in 1887; his affair with a former lady-in-waiting to the Queen of Württemberg, their evening rendezvous 'in the Catholic cemetery at Mürzsteg', the attempts of the German ambassador to hush up the scandal when a claim for alimony was subsequently put forward, and the name of the lawyer ('Dr Meissner') upon whose discretion the ambassador relied – almost certainly the same Florian Meissner to whom Mizzi Caspar turned for legal protection, and who had close contact with police chief Krauss. There was nothing sensational about William's alleged sexual ethics; they conformed to the standard casually observed by many officers, Archdukes included. But his conduct was ill-suited to the mood of Providential mission in which he had exalted since his accession. Szeps knew that in Vienna he dared not use such explosive information. At the Crown Prince's suggestion, Szeps forwarded the 'unsavoury article' to Paris, where he had close friends working for *Figaro*: they, too, thought the scoop too hot to print; 'the story' (as Rudolf called it) was not made public until all concerned in it were dead. Yet did no one other than the editors read the unsavoury article? For the Crown Prince it was a dangerous tale to have put in circulation at such a time.

It is difficult to discover who knew what in Vienna during Rudolf's last ten weeks of life. On 19 November he had a bad fall from his horse but insisted on keeping news of the accident secret; and yet it was so serious that, according to a close friend, it 'brought his brains into disorder, at least he complained frequently of headache and stomach trouble'. Francis Joseph did not hear of the fall, nor was he aware of the interest Krauss's agents had begun to take by early December in the secret assignations of Mary Vetsera. So convinced was Krauss that the Crown Prince's affections had shifted from Mizzi Caspar to Mary that when – at Florian Meissner's prompting – Mizzi reported to him further talk of suicide, as well as Rudolf's original conversation in the previous summer, the chief of police merely filed away her sworn statement, cautioning her to keep the matter to herself; Krauss believed she was a cast-off lover over-dramatizing incidents in order to boost her falling esteem. Francis Joseph does not seem to have had any warning of his son's troubled state of mind, and he ignored any physical manifestations of his illness. On one occasion, apparently before Christmas, Crown Princess Stephanie broke the conventions by insisting on seeing the Emperor privately in order to draw his attention to her husband's poor health. Could he not, she asked, be sent away from Vienna on a goodwill voyage around the world? Francis Joseph was unperturbed. 'There is nothing the matter with Rudolf', he replied, 'He is rather pale, rushes about too much, demands too much of himself; he should stay at home with you more than he does'.

The Christmas festivities at the Hofburg were brief that year, for on 26 December the Empress had arranged to go to Munich to console her widowed mother, taking Archduchess Marie Valerie with her. Gifts were exchanged at half past four on Christmas Eve – Elizabeth's 51st birthday – in (as Francis Joseph wrote) 'an intimate family circle, just our children and our little granddaughter'. Rudolf presented his mother with eleven autograph letters by Heine, which he had commissioned Szeps to bring back for him from Paris. That evening the family celebrated Valerie's betrothal to Francis Salvator, with the Crown Prince in his most benign mood. His parents' thoughts were concentrated on their daughter's immediate future. Francis Joseph was sorry for himself; with Elizabeth's departure he was, as he wrote, 'a grass-widower again'. He could not even talk theatre with Katharina Schratt, for she was in quarantine, her son having caught measles; she was not allowed to write to the Emperor, only to send him telegrams. On 29 December, to ease his loneliness, Francis Joseph paid, for the last time, a purely social call on Anna Nahowski in Hietzing.

By the second week in January 1889 his gloom was lifting. He had spent some days at Mürzsteg, hunting not very profitably but in the company of Rudolf, who was outwardly in good spirits; and the Empress and Valerie were safely back from Munich, though he thought Elizabeth tired herself by working too hard at modern Greek. He was himself busy with routine paperwork, notably reports from Hungary on Tisza's army bill, which included a controversial proposal requiring reserve officers to pass a new examination in German. Yet Hungary was not a pressing problem; Tisza could take care of the linguistic nationalists. For Francis Joseph the worst cloud on the horizon was William II's birthday on Sunday, 27 January; he was expected to attend a soirée at the German embassy ('it pleases me little') and preside over a state dinner ('could last too long').

Would the Crown Prince join in the celebrations? The question aroused wide speculation at Court and in the diplomatic corps that week. Rudolf held honorary rank in the 2nd Prussian Lancers; courtesy obliged him to appear at the Embassy reception in his German uniform. On 16 January, however, the twelfth issue of *Schwarzgeld* carried on its front-page 'Ten Commandments of an Austrian': they included 'Thou shalt have no Emperor other than thine own Emperor' and 'Thou shalt not make an idol of Prussia, nor of the Germany over which Prussia rules'. Both in Austria and abroad this decalogue of dynastic patriotism was openly associated with Rudolf, who may well have drafted it. During the following week British, French and Russian diplomats all commented on the Crown Prince's renewed hostility towards Germany; and newspaper articles suggested that he favoured a reversal of alliances, with Austria-Hungary abandoning Germany and Italy in favour of France and Russia. Not surprisingly, Francis Joseph summoned his son to an audience on the morning before the birthday celebrations.

There is no record of what was said. Did the Emperor insist that Rudolf should cut his links with journalism? Did the Crown Prince urge a change of policy at home and abroad? Were 'unsavoury' aspects of his private life questioned? Nobody knows. Voices were certainly raised one court dignitary maintaining that he heard the Emperor shout at his son, 'You are not worthy to be my successor'; and Rudolf appeared to be angry when he left the Hofburg that Saturday morning. It is probable that his father's obduracy threw him into a black mood of frustrated depression from which he never emerged. But he was at the embassy reception next evening, properly turned out as a Prussian Lancer, although complaining that 'the whole uniform is distasteful to me'. Lady Paget, the British ambassador's wife, noticed that, when Francis Joseph arrived, Rudolf 'bent low over his father's hand, touching it almost with his lips'. It was the last meeting between father and son.

Contemporaries who were not at the reception maintain that there were dramatic scenes, with the Emperor pointedly turning his back on his son, and with the Crown Princess and Mary Vetsera glaring at each other 'like tigers ready to spring'. Lady Paget saw no such confrontation and nor did General Beck, though he recognized Mary Vetsera: she left early, he noted, having barely taken her eyes off the Crown Prince, while Beck saw him looking intensely at her on several occasions. That night, however,

Rudolf was with Mizzi Caspar until three in the morning. He had already told his servants he would leave the Hofburg before noon on Monday for Mayerling, having arranged for a small shoot in the neighbouring woods on Tuesday. By 11.50 a police agent spotted the Crown Prince's carriage well south of the city.

Soon afterwards an agitated Countess Larisch sought out the chief of police. She told Krauss that, while she was settling an account at a shop in central Vienna, her companion Mary Vetsera had stepped out of the carriage in which they had been travelling and was driven away by another coachman. The Countess contacted one of Mary's uncles who thought the Crown Prince might be involved: was he, perhaps, at Mayerling? Krauss, who was not unfamiliar with the escapades of Archdukes and their ladies, insisted that his authority extended to neither the Hofburg nor Mayerling. Not until early on Tuesday afternoon, after further visits from Marie Larisch and Mary's family, did Krauss make a report to Taaffe: he had suggested to Alexander Baltazzi that he should travel out to Mayerling, find if Mary was there, but keep the whole affair as quiet as possible, for no uncle would wish to give journalists the chance to sully a niece's reputation. Though Baltazzi ignored this advice and did not go to Mayerling, Taaffe backed Krauss's handling of the problem; as prime minister he welcomed decisions involving him in no action whatsoever.

That Tuesday evening Francis Joseph was disconcerted when Rudolf failed to arrive at the Hofburg in time for a family dinner party. An explanation by the Crown Princess mollified him: she had received a telegram from Mayerling; Rudolf was suffering from a sudden feverish cold and sent his apologies. This thin tale was confirmed by Stephanie's brother-in-law, Prince Philip of Coburg, who had just arrived from May-erling and was due to return there by the early morning train to Baden. He told Francis Joseph that Rudolf had felt so unwell after breakfast that he declined to go shooting with his two guests, the Prince of Coburg and Count Hoyos, the Court Chamberlain. Somewhat sourly, Archduke Albrecht remarked that the Crown Prince had been expected to take the chair at a meeting of the directors of the proposed Army Museum that Tuesday. The visitor's book for 1889, showing the Crown Prince's titles beside a blank space where he was to sign his name, is now an exhibit at the Heeresgeschichtliches Museum.

On Wednesday morning (30 January) the routine of life at the Hofburg slipped naturally into a familiar pattern. By 10.30 the Empress was learning Greek, the Crown Princess practising singing, the Emperor finishing the day's second session of desk work; he was anticipating an hour's relaxation in Katharina Schratt's company, for Elizabeth had invited their 'good friend' to join them at eleven. A cab from the Sudbahnhof arrived at the inner courtyard. From it Count Hoyos stepped down; he sought out the Emperor's adjutant and told him how, a few hours earlier, he and the Prince of Coburg had found the Crown Prince and Mary Vetsera dead in a locked room at Mayerling. Neither Hoyos nor the adjutant wished to break the terrible news to the Emperor – that, they decided, was a wife's responsibility, even though Francis Joseph himself always insisted that Elizabeth should be spared emotional shocks. The Greek lesson was interrupted; and the Empress, though momentarily in a state of collapse, drew on her latent inner strength of character and went to Francis Joseph. Their son lay dead at Mayerling, poisoned by Mary Vetsera, she told him; for that was what she had been led to believe. Soon afterwards, Elizabeth had to receive Mary's distraught mother who, knowing nothing of events at Mayerling, had come to the palace seeking news of her daughter: now she too learnt the grim truth from Elizabeth. Not, of course, the whole truth, for scandal must be avoided: no mention of a second body at Mayerling: no mention of poison. 'Remember' Elizabeth insisted, as she left Helene Vetsera to her grief, 'Rudolf died of heart failure'.

So, too, reported the special editions of newspapers which went on sale in Vienna in the late afternoon. No one believed the announcement: a heart-attack at thirty in a sturdy family with no record of thrombosis? Even before the court physician reached Mayerling for his autopsy, suspicion of an official cover-up was rife; it was compounded by the evasions and contradictions of the following days. On 2 February a revised statement, admitting Rudolf's suicide, did nothing to re-assure the public. Had the liberal-minded reformer prince been murdered by political enemies, it was asked? Had a cuckold husband taken revenge on him, others wondered?

Not all the blame for the initial confusion rests with the Emperor. For twenty-four hours he remained misinformed over what had happened; Hoyos, who had spent Monday and Tuesday nights at an outer annex rather than in the Schloss and knew nothing of Mary's presence until the bodies were found, did not examine the corpses before leaving for Vienna, nor did he see Rudolf's revolver – only an empty glass which he assumed had contained cyanide. Early on Tuesday morning Francis Joseph heard a report from his physician and realized, with horror, that his son had shot himself and, almost certainly, his mistress, too. For advice Francis Joseph turned to his prime minister and friend, Taaffe. At their first meeting it was agreed to keep three objectives in mind: to secure papal permission for a full Christian burial, despite the stigma of suicide; to conceal the presence of Mary Vetsera and her fate from press and public;

and to delve deeply into the immediate past to see if Rudolf's friends in any way shared responsibility for the tragedy.

When the dreadful news first broke, the Empress showed 'fortitude and courage which surpassed the power of words to describe', as the British ambassador reported to London. The aftermath was too much for her. The autopsy indicated some abnormality in Rudolf's skull, suggesting he had shot himself 'while in a state of mental derangement'. This statement was sufficient for the Pope, under some pressure, to approve the full rites of burial; but it distressed Elizabeth. She feared she had brought into the family the strain of insanity which haunted the Wittelsbachs: might she herself become certifiably mad, she wondered? Her desire to hide herself away from the public intensified. Neither Elizabeth nor Valerie went to Rudolf's funeral on 5 February: for one and a half hours they remained in prayer, secluded in a private chapel.

For support in 'accompanying the best of sons, the loyalest of subjects to his last resting place' in the Kapuzinerkirche Francis Joseph turned to his elder daughter, Gisela. *The Times* reported:

'During the service the Emperor stood perfectly calm, looking about him with quick movements of the head, as his custom is. After the chanting of the *Libera*, however, His Majesty stepped out from his place, walked up to his son's coffin, knelt down beside it, and with clasped hands remained for a moment or two in prayer. This was a moment of poignant emotion for all present. Not a sound was heard. Nobody coughed, not a dress rustled, not a scabbard clanked on the flagstones. An entire stillness prevailed till the Emperor rose from his knees and walked back calmly to his place'.

'I bore up well', Francis Joseph told Elizabeth and Valerie after the funeral, 'It was only in the crypt that I could endure it no longer'.

Five months after the Crown Prince's funeral the Austrian socialist leader Viktor Adler described the Dual Monarchy as 'despotism softened by casualness'. The famous phrase mocked the working of the government system as a whole; but it might well have applied specifically to the handling of the Mayerling tragedy. The macabre conveyance at dead of night from Mayerling to the Heiligenkreuz graveyard in an ordinary carriage of Mary Vetsera's fully dressed corpse, propped up between two of her uncles, was intended by the authorities to frustrate the probing eyes of journalists already suspicious of what lay concealed behind the Schloss's shuttered windows. As soon as Mary had been secretly buried at Heiligenkreuz, Taaffe visited Helene Vetsera to insist that the family ignore the grave 'while so many reporters infested the district', though later she might exhume her daughter's body for burial elsewhere; meanwhile, on the Emperor's orders, she was temporarily to leave the capital.

This command she was prepared to obey, though protesting that she had every intention of letting her daughter's remains lie in peace. Once away from Vienna she could express herself more freely; and she did. Nothing could halt mounting speculation in the capital, in Budapest and the great provincial cities, or across frontiers where Rudolf was better known than any previous Archduke. Emergency censorship, carrying threats to suspend editors and their journals, was employed to stifle the Austrian press. Clumsy attempts were also made to confiscate foreign newspapers – which then, of course, went on sale at black market prices. Within a week a Munich daily paper was linking Mary Vetsera's name with the Mayerling tragedy: but, to the end of Francis Joseph's reign and beyond, the government in Vienna never acknowledged the connection.

Police-chief Krauss, who had been suspicious from the start of Marie Larisch's role, gained an early success. A note from the Countess, apparently referring to Mary's proposed 'disappearance' from the Larisch carriage, was found crumpled in the pocket of a tunic which, a few days previously, Rudolf had left with an artist who was painting his portrait in uniform. Consequently Marie Larisch found herself permanently banished from Court even before the funeral. Other 'discoveries' were less revealing, however. The police investigations assembled a mass of facts, many of questionable relevance. At the same time, on Taaffe's instructions, the credentials of the Crown Prince's friends were critically examined. Even such trusted servants of the Emperor as Bombelles and Latour came under scrutiny: Bombelles produced a letter written by the Emperor Maximilian in the last days before his execution as testimony to his personal probity, and it is now filed away among Rudolf's surviving papers. So, too, are transcripts from books on Russian history, including an account of the coup which brought Tsar Alexander I to the throne and in which his father was, contrary to the son's instructions, murdered. But it would be wrong to assume from such evidence that Rudolf was studying the technique of palace coups; he had been preparing for a projected trip to St Petersburg, for he had never before visited Russia.

At times it seems as if, like an accomplished crime writer, the police allowed red herrings to float on the surface of the evidence so as to make the search for a solution even harder. Why, for example, did they give such attention to Hungarian affairs? Probably because, during the first weeks of the investigation, hostility to Tisza's Army Bill became increasingly vocal and more violent than at the start of the year. Rudolf, who conscientiously took the trouble to speak Magyar in Hungary, was popular in Budapest. In the summer of 1882 he had briefly thought that, like his great-uncle Ferdinand, he might be crowned King of Hungary during his father's lifetime. Archduke Albrecht, however, strongly opposed such a move, arguing that coronation would necessitate a binding oath to uphold the constitution which would hamper Rudolf if he wished, in later years, to reform the character of the Monarchy as a whole; and Rudolf had recognized the strength of this argument. Never would he support any political agitation seeking to broaden the distinction between Hungary and Cisleithania. In the last weeks of his life the Crown Prince was puzzled by the conduct of his friend, Count Károlyi, who spoke out against the Army Bill in parliament after (so the Budapest press said) receiving a letter from Rudolf. The police investigation discovered that, on the fateful 30 January, Károlyi was travelling to Vienna by train to see the Crown Prince when he heard of his death; at once he turned back for Budapest. But were Károlyi's activities worth intensive scrutiny? Clearly he had sought a personal meeting in order to clarify a misunderstood speech and perhaps to give warning of a mounting crisis and it was natural for an eminent magnate to return home when the kingdom was plunged into mourning. A 'Hungarian conspiracy', tempting the Crown Prince into treason, is a figment of the historical imagination.

That particular exercise of the mind continues to find in the Mayerling tragedy a tempting source of speculation, just as it does in the Jack the Ripper murders which took place in London that same winter: the body of the seventh victim of 'the Monster of the East End' was, in fact, found dismembered in Spitalfields at the end of the week in November 1888 when Mary Vetsera made her first visit to the Crown Prince in the Hofburg. It is no coincidence that these contemporaneous mysteries should have aroused sustained interest for so long; they came at a time when, in continental Europe and in Britain, there was a rapid spread of cheap newspapers, with competing rival editors seeking means of gratifying a new appetite for sensation – as, indeed, Taaffe feared and clumsily sought to combat. Each mystery mixed sex and violent death; each echoed disturbing undertones of anti-semitism; each remained 'unsolved'. Soon they passed into lurid folklore, spawning plays and films, novels and ballets. From time to time they are spiced with new theories based on fresh revelations or fashionable taboos: once political 'reasons' for Rudolf's death lost immediate relevancy, there were hints of incest belatedly discovered and, more recently, of a disastrous abortion.

Much about both mysteries is still puzzling; and over the Mayerling tragedy unanswerable questions remain. Why, for example, was there so long a gap between the arrival of the lovers at the Schloss on Monday afternoon and their deaths on Wednesday morning? Why in a farewell letter to Stephanie – written in his old, firm clarity of hand – did Rudolf tell her that he went to his death 'calmly' and as 'the only way to save my good name'? And why did his note to his sister Valerie say 'I do not die willingly'? The British prime minister, Lord Salisbury, at first believed the Crown Prince had been murdered, a notion hastily scotched by Queen Victoria (who was kept remarkably well-informed, both by the Prince of Wales and by Philip of Coburg). Rudolf fired the fatal shots. Yet it is possible that among the many political enemies he made, some were prepared to seek ways of tempting him to kill himself, surrendering to one of the moments of black despair which his illness engendered. Three near certainties stand out: the Mayerling deaths sprang from a suicide pact, agreed before the couple set out from Vienna; Mary Vetsera was devotedly infatuated with her partner in death, whatever the emotions torturing his brooding mind; and the Crown Prince wretchedly accepted that he could never match up to the standards he believed his father expected from him. Rudolf left messages for his wife, mother and sister, as well as for several friends. But, to Francis Joseph's distress, there was no letter of contrition or farewell for him.

The Crown Prince's premature death made as little difference to Austro-Hungarian political history as the anonymous booklets and articles in which he had preached dynastic patriotism. For the diseases eating him away were so grave that he could no more have become a liberal reformer than Germany's enlightened Emperor of a hundred days, Frederick III. But the Mayerling tragedy left a deeper mark on Francis Joseph's personal life than any earlier misfortune. At first he sought to put pained memories aside, resuming his desk-bound routine while telling Katharina Schratt of his worries for the health of the Empress, 'whom I can see is filled with a deep, silent agony'. He talked personally, with sympathy and a measure of understanding, to many sorrowing members of Rudolf's household, trying through them to make sense of the incomprehensible. 'All this does no good at all', he confessed to Frau Schratt on 5 March, 'But one cannot possibly think of anything else, and talking at least brings a certain relief ... The time may come when it is possible to have other thoughts'. Eleven days later he began to exchange theatre news with her: 'You see I am once more taking a certain interest in gossip', he added. From Ischl on Palm Sunday he wrote that in the afternoon he would go grouse shooting – 'and so I am drifting back into old habits and taking up the old life, though things can never be the same'.

One decision Francis Joseph had already taken: Mayerling was to be demolished immediately. As an act of atonement, a chapel was to be built on the site, with a convent of Carmelite nuns. There the Sisters would follow a contemplative life, devoted to intercession by prayer and penance. On All Souls Day (2 November) Francis Joseph travelled out to Mayerling, heard Mass in the new chapel, 'inspected' the cloisters and communal buildings, and was awed by the strict asceticism of the Carmelites. In contrast to the stern simplicity of the conventual buildings, the chapel was intentionally planned to emphasize the devotional unity of the imperial family. Francis Joseph commissioned the Viennese artist Joseph Kastner to paint an ornate fresco above the high altar, which was erected where had stood the room in which Rudolf and Mary Vetsera went to their deaths. Kastner was to show the patron saints of those dearest to Francis Joseph, grouped in adoration of the Holy Trinity. The boy-martyr St Rudolf is prominent in the fresco. So, too, are St Elizabeth of Hungary (whom history recognizes), with St Sophie (whom history does not) behind her; kneeling are the scarcely less obscure St Gisela and St Valery. Kastner also included in the fresco saints associated with the Carmelites and with Habsburg history, as well as the Emperor's own patrons, Joseph and Francis of Assisi. The fresco was (and is) a minor triumph in neo-baroque for, like the craftsmen of Vienna's greatest churches, Kastner's grouping helps focus the eye on the cross, the symbol of expiation. Kastner's fresco is unlikely to have been completed when the Emperor made his first visit. But though Francis Joseph returned to Schönbrunn sorrowful, he was satisfied, conscious that the purpose of his bequest was being truly fulfilled: 'Over everywhere there was a comforting, soothing peace in that lovely countryside', he wrote.

Chapter 17

SPARED NOTHING?

Mayerling left Francis Joseph stunned and shocked. He did not, however, relax the routine of daily business. To pace the treadmill of state was to him a solace for frayed nerves, as his private letters show. Yet there were some problems of government he could not bring himself to discuss. Who, for example, would succeed him on the throne now that his only son was dead? Not a direct descendant, for Habsburg dynastic convention ruled out the possibility of female succession. Technically the Emperor's 55-year-old brother, Charles Ludwig, was the new heir-presumptive but nobody believed he would ever become Emperor-King. Charles Ludwig was as amiably ineffectual and as devoid of ambition as his father had been, though more devout. For the past twenty-eight years he had taken little part in public life and it was assumed that, should Francis Joseph die, he would follow his father's precedent and step aside in favour of his eldest son, Francis Ferdinand, who was born at Graz in December 1863. In fact, the problem of renouncing the succession never arose, for Charles Ludwig died in May 1896 from typhoid contracted on a pilgrimage to the Holy Land; the sacred waters of Jordan might be sprinkled in baptism, but they were not to be imbibed, even in piety.

The Emperor gave no clear indication that he regarded Francis Ferdinand as his successor, either before or after Charles Ludwig's death. The Archduke was not a favourite nephew: while still very young he had added 'Este' (the family name of the former rulers of Modena) to 'Habsburg' in order to inherit the fortune of a distant kinsman, the last Duke of Modena; and, when he was a junior officer, his wild escapades incurred the displeasure of 'Uncle Albrecht', who felt it his duty to inform the Emperor of such matters. Moreover, though Francis Ferdinand might look as strong as an ox, he had inherited from his Bourbon-Sicilian mother the weak lungs which caused her death from consumption when her eldest son was nine years old. The Archduke was first granted sick leave to winter in Egypt in 1885 and not until the spring of 1898 did his doctors finally declare him cured from the last of several tubercular relapses. With such uncertainty over Francis Ferdinand's health, it is small wonder if there were moments when the Emperor seemed to regard his brother Otto as a more likely successor. Nevertheless, within a few months of Mayerling the Archduke was fulfilling official engagements which would normally have been entrusted to the heir to the throne: he travelled to Stuttgart for the silver jubilee celebrations of King Charles of Württemberg, and he accompanied Francis Joseph on a state visit to Berlin. Eventually, in 1891, he undertook the goodwill mission to St Petersburg for which Rudolf had begun to prepare himself shortly before his death.

By then, however, the Emperor had grave doubts over his nephew's temperament. When the news of Mayerling broke, Francis Ferdinand was a major serving with an infantry regiment in Prague and living – like the Crown Prince before him – in the imperial apartments of the Hradčany palace. But a year later he was given command of a Hungarian Hussar regiment at Sopron, a garrison town in western Hungary barely 50 miles from Vienna. The Archduke was sad to leave Prague. By Habsburg standards he was a poor linguist: he had mastered some Czech, but Magyar utterly defeated him. To his fury he found the Hussar officers ignoring army regulations which made German the language of command for the Monarchy as a whole. They persisted in speaking Magyar 'even in front of me', he complained to a friend: 'Military terms were translated into long-winded Hungarian phrases. In short, throughout the regiment, not a word of that German language so detested by the Hungarians'. A responsive, astute colonel might have charmed the less truculent officers into co-operation. But not Francis Ferdinand. He reacted like a frustrated child; his rage knew no bounds. Archduke Albrecht sympathised with him, but he emphasized the need for members of the dynasty to cultivate the trust of every nationality. Such counsel was wasted: Francis Ferdinand's experiences at Sopron left him with a firm impression that all Hungarians, irrespective of social stature, were treasonable rogues. This conviction he never lost. His incandescent temper soon made the prejudice public, with ominous consequences for the dynasty as a whole: for, over a period of some twenty years, the personal authority of the Emperor-King among his Hungarian subjects was diminished by their fear that his heir would remain a rabid anti-Magyar once he came to the throne.

Hungary was in political turmoil during much of the last decade of the old century. Throughout 1889 Kálmán Tisza's army bill continued to provoke unrest in the capital. As a concession to Magyar nationalism, on 17 October Francis Joseph authorised two changes of name: the Imperial-Royal War Ministry of the Empire in Vienna would henceforth be known as the 'Imperial and Royal War Ministry', while the Imperial-Royal Army similarly became the Imperial and Royal Army. These trivial changes, replacing a hyphen by a conjunction and omitting the word 'empire', were regarded by Francis Joseph as 'almost laughable' but in Budapest they were interpreted as confirmation that the sovereign regarded the two parts of his Monarchy as linked solely by mutual consent. This gesture helped secure the passage through parliament of the unpopular army bill and brought a momentary calm to the streets of the capital. But Kálmán Tisza knew that his days of power were over. He no longer commanded the political following of earlier years. When, in March 1890, a further storm broke in parliament he decided to leave office.

Francis Joseph was in residence at Budapest throughout February and well into March that year. He found the politicking of the Magyar parliamentarians around him 'disagreeable': 'The Opposition deputies attack the prime minister with extraordinary rudeness and there is a colossal uproar at times', he wrote to Katharina Schratt. After a relatively stable fifteen year association with the same prime minister he found it hard to accustom himself to a new man. He appointed Count Gyula Szapáry, a cautious conservative, to succeed Tisza, but with little hope of any lasting political calm for Szapáry had no great support in parliament. His gloom was justified. The era of strong Magyar leadership – first Andrássy and later Tisza – was at an end. To Francis Joseph's dismay, over the next fifteen years, he had to find a new Hungarian prime minister on no less than six occasions.

He arrived back in Vienna on 17 March to face fresh problems. In the previous summer the Paris Congress of the Second International summoned socialists and trade unionists on both sides of the Atlantic to observe May Day as a proletarian festival of unity. Since May Day had long been celebrated in the German lands as a spring festival it was easy for Viktor Adler, the Jewish intellectual who led the Austrian socialist movement, to implement the Paris Congress's resolution. He urged trade unionists to hold meetings of 'a popular character open to the public' on 1 May 1890, though only in the morning: in the afternoon everyone should enjoy 'Nature's springtime'. Adler's innocuous call alarmed the Emperor, who could never forget the spring events of 1848 and the ease with which street demonstrations sparked off revolution. Francis Joseph summoned several meetings of ministers in Vienna, presiding over them himself and insisting that Taaffe should take strong action to check the spread of dangerous beliefs. Troops and police were put on the alert in every major city.

As May Day drew nearer, there was a flutter of apprehension in the capital: windows were shuttered; food hoarded for fear that roads from the countryside into the markets might be cut; in the Prater iron railings were removed so as to give cavalry horses freedom of manoeuvre if the mood of the demonstrators turned ugly. Yet the day passed as peacefully as in earlier years. A show of anti-capitalist solidarity brought thousands out to the Prater, processing down the Hauptallee behind a cluster of red flags. But troops and police reserves were kept discreetly in their barracks; with holiday sunshine in such a place at such a time the miasma of protest did not hang long in the air. There was no trouble in the smaller industrial towns of Austria, while in Bohemia and Moravia the response to Adler's call for peaceful demonstrations was lessened by an uneasy Czech awareness that the social democratic movement remained overwhelmingly Germanic in leadership. Francis Joseph's fears proved groundless.

Yet, though he exaggerated the risk of socialist upheaval, the Emperor was right to alert Taaffe's government to the threat posed by mass politics taking to the streets. For it was by now clear that the Reichsrat was no longer an effective safety-valve: the two chambers were too limited in composition and the deputies easily tempted to indulge themselves in rarefied rhetoric over matters remote from public concern. On the other hand, beyond the confines of parliament Schönerer's followers missed no opportunity to flaunt their Pan-German enthusiasm: even the announced intention of ex-Chancellor Bismarck to come to Vienna for his son's wedding was enough to worry the Emperor: 'I hope that Schönerer and company will not make too much trouble for us', he wrote to Katharina Schratt as the arrival of 'the devilish old Imperial Chancellor' drew nearer. But, far more pernicious than all this Pan-German rowdiness, was the rapid spread of anti-semitic feeling at a time when thousands of Jewish families, persecuted in Tsarist Russia and Roumania, were seeking refuge in Austria. The Emperor had no hesitation in condemning all attacks on Jewry: his great-great uncle, Joseph II, had issued patents of toleration in the 1780s; and the Jews were formally emancipated in Austria and in Hungary for the past quarter of a century. Now Francis Joseph looked with particular misgiving at the increased support given to Karl Lueger and his Christian Social Party. 'Every anti-Semitic movement must be nipped in the bud at once', the Emperor told Taaffe, after reading early reports of racial unrest, 'You will immediately have any anti-Semitic assembly dissolved. The Jews are brave and patriotic men who happily risk their lives for emperor and fatherland'.

But Taaffe, like Tisza in Hungary before him, was losing his grip on government: the 'Iron Ring' coalition was twelve years old and showing rust around the edges. His ideal political balance always rested on reconciliation between Czechs and Germans, first in Bohemia and Moravia, later in Cisleithania as a whole. A complicated educational and legal compromise (the *Punktationen* of 1890), settled with the 'Old Czech'

Party, seemed to bring the prime minister's plans to fruition. Taaffe, however, miscalculated: he had ignored the pace of social change in the Czech provinces. The Old Czechs had become yesterday's men: the initiative lay with the 'Young Czechs', radical militants ready to respond in kind to Schönerer's provocation, both in Bohemia-Moravia and in Vienna. They rejected the *Punktationen* and all talk of further compromise. In 1891 they began to win striking electoral successes. Both Taaffe and the Emperor were alarmed, not so much at changes in party affiliation as at the increase of nationalist feeling shown each time Czech and German townsfolk prepared to vote.

At this point Taaffe's minister of finance, Emil Steinbach, put forward an ingenious proposal: he urged the prime minister to broaden the franchise in elections for the lower house of the Reichsrat. Steinbach argued that in Cisleithania intensive nationalism was a middle class phenomenon and to give the working classes a voice in parliament would thus constrain the nationalistic antagonism which threatened the structure of the Monarchy. Taaffe was not easy to convince but, early in 1893, he was won over. To his surprise he found Francis Joseph not simply prepared to listen, but readily receptive: he welcomed the proposed extension of the franchise; in both the countryside and the smaller towns, the Emperor had always found loyal support from the least sophisticated of his subjects. Steinbach was accordingly instructed to prepare a suffrage bill which would have given the vote to almost every literate male in Cisleithania over the age of twenty-five. But Steinbach was not allowed a free hand: he was to draw up the bill in great secrecy, so as to prevent a protracted political crisis; and he was to preserve the complicated electoral system by which the proportion of deputies was stacked heavily in favour of the large landowners and the chambers of commerce.

The Emperor did not expect Steinbach's draft proposals to cause trouble; he was in Hungary again when the franchise reform was announced in Vienna. It was ill-received. Taaffe found every existing parliamentary group opposed to the scheme – except, strangely enough, the Young Czechs – and his coalition partners resigned from the government. There was resentment that the proposals were sprung unexpectedly on the party leaders, who were afraid that a wider suffrage would destroy old established power bases. Might it not advance the socialist cause, they argued? As the links in the Iron Ring began to fall apart, Francis Joseph hurried back to Vienna on 28 October. Taaffe, who had recently celebrated his sixtieth birthday, was a tired man. Technically, the Emperor dismissed the Count from office – an action for which Francis Joseph has been accused of deep ingratitude towards an old friend who had served him for fourteen years. But this charge is unmerited. Although Taaffe was in no hurry to go, he recognized that, sooner or later, he would have to tender his resignation, for he had no hope of forging a new coalition 'ring'. Significantly, after his fall, Taaffe showed no bitterness towards the Emperor; only towards ministerial colleagues who deserted him.

Francis Joseph's reactions to the crisis are interesting. He would have liked to appoint another 'Emperor's Minister', with no party affiliation whatsoever, and both Archduke Albrecht and General Beck recommended the Governor of Galicia, Count Casimir Badeni, who had pleased the generals by his strength of purpose during the Russian war scares of the previous decade. The Emperor, however, felt bound to allow the political leaders who broke the Iron Ring an opportunity to form a coalition of their own; and on 5 November 1893 Prince Alfred zu Windischgraetz, a grandson of the 'emperor-maker' of 1848, accepted the challenge. Once again, however, Francis Joseph imposed a condition: the Steinbach plan must not be dropped, for he was convinced that when an emperor accepted the principle of a reform it ought never to be cast aside in response to criticism in the Reichsrat. Instead, Steinbach's draft bill was referred to a parliamentary committee for close scrutiny and discussion.

In the end, the Windischgraetz coalition achieved little. Confusion between the party leaders led to a dispute in Styria which stirred up latent antagonism between the chief nationalities over the funding of Slovene language classes for secondary school pupils in the predominantly German town of Cilli. This affair, magnified out of all proportion to its significance, split the government and forced Windischgraetz out, after a mere twenty months in office. A stop-gap prime minister, Count Erich Kielmansegg, barely had time to soothe the Slovenes before belatedly making way in September 1895 for the much-respected Governor of Galicia, Count Badeni.

But, to Francis Joseph's dismay, by the middle of the decade Austrian politics were caught in a cycle of change as dramatic as in Hungary; after Taaffe's downfall, there were eight different heads of government in Vienna in seven years. Had the Emperor followed the advice of Albrecht and Beck and appointed Badeni to succeed Taaffe in 1893, the Polish aristocrat might well have emerged as a strong, non-party prime minister, for he possessed considerable personal skills. As it was, however, Badeni's prospects for extricating Francis Joseph from the parliamentary morass were hampered by two unexpected developments: the fall of Kálnoky, and his replacement as foreign minister by a Polish aristocrat; and the rapid rise in influence of Karl Lueger, both in the affairs of the capital and the political life of Austria as a whole.

By the spring of 1895 Gustav Kálnoky had been foreign minister for thirteen and a half years, almost as long a time-span as the premierships of Taaffe or Tisza. The Moravian landowner seemed a solid pillar of the state; he was automatically the chairman of ministerial conferences in the absence of the Emperor and principal arbiter of differences between the two governments of the Monarchy. Kálnoky was not popular with his colleagues nor with the diplomatic corps, for his aristocratic haughtiness never thawed in human contact, nor did he make much effort to conceal his clericalist political sympathies. But in his years at the Ballhausplatz Kálnoky achieved much: a strengthening of the alliances with Germany and Italy; closer co-operation with Britain over the problems of the eastern Mediterranean; and, above all, the maintenance of good relations with Serbia, Roumania and Bulgaria so as to limit the spread of Russian influence in the Balkans. He was, however, exasperated by the confused internal politics of the Monarchy. Neither the Emperor nor Taaffe told him of Steinbach's proposed franchise reforms; Kálnoky heard of them first from the King of Greece in a casual conversation. And for several years he was in conflict with the parliamentarians in Budapest, for the Magyars thought his policies encouraged Serbian and Roumanian irredentism. His contempt for Hungary's politicians, often expressed aloud, brought him an open rebuke from the prime minister in Budapest in May 1895. Kálnoky at once tendered his resignation to Francis Joseph, who accepted it with unflattering alacrity.

In Kálnoky's place, the Emperor appointed Count Goluchowski, son of the wealthy Polish aristocrat responsible for the October Diploma thirty-five years before. In domestic politics Goluchowski 'the Younger' (born four months after Francis Joseph's accession) was as conservative as his predecessor and no less suspicious of Hungarian party politics; but there was much to be said in his favour, notably his personal charm of manner. Nevertheless, Goluchowski's presence at the centre of affairs in Vienna made Badeni's task more difficult. When Badeni included in his ministry two more compatriots – one of whom became Austrian minister of finance – it is hardly surprising if the Viennese Press began to hint at a Polish takeover of government. That at least was the contention of Karl Lueger and his Christian Social Party. And by the autumn of 1895 what Lueger said was of considerable importance in Austrian politics.

To Francis Joseph, Lueger came as a new and unwelcome phenomenon. He was a vote-catching demagogue who exploited the hopes and prejudices of the 'little man in the street' to climb to the top in municipal affairs and, from a narrow power base in the capital, sought to make or brake successive governments. In 1895 he was fifty-one, a radical Catholic lawyer from the Landstrasse district of Vienna, a city councillor for the past twenty years and a deputy in parliament for ten. Though at first a

German Liberal, he won support from a wealthy group of clericalists, headed by Prince Liechtenstein. Their patronage enabled Lueger to build up the Christian Social Party on a basis of loyalty to the Habsburgs as a German-Austrian dynasty, hostility towards 'Jewish capitalism', and respect for the five encyclical letters of Pope Leo XIII which updated the social teachings of Roman Catholicism. 'Handsome Karl' was as good a rabble-rouser as Schönerer, over whom he had three advantages: a more positive programme; an efficient party machine; and a constituency in the capital, whereas Schönerer represented the Waldviertel, the Pan-German district which was the boyhood homeland of Adolf Hitler (born at Braunau-am-Inn in 1889, eleven weeks after Mayerling).

Under Lueger's leadership, the Christian Socials gained an inconclusive municipal electoral victory in June 1895. A second election, three months later, proved more decisive; they won twice as many seats on the Vienna City Council as the German Liberals, who had dominated the capital's politics for several decades. Francis Joseph was appalled: he feared that inflammatory speeches against the Jews would cause greater violence in the streets than Schönerer's followers ever provoked – and he had no doubt that the Schönerer mob would back any mass anti-semitic demonstrations Lueger might encourage. So serious was the prospect that several wealthy Jewish financiers hinted that a Lueger municipal regime in the capital would force them to move their financial institutions away from Vienna to Hungary. The Emperor had the constitutional right to refuse to confirm the election of a Mayor of Vienna if he thought him a danger to the well-being of the state; and in the early autumn he made it clear to Kielmansegg, the outgoing premier, that 'so long as I rule, Lueger will never be confirmed as mayor of my imperial capital'. He rejected a second mayoral victory by Lueger in late October. Badeni, the new prime minister, had shown scant respect for democratic votes in his seven years as Governor of Galicia; his advice strengthened the Emperor's own inclinations. On 13 November he again vetoed Lueger's re-election: the council was dissolved and the city's administration entrusted to an imperial commission of fifteen nominees.

On that November evening, there was some risk of bloodshed in the streets of the capital. One group of supporters wished to storm the Rathaus but were restrained by Lueger himself; ominously another group headed for the Hofburg, but were turned away by the police. The demonstrators were not hostile to the Emperor in person; they seem to have thought he was badly advised: 'Out with foreigners', 'Back to Galicia' were popular slogans. Even so, for the next few days, when Francis Joseph drove down the Mariahilferstrasse on his way to and from Schönbrunn, the customary 'hurrahs' and polite salutes were missing; he made the

journey in a silence he had not experienced since the dark weeks which
followed Solferino. The stock exchange in Vienna remained nervous,
with the worst panic selling since the *Krach* of 1873. New municipal
elections would be held in February or March and there would be parliamentary elections a year later. Despite his repeated assurances that he
would protect all his subjects, would a staunch Catholic like Francis
Joseph continue to resist the growing strength of the Christian Social
Party?

He was certainly puzzled. 'Among the highest social circles anti-semitism is an extraordinarily widespread disease and the agitation is unbelievable', he wrote to Elizabeth in Munich at the end of December 1895;
he enclosed letters which he had received from their younger daughter
and from one of the older aristocratic families 'in which Lueger and his
party were recommended to me most warmly'. He admitted that 'the basic
foundation' of Lueger's beliefs 'is intrinsically good', but the excesses are
terrible'. Badeni, too, was under pressure; and both he and Lueger
were troubled by the mounting support for Adler's Social Democrats as
parliamentary elections came nearer. At a secret meeting between the two
men it was agreed that the prime minister would ask the Emperor to
receive Lueger in a private audience at which he would affirm the movement's loyalty and his personal intention to act with restraint as Mayor.

Francis Joseph and Lueger talked at great length on 27 April 1896, at
a time when Francis Joseph was primarily concerned with Hungarian
affairs. A tacit understanding was reached: the Emperor would appoint
one of Lueger's lieutenants as interim Mayor, to hold office until the
Christian Socials had shown their administration to be constructive and
not discriminatory. Lueger would then become Mayor. Meanwhile the
Christian Socials would maintain only formal opposition to Badeni's
proposals in parliament, notably over the passage of the modified version
of Steinbach's franchise reform, to which the Emperor continued to attach
great importance. The Christian Social council duly took office in Vienna
in the last week of May 1896 and eleven months later Francis Joseph at
last ratified Lueger's appointment as Mayor. By then, Badeni's franchise
bill had become law, and elections in March 1897 gave Austria a new
Reichsrat, containing 425 deputies from 25 political parties. The franchise
reform was hardly democratic: it allowed five and a quarter million male
voters over the age of twenty-four and with a fixed residential qualification
of six months to elect 72 deputies to the lower house; the remaining 353
members were returned by one and three quarter million electors voting
in their four traditional privileged spheres.

Party politics, whether in Vienna's city council, in the Reichsrat, or in
Hungary's parliament, remained distasteful to Francis Joseph. Not least,

they tied him even longer to his desk and entailed more and more audiences for him. His daily routine was formidable: a first session spent in reading reports in his study at five in the morning, followed at eight o'clock by a series of meetings with the head of his military chancellery, the foreign minister or a senior official from the Ballhausplatz and with other ministers concerned with topical problems. Twice a week, at ten o'clock, whether he was in Vienna or Budapest, the Emperor held a general audience: on these occasions, on the average, he would speak to a hundred people individually. Further audiences would continue in the afternoons, after he had studied police reports and a digest of the morning newspapers. As in earlier years of the reign, Francis Joseph dutifully attended official functions in both parts of the Monarchy, his duties increased by the absence of a Crown Prince and the ill-health of Francis Ferdinand. He continued to study the details of military exercises, even adding to the obligations which he felt bound to accept. For he now made a point of joining his ally William II at German manoeuvres, a gesture which William reciprocated, sometimes coming to Austria-Hungary three or four times in the year. These attentions of his German ally were an additional burden; Frances Joseph remained ill-at-ease when exposed to the neo-Hohenzollern swagger and bombast which William affected during the first years of his reign. When Archduke Albrecht died in February 1895 Francis Joseph was sad at losing a kinsman on whose counsel he relied heavily for over thirty years. The grandeur of the state funeral moved him deeply, but he admitted ruefully to Katharina Schratt that preparations for the ceremony were exhausting: 'I had to drive five times to different railway stations to receive foreign guests, clad four times in foreign uniform and once in Austrian ... With the constant putting on and putting off, I could vividly imagine just how agreeable a play must be with many costume changes in it!'.

It would have been unthinkable to shirk the duties of kingship and yet, sadly, the Emperor was left increasingly to sustain them on his own. After Mayerling the Empress Elizabeth allowed the darkness of grief to blanket her world. Melancholia stifled the poetic imagery of the previous decade. Her elder daughter, Gisela, was so alarmed that she warned Valerie to take especial care of their mother when visiting the waterfalls at Gastein, in case she should throw herself into the torrent. But such fears misunderstood Elizabeth's temperament. She wished the world to know of her self-reproach, her regret that she had never understood her son's needs; intruders into the privacy of her soul should find contrition in as much of her fading beauty as she revealed to probing eyes. Always she dressed in mourning, though she rarely appeared at ceremonial functions and was reluctant to sit as a hostess at dinner with visiting state dignitaries.

At the first Court reception graced by the Empress – two years after Rudolf's death – the wife of the British ambassador noted that she was dressed almost like a nun, heavily veiled, with a necklace of black beads which seems to have resembled a rosary, although with the cross replaced by a medallion containing a lock of her son's hair.

In the first shock of the Mayerling tragedy Elizabeth curtailed her foreign wanderings, seeking rest in Hungary or the Dolomites until after the marriage of Archduchess Marie Valerie – a quiet affair at Ischl on 30 July 1890. But, once Valerie had settled with her husband near Wels (where he was serving in a dragoon regiment), the Empress saw no reason to keep up the pretence of Court life. She travelled, not simply to Bavaria or down the Adriatic to Corfu, but to Switzerland, the French Riviera, the Azores and north Africa. She dreamt of setting out on a world cruise in a chartered sailing ship: someone had told her she would find Tasmania attractive. But, to the relief of her faithful household, she accepted that such a voyage was now beyond her physical strength.

Ever since her visit to the Isle of Wight in 1874 the Empress repeatedly urged Francis Joseph to join her on a vacation, shaking off the last coils of Court life for once. At last, in March 1893, she persuaded him to join her for a fortnight in Switzerland, staying in a hotel at Territet, near Montreux. Yet, though they enjoyed walks together, out to the Castle of Chillon or up the mountain foothills behind the lake, the Territet visit was not really a holiday for him. His hopes of remaining incognito were dashed within twenty-four hours, when the hotel proprietor proudly flew the black and gold imperial standard from his flagpole; and, a day later, the Emperor had to spend the whole morning in the hotel dealing with the official papers a courier brought him from Vienna. Moreover, though the Swiss holiday momentarily lifted his flagging spirits, he was sad at the thought that, on leaving Territet, he would not see Elizabeth again for at least six weeks. 'No joy, only loneliness awaits me in Vienna', he admitted in a private letter sent a few hours before setting out on his homeward train journey.

During these long and increasingly frequent weeks as a grass-widower, Francis Joseph was dependent on the companionship of Katharina Schratt, though she was herself often away from the capital. In the bitter aftermath of Mayerling her good sense and sympathy had steadied the Empress's nerves as well as giving him a certain comfort and, with Elizabeth's agreement, he responded gratefully and generously to her gestures of support and understanding. A codicil added to Francis Joseph's will in March 1889 pledged a legacy of half a million florins to the Court actress Katharina Kiss von Itebbe (neé Schratt) 'to whom I am bound by the deepest and purest of friendships and who has always been loyally and faithfully at my side and at that of the Empress during the hardest moments of our life'. At the same time, with the Emperor's support, she purchased a delightful villa at Hietzing overlooking the botanical gardens of Schönbrunn, in what was then the Gloriettegasse. The house was only four doors uphill from the Nahowski home, a source of occasional embarrassment; but it was close enough to the palace for the Emperor frequently to follow the practice which he had begun at Ischl of inviting himself to breakfast, after which the two friends would stroll in the grounds of Schönbrunn itself. As the Empress went out of her way to show her approval of 'the friend', these walks and talks were not in themselves a source of scandalous gossip. Only Archduchess Marie Valerie strongly disapproved of the way in which her father exchanged confidences with '*die Schratt*', and her mother treated her as a family friend.

Relations between Emperor and actress were not always smooth. He was uneasy at her continued friendship with Ferdinand of Bulgaria and irritated by her occasional attempts to secure a more rewarding post in the diplomatic service for her, discreetly distant, husband – who in 1892 was at last transferred from the consulate in Tunis to Barcelona. Most of all Francis Joseph was angered by Katharina's insistence on making a balloon flight over Vienna in June 1890, which received much publicity in Austrian newspapers. He thought the flight dangerous, and he was particularly displeased that her companion should have been Alexander Baltazzi: 'That you made the aerial trip under his auspices means nothing to me, I assure you', Francis Joseph wrote to her from Hungary, 'but in the eyes of the malicious world it will harm you, for the newspaper concentration on his presence underlines the fact that the Baltazzi family is not welcome in all circles since our disaster'. Though he was momentarily afraid that this scolding might end their friendship, he need not have worried; with disingenuous sincerity Katharina assured him that, when next she took to the air, she would keep the matter secret so as to cause him no disquiet.

There were other troubled moments, too. On one occasion in June 1892 – a time when the Emperor was concerned over the Pan-German response to Bismarck's visit to the capital – Francis Joseph 'could hardly sleep at night' after hearing from Katharina that her 12-year old son, Toni Kiss, had received at school an anonymous obscene letter slandering his mother. The Vienna police chief was alerted; the financier Eduard Palmer asked to serve as a discreet go-between, interviewing Toni (who did not understand the implications of the letter), his mother, and the police chief; and the Empress was at once consulted by letter. No prosecution followed; and it was the Empress who responded most sensibly to the whole affair; for when Francis Joseph and Elizabeth were in residence at Ischl that summer and Frau Schratt and her son were invited to take tea at the imperial villa, the Empress took Toni Kiss aside for a walk through the gardens, praising his mother and emphasizing the value of the support she gave the Emperor and herself in the saddest months of their married life.

Unlike his mother and his younger daughter Francis Joseph did not keep a detailed journal. As a substitute for a daily record of this character, he would send long letters to the two women closest to his heart. To the Empress he normally wrote every other day during her travels. Between September 1890 and September 1898 no less than 474 of these letters have survived, clear testimony both to his diligence as a correspondent and to the frequency of her absence from Court. Few make interesting reading: they record the weather, the statistics of his audiences, the seating plan of the formal dinners which she was so relieved not to attend, his comings and goings, news of their daughters and of much loved 'little Erzsi', who lived with the Crown Princess out at Laxenburg and is mentioned on more than seventy occasions. In considerable detail, the letters describe visits to *die Freundin* in the Gloriettegasse, the walks they took together, the progress of Toni Kiss (more than 30 mentions), his meetings with Katharina's cousins and aunt, and all the intimacy of the bourgeois existence which meant so much to him. Occasional entries suggest that the Emperor's interests were broader than many writers concede: he was, for example, fascinated by the invention of the 'Edison phonograph', on an early version of which he heard, very clearly, a German band playing the *Radetzky March*. His theatre visits were not limited to the plays in which Katharina Schratt appeared. Most unexpectedly, on 19 January 1897, he wrote: 'At five o'clock I dined alone and afterwards I went to the second performance of *The Wild Duck* by Ybsen (*sic*), a curious modern piece, uphill work, but excellently presented'. Did the title tempt the marksman in Francis Joseph to the theatre that evening? The letter says nothing of the actors, but 'a new 16-year-old actress, Fraulein Medelski playing a 14-year old maiden showed a remarkable talent and acted very well'. Did he, one wonders, stay for the last scene, in which 'the maiden' shoots herself in her inner sanctuary?

His other correspondent, Katharina Schratt, received more than two hundred letters from the Emperor during the same eight year period (September 1890 to September 1898). They are lighter in character and tinged with mocking self-pity but they reveal more about his inner feelings. Surprisingly they show the onset of a timidity he did not possess before the buffeting of misfortune in his middle years: 'The Empress restarts the sea-voyaging – for me a constant anxiety and worry', he wrote in the autumn of 1890; and he was to warn Katharina, not only against balloon ascents, but against excursions to the glaciers, against mountaineering ('let me remind you that, for safety's sake, you promised me not to climb to the peak of the Dachstein') and, in April 1897, against the risks of falls when bicycling, which was 'a real epidemic' that spring and a pastime much favoured by his daughter, Gisela, three years Katharina's junior.

These letters also preserve his sense of incredulity at what he saw around him during holidays with the Empress on the French Riviera. He first joined her at Cap Martin, near Menton, for a fortnight in March 1894; they were there for a week in February 1895, and for nearly three weeks a year later. A fourth visit in March 1897 was, he said 'ruined by anxiety about the Empress's health' but the earlier vacations were happy affairs; they brought liveliness and colour back to his daily existence.

As at Territet he was fascinated by hotel life, though he contributed little to it: 'I dined in our suite at 7 o'clock', he wrote on arrival in 1896, ... and soon went to bed, lulled to sleep by music from the hotel lounge'. He visited the gambling rooms at Monte Carlo in 1894, but he thought there were too many onlookers for him to chance his luck. Best of all on the Riviera he liked the 'wonderful gardens' at Cannes. A year later he thought the Riviera 'full of Englishmen' and caught sight of Mr and Mrs Gladstone walking in the hotel grounds, but he showed no desire to meet one of Austria's consistently stern critics: why darken a holiday?. 'We try all kinds of restaurants and are really eating far too much and too varied a fare', he told Katharina at the close of the first holiday at Cap Martin, 'After all, the prime purpose of life here consists only in eating. With which sparkling observation I end my letter'.

Inevitably business of state intruded on the holiday mood in March 1896, when the Emperor met the head of a republic for the first time, exchanging visits with President Felix Faure, who was on an official tour of the Alpes Maritimes. Francis Joseph admired the bearing of the Presidential escort of cuirassiers, 'with trumpeters blowing'. He enjoyed watching the French fleet at sea from the Corniche and amused himself by scrambling up to a vantage point for a surreptitious assessment of Alpine infantry as they carried out field exercises with live ammunition. He found, with apparent surprise, that this stretch of the Third French Republic's coastline provided a winter haven for many royal dignitaries: among them he entertained members of his own family, Romanov Grand Dukes, the Prince of Wales, and his old friend, the Empress Eugenie. Queen Victoria was there, too. On 13 March 1896 Francis Joseph and Elizabeth visited her at Cimiez, the only occasion in her life when she 'received the Emperor and Empress of Austria' together. It was, the Queen reported to her prime minister, a 'cordial' meeting: she noted, with satisfaction, the Emperor's confidence in Goluchowski as a foreign minister and his optimism at the prospects for lasting peace in Europe.

Soon after the visit to Cimiez Francis Joseph returned to Vienna, ready once more to face the problems raised by Lueger's meteoric rise in popularity. At the same time Elizabeth sailed to Corfu, still intent on mastering modern Greek, but anxious also to build up her strength in order to meet the challenge of a formidable programme of royal events in the months ahead. For the year 1896 marked the thousandth anniversary of the coming of the Magyars to the Danubian plain and Budapest remained en fête from spring to autumn.

These millennial celebrations, originally planned during the primacy of Kálmán Tisza, were of crucial political importance to the stability of the Dual Monarchy as a whole. They could either confirm Hungary's economic self-sufficiency and cohesion or spark off even worse friction between the master nation and the kingdom's Roumanian and Slav minorities. Tension had grown during 1895 after the appointment in January of a Hungarian Liberal Government headed by a convinced believer in Magyarization, Baron Bánffy. At the same time, the ascendancy of Lueger's Christian Socials in Austria threatened the economic Ausgleich on the eve of its decennial re-assessment, which was due in 1897; for the Christian Socials in Vienna constantly attacked 'greedy Magyar politicians', whom they alleged were in the pay of 'Jewish bankers', hostile to the Catholic church. On every count it was essential for Hungary's King and Queen to tread warily during the weeks of grandiose celebration. And this they did well.

The festivities began on 2 May 1896, when Francis Joseph and Elizabeth opened the Millennial Exposition of Hungarian achievement in the Városliget, the town park of Budapest. The setting recalled the World Exhibition of 1873 in the Vienna Prater, although the most striking building erected for the occasion was not a great rotunda but the Vajdahunyad Castle, an architectural mélange of more than twenty different 'Hungarian' styles, from Romanesque to Baroque. To convey visitors from the inner city to the park the municipal authorities made proud use of a technological innovation, unknown in Europe outside London – an underground railway, running for the most part only a few feet below the surface of Budapest's smartest boulevard, Andrássy-Út, and stopping at eight stations. Francis Joseph made the journey, in a specially decorated imperial carriage, on 6 May, four days after the first trains ran, but Elizabeth did not accompany him. She had felt overwhelmed by 'all that splendour and pomp' at the opening of the exhibition and, as she wrote to her daughter, she was saddened by memories of earlier grand occasions, when she had Rudolf beside her. King and Queen attended a thanksgiving Mass in the coronation church that same week and Francis Joseph stayed on in the city for other festivities. Early in June they were together again for the opening of a new wing to the royal palace in Budapest and for a solemn procession in which the Holy Crown of St Stephen and the coronation regalia were borne across the Danube to the Parliament House and back to the Crown Room beneath the palace dome. In September, when Francis Joseph joined the Kings of Roumania and Serbia at Orsova for the opening of the canalised section of the Danube through the Iron Gates, some attention was paid to the sensitivities of Hungary's minority nationalities, but for the most part the celebrations boosted Magyar nationalism. Bánffy's Liberals easily won a general election in the late autumn, but it was an ugly campaign, with more than thirty people killed in riots or scuffles.

The millennial festivities re-affirmed their Queen's unique hold on the affections of the Hungarian people. Francis Joseph, however, still did not trust Magyar loyalty, especially at a time when there was such widespread commemoration of Kossuth's activities fifty years before. A conflict over the relative contributions of the two halves of the Monarchy to the common budget continued throughout 1897: the Delegation from the Reichsrat in Vienna argued that, since the Milleniary Exhibition had emphasized the great economic progress made by Hungary, parliament in Budapest should now meet 42 per cent of common expenses rather than the 31.5 per cent agreed in 1867 by the original Ausgleich. The Hungarians, on the other hand, maintained that the 1867 level was always too high and they resented the possibility of having to subsidise backward areas of Cisleithania. A powerful rearguard action by the Hungarian Liberals delayed settlement of this tiresome question until the closing months of 1898, with the Hungarian quota finally raised to a mere 34.4 per cent of total expenses. Gloomily Francis Joseph noted that the Bánffy Government expected the anniversaries of the Hungarian revolution to be marked by public holidays. It was an odd situation; for the Emperor-King himself still had paintings on his palace walls which showed the valour of Austria's whitecoats in crushing Kossuth and his rebels during the first year of the reign.

There was, too, the delicate problem of how to celebrate the Golden Jubilee of Francis Joseph's accession, which would fall on 2 December 1898. Here he had at least hoped he would have backing from a firm government in Vienna, especially when in the spring of 1896 Badeni and Lueger reached their informal agreement over the franchise bill. But Badeni made an appalling political miscalculation. In order to win Czech support in the contest with Hungary over the tax quota, he issued language ordinances for Bohemia and for Moravia in April 1897: from July 1901, every civil servant in each of these provinces would have to be bi-lingual in German and Czech; and in lawsuits, the language of the plaintiff was to be used at every level, from magistrate's hearings to the supreme court of appeal.

The Badeni Ordinances gave an enormous advantage to educated Czechs, most of whom spoke and wrote German as well as their native language. On the other hand few Germans, irrespective of their home province, spoke any of the minority Slav languages. What if the Language Ordinances were extended to other provinces? Would German bureaucrats have to become proficient in Slovene or Ruthene or Polish or Italian? To say that the Badeni Ordinances were fought tooth and nail in the Reichsrat is almost literally true: sometimes punches were thrown, sometimes inkpots. A Pan-German deputy who described the ordinances as 'a piece of Polish rascality' accepted a challenge from the prime minister, and in the subsequent duel wounded Badeni in the arm. Most of the disorder was in central or suburban Vienna, but there was serious rioting in Graz, where the Slovene minority was conscious of racial kinship with the Czechs. Lueger led 'Out with Badeni' demonstrations in the capital; and by the last weekend in November military guards patrolled the Ringstrasse and the inner city. If the German ambassador is to be believed, 'Frau Kathi' Schratt – who normally avoided political matters – implored Francis Joseph to get rid of Badeni before the troubles worsened. At all events, the Emperor decided to sacrifice the prime minister for the sake of good order on the streets. On 28 November 1897 Badeni was dismissed, the only minister forced from office by public opinion during the reign.

Yet, though the Emperor might sack a particular man under popular pressure, he obstinately refused to concede changes in the law. Two more years went by before he admitted that the Language Ordinances were administratively impossible to observe and withdrew them. The effect of all this political skirmishing was to weaken the central authority in Vienna. Instead of approaching the critical anniversary year of 1898 with a strong government, as he had hoped, Francis Joseph was forced to work with stopgap administrations, headed by five different incumbents in some twenty-five months.

The only wise inner counsellor to whom the Emperor could turn in 1897–98 was Count Goluchowski, the second of his chosen Polish aristocrats, in the Ballhausplatz. As foreign minister, Goluchowski patiently worked for improved relations with Russia, establishing the principle that Vienna and St Petersburg would work in harmony in the Balkan lands rather than take advantage of each other's problems to destabilise so sensitive a region. In his secondary role, as de facto chairman of ministerial councils held in the sovereign's absence, the easy-going Goluchowski was of great service to the dynasty, since he was able to reduce the chronic tension between the successive prime ministers of the two parts of the Monarchy. Goluchowski's hostility towards the Language Ordinances are more likely to have tipped the balance of Francis Joseph's judgment against Badeni than any prompting from Katharina Schratt.

One important decision, however, probably owes more to Vienna's Mayor than to any individual minister: the Golden Jubilee was to be celebrated in anticipation, not simply left for a winter's day in December; the festivities would begin in the spring, thereby ensuring that attention was drawn to the dynasty during months when more radical spirits might wish to recall the deeds of the 1848 revolutionaries. In mounting commemorative festivals Vienna sought to outshine Budapest. Thousands could flock to the newly completed Volksprater amusement park, where Francis Joseph and Lueger stood side by side as the great Ferris Wheel began its first majestically slow rotation. On 7 May the Emperor opened a Jubilee Exhibition in the Prater itself; he came again on six other days before midsummer; and on 9 May, accompanied by both the Mayor and Cardinal-Archbishop of Vienna, he inaugurated the *Stadtbahn*, a more extensive urban railway system than in Budapest, though not technically an 'underground'. Seventy thousand schoolchildren paraded down the Ringstrasse to greet their Emperor on 24 June: 'It was a joy to see how they smiled at me and to hear the enthusiasm with which they shouted', he wrote to Katharina. A few days later he was hailed by 4,000 huntsmen gathered at Schönbrunn. Yet there was one striking difference between these celebrations and the millennial festivities in Budapest: the Empress took no part in them. The last state occasion which she graced with her presence was a gala dinner at the Hofburg in honour of Tsar Nicholas II and his Empress on 27 August 1896, during a visit which promoted Goluchowski's ideal of an Austro-Russian entente. Thereafter Elizabeth's doctors insisted that, for the sake of her health, she should retire into private life.

For two years Francis Joseph was constantly uneasy over his wife's health and well-being. She was anaemic, and yet insisted on rigorous dieting, sometimes eating no more than half a dozen oranges in the course of a day. There were new anxieties, too: her face was pocked with a rash she found impossible to conceal and doctors who examined her were concerned at an apparent dilation of the heart. When Katharina Schratt was about to visit the Empress at Cap Martin in March 1897, Francis Joseph warned their friend in advance: 'If you should be shocked by her appearance, which unfortunately is very bad, please do not show it'.

A few weeks later tragedy again struck Elizabeth. On 4 May 1897 her youngest sister Sophie, married to the Duke of Alençon, perished in the fire which swept through a charity bazaar at the Rue Jean-Gujon in Paris, killing 200 people: 'In all its circumstances' the fire 'is more terrible than anything that has happened this century', the British prime minister wrote to Queen Victoria. The shocking news from Paris, and the grisly newspaper reports which followed it, almost unhinged Elizabeth; once more her mind seems to have turned round upon itself, bringing to the surface of her consciousness old griefs and past remorse. She travelled more restlessly than ever – to Biarritz, to the Riviera, to the German spas. In the spring of 1898 Francis Joseph joined her at Kissingen for ten days. They were together for a fortnight at the height of summer in Ischl. But on 16 July Elizabeth set out for a new cure at Bad Nauheim. They never saw each other again. Fittingly their romance ended where it began, in the mountain valleys of the Salzkammergut.

Francis Joseph remained at Ischl until the last week of August. Then, after a brief visit to Schönbrunn and a sad walk in the gardens of the Villa Hermes worrying about the health of its chatelaine, he was off to southern Hungary, to watch autumn manoeuvres along the Danube frontier with Serbia. Still he found time to write every other day to Elizabeth, the letters following her from Nauheim into Switzerland. He was back in Vienna on Friday, 9 September, attending to urgent Austrian affairs, for he planned to leave for Gödöllö the following evening. Early on Saturday morning he wrote to Katharina letting her know that he had 'thank God, really good news from the Empress', who was 'enjoying ... the pure, invigorating mountain air' of Switzerland. But at half-past four that afternoon his adjutant arrived with a telegram: it contained, he said, 'very bad news'. At once, the Emperor assumed it was from Geneva, for worry over Elizabeth's health remained uppermost in his mind. The message, however, reported not the Empress's sudden collapse, but that she had been 'injured'. Francis Joseph was both alarmed and puzzled: what could have happened? Within minutes a second telegram arrived and the terrible truth broke upon him: Sisi had been stabbed by an Italian anarchist as she walked to a lake steamer in front of the Hotel Beau Rivage at Geneva; she lost consciousness and died within minutes of the attack. '*Mir bleibt doch gar nichts erspart auf dieser Welt*', Francis Joseph exclaimed in deep grief: 'So I am to be spared nothing in this world!'. And then, so the adjutant reported, he said softly, as if speaking to himself, '*Niemand weiss, wie sehr wir uns geliebt haben*': 'Nobody knows the love we had for each other'.

Chapter 18

THE BELVEDERE

'With whom better can I speak of the lost one than with you?', Francis Joseph wrote to Katharina Schratt on 12 September, thanking her for cutting short a holiday to hurry back to Hietzing and visit him in Schönbrunn. Throughout that autumn his grief was so deep that he went through the daily routine of administration like an automaton, waiting for the hours when he could talk and talk and talk about the Empress, sometimes to his daughters, more often to the friend. Inevitably, the festivities to celebrate the Golden Jubilee were cancelled, as mourning enveloped Court life. His daughters sought to sustain their father; but 'faced with such pain I am powerless to help', Valerie wrote in her journal. She was, of course deeply saddened herself and, being extremely devout, she was worried by the thought that her mother had lost consciousness before receiving the last rites. With encouragement from a Jesuit chaplain, she urged her father to go regularly to confession, dedicating himself anew to God for the sake of the Empress's immortal soul. Of this practice, the family friend did not approve. 'They never stop worrying the poor old gentleman', Katharina Schratt told Philip Eulenburg, the German ambassador, who was fast becoming her confidant: 'All this talk about prayer and repentance gets on his nerves ... I say to him, "There's little point in Your Majesty going to confession when you have no sins on your conscience to confess"'.

No sins, perhaps; but the continued relationship with *die Schratt* was in itself ambiguous; and his strait-laced younger daughter and her husband had every intention of discouraging it. Over the past decade the openness of Elizabeth's friendship with Katharina to some extent curbed slanderous gossip. The Empress invariably treated their friend generously. Earlier that year, she had told her that, to mark the Golden Jubilee, a special medal – the Elizabeth Order – would be struck: and she would be among the first to receive it. The medal was, indeed, struck; but when the list of recipients was published it did not include Frau Schratt's name.

Katharina raised the question with the Emperor, reminding him of the Empress's promises. She should have known her sovereign better. Over such matters Francis Joseph was adamant. Blandly he explained that what would have been natural when the Empress was alive was now out of the question; he could not himself bestow on her an Order honouring his wife without setting tongues wagging so viciously as to cause her pain. Katharina was hurt, much more deeply than Francis Joseph realized since she made some effort to conceal her sense of injury, inwardly blaming Archduchess Marie Valerie for the humiliating disappointment. By the end of the year a rift had opened in the long friendship.

Over the following eighteen months, the rift became a chasm, with the Emperor declining to intervene in rows between the Court actress and the director of the Burgtheater. In July 1900 she sent from Paris a letter of resignation from the Burgtheater company: to her surprise it was accepted. She was in her forty-seventh year; her nerves were shattered and her absent husband still running her into debt. Moreover the disapprobation of the Archduchess's household froze the spontaneous warmth which had brought such enchantment to meetings with the Emperor in earlier years. The letters of Eulenburg, a waspish commentator on any social scene, even gave the impression she was finding 'the poor gentleman' rather a bore. At last, in Ischl immediately after Francis Joseph's seventieth birthday celebrations, she told him that she felt their close companionship must come to an end. Almost immediately she left for Gastein, going on to Munich and Paris and Lucerne and Florence; faithful letters pursued her across Europe. Occasionally she replied to him – as when she let him know that in the Pavilion of Sport at the Paris Exhibition he was accorded a life-size photograph, together with an updated tally of his marksmanship: 48,345 head of wild game had fallen to the sharpness of his eye and the steadiness of his hand. But for much of the time the Emperor was left to gather news of his 'dearest friend' from other sources, such as Eduard Palmer or even her son, Toni Kiss. He was at times a very lonely old gentleman.

Rather surprisingly, Archduchess Marie Valerie seems to have hoped that her father would re-marry. An Empress at Court would focus high society on the imperial family once again; he might even still have a son to succeed him. Many earlier Habsburgs had declined to remain widowers; and both his grandfather, Emperor Francis, and his own brother, Charles Ludwig, married three times, with the last nuptials in both instances celebrated on the eve of their fortieth birthdays. There is, however, a difference between nearly forty and nearly seventy. Although embassy gossip induced Eulenburg to take the possibility of re-marriage seriously, it was never likely and when, long before her voluntary exile,

Katharina Schratt passed the rumours on to the Emperor, Francis Joseph was amazed at such credulity. 'You can tell Count Eulenburg from me that, whatever people may say, I have no intention of marrying again', he said firmly. At seventy Francis Joseph wished life to run smoothly along familiar grooves, like the electric tramcars Lueger was bringing to Vienna's streets; no jumping of tracks through a sudden switch of points; just a steady journey to the terminus, with a bell ringing to clear the path ahead.

Sometimes, however, the journey was impeded by an unexpected obstacle. One such hazard, encountered at high summer in 1899, was the Archduchess Isabella. For several years this formidable wife of his second cousin, the Duke of Teschen, had convinced herself that the heir presumptive sought marriage with her eldest daughter; for why otherwise should Francis Ferdinand so often fish for invitations to her castle at Bratislava? Isabella was flattered: to have a daughter groomed as the next Empress-Queen would at once lift the standing of the parents in Europe's spas and capital cities. But when, in that July, the doting mother could not resist the temptation to open a locket hanging from the chain of a gold watch which the Archduke had left beside her tennis court, she made an unwelcome discovery: she was confronted with a miniature picture, not of her daughter, but of her lady-in-waiting, Countess Sophie Chotek, his occasional doubles partner. Indignantly Archduchess Isabella at once informed the Emperor of such scandalous deception.

To Francis Joseph her complaint was most unwelcome. Private affairs were already intruding on public business: the widowed Crown Princess Stephanie wished to marry a Hungarian nobleman, Count Lonjay. The Emperor did nothing to impede her re-marriage, which was celebrated at Miramare in March 1900, but it posed difficult legal problems, not least concerning Stephanie's status. While he was personally sympathetic towards his widowed daughter-in-law, Francis Ferdinand remained antipathetic to him. Moreover, the fuss over Sophie Chotek erupted at a particularly bad time, politically: she came from Bohemian nobility, and he was under pressure from several aristocratic families to scrap Badeni's Language Ordinances and come down firmly in support of his German subjects in their fight against Czech linguistic claims. Not unnaturally Francis Joseph was inclined at first to dismiss the whole Chotek affair as the passing infatuation of an Archduke with a wandering eye for a demure woman with a warm smile and a good figure. But it was more serious than that. To the Emperor's consternation, Francis Ferdinand insisted he had been in love with Countess Chotek for five years. He wished to marry her. Over the autumn and winter months no peremptory summons to the Hofburg or sharp letters from his brother Archdukes could persuade him otherwise.

Dynastically the marriage was out of the question, by Francis Joseph's reckoning. The Countess's family were good, loyal Bohemian aristocrats; her father was the diplomat in Brussels who had helped negotiate the marriage settlement for Rudolf and Stephanie; but the Choteks were not of sufficiently high social ranking to give the Monarchy its next Empress. At last Francis Ferdinand's step-mother interceded with the Emperor, inducing him to accept the only way in which his nephew could remain heir-presumptive and marry the woman he loved. With a heavy heart, the Emperor reconciled his conscience to accepting the principle of a morganatic marriage, excluding any offspring from succession to the throne. On 28 June 1900, at a ceremony in the Hofburg, the Emperor summoned fifteen senior Archdukes, the papal nuncio, the Cardinal-Archbishop, foreign minister Goluchowski and all the senior court officials to hear Francis Ferdinand solemnly renounce under oath all claims of his proposed wife and children for the rights of status or inheritance accorded to 'a marriage between equals'. The wedding took place a few days later at the castle of Reichstadt, in Bohemia: it was attended by neither the Emperor nor any of the Archdukes. Francis Ferdinand and his 32-year old wife made their principal home at Konopischt, a fortress thirty-four miles outside Prague, which the Archduke had purchased in 1887 and converted into a delightful home with rose gardens famous throughout the continent; they looked best, it was said, from the window of Francis Ferdinand's lavatory, on the third floor of the castle.

Once the morganatic settlement was legalized, the Emperor behaved perfectly correctly towards his heir-apparent. He gave the bride a diadem and raised her to princely (but not royal) rank as Princess von Hohenberg. Francis Ferdinand, more fortunate than poor Rudolf, was given the loveliest of Vienna's baroque palaces, the Upper Belvedere, as an official residence; and he had the personal wealth to allow 'Soph' (as he called the Princess) to create within this splendid museum piece rooms in which it was possible to enjoy family life. Two months after the wedding Francis Joseph officially received 'my nephew's wife' for the first time: he thought her 'natural and modest, but ... no longer young'. Three weeks later he returned the visit, to see Prince Eugene's garden palace – Vienna's counterpart to Blenheim – acquiring the comforts of domesticity. The marriage was an extremely happy one: a daughter, born a year after the wedding, was given her mother's name; a son, Maximilian, followed in September 1902 and a second son, Ernest, in May 1904. That summer Francis Ferdinand could write contentedly to his step-mother: 'By far the wisest thing I ever did was to marry my Sophie. She is everything to me: my wife, my doctor, my adviser – to put it in one word, my whole happiness'. And he went on to describe evenings 'spent at home': 'I smoke my cigar and read the papers, Sophie knits, and the children tumble about, pulling everything off the tables – it's all so delightfully cosy'.

Yet, despite such rare family happiness, official protocol inflicted a series of humiliations on the Princess von Hohenberg. A year after their marriage she could not attend a gala dinner given by her husband at the Belvedere in honour of the German Crown Prince. When the Archduke was within the Belvedere, sentries stood guard at the gates: when he left the palace, the sentries were withdrawn, even though his wife and eventually his children, remained in residence. While he was driven about Vienna in an imperial 'Viktoria' or 'Mylord' with gold-rimmed wheels, his wife and children had to make do with an ordinary carriage. At the opera or the theatre the Archduke would be seated in a separate box from Sophie, and he could never escort her into a state dinner or ball. These social restraints cannot have surprised Francis Ferdinand, for when he accepted the limitations of a morganatic union he well knew the rigidity of convention and protocol at the Habsburg Court; but it was natural for him to look with sympathy on foreign princes who treated Sophie with the respect which he was sure she deserved. When William II – at the prompting of his Chancellor, Prince Bülow – went out of his way to flatter the Princess von Hohenberg during a visit to Vienna in the autumn of 1903, the German Emperor ensured that he could count on the Archduke's friendship and support during the remaining eleven years of his life.

The trivialities of protocol which governed the family's daily existence at the Belvedere were part of a fossilized routine followed by the Court as a whole. Little had changed at the centre of affairs in the last twenty years. In particular, as the nineteenth century came to an end, the isolation of the dynasty from the cultural life of the capital became more and more apparent. The break was made dramatically clear in 1898 when a young architect, Adolf Loos, writing in the *Neue Freie Presse*, attacked Ringstrasse Vienna as an architectural fake, a false facade giving a Renaissance splendour to buildings which lacked a character of their own. In that same year of the Golden Jubilee, barely a quarter of a mile across the Ringstrasse from the Opera, the *Sezession* building was opened; it was (and is) a defiantly modern 'Grove of Art' built in a neo-Assyrian style to house the works of young artists who had 'seceded' from the conventional work favoured by the Academy of Fine Arts. 'To the age its art, to art its freedom' ran the gilt lettered inscription above the main entrance to the *Sezession* exhibition hall.

Yet although the young artists gloried in the modernity of free expression, bringing to Vienna some of the individualism and vitality of the Impressionists, their recognized leader was Gustav Klimt; he was thirty-six in the year of the first exhibition, and had made his name under imperial patronage, assisting Makart at the Hermes Villa and completing several frescoes for the main stairway of the Burgtheater. It is hardly surprising if Francis Joseph had little interest in the innovative work of the *Sezession* artists, and even less for their younger and angrier successors; but, probably because he had always been artistically a detached and slightly puzzled outsider, he accepted *art nouveau* as a phenomenon which might please others, though not himself. While Francis Ferdinand puffed and fumed at the scandalous lascivious lines in Klimt's later work, the Emperor made no protest. He was prepared to spend an hour and a half examining 'applied modern art' at a museum in Vienna before deciding that 'my taste' did not extend to exhibits 'tinged with the *Sezession*'. Many times as his carriage brought him into the city from Schönbrunn he must have seen the *Sezession* exhibition hall, yet it never seems to have aroused his anger. He accepted, too, the functionalism of Otto Wagner's Stadtbahn stations. Only in 1911 was his architectural taste seriously offended: for he intensely disliked Adolf Loos's 'house without eyebrows', the plain fronted building which had no window frames and no ornamentation, built on the corner of the Michaelerplatz. Nothing disturbed his faith in the enduring qualities of all that was familiar to him so much as this '*Looshaus*', standing provocatively across the road from the windows of one of the Hofburg's newer wings: 'Pull the curtains', he ordered, as if turning his back on the future.

At the start of the century it had looked as if he wished to turn his back on parliament, too. 'We are the laughing-stock of Europe' he remarked sharply after an unedifying outburst of fighting between rival nationalists in the Reichsrat. There is a well-known picture of deputies in Vienna's lower chamber banging gongs, clashing cymbals and blowing trumpets in order to silence spokesmen with whom they disagreed. In order to secure the passage of legislation in Cisleithania, the Emperor was forced to make use of emergency decrees, originally proposed by Schmerling but authorized by Article XIV of the 'December Constitution' in 1867: the sovereign could enact measures essential to maintain effective government in the absence of Reichsrat approval. Nevertheless, Francis Joseph was by now sufficiently versed in the art of ruling not to hanker for the autocracy of earlier years, however much the parliamentary system might appear paralysed.

The Emperor favoured a double approach to the protracted political crisis: administration by a dexterous non-party prime minister, who would reduce nationalistic tension by offering material improvements; and a gradual movement toward genuine universal male suffrage. He seems to have accepted the belief that national sentiment was an indulgence practised by the educated middle classes and of little relevance to the lives of the majority of his subjects. If in some industrialized regions, there was an increase in socialist representation, a 'red peril' bogey would frighten the nationalistic parties into co-operation with the dynasty.

The most successful of Austria's bureaucrat prime ministers was Ernst von Koerber, to whom Francis Joseph turned in January 1900 after the final withdrawal of Badeni's Language Ordinances. Koerber at once launched a public works programme which brought new roads, railways and canals to districts whose parliamentary deputies were induced to give him their support in the chamber. At the same time, there was a rapid spread of social welfare projects and a drastic reduction in police surveillance and press censorship. But Koerber was no parliamentarian. Sniping attacks on him in the chamber by rival German and Czech groups, each complaining he favoured the other, left him exhausted. At Christmas in 1904 after five years of improvisation, Koerber stepped out of politics. Francis Joseph began the new year by assessing seriously the prospects for electoral reform and looking for another non-party prime minister to carry it through.

From much that has been written about the septuagenarian Francis Joseph, it seems remarkable he mustered the energy to seek new policies at such a time. Legend represents him as a tired old man living in the past. For this image, he was himself partly responsible; not surprisingly, the buffetings of misfortune often plunged him into deep self-pity. 'You will find me aged a lot and feebler in mind', he wrote to Katharina Schratt in the spring of 1902, when there was a prospect of her returning to the Gloriettegasse, 'My one pleasure in your absence has been my seven grandchildren who, with Valerie, have spent some weeks with me at Schönbrunn. The older one gets the more childlike one becomes, and so I am coming closer and closer to them and their company'. Soon afterwards the old friendship was renewed. Katharina had the doubtful delight of again entertaining her sovereign to breakfast in Ischl at a time when sensible actresses were soundly asleep. As a concession to advancing years – hers rather than his – the breakfast hour at Hietzing was subsequently pushed back to nine.

Physically Francis Joseph was still a fit man. Mentally he was no less and no more receptive than at the height of the reign. To his satisfaction he was able to stay 'long in the saddle' during the autumn manoeuvres of 1902; and it is clear he continued to insist that all army matters and the general conduct of foreign affairs were questions for him to study in detail alone and decide for himself. He retained an elevated concept of the dynasty's role in Austria's past, sharply defined in his mind and, as he believed, incapable of comprehension by nobility or commonalty alike.

The letters to Katharina Schratt show that he was glad to hear his friend would make guest appearances on the stage; but he received icily the news that she had accepted the title role in a new play about his revered ancestor, Maria Theresa, to be presented at the Deutsches Volkstheater in Vienna. Someone leaked the good publicity that 'our Kathi' – as the *Oesterreichische Illustrierte Zeitung* called her – would wear her own jewellery, which was said to comprise gifts from the Emperor. Although the play had a glittering first night in the third week of October 1903, it was not a great success. Pointedly Francis Joseph did not visit the theatre during its short run.

For much of that autumn of 1903 he remained in Hungary, where hopes of raising more recruits to the army by a revised military service bill were running into serious trouble. Over the preceding seven years party loyalties had changed considerably in the kingdom. The Liberals, the government party since their formation in 1874–5, were challenged by the rapid rise of a Party of Independence, led by Ferencz Kossuth, son of the great revolutionary (who, from exile, had remained an influence on politics right up until his death in 1894). By 1903 the Independence Party was concentrating its activities on creating a national Hungarian army which would be controlled from Budapest rather than Vienna, with no regiments quartered outside the kingdom, and with Magyar as the language of command; meanwhile, the Party was disinclined to allow more Hungarians to be called up for service in the joint army. So vociferous was the Opposition that it provoked scenes in the Budapest parliament reminiscent of the recent unrest in the Reichsrat. In June and August 1903 two successive Hungarian prime ministers were forced to resign because they could not conduct parliamentary business in such an atmosphere.

At this point Field Marshal Beck, the Emperor's military confidant for more than a third of a century and Chief of the General Staff since 1881, drew up the first plans for *Fall U[ngarn]* 'Case U.': Austrian troops from Vienna and Graz would move swiftly into Hungary and occupy Budapest, while other units from Przemysl, Zagreb and Lvov converged on central Hungary. Archduke Francis Ferdinand, though in conflict with the General Staff over many matters, warmly supported the proposed military coup. His uncle, however, saw in 'Case U.' the torch which would ignite Hungary and revive the tragic conflicts with which his reign had opened; Beck's contingency plan was put into cold storage, to receive serious consideration again two years later. But while the Emperor shrank from the risk of civil war, he did not intend to loosen his grip on the imperial and royal army, which he regarded as the keystone of the Dual Monarchy.

It was for this reason that, on 16 September 1903, he issued an Order of the Day from Chlopy, his headquarters for autumn manoeuvres in Galicia. The Chlopy Order emphasized the unity of the army: 'Loyal to its oath, my entire army ... must be imbued with that spirit of unity and harmony which respects national characteristics and stands above all antagonism so as to make use of the qualities of each *Volksstamm* (racial group) for the benefit of all'. Unfortunately the Magyar version of the Chlopy Order used *néptörzs* (tribal group) for *Volksstamm*; and the sensitive Hungarian nation resented being downgraded as a tribe. So angry were the subsequent scenes in the Hungarian parliament that Francis Joseph had to spend several weeks in residence at Budapest and Gödöllö, papering the cracks in the Ausgleich settlement with exemplary patience. He conceded the authorization of Hungary's national flag to be flown alongside the imperial flag over military establishments and he allowed Hungarian officers the right to transfer to regiments stationed within the kingdom. In desperation Francis Joseph turned to István Tisza, son of the former Liberal prime minister, and on 31 October 1903 he was able to form an administration pledged to uphold a reformed settlement with Vienna. But, despite Tisza's good intentions, the Opposition's filibustering tactics continued to make a mockery of parliamentary government, although it did at least accept a compromise over the recruitment proposals.

There was no Article XIV in the Hungarian Constitution, permitting rule by emergency decrees. Tisza was therefore at a loss as to how to prevent the country from falling into anarchy. He thought the Opposition parties had discredited themselves by their behaviour in the chamber and would be rejected in a snap election. But this device, tried in January 1905, rebounded disastrously against Tisza: the Liberals were defeated. The Party of Independence emerged as the largest single group in a 'Coalition of National Parties'. Their terms for forming a government involved a greater change in the character of the Monarchy than the Emperor-King was prepared to accept.

Again Francis Joseph came under strong pressure to stage a military coup. But he would not give his assent to 'Case U'. In June 1905 he ordered the formation of a non-parliamentary government under a Hungarian soldier of unquestionable loyalty, the former commandant of the Royal Guard, General Geza Fejérváry. But the crisis dragged on. Ominously, four days after his birthday, Francis Joseph broke precedent by presiding over a council of ministers at Ischl, where detailed study was made of the military options. On 23 September he summoned the Hungarian politicians to Schönbrunn and told them bluntly that, if they wished to constitute a government, they would have to drop from their programme all legislation concerned with language of command or changes in the army structure: these matters, he emphasized once more, remained strictly the concern of the sovereign. They would also have to pledge themselves to pass the proposed budget, to approve a new army bill providing more recruits, and to modify the economic relationship between Hungary and Cisleithania only after agreement in the Delegations, as stipulated in past negotiations. Francis Joseph would not discuss these matters with the Hungarian delegates; they were to see Goluchowski, since he was the responsible co-ordinating government minister. The meeting ended five minutes after it began.

Despite such tough talk, Francis Joseph was uncertain how these over-excited Hungarian politicians would react to what was virtually an ultimatum. Nine days after the 'five minute audience' he was still in doubt, writing from Schönbrunn to Katharina Schratt (in Baden-Baden) to complain that he had been unable to go hunting in Styria, as he planned: 'Unfortunately I must stay on here and worry and fret about Hungary: but I am not going to give way . . .' Two months later he authorized the next step forward. Fejérváry's minister of the interior published the text of a proposed reform bill. It would have raised the size of the Hungarian electorate from one million to two and half million, thereby swamping Magyar voters under a flood of newly enfranchised Roumanians, Slovaks, Serbs and members of other minorities. Such a measure meant the end of the built-in Magyar majority in Hungary's parliament.

The threat was taken seriously by the Coalition leaders. Rather than face such a future, they chose to come to terms with their king. A Hungarian government of all-the-talents was formed in April 1906 under Alexander Wekerle, a Liberal of no strong party commitment. The electoral reform bill was not enacted. An appropriate, dignified calm returned to Budapest's impressive parliament house. Bluff, and a strong hint of political blackmail, had given the seventy-five year old Emperor-King a sound victory. Yet he was neither elated nor confident. 'I have been busier than ever with the makeshift solution of the crisis over Hungarian rights and am very tired and cannot prevent my nerves from being on edge', he wrote to Katharina Schratt on the Wednesday in Holy Week, with two days of penitential observance ahead of him; 'God will help us further, but I see still more fights looming up', he added.

By now he had a new cause for concern: the heavy shadow of the heir-apparent darkened the political scene. Francis Ferdinand was too forceful a personality to be content with deputizing for the Emperor on state occasions. Yet, though an admirable family man, he lacked those easy graces which win popular acclaim. Basically he mistrusted people: 'On first acquaintance I look upon everyone I meet as being a scoundrel', he told the Chief of the General Staff. After his marriage his prejudices intensified, despite his wife's calmly reasonable outlook on life: he remained anti-Semitic, anti-Magyar, anti-Italian. It is hard to escape the feeling he would have become a disastrous Emperor had he succeeded to the throne. Yet he prepared for that day more assiduously than poor Rudolf. From 1901 onwards he built up a personal intelligence service at the Lower Belvedere, the lesser of the complementary palaces built for Prince Eugen and originally intended as administrative offices. In January 1906 he persuaded the Emperor to accept the machine he had created as a Military Chancellery. Under Major von Brosch's supervision it grew into a team of fourteen officers who prided themselves on greater knowledge than the Emperor's Military Chancellery and on smoother efficiency than the General Staff. They recognized – Brosch in particular – the need for 'finesse and tact' in working with a man of such 'explosive energy'.

Though Francis Joseph was frequently exasperated by his nephew and irritated by his bustling restlessness, he treated Francis Ferdinand with punctilious respect: he knew from his own early months with Grünne that an heir to the throne needed access to official papers and, from the spring of 1906 onwards, copies of all important documents and despatches were sent regularly from the war ministry, and often from the Ballhausplatz, to the Lower Belvedere. Not that the Archduke was often in Vienna to receive them: Brosch later calculated that Francis Ferdinand was away from the capital for 200 days a year, on the average. He expected his office to feed him with paperwork wherever he might be. His particular interests were in the armed services (and notably in the navy), in maintaining good relations with Berlin and St Petersburg, in what he regarded as the nefarious intrigues of Hungary's politicians, and in preserving historic churches and buildings. At the same time, Francis Ferdinand turned for political guidance to a circle of advisers including right-wing representatives of the Czech, Roumanian and Croat minorities. In Austria itself the Archduke's sympathies were with Karl Lueger, whom at one time he was expected to appoint as prime minister or even as Chancellor, should he succeed in changing the political structure of the Monarchy.

Francis Joseph welcomed the Archduke's interest in military affairs. He was relieved that Francis Ferdinand seemed pleased to don an Admiral's uniform (the Emperor never had one himself) and launch battleships in Trieste or visit fleet anchorages down the Adriatic. But Francis Joseph was suspicious of the Archduke's politics, which were as conservative as his own beliefs but more narrowly clericalist and far more aggressively authoritarian. It was disconcerting for the Emperor to find, after all these years, a shadow court functioning in Vienna, with ambassadors discreetly keeping in touch with the man whom they believed must surely soon be called to the throne. Francis Joseph treated the emergence of the Belvedere as an alternative political centre as if it challenged his whole concept of the Monarchy. He had no intention of sharing the responsibilities of government with Francis Ferdinand. Sometimes he seems deliberately to have looked for an alternative policy to anything which the Archduke was believed to favour.

Yet it was obvious that men of talent with an eye to the future would be drawn towards the Belvedere. Not all, however, were young, for Francis Ferdinand himself was forty-two at Christmas in 1905. One of the Archduke's earliest associates and wisest counsellors during the crisis over his marriage was Baron Max von Beck (who was totally unrelated to his namesake, the distinguished soldier). Max Beck had such obvious gifts as a constitutional lawyer and patient negotiator that in June 1906 the Emperor invited him to head the Austrian government, an appointment made without consulting Francis Ferdinand, who was abroad at the time. Beck successfully carried through the electoral reforms in Cisleithania which Francis Joseph had long contemplated: universal male suffrage was instituted in January 1907, in time for the Christian Socials and their allies to emerge as the largest single party at the May general election for the Reichsrat. He also succeeded in working out an acceptable commercial Ausgleich with the Hungarians in 1907. But neither of these achievements pleased Francis Ferdinand: he mistrusted universal suffrage in the 'Austrian' half of the Monarchy as opening a door for socialism; and he regarded even the slightest concessions to Hungary's politicians as tantamount to treason. Francis Joseph seems to have hoped that in appointing an old friend of the Archduke as prime minister he would have a tactful intermediary between the Hofburg and the Belvedere. In this he was disappointed: Francis Ferdinand never forgave Max Beck's apparent apostasy. The so-called 'Belvedere Cabal' joined the Christian Social politicians in November 1909 to force the ablest of Francis Joseph's later prime ministers out of office.

Over military affairs Francis Ferdinand showed a sounder judgment than in politics. To some extent he became what 'Uncle Albrecht' had once been, a prodder-general to the military establishment, seeking to combat stagnation in a decade of rapid change. The Archduke's activities did not endear him to Field Marshal Beck, who shared the Emperor's slightly contemptuous assessment of the Archduke's qualities. There was, for example, a wide difference in their attitudes to the significance of the internal combustion engine. Francis Ferdinand early saw the advantages of a car during his indefatigable travelling between isolated garrison towns and along distant frontiers. To Field Marshal Beck, on the other hand, the motor-car was 'a pretty pastime for aristocratic lazybones and Jewish sportsmen; no use for the army'. Francis Joseph's innate conservatism inclined him to agree with Beck: the Emperor visited the Sixth Automobile Exhibition in Vienna in 1906, but he only drove in a car for the first time in August 1908, at King Edward VII's prompting during a visit to Ischl. A year later he sat beside William II in a half-open car at the last autumn manoeuvres they attended. At heart he was convinced that cars had no place with an army in the field: did they not, after all, frighten the horses? Yet Francis Joseph had seen so many changes in transport during his lifetime that he had no wish to reject the latest innovations out of hand. On 18 September 1910 he agreed to be driven by car thirty miles out to the Steinfeld flying field at Wiener Neustadt, where he inspected biplanes and monoplanes and talked to pioneer pilots. A photograph caught an expression of incredulity on the wizened face, as if he was as puzzled as sixty-five years earlier, when he stood beside Radetzky to watch military balloons ascend above the amphitheatre in Verona. Perhaps there was a future in military aviation: he was too open-minded to dismiss all of his nephew's proposals for modernizing the army.

On one particular occasion, four years before his visit to the flying field, the Emperor accepted that Francis Ferdinand was right and he was himself mistaken. In August 1906 the Emperor travelled to Teschen for cavalry manoeuvres in the foothills of the Beskid mountains. At the same time, Francis Ferdinand was sent as his uncle's representative to observe combined sea and land exercises in the northern Adriatic. While the Emperor was satisfied with all he saw, his nephew was shocked by the total lack of co-ordination between artillery, infantry and fleet. In a devastating report, carefully detailed with material fed to him by Brosch's staff in the Lower Belvedere, the Archduke recommended the dismissal of the war minister and Beck's retirement as Chief of the General Staff. Reluctantly the Emperor decided he must agree with his nephew. He would have to look for a new war minister; more importantly he must find for the first time in twenty-five years, a new Chief of the General Staff.

At almost the same time that autumn Count Goluchowski, a tired man exasperated by the attitude of Hungary's political leaders, let the Emperor know he had decided he must give up the foreign ministry. Francis Joseph had little doubt whom he wished to see as Goluchowski's successor; he had the highest opinion of Baron Aehrenthal, the ambassador at St Petersburg for the past seven years. With his attention thus concentrated on the Ballhausplatz, he was prepared to give his nephew a freer hand in finding incumbents for the two military posts than at a less pressing moment. For the war ministry the Archduke had a ready candidate in Baron von Schonaich (who, in fact, soon offended his patron by over-leniency towards Hungary); but General Conrad von Hötzendorf, the soldier whom he wished to take Beck's place, was reluctant to give up a field command and assume the greatest of all staff responsibilities. Only after being browbeaten by the Archduke in two long audiences at the Belvedere did Conrad accept that it was his duty to take up the post. The Emperor formally gazetted him Chief of the General Staff on 18 November 1906, three and a half weeks after Aehrenthal took up his duties as foreign minister. Not for over thirty years had Francis Joseph made so momentous a change of personnel at the head of affairs as in his appointments of Aehrenthal and Conrad. With a semblance of dignity restored to Hungarian politics and parliamentary government refurbished in Vienna, it seemed as if a new dynamism was beginning to power the old Monarchy. But how soon would it blow a fuse?

Chapter 19

TWO JOURNEYS TO
SARAJEVO

By 1906 it was forty years since Francis Joseph had been at war. His subjects were enjoying a longer period of external peace than under any previous Habsburg rulers. Few serving officers could remember the fluctuating fortunes of a military campaign, those dashed hopes which their Emperor recalled all too vividly. Yet there were signs that these halcyon days might already be numbered. From about 1900 onwards a new mood crept into the politics of the Balkan states: young, ambitious army officers – first in Serbia, later during the decade in Bulgaria, Greece and even Turkey – banded together in pressure groups which imposed nationalistic policies on their respective governments. Goluchowski warned Francis Joseph of the mounting danger from Belgrade at the turn of the century, though he assumed that any crisis could be localized. 'Should anything serious happen in the Balkans and the Serbs follow a policy we do not like, we shall simply strangle Serbia', he explained to the German ambassador as early as January 1901.

The first dramatic episode took Francis Joseph by surprise, though not perhaps his ministers. In the small hours of 11 June 1903 King Alexander Obrenović of Serbia and his Queen were butchered by a group of rebel army officers and their naked, mutilated bodies thrown from the palace window in Belgrade. The conspirators invited the head of the rival dynastic clan, Peter Karadjordjević, to return from exile and ascend the throne. Great Britain and the Netherlands, shocked by the savage act of regicide, broke off diplomatic relations with Serbia and declined to renew them for three years. But Austria-Hungary, with posts along the Danube directly facing Belgrade, could not treat the change of dynasty with such lofty disdain. Francis Joseph hesitated. Were the Serbs about to embark on policies Vienna would 'not like'? Had the time come to 'strangle Serbia'? Or would Peter, who was almost sixty in 1903, prove a strong ruler, willing to reject the dangerous policies advocated by the younger generation? The Emperor decided to give the new regime in Belgrade an opportunity to form a stable government. He became the first monarch to recognize Peter I as King of Serbia.

Francis Joseph believed that the surest way of maintaining peace in the Balkans was to work closely with St Petersburg, preserving the Austro-Russian entente attained at the end of the old century. A meeting between the Austrian and Russian rulers, with their foreign ministers, at Mürzsteg in October 1903 agreed to put joint pressure on Sultan Abdulhamid to accept international policing and administrative reform in Macedonia, the most troubled of his Balkan provinces. By 1906, however, Francis Joseph could wonder if the loose understanding with Russia had gone far enough. He was becoming increasingly suspicious of the Belgrade government and the influence of Pan-Serb agents operating beyond Serbia's frontiers. In the autumn of 1905 meetings of Croatian politicians at Rijeka and leaders of Austria-Hungary's Serbian minority at Zadar passed resolutions in favour of Serbo-Croat collaboration against 'the anti-Slav Habsburg dualists'; and sympathy for these resolutions was expressed in Belgrade, much to the irritation of both the Austrian and Hungarian prime ministers. The Serbian government seemed determined to lessen the kingdom's dependence on Austria-Hungary and affirm a sense of Slav, Orthodox brotherhood. A customs union between Serbia and Bulgaria, made public in January 1906, was seen in Vienna as a breach of Austro-Serbian agreements which had long regulated commerce. To Francis Joseph's indignation, the Serbs then placed a huge arms order with the French firm of Schneider-Creusot rather than with Skoda in Bohemia, as in the past. The Serbs, it was decided, must be brought to heel: the Emperor approved the imposition of economic sanctions; Austria-Hungary's frontiers were closed to imports of Serbian pigs and cattle, living or slaughtered.

This 'pig war' proved a disastrous shift of policy, hardening the two government's mutual hostility. Although 80 per cent of Serbia's exports had gone to Austria-Hungary, the sanctions did not bite: the Serbs found new markets and alternative routes, notably through Salonika. The pig war dragged on for four years: anti-Habsburg feeling intensified among the Serbian peasantry inside and outside the Dual Monarchy, particularly in occupied Bosnia-Herzegovina. The incoming Chief of the General Staff, Conrad von Hötzendorf, had seen active service against the Muslim militia in 1878 and brought to his new post a sabre-rattling belligerence. He chafed at the continuance of these ineffectual sanctions: the Balkan problem, he wrote a week before Christmas in 1907, 'must be resolved in grand style by the annexation of Bosnia-Herzegovina and Serbia'.

Francis Joseph did not agree with Conrad. Under no circumstances would he risk a protracted and expensive military campaign. His new foreign minister, Aehrenthal, also stopped short of advocating armed intervention, but he regarded some re-ordering of the Monarchy's Balkan policies as essential. Long-nurtured plans for railway construction were made public in January 1908 and, with the Sultan's assent almost certain, Aehrenthal announced in Budapest that a line would be built through the Sanjak of Novibazar linking Bosnia with the main Turkish trunk routes and eventually with the port of Salonika, then the second largest city of Turkey-in-Europe. At the same time Aehrenthal was giving close attention to the possible incorporation of Bosnia-Herzegovina in the Monarchy. To make the political transference of sovereignty and the railway project palatable abroad he favoured the withdrawal of army units from the towns they had occupied in the Sanjak for thirty years. Yet for Aehrenthal to carry through these radical changes, three pre-conditions were essential: an agreement with Russia; the concurrence of Conrad and the army chiefs; and the formal approval of the Emperor.

In Andrássy's day Francis Joseph followed expedient twists of policy during the Eastern Crisis with minute attention, even if he failed to understand issues in dispute. Now, in 1908, he believed he was still consulted as much as ever, for there was no diminution in the number of papers requiring attention on his desk and his ministers and generals reported personally to him whether he was in Vienna, Budapest or even Ischl. 'Today I am absolutely in no position to ask you to visit me', he told Katharina Schratt in May; 'in the trouble, excitement and rush these days', he explained, 'I cannot find a moment to set aside in advance for me to talk quietly with you'. Yet, though Aehrenthal and Conrad might ply the Emperor with memoranda, they increasingly behaved as if he were in virtual retirement. Conrad in particular consulted the 'alternative Court' at the Belvedere before submitting proposals to his sovereign; and the foreign minister seems to have assumed that the Emperor would automatically approve action already agreed around the ministerial council chamber. But Aehrenthal knew that the Emperor expected to be well briefed on major adjustments to the balance between the Great Powers. In early July 1908 he therefore kept Francis Joseph carefully informed of an apparent change in Russian policy, a diplomatic 'bargain offer' from Alexander Izvolsky, Nicholas's foreign minister for the past two years: if Aehrenthal supported Izvolsky's attempts to secure revision of the Straits Convention (so that Russian warships might pass through the Bosphorus and Dardanelles in time of peace), Russia would not object to the annexation of Bosnia-Herzegovina and the Sanjak of Novibazar.

At first, both Francis Joseph and his minister were suspicious of the proposed bargain. But events in Constantinople caused second thoughts.

In late July the Young Turk revolution, which had begun in Macedonia and spread to the Sultan's capital, induced Abdulhamid to restore the Constitution of 1876, a short-lived experiment in parliamentary government. Aehrenthal was immediately alarmed: what would happen if the Young Turks announced the holding of elections in Bosnia and in Herzegovina for an Ottoman assembly? And how far would the balance in the Balkans be changed if they called for the return of deputies from tributary states such as – in Europe – Bulgaria? When faced by these uncertainties, Aehrenthal recommended the annexation of Bosnia-Herzegovina. He also advocated a change in Balkan patronage, by which Austria-Hungary would back Russia's traditional client, Bulgaria, in any disputes with Serbia. Francis Joseph approved: Aehrenthal was to sound out Izvolsky privately.

On 19 August Aehrenthal told his ministerial colleagues that he could carry through the annexation without arousing the hostility of Russia and with support from Austria's German and Italian allies. Although the two prime ministers were hesitant, Aehrenthal brushed all objections aside, confident of the Emperor's support. He met more opposition from the Belvedere; Archduke Francis Ferdinand doubted if the Dual Monarchy was sufficiently unified in purpose to absorb two provinces with so many conflicting races and religions. He made the important stipulation that Bosnia-Herzegovina must become the joint responsibility of both partners in the Dual Monarchy: 'If Hungary claims the territories for the Crown of St Stephen (as will certainly happen) this must under no circumstances be conceded, even at the cost of abandoning annexation and leaving things as they are', Francis Ferdinand wrote from army manoeuvres, after talks with the Chief of the General Staff. Significantly the Archduke added a further warning: 'I am utterly opposed to all such shows of strength, in view of our sorry domestic affairs ...', he wrote, 'I am against mobilization, and I think we should merely heighten our military readiness'. These were not the views of the Archduke's former protégé, General Conrad.

Aehrenthal met Izvolsky at Buchlau, a shooting-lodge in Moravia, on 15 September, taking up the Russian's earlier 'bargain' terms. No written record was made of their conversations; later accounts by the two participants show discrepancies – to which historians have, perhaps, given undue attention. Izvolsky certainly did not realize that the Austrians were in a hurry because they were worried by the new political vitality in Constantinople. Similarly, Aehrenthal failed to appreciate Izvolsky's difficulties, not knowing that the Russian foreign minister was acting virtually on his own, without backing from the Tsar or the government in St Petersburg, and without consulting Russia's ally, France, or the new

Entente partner, Great Britain. Francis Joseph for his part did all that Aehrenthal expected from him. He even received Prince Ferdinand of Bulgaria with full royal honours in Budapest in late September, though nothing could overcome his basic mistrust of 'the Coburg' as a person. But it was on 6 October 1908 that the Emperor took the decisive step, signing a proclamation addressed to the peoples of Bosnia-Herzegovina; they were told that, as they deserved an autonomous and constitutional government, he had decided to extend his sovereignty so as to include their two provinces within his Empire. At the same time he sent a letter to Aehrenthal, intended for immediate publication, in which he announced that 'to show the peaceful intentions which have inspired me to take this inevitable step' he was ordering the immediate withdrawal of his army from the Sanjak of Novibazar. Meanwhile, in Sofia, Prince Ferdinand had jumped the gun by asserting his country's total independence of the Ottoman Empire on 5 October and proclaiming himself 'Tsar of the Bulgarians' (a title downgraded to 'King' under Austrian pressure).

By annexing Bosnia-Herzegovina the Emperor at last acquired two provinces, his only territorial gains in a long reign. The cost was greater than he had anticipated. For the timing of the annexation left Francis Joseph out of step with every other ruler in Europe, except the precipitate Foxy Ferdinand. The German Emperor, William II, was appalled: 'I am deeply offended in my role as an ally not to have been taken into His Majesty's confidence!', he wrote stuffily in a marginal note to a despatch drafted by Chancellor Bülow. Reaction elsewhere was more dramatic. There were anti-Austrian demonstrations in several Italian cities; the Turks withdrew deposits from Austrian banks, refused to unload Austrian ships, and boycotted goods imported from the Monarchy. Five days after the annexation was announced, ten thousand people demonstrated against Austria-Hungary and Bulgaria in the streets of Salonika, the port which Aehrenthal hoped to develop as the Trieste of the Aegean. The British complained of Aehrenthal's recklessness, the Russian press and people maintained a bitter campaign against the government in Vienna, while Izvolsky insisted that Aehrenthal had deceived him at Buchlau. The Serbian heir-apparent and the most influential Serbian Radical politician, Nikola Pašić, travelled to St Petersburg to win support from Russia's Panslavs; in Belgrade itself 120,000 reservists were mobilized and a national defence organization (*Narodna Odbrana*) established to sustain the Serb loyalties of compatriots in Bosnia-Herzegovina by subversive propaganda and sabotage. Politically the annexation left the Dual Monarchy isolated in Europe.

Francis Joseph backed every move made by Aehrenthal to keep the peace. The Turks were offered money for the loss of two provinces which had long been developed as virtual colonial protectorates. The Emperor gave personal assurances to Nicholas II and to William II that he 'cherished no designs of conquest at the expense' of Serbia and Montenegro, even should one or other of the kingdoms violate his territory and provoke a punitive expedition. Tension gradually relaxed; and the crisis was finally resolved in March 1909 by quiet diplomacy, in which Aehrenthal himself and British and Italian intermediaries all played their part, though much of the credit was claimed by Chancellor Bülow in Berlin.

Ultimately the whole affair strengthened rather than weakened the Austro-German connection, as had seemed likely when William complained of lack of consultation, back in October. The external threat, especially from Russia, favoured close co-operation between the Austro-Hungarian and German chiefs of staff, a link neglected during the past eighteen years. Exchanges between Conrad and the younger Moltke, which began in January 1909, continued long after the crisis was over. More immediately, however, it was the intervention of the German foreign ministry which left an impact on events. For, at almost the last moments in the crisis, while Izvolsky was prevaricating, a telegram in Bülow's name demanded from St Petersburg a clear 'yes' or 'no' response: did Russia recognize the annexation? This near ultimatum was unnecessary. Consent would soon have come, once the Russians devised ways of saving face. Now they were denied any such consolation: Izvolsky appeared to give way under threats from Germany's 'mailed fist'.

William II was well-satisfied. He believed he had checked Austria's drift into dangerous isolation; and he did not intend to release Francis Joseph from the bonds of Hohenzollern friendship. Eighteen months later, William made an impromptu speech in the Rathaus during a visit to Vienna: the Austrian people were told that they, and Europe with them enjoyed peace that year because he had stood 'shoulder to shoulder ... in shining armour' beside their 'august and venerable' monarch during the crisis over Bosnia. The speech irritated Francis Joseph; he did not seek a close relationship with militaristic Prussia. Privately he remarked that, in 'this ostentatious display of the sharp blade of Germany's sword' he sensed danger.

After twenty years of partnership, Francis Joseph still found his German ally personally antipathetic. William tried to endear himself to his brother sovereign, though at times with a patronizing manner almost discourteous in its impact. Unfortunately his frequent presence in Vienna often recalled a past which intruded uneasily on Francis Joseph's peace of mind, particularly the last twelve months before Mayerling and Rudolf's anger at the poses struck by Germany's Emperor on his accession. There were, too, other sad echoes: in 1907 William purchased the Achilleion for a million marks from Archduchess Gisela, who could find no delight in the marble palace among the cypresses and ilex trees which she had inherited from her mother. It became natural for him to sail back from Corfu to Trieste or Pola and break his journey in Vienna. Occasionally his guest's enthusiasm for his island refuge grated on the old widower's sensitivities, opening sore wounds in a starved heart. Yet William was ready to pay homage to Francis Joseph as the head of a great dynasty. On 7 May 1908 he led a deputation of German rulers who travelled to Schönbrunn to greet the Emperor on his Diamond Jubilee. After William conveyed their joint congratulations, Francis Joseph received each prince individually. As he felt obliged to change into the uniform of any of their regiments in which he enjoyed honorary rank it proved to be a long ceremony.

The princes' visit anticipated the anniversary of his accession by seven months, for once again the festivities began in the spring rather than in the gloom of short winter days. On 21 May 82,000 schoolchildren – 12,000 more than in 1898 – gathered on the lawns of Schönbrunn: 'The older I become the more I love children', Francis Joseph remarked, as he waved to them from the balcony. Three weeks later there was a historical pageant along the Ringstrasse, which evoked for the Emperor poignant memories of the silver wedding festivities nearly thirty years before. By early December, with the uncertainties of the Bosnian Crisis weighing on his mind, Francis Joseph looked weary, but he acknowledged a further round of tributes. On 1 December the younger members of the dynasty serenaded him with garlands and bouquets in the private theatre at Schönbrunn; and on accession day itself Francis Ferdinand conveyed the joint congratulations of the Archdukes and their families assembled in the Hofburg, much as had William II for the German princes seven months before. When a few hours later the Emperor attended a short gala at the Opera, the Viennese hailed a father figure they held in affectionate respect. By contrast in Bohemia there were violent demonstrations against the dynasty, with cries of 'Long live Serbia' in a menacing show of Slav solidarity. For twelve days Prague remained under strict martial law.

Yet police reports of increased unrest among the national minorities left Francis Joseph unperturbed. The Emperor never showed any fear of sudden death, treating the threat of assassination as an occupational hazard. No Austrian Habsburg, whether ruler in Vienna or heir to the throne, had fallen a victim to the politics of murder. Accordingly when, in February 1910 General Marijan Varešanin, the Governor of Bosnia, proposed that an imperial dignitary might pay a state visit to the newly annexed provinces, the Emperor himself was anxious to make the journey, even in his eightieth year. Early in March it was announced in the Press that Francis Joseph would visit Bosnia-Herzegovina between 30 May and 5 June. Would-be assassins were thus given eleven weeks in which to complete their plans.

Rumours of a conspiracy reached the Austro-Hungarian embassy in Paris in mid-May: a police informer claimed to have overheard southern Slav anarchists talking of a plan to kill the emperor at Mostar, the capital of Herzegovina. A similar report, again mentioning Mostar, was received at the legation in Sofia. Some precautions were taken, but the authorities still believed that any attempt on Francis Joseph's life would be made in Sarajevo rather than any other town. Close surveillance of travellers into the city was ordered, more than a thousand uniformed police were in the streets, together with a double line of troops along the Emperor's route. Before leaving Vienna, Francis Joseph approved of the arrangements. 'It is to be hoped it will not be too hot in Bosnia', he wrote to Katharina Schratt on the eve of his departure, 'You will see from the arrangements ... that the rush could be worse and that my decrepitude has been taken into consideration ... I commend myself to your prayers throughout the whole Bosnian expedition'.

Francis Joseph arrived at Sarajevo at mid-afternoon on 30 May 1910, his train having stopped at several small stations in Bosnia so that his new subjects could see their Emperor from a respectful and safe distance. He stayed in the Bosnian capital for four nights, driving through the city in an open carriage on four occasions and out to the spa at Ilidze in a car. There was a military review, at which he took the salute sitting superbly upright in the saddle. He watched torchlit festivities for the young from the balcony of the Konak, Governor Varešanin's official residence, and left for Mostar elated by the apparent enthusiasm of his new subjects.

He was at Mostar for only a few hours on 3 June, before boarding the specially decorated imperial coach of the Bosnian Railways for Vienna. 'It all went better than I had expected', he told Katharina Schratt with relief and characteristic understatement on his return. Others concerned with organizing the visit preferred to use superlatives. 'A triumphal progress', reported General Appel, commander of 15 Corps, in a letter to the head of Francis Ferdinand's military chancellery. The Emperor's success prompted Appel to an afterthought: why should not the Archduke come to Sarajevo, the general suggested in a postscript? He could bring his wife and children with him and stay at Ilidze. It would 'give the population great joy', Appel wrote, adding confidently, 'I will vouch for the security of such a visit with my head'.

Within ten days of Appel's letter and Francis Joseph's return home, shots were fired at Governor Varešanin as he rode back to the Konak

after opening the newly instituted provincial assembly in Sarajevo. Varešanin was unhurt and his assailant, a law student named Bogdan Žerajić,
killed himself with his last bullet. Investigations showed that Žerajić had
tracked the Emperor throughout his visit and was himself trailed by three
suspicious detectives in Sarajevo while Francis Joseph was in the city. One
of Žerajić's friends said that Bogdan had told him he was so close to
Francis Joseph at Mostar railway station that he could almost have touched
him; and yet the inner compulsion to pull out his revolver and turn it on
the Emperor at that moment was lacking. Subsequently Žerajić was so
disgusted with himself, and so unable to account for his hesitancy, that
he made his futile attempt to kill Governor Varešanin instead of his
sovereign and chose suicide as an act of martyrdom. In death Žerajić did,
indeed, become a hero of *Mlada Bosna* (Young Bosnia), a militant force
linked with the *Narodna Odbrana* movement which attracted support
from schoolboys and students.

By now, except in these southern regions and in Prague, Francis
Joseph enjoyed more personal popularity than at any time in his reign;
he had the rare distinction that summer of unveiling statues of himself.
Foreign visitors, too, recognized him as a 'presence that pervades the
entire feeling of life' in Vienna. A distinguished American observer,
ex-President Theodore Roosevelt, was able to judge for himself the
reality behind the popular image of 'the old gentleman'. It was seven
weeks before his journey to Bosnia that the Emperor met a President
of the United States for the only time in his life. He received Theodore
Roosevelt in private audience on 15 April 1910, when he is said to
have called himself 'the last monarch of the old school'. The ex-
President's account of the conversation is slightly different: he 'did not
strike me as a very able man, but he was a gentleman', Roosevelt recalled
soon afterwards; 'He talked very freely and pleasantly, sometimes about
politics, sometimes about hunting; ... he said that he had been
particularly interested in seeing me because he was the last representative
of the old system, whereas I embodied the new movement'. Roosevelt
was invited to dine at Schönbrunn: an interesting occasion, he wrote,
marred by 'one horrid habit'; for when 'fingerbowls were brought on,
each with a small tumbler of water in the middle, the Emperor and all
the others proceeded to rinse their mouths and empty them into the
fingerbowls'.

Archduke Francis Ferdinand, meeting the President at King Edward
VII's funeral a month later, complained in a letter to his uncle that
'Rooseveldt' (*sic*) lacked 'court manners'; he was 'enormously witty, or
to put it more clearly – impertinent'. Francis Joseph, on the other hand,
has left no criticism of his visitor's behaviour. Long experience of other

nation's customs gave him a certain tolerance. He respected the United States as a federation of peoples functioning effectively without any need for a unifying dynasty. By emphasizing the solemn bonds of a historic flag and a secular constitution, the American nation had already made 'the new movement' traditional. But such ideas were not, he thought, for Europe. He could not hope to explain to Theodore Roosevelt his conviction that 'the old system' which he exemplified rested on divine sanction. For Francis Joseph, dynasty and supranational Empire remained twin pillars of a just society based upon a predominantly Christian moral order.

In this sunset of the reign he was, perhaps, 'an anachronism' – as he once himself admitted. Politicians whom he consulted complained that proposals they advanced were countered by preconceptions dating back to Schwarzenberg's time. But this was a superficial criticism; long experience and common sense gave him a more detached insight into human problems than his younger ministers or generals, particularly in matters referred to him by the courts of justice. Yet the world around him was changing rapidly, and not every visitor to Vienna was a respectable champion of the established order. Adolf Hitler, a thin and hungry bearded drop-out, was standing in the Ringstrasse when in March 1910 the Emperor rode to St Stephen's Cathedral for the funeral of Karl Lueger. Also in Vienna in these years was Leon Bronstein (alias Trotsky), who was to be joined briefly by an ex-seminarist with the revolutionary pseudonym of 'Stalin'. But, though the authorities showed a passing interest in 'Herr Bronstein', the two more ominous names in this sinister trio went unnoticed in the crowd.

Despite his attachment to the 'old system', Francis Joseph allowed his mind to recognize that familiar certainties of belief were being called in question throughout this first decade of the century. He had himself received in special audience Dr Sigmund Freud, when the University of Vienna belatedly found a professorship for the pioneer champion of psychoanalysis. He knew, too, that among intellectuals there was a strong current of sceptical agnosticism: a newly commissioned army officer now had the right to declare himself '*konfessionslos*', unattached to any denomination. Nevertheless, the decennial census of 1910 showed that 65.9 per cent of his subjects were Roman Catholics. So, demonstratively, was their sovereign. Each summer successive rulers in Vienna had followed the Holy Sacrament as it was born in procession through the Graben to St Stephen's Cathedral on the Feast of Corpus Christi. That tradition Francis Joseph maintained with great solemnity as late as the summer of 1912. However deep the intellectual ferment of new ideas in his capital might be, there was no wavering in the Emperor's public affirmation of the baroque Catholicism he had inherited from an earlier age.

In August 1910 he celebrated his eightieth birthday, like so many other ones, among the mountains of the Salzkammergut. Seventy-two members of the dynasty joined him at Ischl – officially *Bad* Ischl for the past four years. There was a family dinner in the principal salon of the Kurhaus, for the two-storeyed yellow ochre Kaiservilla was too compact for such a gathering; it was a relaxed country house, with balustraded wings and a colonnaded portico looking out across a single jet fountain and neat lawns to rising parkland filled with conifers and the steeper slopes of the Jainzenberg, with an unbroken line of higher peaks behind. Antlers and stuffed trophies recalled hunting forays; even the waste-paper basket beside the Emperor's bureau seemed to be held steady by the paws of a small bear he had once shot. At eighty Francis Joseph was almost resigned to hanging up his guns. Almost, but not quite; he still hoped to rise again to the silent challenge of stalking the Alpine slopes.

During his visit to Sarajevo, old Turks who knew and respected good horsemanship admired his skill in the saddle; surely, they insisted, he could not be so old as they were told; their Emperor rode like a man in his fiftieth year, not his eightieth. Physically, however, he was frailer than he appeared to distant onlookers. He had long suffered occasionally from bronchial asthma and in April 1911 he fell seriously ill. Immediately after Easter, he travelled to his daughter Marie Valerie's home at Wallsee, on the middle Danube. The weather was cold; he had recently followed a Lenten abstinence by his customary observance of the full Holy Week discipline of fasts; and, with damp mists drifting in from the river, he lacked the strength to throw off a persistent cough. Soon he was forced to remain in bed. His doctors were alarmed. Archduke Francis Ferdinand, as heir apparent, was alerted.

Even while confined to a sick room at Wallsee, the Emperor insisted on having official papers brought to him each morning. His Austrian lands were in political turmoil in this summer of 1911 with the conflict of Czechs, Poles and Germans forcing an early and indecisive election in mid-June. For the first time since 1905 the government had to resort to Article XIV of the constitution, imposing essential legislation on this occasion at the decree of a sovereign who many believed would not survive the onset of winter. At the same time there was a new vitality in the political life of Budapest, where István Tisza had emerged as Hungary's strong man, although he did not become prime minister again until June 1913. Tisza's 'Party of Work' favoured reforms, closer collaboration between German-Austrians and Magyars, and no concessions to national minorities or to the southern Slavs in autonomous Croatia. Although critical of Tisza's sternly Calvinistic style of government. Francis Joseph appreciated his qualities of leadership. Archduke Francis Ferdinand did not; the head of his military chancellery in the Belvedere recommended that, should he succeed to the throne, he must delay swearing to uphold Hungary's rights until he had imposed a revised constitution on the kingdom. Such proposals were not made public but it was with genuine relief that Tisza welcomed his king to Hungary when, in June, Francis Joseph exchanged convalescence at Wallsee for recuperation at Gödöllö.

By October 1911 he was fit to travel the forty miles from Vienna to Schwarzau, where his great-nephew (and eventual successor), Archduke Charles, was to marry the 19-year old Princess Zita of Bourbon-Parma. An early newsreel shows the Emperor in good spirits, caught in lively conversation with the bridegroom's mother, though he stoops forward to hear what she is saying and, in profile, his face is deeply lined. The early camera work may accentuate the jerk of his head, the appraising glance with which he looks about him, but he smiles readily and the film conveys an impression of surprising alacrity: here is a great-uncle at ease, and thoroughly happy. Perhaps Francis Joseph enjoyed himself too much that Saturday in the deceptive autumn sunshine at Schwarzau, where the wind came down the valley from the slopes of the Raxalpe; for he caught a chill which lingered through the remaining weeks of the year. Archduke Francis Ferdinand decided that his family should spend Christmas at the Belvedere rather than in distant Konopischt.

Francis Joseph's relapse came at a critical moment in world affairs. Three weeks before the Schwarzau wedding the Italians, complaining of Turkish maltreatment of their merchants, invaded Libya, the Ottoman provinces of Tripolitania and Cyrenaica. Austria-Hungary as an essentially conservative Great Power, deplored the colonial adventure of its ally: war with Turkey might soon spread to the Adriatic, for the Italian port of Brindisi was nearer to Ottoman Albania than southern England to Normandy; and a campaign in Albania would ignite the Balkans. Conrad von Hötzendorf at once proposed an immediate Austro-Hungarian attack on Italy, seeking quick victories in order to advance the southern frontiers to Verona and the line of the River Piave and to assert the Monarchy's role as arbiter of affairs in the Balkans and eastern Mediterranean.

Aehrenthal was aghast at Conrad's folly. On the day after the Schwarzau wedding the foreign minister drafted a formidable indictment of the Chief-of-Staff which he presented to the Emperor, who had already taken Conrad to task more than once for his bellicose views. On 15 November, as soon as his health was up to the strain of renewed argument, Francis Joseph summoned Conrad to a private audience. Attacks on Aehrenthal for his attitude towards Italy and the Balkans were attacks on himself, he told Conrad: 'These pinpricks, I forbid them! ... Policy? It is *I* who make it ... *My* Minister for Foreign Affairs conducts *my* policy ... a policy of peace'. Conrad did not give up the fight but when he returned a fortnight later for another audience, the Emperor relieved him of his post as Chief-of-Staff. He was succeeded by General Blasius Schemua, a competent officer of limited experience, free from his predecessor's obsessive Italophobia.

Yet while Francis Joseph was prepared to re-affirm his authority in a man-to-man confrontation with a difficult general, he did not feel able to summon a meeting of ministers to co-ordinate policy. In the critical weeks of the Franco-Prussian War of 1870 the Emperor had presided over five ministerial conferences in twelve days, but he never attended any of the thirty-nine meetings of the Council of Ministers for Common Affairs convened during the last three and a half years before the First World War. When, on 6 December, the council met for the first time since Conrad's dismissal it was Aehrenthal who emphasized the need 'to stand should to shoulder with our alliance partners', Germany and Italy. The ministers were not impressed by the military capabilities of their southern ally since three army corps were needed to subdue Tripolitania and the Turks were still offering vigorous resistance. The principal purpose of the council meeting was to determine the military budget for the following year. It was acknowledged that the long period of European peace was coming to an end but the ministers sought, so far as possible, to keep expenditure down; they hoped to economize by ignoring Conrad's earlier pleas for arms and re-deployment at the head of the Adriatic.

By the time that Francis Joseph finally approved the ministers' decisions – on 7 January 1912 – he knew he would soon have to find another foreign minister; Aehrenthal was losing a courageous fight against leukaemia. Remarkably, the minister battled on to the end, seeking especially to prevent war coming to the Balkans. Individual diplomats warned Vienna that the Balkan States themselves would form a league, backed by Panslav agents independently of official Russian policy. Aehrenthal discounted this possibility: he thought the hostility between Serbs and Bulgars too deep, and the mistrust of the Balkan politicians too explosive, for such an alliance.

When on 17 February 1912 Aehrenthal died, the Emperor chose as his successor Leopold von Berchtold, ambassador in St Petersburg for four years. The new minister was more naturally at ease escorting society ladies from the paddock to the grandstand at Freudenau racecourse, with field glasses bumping the left hip, then seated in his Ballhausplatz study ready to receive an ambassador. He lacked the expertise of Goluchowski or Aehrenthal, and he knew it. 'When I took over the ministry I had no notion of the southern Slav question', he frankly admitted to the German ambassador in Vienna shortly before Christmas, 'One must have lived here to understand it'. Almost too eagerly he would turn for advice to senior officials in the ministry, have second or third thoughts, and pirouette on an agreed policy. Yet Francis Joseph never realized Berchtold's limitations, possibly because (as with Taaffe) the Emperor interpreted a laid-back manner as a sign of competent mastery rather than concealed fumbling. At one time during the Balkan crises he thought so highly of his conduct that he shook Berchtold warmly by the hand, a rare gesture of confidence from a man who shunned human contact. Berchtold enjoyed one fortuitous advantage; his wife was a girlhood companion of Sophie Chotek (who, in 1909, the Emperor had created Duchess of Hohenberg). This friendship made the Berchtolds welcome guests at the Belvedere and Konopischt.

By the autumn Berchtold was immersed in the full complexity of Balkan politics. It was nearly forty years since Francis Joseph first entertained Nicholas of Montenegro at the World Exhibition in the Prater, receiving the down-at-heel princeling with condescending approval. In four decades Nicholas's fortunes had changed. He was now a ruler of stature, vain, sly and ambitious, a self-proclaimed King since August 1910 and patriarch of an impressive family; his sons-in-law included the Kings of Italy and Serbia and four Russian Grand Dukes. When in June 1912 Nicholas paid a three day visit to Austria, the Emperor was at the Sudbahnhof to welcome him with full royal honours. The Viennese public found it hard to accept Nicholas or his kingdom at face value: the 'Pontevedro' of *The Merry Widow*, Lehar's light-hearted triumph at the Theater an der Wien, seemed to parody the black mountain, while the operetta's hero, like Nicholas's predecessor and his heir, was named Danilo. Nevertheless at Schönbrunn and in the Ballhausplatz the Montenegrin question was taken very seriously indeed: a possible union between Serbia and Montenegro would give Belgrade a strong position on the Adriatic and also block Austrian railway projects through the Sanjak; and an invasion of Turkish Albania might gain Montenegro an expanded coastline and, in the lower Boyana River south of Scutari, a waterway which could be canalized and developed as a southern Slav port. Francis Joseph flattered Nicholas during his visit, even making him honorary colonel of an infantry regiment. But over his immediate intentions in the Balkans Nicholas kept his cards close to his chest.

Four months later the King played an ace. On 8 October 1912 Nicholas declared war on the Ottoman Empire, sent his small army into the Sanjak and Turkish Albania, and called on other Balkan governments to emulate

Montenegro. Serbia, Bulgaria and Greece followed suit, massing armies more than twice as large as the Sultan could hope to put into the field. Within five weeks the Turks were driven out of the whole of Europe except for Constantinople and its hinterland, Edirne (besieged by the Bulgarians), Ioannina (besieged by the Greeks) and Scutari in Albania (besieged by the Montenegrins). The Serbs won a victory at Kumanovo, the Bulgarians at Kircasalih, and the Greeks entered the coveted port of Salonika. No less alarming to the authorities in Vienna was the capture by the Serbs of two small Albanian ports, Durazzo and San Giovanni de Medua. On 3 December an armistice brought a halt to operations, except around Ioannina; within a fortnight peace talks opened at St James's Palace, London. Much credit for bringing the combatants to the conference table lay with Berchtold and Francis Joseph's ambassadors.

The Emperor was determined not to be hustled into any conflict. 'I don't want war', he told his ministers at the end of November 1912, banging his fist on the table, 'I have always been unlucky in wars. We would win, but lose provinces'. But there was a persistent military pressure group in Vienna, backed up by General Oskar Potiorek, who in May 1911 had succeeded Varešanin as Governor of Bosnia-Herzegovina. During the late autumn Potiorek pressed for mobilization and the despatch of more and more troops to the two provinces; and on each occasion Francis Joseph rejected his requests. Eventually, on 28 October, the ministerial council agreed to ask the Emperor for a gradual increase of troops, calling up certain reservists without intensifying the crisis by ordering mobilization. Priority was given to Bosnia-Herzegovina and southern Hungary but by late November the steady build up of troops in Galicia, facing the Russians, was causing alarm among civilians in Cracow and Lvov. In the Belvedere, Archduke Francis Ferdinand remained in favour of peace throughout October and November, but with the coming of the armistice he was alarmed by reports of patriotic belligerence in Belgrade and gave serious consideration to a pre-emptive strike. He had become critical of General Staff planning; on 7 December he induced Francis Joseph to re-instate Conrad von Hötzendorf as Chief of the General Staff. Both the Emperor and the Archduke were soon to regret the return of such a dangerous military schemer to the centre of affairs.

Berchtold, like Francis Ferdinand, was worried about the mood in Belgrade. He was also troubled by the war hysteria in several Austrian and Hungarian newspapers; and in particular by public indignation at the alleged atrocious behaviour of the Serbs towards the consul in Prizren, Oskar Prochaska. On 11 December, almost before the reinstated Conrad had unfolded his Balkan maps, Berchtold visited the Belvedere for a long discussion with the Archduke, whom he found in a state of great excitement and pressing for an immediate attack on Serbia and Montenegro. Later that same day, at Berchtold's request, the Emperor presided over a top-level meeting of ministers at Schönbrunn. Since neither Conrad nor the war minister (General Krobatkin) were present it was not technically a war council. In their absence the case for military action was put by the Archduke, while Berchtold argued against any adventures on the eve of the St James's Palace Conference and the Austrian finance minister complained of the expense of any campaign. The Emperor listened to the exchange of views in an 'unusually serious, composed and resolute' mood, according to Berchtold's diary entry. After an hour of concentrated discussion he took a firm decision: there must be no military adventures; full support should be given to the peacemakers in London.

Significantly Francis Ferdinand at once accepted his uncle's ruling. Throughout the following year he worked in harness with Berchtold. Conrad, however, remained obstinate. As soon as he heard of the meeting on 11 December, he refused to take the Emperor's decision as final: he insisted the Chief of the General Staff and the war minister repeat their conviction that only a short, victorious campaign against Serbia and Montenegro would allow Austria-Hungary to impose an acceptable settlement in the western Balkans, and the war minister agreed with him. Dutifully, Berchtold sought an audience two days after Christmas in order to clarify the Emperor's attitude. He found Francis Joseph unswerving in his commitment to peace. Conrad and Krobatkin were left fuming at what they considered a lost opportunity.

Bulgarian intransigence at the conference table led to a resumption of fighting in the Balkans from early February to mid-April 1913, when the diplomats once again began to try to patch up a peace settlement in London. To the Emperor's dismay, the Austrians found themselves consistently outvoted at the conference, receiving little support from Germany or Italy, despite a recent renewal of the Triple Alliance. Only over Scutari did the Austrians have any success: the Great Powers in conference assigned Scutari to an independent Albania. King Nicholas thought otherwise: neither Montenegrins nor Serbs would lift the siege of Scutari. Again Conrad wished to send the army forward, confident that Europe would allow the Monarchy to implement conference decisions: again he was restrained by the Emperor, the Archduke and Berchtold. However, to Francis Ferdinand's satisfaction, the Austro-Hungarian navy, of which he had long been a staunch patron, was allowed to flex its muscles: on 20 March three battleships, two cruisers and a flotilla of smaller vessels took up position off Ulcinj. But the blockade of a little used stretch of coast had no effect on the fighting around Scutari, nearly 20 miles up river. Nicholas was unimpressed; nor did he respond when

315

at the end of the month three British and two Italian warships joined the squadron. To Vienna's chagrin, the Montenegrins and Serbs tightened the noose around Scutari and on the night of 22–23 April the Turkish commander surrendered the town to King Nicholas. There was intense fury in Vienna. For a week it seemed as if Conrad would be allowed to implement *Fall-M*, his plan to overwhelm Montenegro with 50,000 troops thrusting down the River Drina from Bosnia. Francis Joseph at once authorized Governor Potiorek to proclaim a state of emergency in Bosnia-Herzegovina, putting the army on a war footing in the two provinces.

Tripod masts on a distant horizon meant nothing to King Nicholas, but the rumble of gun carriages across the frontier and the glow from camp-fires in a night sky were warnings he understood. By 4 May Berchtold was able to tell Francis Joseph that the Montenegrins were pulling out of Scutari and he expected the Serbs to withdraw from Durazzo and San Giovanni di Medua. On 14 May a British colonel arrived in Scutari at the head of an international commission charged with delineating the frontiers of a newly independent Albania. To Conrad's intense annoyance it was assumed at Schönbrunn and the Belvedere that the war clouds had lifted. The Chief of the General Staff still believed he should be allowed to implement, not only *Fall-M*, but *Fall-B* as well, the plans he had first drawn up six years before, providing for a general offensive in the western Balkans to destroy both Serbia and Montenegro as independent kingdoms.

Fortunately for Francis Joseph's peace of mind during these taxing winter months, the conflict between the nationalities had become less intense. Much of the credit for this mellowing of old antagonisms lay with the Czech political 'realist' Thomas Masaryk, professor of philosophy at Prague university for a quarter of a century. Although Masaryk had virtually no party following in the Reichsrat, he was widely respected by intellectuals inside and outside the Monarchy for promoting a disciplined ethic of citizenship and a fundamentally federalist ideal of democratic government. Under his influence a political compromise had been achieved in Moravia in 1905, with Germans and Czechs accepting equal status in the provincial legislature and administration, and by the beginning of 1913 similar settlements gave some grounds for optimism in the Bukovina and Galicia. Personally Masaryk still had hopes of winning support for a Moravian-type compromise in neighbouring Bohemia and gradually educating the 'Austrian' politicians to accept reforms which would unify the Monarchy as a whole. The Emperor respected Masaryk's personal integrity and fundamental loyalty, though he recognized that anything achieved in the Austrian and Czech lands would have little effect on the nationality question within Hungary. There was, however, a certain tranquillity in 1913 within the Budapest parliament, imposed by István Tisza. Since out of nearly four hundred members of the lower house only 18 were non-Magyars, this appearance of calm did not reflect the general mood of the kingdom. Tisza was a man of intelligence who realized he needed to show a willingness for reform, if only to quieten the outcry against Magyar domination which he anticipated Francis Ferdinand would encourage on his accession. Yet Tisza offered few concessions: approaches to the Roumanians of Transylvania kept their politicians talking but achieved little, while a token gesture towards the Zagreb Diet met with no response from the deeply mistrustful Croats. For the moment, however Tisza's grip on affairs freed Francis Joseph from any pressing worries in Hungary.

Physically 'the old gentleman' needed any respite which the uncertainties of this troubled year might offer him. The strain of months of chronic crisis had been considerable. After a bad attack of bronchitis in the autumn of 1912 the Emperor remained under strict medical supervision from the court physician, Dr Joseph von Kerzl, who insisted that he should spend most of his time at Schönbrunn, where the air was clearer than in the city; and for the last four years of his life Francis Joseph travelled to the Hofburg only for official business and ceremonial occasions. Although he spent a few days at Wallsee with Marie Valerie and her family, he was rarely seen in public during the winter of 1912–13 or the early spring. Apart from his happiness at being with the youngest Habsburgs, he still found contentment in Katharina Schratt's companionship. By now she was a widow approaching sixty, and there were even silly tales that the Emperor had secretly married her. The memoirs of Francis Joseph's valet, Eugen Ketterl, originally published thirteen years after his master's death, show that the relationship between the retired Burg actress and her sovereign remained unchanged throughout these final years. Since Ketterl was writing while Frau Schratt was still alive, it is possible his account exaggerates her influence on the imperial household. But there is no reason to doubt Ketterl's picture of the lonely Emperor awaiting a visit from his old friend in pleasurable excitement, 'restlessly starting out of his chair to go to the bedroom and brush his hair or comb his side-whiskers'. Katharina Schratt gave him the material comforts he always neglected, such as a dressing gown or a rug to place beside his iron bedstead; and when Dr Kerzl banned strong cigars she found mild ones for him to smoke, in stubborn half-defiance of medical counsel. Summer evenings – again according to Ketterl – would bring the Emperor an invitation to a private dinner party at no. 9 Gloriettegasse, where his hostess would see that one of the popular quartets from the Grinzing *heurigen* was on hand to play familiar Strauss waltzes or newer tunes from Lehar's operettas in the seclusion of her terraced garden.

Yet there can have been few relaxed evenings of entertainment for him in this last full summer of peace. The news from the Balkans remained bad. Moreover he was shocked by a scandal at a high level in the institution upon whose absolute loyalty he set greatest store. In the early spring of 1913 Conrad was informed that German counter-intelligence believed there was a Russian spy in the Austro-Hungarian General Staff: and on 24 May he was told by senior officers, whom he had ordered to investigate the allegation, that the traitor had been identified as Colonel Alfred Redl, chief-of-staff to the 8th Army Corps in Prague. He ordered a small 'commission' of Redl's brother officers to provide the traitor with a loaded revolver and give him an opportunity to judge himself alone. Soon after midnight the officers confronted Redl in a room of an inner city hotel, the Klomser, no. 19 Herrengasse. Redl, left alone, shot himself forty minutes later.

Like Mayerling, the Redl Affair has been over-dramatized on stage and screen. Redl, a 49-year old bachelor from a German middle-class family in Galicia, had been a staff officer for nineteen years. Before going to Prague he was head of counter espionage in the *Evidenzburo* (Vienna's equivalent of London's MI5). A belated investigation revealed that because of his homosexual predilections and taste for a luxurious life style, Redl was blackmailed by the Russians, whom he supplied with information about staff plans and the identity of Austro-Hungarian spies; his activities may have contributed to the setback in Serbia and Galicia on the outbreak of war, though they did not make defeat certain.

Of more immediate consequence was the bungled attempt to hush up the scandal – again reminiscent of Mayerling. Redl was well known in society; a perceptive journalist, Egon Erwin Kisch, soon saw through the bland statements which followed the suicide, alerting newspapers in Berlin and Prague. Within a week of Redl's death alarming rumours of treachery, sexual perversion and corruption were circulating in Vienna, while in Budapest the Magyar press was especially hard on the army. 'The Colonel Redl treason case shocks public opinion', wrote the German-Austrian parliamentarian Joseph Redlich in his diary as early as 2 June. Conrad had given a full report of the affair to Francis Joseph on the previous day, after a preliminary conversation four days earlier. The Emperor agreed that it was right for Redl to have been encouraged to kill himself rather than for the authorities to bring him to trial and thereby undermine confidence in the military establishment – 'to save the army from worse dishonour', as Conrad explained to Joseph Redlich.

Francis Ferdinand, on the other hand, attacked Conrad for his bumbled handling of so explosive an issue. The Emperor supported the General, especially once it was clear that the Archduke's main complaint was over Conrad's complicity in urging Redl to take his life; what was a mortal sin to a devout Catholic was traditional in the army code of honour for which Francis Joseph always showed respect. There were other differences, too, between uncle and nephew. The German initiative in unmasking Redl particularly rankled with the Emperor; no action was taken against Redl's immediate superior, Colonel von Urbanski, a protégé of Conrad and later his biographer. Not unreasonably, the Archduke argued that Urbanski should have been aware that Redl was a security risk: where, after all, did the Colonel acquire money to purchase a Daimler touring phaeton motor car which was the envy of his colleagues? But Francis Joseph sympathized with Urbanski. He disliked probing inquiries into private affairs: serving officers could not marry without their sovereign's permission, Urbanski himself spending several years on a waiting list because the regulations stipulated that, at any one time, half the officers on the General Staff must be celibate; but so long as officers did not compromise themselves with rankers or neglect their duties for the favour of dubious mistresses, the Emperor saw no reason to question their behaviour.

Francis Joseph was anxious to limit the demoralizing effect of the Redl scandal on his army. Officers and rank-and-file must continue to project imperial grandeur, accepting him as a paterfamilias, stern and exacting, but also protective of their way of life. Throughout the summer and autumn he once more emphasized the links of army and dynasty, taking care to give public affirmation of his confidence in the heir apparent, whatever his private doubts. In August he therefore appointed Francis Ferdinand as his military surrogate, making him Inspector General of the Army, a post held by only one previous incumbent, Archduke Albrecht. But as the centenary of the battle of Leipzig drew near, the Emperor made it known that he would himself take the salute in the Schwarzenbergplatz at a parade to commemorate the allied triumph over Napoleon. Thoughtfully on 16 October, a raw autumnal morning in Vienna, a small Persian carpet was spread on the pavement at a corner of the square. Such coddling did not meet with his approval. Photographs, taken as the regiments filed by, show Francis Joseph standing erect, with drawn sword lowered at the salute – and his feet disdainfully placed well behind the carpet.

The Leipzig centenary celebrations, though arranged long before October 1913, fortuitously acquired a topical significance: in that week, for a third time in ten months, it seemed likely that the troops on parade would soon be entrained for the South, marching into Serbia or Montenegro. During the summer the balance of Balkan power had shifted decisively in Serbia's favour when the recent allies fell out over the partition of Macedonia. In early July Bulgaria was defeated in a brief campaign rashly initiated by King Ferdinand and entangling his strategically divided forces with his ex-allies (Serbia and Greece), with Roumania in the north, and with rejuvenated Turkish troops, determined to recover Edirne. Victory made the Serbs overreach themselves. Success on the battlefields intensified the influence of the Black Hand, a secret society established in May 1911 among young army officers in Belgrade and pledged to bring about the union of Serb minorities in the Habsburg and Ottoman Empires with their kinsfolk in independent Serbia. With the army having already doubled the size of the Serbian kingdom, it was difficult for any government in Belgrade to urge caution and restraint. The Black Handers had established a newspaper of their own, provocatively called *Piedmont*, to give Vienna due notice of the role they envisaged for Serbia in creating a unified southern Slav state. The warning was not lost on an Emperor whose formative years coincided with Piedmont's bid for primacy in the Italian *Risorgimento*.

Yet was Nikola Pašić, prime minister and foreign minister in Belgrade from 1910 onwards, Serbia's Count Cavour? In the first days of October the policy makers of Vienna had an opportunity to judge for themselves, for Pašić travelled to the Austrian capital, ostensibly to re-assure Berchtold and the Emperor over alleged Serbian subversion in Croatia. The visit was not a success: the Serbs had still not evacuated Albania, and in the early autumn it was reported they were reinforcing their regular troops in the disputed territories. Pašić showed no wish to talk about Albania; and his evasiveness was exploited by Conrad and the militarists among the ministers. Significantly the 'war party' was now reinforced by István Tisza, who saw Pašić's journey as a sign of appeasement; the time had come, he thought, for harsher measures against Serbia.

On 13 October an informal meeting of ministers in Vienna, with Conrad co-opted so as to give military advice, recommended a short and sharp action which would bring the Serbs to heel. Archduke Francis Ferdinand, deeply mistrustful of Tisza, urged caution; but his uncle, who was rapidly losing patience with the whole affair, agreed with Tisza. On the day after the Leipzig centenary parade, at a time when newspaper editorials in Vienna and Budapest struck a warlike tone, Francis Joseph authorized Berchtold to send an ultimatum to Belgrade, handed over to Pašić on 18 October: the Serbs were given eight days in which to evacuate Albanian territory or face unspecified consequences. Pašić, finding no support for any concept of Slav solidarity from St Petersburg, speedily gave way and by 26 October the Serbs were out of Albania. The crisis had a twofold consequence: in Belgrade it intensified the hidden conflict between the Black Handers and the prime minister whom they now accused of weakness; and in Vienna it showed that armed threats – the 'brinkmanship' of a later generation – brought a swift response from a government which tended to treat the pleas and prods of cautious negotiation with contempt. Neither Francis Joseph nor his foreign minister knew of Pašić's difficulties with the Black Hand; but the effectiveness of diplomacy by ultimatum was too self-evident for them to ignore in any future Balkan crisis.

Foreign observers, and some Austrian members of the Reichsrat, assumed that Francis Ferdinand and his 'Belvedere circle' favoured war. The Archduke, however, was in many ways better informed than his uncle, though his judgment was always clouded by Magyarophobia. He knew that there were deficiencies in the army, and he no longer held the high opinion of Conrad which had first brought the General to the key post he retained so long. The Archduke had such a thundering row with his former protégé during the autumn manoeuvres of 1913 that Conrad went on sick leave. Although the General's apologists maintain that the dispute was caused by his failure to hear Mass during manoeuvres rather than by any military matter, relations between the two men remained strained throughout the winter. Yet there was no doubting the tenacity of purpose with which the Archduke fulfilled his duties as Inspector General of the Army. Even before the October war crisis, he had accepted an invitation from Governor Potiorek to go to Bosnia in the summer and watch army exercises in the newly acquired provinces. Francis Joseph welcomed the proposed visit. In mid-March 1914 it was confirmed that the Archduke would attend manoeuvres of 15th and 16th Army Corps in the Bosnian mountains in June; he would then pay a state visit to Sarajevo, accompanied by his wife, the Duchess of Hohenberg. In 1911 when the Archduke had considered making such a journey he sought advice from a leading Croat who warned Francis Ferdinand's envoy, 'I know the Serbs. I know that they will wait for him in ambush as murderers'. Now, three years later, the Serb students were given a clear three months in which to contact the Black Handers and co-ordinate their plans.

Throughout the winter of 1913–14 Francis Joseph's health caused no particular alarm, although his obstinacy must have exasperated Dr Kerzl. On one occasion, having heard that his exact contemporary General Beck had broken an arm, the Emperor visited his old confidant at his apartment in Vienna and insisted on climbing three flights of stairs rather than make use of the lift. By now, however, excursions of any kind were rare. But he did visit the annual exhibition in the Wiener Künstlerhaus on the first day of spring. Two days later he rode in a carriage from Schönbrunn to Penzing Station with Emperor William II who, as usual, had broken his journey to Corfu in Vienna. But, as three years before, Francis Joseph fell seriously ill with chronic bronchitis immediately after Easter. The first medical bulletin was issued on 20 April; not until 23 May did Dr Kerzl decide that daily reports were no longer necessary. For the last ten days of April Archduke Francis Ferdinand, who was with his family at Konopischt, kept an engine under steam at the nearest railway station, ready to take him to the capital should his uncle's condition worsen. By the third week in May Montenuovo, the Lord Chamberlain, could tell the controller of the Archduke's household that 'if everything develops normally, by the end of June' the Emperor's 'health will be completely recovered'. Yet the illness left Francis Joseph weak. For once, even the routine business of government suffered. Normally he would read, annotate and approve reports of ministerial council meetings within a fortnight; but he was unable to complete work on the papers for the 24 May session until 11 July. The meeting had discussed ways of keeping control of proposed Balkan railway routes in the newly enlarged Serbia; by the second week of July, the topic was a historical irrelevancy.

In mid-May Archduke Francis Ferdinand seriously considered cancelling his journey to Bosnia-Herzegovina because of 'the state of His Majesty's health'. By 4 June, however, Francis Joseph was fit enough to receive the Archduke in audience at his customary early hour; and they appear to have met again on 7 June, once more at a quarter to eight in the morning, when they talked for some forty-five minutes. Ought the Sarajevo visit to be postponed? Francis Ferdinand's own health was suspect and he was having second thoughts over the wisdom of a state occasion, requiring ceremonial uniform, under Bosnia's midsummer heat. Moreover, as on the eve of the Emperor's journey to the two provinces, reports were coming in from several sources of a conspiracy and plans for assassination. No one knows what was said between uncle and nephew. According to Francis Ferdinand's elder son, the Emperor was against the visit but his father felt duty bound not to disappoint the army commanders; according to the later Empress Zita, 'the Emperor made it quite clear that he desired the Archduke to go'; but the most likely reaction is that recorded by General Conrad, who states that Francis Joseph merely told his nephew, 'Do as you wish'.

Emperor and Archduke did not meet again. Francis Joseph was eager to set out for Bad Ischl, but he was still in residence at Schönbrunn on 18 June, when he presented new colours to the Wiener Neustadt military academy. By then Francis Ferdinand was at Konopischt, where he had received in the previous week both Emperor William II and, immediately afterwards, Count Berchtold and his wife. Later commentators have read a sinister significance into these meetings, seeing them as evidence that the German Emperor had written off Francis Joseph and was re-shaping a future Europe with his sabre-rattling Austrian friend. Francis Ferdinand and William did, indeed, discuss Balkan affairs as well as the beauty of the Konopischt rosarium. Since the Tsar's armies were not yet ready for war, it might be well for Austria-Hungary to pursue a firm policy in the Balkans before the situation deteriorated again, William thought; but his general observations were strangely oblique. He took greater trouble in explaining away remarks made to his host at Miramare a few weeks earlier when, having been poorly briefed on the Archduke's prejudices, he had gone out of his way to commend the statesmanlike qualities of István Tisza.

After the visits of the German Emperor and Berchtold, the Archduke enjoyed a few days of family peace. The gardens of his estate were opened for the first time to the people of Bohemia. In his role as squire of Konopischt, he moved easily among his visitors, pleased by the appreciation of both Czechs and Germans for the roses of which he was so proud. But by Tuesday, 24 June, he was at Trieste: that morning he boarded SMS *Viribus Unitis* to sail down to Metković, while Francis Joseph was preparing to set off at the end of the week for Bad Ischl and the good mountain air of the Salzkammergut. In Sarajevo a group of young assassins were studying the detailed itinerary of the coming visit, which the authorities had circulated several days before. Security precautions were far slacker than for the Emperor's visit. Care had been taken to make sure that a quartet was on hand to play 'light Viennese music' for the state visitors at lunch; but there is no evidence that Governor Potiorek realized the significance of the date chosen for the Archduke's processional drive through the heart of Sarajevo: Sunday, 28 June, was Serbia's National Day.

By noon on Saturday the military exercises in Bosnia were over. In the late afternoon a telegram from Ilidze, the small spa a few miles outside Sarajevo, reached Bad Ischl: the Archduke was glad to let the Emperor know that the bearing and efficiency of both army corps had been 'outstanding beyond all praise'. 'Tomorrow I visit Sarajevo, and leave in the evening', the telegram ended. Some eighteen hours later, in the bright sunshine of a Sunday morning, a telephone message reached the Kaiservilla. It was received by Count Paar, who had been duty adjutant at the Hofburg in 1889 when Hoyos arrived from Mayerling and who in 1898 had broken to the Emperor the 'grave news' from Geneva. Now Paar brought him grave news from Sarajevo: the Archduke and the Duchess of Hohenberg had been killed by pistol shots. Later reports gave more details: the visitors had survived a bomb attack earlier in the morning; and on this second occasion their chauffeur, having taken a wrong road on the quayside by the river, was about to reverse when, with

323

the car stationary, a Bosnian Serb student was able to fire at his victims from less than five feet away. Subsequently it was discovered that the student, Gavrilo Princip, was only one of six assassins roaming the streets of Sarajevo that morning.

On hearing of the murders the Emperor is said to have 'slumped in the chair at his desk' before pacing the room in great agitation and saying, almost to himself, 'Terrible. The Almighty is not to be challenged ... A higher power has re-established the order which I, alas, could not preserve'. This familiar tale derives from what Count Paar, the sole witness of his master's grief, told Colonel von Margutti, his deputy, who then wrote up his account ten years later. The harsh comment, with its echo of old worries over the intrusion of a morganatic marriage in what the Emperor regarded as a divinely ordained line of dynastic descent, seems so artificially stilted as to be apocryphal. On the other hand, the news broke on a Sunday, at a time when the unfathomable workings of Providence may have been close to the surface of his shocked mind. Next day he was back at Schönbrunn, sad but self-composed, gratified at being met at the railway station by his great-nephew, Archduke Charles, now heir to the throne, the fifth of the reign. Archduchess Marie Valerie hurried to Schönbrunn to be with her father. She found 'Papa amazingly fresh', as she wrote in her journal, though he was 'shocked, with tears in his eyes ... when he spoke of the poor children'; but he had more confidence in the tact and skills of the new heir than in the murdered Archduke. 'For me it is a relief from a great worry', he admitted to his daughter, thinking of the fate of the dynasty. No one in the family circle foresaw that the event which they mourned as a personal tragedy was for Europe as a whole a cataclysmic disaster.

Chapter 20

WAR

'Terrible shock for the dear old Emperor', King George V commented in his journal on 28 June 1914: 'Poor Emperor, nothing is he spared', echoed his consort, Queen Mary, a few days later. 'The horrible tragedy', as the Queen described the Sarajevo murders, appalled the European courts. In London the Duke of Connaught, Queen Victoria's surviving son, made ready to set out for the funeral. In Brussels King Albert I proposed to go in person. So, too, did Emperor William II who put an abrupt end to the Elbe regatta, ordering his warships to lower their ensigns to half-mast as soon as the news broke. The general dismay abroad was in sharp contrast to reaction within Austria-Hungary. 'No mood of mourning in the city; in the Prater, and here with us at Grinzing, music everywhere on both days!', Joseph Redlich noted in his diary on Monday, 29 June; and the indifference of Vienna was surpassed in Budapest, where little attempt was made to disguise the widespread relief at the death of an Archduke notorious for having hated everything Magyar.

The coffins of the victims reached Trieste aboard SMS *Viribus Unitis* on the evening of 1 July. By then embassies and legations in Vienna had been advised that the Emperor's poor health precluded his acting as host to any gathering of European sovereigns; the funeral ceremonies in the capital would therefore be limited to a single day. In accordance with the Archduke's instructions interment would follow not in the Kapuzinerkirche but at Artstetten, his estate in Lower Austria, where in 1909 he had supervised the building of a 'light and airy' family crypt. The coffins reached the Sudbahnhof from Trieste at 10 p.m. on 2 July and left the Westbahnhof again shortly after ten on the following night for Pöchlarn, a country railway station two miles from Artstetten, but on the opposite bank of the Danube. The obsequies in Vienna were therefore compressed within a mere twenty-four hours.

Francis Ferdinand's secretary, Baron Morsey, and several members of the Belvedere circle were incensed that the Archduke and his wife had been given a 'third class burial'. For this final insult they blamed the Lord Chamberlain, Prince Montenuovo, an old personal enemy of the dead couple and himself descended from a morganatic marriage – his grandmother was the widowed Empress Marie Louise who had not been buried beside his grandfather, Count Neipperg. The unimaginative Montenuovo was a stickler for protocol and, in this instance, had no precedent to follow. He refused to concern himself with what happened after the special funeral train pulled out of the Westbahnhof, since Artstetten was a private residence, outside the Chamberlain's jurisdiction; and no one could blame Montenuovo or anybody else for the violent thunderstorm which so terrified the horses in the funeral cortège between Pöchlarn and Artstetten that they almost plunged the coffins into the Danube. Moreover, while the Lord Chamberlain might legitimately be criticized for limiting the lying-in-state at the Hofburg chapel to a mere four hours, it is hard to see what other action he could have taken once it was conceded that the Emperor's physical frailty made it essential to act as speedily as dignity permitted. But, as early as 5 July, the *Reichspost* (a daily newspaper sympathetic to the Archduke's political views) asked in an editorial 'why, according to the original arrangement, the funeral was so startlingly simple, and so insulting to a grieving people?'. Two days later the *Wiener Zeitung* published a letter from Francis Joseph to the Lord Chamberlain in which he commended Montenuovo's handling of the 'extraordinary duties' which followed 'the passing away of my beloved nephew'. Did Francis Joseph feel that he was himself to blame for denying the murder victims full honours? There could, of course, be no public criticism of the Emperor's conduct. Privately, however, one of Francis Ferdinand's aides-de-camp noted that, during the fifteen minute Requiem, Francis Joseph glanced around the chapel 'with complete indifference and the same unmoving glacial expression he showed towards his subjects on other occasions, too'.

Berchtold, who had seen Francis Joseph for the first time since the tragedy on 30 June, thought the Emperor deeply shaken. His eyes were moist and, unusually, he greeted the foreign minister with a handshake and invited him to sit down beside him. Something would have to be done about the Serbs, the Emperor conceded, for the first reports from Governor Potiorek in Sarajevo suggested the involvement in the conspiracy of military officials in Belgrade. Francis Joseph told Berchtold that he wanted to know from István Tisza how the Hungarians would react to a military confrontation; and he wondered how far Vienna could rely on support from Berlin. Tisza, whom the Emperor saw later that Tuesday, favoured forceful diplomatic pressure on Serbia, taken after consultation with the other leading European Powers but he deplored any moves which involved a risk of war. On reflection, Francis Joseph thought 'the time for military action not yet ripe'. Nevertheless, he sent a personal letter to Emperor William II, blaming Panslavism for the murders; the letter also sought German support in keeping King Carol I of Roumania loyal to his secret attachment to the Triple Alliance and in securing the collaboration of Bulgaria, so that 'the band of criminal agitators in Belgrade' should not go 'unpunished': 'Serbia must be eliminated as a political power-factor in the Balkans', Francis Joseph wrote.

Significantly, however, he avoided any use of the word 'war'. The Emperor's letter was entrusted to a personal envoy, the young Count Alexander Hoyos (the only German-Austrian among senior officials in the Ballhausplatz that year) who also took with him to Berlin a long memorandum on general policies over Balkan affairs, completed by one of Berchtold's senior advisers four days before the assassination and hurriedly updated. The letter was presented to William II by the Austro-Hungarian ambassador at Potsdam on Sunday, 5 July, almost a week to the hour after the Sarajevo murders. Hoyos remained in the German capital for two days of discussion with senior policy makers in the Wilhelmstrasse. His remarks, which were supplemented by reports reaching Berlin from the ambassador in Vienna, suggested that Berchtold was more warlike than his sovereign and may have strengthened the feeling in Berlin that if a general European conflict was unavoidable, it must come 'now or never', at a time when Germany could rely on Austria-Hungary to accept the full commitments of the military alliance. On the evening of 6 July Berchtold duly learnt by telegram from Berlin that 'over Serbia' Austria-Hungary could 'always count' on German support as 'a faithful ally and friend'; and this German offer of 'a blank cheque' was confirmed by the young and enthusiastic Hoyos when, soon afterwards, he arrived back at the Ballhausplatz.

Next morning Francis Joseph resumed his interrupted holiday at Bad Ischl. He remained in the Salzkammergut throughout these three weeks of mounting tension in Europe. There is no clearer illustration of the extent to which age had withered the hand of autocracy than the Emperor's withdrawal from the centre of affairs at such a time. When war loomed in 1859 and 1866 he kept in constant touch with his generals and ministers, and in the summer of 1870 he presided over five Crown Council meetings in twelve days while weighing the merits of neutrality or intervention in the Franco-Prussian War. Now, in July 1914, he was absent from every conference of ministers. He had with him at Bad Ischl only a small personal staff. They were accustomed to conducting urgent business by telegraph during the annual sojourn at the Kaiservilla and, unlike their sovereign, they were even prepared to make use of the telephone. But if a minister or general sought an audience with the Emperor he had to allow five hours for the journey from the capital to Bad Ischl, and another five hours to travel back and report to his colleagues. Berchtold, Conrad and the two prime ministers therefore had greater freedom to shape policy in July 1914 than any of their predecessors earlier in the reign. Moreover, there was no 'shadow court' to influence policy, for the Belvedere circle disintegrated as soon as Francis Ferdinand was killed, and Archduke Charles was too young to have built up a following of his own.

Yet no decisive step towards war could be taken without the Emperor's written consent. Berchtold therefore found it necessary to travel down to Bad Ischl as early as Wednesday 8 July, barely twenty-four hours after Francis Joseph left Schönbrunn. For on the Tuesday on which the imperial railway train was heading south the foreign minister presided over a vital meeting of the 'Council of Ministers for Common Affairs' at the Ballhausplatz. There, despite opposition from Tisza, it was decided to prepare a harsh ultimatum to be sent to Serbia in full expectation that the terms would prove unacceptable and war follow along the middle Danube and the mountainous borders of Bosnia.

Berchtold spent Thursday, 9 July, at the Kaiservilla discussing Tuesday's council meeting in great detail. Francis Joseph at once saw the significance of Tisza's continued striving for peace. He therefore pressed Berchtold to settle the disagreement with Hungary, for he wished his ministers to agree on a united policy at such a time of crisis. Personally the Emperor agreed with Berchtold's 'opinion that a peaceful solution of the crisis would be worthless without positive guarantees that the Pan-Serbian movement will ... be suppressed on the initiative of Belgrade'. He was not prepared for a long series of diplomatic exchanges; but, like Tisza, he refused to rule out the possibility of a peaceful solution if the Serbian authorities had the good sense to fulfil the conditions laid down in Vienna. Neither the Emperor not his ministers seem to have realized that, four days before the Sarajevo murders, Nikola Pašić secured the dissolution of parliament in Belgrade and announced that the first general election in the recently enlarged kingdom would be held early in August. Throughout the July crisis Pašić was therefore fighting an election campaign among a proud people who would certainly reject his Radical Party if its leader bowed to foreign demands.

Tisza, too, was sensitive to public opinion, even though elections were not imminent in Hungary. The 'Austrian' prime minister, Karl Sturgkh, could take decisions without worrying about parliament, for the Reichsrat had been prorogued in March 1914, mainly because of obstructionism by Ruthene and Slovene deputies, and it was not to meet again until after

Francis Joseph's death. But the lower chamber in Budapest sat throughout July, making it necessary for István Tisza to spend an increasing number of days in Hungary. He spoke in parliament on several occasions and was therefore able to sense for himself the mounting desire of the people for some decisive move against the Serbs. At the same time, Tisza knew that most Magyar magnates agreed with him in arguing against the inclusion of more Slavonic peoples in the Monarchy: ideally Karadjordjević Serbia would be crushed and a puppet 'colonialized' kingdom created, ruled either by an Austrian Archduke or a German prince sympathetic to Hungary's commercial needs. So delicate was the political balance among the Hungarian parties that Tisza preferred to keep a personal envoy in Austria, someone who could represent his views to Berchtold and Conrad in Vienna and, when necessary, take the royal road to Bad Ischl.

This task Tisza entrusted to Count István Burian, for nearly ten years before 1912 the common finance minister, a post with special responsibilities inside Bosnia-Herzegovina; he understood the problems posed by Pan-Serb agitation in the provinces and sympathized with Governor Potiorek. But Burian, who possessed the mind of an obstinate legalist and had no liking for compromise, did not agree with Tisza's stand against a harsh ultimatum. Hardly had Berchtold returned to Vienna from the Kaiservilla than Burian set off in the opposite direction. He reported to Tisza – back in Vienna from Budapest by 14 July – that he found Francis Joseph ready to judge the situation calmly and firmly, 'holding out to the bitter end'. Burian's account of the mood at Bad Ischl swayed Tisza's assessment of the crisis, inclining the Hungarian prime minister towards acceptance of a military rather than a diplomatic solution. At the same time Tisza was impressed by the repeated assurance of support received by Berchtold from Berlin. There was no danger of Austria-Hungary being left in isolation, as in 1908, after the announcement of the annexation of the provinces. By the start of the third week in July the foreign minister could see that Hungarian opposition to his war policy had evaporated.

On Sunday, 19 July, Berchtold convened a council of ministers at his home. The meeting agreed that a strongly worded ultimatum should be presented in Belgrade on the following Thursday afternoon, giving the Serbs forty-eight hours to accept the Austro-Hungarian demands, and providing for mobilization in a week's time. By then the harvest would be gathered in and regiments, depleted by 'harvest leave', up to strength again. Yet Tisza still showed an independence of spirit. He insisted that, as soon as the victory was won, no Serbian territory would be annexed by the Monarchy; he still hoped that, if a public declaration was given in Vienna that 'we have no intention of annexing any territory', Russia might be persuaded to stand aside.

First reports of the council's resolutions reached the Kaiservilla on Monday morning, by telephone or telegram. Francis Joseph discussed them at length with Count Parr, his principal adjutant. Colonel von Margutti's account suggests that both men remained convinced throughout the week that any war could remain localized. The Emperor seems to have assumed Serbia would give way under pressure, as in the Balkan Wars. There is, however, also evidence that Francis Joseph believed Berchtold was gambling on Russia's reluctance to risk a war which would spread like a grass-fire from the Balkans to the Baltic and that, as an ex-ambassador in St Petersburg, he knew the limits of official backing for Panslavism.

Yet when, on Tuesday, Berchtold arrived at the Kaiservilla and handed Francis Joseph a copy of the ultimatum, the Emperor was surprised by the severity and precision of the demands. The Serbs were required, not merely to condemn and forbid 'the propaganda directed against Austria-Hungary' and dissolve 'the society called *Narodna Odbrana*', but also to consent that Imperial and Royal officials should 'assist in Serbia in suppressing the subversive movement'. If, on receiving the ultimatum, Pašić should turn for support to the Russian Government and be rejected, the world would see that Panslavism was an empty sentiment, politically of no value whatsoever. Francis Joseph at once saw that St Petersburg's reaction to the ultimatum was of great significance. 'Russia cannot possibly swallow a note like this', he remarked. Yet he did not question the soundness of Berchtold's judgment or the collective wisdom of his ministers. If they were untroubled by the Russian threat, why should he be? No attempt was made to tone down the demands. At six o'clock on the evening of Thursday 23 July, the Austro-Hungarian envoy in Belgrade handed to the deputy prime minister a 48-hour ultimatum which would have virtually reduced Serbia to an Austro-Hungarian dependency. London, Paris and St Petersburg were officially notified by Francis Joseph's ambassadors on Friday morning, some fifteen hours later. That afternoon there was in these distant capitals, for the first time, an apprehension that a general European war was imminent. The Serbian Government had received, as Churchill wrote, 'an ultimatum such as never had been penned in modern times'.

No answer from Belgrade reached Bad Ischl (or, indeed, Vienna) on that Friday, nor on Saturday morning. The Emperor followed his customary routine, busying himself with trivialities of etiquette, even on holiday. The Duke of Cumberland, once Crown Prince of Hanover, was expected to luncheon on that Saturday and Francis Joseph insisted on giving his staff precise written instructions on the Court courtesies to be observed for the elderly exile and his family. But he was ill-at-ease, pacing the terrace of the villa with his hands behind his back. When his guest arrived he was unable to keep conversation flowing at the luncheon table, for he had resolved not to talk of the crisis and no topic other than the uncertainty of the passing hours filled his mind.

Others waited anxiously in Bad Ischl, too. Katharina Schratt was at the Villa Felicitas, her summer home for a quarter of a century. General Krobatkin, the war minister, and Leon von Bilinski, the common finance minister, had made the journey down from Vienna so as to give the Emperor advice at this crucial time; and Berchtold was on hand, staying at the Hotel Bauer, on the lower slopes of the Kalvarienberg, a hill half a mile from the Kaiservilla, across the Ischl River. At a quarter past six the foreign minister decided that no news would come that evening and left the hotel for a walk on the hills. But before seven o'clock the war ministry telephoned from Vienna. Margutti took the message: the Serbs had rejected the ultimatum; the staff of the Legation in Belgrade had crossed the Danube to the safety of Zemlin, twenty minutes away in Croatia. 'So that's that,' Francis Joseph sighed, when Margutti handed him the message. For a few moments he sat dim-eyed at his desk, silently brooding: then, as if clutching at one last straw, Margutti heard him mutter to himself, 'Now that is a break of diplomatic relations; it doesn't necessarily mean war'. He stood up and called for 'the foreign minister – at once, at once'. Hurriedly Berchtold was brought back from his stroll on the hillside. Krobatkin and Bilinski joined him at the Kaiservilla, but they brought Francis Joseph little comfort; he agreed to sign the order for mobilization against Serbia. 'Later than usual' on that Saturday evening Katharina Schratt looked out from the verandah of the Villa Felicitas and saw the Emperor was crossing her private bridge, haltingly and with a weary stoop. 'I have done my best but now it is the end', he told her.

Still, however, Francis Joseph lingered in Bad Ischl. On Sunday he was told that Marshal Radomir Putnik, Serbia's most distinguished soldier and likely commander in the field, had been detained in Budapest while seeking to return home from a spa in Bohemia where he had been taking the waters. The Emperor's sense of chivalry was affronted by the news: orders were immediately sent to Budapest for Putnik to be released, provided with a special train, and allowed back across the frontier to take up his duties in Belgrade. Was there still an element of make-believe in the whole crisis? It is possible that had Francis Joseph returned to Vienna when war clouds closed in he would have seen, as did William II in Berlin, that the Serbian reply to the ultimatum was not unreasonable; the only point firmly rejected was the participation of Austrian officials in policing activities on Serbian soil – an issue scarcely providing a pretext for even a localized war. Yet had Francis Joseph been at Schönbrunn could he have held back his ministers and generals? A quarter of a century later William II explained that in 1914, 'the machine ... ran away with me'. Why should Francis Joseph have fared better in dealing with Conrad than William II with the German Chief-of-Staff, Moltke? The one person who, in an earlier crisis had shown the strength and stature to apply brakes to the machine, lay dead in the crypt at Artstetten.

War was declared on Serbia on Tuesday, 28 July. Next morning two monitors from the Austro-Hungarian flotilla on the Danube began to bombard Belgrade. Only on that Wednesday did Francis Joseph order preparations to be made for the Court's return to the capital. For him it seemed unthinkable to take a holiday when his subjects were at war. Yet he left Bad Ischl early on Thursday, 30 July, with a great inner sadness; he knew it was unlikely that his senses would ever again sharpen to the fresh morning beauty of the mountains or allow the rising mist rolling back up the valley to lift the burden from an aching heart.

The illusion that the war might remain localized as an expanded Balkan conflict persisted in Vienna, despite ominous reports of troop movements around Moscow and Kiev. Except for the token participation of an auxiliary corps on the flank of Napoleon's *Grande Armée* in 1812, the Habsburg armies had never been at war with Russia and there was a reluctance to accept Tsar Nicholas II as an enemy. But war plans, long prepared and well matured, precluded diplomatic improvisation which might have called a halt to the war after a punitive assault on Belgrade. When, on 30 July, Russia ordered general mobilisation behind the long frontier from the Baltic to the Black Sea, neither Germany nor Austria-Hungary could ignore the threat and next day both governments put their armies on a war footing. Fighting broke out along Germany's eastern frontier on 1 August, followed by an invasion of Luxembourg and Belgium and, on 3 August, a German declaration of war on France. Only under German pressure did Francis Joseph agree to go to war with Russia on 6 August. To the Emperor's dismay the tightening of the bonds between the entente partners led Great Britain to join France in declaring war on Austria-Hungary on 12–13 August, even though there was little sympathy for Serbia in London and no clash of interests between Vienna and the Western Powers. Both Italy and Roumania stayed neutral, insisting that their treaty commitments obliged them to support Germany and Austria-Hungary only if these empires were the victims of aggression. Early in November 1914 the Ottoman Empire entered the war on the side of the Central Powers, although as a junior partner – or client – of Germany rather than of Austria-Hungary.

By temperament and conviction Francis Joseph always regarded himself as a soldier. Age, however, necessarily diminished his exercise of military authority: 'if only *I* could have been with my army', he was to remark to Field Marshal von Mackensen in the last year of his life. Since the Emperor believed that a member of the dynasty should lead his troops into battle, he appointed as commander-in-chief, Archduke Frederick, the 58-year old nephew of Archduke Albrecht. Two other Habsburg Archdukes, Eugen and Joseph, also held the rank of Field Marshal, while the heir to the throne, Archduke Charles, gained military experience as an itinerant staff-officer, his soldiering hampered by strict orders from the Emperor that he should not be posted to any sector where his life would be in danger. Effective leadership of the army was entrusted to the Chief of the General Staff, Conrad von Hötzendorf, an over-rated strategist with an obsessive desire to take the offensive. Supreme army headquarters (AOK) were established by Conrad in the fortress of Przemysl. At Schönbrunn the Emperor retained a skeleton military chancellery, which was still headed (after twenty-five years in the post) by General Alfred Bolfras. Apart from the narrowly bureaucratic routine of administration, there was little for Bolfras or the Emperor to do, except to study and assess reports from the two battle fronts, in Serbia and Galicia.

They made sorry reading. As Francis Ferdinand had repeatedly warned, the *k-und-k Armee* lagged behind the armies of the other great continental powers; it was especially weak in artillery. Moreover Conrad gravely bungled his original war plans: on 25 July he ordered maximum concentration against Serbia, even though he had assured his German allies that, in the event of war with Russia, most troops would be sent to Galicia and, on 1 August, this promise was repeated by Francis Joseph in a personal message to William II. The effect of Conrad's 'adjustment' to the war plans was to deprive both fronts of the Second Army in the first weeks of the war: the twelve infantry divisions of the Army were already heading southwards for the Danube when, on 31 July, Conrad sought to recall them for service in Galicia, an about-turn rightly described by the railways section of the General Staff at the time as 'causing endless complications'. Eventually six divisions of the Second Army arrived on the north-eastern frontier to help cover Lemberg (Lvov), the fourth largest city in the Monarchy and capital of Galicia; the other six divisions were engaged in the south, some 600 miles away, probing Serbian defences along the River Sava. General Potiorek, now field commander of the Austro-Hungarian forces in the Balkan sector, originally hoped to present a defeated Serbia to Francis Joseph as a birthday gift on 18 August. By then, however, his troops were no longer making progress against the Serbs and within a few days he was forced to pull every division back across the frontier. In Galicia initial successes by the First Army and the

Fourth Army were soon offset by three weeks of heavy losses in the battle of Lemberg, which on 3 September fell to the Russians.

For the 'old gentleman' in Schönbrunn the news from the battle fronts came like some nightmare recollection from a past he would rather have forgotten. He was bitterly pessimistic, even from the earliest days. When, on 17 August, the Archduchess Zita spoke enthusiastically to him of hopeful reports from the River Bug he replied, cynically, 'My wars have always begun with victories only to finish in defeats. And this time it will be even worse and they will say of me, "He is old and cannot cope any longer". The revolutions will break out and it will be the end'. Next day he received a telegram of birthday congratulations in French from the Roumanian chief-of-staff who hoped he 'will bear up against the shocks inherent to all wars, even the happiest ones'. 'Well meant, of course,' Francis Joseph commented, 'But is it going to be a happy war for us? Already all the signs seem to point the other way'.

Experience, on the other hand, emphasized the need for patience. Five days after the shock fall of Lemberg the Emperor sent a warning to Archduke Frederick: he should not punish defeated senior officers too severely 'because today's unlucky commander may well be victorious tomorrow'. Yet, as winter succeeded autumn, it became clear that his armies were locked in disastrous campaigns in the south and the east. Belgrade fell on the sixty-sixth anniversary of Francis Joseph's accession, but the city was recaptured by the Serbs eleven days later as Putnik mounted a counter-offensive which threw the invaders back across the frontier for a second time. In Galicia a Russian advance on Cracow was brought to a halt and in the Bukovina Czernowitz was recaptured, but these successes were gained only at enormous cost. By the end of the year four-fifths of the pre-war trained infantry in the Austro-Hungarian army lay dead, or were recovering from wounds, or were held captive by the Russians.

During these grim months the Emperor rarely moved outside Schönbrunn. For security purposes the parkland close to the palace had been closed to the public and the Viennese saw so little of their sovereign that there were rumours he was dead or totally senile. In late September he visited, on separate occasions, hospitals hastily set up at the Augarten and within the inner city at the Fichtegasse. He was not greatly concerned over changes which strengthened the hands of military authorities at the expense of the civil courts; and he accepted the establishment of 'military zones' where the army exercised virtually all administrative powers. Not all these 'military zones' were near the front line; they included districts in Silesia and north-eastern Moravia where the greatest danger came not from invaders a hundred miles away but from 'unpatriotic' dissident demonstrators. Yet, though the Emperor was unconcerned over such matters, he was deeply conscious of the impact of war on his least fortunate subjects. The fighting in the East was ravaging one of the Monarchy's richest granaries, making industrialized Austria more and more dependent on food from Hungary. At the same time, fear of the Russian invader had forced many Jews in Galicia to flee westwards and seek safety in the capital, a migration which caused Mayor Richard Weiskirchner to propose that the refugees should be moved to camps in Moravia. The Emperor, however, was adamant: 'If Vienna has no more room for refugees', he told Weiskirchner, 'I shall make Schönbrunn available for my Jewish subjects'. Nothing further was said of camps in Moravia.

Christmas, Francis Joseph remarked to Katharina Schratt with typical simplicity, was a wretched occasion that year, for he could not help thinking of the 'jolly' days of old. Yet it was not only nostalgia which saddened him. He was convinced that the war was going to spread: soon, he told Count Parr, 'Italy will join our enemies', setting an example for Roumania to follow. Even in the first week of the war the Italians had sought cession of the Trentino as compensation for Austria-Hungary's anticipated expansion in the Balkans, a request disdainfully rejected in Vienna. By the coming of the new year Sonnino, Italy's foreign minister, was seeking Istria as well as the Trentino. Berchtold recommended concessions in order to prevent Sonnino striking a bargain with the Entente allies, but Francis Joseph and Conrad were united in their refusal to 'buy off' Italy. The Emperor had reverted to the attitude he assumed in early 1866 when, as Bismarck drew a tighter noose around the Monarchy, he would not consider handing over Venetia so as to save his army from a two-front war. In despair Berchtold resigned office on 11 January 1915, and went on active service as a staff-captain. On 8 March, for the last time, Francis Joseph presided over a ministerial council, summoned to discuss the threat from Italy; he backed Berchtold's successor, István Burián, in refusing to surrender 'one square metre'. Sonnino followed his earlier inclination of striking a bargain with London, Paris and St Petersburg. The secret Treaty of London of 26 April 1915 offered Italy such great gains in the Trentino, along the Adriatic and in Asia Minor that, a month later, Sonnino persuaded King Victor Emmanuel III to go to war with Austria-Hungary. The *k-und-k Armee* was thus given a third front to defend from invasion; and the Emperor focussed weary eyes on maps of the Dolomites, the Venetian plains and the head of the Adriatic: it was more natural to be fighting Italians than Russians. Rivers and mountain contours were all too familiar to him, though there were railway junctions where he had changed horses in earlier years and the Quadrilateral was now in enemy hands. Yet two fortresses, Peschiera and Verona, were within thirty miles of the Austrian frontier and marked on the map beyond them were the names of Custozza (for victory) and Villafranca (for peace).

Archduchess Zita, who with her two children had moved into Schönbrunn when her husband Charles went to the wars, found Francis Joseph increasingly looking back to the early years of the reign. Many years later she recalled that 'he confessed to a feeling that, ever since 1848, the Empire was like a volcano which was uneasily sleeping'. By the spring of 1915 there were ominous signs of imminent eruption. The civil authorities in Prague suspected the existence of an extensive network of secret societies linked with exiles in the West and, in particular with Masaryk, by now a dedicated antagonist of the Habsburgs. The Russians, too, were exploiting Czech and Ruthene dissidence. Propaganda leaflets had been circulating in Bohemia and Moravia throughout the winter and in mid-April the Emperor learnt with dismay that almost all the officers and men in the 28th Prague Infantry Regiment had gone over to the enemy during a battle around the village of Stebnicka Huta at the beginning of the month. There was a steady flow of deserters from Slav units fighting in the Carpathians that spring.

But the volcano did not erupt after all. Militarily the summer of 1915 held out some prospect of final victory. The Italians, whom London and Paris hoped would open up a new front of major strategic significance, made scant impact on the war: in two thrusts towards the River Isonzo they gained little territory, for the Austrian defences were sound. By contrast, an offensive launched in Galicia by the German and Austro-Hungarian armies on 2 May was so successful that in ten weeks the Russians were forced to evacuate almost all the Habsburg lands gained over the previous eleven months. The good news from the East was a tonic to morale in the capital. On 24 June 1915 Francis Joseph came out on to the palace balcony at Schönbrunn to acknowledge cheers from a crowd celebrating the re-capture of Lemberg: press photographs show the Emperor looking happily down on a throng of civilians, dressed as if about to enjoy a summer's day in the Prater, while army officers mingle with them in service uniform: sharing the balcony with the Emperor are Mayor Weiskirchner and Archduchess Zita who holds aloft her two-year-old son Otto, next in line of succession to his father as heir to his great-great uncle's throne.

Later that year came more news of victory. In the third week of October Bulgaria entered the war on the side of the Central Powers and, by the end of November, German, Austro-Hungarian and Bulgarian armies had overrun Serbia, thus fulfilling Vienna's original war aim. Francis Joseph knew, however, that these triumphs, in the East and the Balkans, had been achieved only with German collaboration and under German leadership. An attempt by Conrad to boost Austro-Hungarian pride by gaining a further victory against the Russians in a 'solo' campaign – the *Schwarzgelbe* autumn offensive – ended in disaster on 14 October: the AOK reported 130,000 casualties; significantly, another 100,000 men were taken prisoner, though it is impossible to establish how many defected voluntarily. And to add to the winter's gloom there had been a poor harvest in Hungary. It was enough to feed the kingdom but not to supply regions of the Monarchy already denied Galician wheat; and the Austrian provinces were made dependent on Germany for bread.

The Emperor realized earlier than his ministers the significance of these events: military necessity and economic restraint were robbing the Monarchy of all independence of action. There was a genuine danger that Austria-Hungary might soon become tied as closely to Germany as Bavaria to the North German Confederation under Bismarck's primacy in the four years separating Sadowa from Sedan. This new, satellite status for the Monarchy was first shown clearly in a hardening of attitude in Berlin against earlier proposals from Vienna for a Habsburg solution of the Polish Question. As late as January 1916 a meeting of the council of ministers, discussing the Monarchy's war aims, still assumed that, when the Tsar's Empire collapsed, most of Russian Poland would be united with pre-war Austrian Galicia in a Catholic Polish Kingdom, incorporated in the Dual Monarchy. Such hopes were soon frustrated by Germany's frankly annexationist programme in the East and over the following ten months Francis Joseph was forced to agree to plans for the establishment of an 'independent' Polish kingdom, administered by Prussians though protected by a Hohenzollern-Habsburg condominium.

Two brief successes in January 1916 bolstered Conrad's diminishing authority in Vienna: Montenegro was overrun and a firm foothold established in northern Albania; and in the Bukovina the Austrians could claim a defensive victory when a Russian attack was repulsed with heavy enemy losses. Conrad, always an Italophobe, now argued that the Monarchy stood to gain more in Italy (where there would be no competition from German interests) than in the East. Accordingly he gained hesitant support from the Emperor for a spring offensive in Trentino, designed to strike southwards to the plain of Vicenza and cut off the main Italian armies concentrated between the rivers Tagliamento and Isonzo. Nine experienced divisions were taken out of the line in Galicia and the Bukovina and transported across the Monarchy in early March for concentration in the Sugana valley, at the head of the railway route from Trent to Padua.

Such movement of men and equipment could not be kept secret. The Italian High Command knew of the military build up as early as 22 March. Russian intelligence, too, discovered that élite troops were no longer facing the South-West Army Group on the River Dniester, information of great interest to their staff planners and at once invalidating Conrad's assurance to Francis Joseph that he had no cause for worry over the re-deployment of his army. Heavy snowfalls made Conrad postpone his much-advertised offensive until 15 May. At first all seemed to go well. A massive concentration of heavy guns blasted a path ahead for the best troops remaining in Francis Joseph's army. Within a fortnight the gunners were training their sights on Italian positions in the last foothills before the open plain. But there, on 2 June, the advance ground to a halt. The artillery had only enough shells left for a few days of action. Before fresh supplies of ammunition could complete the journey down a single track railway through the mountains, the Italian commander, Marshal Cadorna, had re-deployed half a million men for a counter-offensive which by 1 July won back much of the lost ground. More dramatically, on the night of 4 June, Conrad's headquarters heard that the Russians had launched a great offensive, stretching from the Pripet Marshes southwards to the Bukovina and striking at that weakened sector of the Front over which the Emperor expressed the deepest concern. Conrad had committed the greatest military blunder of any Austrian commander since Gyulai abandoned Milan after the battle of Magenta. In its consequences his decision to withdraw nine divisions from the Eastern Front surpassed his folly in having left the Second Army divided and train-bound during the first weeks of war. A Crown Council meeting in Vienna on 29 June, showed the hostility of the ministers towards the Chief-of-Staff. Remarkably, however, Conrad remained at his post until after Francis Joseph's death. He survived, not because he retained his sovereign's confidence, but because the Emperor was too old and too out of touch with the officer corps to find a successor.

The Russian assault in Galicia and the Bukovina – 'Brusilov's Offensive', as it is remembered in history – almost brought Austria-Hungary to final defeat. Within a month Brusilov had established a corridor 200 miles wide and in places 60 miles deep, bringing the Russians back to the eastern slopes of the Carpathians before, in September, the offensive lost its momentum. The change of fortune tempted Roumania into the war in August, fighting in Latin solidarity with Italy and France against the Central Powers who had been her allies for so many years during the long peace. Briefly Roumanian troops invaded Transylvania, penetrating some fifty miles across the frontier and threatening an advance into the Hungarian Plain. But, once again, all was reversed by German intervention.

By the late autumn, order was restored on the Eastern Front: General Falkenhayn mopped up the Roumanian units that had so rashly entered Transylvania; Field Marshal von Mackensen struck swiftly northwards from Bulgaria to the heart of the Roumanian kingdom. Francis Joseph admired Mackensen as a strategist and respected him; it is probable he would have accepted him as Conrad's successor. As it was, the Emperor agreed on 6 September to a unified command for the Central Powers with ultimate military authority entrusted to Hindenburg and Ludendorff.

Though desperately tired by now, Francis Joseph tried to follow in detail all the changing fortunes of war and its impact on his peoples. He may have suspected that the Austrian prime minister, Count Stürgkh, was concealing from him the deep distress in the capital, the lack of bread and milk and potatoes. From Katharina Schratt he knew that food supplies were uncertain and that distribution was far from perfect. A curious natural disaster led him to unburden his mind to his military aide, Baron von Margutti. At the beginning of July, with bad news coming constantly from the Eastern and the Italian Fronts a whirlwind swept through the town of Wiener Neustadt causing havoc to several military establishments, the airfield and factories. At once Francis Joseph sent Margutti to the town, with orders to give him a detailed report that evening.

On his return, however, Margutti found the Emperor with more on his mind to discuss than the damage in Wiener Neustadt. He seems to have treated the whirlwind as an omen, and he found relief in discussing the day-to-day problems of the Monarchy with a brother officer, thirty-nine years his junior. 'Things are going badly with us', he said in the end, looking deeply depressed, 'perhaps even worse than we suspect. A starving people cannot put up with much more. Whether and how we get through the coming winter remains to be seen. But I am determined to call a halt to the war next spring. I will not let us drift into irretrievable rack and ruin'. To Katharina Schratt the Emperor spoke, too, of his determination to seek peace before it was too late to hold the Empire together. Yet did he believe he would still possess the freedom of action within the alliance to impose peace? Above all, did he really believe he had the time and strength to check the drift into ruin? For the Emperor who spoke with such certainty to Margutti was only five weeks away from his eighty-sixth birthday.

Chapter 21

SCHÖNBRUNN 1916

In the late afternoon of 21 October 1916 Emperor Francis Joseph received the first reports of yet another violent death, though not on this occasion in his own family. Shortly before half-past two Friedrich Adler, who was the son of the veteran socialist leader, had gone up to Count Stürgkh's table at the Hotel Meissel-und-Schadn in Vienna's Neuermarkt as the prime minister was finishing lunch and fired three shots from a revolver at his head, killing him instantly. 'Down with absolutism! We want peace!', Adler shouted out before being seized and handed over to the police by another diner in the restaurant, Franz Aehrenthal, brother of the late foreign minister. Friedrich Adler – in personal life the gentlest of men – had every intention of being arrested and, at his trial, securing the widest possible publicity for his views.

The Emperor was shocked by the news. He did not hold Karl Stürgkh in particular esteem: the Count was a pedantic bachelor in his late fifties, with nothing to mark him off from other senior servants of the state except his height, for he was 2 metres tall (6 feet 7 inches). What troubled the Emperor was that a young, well-known intellectual should have felt the need to assassinate a minister of such little personal significance. He began to wonder if his darkest fear was now an imminent possibility. Were 'the things', of which he had spoken to Margutti, much worse than he suspected? Was Adler releasing the blind fury of anarchy? Would revolution paralyse the Monarchy while his armies were at war? Desperately Francis Joseph sought reassurance from his ministers. They convinced him that poor Stürgkh's chief failing was his refusal to contemplate the recall of parliament, thereby denying the political opposition a forum to express doubts over the conduct of the war; he had even boasted of having put the Reichsrat to good use at last – as a hospital. His murder was a terrible protest against rule by decree, as permitted by the notorious 'Article XIV' of the 1867 Constitution. In the evening the Emperor turned to the ablest political manipulator among Stürgkh's immediate predecessors, Ernst von Koerber, who had shown how to strike bargains between Germans and Slavs a dozen years back. Koerber was not, like Tisza in Hungary, a skilled parliamentarian but he would clear the hospital beds from the chamber and pump a little oxygen into Austria's constitutional life.

Winter came early that year over most of central Europe: at Schönbrunn there were damp days in late October, and a bitter wind. With the turn of the month, the first snow clouds swept in from the Marchfeld. It was a fortnight before Koerber had completed his talks with party leaders from the Reichsrat elected in 1911, and in the palace long political discussions, following each morning's assessment of reports from AOK and individual field commanders, left the Emperor exhausted. On his desk each day there was a mass of paperwork, including detailed proposals for an independent Polish kingdom and a new autonomous status for Galicia. It is probable, too, that there were dark moments for him in his inner life for, as earlier letters show, Francis Joseph always observed one solemn occasion in this fortnight – All Souls Day – in a mood of intense spiritual contrition, his thoughts deeply concerned with the 'departed ones', especially Rudolf and Elizabeth. Not surprisingly, under the shock, strain and introspection of these long wintry weeks his health began to fail once more. Persistent bronchitis in the last days of October led to fits of coughing, followed by a fever on 6 November and intense weariness. Dr Kerzl recognized similar symptoms to the post-Easter illnesses of 1911 and 1914. By the end of the week there was little doubt that the Emperor was suffering from pneumonia. On the afternoon of Saturday, 11 November, a warning telegram was sent to the heir to the throne who was in eastern Saxony, after visiting Hindenburg's headquarters on the Eastern Front. By Sunday evening Archduke Charles was at Schönbrunn, only to find the Emperor in much better health. As in 1914, he seemed to be shaking off the fever. On Wednesday the improvement was so marked that his daughters hesitated over coming to Schönbrunn in case the gathering of the family should lower their father's will to fight. But Wednesday's gleam of hope was too feeble to throw a clear light forward. His temperature began to climb again on Friday night and Dr Kerzl sought urgent advice from pulmonary specialists in Vienna's famous hospitals.

Sunday, 19 November, was the festival of St Elizabeth of Hungary, Sisi's patron saint. Sixty-three years ago that day a special envoy from Vienna had arrived in Munich with a diamond brooch, shaped like a bouquet, as a gift from Francis Joseph to the princess he was to marry in the spring; and other presents followed on each St Elizabeth's Day of her life. This year her widowed husband heard Mass in his study, for he was not well enough to go down to the chapel. In the afternoon Katharina Schratt came to visit him from Hietzing, where she presided over a convalescent home for officers wounded at the Front. The 'dear good friend' talked of the past, and especially of the Empress. At times she found Francis Joseph too weak to follow her conversation or reply to her. As she left for the short walk back to her villa, Dr Kerzl asked her not to come back on Monday, as the Emperor needed a day of complete rest. By now the wings of death cast lengthening shadows on Schönbrunn.

Archduchess Marie Valerie was at the palace, intent on ensuring that her father received the Church's full spiritual ministrations. Also with him was his granddaughter, Erzsi, the 36-year old Princess von Windischgraetz, whose company had cheered him in the lonely years after Mayerling and Geneva. He refused to be confined to bed: he coughed less if he sat upright, he said. Despite Kerzl's pleas for rest and quiet, the Emperor was determined to continue with his daily tasks. Archduke Charles and Archduchess Zita visited Francis Joseph's study shortly before midday on Tuesday, causing him passing concern because he had no opportunity to put on his military tunic before the Archduchess entered the room; he remained a stickler over conventions of dress. He commented on good reports he had received from the Roumanian Front, but his visitors were surprised to find him studying recruitment papers, even though his body temperature was 102°F (normal 98.4F), or 39.5C (normal 37°C). The work, however, was too much for him. In the early evening he admitted feeling extremely ill and he was persuaded to allow his valet, Eugen Ketterl, to help him to bed. But there was, he thought, much paperwork which still required his scrutiny and signature; perhaps it could wait for one more day. 'Has Your Majesty any further orders?', Ketterl asked before withdrawing. '*Morgen fruh um halb vier Uhr*', a failing voice replied with indomitable insistence ('Tomorrow morning, at half past four').

They were not, however, his last words. As Ketterl helped him sip some tea, the Emperor faintly mumbled one final question, 'Why must it be just now?' He was barely conscious when a Court chaplain administered the rite of extreme unction. Half an hour later a fit of coughing shook the frail body, and then all was silent. Emperor-King Francis Joseph I died at five minutes past nine in the evening of 21 October 1916, only one long corridor and eighty-six years from the room in which he was born.

Joseph Redlich, entering up his journal out at Grinzing, could see no signs of sorrow for the deceased nor of joy in welcoming his successor: 'A deep tiredness, akin to apathy, hovers over Vienna', he wrote. Every day brought tidings of death to families in the city and there were fears for food and fuel supplies as the third winter of war tightened its grip on a hungry people. But they mourned the passing of 'the old gentleman', nevertheless. The Emperor's loyal subjects filed out to Schönbrunn, where for three days his body lay in simple state. On the Monday after his death they stood silently in streets covered with thin snow as eight black horses with trim black plumes between their ears hauled the massive funeral hearse into Vienna to rest, in full magnificence, in the Hofburg chapel.

Court ceremonial prescribed that a sovereign's body should not be buried until nine days after his death and Montenuovo, the Lord Chamberlain, was there to ensure that what was hallowed by tradition should be observed, even under the exigencies of war. A peace time funeral would have brought Europe's crowned heads to Vienna and won for Francis Joseph more charitable obituaries than the French and British Press chose to publish that November: in London Northcliffe's *Weekly Dispatch* even rebuked Fr Bernard Vaughan (brother of the late Cardinal-Archbishop) for praying for the soul of an enemy emperor at Mass in Westminster Cathedral. Germany's ruler, William II, came to Vienna on 28 November and joined the new Emperor Charles in prayer beside the bier, but he did not remain in the city for the final obsequies two days later.

Few troops could parade on 30 November, the day of the funeral, for the Imperial and Royal Army was heavily engaged on three battle fronts. Apart from the Life Guards detailed to escort the hearse, there was only a single battalion of infantry in the city. It was therefore decided, that in the absence of the army, the people of the imperial capital should have one last opportunity to salute the sovereign who had re-shaped the city's outer form. Instead of conveying the coffin directly from the Hofburg chapel to the cathedral, the great hearse followed a route which recalled, on that grey November afternoon, finer days of past pageantry. From the Hofburg the funeral procession moved out through the Burgtor, where Francis Joseph had stood on *Makart-Festzug* in 1879, turned left in front of the statue of Maria Theresa he had unveiled, passed the Opera House, crossed the innermost side of the Schwarzenbergplatz, where he had taken the salute at the Leipzig centenary, and completed a half-circuit of the Ringstrasse, which he had opened with Elizabeth beside him on May Day in 1865. At last the procession turned up the Rotenturmstrasse to the metropolitan cathedral of St Stephen for a final blessing from Cardinal-Archbishop Piffe. After the short service in the cathedral Emperor Charles, Empress Zita and Crown Prince Otto were joined by three kings – Ludwig III of Bavaria; Frederick Augustus of Saxony; Ferdinand of Bulgaria – to follow on foot the funeral chariot as it moved slowly from the cathedral by way of the Graben and the streets of the inner city to the

Kapuzinergruft, the crypt of the Capuchin Church in the Neuermarkt, where more than 140 members of the dynasty were entombed in the imperial vault. Tradition required Montenuovo, as Lord Chamberlain, to knock on the closed door of the crypt, which a Capuchin monk refused to open so long as Montenuovo craved admission for the Emperor-King's body, proclaiming Francis Joseph's full sovereign dignitaries on the first occasion and his more compact title of Emperor-King on the second. Only at the third knocking ceremony, when dynastic pretensions were laid aside and entry to the crypt sought for 'Francis Joseph, a poor sinner who begs God for mercy', did the great door swing open and pall-bearers carry the coffin to rest between the tombs of the Empress Elizabeth and Crown Prince Rudolf.

This final humbling moment of any Habsburg interment has always attracted most comment, and Montenuovo made certain that the age-old ritual was duly fulfilled. Yet the 'poor sinner' had ruled the Monarchy longer than any predecessor and in one respect Francis Joseph's obsequies acknowledged the unique character of the reign. For they did not end with the departure of the last mourners up the stairs from the imperial crypt. The 68th anniversary of his accession at Olmütz fell on 2 December 1916, just two days after the funeral, and a final Solemn Requiem was said in the Hofburg chapel, attended by the imperial family and the Court dignitaries. Only then did his subjects accept that the reign of Francis Joseph I was at an end and an era of Europe's history drawing to a close. Few could remember any other sovereign at the head of affairs in Vienna.

Chapter 22

INTO HISTORY

Within two years of Francis Joseph's death the Dual Monarchy became a cast-off relic of history. The good intentions of Emperor Charles – his proposals for a federalist restructuring of his realm and, in particular, his desire for an early negotiated peace – were frustrated by the sheer weight of powerful interests massed against their attainment. Austria-Hungary was so closely integrated militarily with Germany that Vienna lost all independent diplomatic options. Charles was to see his armies gain striking victories, when backed by Germany, on the Italian Front and against Russia. But after August 1918, when the allies and their American associates broke the German army in the West, Hindenburg and Ludendorff could spare neither men nor material for other theatres of war: General Franchet d'Espérey's multinational army in Salonika knocked out Bulgaria and began to advance from Macedonia into Serbia and Hungary; the Italians regained the military initiative along the River Piave. The governments in Vienna and Budapest had no answer to the sustained propaganda of their enemies in favour of self-determination and of new frontiers drawn 'along clearly recognizable lines of nationality'. The volcano of fanaticism, which Francis Joseph had feared since 1848, finally erupted almost seventy years to the day after the Habsburg Court found refuge from revolution at Olmütz.

On 11 November 1918 Emperor Charles signed at Schönbrunn a message to his peoples renouncing all participation in the affairs of state. He never abdicated, but retired with the Empress and their children to the shooting-lodge of Eckartsau, in the Marchfeld to the north-east of the capital; in March 1919 the family crossed into Switzerland. Members of the dynasty were excluded from Austria by law unless they gave a declaration of loyalty to the republic. Twice in 1921 Emperor-King Charles tried to regain his Hungarian throne from Admiral Nicholas Horthy, who in 1920 had been elected Regent by parliament in Budapest; he was defeated, in part by the hostility of Hungary's neighbours, but also by Horthy's reluctance to hand authority back to his King. Tragically, in the following spring, the exiled Emperor contracted pneumonia on Madeira and died on 1 April 1922, four months short of his thirty-fifth birthday. His eldest son, Archduke Otto (born in November 1912) became claimant to his titles.

By the time of Charles's death the lands he had inherited from Francis Joseph were shared out between seven independent states: the new republic of Czechoslovakia; a resurrected Poland; the kingdoms of Italy, Roumania and 'of the Serbs, Croats and Slovenes' (not called Yugoslavia officially until 1929); a kingdom of Hungary, reduced to a third of its area; and a rump republic of 'German' Austria, of which more than a quarter of the population lived in Vienna. In most successor states there were no regrets at the passing of the Monarchy: Habsburg properties were confiscated; insignia torn down. Yet a few officers of the Imperial and Royal Army remained attached to the dynasty, from both sentiment and a deep mistrust of nationalism. Thus the war hero Colonel Anton Lehar, younger brother of the composer Franz Lehar, could list Czechs, Hungarians, and German-Austrians among his immediate ancestors and denied that he possessed any single nationality: he was, he declared in 1921, a 'Habsburg subject'. Such loyalty made Colonel Lehar ready to stage-manage Charles's abortive bids to recover his crown in Budapest.

Sentiments elsewhere were shaped by different considerations. The re-ordering of Europe after the war brought unexpected hardship to many families in Vienna, especially those dependent on Habsburg state pensions or wage-earners made redundant when the imperial civil service withered away. New frontier barriers led to food shortages and carefully invested savings were hit by runaway inflation, with the cost of living multiplying twenty times between Christmas 1921 and Christmas 1922. Inevitably there was nostalgia for Francis Joseph's golden age of peace and security, back beyond the turn of the century. There were critics who argued that the Emperor's rigid conservatism, and especially his retention of the 1867 settlement virtually unchanged, had brought the Monarchy to disaster. But a spate of memoirs emphasized the good qualities of the 'old gentleman' at Schönbrunn – the compassion which he disciplined his emotions to conceal, choosing to appear callously indifferent rather than risk diminishing the grandeur of imperial sovereignty; the simplicity of his personal tastes and conduct; the sense of duty, which bound him to his desk as he sought expedient ways of guiding his subjects towards enlightened democracy. Margutti's detailed reminiscences of the Emperor's later years went on sale as early as the summer of 1921; they confirmed the widespread belief that he 'had long made the preservation of peace his sacred duty' and emphasized how 'horrified' he had been at his inability to control events in the wake of the Sarajevo murders. This was what a chastened generation, wistfully regretting a lost youth, wished to hear.

There was no orchestrated campaign reviling Francis Joseph. On the other hand, while respecting the person of the Emperor, it became fashionable to pour scorn on the structure of Imperial and Royal institutions. Robert Musil's novel *Der Mann ohne Eigenschaften* (The Man without Qualities), of which the first volume appeared in 1930, introduced the intellectuals of central Europe to 'Kakanien', an ironic name for the Dual Monarchy, based on the k.u.k (*kaiserlich und königlich*) abbreviation in common usage during the Ausgleich era. Musil's incomplete epic was a satirical portrayal of life in Vienna on the eve of the First World War. The book's anti-hero, Ulrich, is in 1913 appointed secretary of a committee given five years to prepare accession celebrations for Francis Joseph (seventieth anniversary) and William II (thirtieth anniversary). The main characters are meretricious social climbers and Kakanien an Empire kept in being only from force of habit, but Musil – an army captain who had distinguished himself on the Italian Front – stopped short of making the Emperor a figure of ridicule. Just as Queen Victoria's biographer Lytton Strachey blunted his iconoclastic pen in a growing respect for his subject, so Robert Musil became captivated by Francis Joseph's prestige in his later years. Nor was Musil the only writer to succumb to nostalgia for Imperial Austria. Joseph Roth, too, attacked the shallow decadence of Habsburg society throughout much of Francis Joseph's reign, but he believed its false values were held in check by the authoritative father figure at Schönbrunn. Roth went further than Musil in open admiration of the Emperor: Francis Joseph's sense of honour and soldierly obligations relieve the gloom of *Radetzkymarsch*, published in 1932; and he is, in effect, idolized in two of Roth's later novels, *Die Büste des Kaisers* and *Die Kapuzinergruft*.

The Emperor's younger daughter Archduchess Marie Valerie, who had pledged loyalty to the republic and settled in Lower Austria, did not live to see her father's memory enshrined in bitter-sweet legend: he died at Wallsee in September 1924. Her sister, Archduchess Gisela, remained in Bavaria, dying in Munich in July 1932, a fortnight after her seventy-sixth birthday. Francis Joseph's children were therefore spared the spectacle of Hitler's ascendancy over the German lands, Schönerer-ism run hideously rampant. Katharina Schratt, however, was in Vienna at the time of the Anschluss, defiantly ordering the blinds of her windows overlooking the Kartnerring to be kept closed on the day Hitler entered the city: she died in April 1940 at eighty-six, thus completing a span of life four months longer than the Emperor's. Two of his great-nephews – the tragic sons of Francis Ferdinand and Sophie Chotek – were sent to Nazi concentration camps; both survived, though neither lived to reach the age of sixty. Crown Prince Rudolf's widow, Stephanie (Princess Lonjay), settled with her second husband on his estate at Oroszvar, in western Hungary, until forced to flee from the advancing Red Army; they found sanctuary near Györ, in the Benedictine abbey of Pannonhalma, where Stephanie died in August 1945. Rudolf and Stephanie's daughter, the Emperor's favourite grandchild 'Erszi', divorced Prince Otto von Windischgraetz in 1924 and made her home in the Hutteldorf district of Vienna. There, in May 1948, she married Leopold Petznek, a socialist who served as Speaker of the lower chamber of parliament; she died at Hutteldorf in March 1963, in her eightieth year.

During the last quarter of her life Elizabeth Petznek saw her grandfather's capital both devastated and magnificently rebuilt. Five days of intensive fighting in April 1945 was followed by ten years of Four Power occupation, for the last allied troops did not pull out of Austria until October 1955. By the end of the decade, however, visitors flocked to Vienna in greater numbers than ever before, and the restored showplaces of Francis Joseph's reign – the Opera House, the Burgtheater, the magnificent facades along the Ringstrasse – were ready to welcome the tourist invasion which came with cheaper and speedier ways of travel. In 1906 a British traveller, Colonel Barry, had declared that no one could cross the inner square of the Hofburg 'without the heart for a moment standing still at the salute: for behind yonder windows lives the man who, as husband, father, emperor, presents to the world the noblest instance of a modern martyrdom'. Later sentiment, of course, does not brim over so readily with hyperbole, and if today's tourists glance up at the window from which Francis Joseph would catch a glimpse of his 'dear friend' on her way to Mass, they will find there only the empty reflection of car roofs from the courtyard below. But, though denied a live Habsburg peepshow, visitors to the Hofburg or Schönbrunn rarely fail to sense the aura of spacious splendour in the apartments through which they trail; even the Kaiservilla at Bad Ischl preserves an impression of majesty relaxed in tranquillity.

More than once, an anniversary or solemn occasion has conjured up a passing image from the Habsburg era. In 1982, for example, the exiled Empress Zita, who had spent long days with Francis Joseph during the war, was allowed to make three visits to Austria after sixty-three years abroad – and at the age of ninety. Tens of thousands of well-wishers greeted her in the capital after she attended a packed service of thanksgiving in St Stephen's Cathedral. When, seven years later, the Empress died from pneumonia in Switzerland, her body was brought to Vienna for a semi-state funeral on 1 April 1989. The coffin was conveyed from

St Stephen's to the Capuchin Church on Francis Joseph's massive funeral hearse, and the threefold ritual supplication for admitting the body of a 'poor sinner' to the crypt was heard for the first time in the republic. Then, the procession over, the hearse was taken back to Schönbrunn and trundled into the Wagenburg – the coach museum next to the palace – to go on show again as an artefact of history. Does contemporary Austria at times appropriate the spectacle of Francis Joseph's Empire to enhance its sense of national identity? At all events, though Maria Theresa may be the most respected of Habsburg monarchs, Francis Joseph continues to attract more personal sympathy than any other ruler in continental Europe since the Napoleonic upheavals. His cult matches the widespread appeal of Queen Victoria within Great Britain.

The Emperor would have been surprised at the durability of the legend, for he was a modest man, aware of his shortcomings. Cynics might say his name commands respect in today's Vienna because he remains good business (as he was in towns across the Monarchy throughout his later years). Yet there are better reasons than commercial gratification for honouring Francis Joseph's memory. Long experience of the eleven peoples grouped together under his rule gave him a deeper feeling for the dynasty's supranational mission than his critics admit. Margutti, serving as a Boswell to his Samuel Johnson, made notes of the table talk at breakfast in Gödöllö on an autumn morning in 1904: 'The Monarchy is not an artificial creation but an organic body', Francis Joseph claimed, 'It is a place of refuge, an asylum for all those fragmented nations scattered over central Europe who, if left to their own resources would lead a pitiful existence, becoming the playthings of more powerful neighbours'. Ninety years later, it is the eleven peoples who are fragmented and seek asylum.

NOTES AND SOURCES

Unless otherwise stated works in English are published in London. FJ throughout Notes and Sources stands for Francis Joseph.

Abbreviations of titles:

AHY: Austrian History Yearbook (Rice University, Texas, 1965–   )

Bourgoing: J. de Bourgoing (ed.) *Briefe Kaiser Franz Joseph an Frau Katharina Schratt* (Vienna, 1949)

Conrad: F. Conrad von Hötzendorf, *Aus meiner Dienstzeit 1906–1918* (Vienna, Berlin, 1921–25)

Corti, *Kind.*: E.C. Corti, *Von Kind bis Kaiser* (Graz, 1950)

Corti, *Mensch.*: E.C. Corti, *Mensch und Herrscher* (Graz, 1952)

Corti and Sokol: E.C. Corti and H. Sokol, *Der Alte Kaiser* (Graz, 1955)

Ernst: Otto Ernst, *FJ I in seinen Briefen* (Vienna, 1924)

FO: Foreign Office Papers in Public Record Office, Kew.

G-H: E. Glaise von Horstenau, *Franz Joseph Weggefährte. Das Leben des Generalstabchefs Grafen Beck* (Zurich, Leipzig, Vienna 1930)

GP: J. Lepsius, et al.: *Die Grosse-Politik der Europäischen Kabinette* (Berlin, 1922–27)

Ham. *El.*: Brigitte Hamann, *Elisabeth, Kaiserin wider Willen* (Vienna and Munich 1982)

Ham. *Rud.*: Brigitte Hamann, *Rudolf-Kronprinz und Rebell*, Revised paperback edition (Munich 1991)

Ham. *Schr.*: Brigitte Hamann (ed.), *Meine liebe, gute Freundin! Die Briefe Kaiser FJs an Katharina Schratt* (Vienna, 1992)

HHSA: Haus-, Hof-, und Staatsarchiv, Vienna.

HM: Adam Wandruszka and Peter Urbanitsch (eds) *Die Habsburgermonarchie 1848–1918:-(4):* Vol. 4. *Die Konfessionen* (Vienna, 1985)

(5): Vol. 5. *Die bewaffenete Macht* (Vienna, 1987)

(6): Vol 6, pt. 1. *Die Habsburgermonarchie im System der internationalen Beziehungen* (Vienna, 1989)

Macartney: C.A. Macartney, *The Habsburg Empire, 1780–1918* (1968)

Margutti: A. von Margutti, *Vom Alten Kaiser* (Leipzig, Vienna, 1921)

Mitis: Baron von Mitis, *Life of Crown Prince Rudolph of Habsburg* (1930)

Nostitz: G. Nostitz-Rieneck (ed.) *Briefe Kaiser FJs an Kaiserin Elisabeth* Two volumes (Vienna, 1966)

OUA: L. Bittner and H. Uebersberger (eds) *Oesterreich-Ungarns Aussenpolitik von der bosnichen Krise 1908 bis zum Kriegsausbruch 1914,* 9 vols (Vienna 1930)

POM (i): H. Rumpler (Gen. ed.), *Die Protokolle des Österreichischen Ministerrates, 1848–1867* (Vienna 1973–)

POM (ii): Gyözö Ember, (Gen. ed.), *Die Protokolle des gemeinsamen Minsterates der ö-u Monarchie, 1867–1918* (Budapest, 1966–)

Roth.: Gunther E. Rothenberg, *The Army of Francis Joseph* (West Lafayette, Indiana, 1976)

Rud. HHSA.: Papers of Crown Prince Rudolf in HHSA.

Schnürer: E. Schnürer (ed.), *Briefe Kaiser FJs an seine Mutter* (Salzburg, 1930)

Soph. Tb. HHSA: Diaries of Archduchess Sophie in HHSA

Chapter 1 Schönbrunn 1830

For Schönbrunn and Vienna in general in 1830 see chapters 2 and 3 of R. Waissenberger, *Vienna in the Biedermeier Era* (1986), pp. 29–91: Fertbauer's portraiture, ibid., p. 183. On the Duke of Reichstadt in Austria see J Bourgoing, *Le fils de Napoleon* (Paris, 1950); his friendship with Archduchess Sophie, p. 343ff. Sophie's correspondence with her mother during pregnancy and on FJ's birth, see Corti, *Kind.* pp. 22–33, supplemented by Ernst, pp. 42–44. Metternich and 1830 revolutions: R. Metternich, *Mémoires . . . par le P. de Metternich* (Paris 1880–84, hereafter cited as Metternich Memoirs), Vol. 5, pp. 7–23; A. Palmer *Metternich* (1972), pp. 246–7; Macartney pp. 232–3. Corti, *Kind.* for Archduchess Marianna (pp. 133, 134), Sophie's reactions to Ferdinand's marriage (pp. 33–42), and for FJ's first visit to Ischl (pp. 43–44). For 'dear Ischl' in 1901, Ham., *Schr.* p. 471. Cholera epidemic, Corti, *Kind.* p. 43; and, in Hungary, Macartney p. 243 and István Deák, *The Lawful Revolution, Louis Kossuth and the Hungarians* (New York, 1979), pp. 21–22. For Coronation Diet of 1830: G. Barany, *Stephen Széchenyi and the Awakening of Hungarian Nationalism* (Princeton, N.J., 1968), pp. 269–70. On Reichstadt and birth of Maximilian: Corti, *Kind.* pp. 40–42, 55–60; Bourgoing, *Le fils.* pp. 350–1; J. Haslip, *Imperial Adventurer, Emperor Maximilian of Mexico and his Empress* (1971) p. 18. Marie Louise's visit to Francis Joseph's nursery: a contemporary letter in M.L.W. von Stürmfeder, *Die Kindheit unseres Kaisers* (Vienna 1910), p. 54, with other references to Reichstadt and his young cousin, pp. 15, 16, and 48.

Chapter 2 A Biedermeier Boyhood.

Many extracts from Archduchess Sophie's letters to her mother are in Corti, *Kind.* pp. 104–93, which also reproduces the Waldmüller portrait, facing p. 24. On Rauscher, HM (4), pp. 22–4, 52–3. Nursery recollections of the years 1830–

40 may be found in the letters in Louise von Stürmfeder's *Die Kindheit unserer Kaisers*, cited above; copies of this book are rare in England, but it is in the British Library. FJ's letters to his brother Maximilian, 1837–44, are printed in Ernst, pp. 55–75 and include facsimiles of some childhood drawings. Dismay at Emperor Francis's failing health in contemporary diaries: Kübeck, 6 October 1834, K. von Kübeck, *Tagebucher* vol I (ii) p. 532; Mélanie Metternich, 25–28 February 1835, Metternich Memoirs, vol. 5, pp. 645–8. Francis's death and testaments: A. Palmer, *Metternich*, pp. 268–9; Macartney p. 255. FJ and his grandfather's memory: Frances Trollope, *Vienna and the Austrians* (Paris, 1838), Vol 2., p. 300. On Bombelles, Macartney p. 409. For FJ's educational programmes, Ernst pp. 38, 48–51. Some letters in French from FJ to his mother are in Schnürer: in July 1838 p. 24; and the 'made us laugh' letter of May 1841, p. 32. For the 'loveliest valley I have seen', see Schnürer 9 September 1844, p. 44. Italian lithographs are reproduced in Corti, *Kind.* facing p. 241. 'Herr Lanner's music', 26 May 1841, Ernst p. 68. FJ's apparent enthusiasm for Jenny Lind's singing is noted in his mother's diary, Soph. Tb. HHSA, 20 February 1847. Fanny Elssler in 1846: Corti, *Kind.* p. 223; Ivor Guest, *Fanny Elssler* (1970), pp. 216–7; and for FJ's lasting admiration for her, Schnürer, 29 April 1851 no. 133, pp. 161–2. On Schreyvögel and Grillparzer see Ilsa Barea, *Vienna* (1966). Weissenberger's *Vienna in the Biedermeier Era* covers theatres on pp. 232–43 and also provides a copiously illustrated examination of Biedermeier culture in general. Archduke Albrecht's comment in 1844, Corti, *Kind.* p. 211. For Italian tour of FJ and his brothers in 1845: Schnürer, 7 September from Belluno, p. 55; 12 September from Verona ('balloon'), p. 59; 19 and 25 September from Venice, pp. 60–2; J. Haslip, *Imperial Adventurer*, pp. 28–31. On the *Staatskonferenz*: Macartney, p. 256; A. Palmer, *Metternich*, pp. 274–6; Alan Sked, *The Decline and Fall of the Habsburg Empire 1815–1918* (1989), pp. 26–30; and for Sophie's views on it, Corti *Kind.* p. 165. FJ's first train journey, Metternich Memoirs vol. 6, p. 242. FJ's diary entry on fifteenth birthday, Schnürer p. 57. Letters in Schnürer for FJ's boyhood friendships: Charly Bombelles in 1842 p. 34, and 1843 p. 41; Francis Coronini in 1845 p. 55; Albert of Saxony in October 1844 (p. 49) and warm September 1847 p. 82; Taaffe not mentioned until 1847 (p. 74), but, with Denes Széchenyi, he was FJ's close companion at Christmas 1845 (Corti, *Kind.* p. 229). FJ and Hungary, 1847: Schnürer 15 & 16 October, nos. 64 & 65 pp. 83–4; 'terrific agitation' 13 November, p. 85. On Sophie and FJ in closing months of 1847, Corti, *Kind.* pp. 244–5. Her diary (Soph. Tb. HHSA) for 20 December comments both on the preparations for *Wirrwarr* and the contrasting attitudes of her sons. Corti's *Kind.* reproduces the cast list of *Wirrwarr*, between pp. 272–3. For comments on performance: Soph. Tb. HHSA, 9–10 February 1848; Mélanie's journal, Metternich Memoirs, vol. 7, p. 534. A translation of the (1788) text of *Wirrwarr* was published in Cambridge in 1842, under title of *The Confusion, or The Wag*.

Notes and Sources

Chapter 3 Year of Revolution

Court faction: the American historian is Gunther Rothenberg, see Roth. p. 23; cf Metternich Memoirs vol. 7, p. 533. For Moehring and Sophie's role in these events, see Macartney p. 325 and Corti, *Kind.* p. 231; her pessimism is shown in diary entries for 2 and 31 December 1847 (Soph. Tb. HHSA). Political horoscope for 1848: Metternich Memoirs vol 7, pp. 569–72. On Kossuth and developments in Hungary: István Deák, *Lawful Revolution*, pp 91–99 supplementing Macartney, pp. 323–5. Sophie's diary entries (Soph. Tb. HHSA): 9 March, parallels with French Revolution; 16 March, events of preceding four days; 2 April, drive with FJ in the Prater; 15 April, assessment after FJ's return from Pressburg; 19 April, meeting with Windischgraetz. Archduke John on Metternich and subsequent events, H von Srbik, *Metternich, der Staatsmann und der Mensch* (Munich, 1925), vol. 2, pp. 263–82; Metternich's fall A. Palmer, *Metternich*, pp. 309–11. FJ and Bohemia, Macartney pp. 349–50. Sophie's letter to Radetzky, 22 April 1848: Corti, *Kind.* p. 276. For FJ's 21 letters from the Italian Front in 1848 see Schnürer, pp. 88–109: 'eagle over Turin', no. 69 from Bozen, 27 April; 'cannon-balls', no. 76, from Verona, 6 May; cf. Oskar Regele, *Feldmarschall Radetzky* (Vienna and Munich 1957), pp. 285–87 and R. Kiszling, *Die Revolution in Kaisertum Oesterreich* (Vienna, 1949), vol. 1, pp. 116–21. On Vienna in May 1848: ibid., p. 128; Walter pp. 49–94; cf. contemporary warnings from Stratford Canning to Palmerston, 30 April 1848, FO 181/215. Further assessments from Canning at Vienna and Trieste in May, in FO 78/733. 'Mouse in trap' Soph. Tb. HHSA, 16 May 1848; escape to Innsbruck, Corti, *Kind.* pp. 289–91 and Kiszling, *Revolution vol.* 1 pp. 131–3. For Grünne's ascendancy, Corti, *Kind.*, pp. 297–99. FJ and Bavarian cousins in Innsbruck: ibid. p. 300 and Corti, *Elizabeth, Empress of Austria* (1936), p. 24. Bohemia: Stanley Pech, 'The June Uprising in Prague, 1848', *East European Quarterly* (1968), vol 1, pp. 341–70. Radetzky and Grillparzer, Macartney, p. 342; O. Regele, *Radetzky* pp. 464–6. For FJ's projected visit to England, Corti, *Kind.* pp. 304–5. FJ's eighteenth birthday, ibid., p. 306; 'that admirable Jellačić, ibid., p. 307. On Radetzky and Latour, HM vol. 5 pp. 8–9. For Batthyány and Jellačić, Macartney, pp. 387–92. Windischgraetz's contingency plan, Walter, p. 192 and Corti, *Kind.* p. 308; 'caravan', ibid., p. 313. Events of 6 October and murder of Latour, Kiszling, *Revolution* vol. 1, pp. 239–48. Army's attack on Vienna, R.J. Rath, *The Viennese Revolution of 1848* (Austin, Texas, 1957), pp. 355–8; WJR trinity, HM vol 5, pp. 1–10; Walter p. 224. Formation of a government: Kiszling, *Fürst Felix zu Schwarzenberg* (Graz-Cologne 1952), pp. 50–3; Macartney p. 406, for Hübner's assessment and Kremsier speech. Windischgraetz and the Empress, Walter pp. 262–4. On FJ's accession: Soph. Tb. HHSA, December 1848; Kiszling, *Revolution* pp. 311–20; Corti, *Kind.* pp. 328–32, including extracts from Ferdinand's journal. For Hungarian dissent: Deák, *Lawful Revolution*, pp. 205–6. On FJ's participation in glass-breaking: French quotation from Soph. Tb. HHSA; her fuller account in a letter to her brother is used by Corti, *Kind.* pp. 343–4.

Chapter 4 Apotheosis of the Army

On Schwarzenberg's policy in general see Kenneth W. Rock, 'Felix Schwarzenberg, Military Diplomat', AHY no. 11 (1975) pp. 85–100. For the invasion of Hungary: Kiszling, *Revolution* vol. 2, pp. 12–14. 'Grace of cannon' exchanges: Sked, *Decline and Fall*, p. 142–3, citing Walther and providing a good summary of events at Kremsier; and Macartney, p. 422. Novara campaign: HM (5), pp. 333–4; Kiszling op. cit., pp. 146–51. Battle of Kapolna and Hungarian counter-offensives, ibid., pp. 46–68. For the reluctant negotiation of the dynastic alliance against Hungary see K. W. Rock's article, 'Schwarzenberg versus Nicholas I, Round One', AHY no. 6/7, 1970/71, pp. 109–42 and Ian Roberts, *Nicholas I and Russian Intervention in Hungary* (1991), pp. 106–27. Fall of Windischgraetz: Kiszling, *Schwarzenberg*, p. 89; Kiszling *Revolution*, vol. 2, p. 77; FJ's letter of dismissal, J. Redlich, *Emperor Francis Joseph* (1929), p. 55. FJ's sentimentality: letter to his mother, Schnürer 19 April 1849, p. 111. FJ becomes supreme commander, Roth. pp. 39–40; and Nicholas I, E. Andics, *Das Bündnis Habsburg-Romanovv* (Budapest, 1963), pp. 372–5. FJ at Raab, Kiszling, *Revolution* vol. 2, pp. 187–88; Maxmilian's account, Corti, *Mensch.* pp. 33–34; Schnürer 29 June 1849, p. 119. On Vilagos, Roberts pp. 179–82; Macartney p. 430. On FJ and Haynau, ibid., pp. 431–2: Corti, *Mensch.* pp. 44–6. Radetzky fêted, Regele, *Radetzky*, pp. 466–7. On General Hess and Grünne, Roth. pp. 39–40, HM (5), p. 25, and FJ to his mother, 18 September, Schnürer, p. 131. 'Apotheosis of the army', F. Walter, *Aus dem Nachlass … Kübeck* (Graz-Cologne, 1960), p. 34. Schwarzenberg's German policy: Sked, *Decline and Fall …* pp. 150–7; F.R. Bridge, *The Habsburg Monarchy among the Great Powers, 1815–1918* (New York, Oxford, Munich 1990), pp. 45–8; Kiszling, *Schwarzenberg*, pp. 156–65. On Kübeck and the constitutional changes of 1851, Redlich, op. cit., pp. 83–8; Macartney, pp. 452–3; Walter pp. 438–42; Sked, op. cit., pp. 147–9; FJ to his mother, 26 August 1851, Schnürer p. 166. Provincial tour, 13 May 1850, Schnürer p. 136; 'mood grows worse' and 'church parade', 1 and 5 September, 1850, Schnürer pp. 139–40. FJ dancing, Corti, *Mensch.* pp. 69–70. Habsburgs and fleet: HM (5), pp. 687–92; FJ at sea May 1850, Schnürer, p. 137; storm of 1852, 6 March 1852 Schnürer, pp. 175–6 and Corti, *Mensch.* pp. 90–91. FJ visits Metternichs, Metternich Memoirs, vol. 8, p. 117; 'faithful pupil', Corti, *Mensch.* p. 87. Sylvester Patent; Macartney, pp. 454–6. Schwarzenberg's death: Kiszling, *Schwarzenberg*, pp. 202–3. 'My greatest minister', for FJ's use of the phrase in 1907, see Rock article, AHY no. 11 (1975), p. 87. FJ's comments to his mother, 6 April 1852, Schnürer, pp. 176–7.

Chapter 5 Marriage

For FJ's romantic attachments, Corti, *Mensch* pp. 101–3; Ham., *El.* pp. 24–25. 'elegant seat', J. Haslip, *The Lonely Empress* (1965) p. 37. Libényi: Corti, *Mensch.* pp. 106–7; J. Haslip, *Imperial Adventurer*, pp. 62–3; Archduchess Sophie's diary entries for late February 1853 and for anniversary references in later years, notably in 1871 and 1872, Soph. Tb. HHSA. Leopold I to Queen Victoria, 3

June 1853, *Letters of Queen Victoria*, First Series, Vol. 2, pp. 447–8. Sophie's invitation to her sister and the journeys to Ischl, Corti, *Elizabeth*, pp 32–33; Ham. *El.* pp. 31–2. Both of these books cover the engagement, from Sophie's letters; the general course of events is confirmed by her diary entries (in French), 18–21 August 1853, Soph. Tb. HHSA; see also Corti, *Mensch.* pp. 121–5. Desk-bound existence', FJ to Sophie, September 1853, Schnürer p. 208. On Eastern Question problems in the background: Paul W. Schroeder, *Austria, Great Britain and the Crimean War* (Ithaca, 1972), pp. 77–82. FJ's letters to his mother for his courtship of Elizabeth in Schnürer: 17 October 1853, pp. 215–6; Christmas festivities, 27 December 1853, pp. 218–20; 'wonderful sunny day', 13 March 1854, p. 222. Background diplomacy; FJ at council of ministers: 23 and 31 January, 22 and 25 March, POM (i) vol 3 pt. 3, pp. 419–40; Paul Schroeder's article, 'A Turning Point in Austrian History in the Crimean War: the Conference of March 1854', AHY, vols, 4–5, (1968–9), pp. 159–202; the Austro-Prussian alliance of 20 April 1854, Bridge, op. cit., p. 54. Re-decoration of Vienna before the wedding: *The Times*, 26 April 1854. Mishap to crown: Soph. Tb. HHSA, 18 April 1854; Ham. *El.* p. 68 for repairs. Landing from Danube steamer, *The Times* 28 April 1854; Walter, *Aus ... Nach. Hübner*, vol. 1, p. 229. Wedding: *The Times* 2 May 1854; Soph. Tb. HHSA, 24 April 1854 (and for early married days entries of 25 and 27 April). For Renz: Corti, *Elizabeth* p. 54. Riding in Laxenburg, J. Haslip, *Lonely Empress*, p. 79.

Chapter 6 'It Is My Pleasure...'.

FJ's council meetings in first weeks of marriage: POM (i) vol. 3. pt. 3, pp. 441–6. Elizabeth's later accounts of Archduchess's behaviour: in Marie Festetics's diary for 1872, Budapest archives, cited by both Corti (*Elizabeth*) and Brigitte Hamann (Ham. *El.*). Parrots: Corti, op. cit., p. 57. Corpus Christi procession: Soph. Tb. 15 June 1854 HHSA. FJ swimming: letter to his mother 28 June 1854, Schnürer, p. 225. Army preparations: HM (5) pp. 340–2; Roth. pp. 50–51. Ministerial conference of 19 May 1854: POM (i) loc. cit. and W. Baumgart (ed.), *Oesterreichische Akten zur Geschichte des Krimkriegs*, vol. 2, pp. 173–81; and diplomatic aftermath, HM (6) pt. 1, pp. 215–8. Nicholas I's disillusionment, Roberts, op. cit., p. 228 and p. 275; FJ to his mother, 'our future lies in the East', 8 October 1854, Schnürer, p. 232. Four Points and subsequent diplomacy: Schroeder, op. cit., pp. 132–226; Baumgart, *Akten* vol. 2, pp. 290–3; Bridge, op. cit., p. 55; A.J.P. Taylor, *The Struggle for Mastery in Europe* (1954), pp. 55–70; A. Palmer, *The Banner of Battle* (1987), pp. 185–6 and 192–3. Russell on FJ: Lord John Russell to Clarendon, 6 March, 1855, Public Record Office, Kew, 30/22/18. Pola as a naval base: HM (5) pp. 724–7. Maxmilian's views while in command of the fleet, chapter 5 of J. Haslip's *Imperial Adventurer*. For ministerial council on *Credit Anstalt* foundation, 9 October 1855, POM (ii) vol. 3 part 4, pp. 140–44. Bruck's achievements: Macartney, pp. 460–1 and 468–9, critically re-assessed by David F. Good, *The Economic Rise of the Habsburg Empire, 1750–1914* (Berkeley and Los Angeles, 1984), pp. 81–8. Re-building of Vienna: Ilsa Barea, *Vienna* pp. 234–9. Concordat: HM (4) pp. 25–34. Telegram on signing of Concordat, 18 August 1855: Schnürer, p. 243. Maximilian's quest for a bride and marriage: J. Haslip. op. cit. pp. 86–101; Corti, *Mensch.* p. 192. FJ criticizes his mother's possessive care for his daughters, 18 September 1856, Schnürer, p. 256. Visit to Lombardy-Venetia: ibid., pp. 258–63; Ernst, pp. 90–6. Visit to Hungary and death of eldest child: Schnürer, pp. 267–71 and p. 280; Corti, *Mensch.* p. 189; Ham. *El.,* pp. 118–21. Sophie on Charlotte's charm: Soph. Tb. 4 August 1857, HHSA. Birth of Rudolf: Ham. *Rud.* pp. 15–17; 'not exactly beautiful', 9 September, 1858. Schnürer p. 286.

Chapter 7 Italy without Radetzky

Radetzky's funeral: Horace Rumbold, *Recollections of a Diplomatist* (1902), vol. 1, pp. 263–4. 'Radetzky was disobedient': Maxmilian to his mother, W.A. Jenks, *Francis Joseph and the Italians* (Charlottesville, 1978), p. 146. The section in Jenks's book on Maximilian in Lombardy-Venetia is useful, especially pp. 140–9 which include extracts from FJ's letters to him. 'Counting on loyal support', Ernst p. 113. Events leading up to the war and FJ's excessive confidence in Buol: Roth., p. 52; Corti, *Mensch.* pp. 220–21. For FJ's hostility towards Prussia, see his letter to his mother, 16 June 1859, Schnürer p. 292. On Gyulai, HM (5) pp. 343–5. For FJ, Metternich and the appointment of Rechberg, A. Palmer, *Metternich,* p. 358 and Corti, *Mensch.* p. 223. On Sisi and FJ's departure for the wars: Soph. Tb. 29 May 1859 HHSA; Ham. *El.* pp. 131–3; Corti, *Elizabeth* p. 78. FJ's letters from the Italian Front to Elizabeth in Nostitz vol. 1, pp. 9–36: 'selfsame room', 31 May, p. 9; 'no place for women', 2 June, p. 11; dismissal of Gyulai, 17 June, p. 22; 'pull yourself together', 7 June, p. 14; no riding with Holmes, 13 June, pp. 19–20 (cf. Corti, *Elizabeth* p. 80); long meeting with Rechberg, 20 June p. 24 (see Corti, *Mensch.* p. 231 for the report Rechberg brought to FJ). FJ's account to Sisi of losing the battle of Solferino, letter of 26 June, Nostitz vol. 1, pp. 26–8; Maximilian's account to Charlotte. see J. Haslip, *Imperial Adventurer,* p. 119. Napoleon III's reactions to Solferino and his desire for peace: Jasper Ridley, *Napoleon III and Eugenie* (1979), pp. 450–5. Extensive coverage of Villafranca meeting by journalists: *The Times,* 19, 20, 21 July 1859. See also for the Italian campaign, Roth. p. 54 and the critical memoirs of Anton Mollinary, *Sechsundvierzig Jahre im österreich-ungarischen Heere,* vol. 2, pp. 45–7 and 60–4. FJ's return to Vienna and the depressed mood of the capital: Corti, *Mensch.* pp. 242–9.

Chapter 8 'Power Remains in My Hands'.

Viennese newspapers, cited Ham. *El.* p. 140. Laxenburg Manifesto and subsequent constitutional experiments: Macartney pp. 496–8 and Corti, *Mensch.* pp. 241–2. Bruck's suicide, ibid., pp. 256–7. FJ's hostility to constitutionalism, 1860: Macartney p. 499. For October Diploma, Corti, *Mensch.* p. 263. 'Power remains in my hands', FJ to his mother, 2 October 1850, Schnürer p. 300.

Archduchess Sophie at Empress's 22nd birthday celebrations: Soph. Tb. 24 December 1859, HHSA. Elizabeth's illness; Ham. *El.* p. 148; Corti, *Elizabeth*, pp. 84–7. Warsaw meeting 1860: W.E. Mosse, *The European Powers and the German Question* (1958), pp. 87–9. Extract from modern biographer on Empress's illness and outside physician: J. Haslip, *The Lonely Empress*, p. 141. 'Shattered by the news': Soph. Tb. 31 October 1860, HHSA. Empress at Antwerp: King Leopold to Queen Victoria, 22 November 1860, *Letters of Queen Victoria* (Series 1), vol. 3, p. 414. 'Eats dangerously little': Louis Rechberg in private letter, cited Corti, *Elizabeth* p. 88. Hungarian affairs and fall of Goluchowski: Macartney, pp. 509–11. FJ at council sessions preparing February Patent 1861; POM (i) vol. 5, pt. 1 pp. 3–5 and 32–61, with agreed text of Patent, pp. 61–6. FJ's insistence on safeguarding his prerogatives, 28 February 1861, ibid., p. 111. FJ and preparation of speech from throne: ibid., pp. 291–300 and 305–6. Empress's return from Madeira: Ham. *El.* pp. 156–7; Corti, *Elizabeth*, pp. 92–3. FJ, his ministers and troubles in Croatia and Hungary, councils of: 6 May 1861, POM (i) vol. 5, pt. 2, pp. 28–33; 9 September, ibid., pp. 460–66; 27 October, ibid., pp. 458–66; and ('disciplining Hungary') 1 November, ibid., pp. 469–73. FJ's Corfu visit of 1861, in letters to his mother: going to Corfu, 30 September, Schnürer p. 305; impressions of Corfu, 15 October, pp. 308–9. Hübner comment on FJ's happy married life at Venice, Corti, *Mensch.* p. 276. Countess Esterházy's dismissal: J. Haslip, *Lonely Empress*, p. 159; Soph. Tb. 27 January and 28 January 1862, HHSA; cf. Archduchess's comments in letters quoted in Ham. *El.* p. 164. Pictures of beautiful women: Corti, *Elizabeth*, p. 96. Dr Fischer's diagnoses and cures: Ham. *El.* pp. 164–8. Start of Mexican imbroglio: E.C. Corti, *Maximilian and Charlotte of Mexico* (1928); L.A.C. Schefer, *La grande pensée de Napoleon III* (Paris 1939); J. Haslip *Imperial Adventurer*, pp. 137–62; J. Ridley, *Napoleon III and Eugenie*, pp. 498–509. FJ 'hungry for mountain air', 11 August 1862, Schnürer, p. 311. Elizabeth's welcome in Vienna, Ham, *El.* pp. 172–3. FJ and Rudolf at Wiener Neustadt, Corti, *Mensch.* p. 282. Ball on 26 February 1863: Hans Pauer, *Kaiser Franz Joseph I, Beitrage zur Bild-Dokumentation seines Lebens* (Vienna and Munich, 1966), no. 115, p. 164.

Chapter 9 In Bismarck's Shadow

For 1852 meeting of FJ and Bismarck: A. Palmer, *Bismarck* (1976), p. 50. 'Shift centre of gravity to Hungary', Karolyi to Rechberg, 5 December 1862. E. Brandenburg (ed.), *Die auswartige Preussens Politik* (Berlin 1930), vol. 3, no. 60, p. 100. Assessment of Bismarck's approach by FJ and ministers, 16 December 1862, POM (i) vol. 5, part 5, p. 117. Bismarck's vacillations: A. Palmer, op. cit., p. 81. The Frankfurt Congress of Princes; ibid., p. 86; Bridge, op. cit., p. 75; Corti, *Mensch.* p. 292–7. FJ's letters to his mother about the *Furstentag*: 'last chance for Germany's rulers' 13 August, Schnürer p. 320; a success, 2 September, ibid., pp. 322–4; FJ's difficult meeting with Queen Victoria, 11 September, ibid. p. 326. Military and naval action against Denmark: Roth. pp. 64–5; HM (5) pp. 345–6 and 694. FJ and Mexico, Corti, *Mensch.* pp. 299–300 (with Schnürer p. 302

for his continued mistrust of Napoleon III); Maximilian's problems, Corti, *Maximilian and Charlotte* (1928), pp. 384–99, J. Haslip, *Imperial Adventurer*, pp. 195–216. Alliance with Prussia 'the only sensible policy', FJ to his mother, 2 August 1864, Schnürer, pp. 333–4. Bismarck 'trying to frighten people with words', FJ to Albert of Saxony, 16 February 1864, Ernst, p. 160. On the Schönbrunn conversations: C.W. Clark, *Franz Joseph and Bismarck* (Cambridge, Mass. 1934), pp. 573–5 and the critical analysis of available evidence in H. von Srbik, *'Die Schönbrunnen Konferenzen von August 1864'*, *Historische Zeitschrift* (Berlin-Munich, 1935–6), vol. 153, pp. 43–88. On Rechberg, Biegeleben and Mensdorff: Bridge, op. cit., pp. 77–9: HM (6) pt. 1 pp. 55 and 67; H. Friedjung, *The Struggle for Supremacy in Germany* (1935) pp. 64–8. FJ's talks with Deák, 1864–5, Macartney, pp. 537–9, 541. Convention of Gastein: A. Palmer, op. cit., pp. 104–5; Friedjung op. cit., p. 75; Clark, op. cit., p. 190. For military preparations and FJ's attitude to the needle-gun: Macartney p. 534; HM (5) pp. 56–7; O. Regele, *Feldzugmeister Benedek* (Vienna-Munich 1960), pp. 372–4. FJ and British ambassador: Bloomfield to Clarendon, 20 January 1866, FO 356/37, extracts in Corti, *Mensch.* p. 332. FJ and ministerial council, April 1866, POM (i) vol. 6, pt. 2, PP. 3–16, 36–40, 45–7, 57–61. Benedek and Krismanic, Regele, op. cit., pp. 396–405; Roth, pp. 67–73 (and for whole campaign). 'Must have a result', FJ to his mother, 11 May 1866, Schnürer, p. 355. FJ's stubbornness over Venetia and treaty with France: council of 11 June 1866, POM (i) vol. 6, pt. 2, pp. 135–9. Gordon Craig, *The Battle of Königgrätz* (1965), pp. 99–175 for the campaign and its climax. Regele, op. cit., pp. 385–447 for Benedek's unfortunate role. On Beck in 1866: G-H, pp. 99–132. For a critical comparison of the Italian and northern campaigns, see the diary and letters of General Karl Moehring, printed as an appendix to Adam Wandruszka, *Schicksaljahr 1866* (Graz-Cologne-Vienna 1966). Tegetthoff's victory at Lissa, HM (5) pp. 696–706. Ceasefire and preliminary peace with Prussia; FJ at ministerial councils of 26–27 July, POM (i) vol. 6 pt. 2, pp. 174–8 and 194–6; Bismarck's difficulties, A. Palmer, op. cit., pp. 122–4. 'We shall withdraw completely from Germany', FJ to Elizabeth, 23 July, 1866, Nostitz, vol. 1, p. 49. 'Refined double-dealing', FJ to his mother, 22 August 1866, Schnürer. p. 247.

Chapter 10 The Holy Crown of St Stephen

'Praise to God a thousand times over', Soph. Tb. 22 April 1865, HHSA. For Fanny Angerer, Ida Ferenczy, and Winterhalter portrait cf. Ham. *El.* pp. 199, 203–7, 218–9, 230–2; J. Haslip, *Lonely Empress* pp. 180–5; Corti, *Elizabeth* pp. 105–6, 171. Rudolf and wild boar: ibid., p. 110. Elizabeth's Ischl ultimatum of August 1865: mentioned, ibid., p. 111, printed in full from Munich archives, Ham. *El.* p. 181. Andrássy and Elizabeth in January 1866: ibid., pp. 226–7; Eduard von Wertheimer, *Graf Julius Andrássy, Sein Leben und seine Zeit* (Stuttgart 1910–13), vol. 1, p. 214. FJ to his mother on Elizabeth in Hungary, 3 and 17 February 1866, Schnürer, pp. 348 and 351. Elizabeth's letters to FJ during the 1866 War, pressing the Hungarian cause, Corti, *Elizabeth* pp. 126–27. FJ's reply to Elizabeth, 17 July,

Nostitz, vol. 1, pp. 39–40. Exchanges between the imperial couple are summarized in Corti, *Elizabeth*, pp. 127–34, with FJ's letters printed in full, Nostitz, vol. 1, pp. 40–67, notably his warning to her that he had no money to purchase Gödöllö (9 August; p. 58) and his concern over presence of 'Her Mexican Majesty' at Trieste (26 August, p. 65). For appointment of Beust, see FJ's council held at Prague, 28 October, POM (i) vol. 6, pt. 2, pp. 281–7, and F.F. Beust, *Memoirs* (1867) vol. 1, pp. 313, 328, 339. 'No war for a long time ahead', Bridge, op. cit., p. 87. FJ at ministerial council of 1 February 1867: POM (i) vol. 2, pt. 6 pp. 300–10. On the agreed form of the Ausgleich and the settlement with Croatia: Macartney pp. 551–64 and, for an assessment of later commentaries, see Sked, *Decline and Fall* pp. 187–92. On the Holy Crown, its burial and later fate: Ian Roberts op. cit., p. 193; Wertheimer, op. cit., vol. 1 pp. 293–5. For the gift of Gödöllö: Corti, *Elizabeth*, p. 137; 'right good cheer', ibid., p. 139. Material showing the Crown Prince's boyhood idolization of Andrássy is preserved with his later papers, Rud. HHSA, K(arton) 12. Concern over fate of Maximilian at time of Hungarian coronation: Corti, *Mensch.* pp. 391–2; *The Times*, 3 June, 1867. Death of Archduchess Mathilde: Ham. *El.* p. 265; Corti, *Mensch.* pp. 392–3. Hungarian Coronation: *The Times*, 12 June 1867; French press quoted, J-P. Bled, *Franz Joseph* (English translation: Oxford, 1992) pp. 153–4; Crown Prince's account, B. Hamann, *Kronprinz Rudolf ... Schriften; Majestat, ich warne Sie* (Vienna and Munich, 1979, hereafter cited as 'Rudolf, *Schriften*)' pp. 387–8. Elizabeth on the martyrs of Arad: Wertheimer op. cit., vol. 1 p. 271. FJ and news of Maximilian's death: Corti, *Mensch.* pp. 397–8. Sophie in mourning for 'my beautiful son', Soph. Tb. 31 December 1867, HHSA. 'Perhaps I am with child': Corti, *Elizabeth*, p. 145. Salzburg visit: *The Times*, 19–24 and 27 August 1867; Hans Wilczek, *Happy Retrospect* (1934), pp. 42–7; Beust, op. cit., vol. 2, pp. 33–6. Diplomatic significance: A.J.P. Taylor, *The Struggle for Mastery in Europe* (1954), pp. 185–6; Bridge, op. cit., pp. 88–9. Eugenie and Archduchess Sophie: Soph. Tb. 19 August 1867, HHSA. Elizabeth informs Eugenie of her pregnancy: H. Kurtz, *Empress Eugenie*, p. 223. FJ's letters from Paris, Nostitz, vol. 1, pp. 68–79: beauty of Paris, p. 72; King Ludwig pp. 73 and 76; Prince Imperial and Crown Prince contrasted (postscript to 30 October letter), p. 75. For the December Constitution, Macartney pp. 560–2. Elizabeth's return to Hungary for her confinement: Corti, *Elizabeth* pp. 149–51. Birth of Marie Valerie, FJ's letter of 23 April 1868, Schnürer pp. 366–7.

Chapter 11 Facing Both Ways

FJ's pleasure in swimming: letter to his mother 3 August 1870, Schnürer, p. 374. Church-State relations and disruption of the Concordat: HM (4), pp. 38–9, 41–3, 51–7; F. Engel-Janosi, *Oesterreich und der Vatikan* (Graz-Vienna 1958), vol. 1, pp. 145–50. Empress at opening of Vatican Council: Corti, *Elizabeth* p. 163. FJ tells Sophie of ending of Concordat, 25 August 1870, Schnürer p. 377. Czech Fundamental Articles: Macartney, pp. 513–4; A.J. May, *The Hapsburg Monarchy 1867–1914* (Cambridge, Mass., 1965 edition), pp. 60–62; A.J.P. Taylor *The Habs-*

burg Monarchy (1948 edition) pp. 145–8; fullest survey in A.O. Zeithammer, *Zur Geschichte der böhmischen Ausgleichversuche,* 1865–71 (Prague, 1913), vol. 2, pp. 4–59. Krisvosije Rising: Roth. p. 86; Theodor von Sosnosky, *Die Balkanpolitik Oesterreich-Ungarns seit 1866* (Stuttgart, 1913), vol. 1, pp. 71–90. On FJ's eastern tour: Beust, op. cit., vol. 2 pp. 126–62. For FJ's 12 letters 'from the East' see Nostitz, vol. 1, pp. 82–148: 'in Stamboul', pp. 84–7; Sultan's horse, p. 88; Hellespont, p. 96; Athens and Piraeus, pp. 97–9; in Holy Land, pp. 103–9; embarkation at Jaffa, p. 110; ball at Ismailia, pp. 125–6; climbing pyramid, pp. 140–1. For written exchanges between Empress Elizabeth and FJ during his tour: Corti, *Elizabeth,* p. 162. Report of opening ceremonies of Suez Canal: *The Times,* 30 November 1869. For an entertaining account of the festivities: Marie des Garets, *Auprès de l'Impératrice Eugénie* (Paris 1928) pp. 140–50. 'Resident guest in the Hofburg': long extract from *Neues Wiener Tagblatt* of 3 March 1870 in Ham *El.* p. 278. For Albrecht, Kuhn and Austro-French staff talks: most detailed account is in the reminiscences of the senior French officer, General B.L.J. Lebrun, *Souvenirs Militaires, 1866–70* (Paris 1895), pp. 69–172; but see also Roth. pp. 87–8, Bridge, op. cit., pp. 95–7 and G-H, pp. 162–73. See, in general, the article by F. Engel-Janosi, 'Austria in the Summer of 1870', *Journal of Central European Affairs,* volume 5 (Boulder, Colorado, 1945–46), pp. 335–53. FJ presides over council, 18 July 1870: minutes in HHSA, PA XL/285, a box which also contains accounts of the important council meetings of 9 August and 22 August (with Andrássy's insistence on being a 'bulwark against Russia'). Archduchess Sophie's sorrow at south German backing for Prussia: Soph. Tb. 27 July and 5 August 1870, HHSA. FJ to his mother on 'catastrophe in France', 25 August 1870, Schnürer, pp. 377–8. Archduchess on Napoleon III's vacillation: Soph. Tb. 3 September 1870, HHSA. FJ, Beust and ministerial council of 11 September 1870: minutes HHSA PA XL/285; and cf. Beust, op. cit., vol. 2 pp. 179–90. 'A very dark future.': FJ to his mother, 23 October 1870, Schnürer, pp. 380–1. Russia and Black Sea crisis: discussed by FJ and ministers at council of 14 November 1870, minutes in HHSA PA XL/285. Beust memorandum of 18 May 1871; quoted Corti, *Mensch.* p. 447; see also Bridge, op. cit., p. 100. Meetings of FJ and William I, ibid., pp. 101–2; Corti *Mensch.* pp. 448–50. Replacement of Beust by Andrássy: ibid., p. 453; Beust, op. cit., vol. 2, pp. 292–7. Merano sojourn and Rudolf: Soph. Tb. 5 October 1870 HHSA; for context, see Ham. *El.* p. 297. 'Worthless shining lights', Soph. Tb. 31 December 1871 HHSA. Gisela's betrothal: FJ's last letter to his mother, 7 April 1872, Schnürer pp. 384–5. Sophie's final days: entries in journal (Soph. Tb. HHSA) until 1 May 1872. For her death: Ham. *El.* pp. 304–6. Festetics record of Elizabeth's reminiscences, ibid., p. 308.

Chapter 12 A Glimmer of Light

On Strauss and the first performances of the Blue Danube: Peter Kemp, *The Strauss Family* (Tunbridge Wells, 1982), pp. 69–71; Ilsa Barea, *Vienna,* pp. 204–5. Spread of banking and commercial enterprise: May, op. cit., pp. 64–7; Macartney pp. 606–7; but cf. D.F. Good, op. cit., pp. 86, 170–9, 204–8. For economic penetration of Turkey-in-Europe: A. Palmer, *The Decline and Fall of the Ottoman Empire* (1992), p. 238. For Schäffle on FJ: A.E.F. Schäffle, *Aus meinem Leben* (Berlin 1904–05), vol. 2, pp. 69–70; and for Schäffle's theories, E. Crankshaw, *The Fall of the House of Habsburg* (1963), pp. 254–5. Gisela's wedding: Corti, *Elizabeth*, p. 184. For the World Exhibition: ibid., pp. 184–91 and cf. the contemporary diaries quoted by Corti, *Mensch.* pp. 466–7, 469–70. For Freud's interest in the World Exhibition, see Ronald W. Clark, *Freud, the Man and the Cause* (1980), p. 30; his description of the opening procession is cited by Clark (pp. 32–3) from an account in Freud's 'Early Unpublished Letters', *International Journal of Psychoanalysis*, vol. L. (1969), p. 423. 'Black Friday' in 1873: Corti, *Mensch.* p. 467; effects of the 'Crash', Macartney, pp. 608–9, 616–18 and the later chapters of Schäffle, op. cit. FJ's Silver Jubilee celebrations: Corti, *Mensch.* pp. 475–6; Brigitte Hamann, *Rudolf, Der Weg nach Mayerling* (Vienna-Munich, 1988), p. 34; J. Haslip, *The Emperor and the Actress* (1982), pp. 18–19; Ham. *Schr.* p. 19. FJ and Press criticism: Ham. *El.* pp. 323–4. FJ a grandfather: Corti, *Mensch.* p. 477; J. Haslip, *Lonely Empress*, p. 257. Confessional Laws of 1874; May, op. cit., pp. 63–4. Four letters from FJ to Elizabeth during his St Petersburg visit of February 1874: Nostitz vol. 1, pp. 149–56. The Gabrielle incident fullest treatment in Corti, *Elizabeth*, pp. 198–205 (based on Fritz Pascher's papers). Empress on Isle of Wight, ibid., pp. 207–10; Roger Fulford (ed.) *Darling Child* (1976), p. 145. 'What a pity you cannot come': Corti, *Elizabeth*, p. 210 and Ham. *El.* p. 33. Prague and death of Ferdinand: Corti. *Mensch* p. 487. Domestic arrangements of Habsburg palaces: Princess Stephanie, *I Was to be Empress* (1937), pp. 151–2.

Chapter 13 The Herzegovina and Bosnia

General background, see Noel Malcolm, *Bosnia: A Short History* (1994). Mollinary's informative letters to his wife are the basis of the chapters in his second volume of memoirs, covering these events: A. von Mollinary, *46 Jahre.*, vol. 2, especially pp. 281–4. Two British Academy Raleigh Lectures clarify the Balkan crises: 1931 lecture by H.M.V. Temperley, 'The Bulgarian and other Atrocities 1875–8', *Proceedings of the British Academy*, Vol. 17, pp. 105–47; 1932 lecture by R.W. Seton-Watson, 'The Role of Bosnia in International Politics, 1875–1914' ibid., pp. 335–68. Military plans for seizing the provinces: Mollinary, vol. 2, pp. 305–6; Bridge, op. cit., p. 112. Starcević and Strossmayer: R. Kiszling, *Die Kroaten*, (Graz, 1956) p. 67. Andrássy's attitude: I. Dioszegi, *Hungarians in the Ballhausplatz* (Budapest, 1983), pp. 60–72; Wertheimer, *Andrássy*, vol. 2, pp. 258–61: German ambassador, L. von Schweinitz, *Denkwürdigkeiten des Botschafters General von Schweinitz* (Berlin 1927), vol. 1 pp. 309–10. Text of Schönbrunn Convention: Bridge, op. cit., pp. 381–2. On Kállay: Seton-Watson lecture cited above, pp. 342–4; Dioszegi, loc. cit.; his later career, Macartney, pp. 742–3. 'Blessed is the rifle' ballad: Temperley lecture cited above, p. 109. FJ's letters from his Dalmatian visit: Nostitz vol. 1, pp. 159–79. 'Local ... Panslavism' Consul Taylor to Lord Derby, 15 May 1875, FO 7/860/5. Spread of rising and Andrássy's attempts to calm down the crisis: R. Millmann *Britain and the Eastern Question*

1875–78 (1979), pp. 13–26; D. Harris, *Diplomatic History of the Balkan Crisis* (Stanford 1936), pp. 428–33. For Andrássy Note: B.H. Sumner, *Russia and the Balkans, 1870–1880* (Oxford, 1936), p. 152. FJ at Reichstadt: ibid., pp. 172–6 and 583–8; Wertheimer, op. cit., vol. 3, pp. 320–5. Text of Tsar Alexander's speech, 11 November 1876: Sumner, p. 227. Beck on war to avenge Világos: G-H p. 200. Albrecht and Beck appeal to FJ to maintain peace: ibid., p. 191 with background in HM (5), pp. 360–3. 'Compact Slav state . . . is out of the question': quotation from the Tsar's chancellor, Gorchakov, 5 December 1876, Sumner, p. 285. FJ on 'It is my policy': HM (6), p. 45. Tsar's tougher tone: Sumner pp. 428–32. Ministerial council of 15 January 1878: Wertheimer, op. cit., vol. 3, pp. 61–3; G-H pp. 196–8. Ministerial council of 24 February 1878: Wertheimer, vol. 3, pp. 76–9; G-H p. 201. Andrássy to Kálnoky on 'conflict or conference': 28 January 1878, GP. vol. 2, no. 303. Possible congress at Baden-Baden: Sumner pp. 434–5. Ignatiev in Vienna and FJ's comment on him: ibid., pp. 444–56; FJ to Albert of Saxony, 25 March 1878, Ernst, p. 175. FJ 'overjoyed': Rudolf to Latour, 13 August 1878, Rud. HHSA 16. 'Headed by a military band': Wertheimer, vol. 3, p. 153. Military plans and campaign problems in occupation of the provinces: Roth. pp. 101–2. For origin of 'Emperor never understand Eastern Question' remark, see Bridge, op. cit. p. 130. Andrássy insists on adhering to treaty terms: minutes of ministerial council on 24 August 1878, HHSA PA XL/290; and cf. his remarks at later council meetings on 11 October and 16 November, with minutes in same HHSA file. Andrássy's abortive attempt to resign, placed in a general context: Bridge, op. cit., p. 132. For Bismarck and Andrássy's resignation: Bruce Waller, *Bismarck at the Crossroads* (1974), chapter 8, especially pp. 190–3. Text of Austro-German Dual Alliance: appendix to Bridge, op. cit., pp. 382–4. Later Austro-Hungarian administration in Bosnia-Herzegovina: Macartney, pp. 740–8, supplemented by Robert Donia, *Islam under the Double Eagle 1878–1914* (New York, 1981), Peter Sugar, *The Industrialization of Bosnia-Herzegovina 1878–1918* (Seattle 1963), and Noel Malcolm, op. cit., pp. 136–55.

Chapter 14 Father and Son

A facsimile of the Crown Prince's military service record with 36th Infantry Regiment is in B. Hamann, *Rudolf, Der Weg nach Mayerling*, p. 57. An extract from *Funfzehn Tage auf der Donau* in Rudolf, *Schriften*, pp. 296–7. British royal family and Rudolf in 1877–78: Richard Barkeley, *The Road to Mayerling* (1958; hereafter cited as Barkeley), pp. 40–1, making use of the Royal Archives. Letter from Chester: Rudolf to Latour, 27 January 1878, Rud. HHSA, K16. His pamphlet on the Austrian Nobility: Rudolf, *Schriften*, pp. 19–52. His views on Joseph II, ibid., pp. 235–54. General Beck on Rudolf: G-H pp. 230–1. Crown Prince's Jewish romance in Prague: Ham. *Rud.* pp. 152–6; Barkeley pp. 52–3. His lecture on battle of Spicheren: see the military service record, cited above; Ham. *Rud.* p. 242; Rudolf to Latour, 4 April 1879, Rud. HHSA K16; for modern assessment of the battle, Michael Howard, *The Franco-Prussian War* (1960), chapter 3, pt. 2. 'All the beautiful women of Vienna.': Mitis, pp. 200–1. FJ's Silver

Wedding: Corti, *Mensch* pp. 526–7; Corti, *Elizabeth* p. 238; Ham. *El.* p. 358. Rudolf's satisfaction with regimental command: Mitis, p. 63. His letters to Latour in Rud. HHSA K16, cover Croat-Magyar relations (8 October 1878), Taaffe and the Czechs (13 October 1878), and social democracy (31 January 1879). Formation of Taaffe ministry and 'muddling through': Macartney pp. 611–15. FJ, Rudolf and Taaffe: Crown Prince to Latour, 30 October 1879. Rud. HHSA K16; Mitis, pp. 54–5; Ham. *Rud.* pp. 139–42, 146, 150–4. FJ and Helene Vetsera: Corti, *Elizabeth* p. 241, citing Marie Festetics's diary of 3 December 1879. FJ's meeting with Anna Nahowski: Ham. *Schr.* pp. 16–17; and Friedrich Saathen (ed.), *Anna Nahowski und Franz Joseph* (Vienna, 1986). On Rudolf's engagement, Princess Stephanie, *I Was To Be Empress*, pp. 89–90. Elizabeth receives telegram at Claridge's, Corti, *Elizabeth*, p. 244. Further correspondence of Crown Prince and Latour in 1880–81 in Rud. HHSA K16 includes: engagement telegram, 7 March; Stephanie 'comely', letter of 7 March; 'intoxicated with happiness', letter, 11 March; 'patriotism here is colossal', 5 April (cf. Mitis p. 202); Elizabeth at Red Cross meeting, 8 June (but for criticism of his mother, see Barkeley pp. 82 and 84); and his letter of 11 February 1881 attacking Taaffe and Cardinal Schwarzenberg and expressing his preference for a Jewish headmaster rather than a clericalist. Parts of this letter are in Barkeley and in Mitis; see also for his views, Ham. *Rud.* p. 166. Rudolf's wedding: ibid., p. 162; Corti and Sokol, pp. 14–15; Stephanie, op. cit., pp. 104–11, with Laxenburg references pp. 112–3. Memorandum on situation in Austria: Rudolf: *Schriften*, pp. 56–78. The long letter to Latour of 2 December 1881, praising Stephanie and criticizing the views of FJ, is in Rud. HHSA K16; a translation forms an appendix to Mitis (pp. 205–7) and it is extensively quoted in Barkeley, pp. 81–4. The Haymerle years: Macartney, p. 594; Bridge, op. cit., pp. 136–49 (with text of Three Emperors' Alliance, pp. 384–6). Rudolf, Szeps and Clemenceau: Barkeley, pp. 113–7, 119–24, 125–6, 160–2; Mitis, pp. 203–5; Bertha Szeps, *My Life and History* (1938), pp. 94–7, 110–11. Rudolf's 'way of talking': Princess Louise of Belgium, *My Own Affairs* (1921), p. 106. 'Waclav' as possible child's name: Stephanie op. cit., p. 144. Birth of daughter 'Erszi', ibid., pp. 145–6: and FJ's reaction Barkeley p. 91.

Chapter 15 Golden Epoch

A comprehensive record of FJ's public duties is in Hans Pauer's, *Kaiser Franz Joseph I,* a chronological guide to the pictorial documentation of the reign: for the 1880s, pp. 191–205. FJ and Queen Victoria at Innsbruck; journal entry for 23 April 1888, G.E. Buckle, (ed.), *Letters of Queen Victoria,* Series 3, (1930), vol. I, p. 400. For FJ's Kálnoky and the Skiernewice meeting: Corti and Sokol, p. 49; Bridge, op. cit., pp. 164–5; and correspondence between FJ and Kálnoky for July 1884 in HHSA PA 1/460 Liasse 22a. Milan of Serbia and his dependence on Vienna: A.F. Pribram, 'Milan IV von Serbien und die Geheimvertrage Österreich-Ungarns mit Serbien 1881–9', *Historische Blätter* (Vienna 1921), pp. 464–94; supplemented by material on Serbian problems, HHSA PA 1/456. Liasse 5. Italian state visit to Vienna: Stephanie memoirs, pp. 126–9; Ham. *El.* p. 212. FJ's visit to Trieste and the Oberdank affair; Corti and Sokol, pp. 30–1 and 34–5; Corti, *Elizabeth* pp. 256–8; Alfred Alexander, *The Hanging of Wilhelm Oberdank* (1977). FJ's reaction to Ringtheater fire: Corti and Sokol, p. 20. Villa in the Tiergarten at Lainz and the Titania theme: Ham. *El.* pp. 440–3. Susanne Walther (ed.) *Hermesvilla* (Vienna, 1986), an excellent brochure produced by Vienna's Historische Museum, with contributions by the editor, by Renates Kassal-Mikula on the architecture of the villa, and by Gunther Martin on the Empress and the villa. Elizabeth's excessive walks: Corti, *Elizabeth*, pp. 259–63; Stephanie memoirs, p. 173. 'Eagle' Ludwig and 'seagull' Elizabeth: see Ham. *El.* pp. 412–39. Dr Brigitte Hamann has edited Empress Elizabeth's 'poetic diary' for this period: *Kaiserin Elisabeth. Das Poetische Tagebuch* (Vienna 1984). FJ on Elizabeth in Ithaca: his letter to her of 1 November 1887, Nostitz, vol. 1, p. 190. FJ's first visit to the Hermesvilla: Ham. *El.* p. 443. FJ and purchase of the Achilleion: Corti, *Elizabeth*, p. 308. FJ's generosity to Helene Nahowski: Saathen (ed.), op. cit., pp. 118–9; Ham. *Schr.* pp. 159–60. Married and professional life of Katharina Schratt, 1873–83: J. Haslip, *Emperor and Actress*, pp. 20–34; Ham. *Schr.* pp. 19–25. FJ at Angeli's studio; ibid., p. 28; Kremsier meeting, Bridge, op. cit., pp. 167–8, 170; Crown Prince's reactions, Mitis, p. 247; Stephanie memoirs, pp. 188–9; Empress's view, Ham. *El.* pp. 533–5. The Bulgarian crisis of 1885: C. Jelavich, *Tsarist Russia and Balkan Nationalism* (Westport, Conn., 1978), pp. 315–43. Andrássy memorandum: Bridge, op. cit., p. 170. FJ and K. Schratt at Frauenstein 1886: Ham. *Schr.* pp. 31, 34, 37; J. Haslip, op. cit., pp. 38–40. 'Chatting ... at Frauenstein': reminiscence in FJ's letter to K. Schratt, 23 November 1886, Ham. *Schr.* p. 38. Anna Nahowski in 1886: ibid., p. 36 and Saathen, op. cit., pp. 110–1. Elizabeth and Ludwig's death: Ham. *El.* pp. 424–9; Corti, *Elizabeth*, pp. 279–84. Elizabeth visits Brundlfeld mental institution: ibid., p. 285. Kaulbars mission and its background: A. Palmer, *Chancelleries of Europe* (1983), pp. 192–3. 'Unthinkable for Austria-Hungary': Kálnoky cited by Aehrenthal in a 166 folio memorandum on Austro-Russian relations 1872–94, drawn up in May–June 1895, HHSA PA 1/469. Contingency plans for war with Russia: G-H pp. 301–6. Strength of war party in Vienna: Roth. pp. 115–6; Rudolf and war party, G-H pp. 308–14. FJ's letters to K. Schratt, Christmas 1886: pleased to see her name on posters, 25 December, Ham. *Schr.* p. 39; 'the prospect is poor', 1 January 1887, ibid, p. 40. Elizabeth's New Year's Night poem, *Poetische Tagebuch*, pp. 138–9. FJ's views on Ferdinand of Saxe-Coburg: J. Haslip, op. cit., pp. 54–6. For the Prince generally: Stephen Constant, *Foxy Ferdinand* (1979), pp. 91–129. FJ's life at Ischl in 1887: Ham. *Schr.* pp. 60–5, with manoeuvre references in two later letters, pp. 65–7. Elizabeth at Cromer: recollection of Compton Mackenzie, *My Life and Times, Octave 1* (1963), p. 144; verses in *Poetisches Tagebuch*, pp. 216–39, with 'backward glance' from Ischl, p. 257. FJ's letters to K. Schratt 1887–8: 'champagne glasses' for Catherine's Day (25 November) and 'to see you would make me happy', 29 November 1887, Bourgoing p. 75, (extract in Ham. *Schr.* p. 69); 'looked up at my window', 6 January 1888, ibid., pp. 78–9; reply to 'letter of meditation', 14 February 1888, Ham. *Schr.* pp. 77–8; Bourgoing pp. 84–7 (cf. J. Haslip op. cit., pp. 69–70); 'frankness is best' and 'Tyrolean garden', 18 February

1888, Ham. *Schr.*, pp. 81–3. Rudolf to Stephanie on Szeps and the Schönerer troubles: Stephanie memoirs, pp. 223–6; supplemented by letter from Rudolf to Bombelles, 8 March 1888, Rud. HHSA K 16 in which he says he thinks Vienna is 'the right place to be at this time'; see also Ham. *Rud.* pp. 406–7; and Andrew G. Whiteside's penetrating study, *The Socialism of Fools; Georg Ritter von Schönerer and Austrian Pan-Germanism* (Berkeley, 1975). Unveiling of the Maria Theresa monument: Corti and Sokol, pp. 103–4; Corti, *Elizabeth* pp. 303–4; *Poetisches Tagebuch* pp. 339–44; FJ. to K. Schratt, 15 May 1888, Ham: Schr. p. 91.

Chapter 16 Mayerling and After

'Settle at Mayerling': Rudolf to Bombelles, 27 July 1887, Rud. HHSA K12. Descriptions of Wienerwald are from the 1888 Lower Austria volume of the Crown Prince's survey of Austria-Hungary: Rudolf, *Schriften*, pp. 351, 352. Opening of Electrical Exhibition: Hamann, *Rudolf, Der Weg...* p. 48. Army bicycle corps: ibid., p. 62; HM (5) pp. 434–5. Inspector-General of Infantry: ibid., pp. 365–6; Ham. *Rud.* pp. 259–62. 'Different from my relations' Rudolf to Bombelles, 4 April 1883, Rud. HHSA K12. FJ 'knows everything': Rudolf to Francis Ferdinand, November 1884, cited from Archduke's papers by Lavender Cassels, *The Archduke and the Assassin* (1983) p. 14; for military private affairs within FJ's cognizance, cf. I. Deák, *Beyond Nationalism*, p. 141 and p. 143. Mizzi Caspar: Judith Listowel's *A Habsburg Tragedy* (1978), gives a clear impression of her (notably pp. 123–5 and 246–7 and 253–4); Lady Listowel makes use of information from Dr Walter Hummelberger, who knew Mizzi's step-sister. See also the semi-official police compilation, *Das Mayerling Original* (Munich, Stuttgart, Vienna, Zurich, 1955), p. 45. Rudolf's mixed feelings towards Stephanie, critical but not unsympathetic: letter to Bombelles, 21 July, 1886, Rud. HHSA K16. For Rudolf and Stephanie in Galicia and Bosnia-Herzegovina: Hamann, *Rudolf: Der Weg...* pp. 90, 102–3, 106–8. For Stephanie on Rudolf's illness, his recuperation on Lacroma and his increasing dependence on morphine, see her memoirs, pp. 206–8. Shooting incident: Mitis, pp. 47–8; Barkeley (pp. 156–7) rightly points out that Mitis's version depends on testimony 40 years later; Listowel, pp. 168–70 emphasizes the event. Hunting in Styria in 1889: there is a hurriedly written letter from Rudolf at Mürzsteg on 2 January 1889 to the journalist Berthold Frischauer in Rud. HHSA K16 (fol. 52 of the Frischauer correspondence). 'In most cheerful spirits', FJ reminiscing to K. Schratt, 5 October 1889, Bourgoing p. 174. The 'Julius Felix' open letter: Rudolf, *Schriften*, pp. 191–227. 'Lynchpin of the German alliance': FJ to Albert of Saxony, 14 December 1887, Ernst p 184. Rudolf's anonymous obituary of William I: Rudolf, *Schriften*, pp. 187–90. Boyhood relationship between William II and Rudolf: see the German Crown Princess's letters to Queen Victoria in 1873, R. Fulford (ed.), *Darling Child* pp. 73, 85, 88–9 and William II, *My Early Life* (1926), pp. 71–3. William borrows money from Rudolf on his visit to Vienna: Ham. *Rud.* p. 335; Stephanie's memoirs p. 143. Rudolf's ironic letter of August 1888 to Szeps about William II, cited from Rud. HHSA K17, Ham. *Schr.* p. 360. Hussar Temple episode: Barkeley, p. 218; Listowel, op. cit., p. 206. Lyrics of two *Heurigenlieder* for Mizzi: Rudolf, *Schriften*, pp. 276–7 (facsimile p. 278). Prince of Wales in Austria: Philip Magnus, *King Edward the Seventh* (1964), pp. 207–11; 'indefatigability', Stephanie's memoirs, p. 238; FJ and the 'fat man' on manoeuvres: letter to K. Schratt, 16 September 1888, Ham. *Schr.* p. 101. FJ and William II's state visit: Rudolf to Kálnoky, 29 September, 1888, Rud. HHSA K16; Stephanie's memoirs, p. 239; FJ 'extremely nervous', letter to K. Schratt, 5 October 1888, Ham. *Schr.* p. 103. Prince of Wales on seeing Mary Vetsera at Burgtheater gala: letter to Queen Victoria, cited from the Windsor archives by Barkeley, pp. 205–6, and written after the Mayerling tragedy. Marie Larisch, *My Past* (1913), pp. 170–208 give her version of events; on Larisch see Barkeley, pp. 209–11. Mary Vetsera's account of events on 5 November 1888 and subsequently, first appeared in Helene Vetsera, *Denkschrift*, (privately printed 1889, re-printed Reichenberg 1921); some of her manuscript is in facsimile in *Das Mayerling Original*, but Mary's original letters have never been made public. Sarah Gainham believes the Prince of Wales was misled (*Habsburg Twilight*, p. 16), deeply mistrusts the Vetsera *Denkschrift* (pp. 13, 25–6), and thinks the affair began earlier. For FJ's activities on 5 November 1888, see his letter to K. Schratt, 6 November, Ham, *Schr.* p. 111. For growing Hungarian army discontent: Macartney p. 695. FJ and Empress at Miramare 1888: Corti, *Elizabeth* p. 309. *Schwarzgeld* and Rudolf: Mitis, p. 109 plays down his role, but cf. Ham. *Rud.* pp. 372–8; see also Rudolf, *Schriften*, pp. 230–2. For Drumont's attack and *Epoca*: Barkeley, p. 198 and Ham. *Rud.* pp. 397–8. Rudolf's 'unsavoury article' about William II is printed in Rudolf: *Schriften*, pp. 228–9. Fall from horse; Barkeley p. 277. FJ does not believe Rudolf is ill: Stephanie's memoirs, pp. 240–1. Christmas at the Hofburg 1888: Corti, *Elizabeth*, pp. 310–11; FJ to K Schratt, 24 and 31 December, Ham, *Schr.* pp. 117–9; Saathen, *Nahowski*, p. 139; FJ to Elizabeth, 31 December, Nostitz, vol. 1, pp. 203–4. FJ's gloom at prospect of William II's birthday celebrations: letter to K. Schratt, 26 January 1889, Ham. *Schr.* p. 122. Title page of 12th issue of *Schwarzgeld* reproduced in *Hamann, Der Weg...* p. 120. For FJ's angry scene with his son and events of 29–31 January in Vienna and Mayerling, I have used books already cited by Barkeley and Listowel, together with: Corti and Sokol, pp. 116–8; Ham. *Rud.* chapter 14; Corti, *Elizabeth*, chapter 13; facsimiles in *Das Mayerling Original*; Walpurga Lady Paget, *Embassies of Other Days* (1923), vol. 2, pp. 464–6; and Hoyos's report, as printed in Mitis, pp. 273–86. Rudolf's funeral: *The Times*, 7 February 1889. For Victor Adler's speech of July 1889: Crankshaw, op. cit., p. 297, citing Adler's *Aufsätze, Reden und Briefe*. Rud. HHSA K. 21 contains papers put together after the Mayerling tragedy; among them is material submitted by Bombelles to clear his name (including two letters from Maximilian, 1866 and 1867) and German language extracts from works on Russian history prepared for Rudolf in late 1888, including an account of the murder of Tsar Paul. Rudolf's farewell letter to his wife: Stephanie's memoirs, p. 248; facsimile in Hamann, *Der Weg...* p. 124. FJ to K. Schratt after the tragedy: 'talking brings relief', 5 March, Bourgoing, p. 135; 'interest in gossip', 16 March, Ham. *Schr.* p. 148; 'taking up the old life', 14 April, Bourgoing, p. 165. FJ described visiting Mayerling on All Souls Day 1889 in two letters to K. Schratt, 3 November, Ham. *Schr.* pp. 189–90('soothing peace'); to Elizabeth, 6 November, Nostitz, vol. 1, pp. 205–6 (awed by Carmelite devotion).

Chapter 17 Spared Nothing

Fate of Charles Ludwig: Corti and Sokol p. 207. Francis Ferdinand's early life: L. Cassels, *Archduke and Assassin*, pp. 8–27; G. Brook-Shepherd, *Victims at Sarajevo* (1984) pp. 9–20. Relations between FJ and Francis Ferdinand after Mayerling: R. Kiszling, *Erzherzog Franz Ferdinand von Österreich-Este* (Graz-Cologne, 1953), pp. 18–20: Margutti, pp. 123–32. Francis Ferdinand's fury over use of Magyar language: G-H, pp. 476–7. Hungarian army bill: Deák, *Beyond Nationalism*, p. 66; Macartney, p. 698; Corti and Sokol, pp. 140–1 FJ on 'almost laughable' changes: letter to K. Schratt, 20 October 1889, Ham. *Schr.* p. 186. FJ on rudeness of Hungarian parliamentarians: letter of 26 February 1890, ibid., p. 210. May Day alarm: Barea, *Vienna*, pp. 311–12; and the detailed study by Harald Troch, *Rebellensonntag, Der 1 Mai zwischen Politik, Arbeiterkultur und Volksfest* (Vienna 1991). FJ and the Bismarck family wedding: letter to K. Schratt, 17 June 1892, Ham. *Schr.* p. 263; cf. A. O. Meyer, *Bismarck, der Mensch und der Staatsmann* (Stuttgart, 1949), pp. 691–93. FJ to Taaffe condemning anti-semitism: N. Vielmetti, *Das Österreichisches Judentum* (Vienna and Munich, 1974), p. 118. For the Czechs and the *Punktationen*: E. Wiskemann, *Czechs and Germans* (2nd ed. 1967), chapter 5, especially, p. 35. FJ, Taaffe's fall and suffrage reform Macartney pp. 659–61; May, op. cit., p. 226. Cilli problem: ibid., p. 323; Macartney pp. 663–4. For FJ, the fall of Kálnoky and the rise of Goluchowski: Bridge op. cit., pp. 205–8. On Karl Lueger's election and FJ's opposition; Richard S Geehr, *Karl Lueger, Mayor of Fin-de-Siècle Vienna* (Boston, 1991), pp. 89–95; John W. Boyer, *Political Radicalism in Late Imperial Vienna* (Chicago, 1981), pp. 362–2 and 374–6; and for an objective assessment of Lueger's achievements, Gainham, *Habsburg Twilight*, pp. 65–90. FJ on anti-semitism as a 'disease': letter to Elizabeth, 30 December 1895, Nostitz, vol. 2, p. 111. FJ ratifies Lueger's appointment: Geehr, p. 99 and Boyer, pp. 409–10. Analysis of election: Macartney pp. 362–3. FJ on Albrecht's funeral: letter to K. Schratt, 27 February 1895, Ham. *Schr.* pp. 322–3. Gisela's warning to Valerie: Corti, *Elizabeth*, p. 329. Return of Empress to court life: J. Haslip, *Lonely Empress*, pp. 416–7. For FJ's reactions to life at Territet: Ham. *Schr.* pp. 273–6 FJ's codicil to his will, favouring Schratt: J. Haslip, *Emperor and Actress*, pp. 119–21. FJ and Baltazzi balloon flight: ibid., pp. 138–9 and Ham. *Schr.* pp. 213–4. FJ unable to sleep because of slanders on K. Schratt, ibid., pp. 264–7; fullest treatment of the affair in J. Haslip, *Emperor and Actress*, pp. 147–50. FJ mentions 'Edison phonograph' in letters both to K. Schratt (= November 1889) and to the Empress (6 November): Ham *Schr.* p. 190 and Nostitz, vol. 1, p. 206. For FJ and Ibsen's *Wild Duck*: letter to Empress, 19 January 1897, Nostitz, vol. 2, p. 214; FJ anxious over Empress's sea voyages: 5 September 1890, Ham. *Schr.* p. 327; complains of bicycling mania, 13 April 1897, Ham. *Schr.* p. 364. FJ's Monte Carlo visit in 1894, ibid., p. 295; 'Soon to bed', 25 April 1896,

Bourgoing, p. 320; sees Gladstone, February 1895, ibid., p. 305 and Ham, *Schr.* p. 319; on Riviera eating habits, 12 March 1894, Bourgoing, p. 294 (with extract, Ham. *Schr.* p. 299). French fleet, Alpine infantry, presidential trumpeters, 5 and 7 March 1896: Ham. *Schr.* pp. 334–6. FJ and Empress to Cimiez: Queen Victoria to Lord Salisbury, 21 March 1896, *Letters of Queen Victoria* (3rd series) Vol. 3, p. 36. Hungarian millennial celebrations: Corti, *Elizabeth* pp. 357–8; Corti and Sokol, p. 206; May, op. cit., p. 363. Hungarian political crisis in 1897: Macartney pp. 700–01. Badeni Ordinance and subsequent unrest: ibid., pp. 663–4; May, pp. 325–8; P. von Eulenburg, *Erlebnisse an deutschen und fremden Höfen* (Leipzig 1934), vol. 2, pp. 210–12; J. Haslip, *Emperor and Actress* pp. 195–6. For FJ and Lueger at Stadtbahn opening: Hans Pauer, op. cit., p. 234. FJ. and schoolchildren: in 1898: letter to K Schratt, 26 June 1898: Ham. *Schr.* p. 384. Warning from FJ to K. Schratt about Empress's poor appearance, 3 March 1897, ibid., p. 358., 'More terrible than anything this century': Salisbury to Queen Victoria, 7 May, 1897, *Letters of Queen Victoria*, ser. 3, vol. 3, p. 159. Effect of fire tragedy on Empress: Corti, *Elizabeth*, p. 363. Elizabeth's visit to Geneva and her murder: ibid., pp. 365–84; Ham. *El.* pp. 596–600; see also Ham. *Schr.* p. 389. The earliest record of FJ's use of the phrase 'spared nothing' (in German) appears to be in an account of Goluchowski's conversation with the British ambassador, Rumbold to Queen Victoria, 11 September 1898, *Letters of Queen Victoria*, ser. 3, vol. 3, pp. 277–8.

Chapter 18 The Belvedere.

FJ's letter to K. Schratt of 11 September 1898: Bourgoing p. 367; Ham. *Schr.* p. 390. Marie Valerie's reaction; J. Haslip, *Emperor and Actress*, pp. 206–7. For Order of Elizabeth: ibid., pp. 208–9; Ham. *Schr.* pp. 396–400. FJ 'no intention' of marrying again: J. Haslip, p. 214. Archduchess Isabella and Sophie Chotek: the tennis-court incident was first printed by the Archduke's former secretary, Paul Nikitsch-Boulles, *Vor dem Sturm, Errinerungen an ... Franz Ferdinand* (Berlin, 1925), pp. 21–2; later treatment in Brook-Shepherd, *Victims at Sarajevo*, pp. 62–3. On Konopischt: ibid., p. 90. FJ and Archduke's marriage: ibid., pp. 78–81; Corti and Sokol pp. 252–61; and the biography of the Archduke's legal adviser, Max von Beck by J.C. Allmayer-Beck (Munich and Vienna, 1956), pp. 47–55. FJ thinks Sophie Chotek 'natural and modest': Corti and Sokol p. 263. Francis Ferdinand on 'wisest thing I ever did': T. von Sosnowsky, *Erzerhog Franz Ferdinand* (Vienna and Munich 1929), pp. 35–6 (and cf. Brook-Shepherd, p. 92). William II to Francis Ferdinand on his wife: Prince Bülow, *Memoirs, 1892–1903* (London and New York 1931), p. 614. For Loos, FJ and the Sezession: Carl Schorske, *Fin de-siècle Vienna; Politics and Culture* (1979) pp. 217–20 and 338–40; A. Janik and S. Toulmin, *Wittgenstein's Vienna* (1973) pp. 90–8; Barea, *Vienna*, pp. 257–8; Gainham, *Habsburg Twilight*, pp. 201–2. Noisy scenes in Vienna parliament: May, op. cit., pp. 333–4. On Koerber: ibid., 334–7; Macartney, pp. 667–9. FJ 'aged a lot': letter to K. Schratt, 12 May 1902, Bourgoing, p. 438. FJ, K. Schratt and the Maria Theresa play: Ham. *Schr.* pp. 487–90; J. Haslip, *Emperor and Actress*, p. 242. Rise of Hungarian Independence Party: Macartney pp. 693, 695, 700 and 760–3; Tibor Zsuppan's contribution to Mark Cornwall (ed.), *The Last Years of Austria-Hungary* (Exeter, 1990), p. 69. Case U (*Fall U*): G-H 404–6; Roth. pp. 134–5. FJ's Chlopy Army Order of 1903: G-H p. 403; I. Deák *Beyond Nationalism* p. 69. FJ's 'five minute audience' and its background in Hungary: Macartney pp. 761–2; minutes of the ministerial conference at Bad Ischl, 22 August 1905, POM (ii) ser. 2 Vol. 5, pp. 445–60. FJ 'not give way' and 'busier than ever over Hungarian rights': letters to K. Schratt, 2 October 1905 and 11 April 1906, Ham. *Schr.* pp. 504 and 510 (cf. Bourgoing, pp. 383 and 385). Francis Ferdinand's mistrustful nature: Conrad, vol. 1. p. 338. On Brosch: Brook-Shepherd, *Victims at Sarajevo*, pp. 119–21; L. Cassels, op. cit., p. 80. There is a study of the archival material on the Archduke's military chancellery by Rainer Egger, *Mitteilungen des Österreichisches Kriegsarchivs*, vol. 28 (Vienna 1975), pp. 141–63. On Max Beck as prime minister: May, op. cit., pp. 338–9; Allmayer-Beck's biography (especially pp. 169–85) and Lother Höbelt 'Austrian Pre-War Domestic Politics' in Cornwall's *Last Years . . .*, pp. 52–4. Austrian internal politics: W.A. Jenks, *The Austrian Electoral Reform of 1907* (New York, 1950); and John W. Boyer, 'The End of the Old Regime: Visions of Political Reform in Late Imperial Austria', *Journal of Modern History*, vol. 58 (Chicago, March 1986), pp. 159–93. For FJ and cars: I. Deák, op. cit., pp. 70–1 (including F.M. Beck's comment). See also H. Pauer, *Kaiser FJ*: pp. 280–1 (Ischl, 12 August 1908); 294 (manoeuvres, 8 September 1909) and photograph 148 between pp. 336–7 for FJ at 1910 Air Show. Archduke's criticism of 1906 manoeuvres: HM (5) p. 133 and Brook-Shepherd, op. cit., pp. 138–9. Appointment of Aehrenthal and Conrad: Bridge, op. cit., pp. 268–9; Roth. p. 137–42; G-H 432–5; Conrad vol. 1. pp. 33–7.

Chapter 19 Two Journeys to Sarajevo

Goluchowski on 'strangle Serbia': Eulenburg to Bülow, 6 January 1901, GP Vol 18(i) no. 3443. Belgrade palace murders and diplomatic consequences: W.S. Vucinich, *Serbia between East and West, The Events of 1903–1908* (Stanford and London, 1904), pp. 46–60 and 75–80. Conrad's memorandum of December 1907: Conrad, vol. 1, pp. 522–3. On the Sanjak Railway: A.J. May, 'The Novibazar Railway Project', *Journal of Modern History* (Chicago, 1938), vol. 10, pp. 496–527; S Wank, 'Aehrenthal and the Sanjak of Novibazar Railway Project', *Slavonic and East European Review* vol. 42 (1964), no. 99, pp. 353–69. 'Trouble, excitement and rush': FJ to K. Schratt, Bourgoing, p. 470. FJ's reaction to Izvolsky's offer in July 1908 OUA vol. 1, no. 9; Bridge, pp. 279–80. For Young Turk Revolution: A. Palmer, *Decline and Fall of Ottoman Empire*, pp. 196–210. Ministerial Conference of 19 August, 1908, OUA vol. 1, no. 40. Francis Ferdinand on Hungarian claims: Brook-Shepherd, op. cit. p. 176, citing Chlumecky, *Wirken und Wollen*, pp. 98–9. On the Buchlau talks: Aehrenthal's version OUA vol. 1, no. 79; Bridge, op. cit., pp. 282–4, updates Taylor, *Struggle for Mastery*, pp. 451–2. FJ and Ferdinand of Bulgaria: OUA vol. 1, no. 87; J. Haslip. *Emperor and Actress*, p. 255.

FJ's formal annexation of provinces: OUA vol. 1, no. 146. William II 'deeply offended': minute written 7 October 1908, GP vol. 26, no. 8992. For FJ's denial of 'designs of conquest': FJ to Nicholas II, 28 January 1909, OUA vol. 1, no. 935. On Austro-German military talks: Norman Stone. 'Moltke and Conrad: Relations between the Austro-Hungarian and German General Staffs 1909–1914', in P. Kennedy (ed.) *The War Plans of the Greater Powers* (1979), pp. 222–51 (reproduced from *Historical Journal* vol. 9, no. 2). 'Yes' or 'no' telegram: Bülow to Pourtales, 21 March 1909, GP vol. 26 (ii), no. 9460. On FJ and William II: A. Palmer, *The Kaiser* (1978,) p. 139. FJ's diamond jubilee: Corti and Sokol, pp. 321–4. Prague protests: May, op. cit., p. 415. FJ's visit to Bosnia: V. Dedijer, *Road to Sarajevo*, pp. 236–41; L. Cassels, op. cit., pp. 110–12, 114–15, and her Chapter 12 in general. 'Not too hot in Bosnia': FJ to K. Schratt, 26 May 1910, Bourgoing, p. 47 (and Ham. *Schr.* pp. 518–9); J. Haslip, *Emperor and Actress*, p. 257. Appel's report to Francis Ferdinand's military chancellery cited, from the Vienna Kriegsarchivs, by L. Cassels, p. 112. FJ's pervading presence: J.P. Barry, *At the Gates of the East* (1906) p. 79. Roosevelt's audience with FJ: J.D. Bishop, *Theodore Roosevelt and His Times* (New York, 1920), vol. 2, p. 216 (cf E.F. Morris (ed.) *Letters of Theodore Roosevelt* [Cambridge, Mass. 1954] pp. 369–70). Archduke's criticism of Roosevelt: report of 25 May 1910, quoted from his papers in HHSA by Dedijer, p. 98 and dated in Brook-Shepherd, *Victims.*, p. 282. Hitler and Lueger's funeral: A. Hitler, *Mein Kampf* (first English translation, 1939), p. 113; see also Alan Bullock, *Hitler and Stalin, Parallel Lives* (1991) p. 44. For Bronstein/Trotsky see Berchtold, as quoted by Taylor, *Struggle for Mastery*, p.xxxiv. FJ and church festivals: Margutti, pp. 225–7. Religious observance census figures: I. Deák, *Beyond Nationalism*, p. 171. FJ celebrates 80th birthday: Corti and Sokol p. 356; illness, ibid., p. 368. Austrian domestic problems 1911: Lother Höbelt in M. Cornwall's *Last Years of Austria-Hungary*, pp. 54–7; Macartney, pp. 796–8; May, op. cit., pp. 428–30. Tisza and Hungary, ibid., pp. 439–45. FJ at Charles and Zita's marriage: Reinhold Lorenz, *Kaiser Karl und der Untergang der Donaumonarche* (Graz, Vienna, Cologne, 1959), pp. 92–5; G. Brook-Shepherd, *The Last Habsburg* (1968), pp. 22–4 and his *The Last Empress* (1991), p. 19. Conrad proposes attack on Italy, 24 September 1911, OUA vol. 3, no. 2644. Aehrenthal's response in memorandum to FJ, 22 October, OUA vol. 3, no. 2809. Conrad's audience with FJ, 15 November, and later dismissal: Conrad, vol. 2, p. 282; HM (5) p. 140. Ministerial Council, 6 December 1911, HHSA PA XL/310, extracts only in OUA vol. 3, no. 3057. (HHSA minutes show ministers critical of Italian ally, as 3 army corps were needed to subdue Tripolitania). FJ chooses Berchtold: Bridge, op. cit., p. 312; S. Wank, 'The Appointment of Count Berchtold as Foreign Minister', JCEA, vol. 23, July 1963. Berchtold professes ignorance of South Slavs: Tschirschky to Kiderlen-Waechter, 6 December 1912, GP vol. 33, no. 12487. Berchtold and Archduke's family: R.A. Kann, 'Francis Ferdinand and Berchtold, 1912–14', S.B. Winten (ed.) *Dynasty, Politics and Culture* (Boulder, Colorado 1991), pp. 105–50. Nicholas of Montenegro in 1912 J.D. Treadway, *The Falcon and the Eagle; Montenegro and Austria-Hungary* (West Lafayette, Ind., 1982), pp. 72–101. Balkan Wars: B. Jelavich,

History of the Balkans (Cambridge, 1983), vol. 2, *Twentieth Century*, pp. 95–100; A. Palmer, *Decline and Fall of Ottoman Empire*, pp. 215–8. FJ says 'I don't want war', Fritz Fellner (ed.) *Schicksalsjahre Osterreich, 1908–1919: Das Politische Tagebuch Josef Redlichs* (Graz, 1953–54; hereafter cited as Redlich *Tagebuch*), 29 November 1912, vol. I, p. 183. Ministerial Councils of 28 October and 8 November, 1912, on war preparadness in annexed provinces: HHSA PA XL/310. FJ re-instates Conrad: his vol. 2, pp. 373–9. Prochaska affair: Bridge, op. cit., p. 318; HM (6)i p. 491. Berchtold on events of 11 December 1912, Hugo Hantsch, *Leopold Graf Berchtold* (Graz, 1963), vol. I, pp. 360–4. His audience with FJ, 27 December: S.J. Williamson, *Austria-Hungary and the Origins of the First World War* (1991), P. 131, citing unpublished section of Berchtold's diary. Scutari crisis; ibid., p. 136; Redlich *Tagebuch*, (21 March 1913), vol. I, pp. 192–3; Conrad vol. 3, pp. 226–30. Conrad wishes to implement earlier war plans: pp. 252–66. Attitudes of Masaryk, István Tisza: C.A. Macartney and A.W. Palmer, *Independent Eastern Europe* (1962), pp. 20–22; supplemented by Eva Schmidt-Hartmann, *Thomas G. Masaryk's Realism* (Munich, 1984). On FJ, Tisza and the Roumanians: Ottokar Czernin, *In the World War* (1919) pp. 76–86. FJ's concern for his appearance before visits of K. Schratt: E. Ketterl, p. 107; his relaxed moments with Grinzing musicians, ibid., p. 108. Basic to the Redl Case are E.E. Kisch, *Der Fall des Generalstafschef Redl* (Berlin 1924), and Robert Asprey, *The Panther's Feast* (New York, 1959); see also S. Gainham, *The Habsburg Twilight*, pp. 142–60; Conrad, vol. 3, pp. 338–80; Redlich *Tagebuch* (26 June 1913), vol. I, pp. 201–2; and Norman Stone's chapter on the Austro-Hungarian intelligence services in Ernest May (ed.), *Knowing One's Enemies* (Princeton, NJ, 1984), especially p. 43. Conflict between FJ and the Archduke over Redl affair: Conrad, as cited above; and L. Cassels, *Archduke and the Assassin*, pp 157–8. FJ increases Francis Ferdinand's military authority: ibid., p. 143; Roth. p. 170; HM (5) pp. 367–9. FJ and Leipzig centenary: see photographs in Franz Hubman, *The Habsburg Empire* (1972), p. 298. Serb officers' pressure group and Black Hand: A. Palmer, *The Lands Between* (1969), pp. 112–16, 116–7; Dedijer op. cit., pp. 371–81; and B. Jelavich's 'What the Habsburg Government knew about the Black Hand', AHY vol. 22, pp. 131–50, including five reports from the military attaché in Belgrade. Pašić in Vienna: Minutes of ministerial council 3 October, 1913: HHSA PA XL/311 (partly printed OUA vol. 7, no. 8779); Berchtold memorandum, OUA vol. 7, no. 8813; Griesinger to German Foreign Ministry, 7 October 1913, GP vol. 36 (i) no. 14157. Ultimatum to Belgrade, 17 October 1913; OUA vol. 7, no. 8850. Archduke and Conrad's non-attendance at Mass: L. Cassels, op. cit., p. 158. First proposals that Archduke should visit Sarajevo: ibid., pp. 143–44; Conrad, vol. 3, p. 445. FJ chooses to walk up the stairs: G-H, p. 442. FJ's illness in spring of 1914: Brook-Shepherd, *Victims*, p. 259; Corti and Sokol, p. 408. Council of ministers on 24 May, 1914: HHSA PA XL/311. FJ's final audiences with Francis Ferdinand: Brook-Shepherd, *Victims*, p. 222. William II and Archduke in 1914: ibid., pp. 228–32; A. Palmer, *The Kaiser* pp. 163–4; Dedijer, op. cit., p. 158; Williamson, op. cit., p. 164. Detailed accounts of the events in Sarajevo are in Brook-Shepherd, Cassels and Dedijer; see also

Joachim Remak, *Sarajevo* (1959), who cites (p. 106) telegram from the Archduke to FJ, 27 June. FJ informed of assassination: Margutti, pp. 147–8. Marie Valerie on her father's reaction: Corti and Sokol, p. 413.

Chapter 20 War

British royal sympathy for FJ: James Pope-Hennessy, *Queen Mary* (1959), pp. 485–6. 'No mood of mourning', Redlich *Tagebuch*, 29 June, vol. 1, p. 235. Baron Morse and the 'third class burial': Brook-Shepherd (*Victims.*, p. 261) writes that the phrase 'crops up repeatedly' in the manuscript diary of the Archduke's secretary, Morsey; and cf. Immanuel Geiss, *July 1914*, p. 56 for other use of the phrase. Brook-Shepherd (pp. 261–9) and Remak, op. cit., (pp. 166–81) give detailed accounts of the prolonged obsequies, from Trieste to Artstetten. Berchtold on FJ's reactions: Hantsch, *Berchtold*, vol. 2, p. 559. 'Time not yet ripe': Macartney p. 807; for Tisza and opinion in Hungary: N. Stone, 'Hungary and the Crisis of July 1914', *Journal of Contemporary History* (1966), vol. 1, pp. 153–170. 'Serbia must be eliminated': FJ to William II, 2 July 1914, OUA vol. 8, no. 9984. The Hoyos mission: S.R. Williamson, op. cit., pp. 195–6; Geiss, op. cit., pp. 70–81. Pledge of support to FJ from Berlin: Szögyeny to Berchtold, 6 July 1914, OUA vol. 8, no. 10076. Ministerial council of 7 July: minutes, OUA vol. 8 no. 10118 (excerpt, Geiss, pp. 80–7). FJ receives Berchtold at Ischl: Berchtold's diary entry for 9 July in Hantsch vol. 2, p. 570; Tschirsky to Jagow, 10 July, 1914, printed as document 16 in Geiss, op. cit., pp. 106–8. Ministerial council of 19 July: minutes, OUA, vol. 8 no. 10393; FJ's first response to report of meeting: Margutti, pp. 397–9. Austrian demands on Serbia, OUA vol. 8, no. 10395 (but see no. 10526 for final note handed to Serbia). FJ, Russia and ultimatum: R.A. Kann, 'Emperor Franz Joseph and the Outbreak of World War I' in S.B. Winters (ed.) *Dynasty, Politics and Culture*, pp. 283–310. Churchill's comment on ultimatum: Winston S. Churchill, *The World Crisis* (1938 edition), vol. 1, p. 155. Duke of Cumberland and other visitors to FJ: Margutti: pp. 401;2: 'That's that', ibid., p. 404. 'I have done my best': J. Haslip, *Emperor and Actress*, p. 267. William II unable to control events: A. Palmer, *The Kaiser*, pp. 170 and 224. FJ's departure from Bad Ischl: Margutti, p. 411. Bungling of war plans by Conrad: Stone, 'Moltke and Conrad' in P. Kennedy (ed.) *War Plans of the Great Powers*, pp. 237–40 and p. 249. 'My wars have always begun with victories': Empress Zita's reminscences of FJ as reported by Brook-Shepherd in *The Last Habsburg*, p. 29 and *The Last Empress*, p. 39. 'A happy war for us?': Margutti, pp. 417–8. FJ and Jewish refugees: A.J. May, *The Passing of the Hapsburg Monarchy*, 1916–18 (Philadelphia, 1968), vol. 1, p. 311. FJ at Christmas 1914: Margutti, p. 431. The Italian problem: L. Valiani, *The End of Austria-Hungary*, pp. 62–71 (1973), and his 'Italo-Austro-Hungarian negotiations 1914–15', *Journal of Contemporary History* (1966), vol. 1, pp. 113–36; Bridge, op. cit., pp. 348–52. FJ presides over his last council of ministers, 8 March 1915: M. Komjathy, *Protokolle des Gemeinsamen Ministerates ... 1914–18* (Budapest, 1966), pp. 215–32. FJ's 'volcano' metaphor: Brook-Shepherd, *Last Empress*, p. 37. Stebnicka Huta desertions:

Z.A.B. Zeman, *The Break-Up of the Habsburg Empire 1914–1918* (1961) pp. 55–7. FJ celebrates re-capture of Lemberg: Hans Pauer, *Kaiser FJ*, p. 327. Conrad's *schwarzgelbe* offensive: Roth. pp. 194–5. FJ and the Polish Question: Fritz Fischer, *Germany's Aims in the First World War* (1967), pp. 236–45; Zeman, op. cit., pp. 100–09. Frustrated Trentino offensive: Gerhard Artl, *Die österreichische-ungarische Sudtiroloffensive 1916* (Vienna, 1983), especially pp. 182–3. Effects of Brussilov's offensive: Macartney, p. 818; Roth. p. 198; Redlich *Tagebuch* (20 June 1916) vol. 2, p. 123. Germany imposes unified military command: 'Silberstein, *The Troubled Alliance; German-Austrian Relations, 1914–17* (Lexington 1970), chapter 13. Weiner-Neustadt whirlwind and FJ's determination to call a halt to the war: Margutti, p. 448.

Chapter 21 Schönbrunn 1916

Stürgkh's assassination is vividly described from contemporary sources and interviews: R. Pick, *The Last Days of Imperial Vienna* (1975), pp. 1–9. Archduke Charles's movements: K. Lorenz, *Kaiser Karl*, pp. 221–3; Brook-Shepherd, *Last Habsburg*, pp. 44–5. Last visit of Katharina Schratt: J. Haslip, *Emperor and Actress*, p. 270; Bourgoing p. 475. FJ's death: Corti and Sokol, pp. 467–9; Margutti, pp. 454–5; Ketterl, p. 251. Reaction to death: Redlich *Tagebuch* (21 November 1916), vol. 2 p. 156; in allied capitals, Harry Hanak, *Great Britain and Austria-Hungary during the First World War* (1962), pp. 211–13, citing *Weekly Despatch of 3 December 1916* for criticism of Fr. Vaughan. Burial processions: Margutti pp. 456–7; Lorenz, op. cit., pp. 227–8. Solemn Requiem on anniversary of FJ's accession: Margutti, p. 458.

Chapter 22 Into History

The second half of Barbara Jelavich's *Modern Austria* (Cambridge, 1987) covers the years 1916 to 1986. For the peace treaties of 1919–20 and their effect on central Europe: Macartney and Palmer, *Independent Eastern Europe*, pp. 97–198. On Anton Léhar's Habsburg loyalty: I. Deák, *Beyond Nationalism*, p. 219. Robert Musil's *Der Mann ohne Eigenschaften* was translated into English by Eithne Wilkins and Ernst Kaiser as *The Man without Qualities* (1953): David Luft's critical study, *Robert Musil and the Crisis of European Culture* (Berkeley, 1980) seems to suggest that Musil interpreted the mood of 1913–14 in terms of a highly individualistic Weimar-Vienna cultural Anschluss. An American edition of Joseph Roth's *Radetzkymarsch*, translated by Eva Tucker was published in Woodstock, New York, 1983. J.P. Barry, *At the Gates of the East* (1906), saluted the modern martyr in the Hofburg, p. 90. For Empress Zita's return to Austria in 1982: Brook-Shepherd, *Last Empress*, p. 323; her funeral in 1989, ibid., pp. 329–34. FJ's table-talk on the Monarchy as 'a place of refuge', Margutti, pp. 261–2.

ALTERNATIVE PLACE NAMES

The first name given below is the one normally used in the book. Abbreviations:–
A. Albanian; Cz. Czech or Slovak; E. English; G. German; H. Hungarian; I.
Italian; P. Polish; R. Roumanian; Rus. Russian; SC. Serbo-Croat; Slov. Slovene;
T. Turkish.

Bolzano (I): Bozen (G)
Bratislava (Cz); Pressburg (G);
 Pozsony (H)
Brno (Cz); Brünn (G)
Buda (H); Ofen (G)
Cracow (E); Kraków (P); Krakau (G)
Cilli (G); Celje (Slov)
Cluj (R.); Kolozsvár (H);
 Klausenburg (G)
Corfu (I); Kerkyra (Greek)
Czernowitz (G); Chernovtsy (Rus);
 Cernauţi (R)
Dubrovnik (SC); Ragusa (I)
Durrës (A); Durazzo (I)
Edirne (T); Adrianople (E from
 Greek)
Fiume (I); Rijeka (SC); Reka (Slov)
Franzensbad (G); Františkovy Lázně
 (Cz)
Györ (H); Raab (G)
Komárom (H); Komorn (G);
 Komárno (Cz)
Königgrätz (G); Hradec Králové
 (Cz)
Konopischt (G); Konopište (Cz)
Kotor (SC); Cattaro (I)
Kremsier (G); Kromeriz (Cz)
Lemberg (G); Lwów (P); Lvov (Rus);
 Lviv (Ukrainian)

Lissa (I); Vis (SC)
Ljubljana (Slov); Laibach (G)
Merano (I); Meran (G)
Novi Sad (SC); Ujvidék (H); Neusatz
 (G)
Olmütz (G): Olomouc (Cz)
Pilsen (G); Plzeň (Cz)
Pola (I); Pula (SC); Pulj (Slov)
Prague (E); Prag (G); Praha (Cz)
Reichstadt (G); Zákupy (Cz)
Ruschuk (G and T); Ruše (B)
Salonika (E); Thessaloniki (Greek)
San Giovanni di Medua (I); Shengjin
 (A)
Scutari [in Albania] (I); Shkodra (A)
Sopron (H); Oedenburg (G)
Split (SC); Spalato (I)
Szeged (H); Szegedin (G)
Temesvár (H); Timişoara (R)
Tisza river (H); Theiss river (G)
Ulcinj (A); Dulcigno (I)
Vienna (E); Wien (G); Bécs (H);
 Videň (Cz); Dunaj (Slov)
Vlonë (A); Valona (I)
Vltava river (Cz); Moldau river (G)
Zadar (SC); Zara (I)
Zagreb (SC); Agram (G); Zágráb (H)
Zemun (SC); Semlin (G)
Znaim (G); Znojno (Cz)

INDEX

(abbreviations: FJ = Francis Joseph, E = Elizabeth, F. Ferdinand = Francis Ferdinand, A-H = Austria-Hungary, B-H = Bosnia Herzegovina, PM = Prime Minister)

Abdulaziz, Sultan: 160, 169, 170, 202
Abdulhamid II, Sultan: 160, 205, 209, 301, 303
Achilleion palace, Corfu: 235, 306
Adler, Viktor: socialist leader, 262, 269, 340
Aehrenthal, Count Aloys: foreign minister, 298–9, 302–5; and Italy, 311–12; dies, 312
Agriculture: Austro-Hungarian, 181, 187
Albania: 311; in Balkan Wars, 314–16, 320
Albert of Saxony, cousin of FJ: 23, 252
Albrecht, Archduke, cousin of FJ: 20, 103, 115, 188, 256; in 1848 revolt, 30–33; in Austro-Prussian war, 142–3, 145; and Franco-Prussian war, 173–4; and Eastern crisis, 204, 206; and Rudolf, 215, 247–8, 263–4; and F. Ferdinand, 267, 268; dies, 276
Alexander II, Tsar: 175, 176; meets FJ (1860), 120; FJ visits, 190–91; and Eastern crisis (1875–8), 203–6
Alexander III, Tsar: 240; meets FJ, 231, 237–8
Alexander of Battenberg, Prince: 238, 240
Andrássy, Count Gyula: 55, 174, 187; E supports, 150–52; Hungarian PM, 154, 156–9; and Czechs, 168; foreign minister of A-H, 177, 183, 190–91; and Eastern crisis (1875–8), 199–206; resigns, 211–12; achievements of,

212–13; and Balkan crisis (1885), 238
Angeli, Heinrich von, artist: 257
Angerer, Fanny, E's hairdresser: 148
Anna of Prussia, Princess: FJ and, 66
Anti-clericalism: Austrian, 189–90; Rudolf's, 222
Anti-semitism: 187, 270, 274–5; in Vienna, 244, 252, 256–7, 281
Army: FJ and, 20, 25; Italians in, 21; in Italian campaign (1848); 33, 35–7; FJ supreme commander of, 52, 56–7; mobilized, (1854–5) 73, 81–2, (1866) 142; in Italian war (1859), 103–4; FJ commands at Solferino 109–10; modernization of, 140, 141, 238; in B-H, 210; Hungarians in, 268–9, 293–5, Redl scandal in, 318–19, in World War I, 333–4
Army Bill (1889): 256, 258–9, 263
Augustinerkirche, Vienna: imperial marriages in, 77, 184–5, 222
Austria, empire of (1830): 5; and Crimean War, 81–5; in Italian war (1859), 102–13; in Schleswig-Holstein crisis, 133–4, 137–8; relations with Prussia, 140, 141–2
Austria-Hungary: Dual Monarchy established (1867), 154–9; and Franco-Prussian War, 174–6; and B-H, 197–8, 207–11, 213, 225, in Eastern crisis (1875–8), 201–7; relations with Italy, 231, 311–12; relations with Russia, 237–8, 283, 301–2; in Balkan crisis (1885–6), 238,

Austria-Hungary—*cont*
240, 241; relations with Serbia, 300–1, 304–5, 320–21; and German alliance, 305; and Balkan Wars, 314–16, 319–20; in World War I, 332–41
Austrian Republic: 346–9
Austro-Prussian war (1866): 142–7
Autocracy: FJ exercises (1851–61), 62–3, 80, 85, 117–18, 123; FJ prefers, 166

Bach, Alexander, minister of justice: 42, 45, 50, 59, 60, 89, 115
Badeni, Count Casimir: PM, 272–3, 275; language ordinances of, 282–3
Balkan Wars, (1912–13): 313–16, 319–20
Balkans, crisis in (1885–6): 238, 240, 241
Ballhausplatz, Austrian foreign ministry in: 139, 177
Baltazzi, Alexander, uncle of Mary Vetsera: 260, 262, 278
Baltazzi, Aristide, uncle of Mary Vetsera: 253
Baltazzi, Hector, uncle of Mary Vetsera: 253, 262
Banking: 87–8, 181–3; crisis in (1873, 186–7
Batthyány, Count Lajos, Hungarian PM: 37, 41, 42; executed, 55
Beck, Baron Max von, PM: 297
Beck, General Frederick von, CGS: 143–4, 174, 197, 204, 321; and Rudolf, 215–16, 259; and Hungary, 293; and F. Ferdinand, 297–8; retires, 298
Belcredi, Count, Richard, PM: 141, 152, 154
Belvedere palace, Vienna: F. Ferdinand's home, 289–90
Benedek, General Ludwig von: 36; at Solferino, 109–10; in Austro-Prussian war, 142, 143–6
Berchtold, Count Leopold von, foreign minister: 312, 322; and Balkan Wars, 313, 314–16; and declaration of war, 326, 328–9; resigns, 335
Berlin: Treaty of (1854), 74; Congress of (1878), 206–9; Treaty of (1878), 207–9; FJ's state visit to, 268
Beust, Count Ferdinand: foreign minister, 153–4; PM, 154–5, 161–2, 168, 169, 176–7; and Franco-Prussian war, 174, 175

Biedermeier culture: 18–20
Bismarck, Prince Otto von, German chancellor: policy of to Austria, 130–34, 137, 141–2, 145; visits Vienna, 130, 137–8, 270; policy of to A-H, 177, 212–13; and Congress of Berlin, 207
Black Hand, Serbian secret society: 320–21
Blue Danube waltz: 180–81
Bohemia: 155; FJ governor of, 34; FJ visits, 61, 192–3; FJ's 'assignations' in, 65; nationalism in, 167–8, 218, 270, 283, 306
Bombelles, Count 'Charly': 23, 26; and Rudolf, 216, 263
Bombelles, Count Heinrich: FJ's tutor, 15–16, 24
Bosnia: 66, under Ottoman Empire, 195–7; F. Ferdinand visits, 321–4
Bosnia-Herzegovina: A-H and, 197–8; unrest in, 199–200; A-H occupies, 207–11; annexation of, 213, 225, 301–5; FJ visits, 306–8, and Balkan Wars, 314, 316
Bratislava: 8, 25, 29; 1848 revolt in, 32, 34–5
Britain: and A-H, 240–41; at war with A-H, 332, 343
Brosch, Major von: F. Ferdinand's aide, 296, 298
Bruck, Baron Karl von: minister of commerce (1849–50) 45; finance minister (1855), 87, 115; suicide of, 117
Budapest: 24, 49; state visits to, (1857) 94–5, (1866) 141, (1896) 281–2; E at (1866–7), 145, 151–2, 157, 163; coronation in (1867), 157–9; rebuilding of, (1883), 229, FJ in (1889), 255; underground railway in, 281
Budapest Conventions (1877): 204–5
Bulgaria: 207, 303, 304; under Ottoman Empire, 202; in crisis (1885–6), 238, 240–2: in Balkan Wars, 314–16, 320; joins A-H in war, 336; collapses, 345
Bülow, Bernhard von, German chancellor: 304–5
Buol-Schauenstein, Count Karl, foreign minister, 66, 99; and Crimean War, 73, 82, 83–4; and Italian war (1859), 103–4

Burian, Istvan: finance minister and foreign minister, 329, 335

Cap Martin, France: FJ and E stay at, 280
Carinthia: 5; state visits to, 92
Carol I, K. of Roumania: 242
Caroline Augusta, consort of Francis I: 3–4, 76
Caspar, Mizzi, dancer; and Rudolf, 248, 251–2, 258, 260
Cavour, Camille, PM of Piedmont: 93, 99–101, 102–3
Censorship: 30, 33
Charles Albert, K. of Sardinia-Piedmont: 33, 39, 43, 51
Charles, Archduke, great-nephew of FJ: marries, 311; becomes heir, 324; in World War I, 333, 336; and FJ's last illness, 341–2; Emperor, 343, 345; dies, 346
Charles, Archduke, great-uncle of FJ: 15; dies, 25
Charles Ludwig, Archduke, brother of FJ: 13, 26, 161, 185, 217; and E, 38, 69; marries, 91, 287; dies, 267
Charlotte, Belgian Princess, 101, 102; marries Maximilian, 92, 95–6; and Mexican empire, 135–6, 153; mental collapse of, 157
Cholera epidemics: (1831), 9; (1873), 186
Chotek, Count Bohuslav: Austrian envoy in Brussels, 220, 289
Chotek, Countess Sophie: 313, marries F. Ferdinand, 288–90; death of, 323–4; burial of, 325–6; sons' fate, 347–8
Cisleithania: 155, 189
Clemenceau, Georges, French statesman: and Rudolf, 225–6
Compromise (settlement of 1867): 154–9
Concordat, Austrian: 88–91, 166; annulled, 167
Conrad von Hötzendorf, General Franz: CGS, 299; and Balkans, 301–3, proposes attack on Italy 311–12; reinstates as CGS, 314; and Balkan Wars, 315–16; and Redl case, 318–19; and Serbia, 320, 321: war plans of (1914), 328; in World War I, 333–8
Constantinople: FJ visits, 169, 170

Constitutions, Austrian: proposed (1848), 29–30, 34, 35, 37, 45; 'Stadion' (1849), 50–51, 57; 'Sylvester Patent' (1851), 62; (1859–60), 115–18; October Diploma (1860), 122; February Patent (1861), 122–3; December Constitution (1868), 162–3: Austro-Hungarian: franchise under, (1897) 271–2, 275, (1907) 297: Hungarian: (1848), 29, 32, 47; (1849), 51; 1867 Compromise, 154–9
Corfu: E in, 123, 124; FJ visits, 124–5
Coronation, Hungarian: 157–9
Coronini-Cronberg, Count Johann: FJ's chamberlain, 15
Cracow: 32, 57
Crenneville, Count Franz: 143, 144
Crimean War: Austria and, 73–4, 81–5
Croatia: in 1848 revolt, 32–3; 42, disaffected, 124; and Yugoslav ideal, 198
Croats: in empire, 85; and 1867 Compromise, 155; and Serbs, 301; and Hungary, 317
Cromer, Norfolk; E visits, 242–3
Custozza, battles of: (1848), 39; (1866), 143
Czech language: 282–3, 288
Czechs: in empire, 5; in 1848 revolt, 33, 34, 38–9; in Austrian army, 111; and October Diploma, 122; and 1867 Compromise, 155; nationalism of, 167–8, 218, 270–71, 316

Dalmatia; 195, 197; FJ visits (1875), 200–1
Danube, R., 34–5, 71, 73, 76, 83, 169, 209
Danubian Principalities (Moldavia and Wallachia): 82–3, 176
Deák, Ferencz, Hungarian reformer: 41, 122, 139–40, 150–51, 154
Debrecen: 49, 51, 95
Dresden: Austro-Prussian conference in (1850), 58–9
Dubrovnik: 200–1

Eastern crisis (1875–8): 199–207
Economy: Austrian, (1850), 58; (1855), 87–8; (1859) 102, 116–17; Austro-Hungarian, flourishes, 181–2, 228; in crisis (1873), 186–7; Hungary and, 282

Edward VII, K., as Prince of Wales: 189, 191, 214, 222, 280; visits Vienna, 185, 252–4; visits Ischl (as king), 298
Elise, Q. of Prussia, aunt of FJ: 69, 71
ELIZABETH, Empress and Queen:
Life (chronological): as child meets FJ, 38; wooed by FJ, 69–73; wedding, 73; dislike of court life, 77–8, 81, 123–4, 188–9; becomes mother, 91; accompanies FJ to Italy and Hungary, 93–4; mourns firstborn child, 95–6; birth of son, 96; and Italian War (1859), 105, 107, 112; first withdrawal from public life, 119, 123–4; resumes court life, 127–9; reconciliation with FJ, 148; likes Gödöllö, 152, 157, 170, 187; crowned Queen of Hungary, 157, 159; goes to Buda for birth of fourth child 163; declines to join FJ's tour in the East, 169–70; World Exhibition 187; Silver Jubilee 188–9; 'Gabrielle' escapade, 191; Silver wedding, 217; Rudolf's betrothal and marriage, 220–3; patronage of Red Cross, 221; shares dangers of FJ's Trieste trip, 231–2; delight in Hermes Villa 232–3; prefers Corfu, 235; commissions Schratt portrait for FJ, 237; visits Brundlfeld asylum, 240; Maria Theresa Monument, 245; 51st birthday, 258; breaks news from Mayerling to FJ, 261; reactions to the tragedy, 266, 276–7; constant travelling worries FJ, 279; in Hungary for Millenial Celebrations, 281–2; at last state function (1896), 284; shocked by sister's death, 284–5; murdered, 285
Appearance: 69, 70, 73, 77, 148–9
Character: 70–1, 72, 78, 219, 226, 232
Finances: 194
Health: 119–22, 125–7, 187–88, 233, 239–40, 241, 276–7, 284
Interests and pursuits: classical Greece 226, 233, 234, 235; fencing 233; Greek language (modern), 125, 258, 261, 281; Heine cult, 226, 234, 237, 242, 258; horses and hunting, 72, 78, 108, 193, 232; Magyar culture, 94, 125, 150, 151, 152; Titania fantasies, 232, 234; verse writing, 70–1, 234, 241, 242–3, 245; walking 233
Journeys abroad: Corfu, 123–4, 235, 243, 277, 281; England, 192, 215, 221, 233, 242–3; French Riviera, 280, 285; Ithaca, 234; Madeira, 121–2; Rome, 166, 173; Switzerland, 277, 285
Personal relations with: Andrássy, 150–1, 157; Fanny Angerer, 148; sister-in-law Charlotte, 95, 136–7; Eugenie 161, 169–70, 171; Ida Ferenczy, 148, 177, 191; Marie Festetics, 177, 179; daughter Gisela, 96, 125, 163–4, 177–8, 184–5, 189, 239, 276; Marie Larisch, 254; Ludwig II of Bavaria, 234, 239; Rudolk, 119, 125, 148–9, 157, 163–4, 221, 245, 265; Katharina Schratt, 237, 239, 243, 278–9, 286; Archduchess Sophie, 69–70, 73, 77–8, 81, 95–6, 105, 119–20, 126, 177–79; Stephanie, 221–3, 231; daughter Marie Valerie, 177, 192, 234, 239, 240, 243, 258, 277, 278; Queen Victoria, 192, 243, 280
Religion: 81, 166
Elizabeth, Archduchess, daughter of Rudolf: 227, 342, 348
Elizabeth of Modena, Princess: FJ and, 65–6
Elssler, Fanny, ballerina: 17–18
England: Rudolf visits, 214–15, 248
Eötvös, Baron Josef, Hungarian reformer: 122
Erfurt Union of German states (1850): 58
Esterházy, Count Moritz, Austrian minister: 139, 140, 141
Esterházy, Countess Sophie, Mistress of Robes: 71, 123, 126
Eugenie, French Empress: 161–2, 169–70, 171–2
Eulenburg, Count Philip zu, German ambassador in Vienna: 286–7

Faure, Felix, French President: 280
February Patent (1861); 122–3, 128, 141
Fendi, Peter, painter: 19–20
Ferdinand I, Emperor, uncle of FJ: 3, 31, 32, 34–5, 39, 42, 113, 134, 167; crowned K. of Hungary, 7–8; succeeds, 14–15; abdicates, 45–7; dies, 193
Ferdinand, K. of Bulgaria: 241–2, 278, 304, 343

Ferenczy, Ida, E's lady-in-waiting: 148, 177, 191
Festetics, Countess Marie, E's lady-in-waiting, 177, 219, 221
Fischer, Dr: E's doctor, 126, 127
France: and Habsburg empire, 1–2; revolutions in, (1830) 6–7, (1848) 29; in Italian war (1859), 103–13; relations with Austria, 142–3, 160–2; relations with A-H, 173; at war with Prussia, 175–6; at war with A-H, 332
Franchise, extension of: 271–2; (1897), 275; (1907), 297
Francis I, Emperor, 1–5, 287; dies, 14–15
Francis Charles, Archduke; father of FJ, 3–4, 10–11, 15, 22, 31–32, 47, 161; dies, 207
Francis Ferdinand, Archduke: 161, 248, 253, becomes heir, 267–8; anti-Hungarian, 268, 311; marries, 288–90; political activity of, 295–7; and armed forces, 297–9; and B-H, 303, and President Roosevelt, 308; and Balkan Wars, 314–15; and Redl case, 318–19; and visit to Sarajevo, 321; burial of, 325–6; sons' fate, 347–8
FRANCIS JOSEPH, Emperor and King
Life (chronological): birth, 4–5; nursery years, 7–15; formal education, 12, 15, 16, 19, 23; initiation into the army, 20–21; first train journey, 23; a reluctant actor, 26; and coming of 1848 revolutions, 30–5; admitted to inner government, 31; appointed Governor of Bohemia, 34; on active service under Radetzky, 35–7; with court at Innsbruck, 37–8, 40; meets E. as child, 38; proposed English visit abandoned, 40; reaches age of majority, 40; accompanies court to Olmütz, 43; accession, 46–8; and counter-revolution, 50–3, 55, 57; meets Nicholas I, 53–4; at 'burning bridge of Raab', 54; and Reichsrat proposals 1851, 59–60, 62; life endangered at sea, 61; mourns Schwarzenberg, 62–3; seeks a wife, 65–6; survives assassination bid, 66–7; betrothal to E., 68–71; marriage, 76–7; spoils E., 78; Crimean War, 82–5; re-building of Vienna, 88–9; becomes father, 91; eldest child dies, 95; Rudolf's birth,

96; Italian War (1859), 102–13; at Solferino, 105–11; at Villafranca, 112–13; abandons absolutism, 114–16, 118, 122–23; abrupt dismissal of Bruck, 117; rumoured attachment to a Polish countess, 120; and E's recuperation on Madeira, 121–2; and Hungarian moderates, 122, 139–40; Reichsrat, 122–3, 128, 140–1, 163, 205; and Mexico, 126–7, 134–7, 157–8; welcomes E's return to Vienna, 127–9; conclave of German princes (1863), 131–3; Schleswig-Holstein crisis (1863–5), 133–4, 137–8, 140;Schönbrunn talks (1864), 138; rise of Belcredi, 141; army modernisation, 141, 142, 146, 297–8; War of 1866 141–7; reconciled with E, 148; negotiation of 1867 Compromise, 151–6; and Beust 153, 154, 169, 176–7; Hungarian coronation, 156–9; Maximilian's death 160; Salzburg talks, 161; birth of Marie Valerie, 163–4; fails to secure agreement with Czechs, 167–8; significance of visit to the East, 169, 170, 173; Franco-Prussian War (1870) 173–6; and Andrássy as foreign minister, 177, 183, 199, 206–13; death of his mother, 179; learns economics from Schäffle, 182–3; World Exhibition of 1873, 183, 185–5; Vienna stock market crash, 186–7; Silver Jubilee, 188–9; becomes grandfather, 189; and anti-clericalism, 190; Dalmatian tour, 195; and Strossmayer's policies, 198–9; Eastern Crisis (1875–78), 201–10; and status of B-H, 209, 211, 213, 304; has Taaffe as head of government, 211, 218; Silver Wedding 217; Rudolf's marriage 222–3; Kálnoky as foreign minister, 225, 273; fulfils official duties, 230–1; Oberdank conspiracy, 231; presents E with villas in Tiergarten and Corfu, 232–5; Eastern Crisis of 1884–6, 238, 240; hostility to Pan-Germans, 244, 251, 256, 270; and Maria Theresa monument, 244–5; dislikes Baltazzi family, 253, 278; Tisza's Hungarian army bill, 256, 263, 268–9; last meeting with Rudolf, 259;

FRANCIS JOSEPH, Emperor and King
Life (chronological)—*cont*
    Mayerling tragedy, 261–5; at Rudolf's
    funeral, 262; hears Mass at Mayerling,
    265–6; reluctance to recognize new
    heir-apparent, 267–8; fears socialist
    May Day, 269–70; rise of Lueger 270,
    273–5; praises Jewish subjects, 270,
    335; supports wider suffrage, 271, 273,
    275, 291, 297; alleged ingratitude to
    Taaffe, 271–2; Hungarian
    Millennium, 281–2; Golden Jubilee,
    282–3, 284, 286; and fall of Badeni,
    283–4; learns of E's murder, 285;
    rejects idea of re-marriage, 287–8; and
    F. Ferdinand's marriage, 288–9; vetoes
    military action in Hungary, 293, 294–
    5; issues Chlopy Order of the Day,
    294; gives Hungarians 'five minute
    audience', 295; first car ride, 298; at
    flying show, 298; approves
    appointment of Aehrenthal and
    Conrad (1906), 298–9; reacts to Pan-
    Serb agitation, 301–2; welcomes
    acquisition of B-H, 302–5; Diamond
    Jubilee, 306; visits Sarajevo and
    Mostar, 307–8; entertains T.
    Roosevelt, 308; 80th birthday
    celebrated, 310; filmed at marriage of
    Archduke Charles, 311; asserts
    personal control over foreign policy,
    312; appoints Berchtold foreign
    minister, 313; opposes war in 1912,
    314, 315; respects Masaryk, 316; Redl
    Affair, 318–19; at Leipzig centenary
    parade, 319; threatens Serbia with war
    over Albania (1913), 320–1; approves
    F. Ferdinand's visit to Bosnia, 321,
    322; personal reaction to Sarajevo
    murders, 324, 325, 326; and
    archduke's burial, 326; in 1914 war
    crisis, 327–31; orders release of
    Putnik, 331; sceptical of war news,
    334, 336, 339; chairs war council over
    Italy (1915), 335; accepts Polish
    kingdom and unified command 337,
    339; hopes to end war in 1917, 339;
    and Stürgkh's murder, 340–41; last
    days and death, 342; funeral, 343–4;
    posthumous assessments, 346–9
Appearance: 9, 20, 25, 67–8, 130, 165,
    243–4, 312

Character: 19–20, 23, 52, 128, 166, 224,
    230, 239, 243–4
Finances: 193–4
Health: 9, 292, 310, 311, 317, 321, 332,
    341–2
Interests and pursuits: artistic patronage,
    19, 217, 230, 232, 235, 237, 291;
    dancing, 17–18; drawing, 17;
    horsemanship and hunting, 12, 20, 23,
    24, 66, 191, 194, 235; letter-writing,
    16–17, 105, 170, 279–80; rock-
    climbing, 127, 172; shooting wildlife,
    127, 194, 235, 250, 265, 287, 310;
    smoking, 40, 112, 194; swimming, 81,
    165; theatre, 17, 162, 229, 255, 279,
    293; touristic delights 170–72, 280;
    urban landscape 229–30
Personal relations with: Albert of Saxony,
    23, 153, 250; cousin FM Albrecht 20,
    22, 33, 174, 226, 260; Andrássy 151–
    2, 157, 168; Charles Ludwig, 23, 26,
    69, 217, 267; Prince of Wales (Edward
    VII), 191, 252; granddaughter
    Elizabeth ('Erzsi'), 227, 258, 277;
    Eugenie 162, 171–2; Francis I, 14–15;
    F. Ferdinand 251, 267–8, 288–9, 296,
    298, 308, 314, 315, 318–9, 321–4;
    Grünne, 38, 42, 56, 59, 115;
    Maximilian, 13, 17, 21, 23, 25–6, 54,
    61, 66, 86, 101, 102, 115–16, 126–7,
    134–7; Metternich family, 22–4, 26,
    62, 105; Anna Nahowski, 330, 235–6,
    239, 258; Reichstadt (Napoleon II),
    11; Rudolf, 128, 132, 150, 163–4, 214,
    218, 219, 223–4, 226–7, 247–50, 252–
    3, 257, 259, 265; Katharina Schratt,
    236–7, 238–9, 241, 242–5, 252–3, 255,
    258, 260, 265, 270, 276, 277, 279–80,
    283, 284, 286–7, 292, 293, 295, 302,
    307, 317, 331, 335, 339, 342;
    Archduchess Sophie, 9, 12–14, 25–6,
    31, 48, 52, 57, 68, 69, 60, 78, 81, 92,
    95, 96, 105, 118–19, 126, 133, 175–6,
    178–9; Stephanie 222, 258, 288; Taaffe
    family, 23, 25, 218, 271; daughter
    Marie Valerie, 249, 258, 310, 324;
    Queen Victoria, 133, 231; William II,
    251, 252–3, 257, 259, 276, 304–6
Religion: 16, 65, 88, 89–91, 166–7, 171,
    190, 261, 265–6, 286, 310, 324, 341,
    342
Journeys outside Empire: Bavaria, 72, 73,

74, 120, 123; Corfu, 124; 'the East' (Constantinople, Jerusalem, Athens, Suez Canal, Cairo), 169–73; French Riviera, 280; Paris 162; Russia 190–91; Territet, 277; Warsaw, 54, 72, 120; Views and ideas on: anti-semitism, 270, 275; 'applied modern art' (*Sezession*), 291; army officer's role in Empire, 247, 319; constitutional government, 60, 118, 224; Ibsen as dramatist, 279; organic composition of Monarchy, 349; parliamentary politics, 128, 205, 269, 270, 271, 275–6, 291; Southern Slav problem, 190, 199, 300–01; U.S. constitution, 311

Franco-Prussian war (1870–71): 174–6

Frankfurt: German princes meet at (1863), 132–3

Frederick III, German Emperor: 16, 133, 145, dies, 251

Frederick William IV, K. of Prussia: 28, 57–8; meets FJ, 72

Freud, Dr Sigmund: on World Exhibition, 184, 185; meets FJ, 309

Garibaldi, Riciotti: 172

Gastein, Convention of (1865): 140

Geneva; E killed at, 285

German Austrians: 5; in Austrian army, 110; and 1860 constitution, 122; anti-Czech, 168, 218, 270–71, 283

German Confederation: Austro-Prussian rivalry in, 131–4, 137–8, 141–2; dissolved, 146

German Empire: relations with A-H, 176–7, 212, 305

Germany: 1848–9 revolution in, 57; federalism in, 58; liberalism in, 124

Gisela, Archduchess, daughter of FJ, 91, 92, 95, 96, 123, 125, 163–4, 262, 276, 347; marriage of, 177–8, 184–5; daughter born to, 189

Giskra, Karl, minister for home affairs: 186

Gödöllö palace, Hungary: 152, 157, 167, 177, 187, 189, 255

Goito, battle of (1848): 33

Goluchowski, Count Agenor (elder), minister of interior: 115, 116–17, 122

Goluchowski, Count Agenor (younger), foreign minister: 273, 283–4, 295; resigns, 298; and Serbia, 300

Gondrecourt, Major-General Ludwig, Crown Prince Rudolf's tutor, 149–50

Gorchakov, Prince Alexander, Russian chancellor: 190, 202–3

Görgei, Arthur, Hungarian general: 50, 51, 54–5

Graz: FJ visits, 61

Greif, SIS, imperial yacht: 170–72

Grillparzer, Franz, Austrian poet: 2, 39, 68

Grünne, Count Karl: 35, 105; FJ's chamberlain, 38; advises FJ, 40, 51, 56, 59, 82, 85, 101, 104, 114–15; E and, 71, 124

Györ, battle of (1849): 54

Gyulai von Maros-Nemeth, Count Francis: 94, 101, in Italian campaign (1859), 103–4, 105–7

Habsburg dynasty: 5

Hauslaub, Colonel Franz von: 16

Haymerle, Baron Heinrich, foreign minister: 211, 223–4

Haynau, Baron Julius von: in Hungarian campaign, 52, 53–4; military governor of Hungary, 55, 57; recalled, 59

Heiligenkreuz Abbey: 246, 262

Heine, Heinrich, poet: 234, 237

Helen of Bavaria, cousin of FJ, 38, 66, 119, 124, 160; visits Ischl (1853), 69–70

Hermes Villa, Vienna: built for E, 232–5

Herzegovina: in Ottoman empire, 195–7 (*see also* Bosnia Herzegovina)

Hess, Baron Heinrich, army QMG: 56, 82–3, 104, 105, 107, 108

Hirsch, Baron Moritz: financier, 252

Hitler, Adolf: 274, 347; in Vienna, 309

Hofburg palace, 14; amateur theatricals in, 26–7; redecorated, 57; FJ's wedding festivities in, 77

Hohenwart, Count Charles von: and Czechs, 168

Holy Crown of St Stephen: 156–7, 158, 282

Honved (Hungarian national defence force): 42, 43, 50

Hoyos, Count Alexander, diplomat: 327

Hoyos, Count Joseph, Court chamberlain: 260–61

Hradčany castle, Prague: 10, 47, 167, 227

Hübner, Baron Joseph von; Austrian ambassador in Paris, 101, 125
Hungary: in empire, 8, 24–5, 85; kingdom of, 7–8, 47; 1848–9 revolt in, 29, 32, 41–2, 49–53, 55; state visits to (1857) 94–5, (1896) 281–2; nationalism in, 122, 124, 139–40, 256, 263–4, 268–9, 293–5; E visits (1866–7), 150–52, 157, 163; subject nationalities in, 189, 317; in Eastern crisis (1875–8), 198–9, 204; and coming of war 328–30

Ignatiev, General Nikolai, Panslav: 203–4, 206–7
Innsbruck: court at (1848), 37, 40
Ischl: FJ first visits, 9–10; FJ hunts at, 61, 235; FJ and E. betrothed at, 68–71; FJ's birthday at, 236; last visit of FJ and E to, 285, FJ's eightieth birthday at, 310; FJ at (1914), 327–332
Ismail, Khedive of Egypt: 169
Italians: in empire, 5, 20–21
Italy: in 1848 revolt, 29, 33, war of 1859 in, 102–13; Risorgimento in, 120; kingdom of established (1861), 125; allies with Prussia against Austria, 141–5; relations with A-H, 190, 231; invades Libya, 311–12; neutral (1914), 332; at war with A-H, 335
Izvolsky, Alexander, Russian foreign minister: 302–5

Jellaçić, Colonel Josip, Ban of Croatia: 57, 77, 198; in 1848–9 revolt, 33, 42, 43–4, 46, 49, 53
Jews: in empire, 116; in A-H, 270, 335; Rudolf and, 252, 256–7
John, Archduke, great-uncle of FJ, 15, 22, 30, 31, 38
Joseph Archduke, great-uncle of FJ: 8, 15; dies, 24
Juarez, Benito, President of Mexico: 126, 157–8, 160

Kállay, Count Benjamin: 199–200, 213
Kálnoky, Count Gustav, foreign minister: 225; and Russia, 237–8; and Balkans, 240–41; resigns, 272–3
Kapuzinergruft, Vienna: 25, 193, 262, 344, 347, 349

Karl Theodore of Bavaria, brother of E: 127
Károlyi, Count Alois, Austrian envoy in Berlin: 131
Károlyi, Count Pista, Hungarian nationalist: 256, 264
Kastner, Joseph, artist: 266
Kerzl, Dr Joseph von, FJ's doctor: 317, 321–2, 341, 342
Ketterl, Eugen, FJ's valet: 342; memoirs of, 317
Kisch, Egon, journalist: 318
Kiss von Itebbe, Nicholas, husband of Katharina Schratt: 236, 278, 287
Kiss von Itebbe, Toni, son of Katharina Schratt: 236, 278–9, 287
Kissingen: E at, 127, 148; E and FJ at, 285
Klimt, Gustav, artist: 235, 290–91
Koerber, Dr Ernst von, PM: 292, 341
Kolowrat-Liebsteinsky, Count Franz, minister of state: 22–3, 28, 32, 34
Königgrätz, battle of (1866): 144–5
Konopischt castle, Bohemia: 289, 322–3
Kossuth, Ferencz, Hungarian nationalist leader: 293
Kossuth, Lajos, Hungarian revolutionary: 24–5, 29–30, 42, 47, 49, 51, 55, 110–11, 139, 156, 293
Kotor, Dalmatia: 169, 195, 201
Kotzebue, Augustus, dramatist: 26
Krauss, Baron Alfred von, Vienna police chief: 248, 257–8, 263
Kremsier: Reichstag at, 44, 49–51; Austro-Russian conference at (1885), 237–8
Krismanić, General Gideon: 142–4
Krobatkin, General, war minister: 315
Kübeck, Baron Karl von, Metternich's assistant: 46, 47, 57; drafts constitution, 59–60, 62
Kuhn, Baron Franz, war minister: 173–4, 175

Language Ordinances: 282–3, 292
Lanner, Joseph, composer: 17–18
Larisch, Countess Marie, niece of E: 254–5, 260, 263
Latour-Baillet, Count Theodore von, war minister: 36, 42–3
Latour von Thurnburg, General Joseph, Rudolf's tutor: 150, 214–15, 221, 223, 263

Laxenburg Manifesto (1859): 115–16
Laxenburg palace: 10, 114–15, 222–3; E
  at, 78, 91, 95–6, 108, 123–4
Lehár, Colonel Anton: 346
Léhar, Franz, composer: 313, 318, 346
Leipzig, battle of, centenary: 319
Leopold I, K. of Belgians: 94, 121, 134;
  visits Vienna, 67–8
Leopold II, K. of Belgians: 220
Leopold, Prince of Bavaria: 178, 184–5
Lesseps, Ferdinand de: 171
Libényi, Janos, assassin: 66–7
Lissa, naval battle of (1866): 145
Ljubljana: FJ visits, 61; state visits to, 92
Lobkowitz, Prince Joseph, FJ's adjutant-
  general: 41, 42–3
Lombardy: in empire, 5; 1848 revolt in,
  29, 33, 39; 1849 campaign in, 51; FJ
  visits, 61; under Radetzky, 86; state
  visits to (1857), 92–3; under
  Maximilian, 99–100; ceded to
  Piedmont (1859), 113, 138, 141
Loos, Adolf, architect: 290–91
Lower Austria: in empire, 5; in 1848
  revolt, 30
Ludovika, Duchess in Bavaria, aunt of
  FJ: 38, 66, 119, 126; visits Ischl (1853),
  68–70; and daughter's marriage to FJ,
  73, 74, 77–8
Ludwig II, K. of Bavaria: 226, 234;
  suicide of, 239–40
Ludwig, Archduke, great-uncle of FJ: 15,
  22, 31, 40
Ludwig Victor, Archduke, brother of FJ:
  48, 91, 161, 186
Lueger, Karl, Mayor of Vienna: 256,
  270, 272, 273–5, 283, 284, 296, 309

Macedonia: 301, 303, 320
Magenta, battle of (1859): 107
Magyar language: 8, 268, 293–4; FJ
  learns, 24–5, E learns, 94, 150, 157
Magyar Millenium in Budapest (1896):
  281–2
Makart, Hans, designer: 217, 235
Mantua: 36, 107, 113
Margaretha of Saxony, Princess: 91; dies,
  101
Margutti, Albert von, FJ's aide: 330, 331,
  339, 346, 349
Maria Anna of Savoy, consort of
  Ferdinand I: 8, 31, 45, 47, 167, 193

Maria Theresa, Empress: 1, 293;
  monument to, 244
Marianna, Archduchess, aunt of FJ:
  disfigured at birth, 4, 81
Marie Louise, consort of Napoleon I: 2,
  11; dies, 25
Marie, Q. of Naples, sister of E: 120,
  191
Marie Valerie, Archduchess, daughter of
  FJ: 163–4, 278, 317, 324, 342, 347;
  accompanies E, 177, 192, 239, 241;
  marriage of, 249 256, 258, 277; after
  E's death, 286–7
Masaryk, Thomas, Czech statesman:
  316
Mathilde, Archduchess: 158
Maximilian, Archduke, brother of FJ: 11,
  46; as child, 13; and Italy, 21; in
  Hungarian campaign (1849), 54; and
  navy, 61, 86, 134; and attempt on FJ's
  life, 67; marries, 92, 95; governs
  Lombardy-Venetia (1857), 94, 99–
  101; and Italian war (1859), 111;
  liberal views of, 115–16; and Mexican
  empire, 126–7, 132–7, 152–3;
  captured, 157–8; executed, 160
Maximilian, Duke in Bavaria, E's father:
  71; dies, 256
Maximilian, Prince of Thurn and Taxis:
  119, 124, 132, 160
Mayerling, Schloss: 226; tragedy of, 260–
  5; convent of, 266
Meissner, Florian, lawyer: 248, 257
Mensdorff-Pouilly, Count Alexander,
  foreign minister: 139, 141
Metternich, Prince Clemens von,
  chancellor: 2, 6–8, 15, 22–25, 57, 60,
  98–9, 168; resigns (1848), 28–32;
  returns to Vienna, 61–2; advises FJ,
  72, 104–5
Metternich, Princess Melanie von: 23,
  25, 28, 61–2
Metternich, Richard von: 23–4, 26;
  Austrian ambassador in Paris, 131,
  143, 174
Mexico: Maximilian invited to rule, 134–
  6, 152–3, 157–8
Milan: 21, 33; state visits to (1857), 93;
  rebuilding of, 99, Austria loses (1859),
  107
Miramare villa, Trieste: 86, 92, 123, 136,
  157, 172–3, 231, 256, 288

Mollinary, General Anton: 195, 202
Moltke, Field Marshal Helmuth von, Prussian commander: 141, 146
Montenegro: 201–4; in Balkan Wars, 313–16
Montenuovo, Prince Alfred, Lord Chamberlain: 322, 326, 344
Moravia: 41, 43, 155, 270, 283; settlement in, 316
Mostar: FJ in, 307, 308
Munich: FJ visits E at, 72, 73
Murad V, Sultan: 160
Mürzsteg: 253, 257, 258
Musil, Robert, novelist: 347

Nahowski, Anna, friend of FJ: 220, 235–6, 239, 258
Napoleon I: 1–2
Napoleon II: *see* Reichstadt, Duke of
Napoleon III: 165, 171–2; and Italy, 100–101, 143, and Italian war (1859), 102–3, 109, 111–13; and Mexico, 126, 134, 135, 152–3; and Austro-Prussian war, 144, 145; visits Austria, 160–61; in Franco-Prussian war, 175
Napoleon, Prince Imperial: 162
National Guard, in Vienna: 37, 40
Navy: 61, 134, 145, 298; modernized, 86; in Albanian crisis (1913), 315–16
Nehammer, Karl, Rudolf's servant: 226
Neue Freie Presse: 290
Neues Wiener Tagblatt, liberal newspaper: 114, 185, 244; Rudolf and, 225, 250–51
Nicholas I, Tsar: 39, 58; intervenes in Hungary, 53–5; meets FJ (1849), 54, (1853) 72; relations with FJ, 62, 83
Nicholas II, Tsar, visits Vienna: 284
Nicholas, Prince (King) of Montenegro: 201, visits Vienna, 312; in Balkan Wars, 313–14
Novara, battle of (1849): 51
Novibazar, Sanjak of: 197, 209; railway in, 302; in Balkan Wars, 314

Obrenović, Alexander, K. of Serbia: 300
Obrenović, Milan, Prince (King) of Serbia: 199, 231, 253
O'Brien, Thomas, *Times* correspondent in Vienna: 74, 76
October Diploma (1860): 118
Olmütz: court at (1848–9): 43–9; FJ's

accession at, 47, 52; FJ meets Tsar at, 72; Austrian headquarters (1866), 143
Orsini, Count Felice, Italian terrorist: 100
Otto, Archduke, nephew of FJ: 161, 268
Otto, Archduke (Dr Otto von Habsburg): 343, 346
Ottoman empire: 66; Russia and, 71–2; and Eastern crisis (1875–8), 195–7, 202–9; A-H and, 209–11, 304–5; and Balkans, 303–3, 304–5; in Balkan Wars, 313–14, 320; in World War I, 332

Paar, Count Eduard: 323
Paget, Lady, British ambassador's wife: 259
Palmer, Eduard, banker: 236, 278, 287
Pan-German movement: 33, 34, 238, 253–4, 270; riot of, 244–5
Pan-Slav Congress (1867): 167
Panslavism: 38–9, 174, 200–1, 203–4, 327, 330
Papal States: 29, 113
Paris: FJ's state visit to, 161–2; Treaty of (1856), 85, 176
Parliaments: Austrian Reichstag, (1848), 39–40,44, 45, 47; (1849), 49–50 (after 1850 *see under* Reichsrat); Hungarian Diet, 24–5, 29, 32, 34–5, 39, 141; Hungarian (from 1867), 154, nationalists in, 293–5; provincial, 116, 118
Pascher, Fritz: with E at masked ball, 191
Pašić, Nikola, Serbian PM: 304, 320–21; in July crisis (1914), 328
Paskevich, Marshal Ivan, Russian commander: in Hungary, 54–5
Peschiera: 36, 37, 113
Peter I, K. of Serbia: 300–1
Philip, Prince of Coburg: and Mayerling, 260–61
Piedmont: at war with Austria (1859), 102–13
Pillersdorf, Baron Franz von, minister of interior: 34, 44
Pius IX, Pope: 21, 166, 190
Plener, Ignaz von, finance minister: 117
Polish Question: 7, 32, 122, 133, 337, 341
Possenhofen, Schloss, Bavaria: 72, 73, 119–20, 127

Potiorek, General Oskar, governor of B-
H: 314; in war crisis (1914), 326;
during war, 333

Prague: 10, 52; in 1848 revolt, 33, 38–9;
martial law in (1849–53), 57, 67;
nationalism in, 167; FJ visits, 167, 193;
rebuilding of (1867), 182, (1883),
229; Rudolf serves at, 214, 218, 221–
3; F. Ferdinand serves at, 268; Treaty
of (1866), 146

Prater, Vienna: 6, 34, 35, 78; World
Exhibition in, 184; FJ's Golden Jubilee
in, 284

Princip, Gavrilo, Bosnian Serb assassin:
324

Prussia: relations with Austria, 57–8, 74,
103, 111, 130–33, 141–2; invades
Schleswig, 133–4; at war with Austria
(1866), 142–7, at war with France
(1870–71), 175–6

Putnik, Radomir, Serbian Marshal: 331

Queretaro, Mexico: 160

Radetzky, Field Marshal Joseph: 20–21,
33, 40, 44, 77; in Italian campaign
(1848–9), 35–7, 39, 51; takes Venice,
55–6; governs Lombardy-Venetia, 57,
84, 85–6, 93–4, funeral of, 98

Radetzky March: 56, 98, 279

Radowitz, General Joseph von, Prussian
PM: 58

Railways: Balkan, 169, 197, 302,
Budapest underground, 281; Vienna
Stadtbahn, 284, 291; Vienna–Trieste
(*Sudbahn*), 87

Rainer, Archduke, cousin of FJ, 115;
PM, 122–3

Rauscher, Cardinal Joseph von, 12, 16,
90, 117, 166, 184; marries FJ and E,
77

Rechberg, Count Johann, foreign
minister: 105, 108, 115–17, 131, 135–
6; and Bismarck, 137–8; resigns, 139

Redl, Colonel Alfred: scandal of, 318–19

Redlich, Joseph, parliamentarian: on
Redl case, 318; on news of Sarajevo,
325, on FJ's death, 342

Reichsrat: (1850–51), 59–60, 62; (1860),
116–18; (1861), 123; (1862), 128;
dissolved (1865), 141; (1868), 163;
and Eastern crisis (1875–8), 205, 211;

Bohemian parties in, 218; failure of,
270, 291; prorogued (1914), 328

Reichstadt: Agreement of (1876), 203–
4, 205–6; F. Ferdinand's wedding at,
289

Reichstadt, Duke of, son of Napoleon I:
2, 10–11

Renz, Ernst, circus rider: 78

Revolutions: (1830), 6–7; (1848), 29–48

Rieger, Franz, Czech nationalist: 167

Risorgimento, Italian: 118, 120

Rodić, General, governor of Dalmatia:
195, 200, 201–2

Roosevelt, Theodore, US President:
meets FJ, 308–9

Roth, Joseph, novelist: 347

Roumania: 209, 240, 241; allies with A-
H, 238; in Balkan Wars, 320; in Triple
Alliance, 326; neutral (1914), 332; at
war with A-H, 338–9

Roumanians: 317; nationalism of, 169

Rüdiger, Bishop of Linz: 166

Rudolf, Crown Prince: born, 96; youth
of, 119, 123, 125, 128, 163–4, 177–8,
185; education of 149–50; and
Hungary, 157, 263–4; at Hungarian
coronation, 158; army service of, 214–
18, 222–3, 226, 247–8; intellectual
pursuits of, 214–16, 247; sex life of,
216, 248–9; marriage of, 217, 220–23,
226–7; political writing of, 218–19,
223–6, 250–51, 256–7, 259; relations
with parents, 188, 209, 223–4, 226–7,
240, 248–50, 258–9, 265; ill, 245, 249,
257–8; buys Mayerling, 246; and
William II, 251, 257; suicide plan of,
251–2; and P. of Wales, 252–4; meets
Mary Vetsera, 253–5; and Jews, 256–
7; death, 260–6

Rumbold, Horace, British diplomat 98

Ruschuk, Bulgaria, FJ at: 170

Russell, Lord John, British foreign
secretary: 84, 94

Russell, William Howard, *Times*
correspondent: 143, 145

Russia: relations with Austria (1854)
82–4; relations with A-H, 174–6, 212,
237, 283, 284, 302–5; FJ visits (1874),
190–91; and Eastern crisis (1875–8),
202–7; and Balkan crisis (1885–6),
240, 241; at war with A-H, 332

Russo-Turkish war (1877): 205–6

Saint Stephen's Cathedral, Vienna: 67, 343, 348–9
Salisbury, Robert, Marquis of, British foreign secretary: 207–8, 265
Salonika: 302, 304, 314
Salvator, Archduke Francis: 249, 258
Salvator, Archduke Johann: 210
Salzburg: 161, 177
San Stefano, Treaty of (1878): 206–7
Santa Lucia, battle of (1848): FJ at, 36
Sarajevo: 197; FJ visits, 307–8; F. Ferdinand's fatal visit to, 321, 322–4
Schäffle, Professor Albert, minister of commerce: 182–3
Schemua, General Blasius, CGS: 312
Schleswig-Holstein crisis (1864): 133–4, 137–8, 140
Schmerling, Baron Anton von, PM: 59, 122, 128, 131, 140–41
Schönaich, Baron Franz von, war minister: 298–9
Schönbrunn, Convention of (1873): 199
Schöbrunn palace: 1–2, 10–1, 40, 43, 53, 341–3, 345; Austro-Prussian talks at, 138; ministerial conferences at, 175
Schönerer, George von, Pan-German, 238, 244, 270, 274
Schratt, Katharina, actress: 188, becomes FJ's friend, 236–9; FJ writes to, 241, 243–5, 254–5, 265, 276, 280, 283, 285–6, 295, 302, 307; relations with FJ, 258, 277–9, 286–7, 292–3, 317–18; and coming of war, 331; last visit of to FJ, 342, last years of, 347
Schwarzau: Archduke Charles' wedding at, 311
Schwarzenberg, Prince Felix: 36, 39, 53, 55; PM (1848), 44; and Ferdinand's abdication, 45–7; policies of, 49–50, 57–9; and FJ, 52, 54, 59; dies (1852), 62
Schwarzenberg, Cardinal Frederick von: 90, 166, 221–2
Schwarzgeld, liberal weekly: 256–7, 259
Scutari (Albania): 314, 315–16
Serbia: 199, 209, 213; at war with Turks, 202–4; relations with A-H, 231, 301, 304–5, 320–21; at war with Bulgaria, 238; military coup in, 300–01; in Balkan Wars, 313–16, 319–20; in July crisis (1914), 326–8 (*see also* World War I)

Serbs: 169; in 1848 revolt, 41–2
Sezession, artistic movement: 290–91
Sidonia of Saxony, Princess: FJ and, 66
Silesia: 138, 143, 168
Slovenes: in empire, 5, 86, 283; and language question, 272
Socialism: 187, 238, 256, 269–70
Solferino, battle of (1859): 108–10
Sophie, Archduchess, daughter of FJ: 91, 92, dies, 95
Sophie, Archduchess, mother of FJ: 3, 6, 8, 23, 48; and children's births, 4, 11; and Duke of Reichstadt, 10–11; in FJ's youth, 9–10, 12–13, 15–17, 25–6; political activity of, 21–2, 28, 35, 37; in 1848 revolt, 30–31; 39, redecorates Hofburg, 56–7; and FJ's marriage, 64–6, 68–71, 73, 77–8; and E, 81, 105, 119, 127, 148, 177; and family marriages, 91–2, 95–6, 178; and Mexican empire, 134; and Maximilian's death, 160, 161; and Franco-Prussian war, 175–6; dies, 178–9
Sophie, Duchess of Alençon, sister of E: dies, 285
Staatskonferenz (Regency council): 22, 31
Stadion, Count Francis, interior minister: 45, 50–51, 59
Stalin, Joseph: in Vienna, 309
Steinbach, Emil, finance minister: 271
Stephanie, Crown Princess: marries Rudolf, 220–23; memoirs of, 226, 233; and Rudolf, 226–7, 249, 258, 260; remarries, 288; last years of, 348
Stephen, Archduke, cousin of FJ, Palatine of Hungary: 25, 32, 35, 41, 42
Strauss, Eduard, composer: 222
Strauss, Johann (elder), composer: 18, 56
Strauss, Johann (younger), composer: 180–81
Strauss, Joseph, composer: 96
Strossmayer, Bishop Joseph: 166, 198–9
Stürgkh, Dr Karl, PM: 328, 339, 340
Stürmfeder, Baroness Louise von: FJ's governess, 12–13
Styria: 5, 92
Suez Canal: FJ at opening of (1869), 169–70, 171–2

Széchényi, Dénes: 23, 26
Széchényi, Istvan, Hungarian statesman:
  41
Szécsen, Count Nicholas, Hungarian
  politician: 118, 122
Szeps, Moriz, newspaper editor: 225–6,
  244, 257

Taaffe, Count Eduard: early friend of FJ,
  23–24; deputy PM, 154, 168; PM,
  211, 230, 231; and Czech nationalism,
  218–19, 222; and Rudolf's death, 261,
  262, 263; resigns, 270–2
Tegetthof, Admiral Wilhelm von: 134,
  145, 160, 197
Territet, Switzerland: FJ and E stay at,
  277
The Times: on FJ's marriage, 74, 76–7;
  on Hungarian coronation, 158–9; on
  Rudolf's funeral, 262
Theresianum (palace and academy),
  Vienna: 74, 244
Three Emperors, League of: 199, 202–
  3, 211, 225, 231, 237–8, 241
Thun-Hohenstein, Count Leo, minister
  of education: 90, 101
Tisza, Istvan, Hungarian PM: and
  Serbia, 320, in war crisis (1914), 328–
  9
Tisza, Kálmán, Hungarian PM: 225,
  240, 256, 268–9, 294, 317; reforms of,
  310–11
Transylvania: 50, 155, 317; martial law
  in (1849–50), 57
Trieste: 153, 172, 229; Maximilian at, 61,
  86; importance of, 86–7; state visits
  to, 92, 231
Triple Alliance (1882): 231, 241
Trotsky, Leon: in Vienna, 309
Tyrol: 5; FJ visits, 17

Umberto, K. of Italy: 231
Urbanski, Colonel: 319

Varešanin, General Marijan, governor of
  Bosnia: 306–8
Városliget Park, Budapest: Millennial
  Exposition in, 281
Vatican Council (1869–70): 166
Venetia: 5; FJ visits, 20–21, 61; 1848
  revolt in, 29, 33; under Radetzky, 86;
  state visits to (1856–7), 92–3; under

Maximilian, 99–100; in Italian
  Confederation, 113, 125; and Italy
  (1866), 142–4, 146
Venice: 33; FJ visits, 20–21; surrenders
  to Austria (1849), 55–6; state visit to
  (1856–7), 93; E visits (1861), 125–6;
  FJ visits K. of Italy in (1875), 190
Ventnor, Isle of Wight: E at, 1927
Verona: 35–6; FJ visits, 20; FJ's
  headquarters (1859), 105–6, 108
Vetsera, Baroness Helene: 219, 254–5,
  261, 262–3
Vetsera, Mary: 219; and Rudolf, 253–5,
  259; death of, 260–3
Victor Emmanuel II, K. of Piedmont
  (Italy): 101–2, 107; visits Vienna, 186;
  FJ visits, 190
Victoria, Q.: 121, 165, 214–15, 231, 265;
  FJ visits at Coburg, 133; E and, 192;
  FJ and E visit in France, 280
Vienna: celebrates FJ's birth, 6; cholera
  in, 9, 186, theatre in, 18, 187; 1848
  revolt in, 30–32, 34, 37, 40–1, 42–4;
  martial law in (to 1853), 57, 67; FJ
  distrusts, 61; attempt on FJ's life in,
  66–7; FJ's marriage in, 74–7; peace
  talks in (1855); 84–5; rebuilding of
  (1857–88), 88–9, 182, 186–7, 229–30,
  244; celebrates Rudolf's birth, 96–7;
  hostile to FJ (1859), 108, 111–14;
  sympathetic to E, 127–8; Opera
  House, 182; World Exhibition in
  (1873), 183–6; celebrates Gisela's
  wedding, 185; stock exchange crash
  in (1873), 186; FJ's Silver Jubilee in,
  188; celebrates FJ's silver wedding,
  217; music in, 228–9; Maria Theresa
  monument unveiled, 244–5; May Day
  (1890) in, 269–70; celebrates FJ's
  Golden Jubilee, 284; FJ's Diamond
  Jubilee in, 306; Leipzig centenary in,
  319; after World War I, 346; after
  World War II, 348 (*see also* Lueger,
  Karl)
Vienna Press, 189, 318
Vienna, Treaty of (Dual Alliance, 1879):
  212–13, 231
Villafranca: 107; Peace of (1859), 112–
  13
Votivkirche, Vienna: 67, 88

Wagner, Otto, architect: 291

Waldmüller, Ferdinand, painter: 13, 19
Wallsee: FJ ill at, 310
Warsaw: 54, 72, 118, 120
Wekerle, Alexander, Hungarian PM: 295
Welden, Baron von, army commander: 51–2, 53
Welden, Baroness Caroline von: Crown Prince Rudolf's nurse, 123, 125–6, 149
Weyl, Joseph, librettist: 180–81
Wiener Neustadt: military academy at, 128, 322; airfield at, 298; whirlwind devastates, 339
Wiener Zeitung, 50, 71, 326
William I, German Emperor: 103, 111–12, 130, 132–3, meets FJ, 120, 137–8, 177, 203, 231; visits Vienna, 186; dies, 244
William II, German Emperor: 222; and Rudolf, 250–51, 256–7; visits Vienna, 252–3, 321; visits A-H, 276; and F. Ferdinand, 290, 322–3; and B-H, 304; irritates FJ, 305–6; pays last respects to FJ, 343
Windischgraetz, Prince Alfred: 25, 77; in 1848 revolt, 31–32, 35, 41, in Prague revolt, 38–9; takes Vienna, 43–4,

political activity of, 43–6, 50; in Hungarian campaign (1848–9), 47–9, 50–52; fall of, 51–2
Winterhalter, Franz, painter: 148–9
World Exhibition, Vienna (1873): 183–8
World War I: July crisis (1914) and, 326–31; spreads rapidly, 332; Serbian campaigns in, 333–4, 336; Eastern Front in, 333, 336–7, 338; Italian Front in, 335, 337–8; Roumanian Front in, 338–9, 342; burden of on A-H people, 334–5, 339; aftermath of, 345–6

Yugoslav ideal: 198–9

Zagreb: 32–33, 198; rebuilt, 229; Rudolf visits, 250
Zerajić, Bogdan, Bosnian Serb terrorist, 308
Zita, Archduchess: 322, 336, 342; marries, 311; as Empress, 343, 348–9
Zollverein (German customs union): 58, 87
Zumbusch, Kaspar von: sculptor, 245
Zurich, Treaty of (1859): 116